汉英对照

# 白门柳

## 第一部 夕阳芳草 上

# Willows of the White Gate I

## Romance in the Setting Sun

### Part 1


刘斯奋 著 褚东伟 译

by Liu Sifen translated by Chu Dongwei



广州新华出版发行集团

广州出版社

GUANGZHOU PRESS

**图书在版编目（CIP）数据**

白门柳. 第一部, 夕阳芳草 ：汉英对照 / 刘斯奋著 ； 褚东伟译. -- 广州 ：广州出版社, 2025. 6. -- ISBN 978-7-5462-3897-5

Ⅰ. I247.5

中国国家版本馆 CIP 数据核字第 2025CB8928 号

**书　　名** 白门柳·第一部·夕阳芳草（汉英对照）
Baimenliu Di-yi Bu Xiyang Fangcao (Hanying Duizhao)
**出版发行** 广州出版社
（地址：广州市天河区天润路 87 号 9 楼、10 楼
邮政编码：510635　网址：www.gzcbs.com.cn）
**出 版 人** 柳宗慧
**项目统筹** 李良婷
**责任编辑** 梁惠明
**责任校对** 王俊婕
**印刷单位** 东莞市信誉印刷有限公司
（地址：东莞市南城区水濂澎洞工业区 C 区
邮政编码：523000　电话：0769-22400139）
**规　　格** 880 毫米 ×1230 毫米　32 开
**印　　张** 39.5
**字　　数** 982 千
**版　　次** 2025 年 6 月第 1 版
**印　　次** 2025 年 6 月第 1 次
**书　　号** ISBN 978-7-5462-3897-5
**定　　价** 158.00 元（上下册）

发行专线：（020）38903520　38903518　38903521

錢謙益
一紙降書
尚費難倉皇
北去寸身卑相憐
柳是隱何及拂水山莊
退步遲徐復詩甲申斯齋寫

迫人青氣雜衣香
變服乘輿半野堂
去竟國亡出士節
堅堅池水凜於霜
徐續詩
柳如是

冒襄
秣陵兵亂此潛藏載得浮名
姬亦可傷頭白故園風雨夜
尚疑飄泊在錢塘

董小宛
影梅還憶此情無手書妝台半路途
為難莫臨神樂觀梅花萬樹一時枯
錄舊詩甲申斯齋寫

阮大铖
石巢深处似幽囚，檀板歌残十七秋。冠带昨蒙新主赐，声兴刑狱报清流。
徐溪诗 丁酉 斯斋

黄宗羲
黄竹灘頭
坐故廬東
南兵革勝
長思蒼生害
地翻天覆且著書
徐俊詩
斯喬寫

陳貞慧
若許秦淮重執手十年回首聽歌吟

吴应箕

余懷

史可法
白门一去尚低徊坐
失编排究可哀此日
淮扬非乐土幕中谁
识故人来
徐续诗甲申斯奋写

馬士英

顧眉
風月秦淮酒半醺清歌鸞步遏行雲
佳人一去山河異此曲他年可得聞
右錄徐俊詩甲申歲斯高寫

李十娘

龚鼎孳

柳敬亭

# 译者序

## 一、为什么《白门柳》值得翻译?

2021 年 4 月，我胆战心惊地接受了《白门柳》第一部《夕阳芳草》的翻译工作，要用一到两年的时间完成。

对于一个人来说，一年三百六十五天、两年七百三十天，他也许不会意识到用一两年时间翻译一本书意味着什么；对我来说这意味着至少我的生命有八十分之一（如果我有那么幸运）的时间要围绕着这本书打转。所以这本书必须要有充分的理由让我来翻译它，它要能够让我的这段人生重要时光有意义。

随着年龄的增加，我开始对未来的日子格外珍惜，无谓的事情不会去做，不该认识的人不去结识，提高生命的质量是最重要的。翻译一本书不仅意味着对别人的承诺，更重要的是对自己的承诺。我在翻译这条路上做过不少事，其中大部分我都很满意。

当初跟随王友贵先生读翻译方向的博士的时候，我就发誓要追踪英译大师林语堂的足迹，毕业时要获得写出漂亮英语书、翻译出漂亮英语作品的能力；不把博士毕业论文写成千篇一律的“八股文”，而是让它成为一本开卷有益的英语好书，这些后来证明我都做到了，非常对得起自己。

《翻译家林语堂》是我自豪的一本英语书，《慧能的智慧——〈六祖坛经〉英译及其他》是我自豪的一本英译书，在美国和中国香港的英文杂志上发表的当代小说作品我都可以大大方方地拿出来给人看。在这条路上，没有鲜花和掌声，但自己在双语语言艺术和精神世界的探险所获得的刺激和成就感、满足感相信是很多人体验不到的。

也是因缘际会，这次有机会结识刘斯奋先生并承担《白门柳》第一部《夕阳芳草》的英译工作，这是我生涯中接受的又一次挑战。

《白门柳》在中文世界的地位自不必说，作为现当代中国文学的经典之作，它理所当然应该走向世界，不必等着西方人按自己的意识形态和文学趣味来索取，而走向世界的第一步是走向英语世界。它是关于十七世纪中叶中国大地朝代更替时期的巨幅历史画卷，画工精良，承载的文化信息量巨大，又有大量的典故和诗文，翻译这样鸿篇巨制的传世之作正好是对我前半生英语学习和翻译知识经验的大练兵，我会以对经典和中国文化及语言文字的敬畏之心、以与英语世界读者站在同一平面对话的姿态认真翻译好这本书，让译作既呈现出原汁原味的中国文化的魅力和语言文字之美，同时又以晓畅的英语走入世界范围内英语读者的心。

翻译成英文的中文现代文学作品，能够翻译好的，全世界屈指可数，不管是西方翻译家还是中国及华人翻译家。我很高兴自己的学术积淀已经允许我胆战心惊地接受这本书的英译工作，在一两年时间里，这项工作让我远离焦虑而进入另外一个世界，穿越到明朝末年，穿越到世界各地的读者身边，像坐过山车一样紧张而兴奋，能够参与这样一项了不起的工作本身就是值得骄傲的事情，我想象着自己是一个文化英雄，勇敢地一步一步往前走，时而停下来，时而快马加鞭。

在这个即使成功按世俗的标准也算不了什么的领域，所有在这条道路上默默奋斗的人都是对文学艺术和翻译艺术有着特殊情感的人，都值得我们去肯定。

文学是跨越国界的，在我国历史上，翻译自国外的文学作品曾经成为中国作家成长的养分，虽然细读那些翻译过来的书会发现各种各样的问题，读起来特别舒服的不多，但中国翻译家是可敬的，他们大多对原作保持着敬畏之心，不去大肆篡改，所以读者读到的作品虽然时常因为译者的功力问题显得生涩却能够在某种程度上保持原作的面貌，这些作品持续地为读者接受。

翻译得不是十分好的书为什么持续被阅读，被不断地追捧？因为一个翻译作品的地位是由其原作在产生之地的文化中的地位确定的。一部经典之作，就应该用对待经典的态度去翻译，不能够为了讨好读者而去大肆篡改。我就是保持着这样一种同理心在对《白门柳》第一部《夕阳芳草》进行英译的。

## 二、中国文学英译是不断升高天花板的行动

2012 年，我在美国访学期间，莫言获得诺贝尔文学奖的消息传来，顿时莫言作品在国内再度掀起阅读的浪潮，一时洛阳纸贵，我很好奇与国内的狂欢相比，美国人是怎样对待这个来自中国的新科诺奖得主的。去美国亚马逊网站上查看，首页没有什么变化，检索到的莫言作品上面都加了一个戳“诺奖得主作品”，再看销量，也没有跃居畅销书之列，这与我的期待落差很大。继续检索下去，发现中国作家作品的英译本很少。后来了解到，美国人基本上只读美国书，把普利策奖和美国国家图书奖看得比诺贝尔文学奖还重要，就如他们只打美式足球，对世界杯不是很感兴趣一样，所以每年在美国出版的翻译书只约占他们出版总量的百分之三。失望之余我也看到了我的机遇。这也许是我学术生涯提升的一个契机。

如诗人罗伯特·弗罗斯特（Robert Frost）所说，面前有两条路，我选那条较少人走的。从此我的工作中心便转移到了中国文学英译上来。当然，这对我来说也不是白手起家，早在 1995 年我二十几岁的时候就在《英语知识》杂志上发表朱自清散文《匆匆》英译，2002 年的时候还在清华大学举办的那次韩素音青年翻

译奖比赛中获得了第五名的成绩（当时汉译英组的比赛题目是翻译王佐良散文《想起清华种种》），这些证明我是有些早期积淀的。后来，三十来岁的时候被林语堂的《吾国吾民》和《生活的艺术》所吸引并感动，原来中国人的英文是可以提升到这个档次的，从此更加发奋读书，追寻大师的足迹，努力要实现用英语做事的理想。那段时期的学习和研究就形成了英文版的《翻译家林语堂》一书，现在已经断售了，建议读者去图书馆找来看看，相信一定会有收获。

文学翻译涉及译者的艺术视野、艺术灵感、艺术素质、语言能力等多方面的问题，本身就不是一件简单的工作。翻译总是在不完美中实现的，即使是翻译成母语已经是很难的事情。如我于2019年在上海交大举办的张炜作品翻译国际研讨会上发言所说：一个严肃的文学作品，它的构成一定有三个方面，“义”“质”和“文”，即目的、内容和形式。一个作品就是一个艺术品，是作家创造力的结晶体，其产生的过程是作家通过主观活动把自己要表达的思想或情绪用自己所掌握的语言资源以很细腻的、有效的方式构建而成的某种完整的载体。作品翻译的时候，对于翻译家来说，“义”“质”是客观的存在，“文”也有其客观的脉络和纹理；理想的翻译应该是跨语言的复写，而不应该是另起炉灶。在翻译一个作品的时候，翻译家与作家同类，却不是作家，翻译与创作有着相关甚至部分相似但截然不同的特性。一个严肃的翻译家，他的工作应该是跨语言复制出一模一样的作品，而不应该是篡改作品、制造出自以为是的新作品。其工作的重心和着力点在“文”。古人所谓“言之无文，行之不远”，对于翻译家来说，就是要精工细作，雕琢出与原文相配的“文”。作为一个完整的艺术品，好的原作有其内聚性，有其内在的脉络和纹理，以一定的节奏和气势在自然地流动，在复制原作的工作中，除了外部强力指使之外，翻译家没有权力增加、删除、变造任何文字。

原作是翻译的唯一标准，别无其他标准。这就是《诗经》中所谓的“伐柯伐柯，其则不远”。一个优秀的翻译家必须在文本中忘记自我，他不应该有自己的声音（即便自身也可能是个优秀的创作家，但他创作家的身份和作品的翻译无关），不应该有自己的风格，如果说他可以有自己的风格，那就是可以跟着不同作品的风格千变万化。翻译家不需要能够创造出和作家一样的作品，但他一定需要作家在语言文字方面的一些感觉或者灵性；翻译是艺术，翻译艺术自然也就要求译者有艺术直觉，用一位美国翻译家兰德斯（Landers）的话来说就是“对细微之处的高度敏感”。翻译家所需要的，除了语言能力和知识之外，最重要的是一种气韵和学术精神，也就是灵性和认真。

前辈翻译家是可敬的，因为他们的工作吃力不讨好，翻译得好是原作者的功劳，翻译得不好都是他们的错，但是他们还是忘我地工作着。我们去读翻译成中文的外文书，读着舒服的本来就不多，如果对照原文，既舒服又和原文能够准确地对照起来的更是少之又少。正是文学翻译所具有的挑战性吸引了一代又一代的翻译家奋不顾身地投入到这项伟大的事业中去。然而，就是这些翻译过来的书成为我们一代又一代作家们的养分，可见人类的灵魂和情感最终还是能够跨越语言障碍实现沟通的。在中国现代化的进程中，谦虚的中国人翻译了大量的英语文学作品，可以说，在文学翻译方面，我们是翻译大国，积累了大量的翻译经验，因为翻译的体量、基数比较大，总有一些资质比较好又非常认真的译者能够翻译出一些优秀的作品，甚至一部作品被一而再再而三地翻译，优秀的翻译作品总数还是不小的。

中国文学作品的英译，特别对于英语是外语的中国译者来说，更是一项“逆天”的行动。

中国文学英译有个“非母语”魔咒，国际上有个简单化的规矩，就是翻译应该遵循译入母语的惯例。这一规矩是约束普通译者的，对于天才翻译家是不适用的。古代有鸠摩罗什，近代有泰戈尔、易卜生、林语堂、杨宪益、金隄等，都不受这种约束，何况在现在一切互联的世界上，国界实际上已经不再分明，哪里出生已经不重要，中国的中英双语人数已远远超过“五眼联盟”国家人口，很多人从小就练就了“英语童子功”，而“五眼联盟”国家的人也不是人人都有文化的，不去尝试，你怎么知道自己不是天才呢？再者，随着大数据和人工智能技术的应用，历史上的翻译成果被大量利用，应该说现在的中国人有机会比前辈们做得更好。

所以，在中国和平崛起，文化自信不断提升，中国文学英译环境、模式和出版模式日趋多元化，中国本土英译和出版力量不断崛起的大背景下，中国文学英译，中国人不仅能做，而且能够做得越来越好。英语有个成语叫 pushing the envelope，意思是不断突破，把不可能变为可能，中国人英译中国文学，本来被人认为不可能的事情，许多人做了，而且未来有更多的人会做得更好，通过这种工作，我们也能够看到人类智能的伟大。

## 三、《夕阳芳草》在国内出版双语版有什么意义

这本书是翻译给全球英语读者看的，因为它对中国的双语读者有价值，所以我们率先在中国出版双语对照版。我曾经有个希望，就是大湾区能够打造一个国际英语出版中心，并不只是面向英语国家，而是面对全球的英语读者出版“英语普通话读物”，希望这本书是个有益的开始。

这本书有一个作用就是帮助破除“英语思维”的迷思、树立使用同一文化内核进行双语切换的意识。记得有位同事说他的一个商务英语全英班的学生去银行面试回来后感觉不太好，因为面试官用中文问了他一个专业的问题，那个问题他知道怎样用英语回答，却不知道用中文怎么说。这个就是所谓的纯英语思维的弊

端，涉及培养的人才是为谁培养，学来的英语到底是应用于纯英文场景还是双语环境的问题。道理很简单，输入什么就能产出什么，没有输入就没有产出。在英语学习的早期阶段，我们会常常听到培养“英语思维”的说法，这个说法本身是有一定道理的。我记得最清楚的一句话是高中英语课本上的一句马克思学外语的心得：“当你说本族语的时候就要像本族人一样说话，当你说外语的时候就要像外国人一样说话。”这其实就是积累说话的套路，需要的时候直接调动外语无须通过翻译。这样做对于应付日常生活和工作场景无疑是对的，但是对于双向交流场景中的复杂的文化与思想交流来说又是远远不够的，一个人在跨文化交际中，他不可能回避翻译问题，即使是他同时精通中文和英文，他可以在中英文之间进行切换讲不同的事情，但如果让他用中英文讲同一件事情，他就没有那么潇洒自如了。

跨语言、跨文化交流本身就是翻译，但不是每个人都是翻译家，如果通过阅读中国的文字翻译成的英语文本直接向大脑输入大量信息，使用时不假思索地直接调用势必有事半功倍的感觉。中国人走出去谈中国，如果要有深度就必须依赖来自中国的、关于中国的英语文本的积淀而不是依赖于外国人写的、经过过滤的、关于中国的文字。

《夕阳芳草》在国内出版双语版的第二个意义就是在中国和平崛起、文化软实力和文化自信不断提升的情况下，增强中国人在中国文学英译方面的话语权。

我在张炜作品翻译国际研讨会上还说，中国文学与英语世界文学在交流方面有很大的不平衡性，特别是当代小说作品，具体体现在英语世界被翻译和传播的中文作品不管从量还是质的方面都与翻译成中文的当代英语世界的作品不能相比，整体上来讲，英译作品还是停留在比较低的层次。虽然近些年中国当代小说英译数量有明显的增长，但是根本面貌还没有改善。英语世界的知名作家的作品往往迅速地被翻译成中文，而即使是中国最一线的作家的优秀作品也未必被大规模地翻译成英文。这当然涉及着复杂的文化关系，和作品本身是否真的优秀关系不是很大。但是，在现有的翻译作品中普遍存在的翻译质量问题，无疑是制约中国当代小说作品被更多的英语世界读者接受、让出版商无法提高热情的重要因素之一。翻译质量上，英语世界小说中译有着悠久的传统，读者群体庞大，翻译人才基数也庞大，翻译批评界也经常炮火猛烈，虽然译作质量仍参差不齐，但是优秀译作的绝对数量还是很大。不少作品还不断地被重译，推陈出新。优秀译作、相关的学术批评以及出版社的编辑能力使中译的英语文学一直整体上保持着较高的水平。反观英语世界，热爱翻译文学的读者本来就少，本土以英语为母语的翻译家也很少，精通双语的华人翻译家是一支重要的力量，但是这样的人也不多；虽然有个别翻译家翻译了很多作品或者翻译质量很高，但是人才基数太小，好的译作自然是凤毛麟角。个别翻译家能单枪匹马“承包”整个中国当代文学的情况对于翻译家本人来说是值得敬畏的一件事，但站在中国文学的翻译和传播的整体视角来看，这显然反映了一种窘境。改革开放四十多年来，中国大陆地区也积累了大量的中英双语人才，其中的优秀者具有翻译出优秀英语译文的能力，但相关的环境和平台还不成熟，很多东西还停留在翻给自己人看的阶段。在国际图书市场上，很多英译的作品还是很稚嫩，质量停留在中国大陆普通大学生英译中习作的水平，漏洞百出，不能细读，经常是若有所云而不知所云。现阶段，中国当代小说作品英译还没有走出初级阶段——追求被翻译的数量，作品能够被翻译出来在英语世界见光已经很幸运。

我们显然不能满足于此，我们应该向更高的层次进军，应该在有更多的作品被翻译成英文的同时追求高质量的有效翻译。初级阶段对译者的要求很低：看得懂中文、写得出说得过去的英文便可。满足这两项要求的译者已经门可罗雀，但我们必须往更高的层次走，用优秀的译作引领读者和翻译人才。只要是真正有价值、值得翻译的作品都应该被当作严肃的文字严肃对待，而不是被当作可以随便阉割、篡改或敷衍了事的东西。为此，翻译家需要有学者的素养、工匠的精神和艺术家的敏感。从一定意义上讲，翻译一部作品要远远难于创作一部作品。翻译的创造活动价值也就在于此。简言之，文学翻译是语言艺术工作，它服务于文学艺术，是文学作品价值倍增的翅膀。文学翻译已经很难，文学英译更是难上加难，翻译家应在克服困难中不断提升自己的艺术水平。中国文学英译作品在英语国家出版时不断被选择和阉割，负责主要工作的中国和华人译者经常在合作翻译中处于服从和被支配的地位，可是中国拥有庞大的双语阅读群体，英语已经不再专属于英语国家，中国文学英译操之在我也势在必行。在今天，中国和华人译者作为中译外主体，使用英语作为第二语言者从事中国文学英译工作比历史上任何时期更具现实性、可行性，中国文学英译可以以中国和华人译者为主体（而不是作为英语母语译者的附庸，名字写在外国译者后面作为第二译者仅仅是因为他们能够美化译文），生产以全球英语读者为对象而不是英语国家读者的核心版本，然后根据市场细分与本地化的需要进行一些微调工作，采用“用国际英语（Global English）进行翻译、凸显中国特色（national color）”的翻译路径。

对于翻译学习者来说，采用英汉对照的形式（虽然这样的方式会让译者的个别缺点和错误无所遁形）可以方便读者研究中英文转换规律。我可以负责任地说，本书中绝大多数的文字可以用作文学翻译的范例，还可以帮助翻译学习者掌握中英文转换规律，有兴趣的读者不妨自行选择部分内容进行翻译然后对照英译文进行阅读与思考，相信您的思路和对自己习作的判断能力会有大幅提升。如果您能够意识到那么多困难原来都是可以克服的，真是天无绝人之路，能够发现有些地方自己可以处理得更好，相信您今后的翻译会更有方法，自信心也会大大提高。

开卷有益是我的希望，如果您感觉能够受益，那是我极大的欣慰，这一两年的付出也就值了。

最后，值得提出的是，《白门柳》第一部《夕阳芳草》的翻译出版可能开启当代中国文学作品翻译出版的一个新的模式，是中国作为文明大国展现文化自信和文学自信的一个标志性事件，从这个意义上讲，通过这部历史小说的翻译出版，我们也在创造历史，作为这次文化事件的策划者，安徽彬蔚鸿雅文化传播有限公司及出版家金学军先生也必将被载入史册。

另外，我要感谢加拿大翻译家阿瑟林·查尔斯（Asselin Charles）先生主动索取书稿并在认真阅读后给予充分肯定并提供一些中肯的参考意见。

褚东伟

二〇二五年二月十九日

红日又西沉，白浪长东去。

——辛弃疾《生查子·题京口郡治尘表亭》

时缤纷其变易兮，又何可以淹留！

兰芷变而不芳兮，荃蕙化而为茅。

——屈原《离骚》

Again the red sun sinks in the west,

And unstoppable are the white waves going east.

From "Written for the Chenbiao Pavilion in Jingkou, Prefectural Capital, to the tune of *sheng zha zi*" by Xin Qiji

Time changes in a chaotic flux,

And what is there that can be left?

Orchids degrade and lose their fragrance,

And sweet grasses downgrade and become satintails.

From "Sorrows of an Exile" by Qu Yuan

# 主要人物表

| | |
|---|---|
| 钱谦益 | 字受之，号牧斋，东林党后期领袖，曾任礼部右侍郎 |
| 柳如是 | 名是，字如是，号河东君，明末盛泽名妓，钱谦益之宠妾 |
| 陈夫人 | 钱谦益之妻 |
| 钱孙爱 | 钱谦益之子 |
| 陈在竹 | 钱谦益妻舅 |
| 钱　曾 | 字遵王，明末诸生，复社成员，钱谦益族孙兼学生 |
| 顾　苓 | 字云美，明末诸生，复社成员，钱谦益学生 |
| 冯　班 | 字定远，明末诸生，复社成员，钱谦益学生 |
| 瞿式耜 | 字起田，号稼轩，东林派官员，曾任户科给事中，钱谦益之门生 |
| 冒　襄 | 字辟疆，明末诸生，复社四公子之一 |
| 董小宛 | 名白，字小宛，明末秦淮名妓 |
| 冒起宗 | 时任衡、永兵备使者，冒襄之父 |
| 董子将 | 青楼篾片，董小宛之父 |

# Characters

**Qian Qianyi**, also known as Shouzhi (courtesy name) or Muzhai (literary name; often addressed as Elder Mu): last leader of the East Wood Party, once Right Vice Minister of the Ministry of Rites

**Liu Rushi**, given name Shi, courtesy name Rushi, also known as Lady of River East (literary name): famous courtesan of late Ming dynasty from Shengze Town, favorite concubine of Qian Qianyi

**Lady Chen**: wife of Qian Qianyi

**Qian Sun'ai**: son of Qian Qianyi

**Chen Zaizhu**: brother-in-law of Qian Qianyi

**Qian Zeng**, also known as Zunwang (courtesy name): student of the imperial schools system at the end of the Ming dynasty, member of the Fushe, grandson of Qian Qianyi's brother and student of Qian Qianyi

**Gu Ling**, also known as Yunmei (courtesy name): student of the imperial schools system at the end of the Ming dynasty, member of the Fushe and student of Qian Qianyi

**Feng Ban**, also known as Dingyuan (courtesy name): student of the imperial schools system at the end of the Ming dynasty, member of the Fushe and student of Qian Qianyi

**Qu Shisi**, also known as Qitian (courtesy name) or Jiaxuan (literary name): government official affiliated with the East Wood Party, student of Qian Qianyi, once served as Royal Liaison Officer of the Department of Revenues

**Mao Xiang**, also known as Pijiang (courtesy name): student of the imperial schools system at the end of the Ming dynasty and one of the Four Young Men of the Fushe

**Dong Xiaowan**, given name Bai, courtesy name Xiaowan: famous courtesan on the Qinhuai River in late Ming dynasty

**Mao Qizong**: father of Mao Xiang, imperial commissioner to Hengyang and Yongzhou

**Dong Zijiang**: father of Dong Xiaowan, a hanger-on of bawdy houses

张明弼　字公亮，时任浙江按察司照磨，复社成员，冒襄之盟兄

刘履丁　字渔仲，明末贡生，复社成员，冒襄之盟兄

黄宗羲　字太冲，明末诸生，东林党人黄尊素之子，复社成员

陈贞慧　字定生，明末诸生，复社四公子之一

吴应箕　字次尾，明末诸生，复社重要成员

侯方域　字朝宗，明末诸生，复社四公子之一

方以智　字密之，时任翰林院编修，复社四公子之一

梅朗中　字朗三，明末诸生，复社成员

顾　杲　字子方，明末诸生，东林党领袖顾宪成之侄孙，复社成员

周　钟　字介生，明末诸生，复社成员

余　怀　字淡心，明末诸生，复社成员

**Zhang Mingbi**, also known as Gongliang (courtesy name): member of the Fushe, sworn brother of Mao Xiang, clerk of the Department of Justice of Zhejiang Province

**Liu Lüding**, also known as Yuzhong (courtesy name): member of the Fushe, sworn brother of Mao Xiang, a selected candidate for the imperial recruitment examination at the end of the Ming dynasty

**Huang Zongxi**, also known as Taichong (courtesy name): student of the imperial schools system at the end of the Ming dynasty, son of East Wood Party member Huang Zunsu， member of the Fushe

**Chen Zhenhui**, also known as Dingsheng (courtesy name): student of the imperial schools system at the end of the Ming dynasty, one of the Four Young Men of the Fushe

**Wu Yingji**, also known as Ciwei (pronounced Tse-wei, courtesy name): student of the imperial schools system at the end of the Ming dynasty, an important member of the Fushe

**Hou Fangyu**, also known as Chaozong (courtesy name): student of the imperial schools system at the end of the Ming dynasty, one of the Four Young Men of the Fushe

**Fang Yizhi**, also known as Mizhi(courtesy name): editor of Hanlin Academy, one of the Four Young Men of the Fushe

**Mei Langzhong**, also known as Langsan (courtesy name): student of the imperial schools system at the end of the Ming dynasty, member of the Fushe

**Gu Gao**, also known as Zifang (courtesy name): student of the imperial schools system at the end of the Ming dynasty, grandnephew of East Wood Party leader Gu Xiancheng, member of the Fushe

**Zhou Zhong**, also known as Jiesheng (courtesy name): student of the imperial schools system at the end of the Ming dynasty, member of the Fushe

**Yu Huai**, also known as Danxin (courtesy name):student of the imperial schools system at the end of the Ming dynasty, member of the Fushe

**张　岱**　字宗子，明末诸生，复社成员

**郑元勋**　字超宗，明末诸生，后中进士，复社扬州地区社长

**熊明遇**　字良孺，东林派官员，时任南京兵部尚书

**史可法**　字道邻，东林派官员，时任漕运总督兼凤阳、淮安、扬州巡抚

**周　镳**　字仲驭，东林派官员，曾任南京礼部主事

**徐石麒**　字宝摩，东林派官员，时任刑部左侍郎

**冯元飙**　字尔弢，东林派官员，时任兵部左侍郎

**吴伟业**　字骏公，号梅村，复社成员，时任詹事府谕德

**龚鼎孳**　字孝升，号芝麓，复社成员，时任兵科给事中

**周延儒**　字玉绳，时任内阁首辅

**马士英**　字瑶草，曾任宣府巡抚

**Zhang Dai**, also known as Zongzi (courtesy name): student of the imperial schools system at the end of the Ming dynasty, member of the Fushe

**Zheng Yuanxun**, also known as Chaozong (courtesy name): student of the imperial schools system at the end of the Ming dynasty, later passed the imperial recruitment examination and became a *jinshi*, president of Yangzhou Chapter of the Fushe

**Xiong Mingyu**, also known as Liangru (courtesy name): government official affiliated with the East Wood Party, Minister of the Ministry of War in Nanjing

**Shi Kefa**, also known as Daolin (courtesy name): government official affiliated with the East Wood Party, chief executive officer of water transport and Governor of Fengyang, Huai'an and Yangzhou

**Zhou Biao**, also known as Zhongyu (courtesy name): government official affiliated with the East Wood Party, former clerk of the Ministry of Rites in Nanjing

**Xu Shiqi**, also known as Baomo (courtesy name): government official affiliated with the East Wood Party, Left Vice Minister of the Ministry of Punishment

**Feng Yuanbiao**, also known as Ertao (courtesy name): government official affiliated with the East Wood Party, Left Vice Minister of the Ministry of War

**Wu Weiye**, also known as Jungong (courtesy name) or Meicun (literary name): member of the Fushe, teacher of morality to the prince at court

**Gong Dingzi**, also known as Xiaosheng (courtesy name) or Zhilu (literary name): member of the Fushe, Secretary of Military Supervision

**Zhou Yanru**, also known as Yusheng (courtesy name): the Prime Minster

**Ma Shiying**, also known as Yaocao (courtesy name; often addressed as Elder Yao): former Governor of the border town of Xuanfu

阮大铖　字集之，号圆海，魏忠贤阉党余孽，曾任光禄寺卿

顾　眉　字眉生，明末秦淮名妓

李十娘　名湘真，字雪衣，明末秦淮名妓

徐青君　明中山王徐达后裔，南京巨富

计　成　字无否，明末著名园林建筑师

李　宝　钱谦益亲随仆人

冒　成　冒襄亲随仆人

黄　安　黄宗羲亲随仆人

毕石湖　浙东帮商人头领

陆卖婆　女帮闲

张　秀　苏州土豪

郝思平　苏州讼棍

**Ruan Dacheng**, also known as Jizhi (courtesy name) or Yuanhai (literary name; addressed as Elder Yuan): a remnant of the treacherous eunuch Wei Zhongxian's party, former secretary of the Department of Ceremonies

**Gu Mei**: also known as Meisheng (courtesy name): famous courtesan on the Qinhuai River in late Ming dynasty

**Li Shiniang**, original name Xiangzhen, also known as Xueyi (courtesy name): a famous courtesan on the Qinhuai River in late Ming dynasty

**Xu Qingjun**: a descendant of Xu Da, Prince of Zhongshan, one of the richest men in Nanjing

**Ji Cheng**, also known as Wufou (courtesy name): a famous landscape architect in late Ming dynasty

**Li Bao**: Qian Qianyi's servant

**Mao Cheng**: Mao Xiang's footman

**Huang An**: Huang Zongxi's footman

**Bi Shihu**: leader of East Zhejiang merchants

**Vendor Lu**: female helper

**Zhang Xiu**: local tycoon in Suzhou

**Hao Siping**: a legal parasite in Suzhou

# 目 录

# Table of Contents

# 引　子

在幽深的山谷里，有一株被人遗忘的梅树。

这株山南常见的红梅，是在一个雷电交加的暴风雨之夜，被猝然暴发的山洪冲到谷底来的。同它一块冲下来的其他梅树，都压在坍塌的岩层底下了。只有这一株，因为长得特别粗大硕壮，侥幸地活了下来。不过，它受到的伤残是如此厉害，以至整个躯干像从当中挨了一斧头似的，可怕地劈裂开来。伤口的部位，结痂累累，永远无法重合了。它的半爿已经死掉，剩下黝黑朽烂的一段木橛，另外半爿艰难地扭曲着，又挣扎着坐了起来，却再也直不起身子。于是，它就这么弓着腰，坐着，过了一年又一年……

渐渐它变得很衰老了，连南方吹来的熏风，也不能使它恢复一点活力。一年到头似乎都沉浸在冥思默想当中——它在想什么呢？是回忆无忧无虑的儿时光景？是重温辛酸而甜蜜的少年春梦？还是追抚凌霜傲雪的壮岁情怀？这些都无从知道。只是，它的枝干一天天地干枯下去，它的花朵和叶子也一年比一年稀少了。

有一阵子，它好像已经死掉。不过，冬至过后，山南的梅花纷纷开放，它那粗糙僵硬的枝丫上，冷不丁又开出一朵憔悴的小花。看上去，就像一个奄奄待毙的老人，忽然睁开了一只发红的、黏滞的眼睛……

当年洪水滔天、山崩地裂的可怕一幕，想必还时时浮现在它的眼前。它无法理解，那一场埋葬了它的理想、青春和最优秀伙

# Prologue

In the deep valley, there used to be a forgotten plum tree.

This red plum tree, common in the south of the mountain, was washed to the bottom of the valley by a sudden flash flood on a stormy night with thunder and lightning. The other plum trees washed down with her were all crushed under the collapsed rock strata. Only this one, because she was very large and strong, survived by chance. However, she was so badly wounded that her torso split apart appallingly as if she had been severed by an axe. Layers of scabs formed where she was wounded and healing was impossible. One half of her was dead and only had a dark and decayed wooden prong left, and the other half, twisting with pain, finally stood up but could never return to her straight posture. So, she had to sit with a hunchback year in and year out.

Over time, she grew old and withered, and even the southerly winds couldn't bring any vigor to her. Throughout the year, she silently sat there, lost in thoughts. What was she thinking? The innocence of childhood? The bitter-sweet romance of youth? Or the glorious ambitions of adulthood? There was no way to know. What was known was her branches dried up day by day and her flowers and leaves were becoming sparser year by year.

For a while, she looked dead. However, after the winter solstice, the plum trees in the south of the mountain bloomed one after another, and a haggard little flower appeared suddenly on one of the callous and stiffened twigs, as if a dying old man suddenly opened a red, sticky eye.

The terrible scene of flood and landslide years ago must have recurred before her eyes from time to time and she wondered what

伴的奇祸巨变，是受着什么样一种力量主宰？又为什么偏偏降临在自己的头上？！这终古难平的怨愤，像利爪揪扯着它的心。每逢风雨之夜，它就会转侧难眠，巍巍颤颤地抖动着那只瘦骨嶙嶙的独臂，发出凄厉的呼啸，咒骂命运的不公和天地的无情……

有一天，一位踽踽独行的旅人经过这里，这株悲惨的老梅树引起了他的惊异。他绕着它反复端详了半天，最后坐下来，抚摸着老梅巨大而支离的躯干，默默地用心声同它交谈了很久、很久。直到红日西沉，徐徐升起的暮霭使山谷变得一片苍茫，他才站起来，抖一抖衣服上的泥土，背起行囊，大步走去。

自此之后，老梅树安静了，它更加沉默。有好几年，它不再开花，也不再长叶，仿佛打算就此长眠下去……可是，一种缓慢的转机终于来临——那已经死掉、铁石般坚韧的表皮，有如一领沉重的护甲，本来紧紧地裹住老梅树的躯体，竟无声地坼裂了。开始是不显眼的一道缝，不久，裂缝扩大了，接着又出现了第二道、第三道……看来，老梅树正从身体内部拼命向外挤迫。它在力图摆脱老死的皮层对于剩余生命的窒息，摧毁与生俱来的这一部分身体对另一部分身体的横蛮禁锢！这真是一场惊心动魄、悲壮绝伦的自我搏杀。夜深人静时，山谷里老远就听见那发自心肺的沉重喘息和含泪的嘶喊。最后，老梅树被自己弄得皮开肉绽，遍体鳞伤。有一次，它偶然在月光下看见自己丑恶不堪的影子，竟害怕得浑身发起抖来。

终于，又硬又厚的坚甲瓦解了，剥落了！

而它，这梅树，仍旧是蜷曲受苦的姿态，仍旧是残缺支离的躯体，可它已经获得了新生。几年后，它出乎意料地抽出数十丫粗壮碧绿的新枝，接着，小骨朵儿似的蓓蕾就密密麻麻地爬满了枝头。在一个凄清微冷的冬晨，它终于开出了满树璀璨的繁花。

kind of power had led to the strange catastrophe that buried her ideals, youth, and companions altogether and why that catastrophe had fallen on her head. This long-lasting grievance gripped her heart like a sharp claw. On every stormy night, she turned and tossed without falling asleep, shaking her skinny arm that remained, screaming loudly, damning the injustice of destiny and the ruthlessness of the lords of heaven and earth.

One day, a lone traveler passed by, and this poor old plum tree caught his attention. He moved around her and regarded her from all sides. Then he sat down, and, caressing her huge and broken torso, conversed with her in the silent language of the mind for a long, long time, until the red sun had sunk in the west and the slowly rising evening clouds enveloped the valley. Then he stood up, shook off the mud on his clothes, took up his luggage, and went on his way.

The old plum tree quieted down and became even more silent than before. For years, she bore no flowers or leaves, as if intending to sleep forever. However, a turning point finally crept in. Her dead skin, hard as iron and wrapping its body like a heavy armor, stealthily cracked open. It was an inconspicuous crevice at first, but soon the opening widened. Then appeared a second opening and then a third ... Obviously, the old plum tree was exerting herself to shake off the old, dead skin that suffocated her remaining life and free one part of the body from the imprisonment of another. This was really a thrilling, tragic life-and-death battle with herself. In the dead of night, her heavy gasps and teary cries reverberated in the valley. In the end, the old plum tree was badly wounded by herself, her skin broken and flesh gaping. Once, she saw her own ugly shadow in the moonlight and trembled with fear.

Finally, the hard and thick armor disintegrated and peeled off.

Though she was still curled up in agony, her body maimed, she had gained a new life. A few years later, she unexpectedly begot dozens of new, green and thick twigs, which were soon covered with tiny little buds. On a bleak and chilly winter morning, she finally bloomed with beautiful flowers.

瞧，它如今有多美啊！山南的梅花浓艳如火，山北的梅花晶莹如雪，它呢？既不是红色，也不是白色，而是一种恬静柔和的绿色。无疑这绿很轻，很淡，骤眼一看，你会错认这是一株白梅，须得把它同真正的白梅放在一起，才会分明显出它其实是绿的。更为特别的是，阳光下看，它还不怎样，而当天色昏暗，或是在夜里，它的每一片花瓣，都会幽幽地发出光来。这时，它仿佛不是一株梅花，而是一位美丽的精灵。轻风吹过，微光颤颤，它便轻盈地舞蹈起来……它的香气也不寻常，细细的，凉凉的。在满山红梅浓烈的香气包围中，仿佛一下子就消失了。可是，你仔细嗅嗅，那凉凉的香气又冒出来，愈久，愈烈，愈鲜明。末了，你就只嗅到这一种凉凉的细香了。

消息很快传扬开去。人们成群结队来观看这株幽谷奇葩。荒凉寂静的山谷顿时热闹起来。丛生的杂草之间，不久便踏出一条一条的路径。风雅之士们甚至在花下排开筵席，疏疏地点上几盏灯烛，作长夜之赏。它成了诗中的佳题，画中的尤物，以至香闺中的腻友。人们经常地提起它，再三地宣扬它，把它说得出类拔萃，超凡绝俗，神而又神……

可怜的梅树是多么激动呀！它吃惊，怀疑，不知所措，终于快活得哭起来了。

从此，它变得十分辛苦忙碌。络绎不绝的来客令它简直应接不暇。为着不使每一个人失望，它一天到晚殷勤地微笑着，尽量舒展开繁密的新枝，毫不吝惜地把异彩和奇香奉献给四方八面。

How beautiful she was now! The plum blossoms in the south of the mountain were as red as fire, and those in the north of the mountain were as white as snow. What was the blossom on this plum tree like? It was neither red nor white; it was of a quiet and soft green. Undoubtedly, this green was the lighter kind. At first sight, you would mistakenly believe that this tree was a white plum tree, and one had to put her together with a real white plum tree to tell that she was actually green. More interestingly, she was nothing out of the ordinary when viewed under the sun, but when the sky became dim or night fell, every petal would start to glow. Then, she looked more like a beautiful apparition than a plum tree. When a breeze came, she swayed lightly like a beautiful dancer adorned with sparkling jewels ... The gentle and cool fragrance was of an unusual kind too. It wafted into the air and then quickly disappeared into the strong fragrance of the blossoms of the red plum trees that populated the mountain. However, if one sniffed hard enough, that cool fragrance immediately came back, and the longer one sniffed, the stronger it got and the more palpable its presence. In the end, there was no other smell left in the nostrils than this gentle and cool fragrance.

Word spread quickly. People came in droves to admire this wonderful blossom in the deep valley. The desolate and quiet valley was suddenly alive. Amidst the lush growth of weeds, a path soon formed. Some men of an artistic bent even arranged a banquet under the tree, with a few lamps and candles scattered here and there, for a night-long viewing party. She thus became a poetic inspiration, a favorite subject for painting, or even a bosom friend of the young ladies in their boudoirs. People tirelessly talked about her, never sparing in their praise as if she were a great legend ...

How excited the poor plum tree was now! Surprised, perplexed and nonplussed by the sudden turn of fate, she burst into tears with joy.

From then on, she became busy as hell. The constant stream of visitors simply overwhelmed her. In order not to disappoint anyone, she smiled diligently all day long and extended the dense, newly grown branches as best as she could to generously share her splendor

只怕不够表达自己的感激和热诚，第一次花朵凋落后，它紧接着又开出了第二次繁花。这下，引起的轰动更大。游客们纷纷去而复来，都要躬逢这梅开二度的难得盛事。山谷里愈加熙来攘往，挨挤不开。各式各样的茶寮、货摊、食担、杂耍乃至戏棚，都竞相出现，热闹的景象赛过盛大的庙会。到后来，连远近的达官贵人们也不惜降贵纡尊，携眷而至，说是“与民同乐”。于是，又有人竭力凑兴，悬出厚赏，为梅花征求名号品题。据说，由于争议纷纭，始终悬而未决……

花团锦簇的日子过得飞快。渐渐，梅树又感到了一种寂寞，一种美中不足。不知为什么，它越来越经常地想起了过去，想起它走过的那一条苦难的、坎坷的道路。它忽然觉得，它有好多好多故事，准备向人们述说。这些故事无疑并不美丽，甚至也不动听，但一个一个都那样真实，那样亲切，那样重要！与眼前的一切相比，似乎实在得多，也有意思得多。梅树很奇怪自己竟会把它忘却了这么长久。现在每回想一次，它都止不住心头发颤，热泪盈盈。啊，应当向人们一一讲出来，讲出来！

于是，它这样做了。但人们的反应却如此冷淡！他们一个劲儿地盯着美丽的花朵，露出不胜倾倒的神情，然后，以突然爆发的喝彩，打断了梅树用微弱、发抖的声音说开了头的故事……

梅树又一次地吃惊、迷惑，无可奈何地沉默了。但没有灰心，它忍耐着，等待着，年复一年地开出更盛更美的花朵。它的名气传得更远了，慕名者从千百里外不绝涌来，以一瞻风采引为毕生

and fragrance with people coming from all directions. Afraid that she was not doing enough to express her gratitude and enthusiasm, when the blossom withered, she bloomed again. Then, she caused a greater sensation. Visitors returned one after another, all to celebrate the rare event of the second flowering of the plum tree. The valley bustled with more activity as more people packed into this small remote corner. Tea sheds, kiosks, food vendors, jugglers, and makeshift theaters competed for business, making this place livelier than a grand temple fair. Later, even high-ranking officials from far and near condescended to visit this remote corner with their family members, saying that they were here to share in the joy of the people. And then, some people added to the fun by offering a generous reward to solicit a special name and a tribute for the blossom of this plum tree. It's said that a decision was never made because no consensus was ever reached.

The days garlanded with flowers flew fast. Gradually, the plum tree felt lonely again and thought something was lacking. Somehow, she couldn't help thinking of the past, of the painful and bumpy road she had traveled. Suddenly, she realized that she had a responsibility to tell all her stories to the visitors. Those stories were undoubtedly not beautiful at all, not even pleasant to hear, but every one of them was so real, so close, and so important. Compared with what she had now, her past experience was much more real and much more interesting. The plum tree was puzzled why she had forgotten them. Every time she thought of them, her heart couldn't help but tremble and tears overflowed her eyes. Yes, she should tell the stories. She should tell them one by one.

So she did. But the reactions were cold. People kept staring at the beautiful flowers with an overwhelmed expression, and then, with a sudden burst of applause, they interrupted the story the plum tree had just started telling with a faint, trembling voice.

The plum tree was surprised, puzzled once again and helplessly fell silent. But she was not discouraged; she endured, waited, and bloomed more splendidly each year. Her fame spread even farther, and admirers flooded in from thousands of miles away to have a glimpse of her grace as a blessing one might have only once in a lifetime.

幸事。然而看客如云，流年似水，它所期待的、愿意倾听它的心声的知音者，却始终没有出现……

哦，也许这样的人是有的？也许他只是不了解梅树的心思？也许他混杂在众多的围观者当中，梅树没能辨认出来？也许他根本挤不进密密层层的人墙，只好站在远处看上几眼，就走了……谁知道呢！

梅树明显地憔悴了。它变得心灰意冷，闷闷不乐，一天到晚像失魂落魄似的，连一年一度的花期，也没有心思料理了。

在又一个冬天来临的时候，它静悄悄地死了。

震惊的游客深为失望，痛惜不已！他们流连凭吊了许久，依依不舍地散去，从此不再来。

古老的山谷渐渐又恢复了昔日的荒凉冷寂。待到游人踏出的路径重新长起离离的芳草，梅树的遗骸也朽败、霉烂，化为尘土之后，一切便像从来没有发生过，也没有存在过一样。

然而，心上的痕迹是不容易抹平的。慢慢地，在当地居民中间，传出了一种说法——

那株梅树其实还在。只要遇上天阴下雨的时节，或者月色朦胧的夜晚，山谷中迟归的樵夫和狩猎的山民常常会看见，那株梅树忽然又在老地方出现了。他们甚至看得清枝头上淡绿的花朵，嗅得着那凉凉的幽香。当他们试着走近去，一切便像烟雾似的消逝了。

于是，当地的人们说：这是那株梅树的影子，是它的灵魂。它不肯死心，还在守候着，要将它的故事告诉一个愿意把它写下来的人……

However, the crowds were merely drifting clouds, and the years were no more than flowing water. The confidant that she was expecting and who was willing to listen to what her heart was ready to share never appeared.

Well, maybe there was such a one. Maybe he simply didn't know what a plum tree was thinking. Maybe he had been here in an admiring crowd, but she hadn't recognized him. Probably unable to penetrate the dense layers of the human wall, he had stood in the distance and taken a few glances, and then left. Who knows?

The plum tree was emaciated. She was downcast and gloomy all the time, as if her soul had been lost, and had no mind to attend to her duties in the flowering period that came only once in a year's time.

When another winter came, she died quietly, leaving tourists disappointed and distraught. They lingered for some time, reluctantly dispersed, and never came again.

The ancient valley gradually returned to its former desolation and cold silence. When the path made by human footprints was repopulated with fragrant grass and the remains of the plum tree had decayed, disintegrated, and turned to dust, it looked as if nothing had ever taken place or had ever been.

However, the imprints on the heart were not to be easily erased. Over time, among the local residents, there grew a speculation:

The plum tree was actually still there. On a day overcast with rain or a hazy moonlit night, the woodmen and hunters in the valley returning home late would often see the plum tree had suddenly reappeared in the old place. They could even see the light green flowers on the branches and smell the cool, mysterious scent. But when they tried to get closer, the vision faded away like a mist.

So, the locals said, "This is the trace of the plum tree and her very spirit. She's not given up. She's still waiting for someone who'll come to hear her stories and write them down."

# 第一章
# 谋复出贿通首辅，巧机变宠夺专房

## 二妾争宠

偏西的早春阳光，透过窗外竹树丛的间隙，把斑斑驳驳的影子，铺洒在梅花暖帘上。每当轻风摇动翠竹，那一帘碎影，便像溪水般来回流淌。地板上厚厚的红氍毹[①]，衬托着褐色的雕花窗棂和紫檀木桌椅，使这房间的基本色调显得十分和谐；而华美的泥金描花草围屏，映衬着大铜火盆里通红的炭火，又增加了寝室的温暖和宁帖；粉壁上那帧独一无二的北宋院画人物，颇有分量地暗示出主人的趣味和家世；在画的下面，还摆着一张式样素雅的古琴，两架收拾得纤尘不染的线装书；一只装饰着走兽图形的景泰蓝博山炉，正袅袅地吐出沉檀的烟缕，淡薄的、若有若无的幽香在房间里浮荡……这间小小的、整洁舒适的闺房，虽然是用绫罗锦绣和金玉器皿布置起来，显得奢华而富丽，却依然保持着高雅的气息。这里看不见一样多余的摆设，也没有一样是可以缺少的，即便是一根雀翎、几片绿叶，都经过精心的挑选，反复的比较，被安插到最恰当的位置上。

躺在悬着流苏锦帐的月洞式门罩架子床上的柳如是，靠着白

① 氍毹：一种织有花纹图案的毛毯，古代产于西域。

Chapter One

# In Which Qian Qianyi Planned for a Comeback to Politics through Bribery and His Concubine Liu Rushi Secured Exclusive Favor through Trickery

## Two Concubines at War

Through the gaps of the bamboo grove outside the window, the early spring sun in the early afternoon dappled the plum-blossom thermal curtain with spots and strips of light. When a breeze shook the bamboos, those spots and strips of light moved like ripples in a stream. The thick red rug on the floor, complimenting the brown carved window lattices and the red sandalwood tables and chairs, gave a strong sense of harmony of color; and the folding screen with a gilded floral scene, together with the red, hot charcoal fire in the large bronze brazier, gave a sense of coziness and quiet in the bedroom; the unique Northern Song dynasty court portrait on the white wall indicated the owner's taste and family background; under the painting was a simple and elegant zither and two bookshelves neatly packed with thread-bound books; a cloisonné Boshan incense burner painted with animal figures was spitting out whiffs of heavy sandalwood smoke, and a light, ethereal fragrance floated in the room. This small, tidy, and comfortable boudoir, although lushly decorated with silk fabric and extravagantly equipped with gold and jade utensils, retained an air of simple elegance. There was nothing redundant here, and nothing less than necessary. Even a bird feather or a green leaf was the result of careful selection and was placed in the most appropriate position.

Reclining in the canopy bed with a round moon-shaped front opening and draped with tasseled and brocaded mosquito netting, Liu

缎红花软枕，斜瞅着那一帘竹影，渐渐觉得目眩起来。她重新把眼睛闭上一会儿，从大红云缎被底下，慢慢地伸出来一只雪白的胳膊，然后，又伸出另外一只，悠悠地舒展了一下身子。

十四岁的丫环红情，听见响动，踮着小脚儿从围屏后面转出来。她长着一张苹果样的小圆脸，和一双灵活的眼睛。看见女主人打算起床，她就走近前去，轻轻地把柳如是扶起来，又从暖笼上取下一件绿绒女衣，替女主人披在身上；然后，走到靠门内侧的一张八仙桌旁，用一只仿成化斗彩葡萄纹茶盅，细细地沏了一杯酽茶，送到柳如是手中，含笑请安道：

"夫人，您醒了，睡得可好？"

柳如是没有回答。她远远地瞟着窗前的一张紫檀木书案。那上面不知什么时候放了一张诗笺。她心不在焉地揭开茶盅的盖子，凑在嘴边轻轻地吹着热气，问道：

"老爷——又作诗了？"

"啊，老爷又作了两首七律，真好！早一阵子着人送进来的。婢子见夫人正睡着，没敢惊动，就搁在书案上了——夫人您这就看？"

柳如是摇摇头，啜了一口茶。这是她平日爱喝的兰雪茶，泡冲时又加进一点松萝茶叶，使茉莉的香味稍煞，而茶味更酽。她含着茶，就在红情捧来的唾壶中漱了口，抱着膝盖，又出了一会子神，终于掀开锦被，把两条腿儿垂落在床沿上。等红情服侍她穿好衣裳，裹好了脚，又把一双瘦才半指的红绣鞋儿替她套上之后，她就扶着红情的肩膀，踩着花梨木脚踏，款款地走下地来。

Rushi, supported on the back by the soft white satin pillow embroidered with red flowers, looked obliquely at the curtain with bamboo shadows and was gradually dazzled. She closed her eyes again, and slowly stretched out a snow-white arm from under the big brocaded red-cloud satin quilt, then the other one and then her whole being.

Hongqing, the fourteen-year-old maid, heard the movement and tiptoed to her from behind the privacy screen. The maid had a small round face like an apple and a pair of flexible eyes. Seeing that her mistress was about to get up, she went over and gently helped her up. She took a green velvet dress from the clothes warmer and put it on her mistress; then, she walked to the eight-seat square *baxian* table① close to the door and made a cup of thick tea with an imitation Chenghua era grapevine-patterned ceramic cup and brought it to Liu Rushi's hands, smiling and saying, "Mistress, now you're awake. Did you sleep well?"

Liu Rushi didn't answer, her eyes on a red sandalwood desk at the window. Some poetry sheets had newly appeared on it. She lifted the lid of the tea cup absent-mindedly, and, gently blowing away the heat, asked, "Are these new poems from his lordship?"

"Yes, his lordship has written two more seven-character four-liners. It's really nice. They were sent in a moment ago. I dared not disturb your sleep, so I put them on the desk. Do you want to read them now, my lady?"

Liu Rushi shook her head and took a sip of tea. It was Blue Snow, her favorite tea. Some *songluo* tea had been added to make it taste more like tea than jasmine. She held the sip in her mouth for a brief moment and, after rinsing her mouth, spat it into the spittoon held by Hongqing; then she hugged her knees and hesitated for a while before she lifted the quilt and dropped her legs over the edge of the bed. Aided by Hongqing, she slowly dressed up, bound her feet, and donned her tiny red embroidered shoes; then, hand on Hongqing's shoulder, she put her feet on the rosewood foot stool and landed majestically on the ground.

---

① A *baxian* table literally means "a table for eight immortals".

她是一个二十五岁的标致女人，因为长得娇小玲珑，看上去还要年轻一点——一头又黑又亮、缎子似的丰厚柔软的长发，椭圆形的、异常白净细嫩的脸蛋，一双顾盼含情的细长眼睛，在远山般弯曲的眉毛下，流动着美妙动人的波光。光洁平整的前额，使她的脸容显得高雅；微微张开的鼻翼和紧闭的小巧的嘴唇，又使她有一种果决的、桀骜不驯的神情。她生性耐冷，虽然正是春寒料峭的天气，也只穿了一身薄薄的暗花紫绒衣裙，越发见得轻盈俏丽。去冬以来，她一直都在闹病，举止之间，时时显出娇弱不胜的样子。

她不慌不忙地走到窗下的紫檀木书案前，拿起了那页诗笺，看见上面写着：

**献岁书怀二首**

香车帘阁思葱茏，旋喜新年乐事同。
兰叶俏将回淑气，柳条刚欲泛春风。
封题酒瓮拈重碧，嘱累花幡护小红。
几树官梅禁冷蕊，待君佳句发芳丛。

香残漏永梦依稀，网户疏窗待汝归。
四壁图书谁料理？满庭兰蕙欲芳菲。

A great beauty of twenty-five, she looked younger for her age, because she was petite with long glossy dark hair, which was thick and soft like satin, an oval, white, immaculate face, and a pair of affectionate narrow and long eyes, under whose arched brows flowed a sparkling river. The smooth and flat forehead gave her face a sense of elegance; the slightly open nose wings and the small, tightly closed lips gave her a determined and unruly look. Being cold-tolerant, she was only wearing a thin purple embossed velvet dress on this chilly spring day. That made her look all the more dainty and attractive, but having been ill since last winter she appeared weak and fragile.

She walked unhurriedly to the red sandalwood desk at the window and picked up the poetry sheets, which read:

**Two Lyric Poems Written in Celebration of the New Year**

*The world is exuberant with green life again.*
*Everyone is joyous, be they in the chariots, or in the curtained chambers.*
*With the coming of the new year*
*Quietly return the old fervour.*
*The orchids have regained their good energies.*
*The willows are brimming with spring breeze.*
*To the garden banner*
*A big jar of wine I proffer*
*With a note saying, would you please*
*Take good care of the little red buds on the plum trees?*
*If you ask, why don't they open now?*
*Without your magic lines, how can the cold stamens and pistils make their metamorphoses?*

*The incense is spent and the dream still lingers after a long long night.*
*In the house of carved doors and windows*
*I wait for your return.*
*Only you, and no one else, can look after the books on the shelves.*
*And the orchids can't wait to display themselves.*
*To the tune of the "Song of the Plum Blossom"*

梅花曲里催游骑，杨柳风前试夹衣。
传语雕笼好鹦鹉，莫随啁哳羡群飞。

诗后有一则附注：

辛巳冬，河东君赴姑苏疗疾，越岁未归，不胜蒹葭之思。诗以促之。越三日，谦益舣舟姑苏，迎返常熟。眷眷此情，耿耿是心，河东君当能察之也。

下署：谦益，崇祯十五年壬午元旦

柳如是的目光在最后几句附注上逗留着，终于哼了一声，把诗笺放在一边，随即在书案前坐了下来。她先歪着脑袋，对镜子端详一下自己的影子，特别仔细地察看了眼角和嘴边。直到证实这些地方依旧滑嫩光洁，并没有出现哪怕一丝皱纹，她才放下心来，伸出两根纤长的手指，在脸上的一小块枕衾压出来的嫣红痕迹上轻轻揉搓着，一边转动着脖颈，使自己的面影以各种不同的角度和表情，反映在镜子里。末了，她似乎被自己依然娇艳动人的风韵逗弄得快活起来，便把头一仰，对红情说：

“嗯，来吧！”

*The patrols on horseback charge forward.*
*In front of the breeze*
*The willows try on their new garments brightly colored.*
*My good parrot in the carved cage and genius in mimicking human words!*
*Don't lower yourself to chitter-chatter and fly with the flocking birds!*

At the end of the poems was a postscript, which read:

*Dedicated to my beloved Lady of River East as a reminder of my humble request for your kind return from Gusu City, where you went for medical treatment in the winter of the Year of Xinsi*①②*. Three days from now, I'll stop my boat at Gusu to welcome you back to Changshu. My fair lady, please understand how much I love you and how much I miss you.*

Signed and dated: *Qianyi, Day One of the fifteenth year of the reign of Emperor Chongzhen, the Year of Renwu*③

Liu Rushi's eyes settled on the last lines of the postscript, and then with a "humph" put the poetry sheets aside and sat down at the desk. Tilting her head, she looked herself in the mirror with special attention to the corners of her eyes and mouth until she was sure they were smooth, clean, and unblemished without a wrinkle; relieved, she stretched out two slender fingers and gently rubbed the reddish mark, an imprint of the bed on her face, while slowly shifting her neck so that her face was reflected in the mirror from various angles and with all kinds of expressions. In the end, apparently enlivened by her own charms that were as good as ever, she raised her head and said to Hongqing, "Hey, come over!"

---

① the Year of Xinsi: AD 1641

② People of the Ming dynasty did not use the Gregorian calendar, so they couldn't possible speak of a Chinese year as "AD 1641". Hence the square brackets. Where possible, conversions are made into the Gregorian calendar for the convenience of the reader.

③ Day One of the fifteenth year of the reign of Emperor Chongzhen, the Year of Renwu: January 30, 1642

红情起初听见女主人“哼”的一声，止不住心头一跳，捉摸不透是吉是凶，正有点惴惴不安。这会儿她连忙答应一声，把几上一只镶嵌着螺钿和玛瑙的梳妆匣子移过来，开始动手替女主人把睡乱了的发髻拆散，小心翼翼地把瀑布般倾泻下来的丰厚长发捧在怀里，然后拣起一把象牙大梳，梳理起来。她生怕把女主人扯痛了，下梳很轻，很慢，一边梳，一边笑着说：

“不是婢子又爱说嘴，夫人这头头发，真是越来越漂亮好看了，又黑、又密、又匀净。梳子下去，像到了水里似的，自自然然就顺溜了，半点儿劲也不费。婢子见的人也不少，可从来没见过夫人这样的好头发！”

说着，她偷眼觑了觑镜子，发现女主人半眯着眼睛，像在沉思，对她的恭维讨好似乎根本没有留意。红情于是揣摩刚才那一声冷笑，大约不是冲自己来的。她暗暗松了一口气，闭嘴不说了。

然而，当她打算移开眼睛，却忽然发现，女主人威严的目光，正从镜子里怀疑地盯着她。

“嗯，你做什么？”柳如是问。

红情的脸顿时涨红了，“没、没做什么呀！”她惊慌地说。

“刚才，你说什么来着？”

“刚才？哦，刚才婢子是说，夫人这头头发……好看……”于是，她把刚才的话，连忙又重述一遍。

柳如是默默地听着，脸色这才渐渐平和下来。可是只一忽儿，她又重新皱起眉毛。

“嗯，这也罢了。”她说，“我问你，我叫你去打听的事，你去了么？”

“啊，婢子已经打听回来了，正要向夫人禀告。”红情赶紧说道。

“怎么样？”

“听说朱姨太还在闹，今儿吃罢午饭，她就把少爷叫到后楼

When Hongqing heard her mistress's humph, at first her heart pounded, not knowing whether it was good or bad. "Yes, my lady!" she answered, and hurried to transport the dressing boxes inlaid with onyx and polished seashells from the bedside table to the desk; she untied the mistress's bun, which was messy from sleeping, and, cautiously holding the cascading thick long hair in her arms, picked up a large ivory comb to groom it. Afraid of hurting her mistress, she applied the comb softly and slowly, and as she combed her mistress's hair, she smiled and said, "I'm not flattering you. Your ladyship's hair is really getting more and more beautiful, more and more attractive. It's dark, dense, and smooth. When you use the comb, it travels down smoothly, as if it were flowing with water. I've seen a lot of ladies, but none with such good hair."

As she spoke, she glanced at the mirror and found that the mistress was half-squinting her eyes, as if in contemplation, totally oblivious to the flattery. Realizing that the sneer just now was probably not directed at her, she secretly breathed a sigh of relief and closed her mouth.

However, when she was about to remove her eyes, she suddenly found that her mistress's piercing eyes were staring suspiciously at her from the mirror.

"Hey, what did you do?" Liu Rushi asked.

Hongqing's face flushed suddenly. "Nothing," she said in a panic.

"Just now, what did you say?"

"Just now? Um, just now I said, your ladyship's hair is beautiful." She nervously repeated what she had just said.

Liu Rushi listened silently and her countenance gradually softened. But in a short while, she frowned again.

"Well, let it be," she said. "Let me ask you, did you go and inquire about the matter as I told you to?"

"Yes, I did, my lady. I asked about it and was just about to tell you," Hongqing said quickly.

"What was it like?"

"I heard that Lady Zhu is still fussing over it. After lunch, she

上去，又哭又叫的，骂了许多难听的话，还摔了好些家伙。”

“她都骂些什么？”

“这……婢子可就、可就不知道了。”

“哼！”柳如是眼睛一瞪，猛地回过头，却不提防带动了头发，慌得红情连忙跟着踉跄了一步。不过，当她重新站稳之后，柳如是已经把自己控制住了。她醒悟到，朱姨太骂她的话，其实不用问也可想而知是些什么内容，难怪红情不敢当她的面复述出来。

“那么，还有其他的人呢？他们怎么说？”她悻悻然问道。

红情惊魂初定，她生怕女主人责怪，不敢再隐讳，便把打听到的消息一五一十都禀报出来。她说，由于最近柳如是同三房朱姨太的争宠愈演愈烈，特别是前些日子，柳如是到姑苏“治病”期间，向老爷——前礼部右侍郎、现罢官在家的钱谦益——提出一定要把朱姨太驱逐出府之后，钱府上下，如今已经分成了两派。一派支持朱姨太，一派支持柳如是；此外，谁也不帮，站在一旁瞧热闹的也还不少。自然，老爷是一心护着柳如是的，老爷的那班子门客，以及府里那些同朱氏有仇怨的人也一样。不过由于朱姨太进府的日子长，人熟地熟，加上又是钱家唯一的少爷的生母，所以总的来说，眼下还是支持她的人居多。像大总管何思虞两口子、侄孙少爷钱曾、大丫环月容这些人，都是朱派。大太太陈氏，表面上不偏不倚，据说也是支持朱氏的。在她的影响下，陈家的那一伙亲戚，也都成了朱派。正因为有这些倚仗，朱姨太才敢扯破脸皮大吵大闹。此外，还有消息说，常熟城里那些同钱谦益一向有矛盾，而对钱谦益与柳如是的结合尤其不以为然的乡绅，如

summoned the young master to the back house. In front of him, she cried and screamed curses, and smashed everything she saw."

"What kind of curses?"

"That—I—I don't know."

"Humph!" said Liu Rushi, her eyes bulging with anger. She turned to Hongqing abruptly, without realizing her hair was moving with her head. Hongqing hurried to move with the hair. However, when Hongqing staggered to her feet, Liu Rushi had steadied herself. She could figure out what the curses were like without being told. Understandably, Hongqing dared not repeat them.

"Then, what about the others? What did they say?" she asked dejectedly.

Recomposing herself, Hongqing didn't dare to hide anything and reported every detail, afraid that otherwise her mistress might be angry. As the rivalry between Liu Rushi and Lady Zhu, concubine of Qian Qianyi, intensified, especially after Liu Rushi proposed during her "medical treatment" in Gusu that Qian Qianyi, ousted former Right Vice Minister of the Ministry of Rites, should banish Lady Zhu from the residence, the House of the Qians had now been divided into two camps, those supporting Lady Zhu and those supporting Liu Rushi; there were also quite a few who stood by and watched without taking sides. Naturally, his lordship was on the side of Liu Rushi, and so were his patronees and those who hated Lady Zhu. However, Lady Zhu had more supporters at the moment because she had been in the house for a long time and knew it inside out, and also because she was the birth mother of the only heir to the Qian family. People like chief steward Mr. He Siyu and his wife, Mr. Qian's grandnephew Qian Zeng, and Yuerong the head maid were all Zhu loyalists. Lady Chen, wife of Mr. Qian Qianyi, appeared unbiased and impartial on the surface but was in fact backing Lady Zhu behind the scenes. Under her influence, all the Chens were Zhu supporters. It was precisely because of these supporters that Lady Zhu dared to make big noises, disregarding any sense of decency. In addition, it was said that the squires in Changshu who had bad blood with Qian Qianyi and were especially disapproving

今都在盯着钱府内的这一场争斗，扬言倘若钱谦益敢驱逐朱氏，他们就要联名写状，声讨钱谦益伤风败俗，不顾廉耻，把他弄个名声扫地……

在红情这一次述说的当儿，柳如是始终静静地听着，再也没有打断她。不过，她仍然不止一次竖起了眉毛，瞪大了眼睛，脸蛋也一次一次因发怒而憋得通红。直到红情说完了好一会儿，她仍然咬着牙，现出恶狠狠的神色。

看见女主人这样子，红情又害怕起来。她十分清楚女主人脾气急躁，担心会迁怒自己，正想说上几句赔小心的话。然而，没等她说出口，柳如是已猛地站了起来。这一次，红情有了准备，等柳如是使劲夺回头发时，她就连忙松了手。

柳如是把头发紧紧攥在手里，开始像一只被困在笼子里的野兽似的，急速地走来走去，嘴里愤愤地问：

“那么老爷呢？老爷他怎么样？”

“哦，老爷，老爷……”

“算了！”红情讷讷的样子，愈加激起柳如是的怒火。她咬牙切齿地说，“什么‘眷眷此情，耿耿是心’，哼，说得好听！亏他还有脸写在纸上，巴巴地送来给我！也不打听打听，老娘是什么人，会信这一套！去——”她一把抓起案上那张诗笺，用力朝地下一摔，“把这破纸片儿给他退回去，就说本夫人不要！”

“是！”红情连忙答应，但是却迟疑着。

“去呀！”柳如是瞪大眼睛喝叫。

红情哆嗦了一下，不敢再违拗。她赶紧捡起诗笺，急急忙忙地向外走去。

红情穿过花木扶疏的庭院，刚走到月洞门前，却意外地发现钱孙爱少爷——一个十四岁的少年，不知为什么没有人跟随，正

of the union of Qian Qianyi with Liu Rushi were now keeping close watch over the battle in the house of the Qians. They had declared that if Qian Qianyi dared to expel Lady Zhu from the house, they would jointly write a statement to condemn his depravity and destroy his reputation altogether.

As Hongqing narrated the details, Liu Rushi listened quietly with no interruption but from time to time raised her brows, her eyes bulging and her face flushing with increasing anger. Long after Hongqing finished speaking, she was still gritting her teeth with indignation.

Seeing her mistress like that, Hongqing was scared again. Knowing full well that her mistress was short-tempered and worrying that the anger might be directed at her, she was going to offer a few words of comfort. Yet, before she said anything, Liu Rushi stood up abruptly. This time, Hongqing was prepared and quickly let go of the hair in her hands when Liu Rushi pulled it from her.

Liu Rushi clasped her hair tightly in her hands and began to pace the floor like a beast in a cage. She asked angrily, "Then, his lordship— what about his lordship?"

"Um, his lordship, his lordship—"

"Forget it!" Hongqing's stutter further infuriated Liu Rushi, who gritted her teeth and said, 'How much I love you and how much I miss you—, ' huh, what beautiful words! And he has the audacity to write it on paper and send it to me! He should have asked around to know that I'm not the kind of person to be fooled like that." She grabbed the poetry sheets on the desk, and threw them to the ground, saying, "Go and return the damned sheets of paper to him, and tell him that I don't need them."

"Aye, my lady!" Hongqing said, but her feet didn't move.

"Go!" Liu Rushi yelled with bulging eyes.

Hongqing shuddered with fear and dared not hesitate any longer. She quickly picked up the poetry sheets and hurried out.

The servant girl walked through the courtyard landscaped with flowers and trees to the door with a moon cutout, when suddenly she saw Qian Sun'ai, fourteen-year-old son of Qian Qianyi, who was peeping in

独自一人探头探脑地朝里张望。一见红情，他那焦急的脸上顿时现出获救的神情。

“哎，柳太太——起来了么？”他急匆匆地问。

这位钱孙爱少爷，是柳如是的对头朱姨太所生，也是钱家唯一的少爷。平日锦衣玉食，百般宝爱自不必说。按理，他应当长得又肥又壮；但是偏不，这位少爷自幼便羸弱多病，长大后，那张还算清秀的脸上，总是血气不足，一双肩膀又窄又小，身子还仿佛有点佝偻。不知为什么，每当瞧见他那又细又长的脖子上，支着一个晃晃悠悠的小脑袋，红情就忍不住想笑。不过，她此刻却没有这种心情。

“咦，少爷，你怎么还敢到这儿来？你不怕朱姨太知道？”红情站住脚，吃惊地问。她很清楚朱姨太对于儿子到我闻室来，是多么地深恶痛绝，更何况是眼前这种时候。

“你别管！”钱孙爱摇一摇头，“我只问你，柳太太起来没有？”

“嗯，你要见她？”

钱孙爱点一点头。

“干什么哩？”

“有事！”钱孙爱不耐烦地说。

要在往常，红情就替他通报了。可是今天她看见钱孙爱身边没有人跟着，胆子就大起来：

“先告诉我！”

“不！”

“那我不给你报！”红情傲然地把手中的诗笺一扬，“夫人派我去干事哩！”

“哎，别，你别……”看见红情要走，钱孙爱慌了，连忙拦

from the outside, unattended by anybody. At the sight of Hongqing, his anxious face suddenly had the expression of being rescued.

"Hey, is Lady Liu up?" he asked hurriedly.

This young master called Qian Sun'ai, born of Liu Rushi's rival Lady Zhu, was the only male heir to Mr. Qian Qianyi. Needless to say, he had the best clothes and the best food as a pampered child of his father. It would stand to reason if he were big and strong, but he was not; instead, this young master of the house had been weak and sickly since childhood. When he grew up, he had a nice face, but it was always in lack of blood; his shoulders were narrow, and he was a little hunchbacked too. For some mysterious reason, whenever she saw that small dangling head on a thin and long neck, Hongqing couldn't help but want to laugh. However, she didn't feel like laughing at the moment.

"Hey, young master, why do you dare to come here? Aren't you afraid that Lady Zhu will find out?" Hongqing stopped and asked in puzzlement. She knew very well how much Lady Zhu hated the young master's visits to the Wowen Chamber, particularly under the present circumstances.

"It's none of your business!" Qian Sun'ai shook his head and said. "I'm just asking you, is Lady Liu up?"

"Yes, she is. You want to see her?"

Qian Sun'ai nodded.

"What for?"

"Something," Qian Sun'ai said impatiently.

Previously, every time he came, Hongqing would go in to report his coming, but today, seeing Qian Sun'ai was unaccompanied, she was emboldened.

"Tell me first," she said.

"No, I won't."

"Then I won't report your coming to her ladyship," said Hongqing. She waved the poetry sheets in the air proudly. "Her ladyship has a job for me."

"Don't go, please don't —" said the boy. Seeing Hongqing was about to leave, Qian Sun'ai hurriedly reached out to stop her. Then he

住她，随即低下头去，犹疑了一阵，终于低声说：

“我、我想求她，别、别把我娘赶出去……”

红情本来已经摆出一副捉弄人的样子，听了这话，神情顿时变了。她怔怔地瞅着钱孙爱，半天，轻轻地叹一口气，说：“只怕、只怕她不会答应。”

“啊，为什么？”

红情动了动嘴巴，但临时又改变了主意。“好吧，我替你去报！”她说，转身向里走去。

钱孙爱呆呆地目送着，渐渐又变得紧张起来。他大瞪着眼睛，脸色也更加苍白；随后，就开始神经质地来回走动……

好大一会儿，从那间垂着梅花暖帘的闺房里传出了柳如是可怕的吼声：

“不见，不见！谁也不见，让他滚！”

钱孙爱浑身一抖，像一只受惊的兔子似的呆住了。他那双圆溜溜的眼睛渐渐现出一种恐惧的神色。突然，他抱着脑袋，逃也似的跑了开去。

## 书房训子

钱孙爱急急忙忙地走着，出了东偏院的门，向左一拐，走进备弄里来。直到我闻室那边的声响完全听不见了，他才如释重负，舒了一口气，放慢脚步。

长长的备弄从后楼一直伸向前门，两边都是高出屋脊的黑瓦白粉墙，把宅第的正院同右边的一爿院落分隔开来。墙上每隔几步就有一个漏窗，漏窗外，正院的高堂华屋和左院的亭轩花树历历可见。这宅子又大又深，尽管住着老幼尊卑数十口人，仍旧十分幽静。特别是这条备弄，主要是供夜间巡逻和防火用的，白天

lowered his head, and after a moment of hesitation, said in a low voice:

"I—I want to beg her not—not to drive my mother out—"

Hongqing, who was going to tease him, suddenly became serious. She stared at Qian Sun'ai expressionlessly, and after a long while, heaved a soft sigh. "I'm afraid, I'm afraid she won't agree," she said.

"Aah, why?"

Hongqing moved her mouth, but instantly changed her mind. She said, "All right, I'll report your coming." Then she turned and walked rapidly to the Wowen Chamber.

Qian Sun'ai watched blankly as she went in and became increasingly apprehensive, his eyes wide open and his face even paler than before. Then, he started to pace back and forth restlessly.

A long while later, from inside the boudoir draped with a plum-blossom thermal curtain came Liu Rushi's terrible roar:

"No, no way! I won't see anybody at all. Let him get out of here!"

Qian Sun'ai gave a shudder and stood still like a frightened rabbit. A look of fear crept into his big round eyes. Suddenly, he took flight with his head in his hands.

## Great Expectations of a Father

Qian Sun'ai quickly exited the east sideyard, turned left, and walked into the narrow lane. It was not until the sound from the Wowen Chamber completely disappeared that he was relieved and slowed down his footsteps.

The long narrow lane, stretching out from the back house to the front door, flanked on both sides by white walls capped by black tiles and rising above the ridge of the roofs, separated the main courtyard of the residence from the sideyard on the right. Every few steps along the way there was a transparent window. Through the transparent windows one could clearly see the grand houses of the main courtyard as well as the pavilions, houses, flowers, and trees in the left sideyard. Though there were dozens of people living in it, this big and deep mansion was quiet, especially in this narrow lane, which was mainly used for night patrol and fire protection and seldom visited during the day. At the moment,

走的人本来就不多，这会儿更是连个人影也看不见。钱孙爱听着自己的足音在青石板上橐橐地回响着，不由得害怕起来。他赶快从最近的那个侧门往里一钻，回到正院里头。

刚才在我闻室所受的惊吓，一直不曾消失，而且愈来愈变得像一团破布似的堵塞在心头。这使钱孙爱感到伤心、困惑，摆脱不开。说实在话，这一次，他虽然是为朱氏求情而来，而作为生母，朱氏对儿子也一向极其钟爱，百般纵容，但奇怪的是，他对朱姨太却始终缺乏亲近之感。而且，朱姨太越是把他当成心头肉、掌上珠，她在儿子心目中的地位反而越低。特别是当钱孙爱逐渐懂事之后，朱氏的专横、鄙俗、愚蠢和唠叨，都叫他感到受不了。仅仅由于纲常礼教的训诲和约束，才使他从理智上觉得应当尊敬她、维护她，站在她的一边。

诚然，钱孙爱还有另外一位看着他长大的女人，那就是大太太陈夫人。陈氏对于钱家的这位唯一的少爷，自然也十分疼爱。按照钱氏的家规，陈夫人才是钱孙爱名正言顺的“母亲”。不过，这位老太太是个秉性懦弱的女人。她过去受二房的王姨太欺负，王姨太被朱姨太逼回娘家之后，她又受朱姨太的欺负。无可奈何之余，陈夫人迷信上了佛法，一心一意地埋头诵经、吃素，还招了一个名叫解空的老尼姑来家里住着，一天到晚讲经参禅，对家里的事情不闻不问，同钱孙爱也慢慢疏远了。今年元旦过后，陈夫人知道钱谦益到苏州去把柳如是接回常熟来，她就领着解空回娘家去，说是打算在那边多住些日子——已经走了好几天了。

如果说对这两位母亲，钱孙爱都缺乏强烈的亲近感的话，那么，他对于住在我闻室的这一位“母亲”柳如是，却怀有一种莫

there was no single soul in sight. Hearing his footsteps reverberating on the bluestone slabs, Qian Sun'ai quivered with fear, so he quickly veered through the nearest side door and returned to the main courtyard.

The fright from the Wowen Chamber stayed with him like a rag clogging his heart. Qian Sun'ai felt sad, confused, and helpless. Curiously, although he came here to plead for Lady Zhu, who, as his birth mother, loved and pampered him with a passion, he had never felt a close affinity with her. In fact, the more Lady Zhu regarded him as the flesh of her heart and the jewel in her palm, the lower her status in her son's mind. As he grew older and began to understand things, her bossiness, vulgarity, stupidity, and nagging became increasingly unbearable. Bound by the Confucian teachings of filial piety and moral propriety, however, he felt obliged to respect, protect and standby her.

Indeed, Qian Sun'ai had another mother, who had participated in his upbringing, and that was Lady Chen, First Lady of the house, who naturally was also very indulgent of the only young male heir to the Qian family. By the Qian family tradition, Lady Chen was Qian Sun'ai's legitimate mother. However, this old lady was born a meek woman. She was first a bullying victim of concubine Lady Wang, Second Lady of the house, then fell victim to Lady Zhu's bullying after Lady Wang was forced to return to her natal home by Lady Zhu. In desperation, Lady Chen turned to the Buddhist faith and wholeheartedly followed the practice of sutra-chanting and eating vegetarian. She even went so far as to invite an old nun named Xiekong to live with her. The two women were so absorbed in the sutras and meditation sessions that Lady Chen paid no attention to anything in the house. Naturally, she gradually alienated herself from Qian Sun'ai. After New Year's Day, having learned that Qian Qianyi had gone to Suzhou to bring Liu Rushi back to Changshu, Lady Chen went back to her natal home with Xiekong, saying that she planned to stay there for a long time, and it had been quite a few days since.

If Qian Sun'ai lacked a strong sense of affinity with these two mothers, he had an inexplicable liking for Liu Rushi, the "mother" who lived in the Wowen Chamber. Although Liu Rushi ruthlessly

名其妙的好感。尽管柳如是蛮横地要把朱姨太赶出府去，刚才又是那样粗暴地对待他，但是钱孙爱仍然感到对她恨不起来，这一点使他十分苦恼。这位柳如是，听说本是苏州府盛泽镇一位很有名的妓女，半年前，才由他的父亲把她娶回家里来。钱孙爱清楚记得，当他第一次看见这位新母亲时，她的年轻，她的美丽，她笑眯眯地瞧着他时那种又高傲又挖苦的神情，都叫他害臊得不得了，以至赶忙低下头去，不敢再看她。几天之后，他在好奇心的驱使之下，到东偏院那一幢小小的、特地为柳如是新盖的我闻室去，想再看一看这位美丽而又神秘的女人。柳如是仍旧用那种又高傲又挖苦的神气瞅他，还不客气地说他像个小痨病鬼。可是，当钱孙爱又害臊又生气，打算立即逃出去时，柳如是却笑眯眯地捉住他的手，态度又变得十分亲昵，并把他留下来玩耍。在随后的一个多月里，钱孙爱在柳如是那儿学会了许许多多有趣的玩意儿——射覆啦，投壶啦，猜枚啦，掷骰子啦，唱小曲啦，用墨把脸抹黑跳胡旋舞啦，钱孙爱又惊又喜，越玩越着迷。从此，只要父亲不在家，他就跑到我闻室去，缠着柳如是玩这玩那。由于笨拙和怯懦，他常常遭到柳如是的嘲骂和捉弄，还挨过她打。但是，钱孙爱毫不怨恨，他怕的是柳如是不理睬他，把他赶出去，不准他再来。事实上，很快地，钱孙爱就被禁止到我闻室去了。不过并不是柳如是这样做，而是他的亲娘朱姨太。当朱姨太发现她的宝贝儿子竟然也被那骚狐狸“迷”上了，登时又惊又气。她立即率领仆婢气势汹汹地赶到我闻室，把钱孙爱“抢”了出来，还同柳如是大吵大闹了一场。不用说，自从那一次之后，钱孙爱的快活日子便宣告结束了。

钱孙爱叹了一口气，他弄不明白，在他看来应当和睦相处的

tried to drive Lady Zhu out of the mansion and treated him so rudely just now, Qian Sun'ai felt he was unable to hate her. That feeling troubled him. The woman called Liu Rushi was said to have been a well-known prostitute from Shengze Town, Suzhou Prefecture. She had been married to his father six months ago. When he first saw this new mother, he was captivated by her youth, beauty, and the arrogant and sarcastic expression in her smiles; he blushed and hurriedly lowered his head when she looked at him. A few days later, driven by curiosity, he went to the small house in the sideyard on the east wing specially built for Liu Rushi to see this beautiful and mysterious new mother. Liu Rushi still regarded him with that kind of arrogant and sarcastic expression, and said ungraciously that he was like a little tuberculosis patient. However, when Qian Sun'ai was about to flee in embarrassment and disappointment, Liu Rushi grabbed his hand with a genial smile and asked him to stay and play with her. In the following month or so, Qian Sun'ai learned a lot of interesting things from Liu Rushi—guess-what-it-is, hit-into-the-decanter, guess-my-hand, throwing dice, singing ditties, the barbarian spinning dance with an ink-smeared face, et cetera, et cetera. Qian Sun'ai was overwhelmed with surprise and joy, and the more he played, the more fascinated he was. From then on, as long as his father was not at home, he would run to the Wowen Chamber and begged Liu Rushi to play these games with him. Because of his clumsiness and timidity, he was often mocked and teased by Liu Rushi, and even beaten by her. However, Qian Sun'ai bore no grudge against her, afraid that she would stop playing with him, drive him out, and forbid him to come again. In fact, soon afterwards Qian Sun'ai was banned from coming to the Wowen Chamber, not by Liu Rushi, but by his birth mother Lady Zhu. When Lady Zhu discovered that her own son was enchanted with the skanky, lecherous fox spirit, she was shocked and infuriated, so she immediately descended on the Wowen Chamber with her men and women servants and snatched Qian Sun'ai away, after a big row, of course. Needless to say, that was the end of Qian Sun'ai's fun days.

Qian Sun'ai sighed. He didn't understand why these two women

这两个女人，何以竟会变得像仇人冤家似的势不两立，一天到晚争吵不休，恨不得把对方一口吞下去。如果不是这样，该有多好！不过，他明白这是不可能的。他从朱姨太的口中知道，柳如是现在正千方百计要把他亲娘挤出去，她已经向父亲声言，要是朱氏不走，她宁可重回盛泽！钱孙爱为这事忧心忡忡，焦虑不已。刚才他摆脱了身边的跟随，私下去求见柳如是，谁知却碰了一鼻子灰！钱孙爱觉得，凭着朱氏是自己的生母这一点，父亲最终大概不会把她驱逐出府，也不会放柳如是走；但是指望这两个女人和好起来，只怕是比登天还难了。

钱孙爱感到了一种悲哀，如同被人遗弃了似的，没有一个人关心他、明白他。他心头一酸，几乎掉下泪来。他停住脚步，站在悬着“半野堂”横匾的大厅前，瞅着屋檐上啁啾营巢的一双燕子，怔了半天，终于没精打采地折回来，朝西偏院走去。

通往西院的门影里，坐着几个上了年纪的妇人，她们是些看守门户的女仆，也有个把寄食的穷亲戚。她们闲日没事，照例坐到这地方来，一边摆弄着手里的活计，一边嘁嘁喳喳地起劲谈论着什么。看见钱孙爱走来，这伙人都一齐住了口，纷纷站起，向小主人亲热地问好。钱孙爱心里正烦恼，低着头只管走过去。

钱孙爱一踏进西院，就听见有人叫他。抬头一看，原来钱谦益的贴身仆人李宝，还有自己的书童张卉儿正沿着复廊急急地朝他走过来。

“少爷，你上哪儿去了？找得小人好苦——老爷叫你去呢！”李宝一边说，一边站住行礼。

听说父亲传唤，钱孙爱有点意外。不过他也懒得打听，点点头，一声不响地跟着李宝走。

who should live in harmony became enemies and bickered all day long, ready to eat each other alive with one gulp. How beautiful it would be if it weren't like that! However, he soon knew it was not possible for them to live at peace. He learned from Lady Zhu that Liu Rushi, having sworn to his father that she would return to Shengze if Lady Zhu didn't leave the house, was now doing everything possible to push his mother out of the house. This matter greatly worried him. So, just now he got rid of his servant to see Liu Rushi in private. Yet to his disappointment, all he got was such a rebuff. He felt that his father would neither banish his birth mother from the home nor let his new mother go, but he also knew that to let the two women reconcile with each other would be as hopeless as to climb to the sky.

He was gripped by a sadness as if he had been abandoned by all the others, none of whom had ever cared about or understood him. His heart broke, tears rolling in his eyes. He stopped and stood in front of the main house where hanged a horizontal plaque which said Half Wild Estate. He looked blankly at the pair of swallows chirping in the nest on the eaves for a long time before he finally turned back and walked listlessly towards the west sideyard.

In the doorway of the west sideyard sat a few elderly women, who were either housemaids or poor relatives seeking food and shelter. Not having much to do, they gathered and sat here as usual, fiddling with something in their hands while chatting vigorously about something. Seeing Qian Sun'ai coming, the bunch of old women stopped talking, stood up one after another, and greeted the little master affectionately. Qian Sun'ai ignored them and continued his entry with a drooping head.

When he stepped into the west sideyard, he heard someone calling him. He looked up and it was his father's body servant Li Bao and his own page boy Zhang Huier walking hurriedly towards him along the sidewalk of the corridor.

"My young master, where have you been? I've been looking for you for ages. His lordship wants to talk to you," said Li Bao with a bow.

Hearing his father summoned him, he was surprised but didn't ask why. He simply nodded his head and silently followed Li Bao.

当钱孙爱登上荣木楼的二楼，来到他父亲的书房——匪斋里的时候，钱谦益正低着头，在看一封信。他用威严的鼻音“唔、唔”地答应着儿子的问安，随手指一指靠窗的几张花梨木椅子，让他坐下，眼睛始终没有离开手里的信件。

这是钱谦益的妻舅陈在竹从京师带回来的一封信。信的内容是如此重要，如此令钱谦益错愕为难，以至他已经反复看过四遍，仍旧拿不定主意该怎么办。这会儿他又仔细地从头再看一遍。

信是一位正在朝廷做官的朋友写来的。一个多月前，钱谦益派陈在竹带了七千两银子到北京活动，希望能获得复官起用的机会。陈在竹找到这位朋友，承他帮忙，与内阁首辅周延儒搭上了线。陈在竹把银子花了个干干净净，最后就带回来这样一封信。

在明朝后期，人们写信的习惯，除了一份正文之外，还有所谓“副启”。副启是一种不具名的信，用以请托办事或谈机密事宜。本来只通行于官场，后来就成为一种繁文缛节，不管有没有特别的话要说，一律都要有副启，否则就会被认为不恭、不厚，副启甚至有多至三四封的。现在钱谦益手里的这封信，也有三封副启。不过，这一次倒不是那位做官的朋友故意多礼，而是因为他要谈的事情确实涉及许多机密，不可告人，也不便署名的缘故。

信的正文照例是些寒温起居的客套话，钱谦益也懒得再看。他拿起了第一份副启。

这上面的内容，谈的是关于明王朝当时抵御“建虏”——山海关外清兵的进攻，以及对“流寇”——李自成、张献忠等部的

When he climbed to the Fei Chamber, his father's study on the second floor of the Hibiscus House, the old man was bending his head reading an epistle. Qian Qianyi answered his son's greeting with a stern nasal sound—um, um—and pointed his finger at a rosewood chair by the window to mean "sit" while his eyes never left the epistle in his hand.

This is an epistle brought back from the capital by Qian Qianyi's brother-in-law Chen Zaizhu. The message in the epistle was of such great weight that the old man was obviously astounded and puzzled; he was at a loss as to what to do, having read it four times. At this moment, he was reading it for fifth time.

The epistle was written by a friend who was an official in the imperial court. A month ago, Qian Qianyi sent Chen Zaizhu to pull the strings in Beijing with seven thousand taels of silver, hoping to get the opportunity to be reinstated to office. Chen Zaizhu found this friend and through him connected with Zhou Yanru, the Prime Minister. Chen Zaizhu spent all the money and finally brought back such an epistle.

In the late Ming dynasty, an epistle often carried side letters. A side letter is in fact an unsigned letter to ask for a favor or send a private message. Originally only used in official circles, it gradually developed into a kind of red tape. Whether there was a special message to convey or not, the side letter became a must, otherwise it would be regarded as ungracious and disrespectful, and sometimes an epistle might carry as many as three or four side letters. The one in Qian Qianyi's hands now had three side letters. However, this time around, it was not that the powerful friend was being polite, but that the things he was going to say did involve a lot of secrets not to be told to anybody and it was simply inconvenient for him to affix his signature.

As usual, the epistle itself was merely a ritual with inquiries about the weather, how things were, and so on and so forth, and Qian Qianyi didn't bother to give it another reading. He picked up the first side letter.

It was an update on the Ming court's defense against the barbarians from Jianzhou—the Qing soldiers north of the Shanhai Pass—and the guerrilla bandits—the peasant rebels led by Li Zicheng and Zhang Xianzhong. In a nutshell, it said, Jinzhou, an important

农民起义军作战的一些最新消息。大意是说：自从山海关外的门户重镇锦州遭到清军的大举围攻，朝廷派蓟辽总督洪承畴率八总兵步骑十三万出关拒敌，于松山至查山一线大败，几乎全军覆没以来，洪承畴率残兵万余退守松山城内，被清军重重围困已达三月有余，形势日见危殆。现在唯一的希望是前往救援的军队能够尽快突破重围。否则松山一失，锦州亦势难支撑，如果锦州也落入清军之手，那么山海关的形势就岌岌可危了。

钱谦益看到这里，不由得冷笑一声，心里说道："做梦！"驰援的军队开赴松山已有一两个月，他们的将领徘徊不前、畏敌如虎的情况，钱谦益屡有所闻。如果真能突破重围，也不会拖到今天了。他算定松山的陷落只不过是早晚的事。于是，他不由得大为感慨地想起，早在两个月前，他曾经上书当道，建议从援军当中分出一半兵力，乘船从海路分进合击，形势就会不同。可惜竟不能用！

信中接下去谈到南方流寇日益猖獗，朝廷自去年督师杨嗣昌畏罪自杀，总督傅宗龙战死，剿寇军事一再受挫。继福王、襄王死难之后，唐王也于南阳殉国。李自成连陷许州、禹州等十余城，再度进围开封。幸而最近朝廷重新起用孙传庭为兵部侍郎，令他

gateway town outside Shanhai Pass, had come under siege by the Qing army. The imperial court had sent Jiliao governor Hong Chengchou to resist the enemy north of the Shanhai Pass with one hundred and thirty thousand troops on foot and horseback, but unfortunately, the troops had been defeated and almost wiped out on the front line between Songshan and Chashan. Hong Chengchou and the ten thousand plus survivors had retreated to inside Songshan City, which since then had been besieged by the Qing invaders for more than three months, and the situation was increasingly dangerous. The only hope now was that the troops going to their rescue could possibly break through the siege as soon as possible. Otherwise, if Songshan was lost, Jinzhou would hardly hold out long. If Jinzhou also fell into the hands of the Qing troops, then the Shanhai Pass would be precarious.

Qian Qianyi couldn't help but sneer when he saw this, and said in his heart, "In your dreams!" The reinforcements had been dispatched to Songshan one or two months ago, but Qian Qianyi had heard their commanders were dragging their feet for fear of the enemy. If they had been able to break through the siege, they would not have delayed it to this day. Thinking that the fall of Songshan was only a matter of time, he couldn't help but recall with a huge sigh that, as early as two months ago, he had petitioned to those in power that the reinforcement troops should be sent by boat to launch an amphibious offensive. If his advice had been taken, the situation would have been very different. It was a pity that it hadn't been adopted.

The letter went on to talk about the increasing activity of the guerrilla rebels in the south. Since the suicide of Commander Yang Sichang in fear of punishment and death of Governor Fu Zonglong in battle, the military offensives against the rebels had met with further setbacks. Following the deaths of the Prince of Fu and the Prince of Xiang, the Prince of Tang was martyred in Nanyang. Li Zicheng, after successively capturing more than ten cities, including Xuzhou and Yuzhou, went on to lay siege to Kaifeng. Fortunately, the imperial court recently reinstated Sun Chuanting as Vice Minister of the Ministry of War and decreed that he should lead the capital army to reinforce

督京师军驰援开封，保定总督杨文岳亦发兵会剿，闯贼大败，死伤过半，现已溃散南窜，相信不日可望剿平云云。

钱谦益又不禁摇摇头，他根本不相信李自成会很快被“剿平”。据他所得的消息，李自成主动解围后，已南克襄城，复攻西华，正包围左良玉于郾城。想到这些在朝大臣，竟然如此盲目乐观，轻信前方送去的虚假捷报，钱谦益不禁又好气又好笑。他丢下这份副启，拿起下面一封。

这一封写得比较简略，主要是说，自从周延儒重新进入内阁，当上首辅之后，颇思振作有为，举措处事，能够顺从众意，对于东林党旧人，也想捐弃前嫌，倾心相结。现在他位高权重，很受皇上信用。

信到此便终止了，但友人的用意不难理解。他是在暗示钱谦益，现在确实存在着一个机会，而成败的关键则操在周延儒的手中。钱谦益如果想获得重新起用，对于这位周相公的要求是不能不认真加以考虑的。不过，钱谦益却明白，周延儒现在之所以愿意捐弃前嫌，并非由于此公有什么恢宏大度，实在是由于他的这一次东山再起，全赖朝廷中东林、复社一派的人，暗中给他帮了忙、出了力的缘故。

第三封副启，钱谦益看过的次数最多，也看得最仔细。他不必再看，信中的字句也还记得清清楚楚。

在这封副启中，友人代周延儒向钱谦益提出一项政治交易——周延儒愿意在钱谦益复官起用的事情上帮忙；不过，作为

Kaifeng. Meanwhile, governor of Baoding Yang Wenyue also sent his troops to crack down on the outlaws. As a result, the rebels led by Li Zicheng, the self-proclaimed King Charger, were defeated, with more than half of them killed or injured. The remnants scattered and went south. They were expected to be completely wiped out in no time ...

Qian Qianyi couldn't help but shake his head, not believing that Li Zicheng was something to be wiped out any time soon. According to the information he had received, after giving up the siege, Li Zicheng went south and captured Xiangcheng and Xihua and at the moment was surrounding Zuo Liangyu at Yancheng. Thinking of the blind optimism of these ministers in court credulously believing the false positives sent from the front, Qian Qianyi couldn't help being angry and amused at the same time. He dropped the side letter and picked up the next one.

This one was relatively brief, to the effect that since Zhou Yanru re-entered the Cabinet and became Prime Minister, he had been very eager to do something great, to the satisfaction of all, and for that end, he was ready to make up with former comrades in the East Wood Party. Now, he had a high position and was the emperor's trusted man.

The side letter ended abruptly, but the intention of the friend was manifest. He was implying to Qian Qianyi that there was indeed an opportunity at the moment and that the key to success lay in Zhou Yanru's hands. If Qian Qianyi wanted to be reinstated to office, he should seriously consider Mr. Zhou's condition. In Qian Qianyi's eyes, however, Zhou Yanru was now willing to give up his old grudges not because of magnanimity, but because his political comeback this time indeed had been the result of secret joint efforts of members of the East Wood Party and the Fushe (Restoration Society).

Having read the third side letter more times than the other ones and more carefully, Qian Qianyi didn't need to have another look. He remembered every word of it.

In this one, the friend proposed a political deal on behalf of Zhou Yanru to the effect that Zhou Yanru would help Qian Qianyi get reinstated to office and that in return, Qian Qianyi should use his

回报，钱谦益必须设法运用自己在东林党人和复社成员当中的强大影响，停止对一个名叫阮大铖的人的激烈攻击，并且不再在政治上与之为难。信的最后几句是这样写的：

> 阮圆海虽名在逆案，第念彼尚无大过。今闻复社诸生，日夕汹汹，必欲置之死地而后快。圆海惶惶不可终日，情殊可悯。语云：君子不念旧恶。足下又何惜反掌之易，不放彼一线生路耶？

信中的这个“圆海”，就是阮大铖的别号。此人在天启皇帝朱由校在位时，做过光禄寺丞，因为阿附大宦官魏忠贤的“阉党”，参与迫害反对宦官专政、主张开明政治的东林党人。所以到了崇祯皇帝朱由检即位，严厉究治魏忠贤，阉党之徒纷纷遭到斥逐，阮大铖也名列“逆案”，被革去官职，灰溜溜地跑回家乡怀宁。后来家乡闹农民暴动，安身不住，他只好又跑到当时称为“留都”的南京去当寓公。可是此人不甘寂寞，仗着有的是钱，在南京库司坊内建了一座雕梁画栋的“石巢园”，天天在那里大摆筵席，轻歌艳舞，招揽宾客，还组织了一个名叫“中江社”的小集团。他眼见明王朝内忧外患日益严重，急需懂得军事的人才支撑危局，于是也装模作样地说剑谈兵，吹得天花乱坠，希图博得“知兵”的名声，东山再起。没料到这一来，可就激怒了聚集在南京城里的一批“复社”的士人。

复社是继东林党之后出现的又一个江南士大夫以文会友的团体，成立于崇祯五年，由太仓人张溥、张采合并江南若干文社组

great influence among members of the East Wood Party and the Fushe to stop their fierce attacks on a man named Ruan Dacheng and all political hostility toward him. The side letter ended with:

*Although Ruan Yuanhai is listed as a treasonist, I know he's committed only a minor offense. Now, I hear that some members of the Fushe are vehemently pressing for his death day and night before being satisfied. Yuanhai is worried for his life. The Analects says: "A man of noble character harbors no old grudges." Why not use the influence in the palm of your hand to spare his life while it is such an easy thing to do?*

The Yuanhai in the letter is the literary name of Ruan Dacheng, who was a secretary of the Department of Ceremonies during the reign of Zhu Youxiao, the Tianqi Emperor, and in order to court favor with Eunuch Wei Zhongxian participated in the persecution of East Wood members who opposed the castrate's dictatorship and advocated liberal politics. So, when Zhu Youjian, the Chongzhen Emperor, came to the throne, Wei Zhongxian was severely punished, and his followers were banished one after another. Ruan Dacheng, listed as a treasonist and ousted from office, ingloriously ran back to his home in Huaining. Later, a peasant uprising took place in his hometown. Unable to stay there, he had to go to Nanjing, referred to as the Legacy Capital at the time, to live as an exile. But this guy simply would not be reconciled to loneliness. Having enough money to spend, he built the Stone Nest Garden in Kusifang. Under the carved beams and amid the painted pillars he banqueted every day with music and dancing performances, and even organized a clique called the MidRiver Society. Seeing the Great Ming, faced with increasing challenges from within and dangers from without, was in urgent need of military talents to cope with the crisis, he started to talk about war to build a reputation as a war strategist so that he would see a political comeback one day. That unexpectedly drew the fury of members of the Fushe in Nanjing.

The Fushe was founded in AD 1632, the fifth year of the reign of Emperor Chongzhen, a new literary society of the gentry scholars

成。复社名义上是“兴复古学，将使异日者务为有用”，实际上是继承东林党的开放言路、改良政治的主张。复社中的不少骨干成员，就是东林党人的子弟，他们与东林党人士互相呼应，在江南一带造成了极大的政治势力。这些人气愤不过阮大铖的嚣张放肆，曾在崇祯十一年，由顾杲、吴应箕、陈贞慧、黄宗羲等一百四十人联名起草了一份《留都防乱公揭》，历数阮大铖的罪状，揭露其阴谋野心，满城张贴分派，鸣鼓而攻，弄得阮大铖在南京安身不住，只好逃到郊外的牛首山下躲起来。但他仍然不甘心，这一次，瞅准周延儒再度入阁拜相，花费应酬甚多，他一家伙就送了一万两银子。周老头儿受了这一份厚礼，当然不能不有所报答，于是也乘着钱谦益有求于他，提出了这样一桩政治交易。

钱谦益慢慢地把信叠整齐、折好，重新装回封套里。以他的老于官场世故，对于这一类的弄权纳贿、私相授受的勾当，早已熟悉得很，所以并不特别吃惊。不过，他仍然感到有点气愤：周老头儿这一次重新上台，明明是靠的东林的力量，谁知他却不知感恩，仍然向自己提出这样狠辣的条件。钱谦益深知此事非同小可，虽说他现在是东林党仅存的几个领袖之一，在士林中享有很高的声望，但是阮大铖是东林公敌、逆案罪人，要复社那一班士子放弃对他的攻击，让他能够东山再起，真是谈何容易！弄不好，

in the River South region after the advent of the East Wood Party as a combination of multiple literary societies in the region, effected by Zhang Pu and Zhang Cai of Taicang City. The Fushe was in name to "learn from the past for future use" but it actually inherited the East Wood propositions of open speech and better government. Many of the key members of the Fushe were sons of East Wood members; they echoed the East Wooders to create a great political presence in the River South area. Infuriated with Ruan Dacheng's presumptuousness and impudicity, these men issued a joint statement called "Public Denunciation of a Treasonist in the Legacy Capital" in AD 1638, the eleventh year of the reign of Emperor Chongzhen, signed by one hundred and forty of them, including Gu Gao, Wu Yingji, Chen Zhenhui, Huang Zongxi, among others, citing Ruan Dacheng's crimes and exposing his evil intentions; this document was posted and distributed all over the city causing a big stir. Consequently, Ruan Dacheng was unable to live in Nanjing anymore, so he had to go into hiding at the foot of the Cow Head Mountain in the suburbs. Yet, Ruan Dacheng was still not reconciled to his fate. Seeing Zhou Yanru once again entered the Cabinet—this time as Prime Minister—and needed money to build connections, he immediately donated ten thousand taels of silver without hesitation. Having received such a generous donation, Old Man Zhou of course felt obliged to repay Ruan Dacheng, so he took the opportunity to propose a political deal when Qian Qianyi sought help from him.

Qian Qianyi slowly tidied the pages, folded them, and put them back in the envelope. Having been in politics long enough, he was rather familiar with this kind of power-for-gain game, so he was not particularly alarmed. However, he still felt a little angry. Old Man Zhou had come back to power this time through the influence of the East Wooders, but instead of showing gratitude he was making such an unreasonable demand. Qian Qianyi understood it was no trivial matter. Though he was one of the remaining few East Wood leaders much revered by the gentry scholars, it was by no means easy to persuade the Fushers to stop attacking Ruan Dacheng and help with

自己就有可能身败名裂，连老本都会赔个精光。想到这里，钱谦益不禁烦躁起来。他站起身，背负着手，开始在屋里来回走动。

钱谦益是个瘦高个儿，黝黑的脸膛，高耸的鼻梁，一部威仪凛凛的花白胡子。他去年刚做过六十大寿，头发是全白了，而且左耳背得厉害，听人说话时，总是侧起脑袋。不过，他身子骨还相当硬朗，一双细眯眼睛也尖利有神。头戴方巾，脚下珠履，大概是为着显得年轻些，他穿了一身藕色莽绒阳明衣。

钱谦益在室中来回踱了一阵，突然站定，用洪亮的嗓门喊道：

“来人！”

仆人李宝应声出现在门口。

“你去，马上把陈在竹、钱养先两位老爷给我请来。”

“是！老爷。”因为怕主人听不清，李宝大声答应着，然后将一叠拜帖呈了上来。

钱谦益翻了翻，一共有五六份之多，看名字都不认识，估计是些慕名进谒的士子，便说道：“我知道了。这会儿没工夫见他们，帖子留下，告诉他们过些日子再来吧。”

李宝答应了，又大声说：“工部严老爷从姑苏来，说是专程来拜望老爷，现住在馆驿里，刚才派人来打听老爷什么时候得空，严老爷要亲自趋府拜候。”他不等钱谦益发问，又补充说：“严老爷的拜帖刚才也呈给老爷了。”

钱谦益倒没留意有这样一份拜帖。他把那叠帖子重新翻了翻，果然找到了。他轻轻摇着拜帖，沉吟了一下，说道：“你告诉来人回禀严老爷，就说不敢有劳严老爷车驾，明早我亲自上馆驿拜

his reinstatement to office, because Ruan Dacheng was a treasonist and public enemy to the East Wooders. There was the risk that his reputation would be ruined and he would lose everything. Thinking of that, Qian Qianyi became ill at ease. He stood up, and, with his hands on his back, began to pace the room.

Qian Qianyi was a tall and thin man with a dark face, a high nose, and a majestic gray beard, who had just celebrated his sixtieth birthday the previous year. His hair had completely grayed, and his hearing in the left ear was so poor that he always tilted his head when listening to people. However, his bones were still quite strong, and his squinting eyes were animated and sharp. He wore a square headscarf on his head and a pair of beaded shoes on his feet, and probably to look younger, a lotus-colored velvet *yangming* robe.

Qian Qianyi paced back and forth in the room for a while, then suddenly stood still and shouted at the top of his voice,

"Someone come in!"

His servant Li Bao appeared at the door in no time.

"Go, go get Mr. Chen Zaizhu and Mr. Qian Yangxian immediately."

"Aye, my lord," Li Bao said in a loud voice so that his master could hear him. Then he presented a stack of calling cards to the old man.

Qian Qianyi flipped through the cards. There were five or six of them. The names were unfamiliar ones. Probably they were some young scholars who called to make his acquaintance. He said, "Noted, but I have no time to see them at the moment, keep the cards and tell them to come later."

Li Bao nodded and said loudly, "Mr. Yan of the Ministry of Industries comes from Gusu to see your lordship. He's now staying in a lodge. Just now his servant came to find out when your lordship is free so that Mr. Yan can call in person." Without waiting for Qian Qianyi to ask, he added, "Mr. Yan's calling card is among the ones I gave you just now."

Qian Qianyi hadn't noticed such a calling card. He flipped through the stack of calling cards and found it. He waved it gently and thought for an instant. Then, he said, "Ask the servant to tell Mr. Yan that it's

望他。”

李宝答应了，但仍旧不走。钱谦益皱着眉头问：“还有什么？”

李宝又禀告说：“崇明县盐户孙振南前两日派人送赆仪来，布政张老爷也派来送礼的人，现还在客房里住着，等老爷示下。”

钱谦益一听，不觉生起气来：“混账东西，叫何总管打发他们就完了。这些小事也值得拿来禀告！”

等到李宝退出去之后，钱谦益转过脸来，眼光这才落到了儿子的身上。

钱孙爱斜靠在椅子上，呆呆地望着窗外尚未返青吐芽的小树林，脸上现出一派茫然的神气，对于父亲刚才的举动，根本就没有留意。

钱谦益默默地瞅着儿子。近半年来，因为筹划起用的事情——请托、应酬、措置款子、打听消息，花去他不少精力和时间；待到腾出身来，又忙着去陪伴新婚的如夫人柳如是，所以，他实在有好长时间没有仔细打量过儿子。现在，他发现儿子好像又消瘦了些，脸色更苍白了，身子还有点儿佝偻……一阵莫名的悲戚之感，忽然涌上了钱谦益的心头。他想到，自己今年已经六十一岁了，早年也生过三个儿子，但都没能养下来，好容易到了四十八岁那一年，才由朱氏替他生下这么一个儿子。常熟钱姓他们这一房，几代都是一子单传，看来轮到自己，也仍然改变不了这种命运。本来，只要有一个儿子，就可以不必再担忧将来祖宗祠墓无人祭扫，自己也不至于成为“若敖之馁鬼”。但是，还得想到，钱家眼下这偌大产业，将来就要全部压在儿子这一副又软又嫩的肩膀上，他——能承受得起么？这孩子自幼单弱多病，

too much bother for him and I'll go to the lodge tomorrow morning."

Li Bao nodded but didn't leave. Qian Qianyi frowned and asked, "What else is there?"

Li Bao said, " Sun Zhennan, a salt dealer in Chongming County, sent a man here with a tribute two days ago, and Mr. Zhang, the chief executive of the province, also sent a man here with a tribute. They're still staying in the guest rooms waiting for a reply message."

When Qian Qianyi heard that, he became angry, saying, "Tricksters! Ask the chief steward to send them away. Don't tell me such trivial things."

After Li Bao withdrew, Qian Qianyi turned around and his eyes fell on his son.

Qian Sun'ai was reclining in the chair, staring blankly at the small woods outside the window that hadn't yet returned to its greenness, with a dazed expression on his face, oblivious of what was going on.

Qian Qianyi looked at his son in silence. Over the past six months, preparation for the reinstatement to office—seeking help, building connections, finding money, collecting intelligence—had taken much of his time and energy, and then there was his newly wedded concubine Liu Rushi; he had had very little time to see his son clearly. Now, Qian Sun'ai looked even thinner than before, his face was paler and his back was slightly hunched. An inexplicable sense of grief crept into Qian Qianyi's heart. He was sixty-one years old now. He had had three sons in his early years but none of them had survived; not until he was forty eight did he beget this one, who was born of Lady Zhu. His family line, a branch of the Qian clan in Changshu, had been continued for generations on the basis of a single male heir and it looked now it was unlikely to change in his generation. In fact, as long as he had a son, he would no longer have to worry that the ancestral shrines and tombs would see no worshipers and cleaners in the future and that he would become a hungry ghost like a member of the annihilated Ruoao family. But given the vast estate of the Qians, would the soft and tender shoulders of this son of his be up to its weight at all? The boy, born timid and having been weak and fragile since childhood, didn't quite

性情又怯懦，完全不像个“克绍箕裘”的人物……

钱谦益不禁暗暗叹了一口气，觉得“命运”这个东西真是难以捉摸。自己一生营营役役，机心用尽，总算弄到今天这样一个“东林领袖”“文坛祭酒”的显赫地位；而且，把父祖辈传下来的一份家业，又扩大了好几倍，满以为上可无愧钱氏列宗之灵，下可振兴子孙于后世了。但是，命运给自己安排的继承人，却偏偏是这样一个角色。自己一生枉自逞强，到头来又安知不是为他人作嫁衣裳！一刹那间，他心灰意冷，感到从未有过的疲倦和衰弱。他摇摇头，竭力想摆脱这种不愉快的思绪，于是勉强打起精神，提高声音问道：

“你——来了么？很好。嗯，这会子你觉得身子好些了么？可吃的什么药？”

仿佛从遥远的思路上被呼唤回来似的，钱孙爱转过脸来，呆呆地望着父亲，好一会儿，才清醒过来。他站起身，重新向钱谦益行礼、请安。

“嗯，问你觉着身子可好，吃的什么药哩！”钱谦益发觉儿子显然没有听清他刚才说的话，于是又重复了一遍。

“孩儿觉……觉着好些了。不敢有劳爹爹挂心。孩儿这会子吃的是三清一气丸。”钱孙爱恭恭敬敬地回答。他一向很畏惧他的父亲。虽然父亲对儿子并不特别严厉，可是钱谦益那种旺盛的精力，那种咄咄逼人的气势，却使钱孙爱同他相对时，总受到莫名的威胁，有一种被压倒的感觉。

“什么丸？”钱谦益没有听清。

钱孙爱又重复一遍药丸的名字。

钱谦益皱着眉毛说：“怎么取这么个刁钻古怪的名字！唔，你可要仔细着，有些个庸医没本事，专靠弄这些名堂骗人。银子花得不少，其实呢，全是白费！”

look like someone who could take over his enterprise.

Qian Qianyi couldn't help but heave a silent sigh, feeling that destiny was really something elusive. Having spent his whole life calculating and bustling about, he had finally come to prominence by becoming the East Wood leader and master of ceremony at the literary altar; moreover, he had made the family estate handed down from his father and grandfather several times larger. Proud that he was worthy of his ancestors, he had thought his line of the Qian clan would be revitalized hereafter. However, fate had given him an heir like this. All his efforts throughout his life were very likely to come to no end and would only serve to benefit others. In an instant, he was disheartened and felt tired and worn out like never before. He shook his head and tried to get rid of this unpleasant thought, so he forced himself to cheer up, raised his voice and asked:

"So you're here. Good. Um, are you feeling better now? What medicine are you taking?"

As if being called back from a distant train of thought, Qian Sun'ai turned around and looked at his father blankly for a long time before waking up. He stood up, bowed and greeted his father again.

"Well, I asked if you feel better and what kind of medicine you're taking," said Qian Qianyi, realizing that his son had obviously not heard what he had just said.

"I'm feeling—feeling better. Thank you Dad for your kind concern. I'm taking the Three Qing One Qi pills," Qian Sun'ai replied respectfully. He had always been in awe of his father. Although his father was not particularly strict with him, Qian Qianyi's vigorous energy and aggressive manner had always made Qian Sun'ai feel inexplicably intimidated and suppressed.

"What pills?" Qian Qianyi didn't hear clearly.

Qian Sun'ai repeated the name of the pills again.

Qian Qianyi frowned and said, "How can there be such a tricky and weird name? Well, you have to be careful. Some quack doctors are no good and they deceive people with such names. Such prescriptions are expensive but in fact useless."

“这是喻先生开的方子。要是爹爹觉着不妥，回头孩儿就对他们说不吃了。”

“嗯，吃着吧，先吃着吧！真的不好，再换不迟。”停了停，他又补充说，“若是喻嘉言开的方子，怕倒是有效的。”

“是。”钱孙爱恭敬地应诺着。

这样说过之后，有好一阵，父子二人谁也没有再开口。钱孙爱低头站着，钱谦益又开始在屋子里走来走去。他瞥见家人李宝在窗外的走廊里朝这边张望，可是没有理他。

“你——今天见过你三娘么？”终于，钱谦益打破沉默，换了一个话题。

“孩儿每天都向娘请安的。”

“唔，很好，很好。”钱谦益心不在焉地点着头，管自考虑着。“可是——”他突然说，“你三娘不好，很不好！”他的语气有一点急促，同时迅速地看了儿子一眼。

钱孙爱低着头，没有吱声。

也许因为看不出儿子的表情反应，钱谦益有一点着急。他咳嗽一声，加重了语气：“听说她这几天尽在闹，闹！闹得很不成话，还骂出许多极其难听的话。我真不明白她怎么会变成这种样子！我们这样的人家，岂能让她一个劲地胡闹，这成何体统！”

钱谦益一边说，一边目不转睛地盯着儿子，希望能看出他对这件事的态度。可是钱孙爱还是低着头，闭着嘴，身子又开始神经质地颤抖起来。

看见儿子这个样子，钱谦益有一点失望，也有点生气。但他仍旧隐忍着，又说道：“我乃念你三娘服侍我许多年，又有抚育你长大成人这份功劳，本不想与她多计较，更不想为难她。只要她能安分克己，和衷御下，虚心敬诚，不惹是生非，让我这把老骨头安安稳稳再活上几年，我也就心满意足了。可是她却不识大体，不知通变——嗯，我听说这些年来，她背着我弄权揽财，徇

"It's a prescription by Doctor Yu. If Dad doesn't think it's good, I'll tell them I'll stop taking it."

"Um, go on taking it before we find anything better. If it turns out to be no good, switch to another medicine," he said. After pausing for an instant, he added, "If it's Yu Jiayan's prescription, I gather it'll be good."

"Yes, Dad," Qian Sun'ai responded respectfully.

After that exchange, for a long while, neither father nor son spoke. Qian Sun'ai stood with his head down, and Qian Qianyi started pacing the room again. He caught sight of servant Li Bao looking in from the corridor outside the window but ignored him.

"Have you—have seen your Third Mother today?" Finally, Qian Qianyi broke the silence with another subject.

"I pay respects to my Third Mother every day."

"Well, good, that's good." Qian Qianyi nodded absentmindedly, thinking to himself. "But—" he said suddenly, "your Third Mother is not good, not good at all." He spoke bluntly and cast a quick glance at his son.

Qian Sun'ai was silent, his head bent.

Qian Qianyi was a little anxious, maybe because he couldn't see any change in his son's expression. He coughed and said in a harsher tone, "I hear she's having explosions of temper these days, making terrible scenes, yelling and cursing. I really don't understand how she's become like this. How can a home like ours allow her to keep destroying? What an inglorious thing!"

Qian Qianyi stared at his son intently, hoping to see his attitude. Qian Sun'ai still kept his head bent and his mouth closed, and his body began to shiver nervously again.

Seeing his son like this, Qian Qianyi was a little disappointed and a little angry too but held himself in check. He continued, "Since she's attended me for so many years and has brought you up, I don't want to be too harsh on her, nor do I want to make things difficult for her. I would be more than happy if she could be humble and kind and let me live longer. But unfortunately, she stubbornly refuses to submit herself to the good of the family—um, I've heard that, over the years, she's done many bad things—power plays, extortion, taking

私纳贿，跋扈凶悍，做了许多不好的事，大大辜负了我对她的信赖和厚望！今天又放肆到连我都敢骂，这还了得！”钱谦益把桌子一拍，生气地瞪着钱孙爱，“而你——你是她的儿子，年纪也不小了，怎么就不规劝于她！你平日读的圣贤训诲，都读到哪里去了？嗯？”

没想到父亲突然把怒火倾泻到自己的头上，钱孙爱吓得一抖，“扑通”跪在地上。

“爹、爹爹息怒，孩儿知、知罪了。”他惊惶地一瞥，不敢接触钱谦益严厉的目光。

“我膝下就只你这么一个孩儿，钱氏的家业将来就全靠你来承担。可是你如此不长进，教为父怎样放心得下！又何以告慰列祖列宗于九泉？”钱谦益怒气不息。

“启、启禀爹爹，孩儿其、其实也劝过三娘……”

“劝过她，你？那么——你是怎么说的？”

“孩儿请三娘不要再生气，不要骂……”

“唔，她呢？她可听从？”钱谦益的语气中不无期待。

钱孙爱苦恼地摇摇头。

钱谦益露出失望的神色。他又开始急速地走来走去，喃喃地说：“这个悍妇，这个悍妇！”他忽然停下来，望着钱孙爱，“所以，为父现在决定，把你三娘搬出半野堂，到城东旧宅去住些时候，让她闭门思过。什么时候改过了，什么时候再搬回来。你——可听明白了？”

钱孙爱大吃一惊，顿时觉得心里像钻进了一群耗子似的乱得很。好半天，他才嗫嚅地问：“那、那么孩儿？”

“你当然不必跟着你三娘！”

“可，可孩儿宁愿跟着三娘去的！”钱孙爱忽然伛下身去，哭起来。

bribes, bullying, and brutalities—that are against my trust and high hopes. Today, she's gone so far as to even swear at me. This shouldn't continue!" Qian Qianyi slapped his hand on the table and stared at Qian Sun'ai angrily, saying, "And you—you're her son, and you're no small kid. Why don't you talk her into reason? Where are the teachings of wise men that you've read? Huh?"

Not expecting his father to suddenly shift the anger to him, Qian Sun'ai shuddered with fear and, plop, his knees fell to the ground.

"Dad, don't be angry at me. I'm sorry for my mistake," he begged. He glanced at his father in panic, not daring to see the old man's stern gaze.

"You're my only son and the sole heir to the estate of the Qians. If you refuse to grow up like this, how can I not worry? How can I comfort our ancestors in heaven?" said Qian Qianyi, his anger not appeased.

"Dad, I've actually talked to Third Mother—"

"Did you? So—what did you say?"

"I asked Third Mother not to be angry and not to swear at people—"

"Well, what did she say? Did she listen?" said Qian Qianyi in an expectant tone.

Qian Sun'ai shook his head in distress.

Qian Qianyi gave him a disappointed look. He started pacing about again, murmuring, "What a shrew! What a shrew!" He suddenly stopped and looked at Qian Sun'ai, saying, "So, now I decide to let your Third Mother move out of the Half Wild Estate and stay in the old house in the east of the city for a while so that she can reflect on her mistakes behind closed doors. She'll be allowed to move back when she's reformed. You—do you understand?"

Qian Sun'ai was taken aback, and suddenly felt as if a host of mice had got into his heart and created a mess therein. After a long while, he moaned, "Then, then I—?"

"Of course you don't have to go with your Third Mother."

"But, but I want to go with her!" Qian Sun'ai suddenly knelt on his knees and started to cry.

“胡说！”钱谦益厉声呵斥道，“你年纪也不小了，该明白事理。你要跟她去，那么，我问你，你打算置为父和你母亲于何地？再者，”他停了停，稍稍缓和了口气，“你是钱家的唯一传人，也该跟在我身边经些历练才是。”

钱孙爱眼泪汪汪地瞧了父亲一眼，不敢再坚持了。其实，真的让他迁出半野堂，去终日陪伴他的那位恣睢暴戾的三娘，钱孙爱也是不愿意的。他只是觉得三娘很可怜，父亲也忒狠心。他张了张嘴，还想说几句什么，但一触到父亲冰冷的目光，所有的勇气便都消失了。他像泄了气的皮球似的伏在地上，哽咽着说：“但凭爹爹做主……”

“嗯，这就很好！”钱谦益满意地点点头，“这样才像我的儿子。识大体，知通变，不因私爱而惑其心志，很好。起来吧！”说着，他走前两步，把钱孙爱扶起来。

由于终于说出了几天来一直困扰着他的这个艰难的决定，钱谦益觉得有一种解脱般的轻松。特别是得到了儿子的理解，使他很高兴。由于某种说不清的、然而又是强有力的原因，他认为，在这种事情上，儿子的理解和支持，对于他来说是重要的。尽管钱孙爱站起来时，脸上分明地表露出痛苦的神情，眼睛还含着泪，可是钱谦益却装作没看见。现在，他觉得应当用什么方式抚慰一下儿子，兼以表示父亲的慈爱。他做了个手势，让儿子等着，然后，转过身向隔壁的一个房间走去。

这是一间很大的藏书室，堆满了各种各样的图书典籍，有装在书套中的，也有保存在木匣子里的。钱谦益曾经花了大半辈子光阴，不遗余力地搜求各种珍本和善本书籍。在这些藏书中，有不少属于宋版和元版的稀世珍品。对于这批财富，钱谦益一向十分自豪，极为宝爱，轻易不让人参观借阅。现在，他一边在排列得过于拥挤的书橱之间困难地转动着身子，一边想着：这房子太

"Nonsense!" said Qian Qianyi, reprimanding his son in a harsh tone. "You're no kid anymore and you should know better. If you go with her, then, I ask you, where do you plan to put your father and your real mother? Besides," he paused, and eased his tone a little, saying, "you're the only heir to the Qian family and you should follow me around for some experience."

Qian Sun'ai glanced at his father with tears in his eyes, and dared not insist anymore. In fact, he didn't really want to move out of the Half Wild Estate to live with the tempestuous Third Mother all the time. Feeling pity for Third Mother, to whom his father was too cruel, he opened his mouth and wanted to say something, but as soon as he met his father's icy-cold gaze, all his courage disappeared. Kneeling on the ground like a deflated leather ball, he sobbed, "I'll listen to you, Dad."

"Excellent!" Qian Qianyi said, nodding in satisfaction. "This is how my son should look like. Knowing what's for the general good, capable of adapting to a changing situation, not confused in the mind by personal preferences. Excellent! Get up!" As he spoke, he walked two steps forward and helped his son up.

As he finally spoke the difficult decision that had been troubling him for days, Qian Qianyi felt relaxed as if he had just been liberated. He was particularly happy that he had the understanding of his son. For some inexplicable but powerful reason, he believed that his son's understanding and support were crucial in this matter. Qian Sun'ai had a painful expression on his face and tears in his eyes as he stood up, but Qian Qianyi pretended not to see it. Feeling that he should find some way to comfort his son and show the love of a father, Qian Qianyi gestured for Sun'ai to wait, then turned and walked to a room next door.

It was a large library filled with all kinds of books, old and new, some in bags and some in wooden boxes. Qian Qianyi had spent most of his life—sparing no effort—looking for various rare books and authentic editions, of which, many were rare treasures from the Song and Yuan dynasties. He had always been very proud and immensely fond of this wealth of collections, which he had rarely allowed anyone to see or borrow. Now, while maneuvering with difficulty among the

小，该建一座新的藏书楼了。他弯下身子，从专门收藏珍本和善本典籍的那几口书柜里，小心翼翼地搬出一套用楠木匣子装着的宋版《倚松老人集》，才走出几步，又折回去。他踌躇了一下，终于把这套宋版的放回原处，改换了一套元刻大字本的《韩诗外传》捧到外面来，又从紫檀木书案上拿起一只古玉簪瓶，一并放在儿子面前，说："这是为父心爱的两件宝物，现在传授与你。今后，你须刻苦自励，潜心学问，虚怀敏求，慎终如始，将来'采芹''入泮'，克绍箕裘，方不负为父的一番训育深心——听明白了么？"

看见儿子垂手聆诲，眉宇之间似乎有悚然之色，钱谦益暗暗感到满意。

他相信，经过自己这一番恩威并施，钱孙爱内心纵有不满，也必然消解，而且会感奋努力，自强上进。他停了一下，终于说道：

"去吧！"

然而，当钱孙爱叩谢了父亲，费力地捧着那一部《韩诗外传》和那只古玉簪瓶，转过身慢慢走出去的时候，钱谦益目送着儿子那瘦削、佝偻的背影，心里不由得又一次涌起了先前那种忧心忡忡的感觉：将来，他当真能够"克绍箕裘"，光宗耀祖么？

……

"启禀老爷，钱、陈两位老爷已经来到，在外间等候多时了。"家人李宝的声音在他的耳边响起来。

钱谦益定了定神，立即想起眼前还有更为要紧得多、也棘手得多的事情，正亟待作出决断。于是，他把思绪从儿子身上收回

overcrowded bookcases, he thought, "The library is too small. It's time to build a new one." He bent down and out of special bookcases for rare and exquisite editions took out a Song dynasty edition of *Collected Poems of an Old Man Leaning Against a Pine Tree* by the Song dynasty poet Rao Jie encased in a *nanmu* box. He hesitated for an instant and finally put the Song dynasty book back in place. In its stead, he took out a Yuan dynasty big-font lithograph of *Hanying's Poetic Biographies* and then picked up an ancient *yuzan* bottle from the red sandalwood writing desk. He put them in front of his son and said, "These are two treasures I like best. I'm passing them on to you. From now on, you shall get inspired, devote yourself to learning with humility, diligence, and perseverance. You shall get admitted to the county school and carry on the family tradition. Only by so doing can you live up to my expectations. Do you understand?"

Seeing his son listening with hands down and deference in the eyes, Qian Qianyi was satisfied in his heart of hearts.

He believed that through his ministering of both compassion and authority, even though Qian Sun'ai was not happy at heart, the boy would eventually come to terms with himself and strive for self-improvement. He paused and finally said:

"You can leave now."

Qian Sun'ai thanked his father, turned and slowly walked out, laboriously carrying *Hanying's Poetic Biographies* and the ancient *yuzan* bottle in his hands. As Qian Qianyi watched his son's thin, hunchbacked form from behind, he couldn't help but feel the same anxiety he had felt previously: Will the boy really be able to carry on his father's cause and bring honor to his ancestors?

...

"Your lordship, Mr. Qian and Mr. Chen have already arrived and have waited in the parlor for quite some time," came the voice of servant Li Bao.

Qian Qianyi recollected himself and remembered that there was a much more urgent and much more thorny matter awaiting his decision. So he withdrew his thoughts from his son. Although he was a

来，虽然已经有点疲倦，但仍旧振作起精神，略为整理一下衣冠，说道：

“请！”

## 共议难题

客人们很快就出现了。

走在前面的是陈在竹。他身材矮胖，方脸，大嘴，小小的眼睛，淡淡的眉毛，无论什么时候都摆出一副乐呵呵的样子。在一般人眼里，他性情爽直，胸无城府，只有钱谦益等少数几个人才知道，此人其实计智深沉，精明强干，含而不露。他是钱谦益正室夫人陈氏的同胞兄弟，曾经替钱谦益办过几件极其棘手的大事，所以钱谦益对这位妻舅一向十分倚重。

走在后面的，是钱谦益的同族兄弟钱养先。他有着与钱谦益同样的黑脸膛和高鼻梁，只是更高更瘦，一双眸子滴溜溜地转个不停。早些年，他也常替钱谦益跑码头，近年因为犯了很重的风湿症，少出去走动了。现在，他扶着一根藜杖，一边走，一边习惯地用手背捶打着腰眼。

因为是至亲常客，钱谦益也不多礼，彼此揖了一揖，就分宾主坐下。老仆钱升奉上茶来，钱谦益知道陈在竹在品茶上十分讲究挑剔，问明是“毛尖”，便摆摆手，吩咐换过三两银子一斤的“岕片”。陈在竹点着头，一边从钱升手里接过茶，一边笑嘻嘻地问：

“钱升，你孩儿入了学，你如今便是秀才的老爹了。你不回家去享清福，还在这儿穷忙作甚？”

little tired, he mustered all the energy he could, tidied his clothes, and said:

"Welcome them in!"

## A Matter of Great Importance

The guests showed up soon.

In front walked Chen Zaizhu, a short and stout man with a square face, a big mouth, small eyes, and faint eyebrows, always wearing a cheerful look. In the eyes of most people, he was simple without guile. Only a tiny few, such as Qian Qianyi, knew that this person was actually deep-minded, smart and capable without showing it. Brother to Qian Qianyi's wife, he had solved some thorny problems for his brother-in-law, who therefore had always held him in high esteem.

Behind walked Qian Yangxian, Qian Qianyi's cousin on the paternal side, who had the same dark face and tall nose as Qian Qianyi but was taller and thinner and whose eyes rolled nonstop. In the early years, he had often run errands for the cousin, but in recent years, he had rarely done so due to severe rheumatism. Now, he was walking with a pigweed cane and frequently beating the center of his back with the back of his hand as a matter of habit.

Because they were close relatives and frequent visitors, there was no need for ceremonies; the guests and the host bowed to each other and sat down. Old servant Qian Sheng brought tea. Knowing that Chen Zaizhu was very picky about tea, Qian Qianyi asked what it was, and upon learning it was *maojian*, he waved dismissal and asked for *jiepian*, which was worth three taels of silver per catty. Chen Zaizhu nodded his head, smiled and asked as he took over the tea from Qian Sheng's hand:

"Qian Sheng, now that your son has been admitted to the county school, you're now father of a *xiucai*① degree holder. Why are you still here instead of going home and enjoy old age?"

---

① *Xiucai* is a junior degree. The word literally means "a young man of extraordinary talent".

钱升正把一杯茶送到钱谦益手里，听了这话，就偏过平扁多皱的脸，不高兴地说："舅老爷，旁人想赶我走还罢了，连你老也赶我？若早知到头来会这样子，当初我一准不叫他去读什么书！"

"咦，这可奇了！"钱养先插进来，"这可是你前世修得的福气，多少人都巴望不来哩，你倒不高兴！"

"是嘛，没准儿你那孩儿今年便考上个举人，明年再中个进士。到其时，你可就是老太爷了。只怕我们巴结都巴结不上哩！"陈在竹依旧笑嘻嘻的，也不知他是挖苦还是真心。

"由他举也罢，不举也罢，反正我老钱升还是老钱升，还是在这儿服侍老爷太太！"钱升涨红了脸，固执地说，随即转过身，噔噔噔地走出去了。

"嗬，好家伙！"陈在竹倒惊奇起来，"瞧样子他还真是王八吞秤砣——铁了心哩！"

钱谦益靠在椅子上，本来一直没吱声，这会儿抬了抬眼皮，发现陈在竹在瞅着他，便含糊地说："自从去年，我替他孩儿落了籍之后，就没再拿他当奴仆看待。可他自小伺候我惯了，所以……"

"哎，似他这等忠心不贰的，如今世上是越来越少了。"钱养先显得颇有感慨，"倒是到处听说奴婢得势，便翻脸不认主子的，哪怕你于他恩义再重，也全不中用，甚至有恣意殴詈、操戈入室的。所以嘛，这老钱升，你别说，还真算是难得喽！"

这样说过之后，两位客人便一齐沉默下来。因为他们知道，钱谦益急急忙忙地把他们呼唤来，决不会无缘无故，必定有什么要紧的事情。所以，现在他们都望着主人，等待他开口。

可是钱谦益尽自沉默着。因为一来，钱升和李宝还在进进出

Qian Sheng was delivering a cup of tea to Qian Qianyi. Hearing that, the flat, wrinkled face turned to Chen Zaizhu and said sulkily, "My lord! Everyone wants me to go. Now, you're joining them to drive me away. If I had known it would have been like this in the end, I wouldn't have allowed my son to go to the county school."

"Well, this is strange indeed," Qian Yangxian cut in. "It's a blessing you cultivated in your previous life, the envy and jealousy of others, and yet you're not happy."

"Yes, indeed! Maybe your son will earn a *juren* degree this year and a *jinshi* degree next year. By then, you'll be the revered old man of a high official, and I'm afraid we won't have the honor of your company," said Chen Zaizhu, still smiling, with sarcasm or sincerity.

"It makes no difference whether or not he'll get a *juren* degree or whatever. I'll still be Qian Sheng here to serve my lord and ladies." Qian Sheng said resolutely, blushing, and then turned around and walked out, thump, thump, thump.

"Wow, good for him!" Chen Zaizhu exclaimed in surprise. "It looks like he's really a good bastard, a turtle that has a heart of iron because he's eaten a scale weight."

Qian Qianyi, who had been reclining in his chair silently, raised his eyes. Seeing that Chen Zaizhu was watching him, he murmured, "Since I relieved his son of servitude last year, I've not treated him as a servant anymore. But having been used to serving me since childhood, he—"

"Good for you! There're fewer and fewer loyal servants like him nowadays," said Qian Yangxian, who looked quite moved. "It's heard everywhere that servants and maids turn their backs on their masters after their change of status no matter how well they've been treated, and in the worst cases, turn against and abuse their masters. So, congratulations on having a good servant like Qian Sheng!"

Then, the two guests went silent, because they knew that Qian Qianyi hurriedly called them in not without a reason. Now they both looked at the host, waiting for him to speak.

But Qian Qianyi remained silent. For one thing, Qian Sheng and

出地张罗茶点；二来，钱谦益觉得要谈的这件事，实在非同一般。尽管眼前这两个人都是追随自己多年的心腹，他也不打算立即和盘托出，但是该怎么向他们谈，谈到什么程度，他都未曾考虑清楚，所以始终还在迟疑。

看见主人的这副神气，陈在竹和钱养先知道他还需要时间考虑，也就不去催促他。钱养先拿起杯子，慢悠悠地呷了一口茶，忽然笑着说："方才，有个客人从姑苏来，说起一件时闻，倒是有些意思。"

陈在竹乐呵呵地瞅着他，蛮有兴趣地问："噢？愿闻其详。"

钱养先又呷了一口茶，看看钱谦益，又看看陈在竹："嗯，不知二位——可听说过陈圆圆？"

"怎么不知道！"陈在竹快活地眨巴着小眼睛，"陈圆圆么，姑苏城里烧得红半边天的小娘！色、艺、才，堪称三绝！前年在虎丘山塘，我还见过她一面。嘿，一出弋阳腔《红梅记》，演得是'如云出岫，如珠在盘，令人欲仙欲死'！……嗯，对了，这几句还是如皋冒辟疆的品评。听说，辟疆同圆圆已经有约，早晚要把她娶回去——冒辟疆，平心而论，也算得翩翩浊世佳公子，配圆圆嘛，倒是还配得起——可是，怎么了，她？"

钱养先把茶杯往几上一放，叹息说："闹出大乱子了！"

在一旁拈着胡子，似听非听的钱谦益，眼皮儿跳动了一下，转过脸来。

钱养先接着说："这——说来只怕也是一场冤孽。正因那陈圆圆自恃容华绝代，歌舞无双，架子拿得挺大，名头也愈来愈响，不料就犯上了煞星。这煞星不是别人，乃系当今国丈爷田弘遇。

Li Bao were still preparing tea and light refreshments; for another, Qian Qianyi felt that the matter to be discussed was of great weight. Although the two men in front of him belonged to his circle of intimates and had followed him for many years, he didn't intend to immediately tell them everything; he hesitated as he hadn't decided how to broach the subject and how far the discussion should go.

Seeing the host's expression, Chen Zaizhu and Qian Yangxian knew that he still needed time to think, so they didn't urge him. Qian Yangxian picked up his cup, slowly took a sip of tea, and suddenly smiled and said, "Just now, a visitor from Gusu said something interesting."

Chen Zaizhu looked at him in good cheer and asked with great interest, "Oh? Let's hear it."

Qian Yangxian took another sip of tea and looked at Qian Qianyi, then Chen Zaizhu, and said, "Um—have you two heard of Chen Yuanyuan?"

"Yes, of course!" Chen Zaizhu blinked his small eyes animatedly and said. "Chen Yuanyuan, the hot young girl that sends the entire Gusu City burning with her beauty, talent, and intelligence. I happened to see her on Canal Street at Tiger Hill the year before last. Her performance in the Yiyang Opera play *The Story of the Red Plum* was 'like a white cloud rising from the mountains or a pearl rolling on a plate, an ethereal, enchanting experience indeed!' By the way, they're the words of Mao Pijiang of Rugao City. I heard that Pijiang has promised Yuanyuan that he'll marry her sooner or later. Mao Pijiang, in all fairness, is a dandy yet a good match for Yuanyuan—but what happened?"

Qian Yangxian put the teacup on the table, sighed, and said, "Something very bad happened."

Qian Qianyi, who had been fiddling with his own beard and listening absentmindedly, was jolted and turned to Qian Yangxian.

Qian Yangxian went on to say, "It is, I'm afraid, bad karma. Chen Yuanyuan, proud of her peerless beauty and unrivaled talent for singing and dancing, is becoming more and more inaccessible and more and more famous, but unfortunately, she's run into an evil star. This evil star is none other than Tian Hongyu, father-in-law of His Majesty

前些日子，田皇亲派人到姑苏采买女孩子，闻得圆圆之名，就指定要买她。吓得圆圆东躲西藏，多亏有几个相好的孤老，甘愿为她效力，鼓噪起好几百个闲汉泼皮，日日守护着圆圆，还揎拳捋袖，舞枪弄棒，要同田府的人厮拼。如今这事闹到苏州府里，那田府的门客天天上衙门逼着要人，把知府大人急得斗昏鸡似的，团团乱转。这事还不知如何了局哩！”

陈在竹把脑袋摇得像个拨浪鼓：“哎，哎！那田皇亲可是好斗的？他的女儿是皇上最宠爱的妃子。圆圆这一回，只怕是劫数难逃了。”

“这倒也难说。”钱养先眨眨眼睛，“想那陈圆圆既以色、艺、才自恃，只怕一入田府，便立蒙眷爱，宠夺专房，从此享不尽的荣华富贵。此番小劫，又安知非福？”

“可是那田弘遇是个粗蠢不过的俗物。”钱谦益忽然开口说，“纵然权倾朝野，富可敌国，其奈不解情趣何！只怕圆圆到底还是明珠暗投。”

他的口气透着烦恼，没有瞧客人，神情越来越阴暗。末了，他站起来，在屋子里转了一圈，意兴萧索地负手低吟道：

“侯门一入深如海，从此萧郎是路人……”

陈在竹眨巴着眼睛，忽然哈哈地笑起来：“罢罢罢，这可真是‘多情却被无情恼’了，其实，‘圆圆’也罢，‘方方’也罢，萧郎也罢，冒辟疆也罢，我们又怎管得着人家被窝里的事情？来，还是喝茶正经。待会儿，我也有一件时闻，只怕姐夫更有兴趣哩！”

钱养先眼珠子一转，也说：“正是正是，还是喝茶，喝茶。”

the emperor. A few days ago, the emperor's relation sent an agent to Gusu to buy a girl. After hearing the name of Yuanyuan, the agent decided she was the one to be bought. Yuanyuan was so scared that she went into hiding, and a few elderly friends organized hundreds of thugs and idlers to guard her, and, clenching their fists, rolling up their sleeves, and waving swords and sticks, they were ready for a fight with the Tians. The prefect was totally at a loss as to what to do, like an embattled fighting cock. There's no knowing how things will end."

Chen Zaizhu shook his head like a rattle and said, "Poor girl! The emperor's relation Tian is not to be reckoned with. His daughter is the emperor's favorite concubine. This time, I'm afraid that there's no escape for Yuanyuan."

"It's hard to tell," Qian Yangxian said, blinking his eyes. "Given her beauty, talent, and intelligence, Chen Yuanyuan will immediately become the favorite concubine and get all the attention as soon as she enters the mansion of the Tians and live happily ever after. Who knows if this kidnap is not a blessing in disguise?"

Qian Qianyi suddenly opened his mouth and said, "But Tian Hongyu is an idiotic, vulgar creature. In spite of his mighty power and great wealth, he's boring as hell. I'm afraid Yuanyuan is after all a pearl for a swine," he said, with a hint of vexation in his tone, his expression getting increasingly gloomy.

In the end, he stood up, paced back and forth, and groaned bleakly with his hands behind his back:

"Deep is the mansion of a peer. From now on Xiaolang my beau will become a stranger."

Chen Zaizhu blinked his eyes and suddenly laughed out loud. "Hey, let it go, let it go! Stop the pining-for-a-lost-love thing. In fact, whether it's Yuanyuan, or Fangfang, or Xiaolang, or Pijiang, their business under the blanket is not our business. Come, come, our correct business is to sip tea. Brother-in-law, I have some news for you to hear. I'm sure you'll be interested," he said.

Qian Yangxian rolled his eyes and said, "Exactly! Let's go on sipping tea."

在他们说话的当儿，钱升和李宝已经在八仙桌上摆出来一席茶点：两把宜兴砂壶，分别泡着重新换过的毛尖、岕片，三只极细的成窑杯子，在桌上摆成了品字形；当中是七八个小碟子——水饺、烧卖、馅儿饼、扁豆糕、蜜橙糕、韭盒、春卷摆了一桌。这时，钱谦益也回过神来，于是请两位客人入席，又对钱升和李宝说：“你们到外间侍候着吧，有事我会叫你们。”

钱升、李宝退了出去。席上这三个人喝着茶，各自吃了一两件点心。钱养先催促说：“竹翁，你到底又有什么好时闻？”

陈在竹嘴巴里正塞满了蜜橙糕儿。他啊啊呜呜地点着头，眨着眼，好容易把糕儿咽下去，又呷了一口茶，这才说道：“不是大得不得了的事，不过，却也可骇可叹——我去岁在京里时听说，前年孟冬祭太庙，群臣先至殿门外候驾。其时殿门未开，忽闻内有异响，众人正惊疑间，只见殿门大开，十余位龙袍帝冕的伟丈夫，从内徐徐走出，转眼不见；再看殿门，又复紧闭如故。当时见者，俱惊骇不敢言。及至皇上驾到，行礼之时，忽然殿内怪风卷起，灯烛全灭。陪祭群臣，无不失色俯伏；皇上亦因此惊悸成疾，下体软麻，不能行立，治理百余日方始痊愈。及至去岁周阁

While they were talking, Qian Sheng and Li Bao got tea and refreshments ready on the *baxian* table. Two Yixing clay pots with newly made *maojian* and *jiepian* tea, three exquisite Chenghua Period[①] government kiln teacups that formed a triangle on the table, and seven or eight small plates in the middle with boiled dumplings, *siu mai*, stuffed cakes, hyacinth bean pudding, orange pudding, chives pockets, and spring rolls. So, Qian Qianyi recollected himself and invited the two guests to the table and said to Qian Sheng and Li Bao, "The two of you wait outside. I'll call you when I have something for you to do."

Qian Sheng and Li Bao withdrew. At the table, the three men started to drink tea and each ate one or two refreshments. Qian Yangxian said expectantly, "So, what's the big news, Brother Zaizhu?"

As his mouth was stuffed with orange pudding, Chen Zaizhu kept nodding his head with a broken, muffled voice, his eyes blinking, and after a long while, finally gulped down the pudding; then he took a sip of tea and said: "It's not a terribly big thing, but it's alarming enough. This is what I heard in the capital last year: His Majesty the emperor was going to offer sacrifices to the Imperial Ancestral Temple in the first month of winter the year before, and the court officials gathered at the temple gate to await his arrival. The gate of the temple was not opened yet. Suddenly, there came a strange noise from inside. As everyone wondered what was happening, the gate opened wide, and more than a dozen majestic men in dragon robes and imperial crowns walked out and disappeared in the blink of an eye. They looked at the gate again only to see it was as tightly closed as before. Those who saw it were so alarmed that they became dumbfounded, not daring to speak a word. When the emperor arrived and paid tribute to his ancestors, suddenly a ghostly wind rose and swirled in the hall and the lamps were all extinguished. All the accompanying court officials fell down on their knees in panic; the emperor became ill from the shock and his lower body went numb. He was paralyzed for more than a hundred days before recovering from it. Last year, Premier Zhou was

---

① Chenghua Period: AD 1465–1487

老再相，祭庙之日，却是天气晴和，亦无异象，闻得龙颜甚喜，对左右叹道，‘周阁老毕竟是有福之人！’”

陈在竹说完，啜了一口茶，又夹了半块蜜糕放进嘴里嚼着，脸上仍旧乐呵呵的。他故意不加注解，知道钱谦益必定领会他的意思。

果然，钱谦益变得沉思起来。他转着手里的成窑杯子，仿佛在研究上面的纹理，好一会儿，终于慢慢地说：“在竹说得不错，这一次，只怕非得打通周老头儿的关节，不过……”他沉吟起来，又顿住不说了。

“不过什么？”陈在竹含笑盯着他，“是不是周老头儿出下了难题儿？而这道难题儿，又与那个‘裤子裆里’的老兄有点关系？”——因为阮大铖住在南京的库司坊内，当时痛恨他的人便取了个谐音，把他叫作“裤子裆里阮”。

听陈在竹一语点破底细，钱谦益不禁有点愕然。他迟疑地说：“……嗯，在竹，你竟是都知道了？”

陈在竹哈哈一笑：“我也是瞎猜！临离京时，贵友再三叮嘱我说：‘周相公的意思是，希望东林方面不念旧怨，请牧翁千万玉成此事。’当时，我就猜到几分。现在阿兄这样一问，我竟是猜对了哩！”

钱谦益眨眨眼睛，叹了一口气：“在竹真是奇才！有你们二位相助，我复何忧？不过，此事成功之望甚微，我看不提也罢。”

他顿了一下，看看陈在竹和钱养先，又缓缓说道：“我知道老周一向对我疑忌甚深，现在他说愿意捐弃前嫌，汲引于我，只怕其实并无诚意。只是碍于他的这次复出，是靠了东林之力，不

reinstated to office and the day sacrificial offering was made to the Imperial Ancestral Temple, the weather was nice and accommodating. Upon hearing it, the emperor was delighted and said to his attendants on his sides, 'Premier Zhou is a blessed man indeed!'"

After Chen Zaizhu finished speaking, he took another sip of tea, and put a slice of orange pudding into his mouth, his face still cheerful. He didn't offer any explanation, knowing that Qian Qianyi definitely understood his meaning.

Sure enough, Qian Qianyi became contemplative. He turned the Chenghua cup in his hand, as if studying its texture, and finally said slowly, "Zaizhu is right. This time, I'm afraid I'll have to enlist the support of Old Man Zhou, but—" His voice trailed off in a mumble and then stopped.

"But what?" Chen Zaizhu gazed at him with a smile, "Did Old Man Zhou create a problem for you? And this problem has something to do with the 'guy in the crotch of the pants'?" Because Ruan Dacheng lived on Kusifang in Nanjing, men who hated him called him by a nickname that contained a near homophone "Ruan in the *kuzidang* (crotch of the pants)."

Qian Qianyi was shocked to hear Chen Zaizhu speak the secret. He said after some hesitation, "Zaizhu, how come you know everything?"

Chen Zaizhu laughed and said, "It's just a blind guess. When I left the capital, your friend repeatedly said to me, 'Premier Zhou hopes that East Wood should forgive and forget and that Mr. Qian can intervene to make it happen.' At that time, I guessed it would be so. And now your asking confirms my guess."

Qian Qianyi blinked his eyes and said with a sigh, "Zaizhu is a genius indeed. With the help of the two of you, why should I worry? However, there's little hope of success in this matter, so I don't want to mention it."

He paused to look at Chen Zaizhu and Qian Yangxian, then said, slowly, "I know that Old Man Zhou has always been on guard against me, and now he says he's willing to give up his grudges and help me. I'm

得不敷衍情面，却又故意提出这么一道难题，使我知难而退罢了！”他捋着垂到胸前的花白胡子，脸上现出嘲讽的神色，“我同这位周大相公打交道，也不自今日始，可以说是知己知彼喽！总而言之，只要他周延儒在朝廷一日，我钱某便安分守己管领山林一日就是。”

陈在竹和钱养先对望了一眼，不明白钱谦益何以忽然说起丧气话来，诚然，钱周之间，素来存在私怨。这种私怨，一直可以追溯到崇祯二年，当时东林党的一些重要人物如顾宪成、高攀龙、李三才、杨涟、左光斗、邹元标、黄尊素等人，已经在激烈的党争中相继死去，钱谦益作为幸存下来的有声望成员，便被推出来争夺内阁的职位。谁知遭到心怀嫉妒的礼部尚书温体仁和礼部右侍郎周延儒的敌视，他们二人联起手来，翻出天启元年钱谦益在浙江主持乡试时，被人指控与举子内外串通、纳贿舞弊的糊涂旧账，在皇帝面前参了一本。结果，钱谦益不但入阁拜相的好梦成空，连礼部右侍郎的乌纱帽也被革掉，一个跟头跌回老家常熟来。到如今，已经整整一十三年了。相反，在此期间，温体仁和周延儒却相继入阁，高居首辅。这些年来，他们对钱谦益一直非常注意，压制打击不遗余力，深恐他有复出的机会……这些情况，陈在竹和钱养先是知道的。不过，官场当中的关系本极复杂，敌我恩怨之间，原没有永久不变的格局。譬如周延儒过去同东林作对，

afraid that he's not that sincere. It's just a perfunctory gesture. He makes it because his recent comeback to power is the result of East Wooders helping him, but meanwhile he's created such a great hurdle to make me retreat." He stroked the gray beard that fell to his chest, with a mocking look on his face, saying, "Premier Zhou is no stranger to me. It can be said that we know each other only too well. In a word, as long as Zhou Yanru is in court for one more day, I, the guy surnamed Qian, will have to behave and stay a recluse in the woods for one more day."

Chen Zaizhu and Qian Yangxian glanced at each other, not understanding why Qian Qianyi suddenly made such a gloomy remark. Indeed, there had been a private grievance between Qian Qianyi and Zhou Yanru, and this private grievance could be traced back to AD 1629, the second year of the reign of Emperor Chongzhen. At that time, some important figures of the East Wood Party, such as Gu Xiancheng, Gao Panlong, Li Sancai, Yang Lian, Zuo Guangdou, Zou Yuanbiao, Huang Zunsu, among others, had already died in fierce partisan battles and Qian Qianyi, as a surviving member of weight, was pushed out to compete for a Cabinet position. Unexpectedly, he was met with hostility from the jealous Minister of Rites Wen Tiren and Right Vice Minister of the Ministry of Rites Zhou Yanru, who joined hands and petitioned to the emperor against him with an old, unconfirmed accusation that he had colluded with a few candidates and taken bribes while presiding over the provincial-level examination in Zhejiang in AD 1621, the first year of the reign of Emperor Tianqi. As a result, not only did his dream of becoming head of the Cabinet evaporate, but also, he was discharged from his position as a Right Vice Minister of the Ministry of Rites, and, thump, he fell back to his hometown Changshu. It was thirteen years since then. On the contrary, during that period, Wen Tiren and Zhou Yanru entered the Cabinet one after the other to become top officials. Over the years, they had paid a great deal of attention to Qian Qianyi and spared no effort to suppress him lest he should have a chance to come back. Chen Zaizhu and Qian Yangxian were well aware of it. However, connections in officialdom were intricately complicated, and there was no permanent friend or

这一次，却因东林的推荐而重新入阁。何况，钱谦益的克星温体仁，已于崇祯九年引疾辞职。如今朝廷上，起用钱谦益的呼声日益高涨。为什么事到临头，钱谦益反而变得如此消极犹疑，畏葸不前呢？这确实使两位心腹族人迷惑不解。特别是陈在竹，他满心以为自己这一次进京，虽然多花了些银子，但总算不辱使命，应当大大记上一功，现在被钱谦益兜头浇了一瓢冷水，心中颇不服气。他于是干咳了一声，清了清嗓子，说：

“姐夫所虑，莫非是复社那一班士子不易对付？那么，小弟已筹之熟矣。依小弟愚见，复社的那班书生真正恨阮圆海的，其实也就是那十个八个爱闹事的角儿。其余的人，有一多半是随大流、瞎起哄罢了。何况，据我所知，便是复社当中，不赞成将阮圆海逼得太甚的，也大有人在……”

“谁？”钱谦益问。

“广陵的郑超宗是一个，还有云间的李舒章、夏彝仲那一班人，为数并不少。”

钱谦益摇摇头：“嗯——说下去。”

“此外，我们常熟，复社中人也不少。只要姐夫一句话，谁敢不遵？”陈在竹急急补充一句，然后，把身子更倾向钱谦益，压低声音接着说，“现在已经知道，三月二十八那天，复社要在虎丘重开大会。这一次大会的主盟，刚好就是郑超宗和李舒章两个。我们何不借此机会，联络郑、李和上面那些人，嗯，自然还可以再多——只要我们派人去游说。到时，就在大会上，揭出值此国家多难之秋，亟宜消除朋党门户之见，和衷共济的大义，连

foe, nor is there permanent love or hate. For example, Zhou Yanru used to be a bitter enemy of the East Wooders, but this time, he re-entered the Cabinet based on their recommendation. What was more, Qian Qianyi's archenemy Wen Tiren had resigned in AD 1636, the ninth year of the reign of Emperor Chongzhen, because of his illness. Now, at the imperial court, the voice was becoming increasingly stronger for Qian Qianyi's reinstatement. Why did Qian Qianyi become so pessimistic and lack confidence when his opportunity came? It really puzzled the two close relations, especially Chen Zaizhu, who was very displeased because instead of being thanked for his successful trip to the capital—expensive as it was—he received a bucket of cold water on his head. He coughed dryly, cleared his throat, and said:

"My dear brother-in-law, are you concerned that the batch of scholars in the Fushe are a problem? I've thought out a plan. In my humble opinion, of the Fushe scholars, there are in fact no more than eight to ten troublemakers who really hate Ruan Yuanhai with a vengeance. The rest of them are mostly noisemakers following the crowd. What's more, as far as I know, many of them don't want to be too unforgiving of Ruan Yuanhai—"

"Who are they?" Qian Qianyi asked.

"Zheng Chaozong in Guangling is one of them, and quite a few in Yunjian, such as Li Shuzhang and Xia Yizhong."

Qian Qianyi shook his head and said, "Well, go on."

"In addition, quite a few in the Changshu chapter of the Fushe. As long as my brother-in-law says something, who would dare not listen?" Chen Zaizhu anxiously added. Then, leaning closer to Qian Qianyi, he continued in a lowered voice, "The Fushe will reconvene on Tiger Hill on the twenty-eighth of March. The head organizers happen to be Zheng Chaozong and Li Shuzhang. Why don't we take this opportunity to contact Mr. Zheng, Mr. Li and those above, um, of course, the more the better? All we have to do is send someone to talk to them. At the meeting, we'll make the point that, at this hour of national crisis, we should forget partisan interests and work for the common good, and then we'll timely bring up the matter of Ruan

带把阮圆海的事情提出来。只要多数人赞成，作出公议，上闻朝廷，那几个爱闹事的刺头儿再要强项，也无济于事了！”

陈在竹一口气说完，目不转睛地看着钱谦益。他由于心情紧张，连经常挂在脸上的乐呵呵表情也不见了。

有好一阵，钱谦益拈须不语，似乎在考虑，然而，终于还是摇摇头。他抬起眼睛，正要说话，忽然看见李宝站在窗外探头探脑，就顿住了。他生气地把桌子一拍，呵斥说：“混账东西，你在那儿干什么？”

李宝连忙走进来，呈上一个拜帖。

钱谦益没好气地接过，瞥了瞥，正想朝李宝直掼过去，仿佛想起了什么，又朝帖子看了一眼，忽然微微变了脸色。他目光朝陈、钱二人一闪，慢慢把拜帖袖在手里，站起来，用漫不经心的口气说：“二位请稍待，我出去片刻便来。”

陈在竹和钱养先目送着钱谦益匆匆走出的背影，有点莫名其妙，只好慢慢地喝着茶，一边谈些没关紧要的事情，一边等候。

谁知足足等了一个时辰，天都快要暗下来了，钱谦益还不回来。两人等得心烦意乱，坐立不安。好不容易才看见李宝匆匆走进来，说：“启禀二位老爷，我家老爷说，他眼下有件要紧的事情绊住了，回不来送二位老爷。请二位老爷先回府去，我家老爷改日当面谢罪。”

陈在竹和钱养先听了，不禁面面相觑，虽然觉得颇为扫兴，但也无可奈何，只好怏怏地一齐起身，出门下楼而去。

## 春闺情浓

不知是由于钱孙爱的意外求见，还是别的缘故，柳如是终于在最后一刻里改变了主意，没再让红情把诗笺退给钱谦益。虽然

Yuanhai. As long as the majority agree and make a joint resolution to be submitted to the imperial court, the troublemakers would go nowhere, however strong their objection."

Chen Zaizhu spoke in one breath and stared at Qian Qianyi intently. The cheerful expression on his face disappeared because of his nervousness.

Qian Qianyi pondered for a long time, stroking his beard but finally shook his head. When he raised his eyes to speak, he noticed Li Bao was peeping in from outside the window. He slapped his hand on the table angrily and yelled, "Idiot! What are you doing there?"

Li Bao walked in quickly and presented a calling card.

Qian Qianyi took it discourteously, glanced at it, and was about to throw it back to Li Bao; then, as if remembering something, he glanced at the card again. Suddenly, his countenance changed. Casting a look at Mr. Chen and Mr. Qian, he tucked the hand with the card into his sleeve, stood up, and said in a flat tone, "My dear sirs, please wait a moment. I'll be back shortly."

Seeing Qian Qianyi left in such a hurry, Chen Zaizhu and Qian Yangxian were a little puzzled. While waiting for his return, they beguiled the time with tea and trivial chatter.

They waited and waited. Two hours passed and it was getting dark. Qian Qianyi didn't come back. The two men became uneasy, not knowing whether they would sit or stand. Finally, they saw Li Bao, who hurriedly walked in and said, "Dear sirs, my master said he's delayed by an urgent matter and he begs your pardon for not being able to see you off. We'd better let you go now and my master will apologize to you in person another day."

Hearing that, Chen Zaizhu and Qian Yangxian looked at each other, utterly disappointed, then stood up, went downstairs and left.

## Husband and Concubine Reconciled

Because of Qian Sun'ai's unexpected request to see her or something else, Liu Rushi finally changed her mind at the last moment and no longer asked Hongqing to return the poetry sheets to Qian

她的怒气仍未平息，但是已经不再像先前那样大发雷霆。她站在大铜火盆前，目不转睛地朝毕剥作响的通红炭火瞅了很久。当她重新转过脸来的时候，那表情又变得安闲而自信了。

她在梳妆台前坐下来，让红情继续替她梳妆。现在，她似乎完全忘记了刚才发生的事，显得特别的愉快，她不停地同红情说着笑话儿，还教她念了两首诗。末了，她随手捡起刚才那张诗笺，把玩了一下，又微微一笑："光顾着教你念诗，倒差点忘了老爷这两首诗。这是我在姑苏治病那阵子，他写了寄给我的。如今改了几个字，又巴巴地送来给我看。不过，这第一首，结句改作'待君佳句发芳丛'，是点着要我酬他。我本来要动笔，这些日子正病着，想了几句，又搁下了。趁着如今有点兴头，不免要还了这笔债。嗯，这里不用你了，给我张罗纸墨去吧。"

说着，柳如是就从红情手中接过梳子，对着镜子自己妆扮起来。她依着当时流行的"雅装"式样，把头发像男子那样，直梳上去，挽成一个堕马髻，垂在后边，两旁插上一对金玉梅花，前面则用金绞丝、灯笼簪，再用两对西番莲花簪，分插两边。由于头发丰厚，又拿了两枝犀玉大簪，横贯在发股上，后面则用点翠卷荷一朵。妆戴好之后，她对着镜子想了想，又在鬓边再加插一朵巴掌大小的珠翠，最后，挑一串珠嵌金玉丁香耳坠戴上。对着镜子又端详了两三遍，她终于觉得满意了，才盈盈地站起来。

红情趁这会子，已经在长几上安排好了宣纸、湖笔，又用那

Qianyi. Although her anger hadn't yet subsided, she no longer let out bursts of temper. She stood in front of the big brass brazier and stared at the crackling and blazing charcoal fire for a long time. When she turned away from the fire, her expression became relaxed and confident again.

She sat down in front of the dressing table and let Hongqing continue to dress her up. Now, she was in good cheer, as if she had completely forgotten what had happened just now. She even joked with Hongqing and taught the maid two poems. Then, suddenly she picked up the poetry sheets, fiddled with them, and smiled, saying, "I was teaching you other poems and almost forgot the ones from his lordship. This is what he wrote and sent to me while I was getting treatment in Gusu. Now he's sending them again with a few changed words. However, the change in the concluding lines—"Without your magic lines, how can the cold stamens and pistils make their metamorphoses" —is evidently a request for a reply poem. I was going to write it some time ago, but since I was still not well, after coming up with a few lines, I had to put it aside. Let me pay the debt while I'm inspired today. Well, you don't have to be here. Just bring me ink and paper."

As she spoke, Liu Rushi took the comb from Hongqing's hand and continued to dress up in front of the mirror. Following the popular elegant style of dressing, her hair was combed straight up like that of a man and at the end woven into a falling-off-the-horse bun, which hung down on the back of the head with a pair of gold-and-jade plum flowers on the sides, and was affixed in the front of her head by gold chains and a lantern-headed hairpin and on each side of her head by a pair of passiflora hairpins. Because her hair was thick, she struck two long rhino-horn pins through the hair strands and put a crystal lotus flower on the back. Having done her hair, she studied herself in the mirror, and then added a palm-sized emerald-and-pearl ornament to the sideburns. Finally, she chose a lilac-shaped gold-and-jade ear ornament embedded with pearls and put it on. After looking in the mirror again and again, she finally felt satisfied and stood up.

During that time, Hongqing put on the writing bench some sandalwood paper, a brush pen, and a seven-eyed ancient Duan

一方有着七颗鹳鸽眼的端州老坑古砚，浓浓地磨了一砚香墨。柳如是径直走过去，拈起一支鸡狼小楷毛笔，在砚台上调弄了一会儿，又仔细拂去落在锦笺上的一点灰尘，略一沉吟，先写出诗的题目——

牧斋夫子见示献岁书怀之作，次韵奉答

她歪着头，端详一下自己瘦长遒劲的书法，觉得还满意，正打算把已经拟好腹稿的一篇七言律诗写上去。忽然，她感到起句中有一个字还欠工稳，于是停了笔，又沉吟起来。

她本以为要换一个字并不难，谁知一连想了七八个字，仍然觉得不妥，便有点焦躁。正思索间，听见有人"哧——"地一笑，她气恼地回头瞪了一眼，蓦地发现，原来是钱谦益老爷站在身后，正偷偷地瞧她写诗哩！

钱谦益抚摸着花白胡子，呵呵地笑着，催促说："咦，写呀，写呀，我这儿正等着拜读哩！"

"你偷看人家，你坏，我不嘛！"柳如是扔下笔，像个小姑娘似的噘着唇儿，扭着身子。

"啊啊，啊啊，夫人生气了，这可不得了啦！"钱谦益故作惊慌地说，"哎，我这厢给夫人赔个礼，好不好？"他笑嘻嘻地说，果真作下揖去。

"不行！"柳如是鼓着腮帮子。

"那——就再添一个礼。"钱谦益说着，又作了一个揖。

"不行！"

"哈哈，莫非夫人要为夫三下其礼？那也未尝不可——"

"不，我要——罚你！"柳如是故意绷着脸儿。

"罚我？嘻嘻，好，好，我打断夫人的诗思，原该受罚！只不知夫人如何罚法？"钱谦益涎着脸，挨了过来。

inkstone filled with newly ground ink. Liu Rushi walked straight over, picked up a small-script brush pen, adjusted it on the inkstone for a while, carefully brushed off some dust on the superfine paper, and, after pondering for a moment, wrote down the title of a poem:

*"A Humble Reply to Mr. Muzhai's New Year Poems Written for Me"*

Tilting her head, she looked at her fine yet vigorous strokes and felt satisfied. She was about to write down the seven-character eight-line poem that had already hatched in her mind when suddenly she realized that one of the characters was not a perfect fit, so she stopped to think of a better one.

She first thought changing one character should be easy, but after trying seven or eight substitutes in a row, she became agitated. As she was racking her brains, she heard a "woah" from someone and turned her head with an angry glare only to see that it was his lordship himself standing behind her furtively watching her writing the poem.

Stroking his gray beard, he smiled and urged her to continue by saying, "Well, go on—go on. I'm waiting to read it."

"You peek at me! You're a bad man. I won't." Liu Rushi dropped the brush pen, pouting her lips like a little girl, swaying her hips.

"Hah, my lady is angry. It's too bad." Qian Qianyi pretended to panic. "I apologize. Please accept my bow, my fair lady. Does that satisfy you?" he said with a grin. Then he really bowed down.

"No, it doesn't!" Liu Rushi puffed her cheeks.

"Then, let me bow again," Qian Qianyi said, giving another bow.

"No, it doesn't!"

"Haha, does my lady want her husband to bow three times? I have no problem with that," he said.

"No. I want to punish you." Liu Rushi pulled a long face.

"Punish me? Haha, okay, okay, I should've been punished for interrupting my lady's poetic outburst. I just don't know how you execute the punishment, my dear lady," Qian Qianyi said, moving his drooling face close to hers.

“哼，我要，我要——对了，我要拔你一根胡子！”

钱谦益蓦地一惊，忙不迭地后退。他用袖子护着胡子，结结巴巴地说：“这，这可使不得！请夫人另出题目，另出题目！”

可是柳如是不由分说，她伶俐地赶上去，按住钱谦益，飞快伸出手，待到钱谦益再想躲闪时，一根长长的白胡子，已经拔了下来。

柳如是用两根纤美的手指，高高举着她的战利品，跳开去，兴高采烈地舞弄着，哈哈大笑。

钱谦益尴尬地眨着眼睛，无可奈何地退到靠墙的一张椅子上坐下来。这时，红情早已知趣地退了出去。钱谦益等柳如是闹够了，笑乏了，才招呼说：“如是，你且坐，我有话要跟你说。”

柳如是闭着眼睛，“嗳”的一声，倒在旁边的一张椅子里。经过刚才这一闹，她已经有点气喘吁吁，胸脯起伏着，略觉苍白的脸颊上，升起了两朵娇艳的红晕，微闭的眼睑上粉光流动，越发显得俏丽迷人。钱谦益呆呆地瞅着她，一时忘记了说话。

“哎，你倒是快说呀！”柳如是催促说。

“啊，”钱谦益定了定神，又瞧了柳如是一眼，不知为什么，轻轻叹了一口气，说，“如是，你又该高兴了。我刚才已经对孙爱说，要把老三迁出半野堂，让她到城东旧宅子去住。往后，这儿再也没有人跟你捣乱了。”

柳如是的眉毛跳动了一下，张开眼睛说：“啊，这么说相公到底拿定主意了？”

钱谦益的脸色变得有点阴沉。他默默地点点头。

“嗯，你告诉了孙爱，他怎么样？”

"Hmm, I want to, I want to—yeah, I want to pull a hair from your beard."

Qian Qianyi was shocked and backed away hurriedly. He covered his beard with a sleeve and said with a stutter, "No, no! That, that can't be done, my lady. Pray use another method—another method."

But Liu Rushi, regardless of the objection, swiftly overwhelmed him and, holding him by one hand, quickly reached out the other. Before Qian Qianyi was able to dodge again, a long white hair had already been pulled off.

Liu Rushi held her trophy aloft in her two slender fingers, jumped away, and waved it in the air, laughing boisterously.

Blinking his eyes awkwardly, Qian Qianyi reluctantly retreated to a chair against the wall and sat down. By then, Hongqing had knowingly retreated. Qian Qianyi waited until the mischief was over and Liu Rushi stopped laughing. Then, he gestured to her and said, "Rushi, sit. I have something to tell you."

Liu Rushi said "aye sir" with her eyes closed and threw herself into a chair nearby. Mischief over, she was gasping for air, her chest rising and falling with each breath, two alluring patches of redness having risen on her palish cheeks, and a feminine charm dancing on her slightly closed eyelids. She became all the more enchanting and all the more captivating to him. He stared at her spellbound, forgetting to speak for a while.

"Why, just say it," Liu Rushi urged.

"Mmm," Qian Qianyi recollected himself and glanced at his love. For some reason he sighed, but then said, "Rushi, you'll be flattered. I told Sun'ai just now that I plan to relocate the Third Lady from the Half Wild Estate to the old residence in the east of the city. From now on, no one in the house will ever make trouble for you anymore."

Liu Rushi's eyebrows twitched. She opened her eyes and said, "Has my dear husband finally made up his mind?"

Qian Qianyi's face became a tad gloomy. He nodded his head in silence.

"Well, what did Sun'ai say when you told him this?"

钱谦益冷冷地说："他还能怎样？莫说他还是个孩子，就是再长几岁，难道还敢违抗父命不成！"他停了停，又补充说："起初嘛，自然是不愿意的，老三毕竟是他的生母。不过，后来经我一番开导，他倒也能体察为父的苦衷。"

柳如是轻轻地摇着头，仿佛在考虑什么。她忽然回过头来："要是——要是我改变主意了呢？"

"嗯，你说什么？"钱谦益似乎没有听清，他把右边那只耳朵侧了过来。

"我说，我要是改变了主意！"柳如是提高声音。

钱谦益盯着柳如是，目光闪动。他忽然放声大笑起来，摇着头说："罢了，夫人又来作弄我了！刚才，我已经领教过你的雅罚，这会儿，腮帮子还疼得慌哩！"

"不，"柳如是认真地说，"刚才我反复思量过了，决意暂且饶过那悍妇，让她留在府里再得意几天。"她站起来，在室内走了几步，"相公这一阵子正在筹划起用的事，妾身不想在这节骨眼儿上，招来外间的物议，耽误了相公的前程。"

钱谦益不再笑了。柳如是的这几句话，正说中了他心中的隐忧。他本是个功名事业心极重的人，早年也曾满怀匡济澄清的雄心大志，只是由于宦途坎坷，迭遭大挫，才变得消沉颓废起来，终日在秦楼楚馆中厮混，结果得了个"东林浪子"的外号。近几年，他因为年纪大了，再像当年那样，到风月场去打滚征逐，已经没有那份精力。对于他来说，最理想的，是有一位既年轻貌美，又多少有点学识才情的女人，整天在身边陪伴他，侍候他，让他可以惬意地消受晚年的"无双艳福"。所以，一年前，当柳如是女扮男装，方巾儒服，亲访半野堂，表示有意委身相嫁的

Qian Qianyi said coldly, "What could he say? He's still a child after all; even if he were a few years older, would he dare to defy his father?" He stopped and added, "At first, he wasn't happy. After all, his Third Mother is his mother by birth. After I explained, he was able to understand the predicament of a father."

Liu Rushi waved her head slowly, as if thinking something, then suddenly turned to Qian Qianyi and said, "What if—what if I've changed my mind?"

"Mmm, what did you say?" asked Qian Qianyi, turning his right ear to her as if he hadn't heard it clearly.

"I said, what if I've changed my mind?" Liu Rushi said in a louder voice.

Qian Qianyi stared at Liu Rushi, his eyes fluttering. Then, he suddenly burst into laughter and said, shaking his head, "Well, well, my dear lady is kidding me again. Just now, I had the honor of experiencing your gracious punishment and my cheeks are still smarting from it."

"No, I'm not kidding you," Liu Rushi said in earnest. "I've thought about it just now and decided to spare the shrew for the time being and let her stay here for a few more days." She stood up and moved a few steps in the room. "My dear husband, you've been busy with the matter of getting reinstated to office, and I as your concubine don't want to incur rumors at this juncture that might damage the prospects of your career."

Qian Qianyi stopped smiling. These few words of Liu Rushi hit the spot in his heart. Originally a man of great ambition, he had had big plans for life in his early years. After all the ups and downs he had been disheartened and become a muddler in places of pleasure with a notorious nickname East Wood Dissipator. In recent years, he was too old to have that energy to roll and make conquests in pleasure lands. For him, the ideal thing was to have a young and beautiful woman with a little learning and talent to accompany and wait upon him all day long so that he would be able to enjoy unparalleled bliss in old age to his heart's content. Therefore, a year ago, when Liu Rushi, disguised as a man with a square headscarf and a Confucian robe

时候，钱谦益的惊异和狂喜，是难以形容的。何况，柳如是的那一份仪容、那一份才智、那一份风情，又绝非寻常风尘女子所能企及。为着报答柳如是的情意，钱谦益决定置原配夫人陈氏于不顾，公然同柳如是举行正式的婚娶大礼；他还吩咐家人称呼柳如是为“夫人”，而不是按常礼称为“姨太”；至于他自己，则称柳如是作“河东君”。这种越轨的行为，引起了盛泽、常熟两地士绅们的大哗。结果去年六月，当钱谦益亲乘彩舟，大吹大擂，把柳如是接回半野堂时，便受到两地卫道之士们的围攻嘲骂，甚至赶着彩船掷砖头，飞瓦片，弄得狼狈不堪。虽说钱谦益毫不在乎，照旧喜滋滋作他的《催妆词》，不过近半年来，外界舆论却于他颇为不利，说他“亵渎朝廷之名器，伤败士大夫之体统”。倘若这一次因为驱逐朱氏，在缙绅中再度引起公愤，闹将起来，传到皇帝耳朵里去，那么，他辛辛苦苦地等待、钻营了十三年的东山再起的机会，就很可能化为泡影。此后，也许就未必再有此机缘了。这种情况，钱谦益事前并非没有考虑过。但是，眼前的这个美丽的女人，在他生活中已经变得如此重要，如此不可缺少，他不忍，也不敢拂逆她的意愿。何况，对于周延儒所提出的那个条件，他又疑惧重重，毫无把握。所以，犹豫再三，钱谦益还是横一横心，决定把朱姨太逐出府去。不过，当他这样做的时候，内心仍旧未能坦然无愧，因为朱姨太毕竟是他唯一的儿子的生

visited the Half Wild Estate and expressed her willingness to marry him, Qian Qianyi was surprised and overjoyed. What was more, Liu Rushi's beauty, talent, and magnetism were absolutely beyond the reach of ordinary "women in the dust". In order to repay Liu Rushi's affection, Qian Qianyi openly held a formal wedding ceremony disregarding the objection of his wife Lady Chen. He even ordered his family to call Liu Rushi *furen*, form of address for a wife, instead of the regular *yitai*, form of address for a concubine while he himself called Liu Rushi Lady of River East. This kind of deviant behavior caused a great uproar among the gentry in Shengze and Changshu. As a result, in June① last year, when Qian Qianyi hired a boat and welcomed Liu Rushi to the Half Wild Estate with great fanfare, he was besieged, ridiculed, and condemned on the way by the defenders of morality in the two places, who even chased after the boat throwing bricks and tiles at it. It was embarrassing. He was in the least bothered and it didn't prevent him from writing his poems A Plea for Immediate Marriage, but in the past six months, public opinion had completely turned against him. People said that he had "desecrated the title and vehicle bestowed by the imperial court and breached the code of conduct of scholar-officials." If this time, should the expulsion of Lady Zhu arouse public outrage among the gentry scholars once again and the emperor hear of it, the opportunity of a comeback that he had been preparing for and waiting for in the past thirteen years would very likely burst like a bubble. It was his last chance. Not that Qian Qianyi hadn't weighed it in his mind. The beautiful woman in front of him had become only too important and too indispensable to his life. He didn't want or dare to go against her wishes. What was more, he was not sure he could ever fulfill the condition set by Zhou Yanru. Therefore, after some hesitation, Qian Qianyi decided to expel Lady Zhu out of the estate. However, when he finally made the decision, he

① June: June in the lunar calendar. For the sake of convenience, the names of the twelve months of the Gregorian calendar are used to mean the Chinese lunar months in this translation unless otherwise self-evident in the text.

母。刚才，他就是怀着这么一种苦恼的心情，把消息告知柳如是的。现在，忽然听见柳如是说出如此知心体贴、顾识大体的一句话，钱谦益不禁深为感动。他沉默了一会儿，点着头说："你——过来。"

柳如是莫名其妙地走到他的跟前。钱谦益伸出一双多皱的、长着老人斑的大手，把柳如是纤弱温馨的小手握住，用深沉的声调说："我很高兴！钱谦益得到你这样的闺中知己，不虚此生了！"

柳如是心中一动，这才恍然领悟钱谦益的心思。她勉强地笑着，眼圈儿却不由得红了，半晌，才慢悠悠地说："只要相公永远记着今日这句话，我就是明儿死了，也是心甘情愿的！"

钱谦益点着头，叹息道："你快别这么说。我知道，我已经是垂暮之年，可你往后的日子还长着呢。不过，你放心，我自会安排得妥妥帖帖，决不会让你这一辈子受委屈的！"

柳如是瞪大眼睛，呆呆地望着钱谦益，忽然"哇"的一声，扑在他的怀里，哭了起来。钱谦益也颇觉恻然。他喃喃地劝慰着，可是柳如是反而哭得更伤心了。她其实是个极不幸的女子，多年的风尘沦落、青楼卖笑的生涯，使她早已看透了人世的丑恶、凶残、冷酷和欺诈。她十二岁那年，被卖到吴江县一个退职内阁大学士家去当婢女，不久就遭到男主人的蹂躏，成为那个行将就木的老头儿的玩物。两年后，因为受到其他姬妾的嫉妒，她几乎被谗害致死。主人把她卖到盛泽的归家院，给一个叫徐拂的名妓做养女，从此正式操起了卖笑生涯。她聪明美貌，很快就走红起来。

was unable to free himself from guilt, because, after all, Lady Zhu was birth mother to his only son. That accounted for the grim mood when he had told Liu Rushi his decision. Now, seeing she was so considerate and obliging, Qian Qianyi was deeply moved. He mused for an instant, then nodded and said, "Come here, sweetheart."

Liu Rushi walked up to him, not knowing what he would do or say. He stretched out a pair of big, wrinkled hands with age spots, held her delicate and warm little hands, and said in a deep tone, "I'm happy and content. Qian Qianyi's life is worthwhile to have a lady soulmate like you."

Liu Rushi's heart throbbed, having finally known what Qian Qianyi had been thinking. She smiled, but the rims of her eyes turned red. After a long while, she slowly said, "My dear husband, as long as you always remember what you've said today, I would have no regrets were I to die tomorrow."

Qian Qianyi nodded his head and sighed, "Stop saying that. I know my days are numbered, but your days are not. However, you can rest assured that I'll arrange everything properly and you'll never have to worry about anything."

Liu Rushi widened her eyes and looked at Qian Qianyi intently. Then she suddenly threw herself into his arms and "waah" started crying with a vengeance. Qian Qianyi was all sympathy. He consoled her in a murmur, but she cried even more violently. She was actually a very unfortunate woman. Years of life as a fallen woman selling laughter in the brothels had enabled her to see through the evils, cruelties, cold-bloodedness, and deceptions of the human world. When she was twelve years old, she was sold to the house of a retired Cabinet member living in Wujiang County to work as a housemaid. Soon afterwards, she was deflowered by her owner and became a plaything of the dying old man. After two years, she almost died of persecution by the old man's wife and concubines. Later, her owner sold her to the Homecoming brothel in Shengze, where she became an adopted daughter of a famous prostitute named Xu Fu and commenced her career as a prostitute. Being smart and beautiful, she quickly

为了保护自己，也为了报复，她开始变得又刁蛮又放肆，经常把那些色迷迷的狎客捉弄得团团乱转，哭笑不得。因了这股狂劲儿，她的名声反而更响了，所到之处，引得那些自命风流的公子名士趋之若鹜，为了获得她的一诗一画，不惜一掷多金。至于为着博取她的青睐而展开的角逐争夺，就更加激烈了。不过柳如是也知道，这种状况是不可能维持太久的，于是，便开始在那些慕名而来的客人当中，物色自己可以托付终身的人。几经挫折和痛苦之后，她选中了钱谦益。钱谦益有的是名望、金钱，而且盛传他很快就会被重新起用，入阁拜相。这对于饱尝卑贱的滋味，因而强烈渴望往上爬的柳如是来说，确是一个理想的从良对象。钱谦益是老了一点，但老年人听话，心眼儿不是那么活，而且懂得疼惜人……事实上，自从嫁到常熟来之后，这大半年，钱谦益对她百依百顺，宝贝得不得了。为着讨她的欢心，老头儿甚至一再牺牲自己的社会名誉而在所不惜。对此，柳如是是十分感激的。正为着不使老头儿过于为难，也为着自己的更高目标——当一个纵无其名也有其实的“阁老夫人”——不致成为泡影，她才断然决定暂时放弃把朱姨娘赶出府去的要求。现在，终于从老头儿口中，得到了这样一个郑重其事的许诺，她怎能不私心大慰。只是想到过去十几年中，自己所付出的种种辛酸的代价，她才又不禁百感交集，悲从中来……

柳如是的这种复杂心情，钱谦益自然是不会理解的。他只把柳如是的眼泪，当作是感激自己的表示。于是他不胜爱怜地抚着柳如是的肩背。等她哭够了，才轻轻地把她扶起来，让她到紫檀木长几前坐下，又替她打开梳妆匣子。他一边看着柳如是重新化妆，一边用了快活的声调说：“哈，我倒忘了告诉你一件稀奇事儿，还要借重你这位‘女元龙[①]’替我出出主意——”他正想说下去，

① 元龙，即陈登，三国时期曹操手下谋士。

became popular. Partly to protect herself and partly to retaliate, she became savagely mischievous and her lecherous pursuers were often caught between tears and laughter. This madness enhanced her reputation. Wherever she went, those self-proclaimed romantic souls of high society flocked to her, throwing large sums of money to get a poem or a painting from her. The competition to win her favor was even more intense. However, she knew that such days would not last long, so she began to look from among her admirers for someone to whom she could entrust herself for life. After several painful setbacks, she finally found Qian Qianyi. The old man was rich and famous, and it was speculated that he would soon be reinstated to office and become a Cabinet minister. He was indeed an ideal husband for a prostitute like her, who had been humbled by life and therefore had a strong desire to go up except that he was a tad too old for her, but an old man knew how to take care of her and would be easy to conquer as he didn't have the fickleness of a young man. Indeed, since she was married to him in Changshu, Qian Qianyi had been very loving and submissive to her for the past six months. In order to please her, he even disregarded damage to his own social reputation. She was very grateful. In order not to make things too difficult for the old man, and in order that her higher goal—to become wife of a minister in substance if not in name—would not evaporate, she decided to give up temporarily her demand that Lady Zhu be driven out of the residence. Now that she had finally obtained a solemn promise from the old man, her selfish heart was greatly comforted, but meanwhile a deep sadness arose as she thought of the bitter price she had paid over the past ten years.

Such a mixed feeling on her part of course would never be understood by Qian Qianyi. He only took her tears to be an expression of gratitude. So, he affectionately stroked her shoulders, and when she stopped crying, gently lifted her up, seated her in front of the red sandalwood table, and opened the dressing box for her. He watched her redo her makeup, and said in a cheerful tone, "Um, I forgot to tell you something curious. I need the help of the genius of the female version of the great strategist Yuanlong—that's what you are—to

忽然看见红情擎着一盏斗色晶灯走进来，就住了口。

红情把灯放在案上，敛衽说："老爷、夫人，夜饭已经开上来了。请老爷、夫人过去用膳。"

柳如是望望窗外，天色果然不早了。她沉吟了一下，说："这会子，我觉得身子怪乏的，也没有胃口，懒得再走过去了。你侍候老爷去用膳吧，回头盛一碗粥，再把小菜也给我送来，就完了。"

钱谦益一听，连忙说："这么着，我也不过去了，你们索性全搬了过来，我就在这屋里同夫人一块儿吃。"

红情答应着，退了出去。

柳如是微微一笑，表示领会到钱谦益的体贴之意。她眼睛一转，提醒说："噢，相公刚才有什么稀奇的事儿要说？"

"哦，是这么回事——刚才，我在西院，正同在竹、养先商议周阁老那封信的事，忽然来了个求见的，我一瞧帖子，倒吃了一惊。你猜那人是谁？竟是阮圆海家的一个清客，叫臧亦嘉，余姚人，是个戏曲班子的教习，不知你可认识？几年前，我在南京见过他一面，差点儿忘记了。这一次，他奉了阮圆海之命，专程到常熟来，喏，给我带来这一封信。"钱谦益说着，从袖子里掏出来一封信，放在桌上，笑着说，"阮圆海在信里说什么他也是进士出身，素知忠君爱国的大义，他过去依附魏阉是不得已，也不曾反对东林，全是一篇鬼话！不过，最后那几句说得倒真切，竟是信誓旦旦，说是'所不改心以相事者，有如此水！'哈哈，这胡子急着重新出头，只怕快急疯了哩！"

know what to do—" He stopped upon seeing Hongqing walk in with a crystal lamp in her hand.

Hongqing put the lamp on the table, and said with a curtsy, "My lord and my lady, dinner is ready. Please move to the dinner table."

Liu Rushi looked out the window. It was indeed late. She hesitated for an instant and said, "I'm not going. I have no appetite because I'm not feeling well. Take his lordship to the dinner table. Just get me a bowl of porridge and some pickles."

Upon hearing it, Qian Qianyi said, "Then, I'll stay with you. Hongqing, just bring all the food here and I'll eat with my wife in this room."

Hongqing said "aye, my lord" and retreated.

Liu Rushi smiled meekly in appreciation of her husband's kindness. She rolled her eyes and said expectantly, "So, what's that something curious you wanted to tell me just now?"

"Um, here it is: just now, when I was discussing the letter from His Eminence the Honorable Mr. Zhou with Zaizhu and Yangxian, suddenly someone requested to see me. I was taken aback when I saw the calling card. Guess who that person was? It was Zang Yijia, a man from Yuyao, a patronee of Ruan Yuanhai. He's director of Ruan Yuanhai's opera group. Do you know him? I met him in Nanjing a few years ago and have almost forgotten him. He was sent here by Ruan Yuanhai to deliver this letter to me," Qian Qianyi said. He took out a letter from his sleeve, put it on the table, and said with a smile, "Ruan Yuanhai says in the letter that as a *jinshi* scholar he knows the importance of loyalty to the emperor and love of country, that his prior submission to Wei the eunuch was a result of the circumstances, and that he's never opposed the East Wood Party, blah blah blah—it's all crap. However, the last few lines are said with sincerity, in which he vows, 'I'll be a loyal servant to Your Eminence, upon the White Water[1]!' Haha, this bastard is so anxious to turn over a new leaf that he's gone nuts!"

---

① "White Water" refers to the Yellow River.

柳如是看了一眼那封信，问："相公同陈家老爷他们商议得怎样了？"

像忽然咬着一只苦果子似的，钱谦益的表情变得懊丧起来。他紧皱着眉毛说："还没个头绪。在竹出了个主意，说是可以利用三月二十八复社在虎丘举行大会之机，联络一帮子人，在会上提出消除门户朋党之见，共扶社稷，并作出公议，上达朝廷。本来么，也不失为一策。只是这一次虎丘大会，两浙的士子估计会来得不少。浙西倒还罢了，浙东的慈溪、甬上那一帮书呆子，却是难轧得很。何况，你也知道，自从天启元年，我主试浙江，闹了那一场公案之后，浙人之于我，已势成水火，又怎能指望这一次他们肯同我联手呢？"钱谦益说完，又连连叹气。

柳如是已经梳妆完毕。她拿着一根玉簪，在案上轻轻地敲着，说："阮圆海既然急急地派人送信来，此事看来不像是周相公有心推搪，只怕有几分真！陈家老爷的献策，也是可用的。至于浙人作对，嗯，确实是一道难题。不过……只要他们并非全都主张对阮圆海赶尽杀绝，事情就有可为……"

钱谦益心中一喜，连忙问："呵，莫非夫人已有良策？"

柳如是摇摇头。她笑起来："瞧相公的着急劲儿，只怕并不在阮圆海之下哩！我一个妇道人家，哪能有什么良策？不过闲着无事，我倒是可以替你想想。"

钱谦益被她打趣，毫不着恼。他喜滋滋地说："我知道夫人不只是个'女元龙'，还是个'女诸葛'，必有奇计妙策，为我分忧！"

Liu Rushi glanced at the letter and asked, "My dear husband, how did your discussion with Mr. Chen go?"

As if he had taken a bitter fruit into his mouth, Qian Qianyi's expression went grim. He frowned and said, "We've got no clue yet. Zaizhu has come up with an idea: The twenty-eighth of March, when the Fushe convenes at Tiger Hill, is a perfect opportunity for liaison with a bunch of scholars to sign a joint declaration on the elimination of partisan bias for cooperation in serving the country, to be submitted to the imperial court. It's not a bad idea in itself. The problem is, this time, there would be a lot of scholars from East Zhejiang and West Zhejiang. West Zhejiang is not much of a problem, but the nerds in Cixi and Yongshang of East Zhejiang are incorrigible. What's more, you know, in the first year of the reign of Emperor Tianqi[AD 1621], I was the head officer for the imperial exam in Zhejiang Province and became involved in a dispute. Ever since then, Zhejiang scholars and I have been like fire and water to each other. How can I expect them to join hands with me this time?" said Qian Qianyi, sighing.

Liu Rushi had finished dressing up. She said, tapping the dressing table with a jade hairpin, "Now that Ruan Yuanhai has asked his servant to bring you the letter in such a hurry, it doesn't seem that Premier Zhou is non-committal. I gather he might be serious. The advice of Mr. Chen is also good. The hostility from the Zhejiangers is indeed a hurdle to cross, but, as long as not all of them insist on a complete elimination of Ruan Yuanhai, there might be a way out—"

Qian Qianyi lit up and asked anxiously, "Well, does my good wife have a good plan?"

Liu Rushi shook her head. She laughed and said, "Look at you! My good husband's eagerness seems in no less measure than that of Ruan Yuanhai. I'm simply a woman. How can I have any good ideas? But when I have nothing to do, I can think about it for you."

Qian Qianyi was not the least annoyed by her teasing. He said, full of smiles, "I know that my good wife is not only a female Yuanlong but also a female version of the wisest Zhuge with extraordinary ideas to solve my problem."

这时，红情和另外一个长得又瘦又小的十二岁丫环绿意，已经把晚膳搬进寝室里来。于是，他们中止了谈话，站起来，一齐朝饭桌走去。

By this time, Hongqing and Lüyi, a thin and small twelve-year-old maid, had moved dinner into the bedroom. So, they stopped the conversation, stood up, and walked towards the food table.

# 第二章

# 冒公子求援尚书府，众社友纷争寒秀斋

## 拜访尚书

钱谦益与柳如是谈话一个月后的一天下午，在远离常熟数百里之外的南京城里，一乘两人抬的轿子，从秦淮河房转出来，匆匆过了贡院，顺着热闹繁华的街道，一直向西行去。

天气晴朗。温暖的阳光从蓝澄澄的天空中斜照下来，把左边一排房屋的阴影，投在宽敞的、青石板铺成的路面上，投在行人的头上、肩上；右边一排店铺的铺面，则沐浴在耀眼的阳光里。这些密密麻麻的店铺，房檐不高，门面挺宽，写着“绸绒老店”“京式小刀”“网巾发客”“画脂杭粉名香官皂”“川广杂货”“西北两口皮货发售”“东西两洋货物俱全”“内廊乐贤堂名书发兑”“万源号通商银铺”等类字样的招牌，琳琅满目。街道上，乘轿子的、跨驴的、步行的人，熙来攘往；来自四面八方的客商，麇集在官廊内，高声叫卖，讨价还价；门前挂着灯笼、供着时鲜花朵的茶

Chapter Two

# In Which Mao the Junior Asked for Help from the Minister of War and Members of the Fushe Contended in Cold Beauty Chamber

## The Minister of War

One afternoon, a month after Qian Qianyi and Liu Rushi had that conversation, in the city of Nanjing, hundreds of *li* away from Changshu, a two-carrier sedan chair came out of the Qinhuai Riverhouse, hurried past the Gongyuan, Imperial Academy of Exams, and went westward along the bustling street.

It was a clear day. Rays of warm sunlight shone diagonally from the blue sky, casting the shadows of the row of houses on the left onto the spacious, bluestone-paved road, and the heads and shoulders of pedestrians whereas the row of shops on the right were bathed in bright sunlight. These densely packed shops with low eaves and wide facades carried a miscellany of signboards like "OLD SILK AND VELVET SHOP", "BEIJING-STYLE KNIVES", "HAIR NET DISTRIBUTOR", "COSMETIC OIL, HANGZHOU POWDER, PREMIUM INCENSE, OFFICIAL SOAP", "SICHUAN AND GUANGXI GROCERIES", "DISTRIBUTOR OF NORTHWESTERN LEATHER", "EASTERN AND WESTERN SEAS IMPORT GOODS", "FAMOUS LEXIANTANG BOOKS SOLD INSIDE", and "TEN THOUSAND SOURCES MERCHANTS BANK". The streets were bustling with sedan chairs, donkey-riders, and pedestrians; merchants from all directions gathered in the public spaces hawked their wares and bargaining with their customers; business was brisk in the tea houses whose facades were decorated with lanterns and

社里，座无虚席，生意兴隆；酒楼上人声鼎沸，笙歌盈耳，随风飘散着哧哧的艳笑和酒肴诱人的浓香……虽然北有“建虏”，南有“流寇”，国家的局面一天乱似一天；江南各府又连年遭灾，“哀鸿遍野”“饿殍载道”一类的消息不断风闻；而且南京城里的米价，也涨到了三两六钱银子一石，为大明开国以来所仅见，但是，这一切似乎都未曾给这个江南最大的都会，投下一丝一毫的阴影。它依旧是那般容光焕发，巧笑迎人，金迷纸醉……

其实，令人不安的影子也不是没有——街上的流民乞丐明显增多了，而且有越来越多的趋势；米铺里，因为无人食用，过去很少出售的大麦、荞麦，现在忽然成了热门货，五千钱一石，仍然供不应求；酒筵歌席之上，那些哗笑哄饮的豪客，会因突如其来的一声悲叹，而举座为之失欢；甚至那些并无事实根据的谣言，也不止一次地使城中的居民们惊慌失措起来……不过，这些看来都无伤大体。正如向巨大的生活旋涡投下了几片枯叶，虽然多少使人感到惨淡和萧瑟，但是随即就被吞没，被包容，成了这个都市光怪陆离的日常生活必不可少的组成部分，一种很自然的色彩，不再引起人们的注目和惊诧了。是啊，天空这么晴朗，春光如此明媚，满城的柳树都开始吐芽了——这些被骚人墨客艳称为“白门[①]秀色”的柳树，有的已经十分古老，其中几株，也许还是太祖皇帝营建应天府城的时候种下的。经历了二百七十余年的漫

① 白门：古代南京的别称。

seasonal flowers; the restaurants were boisterous with noise, music, singing, and with the wind flew sounds of wanton laughter and seductive smells of wine and food. The megacity in the River South seemed to have been totally unaffected by the worsening situation of the country with barbarian invasion in the north and guerrilla bandits in the south; neither was it affected by rumors that countless people were displaced or dead as a result of years of natural disasters in a row in the prefectures south of the Yangtze River, nor by rice prices soaring to three taels and six mace of silver a *dan*①, something never seen since the founding of the Great Ming. It was still as radiant, as welcoming, and as indulgent of pleasure as usual.

In fact, there was evidence that something dark and disconcerting was going on out there. The numbers of refugees and beggars on the streets had obviously increased, and they were growing larger and larger; in the grain shops even the least popular grains such as barley and buckwheat suddenly became hot and were short of demand, selling at five thousand mace a *dan* but still in short supply; drinking and singing at a banquet came to a stop because one of the roaring binge drinkers suddenly heaved a long sigh; from time to time, a rumor without basis arose and caused the residents of the city to panic. However, all these were not concerning enough, as if they were merely a few dead leaves thrown into the huge vortex of life. Although they did give a sense of bleakness and destitution, they were immediately swallowed and assimilated to become an indispensable part of the multi-colored daily life of the city as one of the natural colors worthy of no special attention. Yes, the sky was so clear, the light of spring was so bright, and the willow trees all over the city were beginning to spit buds. These willow trees, called "the beauties of the White Gate" by the romantic souls, could be very old, some of them having been planted when the Taizu Emperor② built Yingtian into the capital

---

① a *dan*: approximately 60-80 kilograms

② Taizu Emperor: Zhu Yuanzhang, founding emperor of the Ming dynasty, AD 1328–1398

长岁月，它们依然青青如昔。如果竟然说大明的一统江山不迟不早，偏偏注定就在他们这一辈人的面前彻底坍塌，眼前这无限的繁华将连同这满城柳色一道灰飞烟灭，这是多么荒唐、愚蠢和不可思议！

是的，这也许就是崇祯十五年早春，南京城里大多数居民的心理。虽然有关“建虏”蹂躏京畿和“流寇”暴虐豫楚的消息不断传来，但在他们的感觉中，那毕竟是遥远的、隔膜的。而且，“建虏”一次一次地来，结果不是一次一次地又退走了吗？至于“流寇”，更是时起时仆，只怕也成不了大气候。尤其重要的是，“建虏”也好，“流寇”也好，哪怕仅仅是他们的影子，都从未在南京城下出现过。这说明南京是可靠的、安全的，纵然真有危险，也还远得很……

然而，也并非一切的人都这样想。譬如说，正沿着繁华热闹的大街匆匆北行的轿子当中，这位默然端坐的青年公子，就完全是另外一种心情。

他名叫冒襄，表字辟疆，是复社的一位重要成员。他出生于如皋县一个数代做官的人家，自幼饱读诗书，才情早发，加上祖辈、父辈在政界、文坛多年积累下来的基础以及各种联系，当他还很年轻的时候，就受到有影响的父执们的称誉和汲引，在同辈中崭露头角；加入复社之后，名气就更大了。他今年才三十一岁。如同那个时代绝大多数的读书人一样，冒襄也把科举入仕看作人生的根本出路。这些年来，他一直在应考乡试，但都没有取中，到如今，仍然是一名秀才。不过，无论是同辈还是长辈都毫不怀疑，他之平步青云，飞黄腾达，只是早晚的事。目前，他与桐城

city. After a long period of more than two hundred and seventy years, they were still as green as before. It would be absurd, preposterous, and ludicrous to say or even to think that the reign of the Great Ming over this unified land should fall apart in their generation, no sooner and no later, and that the never-ending prosperity should be wiped out together with the willows of the city.

Yes, this might be the psychology of most residents in Nanjing in the early spring of AD 1642, the fifteenth year of the reign of Emperor Chongzhen. Although news of northern barbarians—the Jurchens—ravaging the capital region and the terrorization of Henan and Hubei by guerrilla bandits kept coming, they felt it was about something far away unrelated to them. The Jurchens did come again and again, but didn't they withdraw again and again? The guerrilla bandits, who rose and were put down, would not head anywhere either. What was more important was that neither the northern barbarians nor the guerrilla bandits nor even their shadows had ever appeared under the city walls of Nanjing. This meant that Nanjing was safe and dependable; even if there was danger, it was still far away from them.

However, not everyone thought that way. For example, in the sedan chair hurrying north along the bustling street, a young man sitting silently had completely different thoughts.

His name was Mao Xiang, or Pijiang by courtesy name. He was an important member of the Fushe. Born and bred in a political family in Rugao County, he had distinguished himself from among his peers as a widely acclaimed child prodigy well versed in poetry and the classics, praised and endorsed by the influential elders, and had become even more famous after joining the Fushe. He was only thirty-one years old. Like most scholars of that era, Mao Xiang also regarded becoming an official through the imperial examination as the primary route to a successful career. Over the years, he had been taking the provincial-level exam without success. As of this day, he remained a *xiucai*, holder of the lowest degree. However, neither his peers nor elders ever doubted that it was only a matter of time for him to rise to the top and have a successful career. Currently, he and Fang Yizhi of Tongcheng, Chen Zhenhui of

方以智、宜兴陈贞慧、商丘侯方域并称为“复社四公子”。

冒襄受着这些推崇赞誉，事实上他自己也颇为自信，不过他绝不是那种头脑容易糊涂的人。凭着这些年来他周游各地的所见所闻，以及与高官显宦们周旋交往所了解到的情况，他不仅十分清楚国家的局势已坏到什么样的程度，而且，他拿这些情况同历代王朝兴亡的历史对比印证，已经不怀疑，大明的江山正处于风雨飘摇的极险境地，随时都有覆没的可能。他根本不相信，在这场端倪已露的亡国大祸中，南京城会是一爿能逃过劫难的“乐土”。别看它目前似乎还很安宁、可靠，一旦风暴来临，那将是一场席卷一切的惨变——“蔽日旌旗，连云樯橹，白骨纷如雪！”这已经是重复了多少次的历史图景。所以，当轿子走在从三山街到内桥这一段店铺更集中、气象更繁华的街市时，冒襄隔着帘子默默注视着摩肩接踵、嬉笑自若的来往行人，他的眉头不由得皱得更紧了。

不过最近冒襄心情阴郁的原因，还不仅仅在于此。发生在半年前的父亲调职襄阳的那件事，一直在深深困扰着他，使他感到屈辱、痛苦，却不知道怎样才能摆脱。冒襄的父亲冒起宗，本来在湖南担任衡永兵备使者，是个不大不小的三品官。去年秋天，冒起宗忽然接到命令，调他到湖北的军事重镇襄阳，担任总兵官左良玉部的监军。左良玉是临清人，出身行伍，早年在辽东对清军作战，以骁勇受东林党人侯恂提拔；后来在镇压农民军的战争

Yixing, and Hou Fangyu of Shangqiu were collectively known as the Four Young Men of the Fushe.

Amid praises by others, Mao Xiang was quite confident of himself, but he was definitely not the kind of person who was easily carried away. Based on what he had seen and heard through years of traveling in the country, and what he had learned from his dealings with courtiers and high-ranking officials, he not only knew exactly how bad the situation in the country had become, but also, by comparing the present circumstances to the rise and fall of previous dynasties he had no doubt that the Great Ming was now precarious and was likely to crumble at any moment. He didn't believe that Nanjing City would be a safe haven that could escape the imminent catastrophe. At the moment, it looked peaceful and quiet, but once the storm came, there would be a tragic change that would sweep everything away, as a Yuan dynasty poem has it: ... army flags blocking the sun, warships connected to the clouds, and white bones like snow ... A historical scene that had been repeated again and again. Therefore, when the sedan chair was passing the busier and more prosperous section of the market from Sanshan Street to Inner Bridge, Mao Xiang silently watched through the curtain as the pedestrians gleefully rubbed elbows and jostled with each other. His eyebrows were knit tighter and tighter.

However, that was not the only reason for Mao Xiang's current moroseness. His father's transfer to Xiangyang half a year ago had been troubling him. He felt humiliated but helpless. His father Mao Qizong was originally a military emissary to Hengyong in Hunan Province, a middle-rank official. Last autumn, Mao Qizong suddenly received an order that he be transferred to Xiangyang, a place of strategic importance in Hubei, to serve as supervisor to the army led by Chief Commander Zuo Liangyu, who had risen from the ranks. The man from Linqing had fought bravely against the Jurchens in East Liaoning in his early years and was promoted by an East Wood Party member Hou Xun; later, he built a reputation by being relentlessly brutal in the crackdown on peasant uprisings. His influence was

中，以凶悍残暴著名，势力亦日渐增强。他自恃重兵在握，十分骄横跋扈，连朝廷的命令也不大服从。就在冒起宗接到调令之前几个月，襄阳城被张献忠的农民起义军攻破，督师杨嗣昌十万火急调左良玉驰援，可是左良玉为着保存实力，九调九不至，杨嗣昌绝望之余，畏罪自杀身死。现在朝廷竟派冒起宗去监督他。冒起宗明知左良玉决不会轻易就范，弄不好，自己随时随地都有性命之虞，但是格于上命，不敢违抗，只好匆匆赴任。消息传来，急坏了冒襄一家。尤其是冒襄的母亲，日夜哀哭，逼着儿子一定要设法营救。为了这件事，近半年来，冒襄到处奔走投诉，托人疏通说情，请求朝廷把冒起宗调离襄阳。到如今，凡是可能利用的关系，他几乎都跑遍了，银子也花了万把两万，可是事情却有如石沉大海，毫无下文……现在，冒襄又到南京来了。但是他实在不知道，这种请托求告，到底还有没有作用……

轿子轻微地震动一下，停下了。冒襄蓦地惊觉过来。他隔着帘子往外看去，映入眼中的是一道长长的幽静的街巷，一扇黑漆兽头衔环大门，门前踞着一对石狮子。一个年老的门公正坐在台阶前晒太阳。看见来了轿子，他就眯缝着昏花的老眼，偏过脸来。

在长班拿着拜帖上前通报的当儿，冒襄坐着没有动弹。这座年深日久，外观已经略微显得破旧的府第，近半年，他已经来过三次了。主人是个温厚长者，每一次都给予接待，而且答应帮忙。冒襄并不怀疑他的善意和许诺，不过，由于种种缘故，事情尚未

increasing day by day. Emboldened by the military power in his hands, he was haughty and overbearing and even didn't quite obey imperial decrees. Just a few months before Mao Qizong received the transfer order, the city of Xiangyang had fallen to the peasant insurgents led by Zhang Xianzhong. General Yang Sichang ordered Zuo Liangyu to send reinforcements, but Zuo Liangyu defied all nine orders to preserve his own military strength; consequently, Yang Sichang committed suicide in desperation and in fear of punishment. Recently, the imperial court had sent Mao Qizong to supervise such a man. Mao Qizong knew that Zuo Liangyu would never give in easily, and should he fail to handle it well, he would lose his life anytime and anywhere, but since it was a decree from the emperor, he didn't dare to defy it, so he hurried to his post. When the news came, the whole family was worried, especially Mao Xiang's mother, who cried day and night and pressured her son to do whatever he could to save his father. For this matter, in the past six months, Mao Xiang had been running around finding people who could plead on his behalf with the imperial court for his father to be transferred away from Xiangyang. By now, he had exhausted almost all the connections he could use and spent ten to twenty thousand taels of silver, but all efforts so far had been in vain, like a stone sinking into the ocean. Now he came to Nanjing again, but he really didn't know whether such pleading for help was of any use.

The sedan chair jolted to a halt. Mao Xiang woke up from his thoughts. He looked out through the curtain and in front was a long and quiet street lane, a black lacquer gate with a lion head holding a ring in the mouth, and a pair of stone lions crouching in front of the gate. On the steps sat an old janitor basking in the sun. Seeing the sedan chair coming, he turned to it, squinting his dim old eyes.

When the servant went over to present the janitor with the calling card, Mao Xiang sat still without moving. He had visited this age-worn residence three times in the past six months. The owner was a kind elder, who graciously received him every time and promised to help. Mao Xiang didn't doubt his kindness nor his word, but the fact was, for one reason or another the mission was not accomplished yet. Will

办成。自己再三再四地上门催问，会不会使主人感到为难和不快？会不会出现在类似情况下常常会遇到的那种难堪的场面？这种顾虑，冒襄上轿之前就有过，此刻又重新变得浓重起来。他是一个自尊心很强的人，多年来生活上的顺境，使他习惯于别人的礼遇和褒扬，哪怕是一个轻视的眼色，一句暗示的讽辞，都会令他气恼、难受，心里老半天不舒坦……

“启禀少爷，主人有请！”长班的声音在耳边响起来。

冒襄怔了一下，才听清这句话。他松了一口气，点点头，等轿夫打起帘儿，就微微弓起腰，走下轿来。

他是一位异常俊美的儒生，中等身材，衣饰雅致，风度潇洒。他先站在轿旁，转动着一双黑白分明的眼睛，矜持而又冷淡地向周围打量了一下，这才不慌不忙地朝大门右侧那扇便门走去。

“我家老爷请相公书房相见。”已经在门前迎候的门丁行着礼说，随即引着冒襄，经过门厅，从天井里向右一拐，进了一道小门，沿着回廊曲曲折折地走了一阵，来到一处幽静的庭院。庭院里，是一明两暗的三开间书房；沿着墙根莳着些花木，西边角上还有一方水池，围着碧瓦栏杆，池中立着两片姿态奇古的石山，绿竹森然。冒襄无心细看，他匆忙地整理一下衣巾，等院子通报之后，就低着头，拱着手，放轻脚步，从院子揭起帘子的那扇门走了进去。

南京兵部尚书熊明遇，已经在屋里等着他了。

the repeated urging make the owner of the residence feel awkward and annoyed? Will there be the kind of embarrassing scene that often occurs in similar situations? Mao Xiang had had such concerns before getting into the sedan chair, and now they were back again with greater weight. A man of strong self-esteem, he had been accustomed to being praised and treated with deference, because he had had a good life over the years; even a contemptuous wink or a hint of irony would make him feel annoyed and uncomfortable.

"My young lord, his lordship says welcome," came the voice of the servant.

Mao Xiang was woken up from his thinking. He sighed in relief, nodded his head, and when a bearer lifted the curtain, he bent his head and stepped off the sedan chair.

He was an exceptionally handsome young man of medium build, elegantly dressed, and of great decorum. He first stood by the sedan chair, and, rolling a pair of eyes in distinctive black and white, looked around cautiously and placidly, and then walked unhurriedly towards the access door on the right side of the gate.

The janitor, who had been waiting there, saluted and said, "My young lord, his lordship would like to meet you in the study." Then, following his lead, Mao Xiang passed the doorway, turned right from the patio, entered through a small door, walked along the zigzagging corridor for a while, and came to a quiet courtyard. In the courtyard, there was a three-room study with a door to the main room. Some flowers and trees were planted along the root of the walls; and on the west corner was a pond surrounded by blue tile railings and in the pond stood two ancient and exotic stone hills with green bamboos. Mao Xiang was not in the mind for a good look. He hurriedly tidied his gown and turban, and after the janitor announced his coming, he lowered his head, and, clasping his hands and lightening his footsteps, walked in through the door, whose curtain had been lifted by the janitor.

Xiong Mingyu, Minister of War in Nanjing, was already waiting for him in the house.

熊明遇是个须眉皓白的矮胖老头儿，圆圆的、常带微笑的脸上，有一种乐天知命的神气。他是万历二十九年的进士，做过几任京官，也不止一次遭到贬谪和罢免。大半生的宦海沉浮，已经磨掉了他的一切棱角。他最得意时曾做到北京的兵部尚书。十年前，崇祯帝嫌他办事糊涂，革了他的职，直到最近才重新起用，但也无非是让他到南京来坐冷板凳。南京在明代，曾经是开国初年的首都。直到永乐十九年，明成祖朱棣为了抵御北方蒙古族的进攻，才把首都迁到了北京。迁都后，南京原有的一套中央机构形式上仍然保留，称为“留都”。除了没有皇帝外，也同北京一样有皇宫，有吏、户、礼、兵、刑、工等六部，还有国子监等其他部门，不过，北京的六部有实权，所有的事情都集中在北京办；南京的这些官只是闲职，虽然地位很高，但是国家大事轮不到他们拿主意。他们多是一些政治失意，或者被认为年老无用的人。熊明遇也属于这一类。不过，这老头儿倒是个好好先生，同复社一班年轻士子也很谈得来。在冒襄请托的人当中，他是属于真心愿意帮忙的一个，所以冒襄这次到南京，首先就来拜访他。

冒襄撩起直裰的下摆，双膝跪倒，叩下头去：

“老伯在上，小侄给老伯请安！”

The minister was a pudgy old man with a white beard and white eyebrows, and his round, smiling face had a big dose of optimism. Having obtained a *jinshi* degree in AD 1601, the twenty-ninth year of the reign of Emperor Wanli, he had served as an official in the capital several times with ups and downs. The ups and downs as a politician in a good part of his life had worn away all his edges and corners. In his heyday, he had been Minister of War in Beijing. Ten years ago, Emperor Chongzhen was displeased with his lack of judgement in the transaction of affairs and dismissed him from his post; he was re-employed only recently, but it was nothing more than sitting on the cold bench in Nanjing. Nanjing used to be the capital in the early years of the Great Ming. It was not until AD 1421, the nineteenth year of the reign of Emperor Yongle, that Zhu Di, or the Chengzu Emperor, moved the capital to Beijing in order to resist Mongolian invasion in the north. After the capital was relocated, Nanjing's original set of central institutions were symbolically retained and the city was called the Legacy Capital. Except for the absence of an emperor, there was everything else in the Legacy Capital: an imperial palace like that of Beijing, six ministries—Ministry of Personnel, Ministry of Households, Ministry of Rites, Ministry of War, Ministry of Punishment, and Ministry of Industries—as well as institutions such as The Imperial College. However, the six ministries in Beijing had been invested with real power and all matters were transacted in Beijing; the officials in Nanjing had only nominal roles with high titles but no real power to decide on anything of national interest. They were mostly political losers or those considered old and useless. Xiong Mingyu also belonged to this category. However, this old man had a good temperament and got along quite well with the young scholars of the Fushe. Among those whom Mao Xiang had approached, he was the only one who was really willing to help. Therefore, Mao Xiang thought of him first when he came to Nanjing.

Mao Xiang lifted the hem of his robe, knelt down on both knees, and kowtowed, saying, "My dear uncle, please accept a salute from a nephew."

“啊啊，贤侄，何必多礼！”熊明遇满脸堆笑，趋前一步，把冒襄扶起来。两人重新作揖之后，熊明遇做了一个让座的手势，便移动着肥胖的身体，向朝南的一张铺着锦褥的紫檀木炕床走去。

冒襄有礼貌地挨延着。等熊明遇坐定之后，他先告了坐，这才在对面的一张硬木如意椅上坐下来。

以往，熊明遇这当儿就会立即开始寒暄。可是今天，不知什么缘故，直到家人送上茶来之后好一会儿，熊明遇仍然只管默默地、小口地呷着茶，甚至没有看客人一眼。冒襄心里又不安起来：莫非主人对自己的不断来访已经感到腻烦，甚至讨厌，只是格于情面，才不得不勉强接待，所以故意摆出这样的脸色，好让客人自觉难堪，知趣而退？顿时，屈辱羞惭的感觉涌上心头，冒襄的脸又红了。他暗暗打定主意：稍坐片刻，就起身告辞，并且绝口不提请托的事。他觉得，唯有这样，才能多少保持自己的尊严，也等于告诉主人，这只是一次纯粹出于礼貌的例行拜谒，客人本无他求，摆出拒人于千里之外的面孔，其实没有必要……

“哎，贤侄，这一向，你是怎么回事啊？”熊明遇开口了，语气是随便的、愉快的，“怎么许久都不来啦？还有定生、朝宗他们也不来，莫非讨厌我糟老头儿啰唆不成？”

“啊，不敢！只因小侄不来留都已有两月，以致久疏趋候，更兼百事缠身，音书亦稀，不知竟辱老伯挂望，不胜悚愧，尚祈恕罪！”冒襄拱着手回答。

熊明遇点点头：“这就是了。我说呢，我这老朽可没得罪你们复社，怎么一个一个都不见影儿了？抛撇得我老头儿好不冷清！”他继续用开玩笑的口吻说着，同时热切地瞅着冒襄，仿佛

“Hah, my dear nephew, forget about the ceremonies,” said the old man. Xiong Mingyu smiled all over his face, stepped forward, and helped Mao Xiang up. After the two saluted each other, the elder man gestured for the young one to sit and moved his stout body to a south-facing red sandalwood *kang* bed with a brocade mattress.

Mao Xiang politely waited. After the elder was seated and told him to sit, he sat down on a hardwood *ruyi* armchair opposite.

Previously, Xiong Mingyu had used to open his mouth immediately after the guest was seated. But today, for some reason, he was still silent even after his servant brought tea; for a long while he kept sipping tea in small morsels without even looking at the guest. Mao Xiang felt uneasy again. He thought, “Maybe Elder Xiong is simply being polite by receiving me. He must’ve been bored or even annoyed by my constant visits. Is he putting on such a face just to repel me?” Suddenly, a feeling of humiliation and shame rose in his heart, and he blushed again. A decision was made. After sitting for a while, he would get up and take leave, and he would never ask for anything. He felt that the only way to keep his dignity was to pretend that this was just a routine courtesy visit, not one to ask for a favor, so that the host would not find it necessary to put on such a repelling face.

“Hey, my dear nephew, what has happened?” Xiong Mingyu said, his tone casual and jovial. “Why haven’t you come to see me for a long time? Dingsheng and Chaozong are not visiting me either. Are you young chaps tired of this old man’s old rubbish?”

“Oh, no! How dare we! I haven’t come to the Legacy Capital for two months, and since there’re so many things for me to do, I haven’t written you letters as I should. I’m really sorry and ashamed of myself for making you worry. I pray for your forgiveness,” Mao Xiang replied with a bow.

Xiong Mingyu nodded his head, saying, “Now I see. I was wondering why you’ve disappeared one by one leaving me cold and lonely while I haven’t offended the Fushe in any way.” He joked and looked at Mao Xiang concernedly, as if saying: Don’t be discouraged,

在抚慰他：别丧气，小老弟，我很喜欢你，你来了我真高兴!

“定生、朝宗他们也是前几日才回到南京来。还有，太冲也来了。”

“太冲？”熊明遇捋着白胡子，微微仰起脑袋，“莫非就是故世了的余姚黄公尊素的公子，名叫宗羲的？嗯，知道，知道！”

“太冲兄虽身在江湖，却心忧国事，近日颇思将数年潜研默讨之所得，著为一论，上书朝廷。又欲于秉笔之前，与海内贤达，广为奉商。老先生泰山北斗，望重群伦，且久赞中枢，倘能于报最之余，赐以教言，尤为太冲所深望呢！”

“噢，不敢。倒是学生我甚欲一聆太冲兄之匡济宏谋。他既来了，就烦贤侄务必请来一见。”

“老伯传唤，小侄想太冲必定是欣喜趋谒的。”冒襄又拱着手回答。

现在，他的心情渐渐松弛下来。“嗯，主人看来不像是讨厌我。”他想。于是对这位身为高官显宦，脾气却好得出奇的老世伯，忽然变得感激和亲近起来。

## 时局深忧

熊明遇眯缝着眼睛笑着，也在打量冒襄。这位年轻士子虽然来访的次数不多，给他的印象却很好。冒襄的俊美温文、谦恭儒雅，他有求于人时所表现出来的羞赧和不安，都令熊明遇感到满意，对他另眼相看。熊明遇同复社的士子们虽然时有接触，外间

little brother. I like you very much. I'm so glad you've come.

"Dingsheng and Chaozong came back to Nanjing a few days ago. Taichong came too," said Mao Xiang.

"Taichong?" said Xiong Mingyu, who stroked his white beard and raised his head slightly. "Is he Zongxi, son of the deceased Mr. Huang Zunsu? I know him."

He continued, "Though Brother Taichong isn't an official, he's deeply concerned about the affairs of state. Recently, he's been thinking of writing a treatise based on years of research and thinking, and he's going to submit it to the imperial court. Before putting his ideas to paper, he wants to have extensive discussions with the best minds of the country first. Knowing you is greatly revered by all contemporary scholars, who look up to you as Mount Taishan or the Big Dipper for your character and wisdom, and besides, you've been in the center of power for a long long time. If you could spare some time from your busy schedule to offer your guidance, it would be greatly appreciated by Brother Taichong."

"It's very kind of you to say so. I also want to meet him and hear his great ideas. Since he's here in the city too, please ask him to come," said Xiong Mingyu.

"I think he'll be exhilarated to receive your invitation," said Mao Xiang with another bow.

Now, his mind had gradually relaxed. "Um, the host doesn't seem to dislike me," he thought. Suddenly a feeling of gratitude and affinity rose in his heart for this gracious elderly family friend, who was a high-ranking official.

## The Worrying Situation

Xiong Mingyu, squinting his eyes, smiled and looked at Mao Xiang. This young scholar hadn't called many times but had left a very good impression on him. Mao Xiang's beauty, gentility, politeness, and decorum as well as the shyness and nervousness in asking for help were all pleasing to the elderly statesman, who therefore was quite fond of the young man. Xiong Mingyu had met with some of the

甚至把他说成是复社的后台之一，不过，老头儿对于这班年轻人那种锋芒毕露、激烈好名的行为举止和处事态度，却颇不以为然。特别是他们肆无忌惮地议论朝政，讥评人物，得罪的人越来越多。熊明遇担心这样闹下去，总难免有一天要闯出祸来。他知道无法劝说他们，所以近一两年，已经采取了逐渐疏远的态度。他觉得在这一点上，冒襄与他的社友们不同，这个年轻人端庄稳重，沉得住气，也比较听话，正合于自己此时此地的心境。

熊明遇今年六十六岁了。十年前，当他从官宦生涯的高峰跌落下来的时候，他就已经明白，这一生的好运气，算是到此为止。他早就看出来，年轻的皇帝是一位独断多疑、刻薄寡恩的人。自己这种一团和气，事事想当老好人的性格，绝不会得到皇上的欢心。崇祯五年，他仅仅因为说错了几句话，触怒了皇帝，就被勒令“解任候勘”，最后落得个削职还乡。事隔多年，如今又被重新起用，熊明遇心里明白，无非是朝廷临时找不到更合适的人选，才让他出来顶替一下，别说想重新回到昔日的位置上去根本不可能，就是现在这张南京兵部尚书的冷板凳，也说不上能坐多久。好在他乐天知命，抱定做一天和尚撞一天钟的宗旨，日子过得倒也蛮惬意。不过，他却没有失掉保护自己的本能，同大多数正在地位和权势的斜坡上向下滑落的老官僚一样，他对于官场上的同僚们往往怀有一种隔阂和戒备的心理，就像一只行动迟缓但感觉仍然清醒的老猫，时刻都在提防着同类的鬼脸和算计。尽管有时候他的应酬也很忙，可是内心是孤独而寂寞的。在这种情况下，他喜欢同一些尚未涉足官场的年轻士子交往，找他们谈谈，听听他们对时局的看法，接受他们对自己的趋奉的敬意，这往往能使他获得一种快乐和满足。不过，话又说回来，他却不想因此惹来

young scholars of the Fushe from time to time and was even referred to as one of the behind-the-scene operators of the society, but he didn't quite approve of their aggressiveness and the ways they did things. These kids indiscreetly talked about state affairs with biting criticisms and more and more people were offended. He worried that they would get into trouble sooner or later if they went on like this. Knowing that he couldn't dissuade them, he consciously distanced himself from them in the past two years. However, he felt that, in this regard, Mao Xiang was different from the others. This young man was dignified, steady, and patient, and he was more willing to listen, which aligned well with Xiong Mingyu's current state of mind.

Mr. Xiong was sixty-six years old. Ten years ago, when he fell from the peak of his political career, he already understood that the good luck of this life would end there. He had long known that the young emperor was a skeptical, ungracious man, and that given his good nature and goodwill for all he would never win the emperor's favor. In the fifth year of the reign of Emperor Chongzhen[AD 1632], he sent the emperor aflame with a few inappropriate words and was first suspended from office and then ousted altogether. Years later, he was re-employed, but he knew in his heart that he was nothing more than a makeshift arrangement when the imperial court couldn't find a more suitable man. There was no possibility for him to return to his former position. He wasn't even sure how long he would sit on this cold bench as "Minister of War" in Nanjing. With such an understanding, he was happily resigned to fate, and life for him was good in general. However, he hadn't lost the instinct for self-preservation; like most old bureaucrats who had fallen down the slope of status and power, he kept his colleagues at arm's length like a slow but vigilant old cat on guard against the wiles and artifices of other felines. He socialized from time to time but inside he was alone and lonely. Therefore, he liked to associate with some young scholars who hadn't yet set foot in officialdom; talking to them, listening to their views on the current situation, and accepting their more or less flattering respect often gave him a kind of happiness or

横祸，以致把身家性命都赔上去。他记住了十年前的教训：更谨慎一点做人没有坏处。所以，最近他对复社成员的接待，已经变得更有选择，说话也更加小心。复社的年轻头儿如陈贞慧、侯方域等人觉察到了这一点，渐渐便不来了。

刚才，冒襄跨进屋子的时候，熊明遇正苦苦思考着一个问题。这个问题是前几天去牛首山春游的路上，才在他的脑子里突然清晰、尖锐起来的。这个念头一经揭示，竟变得如此狂暴、可怕、无情，以至他几乎再也无法平静下来。他很想找一个人来商讨一下，但是问题的性质非比寻常，必须十分慎重。他打算找一个饱学卓识，具有政治头脑，而且是可靠的、与自己并无利害冲突的人。冒襄的突然来访，正合他的心意，这便是他特别高兴接待冒襄的原因。

“嗯，贤侄来往各地，最近，可听说什么新闻？”熊明遇换了一个话题，问。

“这……也并无特别新闻。老伯想亦知道，各地的灾情愈加重了。山东、河南不必说，此二地已成鬼蜮世界，到处以人肉为粮。听说虽至亲好友，亦不敢轻入人室。安分守己之家，老少男女，相让而食；强梁者，搏人而食；甚至有父杀其子而食……临清米价涨至二十四两银子一石；即如江南各府县，号称富庶之苏杭二州，去岁以来，亦饿死居民无数。每日移葬郊外者，络绎于道。杭州太守刘公是汴梁人，于是便有好事之徒，改古诗以为讽刺……”

“噢？怎么说？”

“这——也无非是些轻薄无根之语，徒逞口舌之快，安知不

contentment. However, he was prudent enough not to risk his life. He still remembered the lesson from ten years ago. There was no harm in being more cautious. Recently, he had become more selective in the reception of members of the Fushe and more cautious in speaking. Young leaders of the Fushe, such as Chen Zhenhui and Hou Fangyu, realized this and gradually stopped coming.

Just now, when Mao Xiang stepped into the house, Xiong Mingyu was pondering over a problem. He hadn't been keenly aware of the problem until his spring outing to Cow Head Mountain a few days ago. It had been weighing heavily on him ever after. He wanted to find someone to discuss it with, but the nature of the problem required great caution. He wanted to find someone who was knowledgeable, politically savvy, reliable, and more importantly, had no conflict of interest with him. Mao Xiang just came in time, hence the warm reception.

"Hey, son! You have been going places. Have you heard any news recently?" Xiong Mingyu changed the subject and asked.

"Well, there isn't anything special. I think you already know that the famine is getting worse everywhere. Shandong and Henan are the worst provinces, which have become dungeons, where humans eat humans. It's said that even close relatives and good friends dare not enter each other's houses without precautions. In decent families, members let each other eat first; in families of aggressive individuals, members fight each other to get a morsel of human flesh; in the worst cases, fathers slaughter and eat their own sons. In Linqing, the price of rice has risen to twenty four taels of silver per *dan*. Even in the River South counties and prefectures, including the prosperous Suzhou and Hangzhou, countless residents have died of starvation since last year. Every day, the roads are streaming with corpses to be buried in the countryside. Liu Gong, the prefect of Hangzhou, is from Bianliang, so some mischievous person has changed an ancient poem to mock him—"

"Oh? What is that?"

"Well, it's nothing more than some frivolous and rootless stuff for

是有诬长上。”

“但说来听听不妨。”

“是！闻得是改的南宋林升‘山外青山楼外楼’一诗，道是：‘山不青山楼不楼，西湖歌舞一时休。暖风熏得死人臭，还把杭州送汴州！’”

熊明遇听了，点着头没有作声。这两年，江南各府灾情严重是事实。但他认为，主要原因还是天时不正造成的，况且各衙门正在设法赈济，然而，立即就出现这种意图煽惑的歌谣，把矛头指向了府尊，足见民心之可虑。这样一想，熊明遇的忧虑心情又增加了几分。

“还有，听说松山已经失陷了。”冒襄见熊明遇不表示态度，猜想是他对那首诗感到不悦，便换了话题。

“松山尚未失守。”熊明遇摇摇头，口气很肯定。他的消息自然是准确的。不过，虽则如此，熊明遇也并不认为松山能守得住。甚至毋宁说，近日来困扰着他的那个可怕的问题，多少正与松山的战局有关。他看了看冒襄，解释似的说：“洪经略尚在死守孤城，建虏以倾国之师，围攻数月，至今未能得逞。不过，”他皱起眉头，“倘使诸镇的援兵继续徘徊不进，松山的陷落，只怕也是迟早而已。”

冒襄对主人已经不再存有猜惧之心。听说松山并未陷落，他精神不禁为之一振。但主人接下去的话，又使他颇为泄气。有片刻，他很想说：“对于此等贪生畏死、误国误民之辈，朝廷就当严加惩处，以儆效尤！”可是话到嘴边又缩了回去。不错，要是

the pleasure of talking, utterly disrespectful to an elder and a superior."

"Let me hear it. It does no harm."

"It's a parody of 'A Mountain Beyond a Mountain and a Mansion Beyond a Mansion' by Lin Sheng of the Southern Song dynasty: A mountain is no longer a mountain. A mansion is no longer a mansion. All of a sudden, the singing and dancing on the West Lake come to a stop, and the warm wind blows the stink of the dead far and wide, from Hangzhou all the way to Bianzhou."

After hearing it, Xiong Mingyu nodded his head silently. It was true that the natural disasters in the River South provinces had been very severe in the past two years. He believed that the main reason was bad weather. The local *yamens* were doing their best to provide relief. The appearance of this kind of seditious ballads whose spearhead was directed at the prefect himself showed that the human heart had an element of evil. Thus thinking, Xiong Mingyu was more saddened.

"Also, I hear that Songshan has fallen," Mao Xiang said. Seeing Xiong Mingyu had no comment on the poem, Mao Xiang gathered that the old man was displeased with it, so he changed the subject.

"Songshan has not fallen yet," Xiong Mingyu said, shaking his head, with a certain tone in his voice. His news source was naturally more reliable. However, in spite of that, he didn't think Songshan could hold on. In fact, the weighty problem that had plagued him in recent days was more or less related to the situation in Songshan. He looked at Mao Xiang and said, as if to explain, "Hong Jinglue is still defending the lonely city with his last bit of effort, and the Jurchens have besieged it for months without success. However," he said, knitting his brows, "if the reinforcements from other cities continue to drag their feet, Songshan will fall sooner or later, I'm afraid."

Mao Xiang was no longer suspicious of his host. Hearing that Songshan hadn't fallen, he was relieved, but the immediate comment of the old man disheartened him again. He wanted to say, "Useless cowards! They should be severely punished by the imperial court so that others won't learn from them." Nevertheless, when the words reached his lips, he withdrew them. Yes, if it were a year ago, he might

在一年以前，他或许可以问心无愧地这样大声疾呼。可是如今，他替父亲奔走求告，请求调离剿“贼”的前线襄阳，在别人眼中，又何尝不是贪生怕死的行为呢！

“以往建虏数度入寇，蹂躏畿辅，而终于不敢久留，全仗山海关遏制其后。而松山、锦州乃是山海关之屏障，二城一旦不守，虏骑便可直逼关前，倘有不测，京师岌岌可危了！”熊明遇继续说。

“难道驰援诸镇当中，竟无一忠义敢死之人，肯奋然而前，直撄犬羊之锋，以解松山之危乎？”冒襄终于还是忍不住，忧形于色地问了一句。

熊明遇望了冒襄一眼，又没有作声。因为目前的事实就是如此，令他无从解说。此外，他还不完全同意冒襄的说法，似乎松山陷落之最终不可挽回，责任就在驰援诸镇。熊明遇明白，造成这场惨败的原因和背景要复杂得多。譬如说，当初如果不是皇上密诏洪承畴速战前进，以解锦州之围，兵部也不一再催战，而是坚持洪承畴最初采取的步步为营、以守为战的方略，形势可能就会大不相同。现在到了主力精兵全军覆没以后，再让驰援诸镇以羸弱之师，去进击建虏乘胜之众，正不啻驱群羊入于虎口，除了徒然送死之外，其实无济于事。不过，这已经关涉军事机密，而且直接触及皇上的个人威信，熊明遇觉得不便，也不敢同这位年轻士子深谈下去。所以，他只是含糊地摇摇头，就把话题从松山的战事移开了。

“建虏固然可虑，但本朝心腹之患，只怕实在流寇。”他慢

have been able to speak up like that with a clear conscience. Now, he was pleading for his father's transfer from Xiangyang, the front line of the battle against the insurgents. In the eyes of others, wasn't it too an act of cowardice?

"In the past, when the Jurchens from Jianzhou invaded and ravaged the vicinity of the capital, they didn't dare to stay long, because there was the Shanhai Pass behind them while Songshan and Jinzhou were fortifications of the Shanhai Pass; should the two cities fall, the Jurchen horsemen would go straight to the pass, then the safety of the capital would be in jeopardy," the old man continued.

"Isn't there a single loyal and brave person among reinforcement commanders who's willing to go confront the enemy and break the siege of Songshan?" Mao Xiang finally said, with a worried expression.

Xiong Mingyu glanced at Mao Xiang but didn't speak. The facts as such, he was unable to give more comments. Besides, he didn't completely agree with Mao Xiang, who implied that the reinforcement troops from other garrisons should take responsibility for the imminent fall of Songshan. Xiong Mingyu knew that there was much more to the defeat. For example, if the emperor hadn't sent a secret edict to Hong Chengchou asking him to advance quickly to break the siege of Jinzhou, and if the Ministry of War, instead of repeatedly urging him to fight, had honored his initial strategy of advancing on a step-by-step basis and launching offensive operations with a good defensive mechanism, the situation might have been quite different. Now that the main force had been annihilated, rushing the weaker forces from the other cities into fighting the mighty, victorious barbarian army was like driving a flock of sheep into the mouths of tigers. It was a futile sacrifice of lives. However, since it involved military secrets and the emperor's personal authority, Xiong Mingyu felt he ought not to go on discussing the topic with the young man. Therefore, he just shook his head equivocally and shifted the conversation away from the war in Songshan.

"The Jianzhou barbarians are indeed worrisome, but the real

吞吞地说，胖圆的脸上现出深深的忧虑神色。像当时相当一部分官僚士绅的看法那样，在熊明遇的心底里，其实觉得关外的清兵虽然可怕，至少还可以通过议和输款，求得一个时期的苟安。但是，面对变得越来越强大的农民起义军，他们却感到束手无策。不管是用“剿”还是用“抚”的办法，都已经越来越不奏效。农民军就像一股刚猛无情、飘忽不定的旋风，冲决一切，扫荡一切，正在从王朝大厦赖以矗立的最底一层，也是最根本的一层的基础上，不折不挠地破坏着、轰击着，使他们这些高高在上的老爷们也已经很分明地感到大地的剧烈震动，听到殿基塌陷、梁柱摧折的可怕声响，以致心惊肉跳，再也无法安枕。事实上，自上一年以来，位于河南的重镇开封，就一直受到以李自成为首的农民军的猛烈进攻，几乎失陷。现在李自成虽然暂时解围而去，但随时随地都可能卷土重来。至于以张献忠为首的另一支农民军，则同革里眼、左金王等部联合起来，正在凤阳府境内横冲直撞，摧州陷县，杀死守官。最近一次，竟攻下了离南京不远的盱眙。他们的图谋已经很清楚，就是准备打过江南来。现在熊明遇虽然一面全力防备，但另一面却不知道明早一觉醒来，周围的世界是否还会是今天这个样子。正是这样一种焦虑，近日来把熊明遇弄得不寒而栗，苦恼不堪。他犹疑了一下，终于压低声音问：

“贤侄，依你之见，大明中兴，尚有希望否？”

“哦，老伯是说——”

problem for the Great Ming, I'm afraid, is the guerrilla bandits," he said slowly, with a deep worry on his chubby face. Like many other scholar bureaucrats of that day, Xiong Mingyu believed that the real problem was the increasingly powerful army of peasant insurgents because the Qing soldiers north of the pass, formidable as they were, could at least be stopped through a negotiated settlement. With the peasant insurgents, however, neither suppression nor containment worked like before. The peasant army was like a fierce, ruthless, erratic whirlwind rushing to destroy everything, sweeping everything, unswervingly wreaking havoc from the bottom layer—the most fundamental layer—on which the edifice of the dynasty stood, and these masters of the world intensely felt the violent vibrations of the earth and heard the terrible sound of the collapse of the foundation of the edifice and the breaking of its beams, which scared the hell out of them and deprived them of their good sleep. In fact, since last year, the strategic fortress of Kaifeng in Henan Province had been under fierce attacks from the peasant army led by Li Zicheng, and the city had almost fallen. Although Li Zicheng had temporarily lifted the siege, he might make a comeback anytime soon and from anywhere while the other peasant army, headed by Zhang Xianzhong, united with He Yilong the Popeye, "King of Zuojin" He Jin, and other insurgent elements, rampaged in Fengyang Prefecture, taking the counties into their hands and killing the local officials and, in a recent offensive, even captured Xuyi, a county very close to Nanjing. Their intention was very clear: they were going to take River South. At present, Xiong Mingyu was doing whatever he could in preparation for what was to come, though he didn't know whether the world around him would still be what it was today when he woke up tomorrow morning. Such an anxiety had been torturing Xiong Mingyu these days and had given him cold fears. He hesitated for an instant, finally lowered his voice and asked:

"Son, in your opinion, is there any hope for a rejuvenation of the Great Ming?"

"Uncle, do you mean—"

“嗯，嗯！”熊明遇不等冒襄说完，就急急忙忙地点着头，还做了一个手势，仿佛害怕他说出那个可怕的字眼似的。

冒襄沉吟了一下，谨慎地说：“老伯所虑，小侄亦曾想来。只是浅陋之见，恐怕……”

“哎，贤侄只管直抒所见。”

“是！”冒襄应诺着。他低下头去，沉默了片刻，这才开口：“小侄冒昧胡言，请老伯指教。时至今日，此事只怕已在两可之数！”他顿了顿，似乎要增加这句判断的分量，“其间大患，自然在于建虏与流寇。建虏自天启元年以来，以沈阳为巢穴，内修制度，外行侵伐，十余年间，已骎骎然雄有辽东以北广袤之地；且东降朝鲜，西收蒙古，羽翼之势已成。彼对我朝佯示就抚之意，实则鹰扬虎视，无日不图南进。天启七年至于今，已三度入寇，京畿以及燕、赵、齐、鲁之地，悉遭蹂躏，杀掠极惨。如今更举倾国之师，专攻松、锦，其意在夺取山海关甚明。山海关为京师门户，虎狼之心，意欲何为，实已昭然若揭！至于流寇，崇祯元年，贼众不过万数，地不出陕西一境，而且各股不相隶属；七年之后，已经居然拥众二三十万，扰地遍及秦、晋、川、楚，然官军尚能制之。尔后凶岁连年，饥民大起，兼之朝廷剿抚之策不定，

"Yes," Before Mao Xiang finished asking, Xiong Mingyu hurriedly nodded with a gesture, as if afraid of him saying that terrible word.

Mao Xiang pondered for an instant, and said cautiously, "I have similar concerns, but I don't know whether I'm thinking it right—"

"Well, speak up your mind, son."

"Aye, sir!" Mao Xiang said. He lowered his head and was silent for an instant before continuing. "Then I'll speak what I think. Please correct me when I'm wrong. The situation is moving in either direction," he said with a pause, as if to accentuate his words. "The biggest threats are the Jianzhou barbarians and the guerrilla bandits. In the past ten years, since the first year of the reign of Emperor Tianqi[AD 1621], the Jianzhou barbarians based in Shenyang, through reforms within and expansion without, have amassed a vast territory north of East Liaoniang. They've also subjugated Korea on the East and Mongolia on the West to form the wings of a hawk. On the surface, they're submissive to us, but in reality, they're hovering over us like hawks and staring at us like tigers, ready to pounce on us every day. From the seventh year of the reign of Emperor Tianqi[AD 1627], till today, they've come three times and ravaged the suburbs of the capital and the lands including Yan, Zhao, Qi, and Lu, killing and plundering without mercy. Now, they've gathered all their forces to take Songshan and Jinzhou. Obviously, their intention is to take the Shanhai Pass. The pass is the gateway to the capital, and what these wolves and tigers intend to do is as clear as daylight. As for the guerrilla bandits, in the first year of the reign of Emperor Chongzhen[AD 1628], there were no more than ten thousand of them, and they were confined in Shaanxi Province and isolated from each other. Seven years later, their numbers increased to two or three hundred thousand and they were active in the lands of Qin, Jin, Chuan, and Chu. At that stage, the government army were still able to cope with them. Afterwards, years of famine caused the hungry people to revolt, but the imperial court was in two minds whether to appease them or crack down on them; consequently, the insurgents, after suffering some defeats, have revived and built

遂致贼势蹶而复振，日渐坐大，竟成今日难以制御之局面。且闯、献二贼，尤为悍猾而强，狂悖之志，曾不下于建虏，令人可惊可虑。况且——”冒襄说到这里，微微叹了一口气，“自古以来，未有国乱于内而能攘夷狄于外者。时至今日，国势之危殆，实为历代所罕见。朝廷倘不急图良策，中兴之业，只恐终难有望！”

冒襄说完了。他谦恭地垂下头，等待主人的指教。但是熊明遇却呆呆地坐着，老半天不作声。不错，这一番话的内容，他也曾经零零碎碎地想到过，可是此刻从这位年轻士子的口中，用如此清晰尖锐的语言说出来，仍然使他的内心受到很大震动。有片刻工夫，他的眼前仿佛出现一幅国破家亡的可怖图景：京师的城门纷纷失守，紫禁城里外燃起冲天大火，禁卫军和内侍作鸟兽散。皇上横刀殉国，百官或死或走或降。而他，熊明遇，自然也要一死以报国恩，这似乎是无可选择的。可是他还有一大群妻妾儿女，到时他也许不忍心让他们全都跟着自己去死，那么就会有人活下来，结果命运却极为悲惨……啊，他们将会怎样呢？被杀戮、拘系、蹂躏、凌辱，最后沦落街头，成了贱民、妓女、乞丐！这种可怕的悬想把熊明遇压得透不过气来，他动弹了一下，想摆脱这种重压，结果只是把身子缩作一团，瞪着惊恐的眼睛，喃喃地问：“那么，那么贤侄有何救时良策？”

“啊，只怕说出来更不足污老伯清听了！”冒襄抬起头，看着主人，谦逊着说。他早已等着有此一问，以便把自己的政见向这位德高望重的前辈陈说出来。冒襄同熊明遇毕竟不一样，虽然

such a momentum that it's no longer possible to contain them. The two head insurgents, Li Zicheng and Zhang Xianzhong are especially cunning and ruthless and their madly perverse ambitions are not any lesser than those of the Jianzhou barbarians, causing great alarm and concern. Besides," Mao Xiang said with a slight sigh, "since ancient times, there has been no successful defense against outside invaders with chaos inside. The danger the country faces today is almost unprecedented. If the imperial court doesn't make a good plan now, there's no hope for a national rejuvenation."

After Mao Xiang finished speaking, he humbly lowered his head to wait for the old man's comment, but Xiong Mingyu simply sat blankly and kept silent for a long time. Indeed, such thoughts had come to him in bits and pieces before, but when they came out of the mouth of a young scholar in such clear and concise language, they struck a cord in his heart. A terrible picture of a lost country with displaced people flashed in front of him. The gates of the capital were lost one after another, from inside and outside the Forbidden City rose a conflagration, and the Imperial Guards and the court servants all fled for their lives like panicked birds and beasts. The emperor martyred himself with a sword, and the hundreds of officials either died or fled or surrendered. He, Xiong Mingyu, should choose to die as a martyr, as was his only choice, but he had a wife, many concubines and children, and he didn't want them to die together with him, then some of them would survive, but with no good ending ... Ah, what would become of them? They would be slaughtered, imprisoned, trampled, and humiliated, and finally roam on the streets to become plebeians, or even prostitutes and beggars. This thought of the dreadful suffocated him, so he wriggled to get rid of it, only to find himself shrunk into a ball. He mumbled with panicked eyes, "Then, then, what do you think is the best way to get out of the current crisis, son?"

Mao Xiang raised his head, looked at his host, and said humbly, "Um, I'm afraid it'll sound stupid to you, my dear uncle." In fact, he had been waiting for this question, which would give him a chance to share his political views with the respected elder. After all, Mao Xiang

他清楚地看到国势的危殆，敏锐地嗅到了亡国气息的临近。但是在他的年轻、强健的心里，却未始不觉得这也是一种机会，正好借以试一试自己的本领和力量，毕竟他还从未加以试验过！何况许久以来，冒襄就认为，国事之所以弄到这个糜烂的局面，主要还是由于主持朝廷大计的，大多是一些庸懦之材的缘故。所以，虽然多少觉察到主人的神气不对，但当他开始回答询问时，仍然情不自禁地用了一种几乎是兴奋的，而且多少有点卖弄的语气：

“以小侄愚见，当今之世，风俗陵夷，廉耻道丧，积弊之多，多于牛毛。若就其中一枝一节而改革，徒然虚费时日，而难见效用。实不若以天雄、大黄之猛剂，治其根本。根本一清，枝节便不难改治。所谓根本，无非是正风俗，严纪纲。风俗正，则积弊消；纪纲严，则君信立。积弊消，君信立，则民不易为乱。虽有少数不逞之徒，亦无所施其煽惑之技。如此，则国内可定。国内定，朝廷便可专力而东向，建虏虽强，不足虑也！虽然，此理说来极寻常容易，唯真正施行，又极不容易。其中用人一事，实为一切之关键。用不得其人，虽有良法美意，亦终因重重扞格，寸步难行。故朝廷倘欲求治图强，须得痛下决心，进君子，斥小人。知其为小人者，虽处庙堂之高，亦必斥而去之；知其为君子者，

was different from Xiong Mingyu. To him, the national crisis and the end-of-the-world atmosphere were also an opportunity to put his talent and youthful vigor to some use; after all, he had never used them before. Moreover, he had always believed that the main reason why the Great Ming had got into a disarray was that those administering the affairs of the imperial court were mostly mediocre and cowardly individuals. Therefore, despite Xiong Mingyu's grim expression, when he began to answer the question, he couldn't help using an almost ecstatic and somewhat showy tone.

"In my humble opinion, in today's world, because morality has weakened and the sense of shame and decency is lost, all kinds of ills proliferate. Treating them one by one will take a long time without producing much effect. The ills should be attacked with powerful medicines such as *tianxiong*[①] and *dahuang*[②] at the very fundamental level. Once the fundamental issue is solved, it'll not be difficult to deal with the derivative issues. The so-called fundamental solution is nothing more than restoration of morality and the keeping of good discipline. When morality is restored, the accumulated ills will dissolve; when discipline is well kept, the emperor will be held in awe. If the accumulated ills are eliminated and the emperor is held in awe, insurgence can hardly take place, and a few treacherous people shall hardly have any use for their seditious skills. Thus, peace and order can be restored domestically. Peace and order restored within, the imperial court shall be able to direct all its forces to the east and the Jianzhou barbarians won't be a problem at all. Though the idea is simple, its implementation is difficult. Finding the right men to do it is the key to everything. If the wrong men are used, any grand idea will fail because of communication barriers. Therefore, if the imperial court wants to bring law and order to the Great Ming and make it prosper, it must make up its mind to be close to men of high character and keep away from men of low character. If someone is known to

① *tianxiong*: aconitum carmichaeli debx

② *dahuang*: spenceria ramalana

虽居江湖之远，亦必求而进之。务使举国上下，正气伸张，人才得用。如此，中兴可指日而待矣！”

冒襄越说越兴奋。他的声音高起来，双颊现出激动的红晕，眼睛也在炯炯发光，同刚才进来的时候相比，仿佛换了一个人。

熊明遇仍旧蜷曲着身子，一动不动地坐着，神情显得愁苦而呆滞，先前脸上那种乐天知命的神态，已经看不见了。他默默地听着冒襄的热烈陈说，高谈阔论，并未能够排除他心头的重压。诚然，这位年轻士子的见解不失为堂堂正理，但国家的局面已经到了这一步，要加以实行简直是不可能的。就拿用人一事来说，长期沿袭、继承下来的习惯，以及各种错综复杂的关系，恰似一棵百年老树，盘根错节，早已形成了异常顽固死硬的格局。要改变它，真是谈何容易！弄不好，改革者就会反招其祸。倘若用强力加以改变，只会加速这株老树的倾倒死亡。为今之计，唯有尽量不要触动它，至多也是剪除一些实在无法保留的枝丫，对于其余则尽可能维持、包容，以求得在狂风暴雨中能同命共济。这样，或许还能苟延残喘……不过，熊明遇最近越来越觉得自己是正在过去的人，思想、精力和记性都在一天天衰退。他对于自己的看法也没有那种自信了。“也许，我确实老迈无能了，这些年轻人才气纵横，说不定真有办法把国家从绝路中解救出来？瞧，他们一个个都很有一套，而且信心十足……”这样一想，他似乎产生了一线希望，于是打起精神，专注地侧着耳朵，期待冒襄说出更

be of low character, he must be removed from office, however high his office is; if a man is known to be of high character, he must be found and promoted no matter how far away he resides. The point is to submit the nation to justice with all talents duly recognized. This way, rejuvenation of the Great Ming is just around the corner," Mao Xiang said in one breath.

He became more and more excited as he spoke. His voice rose up, his cheeks flushing with excitement and his eyes shining brightly, as if he were a different person from the one who had entered the residence a moment ago.

Xiong Mingyu was still sitting motionlessly with his body curled up, the expression on his face sad and stiff. The earlier optimistic expression was no longer visible. He silently listened to Mao Xiang's impassioned speech, but that high talk didn't take the burden off his mind. The young scholar's ideas were quite good, but the situation of the country had reached such a point that it was simply impossible to implement them. Take "finding the right men" for example. The old habits and the various intricate relationships were just like a century-old tree, whose intertwined twigs, branches, and roots had formed an unusually stubborn pattern. Changing it is out of the question. Chances were that there would be misfires and the reformers would incur disasters upon their own heads. If reforms were introduced by force, they would only accelerate the collapse and death of the tree. For the good of the day, it was better to leave it alone or at best to trim off limbs that were dead and keep the rest so that the tree would withstand wind and storm as a whole. This way, it might be able to survive for a few more days ... However, he belonged to the past, Xiong Mingyu felt, as his mind, energy, and memory were declining day by day. He was no longer as confident in his own views as before. "Maybe I'm too old to be useful. These young men are so talented that they might have a way to save the dynasty from ruin. Lo and behold, every one of them have a good plan and is confident ..." Thus thinking, he seemed to suddenly have a glimmer of hope, so he cheered up and tilting his ear, listened attentively, expecting Mao Xiang to say something more

加具体的、切实可行的办法来。

可是，冒襄已经说完了。

“嗯，就是这些？”

“是的，小侄冒昧胡言，敬请老伯指教！”

“哦……贤侄所言，自是堂堂正理。不过——”熊明遇沉吟了一下，“老夫尚欲更有请教。譬如，目前饥民盈野，军饷不继，富室囤积居奇，奸人乘机煽惑，这些都适足资乱，未知计将安出？”

这几点，正是目前江南地区的突出问题，也是日夜困扰着熊明遇，使他大感头痛的问题。所以，他特意点出来，满怀期望地盯着冒襄，等待他回答。

“这……也并非没有办法。”这一次冒襄显然没有准备，他变得有点犹疑，脸也开始微微涨红起来。不过，只一瞬间他就恢复了自信，依然用坚定的口吻说：“不过，当今积弊，又何止此数端！小侄愚见，仍以为与其一枝一节求治，实不若治其根本。本正源清之后，旁枝末流之积淤污浊，便可一并荡涤而去。否则今日除之，明日复生，终难有效！”

熊明遇不作声了。他垂着眼睛，感到失望，“到底只是个书生，徒有空论！”他想。室中寂然半晌，熊明遇终于苦笑了一下，开口说道：“贤侄所言，不无道理，只是知易行难，古今如此，贤侄想亦深知。我是老朽无用了，今后祖宗二百七十年的基业，就寄托在尔等一辈的肩上。望尔等少年英俊，各展高才，同心戮力，

specific and more feasible.

However, Mao Xiang had already finished speaking.

"So, it that all?"

"Yes, it is all, my good uncle. Excuse me for speaking my shallow thoughts. Please kindly let me know what you think."

"Um—what my good nephew has said is quite right, but—" Xiong Mingyu paused for an instant and said. "I have some questions to ask. For example, the present circumstances being that there're homeless, hungry people everywhere, that the army doesn't have guaranteed provisions, and that wealthy families are hoarding goods and profiteering, while agitators are taking the opportunity to incite rebellion—all these are cause for disturbance—what's your solution?"

These were the outstanding issues in the River South region; they had been plaguing Xiong Mingyu day and night and were the cause of his headache. Therefore, he cited them in particular. He looked at Mao Xiang expectantly, hoping to get an answer.

"Well, a solution is possible," said Mao Xiang. Obviously unprepared this time, he stumbled and his face started to flush slightly. However, he soon regained his self-confidence, and said in a firm tone, "However, the social ills of today don't stop at these issues. In the view of your humble nephew, treatment of individual issues isn't as good as treatment at the root level. When the root is rectified and the source is clear, the silt or dirt at the tail end can be washed away all together. Otherwise, if you remove it today it will come back tomorrow and all effort becomes useless."

Xiong Mingyu was silent. He lowered his eyes in disappointment. "After all, he's just a book person only good for empty talk," he thought. After a long silence in the room, Xiong Mingyu finally smiled a wry smile and said, "What my good nephew said sounds plausible, but 'knowing is easier than doing,' as has been proven by history, and I think you also understand it well. I'm too old to be of any use, and the two-hundred-and-seventy-year enterprise will rest on the shoulders of your generation. I hope you and the other promising young men can all make full use of your talents and work together to serve the country

匡扶社稷，克成中兴大业，上报君父之恩，下安黎民之望。如此，则天下幸甚，老夫幸甚了！”

冒襄连忙站起来，拱手当胸，恭恭敬敬地说：“老伯训诲，小侄谨志不忘！”

“嗯，坐、坐。”熊明遇随便做了一个手势。冒襄重新坐下之后，熊明遇沉默了片刻，才又开口说：“有一件事，差点儿忘记告诉贤侄——数日前，京里周阁老有信来，说是贤侄上呈朝廷的救父万言书，他已经知道了。令尊调离襄阳一事，已无干碍，邸报不日可下。”

冒襄的眼睛一下子睁大了。这消息来得太突然，完全出乎他的意料，以至一刹那间，他疑心自己听错了。他的呼吸急促起来，结结巴巴地问：“老伯是说，是说……”

“我给贤侄道喜呐！令尊调离襄阳，只是日内之事了。”

冒襄“啊”的一声站起来，激动地向前跨了两步，忽然又自觉失态似的站住了。他惭愧地微笑着，不胜感激地望着熊明遇，脸上现出兴奋、狂喜的神情。忽然，他跪倒地上，向主人叩下头去。

“哎，贤侄，不必如此，不必如此。”

可是冒襄仍旧叩了一个头，又一个头，直到自己认为叩够了，这才躬身站起。

熊明遇无可奈何地摇着脑袋，等到冒襄爬起来的时候，他也就跟着站了起来。

“有了消息，贤侄便该早点回家报个信，免得令堂倚闾挂望。”他信口提示着，接连打了两个呵欠，神情顿时变得委顿下来。虽

and bring about its rejuvenation in the service of the emperor and the fathers and to the expectation of the common people. If so, the nation is in luck, and I as an old man am in luck too."

Mao Xiang immediately stood up, folded his hands to his chest, and said respectfully, "I deeply appreciate your advice, my good uncle. This humble nephew of yours will never forget it."

"Good! Sit, sit," Xiong Mingyu said with a casual gesture. After Mao Xiang sat down again, Xiong Mingyu was silent for an instant before continuing to speak. He said, "There's something I almost forgot to tell you, my good nephew. A few days ago, His Lordship Mr. Zhou the Prime Minister wrote me a letter saying that he had read the ten-thousand-word petition that you had submitted to the imperial court to save your father. The transfer of your father from Xiangyang is no problem now, and the official approval letter will be issued soon."

Mao Xiang's eyes suddenly opened wide. The news came so suddenly that, for an instant, he suspected he had misheard. Breathing rapidly, he stammered, "My—my good uncle, do you mean—mean—"

"Congratulations to you, my good nephew! The transfer of your father from Xiangyang is only a matter of days."

Mao Xiang stood up with an "ahh", took two steps forward excitedly, and suddenly stopped as he became conscious of his own gaffe. He smiled embarrassedly and gazed at Xiong Mingyu gratefully, with a look of excitement, or better put, a look of elation on his face. Suddenly, he fell to his knees and bowed to the host.

"Well, my good nephew, there's no need to be like this, there's no need to be like this."

But Mao Xiang still went on with the kowtowing, one, two, three, and didn't stand up until he thought he had bowed enough times.

Not being able to prevent it, Xiong Mingyu simply shook his head, and when Mao Xiang stood up, he stood up too.

"My good nephew, you should go home immediately to report the good news to your good mother so that she won't be worried about you," Xiong Mingyu said. He yawned twice in a row and his

然冒襄还在不断说着感激的话，可是熊明遇仿佛听见，又仿佛没有听见。他“嗯、嗯”地答应着，竭力地睁大眼睛。直到冒襄终于告辞出门，沿着花树掩映的回廊，走得看不见了，熊明遇还怔怔地站在阶前。“……嗯，应当叮嘱他，绝不能把这次谈话张扬出去，否则只怕彼此都不便……”他模模糊糊地想。

蓦地，熊明遇清醒过来。他定了定神，有片刻工夫，拿不准主意：该不该派人把冒襄追回来？可是随后就抛开了这个念头。因为先前压迫着他的心头的感觉，又重新出现了。在这种越来越巨大而且沉重的压力面前，其余的顾虑似乎都微不足道，无关紧要，甚至是没有意义的了。

“唉，怎么好，怎么好？”他喃喃自语，绝望地仰起脸，久久注视着不远的屋脊上，那一只突出在夕阳之中的、变得血一般鲜红的鸱吻。一会儿，太阳落下去了，鸱吻也恢复了原来灰暗的颜色。熊明遇颓然垂下白发稀疏的脑袋，慢腾腾步下台阶，开始绕着庭院漫无目的地徘徊起来。

## 喜获佳音

蜿蜒贯穿于东水关和西水关之间的十里秦淮，是南京城里最热闹繁华的一条河道，也是江南首屈一指的绮靡浮华、酒色征逐的销金窟。这里有着最豪华奢费的妓院、最舒适优雅的住宅、最富丽堂皇的酒楼和最出色的戏班子。虽然紧靠着秦淮河北岸，就是庄严肃穆的应天府学宫和科举的考场——贡院，可是，这丝毫也不影响秦淮河那花天酒地、纸醉金迷的气氛，而且不如说，正

expression suddenly dimmed. Mao Xiang continued to say words of gratitude. Xiong Mingyu mechanically responded with "um, uh" as he tried to open up his eyes, either having or having not heard those words. Mao Xiang finally said farewell and walked away along the corridor shaded by flowers and trees. Xiong Mingyu was still standing in front of the steps with a vacant look long after Mao Xiang went out of sight. "Um, I should have told him that he must never disclose this conversation to anyone else; otherwise, I'm afraid that it might cause problems for both ..." he thought in the back of his mind.

Then all of a sudden, Xiong Mingyu woke up. He pondered for an instant, but was still unsure whether he should send someone to bring Mao Xiang back. Then he dismissed the idea, because his obsession with the weighty problem came back to him. Compared with the problem, everything else seemed trivial, irrelevant, or even meaningless.

"Alas, what can I do? What can I do?" he muttered to himself, then raised his face in despair and stared fixedly at the dragon head sculpture at the end of the roof ridge that had turned bloody red in the setting sun. After a while, the sun went down, and the dragon head sculpture restored its original gray color. Drooping his head of sparse white hair, he walked slowly down the steps and began to pace aimlessly in the courtyard.

## Good Tidings

The Ten-Li Qinhuai River, which wound between East Water Pass and West Water Pass, was the liveliest and most prosperous waterway in Nanjing and the largest money sinkhole in the River South area with all kinds of temptations. Here were the most expensive and luxurious brothels, the most comfortable and elegant houses, the most magnificent restaurants and the best theaters. Close to the north bank of the Qinhuai River was the solemn Gongyuan, the highest institution of learning in Nanjing and the venue of imperial examinations, which didn't prevent people from having fun on the Qinhuai River. On the contrary, it was exactly the enthusiastic participation of the well-read

是亏了那一班饱读诗书而又自命风流的圣人之徒的热心参与，才使得这醉生梦死的十里秦淮，平添了许多特殊魅力和奇异的色彩。

的确，秦淮河也自有它的非凡之处，别的不说，光是那一弯碧滢滢的、闪烁着柔腻波光的流水，以及沿河两岸，那一幢挨着一幢的精致河房，就足以令人着迷了。这些河房，大都是有着短短的围墙的独家院落。里面的房舍，不论规模大小，全都装饰着雕栏画槛、珠帘琐窗。讲究一点的，还在院子里凿池植树，垒石栽花。每一所河房，都有一个带栏杆的露台，伸出水面，供人纳凉消夏，赏景观灯。河房的主人，有安享清福的名公巨卿，有不愁衣食的高人雅士，有艳名远播的当红妓女；但大多数河房，却是用来出租的。河房的主人经常变换，从在职官员、宫中太监到一般富户商人都有，他们看中秦淮河的优越环境，购置河房，出租牟利。虽然租金十分昂贵，但过往的公子王孙、富商豪客，仍然趋之若鹜。他们在这里会友、接客、谈生意、论诗文，自然，也还要纵酒、豪赌、狎妓、看戏，想出种种方法享乐，把著名的六朝金粉地最浮艳奢华的这一角，舞弄得更加花团锦簇，五光十色。

当冒襄在他下榻的桃叶河房前下了轿，兴冲冲地走进院子的时候，家人冒成——一个干净伶俐、体格健壮的中年汉子从屋子里匆匆迎出来，后面还跟着两个年轻的长班。

“大爷，你回来啦！”冒成和两个长班侧身站过一旁，拱着手问。

冒襄点点头：“嗯——拿二两银子打发轿班。赶快进来，我

disciples of sages and self-styled romantic souls that gave this drunken and dreamy Ten-Li Qinhuai River a special charm and a curious color.

Indeed, the Qinhuai River had its own unique appeal. The clear river water shimmering with soft ripples and the conjoining exquisite riverhouses lining the banks were enchanting enough in themselves. Most of the riverhouses had exclusive courtyards with short walls. Inside, each riverhouse, regardless of its size, was decorated with carved railings, painted pillars, and beaded curtains. The better ones even had a garden with a pool, trees, and an artificial rock hill. Every riverhouse had a balustraded veranda overlooking the river, where the air was cool on a summer night and the view was extensive. The owners of the riverhouses included retired high-ranking officials who were enjoying peace and quiet in old age, celebrities that had no worries about food and clothing, and famous prostitutes too, but most of the riverhouses were for rent and often changed hands between serving officials, palace eunuchs, businessmen, and other fat cats, who, fascinated by the beautiful environment and prestigious location, often bought a riverhouse and rented them out to make a profit. Despite the exorbitant rent, the riverhouses were highly sought after by men with good means, who used them to meet friends, receive guests, negotiate business, discuss literature, drink, gamble, play with prostitutes, and watch plays. Such men could come up with all kinds of ways to enjoy themselves, making the most luxurious part of the famous Land of Golden Powder in Six Dynasties all the more dynamic and colorful.

When Mao Xiang got off the sedan chair in front of the Peach Leaves Riverhouse where he was lodging and joyously walked into the yard, his servant Mao Cheng, a clean, smart, and sturdily built middle-aged man, hurriedly came out of the house to greet him, followed by two houseboys.

"My young lord, welcome back!" Mao Cheng and the two houseboys stood aside and said, clasping their hands in salute.

Mao Xiang nodded his head and said, "Home at last. Get two taels of silver for the chairmen and come back quickly. I have something to tell you." As he spoke, he went on walking into the

有事吩咐你。”他一边说，一边脚步不停往屋里走去。

一直走进起居室，冒襄才停住脚。他习惯地在花梨木炕床上坐下，立即又站了起来，漫无目的地转了一圈，瞅了瞅门外，焦躁地皱起眉头。当冒成轻快有力的脚步声在门外响起时，他就迅速地转过身去。

“嗯，可曾有客来访？”他照例地问。

“吴次尾、陈定生两位相公方才来过，等不及少爷，他们就说先去了，请大爷随后过去。”冒成垂着手说。

冒襄漫不经心地点点头——今天晚上，吴应箕、陈贞慧、侯方域、黄宗羲、梅朗中、张自烈等几位要好的社友事先约定，要在旧院名妓李十娘家的寒秀斋摆酒，替冒襄接风洗尘。刚才吴、陈二人来访，大约是想同他会齐了，一道前去。

“你记着，”他兴冲冲地说，“明儿一早——今晚怕来不及了——你到船行定一条船，赶在明天晚上，最迟后天一早，我们就回如皋去！”

“啊，回如皋？”

“对，事情有眉目了！”

“哦？”

“蠢材！”冒襄的眼睛闪着兴奋的光芒，“老爷调出襄阳的事，快要办成啦！”

“啊，朝廷开恩啦？”冒成惊喜地问。

“嗯……”

“哎呀，谢天谢地！”冒成把脑门一拍，由衷地欢呼起来。这个冒成，本是冒襄父亲跟前的一名仆童，姓张，由于为人乖觉，办事忠心，颇得主人钟爱，被收作心腹，并改姓冒。以往冒起宗

house and didn't stop until he reached the drawing room.

He sat down on the rosewood *kang* bed as was his habit, but immediately stood up; he paced around aimlessly and then looked out the door, frowning in thought. When the brisk and solid footsteps of Mao Cheng sounded at the doorway, he quickly turned to him.

"Um, did we have visitors?" he asked.

"Mr. Wu Ciwei and Mr. Chen Dingsheng came just now. They waited for a while and then left, saying they would go first and meet you there," said Mao Cheng, with his hands on his legs.

Mao Xiang nodded nonchalantly. His friends Wu Yingji, Chen Zhenhui, Hou Fangyu, Huang Zongxi, Mei Langzhong, and Zhang Zilie said that they would meet tonight in the Old Yard at the Cold Beauty Chamber of Li Shiniang to give him a welcome party. Mr. Wu and Mr. Chen had come just now probably because they wanted to meet him first and then go together with him.

"Remember," he said cheerfully. "Tomorrow morning—I'm afraid it's too late tonight—you go to the boat company to book a boat for tomorrow night or the day after tomorrow at the latest. We'll go back to Rugao."

"Aah, we're going back to Rugao?" asked Mao Cheng in surprise.

"Yes. It's done."

"Oh?"

"Blockhead!" Mao Xiang said, his eyes flashing with excitement. "It's done. The matter of getting your old master to be transferred from Xiangyang."

"Aah, is the imperial court that gracious?" Mao Cheng asked in surprise.

"Yes, that's right."

"Oh, thank goodness!" Mao Cheng slapped his hand on his forehead and cheered heartily. Mao Cheng, originally named Zhang, had been a servant boy of Mao Xiang's father. Because he was capable and loyal, his master was very fond of him and changed his surname to Mao. In the past, Mao Qizong had always taken him along while serving government posts in other places. Three years ago, seeing

到外地做官，总要带上他。三年前冒起宗看见儿子名气大了，经常要外出应酬交际，身边缺个得力的使唤，才让冒成跟了冒襄。这半年来，冒成为着老主人的事跟随冒襄四处奔走，着实出力不少。现在忽然听说事情真的办成了，他高兴得简直手足无措。

“哎，那——我们什么时候去接老爷？”他急不可待地问。

“这倒不用忙。不过，也快了！如今，我们要赶快回如皋去，向老夫人报信，免得她日夜盼望——啊，办成了，总算办成了，哈哈！”冒襄开怀地笑着，大步走向窗前，把临河的一扇窗子推开。微冷的、新鲜的气流立即倾泻进来。冒襄愉快地舒展了一下胳膊，用力做了几个深呼吸。“多奇怪！”他想，“这一次，我本没打算来南京，结果不知为什么，还是来了。若留在常州，就什么消息也得不到了！冥冥中像是有神灵指点似的！”

冒成正在拭着发潮的眼角，他低头想了一下，认真地说：“必定是大爷一片孝心，感动神明了！便是小人向常也叨念：像老爷这般忠心为国，老太太这般乐善好施，加上大爷这般敬上惜下，真是一门忠孝。老天爷怎能不保佑？到底是今日应了！可知天道报应，原是分毫不爽的！”

冒襄慢慢地点着头，现出深思的神情。随即，他又笑起来：“哎，你还呆着干什么？快，拿酒来啊！”

“酒？”

“嗯，就把那瓶‘太禧白’拿来，我要喝一杯，你也喝！”

冒成很快就把酒拿来了。他替冒襄满满地斟了一杯，恭谨地

Mao Xiang was increasingly popular and needed a capable hand in socializing, Mao Qizong assigned Mao Cheng to him. Over the past six months, Mao Cheng had indeed been a great help in the transaction of affairs concerning the older master. When he heard that their mission was completed, he was so overjoyed that he didn't know where to put his hands and feet.

"Hurrah! Then, when shall we go to pick up Old Master?" he asked eagerly.

"There's no hurry yet, but it won't be long. Now, we have to go back to Rugao as soon as possible to report the news to the old lady lest she still be worried day and night. Aah, it's done! It's finally done! Haha!" said Mao Xiang. Laughing heartily, he strode to the window on the side of the river and pushed the panels open. A gush of cool, fresh air immediately rushed in. He happily stretched his arms and took a few deep breaths. "It's like a miracle," he thought. "This time, I didn't plan to come to Nanjing, but somehow here I am. If I had stayed in Changzhou instead, I wouldn't have received any news. There must be a divine spirit giving me directions."

Mao Cheng, who was wiping the wet corners of his eyes, thought for an instant with his head lowered, and said in a serious tone, "My young lord, it must be that your filial piety has moved the gods. I've always been praying to the Lord of Heaven: 'My master is so loyal to the country, my mistress is so kind and generous, and my young master is so respectful to elders and so gracious to the younger ones. This family is a perfect example of loyalty and filial piety. Oh, Lord of Heaven, pray bless this good family!' Today my prayers are finally answered. Providence delivers what one deserves."

Mao Xiang nodded his head slowly with a thoughtful look. Then, he laughed again. "Hey, why are you standing still? Come on, get the wine."

"Wine?"

"Yes. Just bring that bottle of Taixi White. I want a cup of it, and you should drink with me."

Mao Cheng quickly brought the wine. He poured a full cup for

说：“大爷是该喝一杯庆贺这喜事。不过这等名贵的东西，小人福薄，却不敢生受。”

“怕什么！”冒襄一挥手，“让你喝你就喝！这大半年，你跟我东奔西走，也着实辛苦。如今事情办成了，也有你一份功劳！来，快喝！”

冒成被催逼不过，只好又斟了一杯——却只得七分满，先谢了赏，双手捧着，诚惶诚恐地喝干了。冒襄这才哈哈大笑，放他去了。

冒襄自己一连干了两杯，随后又把酒杯斟满。他端起酒，向着窗外，一手叉着腰，眯缝起眼睛，兴致勃勃地眺望起秦淮河上的灯火来……

冒成说得不错，冒襄确有一个为人所称羡的家庭。他的家有着高门甲第的豪华，却没有许多富贵之家的那种复杂龌龊的纠纷瓜葛。家中虽说仆妇成群，但真正的骨肉之亲，却只有六口：一位慈和温厚的母亲，一位安分守己的年轻庶母，加上贤淑淳良的妻子和一个才满三岁的儿子；此外，就是冒襄和父亲。父亲长年在外面做官，父子两人难得见面，即使见了面，彼此也情意相投，不存在隔阂。尤其难得的是，无论父亲还是母亲，对于冒襄的行动都很少干涉；对于他的花费挥霍也从不过问。与其说这是溺爱独生的儿子，毋宁说是完全信任他，尊重他。为了这个缘故，冒襄很爱重自己的家庭，特别是对双亲怀着深深的感激之情。他由衷地觉得，自己只有恭谨敬诚，恪尽孝道，才能报答父母的深恩于万一。所以，去年秋天，他接到父亲调职襄阳的消息后，虽然也为难和犹豫过，觉得自己作为复社的一位年轻领袖，平日与社

Mao Xiang, and said respectfully, "My young lord does need a drink to celebrate the good news, but as a poor man I dare not accept your kindness by drinking it because it's such an expensive wine."

"What are you afraid of?" Mao Xiang waved his hand, saying. "If I let you drink, you drink. For the past six months, you've been through all the hardship together with me. Now that the thing is done, you have a share in its success. Come, drink!"

Thus urged, Mao Cheng poured a second cup, but only seventy percent full. He thanked the young master for the reward, held the cup in his hands, and drank it while trembling with gratitude. Mao Xiang laughed and let him go.

Mao Xiang drank two cups at one go, and then filled the cup again. He took up the cup and looked out the window, his hands on his hips. Squinting his eyes, he started to heartily admire the riot of light on the Qinhuai River.

Mao Cheng was right. Mao Xiang indeed had an admirable family. His home had the luxury and comfort of a high-class family, but didn't have the complicated and dirty entanglements of many wealthy families. Although in his family there were many men and women, only six of them were real family members: a kind and loving mother, a young meek "assistant mother"①, a virtuous wife, and a three-year-old son, besides himself and his father. His father being an official serving posts away from home, father and son rarely saw each other, and once they were able to meet, they got along quite well and there was no generation gap between them. What was particularly important was that both parents rarely interfered in his personal affairs and never asked about his extravagant spending. It was more about trusting him and respecting him than about doting on a single son. For this reason, Mao Xiang cherished family very much and was especially grateful to his parents. He wished he could repay a tiny portion of his parents' love of him by being humble, respectful, and filial. After receiving the news of his father's transfer to Xiangyang last autumn he

① assistant mother: father's concubine

友们悲歌慷慨，以天下为己任，如果为着将父亲调离“剿贼”的前线，自己公开出面奔走，会不会招致别人的讥笑和非议？对自己在社里的威信，会不会有什么影响？可是，当他一想到父母对自己恩义深重，就立即觉得责无旁贷了。“哎，无论如何，我不能眼看着父亲去送死！眼下旁人爱怎么想怎么说，一概随他去吧，反正，我总有办法向他们证明，冒襄绝非欺世盗名、贪生畏死的懦夫！”半年前，他就是抱着这样的想法，提起笔来，写了一封情辞哀切的万言书，书中力陈父亲秉性耿介刚直，不会与同僚合作，担任监军，不但于战局无益，反而可能把事情弄糟。他恳请朝廷哀怜自己作为独生儿子的悲苦心情，将冒起宗调任他职。这封书上呈朝廷之后，接下来冒襄就开始了紧张的活动——变卖家产、送礼打点、求人疏通……“哎，如今总算有了结果，母亲知道这个消息，不知该有多高兴呵！”冒襄望着暮色之中渐次闪现的越来越繁密的灯火，又感叹又喜欢，并且再一次微笑起来。他开始想象家里的人听到这个消息之后兴高采烈的情景……

这当儿，冒成已经把洗脸水端来了，一套出门赴会用的干净衣巾，也整整齐齐地摆在椅子上。他轻声呼唤：

“大爷……”

冒襄回过头来，随即想起今晚李十娘家的聚会，便点点头，爽快地放下酒杯，走过去。他先除去方巾，又把直裰脱下，都交给了冒成，然后双手捧起一掬水，俯下脸去，让散发着荼薇露清香的洁净的水同皮肤接触。顿时，一股说不出的舒爽愉快的感觉

was in a dilemma at first, thinking, "As a young leader of the Fushe, I've been declaring solemnly with other members of the society to serve the country heart and soul. Now, if I openly go about to get my father transferred away from the front line of the battle against the bandits, won't it incur criticism and ridicule? Will it damage my reputation in the society?" However, when he thought of his parents' great love for him, he immediately felt obliged to save his father. He said to himself, "Well. No matter what, I can't watch my father go to death. To hell with what others may think or say. No matter what, I can prove to them that Mao Xiang isn't a death-fearing coward that steals a reputation to deceive the world." Thus, half a year ago, he had taken out his brush pen and written a ten-thousand-word urgent petition letter saying that his father, upright by nature, was not good at working with others and as supervisor to the army would probably mess things up instead of being of any help in the war and begging the imperial court to have pity on him as the only son of Mao Qizong by transferring his old man to another post. After the petition letter was submitted to the imperial court, Mao Xiang began his intense activities: selling family property, buying gifts, finding connections ... "Aah, now finally there're results! My mother will be overjoyed to hear the news," Mao Xiang said to himself. The lights went on in the twilight one after another. After months of worry, his heart was now filled with joy. He smiled again and began to imagine how elated other family members would be upon hearing the great news ...

By now, Mao Cheng had brought in wash water, and a clean gown and turban had already been neatly laid out on the chair.

The servant boy called in a low voice, "My young master—"

Mao Xiang turned around, when he remembered the coming gathering at Li Shiniang's place tonight, so he nodded his head, put down his cup and walked over. He removed the square headscarf and took off the gown and gave it to Mao Cheng, and then scooped up some water with his hands and bent down to let the clean water that exuded the fragrance of rosa centifolia perfume come into contact with his skin. Suddenly, an indescribable feeling of comfort and

直透心脾，他不由得呻吟起来。冒成在旁边听见，倒吃了一惊，只当是水太热了。后来，看见小主人并无表示，才放下心来。

这样反复掬洗了几次之后，冒襄才绞干脸帕，不慌不忙地擦起脸来。他仔细地、使劲地擦着，这半年多来洗不净的仆仆风尘，以及脸上所蒙受的耻辱和羞惭之色，仿佛都要在这一番拭擦当中统统清除掉……

“嗯，吴次尾相公他们刚才来，还说些什么？”当脸洗得差不多的时候，冒襄忽然问。

“哦，也没说什么，就是请大爷早点过去，说有事商量。”冒成早有准备地回答。

冒襄明白朋友们所说的“事”是什么。他不再追问，开始在心里盘算起今晚同社友们的聚会来。今天是三月初七，还有大半个月，也就是三月二十八，复社要在苏州虎丘举行建社以来第四次大会。吴应箕已经事先通知他，今晚的聚会，就是要最后再商量一下这件事。冒襄本来是打算参加虎丘大会的，现在他得赶回如皋去，向母亲报告父亲的事情。一来一往，时间就来不及了。不过，冒襄觉得这也没有什么。因为虽说这是复社领袖张溥逝世之后的第一次全社大会，很可能要讨论推举继承人的问题，颇为重要，但是，前些时候社内各派展开激烈的角逐较量时，自己一直无暇参与，置身事外；而争夺的结果，这次大会的主盟一席，又被扬州地区的社长郑元勋和松江地区的社长李雯夺去，自己这一派人被完全排除在外，看来大势已去，再参加，也实在没有多大意思……他打算等一会儿见到吴应箕他们，把自己改变主意的事告诉一声就完了。

pleasure penetrated his heart and lungs, and he couldn't help groaning. Mao Cheng gave a start when he heard it from nearby, thinking that the water might be too hot. Seeing the young master didn't have a problem, he was relieved.

After washing his face several times like this, Mao Xiang wrung his face towel dry and slowly wiped his face. He wiped it carefully and vigorously, as if all the persistent dust and all the humiliation and shame that had stayed there for more than half a year, were going to be wiped out in this single act ...

"Um, what else did the gentlemen say?" Mao Xiang suddenly asked before he was going to finish washing.

"Oh, they didn't say anything particular. They just asked you to go there early, saying that they have something to discuss with you," Mao Cheng answered.

Mao Xiang understood what that something was. He began thinking about the gathering with his fellow Fushers tonight. Today was the seventh of March, and it was more than half a month to go before the twenty-eighth. The Fushe was going to hold its fourth conference since its founding on Tiger Hill, Suzhou. Wu Yingji had notified him in advance that tonight's gathering was to have a final discussion of the matter. Mao Xiang, who had originally planned to attend the Tiger Hill Conference, now had to rush back to Rugao to report to his mother the good news and would not be able to make it to the conference after his trip home, but he didn't think he had anything to lose. Although it was the first general meeting after the death of Zhang Pu, leader of the Fushe, and it was very likely that the issue of selecting a successor was to be discussed, which was quite important of course, it was meaningless for him to attend the conference over which he didn't have much influence, because the leadership seats of the conference had been taken by Zheng Yuanxun, president of the Yangzhou chapter, and Li Wen, president of the Songjiang chapter, after intense competition, in which he had not participated and through which his faction had been marginalized. He decided to tell Wu Yingji and the others about his change of mind and that would be it.

冒襄终于洗完了脸，丢下脸帕，容光焕发地直起身来。冒成已经捧着新衣巾在旁边伺候着。冒襄翻了翻，是一件百幅流云满绣金的浅蓝直裰，一顶蓝色绣红花万字头巾。他觉得还过得去，便点点头，正想让冒成帮他穿上，忽然瞥见那伶俐汉子正眯缝着眼儿在笑。

“嗯，你笑什么？”冒襄一边戴着头巾，一边问，“莫非你瞧我刚才，有什么可笑之处不成？”

“啊啊，小人不敢！”冒成赶忙说，“小人刚才想起了一件事。”

“哦？”

“小人想，老爷这件事有了着落，大爷就能到姑苏去看陈姑娘了！”

冒襄正把一只胳膊伸进袖筒里，听了这话，不由得怔了一下，随即莞尔一笑，说：“该打的奴才，偏你有这许多闲嚼蛆！”

冒成说的这个陈姑娘，就是苏州红极一时的名妓陈圆圆，色、艺、才号称三绝。去年春天，冒襄到湖南去探望当时还在衡州做官的父亲，途经苏州时认识了她。两人一见钟情，并且有了密约。到秋天，冒襄从湖南护送母亲回来的时候，两人又在苏州再一次见面。当时陈圆圆刚刚躲过一次外戚豪家的逼抢，急于从良嫁人；冒襄对于陈圆圆的娟秀慧黠也颇为满意，终于答允娶她。但是恰好这时传来了冒起宗调职襄阳的消息，事情便拖了下来。这半年，冒襄忙着替父亲奔走，一直腾不出手来料理陈圆圆的事，而且也再没有工夫到苏州去过。虽然陈圆圆三番几次来信询问催

Finally, the washing was over. He dropped his towel and straightened up, his face radiant with light. Mao Cheng was already waiting beside him with his new clothing. Mao Xiang flipped it. It was a light blue straight gown embroidered with hundreds of drifting clouds and a blue turban embroidered with red flowers. He nodded his head in approval. Just as he was about to let Mao Cheng help him put it on, suddenly he caught sight of the quick-witted man smiling with squinting eyes.

"Hey, why do you smile?" Mao Xiang asked as he put on the turban. "Did you see anything amusing about me?"

"No, sir," Mao Cheng hurriedly said. "I have just remembered something."

"Oh?"

"I was thinking, now that my old master's matter is settled, you can go to Gusu to see Miss Chen."

Mao Xiang, who was putting an arm into the corresponding sleeve, stood still when he heard this. Then he smiled and said, "You deserve a good beating, garrulous slave!"

The Miss Chen that Mao Cheng mentioned was Chen Yuanyuan, a well-sought-after prostitute in Suzhou, who was famous for her beauty, talent, and intelligence. Mao Xiang had met her when he stopped at Suzhou on his trip to see his father, then an official in Hengzhou. The two fell in love at first sight and secretly agreed to meet again. In the autumn, the two met for a second time in Suzhou when Mao Xiang returned from Hunan escorting his mother home.

At that time, Chen Yuanyuan had just escaped kidnapping by a relation of the emperor and was eager to marry herself off to a good family. Mao Xiang, quite taken with Chen Yuanyuan's graceful beauty and wily intelligence, finally agreed to marry her. However, at almost the same time, news came that Mao Qizong was going to be transferred to Xiangyang, and the matter was put aside. In the past six months, because Mao Xiang had been busy running about for his father, he was unable to proceed with marrying Chen Yuanyuan, and besides, he had never had time to go to Suzhou again. Chen Yuanyuan

促，但冒襄感到不能太过着急。根据这些年来同女人们打交道的经验，他对于自己有着十足的自信。他很了解自己高贵的家世、超群的才华，以及出众的仪容风度，每一样对于女人们都有着巨大的吸引力。在情场角逐之中，他从来都是一位稳操胜券的将军，只有他经常冷淡地拒绝那些为他如痴如狂的女子，而从来没有被任何一个女子拒绝过。即便是同陈圆圆互相玩弄感情游戏的过程中，他的这种信心也从来没有动摇。他不相信陈圆圆还会有什么变卦，以及发生投向别人怀抱那种事。不，他根本不相信！而且，他倒是有意把迎娶的事拖一拖，以免办得过于急迫匆忙，让陈圆圆顺当容易地达到目的，到头来，倒让她把自己看轻了。因此，当冒成提起这件事时，虽然有片刻工夫，他犹疑不决：是否真该先到苏州去看望一下陈圆圆？但最后还是打消了这个念头。“反正已经拖到了今日，再迟十天半月，也是一样的。”他想。

冒襄一声不响，穿戴停当，然后以坚定、清晰的口吻叮嘱冒成：“别忘了明天一早雇船回如皋！”说完，便从桌子上拿起那柄李昭制竹骨、王孟仁画面的名贵折扇，用了一个潇洒优美的动作，轻轻一挥，迈着轻快的脚步，向外走去。

## 乞丐成灾

李十娘是秦淮河的一位名妓。她家的房子坐落在钞库街南，离冒襄下榻的河房，也就一里之遥。那一带，南京人叫作“旧院”，是秦楼楚馆萃集之所。南京城里最有身价的一群妓女，如李十娘、顾眉、李大娘、尹春、范钰、沙才、马娇、顾喜、崔科、葛嫩、李香等等，都在那儿比屋而居，以她们的芳名丽色，招引着四面八方的风流豪客。这会儿华灯初上，正进入了一天当中最热闹快

had written several times to urge him to keep his promise, Mao Xiang thought there was no hurry yet. Based on the experience of dealing with women over the years, he had full confidence in himself, knowing very well that his notable family background, outstanding talents, and unexcelled appearance and demeanor were all appealing to women. In love competitions, he had always been a winning warrior, who had often coldly rejected women crazy for him and had never been rejected by any woman at all. Even in this romantic game with Chen Yuanyuan, his confidence had never wavered. He didn't believe that Chen Yuanyuan would change her mind or throw herself into someone else's arms. No, he didn't believe it would happen at all. Besides, he wanted to put off the marriage so that Chen Yuanyuan would not get what she wanted so easily and despise him for lack of patience. When Mao Cheng broached the subject, he at first thought it was time to meet with her in Suzhou but eventually dropped the idea. "Anyway, since it has been delayed already, a few more days will make no difference," he thought.

After silently dressing up, he said to Mao Cheng in a firm and clear tone, "Don't forget to hire a boat for Rugao early tomorrow morning." Then, he picked up from the table the expensive folding fan with bamboo bones made by Li Zhao and a painting by Wang Mengren, and, gently waving it in a chic and graceful gesture, walked out with brisk steps.

## The Plague of Beggars

Li Shiniang was a famous prostitute on the Qinhuai River. Her house was located at the south end of Chaoku Street, one *li* away from the riverhouse where Mao Xiang lodged. The neighborhood, cluttered with high-end brothels, was referred to as The Old Yard by Nanjingers. The most celebrated prostitutes in Nanjing, such as Li Shiniang, Gu Mei, Li Daniang, Yin Chun, Fan Yu, Sha Cai, Ma Jiao, Gu Xi, Cui Ke, Ge Nen, and Li Xiang, all resided here next to one another, luring romantic men of good means from all places. Now the lamps were lit and the day's most lively and joyous part began. The mellifluous

活的时刻。柔靡妙曼的歌声、琴笛声随着温馨骀荡的春风远远近近地飘送过来，把来往行人的心头撩得痒酥酥的。

与三山街那边不同，这一带的店铺十有七八都是做的吃和玩的生意。一眼望去，酒楼连着酒楼，茶社挨着茶社，在雪亮的明角灯的映照下，一间间都座无虚席，人声鼎沸。那些遍布全街的大小赌场里，更是生意兴隆。人们不仅在这儿赌纸牌、赌骰子，还赌斗鸡、斗蟋蟀、斗鹌鹑；戏棚里锣鼓喧天，正搬演着一出又一出的新剧；妙曼柔媚的昆山腔，在这儿风靡一时。至于依赖这条街市谋生觅食的人，更是五花八门，从占卜相面的、抬轿撑船的、杂耍卖唱的、卖花送果的、修脚篦头的，到清客篾片、和尚道士、师姑卖婆、泼皮闲汉都有。他们一天到晚在街市上出没游转，一心指望在那些衣饰华丽、出手豪阔的客人身上碰碰运气，讨个彩头……

因为终于放下了心中一件大事，冒襄此刻感到多时未有过的轻松。他愉快地、不慌不忙地走着，觉得今天晚上这街市上的灯光分外明亮，人们的脸孔也变得分外亲切、可爱。如果不是一支押送礼品的队伍走过，引起了他的注意，他也许会这样一直走到寒秀斋。然而，他突然想起了一件事，于是停住脚，回头对跟随在后面的冒成说：

“我几乎忘了，熊老伯那儿，我今日去得匆忙，不曾备得礼品。如今事情办成了，这份礼是欠不得的。你赶快回去打点，宁可多花点银子，总要像样些——连夜给送过去。”

“是！”冒成答应着，又问，“现在就去么？”

“嗯！明儿我们要家去，该办的事情还不少。我这儿不过几步就到了，也不用你跟着。待会儿，你打发三儿，要不冒贵过来接我就完了！”

sounds of singing and of *qin* and flute playing came with the warm spring breeze from far and near, titillating the hearts of the passersby.

Unlike the Sanshan Street, most of the shops in this area were in the business of "eat and play". At a glance, one restaurant was connected to another, and tea houses stood side by side; under the shining bright goat-horn lamp, every room was boisterous with guests. Business was even better in the gambling houses on the street. People not only betted on cards and dice, but also on cocks, crickets, and quails; in the open-air theater, amid noisy gongs and drums, new plays were performed one after another; the mellifluous Kunshan-style singing was all the rage here. There were all kinds of people who depended on this marketplace for a living: fortune-tellers, sedan chairmen, boat rowers, jugglers, beggar musicians, flower sellers, fruit vendors, pedicurists, hair-combers, parasites, Buddhist monks, Taoist priests, nuns, old women peddlers, ruffians, idlers ... They wandered around in the market all day long, hoping to try their luck on the generous, gorgeously-dressed customers and win a jackpot ...

Because he was finally relieved of a weighty matter on mind, Mao Xiang felt more relaxed at this moment than he had ever been in a long time. He walked in gay and unhurried steps, feeling that the lights on this street market tonight were brighter than ever and that people's faces were more agreeable and lovelier than ever. He would have walked all the way to the Cold Beauty Chamber like this if he hadn't caught sight of a team of men escorting a batch of gift items. That reminded him of something, so he stopped, turned around, and said to Mao Cheng behind him:

"I've almost forgotten Uncle Xiong. I went in a such hurry today that I didn't carry a gift for him. Now that things are done, I shouldn't owe him the gift. You hurry back to take care of it. Money isn't a problem. Make sure the gift is decent and deliver it to him tonight."

"Yes, my young lord!" Mao Cheng said. "Should I go now?"

"Yes. We'll leave for home tomorrow and there're many things to do. I'll get there in a few steps, and you don't need to follow me. After a little while, you can send San'er or Mao Gui to pick me up."

冒襄重新转过身来。他小心地靠了路边走，以防被身后不断喝道急奔而来的轿子碰着，脸上始终挂着和气的微笑。

然而，渐渐地，一阵嗡嗡的低语在他的身后响了起来，那是一种胆怯的、机械的乞求声。开始这声音很小，断断续续，随后就扩大起来，越来越响，终于成了一片不间断的喧嚷。冒襄吃惊地站住了，回过头去。

在他的身后，不知什么时候已经聚拢了一大群乞丐，全是些年纪幼小的孩童，大的不过十四五岁，最小的只有三四岁。在市肆的灯光下，看上去他们几乎都是一个模样：乱草一样的头发，污秽尖削的脸颊，呆滞的、没有神采的大眼睛。他们有的穿着褴褛不堪的衣衫，有的则赤裸着上身，露出了伶伶瘦骨。几个年纪更幼小的，干脆一丝不挂，在春夜的寒气中瑟瑟发抖。他们全都乞怜地望着冒襄，一个个伸出了黝黑纤瘦的手爪，幽灵似的在他跟前攒动着……

冒襄惊慌地后退一步，厌恶地皱起眉毛，随即又站住了。他想了想，脸色变得平和下来。他习惯地回顾一下，又把手伸进怀里，忽然怔住了。原来，为着省得麻烦操心，他身上从来不带银子，银子一向由冒成或是别的亲随收着，随时随地跟在他身边，替他支付打发。刚才冒成匆匆一走，冒襄此刻身上竟是连一个铜钱也没有。他摇摇头，无可奈何地转动着眼睛，向四面张望，希望能发现一个认识的人。然而，没有。他回过头来，朝那群正怀着不安和希望静静等待着的小乞丐瞅了一眼，忽然，他转过身，迅速地向就近一家酒肆走去。

“店家！”他向坐在柜台后面的一个白发老头儿拱拱手，“我想向宝号借十吊钱应用，权且以此为押，未知可否？”冒襄说着，把从手上褪下来的一枚精金镶翡翠指环，放在柜台上。

Mao Xiang turned around to continue his trip. He kept to one side of the road to avoid the sedan chairs that rushed forward from behind, a gentle smile hanging on his face.

However, a buzz of murmurs rose behind him. It was a timid, mechanical begging sound. At first, it was small and intermittent, but then it grew louder and louder and finally became an uninterrupted din. Mao Xiang stopped in alarm and turned around.

Behind him, a large crowd of beggars had gathered; all of them were young children, as old as fourteen or fifteen and as young as three or four. Under the lights of the market, they all looked the same, with disheveled hair like messy grass, filthy sharp cheeks, and big yet listless eyes. Some of them were dressed in rags, while others were topless, their bones and joints clearly visible. A few younger ones were simply naked, shivering in the cold air of the spring night. Looking at Mao Xiang pitiably, they all stretched out their dark, slender, skinny claws and moved around him like ghosts.

Mao Xiang stepped back in panic, frowning in disgust, but soon stood still. As he realized what was happening, his expression softened into kindness. He looked back habitually and put his hand into the front of his gown. There was nothing in it. Because Mao Cheng had hurried away just now, Mao Xiang was left without a coin. He had never cared to carry money with him, having always had Mao Cheng or another servant at hand to pay for his expenses. He shook his head, and, moving his eyes helplessly, looked around to find someone he knew. However, there was none. He turned his head and glanced at the swarm of young beggars, who were waiting quietly with anxiety and hope, and then turned and quickly walked to a nearby tavern.

"Hi, boss!" He bowed with clasped hands to a white-haired old man sitting behind the counter and said. "I want to borrow ten *diao*[①] from the tavern, and I can use this as a pledge. Is it possible?" Mao Xiang said as he placed on the counter a ring of fine gold with emerald inlay, which he had taken from his hand.

① *Wen* is the smallest unit of money. 1000 *wen* is equivalent to 1 *diao*.

老头儿瞥了冒襄一眼，拿起指环，眯缝着眼睛反复审视了一阵，又抬头重新打量冒襄。终于，他堆起笑容：“好说，好说，敢问尊客高姓大名？要这十吊钱可是急用？”

“小生如皋冒襄，借寓在下边不远河房里，今日因出门匆匆，身上不曾带得有银子，故此相烦老丈相帮。这十吊钱——”他指一指站在街中，正远远地朝这边观望的那群小乞丐，“也一并烦老丈替小生散给他们。明日小生来取回信物时，另有酬谢！”

“哦，冒相公原来欲行善举。小老自应效力，‘酬谢’二字，如何敢当！”老头儿显出肃然起敬的样子。停了停，他看着冒襄，眨眨眼睛，多少有点尴尬地：“这指环，按理也不敢让相公留下，只是……”

冒襄微微一笑：“老丈肯允相帮，小生已感激不尽。指环一定留下，就请赶快施行吧！”

“这——小老就大胆从命了！”老头儿顿时高兴起来，他郑重收起指环，然后拿过纸笔，写了一张字据，双手交给冒襄，又亲自搬了一张椅子，请冒襄坐下，这才转过身，急急走进后面去了。

过了一会儿，两个年轻伙计走出来，搬了两张八仙桌，两张长凳，在店门外摆好，然后，同那掌柜老头儿一起，从后间将十吊钱扛了出来，堆在八仙桌上。

那群小乞丐早已等得万分焦急，瞧见这种架势，也不待招呼，立即“哄”的一声，拥上前来。两名年轻的店伙早已做好准备，他们站在八仙桌前，伸手一拦，把小乞丐们拦住了。

站在桌子后面的掌柜先不忙发放，他清了清嗓子，大声说道：“列位！请听小老一言：近来天时不正，水旱频繁，远近四

The old man glanced at Mao Xiang, picked up the ring, and, squinting his eyes, examined it again and again. Finally, he smiled and said, "No problem, no problem. May I venture to ask your name, sir? Do you have any urgent use for the money?"

"I'm Mao Xiang from Rugao staying for the time being in a riverhouse nearby. Because I've left the riverhouse in a hurry, I haven't taken any money with me. I'll appreciate it if you can help me out," he said, pointing to the swarm of little beggars who were standing in the street and watching them from a distance. "Sir, would you please distribute the money to them? I'll pay you extra for your kindness tomorrow when I come to get my pledge."

"Oh, I see. It's an act of charity from Mr. Mao. How dare I accept any extra?" The old man was all respect. After a pause, he looked at Mao Xiang, and blinking his eyes, said with a tad of embarrassment, "For the sake of respect, I shouldn't keep this ring, but ..."

Mao Xiang said with a gentle smile, "I'm already grateful to you for your kind help, sir. Please keep the ring and get it going."

"Aye, sir," said the tavern keeper. The old man brightened up. He put the ring in a safe place, took out his writing-brush and paper, wrote a receipt, and gave it to Mao Xiang with both hands. Then he got a chair for Mao Xiang to sit before he turned and walked to the back room in quick steps.

After a while, two young waiters came out. They moved two *baxian* tables and two benches to outside the tavern. Then, together with the old boss, they carried a bag of money from the back room and piled the coins on the *baxian* tables.

Seeing this, the swarm of little beggars anxiously waiting rushed forward without being summoned. The two young waiters, ready for such a scene, stood in front of the *baxian* tables and stretched out their hands to stop the little beggars.

The tavern keeper standing behind the tables, not in a hurry to hand out the money, cleared his throat and said loudly:

"Listen up, everybody! Recently, the climate isn't right. Because of frequent floods and droughts, the land is bare everywhere far and

乡，赤地千里，颗粒无收，饿殍载道，满目凄凉，消息交传，已非一日。虽有官府垂念哀怜，百计赈济，唯是饥民日众，杯水车薪，此亦有目共睹。今有如皋冒先生，文名素著，久孚乡望，且饥溺为怀，有口皆碑，偶来留都，目睹时艰，不忍坐视，慷慨解囊，以使嗷嗷待哺之辈，得以苟延残喘，实属功德无量！小老现今于此替冒先生发放，特此布知，所望四方仁人善士，能者效力，富者输财，挽救浩劫于万一……”

老头儿咬文嚼字，滔滔不绝地说了一大篇，一边说，一边还洋洋自得地摇头晃脑，也不管周围的人听得懂听不懂。冒襄不禁惊奇起来，心想：原来这老头儿是念过几天书的，却拿到这当口来卖弄，真是好笑！本来沽屠之辈中略通文墨的，如今也不算稀罕，只是他出口成文，得体堂皇，倒是难得。所以，当老头儿说完，拱着手作了半个罗圈揖，又转身朝冒襄深深一揖时，冒襄就赞许地笑着，做了一个请他发放的手势。

老头儿受了这鼓励，劲头儿越足。他回过头去，瞅着那群小乞丐，威严地说：“现在开始放赈，每人一百文大钱，不许挤抢。谁要挤抢，不光没有，还要老大棒子打开去！”

near with no single grain to harvest, and corpses of people dead from hunger populate the roads. It's a bleak and heart-rending picture. All kinds of bad news mix with each other. Things have been like this for quite some time. The *yamen* is putting up all kinds of relief efforts, which are just a drop in the bucket given the increasingly huge number of people suffering from hunger, as can be seen by everybody. Today, we're honored to have Mr. Mao of Rugao with us, who is a very famous scholar and commands great respect from people in this part of the country. He's also known as a caring person, whose kindness is proverbial. On this current visit to the Legacy Capital, he is sad to see the hardships you've been going through. Out of a generous and compassionate heart, he now decides to offer some help. This money shall stop your hunger for a little while. It's a great act of kindness indeed! Cheers for Mr. Mao! I hereby announce that I'll now distribute the money on behalf of our beloved Mr. Mao. I hope all good people from all places will do their best by doing something for or give something to the people who are suffering ..."

Speaking the language of the learned, the old man uttered a long essay without pause, proudly shaking his head as he spoke, without caring whether the surrounding people understood or not. Mao Xiang was very much surprised. "This old man has had some learning, but showing off learning at a marketplace like this doesn't sound quite right. It's nothing unusual for a butcher or a wine seller to be somewhat literate nowadays, but his ability to speak an essay in an elegant style is indeed rare." When the old man delivered his speech, he pressed his hands together to give the audience a half bow, and then turned to give Mao Xiang a deep one. Mao Xiang smiled approvingly and made a gesture to ask him to start distributing the money.

Having received this encouragement, the old man was even livelier. He turned around, looked at the swarm of little beggars, and said authoritatively, "Now we're starting to give relief, a hundred *wen* for each of you, but no pushing and shoving! Whoever pushes and shoves not only gets nothing but also gets a good beating from a stick."

老头儿这几句话果然有作用，本来做好了猛冲猛抢准备的小乞丐们，顿时变得服服帖帖。他们一个接一个地走上来领了钱，然后，又走到冒襄跟前，叩头称谢。

冒襄和气地点着头，或者做一个让他们起来的手势。他并非第一次做这种善事。三年前，他来南京应乡试时，就曾经在桃叶河房里临时收养过一批流落街头的弃儿，后来又捐了一笔银子，把他们送到寺院去安置。比起那一桩轰动一时的善举来，眼前这种小事实在不算什么。不过，他现在心情极好，“真是不巧，怎么偏偏身上忘了带钱，要不，还可以多放它几两银子的！”他想。于是，他开始盘算着，等父亲的事情一办成，他就派人上扬州，请一个班子，到如皋去唱几天戏，谢神还愿。到时，再像像样样地散它一笔赈……“嗯，虽说这半年来，奔走请托，家产已经变卖了不少，不过，这一笔开销，看来还是省不得的。”这样暗暗决定了之后，他就抬起头，心安理得地瞧酒店掌柜发放。不过，小乞丐实在太多，而且一个比一个肮脏、丑陋，令人瞧着很不舒服。渐渐地，冒襄厌倦起来，任凭他们叩头，懒得再答理。又坐了片刻，冒襄终于站起来，向老掌柜道了别，委托他把事情办完，然后，自己继续往前走去。

冒襄不慌不忙地走着，一边倾听身后伙计们唱筹发放的声音，同时，还感觉得到路人的指点和赞许的目光。他心头洋溢着一种做了善事之后的满足和快乐。这种感觉同先前喝下去的那两盅美酒交融起来，使冒襄的脑袋变得有点晕晕乎乎，脚步也有点轻飘飘的了。

当冒襄来到钞库街，兴冲冲地打算往旧院里走的时候，忽然大吃一惊——他发现，另外一群乞丐已经撵上了他。这一次不光

The old man's words really worked, and the little beggars who were ready to push, shove and grab suddenly became submissive. One by one, they came up to take their share of the money, and then they walked up to Mao Xiang and knelt down to kowtow to him.

While that was going on, Mao Xiang now nodded his head amiably now gestured for the kowtowing beggars to get up. It was not the first time for him to do such a good deed. Three years ago, when he came to Nanjing for the provincial-level examination, he temporarily provided for a group of abandoned children from the streets. Later, he settled them in a monastery, to which he donated a large sum of money. Compared to that sensational act of charity, this one was nothing, but it did give him a sense of pride. "Regretfully, I forgot to take some money when I left. Otherwise, I would give a few more taels of silver to them," he thought. Then, he started to think about hiring a theater troupe from Yangzhou as soon as the business about his father was final to give performances in Rugao for a few days in a row as a tribute to the gods who had answered his prayers. By then, he would give out more relief money ... "While many of the family assets have been sold in the past six months in running around to seek help, such expenditure is absolutely necessary," he thought. Having made up his mind, he lifted his head and watched the tavern keeper handing out the relief money. However, the crowd of little beggars, one dirtier and uglier than another, was not something pleasant to see. Gradually, Mao Xiang got bored and turned a blind eye to their kowtowing. After sitting for a while, he finally stood up, said goodbye to the old tavern keeper, who was put in charge of the matter, and then went on his way.

Mao Xiang walked unhurriedly amid the voices of the waiters behind him and the curiosity and admiration of the onlookers. His heart was filled with satisfaction and happiness that came after doing a good deed. This feeling, blended with the two cups of wine he had drunk earlier, made his head a little dizzy and his steps a little lighter.

Mao Xiang came to Chaoku Street. As he was just going to walk into the Old Yard, he was shocked to find that another swarm of beggars had already caught up with him. This time, it was not children

是小孩，男女老少都有，而且来势汹汹。冒襄稍一停步，他们就马上围上来，大声地乞讨。一阵阵污浊难闻的臭气，从他们破烂的衣衫上散发出来，中人欲呕，冒襄急忙用衣袖掩住鼻子，赶紧往前走。

“那边、那边！”他挥着手说。

“没有了！”“早派完啦！”“哎，相公可怜见……”“求您再行个好，求您啦！”他们七嘴八舌地说，紧追不舍。

冒襄想说：“那我也没有办法啦！”可是，这时候他看见迎面也有几个影子，正向他逼近。他害怕起来，心里一急，猛地站住脚，大喝一声：

“站住！别过来！你们想干什么？啊？想干什么？”

那群乞丐被他这一喝，犹豫着站住了。

“堂堂留都之地，有官有法！莫非你们敢当街行抢不成？”冒襄瞪起眼睛，愤然质问。

乞丐们你看我，我看你，开始退缩了。有的人往后躲，有的人低下头，站在前面的几个，却“扑通”一声，跪了下来。

“请相公息怒，小人不敢冒犯相公，小人都是安分良民，只求相公垂怜开恩……”一个老头儿战战兢兢地叩着头。

“俺……俺们是安、安分良民，俺打河……河南来，那地方吃……吃吃吃人，俺怕，不不不……敢吃，俺可是安……安分良民……”一个高大的汉子结结巴巴地分辩，昏暗中看不清他的脸。

“相公老爷，您可怜可怜这没爹的孩子吧！”一个瘦小的妇人尖声叫着，举起了怀中哇哇大哭的孩子，“我们一家七口死了四个，我同他爹带着他好容易逃出来，他爹给人卖命保镖，上月一去就没回头，听说半道遇上响马，给杀了！哦……丢下我们娘俩，可怎么活哟！……”她痛苦地捶着自己的胸口，号啕大哭起来。

only. They were men and women, young and old, swarming in like a flood. When he stopped, they immediately gathered around him and begged of him at the top of their voices. A foul, nauseating stench came from their tattered clothes. He quickly covered his nose with his sleeves and hurried forward.

"Over there, over there," he said, waving his hand.

"It's over!" "Nothing left!" "Sir, have pity on me ..." "Pray do another favor!" They babbled and trailed after him.

Mao Xiang wanted to say, "Then I can't do anything about it." However, at this moment, he saw several shadows closing in on him from in front. He was scared. In panic, he stopped abruptly and shouted:

"Stop! Don't come! What the hell do you want to do? Hah? What do you want to do?"

The flock of beggars came to a standstill upon hearing his shout.

"This is the Legacy Capital with law and order! Are you going to rob me on the street in broad daylight?" Mao Xiang opened his eyes wide and questioned them angrily.

The beggars looked at each other and started to shirk. Some hid behind, some lowered their heads, and the few standing in front fell down on their knees with a "plump".

"Sir, please don't be angry at us. We're good people asking for your kindness ..." an old man said, kowtowing fearfully.

"We—we're good—good people, from—from Henan Province. There, man—man—eats—man. We're scared. We—we— don't dare to eat humans. We're good—good people—" a large, tall man said stammeringly, his face blurry in the darkness.

"Mister, pray have pity on this fatherless child," screamed a small, thin woman, holding high a crying baby in her arms. "We were a family of seven. Four were dead. His father and I managed to escape with him. Later, his father took up a job as a bodyguard. He left last month and have never come back. I heard that he met some bandits halfway and was killed, leaving mother and son behind. Wooh-wooh, how can we survive?" she cried vehemently, beating her chest in pain.

冒襄默默地听着这些凄惨的哭诉，心情变得沉重起来。他不由得叹了一口气，声音终于缓和下来：“我不怪罪你们，都起来吧。我不是不肯给你们，实在是出来得匆忙，身上未曾带得有，刚才……”他忽然停住不说了，摆一摆手，转身向外就走。

这一次，乞丐们没有再跟上来。冒襄暗暗松了一口气。但他仍然急急忙忙地走，不敢回头再看一眼。

“他说没有，怎么会没有？”

快要走进旧院后门的时候，冒襄听见背后远远传来这么一句。

“唉，算了！”一个苍老的声音，“给不给，还得凭人家喜欢。”

“可是他愣说没有！”一个年轻的声音不服气地反驳，“还唉声叹气，装得倒像！”

“是嘛！”另一个人提高了声音，仿佛故意要让冒襄听见，“他说没有钱，没有钱还能去逛窑子，找婊子？莫非这婊子的 × 肯白送给他不成？”

冒襄猛地站住了。有一忽儿，他几乎不敢相信自己的耳朵。随后，一股无名怒火从心底直冲上来。他恨不得立即走回去，把这些下贱的、根本不值得怜悯的臭叫花子狠狠教训一顿！然而，当他回过头去，接触到那些远远投来的怨毒的目光时，他忽然又感到畏缩、胆怯了。于是，他只好咬咬牙，强忍着满腔怒气，加快脚步，向旧院走去。

## 聚议社事

旧院的前门在武定桥，钞库街是后门。进了门楼，是一道清洁的石板长街，街头有水井，街道两旁排列着窗明几净的小店铺。这些店铺与外间不同，它不卖别的，专卖那些考究精美、香艳风

Mao Xiang was heavy of heart as he listened to the stories of misery. He sighed. "I'm not blaming you. Please get up, all of you," he said in a softened tone. "It's not that I refuse to give it to you. I really left my place in a hurry and didn't carry anything with me. Just now ..." He suddenly stopped with a wave of his hand, turned and left.

This time, the beggars didn't follow him. Mao Xiang secretly breathed a sigh of relief. However, he still walked hurriedly, not daring to look back again.

When he was about to enter the Old Yard through the back gate, from behind him came a loud conversation:

"He said he doesn't have it, so he doesn't have it?"

"Oh, forget it," a rusty old voice said. "To give or not to give is his choice."

"But he simply insisted on saying he doesn't have it," a young voice retorted in disbelief. "He even sighed. He's very good at pretending."

"I agree," said another man in a higher voice, as if deliberately to let Mao Xiang hear. "He said he has no money, but can he go to the brothel and find a bitch if he doesn't have money? Is there a free bitch for him?"

Mao Xiang stopped abruptly. He could hardly believe his ears. A wave of indescribable anger rushed straight up from the bottom of his heart. He wanted to go back immediately and give a good lesson to those base, unworthy, and stinky animals. However, when he turned his head and came into contact with the spiteful gazes cast from a distance, he suddenly was shy and timid again. He could do nothing but walk into the Old Yard with suppressed anger and quickened steps.

## A Private Meeting

The front gate of the Old Yard was on the side of the Wuding Bridge, and on the Chaoku Street side was the back gate. After Mao Xiang passed the gatehouse, he saw a long, clean slate-paved street with a water well at the start and lined with small bright-windowed shops on both sides. These shops were different from the ones

流的玩意儿——名酒佳茶啦，饧糖小吃啦，箫管琴瑟啦，以及金玉首饰、香囊绣袜等等，价钱都挺贵，专做那些多情的妓女、摆阔的狎客们的生意。从店铺旁边那些小巷走进去，是一个接一个的院落，一扇挨一扇窄小的院门。这些带铜环的院门，通常总是半开半闭，虽然垂着一道珠帘，依然看得见里面青石铺地的小小天井，一明两暗的浅浅堂屋，鹦哥儿在架子上声声唤茶，叭儿狗在台阶前呜呜昵客……这便是妓家，南京城里最有名的一批小娘子，就在这儿比户而居。这些流落风尘的女孩子，年纪小的只有十五六岁，大的也只有二十四五岁。她们有不少人，从母亲那一代起，就已经操起了卖笑生涯，入了乐籍，到了做母亲的年老色衰，就由女儿撑起门户。当然，也有本是好人家的女儿，迫于家庭贫困，被卖到火坑里来的。这些女孩儿，从小就受到严格的训练，不仅一个个能歌善舞，晓笛知琴，而且大都粗通文墨。顶冒尖儿的几个，还博览书史，能写一手娟秀的蝇头小楷，作儿首香艳清新的小诗，或者画儿笔花卉翎毛。因了这个缘故，她们的身价，也就与一般妓女不同，不但追欢一夕索资甚巨，而且对于客人，她们也颇为挑剔。等闲俗客，别说是陪酒侍寝那种事，即便是求见一面，也往往很难。虽然如此，却自有那一群自命风流的公子王孙、富商豪客，不分日夜地到这儿来游转厮混，流连忘返，为博得美人的青睐，不惜一掷千金。所以，尽管院门之外饥民成

outside. They specialized in exquisite gadgets or things that added to romance—famous wines, good teas, malt sugar, snacks, flutes and zithers, gold and jade jewelry, sachets, embroidered socks, and the like—all at exorbitant prices and all for amorous prostitutes and their ostentatious clients. Between these shops were small alleys lined with courtyards each having a small narrow gate. These courtyard gates with copper rings were usually half-open and half-closed; although such a courtyard normally had a curtain of beads hanging down, one could still see a small bluestone patio, a small house consisting of a central room and two side rooms, parrots perched on the shelves saying "welcome, welcome", and dogs wagging their tails on the steps ... This was the house of a prostitute. The most famous prostitutes in Nanjing lived here door to door to each other. These fallen girls were as young as fifteen or sixteen and as old as twenty-four or five. Many of them had had mothers selling laughter as registered prostitutes. When the mother was too old to be of any sexual appeal, the daughter inherited her career. Of course, there were also girls of good families who were sold into the "fire pit" when their families were impoverished. All the girls had received rigorous training since childhood. They could not only sing and dance and play multiple musical instruments such as the flute and the zither but also were able to read and write to some measure. The top-notch ones were even well read in the classics and history books and were capable of writing small script in a beautiful hand, composing a refreshing poem or two, or painting some flowers or bird feathers, and for that reason, their worth was greater than that of ordinary prostitutes. Not only did they charge a huge sum of money for a night of pleasure, but they were quite picky about clients as well. An ordinary man found it very hard to get an opportunity to see such a woman, let alone to have her drink and sleep with him. However, hordes of self-proclaimed romantic souls—wealthy businessmen and young men from aristocratic families—wandered around and lingered in this place day and night, spending large sums of money without a grudge in order to court the favor of a beauty. Therefore, despite the swarms of hungry souls outside the courtyard and the constant influx

市，噩讯纷传，院门内仍旧灯红酒绿，莺颠燕狂，一片无忧无虑的景象……

现在，冒襄已经走进了李十娘家的大门，并在鸨母引导下，穿过堂屋，向寒秀斋的后院走去。他硬是把自己的感情控制住了。因为很快就要同社友们相聚，他不想在他们面前显露出任何异常的神色。自尊心告诫他，这种莫名其妙的倒霉事，哪怕是被朋友们询问起来，也将是极不愉快，而且有损脸面的。不过，要做到这一点并不容易，受到侮辱，尤其是受到下贱的乞丐侮辱的痛苦和恼恨，还在咬啮着他的心。幸而鸨母在身边喋喋不休地说话，才多少分散了他的情绪。

李十娘的这个鸨母，是一个胖胖的、已经不年轻的小女人，圆鼓鼓的脸上涂着脂粉。她显然喝过酒，金鱼般突出的眼睛有点发红。她用一条小手帕半掩着嘴唇，时时回头斜瞅着冒襄，一刻不停地说着话。她告诉冒襄：吴次尾和陈定生两位相公已经来了，其余几位还没见影儿。她又说，今天打一大早起，就不歇地有人送帖子来，招十娘去陪酒，其中包括诚意伯刘大人、徽州盐商吴天行这样的大主顾，都一概回绝了，为了让十娘一心一意侍候复社的相公们。接着，她又说到常来旧院走动的那个吹笛子的张魁，因害白癜风，发了一脸。前两日在眉楼，有客人挂了个牌子在门上，写着“革出花面篾片一名”，把张魁臊得什么似的，几天没见他露面，听说是躲起来了。然后，她又立刻说到，旧院门里的绸绒店，新来了十几匹西洋红夏布，薄得蝉翼儿似的，给十娘扯身夏裳正合适，只是价钱满贵，五百钱一尺……

of bad news, inside the courtyard feasting and merry-making went on and on ...

Now, Mao Xiang walked into Li Shiniang's place, and under the guidance of the madam, he walked through the hall to the backyard of the Cold Beauty Chamber. He had kept his feelings under control. Because he was about to meet with his fellow members of the Fushe very soon, he didn't want to show any unusual expression in front of them. Self-esteem told him that such a sudden unpleasant happening simply out of bad luck was inglorious. However, it was by no means easy. The feelings of humiliation and pain the abominable beggars had given him were still biting his heart. Fortunately, the madam's constant chattering beside him distracted him somewhat.

Li Shiniang's madam was a fat, little, over-the-hill woman, her chubby face coated with powder. She was obviously intoxicated, her reddish eyes like those of a goldfish. Half-covering her lips with a small handkerchief, she looked back at Mao Xiang from time to time, talking nonstop. She said, Wu Ciwei and Chen Dingsheng had arrived, but the others were not seen yet. She went on to say, from the early morning, invitation letters kept coming to request the company of Shiniang, including those of big patrons like the Honorable Baron of Sincerity Mr. Liu and Huizhou salt merchant Mr. Wu Tianxing. They were all rejected so that Shiniang could wholeheartedly wait on the young gentlemen of the Fushe. Then, she said, Zhang Kui, the flute player that had frequented the Old Yard had patches of vitiligo all over his face. A couple of days ago, a client hung a sign on the door of Mei's saying "HERE IS A PARASITE WITH A COLORFUL FACE." Zhang Kui was so embarrassed that he hadn't been seen since. He might have gone into hiding. Then, she went on to say, in the silk and velvet shop at the gate of the Old Yard, there were new arrivals—a dozen rolls of scarlet summer linen, which was as thin as a cicada wing. It was just right for a summer garment for Shiniang, but the price was exorbitant, five hundred *qian* a foot[①]...

---

① The Chinese measure is "one *chi*": one *chi* is roughly equal to one foot.

冒襄用心地听着，不时回答一两句。穿过夜色朦胧的后院，来到一座长轩跟前，他步上台阶，立即就听见一个高亢的嗓音在说：

“若真有此事，我吴应箕同他势不两立！”接着“咣当”一响，像是茶杯重重放在桌子上的声音。

另一个人——大约是陈贞慧——像在劝解，但声音低沉，听不大清楚。

冒襄皱了皱眉头，心想：这位炮药性儿的老学长，不知又在发谁的脾气了。他先不忙进屋，转动着身子，把周围打量了一下。一年多没来，他发现轩前那一株枝丫虬结的老梅、两棵高大挺拔的梧桐树还是老样子，只有那十来竿翠竹似乎益发粗壮茂密了些。他记得李十娘对这些翠竹和梧桐爱惜得不得了，每天一早一晚，都要亲自指挥丫环汲来井水，细细地洗刷两次。现在虽然天色昏黑，但是借着从一字排开的冰裂式风窗里透出来的灯光，冒襄仍然可以看见光洁的树干上朦胧的反光……

“不会，哼，我看就是会！”长轩里的吴应箕又猛然叫起来。他显然还要说下去，但是，跟着走上台阶的鸨母已经尖着嗓子通报说：

“十娘，冒公子来啦，快迎接贵客！”

长轩内的谈话停止了，随即响起细碎的脚步声。暖帘一掀，先走出来一个垂髫的丫环。她向客人行了礼，转过身去，双手把帘子举起。过了一会儿，一位身材颀长的靓妆丽人姗姗地走了出来，后面跟着如护法韦驮般健硕魁梧的陈贞慧。

李十娘看见冒襄，就把双袖交叠在腰旁，侧着身子，轻启朱唇，用娇滴滴的嗓音说：

Mao Xiang listened attentively and gave a remark from time to time. After passing through the lighted backyard, he came to a rectangular hallway. As he ascended the steps, he suddenly heard a high-pitched voice saying, "If so, I, Wu Yingji, will be his enemy!" Then there was a bang, like the sound of a teacup landing heavily on the table.

The other man—probably Chen Zhenhui—was comforting him in a low, hardly discernible voice.

Mao Xiang knit his brows, thinking, "Who might it be that has caused this explosive brother to lose his temper again?" He didn't go into the house immediately; instead, he turned and looked around. After an absence of more than a year, he found that the old plum tree with intertwined branches and twigs and the two tall towering sycamore trees in front of the hallway remained the same and the only difference was that the bamboos looked even thicker and denser. In his memory, Li Shiniang cherished these green bamboos and sycamore trees so much that she instructed the maid to cleanse their trunks carefully with well water twice a day, in the early morning and in the evening. Although it was dark, by the lamplight from the row of cracked-ice-style wind windows, Mao Xiang could still see the dim reflections on the smooth tree trunks ...

"It won't? Humph, I think it will!" Wu Yingji screamed again from the hallway. He obviously wanted to continue, but the madam who had followed Mao Xiang up the steps announced in a sharp voice:

"Shiniang, here comes Young Master Mao. Hurry up and meet the distinguished guest!"

The conversation in the hallway stopped, and then came the sound of mincing steps. When the thermal curtain was lifted, a young servant girl came out. She saluted the guest, turned around, and raised the curtain with both hands. After a while, a tall, elegantly dressed beautiful woman came out gorgeously, followed by Chen Zhenhui, who was as burly as Skanda the guardian.

Seeing Mao Xiang, Li Shinian crossed her sleeves at her waist, turned her body sideways, slightly opened her red lips, and said in a cuddly voice:

“公子万福！不知公子光降，请恕奴家失迎之罪！”

冒襄先朝陈贞慧点点头，然后借着帘子里透出的灯光，打量了一下李十娘。他发现以秀美白皙著称的这位当红名妓，自从前些日子传说她病了之后，更加出落得神气清朗、楚楚可怜，便微笑着称赞说：

“‘独旷世而秀群’——多时不见，十娘益发标致了！”

说罢，转身正要同陈贞慧相见，忽然听见有人在台阶下笑着说：

“啊哟，冒公子这等夸奖十娘，连奴家听了都要眼红了！”

大家一怔，回过头去，只见两名丫环提着一双灯笼，正照着一位女郎登上台阶。那女郎头戴貂鼠暖耳，身穿银鼠皮袄，怀里还抱着一只乌云盖雪波斯猫，打扮得雍容华贵，完全是一副大家闺秀的派头。

冒襄认出这是眉楼的女主人顾眉——目前秦淮河上风头最健的一位名妓。她不仅艳名远播，能诗善画，而且交游广阔，靠山众多，同复社的一班人关系尤其拉得好。大约是陈贞慧送了帖子去，所以她这会儿便前来赴会。

冒襄正要答话，站在旁边的鸨母已经半真半假地抢先嚷起来：

“眉娘，你这是吃的哪门子醋哟！姐夫们夸你还夸得少么？如今冒公子才夸了十娘一句，你就想来抢她，我老婆子可不依！”

顾眉已经走上台阶。她笑吟吟地说：“若是别人夸奖十娘，我也不管。只是冒公子这样说了，我可不饶她！”

李十娘显然十分清楚这种逗趣对于制造一种轻快放纵的气氛会有什么作用。她于是蹙起眉毛，叹一口气说：“总是奴家命苦，

"Bliss be with you, my young lord! I didn't know your young lordship was coming. Please forgive me for my late welcome."

Mao Xiang first nodded to Chen Zhenhui, and then looked at Li Shiniang by the lamplight permeated from the curtain. He found that this famous prostitute, known for her great beauty, was more charming and more adorable after her recent illness, so he said smilingly in compliment:

"'Alone in the world, with a beauty unrivalled in the crowd!' You have become more beautiful than ever since I last saw you."

Then, he turned to meet Chen Zhenhui when suddenly he heard someone laughing and saying from below the steps:

"Oh, my! Such a compliment to Shiniang from Mr. Mao is making me green with envy."

Everyone became quiet and turned around. In the light of a pair of lanterns carried by two maids, a young lady was ascending the steps. Wearing mink earmuffs and a silver hamster leather jacket and holding a black and white Persian cat in her arms, the young woman was gorgeously dressed like a real lady.

Mao Xiang recognized that young woman as Gu Mei, owner of Mei's and the most sought-after courtesan on the Qinhuai River. Not only was she famous for her beauty and artistic talent, but she was social as well, with many backers and a wide range of contacts. As a great friend of the Fushers, she had probably been invited to the gathering by Chen Zhenhui.

As Mao Xiang was about to respond, the madam who stood next to him yelled theatrically, "Mei, what kind of vinegar are you eating to make you so sour and jealous? Did my brothers-in-law ever praise you less? Now Mr. Mao has just passed a compliment to Shiniang and you want to take it from her. Let me tell you: there's no way!"

Gu Mei walked to the top of the stairs and said smilingly, "If someone praises Shiniang, I don't care. But I won't forgive her for a praise from Mr. Mao!"

Li Shiniang obviously knew that this kind of teasing was conducive to creating a genial, relaxing atmosphere. She frowned and said with a

好容易得了冒公子一句夸奖，又被眉娘听了去。若是不让与她，只怕从此一个劲儿地撵着，直到阎罗地府都脱不了身。罢罢罢，这句夸奖我也不敢要了，现在就让给眉娘吧！”

“这可使不得！”陈贞慧从旁接口说，一本正经地摇着大而圆的脑袋，“辟疆此赞，也恰如晋人月旦之评，一经品定，便不可移易。不过，眉娘也不须吃醋，小生这里有八字之评，单道眉娘的好处。但不是出自辟疆之口，不知眉娘……”

顾眉连忙说：“能得陈公子一字品评，眉娘便已荣于华衮了！何况八字？”

陈贞慧微微一笑，说：“我这八字也是出于《闲情赋》——‘神仪妩媚，举止详妍。’不知尚差强人意否？”

大家都哄然叫好，倒把顾眉弄得忸怩起来。面对这种欢洽的气氛，冒襄感到又回到了一种熟悉的自由自在的环境里。他忘却了刚才在大街上所受到的困辱，把手中的折扇轻轻一扬，笑嘻嘻地斜瞅着顾眉，吟哦道：

愿在衣而为领，
承华首之余芳。
悲罗襟之宵离，
怨秋夜之未央。
愿在裳而为带，
束窈窕之纤身。
……

然而，没等他念下去，吴应箕低沉缓慢的声音忽然在轩内响起来，使他不由自主顿住了。只听吴应箕吟道：

sigh, "What bad luck for me! Finally, I've obtained a praise from Mr. Mao, but the praise is overheard by Mei. If I don't yield it to her, I'm afraid she'll follow me even when I go to the netherworld. Forget it! I don't dare to receive this compliment. Let me pass it to Mei."

"Oh, no, that shouldn't be done." Chen Zhenhui said from aside, shaking his big and round head solemnly. "This praise from Pijiang is just like a judgement by the First Day of Month Review①. Once a judgement is made, it's irrevocable and non-transferable. However, you don't need to be jealous. I have an eight-word praise here especially for you, but it's not from Pijiang. I'm wondering if you ..."

Gu Mei quickly responded, saying, "If I can get one word of praise from Mr. Chen, I'll be deeply honored, let alone eight words."

Chen Zhenhui smiled and said, "These eight words are also from Tao Yuanming's poem 'Ode to Leisure':'How comely you look! How gracefully you move!' I'm wondering if it's good enough for you."

Everyone applauded, which embarrassed Gu Mei. In such a jovial atmosphere, Mao Xiang felt that he had returned to his natural habitat, forgetting the humiliation he had suffered on the street just now, and gently raising the folding fan in his hand, he looked at Gu Mei sideways with a smile, and chanted:

*"I would be the collar if I were part of your blouse,*
*To receive the scent of your beautiful face from below.*
*But your blouse would be taken off in the evening*
*And I would painfully wait for the end of the long night.*
*I would be a belt if I were part of your dress*
*Winding around your slim waist*
*..."*

Before he could continue, from inside the hallway came the slow, low-pitched voice of Wu Yingji, who chanted:

① The First Day of Month Review is an art activity in the East Han dynasty, in which artists and their works were judged and the results were published on the first day of every month, hence the name.

考所愿而必违，
徒契契以苦心。
拥劳情而罔诉，
步容与于南林。
栖木兰之遗露，
翳青松之余荫。
倘行行之有觌，
交欣惧于中襟。
竟寂寞而无见，
独悁想以空寻。
……

这一段也是《闲情赋》里的句子，可是经吴应箕的口念出来，却凄厉悠长，充满抑郁怨苦的意味，与眼前的快活气氛极不协调。大家你望我，我望你，都停止了打趣，现出惊疑不定的神色。只有陈贞慧显然知道是怎么一回事，他变得沉静下来，终于摆一摆手，招呼大家一道走进轩去。

这是一个长方形的敞轩，四面都是窗户，垂着梅花暖帘。当中一张楠木炕床，两旁摆着几椅，陈列着盆景瓶花。四个高脚的落地烛台上，八支明晃晃的红蜡烛在那里交映争辉。又黑又瘦的吴应箕正倒背着手站在窗前，听见脚步声，他停止了吟哦，慢慢地转过身来。

陈贞慧走进屋里之后，就把冒襄推在左首，同他行礼相见。冒襄再三推让，到底拗他不过，只得告了僭，作过揖。等吴应箕走过来时，冒襄就坚持站了右首，也行礼见过了。因为还有几位

*"Such wishes can't be had*
*And they only pain the heart all the more.*
*Without a vent for the feelings of love*
*In the south woods I take a stroll,*
*And have a rest by a mulan magnolia tree glistening with dewdrops,*
*protected by the shadow of the green pine.*
*If I met you face to face here and now*
*What surprise would I have and what joy!*
*Yet such an encounter never comes*
*And I am still alone with myself,*
*Thinking and searching in vain.*
*..."*

That part is also from "Old to Leisure", but in Wu Yingji's mouth, it became plaintive and melancholy, extremely inconsistent with the current jovial atmosphere. All the people present stopped joking and looked at each other in bewilderment. Only Chen Zhenhui knew what was going on. He quieted down and gestured for everyone to go into the hallway.

It was an elevated rectangular open hallway with windows on all sides draped with plum-blossom thermal curtains. In the middle was a heated *nanmu* bed with tables, chairs, bonsai vases, and potted flowers on both sides. On the four high-footed candlesticks eight bright red candles were competing to shine. Wu Yingji, a thin and dark-complexioned man, was standing at the window with his hands crossed on his back. Hearing the sound of footsteps, he stopped chanting and slowly turned around.

After entering the room, Chen Zhenhui pushed Mao Xiang to the seat of honor on the left and formally greeted him with a salute. Mao Xiang repeatedly declined the offer but seeing he was unable to reject it he finally accept it with an apology and a bow. When Wu Yingji walked over, Mao Xiang stepped to the first seat on the right and greeted him with a salute. Because there were still a few more members of the Fushe to come and they still would have to perform the rituals of greeting, they

社友未到，还要行礼，所以暂时不宽外衣，只分别坐了下来。

这当儿鸨母已经退出去，丫环把茶端上来。李十娘亲手斟了四杯，分别奉给客人和顾眉。最后，她自己也斟了一杯，本来打算走上前去陪客人，后来看见坐在后面的顾眉朝她招手，又看见客人们暂时没有呼唤的表示，便退到顾眉身旁坐下，静静地嗑起瓜子儿来。

三位社友各自品着茶，好一会儿谁也没有开口说话。吴应箕闭起眼睛，仿佛在养神；陈贞慧则沉思地慢慢捋着那部漂亮的长胡子。至于冒襄，还在轩外的当儿，他就听见吴应箕发怒的声音，接着又听见他那显然是抒发忧思的悲吟，进轩后，更发现两位社友神色有点不太对头。他便断定发生了什么事情。不过，对方不说，他也不打算主动去问，“该告诉我，他们自然会告诉我的。”他想。

果然，陈贞慧终于停止了捋胡子，朝冒襄转过脸来。

“辟疆，你从如皋来，一路上，可听说什么新闻？”他问，饱满结实的宽脸上堆起亲切的笑容。

“哦……”一提起新闻，冒襄便首先想到他父亲已获朝廷批准调任的事，心里冲动了一下，想把它说出来，但是又觉得不必显得过于着忙，临时忍住了。他侧着头想了一下，微笑说：“倒有一件——却是个笑话。小弟数日之前，在常州遇见汤允中，他说最近阮胡子被我们禁制得狠了，颇有改悔之意，已经不敢再同我们捣乱，还托人传话，说什么‘有不改心相事者，有如此水！’我听他说得煞有介事，便问他哪里听来的。他说是在扬州时郑超宗亲口对他说的。我又好气又好笑，当场抢白他说，你也是个老

just sat down temporarily without taking their coats off.

By now, the madam had withdrawn, and the maid had brought tea for them. Shiniang poured four cups and presented them to the guests and Gu Mei one by one. Finally, she poured a cup for herself. As she was going forward to accompany the guests, she saw Gu Mei beckoning to her from a back seat; the guests showing no intention of wanting her company for the time being, she retreated to where Gu Mei was, sat down, and quietly cracked melon seeds.

The three members of the Fushe kept sipping tea without further speaking. Wu Yingji sat in repose with his eyes closed; Chen Zhenhui were slowly stroking his beautiful long beard in contemplation. Mao Xiang had heard Wu Yingji's angry voice and plaintive chanting while he was outside the hallway. When inside, he found that the two fellow Fushers didn't look quite right. He was sure something had happened. Yet, since they didn't say it, he didn't care to ask. "They will tell me if they want to," he thought.

Sure enough, Chen Zhenhui finally stopped stroking his beard and turned to Mao Xiang.

"Pijiang, you've come from Rugao. What news did you hear along the way?" he asked, a cordial smile on his wide, meaty, and solid face.

"Oh—" Mao Xiang said with a pause. When he heard the word "news", he first thought of the imperial court's decision on his father's transfer. That was some good news worth sharing, but he held back in order not to appear too enthusiastic. He thought for an instant, tilting his head, and then smiled and continued, "There's one thing—but it's a joke. A few days ago, I met Tang Yunzhong in Changzhou. He said that Beardy Ruan is now quite repentant after being boycotted. He doesn't dare to make trouble with us anymore. You know what? He has even sent us a message, saying, 'I'll unswervingly submit myself to you, upon the White Water!' He said it in such seriousness that I was tempted to ask where he had heard it. He said that Zheng Chaozong had told him in person when they met in Yangzhou. I was both angry and amused. I admonished him on the spot, saying, 'As

复社了，怎么竟相信起这等没根没蒂的话来？漫道阮胡子决不会这等说，就算他真说了，莫非你就相信？你真是个糊涂虫！若是超宗告诉你，超宗更是糊涂虫！”

冒襄一边说，一边想起汤允中被他抢白时的那副尴尬相，就忍不住笑。他准备让陈、吴二人听了，也大笑一场。然而，出乎意料，陈贞慧听了之后，竟然一声不响；吴应箕却突然睁开眼睛，凝视着冒襄，“很好，很好！”他说，随即又把眼睛闭上了。

“嗯，辟疆，还有吗？”陈贞慧不动声色地问。

“这……后来，在来留都的船上，小弟遇到几个年轻士子，他们也在传说这件事，还拿来问我。小弟听得不耐烦，当场训诫了他们一通，叫他们不要乱传……”

“妙，益发妙了！”吴应箕又大声说道，这一次，他没有睁开眼睛。

冒襄莫名其妙地瞅着陈贞慧。后者却朝他做了一个“等一会儿再给你解释”的手势。

“那么，那几个年轻士子的消息，又是从何而来，你知道么？”他继续问。

“这——小弟倒没细问。只记得他们是从姑苏来的，还去过常熟，打算谒见钱牧斋。结果牧斋还真见了他们……对了，仿佛他们还去过扬州。”

“行了！”吴应箕一欠身站了起来，目光炯炯地，“不必再问了，如今已是清楚不过，追源肇始，就是他——郑、超、宗！”

斩钉截铁地下了这个判断之后，他就踱了开去。在此之前，他同陈贞慧显然有过争论，所以这会儿显出有点傲然自得的样子。

“可是，超宗这样做，究竟所为何来？”陈贞慧捋着胡子，沉思地问。

“所为何来？”吴应箕偏过那张长满刺猬似的胡子的瘦脸，尖刻地说，“就为的他心志不坚，见利忘义！发表《防乱公揭》

an old member of the Fushe, how come you believe in such unrooted words? Beardy Ruan would never say a thing like that. Even if he had really said it, should you believe it? You're such a fool. If Chaozong told you this, then Chaozong is more of a fool.'"

Mao Xiang couldn't help laughing as he thought of the embarrassed look when Tang Yunzhong was admonished. He was prepared to see Mr. Chen and Mr. Wu laugh too, but to his disappointment, Chen Zhenhui was silent and Wu Yingji merely opened his eyes and stared at him, saying "Very good, very good!" and then closed his eyes again.

"Mhm, is there anything else, Pijiang?" Chen Zhenhui asked calmly.

"Later—later, on the boat to the Legacy Capital, I met a few young scholars. They had also heard of such a thing and asked me about it. I was tired of the story and admonished them on the spot. I told them not to spread the rumor ..."

"Wonderful! It's getting more wonderful," Wu Yingji said loudly. This time, he didn't open his eyes.

Mao Xiang looked at Chen Zhenhui puzzledly. The latter made a gesture to him, meaning, "I will explain to you later."

"So, where did those young scholars get the news?" he continued to ask.

"This—I didn't ask. I only remember that they were from Gusu and had been to Changshu. They were planning to see Qian Muzhai, who did meet with them ... By the way, they had been to Yangzhou."

"That is good enough," said Wu Yingji, who straightened himself and stood up. He said, with piercing eyes, "I have no more questions. It's clear now that it has been him all along—ZHENG CHAOZONG!"

After giving such a verdict, he paced away. Before that, he obviously had already had an argument with Chen Zhenhui, so he looked a little proud and contented now.

"But, why did Chaozong do that?" Chen Zhenhui stroked his beard and asked thoughtfully.

"Why?" Wu Yingji turned his thin face with a hedgehoggish beard, and said acidly. "Because he doesn't have a strong will and

那一回，让他具名，我瞧他就挨挨延延的不爽快；后来又听说他同那个造园子的计成搞得黏黏糊糊的。计成是什么人？阮胡子家的一名无耻清客！可超宗却巴巴地把计成请到扬州去，帮他造什么影园——我瞧，八成那时他们就勾搭上了！今日之事，可谓由来已久！”

陈贞慧摇摇头，显然并不满意这个解释。不过，他也没有立即反驳，却把脸转向冒襄：

“辟疆，是这么回事——今年三月二十八的虎丘大会，原本推定了是由郑超宗和李舒章两位主持，如今日期将届，小弟怕有变动，前几天路过扬州，特意上影园去访超宗，想打听备办得如何。那天，他正忙着指挥人抄写传单，见了我就兴冲冲地一把扯住，拖到书房里，一五一十说了一大篇，无非是一切准备停当，要我放心之类。末了，还硬要留我吃饭。小弟见他一番盛情，也就没有推辞。不料，席间他却说出几句话来——”

说到这儿，陈贞慧就顿住了。他抬起头，看了看吴应箕，又漫不经意地扫了一眼正坐在靠后那一排椅子上的顾眉和李十娘。

“啊，超宗他说了些什么？”冒襄好奇地问，同时他已经多少猜到是怎么一回事。

可是陈贞慧仍不说话，他又捋起胡子来。机灵的顾眉似乎觉察到了。

“哎，侯相公他们怎么还不来？把人家的腰都坐酸了！”她忽然说，舒展了一下纤细的腰肢，把脸转向十娘，“姐姐，我进来时，瞧见你轩前那一株梅花，还开着几枝。这会儿月亮上来了，暗香疏影，想必清艳得很哩！你陪我去瞧瞧好么？”说着，也不待答应，她就一手抱起波斯猫，一手挽住十娘的胳膊，站起来，

forgets righteousness when seeing a profit. Earlier on, in the signing of 'Public Denunciation of a Treasonist in the Legacy Capital', I saw he was reluctant; later I heard he was very intimate with Ji Cheng, the garden builder. Who's Ji Cheng? A shameless parasite in the house of Beardy Ruan. But Chaozong happily invited Ji Cheng to Yangzhou to help him build the so-called Shadow Park. That probably was when they hooked up. What happened today is part of a long story."

Chen Zhenhui shook his head, obviously not satisfied with this explanation. However, without immediately refuting it, he turned his face to Mao Xiang and said:

"Pijiang, it goes like this: The Tiger Hill Conference on the twenty-eighth of March this year was presumably to be co-chaired by Zheng Chaozong and Li Shuzhang. As the date is drawing near, I visited Chaozong at Shadow Garden the other day to find out how the preparations were going in case there might be some changes. He was busy instructing some people to copy the flyers. When he saw me, he took me by hand excitedly and dragged me to the study. He assured me by explaining in great detail how well the preparations were. In the end, he insisted on keeping me for dinner. Seeing his kindness, I didn't decline his invitation. However, he said something during the dinner—"

At this point, Chen Zhenhui paused. He raised his head, looked at Wu Yingji, and then aimlessly glanced at Gu Mei and Li Shiniang, who were sitting in the back row.

"Aah, what did Chaozong say?" Mao Xiang asked with curiosity, and at the same time he had already guessed what had happened.

Instead of continuing, Chen Zhenhui started to stroke his beard again. The clever Gu Mei seemed to be aware of the situation, spoke suddenly, stretching her slender form. "Why aren't Mr. Hou and the others here yet? My back is stiff from the sitting," she said, then turned her face to Shiniang. "Sister, when I came in, I saw the plum tree in front of your chamber still has some flowers. The moon has risen and it must be very beautiful with the whiffs of scent and the scattered shadows! Will you see it with me?" Without waiting for a reply, she picked up the Persian cat in one hand, took Shiniang's arm in the other

又回头朝陈贞慧嫣然一笑，做了个鬼脸，然后迈着婀娜的步子，双双走出门去。

陈贞慧目送着她俩的背影，微笑着摇摇头。当他转向冒襄，吴应箕已经冷冷地开口了：

“他要我们饶了阮胡子！”

冒襄一惊：“啊，他、他真是这样说？”

“不，他还没有这样说。”陈贞慧连忙更正，“超宗也只是告诉我，阮胡子最近颇思改悔之类，同你在汤允中那儿听来的差不多。不过——”他转过脸，看了看门口，然后走到紧挨着冒襄身旁的一张椅子坐下，凑在他耳边低声说，“席间，他还说到‘门户交争不已，终非社稷之福’，劝我们勿为已甚。还说，这并非他个人私见，吴中、云间诸君子，多有同感云云。”

说到这里，陈贞慧有意停顿了一下，仿佛要让冒襄品味清楚这些话所包含的意思，又像要观察一下他的反应。看到冒襄没有作声，他又接着说：“若是果真如此，这事只怕会闹大。超宗背后，更有何人主使？他们意欲何为？此刻尚不清楚。不过瞧这来势，小弟估计三月二十八虎丘大会，必然有事！我们倘若不欲就范，须得做好应变的准备。子方、朝宗、太冲他们几个，是靠得住的。要先同他们商量，定出个对策来。不过在这儿不行。小弟之意是今晚早点散席，一起回到你下榻的河房去，从长计议，你意下如何？”

冒襄用心地听着，用手指轻轻敲打着方儿，没有立即回答。现在他也感到问题严重——比他原来猜想的严重得多。“吴中、云间诸君子多有同感”，这个“多”究竟多到什么程度？会不会是郑超宗有意夸大其辞？嗯，看来不大可能。郑超宗是个精细小心的人，如果事情不是发展到相当程度，他已经感到有把握的话，

and stood up; then she turned around, smiled and grimaced at Chen Zhenhui before pacing curvaceously out of the room with the other girl.

As they left, Chen Zhenhui watched them from behind and smilingly shook his head. As he turned to Mao Xiang, Wu Yingji said coldly, "He wants us to spare Beardy Ruan."

Mao Xiang gave a start and said, "Aah, did, did he really say that?"

"No, he didn't say it," Chen Zhenhui quickly corrected himself. "Chaozong simply told me that Beardy Ruan has been repenting lately, which is almost the same as what you heard from Tang Yunzhong, but—" He turned his face to look at the door and paced to a chair next to Mao Xiang, sat down and whispered in his ear, "During the dinner, he said, 'The endless conflict between the different factions isn't a good thing for the country.' He warned us not to be too ego-centric. He also said that it's the sentiment of many of the scholars in Wuzhong and Yujian instead of his own personal opinion."

At this point, Chen Zhenhui intentionally paused, as if to observe his listener's reaction or to allow time for the digestion of the meaning of these words. Seeing Mao Xiang's silence, he went on to say, "If that be the case, I'm afraid it will become a big problem. Who's the mastermind behind Chaozong? What do they intend to do? It's not clear at the moment, but judging from the current situation, I can decide that something will happen at the Tiger Hill Conference on the twenty-eighth of March. If we don't want to submit ourselves, we must be prepared for the turn of events. Zifang, Chaozong, and Taichong are reliable. We must first discuss it with them and work out a countermeasure, but not in here. I mean, we shall finish dinner early tonight and go to your riverhouse to think up a counter plan. What do you think?"

Mao Xiang listened attentively, tapping the square tea table with his fingers without answering immediately. Now, he also felt the magnitude of the problem. It was much more serious than he had originally thought. "What is meant by 'it's the sentiment of many of the scholars in Wuzhong and Yujian'? How many is many? Is Zheng Chaozong exaggerating? Well, it doesn't seem likely. Zheng Chaozong is a meticulous and careful person. If things hadn't reached a certain point and he weren't sure of

绝不会贸然向陈贞慧作那样的试探。而且，瞧这阵势，郑超宗也只是个跑龙套的，他背后必定还有牵线的人。不过，最令人弄不明白的，是对方到底出于一种什么样的目的和打算，如此起劲地要为阮大铖开脱？因为对方应当很清楚，这样做，绝对不会得到他们这一群年轻领袖的同意。强行翻案的结果，很可能会导致社内的分裂。然而，令人困惑之处恰恰在这里：他们甚至不惜冒分裂的风险，也要干。这到底是为什么？难道是……冒襄心头忽然一动，脱口而出地问：

“主持今年大会的，还有一个是李舒章？”

“嗯。”陈贞慧点点头，“怎么——”

“今日之事，会不会与他们有关？”

“不会吧，舒章倒不像是那种人。”

“小弟是说，几社——”

冒襄刚把这两个字说出口，陈贞慧的目光忽然闪动起来。他回过头去，瞧了吴应箕一眼。后者的脸色陡然变了，他咬紧牙齿，重重地“哼”了一声。

虽然冒襄没有把话说完，但陈、吴两人都完全明白了他的意思。目前，复社虽说是全国最大的一个文社，但它最初并不是白手起家，而是合并了东南地区十多个小社组成的，其中包括江南的应社、松江的几社、中州的端社、莱阳的邑社、浙东的超社、浙西的庄社、黄州的质社等等。论名声之响、实力之强，除了应社之外，就要数松江府的几社。旧几社的一批人，以杜麟征、夏允彝、陈子龙这样一些有名望的人物为核心，在复社内自成派系，对社事常常保持着独立的见解。在复社的领袖张溥在世时，他们还有所节制；自从张溥于去年五月病逝之后，这种倾向就更加突

himself, he would never have rushed to make such an attempt. Moreover, it's clear that Zheng Chaozong is just playing a small role. There must be someone behind him pulling the strings. What is most puzzling is, what's their intention in so vigorously trying to exonerate Ruan Dacheng? After all, they're very clear that such a proposal will definitely not be approved by the young leaders of the society. Forcibly overturning the case is likely to lead to division within the society. So, it's rather puzzling for them to risk it. What is it all for? Could it be—" he pondered. Suddenly, he thought of something and blurted out:

"This year's conference is co-chaired by Li Shuzhang?"

"Yes," Chen Zhenhui said, nodding his head. "So—"

"Does what happened today have anything to do with them?"

"No, Shuzhang doesn't look like that kind of person."

"What I mean is, the Jishe—"

Just as Mao Xiang uttered the last two words, Chen Zhenhui's eyes suddenly lit up. He turned around and glanced at Wu Yingji, whose face changed abruptly with a heavy "hm" from between his gritted teeth.

Although Mao Xiang didn't finish the sentence, both Chen and Wu fully understood what he meant. The Fushe was currently the largest literary society in the country. It hadn't been started from scratch, but instead was the result of amalgamation of more than a dozen small societies in the Southeast, including the Ying Society in River South, the Ji Society in Songjiang, and the Duan Society in Zhongzhou, the Yi Society in Laiyang, the Chao Society in East Zhejiang, the Zhuang Society in West Zhejiang and the Zhi Society in Huangzhou, among others. In terms of reputation and influence, the Ji Society (Jishe) in Songjiang Prefecture was only second to the Ying Society. Members of the former Jishe, centering around some famous figures such as Du Linzheng, Xia Yunyi, and Chen Zilong, formed their own faction within the Fushe and often maintained a unified position on Fushe affairs—when the late leader of the Fushe Zhang Pu was alive, they had some restraint—and this tendency had become more obvious since the demise of Zhang Pu in May last year. Members

出了。旧几社的一派人，对于老应社的骨干成员如孙淳、吴翻、吴应箕，以及陈贞慧、冒襄、侯方域这些新崛起的青年领袖，尤其不买账。这一次虎丘大会，就是由于他们的反对和阻挠，使吴应箕这一批人争不到主盟者的席位，而不得不让郑元勋——也就是郑超宗出来，同几社系的李雯共同担任主盟。吴应箕等人对此早已十分恼火，私下认为旧几社的那一派人这样做，最终目的是企图夺取复社的领导权。加上在对待阮大铖的问题上，几社那一派人又一向持有不同的见解。现在，会不会是他们从中捣鬼，想利用这件事来进一步打击吴应箕等人的威信？这种可能性确实不能排除。

“如果真是几社，”陈贞慧沉思地说，“那么，虎丘大会上一场剧斗，只怕就在所难免了。”

冒襄和吴应箕也意识到事态严重，他们各自皱着眉头，谁也没有作声。

“自然，这事还仅是猜测，未必便是如此。”陈贞慧继续说，慢慢地捋着长胡子。他抬起头望了望正在沉思默想的两位社友，忽然提高了声调，讥讽地说：“不过，小弟以为他们最好不要出此下策，以免弄巧反拙，自取其败！”

“啊，定生兄是说——”冒襄迟疑地问。

陈贞慧哼了一声：“想替阮胡子翻案，谈何容易！虎丘之上，他们不动则已，若敢动一动这个题目，我管教他这个所谓盟主，当场易人！”

吴应箕慢慢地点着头，坚决地说：“宁为玉碎，不为瓦全！万一不行，小弟也决不容彼辈如愿！”

他这样说了之后，三个朋友有好一会儿都没有再说话。最后，陈贞慧抬起头来，勉强一笑：“不过，小弟还是希望不致如此，

of the former Jishe were particularly unfriendly to the key members of the former Ying Society such as Sun Chun, Wu Zeng and Wu Yingji as well as the newly emerging young leaders such as Chen Zhenhui, Mao Xiang, and Hou Fangyu. It was because of their opposition and obstruction that Wu Yingji, like some others, was denied a fair chance to preside over the coming Tiger Hill Conference. As a result, the likes of Wu Yingji had to ask Zheng Yuanxun to represent them and share the chair with Li Wen, who was affiliated with the Jishe. They were very unhappy, believing that the Jishers had done so with the ultimate goal of seizing the leadership of the Fushe. Previously, in the handling of the Ruan Dacheng issue the Jishers had always had a different voice. This time, were they plotting to further damage the authority of the likes of Wu Yingji by use of this issue? This possibility couldn't be ruled out.

"If so," Chen Zhenhui said musingly. "Then a battle at the Tiger Hill Conference, I'm afraid, will be inevitable."

Realizing the weight of the matter, Mao Xiang and Wu Yingji frowned in silence.

"Of course, it's just a conjecture," Chen Zhenhui continued, slowly stroking his beard. As he lifted his head and looked at the two fellow Fushers, who were musing, he suddenly raised his voice and said sarcastically, "However, I think they'd better not make such a bad move, lest they be too smart and defeat themselves."

"So, Brother Dingsheng, are you saying—" Mao Xiang asked hesitantly.

Chen Zhenhui snorted, "It's not that easy to reverse Beardy Ruan's case. On the top of Tiger Hill, if they should move, if they should dare to make the proposal, I bet I would get the so-called chairmen replaced on the spot."

Wu Yingji slowly nodded his head and said firmly, "I'd rather break like jade than survive like a clay tile. Should such a thing happen, I wouldn't allow them to have their wish either."

After that, the three friends were silent for a while. Finally, Chen Zhenhui raised his head and said with a forced smile, "However, I'm still hoping that this won't happen and that the Fushe won't

以免社局伤残过甚。当然，也要做好准备，以防不测。所以，我们几个，还有子方他们，都一起到虎丘去，瞧瞧到底是怎么一回事。辟疆，你自然也是去的？”

“哦，小弟、小弟只怕去不成虎丘了。”冒襄忽然着忙起来，脸随即红了。

“怎么——”

“家父之事，今日刚得着信息。小弟打算明日赶回如皋，向家母禀告。”冒襄低着头说。于是，他把刚才拜访熊明遇的情形约略说了一遍。

“啊，原来令尊大人已获改调，可喜可贺！”陈贞慧拱着手微笑说。

吴应箕却没有作声。

“那么，”陈贞慧说，仍旧带着微笑，“既然令尊大人的事已见眉目，辟疆兄就更可放心去赴虎丘之会了。令堂大人处，就由贵价[①]回去报信，也是一样的。”

“定生兄有所不知，家母荏弱多病，为此事近半年来又忧伤殊甚，已数度卧床不起，至今汤药未断。且吾家除小弟之外，别无兄弟可奉菽水。弟此次出来，固是万不得已，其实心中日夜不安，如今得此消息，正恨不得身生双翼，飞归慈亲膝前。此外万事，都不是小弟所敢过问的。”

“孝者，人之天性。弟本来也不敢相强，只是眼前此事，关乎社事全局，而且迫在眉睫，弟才冒昧相劝。其实所耽搁者，不过一二十日，还望我兄三思！”

“这……小弟正恐耽搁，才决意不赴会的。”

在一旁瞧着两人对答的吴应箕，显然越来越不耐烦。他终于插进来说：

---

① 贵价：旧时对对方仆从、来使的敬语。

be crippled. Of course, we have to be prepared in case something happens. So, we and the likes of Zifang should all go to Tiger Hill together to see what's happening. Pijiang, I gather you're going there too as a matter of course?"

"Oh, no. I'm afraid I won't be able to go to Tiger Hill," Mao Xiang suddenly appeared uneasy, his face blushing.

"What is up?"

Mao Xiang lowered his head and said, "I've just got the news about my father today, and will have to rush back to Rugao tomorrow and report it to my mother." Then, he recounted his visit with Xiong Mingyu just now.

"Aah, congratulations on your father's transfer," Chen Zhenhui said with a smile.

Wu Yingji was silent.

"Then," Chen Zhenhui said, still smiling. "Since the matter of your respectable father has had a good result, my dear brother Pijiang should be able to go to the Tiger Hill Conference with peace of mind. Let your servant go back home to report it to your dear respectable mother. There's no difference."

"Brother Dingsheng, here's the thing: my mother is weak and sick and has been bedridden several times in the past six months because of worry and sadness. She's still on medication. I'm her only son to serve her meals. I came out this time as a last resort. In fact, I've been feeling uneasy day and night. Now that I've received the news, I wish I could fly back to in front of the knees of my kind mother. I dare not do anything else."

"Filial piety is human nature. I don't dare to contradict your will. Pray excuse me for venturing to say it, because the matter before us is related to the general good of the Fushe and is very pressing indeed. In fact, it requires no more than a delay of ten to twenty days. I hope you can reconsider it."

"But—but it's exactly because of the delay to be caused that I've decided not to go."

Wu Yingji, who was listening to the conversation between the

“辟疆，你别是有点怕吧？”

“啊，我怕？”

“嗯，我瞧你是害怕几社那帮子人，你还怕得罪阮胡子，怕得罪建虏、流寇！”吴应箕的话尖刻得像一把刀子。

冒襄的脸顿时涨得通红，随即冷笑着说：“次尾兄虽欲行激将之法，其奈小弟归家之志已决，非言语所能打动！”

“嘿嘿，又何须吴某来激将？辟疆兄近半年来之行事举止，外间早已啧有烦言。不过，也许辟疆兄充耳不闻罢了。”

“次尾兄！”陈贞慧显然看出势头不对，打算加以阻止。

“不，应当说！也免得辟疆兄他日怪我等知而不言，有失交友之道！有人说，沙场将士舍生忘死，浴血苦战，为大明力撑危局，身为‘复社四公子’的冒先生却为其尊大人调离讨贼前线竭力奔走，公然向朝廷上救父万言书！又说，复社诸子平日倡言忠君爱国，恪尽臣责，以士林表率自命，不知冒先生之所为，是否堪称表率？”吴应箕本来还想说下去，发现陈贞慧正拼命地朝他使眼色，才临时住了口。

冒襄像挨了一记闷棍似的呆住了。对于这一类的责难非议，他虽然已经多少估计到，但是，如今由吴应箕当面说出来，仍然使他受到猛烈冲击，感到羞愤难当。

陈贞慧连忙站起来，摇着手：“哎，没的事！别听次尾瞎说！”他转向吴应箕，继续使着眼色，“次尾，你哪儿听来这些混话？怎么我就没听到？——哎，算了，不谈这事！好端端的自家人，伤了和气，何苦来！”

two, was obviously getting more and more impatient. He finally cut in, "Pijiang, are you afraid of something?"

"Ah, I'm afraid?"

"Well, I see that you're afraid of the bunch of Jishers, afraid of offending Beardy Ruan, afraid of offending the Jianzhou barbarians and the insurgents." Wu Yingji's words cut him like a knife.

Mao Xiang's face flushed immediately, and then he sneered and said, "Although Brother Ciwei wants to prod me into action, my decision to go home has already been made and won't be changed by whatever you say."

"He-he, why should I prod you? Everyone is talking about what you've done in the past six months. Maybe you've simply turned a deaf ear to it."

"Brother Ciwei!" Chen Zhenhui clearly saw that the conversation had gone wrong and tried to stop it.

"No, let me finish lest Brother Pijiang one day should blame us for hiding it from him. They say that while the soldiers on the battlefield have forgotten their lives to save the Great Ming from the crisis, as one of the Four Young Men of the Fushe, Mr. Mao is trying to get his father off the frontline against the insurgents by even flagrantly writing a ten-thousand-word petition to the imperial court. It's also said that while the Fushe scholars are advocating love of country and loyalty to the emperor as everyone's duty, it's doubtful what Mr. Mao has done is a good example." Wu Yingji wanted to say more but finding that Chen Zhenhui was winking at him desperately, he stopped.

Mao Xiang was dumbfounded, as if he had received a sudden blow from a club. Having more or less anticipated this kind of criticism, Mao Xiang still felt a violent blow when challenged by Wu Yingji. He was ashamed of himself.

Chen Zhenhui quickly stood up and shook his hand, saying, "Well, that's not true. Don't listen to Ciwei's nonsense." He turned to Wu Yingji and continued to wink, saying, "Ciwei, where did you hear such crap? Why didn't I hear it? —Well, never mind! Let's not talk about it. We're friends."

# 第三章

# 顾眉娘妙曲钓金龟，阮大铖无聊排新剧

## 当街敲诈

当冒襄遭受乞丐的围困和奚落，好不容易逃进旧院的那个时刻，从大街的东头——利涉桥那边，大摇大摆地走下来四个衣冠楚楚的儒生。头里的一个，三十出头，身材高瘦，长方脸，浓眉毛，长鼻子，浑身透着精明强干的，是已故的著名东林党首领顾宪成的侄孙顾杲。同他并排走着的是一个英俊魁梧，神情骄傲的年轻人，名叫侯方域。他虽然才二十五岁，是“复社四公子”当中最年少的一个，但才华横溢，机敏狡黠，在伙伴们当中却是个出主意的角色。走在他们后面的，一个叫梅朗中，也生得身材高大，表情却开朗而活泼，平日着魔似的爱好着诗歌。另一个的年纪比其余的人都要大，名叫张自烈。他有一部乱蓬蓬的胡子和一张执拗冷峻的脸。

这四个人都是复社成员，冒襄的好友。今天晚上李十娘家的聚会，就是他们发起的。现在，他们一边走，一边谈论着一件什么事情。

“朝宗兄！”梅朗中从后面叫着侯方域的字，“你难道就当真不想想办法？”

## Chapter Three

# In Which Gu Mei Hooked "a Golden Turtle" with a Wonderful Song and Ruan Dacheng Produced a New Play to Pass the Time

## The Gentlemen Robbers

The moment Mao Xiang escaped into the Old Yard after being besieged and ridiculed by the beggars, four well-dressed scholars descended from the east end of the street where the Lishe Bridge was. The one in front was a thirty-something, tall and thin, with a rectangular face, thick eyebrows, and a long nose, radiating with shrewdness and intelligence. It was Gu Gao, grandnephew of the late famous East Wood Party leader Gu Xiancheng. Walking alongside him was a handsome, burly, proud young man named Hou Fangyu, twenty-five, the youngest among the Four Young Men of the Fushe, yet the most talented and the most resourceful—in fact, he was the mastermind of things. Walking behind them, one was named Mei Langzhong, also tall and burly but with a cheerful and lively expression—he loved poetry with a passion—and another was named Zhang Zilie, who, older than the others, had a matted beard and a flat, cold face.

All four of them were members of the Fushe and friends of Mao Xiang. They were the organizers of the event at Li Shiniang's place tonight. As they walked, they were busy talking about something.

"Brother Chaozong," Mei Langzhong called Hou Fangyu's courtesy name from behind, "Don't you really want to think of a solution?"

“哼，我能想什么办法！”侯方域冷冷地说，并不回头，“岂不闻‘天皇圣明，臣罪当……’”他没有说下去。

“可这分明是冤枉的呀！”梅朗中显得很着急，他跨上一步，同侯方域并排着走，“令尊大人忠贞为国，声闻宇内，怎么会跟左良玉交关欺上？”

“啊？”侯方域偏过脸来，“朗三兄说是冤枉吗？这话小弟可不敢说哩！”他嘿嘿地冷笑起来。

“可是令尊大人身陷囹圄已经五载，朝宗兄总得设法营救才是，就像辟疆兄……”

梅朗中大约想举出冒襄为父亲奔走的事来规劝对方，可是马上就被侯方域打断了：

“辟疆？人家是个大孝子，我怎能比他！他为着父亲不去打仗，可以不顾一切。这点小弟自觉惭愧，还做不来。何况——”他顿了顿，语调变得有点酸溜溜，“家父虽说也是二三十年的老官场，可要我从家里拿出几万两银子替他奔走打点嘛，见笑得很，当真也拿不出！”

“这……万一令尊大人在狱中遭逢不测，朝宗兄又岂能自安？”梅朗中有点气急。他显然弄不懂对于父亲的性命安危，做儿子的怎能这样行若无事，置之不理？

侯方域的父亲，就是最初识拔左良玉的那个东林党人侯恂，他本是明朝的兵部侍郎，五年前，被内阁首辅温体仁排斥构陷，逮捕下狱，判成死罪。虽然不久温体仁就垮了台，但这件案子却一直搁着，既不平反也不执行。直到目前，侯恂还在北京坐牢。

"Huh, what can I think of?" Hou Fangyu said coldly, without looking back. "Haven't you read the lines from Han Yu's poem, 'because of the good judgement of the emperor, all law-breaking subjects should be—'" He said.

"But he's evidently wronged!" Mei Langzhong seemed very concerned. He took a step forward and walked side by side with Hou Fangyu. "It's well known that your respectable father is loyal to the country, how can he possibly conspire with Zuo Liangyu to delude the emperor?" he said.

"What?" Hou Fangyu turned his face to Mei Langzhong and said with a sneer, "Dear Brother Langsan, did you say he was wronged? I dare not say that."

"But it has been five years since your respectable father was put into prison. Brother Chaozong, you should try to rescue him, just like Brother Pijiang ..."

Mei Langzhong presumably wanted to cite what Mao Xiang did for his father as an example, but he was immediately interrupted by Hou Fangyu, who said:

"Pijiang? He's a filial son. How can I compare to him? He went out of his way to prevent his father from fighting in the war. I'm ashamed of myself for not being able to do that. What's more—" He paused, and his tone became a bit sour. "Although my father has been an official for twenty to thirty years, if you ask me to take out thousands of taels of silver from my home to fix it, unfortunately, I don't have it."

"But, Brother Chaozong, if something happens to your respectable father in prison, how can you be at ease?" Mei Langzhong said. He was a little angry, obviously puzzled how a son could be so indifferent to his own father's life.

Hou Fangyu's father was Hou Xun, the first of the East Wood Party members to recognize the talent in Zuo Liangyu. He was originally Right Vice Minister of the Ministry of War. Five years ago, framed by Prime Minister Wen Tiren, he had been arrested and sentenced to death. When Wen Tiren soon fell from grace, the case had been put on hold, but there was neither rehabilitation nor execution.

对此，很有几个朋友替侯方域着急，但他本人却反而好像不当一回事，仍旧一天到晚东游西荡，过他公子哥儿的风流快活日子。刚才，梅朗中又一次提起这件事，但侯方域的态度还是老样子，梅朗中不禁生气起来。

这时候，同他们并排着走，一直没有说话的顾杲开口了。

“朗三！”他把长鼻子转过来，微微一笑，“你又何必发急？依我看，朝宗是有道理的，这件事急不来，只有耐着性子等。况且，朝廷目前必不会有不利于朝宗尊大人之举，他虽身陷囹圄，其实安如泰山！”

“啊，何以见得？”

顾杲撇撇嘴：“方今流寇横行，天下糜烂，朝廷所赖者，唯将帅耳。近十年来，老成可用之将，凋零几尽；唯左良玉一镇，强兵劲卒，岿然独存。彼虽骄悍难制，朝廷又安能舍之而不用？至于左镇对朝宗尊大人怀恩感激，逾于寻常，朝廷更早有所闻。所以起码，为羁縻左镇计，朝廷亦必不会有不测之举。而且——”他看了看侯方域，提高了嗓音，“小弟审时度势，朝宗尊大人之复出，已是必然之理，不出数月，当有好音！”

在这段时间里，侯方域一直不动声色地听着，直到顾杲说完了，他才仰起脸，微微眯缝着眼睛，神情显得十分得意。

“哦……”梅朗中如梦初醒。他眨眨眼睛，还打算问一句什么，跟在他们身后的张自烈忽然扯了扯他的衣袖：“你们瞧，那边在做什么？”

大家停止了交谈，一齐抬头望去，只见离文德桥还有一箭之遥的市肆当中，停着两乘轿子，旁边围了一小堆人，一个愤怒的

Hou Xun had been in a Beijing prison up till now. Quite a few friends were concerned, but Hou Fangyu himself seemed nonchalant and still wandered around all day long, living the happy life of a dandy. As his attitude remained the same when this matter was mentioned again, Mei Langzhong couldn't help getting angry.

At this moment, Gu Gao, who was walking side by side with them, spoke up.

He turned his long nose around. "Langsan," he said with a smile. "Why are you angry? In my opinion, Chaozong is right. There's no use making haste. It takes patience. Besides, at the moment, the imperial court will definitely not do anything unfavorable to Chaozong's father. Although he's behind bars, he's in fact as safe as Mount Tai."

"Aah, how is it so?"

Gu Gao curled his lips and said, "Right now the insurgents are everywhere, corruption is rampant, and the imperial court can only rely on the capable military commanders. Over the past ten years, most of the experienced and capable commanders have dwindled away; only Zuo Liangyu's garrison remains and stands intact, with strong and well-trained troops. Although Zuo Liangyu is arrogant and unruly, the imperial court has no option but to rely heavily on him, having lost most veteran commanders in the past ten years. Well aware that General Zuo is greatly indebted to Chaozhong's father, the court won't do anything to the old man's disadvantage. And—" he looked at Hou Fangyu and said in a louder voice. "Judging from the situation, the rehabilitation of Chaozong's father is a matter of course. Within a few months, there should be good news."

During all this time, Hou Fangyu listened quietly. When Gu Gao finished speaking, he raised his face, and, squinting his eyes, looked very proud of himself.

"Oh ..." said Mei Langzhong, as if awakened from a dream. He blinked his eyes and was about to ask something, when Zhang Zilie, who was behind them, suddenly pulled his sleeves and said, "Look, what are they doing over there?"

They stopped the conversation and looked over; in the marketplace

声音在叫：

“你得赔我，赔我！听见没有？”

“赔？叫你让道你不让，这怨谁？”一个冷冷的声音反驳说。

接着，几个人七嘴八舌地附和起来：

“谁叫你挡道？”“是呀！”“不摔你个跟头，够客气了！”“赔？别想——”

“放屁！本相公为何得给你们让道？本相公走本相公的，你们走你们的，你们为何往本相公身上撞？你们为何不给本相公让道？”先前那个人怒气冲冲地说。听口气是一位儒生。

顾杲等四人怀疑地交换了一下眼色。

“是太冲！”顾杲果断地说。他立即加快脚步，赶上前去。其余几个一窝蜂似的跟在后头。

轿旁那几个仆役模样的汉子已经哇哇地乱叫起来：

“啊，瞧他说的！”

“茄子大个星宿，要我们给他让道？”

“笑话，没听说过！”

“咦，咦！可别小看这位相公，兴许人家还真不简单——没听说‘猪圈里的黄牛’嘛！”

这时，周围已经聚拢了好些看客，听了这句促狭的调侃话，都哄笑起来。

那个儒生却不理会哄笑。他很着急地弯下腰，在一小堆东西里翻来拣去。

“哎，完啦，全完啦！”他用带哭的声音叫起来，“你们赔我书，赔我书，听见没有？”他跺着脚大嚷。原来那堆东西是书，不知为什么给乱扔在地上。

但那伙人看来是财势之家的仆役，趾高气扬惯了，又仗着人多势众，他们不再理会儒生。一个头戴瓦楞帽，身穿闪亮绸子衣服的瘦高汉子，像是个管事头儿，他挥了挥手，四个轿夫分别抬

only a stone's throw away from Wende Bridge stopped two sedan chairs, surrounded by a small gathering of people. An angry voice yelled:

"Recompense me! Recompense me! Did you hear me?"

"Recompense you? Why should you stand in the way after hearing the warning? Whose fault is it?" a cold voice retorted.

Then, other men joined in and said:

"Why did you get in the way?" "That's right!" "You should thank me for not running you down heels over head." "Recompense you? Don't even think about it."

"Bullshit! Why should I make way for you? I went my way and you went yours. Why did you bump into me? Why didn't you give way to me?" said the first man angrily. Judged from his voice, he was a young scholar.

The four friends exchanged looks with an inkling of who it was.

"It's Taichong," Gu Gao said decisively. Quickening his pace, he rushed forward. The others followed.

"Listen to what he says!" screamed the men by the sedan chair, who looked like someone's servants.

"A dignitary like an eggplant is asking us to make way for him?"

"What a joke! I've never heard of a thing like this."

"Huh, huh! Don't underestimate this mate. Maybe he's not that simple. Haven't you heard of 'a yellow cow in the pigpen'?"

By this time, quite a few spectators had gathered around them and guffawed when they heard this nasty ridicule.

The young scholar ignored the guffaw. He worriedly bent down to dig through a small pile of things.

"Ay me, finished, they're all finished!" he shouted in a crying voice, stomping his feet. "You must recompense me. Recompense me! Have you heard me?" The pile of things were his books. Somehow, they had been thrown to the ground.

But that gang of men, emboldened by their numbers, simply ignored him. They seemed to be servants of some big family used to being swollen with arrogance. A thin, tall man with a *waleng* hat and shiny silk clothes, who might be a steward, waved his hand, and

起两乘轿子，打算继续走路。那个儒生急了，只见他猛地跳起来，一下子蹿到轿子跟前，大声吼叫：

“站住！”

现在，借着夜市的灯光，顾杲他们已经看清楚，这位儒生果然不是别人，正是他们的社友黄宗羲。今晚的聚会，也有黄宗羲一份。

“嗯，是他！”顾杲迅速地回顾说。他顿时兴奋起来，领着大家兴冲冲地往前挤。

“堂堂留都之地，岂容尔等横行！不赔书，你休想走，有本事，从本相公身上踏过去！”黄宗羲又大叫起来。由于狂怒，他的眉毛现在倒竖着，瘦小的、讨人喜欢的脸扭歪了，常常微笑的嘴角现出两道凶狠的皱纹，一向温文沉静的眼睛里，放射出吓人的光芒，看样子，他当真打算拼命了。

已经起动的轿子，被迫重新停下来。那群仆役你看看我，我看看你，似乎给这个不顾死活的书呆子弄糊涂了，不知道该怎么办才好。

“哎，怎么回事啊？”坐在前头一乘轿子里的那个人，终于生气地发问了。接着窗帘子掀起，露出来一个中年贵公子的脸。

这是一张又大又白的脸。五官端正，甚至可以说清秀，只是每一样都过于小巧玲珑，同整张脸有点不大相配。下巴上挂着疏疏的几根黄胡子。

侯方域一瞧见这张脸，不由得微笑起来。他认识这个人，名叫徐青君，是本朝开国元勋魏国公徐达的后裔。徐达死后追封中山王，他的子孙后代都居住在南京聚宝门内大功坊侧的王府里，如今轮到徐青君的哥哥徐弘基袭封魏国公，兼任南京守备。徐青君闲着无事，仗着家里有财有势，一天到晚花天酒地，走马斗鸡，

the four chairmen lifted the two sedan chairs to move on. The young scholar was worried. He jumped to the sedan chair, and yelled, "Stop!"

Now, by the lights of the night market, Gu Gao and company could see clearly that this young scholar was none other than their fellow Fusher Huang Zongxi, who was here for tonight's gathering.

"Yes, it *is* him," Gu Gao quickly looked back and said. He suddenly became excited and edged forward, followed by his company.

"This is the Legacy Capital, not a place for lawless men like you. If you don't make the books good, walk over my body!" Huang Zongxi shouted again. Because of his fury, his eyebrows were now inverted, his small, likable face became twisted, two ferocious wrinkles appeared at the corners of his mouth that had often worn a smile, and a scary light radiated from his usually gentle and calm eyes. It looked that he really intended to fight them with his life.

The sedan chairs that were moving were forced to stop again. The pack of servants looked at each other, apparently confused by this desperate nerd.

"Hey, what's the matter?" The man sitting in the front sedan chair finally spoke angrily. Then the curtain was lifted to reveal the face of a middle-aged nobleman.

It was a big, white face with regular features, or you could even say with delicate features, except that everything was too dainty and didn't quite match the face. A few sparse yellowish whiskers hung from his chin.

When Hou Fangyu saw this face, he couldn't help feeling amused. He knew the man, who was named Xu Qingjun, a descendant of Xu Da, Duke of Wei, a founding father of the dynasty. Xu Da was posthumously bestowed with the title Prince of Zhongshan. His descendants lived in a palace on the side of the Arch of Honor inside the Treasure Gate in Nanjing. Currently, Xu Qingjun's brother Xu Hongji had inherited the title of the Duke of Wei and was meanwhile serving as Nanjing defense chief. Born into a family of wealth and prestige, Xu Qingjun was an idler doing nothing but drinking, whoring, horse-racing and cockfighting, squandering money like

享乐挥霍。他家本来已经有一所很大的东花园，坐落在教坊旁边。他还嫌不够排场，在中山府附近又建了一座更加富丽堂皇的西园，在里面广蓄姬妾，过着穷奢极欲的生活。用侯方域的话来说，此人的银子多得简直令人“恼火”。所以，现在发现同黄宗羲吵架的主儿竟然是这位大阔佬，侯方域心里就立即打起主意来。他回头看了一眼顾杲，发现顾杲目光闪动，也在瞅着自己。于是，他闭了一下眼睛，点点头。等顾杲也照样做了一遍之后，他们就彼此会心地微笑起来。

这当儿，那管事头儿已经走到轿子旁边，对徐青君躬身行礼说：“启禀二爷，这人实在太不讲理！刚才他在前头走，小的们在后面几乎喊破喉咙，他硬是不让道。是小的怕碰翻了他，惊着二爷，好心伸手扯了他一把。谁想他反倒诬赖小人把他的什么书弄损了，缠着非赔他不可，故此吵闹起来。”

徐青君扫了一眼黄宗羲，和地上那一摊显然是从臭水沟里捞上来的书，不耐烦地说：“什么了不得的事！几本破书，值得多少银子？打发了不就完了，跟他歪缠什么！”

“是！”管事头儿答应着，搔搔脑袋，走回来说，“好吧，我们二爷……”

可是黄宗羲立即愤怒地打断了他的话：“谁要你的银子！我要的是书，书！你听懂了没有？”

“哦，书……那，那是什么样的书？”

“什么样的书！”黄宗羲悻悻地模仿着对方的口吻。由于刚才徐青君把他的宝贝轻蔑地称之为“几本破书”，黄宗羲显然很不服气。他走回来，指着地上的书，生气地、故意让徐青君听见似的大声说：“你听着！就是这套宋版的《潜虚衍义》！宋版！

dust. He had a very spacious residence called East Garden, which was next to the Jiaofang, the Academy of Performance Arts, but thinking it was not big enough, he had built the glamorous West Garden near the Zhongshan Palace, in which he kept a number of concubines and lived a life of extravagance and dissipation. In Hou Fangyu's words, the amount of silver this man had was shocking. Therefore, seeing that the man engaged in a conflict with Huang Zongxi was this super-rich man, Hou Fangyu immediately had an idea. He looked back at Gu Gao and found that Gu Gao was looking at him, eyes flickering. Then, he closed his eyes and nodded his head. After Gu Gao did the same, they smiled knowingly.

At this moment, the steward walked to the sedan chair, bowed to Xu Qingjun and said, "Second Master, this man is too unreasonable. Just now, he was walking in front of us. We shouted at the top of our voices and he refused to give way to us. Afraid of alarming you in case we should run him over, we pulled him aside out of kindness, but who thought he would instead blame us for damaging his books and ask us to recompense him? That's why we quarreled."

Xu Qingjun glanced at Huang Zongxi and the pile of books on the ground that were apparently rescued from a stinking ditch. He said impatiently, "It's not a big deal. How much silver are a few broken books worth? Give it to him and don't get entangled with him."

"Aye, sir!" the steward said submissively. Scratching his head, he walked back and said, "Well, our Second Master ..."

However, Huang Zongxi interrupted him angrily, "Who wants your silver? Give me back the books! Did you hear?"

"Oh, books ... what, what kind of books are they?"

"What kind of books?" Huang Zongxi imitated the opponent's tone bitterly. Since Xu Qingjun contemptuously called his treasure "several broken books", Huang Zongxi was obviously displeased. He walked back, pointed to the books on the ground, said angrily and loudly as if to deliberately let Xu Qingjun hear, "Listen! This is a complete set of the Song dynasty edition of *Qian Xu Yan Yi* (*Studies in the Explorations into the Ubiquitous Void*). The Song dynasty edition!

你懂不懂？我足足在书坊里候了三年，好容易今天买到手，就被你这狗才弄到臭水沟里。你得赔我，赔我！”由于实在心疼，说到后来，他连声音也变了。

管事头儿似懂非懂地眨着眼睛，无可奈何地走回轿子旁边，启禀说：“二爷，他说……”

“混账！不管他，走！”轿子里蓦地大嚷起来。显然，徐青君的公子爷脾气也发作了。

几个仆役巴不得有这句话，连忙指挥轿夫抬起轿子。

站在场外的侯方域一瞧机不可失，他立即捅了顾杲一下，等顾杲猛地蹿出去后，他也跟着跳了出去。梅朗中和张自烈见状，迟疑了一下，也随后走了出来。

正处在危急绝望境地的黄宗羲，突然看见来了救兵，喜出望外，他连招呼都忘了打，连连点着头，用紧张、发抖的声音说：

“你们来得好……他们欺、欺负人！”

“啊？谁如斯大胆，欺负到我复社头上来啦？”顾杲首先大声喝叫。他心思机敏，看见徐府那几个恶仆正在作势猛冲过来，如果不立即把他们吓止住，局面将会无法控制。所以一开口，他就首先把“复社”的名头亮了出来。

别看复社只是以文会友、切磋学问的一个文社，它的成员也多是一些没有功名的读书人，可是它人数众多，背后又有着一班主张开明政治的官僚撑腰；加上近十年来，通过科举考试进入仕途，跻身于各级大小衙门的复社成员，正越来越多，在朝廷和地方已经暗暗形成了一股不可忽视的势力。这批人大胆议论朝政，褒贬人物，强调君子、小人之别，对社会舆论有着很大的左右力量。而一般的官宦人家，则认为它的子弟只要加入了复社，就等

Do you understand? After searching in the bookstores for three full years, I finally got it today, but this dog of yours got it into the stinking ditch. You give it back to me! Give it back to me!" His voice was distorted with pain.

The head servant blinked his eyes in semi-understanding, helplessly walked back to the sedan chair, and said, "Second Master, he said ..."

"Idiot! Leave him alone, let's go!" came a sudden shout from the sedan chair. Obviously, Xu Qingjun's aristocratic temper was aroused.

The servants, who were waiting for their master's command, hurriedly ordered the chairmen to lift the sedan chair.

Hou Fangyu, who was standing nearby, saw the opportunity and immediately poked Gu Gao, and after Gu Gao suddenly leapt forward, he also jumped forward. When Mei Langzhong and Zhang Zilie saw this, they hesitated for an instant and then stepped forward.

Huang Zongxi, who was lonely and desperate, was overjoyed to see the rescue team. Without greeting them, he nodded his head and said in a nervous and trembling voice:

"You chaps have arrived in time ... they, they're bullies!"

"What? Who's so bold as to bully a Fusher?" Gu Gao said loudly. He had a quick mind. Seeing the devilish servants of the Xus rushing forward, he knew the situation would be out of control if he didn't stop them by frightening them with the name of the Fushe.

Though the Fushe was only a literary society in which members met to discuss academic matters and the members were mostly scholars with no official rank, their numbers were large and they were backed by a group of bureaucrats who advocated benign politics. Over the past ten years an increasing number of Fushers had passed the imperial examinations and entered all levels of government to become an unignorable force at court and in the provinces. Besides, by boldly discussing public affairs and openly judging important personages, the Fushers were very influential in shaping public opinion. Families of ordinary officials, thinking obtaining membership of the Fushe for their children was equivalent to getting a guarantee for an official

于拿到了入仕做官的保票，不惜竭力扶持、巴结。所以在江南地区，特别是南京城里，提起复社，几乎是无人不知；各级官府衙门，对复社也优礼有加，轻易不敢得罪。如今顾杲一上场就先亮出招牌，凭借的正是这样一种背景。

这一手也当真奏效，那个管事头儿愕然地站住了，其余几个奴仆见状，迟迟疑疑地都停了下来。

“哦，原来是复社的相公，小人失敬了！”管事头儿呆呆地打量他们一阵，终于不自然地咳嗽一声，堆起了笑容，“不知几位相公有何吩咐？”他拱着手问。

“谁是你们的主人？请他出来！”顾杲又大喝一声。看见对方已被吓住，他暗暗放了心。他不想同这些人多费唇舌。很明白，要实现他同侯方域那个心照不宣的打算，必须直接同徐青君本人交涉才行。

“哦，是，是，呃……不过，相公们如有吩咐，对小人说——嗯，也是一样的。”管事头儿的态度更加恭谨。不过，瞧得出来，他是捉摸对方来意不善，怕出意外，打算挡驾。

顾杲勃然大怒，“胡说！”他厉声呵斥说，“少啰唆，去！”

“嘻嘻，谅你这小老儿有多少斤两，能代替你们徐二爷？”侯方域在旁边嘻嘻哈哈地帮腔，“快，去吧，就说复社的顾杲、黄宗羲、张自烈、梅朗中，还有区区——侯方域在此，恭请徐二公子出来，有话要说！”

侯方域这几句话轻轻巧巧一说出口，周围看热闹的人登时骚动起来。这几个名字都是复社当中响当当的角色——崇祯十一年，复社诸生发表《留都防乱公揭》，声讨阮大铖，署名的共有一百四十人。头一名就是顾杲，第二名是黄宗羲。张自烈、梅朗

path, never hesitated to support and flatter the Fushers. Therefore, in the River South area, especially in Nanjing, there was virtually no one who didn't know the Fushe, and the *yamen* at all levels regarded the Fushe with favor and never dared to offend its members. It was against such a background that Gu Gao spoke of the Fushe first as his calling card.

That strategy really worked. The steward was overwhelmed, and the other servants stopped in bewilderment.

"Oh, gentlemen from the Fushe! I beg your pardon, sirs!" said the steward, who looked at them blankly for a while, and finally coughed an unnatural cough and smiled. "What can I do for you, sirs?" he said, putting his hands together.

"Who's your master? Please ask him to come out," Gu Gao yelled again. Seeing that the servants had been frightened, he was secretly relieved. He didn't want to bother with such men, aware that he should confront Xu Qingjun directly to execute the plan he and Hou Fangyu had tacitly agreed on.

"Aye sir, aye, uh ... but, if you sirs have anything to say, pray tell me. It's the same," the steward said. His attitude was more respectful, but gathering the intention of the other party was not going to be good, he tried to stop them.

Gu Gao became angry. "That's bullshit!" he said sternly. "No shitting. Go!"

"Hee-hee, who do you think you are to act on behalf of your second master Mr. Xu the Younger?" said Hou Fangyu with a chuckle. "Hurry, go! Just say Fushe members Gu Gao, Huang Zongxi, Zhang Zilie, Mei Langzhong, and me Hou Fangyu are here and would like to have a word with Mr. Xu the Younger."

Hou Fangyu spoke calmly, but the spectators around immediately became rowdy. These names were the big ones in the Fushe. Of the one hundred and forty signers of the "Public Denunciation of a Treasonist in the Legacy Capital" pamphlet in AD 1638, the eleventh year of the reign of Emperor Chongzhen, Gu Gao was the first and Huang Zongxi the second, followed by Zhang Zilie and Mei

中也在其内，这件事当时轰动了南京城，不少人记忆犹新。现在，听说眼前这几位儒生，就是当日那些风云人物，都不由得指指点点，低声议论起来。

那个管事头儿似乎也明白对方来头不小，不敢再怠慢拖延。他慌慌张张地走回轿子跟前，照实向徐青君禀告了一遍。然后，他就退开一步，低头垂手，恭候主人出来。

如今，围观的人越来越多。大家知道今晚准有好戏可瞧，都怀着极大兴趣，目不转睛地一齐盯着徐青君的那乘轿子，屏气静息地候着这位花花太岁出场。

谁知大家伸长脖子等了好一会儿，那乘轿子的帘儿仍旧静静地垂着，纹丝不动。别说看不见徐青君的身影出现，甚至连他的声息都听不到。

那管事头儿感到莫名其妙。他望了望绷着脸的顾杲，只好硬着头皮又上前低声禀告一遍。

“不，我不出去！我不要见他们！”轿子里冷不丁尖声大叫起来。

人们吓了一跳，怔住了。当听明白那是徐青君恐惧气急的声音时，便迸发出一阵哄笑。

顾杲同侯方域交换了一下眼色。等周围的目光开始集中到他们身上的时候，他就从长鼻子里冷笑一声，双手交叉在胸前，抬头望着天空，不紧不慢地说：“好吧，徐二公子既然不肯赏脸，我们就恭候到底。反正，今儿这事不分辨个水落石出，徐二公子休想离开此地。”

“要是他徐二爷敢派人回去搬兵，我们复社同人，也自有办法对付——子方兄，你说是吗？”侯方域笑眯眯地对顾杲说。其实，他是担心对方会来这一手，因此预先提出警告，使之不敢妄动。

“哎，要是徐二公子逃回家去，关上大门不出来，那可怎么

Langzhong. Many people still remembered how that incident caused a sensation in Nanjing at that time. Now, hearing the young scholars in front were some of the most influential figures of the day, the spectators watched with great interest and whispered to each other.

Seeing the young scholars in front of him were not to be trifled with, the steward walked back to the sedan chair frightfully and reported to Xu Qingjun. Then, he took a step back, bowed his head, lowered his hands, and waited for his master to come out.

Now, more and more spectators gathered. Everyone knew that there would be a good show tonight, so with great interest, they stared at Xu Qingjun's sedan chair, silently waiting for the great playboy to go on stage.

To their disappointment, the curtain of the sedan chair was still draping quietly with no disturbance while everyone craned their necks and waited. Xu Qingjun didn't appear, nor was there a sound from him.

The steward was nonplussed. He looked at Gu Gao, who was sullen, and then stepped forward and whispered to his master again.

"No, I won't go out! I don't want to see them!" suddenly came a screaming voice from inside the sedan chair.

People were frightened. When they realized that it was Xu Qingjun's fearful and angry voice, they burst into laughter.

Gu Gao exchanged glances with Hou Fangyu. When the surrounding eyes began to focus on them, he let out a cold sneer from his long nose and said unhurriedly, gazing at the sky with his hands on his chest, "Well, since Mr. Xu the Younger refuses to show his face, we'll wait until he does. In any event, if this matter isn't resolved today, Mr. Xu the Younger will never be able to leave this place."

"Even if Mr. Xu the Younger dares to send for help, as Fushers we're not afraid. Brother Zifang, don't you think so?" Hou Fangyu said to Gu Gao smilingly. In fact, exactly because that was something the other party would most likely do, he warned them in advance so that they would not do it.

"But, what if Mr. Xu the Younger runs back home and closes the

办哪？”事先得到侯方域示意的梅朗中，装出一副天真无邪的样子问。

张自烈老气横秋地沉着嗓子：“哼，除非他一辈子不出门，否则，我们总有法子找到他。”

听着社友们一唱一和，夹在他们当中的黄宗羲仿佛忘记了他的那套宝贝书《潜虚衍义》。他睁大眼睛看看这个，瞅瞅那个，露出又惊奇又好玩的神情。

“胡说！叫他们走！我不见他们，我为什么要见他们？”轿子里的徐青君，忽然又大发脾气地叫起来——这是管事头儿见这样泡下去不是了局，又一次劝说主人出来。他却不知道，徐青君深知这班士子厉害，怕得要死，哪里敢出面相见？

然而，这样一来，复社方面的几个人也没有了主意。大家不约而同地把目光集中到侯方域身上。

侯方域依旧纹丝不动地站着，嘴边挂着微笑，显得满有把握。大家见他这样子，只好重新回过头去，继续僵持着。

时间一点一点地过去，周围的看客开始感到不耐烦。有人大声地打呵欠，有些开始走散。终于，侯方域似乎也有点沉不住气了。他向前跨出一步，清清嗓子，正要说话。

就在这时，从事情发生以来，一直没有任何动静的另一乘轿子里，忽然走出来一个人。他大约六十岁不到，中等身材，头戴方巾，有一张质朴的脸，头发胡子都斑白了。他匆匆走向前一乘轿子，隔着帘子同里面的徐青君低声交谈了片刻，然后快步走上前来。

“诸位先生，”他拱着手说，“在下计成有礼了！”说着，深深作下揖去。

顾杲等人本来已经灰心失望，不知如何收场，忽然出现了转机，不禁喜出望外，于是纷纷谦让起来，各自还了礼。

door behind him never to come out?" Mei Langzhong, who had been signaled by Hou Fangyu in advance, asked with a childlike look.

Zhang Zilie said in a fusty voice, "Humph, unless he doesn't come out for the rest of his life, we can always find him."

Hearing the theatrical conversation between his Fushe comrades, Huang Zongxi, opened his eyes wide and regarded them with an expression of amusement and perplexity, leaving his precious set of *Studies in the Explorations into the Ubiquitous Void* in the back of his mind.

"Nonsense! Tell them to leave. I won't see them. Why should I?" yelled Xu Qingjun in the sedan chair with a new burst of anger. Seeing there was no end to this statemate, the steward once again tried to persuade Xu Qingjun to come out, not knowing his master was actually scared of the young scholars and didn't dare to come out.

Now it was the turn of the Fushers to be nonplussed. They unanimously cast their eyes on Hou Fangyu, who didn't move a muscle and appeared confident, with a smile on the corners of his mouth. Seeing him like that, everyone withdrew their gaze and continued to stand in a stalemate.

As time passed, the spectators began to feel impatient. Some yawned loudly and some started to leave the spot. Finally, Hou Fangyu couldn't hold it any longer. He took a step forward, cleared his throat, and was about to speak.

Suddenly, out of the other sedan chair that had been silent all along since the bickering started came a gentleman of medium build with a square headscarf, who, less than sixty years old, had a plain face, a gray beard, and gray hair. He hurriedly walked to the sedan chair in his front, talked in a low voice with Xu Qingjun through the curtain, and then quickly walked forward.

"Gentlemen," he said, putting his hands together, "My greetings! I'm Ji Cheng." As he spoke, he made a deep bow.

Gu Gao and his friends, frustrated and at a loss as to how to end it all, brightened up at the sudden turn of events. They returned the greeting and the bow cordially.

“方才诸位先生要见青君兄，只因青君兄身体欠安，无法下轿相见，不胜愧歉，尚祈诸位先生见谅。”计成说着，又作了一揖。

这一次，顾杲等人交换了一下眼色，都没有作声。

计成接着又说：“青君兄的家仆冒犯了黄先生，还损坏了黄先生的宝籍，青君兄心中十分不安，特请小弟代向黄先生谢罪！”说完了，他朝黄宗羲又是一揖。

顾杲见他左一揖右一揖，没完没了，心里又不耐烦起来。没等黄宗羲作出表示，他就冷笑一声，说：“嘿，难道徐公子打算这样就完了么？”

“哦，不，不！”计成急急忙忙地笑着，“青君兄情愿赔偿黄先生的宝籍。只是宝籍已然破损，原物奉还，急切恐难做到。青君兄意欲加倍偿还所值，请黄先生赐示数目，青君兄无不乐从。”

顾、侯二人捣了大半天的鬼，目的正是要等着这句话。至于这句话是由徐青君本人说出来还是由他的代表说出来，他们倒不在乎。何况，计成事先曾同徐青君商量过，这句话无疑也是姓徐的意思。因此顾杲一听，脸色便缓和下来。可是侯方域却皱起眉毛，现出为难的神色。他回过头，用犹豫的口气问：“太冲，你可都听见了？按说呢，此书实在得来不易，我见犹痛！此议碍难应允。不过，看来事出无意，对方如今确有为难之处，这位计先生又一片好意……唉，你就瞧着办吧！”说着，暗中扯了扯顾杲的衣袖。

顾杲正听得发呆。他猛地回过神来，急急忙忙地说：

“正是正是，我看也只好如此。只是——太冲，可不能太轻饶他！”

Ji Cheng said, "You gentlemen just now wanted to see Brother Qingjun, but since he isn't well, he can't get out of the sedan chair to see you. Please accept my apologies." As he spoke, he made another bow.

Gu Gao and his friends exchanged glances with each other silently.

Ji Cheng bowed to Huang Zongxi and said, "Brother Qingjun is very sorry for the rudeness of the servants and the damage to your books. He asks me to apologize to you on his behalf."

Seeing him making endless bows, Gu Gao grew impatient. Before Huang Zongxi spoke, Gu Gao sneered and said, "Hey, is Mr. Xu going to finish like this?"

"Oh, no, no!" Ji Cheng hurriedly said with a smile. "Brother Qingjun is willing to take responsibility for the damage to Mr. Huang's treasured books. Problem is, the books have been damaged, and it's impossible to recover the damage. Brother Qingjun would like to pay you twice the price of the books. So Mr. Huang, please say the amount and Brother Qingjun will be happy to pay it."

That was what Mr. Gu and Mr. Hou were waiting for after all the bother. They didn't exactly care whether it was from Xu Qingjun himself or his representative. Besides, since Ji Cheng had spoken with Xu Qingjun beforehand and this offer undoubtedly was also the intention of Mr. Xu. Gu Gao's expression eased as soon as he heard it. However, Hou Fangyu frowned and showed a look of befuddlement. He turned around and said, "Taichong, did you hear it? This set of books is so hard to come by that it hurts to see it like this now. Honestly speaking, this offer shouldn't be accepted but since it's an accident and it's really impossible for them to give you back the original books and Mr. Ji is really kind to ... Well, it's your decision now." As he spoke, he pulled Gu Gao's sleeve secretly.

Gu Gao, who was listening attentively, was jolted back to reality and said hurriedly:

"Exactly. I think there's no other choice. It's just that Taichong shouldn't spare him too readily."

梅朗中本是个性情随和的人，他见顾、侯二人都转了口风，也就随口帮腔说：“太冲，事到如今，只有自认晦气，图个善休，不吃亏，也就算了。”

张自烈却没有作声。他显然已经心里有数，正大睁着一双固执的眼睛，在等着看下文。

听见社友们都在纷纷劝说自己，黄宗羲那张瘦小清秀的脸蓦地红了。他低下头去，皱着眉毛想了半天，终于，无可奈何地点了点头。

侯方域一见黄宗羲同意，他立即朝顾杲使个眼色，两个人便一齐走开去，凑着脑袋嘁嘁嚓嚓地商量起来。

黄宗羲抬起头，迷惑地瞧了一眼两个朋友的背影，仿佛奇怪他们还要捣什么鬼。看来，这会儿他已经想通了，脸色渐渐平和下来。他犹疑地瞧着计成，终于走上前去，拱拱手说：“多承计先生周全此事。非是在下有意如此，实在是此书得来不易，一旦失之，实在痛心。适才冒犯车驾，不胜抱歉。”

计成恭谨地笑着，恳切地说：“黄先生言重了！彼此都是读书人，谁不知善本难得！只怪手下人太过孟浪，令人思之扼腕！”

黄宗羲被对方的话又撩动了痛楚，他长长叹了一口气：“不瞒先生说，为此书在下足足候了三年。价钱呢，倒不算太贵，十六两银子……”

话还没有说完，侯方域已经走过来。顾杲却在远处叫：“太冲，你过来！”

黄宗羲朝计成匆匆点一点头，转身向顾杲走去。

侯方域不知道听见黄宗羲刚才的话没有，他若无其事地对计

Mei Langzhong had a mild disposition by nature. Seeing Mr. Gu and Mr. Hou had both changed their minds, he said, "Taichong, now that things have happened, you can only accept the bad luck. You have to get over it and let it go, now that you're somewhat compensated for the damage."

However, Zhang Zilie didn't speak. Knowing what was going to happen, he waited for the next episode with wide open eyes.

As all the Fushe comrades tried to persuade him, Huang Zongxi's thin and beautiful face suddenly blushed. He lowered his head, thought with a frown for a long while, and willy-nilly found himself nodding his head.

Seeing Huang Zongxi had consented, Hou Fangyu winked at Gu Gao, who immediately walked aside to have a private conversation with him.

Huang Zongxi raised his head and puzzledly glanced at the backs of the two friends, as if wondering what more tricks there were in store. By now he had accepted reality and his face had gradually returned to normal. He looked at Ji Cheng suspiciously, stepped forward, and said, putting his hands together, "Thank you for mediating, Mr. Ji. I didn't want to be angry. Those books are too precious for me. I'm sorry to have stood in your way."

Ji Cheng smiled respectfully and said in a sincere voice, "No apologies, Mr. Huang. Both of us are scholars. Who doesn't know rare books are rare? I'm sorry for the impertinence of the servants. I apologize for the damage."

His words touched the sore spot in Huang Zongxi, who heaved a long sigh. "Truth be told, sir, I've been waiting for this book set for three years. The price I paid, however, is not very high. It's only sixteen taels of silver ..." said Huang Zongxi.

Before he finished speaking, Hou Fangyu came over, but Gu Gao called from a distance, "Taichong, come here!"

Huang Zongxi nodded to Ji Cheng, then turned and walked towards Gu Gao.

Hou Fangyu, who might or might not have heard what Huang

成说："计先生，劳烦你了！按说呢，区区一套书，本来也所值无多，唯是这套《潜虚衍义》是极难得的珍本，太冲兄为它足足耗了三年心血，被贵价毁了，实在无法甘心！本拟定要原书索还，如今碍着计先生金面，忍痛允许以值代书。然而，也不能过于草草。"说到这里，他停下来，不慌不忙地伸出一个手指头，斜睨着计成说："这百金之数，只怕比较相宜。"

计成本来一直赔笑听着，这时脸色蓦地变了。他愕然地抬起头："啊，怎——怎么要这许多？"

"怎么是'许多'？"侯方域顿时沉下脸，"这套《潜虚衍义》，据我们所知，极可能就是嘉靖四十一年从严东楼府中查抄出来的那一套，只怕已是海内孤本。百金之值，还是低的呢！"

"可是适才黄先生说，他买下时才花了十六两银子！"计成忍不住争辩说。

侯方域冷冷地道："买下时是买下时，现在是现在。要是徐二公子以为不值百金之价，也可以，就请再寻一套同样的来赔与黄先生；或者——"他挖苦地微微一笑，"计先生家中藏有此书，愿意拿出来代徐公子赔偿，也极表欢迎！"

计成倒抽一口凉气。以自己数十年闯荡江湖的经历，他明白这回碰上了"硬头船"——眼前这个人，绝不是言辞所能打动的。他略一沉吟，终于苦笑着说："此事在下也无能做主。请侯先生稍待，在下回明青君兄，却来作复。"

Zongxi had said, said to Ji Cheng, as if nothing had happened, "Mr. Ji, thank you for the bother. Let's put it this way: a mere set of books isn't worth much in itself, but this set of *Studies in the Explorations into the Ubiquitous Void* is an extremely rare edition. Brother Taichong spent three full years looking for it and your servants have damaged it. You've no idea how painful it is for Mr. Huang. He originally insisted on having the same books but thanks to your intervention, he now agrees to accept a compensation in monetary terms. Even so, the compensation needs to be fair." Having said that, he stopped, put out a finger calmly and said, squinting at Ji Cheng, "A hundred taels of silver I'm afraid is more appropriate."

Ji Cheng, who had been listening with a forced smile, suddenly flushed. He raised his head in astonishment and said, "Aah, why, why do you want so much?"

"What does 'so much' mean?" Hou Fangyu said. His face immediately sank. "As far as we know, this set of *Studies in the Explorations into the Ubiquitous Void* is very likely to be the one that was confiscated from Yan Donglou's residence in the forty-first year of the reign of Emperor Jiajing[AD 1562]. In fact, one hundred taels is below its real value."

"But Mr. Huang said just now that he only spent sixteen taels of silver when he bought it." Ji Cheng instinctively argued.

Hou Fangyu said coldly, "When he bought it was when he bought it, and now is now. If Mr. Xu the Younger thinks that it's not worth a hundred taels, it's okay, but please find exactly the same thing for Mr. Huang; or—," he smiled sarcastically and said, "you have this book in your house and are willing to give it to Mr. Huang as compensation on behalf of Mr. Xu. That's also a welcome solution."

Ji Cheng sucked in a cold breath. Given his decades of experience in the world, he understood that this time around he had run into a "hard-headed boat," which meant the person in front of him couldn't be moved by words. He thought for an instant, and finally said with a wry smile, "That's something I can't decide. Mr. Hou, please hold on and allow me to ask the opinion of Brother Qingjun."

说完，他垂头丧气地转过身，朝轿子走去。

这时，黄宗羲同顾杲匆匆走了过来。黄宗羲大约已经从顾杲口中听说了他们所开的价钱，而且两人之间有过争论，所以此刻的脸色都显得很不好看。当黄宗羲问明侯朝宗已经把索价报给了对方，就顿时气火起来。

“不行，不行！书是我的，你们不能这样做！”他大声地说。

侯方域怔了一下。他迅速地瞥了瞥周围的观众，脸上随即露出习见的轻松愉快的笑容：“太冲兄……”

“算了！”黄宗羲粗暴地打断了他的话，“你们，你们这是要陷我于不义！”他咬着牙说。

侯方域那张英俊、白皙的脸刷地红了。他的眉毛倒竖起来，眼睛也瞪圆了。一句激烈的话显然已经冲到嘴边，然而不知为什么，却没有说出来。终于，他冷笑一声，转过脸去。

“太冲，”一个老气横秋的声音忽然响起来，那是张自烈，他已经好久没有说话，“你先别急，朝宗不过是替你讨了个价，还不知对方怎样还价哩。你要不愿意，待会儿还可以变嘛！”

这句话倒也在理，说得大家都沉默下来，一齐朝对面望去。

这当儿，计成显然已经同徐青君说妥了。只见他不慌不忙地重新走回来，微笑着对大家拱拱手说：“上复诸位先生，这百两之数，青君兄已然认可，并无异议。多劳诸位合力排难解纷之美意，青君兄命在下代他向诸位先生谨表谢忱！青君兄还说，宝籍既是孤本，百两之数，只怕委实有屈黄先生，青君兄愿再加五十两，实赔一百五十两！”

计成这话一说出口，全场顿时轰动起来，有人大声叫好，有

Then, he turned around dejectedly and walked towards the sedan chair.

Huang Zongxi and Gu Gao came over in a hurry. Huang Zongxi's face looked sullen, probably having had an argument with Gu Gao after hearing the asked amount of indemnity. Hou Chaozong said he had already told the other party the amount, Huang Zongxi flared up.

"No, no way! The books are mine. You can't do this!" he said loudly.

Hou Fangyu was bemused. He quickly glanced at the spectators around him, and his usual relaxed smile appeared on his face. "Brother Taichong ..." he said.

"Forget it!" Huang Zongxi interrupted him roughly. "You chaps, you chaps are trying to make me an unrighteous man," he said with gritted teeth.

Hou Fangyu's fair, handsome face flushed. His eyebrows arched, and his eyes shot out. Words of anger had obviously rushed to the lips, but for some reason, he didn't say them. Finally, he sneered and turned away.

"Taichong," came a fusty voice. It was Zhang Zilie, who hadn't spoken for a long time. "Don't worry! It's just an offer and it's not known what the counteroffer is. If you don't like it, you can change it later."

It made sense and everyone became silent and looked over at the other side.

By now, Ji Cheng had clearly obtained consent from Xu Qingjun. He came back unhurriedly, and said, smiling and pressing his hands together, "Dear sirs, the amount of one hundred taels has been approved by Brother Qingjun. He has no objection. Thank you all for your kindness in helping to solve the problem. Brother Qingjun asked me to say 'thank you' to you gentlemen on his behalf. He also said that since the book set is a unique treasure a hundred taels isn't enough to make Mr. Huang happy. He offers to add another fifty taels, and that will make it one hundred and fifty."

After Ji Cheng said that, a sudden commotion arose in the

人疑心自己是不是听错了，一时间议论纷纷，都说徐二公子果然富可敌国，这一手露得着实漂亮，既大方，又够面子。自然，也有人替黄宗羲他们担心：哎，这一来他们可怎么下台啊！

复社的几个人你看我，我看你，都不由得呆住了。他们完全没料到对方会答允得如此爽快，他们还准备讨价还价。然而，眼前的对手却比他们所估计的厉害得多！他不只赔得起，而且还甩得起——你们不是要敲他一百两吗？他甩给你一百五十两！不错，这一回银子是到手了，而且还多出了一半，可是脸面却要他妈的丢尽了！侯朝宗呀侯朝宗，你这才叫弄巧反拙呢！赶明儿传开去，我们复社还拿什么脸去见人？

“哦，这是一百五十两银票，敬请黄相公笑纳！”

计成恭谨的声音在一片喧闹中响起来。原来，那个管事头儿已经即时写好银票，送了过来。

复社的几个人顿时变得有点不知所措。黄宗羲显得更加狼狈，他恨恨地瞪了侯方域一眼，赌气地背过脸去。

周围的人又重新静下来。大家都饶有兴味地注视着，想看看复社的人到底敢不敢接受这张如此烫手的银票。

这时，只见一直在转着眼珠子的侯方域，忽然哈哈大笑起来。他上前一步，一手接过那张银票。

“多谢，多谢！”他拱着手对计成说，“不想徐二公子果然是位快人，侯某至为佩服！不过——”他转向围观的人群，提高了嗓门，“倘若有哪一位认为，今晚我等数人在此之所为，乃是觊觎徐公子的钱财，那又未免太小看我复社了！现今，侯某在此郑重声言：这一百五十两纹银，除开其中十六两仍扣除偿还黄太

watching crowd. Some yelled loudly; some wondered if they had misheard. The spectators talked noisily, hailing it as a graceful, generous act of Mr. Xu the Younger. There were also people who worried about Huang Zongxi and his friends and wondered how they could find an out.

The Fushe chaps looked at each other, confounded, totally unprepared for the ready consent of the other party, who had now left them no room to bargain. Their enemy was way more potent than they had thought. Not only could he afford to pay what they asked for, but he could pay what they hadn't asked for as well. You ask for a hundred taels? That's no big deal. He gives you one hundred and fifty taels without blinking an eye. You'll indeed get the money, which is one half more than you demand, but your face will be lost. Haha, Hou Chaozong, you're just self-defeating! What kind of face do we Fushers have to meet others should the news spread tomorrow?

"Um, Mr. Huang, here is a cheque for one hundred and fifty taels of silver, please accept it," said Ji Cheng in a loud, respectful voice amidst the noise of the crowd. The steward had already written the cheque and handed it over to Ji Cheng.

The Fushe chaps were suddenly at a loss as to what to do. More abashed, Huang Zongxi glared at Hou Fangyu with a resentful look and turned his back on him angrily.

The onlookers quieted down again. Everyone watched with interest, wondering if the Fushers dared to accept such a burning hot cheque.

At this moment, Hou Fangyu, who had been rolling his eyes aside, suddenly burst into laughter. He took a step forward and took the cheque in one hand.

"Thank you, thank you!" he said to Ji Cheng, pressing his hands together. "Mr. Xu is such a man of honor. I'm really impressed, but—" He turned to the crowd of onlookers and said, raising his voice, "If anyone thinks that what we're doing here tonight is for Mr. Xu's money, they're belittling the Fushe. Please allow me to make a declaration: The one hundred fifty taels of silver, minus sixteen taels,

冲先生之书值外，其余一百三十四两，我们分文不取，全部用来赈济饥民！明朝一等兑换到现款，立即交托施粥厂发放！”

侯方域本来就善于辞令，而且声音洪亮，这一番堂堂正正的话，通过他的嘴巴一板一眼，抑扬顿挫地说出来，不但清楚地送进了每一个人的耳鼓，而且扣动着他们的心弦。全场静了一下，忽然震天价响地喝起彩来：

“好啊！”

“真没想到！”

“太妙了！”

“复社就是好样的！”

……

人们用惊喜、钦佩、赞美的语言由衷地欢呼着。这欢呼声远远胜过了刚才计成宣布徐青君的答复时所引起的骚动。它此伏彼起，经久不息，从市肆升腾起来，在秦淮河上空盘旋、回荡，然后远远地飘散开去……

顾杲、梅朗中、张自烈这才松了一口气，暗自叫声“惭愧！”至于黄宗羲，虽然余气未消，但对于侯方域的应变本领也不由得暗暗点头。忽然，他想起了徐青君，连忙转动着眼睛，想寻找刚才那两乘轿子和那一群仆人。可是他再也找不到了——不知什么时候，徐青君一行已经悄悄溜跑了……

## 文酒风流

冒襄因为不肯到苏州去参加虎丘大会，同吴应箕发生了争执，陈贞慧夹在当中，左右劝解。正在不可开交的时候，顾杲、侯方域等人闹闹嚷嚷的声音已经来到了门外。陈贞慧朝冒、吴二人做了个手势，意思是：“你们别吵了，别吵了啊！”然后，他转过身，匆匆迎出门去。

which is the value of Mr. Huang Taichong's book set, that is, one hundred and thirty-four taels, will all be used to help the hungry. The cheque will be cashed tomorrow and the money will immediately be handed over to the alms place."

Hou Fangyu was a good speaker with a loud voice. Such words of grace, spoken with sincerity, resonance, and cadence, not only touched the eardrums of his audience but also their heartstrings. The spectators went silent and then suddenly cheered:

"Hooray!"

"What a big surprise!"

"A wonderful idea!"

"Hooray to the Fushe!"

...

The crowd hailed with surprise, admiration, and sincerity. The sound of cheers far surpassed the commotion caused by Ji Cheng just now when he announced Xu Qingjun's reply. The hails rose one after another without stop from the marketplace, hovered above the Qinhuai River, and then drifted away...

Not until now had Gu Gao, Mei Langzhong, and Zhang Zilie breathed a sigh of relief. They said to themselves, "How can I compare to such a genius?" Huang Zongxi, although still angry, couldn't help but nod his head in appreciation of Hou Fangyu's ability to rise to the occasion. Suddenly, he thought of Xu Qingjun and turned to look for the two sedan chairs and the flock of servants, who had already sneaked away ...

## A Drinking Party in the Courtesan House

Because Mao Xiang refused to go to Suzhou to attend the Tiger Hill Conference, Wu Yingji had an argument with him. Chen Zhenhui, caught in the middle, became the peace-maker. While they quarreled, the noise of Gu Gao, Hou Fangyu and others arrived at the door. Chen Zhenhui made a gesture to Mao Xiang and Wu Yingji to mean, "Stop the quarrel! Stop the quarrel!" Then he turned and hurried out to greet the late comers.

“姗姗来迟，该当何罪？”

刚走到门口，顾杲已经一步跨了进来，陈贞慧就站住脚，拱着手含笑问。

“哈哈，你们瞧！这话向来只有我们问定生，今儿破题儿第一遭，给他占了个先，就这么神气了！”顾杲兴冲冲地叫。

“啊，定生兄，你不知道，我们干了一件何等痛快的事！”跟着走进来的黄宗羲急匆匆地说。他的眼睛闪闪发光，热切地瞅着陈贞慧。要不是侯方域随后就走了进来的话，他必定会马上就把刚才发生的一切告诉陈贞慧。

侯方域拦住了黄宗羲。

“失期当死，请赎为庶人！”他昂然地说，朝陈贞慧一拱手，然后，像变戏法似的，从袖子里掏出那张一百五十两的银票，双手捧着，高举过头：“望乞哂纳！”

陈贞慧微微一笑。这微笑显示着他对于伙伴们这种煞有介事的表演是多么熟悉，而且料定这一次也并无特异之处。他随手接过银票，扫了一眼，蓦地，微笑消失了。他走到灯前，将银票反复地看了几遍，抬起头，怀疑地问：“嗯，这是怎么回事？”

顾杲等人交换了一下眼色，对那张银票所引起的效果显然颇为满意。

同张自烈一起走进来的顾眉，露出莫名其妙的神气。她好奇地凑近陈贞慧身旁，歪着头儿看了一眼，目光随即闪动起来。她用袖子掩着嘴儿一笑，瞅瞅侯方域，又瞅瞅顾杲，好像催促说：“是呀，这可是怎么回事呢？”

“君试思之！”顾杲洋洋得意地卖着关子。

“我如何猜得着！”陈贞慧双手一摊，“终不成是他送你的吧？”

When he walked to the door, Gu Gao had already stepped in. He stopped and said with a smile:

"You're late. What kind of punishment do you think you deserve?"

"Haha, lo and behold! It has always been my question for him. This is the first time for him to get the opportunity to ask me. Look how proud he is!" Gu Gao shouted excitedly.

"Hey, Brother Dingsheng, can you guess what a delightful thing we did?" Huang Zongxi, who followed him in, said anxiously. He looked at Chen Zhenhui with shining eyes. If Hou Fangyu hadn't walked in shortly afterwards, he would have honestly told Chen Zhenhui what had just happened.

Hou Fangyu stopped Huang Zongxi.

"You must be punished for being late!" Hou Fangyu said righteously, saluting Chen Zhenhui with clasped hands. Then, like a magician, he took out the cheque of one hundred and fifty taels of silver from his sleeve and held it over his head with both hands. "I beg you to accept it!" he said.

Chen Zhenhui smiled. This smile meant how familiar he was with such mock-serious performances of his chaps, and he gathered there was not anything special this time. He took the cheque, glanced at it, and suddenly the smile disappeared. He walked to the lamp and examined the cheque again and again, and then, raising his head, he asked suspiciously, "Um, what has happened?"

Gu Gao and company exchanged glances and were obviously quite satisfied with the effect produced by the cheque.

Gu Mei, who had walked in with Zhang Zilie, looked perplexed. She approached Chen Zhenhui, tilted her head and took a glance at the cheque. Then her eyes sparkled. She laughed, covering her mouth with a sleeve, and then looked at Hou Fangyu and Gu Gao as if urging, "Pray tell me what has happened."

"Guess!" said Gu Gao proudly, keeping the suspense.

"How can I guess it?" Chen Zhenhui spread his hands and said. "Is it his gift for you?"

“当然——非也！”

“那么，”陈贞慧苦笑着，“是你们敲诈来的？”

顾杲瞧了瞧侯方域，然后摇晃着脑袋，像吟诵诗书似的：“哎——思过——半矣！”

陈贞慧吃了一惊：“什么？你们这是——真的？”他的语气急促起来，“这、这，我不是早就劝你们，别干这种事！怎么现在又——”

这时候，吴应箕在冒襄身边待不住，他沉着脸走上来，拿过银票看了看，冷冷地说：“原来是此公！为富不仁，取不伤廉，我看无须紧张！”

“定生兄，此事并非尽如你之所料呢！”黄宗羲连忙插嘴说。刚才，他因别人利用他来敲诈徐青君大为恼火；现在，他又急急忙忙替他们分辩了。于是，他连说带比画，把刚才路上发生的事情一五一十地陈述了一遍。

陈贞慧用心地听完之后，想了想，终于无可奈何地点点头，说：“若是如此，总算还无伤大体。只是这一百五十两银子，除扣下书款外，须得尽数拿去放赈才好。”

黄宗羲毫不犹疑地说：“这个自然！”

陈贞慧不放心，又问：“朝宗兄也是此意？”

侯方域笑了一笑：“我么？这一百三十四两足色纹银，小弟之意，是交给眉楼主人，再邀上十娘、赛赛几个，把张燕筑、吴章甫、盛仲文也叫来，与诸公共谋一夕之欢——岂不比拿去放什么劳什子的赈，痛快得多！”

听他这样一说，不但陈贞慧皱起了眉头，连黄宗羲也变了脸色，倒是顾杲收起了开玩笑的神情，他说：

“定生兄，你莫听朝宗混说，我们本来就说定了拿去放赈的。不信，你问朗三！”

"Of course—not!"

"Then," Chen Zhenhui said with a helpless smile. "Is it the booty of a robbery?"

Gu Gao looked at Hou Fangyu, then shook his head and said, as if reciting a poem, "Well, almost there."

Chen Zhenhui was taken aback. "What? Are you serious?" he said, his tone tensing. "Did, didn't I tell you long ago not to do this kind of thing? Why are you doing it again?"

At this moment, Wu Yingji, standing by Mao Xiang's side, came over with a sullen face, took over the cheque, looked at it, and said coldly, "It is this guy. I don't think we need to be nervous for taking it from a rich, inglorious man."

"Brother Dingsheng, the whole thing isn't exactly what you think," Huang Zongxi quickly cut in. A moment ago, he had been pissed off for being manipulated to extort money from Xu Qingjun, but now he couldn't help but defend the action of his company. He gesticulated and recounted what had happened on the road just now.

After hearing it, Chen Zhenhui thought for a while, finally nodded his head with a contemplative expression, and said, "If that's true, there's no harm at all, but the one hundred fifty taels of silver, except for compensation for the book set, must be used for almsgiving."

Huang Zongxi quickly responded, "That's a matter of course!"

Chen Zhenhui, not reassured, turned to Hou Fangyu, and asked, "Brother Chaozong, is that also what you think?"

Hou Fangyu smiled and said, "Me? The one hundred and thirty-four taels of silver bullion, in my humble opinion, should be handed over to the owner of Mei's, where we should have an all-night fun party with Shiniang, Saisai, Zhang Yanzhu, Wu Zhangfu, and Sheng Zhongwen. Isn't it much better than giving alms?"

Hearing what he said, not only Chen Zhenhui frowned, but Huang Zongxi's expression changed as well. However, Gu Gao put away his joking expression and said, "Brother Dingsheng, don't take Chaozong seriously. He's joking. We have all agreed on using it for almsgiving. If you still doubt it, ask Langsan."

梅朗中一进屋，就同李十娘站在一旁，悄悄地咬耳朵，听了这话，他高声答应说：“正是正是，放赈放赈！”

陈贞慧的脸色这才舒展开来。他叹了一口气，说：“非是小弟胆小怕事，有道是树大招风——近数年来，我社声誉日隆，拥护者固然甚多，侧目者亦复不少。更有无耻小人，从中播弄，图谋倾覆社局。向者周之夔、陆文声之事，便是显证。幸赖皇上圣明，未容此辈如意。唯是其心不死，仍时刻窥我错失，思欲一逞。故此我等总要检点行止，勿要授人以柄才好。何况——”他似乎想继续说下去，临时又忍耐住了，只是轻轻摆了一下手。

于是，大家重新行过礼，然后脱去外衣，随意地坐了下来，一边喝茶，一边闲聊。冒襄今晚是主要的客人，所以大家都照例同他寒暄几句。他虽然窝着满肚子委屈，也只好强打精神应酬，不过神色之间，总透着不大自然。幸而后到的几个人随即忙于同顾眉、李十娘打趣说笑，没有觉察。至于黄宗羲，当他发觉吴应箕在场之后，就时时瞅着他，露出亲切的、急于要同他说话的神气。所以，黄宗羲现在便迅速走到吴应箕跟前，并且立即同他谈起来：

“啊，次尾兄！可记得去岁在杭州，我们曾论及田制之事么？”他兴冲冲地说，不待吴应箕答话，马上就接下去，“数月来，小弟思之再三，如欲匡时除弊，唯一之法，便是恢复先王井田之制！”

“哦？”

“小弟以为，当今钱粮匮乏，国用不足，其源盖出于田制之

Upon hearing it, Mei Langzhong, who had been standing aside and whispering with Li Shiniang since he entered the room, said in a loud voice, "Exactly, exactly! Alms, alms!"

Not until then had Chen Zhenhui's expression relaxed. He sighed and said, "It's not that I'm trifling over a small matter, but that a big tree attracts the wind. In recent years, the Fushe has been growing in popularity with more and more supporters but meanwhile there're many people who view us with suspicion as well; furthermore, there're a number of conspirators who are waiting for an opportunity to destroy the society. The Zhou Zhikui and Lu Wensheng libel case is an example. Fortunately, the emperor is wise and has not allowed them to have their wish. Nevertheless, the intentions of such men are not dead. They're lurking there and waiting for our lapse. Therefore, we should always exercise self-discipline and never give them a handle. What's more—" He seemed to want to continue speaking, but temporarily held it back with a wave of his hand.

Then, they saluted each other again, took off their gowns and sat down randomly to sip tea and chat. Mao Xiang was the guest of honor tonight, so everyone exchanged pleasantries with him as was the custom. Although he was full of grievances, he had no choice but to cheer up. His expression, however, always had a tinge of unease. Fortunately, the late comers took no notice of it because they were busy talking and jesting with Gu Mei and Li Shiniang. Huang Zongxi, seeing Wu Yingji was also present, kept looking at him, eager to have a conversation. Now, Huang Zongxi quickly walked up to Wu Yingji and struck a conversation.

"Hah, Brother Ciwei! Remember we talked about the land system when we were in Hangzhou last year?" he said jovially. Without waiting for Wu Yingji's reply, he continued, "For months, I've been thinking about it again and again. If we want to correct things, the only way is to restore the late former emperor's well-field land distribution system."

"So?"

"I think today's lack of money and food in the nation is the result

弊！田制之弊，则在贵戚官绅仗势侵夺民业，遂致官庄之田日广，而小民之田日缩。即以苏州一府而论，几乎至于无地而非官田，民田仅占十五分之一。现今国家困于战乱，用度浩大，赋税日增；而富豪之家，不肯加额，结果便一并征之于小民百姓。小民不堪重负，唯有弃田逃亡。于是乎，不只国家之赋税，年年大量缺额，无法完成；而且逃亡之民，饿死沟壑者有之，倡乱造反者有之，尽成祸乱之源。时至今日，此事已几至积重难返，倘不急图改革，只怕局面一溃，就无可收拾了！”

吴应箕此刻显然没有心思讨论这类问题，他含糊地点着头：“嗯，你是说，恢复井田制……？”

“啊，你听我说呀！”黄宗羲兴奋地叫，全然没有觉察对方的情绪。他深深吸了一口气，开始从井田制的历史和作用说起，然后将它同目前的田制进行比较。他自信地、匆忙地说着，显然打算把几个月来，他对这个问题的研究结果，一股脑儿都摆出来。他并不考虑急急忙忙这样做到底有多大必要，也不考虑在这样一种场合谈论这么严肃的问题是否适宜。他只是觉得这个问题很重要，而自己经过艰苦的努力，为解决这个问题所设想的一套，看来是可行的。他急不可待地要把它说出来，因为它作为一种成熟了的思想，在他的心中已经憋了好些时候了。正如一个足了月的婴儿，要挣脱母体，以大哭大叫向周围宣告他的诞生一样。而婴儿的呱呱坠地是从不理会场合和旁人态度的……

of ills of the current system of land ownership. The ills of the land system make it possible for the privileged to take land away from the common people. As a result, the powerful have more and more land and the average people have less and less land. In Suzhou, for example, there's almost no land that isn't owned by someone with an official background, and land in the hands of farmers accounts for only one fifteenth. Nowadays, in a time of national crisis with so many wars to fight, taxes have to be increased to generate government revenue, but the rich and powerful don't bear the increase and simply shift their responsibility to the small farmers. The small farmers, unable to bear the heavy burden, have no choice but to abandon their land and flee. As a result, the situation is aggravated. The nation's tax revenue has dwindled and the tax goal has never been met; the people who have fled their land starve to death in the gullies or start rebellions. It's a vicious cycle. Today, the ills are such that without a drastic reform, a total collapse will be unavoidable and irrevocable."

Wu Yingji, obviously having no intention of discussing such issues at this moment, kept nodding and said perfunctorily, "Um, you mean to restore the well-field land system ...?"

"Right. Let me finish." Huang Zongxi said excitedly, completely unaware of the other man's attitude. He took a deep breath and began to talk about the history and role of the well-field system, and then compared it with the current system of land ownership. He spoke confidently and hurriedly, obviously intending to lay out the results of months of his research on this issue at one go, without thinking how necessary it was to do so in such haste or whether it was appropriate to discuss such a serious issue on such an occasion. He just thought this issue was very important and that the set of ideas he had hatched was the cure for the current problem. He couldn't wait to share it, because it had been held in his mind as a mature thought for a long time like a baby who wants to break free from the mother's womb and announce his coming to the world by crying loudly upon reaching the end of the pregnancy term without caring about the occasion and the attitude of others ...

然而，黄宗羲并没有能把他的见解陈述完毕。一个十三四岁，长得挺秀气的丫环从屏门后面转了出来。

“各位相公、阿娘，请到花厅入席。”她行着礼说。

黄宗羲怔了一下，犹疑不决地瞧瞧神思不属的吴应箕，终于无可奈何地挥一挥手，闭上了嘴巴，同大家一齐起身，朝后面走去。

花厅的面积不大，同样布置得异常雅洁，当中已经拼起了一张大圆桌，桌上的青花细瓷食具，在灯烛的辉映下熠熠生光。李十娘的鸨母，正领着两个丫环张罗着，看见客人们进来了，她们就一齐上前，敛衽为礼。

客人们走到桌前，就站住了。陈贞慧上前一步，开始给大家定座。因为是相知雅集，也不必弄那些开桌送酒的虚套，只请冒襄坐了首席，依次是吴应箕、张自烈、顾杲、黄宗羲、梅朗中、侯方域。陈贞慧自己坐了下首的主位。李十娘和顾眉，就分坐在冒襄两旁。

鸨母等客人坐定之后，吩咐两个丫环几句，就退了出去。李十娘和顾眉从座位上盈盈站起来，开始给客人斟酒。

“眉娘！”侯方域转脸瞅着顾眉，用了一种愉快的、轻松的声调说，“今儿晚上，我只当你不会来了呢！”

侯方域同顾眉，不久前很要好过一阵子，可是今晚进门以来，他一个劲儿只同李十娘周旋亲热，对于顾眉，却明显地有意回避和冷淡，正式冲着顾眉说话，这还是第一句。

“为什么？”顾眉问，没有停止斟酒，也没有回过头来。

“嘻，还装糊涂呐！自然是龚孝升啰！”

However, Huang Zongxi was unable to finish sharing his views. A thirteen- or fourteen-year-old, good-looking maid turned up from behind the screen door.

"Gentlemen and ladies, please move to the Flower Hall and take your seats," she said with a curtsey.

Huang Zongxi paused, then, wishing to continue, looked at Wu Yingji, whose mind was absent, and finally shut up unwillingly with a wave of his hand. He stood up like everybody else and walked to the back of the screen door.

The Flower Hall was not big, but it was elegantly decorated. A large round table had been set up in the middle with blue and white fine chinaware shining under the candlelight. The bawd of the brothel was busy setting the table with the help of the two maids, and seeing the guests coming in, they stepped forward together and saluted them.

The guests stopped at the table. Chen Zhenhui stepped forward and began to assign the seats. Because it was a gathering of old acquaintances, all formalities were abolished. He invited Mao Xiang to the seat of honor on the left, then Wu Yingji, Zhang Zilie, Gu Gao, Huang Zongxi, Mei Langzhong, and Hou Fangyu to the other guest seats. Chen Zhenhui himself took the host seat on the right. Li Shiniang and Gu Mei sat on the two sides of Mao Xiang. After the guests sat down, the bawd said something to the two maids and withdrew herself. Li Shiniang and Gu Mei rose from their seats and started pouring wine for the guests.

"Lady Mei," Hou Fangyu turned his face to look at Gu Mei, and said in a pleasant, relaxed tone, "I just assumed you weren't coming tonight."

Previously, Hou Fangyu and Gu Mei had been fond of each other, but tonight, he had been only making love to Li Shiniang, obviously neglecting or dodging Gu Mei. This was the first time for him to speak to Gu Mei.

"Why?" Gu Mei asked. She didn't stop pouring wine, nor did she look back.

"Hey, don't pretend you don't know it. Because of Gong

“啐，没有的事！”顾眉红了脸。

侯方域冷笑一声：“没有的事？这事瞒得了别人，须瞒不过我侯方域！”

顾眉不响了。

“什么？孝升？”“孝升怎么了？”“朝宗，怎么回事啊？”大家好奇地追问。

侯方域拿起筷子，从盘子里拣了一颗鸽蛋，放进嘴里慢慢嚼着，一边瞅着顾眉，装出一副欲言又止的神气。

顾眉忽然朝侯方域转过脸来，用她那双又大又深沉的眼睛凝视着他，长长的睫毛微微颤动着。一会儿，她眯缝起眼睛：

“你敢！”她吓唬说，“看老娘不老大耳刮子扇你！”

大家不由得一怔，随即“哄”地笑了。这笑声是欣赏顾眉的大胆放肆，出语惊人。事实上，善于恰到好处地撒野、放泼，正是顾眉显得与众不同的迷人之处。

侯方域却没有笑。在受到顾眉蕴含深意的凝视当儿，他的表情不由自主地变了。一丝自知理亏的愧色，从他那白净的、骄傲的脸上闪现出来。他的嘴角牵动一下，竭力要做出一个微笑，结果却违反本意地避开了顾眉的眼睛。

“十娘准知道，问她好了！”正当大家有点纳闷，梅朗中忽然冒冒失失地说。自从进门之后，他的眼睛大部分时间都围着十娘转。他柔声地问：“十娘，告诉我，唔？”

李十娘脸一红：“奴家、奴家怎么晓得？只怕、只怕侯相公说着玩儿，也未可知……”她讷讷地说，向梅朗中投去责备的一瞥，低下头去。“你真笨，怎么当众问我？眉娘姐姐不肯说的事，我敢揭破她么？”她仿佛这样说。

“嗯，我知道！”一个低沉的嗓音从李十娘身旁响起来，那是张自烈。他的脾气有点孤僻，进门以来几乎没有说过一句话。

Xiaosheng of course."

"No, nothing of that sort." Gu Mei blushed.

Hou Fangyu said with a sneer, "Nothing of that sort? You can hide it from others, but not me, Hou Fangyu!"

No response from Gu Mei.

"What? Xiaosheng?" "What happened, Xiaosheng?" "Chaozong, what's up?" several voices asked at the same time.

Hou Fangyu took the chopsticks into his hand, picked a pigeon egg from the plate, put it in his mouth, and, chewing it slowly, he looked at Gu Mei with an "I will tell them" expression.

Gu Mei suddenly turned to Hou Fangyu and stared at him with her large and deep eyes, her long eyelashes fluttering. After a while, she squinted her eyes and said:

"Don't you dare to say it!" Then, she threatened, "I'll box your ears."

Everyone looked shocked for a moment and then laughed. The laughter was an appreciation of Gu Mei's bold and unrestrained expression of herself. In fact, the ability to release the wildness in her in good measure was what made Gu Mei unique and charming.

Hou Fangyu didn't laugh. Under Gu Mei's meaningful stare, his expression changed involuntarily. A trace of guilt streaked his fair, proud face. The corners of his mouth twitched to make a smile, but instead he found himself dodging Gu Mei's stare against his intention.

"Shiniang must know it. Ask her," Mei Langzhong said abruptly as everyone was wondering what had happened. Since he came in, his eyes had been around Shiniang most of the time. He said in a tender voice, "Shiniang, can you let me know?"

Li Shiniang blushed. "How, how can I know? Maybe, maybe Mr. Hou is kidding, but who knows?" she said shyly. Then, she gave Mei Langzhong a reproachful glance and lowered her head, as if saying, "What a blockhead! How can you ask me in public? Mei doesn't want to say it. Why should I say it?"

"Well, I know it," came a throaty voice from beside Li Shiniang. It was Zhang Zilie. Very much an introvert, he hadn't said anything yet

他这会儿突然开口，大家都感到意外，不约而同地望着他。就连顾眉也收起了放荡不羁的劲儿，疑惑地睁大了眼睛。

张自烈却没有立即说下去，他举起酒杯，呷了一大口酒，不知为什么意态有点萧索。“这是孝升亲口告诉我的。”这样说了一句之后，他又住口不说了，神情却变得越来越颓唐。

“酒！”他指了指杯子。

大家目不转睛地瞧着他，感到惊疑不定。梅朗中慌里慌张地端起酒壶，给他斟酒。

这时，只听张自烈呻吟似的吟诵起来：“舞榭歌台，风流总被雨打风吹去……”

这样吟诵之后，他就一手抓起酒杯，猛地喝下去，随即瞪着眼睛，把正在发怔的朋友们一个接一个地扫视一遍。

“怎么，啊，不明白？”他突然没头没脑地问，一副怒气冲冲的样子。

“啊，莫非眉娘要归龚孝升了？”梅朗中冲口而出地问。他平日嗜诗如命，当然知道张自烈刚才所诵的，是南宋词人辛稼轩的名作《永遇乐》中的几句。

张自烈点点头，长叹一声，说：“孝升同眉娘已有百年好合之约，花烛迎娶，只是年内之事了！”

其余的人本来也隐隐猜到是这么回事，但张自烈正式把它说出来之后，大家仍然忍不住“啊”了一声，随即不知为什么，也像刚才张自烈那样，一个个变得沉默起来。

“孝升”是合肥才子龚鼎孳的字。他在江南文坛中，也是个知名人物，更兼年少得志，八年前就中了进士，在湖北蕲水做了几年县太爷，如今被召往北京，准备另有任用。人人都说他来日

since he came in. When he suddenly spoke, everyone was surprised and looked at him in unison. Gu Mei withheld her wildness and opened her eyes suspiciously.

Zhang Zilie didn't continue immediately. He raised his cup and took a sip of wine with a sullen expression. "Xiaosheng told me himself," he said. Then he went silent again and his expression became dimmer and dimmer.

"More wine please," he said, pointing to his cup.

Everyone puzzledly looked at him without rolling their eyes. Mei Langzhong hurried to pick up the decanter and refilled his cup.

Zhang Zilie started to chant: "All the theaters, all the romance will be gone with wind and rain ..."

Having recited the poem, he grabbed the drinking cup with one hand, drank it at one go, then opened his eyes wide to scan his puzzled friends one by one.

"Why, hah, you don't understand?" he suddenly asked out of the blue with an expression of profound indignation.

"So, do you mean Mei will belong to Gong Xiaosheng?" Mei Langzhong blurted out. A poetry addict, he of course knew what Zhang Zilie had just recited was lines from the famous lyrical poem by the Southern Song dynasty poet Xin Jiaxuan to the musical score of "Blessed Forever".

Zhang Zilie nodded his head with a long sigh and said, "Xiao Sheng and Mei have been engaged. They'll get married this year."

The others had more or less guessed it, but Zhang Zilie's confirmation still surprised them, and for some reason they went silent, as Zhang Zilie did just now.

Xiaosheng was the courtesy name of the talented Gong Dingzi from Hefei. Gong Dingzi was a well-known figure in the literary circles of River South. He was accomplished at a young age, having been awarded a *jinshi* degree eight years ago and served as a county magistrate in Qishui, Hubei Province for a few years. Now he was summoned to Beijing for a new appointment. Everyone said he would have a great future. Gu Mei, who had been eager to leave the brothel

方长，前程无量。顾眉急于选婿从良，她跟侯方域的交情本来不错，但侯方域的态度忽冷忽热，令她无法把握。最近龚鼎孳途经南京，有人便从中撮合，果然一说便成。这在顾眉私心中，是颇为满意的。刚才她阻止侯方域说出来，无非是她还打算向他私下有所解释。到了张自烈说话的当儿，顾眉知道事情藏不住，已经准备着大家起哄，并且想好了一番应付的话。谁知，出乎她的意料，筵席上到头来却是一片静默——陈贞慧和侯方域微微低着头，仿佛在沉思；顾杲吃惊地张大了嘴巴；冒襄和吴应箕各怀心事地皱起了眉毛；张自烈一个劲儿地喝酒；梅朗中的眼光仍不住往李十娘身上溜；后者却垂着头，仿佛在黯然自伤。只有黄宗羲泰然自若，摆出一副事不关己的神气……

顾眉忍不住了。

“哎，怎么啦？莫非这有什么不好？”她诧异地问。

大家如梦初醒地动了动身子，互相交换了一下眼色。

“哦，好极好极！”侯方域首先打着哈哈说，“孝升一代才人，英姿秀发，得眉娘入辅中馈，正所谓鱼水相得。他日龙云俱化，只怕要羡煞我辈了！”

“那你们怎么一个个都板着脸儿，倒像奴家做了什么错事似的？”

“这——”侯方域不自然地笑了笑，“我想大家是有点舍不得你之故吧！”

“啐……”顾眉绯红了脸，“侯相公又开玩笑了！”

“不，朝宗说的是实话！”顾杲一本正经地插嘴说。然后，像征询意见似的望了望在座的人。大家都不自然地点了点头。李十娘的眼圈儿已经开始发红，显出随时要哭的样子。

and live happily ever after with someone, had been fond of Hou Fangyu, but Hou Fangyu's attitude was elusive. Recently, when Gong Dingzi passed by Nanjing, someone did a match-making and they were engaged. It was going to be a happy ending for Gu Mei. Just now, she had prevented Hou Fangyu from speaking it, because she wanted to explain to him privately before making it public. When Zhang Zilie spoke, Gu Mei knew that she couldn't hide it anymore. She was ready to be teased and rehearsed in her mind what to say in response to their teasing. To her surprise, everyone was suddenly quiet. Chen Zhenhui and Hou Fangyu lowered their heads as if thinking something; Gu Gao opened his mouth wide in surprise; Mao Xiang and Wu Yingji knit their brows, each with their own thoughts; Zhang Zilie kept drinking; Mei Langzhong's eyes continued to fall on Li Shiniang while the latter hung her head as if having pity on herself. Everyone except Huang Zongxi, who was unperturbed with an unconcerned look ...

Gu Mei was puzzled.

"Well, what's wrong? Is there anything wrong?" she asked curiously.

They stirred as if waking up from a dream, and exchanged glances.

"Oh, that's absolutely nice," Hou Fangyu said teasingly. "Xiaosheng is a genius with a great future. He's a perfect match for Mei. It's like fish and water, or a white cloud sailing with a majestic dragon. What an adorable match!"

"Then why do you pull your faces as if I had done something wrong?"

"That—" Hou Fangyu smiled awkwardly and said, "I think it is because everyone begrudges losing you."

"Go to hell," Gu Mei blushed and said. "You're teasing me again."

"No, Chaozong is speaking the truth," Gu Gao cut in in a serious tone. Then, he looked at the people present as if asking for their opinions. Everyone nodded stiffly. Li Shiniang's eye sockets started to flush and tears welled up.

顾眉瞧瞧这个，瞧瞧那个，不禁呆住了。

“嗯，你不妨想想，要是今后筵席上少了眉娘，我们会快活么？”侯方域说。这一次，他的语气十分真诚。

“唉，想到今后再也吃不着眉楼的蒸鳗和爆蟹，我现在就难受极了！”梅朗中可怜巴巴地说。

顾杲沉思着点点头：“要是南曲没有了眉楼，只怕就不再成其为南曲了！”

这几句话，正说中了在座的人此时此刻的心情，大家又沉默下来。

渐渐地，响起了轻微的啜泣声。那是李十娘。她掩着脸，背过身子去，瘦削的双肩，在沉香色妆花绒女衣下面可怜地抖动着。接着，顾眉的眼圈儿也红了，她从身边取出一方手帕，开始抹眼泪。梅朗中不安地转动着高大的身躯，瞧瞧这个，又瞧瞧那个，不停地眨巴着眼睛，嘴巴一扁一扁的。忽然，他“哇”的一声，伏在桌上，号啕大哭起来。

其余的人默默地瞧着，一个个脸上现出凄惨的神色，谁也没开口去劝止他们。

就在这当儿，一个愤怒的、着急的嗓音忽然传遍了整张桌子：

“诸君今晚来此，莫非就是为的效‘新亭之哭’么？”

大家回过头去，只见黄宗羲一张瘦小的脸涨得通红，神情显得异常激动。他大声地说：“辛稼轩生当宋室南渡之际，其时偏

Gu Mei was silent, her eyes darting between these friends of hers.

"Well, just think about it, if there's no Mei at the dinner party in the future, will we be happy?" Hou Fangyu said. This time, his tone was very sincere.

"Alas! Thinking that I'll never have steamed eels and stir-fried crabs from Mei's again, I feel terribly sad," Mei Langzhong said pitiably.

Gu Gao nodded pensively and said, "Southern Opera without Mei's, I'm afraid, won't be Southern Opera anymore."

These words represented the sentiment of everyone present. Another silence.

Someone started to sob. It was Li Shiniang, her face covered with her hands, her back facing the wall, her thin shoulders trembling pitiably inside the agarwood-colored jacquard silk dress. Then, Gu Mei's eye sockets also flushed. She took out a handkerchief from her side and began to wipe the tears. Mei Langzhong fidgetily turned his big torso, looking at this person and that person, eyes constantly blinking and jaw dropping and closing. Suddenly, with a wah, he leaned on the table and cried out loud.

The rest of the people watched silently, with a miserable look on their faces, and no one offered words of consolation.

At this moment, an angry, agitated voice suddenly spread across the table, "Are you here tonight to imitate Crying at Xinting[1]?"

Everyone turned to look at Huang Zongxi, whose thin, small face was flushing with a look of vexation. He said loudly, "In Xin Jiaxuan's time, the imperial court of the Song dynasty went to exile in the South. The emperor had no sense of responsibility, the civil officials didn't attend to their duties and the military officers indulged themselves in pleasures. The loyal and the righteous, finding no occasion to serve their nation, let out cries of desperation. Even at that moment of national crisis, Xin Jiaxuan remained loyal as a son of the land, and,

---

① Crying at Xinting: former officials of the West Jin dynasty lamenting loss of country at the New Pavilion

安日久，主上昏庸，文恬武嬉。忠义之士，空怀报国之志，请缨无路，故发此悲愤之声。然而，即令在彼时，辛稼轩亦不过栏杆拍遍，壮怀激烈，未尝一做儿女之态！今我大明祖宗二百七十年基业，仁德广被，恩泽深厚。虽有建虏、流寇交相为患，终未能动摇我天下一统。而况当今圣上，宵衣旰食，励精图治，此正仁人志士用命之秋也！何以诸君不图壮举，反咨嗟掩泣，若不胜情者！岂不怕失笑古人于地下乎？”

这一顿数落激昂慷慨，义正词严，把大家说得你望我，我望你，倒有点不好意思起来。梅朗中赶紧停止号泣，擦干眼泪。

这时候，陈贞慧站了起来。他说：“太冲责备得对！我们快别再效儿女之态了！眉娘天人之姿，偶谪风尘。今日得此归宿，正是可喜可贺。来，我们贺她一杯！”

他说着，拿起了酒杯。大家也纷纷举杯。顾眉显然十分感动。她又是笑又是抹眼泪，给大家一连灌了三杯，鲜润娇美的脸上，顿时升起了两朵红云，越发显得美艳绝伦。座上倒有一大半的人，都情不自禁地被她吸引住了。大家嘴上不说，心里都暗暗妒羡：龚孝升当真是艳福不浅呢！

陈贞慧等李十娘替大家重新斟过酒之后，接着又说：“今夕之会，还有一事值得庆贺——”他把眼睛转向开席以来，一直显得闷闷不乐的冒襄，用严肃、庄重的声调说，“适才辟疆从熊大司马的府上来，得知消息，他尊大人调职改任之事，已蒙当道允准，邸报不日可下。诸位，夫孝悌者，乃君子立身之本。辟疆近半年来，为其尊大人之事，含悲奔走，不遗余力，孝义之声，竦

slapping his hand on the railings, vowed tragically to devote his life to the country. The Great Ming has lasted two hundred and seventy years thanks to the great virtue of the emperors. Despite the invasions of the Jurchens and riots of the insurgents, the foundation of the unified country has never been shaken. Moreover, today's emperor, working from dawn till night every day, strives to rejuvenate the nation, giving an opportunity to men with lofty ideals. Yet instead of committing yourselves to the great cause, you're sighing and crying as slaves of your emotions. Aren't you afraid of being laughed at by our ancestors underground?"

He spoke so righteously that everyone was embarrassed, one looking at another. Mei Langzhong quickly stopped crying and wiped away his tears.

At this moment, Chen Zhenhui stood up. He said, "Taichong is right. Let's stop acting like children. Mei is an angel fallen in the dust. We should all be happy and congratulate her on finding her good destiny. Come, cheers to Mei!"

He said, picking up his cup. Everyone raised their cup. Gu Mei was moved. She smiled as she wiped her tears, and they each drank three cups in a row. Two red clouds appeared on her tender, fair face. She looked all the more beautiful. More than half of the men at the table were enchanted by her charms. They were secretly jealous. What good luck for Gong Xiaosheng to come into possession of such a pretty creature!

Chen Zhenhui continued after Li Shiniang refilled everyone's cup, "Tonight, there's one more thing worth celebrating—" he turned his eyes to Mao Xiang, who had been sullen since the beginning of the dinner party, and said in a serious, solemn voice. "Pijiang has learned in the residence of Mr. Xiong, Minister of War, that the requested transfer of his respectable father to a new post has been approved by the authorities and that the decree will soon be issued. Sirs! Being filial to parents and respectful to elders is the basis of a man of good character. In the past six months, Pijiang has spared no effort seeking help for his father. The voice of filial piety has moved the imperial

动朝堂。此正是我复社君子之本色。可敬可颂。然而，适才听次尾说，竟有若干社外小人，借此为题，妄加攻讦，以图达彼危倾我社之目的，可谓蚍蜉撼树，不知自量！凡我同仁立身于世一日，断不容彼辈猖狂！未审诸位以弟之言为然否？”

陈贞慧的话音刚落，座上立即有几个人大声叫嚷起来：

“当然！”“他们休想得逞！”“辟疆恪尽孝道，堪为同人表率，岂容鼠辈污蔑！”“辟疆，小弟敬你一杯！”“对，对！辟疆兄，我们都支持你！”

在吵嚷声中，陈贞慧把眼光转向吴应箕，显然希望他能有所表示，以消除他与冒襄之间的芥蒂。可是吴应箕一言不发，固执地扭过脸去……

这时候，冒襄站了起来。他谁也不看，沉着嗓子说：“多承诸位仁兄维护，冒襄不胜感激。是非自有公论，小弟在此也无须多言。来日方长，小弟总有机会向世人证明，冒襄绝非欺世盗名、贪生畏死的懦夫！”

几句话，说得斩钉截铁。大家都哄然叫好。在闹哄哄当中，彼此干了一杯，筵席上的气氛终于变得热烈起来。

## 眉娘妙曲

这当儿，一个丫环来上菜，这是一盘白汁鱼块，热气腾腾地散发着诱人的香味。大家举箸，各自尝了一口，都纷纷点头，说这鱼肉的滋味真是鲜极了。梅朗中更是赞不绝口。他笑眯眯地问：

“十娘，这是什么鱼？难为你家厨子烧得这么香！我怎么从不曾尝过这等美味？”

李十娘抿着嘴儿微微一笑，说：“你猜！”

court. Such is the true nature of a Fusher. He deserves praise for that. However, according to Ciwei, there're little men—enemies of the Fushe—who attack us on this ground with the aim of destroying the society. It's like an ant unaware of its own little strength trying to shake a big tree. As long as we live, we won't allow them to run amuck! What do you think, brothers?"

After Chen Zhenhui finished speaking, some of the men at the table yelled:

"Certainly!" "They won't succeed!" "Pijiang's filial piety is a good example for us all. How can he be smeared by the rats?" "Pijiang, cheers!" "Yep! Brother Pijiang, we all support you!"

Amidst the noise, Chen Zhenhui turned his eyes to Wu Yingji, obviously hoping that Mr. Wu could say something to clear up the misunderstanding between himself and Mao Xiang, but Wu Yingji stubbornly turned away his face without saying a word.

At this moment, Mao Xiang stood up. Without looking at anyone, he said in a calm voice, "Thank you for kindly defending me, brothers. I'm very grateful. The public will judge whether I'm right or wrong. There's no need for me to say anything here. There're long days ahead with plenty of opportunities for me to prove to the world that Mao Xiang is definitely not a coward who deceives the world and steals fame," he said confidently.

Everyone applauded. Then, they noisily toasted to one another, and the atmosphere at the banquet finally became jovial.

## The Beautiful Song of a Prostitute

At this moment, a maid came to serve a dish called "fish nuggets in white sauce", which was steaming with a tempting smell. Everyone raised their chopsticks. After tasting it, they all nodded and said that the fish was delicious. Mei Langzhong was full of praise. He smiled and asked:

"Shiniang, what kind of fish is this? You have a wonderful cook! Why have I never tasted such a great dish before?"

Li Shiniang pursed her mouth and said smilingly, "Guess!"

梅朗中又拣了一箸鱼，放进嘴里，闭上眼睛品味了半天，然后睁开眼睛，摇摇头说："嗯，猜不出，猜不出，各种各样的鱼我吃过不少，从没有这种味儿的！"说着，他又拣起一块，打算再度品尝。

"朗三！你这样狂啖不止，还要命不？"顾杲大惊小怪地叫起来，"你知道么，这是河豚！"

梅朗中已经把鱼肉放进口里，一边说："为什么不？这好吃嘛……"蓦地，他全身一抖，停止了咀嚼，瞪大了眼睛："你说什么？"

"这是——河豚！"

梅朗中"啊"了一声，连忙把嘴巴里的鱼肉吐出来，颤着声儿问："这是，这是那种有毒的河豚？"

"废话！天下哪有无毒的河豚——哼，你吃了这许多，这回非中毒不可！"

"啊，可是你，你们……"梅朗中的脸色开始发青，舌头也有点不听使唤了。

"别怕，奴家的河豚毒不死人的。"李十娘微笑着说。

但梅朗中没有听见，他呆呆地坐着，脸上现出古怪的表情。忽然，他用手捂住嘴巴，飞快地站起来，跌跌撞撞地朝外奔去。门外立刻就响起了"啊、啊"的呕吐声。

在座的人都忍不住大笑起来。两个丫环忍住笑，连忙奔出去伺候他，李十娘也站起来帮忙，又是送水漱口，又是递手帕揩脸，来来回回地忙了一阵，梅朗中这才由丫环搀扶着，面色苍白地慢慢走回来。

"朗三，亏你还是个诗翁！岂不闻东坡诗云：竹外桃花三两枝，春江水暖鸭先知。蒌蒿满地芦芽短，正是河豚欲上时——何

Mei Langzhong picked another nugget, put it in his mouth, closed his eyes, and savored it for a long time, then he opened his eyes and said, shaking his head, "No, I can't guess it. I've eaten a lot of fish, all kinds of fish, but I've never had anything like this before." As he spoke, he picked up another piece to savor again.

"Langsan, aren't you afraid to die eating like that?" Gu Gao cried out in a fake fright. "Be careful! It's swellfish!"

Mei Langzhong had put the nugget in his mouth and said, "Why not? It's too delicious ..." Yet, he suddenly shuddered and stopped chewing, his eyes wide open. "Mmm, what did you say?" he asked.

"It's swellfish!"

With an "ahh", Mei Langzhong quickly spat out the fish, and asked in a trembling voice, "Is this the kind of poisonous swellfish as people often speak of?"

"Nonsense! Is there a non-poisonous swellfish in the world? You have eaten too much to be saved."

"Ahh, but you, you ..." Mei Langzhong said, his face beginning to turn blue and his tongue stiffening.

"Don't be afraid! My swellfish doesn't kill," Li Shiniang said with a smile.

But Mei Langzhong didn't hear her. He sat blankly with a strange expression on his face. Suddenly, he covered his mouth with his hands, stood up quickly, and stumbled out. "Aaagh, aaagh, aaagh, aaagh ..." came the sound of vomiting from the doorway.

Everyone present laughed. The two maids held back their laughter and rushed out to wait on him. Li Shiniang also stood up to help. She went back and forth giving him water for him to rinse his mouth, or handing over a handkerchief for him to wipe his face ... After a long while, Mei Langzhong slowly returned with a pale face, supported by the maids.

"Langsan, how come you are a poet? Don't you know the Dongpo's poem: Beyond the bamboo grove, the peach flowers open on three or two twigs. The spring river warms up and the ducks are the first to know. When mugwort spreads across the land and weeds begin

等闲适风雅！像你方才这样狂呕滥吐，岂止大煞风景，若是东坡地下有知，简直会勃然大怒，把你逐出门墙哩！”侯方域一边说，一边向大家递着眼色。

梅朗中苦着脸道：“河豚我是发誓不吃的。况且，我只学唐诗，不学宋诗，苏东坡也无奈我何！”

大家又笑起来。等笑声停止之后，陈贞慧捋着胡子问：

“十娘，我于这河豚亦向来颇有戒心。因闻此物味美而有剧毒，食之不慎，便有性命之虞，所以东坡又有‘拼死吃河豚’之说。不知以何法处置，方能稳妥？倒要领教！”

李十娘还没开口，顾眉在旁边已经“哧——”地笑出声来，她说：

“陈相公，怎么连你也真信了顾相公那句话？——这哪里是河豚肉，这是鱼罢啦！”

陈贞慧“噢”了一声，露出半信半疑的神气。

李十娘连忙说：“这真是鱼。苏东坡诗里说，‘粉红石首应无价，雪白河豚不药人。’便是此鱼了。”说着，又瞧瞧大家，抿着嘴儿微笑说，“诸位相公难道竟不知仪征的‘假河豚’么？”

在座的人中，除了顾杲、侯方域早就知道这不是河豚之外，其余几个也有瞧出不大像的，只是看见顾、侯两个煞有介事地吓唬梅朗中，反弄得糊涂起来，直到这时，才恍然大悟。

陈贞慧偶一回头，瞥见站在一旁侍候的两个小丫环正用袖子掩着嘴儿在笑，就问：“咦，你们两个笑什么？”

两个丫环对望了一眼，其中穿葱绿袄儿的那一个歪着脑袋笑说：

“河豚的眼有毒，吃时须先去眼。这鱼有眼，显见就不是河豚。当初梅相公若是晓得有这分别，也就不会……”她抿嘴一笑，没

to sprout, it's the season for swellfish ... What a leisurely and stylish life! Your vomiting like that just kills the fun time. If Dongpo heard of it, he would be furious and drive you out of here!" Hou Fangyu said, winking at the others.

Mei Langzhong said with a bitter face, "I've sworn never to eat swellfish. Besides, I only study Tang poetry. I've not studied Song poetry, so Su Dongpo can do nothing to me!"

Everyone laughed again. After the laughing stopped, Chen Zhenhui stroked his beard and asked, "Shiniang, I've always been wary of swellfish too. Having learned that it's highly toxic and life-threatening, Su Dongpo wrote in a poem, 'eating swellfish at the risk of life.' Then, how can it be cured in order to be safe? Please educate me."

Before Li Shiniang replied, Gu Mei chuckled and said, "Mr. Chen, how come you're so credulous as to believe Mr. Gu? It's not swellfish. Just common fish."

"Oh," Chen Zhenhui said suspiciously.

Li Shiniang hurried to explain, "It's really common fish. Su Dongpo said in a poem, 'The pink stonehead is priceless, and the snow-white swellfish doesn't kill.' It's that kind of fish." As she spoke, she looked at the others and then continued, pursing her mouth with a smile, "Don't you know there's a kind of fish called fake swellfish in Yizheng?"

Besides Gu Gao and Hou Fangyu, there were a few others who knew it was not swellfish, but they became confused when they saw Mr. Gu and Mr. Hou frighten Mei Langzhong with such seriousness. It was not until then that they became certain.

When Chen Zhenhui turned around, he caught sight of the two maids standing by chuckling, their mouths covered with their sleeves, and asked, "Huh, what are you two laughing at?"

The two maids looked at each other, and the one in the green jacket tilted her head and said with a smile, pursing her lips, "The eyes of swellfish are poisonous. They must be removed first before eating. This fish has eyes, and obviously it's not a swellfish. If Mr. Mei had

有说下去。

黄宗羲把桌子一拍，高声说：“也就不会平白无故地大吐一场了！”

大家怔了一下，随即又笑起来。梅朗中起先还生气地噘着嘴巴，可是到底撑不住，也就跟着笑了。

黄宗羲却没有笑。他感叹地说：“皆因平日不食河豚，便不知其无目的，遂致一旦鱼目当前，竟茫然不识。朱子所言：格物致知。今夕之宴，我于此解又得一证！”

“说起朱子，我又要骂艾千子了！”沉默了许久的张自烈忽然说，“千子口口声声标榜什么‘以欧曾之笔墨，诠程朱之名理’。他全不知程朱的名理，必要身体力行，心有所得，才发而为言。像千子这等不行不思，终日以扯前人讲章为事，又有何名理可言！”

黄宗羲瞧了张自烈一眼，点头说：“很是很是！即便是欧曾之笔墨，也全仗一点真情，喷薄而出，所以波澜开合，汪洋恣肆。千子竟欲以之纳入八股成法之中，讲什么承题、束股，还有什么文章可观呢！”

艾千子，就是艾南英。他是当时的一位八股文名家，门下弟子不少，在士林中颇有影响。艾南英论文的观点，同复社的人一向处于对立的地位，经常辩论争吵，有一两次还动了武。张自烈、吴应箕对艾南英攻击尤其激烈。所以一谈起此人，吴应箕也来了劲。他插进来说：

known the difference, he wouldn't ..." Then she stopped.

Huang Zongxi slapped his hand on the table and said loudly, "—wouldn't have vomited for nothing!"

The others looked shocked and then laughed again. Mei Langzhong pouted in anger at first, but in the end couldn't help laughing too.

Huang Zongxi didn't laugh. He said thoughtfully, "Because I've not had swellfish before, I don't know it doesn't have eyes. Then, once a fish with eyes appears, I don't know it's not a swellfish. As the Confucian scholar Master Zhu said, 'Seeing a thing is the basis for knowing a thing.' Tonight's banquet is another annotation to the maxim."

"Speaking of Master Zhu Xi, I'm going to criticize Ai Qianzi again," Zhang Zilie, who had been silent for a long while, suddenly said. "Qianzi claims that he interprets the theory of names and patterns of the Cheng Brothers and Zhu Xi by using Ou Yangxiu and Zeng Gong's style of writing.' He doesn't know that the 'names and patterns' of the Cheng Brothers and Zhu Xi lies in verbal expression of thinking after doing. Instead of doing and thinking, Qianzi just copies from the ancients. How can he understand the theory of names and patterns?"

Huang Zongxi glanced at Zhang Zilie, nodded and said, "Quite right! Quite right! Even the style of Ouyang Xiu and Zeng Gong is the flow of true feeling in their elegance and abandon. Qianzi wants to incorporate it into the eight-legged essay— 'breaking open the topic', 'receiving the topic', 'beginning discussion', 'initial leg', 'middle leg', 'later leg', 'final leg', and 'conclusion'—in that case, can you expect a good essay?"

Ai Qianzi is the courtesy name of Ai Nanying. Very influential among the scholars, he was a famous eight-legged essay writer with many disciples. His views on essay writing were opposite to those of the Fushers. The two camps often argued and even resorted to physical fights to solve their differences. Zhang Zilie and Wu Yingji were the bitterest critics of Ai Nanying.

“自然时文也未可一概非之。前辈如杨复所等，亦间有发明之见，而千子竟批驳不遗余力。其实近溪、复所之学，艾千子又何曾梦见！”

三个人于是你一言我一语地指摘起艾南英来。顾杲听得不耐烦，瞅个空儿截住他们说：

“哎，够了够了！这些东西拿到书坊去再说。喝了半天酒，行个令如何？”

梅朗中拍着手说：“正是正是，就由子方兄出令！”

顾杲想了一下，正要出令，忽然侯方域把酒杯一放，说：“慢着！”他站起身，去长几上拿过来一面琵琶，微有醉意地敲着铜板蒙面道：

“眉娘词曲，妙绝南中，自今以后，只怕就专让龚孝升一人独听，我辈无分领受了。今夕良辰，已是千金一刻，又安可轻易放过？如今就请眉娘倾喉一吐，令吾辈一畅耳福，然则他日回思，尚差可自慰也！”

大家一听，都纷纷说好。

顾眉笑着说：“侯相公这话，可羞得奴家脸都没处搁了！要说词曲妙绝南中，谁不知第一就数寒秀斋的李十娘！现放着十娘在眼前不请，却偏要拿奴家出丑。奴家纵然不怕出丑，可是若教外人听见，难保不笑话相公所命失人呢！”

“哈哈，你别推托！十娘自然是要唱的，可是今晚头一个偏要点你。皆因你是将‘失’之‘人’，故须先有‘所命’。莫非眉娘如今有了孝升，就把我们这些平日的相好都看轻了么？”侯方域的语气又变得颇为尖酸。

顾眉的脸似乎红了一下，却没有着恼。她挺直身子，坦然说：“好，那么奴家就唱。不过，可有一件，唱过之后，请容奴家就

Therefore, when this man was mentioned, Wu Yingji joined in. He said, "Writings of the natural style shouldn't be dismissed altogether. Scholars in the older generation such as Yang Fusuo have had many original ideas, but Qianzi spares no effort to criticize them. In fact, Ai Qianzi doesn't even have a clue of the kind of learning that Jinxi and Fusuo have."

The three of them traded their criticism of Ai Nanying. After having heard too much of it, Gu Gao interrupted them, saying, "Hey, enough is enough! Save these things for discussion in the study. We have been drinking for a while, how about a 'drinking order' game?"

Mei Langzhong clapped his hands and said, "Good suggestion! Let Brother Zifang issue the orders."

Gu Gao thought for an instant and was about to issue an order, suddenly Hou Fangyu put down his cup and said, "Hold on!" He stood up, went to the tea table and got a *pipa*. He tapped the copper plate and said with a tad of intoxication:

"Mei's voice and music are unrivaled in River South. From now on, I'm afraid that they'll be exclusive to Gong Xiaosheng. At such a precious moment, why should we give up the opportunity to hear them? Mei, may I ask the pleasure of your singing for us now so that we'll have something to remember in the future?"

Everyone agreed.

Gu Mei smiled and said, "Mr. Hou, you're over-praising me. Everyone knows that the best musician in River South is Li Shiniang of the Cold Beauty Chamber. You're making a spectacle of me in front of Shiniang. I'm not being afraid of being a spectacle, but aren't you afraid that others will laugh at you for losing your judgement?"

"Haha, don't shy away! Shiniang is going to sing of course, but tonight you must be the first. Because you're the person to be lost soon, you deserve the priority. You're not taking your old sweethearts seriously because you have Xiaosheng now?" said Hou Fangyu, whose tone became acrid again.

Gu Mei blushed but was not annoyed. She straightened up and said gracefully, "Okay, I'll sing. However, there's one thing, pray

此告退，先家去一步。”

“啊，不行！”“眉娘怎能这就走？”“不能放她走！”几个声音抢着说。

侯方域斜着眼睛，冷冷地问：“为什么？”

顾眉微微一笑，却不回答。

侯方域的眼睛睁圆了，看样子马上就要发作。这时，陈贞慧说话了：

“行啊，君子不强人所难。眉娘今晚既然有事，陪了我们大半天，已是很难得了。唱完曲子，就让她先回去吧。”

由于陈贞慧这样说了，侯方域大约也就觉得不好再发作。他没有好气地把琵琶往顾眉手里一塞，沉着脸回到自己的位子上坐下来。

顾眉始终微笑着。等伺候的丫环把一张方凳端来之后，她就抱着琵琶盈盈坐下来，不慌不忙地把银甲套在手指上，先在弦上熟练地弹出几个音，又把弦柱调弄了一下，校准音调，这才摆好姿势，侧着头儿默了默神，随即十根手指徐徐摆动，弹出一段过门，接着就曼声唱起来。她唱的是汤显祖的名剧《牡丹亭》里《惊梦》一折——

〔绕地游〕梦回莺转，乱煞年光遍。人立小庭深院。炷尽沉烟，抛残绣线，恁今春关情似去年。

〔步步娇〕袅晴丝吹来闲庭院，摇漾春如线，没揣

allow me to excuse myself and go home after I sing."

"No, we won't!" "How can you leave so soon?" "We won't let you go!" said several voices at the same time.

Hou Fangyu tilted his eyes and asked coldly, "Why?"

Gu Mei smiled but didn't answer.

Hou Fangyu's eyes shot daggers. At this moment, Chen Zhenhui spoke.

"Okay, gentlemen, don't force others to do things against their will. It's very nice of Mei to accompany us for such a long time while she has her own business to attend to. Set her free when she finishes singing," he said.

Now that Chen Zhenhui agreed to her leaving, Hou Fangyu kept his temper in check. He thrust the *pipa* into Gu Mei's hands, returned to his seat with a sullen face and sat down.

Gu Mei was smiling all the time. After a maid got her a square stool, she sat down gracefully and put on the silver finger protectors without haste. Then, she struck a few notes expertly, adjusted the pegs and poised herself to play. After tilting her head to collect herself, she slowly moved the ten fingers to play the prelude and as she played she started to sing along. It was "Startled from a Dream" from Tang Xianzu's masterpiece *The Peony Pavilion*.

*[To the tune of "Traveling Around" ]*
*Waking up from my dream*
*I hear the orioles merrily sing.*
*The commotion of springtime titillates my heart.*
*In the small courtyard out of the way I stand.*
*The sandalwood incense has almost burned*
*The last smoke dispersing like a broken thread.*
*Will the new spring be like the last one?*
*[To the tune of "Graceful Steps"]*
*Threads of a spider web fly in the yard,*
*Drifting with the breeze.*
*The bronze mirror standing by*
*Steals a look at my hairbun from aside.*

的菱花，偷人半面，迤逗的彩云偏。步香闺怎便把全身现？

〔醉扶归〕你道翠生生出落的裙衫儿茜，艳晶花簪八宝瑱。可知我常一生儿爱好是天然。恰三春好处无人见。不提防沉鱼落雁鸟惊喧。则怕的羞花闭月花愁颤……

从听说顾眉要唱《惊梦》开始，客人当中那几个通晓音律的行家像冒襄、顾杲、梅朗中等，就顿时来了精神。因为大名鼎鼎的汤显祖，平生写戏专门讲究“意趣神色”“以意为先”，对于宫调音韵，却并不怎么注重。他的这本《牡丹亭》，虽然文辞极为精美，其实却相当难唱；而能够演唱，又不用增改字眼来迁就音乐的，就更加不易。这一层，无形中已经成为衡量演唱者本领的一个尺度。所以，他们都十分留神倾听顾眉吐出的每一个字，看她有没有改动曲文。然而，没有。看来顾眉的本领确实不凡，哪怕是再拗口的字眼，她都能巧妙处理，使它变得流畅宛转，不着痕迹，甚至更有韵味。如今，她已经唱到最吃紧的一段——

〔皂罗袍〕原来姹紫嫣红开遍，似这般都付与断井颓垣。良辰美景奈何天，赏心乐事谁家院？朝飞暮卷，云霞翠轩，雨丝风片，烟波画船。锦屏人忒看得这韶光贱……

*It's such a small space, how can the mirror take a full view of me?*
*[To the tune of "Come Home Drunken"]*
*You believe in colorful dresses,*
*You believe in dazzling jewelry,*
*But you don't know being natural is my style.*
*No one sees me at my best.*
*In front of me, fish forget to swim and sink to the bottom,*
*Birds forget to fly and fall from the sky,*
*The moon goes into hiding*
*And flowers become shy.*

Seeing Gu Mei was going to sing "Startled from a Dream", the ones who knew rhythm and rhyming—Mao Xiang, Gu Gao, and Mei Langzhong—suddenly became animated. The famous playwright Tang Xianzu had always emphasized spirit and meaning but didn't pay any attention to rhythm and rhyming. Although *The Peony Pavilion* was exquisitely written, singing it was very difficult; it was even more difficult to sing it without changing the words to accommodate the music. In fact, it had virtually become a yardstick of a singer's ability. Therefore, they all listened attentively to every word Gu Mei uttered to see if she had changed the lines. Yet she had not. It turned out that Gu Mei's skills were indeed extraordinary. She could handle even the most difficult pronunciations, making them smooth, melodious, natural, and charming. Now, she reached the most difficult part:

*[To the tune of "A Black Robe"]*
*For whom do all the flowers open?*
*The broken fences and collapsed walls!*
*What a beautiful morning!*
*What a beautiful day!*
*Where is my love, where is my beau?*
*Pavilions in the clouds, pleasure barges in the rain—*
*How I love them, love them all!*
*Yet here I am*
*Locked up inside this house, facing the wall ...*

〔山桃红〕则为你如花美眷，似水流年，是答儿闲寻遍，在幽闺自怜。转过这芍药栏前，紧靠着湖山石边。和你把领扣松，衣带宽，袖梢儿揾着牙儿苫也，则待你忍耐温存一晌眠。是那处曾相见，相看俨然，早难道这好处相逢无一言。

〔绵搭絮〕雨香云片，才到梦儿边，无奈高堂，唤醒纱窗睡不便，泼新鲜，冷汗粘煎，闪的俺心悠步亸，意软鬟偏，不争多费尽神情，坐起谁忺则待去眠。

〔尾声〕困春心游赏倦，也不索香薰绣被眠。（天啊！）有心情那梦儿还去不远……

顾眉一点也不费劲地唱着。美妙的歌声从她那小巧玲珑的嘴里不断地倾吐出来，在琵琶的伴奏下，像一串大大小小、晶莹圆润的珠子在花厅里游走、流动、磕碰着，然后又化成一道道清澈的溪流，一条条飘拂的彩带，一群群飞舞的蝴蝶，在听众的身旁耳畔缭绕，盘旋，摇曳……使人恍如置身于一个春风拂面、繁花似锦的园林，看到一位美丽纯真的少女，在热烈地倾诉着她对爱情的渴望和追求……

终于，顾眉唱完了，但是大家静默着，仿佛还神游在歌声所幻化出来的温馨境界之中。陈贞慧首先喝起彩来，大家这才纷纷

*[To the tune of "Flowering Plum"]*
*What a beautiful lass!*
*What a young thing!*
*Finally, finally, I find you in this corner of the world,*
*Having pity on yourself.*
*Let me go over to the white peony grove by the landscape rock.*
*Let me unbutton your blouse and loosen your belt*
*And lie down with you on the grass mat.*
*We're made for each other. United we shall be.*
*Why should there be words when you have me?*
*[To the tune of "Cotton Flakes"]*
*Oh, my sweet dream of love—*
*The storms of passion and thunderbolts of desire—*
*Is thus broken.*
*In cold sweat, I shudder,*
*In the dreamland, I linger.*
*I am so tired and weary without energy.*
*Should I sit in bed?*
*Or should I get up?*
*[Epilogue]*
*A dream, a sweet dream of love,*
*A beautiful dream under an embroidered quilt*
*(Oh, good heavens!) And it's not far away from me.*

Gu Mei sang with perfect ease. The beautiful voice streamed out of her small and exquisite mouth and, accompanied by the *pipa*, it wandered, flowed, and bumped in the Flower Hall like a string of crystal beads large and small and turned into clear rivulets or floating ribbons or flocks of dancing butterflies, hovering above, encircling or waving through the audience, as if they were sitting in a breezy, blooming spring garden listening to a beautiful, innocent young lass wistfully speaking out her yearning for love ...

When Gu Mei finished singing, everyone remained quiet, as if still wandering in the world of music. Chen Zhenhui cheered first, and

回过神，兴奋而热烈地称赞眉娘唱得实在太妙了。

顾眉把拨子插回原处，又脱下银甲，把它连同琵琶一道，交给身旁的丫环，然后略略整理了一下衣衫，这才说道：“多谢各位相公，有污清听了。”又向李十娘说：“愚姐技尽于此，待会妹妹登场，我可就立时相形见绌了。幸亏我这就要走，倒免得到时自惭形秽呢！”说着，她双手接过梅朗中递来的一杯茶，道了谢，一饮而尽。然后，向在座客人深深地福了一福，说：“奴家就此告退，怠慢之罪，尚祈列位相公宽恕！”

顾眉说完，从丫环手里接过那只乌云覆雪波斯猫，抱在怀里，轻轻抚着，却没有立即就走。她瞅着侯方域，仿佛打算说句什么。但是侯方域故意转过脸去。她只好叹了一口气，对冒襄说：“冒相公，奴家大胆，请相公相送几步，不知可使得么？”

因为刚才当众表明了心迹，而且得到了社友们的理解和支持，冒襄的心情已经舒畅了许多。听见顾眉提出这样的要求，他便笑着站起来：“啊，能陪伴眉娘，小生正是求之不得！”说着，他就跟在顾眉后面，出了厅门，由一名丫环提灯照路，穿过长轩，走到院子里去。

顾眉走到水池旁边，就站住了。

“冒相公，你当真不肯到姑苏去么？”她问，偏过身来。

冒襄一怔：“啊，你怎么——”

“奴家听到了，偷听到的！”顾眉微笑着说，卖弄风情地眯起了眼睛。不过，她立即又改变了神情。

“嗯，相公还是尽快赶到姑苏去为好！”她说，严肃地望着冒襄的眼睛。

“啊，为什么？”

others followed, marveling at the wonderful singing of Mei.

Gu Mei inserted the plectrum back in place, took off the silver finger picks and handed them to the maid next to her along with the *pipa*. Then, after tidying her clothes, she said, "Thank you, sirs! I'm flattered by your listening." Then she said to Li Shiniang, "I've done my best. When you're on the stage, I'll be dwarfed immediately. Fortunately, I'm leaving now, so I won't feel embarrassed." She took over a cup of tea from Mei Langzhong with both hands, thanked him, and drank it at one go. Then, she made a deep bow to the guests and said, "Please excuse me for leaving so early. I'm really sorry for having to go now."

Yet she didn't leave immediately after speaking. Instead, she took over the black and white Persian cat from the maid's hands, held it in her arms and stroked it softly. She looked at Hou Fangyu, as if she wanted to say something, but Hou Fangyu deliberately turned away his face. She sighed and said to Mao Xiang, "Mr. Mao, can you please accompany me for a moment on my way back?"

Because Mao Xiang had spoken his mind and won the understanding and support of his fellow Fushe comrades, he was in a much better mood now. Hearing Gu Mei's request, he smiled and stood up, saying, "Ah, what a privilege it is to accompany Mei!" He followed Gu Mei and exited the door of the hall, and, led by a maid lighting the way with a lamp, they passed through the roofed corridor, and walked into the courtyard.

Gu Mei walked to the side of the pool and stopped.

She turned to Mao Xiang and asked, "Mr. Mao, is it true that you don't want to go to Gusu?"

Mao Xiang looked surprised and said, "Aah, how do you—"

Gu Mei smiled and said, narrowing her eyes coquettishly, "I happened to hear it. I was eavesdropping." However, she immediately changed her expression.

"Well, I think you'd better go to Gusu as soon as possible," she said, looking into Mao Xiang's eyes in earnest.

"Aah, why?"

“卞赛赛刚从姑苏来，她告诉我，田皇亲派人到姑苏采买女孩子，点着名儿要圆圆。吓得圆圆东躲西藏，幸得有几个相好的孤老，拼死护着她，买动了一班‘撞六市[①]’日夜轮番守卫，喊打喊杀地要同田皇亲的人放对。这件事如今已经闹到府衙里，是凶是吉，还不知晓呢！”

“你，你说什么？”冒襄的眼睛一下子睁得老大，他失态地一把抓住顾眉的胳膊。

顾眉没有动弹，她斜瞅着冒襄：“奴家劝相公赶快到姑苏去，越快越好。迟了，还能不能见着圆圆，可就难说了——哎，你揪得奴家真紧！”

冒襄“啊”的一声，松开了顾眉的胳臂：“那——圆圆如今在哪儿？她、她还好吧？”

“哎，赛赛说她来的时候，圆圆还没被弄走。不过又过了几日，事情闹成怎么个样子，就不晓得了。而且，赛赛就对奴家说了这些，再多奴家也不知道。总之，相公赶快到姑苏去就对了！”

冒襄显然被这突如其来的消息震呆了。他甚至忘了向顾眉道谢，不由自主地退后几步，靠在水池的石栏上，两眼直瞪瞪地望着前面，一言不发。

顾眉站在旁边，怜悯地瞧了他一会儿，终于，她轻轻叹了一口气，悄悄地移动着脚步，沿着鹅卵石小径向外走去。开始她还不时回顾一下，后来越走越快，不一会儿，就消失在花木繁密的阴影里了。

又过了一会，冒襄才惊醒过来。他茫然地四面望望，发现顾眉已经离去。突然，像被人击了一掌似的，他猛地跳起来，飞快地奔上长轩。可是，当他听见花厅里传来社友们的喧哗和哄笑声

---

① 撞六市：旧指恶少合伙诈骗劫掠，横行霸道。

"Bian Saisai has just come from Gusu. She told me that the emperor's relation Mr. Tian has sent his men to Gusu to purchase a girl. They have named Yuanyuan. Yuanyuan was so scared that she went into hiding. Fortunately, a few elders are offering her protection. They've hired a few street thugs to guard her day and night, threatening to kill anyone who should dare to kidnap her. Now, the case is being heard in the *yamen* of the prefecture and there's no knowing whether things will come to a good end."

"What, what did you say?" said Mao Xiang. His eyes opened wide and unmannerly grabbed Gu Mei's arm.

Gu Mei didn't move. She looked at Mao Xiang obliquely and said, "I think you should go to Gusu as soon as possible, the sooner, the better. If you're late, you'll never see Yuanyuan again. Ouch, it hurts!"

Mao Xiang let go of Gu Mei's arm with an "aah". "Then, where is Yuanyuan now? How, how is she?" he said.

"Saisai said when she left, Yuanyuan hadn't been taken away yet, but since a few more days have passed I don't know how things are now. Besides, Saisai only said this much to me, and I know only this much. In spite of everything, you should go to Gusu as soon as possible."

Mao Xiang was obviously stunned by the sudden news. Forgetting to thank Gu Mei, he involuntarily moved back a few steps and leaned against the stone rail of the pool, without saying a word, his eyes staring blankly straight ahead.

Gu Mei stood by and looked at him pityingly for a while. Finally, she heaved a sorrowful sigh and silently walked out along the cobblestone path. At first, she looked back from time to time, but soon she went faster and faster and in a short while disappeared in the dense shadow of flowers and trees.

Some time later, Mao Xiang woke up from the shock. He looked around blankly and found that Gu Mei had already left. Suddenly, as if being slapped by someone, he suddenly jumped up and hurriedly rushed to the hallway. However, when he heard the noise and laughter

时，脚步就缓慢了下来。终于，他停住脚步，低头沉思了片刻，这才没精打采地一步一步朝花厅走去。

## 闯席求援

阮大铖的私邸石巢园，坐落在城南库司坊里。当街一个派头十足的大门楼，进门是宽敞的天井，高大的厅堂。厅堂后面回廊曲折，门户重重。据说八年前，阮大铖从安徽老家逃难到南京来时，为兴建这所府第，很花了些银子，所以园内不仅恢宏幽深，而且雕栏画槛，绣户绮窗，样样都极备精巧，什么桃花坞啦，芸香小筑啦，枫叶亭啦，梅屋啦，各有各的名目和特色。阮大铖有了这座华美舒适的园林，再加上他家里一流的烹饪、一流的戏班子，便千方百计诱引各方面的人士来歌舞宴饮、说剑谈兵，着实热闹风光了几年。后来受了复社诸生的猛烈抨击，来石巢园的客人因此大减。阮大铖虽然十分恼恨，却也无可奈何。他闲极无聊，只好把心思都用在写作戏本上，什么《桃花笑》《井中盟》《牟尼合》《双金榜》之类的，这几年倒真的弄成了好几个。虽然无非是好看热闹，文辞华美，却因颇能迎合时尚，南京城里的各大戏班都竞相传抄搬演。阮大铖因此又洋洋得意起来，傲然对人说："复社那伙人合力排揎我，真是蠢得很！其实论学识论才情，我阮大铖哪里就比不上他钱牧斋、周仲驭！他们若肯尊我一声'前辈'，复社的局面，只怕还远不止今日的规模身价哩！"

不过，大话虽然好说，阮大铖面对着这一群激烈而又固执的书呆子，却实在毫无办法，所以如今除了写戏订曲之外，他的另一件可干的事情，就是躲在家里侍弄园子。他有的是精力，也有

of his comrades coming from the Flower Hall, his steps slowed down. He stopped, bowed his head and thought for a while, and then listlessly walked back towards the Flower Hall.

## A Man Seeking Help

Ruan Dacheng's private residence, Stone Nest Garden, is located in Kusifang in the south of the city. On the side of the street was a grand gate-house; inside were a spacious patio, a majestic main hall, and a meandering corridor linking the various structures. It was said that when Ruan Dacheng fled from his hometown in Anhui to Nanjing eight years ago, he spent a huge sum of money building this glorious residence. The garden was not only large and deep, but also exquisite with beautifully sculpted pillars, rails, doors, and windows. Every structure, be it Peach Blossom Castle, Rue Cabin, Maple Pavilion, or Plum House, is unique in its own right. This gorgeous and comfortable garden, equipped with a first-class cooking team and a topnotch theater troupe, attracted celebrities from far and near to wine and dine and discuss matters of great importance. It saw several years of good time. After Ruan Dacheng was condemned by the Fushe, Stone Nest Garden had fewer and fewer visitors. Although he was very annoyed, he could do nothing about it. To kill his boredom, he turned to playwriting and wrote quite a few plays in the following years, including *Smile like a Peach Flower*, *Oath in the Water Well*, *The Muni Pearls*, and *Double Bingo*. Although they were nothing more than a good noise with an elegant style, because they catered to the fashion of the time, the major theater troupes in Nanjing competed to stage them. Ruan Dacheng was proud of himself again and said to others, "How stupid the Fushers are to persecute me! In fact, when it comes to learning and talent, Ruan Dacheng is by no means inferior to Qian Muzhai and Zhou Zhongyu. If they had ever respected me as an elder, the Fushe I'm afraid would've long outgrown what it's like today."

However, talking big was one thing, and the reality was that there was nothing Ruan Dacheng could do when faced with this group of fierce and stubborn nerds. So now, besides writing plays,

的是银子，石巢园就此一年到头不得安生，总得由着主人那刁钻古怪的脑瓜子转出点新花样来——今天这儿砌一道短墙，明天那儿改建一座凉亭，要不就是把新采购来的大理名种山茶一口气种它二三十株。可是，过不了十天半月，短墙、凉亭、山茶又忽然失踪，原来的地方说不定已经是石山耸峙、清溪蜿蜒了……

这一次，当徐青君和计成二人，逃脱了黄宗羲、侯方域等人的困阻，气急败坏地闯进石巢园，并由一名家童提着灯笼引路，沿着回廊曲径，向花厅走去的时候，徐青君就发觉，好儿种布置都不同了。一道执圭式的院门也变成了月洞式，害得他有一两次疑心走错了路。要是在往常，走在旁边的计成必定会技痒起来，忍不住指手画脚说这一处改好了，那一处却弄巧反拙，等等。不过，此刻计成却知趣地沉默着，徐青君更是压根儿全无鉴赏的心思。

今天晚上，徐青君算是倒了八辈子霉，天晓得是触犯了哪一路邪神，让他一出门就撞上了复社那一伙瘟生！眼睁睁被敲去了一百五十两银子不算，还被他们当众戏弄侮辱了一场。徐青君不心疼银子，他平日到旧院里去马马虎虎泡上一天，所费的也不止这个数目。他是气恼丢了面子——堂堂中山王府的二公子，在小民百姓面前遭受如此折辱，这口气，徐青君觉得无论如何也咽不下去！不错，他的哥哥魏国公徐宏基，现任南京守备，兵权在握，按理应当可以替弟弟出这口气。不过，徐青君知道这位哥哥官儿虽大，胆儿却小，估计他未必就肯出头去惹复社，说不定，还会被他埋怨一顿。刚才，徐青君在轿子里左思右想，气闷得慌，最

the only other thing he could do was hide at home attending to his garden. Since he had both time and money, Stone Nest Garden had never seen a day of quiet throughout the year, submissively letting the master experiment with his whimsical ideas—building a short wall here today, rebuilding a pavilion there tomorrow, or planting twenty or thirty camellia japonica trees from Dali in one go. However, within ten days or a half month, the short wall, the pavilion, and the japonica suddenly disappeared to give way to a towering stone mountain or a winding rivulet ...

After Xu Qingjun and Ji Cheng broke free from Huang Zongxi and Hou Fangyu, they stormed into Stone Nest Garden in a frenzy of rage. As they walked along the winding corridor to the Flower Hall, led by a boy servant carrying a lantern, Xu Qingjun noticed several new changes had been made. A double-door fence gate had turned into a moon-hole gate, so he constantly felt he was going the wrong way. Ji Cheng silently walked beside him instead of showing off his judgement by gesticulating and commenting on the changes like before, knowing Xu Qingjun was in no mind for art at the moment.

Tonight, Xu Qingjun had had bad luck. He must have offended some demon so that he had run into the bunch of hateful Fushers immediately after he left his residence. Not only was he robbed of one hundred fifty taels of silver, he was also teased and insulted by them in public. Xu Qingjun didn't care about the money. He spent more than that amount every time he went to the Old Yard. He was angry for the loss of face. That the second young master of the dignified Zhongshan Palace should have suffered such humiliation in front of the lowly people was not something he could swallow anyway. He was right. His elder brother Xu Hongji, Duke of Wei and incumbent Minister of Defense in Nanjing, held real military power and in theory should be able to speak for the younger brother. However, Xu Qingjun knew that his elder brother, a high official with a timid character, might not want to confront the Fushe on his behalf. Chances were that his brother would give him a reprimand instead. In the sedan chair just

后忽然想到阮大铖。他素知阮大铖同东林、复社积怨甚深，平日私下里提起复社那伙书生，阮大铖总是气得扯着大胡子发狠。何况此人狡狯机智，一肚子鬼心思，必然乐于替自己出主意报仇。这样一想，徐青君就当即吩咐改道往库司坊来。不料刚才到了门前，门公却告诉他，主人临时出门了。徐青君好不失望。后来，听说阮大铖的同年好友马士英也来了，现正在花厅候茶。徐青君想，先听听马士英的主意也好，便带着计成进来了。

徐青君同计成到了花厅，却不见马士英的影子。一个仆人回话说："马老爷到咏怀堂看排戏去了。"徐青君便不停留，带着计成又赶到咏怀堂来。

咏怀堂内灯火通明。一群小女孩儿正聚在大堂中央的红氍毹上，有的坐在一旁弹琴吹笛，有的正在走场唱曲。戏曲教习臧亦嘉，亲自掌着鼓板。他大约有四十多岁，长得苍白清秀，下巴没有蓄胡子。他全神贯注地掌握着排练，每当发现有人奏错了音调，或是唱错了板眼的时候，他就吃疼似的眯起一只眼睛，同时更加用力地敲击鼓板，仿佛要以此提醒出错的人注意。

不过，徐青君并没有留意这些。他一眼看见马士英正坐在上头的一张花梨木攒牙子翘头案后面，一边看戏，一边自斟自饮，他就气咻咻地叫起来："啊，瑶老！岂有此理，气死人了！"

红氍毹上的演出被扰乱了。伶人们一个个停止了动作，惊疑不定地转过头来。

马士英错愕了一下，看清是徐青君之后，他的神色就恢复了平静。"哦，青君兄。"他淡淡地说，扶着桌子，缓缓地站立起来。

马士英是个蓄着山羊胡子的干瘦老头儿，靠六十岁的样子，大脑门、尖下颏，当中一个骨棱棱的鼻子，表情阴沉而冷峻，经

now, after weighing all the possibilties for a revenge, he suddenly thought of Ruan Dacheng. Ruan Dacheng had deep grievances with the East Wooders and the Fushers and had never spoken of them with a kind word. Besides, this man was full of cunning. So he was just the right kind of person to approach for a good idea to redress the great humiliation. Thinking of this, Xu Qingjun immediately ordered the sedan chairmen to change direction and head for Kusifang. To his disappointment, when he arrived at the gate just now, the janitor told him that the master had left for some urgent business, but he heard Ma Shiying, Ruan Dacheng's friend of the same age, had also come and was now waiting in the Flower Hall. "Maybe I can listen to what Ma Shiying has to say first," he thought. So he came in with Ji Cheng.

Xu Qingjun and Ji Cheng arrived at the Flower Hall, but Ma Shiying wasn't there. A servant said, "Mr. Ma went to the Playhouse to watch a rehearsal." Xu Qingjun hurried to the Playhouse with Ji Cheng.

The Playhouse was brightly lit. A group of young girls gathered on the red rug in the middle of the house, some playing music, others acting. The play director Zang Yijia was beating the drum. He was a forty-something, pale but handsome, with no beard on his chin. All his attention was on his job. Whenever he caught a mistake, he squinted one eye miserably and at the same time beat the drum harder as warning.

Xu Qingjun was not interested in the rehearsal. When he caught sight of Ma Shiying sitting behind a rosewood hall table in front, serving himself wine while watching the show, he shouted at him boorishly, "Hey, Elder Yao! I had a very unpleasant experience."

The performance on the red rug was disrupted. The actors stopped one after another and turned their heads in bewilderment.

Ma Shiying looked startled, but soon relaxed after seeing that it was Xu Qingjun. "Hey, Brother Qingjun," he said calmly, and slowly stood up, propping himself against the table.

Ma Shiying, about sixty, was a bony, thin old man with a goatee, a broad forehead, a pointed chin, and a sharp nose, looking gloomy

常紧抿的嘴角儿，有一道刚愎暴戾的皱纹。他是万历四十七年的进士，曾任右佥都御史，巡抚宣府。崇祯五年因私自盗用公库的钱钞，贿赂权贵，被人参劾，得了死罪，全靠阮大铖为他花了重金打通关节，才改为“免死谪戍”。期满后，他就跑到南京来当寓公。马士英同阮大铖本有“同年”之谊，又多亏阮大铖拼力相救，再加上两人都丢了官，同病相怜，所以一拍即合，很快成了死党，一天到晚凑在一块喝酒行乐，咒地怨天。自然，他们暗地里也没有放松向朝中的当权者积极活动，指望有朝一日重新复官，东山再起……

“瑶老，给小弟出个主意，小弟要狠狠地教训复社那班瘟生！”徐青君走到马士英跟前，拱着手又叫。

马士英疑惑地瞅了他一眼，还了一揖，接着又同计成行过礼。他没有说话，朝旁边的一张空着的平头案做了个让座的手势，自己就在原来的位置上坐了下来。

徐青君不由自主地坐到椅子上，计成也随后坐下了。旁边伺候的小仆童立即端上来几样精美小吃，摆上酒盅，又替他们斟酒。

徐青君抓起筷子，随即又把它扔到桌子上。

“瑶老——”他急切地把脸转向马士英。

马士英抬起一只手，做了个“等一等”的手势，然后，用平静的声调对堂下说：“接着演！”

于是中断了的乐曲又重新开始演奏。红氍毹上的旦角也款摆

and cold. The corners of his mouth were often marked by two deep wrinkles. He was awarded a *jinshi* degree in AD 1619, the forty-seventh year of the reign of Emperor Wanli, and had served as a small-time councilor in the Imperial Supervision College and Governor of Xuanhua Prefecture. In AD 1632, the fifth year of the reign of Emperor Chongzhen, he was impeached for bribery and appropriating public funds and subsequently sentenced to death, but thanks to Ruan Dacheng, who pulled strings by bribing important men above, he was pardoned from the death penalty and exiled to a border town instead. When the restriction was lifted, he continued his exiled life in Nanjing. Ma Shiying and Ruan Dacheng were coevals, and because Ruan Dacheng had done his best to save Ma Shiying and the two sympathized with each other for having lost their government positions they hit it off and quickly became good buddies hanging together all day long, drinking and having fun, cursing the earth and blaming the sky. Naturally, both were trying to influence those in power at court, hoping that one day they would be reinstated and rise again ...

Xu Qingjun walked to Ma Shiying, bowed and said, "Elder Yao, would you please teach me how I can get revenge on the nasty Fushers?"

Ma Shiying glanced at him in bewilderment, bowed back and then exchanged salutes with Ji Cheng. Without speaking, he gestured for Mr. Xu to sit at a flat-topped table next to him and he himself sat down in his original seat.

Xu Qingjun submissively sat down and then Ji Cheng too. The little boy servant who had been standing by immediately brought a few exquisite snacks, put two more cups on the table and filled them with wine.

Xu Qingjun took up the chopsticks, but then slammed them on the table.

He turned his face to Ma Shiying eagerly and said, "Elder Yao—"

Ma Shiying raised a hand and made a "hold on" gesture, and then said to the actors below in a calm tone, "Continue!"

So the interrupted music resumed and the female characters went

着腰肢，走着台步，咿咿呀呀地唱起来。马士英这才偏过脸，不慌不忙地问：“唔，青君兄方才是说——”

徐青君眨眨眼睛，对于马士英的傲慢与冷漠颇为不快，但是却不得不放低了声音。

“瑶老，小弟给复社的人欺负了！”他恨恨地说，于是把刚才路上发生的事一五一十说了一遍。不过，他隐瞒了其中两点：一是不说被诈去的一百五十两银子里，有五十两是自己为着炫耀富有，压倒对方，主动加上去的；二是不说侯方域等人已当众宣布，要把这项银子拿去赈济饥民。

马士英一边看演出，一边心不在焉地听着。但是不久他就转过脸来，眼睛也渐渐睁圆了。终于，他把桌子一拍，怒声说：

“岂有此理！堂堂留都之地，岂容他们如此胡闹！”

“小弟倒不是心疼银子！”徐青君愤愤地说，“只是他们欺人太甚！这口气，小弟怎样也咽不下去！”

本来已经恢复排演的那一班伶人，被马士英一声怒喝，吓了一跳，莫名其妙地又停下了。后来弄明白老爷们的火气并不是冲着他们来的，也没有让他们停演的意思，才犹犹疑疑地又接着演下去。不过经这两番干扰，他们一个个都显得心神不安，接二连三地错步、唱走板，弄得臧亦嘉一个劲儿地皱眉头、叹气。

“哼，如此胁迫敲诈，与当街行抢何异！”马士英怒气不息。

“对，对，他们就是当街行抢、抢我的！”徐青君憋着嗓子叫。看见这个冰冷阴沉的老头儿居然动了真怒，他喜出望外，回头同计成交换了一个眼色，然后，把身子倾向马士英，热切地瞅着对方的脸孔，期待他说出不寻常的话来。

back into motion, singing and dancing with graceful steps. Then, Ma Shiying turned his face and asked calmly, "So, you said—"

Xu Qingjun blinked his eyes. He was irritated by Ma Shiying's arrogance and insolence, but had to comply. "Elder Yao, I've been bullied by the Fushers," he said resentfully in a lowered voice. Then, he recounted what had happened on the way just now. However, he concealed two things. He didn't mention that out of the one hundred and fifty taels of silver taken from him, fifty taels were given out of his own volition because he wanted to show off his wealth and crush the pride of the other party, nor did he say that Hou Fangyu and company had announced in public that they would use the money to feed the hungry.

Ma Shiying listened absent-mindedly while watching the performance, but soon he turned his face to Xu Qingjun with widening eyes. Finally, he slapped the table and said indignantly, "It's outrageous! This is the Legacy Capital, not a lawless place!"

"It's not about the money," Xu Qingjun said exasperatedly. "It's just that they went too far in their bullying of me. I just can't swallow it."

The cast of actors who had resumed the rehearsal were taken aback by Ma Shiying's burst of anger and stopped again in shock and puzzlement. When they found that the anger of the two men was not directed at them and that they had no intention to stop them, they hesitatingly resumed the performance. However, since these interruptions disrupted their frame of mind, they kept making mistakes in singing and stage actions so that Zang Yijia kept frowning and sighing.

"Humph, such extortion through intimidation is no different from street robbery!" Ma Shiying's anger didn't subside.

"Right, right! They openly robbed me on the street!" Xu Qingjun shouted at the top of his voice. Seeing that this cold, gloomy old man had real anger, he was overjoyed and exchanged a wink with Ji Cheng. Then, he leaned towards Ma Shiying and anxiously looked at him, expecting him to say something notable.

可是，马士英说了那两句话之后，就靠在椅背上，垂下眼皮，一动不动，也不再说话。

徐青君眼巴巴地等了好一会儿，渐渐有点不耐烦，正想催问。忽然，马士英又开口了。

“嗯，前几年，”他缓缓地说，没有抬起眼睛，“记得有个叫徐怀丹的，作了一篇声讨复社的檄文，其中列举该社十大罪，道是僭拟天王、妄称先圣、煽聚朋党、妒贤树权、招集匪人、伤风败俗、谤讪横议、污坏品行……嗯，还有、还有……”

“还有‘窃位失节’‘招寇致灾’！”计成提醒说。这篇檄文，当时南京城里城外到处张贴，辗转传抄的也不少，颇轰动了一阵子，计成也曾读过，所以记得。

“嗯！”马士英点点头，依旧耷拉着眼皮，“当时读后，我便觉得他言之过甚，并不足信，复社那班士子再不怎样，好歹也是些读书人，这圣人之言、纲常之教是自幼熟习的，其中不少还是官宦子弟，诗礼传家。污秽之行，容或有之，若说全体如此，而且意在谋逆，却令人觉得兹事太奇，难以置信……”

马士英说到这里就顿住了，仿佛在思索。徐青君却听得糊涂起来，连忙说：“啊，瑶老——”

可是马士英立即挥手止住了他。

“即以第一罪而论，所谓‘僭拟天王’，我以为就必无此事！”他断然地说，睁开了眼睛，“徐怀丹檄文列此为首罪，其所据者，乃系张溥表字天如——‘天如’者，‘如天’也，岂非自比天王？其实大谬不然，大谬不然！‘天如’者，不过取广大普遍之义，虽不免乖张狂妄，却未至于自比天王，若‘天如’便是自比天王，那么足下字‘青君’，岂非自比东帝？足下果然肯应承么？可见，

However, Ma Shiying leaned against the back of his chair, shut his eyes and went silent without moving.

Xu Qingjun waited anxiously for a long time and gradually became impatient. Just as he was going to urge his friend to speak, Ma Shiying suddenly spoke again.

"Well, I remember that a few years ago," he said slowly, without raising his eyes, "there was a man named Xu Huaidan who wrote an article to attack the Fushe, citing ten major crimes of the society: usurpation of the power of the heavenly king, stealing the names of the great sages, partisanism, hunger for power, inciting rebellion, moral depravity, slander, and bad conduct ... Well, there's, there's also ..."

"There's also 'loss of virtue' and 'incurring national crisis'," Ji Cheng said. This article was posted everywhere in and outside Nanjing at that time, and a lot of copies were circulated. It caused quite a stir. Ji Cheng had also read it, so he remembered it.

"Humph!" Ma Shiying nodded his head, his upper eyelids still drooping. "At that time, I had doubts, for, after all, the Fushers are scholars well versed in the works of the sages and know the Confucian code of conduct, many of them born of families of high-ranking officials with a polite tradition. Occasionally, there might be bad deeds, but if you say everyone is so bad and so treacherous it's hard to believe ..." he said.

Then he paused, lost in thought. Xu Qingjun became confused as he listened. He said worriedly, "Hey, Elder Yao—"

But Ma Shiying immediately stopped him with a hand wave.

"For example, the so-called 'usurpation' in the first crime I think doesn't apply," he said unequivocally, opening his eyes. "Xu Huaidan cited it as the first crime. The basis is Zhang Pu's pen name Tianru, 'like heaven,' which is taken to mean he was comparing himself to the heavenly king. That's a great fallacy. 'Tianru' simply means big and vast. Although there's arrogance in it, it's not comparing himself to the heavenly king. If *tianru* were a comparison to the heavenly king, then wouldn't your name *qingjun*, the Green Prince, a comparison to Emperor of the East? Would you accept that accusation? Obviously,

徐怀丹此条，显属捕风捉影、罗织构陷！所列首罪即已如此，其余亦不问可知。所以，该檄文纯属一派胡言，毫无道理，全不足信！”

马士英斩钉截铁地连续下了这三个四字评语之后，就闭紧嘴巴，不开腔了。

徐青君同计成你看看我，我看看你，都被马士英这一席话弄懵了。他们真不明白，马士英方才明明是痛骂复社“无异当街行抢”，何以说着说着，倒全力替复社打抱不平起来？

计成搔搔脑袋，试探地说：“瑶老，依小弟之见，徐怀丹檄文自有不尽翔实之处，不过似乎也并非全无可采……”

“不！”马士英的口气异常坚决，大有不容置辩之概，“大丈夫立身行事，须出以公心。似这等心怀私怨，深文周纳，指鹿为马，欲图一逞，乃是狗彘之行，绝无半点可取！”

徐青君目瞪口呆。他的脸色渐渐变得难看起来，终于悻悻然问：“照瑶老这等说，复社那班人倒当真是正人君子了？”

马士英摇摇头：“这又不然。适才听青君兄说，他们聚众勒索，当街行抢，实在已经形同匪类，哪里有半点君子、正人气味？此事而可为，又何事而不可为！说他们僭拟天王、妄称先圣、煽聚朋党、妒贤树权等等，只怕也是不假。”

他忽然又指斥起复社来，徐青君和计成却愈加摸不着头脑。

可是马士英根本没有注意他们的迷惑表情。“复社并未骂我，我与他们并无旧怨，”他淡淡地说，顿了一下，“我说他们‘僭拟天王’，所据也并非‘天如’二字，乃是依据其本心。他们既

it's a trumped-up charge by Xu Huaidan that has no basis at all. The first crime being thus trumped up, there's no need to investigate into the rest. Therefore, that article is pure nonsense, not to be taken seriously."

After Ma Shiying passed that verdict on the article, he shut his mouth and became silent.

Xu Qingjun and Ji Cheng looked at each other, both bewildered by Ma Shiying's words. They really didn't understand why Ma Shiying suddenly spoke for the Fushers after accusing them of street robbery.

Ji Cheng scratched his head and said probingly, "Elder Yao, in my humble opinion, Xu Huaidan's article isn't well substantiated, but it doesn't seem to be complete nonsense ..."

"Yes, it is!" Ma Shiying said, his tone determined, with no room for dispute. "An honorable man does everything in the name of justice. To trump up charges based on personal grievances, like calling a deer a horse, serves no other purpose than venting one's anger. It's the doing of pigs not to be copied."

Xu Qingjun was dumbfounded. His face gradually became ashen, and finally he asked feebly, "Then, in your opinion, the Fushers are decent men?"

Ma Shiying shook his head and said, "No. That isn't true either. You just said that they robbed in the street as a mob. Then they're really like bandits. What decency is there in what they did? If that could be done what else shouldn't be done? Therefore, it's not wrong to accuse them of 'usurpation of the power of the heavenly king, stealing the names of the great sages, partisanism, hunger for power ...'"

He suddenly criticized the Fushe again. Xu Qingjun and Ji Cheng became even more confused.

Yet he didn't notice their expression at all. "The Fushe has never attacked me and I have no old grudges with them," he said calmly with a pause. "I said that they're usurping the powers of the heavenly king not on the basis of the name *tianru* but on the basis of the nature

敢于当街行抢，可见已具贼性。但凡一个人有了贼心，那么一切贼言贼行，皆可由此发生，故此僭拟天王、妄称先圣、煽聚朋党等等，也就不足为奇了。先朝阳明先生说：‘诛心中贼。’便是此意！”

直到这会儿，计成才多少有点听明白了。他不禁微笑起来：“这马老儿原来刚愎自负得紧，他刚才极力贬斥徐怀丹的檄文，原来是为着显示自己的公正与高明哩！”

徐青君显然还不明白。他不放心地追问：“这么说，复社到底并非君子了？”

马士英冷冷地瞧了他一眼，“当然不是君子！”他说。仿佛因为徐青君仍未领会他的谈话要旨，感到颇不耐烦，他提高了声音：“他们是君子之贼，嗯，君子之贼！”

徐青君这一下懂了。他松了一口气，顿时高兴起来，连连点着头，拿起酒杯：“对、对，君子之贼，君子之贼！哈哈，瑶老，不瞒您说，刚才小弟听您一路说下来，心里还真犯疑，怎么瑶老维护起复社那帮小子来了？没想到最后却藏着这么一篇高论！”

计成也拿起酒杯：“瑶老方才力斥徐怀丹之非，乃是辨本追源，区分公私邪正。这叫作不因持论偶同而恕其心，只此一点，旁人便万万不能及！”

听了这两个人的恭维话，马士英却没有任何高兴的表示。大约他认为自己所说的，乃是导人向善的普通正理；对于普通的道理，是无须加以恭维的。

“瑶老，青君兄今日受此凌辱，你看这事该怎么办？”大家各自饮过一杯酒之后，计成这样问。

of their hearts. Since they dared to rob in the street in broad daylight, it can be seen that they have thieving hearts. Once a man has a thieving heart, then all treacherous words and deeds will follow. So it's not surprising to find they act like kings, pretend to be sages, and incite rebellion. As the late Mr. Wang Yangming who lived in the time of the previous emperor once put it, 'It's the thief in the heart that is to be killed.'"

It was not until now that Ji Cheng started to understand a little. He smiled, thinking to himself, "What a self-important man Mr. Ma is! It turns out that all his criticism of Mr. Xu Huaidan's article serves to prove what fair judgement he has."

Xu Qingjun obviously was still puzzled. He asked probingly, "So, those Fusher chaps are not decent men after all?"

Ma Shiying glanced at him coldly. "Of course they are not," he said, and raised his voice, displeased that Xu Qingjun still hadn't grasped his point, "They're gentlemen thieves, right, gentlemen thieves."

Xu Qingjun suddenly understood. He breathed a sigh of relief and brightened up. Nodding his head repeatedly, he took up the drinking vessel, "Yeah, yeah, gentlemen thieves, gentlemen thieves! Haha, Elder Yao, to be honest with you, just now as I listened to you, I was thinking, 'Why does Elder Yao defend the bad boys of the Fushe?' To my surprise, you have such a powerful argument in the end."

Ji Cheng took up his wine cup and said, "By pointing out Xu Huaidan's faults, Elder Yao means to trace things to the origin and distinguish between good and evil and between interpersonal animosity and public interest. One should distinguish between accepting a point made and accepting the making of a point. No one can compare with Elder Yao in this regard."

Ma Shiying didn't respond to the compliments, probably because he thought what he had said was no more than plain truth, for which no compliment was necessary.

"Elder Yao, what do you think can avenge the humiliation?" Ji Cheng asked after everyone finished a cup of wine.

马士英的目光，这时已经回到了堂下的演出上。他没有立即开口。直到计成疑心他没听见，打算重复一遍时，马士英才反问：“青君兄有何打算？”

“打算么……”徐青君转了一下眼珠子，“哼，小弟、小弟要诛他这心中之贼！”

“噢？”马士英偏过脸来，瞅着徐青君，“倒要领教！”

“这个，这个……”徐青君顿时结巴起来。他刚才只是灵机一动，顺着马士英的话茬儿混说，其实对那一句话的含义不甚了了。他着忙起来，一边支吾着，一边暗中去扯计成的袖子。

计成咳嗽一声，朝马士英拱着手说：“瑶老，诛心中贼，乃是正人心、淳风俗之大计，非一时一日所能奏效。适才青君兄说这话的意思，也是就长远之计而言。至于目前嘛，但能对复社之徒小施惩戒，以雪心头之愤，也就足矣。此事还望瑶老指教哩！”

徐青君连忙说：“正是正是，此等不逞之徒，非得痛加惩戒不可！”

马士英长长地“哦”了一声，似乎颇为失望。他淡淡地说：“惩戒之道，却非我所长。待会儿圆老回来，二位自去请教于他好了！”

## 书房奥妙

马士英的话音刚落，忽然大堂门口有人高声大叫起来：

“哎，不对，不对，不是这样！”

大家一怔，回头望去，原来阮大铖不迟不早，恰巧在这当儿回来了。

阮大铖是个中等身材的胖子，今年也有五十五六岁了，扫帚眉、圆鼻头、大嘴巴，一双乌溜溜的眼睛挺有神采，下巴上挂着

Ma Shiying's gaze had now returned to the performance space below. He didn't answer immediately. When Ji Cheng was going to repeat it in case he hadn't heard it, Ma Shiying asked back, "Brother Qingjun, what do you plan to do?"

"I'm going to—" Xu Qingjun said, rolling his eyes. "Huh, I, I want to kill the thief in his heart."

"Oh?" Ma Shiying turned his face to look at Xu Qingjun, "Let me hear it."

"That, that—" Xu Qingjun suddenly stammered. He said it on the spur of the moment following Ma Shiying's words. In fact, he didn't have much clue about what was meant by 'to kill the thief in the heart'. So he helplessly pulled Ji Cheng's sleeve as he mumbled a reply.

Ji Cheng coughed, bowed at Ma Shiying, and said, "Elder Yao, to kill the thief in the heart is a long-term strategy for the rectification of the human heart and purification of social atmosphere, not a method that produces immediate effect. What Brother Qingjun said refers to the long-term strategy. The immediate concern is how to avenge the humiliation and punish the Fushe boys so that they would not do anything like it again. Please educate us on what to do!"

Xu Qingjun echoed, "Precisely, precisely. They must be punished for what they did!"

Ma Shiying let out a long "ehhh" sound, apparently disappointed. "I'm not good at punishing people. Elder Yuan will be back soon and you can ask him for advice," he drawled out.

## A Private Conversation in the Study

As soon as Ma Shiying's voice fell silent, someone yelled at the entrance of the lobby:

"Hey, no, no, not so!"

Everyone gave a start and looked back. It was Ruan Dacheng coming back just in time.

He was a fat man of medium build, fifty five or six years old, with a pair of broom-like eyebrows, a round nose, a big mouth, a

那部有名的大胡子。他虽然腆着一个大肚子，走起路来却像一阵风。现在他急步地朝大堂中央走来，脸上显出气急败坏的样子。

徐青君和计成站起身，打算同他招呼。可是阮大铖没有瞧见。他走到那群正在演戏的伶人跟前，就站住了。

“咄！停下，停下！”他大声叫。

伶人们立即顺从地停下了。

“你们——”阮大铖的眼睛发怒地圆睁着，胡子一翘一翘地在喘气，“你们这算是演戏？啊！你们这是成心糟蹋我的戏本！”他跺着脚嚷。

伶人们惶恐地动弹了一下身子，一个个都自知有罪地低下头去，不敢接触他霍霍的目光。

“你——”阮大铖指着那个唱小旦的女孩儿说，“‘日正长时春梦短，燕交飞处柳烟低’，这两句宾白你是怎么念的？”随即他自己憋着嗓子，模仿那小旦的声调念了一遍，故意把其中的缺点加以夸张、突出，使之听起来显得异常古怪刺耳。那小旦顿时面红耳赤，战战兢兢地跪下去。

徐青君和计成都撑不住，笑了起来。

阮大铖却绷着脸，“还有你！”他指着另一个唱旦角的少女，“‘曳金铃，绣幕风儿紧，看花影，在纱窗映’这几句，唱得就像猫儿叫！啊——”说着，他也用稀奇古怪的调门儿学她唱了一遍。那旦角面色煞白，极力忍着涌到眼眶来的泪水，也双膝跪倒在地上。

这时候臧亦嘉放下鼓板，走过来拱着手说：“东翁……”

阮大铖猛地回过头：“啊，原来你还在这儿！我只当你也学苏昆生的样，跟东林、复社跑了呢！原来你没有跑，很好很好！那么请问，这个班子你是怎么带的？啊！”

阮大铖家的这个戏班子，原先是由一个名叫苏昆生的老头儿

pair of dark, bright eyes, and a signature big beard hanging on his chin. Although he had a big belly, he walked like a gust of wind. Now he was walking hurriedly towards the middle of the hall with an exasperated expression on his face.

Xu Qingjun and Ji Cheng stood up to greet him. But Ruan Dacheng took no notice of them. He walked over to the actors at work and stopped.

"Duh! Stop, stop!" he yelled.

The actors stopped submissively.

"You—" said Ruan Dacheng out of breath, his eyes bulging in anger, his beard curled up. He stomped his feet and yelled, "Do you call this a performance? Aww! You're ruining my play!"

The actors shuddered and bowed their heads guiltily, not daring to look him in the eye.

"You—" Ruan Dacheng pointed to the girl who played *xiaodan*, a young female role. " 'Days are long and dreams are short. Swallows are high and willows are low.' How did you speak these two lines?" Then, he imitated the *xiaodan's* singing in an exaggerated voice. The actor immediately blushed and fearfully knelt down.

Xu Qingjun and Ji Cheng burst into laughter.

"And you!" he pointed to another *xiaodan* girl and said with a sullen face, "'Golden bell flowers sway in the wind, casting their shadows on the silk screen' sounds like a cat meowing. Aww—" Then he sarcastically imitated her singing. The *xiaodan* actor's face turned pale, and, holding the tears that came to her eyes, she also fell on her knees.

At this moment Zang Yijia put down the drum, walked over, bowed, and said, "My lord, ..."

Ruan Dacheng turned around abruptly, "Ah, so you're still here! I thought you'd run away with the East Wooders and the Fushers, following the example of Su Kunsheng. You have not. Excellent! Then, let me ask you: how did you train these actors? How?"

This opera team of Ruan Dacheng's had been originally coached by an old man named Su Kunsheng, who was a veteran actor and a

调教的。苏昆生是个老戏行，教戏很有一套，阮大铖对他好生优礼。谁知到了崇祯十一年，复社诸生发表《留都防乱公揭》，苏昆生读后，大受震动，当即提出辞职。阮大铖千方百计挽留不住，才改聘臧亦嘉来当教习。这件事，阮大铖一直引为平生恨事，轻易不愿提起。今天他当着许多人的面突然又说起来，臧亦嘉就明白，主人实在是气愤到了极处，才这样急不择言。

“说啊，这个班子你是怎么带的？”阮大铖又大声质问。

臧亦嘉的喉头动了几下，张了张嘴，却没有说出话来。他心里感到很为难：今天这出《燕子笺》演得十分糟糕，这点他当然知道。但是这不能全怪这群小孩子，甚至也不能全怪自己指导不力——座上的几位客人，根本不是在看戏，他们高谈阔论，大嚷大叫，演员和乐工的心思全给扰乱了，就是自己，也集中不起精神来。加上又是刚刚开排的戏，唱、念、做、打全都不熟，结果就弄得一团糟。然而，臧亦嘉十分明白，在这种场合下是不能申辩的，指摘客人的不是，尤其绝对不行。他犹疑了一下，只好拱着手说：

“东翁责备的是，门下管教不严，有辱东翁委托之殷，今后定当改过，尚祈恕罪！”

阮大铖目不转睛地瞪着臧亦嘉。他的嘴巴还在翕张着，可是渐渐地，表情起了变化，绷得很紧的脸开始松弛，凶猛的目光变得阴沉起来。一种心有未甘，但又无可奈何的神情从他的脸上呈现出来。他向四面环顾一下，忽然转过身，朝马士英走去。

“啊哈，瑶老，你来了！”他拱着手说，又轻快地转向徐青君和计成，“青君兄，无否兄，你们也来了！是同瑶老一块来的，

good coach too. Ruan Dacheng had been very good to him. However, in AD 1638, the eleventh year of the reign of Emperor Chongzhen, the Fushe scholars published the joint declaration "Public Denunciation of a Treasonist in the Legacy Capital". Deeply shaken after reading it, Su Kunsheng immediately resigned. Ruan Dacheng did everything possible to retain him, but without success, so he hired Zang Yijia instead. This was a pain of his life, something he would avoid mentioning. Zang Yijia understood that if not for the great anger, Ruan Dacheng would not have mentioned it in front of so many people today.

"Tell me, how did you lead this team?" Ruan Dacheng said aggressively.

Zang Yijia's larynx moved and his mouth opened, but he didn't utter a word. He was in a predicament. Of course he knew today's performance of *Letter from Swallow* had been a disaster, but the kids were not fully responsible, or even he himself was not fully responsible as stage director. The few guests in the audience seats were not watching the show at all. They talked and yelled, and the minds of the actors and musicians were all disturbed. Even he himself couldn't concentrate. In addition, it was a new play that required more training in singing, speaking the lines, making postures, and theatrical combat. As a result, it was a total mess. However, Zang Yijia fully understood that in this kind of situation he shouldn't defend himself and that it was not appropriate to blame it on the guests either. After hesitating for a moment, he bowed and said:

"I'm truly sorry for letting you down. I've been too lenient to the cast and crew. Pray forgive me!"

Ruan Dacheng stared at Zang Yijia without moving his eyes. His mouth was still open, but gradually, his expression changed, his tightened face began to relax, and his ferocious eyes darkened. An expression of resentment and helplessness appeared on his face. He looked around, then suddenly turned and walked towards Ma Shiying.

"Hah, Elder Yao, you're here!" he bowed and said. Then he briskly turned to Xu Qingjun and Ji Cheng and said, "Brother Qingjun, Brother Wufou, you're here too! Did you come with Elder Yao, or did

还是你们先到？”

“是瑶老先到，我们随后才来。”计成回着礼说。

“啊，好、好！”阮大铖点着头，显得很高兴的样子，“好、好！”他反复地说，重新转向臧亦嘉：

“哎，老臧，你可别多心！你教导有方，尽职尽责，我平日都是深知的！只是刚才，刚才——哎，不说它了。总之你我莫逆之交，纵有言语冲撞了你，也请休怪！今儿你们辛苦了半天，想都困乏了，所以唱着唱着就懈怠起来也未可知。今儿就到此为止，你带她们下去好好歇息。回头我叫赵管家称二十四两银子过去，明儿再放一天假，让大伙儿透透气，乐一乐。你臧老爸也歇一歇，来陪我喝酒！”

臧亦嘉恭恭敬敬地答应着，又向客人们一一行礼告辞，领着女孩儿们下去了。

“啊，圆老！几天不见，原来你又有新作！我们瞧了半天，只觉得好，却不曾问得是何名目，倒要请教！”徐青君笑嘻嘻地恭维说。

阮大铖脸一红，一本正经地说：“哦，这个戏的名字叫《燕子笺》——青君兄，你这话可是取笑小弟了。刚才这样子，你还夸演得好？错位、走板不算，就拿刚才演到的这出‘闺痊’来说，一开头就全不对劲儿！那梅香一出场，开口念一段宾白，‘日正长时春梦短，燕交飞处柳烟低’——明明是一派大清晨晓日初升的景象嘛。那梅香是站在闺楼上，本该一边念白，右手撩开帘子，左手这么轻轻一指，一个眼色儿，嘴角儿这么微微一笑：哟，太阳出来了！”阮大铖一边说，一边学着小姑娘的姿态，扭扭捏捏地扮演着，居然惟妙惟肖。“可是方才那唱小旦的，偏生把下颏儿仰得老高，那不成了日上三竿了么？刚才我骂她，也是这个缘故！唉，青君兄，亏你还说好，羞煞我阮胡子！”他说罢，把脑袋摇得像个拨浪鼓似的。

you come first?"

"Elder Yao came first and we came later," Ji Cheng said, saluting back.

"Oh, nice, nice!" Ruan Dacheng nodded, looking very happy. "Nice, nice!" he repeated. Then he turned back to Zang Yijia:

"Hey, Old Zang, don't worry about it. I know you're a good coach. It's just, just now—well, let's forget about it. We're good friends. Excuse me if I've offended you just now. You must've been tired after working for such a long time today. A slip or two is understandable. Let's call it a day! You and the girls need a rest. I'll ask Mr. Zhao the housekeeper to get you twenty-four taels of silver shortly. Tomorrow, the girls will have a day off to go out and have fun, and you can stay in the house and drink with me."

Zang Yijia said aye respectfully, bade farewell to the guests, and exited with the girls.

"Ah, Elder Yuan! It's just a few days since my last visit, and you've written a new play! We watched it for a long time and loved it, but what is it called?" Xu Qingjun smiled and said in compliment.

Ruan Dacheng blushed and said in a serious tone, "Oh, the play is called *Letter from Swallow*. You're making fun of me, Brother Qingjun. You say it's good after seeing it like that. Wrong positions, singing out of tune—take the last act 'Healed in the Boudoir' for example—everything went wrong. When Mei Xiang enters, she says, 'Days are long and dreams are short. Swallows are high and willows are low.' It's the scene of sunrise in the early morning, Mei Xiang standing in the boudoir opens the curtain with the right hand and points out of the window with the left hand as she speaks the lines with a bright look in the eye and a soft smile in the corner of her mouth. Then, she says, 'Lo and behold, here comes the sun!'" As Ruan Dacheng spoke, he vividly imitated the posture of a shy, young girl. "But the young girl just now raised her chin too high, as if it were the midday sun. That's why I reprimanded her. So, Brother Qingjun, aren't you shaming me by saying it's good?" Having said that, he shook his head like a rattle drum.

计成忍住笑，说：“那小旦演得果然不到火候。不过我们只觉得戏文好、曲词美，倒把那做工不足遮掩过了。”其实，计成也同徐青君一样，刚才根本没有留心看戏。

阮大铖这一下却高兴起来。他眉开眼笑地说：“无否兄，你这话可是搔着我老阮的痒处了。不瞒列位说，这《燕子笺》，乃是我平生第一部得意之作。虽不敢自夸能追步汤若士的《玉茗堂四梦》，但同什么《贞文记》《绿牡丹》之类相比，自问还高一筹！”

“圆老，先别顾谈戏了。青君兄还有事要同你商量呢！”马士英站在一旁，看见阮大铖一谈起戏来就像着了魔似的，手舞足蹈，心中颇不耐烦，就截住他说。

阮大铖“哦”了一声，询问地望着徐青君。

徐青君被提醒，脸色顿时沮丧下来。于是，他把被复社诸生欺凌的事，又向阮大铖说了一遍。

阮大铖哼哼哈哈地听完之后，仰起脸，朝大堂楹柱上挂着的一盏八角宫灯愣了会儿神，随即回过头来说：“这里不是谈话之所，且到弟的书房里去，坐下细说如何？”

大家都没有异议，于是由小厮提灯引路，一同离开咏怀堂，沿着曲折的回廊走去。

阮大铖的书房设在一个独立的小小庭院里，是一明一暗的两间平房，外面照例是花草木石，室内却布置得出奇的简朴。特别是里面一间，只有数架图书，一张长榻，几把椅子；书案上除了笔墨纸砚之外，并无任何珍奇玩好之类的摆设。墙壁上也只是正中一面挂了一幅《百子山樵笠屐图》，画中的阮大铖头戴斗笠，脚蹬木屐，一副世外闲人的神气。只是两旁的对联却与这画并不

Ji Cheng held back his laughter and said, "That young girl indeed didn't perform well. We were enjoying the lines and the lyrics and didn't pay attention to the defects in the performance." In fact, just like Xu Qingjun, Ji Cheng hadn't paid attention to the play at all.

Ruan Dacheng was evidently flattered. He beamed with a smile and said, "Brother Wufou, you did scratch the spot. Truth be told, I think *Letter from Swallow* is my best work so far. Although I dare not claim it's anything comparable to Tang Ruoshi's *The Four Dreams of the White Camellia Hall*, compared with *Story of a Chaste and Talented Lady* or *The Green Peony*, it's far better."

"Elder Yuan, don't just talk about plays. Brother Qingjun has something to discuss with you," interrupted Ma Shiying, who was standing by and grew impatient with Ruan Dacheng's self-indulgent, hedonistic ramble.

Ruan Dacheng said "oh" and looked at Xu Qingjun inquiringly.

Xu Qingjun's expression changed upon Mr. Ma's suggestion. He told Ruan Dacheng how he had been bullied by the Fushe scholars.

Ruan Dacheng listened with "uh", "mhm", and then raised his face and stared at the octagonal palace lantern hanging on the pillar of the lobby for a moment. Finally, he turned and said, "This isn't the place to talk. Let's go to my study, sit down and talk about it."

No one objected to the idea, so led by a young servant with a lantern, they left the Playhouse and walked through the winding corridor toward the study.

Ruan Dacheng's study was in a small, independent courtyard. It was a two-room bungalow with one door. The outside was decorated with flowers, plants, trees, and stones like the other places, but the interior was surprisingly simple and crude, particularly in the inner room, which had only a few books, a couch, and some chairs, and no gadgets of interest on the desk except for brush pens, ink, paper, and an inkstone. On the back wall hung a picture captioned "Portrait of Baizi Mountain Woodcutter in Straw Hat and Clogs." In the painting, Ruan Dacheng wore a straw hat on his head and wooden-soled shoes on his feet in the image of a recluse. However, the

相称。那联语是：

有官万事足

无子一身轻

下署：百子山樵并书崇祯十年元月吉日

徐青君是头一次走进阮大铖的书房。他满心以为石巢园到处都是珠帘绣幌，陈设精奇，这书房想必也是极其华美讲究。万没料到竟是如此简朴，甚至寒碜，脸上不禁露出惊讶的神色。

阮大铖一直在留意他的反应，这时看见不出自己的所料，就得意地微微一笑。等大家坐定，仆人重新奉上茶来之后，阮大铖这才不慌不忙地开口说：

“青君兄想必以我这书室简陋过甚为怪了？这里头却有一个道理——前几年，我被复社那伙人逼逐，只有躲到牛首山祖堂寺去住。当时所居僧房，十分简陋，也只这么一所斗室，而且只有两椅一桌，连门也不敢多出。不过说来也怪，偏是这样的陋室中，我反而万虑俱洗，胸无杂念。每夕三更之后，灯前独坐，便飘飘然神游于别样境界，握笔展纸之际，竟是文思喷涌，如有神助，数月之内，一口气写出了《桃花笑》《井中盟》《双金榜》，你道奇也不奇？”

计成“啊”了一声，脱口说道：“莫非这书房竟是依照祖堂寺的模样布置的？”

阮大铖点点头：“不错。由此我悟出一个道理，以往我之所以文思不振，皆因眼前的锦绣珠翠太盛，窒碍了心头空灵之气。故此回来后，我便命人把一应多余陈设尽行撤去，单留下这几样

couplet on the two sides were not in agreement with the subject of the painting. It read:

WITH HIGH OFFICE EVERYTHING COMES
WITHOUT CHILDREN THERE IS NO BURDEN

Signed and dated: *Baizi Mountain Woodcutter, on a lucky day in the first month in the tenth year of the reign of Emperor Chongzhen [AD 1637]*

It was the first time for Xu Qingjun to visit Ruan Dacheng's study. Since Stone Nest Garden was full of beaded curtains, embroidered draperies and exquisite furnishings, he had been prepared to be awed by the grandeur of the study as well. Yet after entering it, he was surprised by its simplicity bordering on sheer starkness.

Seeing his reaction was just as expected, Ruan Dacheng, who had been watching his expression, smiled contentedly. After everyone was seated and tea was served, Ruan Dacheng said calmly:

"Brother Qingjun, are you wondering why my study is so simple and crude? Here's why: a few years ago, I was persecuted by the Fushers and hid in the Zutang Temple in Cow Head Mountain. I stayed in a small, crude monk's room with two chairs and a table, not daring to go out. But strangely, in such a shabby room, I was cleansed of all my worries and there was nothing on my mind. Every night after the third watch, I sat in front of the lamp and let my mind wander in a different world and inspiration came pouring in as I held the brush pen. So I spread the paper sheets on the desk, and as if assisted by a divine spirit, I wrote three plays in one breath in a matter of months: *Smile like a Peach Flower*, *Oath in the Water Well*, and *Double Bingo*. Don't you think it's a miracle?"

Ji Cheng gave an "ah" and blurted out, "So this study of yours is arranged after the room in the Zutang Temple?"

Ruan Dacheng nodded, "Right. From that experience, I realized that my prior lack of inspiration was because the excessive presence of pearls and embroideries had been a hindrance to the release of my free spirit. So after coming home, I ordered my servants to remove all

东西。尔后，哈哈，果然就大不相同！便是这部《燕子笺》，也只费了两个月的工夫，便写出来了。”

徐青君听得张大了嘴巴，连正题都忘记了。他怎么也想象不到，这书房的布置原来有如此奥妙。

马士英冷笑一声，说：“那么圆老倒是该多谢复社才是了！”

阮大铖拍着又肥又圆的膝盖，一本正经地点着头说：“正是正是，他们虽然对我不够客气，可是我现在却不恼他们。要没有他们那一次捣乱，我这四五本传奇，只怕真还未必写得出。说起来，他们可算是我咏怀堂的功臣哩！”

徐青君错愕了一下，随即放心地微笑起来。他想起了方才同马士英谈话的时候，开始也是这样的。“这些老奸巨猾的老家伙，总爱故弄玄虚！”他想，于是用了狡黠的口气问：“圆老，你当真不恨复社？你？”

“当真不恨，当真不恨！青君兄，我劝你也别恨。他们这些人性子是激烈了点，可也不见得便是歹人。譬如他们刚才敲了你一百五十两银子，无非见你有的是钱，同你开个小小的玩笑，其实也不是装进自己的腰包。他们不是转眼就拿去赈济饥民了么！”

“啊，你，你怎么都知道？”

“我什么都知道，什么都知道。我刚才出门，满街的人都在说这件事。赈是他们放的，银子却是你徐二公子的，这谁都知道。没有你徐二公子，他们想放赈也放不成。所以真正做善事的其实是你！他们本想敲诈你，却反而促成了你这桩善举。这也正像我写传奇一样，你又何必恼他！”

the unnecessary furnishings, leaving only these few things. Since then, haha, things have been different. For example, *Letter from Swallow* was written in only two months."

Xu Qingjun listened with a gaping mouth and even forgot the purpose of his visit, utterly fascinated by the story behind the design of the study.

Ma Shiying sneered and said, "Then, you should thank the Fushe, Elder Yuan."

Ruan Dacheng nodded and said in all seriousness as he patted his fat, round knees, "Precisely, precisely. Although they haven't been kind to me, I don't hate them now. If not for the trouble they've created for me, I'm afraid I wouldn't have written the five plays. They've rendered me a great service, so to speak."

Xu Qingjun was jolted by that remark, but soon calmed down and smiled. He remembered his previous conversation with Ma Shiying had also been like that. "These wily old foxes always like making things appear sophisticated and mysterious!" he thought. Then, he asked in a cunning tone, "Elder Yuan, do you really bear no grudge against the Fushe? No grudge at all?"

"I bear no grudge against them, really. Brother Qingjun, I hope you don't hate them either. These men have hot tempers, but that doesn't necessarily mean they're bad people. For example, they've extorted a hundred and fifty taels of silver from you a moment ago simply because they knew you were rich and played a small hoax on you. They were not going to load it into their own pockets. Didn't they use the money to feed the hungry shortly afterwards?"

"Ahh, how do you know?"

"I know everything, everything. I went out just now and everybody on the street was talking about it. They fed the hungry with your money. Everybody knows it. If not for you, they wouldn't be able to perform the act of charity. Therefore, you were the real almsgiver. They intended to extort money from you, but accidentally gave you an opportunity to do a great deed. This is similar to their influence on my play writing. Please pardon them."

徐青君“哼”了一声。“圆老，你这不是在打哈哈吧？”他斜瞅着阮大铖问。

“打哈哈？”阮大铖故作惊讶地说，“不，绝对不是！为什么要打哈哈？我顶顶讨厌打哈哈了！”

徐青君这才真正愣住了。他大惑不解地瞧瞧阮大铖，又瞧瞧马士英。后者此刻端坐在椅子上，默默地捋着山羊胡子，正在闭目养神，摆出一副绝不介入的神气。

“可是我非报此仇不可！”徐青君突然跳起来高叫。

“啊，青君兄一定要报此仇？”

“当然要报！”徐青君那苍白的胖脸竟也被愤怒逼出两片潮红来，他吵架似的说，“我是小人量窄！可没有你圆老的君子大度！也不像你圆老这样、这样——”他噎住了，一下子找不到合适的词句，急得眼珠子乱转，像是要抓住能帮助他说下去的倚仗似的。忽然，他的眼光落在正墙的对联上：

“这样，这样‘有官万事足’！”

阮大铖的脸刷地红了，就像被人无意中戳破了心事似的。可是只一忽儿，他就恢复了常态：“哎，青君兄一定要报仇？这很好，很好！我不反对，更不阻拦，令兄魏国公是留都守备大人，有他，青君兄这仇一定是报得成的！”

徐青君冷笑一声：“这个么，倒不劳圆老指教，小弟自有计较——好，就此告辞！”

徐青君说着，朝马士英和阮大铖拱一拱手，然后把袖子一拂，气哼哼地领着计成往外就走。

“哎呀，青君兄这就要走？不再坐会儿，喝杯酒再去？那，既然如此，就不敢强留了。哎，这边走，这边……”阮大铖唠唠叨叨地说着，一路送了出去。

Xu Qingjun snorted. "Elder Yuan, are you making fun of me?" he asked, looking obliquely at Ruan Dacheng.

"Making fun of you?" Ruan Dacheng said affectedly, "No, absolutely not! Why should I make fun of you? I hate making fun of others."

Now, Xu Qingjun was really confused. He looked at Ruan Dacheng quizzically and then Ma Shiying. The latter was sitting squarely in the chair, quietly stroking his goatee, his eyes closed in repose, with an air of nonchalance.

"But I must avenge myself!" Xu Qingjun suddenly jumped up and shouted.

"Brother Qingjun, are you sure you want to avenge yourself?"

"Yes, of course!" Xu Qingjun's pale, round cheeks flushed. He said as if in a quarrel, "I'm a little man with a narrow mind. I don't have your kind of magnanimity. I'm not like you—" he choked as he spoke, unable to find an appropriate word, his eyes searching here and there as if he were looking for a support. Suddenly, his eyes fell on the couplet of the main wall.

"With your high office, everything comes."

Ruan Dacheng's face blushed as if a sore spot had been touched, but he instantly calmed down and said, "Brother Qingjun, do you really want a revenge? If yes, it's very good. Personally, I won't object nor will I dissuade you from doing so. Your brother Duke of Wei is the defense minister of the Legacy Capital. With his help, revenge is a small matter."

Xu Qingjun sneered and said to the two men, with a clasped-hands salute, "That doesn't have to be taught. Of course, I know it. Well, goodbye!"

Then he flicked his sleeve and walked outward with Ji Cheng, full of anger in his chest.

"Brother Qingjun, are you leaving now? Why don't you stay longer and have a cup of wine? Well, if you insist, I dare not make you stay. This way please, this way ..." Ruan Dacheng mumbled as he saw the guest off.

过了片刻，阮大铖擦着汗，重新走了回来。

“哎，可把这个花花太岁打发走了！”他说，一屁股坐到椅子上。

“嗯，你就真的一个主意都不肯替他出？”马士英问。

“咦！”阮大铖抬起头，一拍膝盖，“我怎能给他出主意？我现在讨好复社还怕来不及，若是给他出主意，万一传出去，那班书呆子还放得过我？现在我就希望这花花太岁出去嚷嚷，说我拒绝了他，这才好哩！”

马士英摇摇头：“他虽是个浮薄纨绔，到底同我们结交了一场。你这样半句好话不说，就轰跑了他，也忒薄情了些。”

阮大铖满不在乎地说：“你只管放心！我包管不出三天，他还得乖乖儿到石巢园来找我们。我瞅准了，他要玩得痛快，他离不了我们！”

“可是他心里必定把我们看作无义小人了！”马士英皱着眉毛。

阮大铖“哼”了一声，生气地嚷：“由他去，由他去！小人就小人！都到这种地步了，再硬充什么王八伪君子，我阮大铖就只有一辈子蹲在南京城里当寓公！”

马士英冷冷地说：“我担心你到底是水中捞月一场空——复社那伙人，你以为他们当真会放过你？”

阮大铖怔了一下，随即摇着头，用恶毒、得意的声调说：“这你就不知道了！刚才，你知道我去做什么？去会一个人。你猜得出这人是谁么？哈哈，不是别个，乃是堂堂东林巨魁、君子们的头儿——钱牧斋的堂兄弟钱养先！”

阮大铖说完这句话，故意停了一下。看见马士英不由自主地收起不以为然的表情，正留神地瞅着自己，阮大铖更加得意：“钱

After a while he returned, wiping sweat.

"Eww! Finally, the playboy is gone," he said as he plopped down into the chair.

"Hoo, you really don't want to give him advice?" Ma Shiying asked.

"Well," Ruan Dacheng raised his head as he stroked his knees. "Why should I? I'm afraid that it's already too late for me to please the Fushers now. If I gave him advice and word spread out, would the nerds let me go? I hope the playboy will go out and tell everybody that I've rejected him."

Ma Shiying shook his head and said, "Although he's a flamboyant boy, he's been a friend after all. It's too ungracious to turn him away like that without a single good word."

Ruan Dacheng said nonchalantly, "Just don't worry! I bet he'll voluntarily come to join us in Stone Nest Garden within three days. I'm sure he wants to have fun and can't do without us."

"But he must think we're all little men without sense of justice." Ma Shiying frowned.

Ruan Dacheng snorted and growled, "Let him go, let him go! So we're little men. So what? Having sunk so low, locked up in Nanjing, should I pretend to be a damned gentleman?"

Ma Shiying sneered, "I'm worried that you'll get nothing, like trying to fetch the moon from the water. Do you think the Fushers will really let you go?"

Ruan Dacheng looked stunned, then shook his head and said in a vicious, triumphant tone, "You just don't know it. Do you know what I did just now? I went to meet someone. Can you guess who this man is? Haha, it's none other than Qian Yangxian, cousin of Qian Muzhai, head of the East Wooders."

Ruan Dacheng paused and became more proud of himself when he saw Ma Shiying had unconsciously withdrawn the disapproving expression and was looking at him intently. "Qian Yangxian brought me a message from Qian Muzhai that said he had communicated my proposal to join hands with the Fushe to other important members,

养先替钱牧斋传话给我，说他已将我诚心相结之意，周知各方，并征得多数人士同意，准备在三月二十八虎丘大会上正式作出公议，让我静候好音哩！哈哈，怎么样，君子们来投降了，没有想到吧？”阮大铖说着，开怀大笑起来。得意的响亮的笑声冲出窗外，吵醒了树上栖息的鸟雀，使它们扑扇着翅膀，啪啪地惊飞起来……

阮大铖笑过一通之后，回头看看马士英，见他仍旧皱着眉毛，现出将信将疑的神气，就站起来，拍拍他的肩膀说：

“瑶老，此事假不了！钱牧斋自从崇祯二年丢了官，整整十三年不能起用，他的心里，只怕比我们还着急呢！有这样一个机会，他怎肯白白放过！我料定，他拼老命也非要把这件事办成不可！你只管放心好喽！”说罢，他兴冲冲地转过肥胖的身躯，望着墙上那副对联，拈着大胡子，摇头晃脑地吟诵道：

“‘有官万事足，无子一身轻’！阮大铖呀阮大铖，你天生奇才，学兼文武，胸罗万卷，满腹经纶，老天爷又怎会让你永远闲却这副好身手？这一天，不是终于来了么！”

and that most of them have agreed. It will be officially approved at the Tiger Hill Conference to be held on the twenty eighth of March, and that all I have to do now is wait for good news. Haha. Lo and behold, the gentlemen have come to surrender themselves. Isn't it surprising?" He laughed after speaking. The victorious laughter broke out of the window, woke up the birds perching in the trees and sent them a-flying in panic.

When Ruan Dacheng finished laughing, he looked back at Ma Shiying. Seeing Mr. Ma was still doubtful with knit brows, he stood up, patted the man on the shoulder, and said, "Elder Yao, you can count on it. It has been thirteen years since Qian Muzhai lost his job in the second year of the reign of Emperor Chongzhen[AD 1629]. He must be more worried than we are. How can he give up an opportunity like this one? I bet he'll do everything he can to be reinstated to office. Set your mind at rest!" Then, he cheerfully turned his fat body and looked at the couplet on the wall.

"'With high office everything comes!' Hey, Ruan Dacheng, you're a rare genius with both physical and intellectual strength. Heaven forbid the thousands of volumes of books you've read and the vast knowledge in your mind lie in waste. Isn't this the day for you to see the light again?" he said, stroking his beard and wagging his head.

# 第四章
# 遇淫威宛娘惊虎口，激义愤书生斥牙行

## 寺内搜人

钱谦益和柳如是到苏州已经两天了。他们没有进城，下榻在阊门外彩云里已故徐太仆家的东园。徐太仆名时泰，万历年间进士。他家是三吴数一数二的巨富，在苏州拥有的园林房产不下七八处之多，这东园是徐太仆暮年静养之所，虽然不甚宽敞，却颇为清静幽雅。钱谦益深喜它境界不俗，出入苏州时，每每在这儿落脚。

由于事先约定要到苏州来聚齐的陈在竹和钱养先一直不见踪影，钱谦益对于这半个月来，他们二人在外间活动的情形至今摸不清底细。眼看已经是三月二十三，再过五天，就是虎丘大会。虽然这两位心腹族人的办事本领都是可以信赖的，但是这一次的使命非比寻常，而且时间紧迫，因此钱谦益始终暗暗悬着一份心，生怕会出什么娄子。

钱谦益的担心，说来也并非多余。一个多月前，他得到内阁首辅周延儒传来的信息，讽示他运用自身在士林当中的威望和影响，设法促使东林、复社方面停止对阮大铖的激烈抨击，改而采

## Chapter Four

# In Which a Young Lady Escaped from a Tiger's Mouth and an Indignant Young Scholar Snapped at the Brokerage House

## Kidnappers at a Monastery

Qian Qianyi and Liu Rushi had come to Suzhou two days ago. Instead of entering the city, they stayed in East Garden, former residence of the late Xu Taipu on Cloud Lane on the outside of the West City Gate. Xu Taipu's real name was Xu Shitai. He was a *jinshi* scholar in the Wanli period [AD 1573–1620]. His family, possessed of no fewer than seven or eight garden-style estates in Suzhou, was one of the wealthiest in the Sanwu area. East Garden had been Xu Taipu's residence in his late years. It was not very large, but it was nice and quiet, a perfect place for old age. Qian Qianyi liked the atmosphere and spent a few days here every time he visited Suzhou.

Chen Zaizhu and Qian Yangxian, who were supposed to meet him in Suzhou, hadn't turned up yet. Qian Qianyi was anxious to know if they had succeeded in their mission after half a month of effort. It was the twenty-third of March, only five days to go before the Tiger Hill Conference. Although he had no doubt about the abilities of the two close relatives, his heart had been hanging in midair, because they had been given too little time for too important a task.

Qian Qianyi's worry was not unnecessary. A month earlier, he had received a message from Prime Minister Zhou Yanru requesting him to stop the East Wooders and the Fushers from attacking Ruan Dacheng

取比较宽容的态度，以此作为他钱谦益复官起用的一种交换条件。当时，钱谦益就颇为犹豫，而且对于周延儒的刁难要挟深为气愤。不过，他苦苦等待、钻营了十三年之后，终于出现这么一个转机，却又无论如何都舍不得轻易放弃掉。他隐隐预感到，这是他的最后机会，如果加以拒绝，他也许将会抱憾终生，死不瞑目。因此，踌躇再三，钱谦益还是横下了心，决定冒险尝试一下。

经过同陈在竹、钱养先，自然还有柳如是，反复磋商研究，钱谦益同意了一个在他看来比较可行的计划。这个计划是这样的：按照他们的估计，替阮大铖开脱的主要阻力，当然是来自复社。不过在复社当中，真正坚决强硬反对阮大铖的，除了少数像吴应箕这样的激烈分子之外，还有就是陈贞慧、黄宗羲、顾杲、侯方域这批东林党人的后代，他们的父祖辈在魏忠贤专权的时代，曾受到严酷的迫害，对于阉党有不共戴天的仇恨，让他们捐弃旧怨，宽恕阮大铖，看来是办不到的。不过，在整个复社当中，以上两类人毕竟是少数，多数的成员，与阮大铖其实没有什么了不得的仇怨，无非瞧着现时在士林当中，骂阉党、斥小人是件时髦的事儿，于是也跟着瞎闹腾，希望借此出出风头，博得个“君子”的美名。近几年来，事实上已经有一些人对这种没完没了的“门户之争”颇感厌倦，流露过和衷共济的想法。如果设法联络第三种人，再通过他们说服第二种人，那么就能够把相当大的一批人争取过来。此外，看来同样重要的是：目前复社的成员虽然人人都以“清流”自居，以“君子”自命，实际上其中却分门立派，各有各的小圈子，利益、打算都不相同。过去已经是面和心不和，自从复社的创始人张溥于去年逝世之后，各派之间的明争暗斗，

by using his influence among the scholars in exchange for support in his reinstatement to office. He had hesitated at first, deeply angry at Zhou Yanru's blackmailing, but on second thoughts he had decided to take the risk. After all, it was the only opportunity after thirteen years of waiting and scheming and he was reluctant to give it up too easily. If he refused, he might regret it for the rest of his life. Therefore, despite the hesitations, he had finally opted to bite the bullet.

After repeated consultations with Chen Zaizhu, Qian Yangxian, and Liu Rushi, Qian Qianyi agreed to a plan that seemed relatively feasible. Thus they had calculated: The main obstacle to exonerate Ruan Dacheng came from the Fushe. Among the hardliners against Ruan Dacheng, besides a few radical elements like Wu Yingji, there were also sons and grandsons of the East Wooders, such as Chen Zhenhui, Huang Zongxi, Gu Gao, and Hou Fangyu. Previously, in the days of Wei Zhongxian dictatorship, their fathers or grandfathers had gone through severe persecution, so their hatred of the eunuch was unshakable. They were unlikely to abandon their old grievances and forgive Ruan Dacheng. However, the above two types of men were after all in the minority, and the majority of the Fushers, having no terrible grudges with Ruan Dacheng, would merely follow the crowd in a craze to be identified as good guys because it was fashionable among the gentry scholars to denounce the party of eunuch Wei Zhongxian and to condemn the bad guys. In recent years, in fact, some of them had become tired of this endless partisan war and had expressed the idea of co-existence. If the party of Qian Qianyi could enlist the support of the third type and through them persuade the second type, they would be able to win over a considerable number of fellow Fushers. In addition, although all the members of the Fushe identified themselves as "in the clear stream" and called themselves "men of noble character," in fact, they were divided into different groups and subgroups, each with its own interests and agendas. Having merely maintained a superficial harmony, the different factions saw their conflicts increasingly intensify after the death of Fushe founder Zhang Pu last year. If they could add fuel to the fire and use

更加日甚一日。如果能巧妙利用他们的矛盾，使之尖锐激烈起来，那么到时又可以争取到一批人。只要把大多数人拉到自己这一边，剩下的少数人士纵然强项顽固，也无济于事了。

基于这样的分析和估计，他们决定首先从两个方面来实施他们的计划：一方面，派钱养先带着几名族中心腹子弟，到扬州去找郑元勋。因为郑元勋曾经向钱养先表露过对于目前这样压制阮大铖有不同看法，加上他又是本届复社大会主持者之一，只要说动他，再通过他去联络说服其余的人，事情就会顺当得多。鉴于平日郑元勋对钱谦益奉若神明，巴结得不得了，估计钱养先此行问题不大。另一方面，则是派出陈在竹，也带着几个得力的子弟，到松江一带去活动，散布吴应箕、陈贞慧等人对旧几社一派人极端不满，认为他们成心拆台，搅乱社局，以便取而代之，因此准备在虎丘大会上同他们摊牌算账的谣言，从而煽动旧几社一派人的愤怒，使之在未来的斗争中即使不倒过来，至少也保持中立。当以上两个方面都办成之后，接下来，就在虎丘大会上，由郑元勋发难，钱家的族人弟子群起响应，提出宽宥阮大铖的主张，并且凭仗多数作出公议，布示四方，上达朝廷。只要能做到这一步，事情就算成功了。最后，根据柳如是的建议，在整个计划进行的过程中，钱谦益都避免直接出面，只在幕后调度指挥。这样，万一事情失败，也不至于严重损害钱谦益的声誉和地位。

这个计划，陈在竹和柳如是都觉得比较切实稳妥，钱养先尤其乐观，认为已是万无一失。受了他们的鼓舞，钱谦益的劲头也

the internecine struggles to their own advantage, they should be able to enlist more supporters. As long as the majority of the Fushers were pulled to their side, the remaining few, no matter how hardlined they were, would not be able to turn the tide.

Based on this analysis of the situation, they decided to implement their plan by taking two simultaneous actions: On one front, they would send Qian Yangxian, together with some most-trusted members of the greater Qian family, to Yangzhou to talk to Zheng Yuanxun, who had once said to Qian Yangxian that he had different views on the current suppression of Ruan Dacheng, and who was one of the organizers of the coming Fushe conference. If they could persuade him and then others through him, things would be much easier. As Zheng Yuanxun worshipped Qian Qianyi like a divinity, they estimated that Qian Yangxian's trip would be a success. On another front, they would send Chen Zaizhu and a few capable young men to Songjiang to spread a rumor: Wu Yingji, Chen Zhenhui and a few followers were extremely dissatisfied with former members of the Jishe, who they thought had intended to upset the order of the Fushe and usurp the power of leadership, and were prepared to lay their cards on the table at the Tiger Hill Conference. The purpose in doing so was to incur the anger of the former members of the Jishe, who would at least remain neutral if not to align with them. When the two things were done, then, at the Tiger Hill Conference, Zheng Yuanxun would speak up and members, relatives, and disciples of the Qian family would echo by proposing to forgive Ruan Dacheng. Then, by the power of majority, the conference would make a joint declaration to be publicized far and wide and submitted to the imperial court. Then, mission accomplished. Meanwhile, following Liu Rushi's suggestion, in the whole process, Qian Qianyi should work behind the scenes and avoid direct appearance in the execution of the plan so that in case of failure Qian Qianyi's reputation would not be damaged.

Both Chen Zaizhu and Liu Rushi thought this plan practical and safe, and Qian Yangxian on a more optimistic note said that it was foolproof. That boosted Qian Qianyi's spirits. In fact, once he got

来了。事实上，一旦摆脱了开始那种犹豫消极的状态之后，他所表现出来的巨大热情和过人精力，使手下的人都为之惊讶。为了推动计划的实施，近一个月，钱谦益已经全力以赴地行动起来。他先修了一封措辞得体而又意思明确的信，托人送往北京，向周延儒表示态度；同时，又再拿出几千两银子作为活动费用，交给陈在竹和钱养先带上，命他们立即分头出发。这之后，他就开始利用他在士林中的崇高声望，一改近几年懒于见客的习惯，对于来访的人士，不论贵贱高低、熟与不熟，一律给予接见，优礼相待；对于他们的请托要求，也尽可能给予满足或帮助，使这些人一个个都受宠若惊、大为感动；受到恩惠的，对他更是满怀感激。消息一传开，又招引来更多的拜访者。以至到后来，半野堂前竟弄得一天到晚轿马不断，城里城外的客店都住满了等待接见的人。钱谦益也不辞劳苦，一边服着参汤，一边抖擞精神接客。在这期间，他自然也想方设法散布例如"虏寇交煎，国事日危，亟宜平息党争，和衷共济"一类的论调，只是回避不提阮大铖这一点。这样一直忙了将近一个月，眼看同陈在竹、钱养先约定的会合日期已到，他才带着柳如是匆匆赶到苏州来。然而，令人不解的是，几天过去了，陈、钱二人却没有一个回来复命，钱谦益就有点担心了。他不由得开始想，自己是不是把事情估计得太简单？事实上吴应箕、陈贞慧那一帮子人数虽少，在复社当中的影响力仍然相当大。加上阮大铖是钦定逆案中的成员，是狗彘不如的阉党儿子，这种观念十多年来已经在人们的头脑里生了根，一旦要加以改变，绝不是件容易的事。何况，士林当中的情况相当复杂，人

rid of his initial doubt and hesitation, he began to exhibit such high spirits and such great gusto that everyone was surprised. To speed up execution of the plan, Qian Qianyi had put up all his efforts in the past month. He had first composed a well-worded letter with a clear message and sent it to Zhou Yanru in Beijing through a friend of his to express his willingness to cooperate; in the meanwhile, he took out a few thousand taels of silver as activity expenses, handed it to Chen Zaizhu and Qian Yangxian, and bade them to go on their trips immediately. After that, he began to make the best use of his high reputation among the gentry scholars. Instead of shutting his door on visitors as he had always done, he received everyone respectfully regardless of status or degree of familiarity and did his best to satisfy their request for help. The visitors felt flattered. Those who had received his favors were particularly grateful. As news spread, he attracted more and more visitors so that, later, in front of the Half Wild Estate, there was a continual train of wagons and sedan chairs all day long, and the inns and lodges in and out of the city were full of men waiting to be received by him. Qian Qianyi, continuously boosting his spirits with ginseng soup, was never tired of receiving visitors. During that period, he took every opportunity to promote the idea of peaceful coexistence and call for an end to partisan struggles for the common good in a time of national crisis caused by barbarian invasion and domestic insurgence, but he avoided mentioning Ruan Dacheng. Thus he busied himself for nearly a month until the agreed date to meet Chen Zaizhu and Qian Yangxian came. Then, he hurried to Suzhou with Liu Rushi. However, what was puzzling was that, after a few days, neither Chen Zaizhu nor Qian Yangxian came back. He started to worry. "Did I underestimate the difficulty?" he asked himself. Despite their small number, Wu Yingji, Chen Zhenhui and their likes held considerable sway in the Fushe. Besides, to change the ingrained conception that Ruan Dacheng, a son of a member of eunuch Wei Zhongxian's party, was a condemned treasonist confirmed by His Majesty the emperor himself was no easy task at all. Furthermore, the scholars were too sophisticated a species to be fooled. Everyone was

人都熟读诗书，脑瓜都会绕弯子，要完全骗过他们并不容易。不错，他们之间确有纠纷，而且相当尖锐。善于利用这些纠纷，固然有可能达到目的；但是反过来，也会恰恰因为这些莫名其妙的纠纷，使再好的计划也葬送掉……

不过，钱谦益内心虽然烦躁，表面上却依然保持从容镇定。他对于下人的态度，甚至比往常更温和一些。今天早上起来，丫环红情失手打破了一只细瓷盅子，把刚炖好的参汤洒了一地毯。要是在平时，钱谦益难免会皱起眉毛申斥两句。可是今天，他只是淡淡地叫她收拾干净，就完了。钱谦益这种“不示人以迹”的处事涵养，自然瞒不过他的那位绝顶聪明的如夫人。只是，即使柳如是，这会儿也在暗暗着急，想不出用什么话来安慰他。而且她还不愿多问，生怕加深了钱谦益的忧虑。所以此刻，当两人在揖峰轩中摆开棋局对弈，钱谦益接连下错了数子之后，柳如是便含笑推开棋枰，说：

“这天气怪困人的，我也没劲儿再下了，想去歇会儿。相公在园子里窝了两天，想必也闷得慌哩，何不到外面散散心？”

钱谦益本来就没有心思下棋，听见柳如是这样建议，他点点头，站起来，等红情服侍他换过衣服之后，便携了一支藜杖，叫了一名小厮跟着，慢慢地走出外面去。

钱谦益来到大门口，就站住了。他扬起脸，朝彩云里南头眺望了一阵，直到断定无论是陈在竹还是钱养先的影子，都不会很快出现之后，才失望地转过身，信步向西园行去。

西园也是徐府的产业，跟东园隔着一截街道。徐太仆死后不久，他的儿子把西园东面的一片住宅舍做了佛寺，取名戒幢寺。

well read in poetry and the classics and was capable of complicated thinking. True that they had disputes among themselves, very serious ones, and it was possible to use the disputes to achieve the goal, but it was precisely because of these inexplicable disputes that the best plan might be ruined ...

Though deep inside he was rather troubled, Qian Qianyi remained calm and collected on the surface and appeared even more friendly to the servants than usual. Early in the morning, Hongqing the servant girl broke a fine porcelain cup and spilled the freshly stewed ginseng soup on the carpet. Instead of frowning and reprimanding the girl, he merely asked her to clean it up and that was all. However, the hiding of his own feelings in front of others didn't dodge the attention of his clever wife-like concubine. Liu Rushi was worried and wanted to offer some words of comfort, but she didn't know what to say nor dared to ask him about his problem lest her asking could only add to his anxiety. Therefore, when Qian Qianyi kept making wrong moves while they played chess in the Yifeng Chamber, Liu Rushi pushed the chessboard aside and said:

"I'm feeling under the weather. I'd better have a break. My dear husband, you've stayed in the house for two days. Why not go out to get some fresh air?"

Not really interested in playing chess, Qian Qianyi nodded his head and stood up when he heard Liu Rushi's suggestion. After he dressed up with the help of Hongqing, he took a pigweed walking stick and slowly walked towards the gate of the garden home, accompanied by a boy servant.

As he came to the gate he suddenly stopped. He raised his head and looked at the south end of Cloud Lane for a while, and when he decided that neither Chen Zaizhu nor Qian Yangxian would appear anytime soon, he turned around disappointedly and walked towards West Garden.

West Garden was also a property of the Xu family, a block away from East Garden. Soon after Xu Taipu passed away, his son turned the east side of West Garden into a Buddhist monastery and named

寺内的住持茂林法师，是一位有道高僧。钱谦益因为常在东园落脚，也就认识了茂林，平日谈经论禅，彼此颇为投契。现在钱谦益想找个人解解闷，便自然想到了他。

正是春天进香的季节，街道上，来来往往净是从四乡赶来进香的客人，有男有女，有老有少，或者乘轿，或者步行，不少人还背着包袱、挑着箩担，在又窄又长的街道上挨着、挤着，那些低矮浅窄的茶馆，生意清淡的香烛店，像着了魔似的，一下子紧张忙碌起来，出现了前所未有的活气。显然，尽管四乡都在闹饥荒，米价腾踊，人心惶惶，但是人们奉祀神灵之心，却丝毫不敢懈怠。他们宁可把裤腰带勒得更紧一点，也要设法拿出尽可能多的香烛和捐赠，再加上更虔诚的祷告和许愿，希望求得神明的垂悯，保佑自己及亲人的福禄康宁……

钱谦益夹在香客当中，来到悬着“戒幢律院”横匾的山门前。他稍稍停留了一下，将门外那些摆卖香烛元宝、胭脂簪珥、牙尺剪刀以至经典木鱼的大小摊档浏览了一遍，发现并无看得上眼的货色之后，才慢慢地踱着方步，走进寺中。

戒幢寺的规模不算太小，一共三进，两边还有别院。寺前的部分本是门厅，现在改成了四天王殿；寺后是藏经阁和僧舍。居中一进的大雄宝殿，是大厅改建的，顶上加了一重飞檐，殿前筑起了露台，气象颇为宏伟。不过这样一来，两侧的厢房便显得低

it Jiezhuang Monastery. The abbot of the monastery, Dharma Master Maolin, was a highly accomplished monk. Because Qian Qianyi often lodged in East Garden, he was acquainted with Maolin and the two developed a friendship by sharing their ideas on meditation and discussing Buddhist sutras. So, when Qian Qianyi wanted to find someone to talk to, he naturally thought of the monk.

It was springtime, the season for incense tribute to the monastery. The street was crowded with pilgrims from the neighboring places; men and women, young and old, some in sedan chairs, some on foot, and many carrying luggage on their backs or with shoulder poles, jostled with each other on the narrow, long street, the low, shabby tea houses and the scarcely-visited incense and candle shops suddenly became alive as if possessed by a spirit. Obviously, despite the famine in the neighboring places, the inflation of rice prices, and the scare and panic, people didn't dare to neglect their worshipping of the gods; they tightened the belts of their trousers to save money so that they would be able to offer as many candles and incense sticks as possible and to give as much donation as possible; such offerings, they hoped, coupled with their pious prayers and sincere wishes, would incur the mercy of the gods, who would bless them and their loved ones ...

Qian Qianyi made his way through the pilgrims and came to the monastery gate, on which hung a horizontal plaque: Jiezhuang Academy of Precepts. He paused for a while and browsed the stalls selling incense, candles, ingots, rouge, hairpins, earrings, ivory rulers, scissors, and wooden fish, and finding nothing interesting, he slowly walked into the monastery.

The monastery was not a small one. It consisted of three main courtyards with two side yards. The front courtyard, originally the entrance hall, had now been turned into the Hall of Four Heavenly Kings; the back courtyard included the library of sutras and the monk's living quarters. In the middle was the magnificent Sakyamuni Hall, which was a remodeling of the grand hall with a cornice added to the top and a terrace built in front of it. In contrast, the rooms on both sides appeared low and cramped, not quite commensurate with

矮局促，不大相称。以往钱谦益也曾一再向茂林住持指出这个毛病，不过茂林听了，总是合十低眉，念一声“阿弥陀佛”，说：“罪过罪过，前次改建大殿，所费之资已抵百户中人之产，贫衲为此事至今不安，怎敢再生妄念！”现在，钱谦益发现两厢的景状依然如故。在殿前的空地上，分男女两边，密密麻麻地坐满了香客；露台上设着一架高脚香炉，炉上香烟袅袅，身躯瘦小而面目慈和的茂林法师身披袈裟，端坐于蒲团之上，正在向善男信女们宣讲佛法。

钱谦益因为耳背，开始听不清茂林说什么，后来走得近了，才听出是在述说《大庄严论经》当中的《尸毗王舍身饲鹰》的故事。故事的大意是说：古时有个尸毗王，精勤苦行，一心向佛。佛祖为了考察他心志是否坚牢，乃命天神毗首羯摩化作鸽子，他自己化作老鹰。鸽子躲到尸毗王的腋下。老鹰赶来索取，尸毗王不允，宁愿割自己身上的肉来换取鸽子的性命。老鹰同意了，但要求割下的肉须同鸽子重量相等。尸毗王命人拿来一杆秤，一边放鸽子，一边割自己的肉。谁知身上的肉一一割尽，仍然未抵鸽子的重量。尸毗王最后举身上秤，表示愿意把整个身子舍献出去。这时大地震动，诸天唱叹，佛祖显形，微笑嘉慰。尸毗王心志愈坚，合十作偈说：

the grandeur of the temple. Previously, Qian Qianyi had repeatedly pointed out this defect to Abbot Maolin, who, upon hearing it, always clasped his hands and bowed with an "Amitabha Buddha!" and went on to say, "What a shame! What a shame! The remodeling of the hall has cost what is worth the assets of a hundred households put together. For that reason I've always been uneasy. How dare I think of anything else?" Now, Qian Qianyi found that the rooms on the two sides remained unchanged. In the open space in front of the temple sat the densely packed pilgrims, men on one side and women on the other side; on the terrace was a tall censer, from which rose wisps of incense smoke. The thin and kind-faced Master Maolin, dressed in a monk's robe, sat squarely on the futon, preaching to the deeply pious men and women.

At first, Qian Qianyi didn't quite hear what Maolin was saying because of his poor hearing; later, when he moved closer, he heard it clearly enough. The master was telling the story of "King Shibi Feeding the Eagle with His Own Body" in the *Kalpanā-manditikā*. The story goes as follows: Long long ago, there lived King Shibi, who exerted himself ascetically with a heart solely devoted to the Buddha. In order to see whether his mind was firm, the Buddha ordered a god named Vishvakarman to turn into a pigeon and he himself turned into an eagle. The pigeon hid under King Shibi's armpit. The eagle came to ask for it, but King Shibi refused him and would rather cut off his own flesh in exchange for the life of the pigeon. The eagle agreed, but set a condition that the weight of the flesh be equal to that of the pigeon. The king agreed and called for the knives and the balance. He began to cut his flesh as he released the pigeon. However much flesh he cut off himself, it couldn't match the weight of the pigeon. Finally, King Shibi decided to give himself up and stepped onto the balance, when suddenly, the earth trembled, the gods in the heavenly realms hailed, and the Buddha Himself appeared with an approving smile. King Shibi's mind was even more determined and he said a gatha, clasping his hands:

我割身肉时，心不存苦乐，
无瞋亦无忧，无有不喜心。
此事若实者，身当复如故。
速成菩提道，救于苍生苦。
……

钱谦益无聊地站了片刻，估计这种讲经不会很快就完。他一心惦记着家里，只怕在他出来这会儿，陈在竹或者钱养先已经回来了，于是便悄悄转过身，打算退出去。这时候，一个长得斯文秀气的中年僧人，穿过人丛，走到了他的跟前。

“不知檀越光临敝寺，有失远迎，望祈恕罪！”那位僧人打着问讯说。

钱谦益“噢”了一声，连忙还礼。他认得这位僧人法名观照，是寺里的知客僧。“不敢，学生偶因小事来苏，下榻东园，闲着无事，前来走走。既是贵寺佛事正忙，学生就不打扰了。”

“檀越千祈留步。敝寺住持长老吩咐，请檀越方丈奉茶，他即刻便来。”知客僧恭敬地挽留。

钱谦益迟疑了一下，觉得不好推托，只得点点头，由知客僧在前引导着，朝方丈室走去。

还没走出大院，突然“哄”的一声，山门外骚动起来，一群香客神色惊惶地从四天王殿奔进了大院。接着，外面一个声音高叫：“前门、后门都把住了！休得放走一个！”

钱谦益微微一怔，不由自主停住了脚步。院子里听讲的香客，还有露台上的茂林法师和执事僧人不知道发生了什么事，都纷纷

*When I have my flesh cut,*
*There's no pain or happiness in my heart.*
*There's neither anger nor worry nor grievance.*
*If it has to be so, let it be so,*
*And I shall go with a calm mind.*
*Let me attain to the way of Bodhi more quickly*
*And save all the living things from their suffering.*
...

Qian Qianyi stood emptily for a while and then decided that this kind of sermon would not end very soon. Thinking that Chen Zaizhu or Qian Yangxian might have already returned, he quietly turned around to leave. At this moment, a middle-aged monk with a graceful appearance made his way through the crowd to greet him.

"I didn't know you were coming. Pray excuse me for failing to welcome you in time!" the monk said with a salute.

Qian Qianyi said "Oh" and returned the courtesy. He recognized the monk as Guanzhao, master of ceremonies in the monastery. "That's very polite of you. I've come to Suzhou for some business and am staying in East Garden. Not having much to do at the moment, I'm out for a walk. Seeing all of you're busy with the Buddhist service, I was thinking I'd better leave," he said.

"Sir, please stay! The abbot asked me to serve tea to you and he'll be here very soon," said the monk.

Qian Qianyi hesitated for a moment, and feeling that it was not polite to refuse, he nodded his head, and guided by the monk, walked towards the abbot's room.

Before they left the main courtyard, a sudden commotion rose outside of the monastery gate, and a crowd of panicked pilgrims rushed into the courtyard from the Hall of Four Heavenly Kings. Then, a voice shouted from the outside, "Close the doors, front and back! No one shall escape!"

Qian Qianyi stopped in alarm. The pilgrims listening to the sermon in the courtyard, as well as Master Maolin and the deacon-

回头朝山门望去。

一会儿，只见堆挤在四天王殿前的香客们忙不迭地向两旁闪开，五六个头戴红黑两色帽子的衙役气势汹汹地走了进来。走在最后的，是个四十来岁的圆脸汉子。他头戴瓦楞帽，身穿鹦哥绿夹绸长袍，脚下三丝官履，一时倒瞧不出他是什么身份。

圆脸汉子来到院子里，就站住了。他叉开两腿，倒背着手，阴沉地转动着小眼睛，朝在场的人们来回扫视了几遍，最后目光停在露台上。

“谁是本寺住持？请出来说话！”他大咧咧地说，声音尖锐刺耳。

知客僧观照离开钱谦益，他快步走到那汉子跟前，打着问讯说：

“檀越光临敝寺，不知有何赐教？”

圆脸汉子翻了他一眼：“你就是住持？”

“不敢，小僧是本寺知客。”

“叫你们住持说话！”

“是！——不敢动问檀越高姓大名，以便小僧通报。”

圆脸汉子“哼”了一声，正想说话，一个衙役忽然走过来，指着大殿说：“金爷，那妮子像是躲进里面去了！”

姓金的圆脸汉子眉毛一耸，喝叫：“快搜！”

几个衙役立即朝大雄宝殿奔去。两廊上的香客，稍微躲闪得慢一些的，都被他们撞得东倒西歪。本来坐在院子里静静听讲的香客，吓得“哄”地站立起来，互相招呼着，拥挤着，都想找个安生的地方躲避。院子里顿时乱了套。

姓金的汉子蓦地大喝一声：“不准乱跑！谁跑就锁谁！”

monk on the terrace, not knowing what had happened, all gazed at the monastery gate.

In an instant, the pilgrims crowded in front of the Hall of the Four Heavenly Kings hurriedly stepped back to the sides, and five or six *yamen* men wearing red-and-black hats came in mightily. At the end was a round-faced man in his forties, wearing a *waleng* hat, a parrot-green silk robe, and official boots of mixed fabric. It was difficult to tell his rank.

The round-faced man came to the yard and stopped. Hands on his back, spreading his legs, rolling his small eyes gloomily, he scanned the crowd back and forth, and finally his eyes stopped on the terrace.

"Who's the abbot of the monastery? Come out and talk to me!" he said loudly in a sharp voice.

Monk Guanzhao left Qian Qianyi, quickly walked to the man, and said with a salute:

"My dear patron, what an honor to have your visit! Is there any instruction?"

The round-faced man cast him a look and said, "So, you're the abbot?"

"Nay, sir! I'm merely the master of ceremonies of the monastery."

"Go get the abbot!"

"Aye, sir! My dear patron, may I venture to ask your honorable name so that I can tell him your coming."

The round-faced man gave a "hum" and was just about to speak when suddenly a *yamen* man walked over and pointed to the hall, saying, "Master Jin, the girl seems to be hiding in there!"

The round-faced man named Jin raised his eyebrows and shouted, "Search!"

Several *yamen* men rushed to the Sakyamuni Hall immediately. The pilgrims in the corridors who dodged too slowly were almost knocked over. The ones who were sitting in the courtyard quietly listening to the sermon stood up in fright and ran toward safety, shouting and jostling. The courtyard was suddenly thrown into a chaos.

The man named Jin yelled suddenly, "Don't run! Whoever runs

站在他附近的香客呆了一下，犹豫着站住了。其余的人没有听见，依旧乱钻乱躲。钱谦益给人挤在栏杆旁边，靠了小厮的大声吆喝和竭力保护，才没有被挤着。他进又不是，退又不是，心中好生懊恼：“早知会碰上这种倒霉事，我便不来了！”他想。同时暗暗纳闷：“这个姓金的不知什么底细，竟然如此骄横，连衙役都听他指派。他们到庙里来不知要搜拿什么人？”

这时候，只见露台上的茂林长老站了起来。他回头朝侍立在身后的几个僧人吩咐了几句。那几个僧人立即分头走下来，开始极力安抚香客，维持秩序。

茂林长老眼见院子里慢慢平静下来，才不慌不忙地步下台阶。他先来到钱谦益跟前，同他行礼相见。略事寒暄之后，茂林便摆摆手，命手下的僧人先把钱谦益送到方丈室奉茶，免得在这儿被人挤着了。钱谦益心里有事，本来无意久留，又碰上这么件意外的是非，更加扫兴，只想快点离开。不过，一来他不想太拂主人之意；二来，觉得在这种情况下，自己一走了之，似乎也不怎么好。于是，他只得点点头，心里却越来越别扭，觉得来苏州这两天，净碰上些倒霉的事，仿佛预兆着此行并不吉利似的。

“喂，你们往哪儿走？”姓金的汉子蓦地吆喝起来。这时，钱谦益正没精打采地跟着一名僧人，打算朝方丈室走去。

“我说了，谁也不许乱跑，你聋了吗？”姓金的汉子看见钱谦益没有停步，他猛地蹦过来，气势汹汹地企图阻拦。

钱谦益站住了。一股无名怒火猛地升腾起来，但他仍然极力

will be handcuffed!"

The pilgrims standing near him were scared and stood still hesitatingly. Others didn't hear him and headed in various directions. Qian Qianyi was squeezed to the railing by the jostling crowd but was unharmed thanks to the yelling and pushing of his servant. Caught amidst the crowd and unable to either advance or retreat, he regretted having come. "If I had known I would be running into such bad luck, I wouldn't have been here," he thought. At the same time he secretly wondered, "Who's this man named Jin that's so powerful that even the *yamen* listens to him? Who are they searching for in the monastery?"

At this moment, Master Maolin on the terrace stood up. He turned around and said something to the monks standing behind him. They walked down immediately and began to pacify the pilgrims and maintain order.

After the courtyard had gradually calmed down, Master Maolin descended the steps calmly. He first came to Qian Qianyi and greeted him with a salute. After a brief greeting, he beckoned to a monk and asked him to take the friend away from the jostling crowd and escort him to the abbot's room for tea. In fact, at this moment, Qian Qianyi just wanted to leave as quickly as possible. He had no intention to stay long as he had something on his mind; besides, the incident just now had aggravated his mood of dejection. However, it was not polite to reject the kindness of a friend, nor was it appropriate to leave at such a moment. So, he nodded his head but felt increasingly bad inside. Nothing had been good since he had come to Suzhou two days ago. He had a premonition that things might not turn out well on this current trip.

"Hey, where are you going?" The man named Jin yelled suddenly as Qian Qianyi followed the monk and walked listlessly towards the abbot's room.

"I said, no one is allowed to move. Are you deaf or what?" Seeing that Qian Qianyi didn't stop, the Jin guy rushed over menacingly and tried to stop him.

Qian Qianyi stopped. An unnamed anger rose, but he tried his

克制着。他缓缓回过头来，冷冷地瞧着姓金的汉子，一言不发。

“哦，这位是常熟的钱牧斋檀越。”茂林长老连忙跟过来介绍说。也许因为看见姓金的来头不小，而且蛮得可以，生怕钱谦益会吃眼前亏，茂林的语气有点急促。

“钱檀越早年官居礼部右堂，又是东林领袖、文坛宗主，京里也是大大有名的！”茂林很快地补充说。他情急之际，不知不觉地用了一种夸耀的口吻，说过之后，才似乎颇以这种“面谀”为可羞，自己反而脸红了。

钱谦益尖利地瞥了茂林一眼。“你是什么人？”他问姓金的汉子，口气依然十分平静。

听说钱谦益曾经官居礼部右堂，那姓金的汉子似乎呆了一呆，但是刚才他的横蛮劲头使得太满，众目睽睽之下很难兜得转来。他瞪了几次眼睛，又使劲地咽了一口唾沫，才勉强地拱一拱手说：“原来是钱老爷，在下金三，是京里国丈府里派来姑苏公干的，适才不知老爷，多有冲撞，休怪！”

金三报出来历，茂林等僧人听起来还不怎样，站在四周静待发落的香客都不约而同打了个寒噤。有人“啊”地叫出声来，立即又惊恐地窒住了。院子里刹那间更加寂静，微风吹拂树木和鸟儿啁啾的声音听来格外分明。

钱谦益顿时醒悟了：“怪不得他如此骄横，还能动用衙役，原来背后是这样一座大靠山！”钱谦益早就听说，国丈田弘遇最近派人到苏州来采买女孩子，名是采买，实际上只要是看上了的，就连逼带抢，也不管对方愿意不愿意。所以近两个月来，弄得姑

best to restrain it. He slowly turned his head, looked at Mr. Jin coldly, but said nothing.

"Oh, this is the monastery's patron Qian Muzhai from Changshu." Abbot Maolin hurriedly came over to introduce him. Seeing that the Jin guy was of no ordinary background and was not prone to civility, he hurried to Qian Qianyi's aid lest his friend be harmed.

"Mr. Qian is a former Right Vice Minister of the Ministry of Rites, head of the East Wood Party and leader of the literary circles. He's very famous in the capital." As he spoke, he unknowingly used a boastful and flattering tone. After realizing it, he blushed, as if quite ashamed of such face-to-face flattering.

Qian Qianyi gave Maolin a sharp glance, then turned to the Jin guy and asked, "Who are you?" His tone was still very calm.

Hearing that Qian Qianyi was a former Right Vice Minister of the Ministry of Rites the Jin guy was overwhelmed, but since earlier he had made too great a show of himself, he now had difficulty making a sharp turn. He helplessly blinked his eyes, vigorously swallowed his saliva, then reluctantly bowed and said, "Oh, it's the respectable Mr. Qian! I'm Jin Third, on an errand from the father-in-law of His Majesty the emperor. Please forgive me for alarming Your Honor."

When Jin Third revealed his identity, Maolin and the other monks were not quite impressed, but the pilgrims waiting for orders shuddered unanimously. Someone yelled "Ah" and immediately choked in horror. The yard became more silent, and the sound of the breeze blowing on the trees and the chirping of the birds were particularly distinct from each other.

Qian Qianyi suddenly understood the situation. "No wonder he's so arrogant and aggressive and even the *yamen* is working for him. It turns out he has a powerful master," he thought. Qian Qianyi had long heard that the emperor's father-in-law Tian Hongyu had recently sent someone to Suzhou to buy a girl. "Buying" was just the word for it. In fact, as long as they set their eyes on a maiden, they would get her by any means, whether she was going to agree or not. Therefore, in the past two months, the whole city had been in

苏城里，市井骚然，人心惶惶。大凡长得好看一些的女孩儿，都设法躲藏起来。那些艳名久著的妓女，就更不用说了。本来，田弘遇贵为国丈，富可敌国，对于流落青楼的女子来说，未始不是一个归宿之所。不过，一来田弘遇府内姬妾众多，而且还在不断增加，别说打算宠夺专房，就是要站稳脚跟也很不容易。二来，田弘遇还有一桩怪脾气，每逢有新人入府，开始他总是优礼迎娶，赐给珠冠蟒服，位列姬妾；但是三四天后，就立即贬为婢仆，呼来喝去，动不动就鞭笞毒打。去年，红极一时的秦淮名妓杨宛叔，被田弘遇抢回去之后，就吃尽了苦头。消息传来，把她的姐妹们都吓坏了。所以今年听说田国丈又派人来物色美女，平日稍有一点艳名的，都躲的躲，藏的藏，生怕跳出火坑之后，却掉进了地狱。眼前这个姓金的，八成就是干的这种勾当。只是，采买女孩子，怎么跑到寺院里来了呢？瞧他们刚才的架势，像是要搜寻什么人似的，莫非那女孩子竟逃进这儿来了么？

“嗯，你来这儿做什么？”钱谦益仍然不动声色地问。弄清了金三是田弘遇手下的一名家仆，钱谦益反而放下心来。他同田弘遇多少还有一点交情，去年田弘遇奉旨到南海进香回来，路经南京时，两人还见过一面。当时钱谦益曾应田弘遇之请，写了一首诗送他。要在平时，冲着这份交情，钱谦益对这个金三自然会改容相见；可是此刻，不知为什么，他却涌起了一股要狠狠教训一下这个狂妄之徒的欲望，这种欲望又因为意识到它的愉快后果而变得强烈起来了。

“这，好教钱老爷得知，在下前两天走失了一个人口，嗯，

panic. Every girl that looked more or less beautiful went into hiding, not to mention the famous prostitutes. Honestly speaking, given his great wealth, Tian Hongyu was not a bad destiny for a fallen girl in a brothel. The problem was, for one thing, he had too many concubines in his mansion and more coming—securing exclusive favor was out of the question and even getting a firm foothold in the house was not possible—and for another, Tian Hongyu had a weird temper: whenever a newcomer entered the mansion, she was welcomed as one of his concubines with a lavish wedding ceremony and given a python dress and a jeweled bridal crown to start with; but after three or four days, she was immediately demoted to a maidservant to be ordered about and whipped at will. The previous year, Yang Wanshu, a famous prostitute on the Qinhuai River, had been taken away by Tian Hongyu and received such treatment. The news came and frightened the other girls. So this year, upon hearing that Mr. Tian was outsourcing for another beautiful young woman, the girls whose names were better known fled into hiding for fear that after jumping out of a fire pit they would fall into a dungeon. The Jin in front of Qian Qianyi was most likely in that business. Yet, what had a monastery to do with the outsourcing of a young woman? A moment ago, Jin and his men had acted as if they were searching for someone. Is the girl hiding in the monastery?

"Well, what are you doing in here?" Qian Qianyi asked stoically. After learning that Jin Third was one of Tian Hongyu's servants, Qian Qianyi was relieved. He was in some measure a friend of Tian Hongyu's. They had met the previous year when the royal relation passed Nanjing on his return trip from his royally commissioned pilgrimage to the South China Sea. Qian Qianyi had even written a poem for Tian Hongyu upon his request. Such a friendship would have made Qian Qianyi change his attitude in normal situations, but not now; for an unknown reason, he was in a good mind to give this vain guy a lesson and such a desire increased in intensity as he imagined what happy results it would achieve.

"My respectable Mr. Qian, a person in our care went missing the

是个女孩儿。有人看见她逃进寺里来，所以进来寻她。”

“什么样的女孩儿？叫什么名字？”

“她叫董白，又叫董小宛，也就十七八岁，鹅蛋脸，大眼睛，一笑俩酒窝，身量嘛，不高也不矮……”金三用手比画着说。

钱谦益不由得“噢”了一声。他不仅听说过这个女孩儿，而且还见过她，认识她。董小宛也是秦淮河的一位名妓，不仅美貌出众，而且心思明敏，琴棋书画固然不在话下，她还学得一手出色的刺绣，唱得一口呱呱叫的曲儿，就是人冷傲点儿，顶不爱凑热闹，人们都说她不像个旧院姐儿，倒像个隐居山林的女高士。

“嗯，找到了吗——这个董小宛？”

金三还没有来得及开口，进入大殿搜寻的那几个衙役匆匆走了出来，像是回答钱谦益的问话似的说：“启禀金爷，没有找到。”

“啊，怎么找不到！”金三发急说，登时拉下脸来。

衙役们你看我，我看你，都没有吱声。

“再给我搜！”金三跺着脚叫。

“是，金爷！”衙役们答应着，迟迟疑疑地走开去。

站在前面的香客不由自主地后退了一下，后面的人跟着骚动起来，随即又怕冷似的挤到一块。

“人这么多，仔细瞧瞧，看看有没有躲在人堆里。还有，那些和尚的房间，都给我里里外外搜一遍！”金三发狠地命令着。

听说要搜查住房，在场的僧人都变了脸色，不约而同地望着茂林长老。

茂林的神色有点尴尬。他显然觉得对方并无官府凭信，便要

other day, a young woman. Someone saw her run into the monastery, so we're here to look for her."

"What kind of a young woman? What is her name?"

"Her name is Dong Bai, or sometimes called Dong Xiaowan, seventeen or eighteen years old. She has an oval face, big eyes, and two dimples when smiling. She's of medium height ..." Jin Third said with a hand gesture.

Qian Qianyi let out an "ah". He hadn't only heard about her but also met her once. She was one of the famous prostitutes on the Qinhuai River. Not only was she a great beauty, she was extremely intelligent as well. Besides the zither, chess, calligraphy, and painting, she was also good at embroidery and singing. Her only shortcoming was her cold pride. She never liked to join others in the pursuit of fun. Everybody said she was more like a female recluse in a forest than a prostitute of the Old Yard.

"Well, did you find her?"

Before Jin Third replied, the few *yamen* men who had entered the temple hurriedly came out and said, as if answering Qian Qianyi's question, "We didn't find her, sir."

"Ah, how come you can't find her?" Jin Third said worriedly. His face sank.

The *yamen* men looked at each other but none spoke.

"Search again!" Jin Third stomped his feet and screamed.

"Aye, Lord Jin!" The *yamen* men said in unison and left hesitantly.

The pilgrims standing in front of them stepped back involuntarily and the crowd panicked and dispersed, but very soon reassembled as if in fear of cold.

"It's a huge crowd here. Take a closer look to see if she's hiding in the crowd. Also, search the monks' rooms inside and out!" Jin Third ordered sternly.

Hearing that the living quarters were going to be searched, the monks lost their countenance and looked at Abbot Maolin in unison.

Maolin's expression was a bit awkward. He felt it humiliating to allow the search to happen—obviously, these men had no official

搜查僧房，实在欺人太甚，但是如果不让搜查，又仿佛寺里真的藏着什么女孩儿似的，传扬开去，更加不得了。他犹豫了半晌，终于叹了一口气，说：“搜吧，还是搜个清楚的好！”

如果金三不下令搜查僧房，或者虽然下令搜查僧房，但茂林长老不是这样回答的话，钱谦益也许就会对这件事罢手不管了。因为，最初他虽然打算教训金三，后来转念一想，迫在眉睫的那件大事还没有着落，实在没有必要去争这份闲气。他还想到田弘遇是当今皇上的老丈人，他的女儿田贵妃是皇上最宠爱的一个妃子。父女二人都是炙手可热的人物。将来自己入京复官之后，许多事情只怕还得仰仗于他，也实在不便得罪。但是，眼前这个姓金的家伙却不见好就收，似乎根本不把自己放在眼内；而茂林长老遭此凌辱，也丝毫没有向自己求援的表示，仿佛看透了自己并无能力保护他似的。这就使钱谦益感到了一种被人藐视的痛苦，而这种痛苦又由于近两天来的等待、烦恼和失望而变得难以忍受。“哈哈，瞧吧，钱谦益！在别人眼中，你已经成了这样一个无足轻重的废物了！”他恶毒、快意地对自己说。同时感到这些天来——不，这十多年来所积存下来的苦恼、怨毒和愤懑开始在胸膛里翻涌，他极力试图压抑它，却反而使它急剧地膨胀起来。

“慢着！”他费力地喊，声音是喑哑的、微弱的。

金三回头看着他，安抚地微微一笑。钱谦益却觉得，这微笑仿佛在说：“老头儿，你就呆着吧！没你的事，你也拦阻不住咱！”

“站住！”钱谦益蓦地怒叫起来，声音大得连自己也有点吃惊，“不许你们胡作非为！”

全场的人，包括金三在内，都愕然呆住了。

“不许你们胡作非为，听见没有？”钱谦益跺着脚又叫。

permission—but if he didn't allow them to search, the monastery would be prone to doubt and scandal as if it had really hidden a young woman. He hesitated for an instant, finally sighed and said, "If you have to search, search thoroughly until you're sure!"

If Jin Third hadn't ordered the search of the monks' rooms, or even though he had but Abbot Maolin hadn't answered that way, Qian Qianyi might have just left it alone, because, although he had wanted to teach Jin Third a lesson, on second thoughts, he didn't find it necessary to be bothered with this triviality while he was concerned with something more urgent. Besides, Tian Hongyu was a father-in-law of His Majesty the emperor and his daughter was the emperor's favorite concubine. Both father and daughter were no ordinary people. If reinstated to office in Beijing, Qian Qianyi would have to rely on the emperor's relation for many things, and offending the old man was obviously not something sensible to do. However, the guy named Jin in front of him showed no sign of giving up, completely ignoring his presence. Abbot Maolin, while suffering such humiliation, didn't intend to ask for his help at all, as if not expecting him to have the ability to offer protection. Qian Qianyi felt the pain of being slighted, and this pain became more acute when he thought of the waiting, the anxiety, and the disappointment in the past two days. "Haha, lo and behold, Qian Qianyi! In the eyes of others, you've become such an insignificant good-for-nothing!" he said to himself sourly. At the same time, he felt that the distress, grievance, and anger accumulated over the past few days, nay, the past ten years began to surge in his chest. He tried his best to suppress them but only inflated them instead.

"Hold on!" he shouted in a weak, raspy voice.

Jin Third looked back at him and gave him a sympathetic smile. That smile seemed to say, "Old man, just stay where you are! It's none of your business, and you can't stop us even if you want to."

"Stop!" Qian Qianyi suddenly yelled, his voice so loud that even he himself was a little surprised. "No messing around here!"

All those present were stilled, including Jin Third.

"No messing around here. Have you heard?" Qian Qianyi

“钱老爷，是这样的——”金三被钱谦益的气势所震慑，他的口气不由自主地软下来，“我们走失人口……”

“胡说！这戒幢寺是清净佛地，这位茂林长老是有道高僧，怎么会收藏你的女孩儿？”钱谦益瞪起眼睛。

“可是……”

钱谦益做了个“不要听”的手势：“要搜查寺院，得有吴县、苏州的牌票！你有吗？要不——”他转向那几个衙役，厉声地说，“莫非你们身上带得有？”

那几个衙役是苏州府派出来协助金三办事的，事先并没有估计到要来搜查戒幢寺，当然也就没有什么牌票。他们一下子被问住了，张了张嘴，却说不出话来。其中也有认得钱谦益的，知道他同知府大人素有交情，在他的跟前，知府大人还得自称一声晚辈，这会儿见钱谦益发了怒，就更不敢应嘴了。

金三却似乎颇不服气，他挺一挺脖子，争辩说：“钱老爷，我们可是给国丈爷办事。这个女孩儿，是国丈爷点着名儿要的，如今走失了，国丈爷责备下来，在下可是吃罪不起！”

钱谦益冷笑一声：“国丈大人么，我也认识，去年他奉旨往南海进香回来，我还跟他见过一面。承他告诉我，他这次赴南海，是代皇上去给观音大士上香，祈求神明保佑贵妃娘娘玉体安康、早生贵子。观音大士当夜已经托梦国丈大人，谕示允可。但是现在——”钱谦益把脸孔一板，声色俱厉地说，“寺里正在进香，

stomped his feet and shouted again.

"Lord Qian, let me explain—" said Jin Third, whose tone immediately softened as he was overwhelmed by Qian Qianyi's mighty anger. "A woman is missing ..."

"Nonsense! Jiezhuang Monastery is a pure land of the Buddha. Abbot Maolin is a highly accomplished master monk. How could he possibly hide the woman you're looking for?" Qian Qianyi's eyes shot out in anger.

"But ..." Jin Third wanted to explain.

Qian Qianyi made a "I won't listen" gesture and said, "To search the monastery, you must have a search warrant from Wu County or Suzhou Prefecture. Do you have one? Or," he turned to the *yamen* men and said sternly, "do you have one?"

The *yamen* men were dispatched by the *yamen* of Suzhou Prefecture to assist Jin Third. Having not anticipated that they would be searching the Jiezhuang Monastery, they didn't bring a search warrant with them. Baffled by the question, they opened their mouths without being able to utter a word. Those who had met Qian Qianyi before knew that he was a friend of the prefect and before him the prefect had to call himself "your student". Seeing Qian Qianyi getting angry, they didn't dare to speak at all.

Jin Third was not resigned. He straightened his neck and argued, "Lord Qian, we're acting on behalf of the father-in-law of the emperor. He specifically asked for this girl but now she's missing. The consequences are huge if we don't make it right for his lordship."

Qian Qianyi said with a sneer, "I know his lordship the emperor's father-in-law. I met him once. It was on his return trip back from his pilgrimage to the South China Sea. He told me that he had gone to the South China Sea on behalf of His Majesty the emperor to offer incense to Bodhisattva Guanyin and pray that the royal concubine be blessed with health and children. He said, Bodhisattva Guanyin had entered his dream that night and had promised him what he had asked for. Yet now," he continued with a stern face, "while incense-offering is going on in the monastery, you're disrupting the sacred ritual and disquieting

你却带了这些人前来骚扰滋事，大闹佛地，万一神明责怪下来，收回许诺，致使贵妃娘娘哪怕有一点儿差池不测，这个罪，你难道吃得起吗！”

这一番申斥，果然把金三吓住了。他望着钱谦益，现出畏怯的、惊恐的神色。终于，他低下头去，额角冒出点点细汗珠子，然而，很快地他又抬起头来：

“钱老爷，您老能担保那个女孩儿必定不在寺里？”

“我——担保！”钱谦益把藜杖朝地上一顿，断然地说。可是，随即他就有点后悔了。因为他知道，倘若这姓金的在别处也找不着董小宛的话，那么回到京里向田弘遇复命时，必定会把找不到董小宛的原因说成是他钱牧斋横加阻挠。如此一来，骄横跋扈的田弘遇就会迁怒到自己的头上，往后的种种是非风波，都可能由此而生。经过刚才的一通发泄，钱谦益现在逐渐冷静下来，开始考虑自己这样做是否值得了。

金三却分明松了一口气：“好，有钱老爷担保，在下就放心了！”他爽快地说，随即满脸堆笑地拱着手，“钱老爷，在下金三，您老什么时候进京，派人呼唤一声，在下便立即过来侍候您老人家——刚才的事儿，请您老千万包涵着点，金三有天大的胆，也不敢骚扰进香，触怒神明！你老不信？这可是真的！将来国丈大人跟前，还仰仗您老多多周全哩！哈哈！真的，您老大人别生小人气……”

他啰啰唆唆地说着，看见钱谦益呆呆地一言不发，他就立即闭了嘴，回头招呼衙役，迅速地退出去了。

周围默默地瞧着的香客们，直到这会儿，悬在半空的一颗心才算着了地。他们开始嗡嗡地交谈着，移动着脚步，叹息、摇头，同时纷纷向钱谦益投来感激和敬重的目光。

the place of the Buddha. If the gods are offended and take back the promise, and as a result, anything bad happens to the royal concubine, can you afford it?"

Such a rebuke scared the wits out of Jin Third. He looked at Qian Qianyi with a timid and horrified look. Finally, he lowered his head and little beads of sweat oozed from the corners of his forehead, but soon he raised his head and said:

"Lord Qian, can you guarantee that the girl isn't hiding in the monastery?"

"Yes, upon my honor!" Qian Qianyi said affirmatively, sticking his pigweed walking stick to the ground. Yet very soon he regretted it, because he knew that if this Mr. Jin couldn't find Dong Xiaowan anywhere else, when he returned to Beijing to report to Tian Hongyu, he would definitely blame his failure on the obstruction of a Mr. Qian Muzhai. Then consequently, the arrogant and peremptory Tian Hongyu will turn his anger on the head of that Qian Muzhai, and all kinds of problems might follow. After the tempest, Qian Qianyi gradually calmed down and began to think whether what he did was worthwhile.

Yet Jin Third breathed a sigh of relief. "Good! Since I have your word on it, I can set my mind at rest," he said in a jovial mood, putting his hands together with an exaggerated smile on his face. "Lord Qian, I'm Jin Third. Whenever you come to Beijing, send a message to me, and I'll immediately come over to wait on you. Forgive me for what happened just now. No matter how daring Jin Third is, he didn't have the courage to disrupt incense-offering and offend the gods. You don't believe it? I'm telling the truth. In the future, from time to time, I shall need you to put in a good word for me in front of his lordship the emperor's father-in-law. Haha! I'm serious. I pray for your forgiveness ..."

Seeing no response from Qian Qianyi, he immediately shut up, turned around to recall the *yamen* men and quickly withdrew.

The pilgrims, who were watching silently, were finally relieved. They began to talk noisily, moving, sighing or shaking their heads, and at the same time cast grateful and respectful glances at Qian Qianyi.

茂林长老合十低眉，念一声“阿弥陀佛”，然后走上来，朝钱谦益深深打了一个问讯：

“多承檀越庇护敝寺，贫僧感激不尽！此处非说话之所，请入方丈奉茶。”

钱谦益没有作声。不知为什么，现在他忽然觉得，茂林那恭敬虔诚的声音里，似乎有一种乖巧的、愚弄的意味。他不由得投去冷冷的一瞥，随即摇摇手，领着小厮一言不发地朝山门外走去。

## 私藏小宛

“相公，你可回来了！再不回来，我可要着人去寻你了呢！”

当钱谦益回到东园，穿过楠木厅，走进他下榻的院落时，柳如是微笑着迎出来这样说。

“唔，有什么事么？”钱谦益步入起居室，把藜杖交给红情，漫不经心地问。

“自然有事，一件不大不小的事呢！”柳如是轻快地走上来，一边帮他脱下外衣，一边说。

“什么事？”钱谦益仍旧沉着脸。

“你猜？”柳如是偏着头儿说，虽然她已经看出钱谦益心绪不佳，却依然想用这种方法逗他高兴。

“嗯，要不是挺要紧的，回头再说吧。”钱谦益的声调里透着烦躁。他离开柳如是，脚步有点蹒跚地朝小书斋走去。

柳如是呆了一下，把外衣交给红情，连忙跟上来：“怎么，哪儿不舒服？”她关切地问，伸手去探钱谦益的额角。

钱谦益摇摇头：“不是，我只觉得，嗯，有点乏了。”他说，慢慢走到一张罗汉榻前，坐了下来。

柳如是顿时忙碌起来。她敏捷地移过一床被褥，让钱谦益靠

Abbot Maolin clasped his hands and said "Amitabha Buddha", then walked up and gave Qian Qianyi a salute. "I'm very grateful for your kind protection. This is not a place to talk. Please move to the abbot's room to have tea."

Qian Qianyi didn't speak. Somehow, he suddenly felt that Maolin's respectful and pious voice had a tinge of shrewdness and trickery. He involuntarily cast a cold glance at the monk, then waved his hand and walked with his servant boy towards the monastery gate without saying a word.

## An Angry Old Man

Qian Qianyi returned to East Garden, walked through the Nanmu Hall, and stepped into the courtyard where he was lodging.

Liu Rushi came out and said with a smile, "My dear husband, you're finally home. If you don't come back now, I'll send someone to find you."

"Well, what's up?" Qian Qianyi asked absent-mindedly as he entered the drawing room and handed his walking stick to Hongqing.

Liu Rushi walked up to him briskly and said as she helped him take off his coat, "Certainly there is something! It's a matter of no small weight."

"What is up?" Qian Qianyi's face was still sullen.

"Guess," Liu Rushi said, tilting her head. Although she could see that Qian Qianyi was in a bad mood, she still wanted to use this method to make him happy.

"Well, if it's not something urgent, let's talk about it later." Qian Qianyi's tone had a touch of irritation. He left Liu Rushi and staggered towards the small study.

Liu Rushi was perplexed. She handed the coat to Hongqing and hurriedly followed her husband. "Why, are you not well?" she asked concernedly, reaching out to feel his forehead.

Qian Qianyi shook his head, saying, "I'm fine, just, um, a bit tired." Then, he walked slowly to an Arhat bed and sat down.

Liu Rushi was immediately busy. She quickly brought a quilt for

上，又弯腰替他脱去鞋子，把他的两条腿搬到榻上，然后回头叫：“红情，沏杯茶来！”

钱谦益点点头，闭上了眼睛。他感觉到柳如是温暖柔软的手在他的前额、脸颊和心窝不停地探测着，抚摸着。这是一种亲切的、怜惜的、令人心神宁帖的接触。钱谦益渐渐觉得轻松了一点。又过了一会儿，他勉强睁开眼睛：

“你要说什么事？”

柳如是摇摇头。她从红情手里接过香茶，送到钱谦益唇边：“没什么打紧的事，回头再说吧！”

钱谦益费劲地支撑起身子，红情连忙走过来帮助他。钱谦益呷了两口茶，摇摇头，表示不要了，随即又躺下去。

“那么，你们不必在这儿侍候了，我要静静躺会儿。”他说，重新闭上眼睛。

柳如是服侍他睡好，盖上被褥，又留神观察了片刻，估计确实不是病，这才直起腰来，把茶杯移放到钱谦益伸手够得着的地方，然后领着红情悄悄地退了出去。

钱谦益一动不动地躺着，他确实感到累了，不过头脑却十分清醒。他心情阴郁地回想着戒幢寺所经历的一幕，并且再一次想到：田弘遇这人实在不好惹，他仗着女儿得宠，一贯骄横弄权、贪赃枉法，不少朝中大臣都得仰仗他的鼻息。论威势，他还在周皇后的父亲周奎之上。倘若他因此怀恨在心，有意跟自己为难，那么今后到了京里，自己的日子就会十分难过，弄不好还会有不测之祸。他越想越懊恼。为了摆脱这种困扰，他只好转而集中精神考虑起这一次的行动计划来。他隐约觉得一切都没有经过认真的推敲掂量，就匆忙草率地作出了决定，其实很不可靠。不过，

Qian Qianyi to lean his back on, bent down to take off his shoes and moved his legs onto the bed, and then turned around and said:

"Hongqing, make a cup of tea!"

Qian Qianyi nodded and closed his eyes. He felt Liu Rushi's warm and soft hands constantly feeling and caressing his forehead, cheeks and chest. It was the kind of congenial, sympathetic, and heart-warming contact. Qian Qianyi gradually eased up. After a while, he struggled to open his eyes and said:

"What were you going to say just now?"

Liu Rushi shook her head. She took the aromatic tea from Hongqing and brought it to Qian Qianyi's lips. "Not a big deal. Let's talk about it later."

Qian Qianyi struggled to sit up. Hongqing hurriedly came over to help him. He took two sips of tea, shook his head, and said it was enough, then lay down again.

"Then, you don't have to wait on me here. I need some quiet," he said, closing his eyes again.

Liu Rushi waited on him until he was asleep, then put a quilt on him and watched for a while. When she was certain he was not ill, she straightened up, moved the teacup to a place where he could reach, and then quietly backed out with Hongqing.

Qian Qianyi lay in bed motionlessly. He was indeed tired, but his head was sober. He gloomily recalled the scene at the Jiezhuang Monastery, and ruminated on it. Tian Hongyu is not somebody to trifle with. Because his daughter is a favorite concubine of the emperor, he's arrogant, abusive and corrupt, without any regard for the law. Many courtiers have to look up to him for survival. In fact, he has more power than Zhou Kui, father of Queen Zhou. Should this relation of the emperor be offended and bear a grudge, life for me would be hard in Beijing and even big trouble would come. The more Qian Qianyi thought about it, the more troubled he became. In order to get rid of the thought, he turned to concentrate on his current action plan. He vaguely felt that he had made a shaky plan because his decision was too hasty without duly weighing the pros and cons. However, he

到底怎么个不可靠，他此刻又说不上来。

房间里很寂静，静得连一点声音都没有。钱谦益虽然闭着眼睛，却分明感觉到窗上的湘妃竹帘子怎样一动不动地垂挂着，淡淡的帘影又怎样投在窗前的紫檀灵芝纹画案上。那案上压着一幅柳如是尚未完成的画——《耦耕堂读书图》。

耦耕堂是钱谦益在常熟城北郊的别墅拂水山庄里的一所山堂，取《论语》里“长沮、桀溺耦而耕”的句意，作为堂名。当年钱谦益眼见复官无望，便构筑耦耕堂，打算约他的老朋友程松圆来一起归隐读书。谁知程松圆到底没有来成，就病逝了。钱谦益此刻忽然想起来这件事，心中的感慨油然而生：是啊，人生但能饮酒读书，优游卒岁，也就大可满足了。终日栖栖遑遑，奔走钻营，空劳心力，实在是何苦来！接着，他又觉得其实连读书也是多余。像程松圆那样，读书一生，胸罗万卷，到头来仍不免于黄土白骨，与草木同朽！干脆如老子、庄子所主张的那样：绝圣弃智、浑沌无知、物我齐一，才是真正的彻底。

这样一想，钱谦益数日来的奔竞之心陡然大减，似乎这一次的图谋成功与否，都没有什么值得介怀了。不错，一切都是虚幻，什么富贵荣华、封妻荫子，无非是昙花一现，转眼成空！人生不

couldn't tell how shaky it was at the moment.

The room was quiet, so quiet that there was no sound of any kind at all. Although his eyes were closed, he could clearly feel how the bamboo curtain painted with the two concubines of the primeval emperor Shun hung motionlessly on the window and how the faint shadow of the curtain was cast on the red sandalwood art table carved with ganoderma motifs. On the art table was an incomplete painting by Liu Rushi captioned "Reading in the Hall of the Farming Duo".

The Hall of the Farming Duo was a building in Qian Qianyi's Waterside Villa in the north of Changshu City. It took its name from a story in the Confucian *Analects*: Two recluses, a tall one and a short one, formed a farming duo. One day, Confucius passed by them and sent his pupil Zilu to ask them the way to the ferry. The tall man asked back, "Who's the one holding the lead rope?" Zilu answered, "Confucius." The tall man asked, "Is it Kong Qiu from the Kingdom of Lu?" Zilu said, "Yes, it is." Then the tall man said, "He should've known where the ferry is given his extensive travels." ... Earlier, seeing there was no hope for being reinstated, Qian Qianyi had built the Hall of the Farming Duo and planned to invite his old friend Cheng Songyuan to study with him. However, Cheng Songyuan had never come. He had died of illness. Thinking of that, Qian Qianyi sighed silently. "Yes, if one can spend his life drinking and reading, free from worry, he should be satisfied. What is the point of bustling around and calculating for personal gain?" he thought. Then, he felt that even reading was unnecessary. A man like Cheng Songyuan, who had spent his whole lifetime reading, in the end would still unavoidably become white bones to be buried in the earth and gradually worn away by natural agents together with the grasses and trees. It was better to act in accordance with the philosophy of Laozi and Zhuangzi—abandoning all clever thoughts to arrive at a state of innocence and oneness with nature.

Thus thinking, his anxiety eased, as if whether or not his action plan would succeed didn't concern him anymore. Yes, everything is illusory. All wealth and glory, and all the imperial favors and

过百年，实在不必为此自缚自苦，一切都听其自然好了。于是，他的情绪渐渐松弛下来，胸口也不再那么堵得慌。他的脑子渐渐变得迷糊，开始沉沉睡去……

蓦地，他惊醒过来。他听见了一种细小的嗡嗡声，那是一只黄色的蜜蜂，不知什么时候闯到屋子里来，却找不到飞出去的路。它焦急地、不停地嗡嗡叫着，在屋子里打转，一会儿飞近卧榻，一会儿又飞开去。起初钱谦益还隐忍着，可是那蜂儿飞来飞去，末后竟然飞到他的鼻子尖上来，而且久久地盘旋着，不肯离开。它仿佛把钱谦益的胡子认作了草丛，而把他的两个鼻孔认作了蜂巢似的，大有在此落脚之意。钱谦益心里一急，猛地跳起来，大叫：

“红情，红情！”

“哎，来啦！”红情慌里慌张地奔了进来。

“蜜蜂，打，打！”钱谦益气急败坏地说。

红情怔了一下，才明白过来，脸上现出“原来是这么个事，好把我吓一大跳”的神气。

“打，快打呀！”钱谦益嚷着。

“哟，原来是只蜂儿。老爷，不用打，待婢子放它出去得啦！”红情说着，走过去，打算把帘子掀开。但是钱谦益冒火了：

“混账东西，叫你打你就打！”

“是！”红情不敢再争辩。她从书架旁抽出一支蝇拂，来回赶了一阵，终于把蜜蜂拂落在地上。

钱谦益走近去，看见那只受伤的蜜蜂还在扑扇着翅膀，试图挣扎着飞起来，他就提起脚，使劲一踏，把它踏扁。

“可恶的东西！”他恨恨地说。

红情的眉毛颤抖了一下，现出不忍的神情。她默默地蹲下去，

hereditary titles are nothing more than a flash in the pan and would come to nought in the blink of an eye. Human life is less than a hundred years, so there's no need to seek self bondage. Let nature run its course. Then, his mood gradually eased, his chest was no longer congested, his mind gradually became clouded and he began to fall asleep ...

Suddenly, he woke up upon hearing a small buzzing sound. It was a yellow bee that had broken into the house some time ago but now couldn't find a way out. It buzzed anxiously, flying to and fro, up and down. Sometimes, it came close to the bed and then left. At first, Qian Qianyi was able to tolerate it, but the bee was so audacious as to fly to the tip of his nose and hovered there for a long time without leaving, as if it had taken his beard for a bush, and his two nostrils for a honeycomb, where it would settle. Irritated by the bee, Qian Qianyi jumped up abruptly and yelled:

"Hongqing, Hongqing!"

"Yes, my lord. I'm coming!" Hongqing hurriedly rushed in.

"A bee! Kill it!" Qian Qianyi said exasperatedly.

Hongqing looked startled and then realized what had happened with a you-have-scared-the-hell-out-of-me-with-such-a-small-thing expression on her face.

"Kill it! Be quick!" Qian Qianyi yelled.

"It's just a bee. My lord, we don't have to kill it. I can let it out," Hongqing said. She walked over to the window, and just as she was going to open the curtain, Qian Qianyi flared up.

"You bastard girl. I told you to kill it. So kill it!"

"Aye, my lord!" Hongqing dared not argue. She drew a fly swatter from the bookshelf, chased after the bee, and finally flicked it to the ground.

Qian Qianyi went over and seeing that the injured bee was still flapping its wings and trying to fly up, he lifted his right foot, stomped it hard, and squashed it.

"Damned creature!" he said in distaste.

Hongqing's eyebrows twitched in pity for the bee. She squatted

用指头把死去的蜜蜂拈起来。

“老爷还有什么吩咐？”她垂着头问。

钱谦益迟疑了一下，问：“柳夫人呢？”

“夫人陪董姑娘去了。”

“董姑娘？哪个董姑娘？”

红情摇摇头：“婢子不知道，婢子只听夫人叫她‘小宛’‘小宛’的。”

钱谦益蓦地一惊：“什么，董小宛！你是说董小宛？”

见主人的神情不善，红情害怕起来，点点头，立即又摇摇头。

“她——什么时候来的？”钱谦益厉声追问，把红情吓得倒退一步。

“就在老爷刚才出门的时候。”

钱谦益愣了一下，猛地把桌子一拍，大声吼叫：“把夫人请来！”

“是！”红情连忙答应。

“让她自己一个人来！”钱谦益接着又说。

等红情飞快地退出去后，钱谦益一屁股坐到椅子上。他万万没有料到，那个累得他在戒幢寺里招惹了一场是非的董小宛，不曾藏在僧房里，却居然躲到自己的住处来了。而这么一件大事，柳如是事先没得到他的首肯，事后也不向他禀告，就自作主张把人收留下来。“太放肆了，进门不过半年，她就敢这样干，往后还了得？”钱谦益怒气冲冲地想。他决定狠狠教训柳如是一顿，让她懂得作为钱家的一名姬妾，应当怎样恪遵闺范：“倘若不严加训责，今天她敢背着我藏个女人，明天难保她就不会藏个男的！”当门外响起柳如是的脚步声时，钱谦益心中的愤怒也上升到了顶点。

down silently and picked up the dead bee with her fingers.

"My lord, is there anything else I can do for you?" she asked with her head down.

Qian Qianyi thought for an instant and asked, "Where is Lady Liu?"

"Her ladyship went to accompany Miss Dong."

"Miss Dong? Which Miss Dong?"

Hongqing shook her head. "I don't know. I only heard Mistress call her Xiaowan," said the maid.

Qian Qianyi was shocked. "What? Dong Xiaowan? You mean Dong Xiaowan?" he said.

Seeing her master's unkind expression, Hongqing became frightened. She nodded, and then immediately shook her head.

"When did she—when did she come?" Qian Qianyi asked sternly. Hongqing was so scared that she took a step back.

"Shortly after you went out."

Qian Qianyi thought for an instant. Then he slammed the table and yelled, "Call Mistress!"

"Aye, sir!" Hongqing quickly responded.

"Let her come alone." Qian Qianyi continued.

After Hongqing hurriedly withdrew, Qian Qianyi sat down on the chair. He never expected that Dong Xiaowan, who was the cause of all the trouble at the Jiezhuang Monastery, instead of hiding in a monk's room, had been hiding in his own residence all along. And for such a serious matter, Liu Rushi hadn't sought his approval in advance, nor had she reported to him afterwards, acting completely on herself. "It's very presumptuous of her to do so. How dare she have the audacity to do such a thing while having been in my family for no more than six months. What wouldn't she be up to in the future?" Qian Qianyi thought angrily. He decided to give Liu Rushi a severe lesson in how to behave as a concubine of his. "If I don't reprimand her and let her hide a woman behind my back today, there's no guarantee that she won't hide a man tomorrow!" When Liu Rushi's footsteps sounded outside of the door, the anger in Qian Qianyi's heart rose to its apex.

柳如是进来了。

显然，她已经从红情那里得知钱谦益大发雷霆的消息，所以走得有点急，不过，神态却十分镇定。

钱谦益陡然回过头来，一句粗暴的话已经冲上嘴边。然而，当他接触到柳如是那坦然、镇定的眼神时，不知什么缘故，他的勇气消失了，一刹那间变得目瞪口呆，不知怎样措辞才好。

柳如是也没有说话，只是用那一双即便在严肃的时候，也显得妩媚动人的细长眼睛，静静地望着对方。

这样相持了一会儿，钱谦益终于移开了视线，咳嗽一声，用不大自然的语调问："听说，董小宛到这儿来了，可有此事？"

柳如是点一点头："是的，我正想告知相公这事。"

"怎么来的——她？"

"她说，有恶人追她，慌不择路，误打误撞逃进来的。"

"噢，是什么人追她？"

"听说是京里田皇亲手下的人，来姑苏买女孩儿的。"

"嗯，田皇亲可是个不好惹的刺头儿啊！"

"……"

"你想，这样合适么？——我是说收留她。"

"好歹我们也是手帕姐妹，相与一场，如今她有难，不好撒手不管。"

"可是，你总该先问问我！"

"那时节，正赶上相公出门了。情势又紧迫，才先让她进来了。随后相公回来，本想告知，又碰上相公身子不适，就没敢……"

"胡说！"钱谦益猛地站起身，铁青着脸吼叫起来。他忍耐了许久，但是自己说一句，柳如是辩解一句，丝毫没有知错认错的意思。而且说到后来，反而像是错在他这个一家之主不该出门，

Liu Rushi came in.

Obviously, she had learned about Qian Qianyi's anger from Hongqing, so she came in a hurry, but her expression was calm.

Qian Qianyi turned around abruptly, and a rude remark rushed to his lips. However, when he came into contact with Liu Rushi's innocent, calm eyes, for some reason, his courage disappeared, and he was suddenly lost for words.

Liu Rushi didn't speak either. She just looked at her husband quietly with the pair of slender eyes that were not any less enchanting in such a serious moment.

After a moment of silence, Qian Qianyi finally looked away, coughed, and asked in an unnatural tone, "I heard that Dong Xiaowan is here. Is it true?"

Liu Rushi nodded and said, "Yes, my dear husband. I was just going to tell you about it."

"How did she—come?"

"She said that she were being chased by bad men and ran into our place by accident."

"Then, who was chasing her?"

"I heard that it was the servants of Mr. Tian, the emperor's relation. They came from Beijing to Gusu to buy a girl."

"Well, the emperor's relation Mr. Tian is not somebody to trifle with."

"..."

"Do you think this is appropriate? —I mean taking her in."

"Well, we were handkerchief sisters in the courtesan house after all. Now she's in trouble and it's hard not to lend her a helping hand."

"But, you should've asked me first!"

"When she came, you had gone out. It was so urgent that I had to allow her in first. My dear husband, I was going to tell you when you came back but stopped when I saw you were unwell ..."

"Nonsense!" Qian Qianyi stood up abruptly and shouted with an iron-gray face. He tried his best to hold himself back, but Liu Rushi was always defending herself without a hint of apology, as if the fault

回来后又不该推说身子累乏，不询问清楚。一股受到冒犯的怒火陡地升腾起来，他终于爆发了：

“你说的没有半句是实话！净拿些花言巧语来文饰狡辩！我们来姑苏不过两天，董小宛怎么知道来这儿找你？就算她是误打误撞，门公又怎么会让她进来？还有，我刚才是身子不适，可是这么大一件事，你就该立即告诉我，而你却乐得装聋作哑，一声不吭。你到底想做什么？你，你眼中还有我这一家之主没有？”钱谦益一边吼叫，一边呼哧呼哧地喘气，黝黑的脸变得更黑，怒火从他的眼睛里可怕地喷射着。他的胡子向两旁张开，露出一排残缺不全的门牙。

柳如是呆住了。她没有料到钱谦益会生这么大的气。自从她进门以来半年多，钱谦益对她总是低声软语，曲意迁就，千方百计讨她的欢心。可是这一次却突然翻了脸，而且激烈之状非同一般。不错，刚才她是隐瞒了一点实情：董小宛本来并不知道她住在这儿。只为这东园的门公，是董小宛的同乡近戚。小宛逃来找他庇护，恰好柳如是碰上了。一时动了昔日之情，才把小宛招进白石小筑里来。不过，眼下钱谦益正在气头上，柳如是担心这样解释，会更加火上添油，所以只好不作声。但她依然不太明白，何以为着这么点事，钱谦益竟至于大动肝火。这可完全不像他平日的处事风度。

“哼！”钱谦益冷笑着说，“你敢情是怕我知道之后，会把她撵出去吧？那么，我现在明白告诉你，我确实不许她留在这儿。你告诉她，让她快点走！”

“啊，为什么？”

“不为什么。总之，她必须赶快离开此地，越快越好！”

were his because he shouldn't have left home as head of the family and upon coming back he hadn't bothered to find out about it on account of being tired. Feeling greatly offended, he finally flared up.

"Not a single word of what you said is true! It's all clever excuses! We've been in Gusu for only two days. How did Dong Xiaowan know you're here? Even if she came here by chance, how could the janitor let her in? Also, I did feel unwell just now, but you should tell me immediately about such a big thing instead of keeping it to yourself. What do you intend to do? Do you still have the head of the family in your eyes?" Qian Qianyi yelled, gasping in short breaths. His swarthy face became darker, and anger spurted terribly from his eyes. His beard splayed to the sides, revealing a row of jagged front teeth.

Liu Rushi was baffled, not having expected Qian Qianyi to be so angry. For more than half a year since she entered the Qian family, her husband had always spoken softly to her, giving her everything she wanted, and doing everything possible to please her. But this time around, his countenance changed suddenly and dramatically. Yes, she did conceal some truth. It was true that Dong Xiaowan hadn't known that she lived here, but what she didn't say was that the janitor of East Garden was Dong Xiaowan's close relative from her hometown. Xiaowan came to him for shelter, and Liu Rushi happened to see her. As an old friend, Liu Rushi felt obliged to accommodate Xiaowan in the White Stone Lodge. However, since Qian Qianyi was at the apex of his anger at the moment, Liu Rushi was afraid that such an explanation would add fuel to the fire, so she had to remain silent. Yet she still didn't quite understand why Qian Qianyi was so angry about such a small matter. It was not like him.

"Humph!" Qian Qianyi said with a sneer. "You're afraid that I may drive her out after hearing it? Well, I can tell you now that I really won't allow her to stay here. You tell her. Tell her to leave as quickly as possible!"

"Ah, why?"

"No reason. She must leave this place as soon as possible, the

“可是，外面有人要抢她……”

“这我不管！”

柳如是的眉毛抖动了一下，看来也有点着恼了。可是，随即她就放弃了这种念头。她走上前去，开始迷人地笑着，扯着钱谦益的衣袖，摇摆着身子，用撒娇的口吻说：“我要你管，我要留下她，我要嘛！”

“不行！”钱谦益的口气斩钉截铁。

柳如是一怔，脸蛋涨得通红。她负气地摔开钱谦益的袖子：“我偏不去说，要去，你自己去！”

钱谦益瞧着柳如是，胡子动了动，想说句什么，可是他终于一跺脚，向外面叫：“红情，红情！”

柳如是急了，她慌忙赶上去，拦住钱谦益：“可是你让她到哪儿去？她刚刚死了亲娘，如今，她自己又病得腻腻歪歪的！”柳如是的口气简直是在哀求了。

钱谦益转动了一下眼睛，对于这个消息似乎感到意外。他停止了呼唤，转过身，慢慢地踱到画案前，对那幅尚未完成的《耦耕堂读书图》默默地瞧了片刻，然后没有瞧柳如是，也没有抬起头，用一种低沉而缓慢的声音说：

“你要我怜悯她，那么有谁来怜悯我呢？……唉，你——还是让她走吧！”

柳如是睁大眼睛听着，似乎有点明白了。她静默下来，呆呆地坐到椅子上，不再提出异议。只是，她的鼻翼在翕动，愈来愈急促。终于，她背过身去，轻轻地抽泣起来……

## 痛失善本

“哼，只要有我黄宗羲在，断不容那伙败类的奸谋得逞，这是毫无疑问的！”黄宗羲抿紧了稍稍向前突出的嘴唇，坚决地想。这时，他正走在苏州城西阊门内的大街上。他走得那样急，以致

sooner the better."

"But, there're men outside waiting to kidnap her ..."

"It's none of my business!"

Liu Rushi's eyebrows twitched, and she seemed a little vexed. But then she kept herself under control. She stepped forward, and, smiling charmingly, pulled Qian Qianyi's sleeve, and said in a coquettish tone, swaying her body, "Please, please, please! Please help her! I want to help her."

"No way!" Qian Qianyi's tone was firm.

Liu Rushi was baffled, her cheeks flushing. She threw away Qian Qianyi's sleeve in anger. "I won't tell her! If you want to, go tell her yourself!"

Qian Qianyi looked at Liu Rushi. His beard moved. He wanted to say something, but finally stomped his foot and shouted to the outside, "Hongqing, Hongqing!"

Liu Rushi was worried. She hurried to stop him. "But where do you let her go? She has lost her mother a short while ago, and now she herself is so sick." Liu Rushi's tone was bordering on pleading.

Qian Qianyi rolled his eyes and seemed shocked by the news. He stopped shouting, turned around, walked slowly to the front of the art table, and silently looked at the unfinished "Reading in the Hall of the Farming Duo" for a while; then, without looking at Liu Rushi or raising his head, he said slowly in a low voice, "You want me to have pity on her, but who will have pity on me? ... Well, you—let her go!"

Liu Rushi listened with wide open eyes as she started to understand the situation. She fell silent and sat on the chair blankly without raising further objections. However, her nosewings began to flutter. Finally, she turned her back and sobbed ...

## Loss of a Rare Book

"Humph, as long as I, Huang Zongxi, am there, I'll not allow the gang of scums to succeed. There's no doubt about it!" Huang Zongxi thought resolutely, tightening his slightly protruding lips. He was walking on the street inside of the West City Gate of Suzhou

胳肢窝下夹着一个青布包袱、正从身后替他打着油纸伞的书童黄安都有点跟他不上。

绵密的春雨在无声地飘洒着，雨水浇湿了石子铺砌的路面，浇湿了街道两旁店铺的黑瓦顶，也浇湿了街上来来往往的油纸伞、斗笠和轿顶，给本来就显得闷闷不乐的行人脸孔，蒙上了一层灰暗的色彩。这一场春雨，按说来得正是时候，要在以往，它多少能给忧惧不安的人心注入一些温暖和希望。可是如今不行了。如今的苏州，这个江南首屈一指的商埠、丝织业的中心、大明帝国空前繁华的一个象征，经过多年来沉重的战费负担的消耗，以及去年夏秋之间那一场横扫三吴地区的大旱和蝗灾的袭击，终于彻底地衰落了，几乎成了一个乞丐塞途、饿殍载道的鬼蜮世界。仅仅在大半年前，那遍布全城的机房里，提花织机还一天到晚地轧轧作响，如今已经难得听到了。那纵横交错的水巷，昔日还飘荡着美妙的吴侬软语和琵琶，如今已经被穷饿无计的呻吟愁叹和失去亲人的哀哀痛哭所代替。至于最热闹繁华的阊门一带，由于商船往来稀少，店铺纷纷闲歇。以往那种百货充盈、游人熙攘的景象也已经荡然无存，只剩下少数的店铺还勉强支撑着门面，那景况也相当惨淡可怜了。只是由于最难熬的春荒已经过去，四乡涌来的饥民开始逐渐离开，加上盛传复社的相公们又要来参加虎丘大会，这对于正在饥寒中苦苦挣扎的市井小民来说，无论如何总是个碰运气、谋活路的机会，于是他们拼着一口气，又想方设法地积极活动起来，才使得萧条冷落的市面，多少恢复了一点活气。

City. He walked in such a hurry that Huang An, the boy servant who was holding an oil-paper umbrella for him and tugging a blue cloth package under one arm, could hardly catch up with him.

The fine but dense spring rain was coming down silently, wetting the pebble pavement, the black tile roofs of the shops, the oil-paper umbrellas, the cone hats, and tops of sedan chairs, and casting a dark hue on the sullen and gloomy faces of the pedestrians. This spring rain, which should have been welcome, was particularly irritating now. Previously, at this time of year, it had always injected some warmth and hope into the worried and fearful hearts. The city of Suzhou, the premier commercial port south of the Yangtze River, center of the silk industry, and a symbol of the unprecedented prosperity of the Great Ming Empire, after years of consumption by war and last year's drought and locust plague that swept the Sanwu area at the turn of summer and autumn, had now declined and almost became an otherly world filled with beggars and corpses. Back half a year ago, the jacquard looms were still rustling in the machine rooms all over the city. Now one could hardly hear that sound. In the criss-crossing water alleys, the soft whispers of the beautiful young ladies speaking in the local dialect and the music of *pipa* had now been replaced by moans of those who had had no food and heart-wrenching cries of those who had lost their loved ones. In the once most lively and prosperous West City Gate area, because of the reduced activity of merchant ships, the shops were mostly closed. The previous scene of bustling tourists and flourishing shops full of all kinds of goods had disappeared. A few shops remained and struggled to maintain the facade, but the overall picture was a bleak one. Meanwhile, there were some positive signs. Spring famine—the most difficult time—had passed, the hungry people from the neighboring places were beginning to leave. It was said that the young scholars of the Fushe would come to meet at the Tiger Hill Conference. In any case, it was a chance for the struggling men and women at the bottom of society to try their luck and find a way to survive, and thanks to their diligence, the depressed market became more or less alive.

不过，此刻黄宗羲却没有心思理会这些，因为最近以来复社内部所发生的事态是如此地严重，简直把他的全部思想都占据了。他是三月初七那天夜里，同朋友们结束了在李十娘家的饮宴，回到冒襄下榻的河房之后，才第一次听说有人试图替阮大铖翻案的。当时，他是那样的吃惊和愤怒。他不仅完全同意社友们认为这桩阴谋的主角是几社的分析，而且拍案而起，主张立即前往松江，向几社之徒大兴问罪之师。只是由于陈贞慧力主持重，再三劝说，他才勉强忍了下来。按照陈贞慧的计划，他们当然决不放过几社那伙败类。但是，考虑到自从前些日子，在争当大会主盟的角逐中失败以来，自己这一派人的影响力已大为削弱，加上另一个主盟者郑元勋看来又已经同几社的人穿上了连裆裤，光凭自己这么几个人，到时也许控制不了局势。为稳妥起见，还必须去请一两位德高望重的东林元老出来压阵。这一点，黄宗羲也是同意的。然而，在讨论到究竟请谁出面的时候，他却同大家发生了争执。他提出钱谦益就住在常熟，与苏州近在咫尺，不妨请他出面；但是多数人不赞成，而主张到金坛去请周镳、周钟兄弟。本来，周氏兄弟都是士林中声誉卓著的人物，又是坚决的反阮派，请他们出面也未尝不可；但是吴应箕等人却因此而排斥钱谦益，把他说成似乎是不可信赖的。这一点，却大大激怒了黄宗羲。他不能容忍任何人藐视和诋毁钱谦益，尤其不相信吴应箕所说的钱谦益似乎也主张宽纵阉党的传闻，因此当场就同他们争吵起来。偏偏对方人多，特别是侯方域和顾杲，说话又尖又损，黄宗羲只有一张嘴巴，争他们不过。他一怒之下，便声言不同他们一道上虎丘。

However, at this moment Huang Zongxi didn't have the mind to pay attention to these, because he was obsessed with the grave situation in the Fushe. Back on the night of the seventh of March, after he returned from the gathering at Li Shiniang's place to the riverhouse where Mao Xiang was lodging, when he heard for the first time that someone tried to reverse the Ruan Dacheng case, he was shocked and deeply angered. Believing like his Fushe comrades that it was the Jishers that had masterminded the conspiracy, he slapped the table and suggested that they go to Songjiang immediately to question the Jishers. Chen Zhenhui counseled caution and persuaded him to be patient and he reluctantly held himself back. According to Chen Zhenhui's plan, they would not let go the Jishe scumbags, but meanwhile they should exercise more caution as they were few in number and might not be able to keep things under control. After their defeat in the competition for dominant roles in the coming conference the influence of their faction had waned. Besides, it seemed that one of the other dominant personages, Mr. Zheng Yuanxun, was evidently colluding with the Jishers. To be on the safe side, they needed to enlist the help of one or two respected East Wood veterans. Huang Zongxi agreed. However, when it came to who they should invite, a dispute began.

Huang Zongxi suggested that they invite Qian Qianyi because the old man lived in Changshu, very close to Suzhou; but most of the others disagreed and proposed they go to Jintan to invite the Zhou brothers: Zhou Biao and Zhou Zhong. To be fair, the Zhou brothers were both reputable figures and resolute anti-Ruanists. It was not a bad idea to ask them to intervene. However, Huang Zongxi was displeased by the rejection of Qian Qianyi by the likes of Wu Yingji, who made an issue of trustworthiness. He couldn't tolerate anyone slighting or slandering Qian Qianyi, and he especially didn't believe the rumor cited by Wu Yingji that Qian Qianyi advocated the pardening of the party of eunuch Wei Zhongxian. So, he quarreled with them on the spot. Unfortunately he was overwhelmed in number by the other side; two of them in particular, Hou Fangyu and Gu Gao, spoke sharply and harshly against Qian Qianyi. Huang Zongxi, with one mouth only,

后来，亏得陈贞慧、梅朗中、张自烈几个竭力劝解，又同意黄宗羲上常熟去把钱谦益也请来，才把这场风波好歹平息下去。

现在，陈贞慧和顾杲到金坛去了，冒襄经过大家劝说，也同意参加大会，但又说有事要办，必须先上常州，独自走了。剩下黄宗羲跟着吴应箕、侯方域、梅朗中、张自烈几个，提前到了苏州，住进皋桥往东不远、一位名叫钱禧的社友家里，打算一边观察动静，一边预做准备。不过，黄宗羲仍然一心想着到常熟去访钱谦益，而且由于想到很快就会同这位老世伯相见，他的心情甚至变得更热切了。

说到黄宗羲同钱谦益的关系，确实与一般人不同。这不仅因为黄宗羲的父亲黄尊素与钱谦益当年同属东林，两家本来就有交情；而且还由于黄尊素被阉党迫害致死后，钱谦益对这位故人之子，多年来一直十分关怀照顾。他看见黄宗羲生活拮据，常常给予资助不必说，还特意把黄宗羲请到常熟家里去住下，将全部藏书向他敞开，让他潜心攻读，同他一道讨论切磋。钱谦益的文章学问，黄宗羲自然是十分敬佩；而黄宗羲的好学深思，见解不凡，也常常使钱谦益大为惊异，于是又不遗余力地向别人推奖揄扬。因为这些缘故，黄宗羲对这位老世伯一直十分感激，把钱谦益当作前辈知己。虽然他早就拜了著名大儒刘宗周为师，但比较起来，博学多才、思想灵活、不拘一格的钱谦益却另有一种特殊的吸引力，使黄宗羲不由自主地对他怀有一种亲近的依恋之情。事实上，

was not their match. In a fit of anger, he declared that he would not go to Tiger Hill together with them. Chen Zhenhui, Mei Langzhong, and Zhang Zilie did their best to appease him but not until they agreed that he could go to Changshu to invite Qian Qianyi did the tempest subside.

Then, Chen Zhenhui and Gu Gao left for Jintan. Though earlier Mao Xiang had agreed to take part in the conference through persuasion by the others, he said that he had to go to Changzhou first and left alone. Huang Zongxi followed Wu Yingji, Hou Fangyu, Mei Langzhong, and Zhang Zilie to Suzhou ahead of schedule. They stayed in the house of a fellow Fushe member named Qian Xi, who lived east of Gao Bridge. The party planned to make preparations while observing the situation. However, Huang Zongxi was still obsessed with his coming visit to Qian Qianyi in Changshu. When he thought that he would be meeting the venerable elder very soon his heart was filled with joy.

Huang Zongxi and Qian Qianyi did have a very close relationship. For one thing, the two families had a long-standing relationship because both Huang Zongxi's father Huang Zunsu and Qian Qianyi belonged to the East Wood Party; for another, after Huang Zunsu died of persecution by "the castrate's party", Qian Qianyi had been very caring to the son of the deceased friend over the years. Needless to say, Qian Qianyi had lent a helping hand when Huang Zongxi was in financial distress. He had invited Huang Zongxi to live in his home in Changshu and given the young man access to all the books in his library. The two often held intellectual discussions. Huang Zongxi admired Qian Qianyi for his writings and great learning while Huang Zongxi's diligence and intelligence often amazed Qian Qianyi, who spared no effort to recommend the young man to others. Therefore, Huang Zongxi had always been very grateful to this friend of his father and regarded him as a confidant despite the age gap. Although the young man was officially a pupil of the famous Confucian scholar Liu Zongzhou, he was very much drawn to Qian Qianyi for the old man's learning, versatility, wisdom, and unconventionality. In fact,

在黄宗羲看来，钱谦益作为当年身受迫害的东林元老，无论是就对阉党的仇恨而言，还是就目前在士林中的威望影响而言，周镳、周钟兄弟都无法与之相比。任凭几社那伙人再嚣张跋扈、再善于蛊惑人心，到时只要钱谦益出面说上一句话，他们的阴谋就一定不能得逞。这一点，恐怕周氏兄弟还未必能做到。

“哦，无论如何，我得赶紧到常熟去，越快越好！”他在心里这样催促自己，不由自主地兴奋起来，脚步也迈得更快了。

这样一直走到吴趋坊。这一带是书坊萃集的地方，大大小小的铺子很是不少。过去黄宗羲到苏州，总要上这儿来转一转，所以并不生疏。不过，现在黄宗羲到这儿来，却不是为了买书，相反是打算把手头一套宋版《潜虚衍义》设法抵押出去。因为他已经有两年多没见钱谦益了，这一次上常熟，不管怎么说，总得办点礼物。但眼下他已经是囊空如洗，别说办礼，几乎连回家的旅费都颇费踌躇。照理说，他也不该弄到这样子，仅仅半个月前，身上还带着五六十两银子。谁知碰上了陈贞慧、吴应箕这伙朋友，三天两日不是饮酒，就是访妓。虽说自有冒襄、陈贞慧这些阔气的公子哥儿做东，可自己也不好意思天天白吃，偶尔也要还上一席两席。这么一松手，转眼工夫就把钱花个精光。自然，他还有一班朋友，但为着请钱谦益出面的事，刚刚同他大吵了一场，现在又低声下气地伸手借钱，黄宗羲无论如何也放不下这个面子。想来想去，最后才想到这部《潜虚衍义》上。这部书半个月前闹了一场风波。后来黄宗羲到底舍不得，把它送到裱褙店去，经过

in Huang Zongxi's eyes, Qian Qianyi, as an East Wood veteran who had suffered persecution at the hands of Eunuch Wei, had a greater hatred towards the castrate's party and greater influence among the gentry scholars than the Zhou brothers. No matter how powerful and deceptive the Jishers were, one word from Qian Qianyi would be sufficient to frustrate their conspiracy. The Zhou brothers would not be able to do it.

"Well, in any case, I have to go to Changshu as soon as possible, the sooner the better," he thought to himself, quickening his steps with eagerness.

He went all the way to Wuqu Street. It was an area packed with bookstores, big and small. He was not unfamiliar with this place because he had visited it every time he came to Suzhou. However, he was here now not to buy books; on the contrary, he had to find a pawnbroker to pawn his set of the Song dynasty edition of *Studies in the Explorations into the Ubiquitous Void*. Because he hadn't seen Qian Qianyi for more than two years, he felt obliged to bring the elder some gifts on his visit to Changshu. The problem was, at the moment his pocket was empty and he even didn't have enough money to travel home, not to mention to buy gifts. Supposedly, he shouldn't have lowered himself to this state. Just half a month ago, he still had fifty or sixty taels of silver on him. Unfortunately, he had run into a group of friends, including Chen Zhenhui and Wu Yingji; they had met to drink or visit prostitutes every two or three days. Although on most occasions it was his generous chaps like Mao Xiang and Chen Zhenhui who paid the bills, he was decent enough to return their favor once in a while by hosting a banquet. Then, the money was gone in the blink of an eye. He had a bunch of friends of course, but having just had a big quarrel with them just now over the proposal to invite Qian Qianyi, he was too proud to lower himself to borrow money from them. After much deliberation, he finally thought of his valuable asset *Studies in the Explorations into the Ubiquitous Void*. It was the book that had caused a disturbance half a month ago. After that incident, unwilling to part with the damaged book, he took it to a paperwork embellishment

那里的老师傅仔细地漂洗、修补，重新装裱，居然奇迹般地大体恢复了原貌。这是目前黄宗羲手头唯一还值点钱的东西，他虽然十二分舍不得，也只好狠狠心暂时押出去。这件事，本来派黄安办就成，可是黄安来了一趟，回去说书坊的老板们刁滑得紧，明明值十六两银子的书，他们竟然只肯出三两四两，最通融的一个也只出到七两。黄宗羲又气又急，把书童骂了一顿，说他不中用，连这点小事都办不好。但骂归骂，到头来，却还得亲自出马。

“无论如何，这套书是十六两买来的，我就得押回十六两！”黄宗羲执拗地想，挥手赶开几个围上来讨钱的小乞丐，又侧身让过了一队扛着棺材号哭而过的送丧行列，这才踏进大来堂书坊的门槛。

这所大来堂，据黄安说，就是愿意出七两银子的那家书坊，瞧门面倒也平常，外面竖着“古今名书发兑”的木招牌，当门一个小小的柜台，四面靠墙壁排列着书架，上面堆满了各种书籍，此外就是一张小方桌和几张椅子、凳子之类，那是供顾客歇脚的。不过，此刻里面却看不见一个顾客，只有一个伙计模样的后生正伏在柜台上打盹。

黄安合上油纸伞，在门槛外甩了几下积在上面的雨水，顺手把它倚在门边上，就走过去摇醒那伙计，说明来意。谁知不巧，书坊老板不在家。问去了哪里，那伙计也说不清；让他派人去找，又诸多推搪地不愿意。最后，黄宗羲听得心头火起，干脆叫黄安

shop. The book was miraculously restored to almost the original shape through the old craftsman's work that involved rinsing, repairing, and outfitting. It was currently the only thing Huang Zongxi had that was worth something. Although he was reluctant to part with it, he had to harden his heart to pawn it to solve his problem. He asked his page boy Huang An to pawn the book, but Huang An came back and said that the owners of the bookstores were all cunning and stingy. They were only willing to lend three or four taels of silver for a book set that was worth sixteen taels. The most generous one only offered seven taels. In anger and frustration, Huang Zongxi scolded the boy for being useless. After the outburst of his temper, he had to go himself.

"This set of books were bought at sixteen taels, so I'll pawn them at sixteen," Huang Zongxi thought stubbornly. He waved away a few little beggars who surrounded him to ask for money, stood aside to dodge a funeral parade with a coffin followed by a crowd of crying mourners, and then came to the threshold of the Dalaitang Bookstore.

The Dalaitang was the bookstore that Huang An said was willing to give seven taels of silver. The storefront was nothing extraordinary. In front of it stood a wooden signboard that said WE SELL AND BUY FAMOUS BOOKS ANCIENT OR NEW. There was a small counter at the door. Against the walls were lined up bookshelves filled with all kinds of books. In the middle was a small square table and a few chairs and stools for customers to rest. At this moment however, there was no customer in sight. A young man who looked like a shop assistant was napping with his head on the counter.

Huang An closed the oil-paper umbrella, flicked the rainwater outside the threshold, leaned it against the door, walked over, woke up the guy, and explained the purpose of their visit. Unfortunately, the owner of the bookstore was not in. Huang An asked where he went, but the guy couldn't tell it; Huang An suggested sending someone to look for him, but the shop assistant refused by giving various excuses. Finally, Huang Zongxi, who had been listening to their conversation, was inflamed. He told Huang An to ignore the shop assistant, took a chair and sat down by the door. Then he ordered Huang An to hand

别理会他，管自移了一张椅子在门边坐下，并命黄安把那套《潜虚衍义》拿过来，一边作最后的摩挲赏玩，一边等候坊主回来。

淅沥的春雨还在不停地下。雨水在门槛外积聚起来，又缓慢地向更低洼的地方流去。这雨已经下了整整一天，街道上的泥尘污垢被洗得差不多了。如今这一小片流动的积雨看上去是清澈和干净的。它被屋檐上不停落下的水滴溅击着，勾画出一长串奇妙的图案。

黄宗羲把《潜虚衍义》从楠木匣子里取了出来。这书共有四册，一色灰蓝色的书衣，有点发黄的宋笺藏经纸书签上，印着书的名称，看上去十分古雅。翻开里页，可以发现这书不仅纸幅版框特别高大，而且字体也挺大，一个个方正工整，刀法圆润，更兼纸色墨汁，粲然夺目，一望而知是宋代浙版书中的精品。美中不足的是，个别书页上，如今留下了一些无法漂洗干净的污痕。这污痕使黄宗羲感到心疼和愤恨，同时又使他对这书更多了一分抱愧和爱惜之情……终于，他长长地叹了一口气，把书合起来，不看了。“虽然不得不暂时把它抵押出去，但是为了答谢钱老伯，也为了不让替阮胡子翻案的阴谋得逞，这是应当的，值得的！”他一边把书重新放回楠木匣子里，一边这样说服自己，又用青布包袱重新把书裹好，搁在膝盖上，抬起头，开始向街上张望。

这条吴趋坊，紧连着阊门大街，虽然也是个人烟稠密、店铺众多的去处，可是街道却挺窄，对面屋子里的情形，可以看得很清楚。书坊的正对面是一爿不小的布店，左侧是间药材铺子，右侧是卖杂货的，再旁边还有几间书坊和别的店铺。这会儿，雨下得小了些，街上的行人渐渐多了起来。黄宗羲看见：两乘轿子踏着水花过去了；一个瞎眼的老头掮着一把胡琴，由一名十三四岁

him the *Studies in the Explorations into the Ubiquitous Void* book set for him to have a final perusal while waiting for the bookstore owner.

Outside, the patter of the spring rain continued. Rainwater built up outside the threshold, and then slowly flowed to the lower places. It had been raining for a whole day, and the streets had been washed clean. The flowing rainwater looked clean and clear. Together with the splashes of water droplets from the eaves it drew a long series of wonderful patterns on the ground.

Huang Zongxi took the *Studies in the Explorations into the Ubiquitous Void* from the *nanmu* box. There were four quaint volumes in gray-blue bookcloth with the title printed on a yellowish label of Song-dynasty scripture paper. On the interior pages, the book content was printed with a small margin and big-font square characters carved expertly on lithographic plates. The ink and the color of the paper formed a clear contrast. One could tell it was among the best of Song-dynasty books printed in Zhejiang Province. The only blemish was that on some pages there were now some stains that would stay forever. Huang Zongxi was pained and grieved to see the stains. He felt guilty and was very sorry to have to part with the book set. Finally, he leaved a long sigh and closed the book in his hand. "I'm sorry to let you go for now, but to repay Uncle Qian's kindness and to prevent the conspiracy to reverse the Ruan case, it's worth it." He tried to persuade himself as he put the book back in the *nanmu* box. Then he wrapped the volumes in the green cloth wrapper and put the bundle on his knees before raising his head to look out into the street.

Wuqu Street was adjacent to West City Gate Street. Although it was also a crowded place with many shops, the street was rather narrow, and everything in the opposite stores could be seen clearly. Opposite the bookstore was a large fabric shop with a herbal store on the left and a grocery store on the right and a few bookstores and other stores further on both sides. At this moment, the rain was a little lighter, and more and more pedestrians showed up on the street. In front of Huang Zongxi two sedan chairs passed by, rainwater splashing from under the chairmen's feet; a blind old musician carrying a *huqin*,

的小姑娘引路，从小巷里慢慢转了出来；三个小孩冒着雨，蹲在房檐下的积水边，在放一只木制的小船；于是又招来一个瓦刀脸的闲汉，指手画脚地从旁充当指导，并以他的油腔滑调，逗引得正倚在就近门边的一个浓妆艳抹的大嘴女人，吃吃地笑个不住。此外，那些肩挑手提，匆匆而过的行人也自然不少。“嗯，书坊老板这会儿也该回来了吧？”黄宗羲想，不由得睁大眼睛，用热切的目光迎着每一个走近来的可疑者，并不时抬起头，向更远的地方眺望。

正当他盼得有点心焦的时候，忽然，街道上响起了一阵杂沓的脚步声，一个衙门公差，手里扬着一张公文模样的纸片，大摇大摆地走过来。在他的身后，还跟着一群各执扁担的挑夫。他们来到书坊正对面的布店前，就站住了。只见那公差走进店去，大声地说了几句什么，随即走出来，朝那群挑夫做了个手势，说：

“快，进去搬！”

挑夫们挤拥了一下，正要往里走，这时，店主人——一个胖胖的中年男子气急败坏地奔了出来，朝那公差一个劲地行着礼说：“头翁息怒，头翁息怒！请听小可一言，此次承值，非是小店有意拖延，实因遭遇荒年凶岁，亏损甚大。这百匹之数，小店已是多方筹措，百计张罗，还望头翁宽限数日，一定如数送到府衙，感激不尽！”

那公差冷笑一声，说：“李老爸，你这话说了也只好当放屁！你要我宽限你，大老爷却不宽限我！你须也知道，这次可是京里周国舅爷着人来姑苏买货，限令今日取齐，便是大老爷也只有顺

led by a thirteen-or fourteen-year-old girl, slowly moved out of a small alley; three children crouched in the rain beside a pool of rainwater under the eaves playing with their toy wooden boats; an adult idler with a brick chisel face was attracted to them and offered to give them guidance, waving his hand here and there as he spoke zealously in such unctuous tones that sent a gorgeously dressed, heavily powdered, and big-mouthed lady leaning on a door close by giggling nonstop. There were quite a few people hurrying past with a heavy load on their shoulders or in their arms. "Well, the bookstore owner should be back now," Huang Zongxi thought, greeting everyone coming his way with expectant eyes and raising his head from time to time to look into the street.

Just as he was growing impatient, he heard a jumble of footsteps on the street, and a *yamen* man came swaggeringly over, with a piece of paper in the shape of an official document in his hand. He was followed by a group of porters each with a shoulder pole. When they came to the fabric shop directly opposite the bookstore, they stopped. The *yamen* man entered the store, said something loudly, then came out, and, gesturing to the porters, said:

"Quick! Go in and get moving!"

As the porters jostled to go in, out came the shop owner, a fat, middle-aged man. He kept saluting the *yamen* man panickedly and said, "I beg your mercy, sir! I beg your mercy! Please kindly take a listen to my explanation. We haven't tallied in the fulfillment of your order. The fact of the matter is, we've suffered greatly in the year of famine, and a hundred units of fabric is no small quantity. We're doing everything possible to get it from various sources and will deliver it to your residence if you could be so obliging as to give us a grace period."

The *yamen* man sneered and said, "Boss, your words are only as good as a fart. You want me to give you a grace period, but the prefect doesn't give me one. You should know that the emperor's brother-in-law Mr. Zhou from Beijing sent his men here to purchase cloth and demanded that everything be ready today. Even the prefect himself has

着他！”

李老板哭丧着脸道：“皆因机房歇业，货源不继，自从传闻周国舅来苏办货，绸缎之价，一夜暴长，竟高出往时一倍有余。小店大亏之后，本微力薄，实在是……”

那公差无动于衷地说：“你本微也罢，本厚也罢，今番该你承值，便是倾家荡产，也得如数办齐！”李老板急了，结结巴巴分辩说：“可是、可是府里分明出过告示，立了碑文，说一应上司按临时之府县公务，照依时价平卖，再不用铺行承值的呀！”

那公差怔了一下，顿时变了脸，大吼一声：“这个，你跟大老爷说去，我管不着！”说完，一挥手，吆喝那群挑夫：“给我搬！”

在他们对答的当儿，黄宗羲一直在目不转睛地注视着。这时他有点明白了：看来，是苏州府责令这布店代购百匹绸缎，可是这布店却因折了本，无力张罗。所以如今官府便派人上门，强行收缴。本来，朝廷过去是有所谓“铺户当行买办”之制，规定各行铺户必须轮流义务当差，替官府采办货物。办货的钱表面上由官府发给，但实际上，却往往并不给足，到底给多少，那就得看当官各人的品性而定，其间伸缩性很大。不足的部分，照例就由各行当值的铺户自己补足。铺户们畏惧官府的势力，只有忍痛认赔。这个制度实行多年，把铺户们逼迫得叫苦连天。有办法的富

to listen to him have his way."

The shop owner said in a sad voice, "Supplies have been discontinued due to stoppage of production. Since news spread that the emperor's brother-in-law, Mr. Zhou from Beijing, was coming to make purchases in Suzhou, prices of silks and satins have doubled overnight. After having suffered a big loss, my store, because it's too small, isn't strong enough to ..."

The *yamen* man said nonchalantly, "It doesn't matter whether you're small or big. This time, it's your turn to take the order and fulfill it. You have to do it even if you have to go bankrupt." The shop owner panicked. He argued with a stammer, "But, but there has been a notice from the *yamen* inscribed on a tone tablet saying that purchases will be made on the basis of current prices instead of flat rates since they're considered emergency procurement by the county and prefecture authorities for government use."

The *yamen* man was silent for a brief moment and then his countenance changed suddenly. He shouted, "Well, say it to the prefect. It's not my concern." Then, he waved his hand and yelled to the porters, "Get moving!"

While they were arguing, Huang Zongxi was watching intently. At this point he somewhat understood what was happening. The Suzhou prefectural *yamen* had ordered the fabric shop to purchase one hundred units of silks and satins on its behalf, but the fabric shop was unable to perform the task because they had suffered a big loss. So the *yamen* came now to forcefully seize the goods in the shop. At that time, the imperial court had a so-called compulsory supplier system, in which all shops had to take turns to serve as a purchasing arm for the government. On the surface, the money for the purchased goods was paid by the government, but in fact, it was never paid in full. How much was paid depended on the character of the official in charge, and there was great room for maneuvering. If there was a deficiency, the store that was "on duty" should make it good. In awe of the *yamen*, the store owners had to accept the loss against their will. This system had been in place for many years, and the shop owners had been

商，就设法投靠官府，逃避差役；没有办法的中小商人，往往被弄到倾家荡产，甚至还有卖儿卖女、投河上吊的。铺户们不堪重负，联合起来实行罢市的事件也屡有发生。后来朝廷看见积弊实在太多，不得不作一些变通，改“当行买办”为“招商买办”和“佥商买办”，还立了碑文。但是看来，此项弊政并未真正革除，只要下面喜欢，照样还这么干。

这当儿，街道上已经围起了一些看热闹的人，把黄宗羲的视线挡住了。他不由得站起来，伸长脖子从人们的头上望过去。他看见那些挑夫在公差的指挥下，正不停地从布店里把一匹一匹的绫罗绸缎搬出来，准备挑走。那个李老板失魂落魄地站在一旁，浑身上下不停地发抖。黄宗羲心中很是不忍，他想了想，回过头，吩咐正站在一旁看得发呆的书童说：

“黄安，你去，请那位头翁过来，就说本相公请他说话。”

“头翁？哪位头翁？”黄安有点莫名其妙。

“喏！”黄宗羲一指那个公差。

黄安眨巴了一下眼睛，显然有点不乐意：“大爷，你又想管……”他噘起嘴巴说。

“叫你去你就去！”

黄安没有办法，只好跨出门，分开围观的人，走前去同那公差说了几句，然后带着他走回书坊来。

那公差是个黑脸汉子，长着一部络腮胡子和两道几乎连到一起的眉毛。黄宗羲迎上前，拱一拱手，正要说话，随即发现门外

complaining about its injustice. Wealthy businessmen who had the means cooperated with the *yamen* and escaped official duties whereas owners of small and medium-sized businesses who didn't have the means were often ruined, and some of them even had to sell their sons and daughters or commit suicide by hanging themselves or plunging into the river. Since the burden was unbearable, industrial action was not unrare. Later, the imperial court saw the ills of the system and made some modifications. The forced supplier mechanism was replaced by the negotiated supplier or appointed supplier mechanism. Stone inscriptions were made to make the change official. However, in practice, the ills were not eradicated. Lower level officials still loved the old ways.

By now, some spectators had gathered on the street and the view was blocked.

Huang Zongxi stood up unwittingly, craned his neck and looked over the heads. He saw the porters, under the direction of the *yamen* man, were busy moving out rolls of silks and satins from the fabric shop to be carried away on their shoulder poles. Mr. Li, owner of the shop, stood aside in despair, trembling from top to bottom. Huang Zongxi couldn't bear to see it. He thought for an instant, then turned around, and said to his page boy, who was watching dumbfoundedly:

"Huang An, go ask the head man to come over, and just say that I want to have a word with him."

"Head man? Which head man?" Huang An was a little bit puzzled.

"That one!" Huang Zongxi pointed to the *yamen* man.

Huang An blinked, obviously reluctant to go. "My young master, do you want to get into other people's ..." he said with a pursed mouth.

"If I ask you to go, just go!"

Huang An could do nothing but obey his young master. He stepped out, separated the onlookers, walked over, said something to the head man, who came to the bookstore with him.

The *yamen* man was a dark-faced guy with a beard and two eyebrows that almost looked like one. Huang Zongxi clasped his hands

那些看热闹的人，已经纷纷转过身来，好奇地瞅着他们。于是，他便把手中的那套《潜虚衍义》往椅子上一放，做了个相让的手势，说：“头翁，请借一步说话。”

那公差睁着眼睛，把他打量了一下，疑疑惑惑地跟着。一直走到距门口最远的那排书架前，黄宗羲才回过头来，瞧着公差的眼睛，恳切地说：“头翁，小生有一句话，不知当说不当说？我瞧这布店生意萧条，情形困窘，倒不像是故意拖延的，头翁何不与人方便，就宽限他几日呢！”

那公差见他是个秀才，起先不知道有什么事，倒有几分恭谨之色，听他这么一说，顿时冷下脸来，摇一摇头，说：“先生有所不知，非是在下不肯通融，皆因此事系府里大老爷亲责下来，要克期办妥，在下也是身不由己！”

“这‘当行买办’，朝廷不是明令裁革了么，怎么如今又在实行？”

公差瞥了他一眼，满不在乎地说：“裁革归裁革，但这些事儿，也只能瞧着办罢咧！譬如今番京里周国舅派人来办货，一封书送到大老爷手里，大老爷还能不用心打点么？这笔钱，公库里开销不了，大老爷又不能自己掏腰包，也只有分摊给各行铺户了。”

黄宗羲厌恶地皱紧了眉头：“可是这些铺户已是患难余生，朝不保夕，还要如此摊派，岂不是要他们的命么？”

公差呵呵地笑起来：“先生也忒老实些！别瞧这些铺户专会装穷叫苦，其实哪一个屋角床底，不埋着一万两万的？你不下狠

to greet the guy, and just as he was about to speak, he found that the people watching the commotion outside had turned around and looked at them curiously. So, he put the set of *Studies in the Explorations into the Ubiquitous Void* on the chair, made a gesture of inviting the *yamen* man inside, and said, "Sir, please take a seat and let's have a talk."

The *yamen* man widened his eyes, sizing him up, and followed his direction suspiciously. When they reached the bookshelf farthest away from the doorway, Huang Zongxi turned around and looked into the *yamen* man's eyes and said earnestly, "Sir, I'm wondering if I may venture to give a comment. I see that the fabric shop isn't doing very well. It doesn't look like they're deliberately delaying things. Isn't it a good idea to be merciful and give him a few days of grace?"

Since Huang Zongxi was a young scholar, the *yamen* man was more or less respectful to him at first, but upon hearing these words, the guy suddenly changed his expression, shook his head, and said, "Sir, please understand that it's not that I'm not merciful but that it's an order from the prefect himself. The matter must be settled in time. I'm not in a position to make decisions."

"Hasn't the imperial court abolished the forced supplier system? Why is it still working?"

The *yamen* man glanced at him and said nonchalantly, "Sure it's abolished, but in practice discretion is exercised. For example, now that the emperor's brother-in-law, Mr. Zhou from Beijing, has sent someone here to make purchases and a letter is delivered to the prefect, can the prefect afford not to take heed to it? The needed money can't be withdrawn from the public treasury, and the prefect can't pay from his own pocket. The only way is to share it among the shops."

Huang Zongxi frowned in disgust. He said, "But these shopkeepers are barely meeting their ends meet after the natural calamities. Isn't such sharing of the burden taking their lives away?"

The *yamen* man laughed out loud, saying, "Sir, you're too innocent. These shop owners are merely pretending to be poor. In fact, every one of them has huge amounts of money hidden in a corner of their house or under the bed. If you don't squeeze hard, how do

劲儿挤，就别指望他拿出来！这事我经历多了，放心，他们完不了，远着呢！”

“非也！”黄宗羲被公差昧着良心的胡说激怒了，“眼下分明是寇虏交煎，天灾频仍，民生忧悴，百业不振。铺户行商，破产者不知凡几！幸能保存者，亦是苦苦支撑，辗转挣扎。须知商贾之业，亦是民生所系，不可或缺，为政者应当爱惜之，振拔之，方是正理！像这等鞭扑敲剥，锱铢不遗，试问百姓尚有何生理，国家尚有何生理？”

他越说越激昂，用力地做着手势。可是那公差显然有大半听不懂，而且不明白黄宗羲为什么会突然如此激动。他大约只觉得这个秀才呆气十足，根本不值得同他纠缠下去，便转过身，做出要离开的样子。然而，没等他迈开腿，就见挤在门外瞧热闹的那些人骚动了一下，一个十一二岁的小男孩跌跌撞撞地奔了进来，一把揪住公差的衣裳，用带哭的声音嚷：

“这是我家的东西！你为什么抢我家的东西？你还我，还我！听见了没有？”

他一边嚷，一边使劲往公差身上撞。

那公差猝不及防，倒闹了个手足无措。当弄清是怎么一回事之后，他就暴怒起来，一巴掌把那孩子扇到一边去，骂道：“小杂种，连你也来寻老子开心！”他还想举脚踢去，临时瞥见黄宗羲愤然的目光，才勉强把已经抬起的一只脚收回来，朝地上狠狠地吐了一口唾沫，大踏步向外走去。

黄宗羲扶住被推倒在自己身上的孩子，睁圆了眼睛，打算大声喝住公差，同他评理。就在这时，黄安惊慌的声音蓦地响起来：

you expect them to take it out? I've experienced this a lot. Don't you worry! It's not the end of the day for them."

"No, you're wrong!" Huang Zongxi was enraged by the nonsense of the *yamen* man speaking against his conscience. "It's clear that with the constant harassment of bandits and barbarian invaders and frequent strikes by natural disasters people are scrambling for a living and businesses are suffering from depression. Countless shops and business firms go bankrupt and close down. A few fortunate ones are struggling to survive. It should be known that the business of merchants is indispensable to the livelihood of the people. It's the responsibility of men in power to protect them and help them. Stripped of everything like this, how can the broad masses of the people survive and how can the nation survive?"

The more he talked, the more agitated he was. As he spoke, he accentuated his words with various gestures. But the *yamen* man obviously didn't have a clue what he was saying, nor was he able to comprehend why Huang Zongxi was suddenly so agitated. Probably because he felt the young scholar was too much of a nerd and not worth his time, he turned around in a posture to leave. Yet before he opened his legs, the onlookers outside stirred and an eleven- or twelve-year-old boy stumbled in, grabbed the clothes of the *yamen* man, and cried in a tearful voice:

"It's our property! Why are you robbing us? Give it back! Give it back to me! Did you hear it?"

As the boy cried, he hurled himself on the *yamen* man, who was caught off guard and was suddenly at a loss as to what to do.

When *yamen* man figured out what was going on, he flew into a rage and sent the boy aside with a slap, saying, "Little bastard, even you're here to make fun of me!" He raised his foot to kick the boy, but seeing Huang Zongxi's angry gaze, he had to take his foot back. Instead, he spat on the ground and walked out in big strides.

Huang Zongxi helped the kid up, who had collapsed onto him due to the *yamen* man's push, opened his eyes wide, and was going to remonstrate with the brute. Just then came Huang An's panicked

“啊呀，大爷，你的书呢？”

黄宗羲心中一跳，回过头去：“什么？”

“书，书，那部书！”

黄宗羲“啊”了一声，连忙奔到他原来坐的那张椅子跟前。顿时，他像吃了一记闷棍似的呆住了——椅子上空空如也，刚才被他随手放在上面的那套《潜虚衍义》已经不翼而飞了。

## 胁迫出头

“超宗兄，不知养先可曾向你言及？学生此次不自量力，意欲替阮圆海向江南诸君子缓颊疏通，实在是欲借此事为契机，了结我朝二十余年的一场公案，消解相仇不已的门户之争。唯是人情陷溺已久，一旦更变，实非容易，稍有差池，便会反招其乱。所谓‘治丝愈棼[①]’，不可不慎！故学生不得已，才出此下策。这也是为天下安危着想。倘若有人因此不谅学生，学生亦唯有甘心受之而已！”

钱谦益说这一番话的时候，正是黄宗羲在书坊失窃的第二天上午。他坐在徐氏东园楠木厅当中的一张紫檀木扶手椅上，用两根指头不慌不忙地转动着腕上的一串念珠，时不时朝坐在对面的客人瞟上一眼。

由于陈在竹和钱养先终于在昨天同时回到了苏州，大半个月来混沌难测的局面顿时明朗起来。钱谦益现在了解到：两位心腹族人这一次分头执行使命，总的来说是意外的顺利。钱养先方面，已经通过扬州的郑元勋，联系了一二十位在社内有一定地位和影响的人物，他们都答应在虎丘大会上，对于停止攻击和压制阮大铖的建议给予支持，并设法对他们的学生和好友做说服疏通

① 治丝愈棼：整理丝不找头绪，越理越乱。喻做事没有条理。

voice: "Oh, my young lord, where's your book?"

Huang Zongxi's heart leapt and he turned around. "What?" he asked.

"Book, book, that book!"

Huang Zongxi let out an "ahh" and hurried to the chair where he had been previously sitting. Suddenly, he was stunned as if he had been struck by a stealth club—the chair was empty, and the set of *Studies in the Explorations into the Ubiquitous Void* he had just put on it was gone.

## A Puppet

"Brother Chaozong, I'm wondering if Yangxian has ever told you about it. Though I'm not qualified to do it, I do want to seek the understanding of the scholars in the River South area in the pardoning of Ruan Yuanhai. This is an opportunity to conclude a public dispute that had lasted for over twenty years and put an end to the factional strife in the intellectual circles. The problem is, bad blood has already formed. To undo things is by no means easy. Any misstep may lead to serious consequences. I have to be very careful to avoid being enmeshed into a bigger mess. So, I've no choice but to make this proposal. It's also for the good of the nation. Should anyone misunderstand me, I'll have to take it without complaint," Qian Qianyi said.

It was on the morning after Huang Zongxi lost his book in the bookstore. Qian Qianyi was sitting in a red sandalwood armchair in the Nanmu Hall of Xu's East Garden, calmly turning a string of rosary beads on his wrist with his two fingers, and occasionally glancing at the guest sitting on the opposite side.

As Chen Zaizhu and Qian Yangxian finally returned to Suzhou at the same time yesterday, the chaotic and unpredictable situation over the past half month suddenly cleared up. Qian Qianyi now learned that the two confidants from the Greater Qian family had carried out their missions without difficulty. Qian Yangxian, through Zheng Yuanxun of Yangzhou, had communicated with more than a dozen men of significance and they all agreed to support the proposal

的工作。至于陈在竹到松江一带散布流言蜚语的结果，也已经促使旧几社那帮子人个个怒气冲天，摩拳擦掌，发誓要同吴应箕、陈贞慧等人大干一场。钱养先还呈上阮大铖的一封亲笔密信，信中除了极力吹捧钱谦益，称他是宰辅长材，众望久归，人阁拜相，是势所必然之外，还再一次表明自己决意洗心革面、投靠东林的“耿耿孤衷”。这一切，都使钱谦益感到满意和放心，很大程度驱散了这些天来一直笼罩在他眼前的愁云疑雾。他又重新变得自信、沉着、精力充沛了。

按照原定计划，在整个行动中，钱谦益都不直接出面，只在幕后指挥，以避免承担万一失败的后果。因此第二步，就必须物色一个能够代替钱谦益在大会上支撑场面、操纵局势的人物。这个人物也已经初步确定，就是眼前这位客人——扬州大名士郑元勋。他是复社在扬州地区的社长，又是本次虎丘大会的两位主盟者之一。何况现在，他实际上已经成了本计划的积极追随者。由他来充当这一角色，正是再合适不过。虽说在钱谦益看来，此人略嫌魄力不足，不过到时有陈在竹、钱养先等人从旁协助，估计问题不大。前一段，钱谦益出于谨慎的考虑，没让钱养先过早地向对方透露，而打算亲自来做这件工作。

现在郑元勋正带着敬畏的神情，专心地在听钱谦益说话。他是一个开始发胖的中年人，有着亮晶晶的脑门和一张圆滑随和的脸。他听得那么留神，以至整个肥大的身躯都紧张地向前倾着，大张着胡须稀少的嘴巴，再加上一双睁得滚圆的小眼睛，使他看

to stop attacking and suppressing Ruan Dacheng at the Tiger Hill Conference and promised to do their best to persuade their pupils and friends. Chen Zaizhu had also succeeded in his rumor-spreading mission to Songjiang. Members of the former Jishe were enraged and vowed to settle accounts with Wu Yingji and Chen Zhenhui. Qian Yangxian also brought a secret letter from Ruan Dacheng, which not only praised Qian Qianyi by saying that Qian Qianyi was made for a Cabinet minister and commanded respect from everybody and that his becoming a Cabinet minister was a matter of course but also reiterated Ruan's determination to turn over a new leaf in his life by submitting to the East Wood Party. All this made Qian Qianyi happy and content and to a large extent dispelled the sorrow and doubt that had been shrouded him for days. Once again he was confident, composed, and vibrant.

According to the original plan, Qian Qianyi was not going to make any presence during the entire operation. He would work behind the scenes to avoid the consequences of failure. Therefore, in the second step, it was necessary to find a man who could act on his behalf to be present and manipulate the situation at the conference. That suitable man was none other than the guest in front of him: Zheng Yuanxun, a famous scholar from Yangzhou. Zheng Yuanxun was president of the Yangzhou chapter of the Fushe and one of the two co-chairs of the coming Tiger Hill Conference. Besides, he had now for all intents and purposes become an active participant of this scheme. It was fitting for him to play this role. Although this man was lacking in leadership skills, he would be up to the job with the help of Chen Zaizhu and Qian Yangxian. Previously, Qian Qianyi, out of prudence, had kept Qian Yangxian from revealing it to Zheng Yuanxun prematurely; he was going to tell Mr. Zheng in person.

Zheng Yuanxun listened attentively to Qian Qianyi with a look of awe on his face. He was a middle-aged man beginning to gain weight, with a shiny forehead and a smooth, amiable face. He listened so attentively that his entire self was leaning forward nervously, and with a sparsely-bearded wide open mouth and a pair of small round eyes, he looked like a frightened goose. This posture caused Chen Zaizhu,

上去很像一只受惊的鹅。这种姿态，引得坐在旁边的陈在竹朝钱养先直递眼色；而坐在另一边的钱曾——一个面孔苍白、神情阴骘的青年儒生，他是钱谦益的族孙和晚年的得意弟子——却侧目而视，满脸瞧不起的样子。

当钱谦益故意顿住话头，等待客人反应的时候，郑元勋立刻站起来，拱着手说："老先生苦心孤诣以谋社稷之安，耿耿丹衷，天日可表！便是晚生也一向以门户之争为忧，只苦于人微力薄，无济于事。今得老先生奋袂前导，晚生不胜欢忭鼓舞，感佩无已！老先生以为晚生尚有可用之处，虽赴汤蹈火，亦不敢辞！"

钱谦益微微一笑，腕上的念珠转得更轻快："超宗兄言重了！学生素闻兄襟怀旷达，见识高远，料知不只必能谅我，而且必能慰我。适才之言，足见肝胆！学生得到超宗兄这么一位良朋，可真是喜欢得很哪！"

"老先生如此嘉奖，令晚生羞惭欲死。老先生泰山北斗，望重群伦，晚生无任钦仰。唯是远处广陵，未得侍奉左右，时时亲炙，常以为恨！"受宠若惊的郑元勋赶紧又说。

钱谦益点点头，捋了一阵胡子，忽然微微仰起脸，朗声吟道：

月华蘸露扶仙掌，
粉汗更衣染御香。
……
金罂玉瓒须携醉，
任是蜂狂总未知！

who was sitting on the one side, to wink at Qian Yangxian, while Qian Zeng, a young Confucian scholar with a pale face and a gloomy expression, one of Qian Qianyi's grandsons and his favorite pupil in his old age, who was sitting on the other side, looked sideways with a look of contempt.

When Qian Qianyi paused and waited for a response, Zheng Yuanxun immediately stood up, bowed, and said, "Your lordship, your devotion to the country heart and soul is great indeed! It's a shining example. I've always been worried about the struggle between the different factions but haven't been able to do a thing due to my limited capabilities. Your kind guidance has given me confidence. I feel much obliged to you, your lordship. If you think there's still some use for me, I'll go for it even if I have to go through fire."

Qian Qianyi smiled slightly and turned the rosary beads on his wrist faster, saying, "I'm flattered, sir! I've always heard that you're broad-minded and far-sighted. As I expected, you're not only able to understand me but also able to comfort me. What you've said proves your wisdom and courage. I'm so happy to have a friend like you, Brother Chaozong!"

"Oh, your lordship, your praise is more than I deserve. Your lordship commands the scholars like Mt. Tai, like the Northern Star! You don't know how much I admire you. Far away in Guangling, I often long to be close to you, to attend you, and to listen to your instructions," said the flattered Zheng Yuanxun.

Qian Qianyi nodded his head, and, stroking his beard, suddenly raised his face slightly, and chanted:

*"Like moonlight sparkling on the dew-receiving copper plate held up by the hand of a Taoist immortal,*

*With the scent of powdered sweat of a royal concubine."*

Then,

*"Gold vessels and jade cups should carry drunkenness in themselves,*

*Totally oblivious to the honey bees running wild."*

他侧过脸，斜瞅着郑元勋：“嗯，学生记得两年前，超宗兄送来的那些《黄牡丹诗》中，好像有这么几句？”

“啊，老先生还记得？”郑元勋的脑门发亮了。提起两年前的《黄牡丹诗》，那可是郑元勋平生第一件得意的豪举。当时，在扬州他家的影园内，开了一株极罕见的黄牡丹，一丛五朵，朵朵大如海碗，复瓣繁蕊，奇丽异常，见者无不啧啧称羡。郑元勋一时动兴，决定大摆筵席，招请四方名士，饮宴赏花，拈韵赋诗。并事先宣布：夺魁者以金杯一双为酬。到时果然宾客云集，着实热闹风光了一场。那批诗，后来就送到常熟，请钱谦益评定。结果广东举人黎遂球所作的十首七律名列第一。这件事，当时轰动远近，传为雅谈。而影园主人郑元勋的大名，也因此不胫而走，传遍了大江南北……

“那一次，全仗老先生俯允主持，遂使荒园雅集，顿增光仪。岂唯黎美周因之声价十倍，便是晚辈也叨光不浅哩！”郑元勋感激地说。

“区区微劳，何足挂齿！”钱谦益摆摆手，示意客人重新坐下。停了一停，他忽然微笑说，“倒是今日之事，学生却要仰仗超宗兄的大力哩！”

“岂敢，但请老先生主持大局，晚生愿供驱策！”

“不，”钱谦益摇摇头，“学生确实要仰仗吾兄！此次学生来姑苏，尚有其他要事，三月二十八，是无法分身赴会了。不过，

He turned his face and looked askance at Zheng Yuanxun. "Well, I remember that there're such lines in *The Yellow Peony Poems* you sent me two years ago."

"Ah, you still remember them?" Zheng Yuanxun's forehead lit up. *The Yellow Peony Poems* of two years ago was the monument to Zheng Yuanxun's first heroic act in his life. Back then, in his Shadow Garden in Yangzhou appeared a very rare yellow peony blossom with a cluster of five flowers each as big as a large bowl and with multiple petals and numerous, showy stamens. Its extraordinary beauty dazzled everyone who saw it. Zheng Yuanxun was so delighted that he decided to put on a big banquet, to which celebrities from far and wide were invited to drink, admire the flowers, and compose poems. He announced in advance, "Whoever composes the best poem will be rewarded with a pair of gold cups." Sure enough, guests swarmed in and he had a sensational moment. That batch of poems were later sent to Changshu to be judged by Qian Qianyi. As a result, Li Suiqiu, a *juren* degree holder from Guangdong ranked first with ten seven-character four-liners. That event caused a huge sensation at that time and was widely talked about. And the name of Zheng Yuanxun, the owner of the Shadow Garden, traveled fast even though it had no legs and in no time was spread all over the country, south and north.

"I'm deeply indebted to you for being so obliging as to agree to be the judge. The little collection of poems from my humble wild garden suddenly appreciated in value because of your graciousness. Not only Li Suiqiu's name grew ten times bigger, but also I myself have benefited a great deal," Zheng Yuanxun said gratefully.

"It was a small help. Don't mention it." Qian Qianyi waved his hand and motioned for the guest to sit down again. After a pause, he suddenly smiled and said, "Yet, now I depend on you for something big."

"I'm afraid I'm not that useful, but I'll be delighted to render my service, your lordship."

"I'm serious," Qian Qianyi waved his head and said. "I do have to rely on you, brother. Since I have other important things to do on this visit to Suzhou I won't be able to attend the conference on the

有兄为我主持一切，学生甚为放心！”

郑元勋仿佛没有听清：“老先生是说、是说，要晚生主……主……”

“不错！”钱谦益的口气很郑重，他停止了转动念珠，“一客不烦二主。此次大会，兄已执其牛耳，就请一并代学生主持此事，正是两全其美。”

郑元勋大吃一惊地噎住了。一种错愕、胆怯、怀疑的神情从他那滚圆的脸上显露出来。他嗫嚅地说：“多、多谢老先生见爱，只怕晚生驽钝下材，难、难以当、当此重任。”

“兄何必过谦！学生既以此为大事，自不欲见其功败垂成。若非深知我兄足副此任，学生也不会贸然相托。况且在竹、养先，还有遵王——”他指一指那位名叫钱曾的青年儒生，“到时都要上虎丘去，他们自会全力襄助足下。”

“只是，只是晚生确实自问无能当此重托，还请前辈另委贤能，晚生愿竭尽绵薄，促其成功。”郑元勋极力推托，由于惊惶，也由于着急，额上冒出了星星汗珠子。

钱谦益沉下了脸：“啊，莫非超宗兄竟如此见弃？老夫废置多年，昏庸老迈，自知不足以动兄台之心，难道兄台也不以社稷苍生为念么？”

郑元勋的眉毛抖动了一下，飞快地瞥了一眼钱谦益：“啊，不敢，不是的……”他畏惧地说。

“那么——”

“呃、呃，实、实在……晚生实在是自知无能，难、难当此重托……”郑元勋掏出一条汗巾，擦着脑门上的汗，抱愧地低下头去。

看见对方如此推托，钱谦益很不高兴。他是这样看的：郑元

twenty-eighth of March. Now with you in charge of things for me, I'm relieved."

Zheng Yuanxun said, as if he hadn't heard it clearly, "Sir, are you saying that you want me to be in charge of ..."

"Yes, I am," Qian Qianyi's tone was solemn. He stopped turning his rosary. "One guest doesn't bother two hosts. Since you're in charge of the conference, to place this matter in your hands is just fitting."

Zheng Yuanxun choked in surprise. A look of astonishment, timidity, and suspicion emerged from his round face. He said with a stammer, "Many, many thanks, sir, for trusting me, but, but, I'm afraid, afraid that I'm not qua-qua-qualified to take this res-responsibility."

"Brother, you're being modest. Since I understand the weight of the matter, of course I don't want to see failure while success is in sight. If I hadn't been well aware of your capability, I wouldn't have rashly entrusted things to you. Besides, Zaizhu, Yangxian, and Zunwang—" he said, pausing to point to a young scholar named Qian Zeng. "They will all go to Tiger Hill by then, and they'll all help you to their utmost," he continued.

"It's just that I really think I'm not up to the important task. May I suggest that your lordship find someone better, and I'll do my best to assist him to ensure success?" Zheng Yuanxun said, giving a feeble excuse, his forehead sweating from panic or anxiety.

Qian Qianyi screwed up his face into a scowl, saying, "Hah, how come you're giving me the cold shoulder? An old man on the cold bench for years, I know I'm unable to persuade you to do things but aren't you concerned about the future of the nation and the fate of the people?"

Zheng Yuanxun's eyebrows twitched. He took a quick glance at Qian Qianyi. "O, I dare not, no ..." he said fearfully.

"So ..."

"Uh, uh, I—I— I'm really aware that I'm not qualified for the job ..." Zheng Yuanxun took out a sweat towel, wiped the sweat on his forehead, and bowed his head embarrassedly.

Qian Qianyi was very displeased with Yuanxun's dodging. He

勋之所以对开脱阮大铖一事表现得颇为热心，无非是想巴结讨好他钱谦益，指望钱谦益将来复职升迁时，能够提携他一把。不错，对在这件事上出过力的人，钱谦益自然不会忘记。不过，既然如此，那就得服从指派，舍得付出代价。这也如同合伙做生意一样，本钱下得愈多的，到头来分得的一份红利才会愈大。然而眼前这位郑大名士，却刁滑得紧，既想图大利，又怕亏本钱。“哼，亏你开头说得好听，一见了真章儿就忙着往后躲。莫非指望我钱某人自个儿拿这把老骨头去拼，好让你们跟着捡现成不成？”钱谦益越想越恼火，他一声不响地站起来，沉着脸，气呼呼地走进屏门后面去了。

这一着显然大出郑元勋的意料。他吃惊地站起身，双手做出挽留的姿势，可是又不敢叫出声来，只是用惶急的眼光，求援似的瞧着在座的三位钱氏族人。

但是这会儿，那三位族人却变得像泥胎木偶似的，全都脸色阴沉地坐着，一声不响。

郑元勋不由得怔住了。渐渐地，他那张滚圆的脸孔由红转白、由白转青。他动了动嘴巴，想说句什么，到底没有说出来，只是呆呆地坐了下去。

看见他这个样子，钱氏三位族人互相递着眼色，又故意挨延了一阵，钱养先才站起来。

“哎，超宗兄，你这是怎么啦？”他走过去，拍着郑元勋的肩膀，“在扬州，我们不是谈得好好儿的？——这次大会，你是

saw it this way: Zheng Yuanxun's enthusiasm for the exoneration of Ruan Dacheng was not genuine. It was simply flattery. The man flattered him in hopes of getting advancement after his reinstatement. Yes, as a matter of course, Qian Qianyi would remember all those who contributed to his reinstatement. Everyone expecting some form of reward in the future would have to take a share of the responsibility, or in other words, to be willing to pay a price. It's like in a joint venture. The more capital you spend, the greater the dividend you'll get in the end. However, the celebrated scholar Mr. Zheng in front is so slick that he wants to make a big profit without risking anything. Humph, you spoke nicely at the beginning, but as soon as we get to the real point, you start to dodge. Are you counting on this bunch of old bones to charge forward and all of you simply pick the ripe fruit? Qian Qianyi became more and more annoyed as he thought about it. He stood up silently with a sullen face and walked to behind the screen door angrily.

Obviously baffled by such a reaction, Zheng Yuanxun stood up, reached out his hands to stop Qian Qianyi from leaving, but not daring to speak, he just looked at the three men of the greater Qian family anxiously, as if asking for help.

Yet at this moment, the three members of the greater Qian family looked like three mud figures, all sitting gloomily without making a sound.

Zheng Yuanxun found himself in a predicament. Gradually, his plump round face turned from red to white, and then from white to blue. He moved his mouth and wanted to say something, but eventually gave up and sat down blankly.

Seeing him like that, the three members of the greater Qian family stared at each other and deliberately kept silent for a while before Qian Yangxian stood up.

"Hey, Brother Chaozong, what's the matter with you?" He walked over and patted Zheng Yuanxun on the shoulder. "Didn't we reach an agreement in Yangzhou? Since you're one of the co-chairs of the conference, you're the best person to be in charge and no one can

主盟，由你出面主持，正是顺理成章，谁也替代不了的！”

陈在竹依旧是那副乐呵呵的样子：“莫急莫急，我算准超宗兄必定应允，只是他还得想想。这么件大事，难怪他要慎重。换了是我，也一样的！”他一边说，一边朝钱曾使着眼色，“遵王兄，你说是么？”

后者却鄙夷地“哼”了一声，算作回答。

听着这三位族人一唱一和，郑元勋的眉头皱得越来越紧。他显然明白，要是坚持不肯应承的话，将会带来什么后果。但是如果应承……

“超宗兄，你到底意下如何？”钱养先催问了。

郑元勋蓦地抬起头，意外地发现，钱谦益不知什么时候又走了出来，正站在屏门边上，一声不响地朝外注视。他刚刚进去时那种凌厉的、愤怒的神气已经看不见了，代之以焦急、担忧和期待的神情，甚至整个人也一下子显出了老态——微弓着腰，吃力地向前倾侧着右耳朵……

“这个，这个……”郑元勋支吾地说。

“唉，莫非真的就是这等为难么？”陈在竹悲天悯人的声音响起来。

“哼，我平生最恨的，就是那种忘恩负义之辈！”一直阴沉着脸的钱曾突然开口了，“这种人，有求于人时就急巴巴地找上门来，反过来让他帮点忙，就半天也放不出一个屁！”

郑元勋拿着汗巾的手抖了一下，停住了。他抬头望了望，希望钱谦益对于手下人这种粗暴无礼的言辞有所干预。然而，令他失望的是，此刻的钱谦益不知是受到钱曾那句话的挑动，还是别有想法，他仍然保持着刚才的站立姿势，但是眼睛里却分明地闪烁着刻毒和冰冷的光芒……

郑元勋心头一震，惶恐地低下头去。半晌，他终于咬咬牙，

replace you," said Qian Yangxian in a congenial tone.

"Don't worry! I'm sure Brother Chaozong will agree, but he needs more time thinking about it. Because it's a matter of great importance, he should give it more thought. If it were me, I would be like him," Chen Zaizhu said in good cheer, winking at Qian Zeng. "Brother Zunwang, do you agree?"

The latter hummed scornfully as an answer.

As the three members of the Qian family spoke in one voice, Zheng Yuanxun's brows became tighter and tighter. He clearly understood what the consequences would be if he persisted in his refusal, but if he agreed ...

"Brother Chaozong, what do you really think?" Qian Yangxian pressed on.

Zheng Yuanxun raised his head suddenly and found that Qian Qianyi had come out and was standing next to the screen door, silently watching them. The exasperated and angry look that Qian Qianyi had worn when he went inside had disappeared and was replaced by an anxious, worried and expectant one. He suddenly looked older, struggling to lean his right ear forward, his back slightly arched ...

"This, this ..." Zheng Yuanxun said stutteringly.

"Hey, is it really such a difficult decision for you?" Chen Zaizhu said in a compassionate voice.

"Humph, I've always hated ungrateful men!" said Qian Zeng suddenly, who had been wearing a gloomy face. "This kind of men come to your door wagging their tails when they need help but once you want some help from them, they don't even give a monkey's fart!"

Zheng Yuanxun's hand holding the sweat towel gave a sudden jerk. He looked up, hoping Qian Qianyi would intervene to stop such rude remarks from his men. However, to his disappointment, Qian Qianyi, either having taken in Qian Zeng's remark or having something else on mind, stood silently, his eyes gleaming with dark, cold light.

Zheng Yuanxun shuddered and lowered his head in trepidation. After a long while, Zheng Yuanxun finally gritted his teeth and said,

说：“好吧，既蒙老先生见爱，晚生从命就是！”

## 牙行凶焰

《潜虚衍义》的失窃，使黄宗羲懊恼得要死。要不是想到自己多少也有一点责任，他简直就会把黄安捆起来，狠狠揍上一顿。如今他已经落得书财两空，走投无路。不过，他仍然不打算转而向朋友们求助，也不肯放弃给钱谦益送一份礼物的计划。“无论如何，我绝不改变，绝不！”他想。昨天夜里，他倒背着手，在屋子里走过来，走过去，苦苦思索了大半晚，终于又想出了一个办法。今天一早起来，他先把黄安反锁在屋子里，声明中午不给饭吃，要书童“枵腹思过”。然后自己就独自出门，打算到阊门外的浙东会馆去碰碰运气。

雨住了小半天，可是堆积着的云朵阴沉沉的，总不肯散。黄宗羲夹把油纸伞，穿过行人不多的大街，出了阊门，走到了一座石砌的拱桥上。这座横跨在护城河上的石桥，有着巨大的拱形环洞，哪怕是载重一二千石的粮船，都可以在它下面畅通无阻地来往。桥的右侧不远，是一个大码头，从那里有水路可以直通大运河。要是在以往，这一带总是泊满了大大小小的商船，熙攘繁忙的景象赛过庙会。可是如今却零落得很了。黄宗羲在桥上停了停，随即记起，这桥上本来躺着一个面目黄肿的女孩，约摸有四五岁，身上一丝不挂，蓬头垢面，肮脏不堪，也不知是谁家丢弃的。前两天黄宗羲经过这里时曾看见过她，如今却不在了。“大概总算碰上好心人，给收留去了吧！”他想，打算继续走路。可是忽然，

"Well, since your lordship decides I'm the right man for it, I've no other choice but to obey."

## The Fangs of a Brokerage House

Huang Zongxi was very upset about the missing of *Studies in the Explorations into the Ubiquitous Void*. If it were not partly his fault, he would tie up Huang An and give him a good flogging. Having lost both the book and the money, he was thrown into desperation. However, he was not going to turn to his friends for help, nor was he going to give up his plan to buy Qian Qianyi a gift. "No matter what happens, I'll never change myself, never!" he thought. The previous night, he had paced back and forth in his room with his hands on his back, racking his brains for a way out and finally figured out something. When he woke up early this morning, he locked Huang An in the house and declared that nothing would be given to the boy for lunch as a punishment which he called "making him good through starvation". Then he went out alone, intending to try his luck at the East Zhejiang Guild outside the West City Gate.

The rain had stopped a long while ago, but the storm clouds were still thick and heavy, refusing to dissipate. An oil-paper umbrella in his hand, Huang Zongxi crossed the largely empty street, exited the West City Gate, and walked to a stone arch bridge. This stone bridge spanning the moat had a huge arched hole. Even a ship with a load of ten or twenty thousand *dan* of grains could pass it unimpeded. Not far to the right of the bridge was a large pier, from where there was a waterway that led directly to the Grand Canal. In the past, this area had always been full of merchant ships, large and small, and the bustling scene had surpassed that of a temple fair. But now it was very much deserted. Huang Zongxi stopped on the bridge as he remembered that there was a girl with a swollen, sallow face lying on the bridge, about four or five years old, unclad, unkempt, and unwashed, abandoned by unknown parents. He had seen her as he passed the bridge two days ago, but she was no longer there now. "Probably she's finally met a kindhearted person and is adopted," he thought. Just as he was going

他又看见了那女孩，原来不知什么时候已经被人移到桥头树下的垃圾堆里。她一动不动地仰面躺着，也不知是死是活，肚子胀得发亮，四肢却似乎开始腐烂，正在往外淌着脓水，一大群金头苍蝇嗡嗡嘤嘤地绕着她打转……黄宗羲心头一震，感到喉头作呕。他连忙别转脸，三步并作两步走下桥头，径直向左走去。

"唉，苍生涂炭，至于此极！可是几社那伙人却不思同命共济，救民于水火之中，反而想方设法去替阮胡子翻案，真是可恶可恨！而定生他们现放着近在咫尺的钱牧斋不去请，却宁可绕道金坛去求周仲驭，也是毫无道理！"他愤愤地想，要办成眼前这桩事的决心更大了。

浙东会馆坐落在南濠，离桥头并不远。当黄宗羲来到那三扇装饰着砖雕的门前，向门公说明有事来访的时候，大门里忽然响起了急促的脚步声。接着，奔出来三个怒气冲天的汉子。为首一个，头戴瓦楞帽，身穿酱色绒衫的，一出门口就站住了。他回过头，指着里面破口大骂说：

"什么狗屁会馆？才钻出裤裆几天？你识得大爷，大爷还不识得你哩！告诉你，大爷这里可是有苏州府发下的牙帖！你胆敢违抗，自有官府同你区处！"

他接着又骂了一些粗鄙难听的话。看见会馆内始终静悄悄的，没有人出来招架，才气昂昂地领着手下人走了。

黄宗羲暗暗纳罕，不知道发生了什么事情，但估计不外是生意上的争执，也就不再理会。等会馆的掌事人迎出来，他就堆起

to continue his journey, suddenly, he caught sight of the girl, who had at some point been moved to the garbage dump under the tree at the bridgehead. She lay motionlessly on her back, alive or dead; her swollen belly sparkled with light but her limbs, dripping with pus, was evidently rotting. A swarm of golden-headed flies were buzzing around her ... Huang Zongxi's heart jerked, and he had a nauseous feeling in the throat. He immediately looked away and quickening his steps he walked off the bridge and turned left.

"Alas, how people are suffering! Yet in such a time of national crisis, the Jishers, instead of doing their best to save the people from fire and water, are trying every means to reverse the case of Beardy Ruan, which is really hateful. The queston is, now that we have Qian Muzhai close at hand, why do Dingsheng and the others insist on making a long trip to Jintan to seek the help of Zhou Zhongyu rather than that of Qian Muzhai?" he thought resentfully, more determined to have his way.

East Zhejiang Guild was located in Nanhao, not far from the bridgehead. When he came to the three-panel gate decorated with brick carvings and explained to the janitor the purpose of his visit, there came a sudden sound of rapid footsteps from inside. Then, three angry men rushed out. The first one, wearing a *waleng* hat and a brown sweater, stood still as soon as he came out. Then he turned to point at the inside and yelled:

"What shitty guild? How many days have you been out of your mother's womb? You know I'm your grandfather, but I don't know you! Let me tell you. I, your grandfather, have a writ from the *yamen* of Suzhou Prefecture! If you dare defy it, the *yamen* will take care of you!"

He then uttered a string of expletives. Seeing that the guild was quiet all the time and that no one came out to parry, he left with his men triumphantly.

Huang Zongxi secretly wondered what had happened, but gathering it was nothing more than an ordinary business dispute, he let it go without inquiring. When the head of the guild greeted him, he put

笑容，上前相见。

会馆的掌事人姓毕，名石湖，是位谦和中透着精明的中年商人。他见黄宗羲既是位在学的相公，又是浙东同乡，便分外殷勤恭敬。他把客人迎到堂上，重新行礼。等黄宗羲在上首的交椅坐定之后，他不敢也坐椅子，扯了张四开光坐墩在下面相陪。

黄宗羲虽然心里有事，但同对方毕竟素不相识，不好意思马上开口，只得一边品着茶，一边先同他天南地北地闲聊，无非是商货行情、家乡近况之类。谈了一阵，毕石湖忽然问：

“先生是余姚世家，不知已故的黄太仆公讳尊素的，同先生怎生称呼？”

“不敢，便是家父。”黄宗羲拱着手回答。

毕石湖“啊”了一声，连忙站起来：“原来先生便是黄公子，小老竟然不知，失敬高贤了！”说着，就要跪拜下去。

黄宗羲慌忙起身扶住，说：“老爹且坐，何须如此！”

可是，毕石湖执意要行礼，双方争持了一会儿，黄宗羲到底拗不过，只得受了他半礼。

“公子，非是小老定要多礼。”等重新坐定之后，毕石湖才解释地说，“小老虽是一介行商，也颇知忠义之理。当年魏阉当国，矿监、税吏横行州县，我工商之民饱受敲剥，惨苦难言，奄奄气尽。是东林诸公不忍坐视，仗义执言，触怒魏阉奸贼，不幸竟以身殉！此等大恩大德，凡我商人之有心肝者，又岂敢一日忘怀！

up a smile and walked over.

The head of the Guild was Bi Shihu, a humble yet quick-witted middle-aged merchant. Since Huang Zongxi was a scholar and a fellow East Zhejianger he was extremely courteous and respectful. He welcomed the guest to the guild with a salute. After Huang Zongxi was seated in the guest chair, Mr. Bi humbly sat down on a stool.

Although Huang Zongxi had something on mind, he didn't venture to speak it immediately because, after all, they had been strangers so far. To start with, he conversed with Mr. Bi about distant things as they sipped sea together, things like prices of goods and recent events in their hometown.

After a while, Bi Shihu suddenly asked, "Since you're from Yuyao, you must be a relative of the late Mr. Huang Zunsu, Secretary of the Royal Stables."

"Yes, he's my father." Huang Zongxi answered with clasped hands.

Bi Shihu let out an "ah" and quickly stood up. "I'm so honored to meet you, my young lord! Pray forgive me for not being prepared for your coming," he said, ready to kneel down to kowtow.

Huang Zongxi hurriedly stood up to stop him, saying, "Please sit down, sir! There's no need for such ceremony."

However, Bi Shihu insisted on kowtowing. Both refused to concede. Huang Zongxi, unable to dissuade Mr. Bi, finally agreed to half of a kowtow.

"My young lord, please understand why I must kowtow to you," Bi Shihu explained after sitting down again. "Although I'm a merchant, I know gratitude and loyalty. Years ago, Wei the Castrate controlled the country, mine supervisors and tax collectors rampaged the prefecture and the county, merchants and entrepreneurs like me were heavily exploited, almost to the brink of bankruptcy. It was the East Wooders who stood up and spoke up for us in the name of justice, and by doing so they offended the castrate and many died of persecution. Any businessman that has a conscience won't forget such a great kindness, even for a single day. Besides, you went to Beijing to vindicate your

又如公子，当年袱被赴京讼冤，于公堂上，为父报仇，手出铁锥，当场击毙阉党爪牙二人，重伤二人。此等大孝大勇，谁人不知，谁个不赞！今日得仰台颜，实是小老三生之幸！”

“啊，老爹言重了，小生愧不敢当！”黄宗羲连忙拱着手，谦逊地说。虽然如此，看到父辈们的业绩，至今仍受到人们的由衷景仰，这毕竟是值得欣慰和骄傲的。他不由得兴奋起来，呷了一口茶，把杯子往方几上一放，说，“老爹，说到工商之民，小生却有一私见：历来为政者俱视工商为末业，而视农为本。时至今日，此说仍牢不可破。遂致禁制之，摧抑之，视为正理。其实，世上若无工匠，这一应民生日用之物，从何而来？世上若无商贾，这一应货物，又安能转运流通？可知农是本，工商又何尝不是本？”

“啊，先生是说——工商皆本？”毕石湖似乎有点意外。看见黄宗羲肯定地点点头，他就变得沉默起来，捋着胡子，半晌，才感叹地说：“不瞒先生，此疑窦存于小老心中，亦已多年，唯是无此自信。今日得先生一语道破，真乃茅塞顿开，心目一豁！”他抬起头，感激而又恳切地说，“公子高才卓识，他日定能飞腾宦海，出秉大政。如此，便是我辈之福了！今日难得公子屈尊下顾，小老无以表敬，意欲略备菲酌，敬奉三杯，祝公子福寿无量！”

“哎，不必了！小生尚有要务在身，即刻便要去了！”由于忽然想起此来的目的，黄宗羲连忙摆着手说。昨天夜里，他苦苦想到的那个办法，就是打算到这儿来，凭借同乡的关系，设法向

wronged father and avenged him in court by killing two of the minions of Eunuch Wei on the spot with an iron spear and severely wounding two of them. Such a great act of filial piety and bravery is publicly known and hailed by all. I'm so much blessed to have the opportunity to see you in person today."

"Hah, you speak too well of me, sir. I feel flattered," Huang Zongxi bowed and said modestly. Even so, seeing what his father had done was still remembered and admired was gratifying enough and gave him a great deal of pride. With heightened spirits, he took a sip of tea, put the cup on the square table, and said, "My dear sir, speaking of entrepreneurs and merchants, I have a private opinion to share with you: Throughout history, those in power have always regarded industry and commerce as auxiliaries and agriculture as the foundation. To this day, it's still the case. Industry and commerce are discouraged or suppressed. In fact, if there're no craftsmen in the world, where do the things we use come from? If there're no merchants in the world, how can all the goods be transported and circulated? Agriculture is the foundation for sure, but industry and commerce also constitute the foundation of our life."

"Ah, my young lord, you mean industry and commerce are also fundamental?" Bi Shihu seemed a little surprised. Seeing Huang Zongxi nodded affirmatively, he went quiet and stroked his beard, and after a long while, sighed, "My young lord, I've been thinking so for many years but have never had such self-confidence to speak it out. Your words hit the point and are enlightening indeed." He raised his head and said gratefully and earnestly, "My young lord, with your knowledge and wisdom, you'll surely be able to rise in the future and handle matters of state. It will be a great blessing to men like me. Now that you stoop to visit us, I shall prepare a humble meal and some wine. Pray allow us to toast to your good health and great future."

Suddenly remembering the purpose of this visit, Huang Zongxi waved his hand and said, "Well, pray don't bother. I have something important to do and will be leaving very soon." The previous night, he had come up with a solution, which was the purpose of his visit. He

商人们通融一笔钱，同时修一封书，说明情况，让对方带回余姚，由家里代为偿还。这么一个变通之策，看来是理应行得通的。他停了一下，正打算提出来，偶一回头，忽然瞥见屏风旁边，有一双混浊而又呆滞的眼睛，正直勾勾地望着自己。那双眼睛嵌在一张青灰色的、油晃晃的脸上。这没有戴帽子、光着一头蓬蓬乱发的人，仿佛在等待机会，看见黄宗羲发现了他，就兴奋起来，扭动着脸孔，先做出一个讨好的笑容，然后弯着腰，缩着肩膀，很快地走出来。

“嘻嘻，大人，你来啦？嘻嘻，小人请大人的安！”他莫名其妙地称呼说，跪下去，“咚咚”地叩了几个头，然后低着头，急急地又问，“嘻嘻，大人，阊门内牙行的汪大元，不知你老可认得？大人若是认得，求大人去说说他，叫他将小人那批海货，早早销发了。求求你，大人，小人求你啦！”说完，他又趴在地上，“咚咚”地叩起头来。他叩得那么使劲，很快，额上就碰出一块紫色的淤血。他却仿佛一点也不觉得痛，仍旧不停地叩下去。

“哎，黄相公不必理他！”大约看见客人被这突如其来的纠缠弄得愕然失色，毕石湖连忙解释说，“他是个疯子！”又回头呵斥道，“马小舍，你怎么又糊涂啦？谁让你跑出来的？回去，快回去！”

但是马小舍却不肯走，仍然一个劲地苦苦哀求，说他是借了高利贷来经商的，家里的老母妻儿都在盼着他早早卖了货物回去。求“大人”无论如何一定要帮他的忙。毕石湖几次喝他不住，还是会馆里的两个小厮闻声出来，才把他半劝半拖地弄进去了。

黄宗羲沉思地目送着。毕石湖显然颇为不安，一再道歉。黄

was going to borrow a sum of money from the businessmen from his hometown and meanwhile send a letter home through them explaining the situation to his family in Yuyao, who would repay the loan on his behalf. Such a solution seemed feasible. He paused for an instant and was about to bring it forward when suddenly he saw a pair of murky and sluggish eyes next to the screen looking straight at himself as he turned around. That pair of eyes were embedded in a pale, greasy face. The man without a hat, his hair unkempt, seemed to be waiting for an opportunity. Seeing Huang Zongxi cast a glance at him, he was excited and twisted his face to make an obsequious smile, and quickly came out, bending forward, his shoulders contracted.

"Hee-hee, your highness, welcome! Hee-hee, your highness, pray allow me to knowtow to you," he said, addressing Huang Zongxi with a puzzling title. Then he knelt down and kowtowed several times. He asked, his head still bent, "Hee-hee, your highness, do you happen to know Wang Dayuan of the brokerage house inside of the West City Gate? If your highness knows him, pray tell him to sell that batch of foreign goods as soon as possible. Pray tell him, your highness. I beg your help." Then, he knelt down again and kowtowed, but he knocked his head so hard that soon a patch of reddish bruise appeared on his forehead. As if feeling no pain at all, he continued kowtowing.

"Well, Mr. Huang, don't worry about him." Seeing his guest stunned by this sudden hassle, Bi Shihu quickly intervened and explained, "He is mad." He turned and shouted, "Ma Xiaoshe, why are you confused again? Who allowed you to come out? Go back, go back!"

However, Ma Xiaoshe refused to leave, still pleading, saying that he was doing business on a usurious loan, and his mother, wife and children were expecting him to sell the goods and go home soon. He wanted "his highness" to help him out by all means. Bi Shihu's shouts didn't stop him. Two servants heard them and came out. They took the madman away partly through persuasion, partly by force.

Huang Zongxi watched pensively as they left. Bi Shihu, obviously quite disturbed by the episode, apologized repeatedly. Huang Zongxi

宗羲摇摇头，表示不介意。

“嗯，方才听这位马……马兄的口气，像也是位客商，不知怎地弄得如此模样？”他转过脸来，瞅着主人问。

毕石湖摇摇头，叹了一口气：“这事说来，也是我们行商的一大苦处。别瞧我们无非载货扬帆，将本图利，自在得很。其实一买一卖，俱受制于牙行。不经牙行，便不能购货，亦不得发卖。那牙行主人，仗着有官府牙帖，坐收厚利不算，还恣意欺侮我们外来行商。大凡商货初到，他也照例宰鸡开宴，召妓演戏，殷勤招待。及至商货入了他仓里，他便任意把持，私行取用自不必说，还每每压住商货，不与你觅主批卖。弄得我们客商，常有坐守数月一年，货物仍未能脱手的。相公试想，我们做行商的，哪一个不把性命全押在这行情涨落上？被他这样一压，好端端的热货，便成了冷货。这不是要了命么！”

“噢？商货跌价，牙行又有何好处？”

“自然也无好处，只是他一味招揽，自己做不来，又不许我们自行批卖。到了货贱时，他便愈加压住不发，却照旧向我们收取仓租牙用。我们这些客商，财雄势大的也有，总是小本经纪为多，哪里受得起他这等簸弄！刚才这个马小舍，便是被他压了九个月，其间催问了无数次，反遭他奚落抢白，一时想不开，便发起疯癫来。如今一见生人，就以为是官府衙门来的。唉，瞧他那样子也着实可怜！”

shook his head and said he didn't mind.

He turned to the host and asked, "Why, from what I just heard, this brother, Mr. Ma, is a merchant from another place. How come he's fallen to such a state?"

Bi Shihu shook his head and sighed, "It's a long story involving one of the biggest problems facing us merchants. In the eyes of others, what we do is nothing more than loading our boats, sailing, and turning a capital into a profit. In fact, every purchase and every sale are subject to the brokerage house. You can't buy or sell goods without going through a brokerage house. The owner of a brokerage house, relying on the official certificate, not only reaps huge profits but also bullies us traders at will. When a batch of goods first arrives, he's all hospitality to the merchant—slaughtering chickens to give a banquet, summoning prostitutes, hiring an opera troupe to give performances ... but as soon as the goods enter his warehouse, you're at his mercy. He'll not only take whatever he likes but often detains the goods and refuses to find buyers for you. As a result, the traders often sit there for months and even a year without selling the goods. Just think about it, my young lord. As a trader, which one of us doesn't bet on market fluctuations? Given his indefinite detention of the goods, the supposedly hot-selling goods eventually become cold. Isn't this taking our lives?"

"Oh? What are the advantages for a broker when prices of the goods fall?"

"Naturally there's no benefit for him either. The problem is, he takes all the goods and forbids us to sell them on our own when he himself isn't able to sell them. When prices fall, he keeps tighter hold on the goods and charges us warehousing fees and management expenses. Among the guest merchants, there're a few rich and powerful ones but most are operating on a small scale with a small capital and can't afford being played like this. Ma Xiaoshe, for example, had his goods delayed for nine months, during which time he talked to him countless times and was rebuked and ridiculed. As a result, he's lost his mind. Whenever he sees a stranger, he thinks it's a *yamen* man. Alas, look at him! A poor man indeed, isn't he?"

黄宗羲平日，对于牙行凭借官府势力欺压客商的劣迹，亦时有所闻。不过，像这样把客商逼疯的，却是头一遭听说。他沉默了一阵，皱着眉毛问：

“这位马兄既遭此不幸，何以不早日将他送回家乡将息料理？也免得他家人悬望。”

毕石湖点点头：“黄相公所言甚是，便是小老也意欲尽早送他归去。只是眼下尚有用得着他处，所以才留下再住数日。”

“啊，一个疯癫之人，尚有何用处？”

毕石湖没有立即回答。他那谦恭随和的脸变得有点阴沉，一双眼睛却异样地亮起来。他瞧了瞧黄宗羲，从紧抿着的嘴唇里吐出三个字：

“打官司！”

“噢？”

“马小舍被他们逼成疯癫，这事我们浙东客商都气愤不过，俱说如今不比往日，既已立了馆，就不能再受他欺压。决意联起手来，同他斗一斗。定要牙行为这事向我会馆赔礼认错；马小舍一应商货损失、汤药使费，得由牙行赔偿；今后我浙东商货到行，均须及时批卖，不得任意稽延。否则，今后一应货物，会馆俱自行觅主发卖，再不经他牙行！”

“这——固然甚好，只是那牙行怕未必便肯？”

“他自然不肯。刚才，还来了三个人上门吵闹。不过，我们已经算计定了，拼着花他一笔银子，把本地几个有力的乡绅请出来主持公道；何况，官府庇护牙行，也不外得了他的使费，只要

Huang Zongxi had heard from time to time of broker firms colluding with the *yamen* to exploit guest merchants, but this was the first time for him to hear a guest merchant had gone mad because of the exploitation. He went silent. Then he asked with a frown.

"Now that this mishap has befallen Mr. Ma, why not send him back to his hometown as soon as possible so that he can be nursed by his family, who wouldn't be worried."

Bi Shihu nodded and said, "You're quite right, my young lord. I also think it's a good idea to send him back home as soon as possible. It's just that he's still needed right now and has to stay for a few more days."

"Ah, what's the use of a madman?"

Bi Shihu didn't answer immediately. His humble and easy-going face became a little gloomy, but his eyes strangely lit up. He looked at Huang Zongxi and uttered three words from his tightly pressed lips, "We want justice."

"Oh?"

"Ma Xiaoshe was driven into madness by them. We guest merchants from East Zhejiang were all angry about this. We all think things are different nowadays now that we've formed a trade guild. Such bullying will no longer be tolerated. We're determined to join hands and fight for justice. The brokerage house must apologize to the guild for this matter; it must compensate Ma Xiaoshe for the loss of his goods and medical expenses; from now on, when a batch of goods of any guild member arrives, the brokerage house should make sure it's sold without delay. Otherwise, in the future, the guild will find buyers and sell goods on our own and we'll have nothing to do with the brokerage house."

"That, that sounds good, but I'm afraid the brokerage house won't agree."

"Of course they won't. Just now, they sent three men here to make trouble. However, we have our plan. We're going to create a fund and invite a few most influential local squires to speak for justice; besides, the brokerage house's protection from the *yamen* comes from

肯花银子，不难买他一个秉公而断！”

黄宗羲想了一下，点点头说：“牙行欺人太甚，不妨与他斗一斗！”他抬起头，奋然道，“小生不才，亦愿为乡里略尽绵薄。在下如今便要到常熟去谒见钱牧斋老先生。钱老先生德高望重，在此间极有力量，若得他一纸关照，不愁官府不秉公审处。这一封书，小生自问还求得来！”

毕石湖一听，喜出望外，连忙站起来，深深作下揖去，说：“若得黄相公援手，正是小人们之大幸！只是劳动不当。”又问，“黄相公所言的这位钱老先生，不知可是曾任礼部右堂的钱大人么？”

“正是。”

“哦！那么，好教相公得知，钱大人眼下不在常熟，他已来姑苏。昨日，小人亦央人引见，前往叩拜，只是钱大人事忙……”

“你说什么？”黄宗羲的眼睛顿时睁大了，“牧老已来姑苏？他、他现在何处？”

“就下榻在离此不远的徐氏东园。”

黄宗羲“啊”了一声，顿时笑逐颜开。他站起来，向主人深深一揖，说：“既然如此，小生这便告辞。不过，尚有一事相求……”

他正想把借钱的事提出来，然而，就在这时，只听大门外蓦地响起一阵呼喊，接着，两个仆人跌跌撞撞地奔了进来，一见毕石湖，就惊慌地说：“老、老爹，不好了，打、打进来了！”

黄宗羲和毕石湖都吓了一跳，同时问：“谁打来了？”

“牙、牙行的人！”

话音刚落，就听外面乒乒乓乓地乱打乱砸起来，几个声音在狂叫：

nothing more than bribery and if we're willing to spend the money, it's not difficult to buy fair judgement."

Huang Zongxi thought for an instant, nodded and said, "The brokerage house goes too far in their bullying of merchants, you might as well fight them." Raising his head, he said indignantly, "I might not be of much use but I would like to do my bit for fellows from home. I'm going to Changshu to meet with Mr. Qian Muzhai, who is a highly respected personage and has great influence here. If he writes a letter, we'll not have to worry about the fairness of the trial. I think I can get a letter from him."

Overjoyed to hear it, Bi Shihu stood up, made a deep bow, and said, "If you can help, we're very fortunate indeed, but meanwhile we're worried if it's too much bother for you." He went on to ask, "Is the Mr. Qian you speak of the Lord Qian who has once served as the Right Vice Minister of the Ministry of Rites?"

"Exactly."

"Oh! Then, I should tell you that Lord Qian isn't in Changshu right now. He has come to Gusu. Yesterday, I went to see him through the introduction of a friend, but he was busy ..."

"What did you say?" said Huang Zongxi with wide open eyes. "Lord Qian has come to Gusu? Where is he, where is he now?"

"He stays in Xu's East Garden, not far from here."

Huang Zongxi let out an "Ah" and suddenly beamed with a broad smile. He stood up, gave the host a deep bow, and said, "In that case, I have to say goodbye now. However, may I ask you a favor ..."

As he was going to broach the subject of borrowing money, a large noise came from outside the door and two servants came stumbling in. "Ma-master! They, they're forcing their way in!" they said to Bi Shihu, panicked.

Both Huang Zongxi and Bi Shihu were taken aback and asked at the same time, "Who is it?"

"The, the broker's men."

Then came the sound of smashing and striking from the outside, ping, pong, ping, pong, and several voices were screaming: "Destroy

“踏平了他！”

“叫他神气！”

“砸、砸！狠砸！”

黄宗羲毫无思想准备，不禁惊得倒退几步，愕然地朝外张望。倒是毕石湖显得比较镇定，他皱起眉毛，果断地一挥手：“关上二门！”随即冲上前去，同仆人们一齐动手，把沉重的二门用力关上。当他们刚刚上好门闩，进攻者已经在外面把门扇撞得“咚咚”直响了。

这当儿，住在会馆里的其他客商听见响动，都纷纷从各个角落里奔出来，有的人手里还拿着随手抓到的扁担和棍棒。大堂上下，转眼间聚起了几十人。当弄清发生了什么事之后，一个个都现出吃惊、愤怒的神色。忍不住的，就破口大骂起来。更有人主张出去同对方拼个你死我活。

正当他们议论纷纷，门扇却猛烈地震动起来。大约进攻者搬来了大圆木，正在从外面撞击。大家吃了一惊，连忙再加了一道门闩，又把大堂上那些紫檀木桌椅搬来，一股脑儿把门顶住。做完这一切之后，毕石湖朝震动不已的门扇瞅了一会儿，然后做手势让大家静下来，他提高嗓门叫道：

“喂！外面的，住手，住手！我们有话要说！”

一连叫了几声，外面却根本不理，相反，撞击得更加疯狂了。幸而这门扇本来就是专为防盗而设，用的是两整块花梨木合成，外裹铁皮，十分坚厚，加上有三道门闩和许多桌椅抵住，一时还不致被攻破。但时间长了，就很难说。大家都感到事态严重，一齐望着毕石湖，等他拿主意。

毕石湖也显得有点紧张，他挥挥手，领着大家退进三门，又合力筑起一道防线，这才说：

everything!"

"Destroy his pride!"

"Smash, smash! Smash hard!"

Huang Zongxi, totally unprepared for such a situation, stepped back in shock, and looked out, dumbfounded. Bi Shihu, however, appeared rather calm. Knitting his eyebrows, he said resolutely with a hand wave, "Close Gate Two!" Then, he immediately rushed forward and worked together with the servants to close the heavy second gate forcefully. As soon as they bolted the gate, the attackers arrived and banged the gate from the outside.

By then, the guest merchants staying in the guild premises had rushed out from every corner, having heard the noise, some of them holding a shoulder-pole or a stick that they had grabbed in a hurry. In an instant, dozens of men gathered in the lobby. When they figured out what happened, they brimmed with shock and indignation. Some swore at the intruders. Some suggested they go out and battle it out with them.

Just as they debated what to do next, the gate shook violently—probably the attackers had brought a big log and were banging it from the outside—and in a panic, they quickly added one more bolt to fasten the gate and moved the red sandalwood tables and chairs in the lobby over to consolidate their defense. That being done, Bi Shihu took a look at the quaking gate leaf, raised his voice and shouted:

"Hey, there! Stop, stop! We have something to say."

He yelled a few times, but there was no response at all. On the contrary, the banging increased in force. Fortunately, this gate leaf, originally designed to prevent theft, was very strong, consisting of two whole planks of rosewood wrapped in iron sheets. In addition, it was held by three bolts and many tables and chairs. So it would hold out for a while. Yet, it was hard to tell how long it would last. Everyone felt the gravity of the matter and looked up to Bi Shihu for the next move.

Bi Shihu also seemed a little nervous. He waved his hand and led the gathering to inside Gate Three. Together they built another line of

“方才，弟已经着人火速去报官。只是，官府何时才派人来，肯不肯派人来，都无从预知。如今之计，要么死守，要么退走。打算不同，处置也不同，事不宜迟，望列位从速决断！”

他的话刚说完，好几个声音同时叫起来：

“许多商货都在馆里，怎么不守？守！一定要守！”

然而也有相当一部分人没有作声，脸上露出畏惧的神色。

毕石湖扫了他们一眼，冷冷地说：“要守，就大家一块守。走一半，留一半，那就别指望守得住。大家瞧着办吧！”

听他这样一说，大家你瞧我，我瞧你，开始嗡嗡议论起来，各摆各的理由，一时间谁也说服不了谁。就在这时，只听外面“哗啦”一声巨响，接着便是进攻者们的狂呼乱叫，显然，二门已被突破了！

一刹那间，三门内的人们像是遭了雷击似的，一个个都停止了争论，在原地呆立不动。

就在这一片死寂当中，忽然，人丛中响起了笑声。那是一阵欢乐的、怪诞的、使人听了毛骨悚然的笑声！接着，一个头发披散的人钻了出来，大声欢呼说：“好了，好了！我的商货回来了！听，大箱子，好大的箱子！哎，你们别摔、别摔，摔坏了我要你赔！”说着，跌跌撞撞地奔过去，开始很着急地把堵在门上的桌椅杂物又推又拉，要把门打开。

大家吃了一惊，当看清那是疯癫了的马小舍时，几个人就连忙奔过去，横拖倒拽地把他弄到一边去。可是马小舍不肯，又是叫又是哭，又是苦苦哀求，那凄厉的声音在庭院上空久久回荡，听得人们都惨然地低下头去……

这时，自从二门被攻破之后，停止了片刻的打砸声忽然又在

defense. Then he said, "Just now, my younger brother sent someone to report to the *yamen*, but there's no knowing when they'll come or whether they'll come at all. We have two choices: either to hold our ground or to retreat. Each choice involves a different action plan. Since it's an emergency, let's make our choice now."

When he finished speaking, several voices screamed in unison:

"We have a lot of goods here. How can we give up? Hold the ground! We must hold our ground!"

Yet, quite a few men were silent, with a look of fear on their faces.

Bi Shihu glanced at them and said coldly, "If we decide to hold our ground, we should do it together. If half of us stay and the other half retreat, there's no hope to succeed in the defense. The decision is yours, men!"

Hearing what he said, the merchants looked at each other and started to debate, each citing his own reasons, but no one was persuaded by anyone else. At this moment, a loud rumbling sound came from the outside, followed by the hilarious shouts of the attackers. Obviously, Gate Two had fallen.

All of a sudden, the men inside Gate Three stopped arguing and stood still as if having been struck by lightning.

In the midst of this dead silence, a laughter suddenly rang from the crowd. It was a joyous, eerie, and creepy laughter. Then, a man with unkempt hair came out and cheered loudly, "Jolly good, jolly good! My goods are back! Listen, a big box, a huge one! Hey, don't drop it, don't drop it. If you break it, you must recompense me!" As he spoke, he came stumbling over and began to anxiously push and pull the tables and chairs and the clutter blocking the gate to open it.

Everyone was taken aback. When they saw it was Ma Xiaoshe the madman, a few of them rushed over and dragged him aside, but Ma Xiaoshe refused to leave. He yelled, cried, and pleaded, his tragic, heart-piercing voice reverberating in the courtyard. Everyone sadly lowered their head ...

Then suddenly, the smashing sound that had lulled awhile after

门外爆发了。大家都吃惊地抬起头来。一个年轻的商人显然悲愤已极，他一拳擂在门扇格上，厉声大叫：

“牙行的狗杂种，实在欺人太甚！若是这一次再轻饶了他，往后我们浙东人就别想在这一方立足了！守，非守不可！”

说着，他一手抄起棍棒，大步走到毕石湖身旁，气冲冲地瞪着大家。人们到了这时，也已再不迟疑，纷纷拿起自卫家伙。

毕石湖看见这种情形，就点点头，说：“既然大家情愿死守，那么好，听我号令——”他刚要说下去，忽然想起了什么，临时又做了一个“等一等”的手势。然后，快步走到正站在一旁沉思地注视着三门的黄宗羲跟前，说：

“黄相公，我们这些人，身家性命都系于这一场争斗，已决意死守。相公是局外人，犯不着同我们一道冒这风险，本馆有一道侧门，与隔壁全晋会馆相通，请相公过去暂避。如何？”看见黄宗羲一声不响地摇摇头，毕石湖迟疑了一下，又说：“相公倾诚相助，本馆十分感激。只是相公是万金之躯，若有什么差池，在下实在担待不起。情事已急，相公若有意援手，出去之后，请速往官府，促他派人前来弹压，小可便毕生感戴大德了！”

可是，黄宗羲仍然摇摇头，他缓缓举起手，指着三门，从牙缝里挤出一句话：“把这门——开了！”

“啊？”

“哼，什么牙行！本相公倒要会一会他们！快——开了！”

the fall of Gate Two broke out again outside. Everyone looked up in fright. A young merchant, in utter indignation, punched the gate leaf grid and screamed:

"The sons of bitches in the brokerage house are going too far in their bullying of us. If we spare them again this time, there'll be no place for us East Zhejiangers in the future. Hold the ground! We must hold our ground!"

As he spoke, he grabbed a stick with one hand, strode to the side of Bi Shihu, and glared at the crowd angrily. At this point, there was no more hesitation and the merchants took up whatever weapons available for self-defense.

Seeing that, Bi Shihu nodded and said, "Since everyone is ready to hold our ground, then, listen up." He stopped as he remembered something and made a gesture to mean "Hang on!" Then, he walked quickly to Huang Zongxi, who was standing aside and watching Gate Three thoughtfully, and said:

"Mr. Huang, our lives and livelihood depend on this battle and we've decided to defend ourselves. You're not in this. It's not fair to get you involved in this risky thing. There's a side entrance that connects our guild to the Quanjin Guild next door. You can go and take shelter there. What do you think?" Seeing Huang Zongxi shake his head silently, Bi Shihu hesitated and said, "We're very grateful for your kind support, but you're a scholar of great learning and I should not let anything happen to you. It's an emergency. If you want to lend us a helping hand, you can go to the *yamen* after you leave and ask them to intervene. I'll be indebted to you for life."

However, Huang Zongxi still shook his head. He slowly raised his hand, pointed at Gate Three, and squeezed three words from his teeth:

"Open the gate!"

"What?"

"Humph, it's merely a brokerage house. Actually, I've been wanting to meet them for a while! Open it! Quick!"

## 心怀鬼胎

钱谦益默默地瞧着已有几分酒意的钱养先一个劲儿扯着郑元勋碰杯，暗自在心里盘算：“如今总算已经万事俱备，只等着大会来开锣了！如果一切顺利，作出公议，应当连夜派人进京，把消息报知周延儒。这样，到五月底，最迟六月中，老周守信的话，就该有所动作。算他再不起劲，也不能拖过今年。否则，我照样有办法把阮胡子再打下去，让他吃不了兜着走！嗯，那么说，就是今年，今年我就出山了！哈哈！”一想到自己苦苦熬了十三年之后，终于又能重立朝班，扬眉吐气，钱谦益心里充满了难以形容的喜悦。他放松身体，靠在椅背上，微微眯起眼睛，开始历历如绘地想象一旦九重诏下，朝野如何额手称庆，亲友们如何奔走相告，门生故旧如何络绎来贺。然后，就是隆重的送别，旅途的应酬，到京之后同僚的迎接，皇上的赐见，出席喜气洋洋的接风酒宴和参与朝房密殿里的各种军机大事……不过，有一件事，他此刻还拿不定主意，就是到时把全家都带进京去呢，还是轻装简从？如果不带家眷，那么把柳如是丢在常熟，却是难以放心得下；但如果让她以“夫人”的名分跟着自己进京，又难免会招来物议……

“启禀老爷，余姚黄太冲先生求见……”一个熟悉的声音在耳畔响起。

钱谦益抬了抬眼皮，发现李宝站在花厅的门口，“嗯，他说什么？谁来求见？”他迟钝地想。蓦地，他回过神来，心中一惊。

## A Heart of Evil

Qian Qianyi secretly calculated, as he silently looked at Qian Yangxian, who, already a little bit intoxicated, kept clinking cups with Zheng Yuanxun, "Now everything is ready. We're just waiting for the conference to kick off. If all goes well and a consensus is made, we should send someone to Beijing the very night to report to Zhou Yanru so that he should be able to do something by the end of May or mid-June at the latest should he be good for his word. Even if he isn't enthusiastic enough, he's not supposed to delay the matter to after this year. Otherwise, I would do something else to defeat Beardy Ruan and by then he would be losing face. This is the year of my comeback, so to speak, ha ha!" Qian Qianyi's heart was filled with indescribable joy when he thought that after thirteen years of waiting he was finally able to re-establish himself in court. Reclining on the back of his chair, he squinted his eyes slightly and began to imagine that once the nine-fold edict was issued how men in court or serving in the provinces would applaud his reinstatement, how his relatives and friends would rush to tell the good news to one another, and how his pupils and old acquaintances would flock to his house to congratulate him. Then, a grand farewell, meeting people during the journey, a warm welcome in the capital by former colleagues, an audience with His Majesty the emperor, attending reception banquets beaming with happiness, and participating in the various military decisions in the secret palace rooms ... but there was one thing he couldn't decide: by then, should he bring his whole family to the capital or should he go alone? If he didn't bring his family to the capital and left Liu Rushi in Changshu, he couldn't set his mind at rest, but if he took her along as lady of the house, he would inevitably incur backbiting ...

"Your lordship, Huang Taichong from Yuyao wants to see you ..." A familiar voice rang in his ears.

Qian Qianyi flipped up his eyelids and saw Li Bao standing at the door of the Flower Hall. "Eh, what did he say? Who is it?" he thought sluggishly. Suddenly, he woke up with a start.

“啊，来、来了、来了多少人？”他失态地站起来问。

“回老爷，只是黄相公一位，并无别人。”李宝回答，有点奇怪地瞧了主人一眼，随即把拜帖递过来。

“什么？”钱谦益急躁地侧着耳朵。

李宝把刚才的话又大声重复了一遍。

“哼，传个话都不清楚，嗡嗡嗡就像蚊子叫！”钱谦益悻悻地呵斥说。弄清楚并不是吴应箕、陈贞慧全伙上门来，他松了一口气，这才瞧一瞧拜帖。的确，如果在这个时候走漏了风声，被对方找上门来同自己吵闹，那可是大大的不妙。不过，虽然如此，钱谦益仍旧怀疑黄宗羲是被对手们派来刺探动静的。他离开座位，一声不响地在室内来回走了片刻，立住脚，瞅了瞅已经停止了谈话，正在一齐望着他的几个心腹，用犹疑不决的口气说：“请黄相公外堂奉茶，我随后便来。”

等李宝答应着退出去之后，钱谦益又皱着眉头，寻思了一下，这才吩咐陈在竹等陪着客人，他自己出了门，慢慢向楠木厅行去。

“……嗯，他若不是来刺探我的便罢，他若真的为此而来，我就干脆给他个矢口否认，看他能奈我何！哼哼，对了，我正愁不清楚他们的动静，趁此机会倒可以反过来摸摸底细哩！”当钱谦益隔着楠木厅的窗棂，望见黄宗羲那熟悉的背影时，他终于暗暗拿定了主意。

钱谦益的这种想法，黄宗羲自然是不知道的。他刚刚在浙东会馆里碰上一场争斗，激于义愤，打算冒险去见那伙暴徒，面斥其非，被会馆的人竭力劝住。幸而，在最后一刻里，官府总算派

"Oh, he's come. How many of them are there?" He stood up and asked awkwardly.

"Your lordship, it's just Mr. Huang alone." Li Bao replied, taking a look at his master curiously, and then handed over the calling card.

"What?" Qian Qianyi eagerly strained his ear to listen.

Li Bao repeated his words in a loud voice.

"Huh, you're buzzing like a mosquito instead of speaking like a human," Qian Qianyi growled. After learning that it was Mr. Huang alone without the company of Wu Yingji and Chen Zhenhui, he breathed a sigh of relief and took a look at the calling card. Indeed, should wind be leaked at this moment and his adversaries find out about what he had been planning, the situation would not be good. Even so, Qian Qianyi still suspected that Huang Zongxi was sent by his opponents to spy on his movements. He left his seat and silently paced back and forth in the room for a while. Then, he stood still, looked at his confidantes who had stopped talking and were looking at him, and said in a hesitant tone, "Ask Mr. Huang to come in and have some tea. I'll come to him shortly."

After Li Bao exited with "Aye, my lord", Qian Qianyi knit his brows and thought for a while. Then, he bade Chen Zaizhu and others to accompany the guest and he himself exited the door and slowly walked toward the Nanmu Hall.

"Well, I hope he's not here to spy on me. If he is, I'll simply deny everything and see what he can do with me. Humph, good, since I don't know what they're doing either, I can take this opportunity to find out about them." When Qian Qianyi saw Huang Zongxi's familiar figure behind the window lattice of the Nanmu Hall, he finally made up his mind.

Huang Zongxi didn't know what Qian Qianyi was thinking, of course. A short while ago, he had accidentally witnessed a brawl in the East Zhejiang Guild, where, out of righteous indignation, he was going to take the risk of confronting the thugs but was stopped by the guild members. Fortunately, a *yamen* man came at the last moment to stop the violence. Yet havoc had already been wreaked and everyone in the

来了衙役，才把暴行制止下来。不过，经过这一场破坏，会馆损失惨重，人心惶惶。黄宗羲犹豫了又犹豫，到底不好意思再开口借钱，只得匆匆告辞，赶到徐氏东园来。好在如今不是上常熟去，算不上专程拜谒，即使不送礼，也勉强说得过去。虽然如此，黄宗羲到底心中不安，总觉得有点对不起这位老世伯似的。

现在，黄宗羲听见了一种熟悉的脚步声。那是他在常熟半野堂读书期间听惯了的、沉稳而又略带几分拖沓的脚步声。他的心跳动了一下，迅速地转过身去。一刹那间，一种热烈的、狂喜的表情，从他那张清秀的小脸显现出来。他用闪闪发光的眼睛瞅着钱谦益，仿佛要拥抱他似的，急切地向前迎了两步，随即弯下膝盖，拜倒在地上。

“哎呀，贤侄！不必多礼，不必多礼！”钱谦益满面春风地迎上前，紧紧抓住黄宗羲的胳膊，用一种亲昵的、不拘形迹的动作，把他扶了起来。

“小侄不知世伯也在姑苏，拜望来迟，望祈恕罪！”黄宗羲拱着手说。他的小脸因为喜欢而发红，目不转睛地瞅着钱谦益。

钱谦益也在微笑着，不住地打量着眼前的世侄，发现黄宗羲除了脸上多了几分风尘之色外，体魄依旧是那般挺拔、健壮。发达的肌肉，从蓝布直裰的胸前、肩头凸现出来。一双秀气的眼睛里，仍旧闪烁着纯真、智慧的光芒。不知什么缘故，每当看到黄宗羲，钱谦益总是不由自主地在心里拿他同自己的儿子孙爱相比，并且油然涌起感叹：我的儿子要是像他，该有多好！那样我就心满意足，把一切事业都托付给他，再用不着以垂老之身，还为着一顶劳什子乌纱而栖栖遑遑、虚耗心力了。何况，他对我实际上

guild hall was agitated. After some hesitation, Huang Zongxi gave up the idea of borrowing money from the guild, hurriedly said goodbye and rushed to Xu's East Garden. Since it was not a visit to the old man's home in Changshu, it didn't exactly count as a special trip to pay tribute to this elder. Therefore, not bringing a gift for this occasion would not constitute a breach of etiquette. Even so, Huang Zongxi felt uneasy as if he were in debt.

Now, Huang Zongxi heard a familiar footstep. It was the kind of heavy, steady, and sluggish footstep that he had used to hear while studying in the Half Wild Estate in Changshu. His heart jerked and he quickly turned around. In an instant, a warm, ecstatic expression appeared on his delicate small face. He looked at Qian Qianyi with gleaming eyes, and as if to embrace the elder, he eagerly took two steps forward, knelt down on his knees and kowtowed.

"Oh, nephew! No need for ceremonies, no need for ceremonies." Qian Qianyi greeted Huang Zongxi with a face full of spring breeze, tightly grasped his arm, and helped him up with a friendly and casual gesture.

"My dear uncle, I didn't know you're also in Gusu, pray forgive me for my late visit." Huang Zongxi said with clasped hands. His small face flushed with delight, and he looked at Qian Qianyi intently.

Qian Qianyi also smiled, and glancing up and down at his friend's son standing in front, he found that Huang Zongxi was tall and fit and energetic just like before. The only difference was the appearance of some worldly dust on his face. The blue robe didn't hide the young man's well-developed muscles that bulged on the chest and shoulder heads. A pair of exquisite eyes gleamed with innocence and intelligence as they had used to. For some reason, whenever he saw Huang Zongxi, Qian Qianyi couldn't help comparing the young man with his own son Sun'ai with a sigh: "If only my son could be like him! Then, I would be happy and content and would entrust everything to my son instead of wasting my time guarding my useless black gauze cap. And this kid is actually so close and attached to me ..." At this moment, such a feeling resurged in Qian Qianyi's heart,

又是这般亲近、依恋……此刻，这种感情又一次在钱谦益心中涌现了，而且比以往更加强烈，使他暂时忘记了从花厅出来一路上的种种疑虑和盘算，只感到由衷的喜悦，仿佛感情当中长期遭受簸弄、伤害的一角，忽然得着了抚慰似的。

“老伯，小侄此次出来，到处听闻老伯行将起复，入赞中枢，真乃令人惊喜不胜哩！”当最初一阵热烈的寒暄过去之后，黄宗羲在椅子上坐下，端起一杯茶，立刻又放下来，兴奋地说。

“噢？”钱谦益不在意地应了一声，仍旧不住眼地打量黄宗羲，并未从刚才的状态中摆脱出来。

“只是周阁老为人贪婪忮刻，未必有此胸襟！倘若又旁生枝节，从中作梗，实在不可不防！”

钱谦益迷惑地望着黄宗羲热切的脸容和圆睁的眼睛，好一会儿弄不明白对方在说什么。蓦地，他清醒过来，随即想起黄宗羲此次来访，可能是奉吴应箕、陈贞慧他们的指派，向自己刺探消息的。这位年轻有为的世侄，其实是窥伺在旁的危险对手。缠绕在钱谦益心头的绵绵情意立时烟消云散了。他警觉起来，沉默了一会，拿起了几上的茶杯，淡淡地问：“嗯，怎么？”

黄宗羲本能地也端起茶杯，但又一次放下了：“周阁老对老伯嫉忌甚深！”他急急地说，向前挪了挪身子，“这些年，他与温体仁交相排斥老伯，天下共知，不必复论。此公无才无德，秉政多年，唯知阿迎上意，未见有尺寸建树；且广纳苞苴，贪赃受贿，较之温体仁，尤为放肆无耻。此次东林诸君子合力举之出山，小侄窃以为失计！虽然如此，此公却未必感恩知报。何况老伯一旦复出，必以斡旋运会、矫正人心为己任，宏谟一展，益见其庸

with a greater intensity than ever before, making him temporarily forget all the doubts and questions he had had along the way from the Flower Hall and giving him a deep satisfaction, as if a chronic spiritual suffering were suddenly redressed.

After they exchanged greetings, Huang Zongxi sat down on the chair, picked up a cup of tea, which he immediately put down, and said excitedly, "My dear uncle, on my current trip, I hear everywhere I go that you'll be reinstated to office as a key member of the Cabinet. I'm really excited for you."

"Oh?" Qian Qianyi replied nonchalantly, still glancing up and down at Huang Zongxi without emerging from his thoughts.

"It's just that Premier Zhou is corrupt and treacherous. He might not have the magnanimity. You must beware his wiles."

Qian Qianyi suspiciously looked at Huang Zongxi's zestful face and wide-open eyes in confusion, and for a while couldn't figure out his intention. Suddenly, he woke up and remembered that Huang Zongxi might have been sent by Wu Yingji and Chen Zhenhui to spy on him. This young promising son of a friend was actually a dangerous opponent watching him. The affection in Qian Qianyi's heart immediately disappeared. He became alert. After being silent for a while, he picked up a cup from the tea table and asked in a quiet voice, "Well, explain."

Huang Zongxi instinctively picked up his teacup but immediately put it down, saying, "The Honorable Mr. Zhou is very jealous of you, my dear uncle." He said anxiously, moving forward. "Over the years, he's worked against you together with Wen Tiren. The whole world knows it, so there's no need to go over the details. This man, who has no talents or virtues to commend him, has been in power for many years. He has no achievements of any kind. The only thing he can do is flatter the emperor. Moreover, he abuses his power and takes bribes, and that considered, he's more brazen than Wen Tiren. Yet now the East Wood scholars are joining forces to restitute him. I think it's definitely a misstep. He'll not be grateful despite everything. What's more, once you're reinstated to office, you're sure to make it your

陋，彼又安能甘心乎！”

钱谦益斜睨着黄宗羲，眼睛里怀疑和戒备之意越来越重。黄宗羲一坐下就大谈周延儒，而且没有一句好评，正刺中了他心中的隐私。“莫非他们真的知道了，却派他来警告于我？”他想。可是，瞧黄宗羲的神气又不大像。于是，他不动声色，照旧淡淡地说：

“老夫起复之说，近来传闻确是不少。唯是凿空之言，均无实据。其实，老夫如今年逾花甲，但得优游林下，于愿已足，这‘兼济’二字，倒也无复萦怀了！”

“啊，老伯安能作如此想！方今天下扰攘，社稷危殆，正是仁人志士用命之秋。老伯雄才峻望，四海共瞻。凡我君子，谁不倾耳侧足以望老伯出秉大政。倘若以小人之故，甘心独善，其如苍生何！”

钱谦益没有回答。黄宗羲这一番话令他颇为感动。他现在已经看出来，这位世侄一片至诚，胸无城府，绝不是为着刺探消息而来的。“可是，他又哪里晓得，我岂是真心的甘于老死山林？相反，眼下正为复出的事殚精竭虑、寝食不安呢！”他望着黄宗羲，默默地想，忽然冒出一个希望：要是这位世侄能站到自己一边，支持自己，那该多好！他是东林的遗孤，又是《留都防乱公揭》的发起人。到时，他如果能够出面表示宽宥阮大铖，那效用自然非比寻常。不过，这办得到么？

“唉，皇上英明天纵，唯于用人一端，却令人百思不得其解！”黄宗羲并不理会钱谦益的沉默，管自愤愤地低声说，“今上并非

responsibility to work with all parties to restore a sense of right and wrong and put things right. By then, how can they be happy seeing themselves pale into insignificance?"

Qian Qianyi squinted at Huang Zongxi, his eyes becoming increasingly suspicious and vigilant. Huang Zongxi touched a secret corner of his mind by talking negatively about Zhou Yanru up front without a single good word. "Have they really heard wind of it so they're sending him to warn me?" he thought. "But his expression didn't look it." So he said in a calm tone:

"There have been a lot of rumors recently about my reinstatement but nothing is confirmed. In fact, since I'm over sixty now I'm very happy to wander in the woods every day and not to be bothered by the affairs of the outside world."

"Why, my dear uncle, pray don't think so. The world now is in turmoil and the nation is in danger. It's an occasion for men with lofty ideals to exert themselves. They all defer to you for your great wisdom, which will guide them through the crisis. Who of us isn't looking forward to your coming out to be in charge? If you think too much of the little men and choose to protect yourself, where's hope for the people?"

Qian Qianyi gave no response, rather moved. He could see this young man was sincere without guile and was definitely not here to spy on him. "But, how can he know that I'm not going to be reconciled to dying in the woods? In fact, I've been thinking so much about my reinstatement that I've been unable to eat or sleep." As he regarded Huang Zongxi in silence, suddenly an idea occurred to him: "If this young man can be on my side and support me, things will be going well. As the orphan of an East Wooder and the initiator of 'Public Denunciation of a Treasonist in the Legacy Capital', if he's willing to stand up and say that he'll forgive Ruan Dacheng, the impact will be great. But is it possible?"

"Woe! Despite the unrivaled wisdom of His Majesty the emperor, the way he employs talents is quite puzzling," Huang Zongxi grumbled, disregarding Qian Qianyi's silence. "His Majesty the

不知东林为君子，却以有一二非君子之人混杂其间，而事事猜疑提防；也并非不知攻东林者为小人，却以其可以牵制东林而不惜重用之。遂致十余年间，君子尽去而小人独存。如此下去，只怕大明真要亡呢！”

钱谦益怔怔地眨着眼睛，似乎没有听清。当他终于弄明白之后，不禁大吃一惊：这世侄竟敢放肆到攻讦起皇上来，这还了得！万一给厂卫的人侦知，便是破家灭门之祸呀！他不胜张皇地向四边望了望，压低嗓门训斥道：

“贤侄，你怎地如此荒唐！这种话也能说的么？亏你还是个圣贤之徒、忠良之后，怎地说出这种反贼流寇一般的悖语狂言来！你莫是不要命了！”钱谦益越说越严厉，他当真动了气：这群书呆子怎地如此不知死活，平日讥评大臣、议论朝政倒还罢了，竟放肆到指摘皇上的不是！这种念头，顶多只能悄悄地想一下——那也是有罪的，他却公然无忌地说出口来！钱谦益觉得黄宗羲的这种情绪十分危险，很想狠狠地呵斥他一顿，教他知道即使在自己面前，说话也应当有分寸。可是，当他看见黄宗羲低着头闷声不响时，口气不知为什么却软下来：“嗯，这话悖谬之极！不过，你在这里说说还不打紧，若到外面去，千万不能！可记住了？”他犹豫了一下，慰解似的说，“只要有我东林、复社诸君子在，嗯，大明亡不了！”

“可是，江南的社局，是越来越不成话了！”黄宗羲爆发似的抬起头来，满脸是苦恼的神情，“沽名钓誉者有之，争权夺利

emperor, not unaware that the East Wooders are good men in general, keeps close watch on them simply because there's one or two bad elements, and not unware that those attacking the East Wooders are little men, relies heavily on them to curb the East Wooders. As a result, for more than ten years, he's been served by little men and no good men. If this continues, I'm afraid that the Great Ming will really go to the dogs."

Qian Qianyi blinked his eyes confoundedly, as if he hadn't heard it clearly. When he finally figured it out, he was shocked. The young man was so presumptuous as to be slandering His Majesty the emperor. It was a crime punishable by death to the whole family should it be known by the Jinyiwei secret agents. He looked around panickedly, lowered his voice and reprimanded Huang Zongxi, saying:

"My dear nephew, why do you go so far? Should you say a thing like that? As a disciple of the sages and a son of a loyal official, how can you say such treacherous things like a treasonist or an insurgent? Don't you fear for your life?" Qian Qianyi spoke with increasing sternness in his tone. He was really angry. How could these nerds be so reckless as to criticize the emperor himself after ridiculing the ministers and vainly commenting on matters of state? Such ideas, should they occur, should only stay in the mind for a moment—even that was criminal—and should never be spoken out the way the young man did. Feeling Huang Zongxi's sentiment was very dangerous, Qian Qianyi was in a good mind to reprimand him more harshly and let him know that he should speak within limits even before his father's close friend. However, when he saw Huang Zongxi was silent with a bent head, his tone somehow softened. "You know, it's utterly wrong to say so. It doesn't matter very much to say it here. Never say it anywhere else. Do you remember?" Qian Qianyi said. He paused and then said assuringly, "As long as there are the East Wooders and Fushers, um, the Great Ming will not go to the dogs."

"But the situation of the Fushe in River South is increasingly bad," said Huang Zongxi. Then, he suddenly raised his head and said, with a distressed expression on his face, "Some are scheming for fame

者有之，同类相残者有之，简直是一塌糊涂！”他的胸膛急剧地起伏着，终于，仿佛抵受不住内心的压力似的，猛地站起身，来回走了几步，突然回过头来，“听说，还有想替阮大铖翻案开脱的！”

钱谦益正想着如何开导黄宗羲，听了这话，心头一震。虽然他刚才还打算把对方拉到自己这边来，可是猝不及防地听到这么一句，仍然像被击中了要害似的，一下子目瞪口呆，不知道该怎么回答。

幸而黄宗羲并未察觉。他忧心忡忡地紧抿了一会嘴唇，然后长长地吐了一口气，开始把三月初七那天晚上，他同吴应箕、陈贞慧等人如何在李十娘家聚会，后来又如何回到冒襄下榻的河房里商议，大家听到消息后如何愤慨，如何认定是旧几社那帮人捣的鬼，以及大家准备在虎丘大会上同旧几社的人大干一场，现在陈贞慧和顾杲已经到金坛去请周镳、周钟兄弟相助等等，原原本本地向钱谦益述说了一遍。末了，他说道：

“郑超宗和几社那帮人竟敢替阮胡子翻案，我黄宗羲第一个放他们不过！但听说社内有不少人还附和其说，不以为非，不以为耻！真不知他们当初入社，所为何来？竟然糊涂若此！”

钱谦益小心翼翼地皱着眉毛，竭力不让自己流露出任何异常的神色。他侧着耳朵，注意地捕捉着黄宗羲说出的每一个字眼，终于，他暗暗吁了一口气——无论如何，对手们当真完全不知底细，岂止不知，还错把旧几社的人当成了攻击的目标，准备大闹一场。啊哈，这正是自己求之不得的一种局面！想到曾经被他估计得极为困难的这件事，竟然进展如此顺利，一切都像有神明在冥冥中扶助似的！钱谦益不觉大为宽慰，但同时又多少有点遗憾。因为他看得出来，黄宗羲也如同吴应箕、陈贞慧一样，是绝不会

and some are fighting for power in a ruthless internecine struggle. It's an utter chaos." His chest heaved up and down, and finally, as if unable to withstand the pressure from within his heart, he stood up abruptly, paced back and forth, and suddenly looked back, saying, "I heard that there're still men who want to reverse the Ruan Dacheng case."

Qian Qianyi was thinking how to make Huang Zongxi think positively. Hearing that, he gave a start. As he was going to persuade Huang Zongxi to side with him, such a sudden remark left him dumbfounded as if he had been hit in a critical spot.

Fortunately, Huang Zongxi didn't notice it. He pressed his lips pensively for a while, then let out a long sigh and started to honestly tell Qian Qianyi what had happened on the night of the seventh of March: how he had met Wu Yingji and Chen Zhenhui in Shiniang's place, how they had discussed the matter later in the riverhouse where Mao Xiang was staying, and how everyone was indignant after hearing the news, how they had concluded that it was the doing of the former Jishers, how they had planned to fight it out with them at the Tiger Hill Conference ... and now Chen Zhenhui and Gu Gao had left for Jintan to enlist the support of the Zhou brothers.

Finally, he said, "If Zheng Chaozong and the Jishers should dare to try to reverse the Ruan case, I, Huang Zongxi, will be the first to take issue with them. But I hear quite a few Fushers are echoing them with no sense of justice or shame. Because these Fushers appear so muddle-headed I'm beginning to doubt their motive in joining the Fushe."

Knitting his brows, Qian Qianyi tried not to show any unusual expression on his face. Tilting his ear, he listened to every word with concentration, and finally heaved a secret sigh of relief. At any rate, his opponents knew nothing about the matter and not only they didn't know it, but also they wrongly identified the former Jishers as a butt of attack and were going for them. "Aha, this is exactly what I want," he thought. What had been thought of as something impossible suddenly went on so well, so he rejoiced in his heart and considered himself lucky. He was much relieved but meanwhile had some disquiet,

在这件事情上妥协的。指望他站过来支持自己，更绝无可能。想到刚才见面之初，自己对于这位世侄所产生的那种不能自抑的感情，钱谦益的内心不禁漾起一丝苦笑。

“不知老伯亦曾听闻此事否？”

黄宗羲的声音在耳边响起。钱谦益一怔，回过神来。他本能地打算加以否认，可是不知为什么，话到嘴边却说不出来，只是在喉咙里“咕噜”了一声。

“哦，原来老伯已有所闻！”

“不！”钱谦益慌忙说。他犹疑了一下，又补充道：“我对此事一无所知！”

这样说了之后，他就把眼睛移开，以免接触对方的真诚的视线。

“原来如此！不过，替阮大铖翻案之事已无可疑。虎丘之上，一场内讧只怕势在难免了！”黄宗羲烦恼地说，“次尾、定生他们都说旧几社那伙人久有独揽大权把持社局之心，小侄本来也不甚相信。不过，看到此次他们如此妄为，分明是存心挑起大纷争，却又令人不得不信！”于是，他又把自从复社领袖张溥死后，旧几社一派人如何妄自尊大，不把吴应箕、陈贞慧等人放在眼里；这一次虎丘大会他们又如何故意拆台，使吴应箕等人当不成主盟；吴应箕等人又如何气愤等等告诉了钱谦益。

钱谦益听完之后，却没有作声。不错，要是早半天工夫听见这个消息，或者这个消息是由别人的口中说出来，钱谦益必然会大慰胸怀。可是，此时此刻，从黄宗羲口中又一次听见这种忧心忡忡的投诉，以及看见他满怀希冀的焦急眼神，钱谦益的心中却有一种空虚茫然之感。

“老伯，小侄此来，意欲有一事相恳，未知老伯能答允否？”

“哦，贤侄只管直说。”钱谦益的态度显得格外和蔼。

“小侄想请老伯亲赴虎丘，平息此番内讧！”

because he could see that Huang Zongxi, like Wu Yingji and Chen Zhenhui, would never compromise on this matter. Chances were small to expect the young man to stand up and support him. Thinking of the strong affection he had felt for the young creature a moment ago, Qian Qianyi couldn't help but give a secret, wry smile.

"My dear uncle, I'm wondering if you've also heard of it."

Huang Zongxi's voice rang in his ear. Qian Qianyi was jolted back from his thought. He was instinctively inclined to say "No" but somehow the word stuck in his mouth and instead he only gave a grunt.

"Oh, you've already heard of it."

"No, I have not." Qian Qianyi said hurriedly. He paused, then added, "I don't know anything about it."

Then, he moved his eyes away to avoid Huang Zongxi's innocent gaze.

"I see. But it's confirmed that they're trying to reverse the Ruan case. An infighting is inevitable at Tiger Hill," Huang Zongxi said in a distressed tone. "When Ciwei and Dingsheng said the former Jishers had had a motive all along to dominate the Fushe, I didn't quite believe it, but seeing their divisive actions, I'm now convinced." Then, he went on to tell Qian Qianyi how the Jishers behaved overbearingly after the death of Zhang Pu disregarding Wu Yingji and Chen Zhenhui, how they conspired to prevent Wu Yingji and his like from becoming organizers of the Tiger Hill Conference, and how infuriated Wu Yingji and his like were.

Qian Qianyi was silent upon hearing it. Yes, if he had heard the news a few hours earlier, or if the news had been broken by someone else, he would definitely have been comforted, but now he felt a sense of emptiness and loss upon hearing it from Huang Zongxi, who complained with a worried look.

"My dear uncle, I've come today to ask you a favor."

"Oh, nephew, just say it straight," said Qian Qianyi in a congenial tone.

"I'm wondering if you can go to Tiger Hill to put an end to the internal strife."

钱谦益蓦地一惊，他失态地站起来，慌乱地说："这，这怎么行？不行！"

黄宗羲奇怪地瞧着钱谦益："小侄看来，到了这一步，除非有德高望重如老伯者出面，已是无人能排解此事。"

钱谦益情急地盯了黄宗羲一眼，使劲地摇头。

"啊，莫非小侄此议有何不妥之处？"

钱谦益又摇一摇头，神情却越来越尴尬和难看了。

"那么，莫非老伯忍心眼见复社毁于一旦不成？"黄宗羲的语气里流露出明显的失望。他显然无法理解，像钱谦益这样一位他素所景仰的东林前辈，何以对于这样一件关系复社存亡的大事，竟然会无动于衷？

"贤侄，是定生、次尾他们让你来的吧？"钱谦益注视了黄宗羲片刻之后，突然冷冷地问。

黄宗羲一怔，摇摇头："不是。次尾他们并不知道老伯来了姑苏。小侄到这儿来，事先也不曾告诉他们。"

钱谦益笑了："贤侄又何必瞒我，此等大事，次尾、定生着你来问我，原也应该！"

"老伯说得是。不过，小侄此来确实不曾告诉他们。"黄宗羲回答得很认真。

钱谦益不言语了，可是冰冷的目光仍旧在黄宗羲的脸上停留了好一会儿。直到断定对方并非说谎之后，他才重新堆出微笑，走过来，拉住黄宗羲的手，用亲昵、诚恳的口吻说："贤侄，不是老夫存心推托。你也知道，老夫以病废之身，待罪山林，虽然深自韬晦，亦难免为朝中小人所侧目。去岁蔡奕琛行贿事发，不

Qian Qianyi was shocked to hear it. He stood up embarrassedly and said anxiously, "Well, I don't think it's a good idea. No, it's not."

Huang Zongxi looked at Qian Qianyi puzzledly, saying, "In my eyes, by now the problem can't be solved without the intervention of a highly respectable person like you."

Qian Qianyi cast an anxious look at Huang Zongxi and shook his head vigorously.

"So, is there anything wrong with my proposal?"

Qian Qianyi shook his head again, but his expression became more awkward.

"Then, my dear uncle, do you have the heart to see the ruin of the Fushe?" There was obvious disappointment in Huang Zongxi's tone. Apparently he couldn't understand why a senior East Wooder like Qian Qianyi, whom he had always admired, should be indifferent to such a major event related to the survival of the Fushe.

Qian Qianyi looked at Huang Zongxi for a moment, then suddenly asked coldly, "My dear nephew, did Dingsheng and Ciwei send you here?"

Huang Zongxi gave a start and shook his head. "No. They didn't know that you're in Gusu. Nor did I notify them of my visit before I came."

Qian Qianyi smiled and said, "My dear nephew, there's really no need for that little white lie. Since it's a matter of great importance, there's nothing wrong with Ciwei and Dingsheng in sending you here to seek my advice."

"You're quite right, my dear uncle, but I've not notified them of my visit," Huang Zongxi answered in a serious tone.

Qian Qianyi was silent, but his icy-cold eyes stayed on Huang Zongxi's face for a while. When he ascertained that the young man was not lying, smiles came back to his face. He came over, took Huang Zongxi's hand, and said in an intimate, sincere tone, "My good nephew, it's not that I'm dodging. As you know, I'm a sick, useless person accused of wrongdoing and exiled to the woods. Although I've been staying away from the world, the little men at court don't let go of me.

肯入狱，竟诬告老夫教唆复社构陷于他。幸赖天子圣明，置之不问。此次若公然出面干预社事，岂非适足授彼以柄？老夫一身不足惜，只怕于社事不唯无补，抑更有害呢！虎丘之会，既然定生已赴金坛请仲驭、介生他们来，纵有大事，他们尽能应付裕如，贤侄倒也不必担忧。”停了停，他斜觑着黄宗羲，又意味深长地补充说，“眼下四海汹汹，人情昏乱，谣言蜂起，往往真假难辨。贤侄须得自有主张，心明力定，勿为他人所蛊惑左右，这也是要紧的！”

Last year, Cai Yichen was caught giving bribes, but in order not to go to prison, he falsely claimed that I had conspired with the Fushe to set him up. Fortunately, His Majesty the wise emperor ignored it. If I openly intervened in the affairs of the Fushe this time, I would be giving them a handle. For me it's no big deal, but for the Fushe, I'm afraid, it does more harm than good. Now that Dingsheng has gone to Jintan to invite Zhongyu and Jiesheng to come, even if something happens at the Tiger Hill Conference, they can deal with it, and you don't need to worry, my dear nephew." After a pause, he looked at Huang Zongxi obliquely, and added meaningfully, "Now the Great Ming is in turmoil and people are not always predictable. With so many rumors flying, it's often difficult to distinguish between what's true and what's false. The most important thing is, my dear nephew, you need to exercise your own judgement and not to be misled by others."

## 第五章

# 争名位兄弟阋墙，辩正邪师生反目

### 圆圆被骗

一连两天的阴雨，使从四面八方聚集到苏州来的复社社友们颇为扫兴。他们大部分时间都被困守在各自的客房里，喝闷了酒，睡厌了觉，各种话题也都谈完了，只好百无聊赖地望着灰蒙蒙的天空皱眉头。有人甚至断言，这次虎丘盛会必定被这鬼天气弄得黯然失色，兴味索然。可是，到了三月二十八这一天，一抹明亮的曙色出乎意料地从天东头冒了出来，接着，沉默了多日的鸟雀也开始吱吱喳喳地啼鸣着，扑棱棱地上下飞蹿。虽然天幕上还浮荡着薄翳，原野上也依旧水气迷蒙，但是曙色深处，一朵嫣红的朝霞蓦地绽开了。它犹如从天孙[1]的织机上飞出的锦缎，不断地涌现着、堆积着，把璀璨的光华投向高天，投向大地，投向炊烟四起的城市。于是，返青的小树林啦，正在开耕的田野啦，城头上的雉堞啦，屋脊上的瓦顶啦，都一齐闪出五彩的光晕。微冷的空气中，有一股清爽的、令人心神愉快的意味。

从大清早起，阊门外码头、接官亭、钓桥一带，就聚拢了各

① 天孙：即织女星。

## Chapter Five

# In Which Two Brothers Fought for Privilege and Teacher and Pupil Became Enemies After an Argument

## Abduction

Two consecutive days of rain had spoiled the fun of the Fushers who had gathered in Suzhou from other places. Most of the time they were trapped in their rooms where they lodged, drinking, sleeping and talking until they were utterly bored. Then, all they could do was to knit their brows and idly look at the grey sky. Some of them even asserted that this coming Tiger Hill event would surely be eclipsed by the ghostly weather. However, on the twenty-eighth of March, a gleam of dawn unexpectedly appeared in the east. Then, the birds that had been silent for many days resumed their chittering and darting. Although there were still a few thin clouds sailing in the sky and the open fields were still misty from the rain, deep in the light of dawn, the tiny, bright, red morning glow suddenly blossomed like a brocade flying out of the loom of the Vega—the weaving star—constantly spilling out and piling up higher and higher to give more and more luminance to the sky, the earth, and the city whose chimneys were smoking. Consequently, the small woods that had come back to green, the farm fields that were being plowed, the turrets on the city wall, and the tiles on the roofs were all emitting colorful halos. So, in the chilly air, there was something pleasant and refreshing.

From early in the morning, all kinds of boats gathered outside

式各样的大小船只。因为几天来，复社的相公们又要大会虎丘的消息，已经传遍了七里山塘，所以船户们都纷纷赶来抢一份生意。其中有一篙一橹的“七里乑[1]”，有双橹的快船，还有重檐走舻、富丽堂皇的沙飞船，一只一只都拾掇得雅致整洁，船身漆着彩纹图案，讲究的还在窗户上嵌上蠡壳，在舱里陈设着香鼎瓶花。掌篙摇橹的，大都是些中青年的船娘。她们的发髻梳得油光水滑，脸上薄薄地施着脂粉，鬓边插着珠翠，雪白的手腕上还戴着明晃晃的镯子，娉娉婷婷地站立在船头上。每当岸上来了客人，她们就七嘴八舌地用苏白招呼起来：

“几位公子阿要上虎丘去白相？介末请坐我的船去好哉，船上有茶喝，有点心吃，交关之舒服稳当，保管公子们满意，好？”

“两位大爷来啊来到苏州哉，我的船又快又稳，上虎丘白相最便当，还有这位大爷，也一起来哉，勿要看介只船小，再坐几个人也勿要紧格！”

“介搭去虎丘，坐船最舒服哉，如果这几位通通要去，我划船相送，价钿一定便宜，好？”

一般外地初来的客人，见了这样如花似玉的船娘，听了这甜美动听的柔声软语，都会顿时心平气和，觉得很难拒绝。老实一点的甚至连价钱也不好意思同她们争论，身不由己地就跨上船去。于是长篙一点，柔橹轻摇，一只画船就离开了码头，欸乃声声，沿着七里山塘，向虎丘荡去了……

当载着复社士子的船只三三两两离开码头的时候，冒襄也乘船到了苏州。同他一块赶来的还有他的朋友——金沙人张明弼。

---

① 七里乑：一种只可坐三四人的“小快船”，常为人短途交通所雇乘。

of the West City Gate, where were the Pier, the Official Reception Pavilion, and the Fisherman's Bridge. In the past few days, the news that the scholars of the Fushe were going to meet again at Tiger Hill had spread all over the Seven-Li Waterway, so the boat owners all rushed here to grab a business opportunity. There were small boats for three or four passengers called "seven-*li* punts" propelled by a pole and an oar, bigger, faster boats propelled by two oars, and luxurious two-storey pleasure boats with double eaves, all neatly and elegantly arranged. The boats were painted with colorful patterns, and the more elaborate ones were even decorated with colorful seashells on the window panes and censers and vased flowers in the cabin. The pole and oar masters were mostly young or middle-aged boat ladies with a gleaming bun on the back of the head and a thin layer of powder and rouge on the face, a pearl-and-jade hair ornament on one side of the head, and a sparkling bracelet on a wrist. They stood seductively on the bows of their respective boats and vied with each other to greet visitors coming their way, with "Young misters, are you going to have fun on Tiger Hill? I'll take you there. Please take my boat. It has tea and snacks. Safe and comfortable. You'll like it."

"Misters, my boat is best for the two of you, fast and safe. Hey, mister, you can take my boat together with them. It looks small, but a few more people is no problem at all."

"The best way to go to Tiger Hill is by boat. If all of you're going there, take my boat together. I'll give you my best rates."

A first-time visitor to the city would be immediately melted by the sweet, melodious voice of such a beautiful lady and find it very difficult to turn her down. A less sophisticated man would involuntarily step onto the boat without trying to haggle with her. Then, splash, with a push by the pole and a rowing of the oar, the painted boat was off the pier and, squeak, squeak, sailed on the Seven-Li Waterway toward Tiger Hill.

As the boats carrying the Fushe scholars left the pier in twos and threes, Mao Xiang also arrived in Suzhou by boat. Together with him was a friend of his, Zhang Mingbi from Jinsha. They didn't immediately enter the city, nor did they go to Tiger Hill directly;

他们没有进城，也没有立即前往虎丘，而是沿着运河一直往南，朝着胥门外的横塘驶去。

冒襄大半个月前离开南京，到常州后，接连收到北京两位熟人的来信，都证实了冒起宗即将调离襄阳的消息。这使他进一步感到宽慰，也使他终于回心转意，修了一封家书，派人先送回如皋，向母亲禀明一切；自己则买舟南下，到苏州来赴复社大会，顺便探望陈圆圆。恰巧在半路上，遇见了正到处寻访他的张明弼。

张明弼是个年近花甲的老头儿，五年前中了进士之后，被派到粤东揭阳去当县太爷，最近因为得罪了上司，又被贬回浙江按察司当个管文书的小官。他觉得没有意思，便借口回家探亲，告了个长假，到处游山玩水，寻朋访友。他同冒襄，还有陈梁、刘履丁、吕兆龙几个，十年前曾在秦淮河的眉楼上义结金兰，立誓以心相许。论起他同冒襄的交情，较之吴应箕、陈贞慧等人更为密切。这一次，张明弼是受了陈圆圆之托，来找冒襄告急的。据他说，由于苏州府出动衙役，那些雇来守护陈圆圆的“撞六市”被捉去了好些人，眼看坚持不住，半个月前，只好又把陈圆圆转移到横塘藏起来……冒襄听了这个消息，起初还摆出满不在乎的样子。直到读了陈圆圆捎来的信中，有“君倘不来，恐成永诀”的话，他才有点着紧起来，听凭张明弼吩咐船家昼夜兼程，总算在今天一早赶到这里。

横塘是个不大的圩镇，离胥门也就六七里的水程。由于靠着运河，往日倒也颇为兴旺；如今却同苏州一样，萧条冷落得很了。冒襄在码头上了岸，吩咐冒成和长班留在船上等候，然后由张明

instead, they sailed toward Hengtang outside of the Xu Gate.

Half a month ago, after Mao Xiang left Nanjing and arrived in Changzhou, he had received two letters from two of his acquaintances in Beijing confirming the news of his father's transfer from Xiangyang. He was greatly relieved and changed his mind, so he wrote a letter and sent a servant to Rugao to report the great news to his mother while he himself booked a boat for Suzhou in the south, where the Fushe Conference was to be held. He would take this opportunity to see Chen Yuanyuan. Halfway to Suzhou, he had come across Zhang Mingbi, who had beeen looking for him.

Zhang Mingbi was an old man in his late fifties. After getting a *jinshi* degree five years ago, he was sent to Jieyang, eastern Guangdong, to serve as the county magistrate. Recently, because he had offended his superior, he was demoted to a lesser post as document clerk in the Zhejiang Provincial Procuratorate. It was a boring job. On the excuse of visiting family, he took a long leave to travel around and meet friends. He had become sworn brothers in Mei's on the Qinhuai River ten years ago with Mao Xiang, Chen Liang, Liu Lüding, and Lü Zhaolong. Of all his friends, he was closest to Mao Xiang, closer than Wu Yingji and Chen Zhenhui. This time, Zhang Mingbi had come to Mao Xiang upon the request of Chen Yuanyuan for some urgent matter. According to him, the Suzhou *yamen* had arrested many of the local ruffians hired to protect Chen Yuanyuan. Half a month ago, seeing that they couldn't hold out for long, Yuanyuan's friends had to transfer her to Hengtang ... Mao Xiang had appeared nonchalant at first after hearing the news. It was not until he read the letter from Chen Yuanyuan that said "if you don't come, you probably won't be able to see me again" that he began to tense up and allow Zhang Mingbi to hurry up the boatman to travel day and night, and finally they had arrived here early this morning.

Hengtang was a small town, only six or seven miles away from the Xu Gate. Because of its proximity to the Canal, it used to be quite prosperous; now, like Suzhou, it was very much deserted. Mao Xiang landed on the pier and ordered Mao Cheng and the footman to stay

弼引路，沿着狭长的小巷弯弯曲曲地走了一阵，来到了一个小小的门楼前。张明弼上前敲门，半天，才有一个老门公出来开门。张明弼早已不耐烦，扯住冒襄就往里走，一边兴冲冲地叫：

“圆圆，圆圆！看我把谁给带来了！”

冒襄跟在后面，想到马上就要同陈圆圆相见，心情也很有点激动：“嗯，大半年不见，又经历了这一番颠沛惊恐，她不知怎样了？还是娇艳如昔么？哎，只怕不免憔悴瘦损了吧？”他想，一边四面张望着，希望尽快见到那张熟悉的、可爱的脸蛋。

张明弼叫了一阵，屋子里静悄悄的，没有任何动静。就连平日的使唤丫环，也不见一个露面。

张明弼同冒襄交换了一个莫名其妙的眼色，直着脖子又叫：“圆圆，圆圆！”

“两位相公不用叫了，屋子里没人。”一个苍老的声音从背后响起，原来那个老门公已经跟了进来。

“啊，没人？上哪儿去啦？”

老门公没有马上回答。他眯缝眼睛打量着冒襄：“敢是小人眼拙，这位相公却似不曾来过？”

“这便是如皋冒辟疆相公！”张明弼说，“今日特地从常州赶来瞧圆姐儿的。门公，你快快把她找回来，我们还有要紧的事哩！”

门公的眼睛一下子睁大了，“啊，你就是那个冒、冒相公？”他神色紧张地问。

冒襄莫名其妙地点点头。

“那么，那么圆姐儿当真不是相公接走的？”

冒襄越加摸不着头脑：“你说什么？我接走圆圆？哪有此事！”

门公直着眼睛瞧了冒襄半晌，喃喃地说：“哎，糟了，糟了，果然不错，上了当了！”

冒襄和张明弼吃了一惊。

“喂，到底是怎么回事？”张明弼生气地追问。

in the boat and wait. Then, with Zhang Mingbi leading the way, he zigzagged through the narrow alleys for a while and came to a small gatehouse. Zhang Mingbi went forward and knocked on the gate. After a long time, an old man came out to open the gate. Zhang Mingbi impatiently took Mao Xiang by the hand and walked in, shouting excitedly, "Yuanyuan, Yuanyuan! See who I've brought!"

Mao Xiang followed. Thinking that he was going to see Chen Yuanyuan soon, he was very excited. "Well, I've not seen her for half a year, and after all the panic, what's she like now? Is she still as beautiful as before? I'm afraid she must be emaciated," he thought as he looked around to see that familiar, admirable face.

Zhang Mingbi yelled for a while but there was no response from the house. There was not even a servant girl in sight.

Zhang Mingbi exchanged a puzzled look with Mao Xiang, and yelled again, stretching his neck, "Yuanyuan, Yuanyuan!"

"There's no use calling, sirs. She's not there." An old man's voice came from behind. The janitor had been following them.

"She's not there? Where has she gone?"

The old man didn't answer immediately. Squinting his eyes he looked at Mao Xiang and said, "If I'm not mistaken, I've not seen you before."

"This is Mr. Mao Pijiang from Rugao," Zhang Mingbi said. "He comes from Changzhou to see Sister Yuan. Mr. Janitor, please find her. We'll have to go soon for some urgent business."

The janitor's eyes widened suddenly. "Ah, are you that Mister—Mister Mao?" He asked nervously.

Mao Xiang nodded in bewilderment.

"Then, then it was not you who took Sister Yuan away?"

Mao Xiang was more confused. "What did you say? I took Yuanyuan away? No, there's no such a thing."

The janitor stared at Mao Xiang for a long while and then murmured, "Oh, no! I have really been deceived."

Mao Xiang and Zhang Mingbi were taken aback.

"Hey, what has happened?" Zhang Mingbi asked angrily.

“这件事，小的也只知个大概——哎，两位相公请坐，待小的禀来。”看见两位客人急躁地摇摇头，门公就叹了一口气，说起来：

“小的听说，这是去年惹下的祸。去年，田皇亲派人来苏州，点着名儿要买圆姐儿，谁知弄了个假的回去，惹得田皇亲大发脾气。故此这一次追得真紧，圆姐儿接连换了好几个地方，都没能躲开他们。凭着几位相熟的相公相帮，买动一班‘撞六市’，同他们放对……”

张明弼不耐烦地打断他：“这些我们都知道了。你只挑要紧的说——后来怎样了？”

“哎，是——后来，后来就躲到这里。那一天，也是这个时辰，小的正在门房里打盹儿，冷不丁有人‘咚咚咚’打门，小的爬起来开门一看，原来是镇上的船户陆小四，后面还跟着个长大汉子。小的问他来作甚？陆小四说：‘如皋冒相公来了，正在码头上的船里，吩咐请圆姐儿即刻过去相见。’又指着那汉子说这就是冒相公的长班，来接圆姐儿的，轿子就在门外。小的平日每常听说，圆姐儿一心一意就是盼的冒相公来，便给他报了。翠影丫头即时出来，把长班叫了进去，说是圆姐儿要问他。小人站在门影里同陆小四正说话哩，就见圆姐儿穿戴整齐，张皇失落地走出来，上了轿，随那长班去了。当时大伙儿都喜欢，说：这下可好了，圆姐儿有救了。谁知呀，圆姐儿这一去，直到天晚也不见回来。大伙儿都有点纳闷，又猜道冒相公带了圆姐儿到哪儿白相。过了四五日，还不见音信。大伙这才着紧起来，四下打听，都不得信儿，去找陆小四，也不知他躲到哪儿去了。后来影影绰绰传

"I don't exactly know, sirs. Please be seated and let me tell you what I know." Seeing the two guests shook their heads worriedly, the janitor sighed and said:

"I hear it all goes back to last year. The emperor's relation Lord Tian dispatched his men to Suzhou to buy Sister Yuan but they went back with an impostor. Lord Tian was furious to find out it was a fake. This time around, they pursued Sister Yuan relentlessly. She kept changing places but still couldn't get rid of them. With the help of some gentlemen she knew well, she hired a few street thugs to protect her ..."

"We know this already. Say what we don't know. What happened afterwards?" Zhang Mingbi interrupted him impatiently.

"Yes, sir! Later, later she hid here. That day, at this hour, I was taking a nap in the entrance room, and knock, knock, knock, suddenly someone pounded the gate. I got up and opened it. It turned out that it was boatman Lu Xiaosi from this town, followed by a large man. I asked him what he came for. He said, 'Mr. Mao of Rugao is here and he's in the boat at the pier. He wants Sister Yuan to go over and meet him immediately.' Then, he pointed to the large man and said, 'This is Mr. Mao's attendant coming to pick up Sister Yuan. The sedan chair is outside the gate.' I had often heard that Sister Yuan was looking forward to seeing Mr. Mao, so I reported it to her. Cuiying the servant girl came out immediately and invited the attendant in, saying Sister Yuan wanted to ask him a few questions. As I stood behind the gate talking to Lu Xiaosi, I saw Sister Yuan, well dressed, came out in a hurry, got on the sedan chair, and left with the attendant. At that moment, we were all happy for her and said, 'Everything's fine now. Sister Yuan is saved.' However, she didn't come back that night. Everyone was a little puzzled, but thinking that Mr. Mao might have taken her somewhere to have fun, we were not worried at first. Four or five days passed. She didn't come back, nor was there any word of her. We started to worry and asked around, but there was still no word of her. Then, we went to look for Lu Xiaosi, who was nowhere to be seen. Later, it was rumored that she had been taken to Beijing by

出言语来，说圆姐儿早被田皇亲的人弄回京里去了，也不知是真是假。今日见了相公，才知圆姐儿真的给骗去了！唉，听说田皇亲性子暴戾非常，圆姐儿这一去，不知是好是歹呢！”

老门公一边说，一边直摇脑袋。冒襄和张明弼却像当头挨了一棒似的，被这突如其来的消息弄得目瞪口呆。

“啊，你……你这话可是当真？”张明弼好容易才挣出一句。

“小人怎敢欺蒙相公！圆姐儿，多好的一位姑娘，最是怜贫惜老。便是小人，平日一吊半吊的，也没少受她的恩惠。可是这世道，偏不让好人安生……”门公伤感地摇着头，抖抖索索地拉起袖子去抹眼睛。

张明弼问不下去了。他眨巴了一会儿眼睛，只好回头征询地望着冒襄：“辟疆，这事你看……”

冒襄冷冷地问：“这事——出了有多久啦？”

“啊，今日是二十八，圆姐儿走的那天，我记得是十八，嗯，回相公，有十天了。”

冒襄哼了一声，走开去，很快又走回来，坐到椅子上。他紧皱着眉毛，一声不响，脸孔渐渐变得通红。终于，他站起来，咬着牙说：

“她、她怎么这样蠢！简直糊涂透顶！这样就上当了！我派人来接她上船？笑话，那时我还在常州，怎么可能，怎么会！真是昏了头，轻轻易易就被骗走了！”

他双手叉在腰间，迈出两步，忽然又停住，冷笑地说：“既然我到了码头，怎么会不上岸，怎么会不进来？却派人来接她？这不明摆着是假的，是圈套嘛！可她竟然就相信了！我叫她安心

Lord Tian's men, but there's no way to know whether it's true or not. Since you're not with her, it appears that Sister Yuan has really been abducted. Alas! Her chances are not going to be good. We all hear the emperor's relation is an unmerciful man."

The old janitor shook his head as he spoke. Mao Xiang and Zhang Mingbi were stunned by the sudden news as if they had had a blow on their heads.

"Aagh? Are, are you telling the truth?" Zhang Mingbi uttered those words with great difficulty.

"How dare I cozen you, sirs? Sister Yuan, what a good girl, is most caring to the poor and the old. Even a man like me has been receiving favors from her from time to time. But this world doesn't allow good people to live in peace ..." The janitor shook his head sadly and tremblingly pulled up his sleeve to wipe his eyes.

Zhang Mingbi found it hard to continue asking. He blinked his eyes for a while and finally looked back at Mao Xiang inquiringly. "Pijiang, what do you think ..."

Mao Xiang asked coldly, "When did it happen?"

"Um, today is the twenty-eighth. The day Sister Yuan left as I remember was the eighteenth. So, it has been ten days since, my dear sir."

Mao Xiang snorted and walked away, but immediately returned and sat down in a chair. Knitting his brows, he kept silence for a while, his face gradually turning red. Finally, he stood up, gritted his teeth and said:

"She—how can she be so stupid? Like an idiot! So gullible! I sent someone to pick her up for a meeting on the boat? A joke! I was still in Changzhou at that time. How was that possible? How was that possible? What a moron to fall so easily into a trap!"

He put his hands on his hips, took two steps forward, suddenly stopped, and said with a sneer, "If I had arrived at the pier, why hadn't I gone ashore, why hadn't I come in person? Sending someone to pick her up? It was obviously a trap but she actually believed it. I told her to wait for me with peace of mind, wait for me, but she doesn't listen

等我，等我，偏不听，自作聪明！现在行啦，一了百了啦！我们还来这儿做什么？昼夜兼程，可是人去楼空了！好吧，我的话你不听，那就算了，我也管不了啦！你自作自受吧！”

冒襄怒气冲冲地叫着，使劲一脚，踢翻了一张挡道的小凳子，开始在堂屋里走来走去。他那白净俊美的脸变得铁青，看上去十分凶狠可怕。老门公被这意外的反应吓住了，不知所措地望着张明弼。后者倒还镇定，他默默地等待着，直到冒襄发泄得差不多了，才劝慰地说：

“辟疆……”

“算了，”冒襄猛地挥了一下手，“没什么意思了，走吧！”说完，他就管自转过身，大步向外走去。

“啊，公子……”

当冒襄跨出堂屋时，听见一个细小的声音在招呼他。

冒襄愤怒地回顾一下，忽然怔住了——门边上，站着一个十四五岁，长得挺秀气的女孩儿，正红着脸，胆怯地、焦急地望着他。冒襄认得，她就是陈圆圆的贴身丫环翠影。

“唔，是你！”冒襄板着脸说，脚步不由自主地停了停。当他打算继续朝外走时，张明弼从里面跟了出来。

“是你，翠影！你还没走？”张明弼惊奇地叫，“哎，你快给我们说说，圆圆是怎样给骗走的！”他回头向冒襄，“辟疆，你何必忙着就走，再问清楚点不迟啊！”

说着，他抓住冒襄的胳膊，把他拖回堂屋里，一边招呼翠影：“进来说话，进来说话！”

翠影所说的情况，同门公也大同小异，只是补充了一些细节——那天听说冒襄来了，陈圆圆高兴得又是哭，又是笑，立即就把来人叫来询问，问冒公子身子可好？老爷的事办得怎样了？

and pretends to be smart. It's all right now. Everything is finished. What are we doing here? We've traveled day and night only to see an empty house. Well, if you don't listen to me, then forget it. It's beyond my reach. Just take whatever comes for your own doing."

Mao Xiang shouted angrily and kicked a small stool that was blocking the way. Then he started pacing around in the drawing room. His fair and handsome face turned iron gray and looked menacing. The old janitor was frightened by the unexpected reaction and helplessly looked at Zhang Mingbi, who stayed calm and waited silently for Mao Xiang to spend his anger before comforting him.

"Pijiang ..."

"Forget it." Mao Xiang waved his hand abruptly. "It's senseless. Let's go." Then, he turned around and strode out.

"Young master ..."

When Mao Xiang stepped out of the main house, he heard a small voice greeting him.

Looking back sulkily, he suddenly froze. By the door stood a good-looking young girl fourteen or fifteen years of age, blushing, and looking at him timidly and anxiously. He recognized her as Chen Yuanyuan's maid Cuiying.

"Oh, it's you," Mao Xiang said with a long face, and stopped involuntarily. As he was going to continue his departure, Zhang Mingbi came out after him.

"It's you, Cuiying! You haven't left with Yuanyuan?" Zhang Mingbi exclaimed in surprise. "Hey, tell us how Yuanyuan was abducted." He turned to Mao Xiang and said, "Pijiang, why should you leave in such a hurry? Let's ask for more details."

As he spoke, he grabbed Mao Xiang's arm and dragged him back into the main house while beckoning to Cuiying, "Come in, come in, tell us about it."

Cuiying's account was similar to that of the janitor except that she added some more details: Hearing that Mao Xiang was here that day, Chen Yuanyuan was so happy that she now wept now laughed and asked the comer a lot of questions: Is the young master well? How are

怎么不派冒成来接？来人说：公子身子挺好，冒成却病得厉害，公子已经让他回如皋去了。老爷的事还没个头绪，眼下公子正急着去见一位世伯，不下船了。请圆姐过去相见，有要紧的话说。当时翠影多少有点疑心，劝圆圆仔细提防些。但陈圆圆说，公子正忙着老爷的事，不能下船只怕也是真的。现在公子派人来接，又说有要紧的话同我商量，去迟了他会生气。所以立时装扮起来，跟来人去了，谁知果真就着了圈套……

翠影最后说："冒公子，适才婢子在门外听你说话，像是很生我家阿娘的气，这可是错怪阿娘啦！多半年来，别人不知，我翠影可最清楚，阿娘哪一天不把公子叨念上几十遍！为了一心一意等公子，她客也不接了，好衣裳也不穿了，三天两头就上江神庙去烧香，求神保佑冒郎身心安泰，老爷早日高迁。可是、可是公子也忒狠心，这多半年，也不给阿娘来个信儿，害得阿娘她背地里不知流了多少泪。婢子就是不解，公子再忙，写几个字的空儿总还是有的呀！"

冒襄起初一直绷着脸，可是听着听着，他的神情不由得变了。这时他猛一慌神，结结巴巴地说：

"我，我……"

"冒公子，你很怪阿娘糊涂，怎么中了田府的奸计，其实，阿娘不是糊涂，她是真怕你哟！"

"啊，怕我？"

翠影叹了一口气："阿娘常说，她实在配不起公子。她老怕公子变心。她还说，公子与众不同，是个心比天高的人，对公子

things going with his father? Why isn't Mao Cheng coming to pick her up? The comer said, "The young master is very well, but Mao Cheng is very sick and the young master has sent him back to Rugao. Since there's no clue yet about the matter concerning his father, the young master is in a hurry to see an old friend of his father and therefore decides not to leave the boat. He wants to meet with you in the boat and tell you something important." Cuiying was somewhat suspicious and advised Yuanyuan to be cautious, but Chen Yuanyuan said, "Since the young master is busy with his father's affairs it's understandable that he can't get off the boat; now that he sends his servant to pick me up and has something important to discuss with me, I shouldn't be late, or he'll be angry." So, she quickly dressed up and left with them. Who would know it was a trap?

Cuiying finally said, "Young master, I heard from the outside just now that you're angry with my lady. You're mistaken about her. For more than half a year—others don't know it but I do—she was saying your name dozens of times every day. She's stopped receiving clients and wearing good clothes and waits for you wholeheartedly. Every other day, she goes to the River Temple to burn incense and pray for you and your father before the River God. But, but you're too cold-hearted. For more than half a year, you've not even written a single letter to her. You've no idea how many tears she's shed behind the closed door. What I don't understand is, are you so busy that you can't even spare a moment to write a few words?"

Mao Xiang had been pulling a long face, but as he listened, his expression began to change. Hearing that, he was embarrased and said with a stammer, "I—I ..."

"Young master, you're blaming Missus for being stupid and falling for the trick of the Tians, but in fact, Missus isn't stupid at all. She's merely afraid of you."

"Ah, afraid of me?"

Cuiying sighed, "Missus often said that she really isn't good enough for you. She was always afraid that you might change your mind. She also said, because you're a man with a great ambition,

表面上不能百依百顺，要不就会给公子瞧不起。所以她平日拿架子，使小性儿，都是一心为的拴住公子的心。可是，每闹一回别扭，她心里就直哆嗦，生怕当真把公子给惹恼了。待到这大半年，公子无音无讯的，她就真的害怕了。所以听说公子派人来接，她再不敢怠慢，即时便去了。谁知偏偏中了奸计！公子，阿娘若不是那样怕你，她也不会……”翠影说到这里，忍不住用双手掩着脸，哀哀痛哭起来。

冒襄呆住了。他万万没有想到，这个令他如此气恼，又如此抛撇不开的陈圆圆，竟是这样一个女人……刹那间，他感到心中一片纷乱，茫然地倒退几步，跌坐在椅子上，懊恨地低下头去。

## 迫问实情

尽管早就到了该出门的时候，郑元勋在他下榻的半塘姜氏别业里，还迟迟地不想动身。他已经换好了衣裳，却长久地站在堂屋中央，怔怔地瞧着被早晨的太阳照得闪闪发亮的乌木门槛，觉得那仿佛是横在脚下的一把剑——也许自己一抬脚就能跨过去，也许反被突然跃起的剑刃割伤足踝……

由于答允在虎丘大会上充当钱谦益的代理人，两天来郑元勋都处于后悔、不安和苦思焦虑之中。如果说，最初他作为一名附和者，还没充分认识到这件事的复杂性和危险性的话，那么现在就完全不同了。他越想越觉得困难很多、风险极大，万一办不成，到头来身败名裂，被士林唾弃的厄运就会无情地落到自己的头上。每当想到自己的半世清名，想到半年来自己暗地里苦心经营的一

completely different from the others, she shouldn't yield to all your demands, or you would look down upon her. Therefore, she often deliberately kept a distance from you and affected some little tempers in order to keep your attention. But every time she had an argument with you, she was uneasy in her heart, fearing you would really be annoyed. Having not heard from you for more than half a year, she was really scared this time. So when she heard that you had sent your servant here to pick her up, she didn't dare to tally and went immediately. How could she know that she was going to fall into a trap set for her? Young master, if Missus weren't afraid of you like that, she would not ..." She sobbed woefully, covering her face with her hands.

Mao Xiang was stupefied. He had never thought that Chen Yuanyuan, who was nasty and addictive, turned out to be such a woman ... In an instant, he felt lost and his mind went blank. He involuntarily took a few steps back, slumped into a chair, and lowered his head in shame.

## Confession

Zheng Yuanxun dallied in Jiangs Villa where he lodged although it was time to go out. Having changed his clothes, he stood in the middle of the drawing room for a long time, staring blankly at the ebony threshold that was shining brightly under the morning sun. He felt that it was like a sword lying under his feet. By lifting his foot he could either step over it or have his ankle cut by the blade of the sword that might suddenly jump up ...

Having agreed to act as Qian Qianyi's proxy at the Tiger Hill Conference, Zheng Yuanxun had been living in regret, fear, and anxiety for the past two days. If at first, as an adherent, he hadn't fully realized the complexity and danger of the task, it was completely different now. The more he thought about it, the more he realized that it was a risky undertaking full of challenges. Should he fail, he would be ruined, and the fate of being spurned by the circle of gentry scholars would murderously fall on him. Every time he thought that

切，很可能会因此被一股脑儿葬送，郑元勋就心惊肉跳，无论如何也平静不下来。

郑元勋十年前就当上了复社在扬州地区的社长。复社的领袖张溥在世的时候，他一直是兢兢业业，勤于职守，丝毫不敢存有非分之想。他只求能保住已有的地位，作为将来的晋身之阶，就心满意足了。谁知天有不测风云，半年前，年纪还不到四十岁的张溥突然病逝。副手张采的魄力、才智都远逊张溥，加上他入仕做官之后，很为朝廷注目，不便公开参预社事。这样，由谁来接替张溥的位置，就成为全社面临的最大难题。而社内各派系的角逐争夺，也就由此而激烈展开。其中，风头最健、名声最响的，自然要数吴应箕、陈贞慧这一派——吴应箕是复社资格最老的学长之一，陈贞慧则是“四公子”之首。他们以东林党人、前礼部主事周镳为后台，在社内一呼百诺，颐指气使，谁都得让着他们三分。对于领袖的金交椅，他们自然不肯放过，而且志在必得。然而，这一派人言行偏激，目空一切，却也招致社内许多人的不满；尤其是旧几社那一批人，对于吴、陈派的飞扬跋扈早就看不顺眼，于是挺身而出，处处同他们作对。旧几社一派人实力也不小，但成员都是松江一带的士子，难免心存地域之见。他们反对吴、陈，固然能争取其他地区一些社友的同情和支持，但想夺取领袖全社的位置，就不是那么轻而易举了。这两派势均力敌，谁

his good name built through a lifetime of effort and everything he had done in the past six months would very likely come to naught because of it, he found his heart racing with fear.

Zheng Yuanxun became president of the Yangzhou chapter of the Fushe as early as ten years ago but when Zhang Pu, leader of the Fushe, was alive, he had always been conscientious and diligent in the performance of his duties and never dared to think of anything more than he deserved. His only concern was to keep his existing position as a rung in the ladder. Yet things often would not go as expected. Six months ago, Zhang Pu, who was less than forty years old, suddenly died of illness. His deputy Zhang Cai was by far not as good as Zhang Pu in terms of experience and talent; besides, Zhang Cai had received a great deal of attention in court ever since he became an official and it was inconvenient for him to openly intervene in the affairs of the Fushe. Thus, who should take over the position of Zhang Pu became the biggest problem facing the whole society and intense competition among the various factions began. Of all the factions, the most active and the best known was naturally the party of Wu Yingji and Chen Zhenhui, Wu being one of the most senior members of the Fushe and Chen being head of the Four Young Men of the Fushe. With the backing of Zhou Biao, an East Wooder and former head of the Ministry of Rites, they had a large following in the society, and everybody had to yield to them more or less. These men were desperately seeking control of the leadership. However, because they were radical in words and deeds and too proud of themselves and contemptuous of others, they had caused dissatisfaction in the Fushe, particularly among members of the former Jishe, who, having long been displeased with the insolence of the party of Wu Yingji and Chen Zhenhui, stepped forward and took issue with them whenever there was an occasion. The members of the former Jishe had considerable influence too, but since they were mostly scholars from the Songjiang area and were limited by their local vision, it was not so easy for them to secure the top spot of leadership to dominate the Fushe though they could likely win some sympathy and support from some Fushers in other localities.

也压倒不了谁。正是面对这样一种形势，一个前所未有的念头，在郑元勋的心中悄悄萌动了。起初，它很小，只是不显眼地冒出一点尖角儿，然而，它是那么可喜，那么逗人，于是，就一天天地生长起来。不过，郑元勋仍然把它保护得很小心、很隐蔽，甚至他的一些最亲近的人，也全不知道。当然，这并不妨碍郑元勋开始积极活动。他本来就有平和、公允、踏实、稳重的好名声。从此，他愈加显得虚怀若谷，礼贤下士，竭力同吴、陈派和几社都保持良好的关系。与此同时，他不放过一切机会，在社友面前表示继承西张夫子[①]的遗志使之发扬光大的决心，以及对社内纷争之局的忧虑和痛心。然后，他就滔滔不绝地大谈重振社局的方针措施——第一、第二、第三……郑元勋很明白，要实现登上领袖宝座的目标，光靠这些还不够，还必须有强大的后台，于是，他又找上了钱谦益……

这些活动是有成效的，这次虎丘大会，他就被推举为两个主盟者之一。这种全社大会，是社内的一种盛典，建社十余年间，总共也才举行过四次。它具有检阅本社力量、决定重大事情，以及扩大声势影响的作用。大江南北，多少士子都以能躬逢盛会为莫大荣耀。至于大会主盟一席，其尊隆程度就更不用说。事实上，过去几次大会，主盟者不是张溥就是张采。所以，这一次谁能当上主盟，可以说，算是半个屁股坐上了领袖的宝座。正因如此，吴、陈派同旧几社一派明争暗斗，异常激烈。郑元勋照例摆出一

① 西张夫子：复社士子对张溥的尊称。

In this battle of equal strength, neither side could overwhelm the other. The situation being such, an idea quietly sprouted in Zheng Yuanxun's mind. At first, it was very small, just a tiny inconspicuous bud, but it was sweet and lovely and grew up day by day. At first, Zheng Yuanxun carefully nurtured it and kept it so secret that even those closest to him didn't know it. Of course, this didn't prevent Zheng Yuanxun from actively acting on it. He had had a good reputation for being humble, fair, practical, and reliable. From then on, he became more humble than ever, treating everyone respectfully, including the nobodies, and tried his best to maintain good relations with both the Wu and Chen faction and the Jishe faction. At the same time, he didn't let go of any opportunity to show his determination to carry forward the cause of West Zhang[①] and express his worry about the infighting within the Fushe. Then, he talked endlessly about ways to revitalize the society: first ..., second ..., third ..., and so on and so forth. Zheng Yuanxun knew very well that to achieve the goal of becoming the leader of the society, these were not enough. He would also need a powerful backing. Then, he went to Qian Qianyi ...

Such activities were fruitful. He was elected one of the two joint chairmen of the Tiger Hill Conference. This kind of society-wide meeting was a great event for every Fushe member and had only been held four times during the ten-odd years since the founding of the Fushe. It was an occasion to showcase the strength of the society, to make critical decisions, and to spread its influence. Across the country, numerous scholars considered it a great honor to attend the grand assembly in person and naturally it was a great privilege if anyone could preside over it. In fact, the previous conferences having been chaired by either Zhang Pu or Zhang Cai, whoever became the chairman of the coming conference was very close to becoming the leader of the Fushe. Because of this, the Wu and Chen faction fought both openly and secretly with the faction of the former Jishers in a

---

① Fushe scholars called Zhang Pu "*xizhang*", which means West Zhang, to avoid direct mention of the name out of respect.

副不偏不倚的姿态，一方面极力稳住吴应箕、陈贞慧等人，另一方面又同几社一派暗中交易。公举的结果，决定由他同旧几社的李雯双双出任主盟。吴、陈派大为愤怒，扬言要抵制这次大会。郑元勋连忙苦苦相劝，又表示情愿把主盟一席让给他们。吴、陈派目标不在郑元勋，自然不肯，可是这样一来，也就暂时不好意思闹下去了。郑元勋稳定了局面，便开始兴冲冲地着手筹备开会的事宜。就在这时，钱养先忽然来到扬州，向他转达了钱谦益要替阮大铖开脱的意思，郑元勋觉得正好乘此机会，进一步巴结讨好这位东林领袖，作为日后的有力靠山，所以立即爽快地答应了。没想到，到头来钱谦益竟毫不客气地把一切责任、风险都推到他的头上……

“哎，我为什么要答允他？我真不该答允他！”郑元勋在心里气急败坏地叫。然而，与此同时，他又分明听见发自心中的另一个冷冷的声音：“你不答应，又会怎样？只要钱谦益在士林中随随便便说上几句不支持的拆台话，你的那一点本钱，也同样赔不起哟！”

郑元勋感到绝望了。现在，他觉得在这个世界上做人真是很难。他的目光不由自主又回到适才那柄“利剑”——门槛上，那“剑身”的光芒似乎更加刺眼了，简直是在朝他嘿嘿冷笑。郑元勋把心一横，抬脚向外迈去。就在这时，他看见身材瘦小的老仆殷报手里扬着一张拜帖，匆匆走了过来。

“禀老爷，周老爷，还有几位相公来拜。”

郑元勋只好把迈出去的一只脚又收回来。他没精打采地接过

fierce battle. Zheng Yuanxun assumed an impartial posture as always. On the one hand, he tried his best to appease the party of Wu Yingji and Chen Zhenhui; on the other hand, he secretly traded with the Jishers. As a result of multiple consultations, he and Li Wen from the former Jishe were going to be joint chairs. The Wu and Chen faction were furious and threatened to boycott the conference. Zheng Yuanxun hurried to pacify them by expressing his willingness to yield his position as co-chairman to them. The target of the Wu and Chen faction was not Zheng Yuanxun, so they naturally refused the offer but meanwhile found it inappropriate to go on protesting. Having the situation in control, Zheng Yuanxun began to prepare for the conference enthusiastically. At this juncture, Qian Yangxian suddenly came to Yangzhou and conveyed to him Qian Qianyi's intention to parden Ruan Dacheng. Zheng Yuanxun immediately agreed, thinking it was a very good opportunity to further curry favor with the East Wood leader, who might become a strong backer of his in the future, but he had never thought that in the end Qian Qianyi should unceremoniously shift all the responsibilities and risks onto his back ...

"Damn it! Why should I have agreed? I shouldn't have agreed." Zheng Yuanxun cried out exasperatedly in his heart. At the same time, he heard a cold voice from inside him saying, "What if you don't agree? As long as Qian Qianyi casually says something to your disadvantage in the circle of gentry scholars, you can't afford its impact with that little amount of capital you have."

Zheng Yuanxun was desperate. Now, he felt the difficulty of living in this world. His gaze involuntarily returned to the "sharp sword" —the threshold—he had noticed just now and the light of the sword seemed to be even more dazzling. It glared and sneered at him. As if having made a resolute decision, Zheng Yuanxun lifted one foot to step out. Just then, he saw Yin Bao, a small, thin, old servant, was hurriedly walking over, holding a calling card in his hand.

"My lord, Mr. Zhou and a few other gentlemen are here to see you."

Zheng Yuanxun took back the foot that was going to cross the

拜帖，问：“哪个周老爷……”突然，像被人卡住了脖子似的，噎住了，只见拜帖赫然写着：

眷侍生周镳

眷社弟周钟、陈贞慧、顾杲顿首同拜

郑元勋怔怔地瞪着帖子，仿佛不认识这几个字似的。接着，他的双手开始微微发起抖来，脑门变得更亮了，后来，竟冒出了星星点点的汗珠子。

“老爷……”一个苍老的声音在身边响起。郑元勋猛一回头，只见殷报正关切地瞧着自己。这个老仆人，跟随郑元勋已有二十余年，一贯忠心耿耿，办事勤快，而且最能体察主人的意思，所以郑元勋待他也特别优礼，轻易不斥责一句。可是，不知为什么，此刻殷报那关切的眼神，那催促的语气，以及那等待回话的姿态，都叫郑元勋感到刺眼，可恶，不是味儿。

“催什么，混账东西！”他爆发似的吼道。可是，话一出口，他就自觉失言，立即顿住了。

殷报却不惊慌。他恭顺地低下头，打眼角斜瞟着主人：“老爷若是不想见客，小的便去回答他们，就说老爷已经……”他故意把“出门”二字说得含糊不清，但相信主人自能领会。

郑超宗目光一闪，但很快又摇摇头。他沉吟了一下，挺直身子，板起脸孔教训说：“我分明在此，岂可谎称不在？这不是骗人么！我每常不是教你，待人接物，这诚、真二字是顶要紧的！此种伎俩对待寻常之客，尚且不可，何况这几位都是我的知交密友，正巴不得他们常来见面亲近哩！”

threshold. He took the calling card listlessly and asked, "Which Mr. Zhou?" Suddenly, he choked as if someone had held him by the neck as he saw that the calling card said:

*Your humble student Zhou Biao, together with his brother Zhou Zhong, Mr. Chen Zhenhui, and Mr. Gu Gao, wishes to have the honor of kowtowing to your lordship.*

Zheng Yuanxun stared at the calling card blankly as if he hadn't recognized those words. Then, his hands began to tremble slightly, and his forehead became more glistening as beads of sweat oozed out.

"My lord—" An old voice rang beside him. Zheng Yuanxun quickly turned his head and saw that Yin Bao was regarding him with concern. This old servant of his, who had been with him for more than twenty years, had always been loyal, diligent, and able to understand the intentions of the master. Therefore, he was especially kind to the servant and seldom criticized him. However, somehow, the concerned eyes, the urging tone, and the posture of waiting for a reply were now particularly annoying, hateful, and unwelcome.

"Don't urge me, you damn fool!" Mr. Zheng exploded. However, as soon as he uttered those words, he regretted it and stopped immediately.

Yin Bao was not worried. He bowed his head obediently and glanced at his master obliquely from the corner of his eye. "If your lordship doesn't want to meet them, I can go and tell them that you've already ..." He deliberately omitted "gone out" believing his master could understand it.

Mr. Zheng's eyes flashed, but soon he shook his head. He pondered for a moment, then straightened up and scolded the servant with a long face, "How can you say I'm not in while clearly I am! Isn't it lying? Didn't I tell you that in dealing with people the most important thing is being honest and sincere. Such a trick shouldn't even be applied to an average visitor; how can it be used on such close friends of mine, whose visits are always welcome?"

说着，他就整一整衣巾，撇下被教训得发怔的殷报，管自摇摇摆摆地向外走去。

郑元勋刚刚迎出门外，客人们所乘坐的轿子也正好到了。轿帘开处，从第一乘轿子里走下来的是周镳。他大约五十上下的年纪，身材瘦小，有着一个硕大饱满的前额，和一张狭小而冷峻的脸，这张脸被一部浓密的络腮胡子遮去了一半，剩下的地方就更小了。在这有限的地方，却安放着一个大得异常的圆鼻子，两道同样浓密的、向前耸出的眉毛，一双瞳仁黑中带绿的眼睛，永远躲藏在眉毛下，咄咄逼人地向外扫视。他是崇祯元年进士，官至南京礼部主事，由于上疏弹劾宦官，触怒皇帝，被削职为民。他在士林中声望很高，对阮大铖一向深恶痛绝，崇祯十一年复社诸生起草《留都防乱公揭》，据说实际上是他出的主意。他头戴四角方巾，穿一领花绒直裰，身体似乎并不好，一下轿子就频频咳嗽，把苍白的、没有血色的脸挣得通红。

紧接着的一乘轿子里走出了复社的元老周钟，他是周镳的堂弟，模样儿却与堂兄没有任何相似之处——甚至正相反。他的脸膛很宽，呈椭圆形，鼻子和眼睛却细长小巧，再配上疏朗的胡子，秀气的眉毛，往往使人误认为他是一位温文儒雅的人。其实不然。据说有一次，他在酒筵上碰见了阮大铖，一言不合，他发起怒来，竟把整桌酒席掀翻在地，摔得稀烂，然后拂袖而去。在这一点上，他显出了与周镳有着相似的性格。不过，这兄弟俩平日的关系并不怎么融洽。两家门下的弟子对立尤其严重，经常互相攻击，争

As he spoke, he straightened his clothes and adjusted his square headscarf, and then walked out staggeringly, leaving Yin Bao dumbfounded.

Shortly after Zheng Yuanxun came out to welcome the guests, they arrived in sedan chairs. As the curtains were lifted, out of the first sedan chair came Zhou Biao, about fifty years of age, with a small build, a broad, prominent forehead, and a narrow, small, and stoic face, half of which was covered by a thick beard, and the rest of which consequently looked even smaller. Interestingly, in that limited space sat a round nose of an unusually large size and two thick eyebrows protruding forward under which hid a pair of greenish black eyes looking out menacingly. He had earned his *jinshi* degree in AD 1628, the first year of the reign of Emperor Chongzhen, and had been a high-ranking official in the Ministry of Rites in Nanjing. Previously, he had been deprived of his post because he had angered the emperor by filing a petition for the impeachment of a eunuch. Though he was now just a commoner, he had a high reputation in the circle of gentry scholars. He had always hated Ruan Dacheng. It was said that he was the mastermind behind the "Public Denunciation of a Treasonist in the Legacy Capital" issued by members of the Fushe in AD 1638, the eleventh year of the reign of Emperor Chongzhen. He was wearing a square headscarf and a sculptured velvet robe. His health didn't seem to be good as he coughed and coughed after getting off the sedan chair, causing his pale, bloodless face to flush.

Out of the second sedan chair came Zhou Zhong, a veteran member of the Fushe and cousin brother of Zhou Biao, to whom he didn't have any resemblance at all—to be more exact, he was the opposite with a wide and oval face, a small nose, slender eyes, a neatly sparse beard, and a pair of fine eyebrows. Therefore, he was often mistaken to be a gentle and refined person. Actually he was not. It was said that once, when he met Ruan Dacheng at a dinner table and had an argument, he flew into a temper and upended the table, and then walked away. In this, he had some similarity to Zhou Biao. However, the relationship between the two cousin brothers was not a very good

吵不休。这一次周钟本不肯来，是陈贞慧一再上门请求，动之以大义，才说服了他一起前来。

周镳一见郑元勋，略拱一拱手，劈头就说："我知道你很忙。我也很忙。但有几句话，一定要说，说完就走，决不碍你的事！"说着，他也不等郑元勋答话，回头瞧了瞧，看见陈贞慧和顾杲也都下了轿子，便说一声："请啊！"带头向大门内走去。

郑元勋很清楚这位周老爷子的脾气，不敢阻拦。他匆匆向其余几个人拱拱手，便转过身，竭力赶上周镳的步伐，在前面毕恭毕敬地引着路，来到了大堂之上。

当大家重新行过礼，分宾主坐下之后，客人们各自啜着茶，没有立即开口说话。周钟等三人显然是等着周镳，而后者却慢慢地抚弄着络腮胡子，从眉毛底下直瞅着郑元勋，仿佛要在开口之前，把对方看个透似的。

终于，周镳把手中的杯子一放。

"听说，阁下荣膺本次大会主盟，真乃可喜可贺啊！"他一本正经地说，听语气，瞧不出他到底是真心道贺，还是故意挖苦。

郑元勋的目光闪动了一下，谦恭地说："啊，这个——实非晚生所愿，只为社友如此推举，迫于无奈……"

"嗯，阁下自问德才胆识，足膺此任么？"周镳却毫不客气，单刀直入地问。

"晚生自知德薄能鲜，难膺此重寄！"

"不错，学生也有同感！"周镳严肃地点点头，"阁下能出

one. Their pupils naturally fell into two opposing camps which often attacked each other and bickered endlessly. This time, Zhou Zhong had refused to come with his cousin at first, but had finally agreed through Chen Zhenhui's constant begging and persuasion.

When Zhou Biao saw Zheng Yuanxun, he bowed slightly, and said up front, "I know you're busy. I'm busy too. But there're a few words I must say to you and I'll leave after I say them. It won't take you much time." Then, he looked back and saw that Chen Zhenhui and Gu Gao had also got off their sedan chairs. Without waiting for a response from Zheng Yuanxun, he said "Please come with me!" and went straight in.

Zheng Yuanxun, knowing very well the temper of Zhou Biao, didn't dare to stop this guest of his. He hurriedly bowed to the others, then turned around, caught up with Zhou Biao, and respectfully led them to the reception room.

They formally greeted each other and sat down. Tea was served. The guests quietly sipped tea and none spoke. Zhou Zhong and the other two were obviously waiting for Zhou Biao to speak first, but Zhou Biao slowly stroked his beard and looked at Zheng Yuanxun from under his eyebrows, as if he were going to see through this person before speaking.

Finally, Zhou Biao put down the cup in his hand.

"I hear that you've become chairman of the conference. It's worth celebrating. My congratulations to you!" he said seriously. From his tone, it was difficult to tell whether he was being sincere or sarcastic.

Zheng Yuanxun's eyes blinked and he said humbly, "Well, that—that's not what I wished for. Since it was the recommendation of our comrades in the Fushe, I had no choice but to accept it ..."

"Well, do you think you're qualified in terms of virtue, ability, courage, and vision?" Zhou Biao asked straightforwardly with no regard for politeness.

"I know I'm not quite qualified with my influence and ability."

"Yes, you're quite right. That's what I think too." Zhou Biao nodded solemnly. "Since you're able to say this, you do have self-

此言，殊不失有自知之明！”他抬起头，仰望着房顶上的大梁，忽然叹了一口气，“大厦将倾，一木已是难支，何况所举之材，又非栋梁乎？复社诸生，何以糊涂若此！”

郑元勋被弄得哭笑不得。本来，从接到拜帖的一刻起，他就估计对方来意不善，所以抱定一个以柔制刚的宗旨，一味地谦恭忍让。谁知道，这位老先生却你谦虚一句，他就实认一句，一点面子都不给。郑元勋的涵养功夫哪怕再好，也不能不有点着恼了。

“哦，晚生自知材非栋梁，只足败事，所以曾恳请次尾、定生二兄，情愿将主盟一席，让与他们。”郑元勋冷冷地说，心想：你心下所想，无非是这么一句话，我干脆替你说出来，看你又怎么样！反正主盟一席，乃是全社公举的，终不成凭我这句话你就能抢了去！

然而，出乎他的意料，只见周镳摇摇头，“这是不行的！”他断然地说，“虽说次尾、定生充任此席，较之阁下似更胜一筹，然而阁下乃公众所举，次尾、定生决无私相取代之理！”

“莫非仲老意欲再行公举，让晚生名正言顺地让贤？那也并无不可！”

周镳似乎并未觉察对方的尖锐语气，摆摆手：“非也，我等意欲助兄一臂之力。”他看了看郑元勋，见他露出惊愕和怀疑的神色，又补充说，“我们不仅不扯你下来，还要把你捧上去，齐心合力扶持你，让你做一个名副其实的复社盟主，你看如何？”

郑元勋忽然笑了：“多承仲老错爱。只是晚生却不敢领教。”

knowledge." He raised his head and looked up at the beam on the roof, and then suddenly sighed, "When a house is going to fall, a single piece of wood is insufficient to prevent it from falling, not to say a piece of wood that is not good for a pillar or beam. How can the Fushe scholars be so stupid as not to understand a thing like this?"

Zheng Yuanxun didn't know whether he should cry or laugh. The moment he received the calling card, he had sensed that his visitors didn't come with a good intention and decided to stay humble and respectful in order to allay their hostility, but it turned out that Zhou Biao didn't give him any face at all by taking his humility to be admitting the truth. Inspite of his self-restraint, he was deeply annoyed.

"Well, I do know I'm not fit for a pillar or a beam and I'm not the right person to do things right. So, I'll beg Ciwei and Dingsheng to take over the chairmanship." Zheng Yuanxun said coldly, thinking, "This is what you want and I'm saying it on your behalf. Let's see what you can do about it. In any case, the chairman seat was decided through consultation in the society. I don't think you can take it away from me merely because I say I can surrender it to somebody else."

To Zheng Yuanxun's surprise, Zhou Biao shook his head and said resolutely, "No, it won't do." Then, he went on to say, "Though either Ciwei or Dingsheng is certainly more qualified than you, you're the choice made through consultation and no private transfer should take place."

"So, are you suggesting there should be another round of consultation so that I can justifiably yield the position to them? It's not a bad idea at all."

Zhou Biao, not having noticed Zheng Yuanxun's sour tone, waved his hand, saying, "No, we want to help you, brother." He cast a glance at Zheng Yuanxun, who had a look of consternation and suspicion, and added, "We're not going to pull you down, but instead we're going to lift you up. We'll work together to support you and let you become a veritable leader of the Fushe. What do you think?"

Zheng Yuanxun suddenly laughed and said, "I do appreciate your

“啊，何以故？”

“仲老试想，那社内盟主一席，何等重要，倘若选非其人，岂唯危及社局，抑更干系社稷之未来，须得极其慎重。晚生虽则愚钝，尚有自知之明。此次虎丘之会，滥充一日主盟，或者尚差可胜任，若论那社内盟主，却绝非晚生所敢希冀呢！”

“嗯，这话不为无理。不过，阁下能有自知之明，便是最大之美德。今后只要大家齐心扶助，这社事一层倒也不必过虑。”

“晚生当真不敢应承！”

看见郑元勋如此坚拒，周镳反而有点着急起来。他沉下脸：“啊，莫非阁下重一身之得失，竟过于天下之安危么？”

然而，郑元勋似乎拿定了主意。听了这句责备，他眼皮儿也不眨一下。相反，周镳越是着急，他越是摆出一副谦恭、惶恐的模样，说什么也不肯答应。倒把那位盛气凌人的周老爷子摆布得恼也不是，哭也不能，僵在那里直翻白眼。

“超宗兄，”看见这种情形，陈贞慧出来打圆场了，“此事关系我社之兴衰，大明之国运，至为重大。若所举非人，后果不堪设想！仲老之议，事前曾经弟等反复参详，一致公认我兄最为合适。我兄才具，较之西张夫子或有不及，但与弟等相比，又胜之远矣！还望勉为其难，勿再推却为幸！”

可是郑元勋仍旧一个劲儿地往后躲，口中逊谢不已。陈贞慧

giving me this undeserved favor, but I don't dare to take it."

"Oh, why?"

"You know how important the leader of the Fushe is. If a wrong person is chosen, not only is the society at risk but the future of the nation is involved. This is a matter of great importance and needs to be regarded with great caution. Though my wits are slow, I have enough self-knowledge. This time, to serve as chairman of the Tiger Hill Conference is already too much for me and I can hardly manage. How can I expect to be the leader of the Fushe? It's definitely not something I dare hope for."

"You're right about that, but the fact that you have self-knowledge is a great virtue. In the future, as long as everyone is working together to help, you shouldn't worry too much about the management of the affairs of the society."

"I really dare not agree."

Seeing Zheng Yuanxun's resolute refusal, Zhou Biao became a little worried. His face sank. "So, you think more of your personal gain or loss than the safety of the nation?"

However, Zheng Yuanxun seemed to have made up his mind. Hearing the reproach, his expression was unmoved. On the contrary, the more anxious Zhou Biao was, the more humble and meek he appeared. He refused to agree no matter what Zhou Biao said. Consequently, the overbearing Old Man Zhou found himself in an awkward position: he could neither lose his temper nor reveal his own weakness by crying; all he could do was roll his eyes helplessly.

"Brother Chaozong," said Chen Zhenhui, who intervened at this awkward moment. "This matter is of utmost importance as it's related to the future of the Fushe and the fate of the Great Ming. If a wrong person were in charge, the consequences would be disastrous. Elder Zhong's proposal has been discussed repeatedly between us and we all think you're the most suitable person. Your credentials might not be as good as those of West Zhang [Zhang Pu], but you're much more qualified than me and many others. Please don't push it off anymore."

Zheng Yuanxun kept saying "thank you" but continued to shirk.

见说他不动，只好朝周钟、顾杲丢了个眼色。于是，那两个也一齐开口相劝。他们都猜想郑元勋拒不应承的原因，是被周镳开头那一番话逼住了，下不来台，倒也着实说了许多恭维推许的话。

就在他们你一言我一语，忙着给主人搬梯子下台的当儿，郑元勋却一直在暗中察言观色。他绝不是傻瓜，也不是那种心气浮躁的人，周镳的盛气凌人固然使他恼火，但更重要的是今天这事来得太突然，太轻易，使他本能地产生了警惕：他既工于心计，自然也时刻提防别人的圈套，特别是此刻他正心怀鬼胎，“啊，我怕就怕他们同我作对为难！要是他们真肯撑我的腰，社内盟主这把交椅，我自然就能稳坐无疑，也用不着再去讨好钱牧斋，替他当箭靶儿，冒身败名裂的风险了。可是，只怕他们未必有此气量。他们八成是已经听到了点风声，生怕有人要借大会替阮圆海开脱，却设了这个圈套来稳住我，一旦事过境迁，再来个翻脸不认账。哼，我又岂会上当！”

这样一想，他就更加咬定牙关，决不应承。瞧他这个样子，客人们都有点束手无策了。周钟首先不耐烦起来，他皱着眉毛，冷冷地说：

“超宗兄，你既一定不肯，也由你！可有一件，听说有人想乘今日社内大会之机，替阮胡子开脱翻案，这是断然不可的！阁下身为大会主盟，这一关可得把稳了！”

“哼，岂止断然不可，有哪个乌龟王八蛋敢这样干，超宗兄

Seeing that Zheng Yuanxun was not going to be persuaded, Chen Zhenhui winked at Zhou Zhong and Gu Gao. Then, they joined him in the persuasion. Thinking Zheng Yuanxun's refusal might have been caused by Zhou Biao's opening remarks, the three men passed him a good number of compliments to give him a ladder for him to climb down.

While they were busy building the ladder for the host to get off the awkward position, Zheng Yuanxun was secretly studying them as he listened. He was no fool, nor was he the impetuous sort. Zhou Biao's domineering stance certainly annoyed him, but more importantly, the proposal came all too suddenly and all too easily so that he had to be instinctively vigilant. He was good at scheming, and naturally he was always on guard against potential traps, especially at this moment, when he had a secret agenda. "Um, I've always been afraid that these men would take issue with me. If they're really going to lend me support, I'm sure to become the leader of the Fushe without any doubt and then I shall no longer curry favor with Qian Muzhai and be his puppet and scapegoat at the risk of my own life and reputation. The thing is, I'm afraid they don't necessarily have the magnanimity. Most probably, they've heard that some Fushers would propose to exonerate Ruan Yuanhai at the Tiger Hill Conference and therefore lay this trap for me so that I can be in their control, and then when the conference is over, they'll go back on their word. Humph, how can I fall into this trap?"

Thus thinking, he kept his mouth even tighter and made up his mind not to accept the proposal. Seeing him like this, the guests were at their wits' end. Zhou Zhong was the first to become impatient. He frowned and said coldly:

"Brother Chaozong, if you insist on not accepting it, it's your choice, but there's one thing: I hear that some Fushers will propose to exonerate Ruan Dacheng and reverse the Ruan Case at the conference. We forbid it. As co-chair of the conference, you'll have to be a good gatekeeper."

"Humph, we not only forbid it but also should excommunicate

就该鸣鼓而攻，把他扫地出门！”顾杲也跳了起来。

郑元勋哆嗦了一下，畏怯地抬起眼睛。虽然他已经多少估计到对方是为此而来，可是一旦证实，他仍旧感到心头震动。

“啊，为阮、阮圆海开脱？谁？不、不会吧！”他结结巴巴地问。

“超宗兄，”陈贞慧不动声色地插了进来，“眼下这消息已传遍了江南，难道兄竟会不知道？”

“哦？小弟实在……”郑元勋本能地想推脱，忽然又顿住了。因为他想起，一个月前，钱养先到扬州转达了钱谦益的意思后，为着制造舆论，他也曾亲口对一些来访者散布过类似的言论，其中好像就包括陈贞慧！

“嗯，难道超宗兄实在不知道？”周钟不动声色地问。

“不，不不，小弟也是听人说……”

“听人说？谁？”

“这——”

“是啊，你到底是听谁说的？”早已停止了翻白眼的周镳也开口了。郑元勋过分惊慌的反应，显然引起了他的怀疑。

郑元勋不说话，额上却渐渐冒出汗来。本来，以他的聪明才智，要是换了往常，他会很容易掩饰过去。然而，眼下的情况，却使他十分为难。本来，如果只有钱谦益那一方来拉拢他，郑元勋为着实现自己的图谋，也许就只有硬着头皮跟他走到底；谁知忽然又来了周镳这一群人，他们手里拿着的，正是郑元勋朝思暮想的那把复社盟主的金交椅，这就使郑元勋变得有点眼花缭乱，心旌摇摇。他自然十分清楚，跟着钱谦益走要冒极大的风险，而投靠周镳却安全可靠得多。但是他又担心周镳他们此议并非出于

whoever dares to do it under the leadership of Brother Chaozong," Gu Gao cut in.

Zheng Yuanxun shivered and raised his eyes timidly. Although he had more or less guessed that his guests were here for this, once it was confirmed, he still felt a shock.

"Oh, exonerating Ruan—Ruan Yuanhai? Who? No, absolutely not!" He stammered.

"Brother Chaozong," Chen Zhenhui cut in calmly. "The news has spread all over the River South area. How come you don't know it, Brother Chaozong?"

"Oh? I really—" As Zheng Yuanxun was instinctively going to deny knowledge of it he suddenly stopped as he remembered that one month ago, after Qian Yangxian went to Yangzhou and told him about Qian Qianyi's plan, in order to create public opinion he himself also spread similar rumors to his visitors, including Chen Zhenhui.

"So, you really don't know it?" Zhou Zhong asked placidly.

"No, not really. It's hearsay from someone—"

"Hearsay from someone? Who is it?"

"It is—"

"Well, hearsay from whom?" asked Zhou Biao, who had stopped rolling his eyes. Zheng Yuanxun's panic reaction obviously aroused his suspicion.

Zheng Yuanxun went quiet, sweat oozing from his forehead. Given his quick wit, he would have easily concealed himself under normal circumstances, but the current situation was different. He was caught in a quandary. Were it Qian Qianyi alone to try to win him over, he would face up to it and follow Qian Qianyi to the end in order to accomplish his own agenda; now suddenly came Zhou Biao and his party holding in their hands the golden chair of the Fushe that he had been longing for. Then, he wavered and oscillated between the two choices. He knew very well that to follow Qian Qianyi meant he would have to take great risks while to submit himself to Zhou Biao was much safer, but he was afraid that Zhou Biao's proposal was not out of sincerity, and for fear of falling into a trap, he pretended not

真心，生怕落入圈套，所以一直故作盘旋，不肯立即应允。不过，要他断然回绝这一桩唾手可得的好买卖，郑元勋还真舍不得。正因为这一连串的考虑，把郑元勋弄得心忙意乱，左右为难。平日的机智灵巧，这会儿竟一点儿也用不上了。

“超宗兄！”看见他默默不语，顾杲脸色阴沉地说，“弟等可是诚心诚意奉足下为主盟，但愿足下也能诚心诚意地对待弟等，否则的话——”

他“哼”了一声，没有说下去。但郑元勋自然明白其中的威胁意味。这些人的厉害，他是深知的，要是惹恼了他们，今后的日子就休想过得安生，就算有钱谦益的支持，自己也未必就坐得稳那把金交椅。可是，若把真相说出来，他们真能谅解自己么？

“莫非超宗兄尚疑心弟等的诚意不成？”像是窥破了郑元勋的心思似的，陈贞慧忽然站起来说，“那么贞慧愿在此表明心迹！”

说罢，他就走到桌子旁，从笔筒里抽出一管笔，双手握住，举到胸前，神情严肃地说：“贞慧若口是心非，当如此管！”双手一使劲，把笔管“啪”地折成两段，丢在桌子上，拍了拍手，说：“仁兄可以相信了吧？”

郑元勋错愕了一下，呆呆地望着桌上那两截笔管。他的眼神渐渐变了，一种果决的光芒从他那双充满疑虑的小眼睛里闪现出来。终于，他点了点头，平静地说：

“好吧，那么小弟就说……”

## 挑拨人心

复社大会的会场，就设在虎丘半山的千人石上。

那是一块绿树环抱的天然巨岩，北广南尖，略呈倒三角形。

to be enthusiastic and didn't agree immediately to cooperate with the Zhou Biao camp. In fact, Zhou Biao had offered him such a good deal that it was impossible for him to reject it categorically. Such calculations disquieted him and put him in a dilemma so that his usual wit lost its power at this moment.

"Brother Chaozong," Gu Gao said with a sullen face, seeing he was silent. "We're recommending you for leader of the Fushe and we hope you can treat us with sincerity as well, otherwise—"

He gave a snort and stopped. But Zheng Yuanxun understood the threat. He knew how powerful these men were. Should they be annoyed, he would not be able to live a peaceful life in the future. Even if he had the support of Qian Qianyi, he would not be able to sit well in the golden chair. However, if he told them the truth, could they really forgive him?

"Dear Brother Chaozong, are you doubting our sincerity?" Chen Zhenhui stood up and said, as if having seen through Zheng Yuanxun's thoughts. "If so, I would like to give you my word for it."

Then, Chen Zhenhui walked to the table, took out a brush pen from the holder, held it with both hands, raised it to his chest, and said solemnly, "If Zhenhui isn't true to his word, he shall be like the handle of the brush pen." Then, crack, he broke the handle into two halves, put them on the desk, rubbed his hands, and said, "Now, can you take my word for it?"

Zheng Yuanxun looked startled and stared blankly at the broken handle of the brush pen on the desk. The expression in his eyes gradually changed, and a resolute light flashed from his small suspicious eyes. Finally, he nodded and said calmly, "Well then, I can tell you ..."

## Discord

The venue of the Fushe Conference was the Thousand People Rock in mid Tiger Hill.

It was a huge, triangular natural rock surrounded by green trees, with one angle on the south and one side on the north. The

岩面平坦开阔，坐得下上千的人，所以叫千人石。石的北面是生公讲台——说是讲台，其实只是山崖上的一块平地，梁代高僧生公曾在台上宣扬佛法，信徒们列坐于千人石上听讲。据说这位生公道行着实高深，连冥顽的石头也被他的讲经感化，竟然点头皈依。这一块点头石，现在就立在讲台东侧的白莲池内。暮春方届，还看不到一个花骨朵，只有满池的荷叶在微风中摇摆着，迎着朝阳，一一举起了圆圆的、半透明的绿盖。

在讲台西侧，紧贴千人石，是一道又高又厚的砖墙。当中一个月洞门，门内奇岩耸峙。下俯深潭，那是剑池——当年吴王阖闾埋剑的处所。走近一瞧，黑幽幽的潭水隐藏在石壁和灌木的阴影之中，很有几分幽邃，几分神秘。而这儿那儿，波光间或一闪，冷森森，颤巍巍，又使人疑心那是远古倔强的剑魂，不耐禁锢的寂寞，正在潭底挣扎跃动，说不定什么时候便会风雷交迸，破水击空而去……

千人石南端的尖角上，是一道宽阔而平缓的登山石磴，连接山下的断梁殿和头山门。这石磴到了千人石便分成左右两股，右边一股上通云岩禅寺和虎丘塔，左边则可以直抵剑池和第三泉。

也不知从哪个年代起，这地方就成为四方游人憩息宴饮的场所。每逢花朝月夕，从云岩禅寺到断梁殿，总是士女如云，联袂接席，挨挤不开。以往复社有两次大会，都把会场设在这里。方圆数亩的千人石上，如今已经铺开了一排一排的垫席，每张垫席

rock surface, flat and open, was able to accommodate hundreds of people, hence its name. To the north of the rock was Shenggong's Podium, which, despite its name, was in fact merely a flat terrace on a cliff, where the Liang dynasty high monk Shenggong once preached the Dharma while the believers sat and listened. It was said that Shenggong's sermon was so good that even a stubborn stone understood it and nodded its head. This nodding stone now stood in the White Lotus Pond on the east side of the podium. It was late spring and the lotuses hadn't budded yet. A pondful of lotus leaves swayed in the breeze like little round translucent green parasols under the morning sun.

On the west side of the podium and close to the Thousand People Rock was a tall and thick brick wall with a moon-hole door. Inside was a garden of strange rocks overlooking a deep pond called the Sword Pool, where King of Wu had buried his sword according to legend. When one moved closer, the dark pond water secluded in the shadows of the rocks and shrubs looked enigmatic and mysterious, but here and there, the water sparkled with a cold, trembling light as if the spirit of the sword of the ancient king were struggling to break its yoke and soar into the sky with wind and thunder at any moment ...

At the tip of the southern angle of the Thousand People Rock was a broad sloping path which led to the second mountain gate known as the Broken Beam Hall and all the way to the First Mountain Gate down below. The stone path forked into two at the Thousand People Rock, the one on the right leading to the Clouds and Rocks Zen Monastery and the Tiger Hill Pagoda above and the one on the left to the Sword Pool and the Third Spring.

Since an unknown time in history, the Thousand People Rock had become a favorite spot for tourists from all places to dine and wine and have a break from the outside world. On days when the flowers were blooming or on moonlit nights, men and women jostled with each other to visit it. Two previous Fushe conferences had been held here. The Thousand People Rock, several acres in size, now was lined with rows upon rows of mats each with a large octagonal bamboo food box

当中，是一个竹制的八角形大食盒，周围摆着壶盏食具。垫席之间的通道上，每隔十来步，就立着一个大肚子酒坛，上面贴着标志酒名的红纸签。阵阵醉人的酒香，正透过启开了的泥封四散飘溢开来。会场正面的边上，一字排开了五张紫檀木八仙桌。那是贵宾席，每桌六把圈椅，桌上也是碗盏俱全，只是不设食盒。会场的两侧，还临时搭起了两个“诗棚”，棚内陈列着些古董字画，并备有纸砚笔墨，专供有诗瘾的社友兴之所至，即席挥毫。站在石磴的口子上望，整个会场的布置称得上简朴无华。那些个灯笼、彩球之类的玩意儿，一概摒弃不用，唯一的装饰是一幅宽一丈、长二丈的白色布幔，从一根斜贯而出的树丫上悬挂下来，上书“复社大会”四个黑色大字，远看近观，都十分庄严醒目。

时候已经不早，会场上东一堆西一群地聚满了等待开席的士子，他们有的围住了远道而来的社友，热心地打听战局新闻；有的挤在诗棚前，命题赋诗，津津有味地品评优劣；还有不少人眼见一时半刻还开不成会，便三五成群地四散开去，或访僧房，或寻古迹，或攀高阁，或俯清流。在这方圆不过二十丈的小山丘上，一下子聚起了这许多方巾儒服的斯文相公，一个个看上去都从容自信，气宇轩昂，早把那些从城里和四乡赶来进香的小民百姓唬得躲藏不迭，只远远地站着，探头探脑地朝这边观看。

当冒襄迈着轻快的步伐，登上最后一级石磴，出现在会场上时，气喘吁吁的张明弼几乎赶他不上。

in the middle and bowls and cups on the sides. In the aisles between the rows of mats stood a big wine jar every ten steps with a red paper label that marked the name of the wine. The intoxicating aroma of wine was wafting out of the newly opened mouths of the wine jars. In the front of the conference space were five red sandalwood *baxian* tables reserved for the very important personages, each with six armchairs and complete with bowls and cups but with no food box. On the flanks of the conference space were two temporary poetry booths, which displayed some antiques, calligraphy works, and paintings and were equipped with paper, inkstone, writing-brushes, and ink for those members who might have poetic outbursts. Seen from the fork of the stone path, the layout of the venue appeared simple and unostentatious. There were no lanterns, no colored balls. The only decoration was a white cloth curtain of ten feet[1] wide and twenty feet long hung from a slanting tree with four big black characters that said "General Assembly of Fushe," which was solemn and conspicuous viewed either close up or from a distance.

It was not early and the scholars had gathered in small groups in the conference venue for the banquet to start. Some of them surrounded those from far away places to inquire about latest developments of the war, others stood in front of the poetry booths to write poetry on given topics or comment on the poems of others, and many others, seeing there was still time before the conference began, scattered in twos and threes to visit the monks, see the historical sites, climb to the pavilions, or overlook the creek. The fact that in this hill of about four thousand square meters suddenly gathered so many mannerly, gorgeous-looking and awe-inspiring scholars in square hats and Confucian robes was astounding to the local pilgrims to the monastery, who stood away and watched.

When Mao Xiang briskly ascended the last step of the stone path and appeared at the conference venue, Zhang Mingbi was panting behind him, unable to catch up.

---

① The Chinese measure is "one *zhang*": one *zhang* is roughly equal to ten feet.

“喂，快点快点！区区几级石磴，你就成了喘月的吴牛啦！”冒襄回头嘲笑地说，脚步不停，表情兴奋而活泼。

张明弼绝望地挥了一下手，低低咕噜了一声，紧赶几步，走到冒襄身旁。

“冒先生、张先生，您二位可到啦！”几名知客立即迎上来，分外热情地招呼：

“一路上辛苦了吧！”

“难得二位先生光临，真是不胜荣幸呢！”

“这边请，请！”

冒襄照旧愉快地微笑着，脚步不停地往前走。一名知客连忙抢上一步，把他们引到贵宾席前。

“哎呀，辟疆、公亮，可把你们给盼来了！刚才我还嘀咕，生怕你们不来呢！”正在来宾中间周旋应酬的李雯，连忙迎上来，满脸堆笑地拱着手说。他是个白面长须、身材魁伟的中年人，举止谈吐颇有长者风度。这次大会，他也是主盟者之一。

“本社大会，弟岂敢自外！何况又是二位社兄主盟，弟等更断无不来之理！”冒襄大声地说。

“呵，呵！”李雯连忙摇着双手，“社兄这等说，可是羞煞小弟了！这‘主盟’二字，再也休提！倒是这次大会，若非列位社兄鼎力提携，只怕定要落空呢！”

“舒章兄何必太谦！荒年凶岁，难为二位主盟居然把这千人之会张罗起来，单只这点魄力，小弟便佩服得五体投地！”

“惭愧惭愧，我们也是穷九牛二虎之力，欲罢不能！简陋之处，列位社兄倒是不要见怪才好！——对了，定生、次尾他们，怎么不见？”

“噢，要来的，要来的。如此盛会，他们岂肯错过！”

……

彼此一一寒暄行礼后，那些先到的名流——书画名家查伊璜、

"Hey, hurry up! It's just a few steps and you're panting like a baffalo," Mao Xiang turned around and said mockingly without stopping, beaming with excitement and pride.

Zhang Mingbi waved his hand in despair, murmured something, quickened his steps, and walked to Mao Xiang's side.

"Mr. Mao and Mr. Zhang, finally you're here." Some ushers greeted them enthusiastically.

"How's your trip?"

"We're so deeply honored to have you here with us."

"This way, please."

Mao Xiang moved forward without stopping, still beaming with delight. One of the usherers hurriedly took a step forward and led them to a table for celebrities.

Li Wen, who was talking to other participants, hurriedly came over, bowed, and said with a smile on his face, "Oh, Pijiang and Gongliang, finally we have you here! I was afraid just now that you were not coming." This middle-aged man with a fair complexion, a long beard and a large build was one of the co-chairs of the conference.

"As a member, how dare I exclude myself from a general assembly of the Fushe? Besides, you two brothers of mine are the co-chairs and I have no reason not to come," Mao Xiang said in a loud voice.

"Oh, you're flattering me," Li Wen hurriedly waved his hands and said. "Brother Mao, I'm embarrassed if you say so. Never mention the word 'co-chair' again. But I have to thank you all for your support, without which the conference is impossible."

"Brother Shuzhang, why are you so modest? The two of you as co-chairs have successfully organized this conference of a thousand participants in such a bad year. This alone gives me reason for admiration."

"That's a great compliment. We're doing everything we can and there's no way to retreat. Please bear with us if things are not good enough. Well, how come I don't see Dingsheng and Ciwei?"

"Oh, they're coming. How can they miss such a grand event?"

After they exchanged pleasantries, the celebrities that had come

合肥才子龚鼎孳、选文名家陈名夏，以及杭州登楼社的严氏兄弟、陆氏兄弟，还有别的名流，都纷纷围拢上来，于是大家又继续招呼、行礼、寒暄……

张明弼照例地应酬着，一边忧心忡忡地留神着冒襄。见他越来越兴奋，高声地说着，无缘无故地发出笑声，并且一再打断别人的谈话，张明弼就更加担心了。他正犹豫着要不要过去关照一下的时候，冒襄忽然朝他转过脸来：

“喂，公亮，郑超宗大盟主迟迟不来‘亮相’，这儿闹哄哄的，讨厌得很，我们不如到上边走走好了！”

他这样大声说完，就毫不客气地把正在同他说话的一位名流撇在一边，走过来，硬拖着张明弼向白莲池走去。

张明弼身不由己地跟着他，小声地埋怨说：“辟疆，这怎么可以——人家正跟你说话哩！”

“哼，管他哩！俗不可耐，连文章都未做通的一个腐儒，却自命什么大名士，我瞧着他那模样就讨厌！”

“嗳，我说辟疆，你也须放宽点心肠才好，事已如此，要善自珍重。”

“嗯，这是什么意思？”冒襄的眉毛竖了起来。

“我是说，圆圆……”

“我不想说圆圆！”冒襄猛地甩脱张明弼的手，怒冲冲地向前走出几步，又回过头，瞪着眼睛，“也不许你提她！”

张明弼噎住了。他皱起眉毛，望着冒襄迅速走去的背影，终于叹了一口气，闷闷不乐地跟了过去。

冒襄和张明弼的背影刚刚消失，吴应箕、黄宗羲、侯方域、

earlier—calligrapher Zha Yihuang, Hefei prodigy Gong Dingzi, anthologist Chen Mingxia, the Yan brothers and the Lu brothers of Denglou Society in Hangzhou and many others—also joined in and it was more greeting, saluting, and exchange of pleasantries.

As Zhang Mingbi politely interacted with the others, he was keeping an eye on Mao Xiang. Seeing Mao Xiang get more and more excited, letting out laughter from time to time for no good reason at all and interrupting others again and again, he became more and more worried. Just as he was thinking whether he should approach Mao Xiang, the latter suddenly turned to him and said in a loud voice:

"Hah, Gongliang, it has been ages and Chairman Zheng Chaozong has not shown up yet. It's too noisy here. Let's go and take a walk up there."

Then, Mao Xiang bluntly left the celebrity that had been conversing with him, walked over to Zhang Mingbi and dragged him towards the White Lotus Pond.

Zhang Mingbi involuntarily followed him, complaining in a low voice, "Pijiang, this isn't good. You're in the middle of a conversation."

"Huh, leave him alone. Very boring person. A doltish pedant that can't write a good essay claiming to be a celebrity. The sight of him makes me sick."

"Well, my dear Pijiang, you have to relax. Now that things have happened, you have to take good care of yourself."

"Eh, what do you mean?" Mao Xiang's eyebrows were erected.

"I mean, Yuanyuan ..."

"I don't want to mention Yuanyuan." Mao Xiang shook off Zhang Mingbi's hand abruptly, took a few steps forward in distemper, turned his head and stared at Zhang Mingbi. "Nor should you mention her name."

Zhang Mingbi choked. He frowned and looked at the back of Mao Xiang, who was quickly walking away, sighed and followed behind gloomily.

Shortly after Mao Xiang and Zhang Mingbi left, Wu Yingji,

梅朗中、张自烈几个，也来到虎丘。他们本来打算一早就到场，以便观察动静，并监视几社那伙人。但是，由于一直不见陈贞慧、顾杲前来会合，也闹不清他们去金坛请周镳、周钟出面的事结果怎样。大家怕万一情况有变化，联系不上，只得继续待在钱禧家里等候。一直等到心急火燎，叹气不止的时候，才得着陈贞慧派人来传话，说周氏兄弟已经请到，但目前有急事，必须赶到半塘去，不进城了，让他们几个先上虎丘。大家听了，虽然有点纳闷，但已经没有工夫深究，赶紧出门。不过，晚来了这么小半天，虎丘上，社友已经到得差不多了，只是由于主盟者郑元勋还不见到场，才耽搁着未曾开席。

吴应箕眼见时间紧迫，可是对会场上的情况还一点都不摸底。事先只估计杜麟征和夏允彝远在北京，陈子龙现在浙江推官任上，大约都不会前来参加大会。但目前千人石上，除了李雯之外，几社其余的几个头面人物也一个都瞧不见。吴应箕不由得心里着急起来。等照例的寒暄客套一结束，他就朝同来的伙伴们使个眼色。侯方域等人立即会意地分散开，走到人丛中去了解情况。

如今，侯方域、梅朗中、张自烈几个都走开了，吴应箕则要留下来监视贵宾席的动静。黄宗羲四面张望一下，也登上左边的石阶，朝三泉亭那边走去。

由于钱谦益到底不肯出面干预今天的大会，这使黄宗羲十分失望，也十分扫兴。本来，他满心以为，像这么一件关系到国家安危、社局兴衰的大事，钱谦益作为东林元老，一定会拍案而起，挺身而出，而且相信只要他一出面，就定能制止这桩卑鄙阴谋。当初，正是基于这样的估计，黄宗羲才那么坚决地主张去请钱谦

Huang Zongxi, Hou Fangyu, Mei Langzhong, and Zhang Zilie came. They had planned to be here early in the morning in order to size up the situation and keep an eye on the Jishers. Because Chen Zhenhui and Gu Gao hadn't turned up yet and they had no idea whether the Zhou brothers had agreed to join them in their plan, they decided to wait in Qian Xi's house lest they should lose contact with each other in case of emergency. As they were anxiously waiting, word came from Chen Zhenhui that he was not going to meet them in Qian Xi's house and they should go to Tiger Hill first as the Zhou brothers, having agreed to be involved, needed to go to Bantang first for some urgent matter and were not going to enter the city. Upon hearing it, they were a little puzzled but nonetheless hurriedly set out without delay. When they finally arrived after several hours of delay, most of the other participants had already come. The opening banquet hadn't started because Zheng Yuanxun, one of the co-chairs, hadn't arrived yet.

There was little time left but Wu Yingji had no idea yet of the situation at the conference venue. As he had predicted, Du Linzheng and Xia Yunyi, who were far away in Beijing, and Chen Zilong, who was serving an official post in Zhejiang Province, didn't come to the conference, but he was puzzled to see that none of the other leading figures of the Jishe were present except for Li Wen. He couldn't help feeling anxious. When the usual greetings were over, he winked at his companions. Hou Fangyu and others immediately understood him and dispersed into the crowd to find out about the situation.

Now, Hou Fangyu, Mei Langzhong, and Zhang Zilie having all left, Wu Yingji stayed to monitor the table of celebrities. Huang Zongxi looked around and ascended the stone steps on the left, and then walked towards the Three Springs Pavilion.

As Qian Qianyi refused to intervene in the current assembly, Huang Zongxi was very disappointed and dejected. He had thought that Qian Qianyi, as a veteran East Wooder, would definitely stand up at such a major event related to the fate of the nation and the survival of the Fushe, believing that as long as the old man came forward the despicable conspiracy would be stopped. Previously,

益，并不惜同吴应箕、侯方域等人大吵了一场。谁知结果却事与愿违。朋友们知道后虽然没说什么，可是黄宗羲却自觉脸上无光。特别是当他试图挽回一下面子，而详细地向大家转述钱谦益不能出面的“理由”时，侯方域那种微微冷笑的表情，更是深深刺痛了黄宗羲。“哼，你们只管笑吧！到时候，我会让你们大吃一惊的！”他气恼之余，这样暗暗地想。

现在，黄宗羲独自走在用砖块砌成的路径上，微皱着眉毛，紧抿着嘴巴。由于意识到这场生死攸关的大较量，只能靠自己和同伴们承当起来，他的心情反而不像前一阵子那样焦虑和烦躁。“是的，他们竟敢拿阮胡子来做题目，真可谓利令智昏！阮胡子是什么东西？一名死有余辜的阉党余孽，一个十恶不赦的卑鄙小人！何况上有钦定的铁案，下有士林的清议，我就不信，在今日的大会上，真会有多少人敢公然附和他们的主张！其实，也不须牧老出面，定生他们去请周仲驭，更是多余的。到时只要我振臂一呼，把是非利害当众一摆，再搬出四年前的《留都防乱公揭》来，声讨他们背盟毁约之罪，就保管能把绝大多数社友争取到我们一边来。这是毫无疑问的！”这样自信地想着，黄宗羲感到浑身充满了力量。他开始想象几社的败类们受到自己严辞痛斥时，那种沮丧惶恐、目瞪口呆的模样，不由得露出快意的、胜利的微笑，脚步也更加轻快有力了。

这样一直走到三泉亭，忽然听见有人高声招呼：

“太冲，太冲！”

他抬头一看，发现亭子里聚着几个儒生，都是从杭州赶来参加大会的同乡。招呼他的那一位叫郑铉，其余几个也都认识。

it had been precisely based on this belief that Huang Zongxi had insisted on inviting Qian Qianyi and even had had a bitter argument with Wu Yingji and Hou Fangyu. It turned out that things didn't go the way he wanted. Although his friends didn't say anything about it, Huang Zongxi felt ashamed of himself. In particular, he was deeply stung by Hou Fangyu's sneering look when he tried to save his own face by explaining why Qian Qianyi was unable to come forward. "Huh, just laugh! In time, I'll surprise you all," he thought to himself vengefully.

Huang Zongxi walked alone on the brick path, frowning slightly and compressing his lips firmly together. Having realized that this life-and-death battle was left to himself and his comrades, he was not as anxious and worried as he had been a while ago. "Yes! They're definitely crazy to raise the issue of Ruan Dacheng. What is Ruan Dacheng? A remnant of the castrate's party, an unpardonable, despicable little man. What's more, with a verdict endorsed by His Majesty the emperor himself and a public condemnation from the gentry scholars, I don't believe there would be a significant number of people to second their proposal at today's conference. In fact, there's no need for Elder Mu to come forward. There's even less need for Dingsheng to seek the support of Zhou Zhongyu. Most conference participants will without a doubt stand on our side if I stand up against the proposal, read the "Public Denunciation of a Treasonist in the Legacy Capital" and condemn those who breach that written consensus." Thus thinking, Huang Zongxi felt energized. As he began to imagine how frustrated, stunned and dumbfounded the Jishe scums would be when severely reprimanded, he couldn't help but give a hearty, triumphant smile, and his footsteps became faster and livelier.

He walked all the way to the Three Springs Pavilion and suddenly heard someone calling him in a loud voice:

"Taichong, Taichong!"

He looked up and saw a few Confucian scholars had gathered in the pavilion, all from Hangzhou to attend the conference. The one who greeted him was Zheng Xuan, and he knew all the others too.

黄宗羲正要了解一下情况，便欣然走过去，彼此在亭子里行礼、寒暄，然后分别在栏杆榻板上坐了下来。

“列位社兄先我而至，不知可听到些新闻么？”黄宗羲环顾大家，微笑地问。

“啊哈，我们能有什么新闻？”一个名叫严津的儒生抢着回答，“新闻就是我们这次都做了傻子！巴巴地一早就赶来，腿也站酸了，眼也望穿了，却还老是不开席。”

“还有，我们一到姑苏，就到处打听你，也不知你躲到哪儿去了，害得我们满城地好找！”他的哥哥严灏也半开玩笑半认真地插了进来，“哼，就凭这个，待会儿非得先罚你三杯不可！”

“对，对，要罚，一定要罚！”好几个人欢声应和。

黄宗羲不在意地摆一摆手：“你们——难道什么也没听说？”他又一次问。

严津迷惑地摇着头：“没有呀！”随即眼珠子一转，“咦，太冲，莫非你听到了什么不成？”

黄宗羲点点头：“听说这次大会，要作出公议，宽宥阮圆海。兄等难道不知道？”

“阮圆海？”严津莫名其妙地问，“哪个阮圆海？”

“莫非是阮胡子？”另一个人问。

“什么，宽宥阮胡子？”“他是什么人！”“这是怎么回事？”好几个声音同时响起来。

“此事已千真万确！”黄宗羲做了个断然的手势，“而且此项奸谋的祸首就是松江几社那伙败类！”

大家“啊”了一声，不知是吃惊还是不懂，都望着黄宗羲发呆。

“幸而此事被我们及早觉察，已经做好准备。”黄宗羲轻快

Because Huang Zongxi wanted to find out about the situation, he gladly walked over to them. After the exchange of salutes and pleasantries, everyone sat down on the railings of the pavilion.

"Dear brothers, since you're here first, is there any news to share with me?" Huang Zongxi scanned them and asked with a smile.

"Haha, what news can we have?"came a quick reply from a scholar named Yan Jin. "The news is that we're all fools this time. We rushed here early in the morning, waited and waited but the opening banquet has not started yet."

"Also, as soon as we got to Gusu, we looked for you everywhere but couldn't find you. Were you hiding from us?" His brother Yan Hao cut in half-jokingly and half-seriously. "Huh, because of this, you have to drink three cups first as punishment."

"Yes, yes, punishment, there must be punishment!" Some others echoed.

Huang Zongxi waved his hand and asked again, unmindful of what they said, "You— haven't you heard anything?"

Yan Jin shook his head confusedly and said "no, nothing" but then, rolling his eyes, he asked back, "So, Taichong, you've heard something?"

Huang Zongxi nodded his head and said, "I hear that this conference would have an open discussion of the issue of pardoning Ruan Yuanhai. Don't you know it, brothers?"

"Ruan Yuanhai?" Yan Jin asked puzzledly. "Which Ruan Yuanhai?"

"Is it Beardy Ruan?" another man asked.

"What, pardoning Beardy Ruan?" "What a horrible person he is!" "How does this happen?" Several voices rang out at the same time.

"It's absolutely true," said Huang Zongxi with a decisive gesture. "And the scums of Jishe in Songjiang are the conspirators."

"Ah?"said the others in unison. They stared at Huang Zongxi with a blank expression of shock or puzzlement.

"Fortunately, it came to our knowledge and we're prepared." Huang Zongxi stood up briskly, and said confidently, "As long as

地站起来，胸有成竹地说，“只要我同盟君子，心明力定，不为所惑，鸣鼓而攻，彼奸谋就必定无法得逞！”

“可是，太冲，这到底是怎么回事啊？”越听越糊涂的郑铉问。他长得又矮又胖，下巴却挂着长到腰际的胡子。

想必其他人也有同感，都不由得点点头。

“哎，你们听我说呀！”黄宗羲兴冲冲地摆一摆手。由于碰上了这批朋友，而且感到完全有把握说服他们，使他们在未来的较量中站到自己的一边，现在黄宗羲夺取胜利的信心甚至更足了。“事情是这样的——”他说。于是，他从大半个月前在秦淮河李十娘家的那一场聚会追溯起，把陈贞慧如何在郑元勋那里听到了消息，他们如何分析研究，得出主谋者就是几社的结论，又如何准备反击，以挫败这个阴谋等等，向大家说了一遍。为了证明推断无误，他特别列举了几社的头头夏允彝的老师张贤登当年如何同东林人士为敌，这些年来几社之徒对社事如何消极敷衍，同大家如何离心离德；张溥死后，他们又如何一反旧态，积极活动，企图篡夺社内大权的种种“劣迹”。末了，他兴奋地环顾着大家：“列位，几社之徒虽则猖獗，但终敌不过我同人君子的浩然正气。弟已料定他们必败无疑！但一场剧斗，恐亦难免。小弟不才，已决意奋然前驱，直撄其锋！不知列位社兄届时亦能投袂而起，助我一臂之力乎？”

在黄宗羲热烈陈说的当儿，朋友们始终静静地听着。这自然是由于他们很想弄清这个消息到底是怎么一回事。不过，当黄宗羲说完之后，他们却你望望我，我瞅瞅你，好大一会儿，没有人作声。

the good men in the Fushe resolutely safeguard our principles with a clear understanding of the situation, their conspiracy will definitely fail."

"But, Taichong, what on earth is going on?" Zheng Xuan asked, who was increasingly confused as he listened. He was short and fat, but had a beard that drooped down to his waist.

Presumably others felt the same way because they all nodded to confirm that they had the same question.

"Well, listen up," Huang Zongxi waved his hand avidly. Since these men were his friends and he was sure that he could persuade them to stand on his side in the coming struggle, he now had even more confidence in winning the battle. "It's like this—" he said. Then, he told them about the gathering at Li Shiniang's place on the Qinhuai River half a month ago—how Chen Zhenhui heard the rumor from Zheng Yuanxun, how they studied the situation and came to the conclusion that the conspiracy was masterminded by the Jishe, how they planned to launch a counter-attack to defeat the conspiracy and so on and in order to prove the correctness of their reasoning, he specifically cited things that had led to the conclusion; how Zhang Xiandeng, teacher of Xia Yunyi and head of the Jishe, was hostile to East Wooders, how unconcerned the Jishers had been about Fushe affairs over the past few years, and how they went against the common goal of the Fushe, and after Zhang Pu's death, how they suddenly became enthusiastic about the affairs of the Fushe and wanted to usurp its leadership. Finally, he scanned his comrades zealously and said, "Gentlemen! No matter how the Jishers are actively pushing for it, they're no match for the good forces in the Fushe. I'm sure they'll be ultimately defeated, but a hard battle is inevitable. Though my strength is limited, I've made up my mind to stand the brunt of the fighting. By then, will you lend me a helping hand?"

While Huang Zongxi was passionately speaking, his friends listened quietly as they wanted to know more about the news, but when Huang Zongxi finished, they looked at each other and none spoke.

“哎，列位，怎么样啊？”黄宗羲忍不住了。

“太冲，”严灏拈着稀疏的黄胡子，迟疑地说，“这事……只怕还须持重为好。”

“怎么？”

“请恕小弟孤陋寡闻，适才听兄说了，方知这阮圆海乃是钦定逆案中人。既然如此，又有谁敢为他翻案？只怕几社他们也是胡乱说笑而已，次尾、定生他们却拿来当真，硬要争这一口气，又何苦来？”

“太冲，”郑铉也接了上来，“小弟早欲劝兄，此类无谓之争，竟是躲开为是。弟见你跟着定生、次尾他们，一天到晚争来吵去，劳心竭力，不知到底有何得益？不如赶早撇开，一心一意把几篇时艺琢磨精熟通透，倒是正经！”

“乖乖，若是当真闹将起来，可不得了！”严津吃惊地笑道。也许想象到一旦纷争大起之后那种不可开交的情景，他兴奋得直眨眼睛，“热闹，嘻嘻，有趣！”他神往地说。

“你就知道瞎起哄！”严灏瞪了弟弟一眼，又劝解黄宗羲，“太冲，同社之内，以和为贵。几社他们纵有不是，要么忍让着点，要么私下说他几句就完了，又何必在今日大动干戈？一则扫了大家之兴，二则传出去，也难免外人笑话。”

“嗯，依弟之见，此事莫非竟是阮圆海造作谣言，意欲蛊惑人心，扰乱我社局么？”一个名叫江浩的黑瘦儒生忽然说。他为人一向沉默寡言，直到这会儿才开口。

“哎，这怎么会！”黄宗羲气急地分辩说，“此事出于郑超宗之口，怎么会是阮圆海之谣言？非是弟等好斗乐争，实因此事关乎社局兴衰，家国存亡，断难坐视。如今奸谋已生，逆象已见，

"Hey, gentlemen, what do you think?" Huang Zongxi broke the silence.

"Taichong," Yan Hao said hesitantly, picking at his own sparse yellow beard. "This matter—I'm afraid—needs to be taken seriously."

"Why do you say so?"

"Please forgive my ignorance. From what you just said, Ruan Yuanhai is a treasonist confirmed by the emperor himself. That being the fact, who would dare to reverse the case for him? I'm afraid that the Jishers are just joking. Yet Ciwei and Dingsheng are taking it seriously and insist on fighting it out. So why the bother?"

"Taichong," Zheng Xuan cut in. "I've been thinking, you should stay away from such a meaningless contention. There's really no good in following Dingsheng and Ciwei to fight others all the time. You may fare better by keeping away from such things and concentrating on polishing your essays."

"Good heavens! Should a battle take place, it would be scary," said Yan Jin alarmedly with a smile. Probably visualizing the scene of the battle, he said excitedly and longingly, "Hooray! It would be a lot of fun!"

"Stop that stupid hollering," said Yan Hao, fixing his younger brother with a stare. Then he said to Huang Zongxi appeasingly, "Taichong, we're all Fushers and should live in harmony. When the Jishers make a mistake, you can either bear with them or criticize them in private. Why bother to fight them in public? A public fight will spoil the fun and should it be known by others we would become a laughing stock."

"Well, in my humble opinion, it's a rumor spread by Ruan Yuanhai in order to confuse our minds and disrupt the order of the Fushe," said a thin, dark-complexioned young scholar named Jiang Hao, a taciturn person by nature.

"No, it's not," Huang Zongxi argued. "Since it's from the mouth of Zheng Chaozong, how can it be a rumor from Ruan Yuanhai? I'm not belligerent but I won't sit back when such a matter involves the existence of the Fushe and the safety of the nation. A conspiracy is

绝非口舌所能挽回。若不痛加惩戒，清扫门庭，则社事更不堪问！列位若不视小弟为狂悖无知之人，还望明鉴此理，同生义愤，存此一段公论，以寒天下乱臣贼子之胆！则社稷幸甚，复社幸甚！”说着，向大家深深一揖。

这么一来，朋友们都不作声了，但仍然露出为难的神气，没有立即表示态度。

看见这种情形，黄宗羲有点着急，也有点失望。他正考虑到底怎样才能说服他们，忽然，传来一阵急促的脚步声，梅朗中气喘吁吁地奔进亭子来。他来不及同大家见礼，就冲着黄宗羲嚷："太冲，原来你躲在这儿，却教我好找！"

黄宗羲见他气急败坏的样子，忙问："朗三，怎么了？"

梅朗中摇着头："不得了，不得了，厉害，厉害！"

"到底是什么事？"黄宗羲发急地问。

"谣言，谣言太厉害了！"梅朗中又是伸舌头，又是挤眼睛。

听清是谣言，黄宗羲才放下心来，"你听到什么？"他皱着眉毛问。

"嗨，可多啦！"梅朗中把胳臂往空中一画，"喏，说是皇上因妖氛日亟，求才心切，曾下旨吏部，命于逆案中择其罪轻者予以甄别，还特地提及阮圆海和冯琢庵，说是俱属有才可用之人。所以无论我辈宽贷与否，这胡子总归是要起用的了！另外又说，西张夫子在世时，其实也早有宽宥阮胡子之想，曾私下与东林诸前辈会商过数次，可惜未及作出公议，便撒手先逝。所以我辈这次公议宽宥阮某，其实也是秉承西张夫子的遗愿哩！"

taking place with obvious signs. Mere talking won't stop it. If the conspirators were not punished and expelled from the Fushe, the damage to the Fushe would be unthinkable. Gentlemen! If you don't think I'm a self-important, ignorant person, please stand with me in the defense of truth and justice. Then, the nation is in good hands and the Fushe is in good hands." He gave a deep bow after speaking.

The friends lapsed into silence, unwilling to voice their position.

Seeing it was like this, Huang Zongxi was worried and disappointed at the same time. As he was thinking how to persuade them, suddenly there came a rush of footsteps, and Mei Langzhong hurried into the pavilion, gasping for breath.

Not bothering with the formalities of greeting, he said to Huang Zongxi in a loud voice, "Taichong, you're hiding here. I've been looking for you for ages."

Seeing him exasperated like that, Huang Zongxi said concernedly, "Langsan, what has happened?"

Mei Langzhong shook his head and said, "Terrible, terrible! It's outrageous!"

"What exactly has happened?" Huang Zongxi asked anxiously.

"A rumor, a terrible rumor!" said Mei Langzhong, his tongue sticking out and eyes staring.

Hearing the word "rumor", Huang Zongxi was relieved. "What did you hear?" he asked, knitting his eyebrows.

"Quite a lot." Mei Langzhong drew an arch in the air with his arm. "The rumor says: In this moment of national crisis, the emperor is eager to seek talent for the country. He has ordered the Ministry of Personnel to discriminate between the transgressors in the treason case and pardon the lesser ones with special mention of Ruan Yuanhai and Feng Zhuoan, whom he says are talented men. Therefore, Beardy Ruan will be exonerated in any event, whether men like us decide to pardon him or not. The rumor also says that when Mr. West Zhang was alive, he had thought of pardoning Beardy Ruan and had discussed the matter with Fushe elders many times but unfortunately he had passed away before a consensus was reached ... therefore, a decision at the

“啊，西张夫子生前已有此意？这，这可是真的？”严津吃惊地问。

“啊哈，连老严也相信了，你看，厉害不？”梅朗中得意地说，“告诉你，这是谣言，谣言！懂么？”

“还有什么？”黄宗羲气哼哼地问。这些离奇的谣言，其卑鄙无耻的程度远远地超出了他的想象，这使他大为愤怒，也大为吃惊。

“哦，还有人说，前些日子阮胡子曾向吴次尾、陈定生二兄当面哭求，发誓从此洗心革面，投靠我社。吴、陈二兄见他一片至诚，已然认可……对了，甚至说阮胡子已加盟我复社了！”

梅朗中说到最后这一句，先自撑不住笑起来。就连其余的人也都纷纷摇头，认为这未免太不可信了。

可是黄宗羲没有笑，他气得脸色铁青，胸口在急剧地一起一伏。蓦地，他大吼一声：

“朗三，我们走！”

梅朗中正同大家嘻嘻哈哈地取笑这些谣言的荒诞不经，被他一喝，迷惑地问：“走？上哪儿去？”

“找几社的败类算账去！”

梅朗中吃了一惊：“什么，算账，眼下便去？”

“怎么，你难道不敢？”

“哎，敢……”

“那么走啊！”

“可是，可是……”

“没有什么可是，说干脆点，你去不去？”黄宗羲不耐烦地瞪大了眼睛。

梅朗中显然不愿意马上就去。但在黄宗羲咄咄逼人的目光下，他却不敢说出来，只是畏怯地问：“就、就光我们两个去？”

黄宗羲沉默了一下。他当然希望眼前这帮人都跟着去，至少

conference to pardon Mr. Ruan is in fact a tribute to Mr. West Zhang."

"Oh, did Mr. West Zhang ever have such an idea while he was alive? Is—is it true?" Yan Jin asked alarmedly.

"Lo and behold! Even Mr. Yan was taken in. Isn't it a terrible rumor?" Mei Langzhong said triumphantly. "Let me tell you, it's a rumor. A rumor, understand?"

"What else did you hear?" Huang Zongxi asked, infuriated and shocked by the absurdity of the rumor and the shamelessness in its making which far exceeded his imagination.

"Oh, it's said that Beardy Ruan begged Wu Ciwei and Chen Dingsheng a few days ago to be admitted into the Fushe, vowing to turn a new leaf in his life ... Brother Wu and Brother Chen, moved by his sincerity, agreed ... and, it's even said that Beardy Ruan has already joined the Fushe."

When Mei Langzhong said the last sentence, he couldn't help laughing and the others shook their heads in disbelief.

But Huang Zongxi didn't find it amuzing. His face was red with anger, his chest rising and falling. Suddenly, he yelled, "Langsan, let's go!"

Mei Langzhong, who was joking with the others about the absurdity of the rumor, was jolted by the yelling and asked confusedly, "Go? Where do we go?"

"Let's go find the Jishe scums and settle accounts with them."

Mei Langzhong was taken aback. "What, settle accounts with them now?"

"Oh, don't you dare to go?"

"Um, of course I dare ..."

"Then let's go."

"But, but ..."

"No buts, just say it, are you going or not?" Huang Zongxi glared at Mei Langzhong impatiently.

Mei Langzhong was obviously unwilling to go right away, but under Huang Zongxi's blazing gaze, he didn't dare to say it. Instead, he asked timidly, "Just—just the two of us?"

Huang Zongxi was silent for a while. Of course he hoped that

能壮一壮声势。然而，令他失望的是，那几个朋友在一旁依旧装聋作哑，毫无表示，有一两个还悄悄地往后躲。“哼，亏他们还自命是复社君子，事到临头就是这样！”他冷冷地想，随即抬起头，傲然地说道：

“两个人又怎样？两个人照样对付得了他们！莫非还怕那伙丑类不成？”

梅朗中趁这当儿也镇定下来。“还是等定生和仲老他们来了再说。要不，也该先告知次尾、朝宗他们。”他说着，挺直了高大的身躯。

黄宗羲冒火了，“用不着管他们，用不着！你听见了没有？”他跺着脚说。

但是梅朗中相当固执：“不告知他们，我是不能去的。”

黄宗羲不再说话了。他狠狠地横了梅朗中一眼，扭头就走。刚刚走下亭子，他又突然折回来，一直走到梅朗中跟前，咬着牙，一字一句地说：

“你听着，从而今起，我们绝——交！”

他重新转过身，头也不回地往亭子外去了。

梅朗中显然没料到老朋友会来这一手，他不胜震惊地瞪视着黄宗羲的背影，随后又求援地望望周围的人。当确信没有人能够搭救他时，他就猛地跳起来，发出一声哀叫，气急败坏地追了出去……

## 僧房戏谑

张明弼尾随着冒襄的背影，离开白莲池，过了养鹤涧，走到了东塔院。这儿离千人石比较远，游人稀少。张明弼沿着幽静的长廊往前走，正考虑着怎样劝说冒襄。忽然，“哄”的一声，从

all the other men present would follow them so that they would at least have the advantage of numbers. However, to his disappointment, they kept deaf and dumb without saying anything, and one or two even quietly stepped backward. "Humph, this is how the self-styled gentlemen of the Fushe act when things happen," he thought coldly, then raised his head and said scornfully:

"Yes, just the two of us. Is there anything wrong with it? Two is enough. Should we be afraid of those little clowns?"

By then, Mei Langzhong had calmed down. "Let's wait for Dingsheng and Elder Zhong. Or at least, we should let Ciwei and Chaozong know first," he said as he straightened his towering figure.

Huang Zongxi flared up. "There's no need to get them involved. No need at all. Did you hear me?" he said, stomping his feet.

But Mei Langzhong was rather stubborn. "I can't go without telling them first," he said.

Huang Zongxi went silent. He gave Mei Langzhong a stern look, turned around and left. Shortly after he walked out of the pavilion, he suddenly turned back and said to Mei Langzhong from between his clenched teeth, counting every word:

"Listen! From now on, we'll have nothing to do with each other."

He turned around and walked out of the pavilion without looking back.

Mei Langzhong obviously didn't expect his old friend to act like this. He dumbfoundedly stared at the back of Huang Zongxi and then looked at the others as if for help. When he was sure that no one would come to his rescue, he jumped up with a sad cry and went after Huang Zongxi exasperatedly.

## In the Room of a Monk

Following on the heels of Mao Xiang, Zhang Mingbi left the White Lotus Pond, passed the Crane Creek, and came to the East Pagoda Garden. It was a quiet place far away from the Thousand People Rock with very few tourists. As he walked along the sequestered corridor thinking about how to persuade Mao Xiang,

一所僧房里传出一阵嬉笑，随即又响起了“啪、啪”的拍桌子声。正伏在窗棂上朝里面窥看的冒襄，听见张明弼的脚步声，就做了个制止的手势，又招招手，让他过去。

张明弼莫名其妙，放轻脚步走到窗棂下。冒襄按了按他的脑袋，让他把耳朵贴在窗上，只听见一个怯怯的声音在里面说：

“啊，那么，可是，可是光着身子的么？”

另一个愉快的声音：“那还用问！你也不想想，这种时候，谁肯穿着衣裳？喂，你肯么？”

又是一阵哄笑，听声音，少说也有七八个人。

张明弼愈加摸不着头脑。这时，冒襄又碰了碰他，指着窗纸上的一个小洞让他看。

张明弼把眼睛凑上去，这下看清了：原来房间当中放着一张八仙桌，四个士子正围在一起打纸牌，当他们用巴掌使劲把牌拍到桌子上时，就发出“啪、啪”的声响。另外还有两个站在旁边观战，其中正在指手画脚地说话的，是个细高挑的儒生，长得相当秀气，一双水汪汪的眼睛，一只高而直的鼻子，再加上两片薄薄的嘴唇，一举手一顾盼都透着一股风流潇洒的劲儿。张明弼认得他名叫余怀，表字淡心，是个有名的浪荡角色。

只听余怀又笑吟吟地说：“话说密之和克咸两个，把姜如须吓了个够，这才把刀一掷，大笑道，‘三郎郎当！三郎郎当！……’”

张明弼心中一动，顿时记起一件事：那是好几年前，莱婺人姜垓在秦淮河旧院，迷上了李十娘，躲在寒秀斋里整整一个月不出来。桐城社友方以智和妹夫孙临两人当时也在南京，知道这事，

suddenly there came a roar of laughter from a monk's room, followed by sounds of slapping the table. Mao Xiang, who was leaning on the window lattice and peeping inside, heard Zhang Mingbi's footsteps and gestured for him to stop before beckoning for him to come over.

Zhang Mingbi puzzledly tiptoed to the window lattice. Mao Xiang pushed his head to the window for him to listen. A timid voice came from inside, "Well, then, were they naked?"

Another voice said joyfully, "You don't need to ask that question. Just think, in such a moment, who would like to have clothes on? Would you like to?"

There was another burst of laughter. Judging from the voices, there were seven or eight men altogether.

Zhang Mingbi became more confused. Then, Mao Xiang touched him again, and pointed to a small hole in the window paper for him to look through.

Zhang Mingbi brought his eyes up to the hole and saw what was happening inside: There was a *baxian* table in the room and four scholars were playing cards together. Every time someone put a card on the table, there was a slapping sound. Beside them stood two onlookers—the one talking and gesticulating was a tall and slender scholar with a pair of watery eyes, a tall and straight nose, and a pair of thin lips and every gesture and every look of his carried the air of a dandy. Zhang Mingbi recognized him as Yu Huai, courtesy name Danxin, a well-known profligate character.

Yu Huai said gleefully, "And, when Mizhi and Kexian scared the life out of Jiang Ruxu, they put down the sword, laughed and said, 'Sanlang is a wanton man. Sanlang is a wanton man.'"

Zhang Mingbi suddenly remembered one thing: A few years ago, Jiang Gai from Laiwu fell in love with Li Shiniang in the Old Yard on the Qinhuai River and stayed in the Cold Beauty Chamber for a month without ever coming out. Fang Yizhi and his brother-in-law Sun Lin, two Fushers from Tongcheng, heard of it and decided to play a joke on him. Good at climbing walls and walking on rooftops, the two men disguised themselves as bandits one night and climbed into

便有心同他开个玩笑。他们两人都学过一点飞檐走壁的本领。一天夜里，他们翻墙进了李十娘家，装作江洋大盗的模样，手执钢刀，直奔卧房，一路喊杀连天，吓得姜垓从被窝里直滚出来，跪在地上哀叫：“大王饶命，莫伤十娘！”还一个劲儿地叩头。方、孙二人把姜垓捉弄够了，这才露出真面目，哈哈大笑。当晚四人摆酒畅饮，尽欢而散。余怀现在讲的，大约便是那件事。

张明弼看了一阵，正想伸直身子，忽然“咣当”一声，冒襄猛地推开虚掩着的门，一步跨了进去。

“哈哈，好啊！肃穆名刹，清净佛地，我道是谁如此大胆，敢躲在这里大讲什么光身子不光身子的！原来是你们这伙圣人之徒！”他虚张声势地大叫。

房间里的人愣了一下，随即欢呼起来：

“辟疆，原来是你！啊，公亮兄也来了！”

“快来，就等着你们呢！”

“啊哈，你们怎么知道我们在这里？”

“这边坐，这边！”

冒襄微微笑着，昂着头，作了个罗圈揖，然后从身边取出一个荷包，朝桌上一摔，兴冲冲地说：“怎么停啦？来，打它十局！”

“不成啦！”

“怎么？”

“我们都输得荷包见底啦！”

“啊？赢家呢？谁是赢家？”

有人一指，“是淡心，还有密之！”

“什么？密之也来啦？在哪儿？”因为看不见人，冒襄转动着脑袋寻找着。

“嗯，是哪儿来的野小子啊，又吵又嚷的，搅得人睡不安生！”一个含混不清的嗓音从人们的背后响起。接着，吱扭吱扭的床榻响，有人翻身爬起来。人们向两旁让开了，露出来一张年轻人的

Li Shiniang's house with swords in their hands and, shouting slogans, went all the way to the bedroom. Jiang Gai was so scared that he rolled out of bed and went on his knees begging for mercy. "I beg your forgiveness, sirs. Pray don't hurt Shiniang." He kept kowtowing as he spoke. Satisfied with their own hoax, Mr. Fang and Mr. Sun revealed their real identities and laughed out loud. That night, the four of them ate and drank and talked until they had enough fun. Yu Huai was probably telling that story.

As Zhang Mingbi was going to straighten up after watching for a little while, clank, Mao Xiang pushed the unbolted door open and stepped in. "Ha ha, good for you! Disciples of the sages talking about naked bodies in a sacred temple in the pure land of the Buddha." He bluffed.

The men in the room were startled and then shouted cheerfully, "Pijiang, it's you! Ah, Brother Gongliang is here too!"

"Come on in. We're waiting for you."

"Why, how do you know we're here?"

"Sit here, please sit."

Mao Xiang smiled slightly, raised his head, saluted them by putting his hands together, and then took out a purse from his side, threw it on the table, and said enthusiastically, "Why stop? Go on, ten more rounds of playing."

"Oh, no!"

"Why not?"

"We have no more money to lose."

"What? Where is the winner? Who's the winner?"

One of them said, pointing, "There're two of them. Danxin and Mizhi."

"What? Mizhi is here too? Where is he?" Not seeing Mizhi, Mao Xiang looked around to find him.

"Well, where does the wild boy come from? So noisy that I can't sleep." From behind these men came an indistinct voice. Then, with the creaking of the bed, someone stood up. The men at the table stepped aside, revealing an elongated face of a young man. It was a

瘦长脸。这是一张结实红润、轮廓分明的脸，粗黑剑挺的眉毛下面，嵌着一双钻石般的黑眼睛，再加上壮硕的鼻子，端正的大嘴，使这张脸显得开朗、聪明，生气勃勃；而此刻它却滑稽地耷拉着，一副没精打采的样子。这就是复社四公子之一，大名鼎鼎的方以智。两年前，他中了进士，官授翰林院编修，一直在北京供职，这会儿不知为什么又跑回江南来，还这等装神弄鬼的模样。

方以智又哼哼唧唧了一阵，然后抬了抬眼皮："啊，辟疆、公亮，是你们哪！"他说着，打了个哈欠："嗯，刚才，你说什么来着？"

冒襄十分熟悉对方的脾气，他把桌子一拍："叫你来斗纸牌！你不是大赢家嘛！"

方以智摇摇头："纸牌，我是不想赌了。要赌，就赌这个——"

他说着，不慌不忙地坐起来，伸手在袖筒里掏了一会儿，摸出一根长长的、小拇指粗细的银管，管的一端打成个小漏斗状，向上翘起，管身上挂着个绣荷包。方以智像变戏法似的，从荷包里拈出一撮金黄色的细丝，填在小漏斗内。他把银管的另一头含在嘴里，又掏出火石，敲着了纸媒，把火凑在小漏斗上，点燃了里面的黄色细丝，小心翼翼地吸了一口。

大家目不转睛地瞧着，不知道他在捣什么鬼。突然，方以智把嘴一张，一股白烟直喷出来，顿时，整个房间里充满了一种刺鼻的恶浊的气味。站在前面的几个人冷不防被这气味一熏，立即咳嗽起来。

方以智似乎因为终于完成了这番困难而危险的表演而松了一口气。他哈哈笑着，跳起来，摇晃着脑袋，一副得意洋洋的样子。

"密、密之兄，请问此为何物？"一个士子结结巴巴地问。

"哼，这叫金丝烟。闽人叫它淡肉果，北人又叫淡巴菰，又

solid, rosy, well-defined face that radiated cheer, wit and vigor with a pair of diamond-like black eyes embedded under the thick, straight, black brows in addition to a prominent nose and a large, well-placed mouth. Yet at this moment those eyes were funnily half-closed, lacking the luster they should have. It was the famous Fang Yizhi, one of the Four Young Men of the Fushe. Two years ago, he was awarded a *jinshi* degree and appointed editor at the Hanlin Academy to serve in Beijing. Curiously, he was now back in River South like an apparition.

Fang Yizhi grumbled for a while, then opened his eyelids. "Ah, Pijiang and Gongliang, it's you two," said he with a yawn. "Well, what did you say just now?"

Mao Xiang, knowing his disposition very well, patted the table and said, "I said you can come to play cards. Aren't you a big winner?"

Fang Yizhi shook his head, saying, "No more betting with cards. If I have to bet, I would like to bet with this—"

As he spoke, he slowly sat up, put his hand in his sleeve and took out a long silver pipe with the thickness of a little finger. One end of the pipe was shaped like a funnel and a little embroidered bag hung from the middle of it. Fang Yizhi conjured up a pinch of golden filaments from the bag and fed them into the small funnel. Then, he held the other end of the silver pipe in his mouth, took out a flint, ignited the tinder, moved the fire close to the funnel, lit the yellow filaments inside, and took a careful puff.

Everyone looked intently, wondering what he was doing. Suddenly, Fang Yizhi opened his mouth and a puff of white smoke burst out. The whole room was filled with a pungent, nasty smell. The few men standing in front caught the smell and immediately coughed.

Fang Yizhi seemed to be relieved upon finishing this difficult and dangerous performance. He laughed, jumped up and swayed his head triumphantly.

"Brother Mi—Mizhi, what's this?" a young scholar stammered.

"Well, it's called golden filaments tobacco. The Fujianese call it *danrouguo*, Northerners call it *danbagu* or *xiangbugui*. If you smoke

叫想不归。小吸可以驱温发散，多吸则会醉人，久服则肺焦，无药可救，吐黄水而死——怎么样？你要试一试？”他把银管朝那士子嘴边一送，吓得那人忙不迭地后退。

“啊，此乃朝廷明令严禁之物，有吸之者，杀无赦哩！”有人惴惴不安地说。

方以智冷笑一声：“若是朝廷不禁，人人均能吸之，那还有何兴味？这也如同闭门读禁书，唯其有此胆量，才算得上我辈中人！嗯，谁敢一试？”

“好，我来试一试！”余怀显然被方以智的话激起了好胜心，首先站了出来。

于是，他在方以智的帮助下，按照刚才的方法，吸了一口，立刻被呛得喉头又痛又痒，咳嗽得眼泪都流了出来。

方以智摇头说：“谁让你不要命地狠吸！须是如我方才的样子，轻吸慢嘘，不唯安然无恙，且觉余味无穷哩！”

由于余怀带了头，其余的人也不甘示弱，纷纷抢着要试。不大一会儿，室内便弄得烟雾弥漫，咳声不止。

方以智忙了一阵，忽然回头看见冒襄一动不动地坐着，正在那里嘿嘿冷笑。

“咦，辟疆，你也来一口如何？”方以智问。

冒襄摇摇头：“一口我是不吸的，要吸，就来打个赌！”

“哦？”

“这东西，不是能吸得人醉么？现在我要同你比拼，一人一口轮流地吸，看谁先醉倒——你敢不敢？”

“这个……”

“你敢不敢？”冒襄站起来，挑战地叫。他兴奋地抓起装钱

a little, it helps dispersing body heat. If you smoke too much it causes intoxication and if you smoke too much in the long run it will burn the lungs with no medicine to cure it and you'll spit yellow water and die. So, do you dare to try it?" He extended the pipe to the mouth of the young scholar, who stepped back in horror.

"Oh, good gracious, it's strictly prohibited by the imperial court. Anyone who smokes it is punishable by death," someone said anxiously.

Fang Yizhi sneered, "If the court doesn't ban it, everyone can smoke it, then where's the fun? It's like reading a banned book behind closed doors. Only with this kind of courage can you be considered a member of our generation. So, who dares to give it a try?"

"Okay, I'll give it a try." Yu Huai stood out first, obviously aroused by Fang Yizhi's words.

Then, with the help of Fang Yizhi, he took a puff in the same manner and was immediately choked. His throat ached and itched and he coughed so violently that tears flowed from his eyes.

Fang Yizhi shook his head and said, "Who told you to take such a mighty puff? If you had taken it in and breathed it out slowly the way I did, instead of having been choked you would be experiencing the thrill now."

After Yu Huai tried it, the others followed. The room was quickly filled with smoke and coughing.

After busying himself for some time, Fang Yizhi turned around and saw Mao Xiang sitting motionlessly with a sneer on his face.

"Hey, Pijiang, don't you want to have a try?" he said.

Mao Xiang shook his head. "No, I won't. If you want to get me to try it, let's make a bet."

"Oh?"

"You said this stuff causes intoxication. Then, I would like to see who gets intoxicated first if the two of us have a competition, taking puffs in turn. Do you dare to bet on it?"

"That —"

"Do you dare or not?" Mao Xiang stood up and challenged him.

的荷包，又重重地摔到桌上。

“哎，辟疆！”张明弼着急地问，“你吸过这、这烟？”

冒襄摇摇头：“没有！”

“那、那可使不得！你没听密之说，此物简直就是毒药一类，不但能醉人，而且能置人于死呢！”张明弼说，一边拼命朝方以智使眼色。

“不错，”方以智犹豫地说，“此物并非善类，不赌也罢。”

“啊，原来你怕醉，怕死！”冒襄逼视着对方，狠狠地挖苦说。突然，他仰头狂笑起来，“可是我不怕！有什么可怕！国家到了这种地步，还有什么希望！说不定哪一天就大祸临头，大家都得完蛋！可是，偏有那等公卿大臣，皇亲国戚，还不知死活，拼命刮民财、买婊子，买不成就抢！无耻，卑鄙，不要脸！哼，还有那些个装得挺像的东林领袖，文坛祭酒，为着讨一顶劳什子乌纱，竟暗地里捣鬼，要替阮胡子翻案开脱，别以为我不知道！”

他又是笑又是叫，用力拍着桌子，泪水糊了一脸，把在场的人都吓怔住了。

只有张明弼十分着急，他显然想劝止，但又不知怎么劝才好。

“哎，辟疆，你说话可得有点证据才行，可不能由着性儿乱说呀！”他跺着脚说。

“什么，没证据？”冒襄瞪着红得可怕的眼睛，把手探进怀里，抽出来一封信，“啪”地甩在桌上。

“这就是证据，顾玉书从京里寄来的，钱牧斋致书周阁老，要替阮胡子开脱！”

“啊……？”

He took up his money bag excitedly and slung it heavily onto the table.

"Hey, Pijiang,"Zhang Mingbi said anxiously. "Have you ever smoked it before?"

Mao Xiang shook his head and said, "Nay."

"Then, then you shouldn't do it. Didn't you hear Mizhi say that this thing is like a poison? It not only intoxicates but also causes death," Zhang Mingbi said, winking at Fang Yizhi desperately.

"Aye," Fang Yizhi said hesitantly. "It's not something good. We'd better not bet."

Mao Xiang stared at Fang Yizhi menacingly and said sarcastically, "Oh? So you're also afraid of intoxication and death?" Suddenly, he raised his head and gave a wild laughter. "But I'm not afraid. What is so scary? The country has reached a point where there's no hope. A catastrophe will happen anytime soon, and everyone will be finished. Yet, some barons, ministers, relatives of the emperor, unaware of the doom, continue to rob the people and buy bitches—if money doesn't work they resort to kidnapping with no sense of shame and decency at all. Humph! Some sanctimonious East Wood leaders and important figures in the literary circles, in order to get a government position, even plot to reverse the case for Beardy Ruan. I know their conspiracy."

He laughed and yelled, pounding the table, his face streaked with tears, and everyone present was frightened and confused.

Zhang Mingbi was worried. He obviously wanted to persuade him to stop but didn't exactly know what to say.

"Hey, Pijiang, you need to speak from evidence. Pray don't make assertions," he said, stomping his feet.

"What? I have no evidence?" Opening wide his horribly red eyes, Mao Xiang put his hand in his robe, took out a letter, and slapped it onto the table.

"This is the evidence. Gu Yushu sent it from Beijing. It says Qian Muzhai wrote to Premier Zhou to ask for the exoneration of Beardy Ruan."

"What ...?"

这消息如此惊人，犹如晴天霹雳，在场的人全都震动了。大家瞧着那封信，有片刻工夫，谁也不敢去碰。

终于，方以智徐徐拿起信件，抽出来看了一遍：“嗯，顾玉书在周阁老的幕中掌管文书，他的话自然是靠得住的。”他神情严肃地皱着眉说：“辟疆，你打算如何处置？”

“我本想告知次尾、定生他们，他们都说要来虎丘，事先约得明明白白的，鬼知道为什么还不来！”

方以智还想问什么，就在这时，门外响起了杂沓的脚步声，郑元勋由一个小和尚领着，急急闯了进来。

“啊，原来兄等在这儿，叫小弟好找！”郑元勋气喘吁吁地擦着脑门上的汗，显然没有觉察到室内的气氛不对。他朝大家草草拱一拱手，立即转向冒襄：

“辟疆兄，定生让弟告知兄，他们不来虎丘了。他们现在要上徐氏东园去访钱牧斋，请兄去聚齐，次尾、朝宗他们都去。”

“啊，为何？他们为何不来？”余怀抢先问。

郑元勋的脸微微一红，躲闪地说：“这……定生只让弟把这话转知辟疆，别的，小弟可就不知道了。”

大家见他这样子，愈加感到意外，也有点紧张，都不约而同地把目光集中到冒襄身上。

冒襄气哼哼地把头一摆，说：“他们既然不来，我也不想去了！”他瞧了瞧方以智，“密之，要不，你替我把这信带给他们。”

方以智神情专注地皱着眉，似乎在沉思。终于，他点了点头。

The news like a bolt from the blue shocked everyone. They stared at the letter but no one dared to touch it.

Finally, Fang Yizhi slowly picked up the envelope, took the letter out and read it. "Um, since Gu Yushu is in charge of the documents in Premier Zhou's office, his words are reliable," he said, knitting his brows. "Pijiang, what do you plan to do with it?"

"I had thought to tell Ciwei and Dingsheng about it. They said they would come to Tiger Hill. We have agreed to meet here but they've not arrived yet," said Mao Xiang.

Just as Fang Yizhi was going to ask further, a clatter of footsteps sounded outside the door.

In came Zheng Yuanxun and a little monk.

Zheng Yuanxun said, out of breath, wiping the sweat from his forehead, obviously unaware that the atmosphere in the room was not right, "Ah, you're here! I've been looking for you for ages." Pressing his hands together hastily, he saluted the gathering and then immediately turned to Mao Xiang.

"Brother Pijiang, Dingsheng asked me to tell you that they are not coming to Tiger Hill. They're now going to the Xu's East Garden to visit Qian Muzhai. They want you to join them there. Ciwei and Chaozong are going too," he said.

"Ah, why? Why don't they come?" Yu Huai asked.

Zheng Yuanxun flushed and said evasively, "That—that I don't know. Dingsheng only asked me to pass this message to Pijiang, and I don't know anything else."

Seeing him like that, the small gathering of men were even more puzzled and a little nervous too, and they all focused their attention on Mao Xiang, who angrily tossed his head to one side and said, "Since they are not coming, I don't want to go either." He looked at Fang Yizhi and said, "Mizhi, would you please take this letter to them for me?"

Fang Yizhi pondered for a while, knitting his brows. Finally, he nodded his head.

# 上门算账

黄宗羲下决心立即找几社的人算账。他一连打听了好几处，问明几社的那伙头头，如今都齐集在千顷云阁上，就领着愁眉苦脸的梅朗中，越过剑池，绕到虎丘塔后面来。

虎丘的前坡比较平缓，后坡却相当陡峭。一道崖壁，平地拔起数丈，千顷云阁，就建在朝西的山崖上。从那里可以远眺天池山的苍然秀色。因为苏东坡有“云水丽千顷”的诗句，就拿来做了阁子的名称。那上面有一个茶社，是本山寺僧开设的，角落里一个小小的柜台，后面坐着一个老和尚，外加一名俗家汉子。炉上烹着上好的三泉水，十来张方桌，错落地摆开在楼面上，桌子上还供着时鲜花朵。平日游人不多时，来这里品茶凭眺，倒也颇为清雅。

当他们快步登上阁楼时，却意外地发现，上面的气氛异乎寻常。一大群儒生，少说也有一二十人，团团围住了当中的一张桌子，一个个神色庄重，静静地伫立着，似乎在等待什么。站在靠前的两个，却是头发蓬乱，衣衫不整，光着脑袋，连头巾也没戴，瞧模样就像跟人家厮打过似的。在桌子后面，坐着几社的两位元老——一位是身材高大的周立勋，他左手抓住椅子的扶手，右手的胳膊肘抵住桌面，揪着胡子在指头上慢慢地缠绕着，一言不发，脸色阴沉得可怕。另一位名叫彭宾，生得短小精悍，也是紧绷着脸，毫无表情。

黄宗羲闹不清发生了什么事，倒迟疑了一下。只见周立勋的目光冷冷地朝他一闪，立刻又回到原来的目标上去，显然不打算

## The Settling of an Account

Huang Zongxi made up his mind to settle accounts with the Jishers immediately. He went around asking their whereabouts and when he learned that the leaders of the Jishe were now all gathered in the Water and Clouds Pavilion, he immediately went along the Sword Pool to the back of the Tiger Hill Pagoda together with Mei Langzhong, who kept his brows knit all the way.

The front slope of Tiger Hill was relatively gentle, but the back slope was rather steep with a high cliff facing west and the Water and Clouds Pavilion was built on top of the cliff. From there, one could overlook the beautiful landscape of Sky Lake Mountain. The pavilion took its name from a line in a Su Dongpo's poem "a thousand acres of water and clouds." There was a tea stall in the pavilion run by the Tiger Hill Monastery, with a small counter in a corner and an old monk sitting behind it and a layman worker helping around. On the stove was a pot of water from the Three Springs. A dozen square tables were spaced out on the floor, and seasonal flowers were placed in the middle of the tables. It was a very quiet and relaxing place for one to sip tea and admire the scenery when there were few tourists.

When they hurried up to the pavilion, they were surprised to find that the vibe was not quite right. A large group of Confucian scholars, at least twenty, were gathered around a table in the middle, each with a solemn expression. They stood quietly, as if waiting for something. The two standing at the front obviously had just come out of a brawl with their hair tousled, clothes disheveled, and heads bare—with no headscarves. Behind the table sat two veterans of the Jishe: one was the tall and thickly built Zhou Lixun, whose left hand was holding the armrest of the chair and who was playing with his beard with the right hand—winding the hairs on his fingers with the elbow pressed against the tabletop. He was silent, with a somber expression on his face; the other one was named Peng Bin, short and smart, also wearing a cheerless expression.

Having no idea what was going on, Huang Zongxi stopped in

搭理；其余的人还有好几个是认识的，也全都对他不瞅不睬。黄宗羲不由得生气起来。“我还没开口，你们倒先摆出这副嘴脸，却想吓唬谁！”他想，挺一挺脖子，正要发问，忽然，“砰”的一响，周立勋一巴掌击在桌子上。

“来而不往非礼也！好，找他们去！”

那群士子显然就等着这么一句，顿时骚动起来，好几个高声在叫：

“对，找他们算账去！”

“非要他们赔礼认错不可！”

“给他们点厉害，看下次还敢不！”

“要他们把侯朝宗那坏小子交出来！”

“对，侯朝宗，一定要交出侯朝宗！”

黄宗羲吃了一惊：朝宗？为什么要找朝宗？莫非朝宗他们已经先动手了？他心里一急，猛地大叫：

“站住，别走！”

已经移动脚步的人群又站住了，纷纷回过头，疑惑地打量着这两位不速之客。

“请问列位，意欲何往？”黄宗羲向前跨出一步，紧盯着周立勋问。

后者“哼”了一声，却不回答。

黄宗羲的眼睛睁圆了，一句激烈的话也涌到了嘴边。

“哎，太冲，是这么回事！”一个尖尖的嗓音慌忙插了进来，接着，人丛中走出一个高颧骨、尖下颏的中年儒生。黄宗羲认得，这是常熟人顾苓。从前黄宗羲在钱谦益家读书时，见他常来走动，而且知道他颇受钱谦益信用。按说此人并不属于几社一派，不知

bewilderment. Zhou Lixun cast him a cold glance and immediately looked away, obviously not intending to greet him. A few others were also his acquaintances but they ignored him too. He became angry. "You put up such faces before I say anything. Do you think you can scare me?" he thought. As he straightened up his neck to ask them, smack, suddenly Zhou Lixun's hand landed on the tabletop.

"Tit for tat. Let's go find them."

The group of scholars, who had been obviously waiting for this command, suddenly became animated, and some of them shouted loudly:

"Aye, let's go and settle the account with them."

"They must apologize and pay for what they've done."

"Teach them a lesson and they'll behave."

"Ask them to surrender Hou Chaozong the bad guy."

"Aye, aye, Hou Chaozong, they must surrender Hou Chaozong."

Huang Zongxi was taken aback. Chaozong? Why are they after Chaozong? Has Chaozong already started to act? He hurriedly shouted:

"Stop, don't go!"

The moving crowd stopped and turned their heads one after another to look at the two uninvited guests suspiciously.

Huang Zongxi took a step forward and said, staring at Zhou Lixun, "Excuse me, sirs! May I know where you're going?"

The latter said "Humph!" but gave no reply.

Huang Zongxi's eyes opened wide, and words of anger crept to his lips.

"Hey, Taichong, let me explain," a high-pitched voice hurriedly cut in, followed by the appearance from the crowd of a middle-aged scholar with high cheekbones and a sharp chin. Huang Zongxi recognized him as Gu Ling from Changshu.

Huang Zongxi, who had studied with Qian Qianyi and seen Gu Ling quite often at Qian Qianyi's residence, knew that Gu Ling was deeply trusted by Qian Qianyi and supposedly was not a member of the Jishe. Therefore, he was puzzled why the man was here mixing

为什么此刻却同他们混在一起。

“太冲兄，是这么回事——”顾苓重复地说，显得有点迫不及待。然而，站在他旁边的一位几社的年轻头头，名叫赵人孩的，一扬袖子，把他给拦住了。

“太冲，此事与你无关。”赵人孩淡淡地说，扁圆的脸上现出傲慢的神情，“你——不知道也罢。”

“什么，与我无关？”黄宗羲冷笑一声，“你们——”

“听我说啊！”赵人孩不慌不忙地整理着袖子，语调里透着怜悯，“本来么，告诉兄也无妨，只是，兄知道了并无好处……”

“啊，为什么？”

赵人孩微微叹息：“这件事说出来，只怕会令兄失望，令兄为难的哟！”

“不，你说，你说！”黄宗羲被对方猫儿玩弄老鼠般的态度激怒了，一张小脸涨得通红。

“那么，兄必定要知道？”赵人孩凝视着他，眼神渐渐变得冷峻起来，“你不怕把自己置于可悲、可笑之境地——当着这许多社友的面？”

“啊？”

赵人孩把声音放得更低，但仍然让周围的人听得清楚：“你——也不怕吴次尾、陈定生二位那些个不可告人的卑污之行公之于众？”

黄宗羲心中一凛：“什么？次尾、定生的卑污之行？他、他们会有什么卑污之行？”他惊疑地想，不由得回头望了一眼，却发现被胁逼而来的梅朗中也在神色慌张地望着他。

“怎么样，不想知道了吧？啊！”赵人孩得意地问，扬声大笑起来。

“不，”黄宗羲固执地说，“我要知道！”

赵人孩把脸一沉：“哼，你不配！”他猛地转过身去，一摆头，

with the Jishers at the moment.

"Brother Taichong, let me explain—" Gu Ling repeated with a little eagerness. However, a young leader of the Jishe named Zhao Renhai, who was standing next to him, flapped his sleeve and stopped him.

"Taichong, this matter has nothing to do with you," Zhao Renhai said calmly, with an arrogant look on his oval face. "You'd better not know it."

"What? It has nothing to do with me?" Huang Zongxi sneered. "You—"

"Let me finish," Zhao Renhai tidied his sleeves calmly and said compassionately. "In fact, there's no harm to tell you, but there's no good for you either ..."

"Oh, why?"

Zhao Renhai sighed slightly. "If you knew it, you would be disappointed and embarrassed."

"No, I wouldn't. Pray say it. Say it." Huang Zongxi was irritated by what he sensed as a cat teasing a mouse and his face flushed.

"So, you really want to know?" Zhao Renhai looked at him fixedly, his eyes gradually becoming stern. "Aren't you afraid to put yourself in a sad and ridiculous situation—in front of so many Fushe friends here?"

"What?"

Zhao Renhai lowered his voice, but still it was loud enough for everyone to hear. "Are you not afraid that the dirty deeds of Wu Ciwei and Chen Dingsheng be made public?"

Huang Zongxi gave a start. "What? The dirty deeds of Ciwei and Dingsheng? What kind of dirty deeds can they have?" He puzzled and instinctively looked back, only to find that Mei Langzhong, who had come with him under coercion, was looking at him in panic.

"So, do you still want to know it, huh?" Zhao Renhai asked triumphantly, and laughed out loud.

"Yes, I do," Huang Zongxi said stubbornly. "I do want to know."

Zhao Renhai's face sank. "Huh, you don't deserve to know."

"列位社兄，走！"等大家开始移动脚步的时候，他又回过头，朝黄宗羲鄙夷地冷笑一声，然后向楼梯扬长走去。

就在这个时候，令人吃惊的事情发生了。只见黄宗羲突然蹦起来，冲到赵人孩背后，粗暴地把他的身子扳过来，用双手抓住他的衣襟。

"告诉我，我要你告诉我！"他狂怒地叫，使劲摇撼着对方。他的脸歪扭着，两眼发出吓人的光芒。在秦淮河畔受到徐青君侮辱时曾经显示过的那种拼命的劲头儿，又一次在他身上显现出来。

在场的人全都惊呆了。赵人孩更是狼狈不堪，他试图反抗，可是黄宗羲自幼练过拳棒的双臂是那样强健有力，使他根本无法挣脱，只能惊恐地叫："啊，你做什么？做什么？"

"太冲兄，不要无礼！"周立勋终于说话了，语气是烦躁的。他朝顾苓做了个手势，"云美兄，你告诉他吧！"

这时，梅朗中同其他几个几社的士子已经清醒过来。他们连忙拥上去，又是拉又是劝，好容易才把赵人孩解救下来。只见他已经吓得面色发白，浑身直打哆嗦。黄宗羲却仍旧红着脸，激怒地嚷："你说，我要你说！"

"哎，太冲，我跟你说！"顾苓慌忙走上前来，"是这么回事，方才，这两位社兄——"他指了指那两个衣冠不整的儒生，"在后山走，迎面碰见侯朝宗领着一帮人，起初也没怎么在意，后来见他们指手画脚，留神一听，原来是在骂人，什么'狗杂种'啦，'王八蛋'啦，还一个劲地朝地上吐唾沫。两位社兄不禁有气，问他为何如此。谁知他们反而骂得更凶，连几社的几位老学长，还有杜老、夏老，全给骂了进去。哎，其辞之荒谬难听，实有不

He turned around abruptly, shaking his head. "Brothers, let's go." When everyone started to move, he turned around and sneered contemptuously at Huang Zongxi, and then walked towards the stairs.

At this moment, something shocking happened. Huang Zongxi suddenly jumped up, rushed to the back of Zhao Renhai, roughly turned him over, and grabbed the front of his robe with both hands.

"You must tell me. I want you to tell me." He yelled furiously, shaking the man hard, his face distorted and his eyes emitting a scary light. The fury he had shown when he had been humiliated by Xu Qingjun on the bank of the Qinhuai River once again came back to him.

Everyone present was stunned. Zhao Renhai was in a sorrowful state. He tried to put up resistance, but the arms of Huang Zongxi, who had practiced martial arts in his early years, were so strong that he couldn't break free at all, so he could only scream in horror, "Oh, my, what are you doing? What are you doing?"

"Brother Taichong, don't be rude." Zhou Lixun finally spoke in an irritated tone. He gestured to Gu Ling and said, "Brother Yunmei, tell him."

By now, Mei Langzhong and a few Jishers had regained their consciousness. They rushed to the two men, intervened and pulled them apart. Zhao Renhai was finally rescued. His face was pale with fright and his whole being was trembling. "Say it. I want you to say it," said Huang Zongxi, still blushing and unappeased.

"Alright. I'll tell you." Gu Ling hurriedly stepped forward. "A moment ago," he said, pointing to the two disheveled scholars. "When I was walking on the back of the hill, I met Hou Chaozong and a bunch of other men. I didn't pay much attention to them at first, but later seeing them talking and gesticulating. I turned my ear to them. It turned out that they were cursing, using words like 'a son of a bitch' and 'bastard' while spitting on the ground. Two fellow Fushers felt annoyed and asked them why they were like that. Unexpectedly, they cursed even more fiercely and even started to damn the elders in the Jishe, and the respectable Mr. Du and Mr. Xia as well. They used such

便复述者！总之，逼得两位社兄忍无可忍，上前去同他论理。他们仗着人多势众，一齐按住两位社兄，把头巾、直裰都剥了去。是小弟同几位社友路见不平，好歹将他们搭救下来，否则，还不知道会遭到何等折辱哩！”

顾苓指手画脚，绘声绘色，一口气地说下来，一边摇着脑袋，现出很不以为然的样子。

“所以、所以列位……如今要去找朝宗问罪？”梅朗中讷讷地问。显然，连他也觉得这件事未免做得太过分，以至很难替侯方域辩护。

“不错！”顾苓停止了摇头，义形于色地说，“朝宗如此胡闹，休说松江社友气愤填膺，便是小弟见了，也难以心服！”说完，却不无担心地溜了黄宗羲一眼。

“这……”梅朗中搔搔后脑勺，瞅着那两个衣冠不整的受辱者，“不知列位打算如何了结此事？”

“起码——”大约是看见黄宗羲低头不语，顾苓神气起来，“要他认错赔礼，偿还损失。还要他立下保状，声明以后永不重犯！”他回头问周立勋和彭宾，“勋老、燕老，是这样么？”

“可是，这是你们自己惹出来的！”黄宗羲蓦地抬起头，爆发地说，“你们——为什么要替阮胡子翻案？为什么？你说！”他大声地问，眼睛里忽然迸出了泪水，“你们凭什么敢这么干？莫非你们不知道阮胡子是什么人？莫非你们忘了《留都防乱公揭》？忘了阉党乱政的奇祸惨变？也忘了东林列位先贤的一腔热血为何而洒？你们到底还算不算复社，算不算君子？！”

大家眼见风波平息，正打算动身下楼，冷不防他又莫名其妙

horrible language that repeating it is embarrasing. The two fellow Fushers couldn't bear it and went forward to argue with them. With the advantage of numbers, they—they held the two fellow Fushers to the ground and stripped them of their headscarves and robes. If I and a few other fellow Fushers hadn't intervened, the consequence would have been unthinkable."

Gu Ling said in one breath, gesticulating and shaking his head in disgust.

"Therefore, dear friends, that's—that's why you're going to take on Chaozong?" Mei Langzhong asked stammeringly. Obviously, even he felt it difficult to defend Hou Fangyu.

"That's right," Gu Ling stopped shaking his head, and said uprightly. "Chaozong's mischief not only infuriated the fellow Fushers in Songjiang, but also disquieted me." Having said that, he nonetheless gave Huang Zongxi a concerned look.

"Then—" Mei Langzhong scratched the back of his head and looked at the two disheveled victims. "What are you going to do with it?"

"At least—" Seeing Huang Zongxi drooping his head in silence, Gu Ling became animated. "He must apologize and pay for the harm and damage, and he must write a guarantee that he'll never do it again in the future." He turned around and asked Zhou Lixun and Peng Bin, "Mr. Zhou and Mr. Peng, is that right?"

"But, you chaps are the cause of the problem!" Huang Zongxi suddenly lifted his head and burst out. "Why do you try to reverse the case for Beardy Ruan? Why? Tell me," He said in a loud voice, tears coming out of his eyes. "How dare you? Don't you know what kind of man Beardy Ruan is? Have you forgotten the 'Public Denunciation of a Treasonist in the Legacy Capital'? Have you forgotten the atrocities of the eunuch's party? Have you forgotten for what the East Wood martyrs have shed their blood? Are you still members of the Fushe? Are you still good men with morals?"

A moment ago, seeing that the storm had subsided, everyone was about to go downstairs and leave the pavilion. Now hearing this

地大吵大嚷起来，都不禁愕然止步，面面相觑。

“太冲，你是说谁要替阮圆海翻案？”周立勋皱起眉毛问。

“你们，就是你们！”黄宗羲一把擦去流到颊上来的眼泪，咬牙切齿地说，“你们为着把持社局，排除异己，不惜借阮胡子的事挑动纷争，以为别人不知道？”

周立勋眨眨眼睛，似乎没听明白他的话。站在旁边的彭宾却显然机灵得多，他“呵呵”地笑起来：“太冲兄，这阮胡子该不该宽宥，可当别论。不过，阁下说此事乃我几社挑起，却是大错特错了！”

这时赵人孩已经从刚才那一阵子狼狈惊恐中恢复过来，他蓦地扯着嗓子嚷叫：

“对，告诉他！把吴次尾、陈定生那档子臭事给他抖明白！”

“竹翁，请你来说吧！”彭宾轻快地向着人丛背后招呼说。

直到这时，人们才发现除顾苓之外，在他们背后，原来还站着另一个不是几社的人。而当这位衣饰讲究、有着一个方形脑袋和一双小眼睛的老头儿不慌不忙地走到前面来时，黄宗羲不禁一怔，因为他忽然认出，这个一直躲在人丛中不露面的人，竟然是钱谦益的妻舅陈在竹。“啊，他到这儿来做什么？谁让他来的？”黄宗羲迷惑地紧盯着，又回头望一眼站在旁边的顾苓，忽然产生了一种不祥的预感，仿佛有什么可怕的事情将要发生似的。

陈在竹也不说废话，只朝他点点头，清一清喉咙，就一本正经地说起来。据他说，早在周延儒复出那阵子，阮大铖就找到吴应箕和陈贞慧二人，哭求宽恕。当时，吴、陈二人见他一片至诚，已是首肯，随后便到扬州去同郑元勋商量。郑元勋知道复社领袖

sudden explosion of Huang Zongxi, they automatically stopped and looked at each other.

"Taichong, who are trying to reverse the case for Ruan Yuanhai?" Zhou Lixun asked, knitting his brows.

"You chaps," said Huang Zongxi, gritting his teeth and wiping the tears that flowed down his cheeks. "In order to get rid of opposition and take control of the Fushe you're stirring up disputes by bringing up the Ruan issue. You think we don't know it?"

Zhou Lixun blinked, as if he didn't understand what Huang Zongxi was saying. Peng Bin, who was standing next to Lixun and who was obviously more quick-witted, laughed and said, "Brother Taichong, whether Beardy Ruan should be pardoned or not is a different matter. One thing is for sure: your accusation of the Jishe is quite mistaken."

At this moment, Zhao Renhai, who had recovered from the panic yelled suddenly, "That's right. Tell him. Tell him all about the dirty deeds of Wu Ciwei and Chen Dingsheng."

"Zaizhu, pray tell him," said Peng Bin, beckoning to a man in the back of the crowd.

It turned out that apart from Gu Ling there was another man standing behind them, who was not a member of the Jishe. When the well-dressed old man with a square head and small eyes unhurriedly stepped forward, Huang Zongxi was surprised to see it was Chen Zaizhu, brother of Qian Qianyi's wife. "Ah? What is he doing here? Who asked him to come?" Huang Zongxi stared at him in puzzlement, then looked back at Gu Ling, who was standing next to him, and suddenly had a premonition that something terrible was about to happen.

Without wasting of time, Chen Zaizhu nodded his head, cleared his throat, and told the story in a serious tone. According to him, as early as when Zhou Yanru was reinstated to office, Ruan Dacheng found Wu Yingji and Chen Zhenhui and begged for forgiveness. Seeing his sincerity, Wu Yingji and Chen Zhenhui agreed and then went to Yangzhou to discuss the matter with Zheng Yuanxun. Zheng

张溥生前已有此意，也觉人才难得，便同意了。其后又普遍征求社内外的意见，绝大多数人都表示赞成。谁知吴、陈二人另有打算，想乘机敲诈阮大铖，开口就是一万两银子。阮大铖因为周延儒复出时，已送了一万两，此时再拿不出，请求削减些。吴、陈二人见他不爽快，顿时就翻了脸，要将这事作罢。是郑元勋看不过眼，好意相劝。吴、陈二人恼羞成怒，索性一不做，二不休，把这赃反栽在郑元勋身上；又恨几社平日不买他们的账，干脆连几社也牵连进来……末了，陈在竹摇晃着脑袋，感慨系之地说："谁想得到，堂堂吴次尾、陈定生为了一万两银子，竟会做出这种事！据说，如今他们在那里虚张声势，要同超宗、几社斯拼，用意仍是想逼阮圆海就范罢了！"

这个消息实在太惊人，黄宗羲和梅朗中固然听得目瞪口呆，在场的那些几社士子，更是一片哗然：

"好哇，原来如此！"

"真亏他们平日装得挺像！"

"啊哈，原来是个伪君子！"

"对，伪君子，伪君子！"

人们大声地叫嚷着，讥笑着，咒骂着，闹哄哄地吵成一片。

陈在竹却不动声色。他瞅了瞅黄宗羲，见他仰着脸，眼睛睁得老大，对于周围的喧闹仿佛充耳不闻，就凑上去，叹了一口气，同情地低声说："太冲，这事牧老也知道了，所以……"

"啊，不！"黄宗羲像给火烫了一下似的，跳开去，"我什

Yuanxun also agreed, knowing that Zhang Pu, the late leader of the Fushe, had had this intention before his death and thinking that the nation was desperately in need of talent. Afterwards, they solicited opinions from inside and outside the Fushe, and the vast majority of scholars agreed too. Wu Yingji and Chen Zhenhui turned out to have other motives. They wanted to take the opportunity to blackmail Ruan Dacheng and asked for ten thousand taels of silver. Ruan Dacheng had already given away ten thousand taels when Zhou Yanru was reinstated to office and was not able to give them that much, so he asked for a reduction. Not satisfied with Ruan's reaction, Wu Yingji and Chen Zhenhui suddenly turned their backs on him and threatened not to help. Zheng Yuanxun, out of a sense of justice, intervened. Wu Yingji and Chen Zhenhui, exasperated, spread the rumor that Zheng Yuanxun blackmailed Ruan Dacheng. Since they hated the Jishe for never taking them seriously, they put the Jishe in the story as well ... Finally, Chen Zaizhu sighed, shaking his head, "Who would think that Wu Ciwei and Chen Dingsheng would do such a thing for ten thousand taels of silver? It's said that their talk of fighting Chaozong and the Jishe now is a mere bluff with the intention to make Ruan Yuanhai yield to their demand."

The revelation was so shocking that Huang Zongxi and Mei Langzhong were dumbfounded upon hearing it, and that it caused an uproar among the Jishers present.

"Unbelievable!"

"They don't look what they are."

"Aha, what hypocrites!"

"That's the word, hypocrites, right, hypocrites!"

The men yelled, sneered, and cursed.

Chen Zaizhu was calm. He glanced at Huang Zongxi, who was completely deaf to the noise around with wide open eyes and a blank expression, and leaned forward, sighed, and whispered sympathetically, "Taichong, Elder Mu also knows about this, so ..."

"No way!" Huang Zongxi jumped away as if burnt by fire.

么都不相信，不！”他直着脖子大叫，奔到周立勋和彭宾跟前，气急败坏地指着他们，“分明是你们要替阮胡子翻案！是你们，你们赖不掉！”他竭尽全力地喊，为的是压倒周围的一片使他感到气愤、屈辱和恐惧的喧嚣。

“是你们！”他又大叫一声，却意外地发现，他的声音变得那样洪亮、清楚，而且孤单。原来，周围的喧闹在一刹那间全都消失得无影无踪了。

他迷惑地回过头去。顿时，他也变成了哑子。不知什么时候，吴应箕领着张自烈、侯方域，还有方以智已经来到了阁楼上。

“太冲，你说错了，不是他们。”吴应箕望着他，平静地说。

## 揭破阴私

柳如是站在起居室的门前，隔着帘子，心烦意乱地朝外面张望。她的眼皮儿因为不安而频频跳动，柳叶样的长眉也皱得越来越紧。当她一次又一次屏住气，尽量支起耳朵，却仍然听不到楠木厅那边的任何动静，就不由得焦躁起来了。

谁能料到会发生这种事——就在钱谦益向陈在竹、钱养先二人布置好一切，把他们打发走了之后，周镳、周钟兄弟，还有陈贞慧和顾杲突然登门拜访。他们为什么而来？何以不迟不早，偏挑这么个节骨眼来？这些，柳如是还不太清楚。不过，凭着直觉，她立即预感到有点不祥。特别是随后钱谦益派人来传话，要她立即通知负责联络的钱曾，把陈在竹、钱养先二人截回来，暂且按兵不动。柳如是就更认定自己的担心绝不是多余的了。

不过，尽管如此，柳如是却没有按照老头儿的吩咐去办。虽

"I don't believe it at all. It's not true." He yelled with his neck straight, rushed to Zhou Lixun and Peng Bin, and pointed at them exasperatedly. "It's clear and unmistakable that it's you chaps who are going to reverse the case for Beardy Ruan. It's you, and you can't deny it," he shouted with all his might to overwhelm the noise around him that made him feel angry, humiliated, and terrified.

"It's you!" he yelled again. To his own amazement, his voice became loud, clear, and distinct. It was because that all the noise around him had suddenly disappeared.

When he puzzledly turned around, he became silent too. Wu Yingji had arrived at the pavilion with Zhang Zilie, Hou Fangyu, and Fang Yizhi.

"Taichong," Wu Yingji looked at him and said placidly. "You're wrong. It's not them."

## A Conspirator Cornered

Standing at the door of the drawing room, Liu Rushi looked out through the curtain. Her eyes twitched with anxiety, and her slender brows knitted more and more tightly together. Again and again she put up her ear and held her breath, but there was still no sound from the Nanmu Hall. She began to worry.

It was not something she had expected. Just after Qian Qianyi arranged everything with Chen Zaizhu and Qian Yangxian and sent them away, the Zhou Brothers—Zhou Biao and Zhou Zhong—came to visit, together with Chen Zhenhui and Gu Gao. Why are they here? Why at such a critical juncture, not sooner or later? Liu Rushi had no idea. By instinct, she immediately felt it a little ominous. Especially when a short while later Qian Qianyi sent word that she should immediately dispatch Qian Zeng to stop Chen Zaizhu and Qian Yangxian on their way and bring them back—they'd better not do anything for the time being—Liu Rushi was even more convinced that her worries were by no means unnecessary.

Yet Liu Rushi didn't follow the old man's instructions. Although she knew that Qian Zeng was waiting in the Yifeng Hall, she decided

然她明知钱曾正守候在揖峰轩内，但还是决定再等一等，看一看。她深知这一次图谋的成败，不仅关系到老头儿能否复出起用，而且也关系到自己后半辈子的荣华富贵。机不可失，时不再来。

地毯上的帘影一点一点地向门外移去，柳如是的忧虑也越来越深。她已经毫不怀疑周镳等人此来，必然与阮大铖的事有关；她只是考虑他们对这件事到底知道了多少，是否全都摸了底去？现在柳如是最担心的是钱谦益胆子太小，被人一吓唬就慌了神。这半年来，她已经摸透了老头儿的脾性，每做一件事，总是瞻前顾后，畏首畏尾，明明心里这么想，做出来却往往是另一回事。这也皆因他平日名声太大，顾虑便不能不多。如果这一次也轻率罢手，让花了许多银子、心血经营的这件事功亏一篑，那就太不值得了。

终于，柳如是觉得，应当设法干预一下楠木厅那边的谈话，给钱谦益打打气，至少也应当提醒他注意。只是，由谁去做这件事呢？自己固然不便抛头露面，但陈在竹和钱养先又上虎丘去了，唯一的就剩下守在揖峰轩里的钱曾。虽说柳如是对于这位“侄孙”一向没有好感，但这会儿却计较不了许多。“嗯，他既是老头儿的学生，又是复社中人，瞧他那副狠巴巴、阴沉沉的嘴脸，肚子里的鬼点子想必不少；何况是个年轻后辈，捅点娄子也不要紧，由他去唱这出戏，倒合适不过。”柳如是沉吟一下，回头吩咐红情到揖峰轩去，把钱曾请过来。然后，她就隔着帘子，用一种信赖的，甚至是亲切的态度同他商量起来……

当钱曾离开东厢的起居室，来到楠木厅的院门时，他受到了一点阻拦，因为钱谦益吩咐李宝守在门外，不准放人进来。可是钱曾用那双能把人看得发毛的眼睛朝李宝一瞪，鼻子里轻蔑地

to wait for a while. She knew that the attempt was not only related to whether the old man could be reinstated to office but also to her own well-being for the rest of her life. It was a once-in-a-lifetime opportunity.

As the shadow of the curtain on the carpet slowly moved outside, Liu Rushi became more and more worried. She was certain that Zhou Biao's visit had something to do with the Ruan Dacheng issue. She wanted to know how much they had already learned from Qian Qianyi. Have they been told everything? She was worried that her old man, who was timid by nature, would tell them everything in a panic when intimidated. Over the past six months, she had known the old man thoroughly. In everything he did, he looked forward and backward, caught between head and tail. When he was thinking one thing, the result was another. After all, he was too famous and he should be cautious. Should he give up again, all the money spent and all the efforts made would be in vain.

At long last, Liu Rushi decided that she should intervene in the conversation in the Nanmu Hall to spirit him up or at least put him on alert. The problem is, who should she send to do it? As a concubine, it was not befitting for her to go. Chen Zaizhu and Qian Yangxian had gone to Tiger Hill. The only person she could think of was Qian Zeng, who was in the Yifeng Hall. Though she had never liked that "grandnephew" she had no choice at the moment. "Well, he's both a pupil of the old man and a member of the Fushe. Look at his ruthless, gloomy face, there must be a host of bad ideas in his mind; besides, he's young and will be excused if he says or does anything wrong. It's fitting to send him over." Liu Rushi pondered for a moment, then turned around and ordered Hongqing to go to the Yifeng Hall and invite Qian Zeng over. Then, from behind the curtain, she discussed the matter with him in an intimate and confiding manner.

When Qian Zeng left the drawing room of the East Wing and came to the door of the Nanmu Hall, he was stopped by Li Bao, who had been told by Qian Qianyi not to let anyone in. Qian Zeng stared at Li Bao with his menacing eyes and snorted contemptuously. Li Bao

“哼”了一声，就把李宝吓退了。他登上厅堂的台阶，听见顾杲的声音在说：

“君子、小人不两立！老伯坚谓并无此事，最好！唯是适才听老伯言语之意，似乎深以所谓‘门户交争’为忧，小侄却不敢苟同！”

钱谦益沉默着，似乎在等待对方说下去。忽然瞧见钱曾闯进来，他的脸上露出惊愕、迷惑和生气的神情。

钱曾不理会老师的目光，他双手交拱在胸前，昂然地说：“闻知周老前辈和列位社兄光临，特来拜望！”

客人们全都认识钱曾，虽然对他的突然出现感到意外，但也只好停止谈话，一齐起身答礼。

钱曾大步走向周镳，朝他深深一揖。周镳料想他照例要行跪见之礼，连忙说：“贤契请起，不必多礼！”一边笑吟吟地弯腰伸出手，准备搀扶。

谁知钱曾立刻直起腰来，居高临下地瞧着周镳，鼻孔里轻蔑地一笑，转身离开了他，走到钱谦益跟前，深深一揖，然后撩起衣裾，后退一步，恭恭敬敬地双膝跪倒，大声说：“弟子曾——参见夫子！”

周镳显然没有防备这一招，他目瞪口呆地僵在那里，好一会儿才讪讪地直起身来，一张瘦脸早已气得通红。

钱曾若无其事地站起来之后，转过身，眯缝着眼睛，把向他怒目而视的客人们挨个儿审视了一遍，然后走向朝东的一排椅子，挨着顾杲坐了下来。

在来客当中，要数周钟顶不喜欢钱曾。看见他闯进来，周钟已经老大不乐意。随后又见他单单向周镳行礼，虽然是存心作弄，

stepped back fearfully. Qian Zeng ascended the steps of the hall and heard Gu Gao's voice saying:

"Good men and bad men are never reconciled. Since you're certain there's no such a thing, I'm relieved. Just now, you said you're deeply worried about the struggles between the factions. I don't think it's necessary."

Qian Qianyi was silent, as if waiting for the other man to continue. When he suddenly saw Qian Zeng rush in, he was shocked, stunned and then angry.

Qian Zeng ignored his teacher's gaze. Folding his hands on his chest he said brazenly, "Dear Mr. Zhou and Fushe brothers, I hear you're here and can't wait to see you."

The guests all knew Qian Zeng. Although they felt his abrupt appearance intrusive, they had to stop the conversation and got up to greet him.

Qian Zeng strode towards Zhou Biao and gave him a deep bow. Thinking he was going to kneel down to kowtow as was the custom, Zhou Biao said, "Please get up, son. No need for ceremonies." He smilingly bent over and stretched out his hand, ready to help Qian Zeng up.

However, Qian Zeng immediately straightened up, looked at Zhou Biao condescendingly and smiled with a snort before he turned and left him, walked up to Qian Qianyi, made a deep bow, then lifted the train of his robe, took one step back, respectfully knelt down on both knees and said loudly, "My dear teacher, accept my kowtowing."

Zhou Biao obviously was caught off guard. He froze there dumbfounded, and it took him a long while to straighten up in embarrassment, his skinny face flushing with anger.

As if nothing had happened, Qian Zeng stood up, turned around, and squinting his eyes, scrutinized one by one the guests glaring at him, then walked to the row of chairs on the east side and sat down next to Gu Gao.

Zhou Zhong disliked Qian Zeng in the superlative degree. Having been displeased by Qian Zeng's intrusion, Zhou Zhong was now even

但是对自己却干脆毫不理睬，仿佛没有瞧见一般，周钟心中更为恼火。只是碍着钱谦益的面子，不便当场发作。按他的脾气，本应立即拂袖而出，但考虑到刚才追问了钱谦益半天，始终问不出个结果，所以只好忍着一口气，朝钱谦益拱手说道：

“牧老，我们还是接着谈，如何？”

钱谦益没有立即回答。他正在琢磨着钱曾突然闯席的用意。他明白钱曾决不会无故而来，很可能是受了柳如是的指派，来协助自己对付这批不速之客的。事实上，刚才自己猝不及防，被对方一下子提出阮大铖的事情，弄得慌了神，差点儿露出马脚。后来见他们并无多少根据，也未提及郑元勋，才定下心来，一口否认有这么回事。可是对方仍旧纠缠不休，一个劲儿寻根问底，逼得自己左右躲闪，正有点儿招架不住。钱曾这么一闯，确实替自己暂时解了围，缓了一口气。此刻，必须抓住这个机会，赶快脱身，否则拖下去，再陷重围就难办了……这样想定之后，他就站起来，拱着手说：

“列位若为阮圆海的传闻而来，那么谦益所知者已全部奉告。所谓谦益主谋云云，纯属无稽之谈。言尽于此，未知列位可以放心否？”

“这——不瞒牧老说，实在是超宗兄如此这般告知弟等，是以未敢放心哩！”周钟突然说道。本来，为着保护郑元勋，他们一直避免说出消息的来源。但是看见钱谦益分明想溜，周钟心里一急，便顾不得许多了。

这一招果然见效，钱谦益的身子微微一震，脸刷地红了。他望了周钟一眼，立刻又移开视线。

“嗯，你说什么？”他哑着嗓子问。

“此事是郑超宗亲口说的！”周钟紧盯着钱谦益，又重复了一遍。

more annoyed to see the young man salute Zhou Biao only, as if he were non-existent. However, in front of Qian Qianyi he had to hold off his anger. He was a man with a temper. Normally, in a situation like this, he would have walked away, but since he hadn't obtained any useful information from Qian Qianyi yet, he had to hold on to his temper.

"Elder Mu, can we go on?" he asked.

Qian Qianyi didn't immediately answer. He was thinking about Qian Zeng's intention, knowing that the grandnephew had come not without a reason—probably he was sent over by Liu Rushi to deal with the uninvited guests. In fact, Qian Qianyi was caught off guard a moment ago by their sudden mention of the Ruan Dacheng issue and almost let the cat out of the bag in a fluster. Since they didn't mentioned Zheng Yuanxun and apparently didn't know much about it, he denied it altogether. However, the visitors continued to press him with more questions, making it difficult for him to evade. Qian Zeng's intrusion did set him free temporarily and gave him some respite. He had to take this opportunity to escape now, or it would be more difficult to escape should he fall under siege again ... Thus thinking, he stood up, bowed, and said:

"My friends, if you're here because of the Ruan Yuanhai rumor, you have everything I know. That I'm the mastermind of the idea is pure nonsense. Now I've told you everything I know, you can set your minds at rest."

"No, we can't. Honestly speaking, we heard it from Brother Chaozong," Zhou Zhong said. They had closely guarded their source of information until now to protect Zheng Yuanxun, but seeing Qian Qianyi was going to get away, Zhou Zhong had to say it as a last resort.

It really worked. Qian Qianyi's body shook slightly and his face flushed. He glanced at Zhou Zhong and immediately looked away.

"Why, what did you say?" he asked in a husky voice.

Zhou Zhong stared at Qian Qianyi and repeated, "Zheng Chaozong said it himself."

钱谦益的脸色开始变成灰白，身体也摇晃起来。他用力抓住椅靠，背过身去，半晌，才嘟嘟哝哝地说：“简直……乱……七八糟！”

客人们互相交换了一个郑重的眼色。陈贞慧很快地站起身，说道：

“牧老……”

然而，就在这时候，朝东一排椅子的末座上，突然响起一阵尖利的笑声。那笑声是如此难听、刺耳，大家倏然回过头去，只见钱曾坐在那里。他已经不笑了。可是那尖锐的、金属般的音响还在人们耳边嗡嗡了好一会儿才消失。

“诸位今日来此，就是为的这件事么？”钱曾抬头望着屋梁，大大咧咧地问。见客人们都沉默着，没有回答，他又说：

“数百里的奔走驰驱，不惮烦的明察暗访，诸君也可谓栖栖遑遑，用心良苦了。只是，如许心思，却未必用得妥当啊！”

“噢，遵王兄如此相责，小弟鲁钝，不识其义，倒要领教！”陈贞慧客气地拱着手问。他看见刚才周钟一点出消息的来源，钱谦益立即慌了手脚，心里知道已经打中了要害。他再不怕钱某人逃到天上去。同时，又发现钱曾突然闯进来，与这件事显然有关；而且这个阴阳怪气的家伙，言语之间似乎并不打算否认实有此事，于是陈贞慧立即决定抓住他作为突破口，彻底挫败对方的阴谋。

这样一种形势，钱谦益同样觉察到了。刚才钱曾一开口，说出那句无异于不打自招的话，钱谦益心里就暗暗叫苦。按照他冷静下来后的想法，这件事当时并无外人在场，而且从派钱养先到扬州去的时候起，一直注意不留下任何物证。他大可以矢口否认，甚至可以倒打一耙，说郑元勋出于想当复社领袖的野心，企图拉自己做靠山，自己没有答允，郑元勋怀恨在心，所以造谣报复。

Qian Qianyi's face began to pale, and his body trembled. He put his hand on the back of the chair and turned his back to his guests and then mumbled, "What—what nonsense!"

The guests exchanged solemn glances. Chen Zhenhui stood up quickly and said:

"Elder Mu, ..."

At this moment, from the end seat of the row of chairs on the east side came a high-pitched laughter. It was sharp, unsettling and unhuman. Everyone looked back. Qian Zheng was sitting there. He had stopped laughing, but that sharp, metallic sound was still echoing in the ears of the guests.

"That's what you chaps are here for today?" Qian Zeng looked up at the roof beam and asked contemptuously. Seeing that the guests were silent and didn't answer, he said, "You have taken the bother traveling hundreds of *li* digging all the way, but I'm afraid, it's not worth the while."

"Oh? Brother Zunwang, I don't understand your criticism. Pray educate me," Chen Zhenhui asked, putting his hands together. Seeing Qian Qianyi panicked upon Zhou Zhong revealing the source of information, he understood that they had hit the spot. He was no longer afraid that Qian Qianyi would escape. He also understood that Qian Zeng's abrupt appearance had something to do with the matter. Judging from the playful tone, he saw that Qian Zeng was not going to deny the fact. So he decided to use the young man as a starting point to crush Qian Qianyi's conspiracy.

Qian Qianyi sensed it. What Qian Zeng had said just now was tantamount to admitting to the plot. He was deeply worried. The arrangement, he thought, hadn't been witnessed by anyone else, and from the moment he sent Qian Yangxian to Suzhou onward, he had always been careful not to leave any evidence of any kind so that in case of exposure he could deny everything and even shift the guilt to Zheng Yuanxun by saying that Zheng Yuanyuan had created and spread the rumor in revenge for his refusal to help him become the leader of the Fushe. Then, the plan would have to be aborted, but at

这样，虽然事情只好作罢，但至少可以确保自己的名声。现在，倘若给钱曾冒冒失失地捅出来，岂不是两头都输个精光？他心里又惊又急，恨不得立即制止钱曾的胡说，可是周镳、周钟和顾杲等人都在一旁虎视眈眈，只要自己举动稍有不慎，就会弄巧反拙。为此，钱谦益不能不十分小心。所以他虽然焦躁万分，也只好眼睁睁地望着钱曾，急切之间，不敢轻举妄动。

至于钱曾，在周钟说出郑元勋来的一刹那间，也颇为震动，而且立即考虑了多种抉择。他绝不是一个愚蠢鲁莽的人，未始不知道一旦直接承认了这件事，会产生什么样的后果。但是他也有他的想法。他认为，老师年逾花甲，余下的机会已经不多了，也许这是最后一次；如果轻易放弃掉，恐怕就未必再有机会，无论对老师、对自己来说，都将是难以补偿的损失。既然现在到了这一步，不如干脆大家摊开来讲个明白，从此放开手脚大干，比之目前这样偷偷摸摸、畏首畏尾反倒强得多。事实上，如今的复社同以往已大不相同，周镳等人未必就能一手遮天。凭着钱谦益的声望和影响，事情不见得毫无希望……这样打定主意之后，钱曾就不理会老师的焦急目光，不慌不忙转过脸，朝四个客人扫了一眼，问：

“眼下建虏猖獗，流寇纵横，国维不张，妖氛日亟。未知诸君子将何以自处？”

对方一开口，就搬出安邦定国、立身济世的大题目，倒也出乎陈贞慧的意料。他想了一下，小心答道：“当此国事蜩螗之秋，凡我君子，自当同心戮力，共扶社稷，以图再造中兴。唯此之故，纵使破家灭身，肝脑涂地，亦在所不惜！”

“说得好！只是诸君又将有何宏谟大略以济之乎？”

least his reputation would not be harmed. Now, should Qian Zeng tell them about his plan out of imprudence, he would lose both the plan and his reputation. Afraid and worried at the same time, he wanted to stop Qian Zeng immediately, but since Zhou Biao, Zhou Zhong, and Gu Gao were all there staring at him, any wrong move would be disastrous. He told himself to be careful and stay calm. Therefore, in spite of his worry, he dared not make a single move. All he could do was look at Qian Zeng and see what he was going to say next.

Qian Zeng was also shocked when Zhou Zhong revealed Zheng Yuanxun as the source of information. He considered several options. Being no fool acting on impulses, he knew the consequences of directly admitting to it, but he had other thoughts as well, knowing as a man over sixty his teacher probably would not have another opportunity; if they let go of this one too easily, the loss for him and his teacher would be irremediable. Now that things had come to such a pass, he would fain lay it bare so that they could proceed with their plan openly instead of doing it surreptitiously. In fact, the Fushe today was very different from what it had been. Zhou Biao and his like were no longer able to take full control of it. With Qian Qianyi's reputation and influence, there was still a ray of hope ... As he made up his mind, he turned to scan the guests one by one unhurriedly, oblivious to the worried look of his teacher.

He asked, "At present, there're invaders in the north and bandits everywhere. The four principles of respectability, righteousness, honesty, and sense of shame, on which the nation is based, are going to the dogs and evildoers run at large. How do you hold yourselves in such a situation?"

That grand discourse about government of the nation and submitting the self to the public good caught Chen Zhenhui by surprise. He thought for an instant and answered cautiously, "In this moment of national crisis, we should all work together for the rejuvenation of the nation without considering ourselves and our families."

"That's well said, but do you have any good plans?"

“宏谟大略，何敢自矜？唯是圣人有云，‘悠悠万事，唯此为大：克己复礼。’克己复礼之第一要务，亦唯亲君子，远小人而已矣！”

钱曾微微一笑：“定生兄此言，固不失为堂堂正论，只是总觉空泛了些。所谓‘大而无当’！以之拿去试策论，课生徒，或许还有点用处；若想以此去抵挡建虏的铁骑、流寇的大刀，小弟担心，却是全不济事！”

陈贞慧的脸陡地涨红了，眼睛也瞪起来，对方的傲慢不逊使他十分恼火。事实上他还从未碰见过敢于用这种可恶的态度向他说话的人。不过，他还是竭力管住自己，冷冷地说：

“如此说来，遵王兄必定另有安邦定国之仙方奇术了？小弟倒要领教！”

“不敢！”钱曾脸上的微笑早已消失得无影无踪，“适才定生兄说过‘同心戮力，共扶社稷’八字，弟以为此意不错，却可惜只说得一半，故仍不免空泛无用，若再添八字，凑成四句，便可差强人意了！”

“敢问是哪八个字？”

“弟这八字便是‘消除党见，唯才是用’！”

“啊！‘消除党见，唯才是用，同心戮力，共扶社稷’？”

“不错！”

“所以阮圆海之禁……”

“应当解除！”

“何时为好？”

“越快越好。”

“就趁今日的虎丘大会……”

“也未尝不可！”

“唔……”

“嗯？”

"Good plans? How dare we claim to have good plans? But our sage Confucius does say 'Of all the things, the most important is to curb our desires and do what's proper.' To curb our desires and do what's proper, the first thing to remember is to be close to good men and keep away from bad men."

Qian Zeng said with a smile, "Brother Dingsheng, what you say is in keeping with the standard teaching but it's empty of substance, 'big and useless' as sage Zhuangzi said. It might be good for a lecture to be given to your pupils but I'm afraid it is completely useless when used to resist the horse-riding invaders or fight the sword-holding bandits."

Chen Zhenhui flushed, staring angrily at Qian Zeng, annoyed by his insolence. He had never met a man speaking with such an abominable attitude before. Trying to keep himself under control, he said coldly, "Thus speaking, Brother Zunwang, you must have a wonderful idea of your own for the restoration of law and order in this nation? Please educate me."

"I dare not to," said Qian Zeng, his smile having disappeared. "Just now you said 'we should work together for the rejuvenation of the nation,' I think it's good, but it's not good enough as it's still empty and useless. I'd like to add more words to make it perfect."

"Pray tell me what words you would like to add."

"And we should eliminate all partisan bias and give every talented man an opportunity."

"We should eliminate partisan bias, give every talented man an opportunity, and work together for the rejuvenation of the nation."

"Correct."

"So, the ban of Ruan Yuanhai from politics—"

"should be lifted."

"When is the time?"

"The sooner the better."

"Let the Tiger Hill Conference today be the time."

"That's not a bad idea."

"Oh—"

"Um?"

突然，陈贞慧放声大笑起来，这是一种终于发现了底细的、压抑已久、至此才得以尽情发泄的大笑。坐在各自的位置上，一直注视着这场谈话的周镳、周钟和顾杲也齐声发出了讽刺的冷笑。只有钱谦益面色苍白，全身因为愤怒而簌簌发抖。他猛地站起来，一拂袖子，打算离开大厅，却被周氏兄弟双双拦住了。

“牧老，何必着急，令高足的高论，很有点‘滋味’嘛！”周钟挖苦地说。

周镳却大惑不解：“这些话他怎么敢说出来？亏他还是复社中人……”

“哼，这小畜生如此放肆狂妄，一派胡言，把我平日的训诲，全不放在心上，简直气死我了！”钱谦益眼看走不脱，只好装出悻悻然的样子，无可奈何地又坐了下来。

这时，只见钱曾傲然站着，嘴角挂着惯常的冷笑，似乎丝毫也没被对手们的笑声所吓住。直到笑声完全平息下来，他才不慌不忙地问：

“定生兄以为阮圆海是何等样人？”

这回，陈贞慧可不再让他神气了。他把脸一沉，反问：“阁下以为他是何等样人？”

“两榜进士，学兼文武，工书史，知兵略，诗词曲赋，样样皆精。早年虽曾失足，近年却并无大过。小弟以为，此等人虽非安邦定国之大材，若论筹边制寇，却也是不可多得之选哩！”

陈贞慧见钱曾仍旧不思收敛，居然荒唐到替阮大铖摆起好来，不由得气往上冲。他厉声说：“非也！阮胡子乃系阉党余孽，乱臣贼子！他奸险狡诈，卑鄙无耻，当年编造《百官图》，谄事魏阉；又复勾结杨维垣，诬陷东林。此天下共知，人神同愤。名列

Suddenly Chen Zhenhui laughed out loud sarcastically. It was a laughter of relief after discovering a great truth. Zhou Biao, Zhou Zhong, and Gu Gao, listening to the conversation in their respective seats, also let out sarcastic laughs. Qian Qianyi, pale and grim, shuddered with anger. He stood up, lifted his long sleeves, and was about to leave the hall, but he was stopped by the Zhou brothers.

"Mr. Qian, no rush. This pupil of yours has a very interesting point," Zhou Zhong said sarcastically.

Zhou Biao was puzzled and said, "As a member of the Fushe, how can he say a thing like that?"

"What a hopeless little beast talking nonsense like that, totally forgetting what I've taught him!" Seeing that he was unable to escape, Qian Qianyi pretended to be angry and reluctantly sat down.

Qian Zeng stood disdainfully with a constant sneer on the corner of his mouth, not at all affected by the sarcastic laughs. When the laughs subsided, he asked undisturbedly,

"Brother Dingsheng, what kind of man do you think Ruan Yuanhai is?"

This time, Chen Zhenhui decided to crush his spirit. He asked with a sullen face, "What kind of man do you think he is?"

"He is a *jinshi* degree holder well trained in the arts and martial arts, well read in history and the classics, with a profound knowledge of war, and good at poetry, song writing, and music composition. He made mistakes in his early years but has very much reformed over the years. He might not be a political genius to handle great affairs of state but he's one of the rare talents that can be employed to fight barbarian invaders at the border and insurgents at home."

Seeing Qian Zeng go even further by ridiculously praising Ruan Dacheng instead of correcting himself, Chen Zhenhui couldn't help becoming angry. He said, "You're quite mistaken, sir. Beardy Ruan is a remnnant of the party of Wei the eunuch. He's a treacherous, shameless treasionist. In the early years he drew the "Pictures of a Hundred Officials" to flatter Wei the Eunuch and colluded with Yang Weiyuan to frame the East Wood Party. All the world knew it

逆案之后，仍不肯敛迹思过，愈肆凶恶，广设爪牙，暗结余党，散布谣言，交关权贵，日夜图谋翻案起用。徒以上赖天子圣明，宸衷英断，下有我仁人君子抨击禁制，彼奸谋方始不售，此实国家之福。阁下名列复社，竟置我同人大义于不顾，出此狂悖叛逆之言，今后尚思立于君子之林么！”

陈贞慧越说声音越大，怒火在他胸中燃烧，热血在他周身沸腾。他深深感到情况的严重和责任的重大。正是这一点，使他的整个姿态充溢着一种大义凛然、悲壮动人之气，以致钱曾也不敢再摆出那种傲慢不逊的样子了。

“倘若定生兄仍一味坚持门户之见，那么小弟只好不说了！”

钱曾摊开双手，做出无可奈何的样子。

“不！”陈贞慧斩钉截铁地说，“这绝非门户之见！此乃小人、君子之分，不得混同！若夫唐之牛李、宋之蜀洛，异在议论，而非流品，可谓之门户之争；至于汉之党人、宦官，今之东林、复社同魏阉及其余孽，均异在流品，势无两立之理！阁下以为阮圆海有才可用，殊不知此种人一旦得势，定必为祸家国，残害忠良。这也是流品使然，无可改易！何况此辈小人，从来只问利害，不思恩义。纵然你今日宽纵于他，又安知异日他不会恩将仇报？到其时身陷囹圄，人头落地，只怕悔之晚矣！”

陈贞慧用力一挥手，结束了谈话。有好一阵子，大厅里变得

and condemned him. After being convicted for treason, he's shown no remorse; instead, he shamelessly goes about building secret connections, spreading rumors, and scheming with figures of influence to reverse his case. Fortunately, His Majesty the emperor is wise and good men like us forbid it. As a member of the Fushe, you disregard the principles of the society by speaking such treacherous words. Are you going to excommunicate yourself from the company of good men in the future?"

Chen Zhenhui's voice became louder and louder as he spoke, the flame of anger burning inside his chest and hot blood coursing through his veins. He felt the severity of the situation and the gravity of his responsibility, and because of that, his entire posture was filled with a sense of righteousness, tragic and moving, so that Qian Zeng didn't dare to put on that kind of arrogance anymore.

"Brother Dingsheng, if you insist on your partisan views, I had better stop saying anything," Qian Zeng said, laying open his hands helplessly.

"No," Chen Zhenhui said categorically. "It's not about partisan views. It's about bad men and good men, black and white. Between Niu Sengru and Li Zongmin in the Tang dynasty, or between the Shu Party and the Luo Party in the Song dynasty, it was a matter of partisan struggle, not a matter of good or bad. Today, the struggle between the East Wood Party and the party of Wei the Eunuch is a matter of good or bad, and there should be no compromise. You only think of Ruan Yuanhai as a talented man who could be of some use but you don't know that when such kind of men once comes into power, they're sure to be harmful to the country and to persecute the virtuous officials as their natural enemies because of their bad character. Besides, such little men are only concerned with their own gains without ever thinking of gratitude. Even if you pardon them today, in time, your kindness will only be rewarded with evil. By the time you're framed by them and your head falls off your shoulders, it will be too late for you to regret having pardoned them."

Chen Zhenhui stopped with a vigorous wave of his hand. For a

一片静默。陈贞慧最后这一番分析，不但使周镳、周钟和顾杲他们暗暗点头，同时也向钱谦益师徒指出了一个他们事先不曾预见到的危险，促使他们不得不有所考虑。然而，也只不过一忽儿，钱谦益抬起头来。他瞧瞧陈贞慧，又瞧瞧座上的其他客人，仿佛下了决心似的，把双手拱在胸前，说："列位君子，适才定生兄一番高论，可谓义正词严，令人闻之气旺！凡我同人，均应如此。遵王之论，显属荒诞不经，不须复言！"说到这里，他向钱曾一瞪眼睛："畜生，还不赶快给我下去！"

钱曾猛地抬起头，张了张嘴巴，似乎还想说什么。可是在老师凌厉的目光逼视下，他终于咬咬牙，站起来，朝客人作了一揖，一声不响地走了出去。

钱谦益这才回过头来，重新堆起笑脸："列位先生都是同道中人，关起门来无话不可谈，只是别拿到外面去乱说就对了。在此，谦益有一管见，意欲请教诸位先生，不知可否？"

他的态度显得特别谦恭，足以使客人们冷静下来，而且无法加以拒绝。

"啊，牧老，你又何必过谦？但有指教，弟等无不洗耳恭听。"周镳说。

"当今寇虏披猖，天下鱼烂。社稷危倾，已是间不容发！所望者，天子圣明，仁人用命，或许尚能有救。我东林、复社诸君子，胸怀忠义，以手援天下为己任。唯是志固甚高，力尚嫌薄，今社外之人，又以门墙严峻、党同伐异而疑我、非我、妒我、远我。此类人绝非阉党余孽，却为数不少。设若不能收彼辈之心，感悦来附，则同心戮力，共扶社稷，到底只是一句空话而已！"

"啊，那么牧老又有何高见呢？"周镳问。由于钱谦益指出

while, the hall was silent. After hearing Chen Zhenhui's analysis, Zhou Biao, Zhou Zhong, and Gu Gao nodded their agreement, and Qian Qianyi and his pupil became aware of a hidden danger and started to ponder. A moment later, Qian Qianyi lifted his head. He first looked at Chen Zhenhui, then the others, and as if having made up his mind, he bowed and said, "Dear sirs, what Dingsheng said is quite to the point. It's mindblowing indeed. All of us should act in accordance with it. What Zunwang said is absurd and let's forget about it." Then, he gave Qian Zeng a cold stare and said, "Beast, go!"

Qian Zeng lifted his head and opened his mouth, as if going to say something, but under his teacher's fierce gaze, he finally stood up, bowed to the guests, and silently exited the hall, gritting his teeth.

Qian Qianyi turned around and put on a smile. "Dear sirs, since we're comrades, we can talk frankly about anything behind closed doors, but remember not to disclose to others what we say here. I have a humble opinion to share with you. Please let me know what you think," he said.

He spoke with such humility that everyone quieted down to listen.

"Elder Mu, please don't be so modest. We're all ears to you," said Zhou Biao.

"At present, plagued by bandits and barbarian invaders, the Great Ming is in great peril. Our hope lies in the wise discretion of the emperor in choosing the right men to govern. Though the East Wooders and the Fushers have lofty ideals and are loyal to the emperor, ready to serve the nation heart and soul, we're a small group of men not quite up to the great task of saving the dynasty from ruin. Many of the non-Fushers, who are not remnants of the party of Wei the eunuch, keep away from us and view us with suspicion, jealousy or hostility because we have built a high wall between us and others and often attack others for holding different views. If we don't unite with them in the service of the Great Ming, in the end all our talk will amount to nothing."

"Then, please educate us, dear Elder Mu," Zhou Biao said.

复社高自标榜，唯我独尊，无容人之量，遂致外人侧目，众心不附，确实打中了目前社局的要害，所以客人们都想听听他到底有什么办法解决这个颇伤脑筋的问题。

看见对手们显出留神倾听的样子，钱谦益暗暗满意。他把态度放得更谦恭，口气更加诚恳："谦益之见，列位未必赞同，此亦无妨，只要彼此心存一个为公之念，其余一切，尽可畅所欲言，坦诚相见。"他把"为公"二字说得特别重，还故意停顿了一下，以便加深对方的印象，然后，才接着说，"社外人士疑我之心，由来已久，非旦夕之间、片言只语所能消除。而国事如此，又断不容我有许多时日，从容解说。以谦益陋见，唯有以非常耸动之举，令彼惊骇震动，见我诚意，始能收事半功倍之效……"

钱谦益说到这里，又看了看客人们，见他们全都默默无言，似在沉思，也猜不透心中在打什么主意。于是，他鼓起勇气，一口气把最后的话说完："昔日汉高祖咬牙封雍齿，诸将反侧之心，遂得以安。今阮圆海一介小人，品格鄙劣，天下共知。唯其如此，倘若我辈稍示宽纵，则反响必大，朝野耸动，以为我辈于阮圆海尚能如此，其余流辈，自不必问矣。如此，则门户之说，不攻自破。门户之说一破，则可以同心戮力，匡扶社稷，建虏流寇，不足虑也！取治取乱，实在我辈一念之间，还望诸位君子三思焉！"

钱谦益刚把话说完，周镳等人还未答话，忽然李宝扬着一张拜帖匆匆走上台阶，站在门外探头探脑。钱谦益正急于听取客人的反应，对于有人在这个节骨眼上来打扰，很不高兴。他朝李宝做了个挡驾的手势，然后回过头，拱着手，征询地盯住了周镳。

Because Qian Qianyi hit the spot by pointing out the self-importance and self-isolation of the Fushers as the cause of hostility from others, his guests wanted to know what good solution he had to the thorny problem.

Seeing his opponents were all ears to him, Qian Qianyi was secretly satisfied with himself. He went on in a humbler tone, "In my opinion—you don't have to agree with me—as long as each of us has the desire to serve the nation, nothing else should be a problem. We can all speak candidly about anything." He accentuated "serving the nation" and paused for an instant so that his guests could hear it more clearly. Then, he continued, "The non-Fushers have been suspicious of us for a long time and the suspicion won't disappear overnight with a few words of explanation. Meanwhile, the current state of affairs doesn't await us. In my humble opinion, only a sensational act can produce a quick effect so that they all see our sincerity. This is the so-called 'to achieve great results with minimal effort'."

Qian Qianyi looked at the guests again. They were all silent, as if thinking something. Then, he mustered his courage to finish what he wanted to say, "In the old days, Emperor Gaozu of the Han dynasty reinstated Yong Chi to office gritting his teeth and then the generals harboring thoughts of rebellion became loyal again. Today, if we can pardon Ruan Yuanhai, who is a well-known little man with a despicable character, it will be sensational news. Both officials at court and in the provinces will be alarmed. Seeing we can pardon a man like Ruan Yuanhai, the lesser wrongdoers will set their mind at rest. Thus, the charge of partisanism will be automatically gone. Then, everyone will be united in the great cause of saving the Great Ming, and the insurgents and barbarian invaders will no longer be a cause for worry. Peace or chaos, it's our choice. Please think it over."

As Qian Qianyi waited for Zhou Biao and the other guests to reply, Li Bao hurried up the steps holding a calling card in his hand and stood outside the door to peep inside. The old man was rather annoyed by this interruption. He gestured for Li Bao to stop, turned around, and, clasping his hands, stared at Zhou Biao inquiringly.

可是周镳却不说话，只是用他那双黑中带绿的眼睛，在眉毛底下古怪地望着钱谦益。其余的客人，也全是一声不响。

钱谦益被周镳瞧得有点不自在，为了掩饰，他竭力装出一副坦然的样子。这时，周钟首先说话了：

“哈哈，姜到底是老的辣！牧老，你这番话，可是比令高足中听多了！”

“啊，介生兄的意思是……”

周钟挥一挥手：“可惜立论虽则有别，宗旨却是一个——替阮胡子开脱！既然如此，尽可直说，又何须辛辛苦苦绕这么个大圈子？学生倒为牧老不值呢！”

“岂止不值，简直欺人太甚！”一直坐着没有开过口的顾杲，突然愤愤地迸出一句。

钱谦益目光一闪，脸上掠过一丝愠色，但立即又忍耐住了。他拱拱手：“列位请勿误会谦益之意……”

然而，没等他说完，周镳突然站起来，一声不响地朝他一揖，转身向外走去。

钱谦益怔了一下，连忙起身，紧赶几步，在门前拦住了他：“哎，仲老，有话尽可商量，何必如此！”

周镳仍旧一声不响，向左一拐，想躲开阻拦，可是钱谦益也跟着向左；周镳又折向右，钱谦益也跟着向右。周镳没有办法了，他跺跺脚，很着急地说：

“牧老，你我道不同不相为谋，还是各自躲开为妙。莫非还要我在此跟你撕破脸皮吵一架不成？”

“仲老不要误会，谦益如此主张，也是为的社稷安危设想，不当之处，尽可批驳。总之谦益自问并无私心，耿耿此衷，天日可鉴……”

钱谦益这话刚一说完，蓦地台阶下有人高声说道：

However, Zhou Biao didn't speak. He just looked quizzically at Qian Qianyi with his greenish black eyes under his brows. All other guests were silent too.

Qian Qianyi felt a little uncomfortable under Zhou Biao's stare. In order to cover up his discomfort, he tried to put on a calm look. At this moment, Zhou Zhong first spoke.

"Haha, the older the wiser. Elder Mu, it's so much more pleasant to hear you than your pupil," said Zhou Biao.

"Oh? Brother Jiesheng, you mean—"

Zhou Zhong waved his hand. "Unfortunately, although the arguments are different, the purpose is one: to excuse Beardy Ruan. That being the case, just put it straight. Why bother beating around the bush? It's a waste of your time."

"It's not just a waste of time. It's an insult to our intelligence," Gu Gao, who had been sitting silently, suddenly burst out angrily.

Qian Qianyi's eyes flickered and a shade of displeasure flashed across his face, but he immediately controlled himself. He bowed and said, "Dear friends, please don't misunderstand me—"

However, before he could finish speaking, Zhou Biao suddenly stood up, bowed to him, turned and walked outward.

Qian Qianyi looked baffled, then hurriedly got up, caught up with Zhou Biao and stopped him in front of the door. "Hey, Elder Zhong, if you have a different opinion, say it. You don't have to go."

Zhou Biao remained silent. He turned to the left, trying to avoid the obstruction, but Qian Qianyi also followed him to the left; he turned to the right, but Qian Qianyi also followed him to the right. Having no way out, he stomped his feet and said anxiously, "Elder Mu, we can't work together because we travel on different paths. We'd better stay out of each other's way. Do you want me to stop being decent and start a huge argument?"

Qian Qianyi said,"Elder Zhong, don't take me wrong. I'm thinking for the safety of the Great Ming. If I'm wrong, your criticism is welcome. Upon my conscience, I'm not thinking for myself ..."

When Qian Qianyi finished speaking, someone down the steps

"只怕未必！"

大家愕然回过头，只见方以智笑吟吟地大踏步走了进来，气急败坏的李宝拼命想阻拦，却怎么也拦他不住。方以智后面，还跟着吴应箕、侯方域、张自烈、梅朗中，只是看不见冒襄和黄宗羲。

方以智走上台阶，笑嘻嘻地朝钱谦益深深一揖，立刻指着李宝告起状来：

"牧老，你这贵价好不惫懒！晚生等有天大的一桩紧急事儿求见，他却死活不放我们进来，分明想诈骗晚生的钱财！你想晚生在盛泽归家院住了半个月，几乎连这身衣裳都给鸨儿剥了去，哪有银子与他。若非晚生斗胆硬闯，岂不误了大事！"

钱谦益一见这个阵势，早已慌了手脚，哪里还有闲心听他打趣。他迟迟疑疑地问：

"贤契过访，不知有何见教老夫？"

"哦，晚生因受辟疆兄之托，要将一封极其紧急之书信呈交周仲老，是以冒昧登门，还祈牧老见谅！"

方以智说罢，在身上前后左右地摸索了一阵，最后才从怀里掏出信来，双手呈给周镳。

周镳不知就里，疑疑惑惑地接过，打开一看，顿时变了脸色。他狠狠地横了钱谦益一眼，"哼"了一声，把信递给了他。

钱谦益心内有鬼，看见周镳神情不善，不禁恐慌起来。他连忙接过信，看见上面写着：

眷社弟顾麟生顿首拜。去岁匆匆进京，未能面别，心常耿耿。复以关河辽阔，通问维艰，遐念昔游，曷胜

said loudly:

"I'm afraid it's not true."

Everyone turned toward the man. It was Fang Yizhi striding in with a grin. Li Bao desperately tried to stop him, but to no avail. Behind Fang Yizhi followed Wu Yingji, Hou Fangyu, Zhang Zilie, and Mei Langzhong. Mao Xiang and Huang Zongxi were not among them.

Fang Yizhi walked up the steps, bowed at Qian Qianyi smilingly, and complained, pointing at Li Bao:

"Elder Mu, this servant of yours is very rude. We have something urgent to discuss with you but he refuses to let us in. It's evident that he wants to take a bribe. As you know, having stayed in the Homecoming brothel for half a month, I have nothing left beside my clothes. There's no money to bribe him with. If I hadn't broken in, there would be serious consequences."

Fang Yizhi's presence was so mighty that Qian Qianyi panicked and asked timidly, without taking the joke:

"Son, please let me hear it."

"Upon the request of Pijiang, I'm taking an urgent letter to Elder Zhou Zhong. Please excuse me for my abrupt visit, Elder Mu."

He fumbled in his clothes for a while, and finally took out a letter from under his arms and presented it to Zhou Biao with both hands.

Not knowing what it was about, Zhou Biao took it over suspiciously. When he opened it, his countenance changed. He gave Qian Qianyi a hard stare and handed the letter to him with a snort.

Qian Qianyi, who had shady thoughts, panicked upon seeing Zhou Biao's unkind expression. He took over the letter, which read:

*Dear friend,*

*Greetings from Gu Linsheng. I apologize for my hasty departure for Beijing last year without saying goodbye to you in person. Since I arrived in Beijing, I've been traveling throughout the country on various errands. In moments when I'm free from my duty, I often become nostalgic and think of my friends back in the hometown. My recent job is to take care of documents and correspondence in the office of His Honorable Premier Zhou. It's a low-ranking job that keeps me busy.*

怅惘。弟近于周阁老幕中，暂掌文牍，营营役役，乏善可陈。唯日前偶见吾乡钱牧斋来书，言及彼已决意向东南诸君子疏通，谋为阮圆海缓颊，中并有“阁下含弘光大，致精识微，目今起废为朝政第一”等语。弟始而讶，继而愤，又继而忧，以为天启之祸，行将复见于今日。故不避利害，驰函奉达，亟望我社同人，急图对策，必不令此奸谋得售而后已……

钱谦益看信的当儿，陈贞慧走到梅朗中身边，悄悄地问：“太冲呢，他怎么不见来？”

“太冲看了此信之后，刺激极深，独自奔下虎丘，不知去向……”梅朗中也悄悄地回答。蓦地，他惊慌地叫起来：

“不好，牧老要倒，快扶住他！”

*There's nothing extraordinary to report to you. The other day, however, I happened to see a letter from our fellow provincial Qian Muzhai that said that he had decided to seek the help of the scholars in the South East for the exoneration of Ruan Yuanhai with words like "Your Highness has a broad vision and a great devotion to detail. You have undertaken the great task of finding talent for the Great Ming, even pardoning talented men who have once made mistakes ..." I was shocked, then angry and then worried. It looks that the calamity of the Tianqi years caused by Wei the eunuch was going to befall the Great Ming again. Therefore, without regarding the safety of myself, I'm writing to let you know it so that our comrades in the Fushe can come up with a method to stop the conspiracy from materializing before it's too late..."*

As Qian Qianyi read the letter, Chen Zhenhui walked over to Mei Langzhong and whispered, "Where is Taichong? I don't see him."

"After reading the letter, Taichong flared up and ran down Tiger Hill alone. I don't know exactly where he went ..." Mei Langzhong whispered back. Suddenly, he screamed panickedly:

"Oh, no! Elder Mu is going to fall. Go help him!"

## 第六章

# 痴情女梦迷病榻，失意人夜访半塘

### 噩梦惊魂

自从被钱谦益撵出东园，冒险回到半塘家中之后，董小宛的病，又加重了几分。

她是在给她娘送葬那天染的风寒，后来一直不大见好。不过前些日子还能勉强挣扎着东躲西藏，这两天她却躺在床上，几乎再没有起来过，一切都由唯一的丫环寿儿给她料理打点。她那丰润漂亮的鹅蛋脸明显地变长了，鲜艳的、小小的嘴唇也失去了光泽。她睁着一双有着长长睫毛的大眼睛，好半天好半天地瞅着屋梁上的燕子巢，不动，也不说话。害得寿儿瞧着瞧着，不由自主就惊慌起来。

在追欢卖笑的风月场中，董小宛是属于那一类为数不多的女子——她自幼沦落风尘，却例外地不曾染上太多的青楼习气。有人曾经挖苦说，这是读书把她读呆了。这话说来也有几分真。她的娘姓陈，本是个贫家女子，卖入青楼当了妓女之后，深感不谙文墨，十分吃亏。任凭你模样儿再俏，对客人再殷勤卖力，终难

Chapter Six

# In Which a Lovesick Girl Was Taken Ill and an Unfortunate Man Visited Bantang at Night

## A Nightmare

After Dong Xiaowan was expelled from East Garden by Qian Qianyi, she ventured back to her home in Bantang. Now her condition worsened.

She had come down with the wind-cold① on the day of her mother's funeral and hadn't recovered ever since. Whereas she had been able to hide herself from view a few days ago, she had been completely bedridden for the past two days. Everything was handled by Shou'er, the only maid. Her plump and beautiful goose-egged face had obviously grown longer, and her bright, small lips had lost their luster. Opening wide her pair of big, long-lashed eyes she stared at the swallow nest on the roof beam for a long time, without moving or talking, so that Shou'er began to fret.

In the pleasure-seeking and merrymaking places, Dong Xiaowan belonged to the unusual sort of young women who had unfortunately been trapped in the dusty world since childhood without developing the habits of a prostitute. Someone had once said sarcastically that she was not smart because she had had too much learning. It was somewhat true. Her mother Miss Chen, born of a poor family, was sold into a brothel at a young age. Knowing the disadvantages of

① wind-cold: "fenghan" in traditional Chinese medicine

攀得上第一流名妓的地位。所以，小宛七八岁起，娘就下决心给她延师授课。小宛生性聪慧，记性儿又好，到了十六七岁上，那些四书五经、诗词歌赋、女训女诫、食谱茶经之类，当真给她熟读了不少。更有一桩，她不光是读，对书中那些圣人之言、闺阃之训还深信不疑，以为那便是天地间的至理。她既自伤沦落，命薄如纸，对于那些古哲先贤、名媛淑女就愈加心深向往，倾慕不已，久而久之，言行举止之间，便不知不觉地学起样来。譬如卖笑人家求之不得的是门庭若市，客似云来；她却偏偏喜欢清静闲适。青楼姐妹们为着成名走红，谁都争着往通都大邑里跑；她却偏偏向往隐居山林。至于碰上男男女女挤坐在一块，又弹又唱，又笑又闹，她就更是愁眉苦脸，打心眼里感到厌烦。这股子清高脾气，同她的身份地位本来很不相称，注定她非倒霉碰壁不可。只是世上有的事情却不能以常理测度，秦淮河上偏有那么一批自命风雅的公子名士，每日家在旧院里鬼混流连，征歌逐色，受着那一个个热得像火盆儿、暖袄儿一般的娘们儿的奉承巴结，都腻烦了。一见了这位空谷幽兰般的董大姑娘，都稀罕得不得了。何况，小宛毕竟也是一位色艺双绝的美人儿。所以，她愈是摆出一副清高冷淡的模样，他们愈是一窝蜂地捧她的场。因了这缘故，董小宛的名声反而不胫而走，一天天地叫响起来，在狎客们的口碑当中，成了与顾眉、李十娘这样一些红角儿享有同等身价的尤物。

不过，这种令多少同行姐妹嫉妒艳羡的成功，并未能改变董小宛的心意。不如说，她因此更加讨厌这种卑贱、屈辱的卖笑生

being illiterate—no matter how pretty you look, and no matter how attentive you're to your clients, you're unlikely to become a famous courtesan if you're illiterate—Miss Chen decided to hire a tutor for her daughter when Xiaowan was seven or eight years old, and the young girl, born intelligent with a good memory, had been very familiar with the Four Books and the Five Classics, the poetry books, Advice to Women, Admonitions for Women, food recipes and literature on tea by the time she was sixteen or seventeen. What was remarkable was that she not only had read but also believed in the words of the wise men and famous women, which she thought contained the ultimate truth in between heaven and earth. While pitying herself for bad luck and paper-thin life, she heartily admired the wise men and virtuous women of the past and over time began to act and speak like them. For instance, while an escort typically loved to welcome visitors—clients one following another—the more the better, she alone loved peace and quiet. The gray house girls vied with one another to go to the big cities to prosper but she alone wanted to live a secluded life in the woods. When men and women jostled together in the couches playing zither, singing, laughing, and frolicking, she was sadder than ever, eyebrows knit and face drawn in sorrow—she was utterly disgusted. Her sense of pride, not befitting her identity at all, was destined to lead her nowhere and create problems for her. However, there're things in the world that cannot be explained by common sense. There were a few self-important narcissistic male celebrities and sons of powerful families muddling along on the Qinhuai River every day, making merry and seeking pleasure. Tired of flattery from girls as hot as blazing braziers or as warm as cotton-padded coats, they all fell in love with the fairylike Miss Dong at first sight, because Xiaowan was not only beautiful but also talented. The more indifferent she was to their advances, the greater the charm she held over them. Thus, her name spread far and near and she became a highly sought-after creature as worthy as Gu Mei and Li Shiniang.

Despite the success, which caused jealousy and envy in the hearts of the other girls of her trade, she hadn't changed her mind.

涯。至少是为着暂时摆脱它，她终于打点行李，离开了秦淮河，搬到苏州城外的半塘来住。三年前，她又随着她娘，到西湖、黄山、白岳一带去漫游，直到前不久，才回到苏州来。谁知就在归途上，娘忽然染上重病，一连请了几个大夫诊治，却全无起色，好容易挨到半塘家中，就死了。小宛悲痛过度，身子便有些不妥，初时还硬挺着办完丧事，不料随后就碰上田国丈派人来苏州采买女孩儿，并且点着名儿要买她，吓得她拖着有病的身子四处逃难。这两天，外间的风声倒是平静了些，听说田府的人已经回京去了。

现在，董小宛斜靠在她的闺房里的一张雕漆八步床上，刚刚吃过药，正闭着眼睛歇劲儿。这间闺房，位于院子当中的一幢二层小楼上，楼下是用竹篱笆围成的院子，满院的梅树，以及几幢模仿乡间茅屋式样建筑的厅堂馆舍，七里山塘就在门前蜿蜒流过。自从黄山归来之后，董小宛便闭门谢客，加上前一阵子又忙于逃难，这宅子一直不曾认真收拾布置。院子里固然杂草丛生，落叶满径，即便是闺房，也处处显出凌乱和不经意。那架大红绸帐，只放下了一半，另一半还挂在钩子上；床靠的一边，随手搭着脱下来的一条裙子；那些平日安放小摆设的地方，至今还让它空着；两幅字画已经长了霉点，却依旧挂在墙上；窗前的镜台蒙上了一层灰尘，周围还堆满了各式各样的药瓶药罐，有的打开了盖子，却忘记随手扣上。也许是因为这个缘故，在这里嗅不到通常名妓闺房里的那种令人骨酥意荡的幽香，有的只是刺鼻的药饵气

Rather, she hated this kind of humble and humiliating career of selling laughter even more. To get rid of it at least temporarily, she finally packed up her things, left the Qinhuai River, and moved to Bantang outside of Suzhou City. Then, three years ago, she decided to travel with her mother and went to places like the West Lake, the Yellow Mountain, and the White Mountain—she had returned to Suzhou only recently. Unfortunately, on the way home her mother suddenly became seriously ill. They called in several doctors, but her mother's condition didn't improve and died upon reaching their home in Bantang. Despite her poor health resulting from the grief, she had been able to see to her mother's funeral, but misfortunes never come singly. The emperor's father-in-law came to Suzhou to purchase a girl and she was the one they were after. So, she fled fearfully and went into hiding with a sickly body. A couple of days later, the situation became less tense as the men sent by the Tians were said to have left for their den in the capital.

Dong Xiaowan reclined in a lacquered canopy bed in her boudoir, eyes closed, taking a respite after taking her medicine. Her boudoir was located on the second floor of a two-storeyed house in the middle of a courtyard on the Seven-Li Waterway defined by a bamboo fence, lined with plum trees, dotted with imitation thatched cottages serving as activity rooms or guest rooms. Since her return from the Yellow Mountain tour, she had kept her door closed for visitors; besides, she hadn't really had time to keep house because she had been dodging her pursuers. As a result, her yard was very much dilapidated, overgrown with weeds and littered with fallen leaves, and even her boudoir showed disorder and lack of care. One half of the scarlet silk mosquito net draped to the floor but the other half was still on the hooks; a skirt had carelessly landed on the curb after its removal from the body of its mistress; the spaces for small gadgets remained vacant; the two paintings tainted by mold were still hanging on the walls; the mirror at the window, having a thick layer of dust, was surrounded by all kinds of drug bottles and containers—some hadn't been closed after being opened—so that instead of the captivating and titillating feminine

味。由于寿儿明显地在设法偷懒，尽管天色已经不早，窗际那一方薄暮晴空正在逐渐黑下去，房间里还迟迟未曾上灯。

不过，这一切，董小宛都没有心思再理会了。经历了十多天的悲伤、疾病和惊吓的折磨，她现在是那样的虚弱，以致周围的一切，在她的感觉之中，都变得那样遥远、隔膜，无关紧要。甚至连身体和四肢，也由于它们的麻木和沉重，仿佛不再属于自己。唯独心还在跳动，肺叶还在呼吸，脑子也仍旧在活动，这些是她还能清晰地感知到的。不过，就连这些部分，似乎也正在衰竭下去……

“哦，莫非我快要死了么？”董小宛冷漠地想，同时有一点惊奇，这一天会来得这么快。“十九岁就死，这是什么意思？”她费劲地思索，可是脑子里却一片茫然。她实在太虚弱了，思路无论如何也集中不起来。而且她愈是努力，它们就愈加变得飘忽不定，终于只剩下一些迷离难辨的迹辙，几乎看都看不清了……

现在，董小宛觉得自己正独自一人，沿着一条难以辨认的小路往前走。这条小路仿佛是悬在空中的一根飘摇不定的带子，周围是黑沉沉的无底深渊，只要稍不留神，就会掉下去摔得粉身碎骨。她心里非常害怕，双腿也在簌簌发抖，可是却不能不往前走。因为她听见有一个亲切的、温柔的声音在不停地呼唤她。她走啊，走啊，也记不清走了多久，只是觉得很累，两条腿也越来越沉重。“啊，看来我是走不到那里的了！得歇一歇，回家……”刚动了这样的念头，她就发现自己已经站在一堵黑沉沉的墙壁跟前，墙上没有门，却有一个小圆洞。她凑近一瞧，看见里面当中放着一张床，一个同自己长得一模一样的女孩子，赤身露体地躺在上面；周围站着一群长得人不像人、野兽不像野兽的东西，正贪婪地盯着那女孩子雪白的身体；一个面目狰狞的、屠夫样的人，把那女孩儿的肉一片一片地割下来，抛给他们。旁边还站着一个中年女人——董小宛认得那是她死去的娘，高高地卷起袖子，手里拿着一把尖刀在等着，把每一个抢到肉的人不人、兽不兽的东

scent typical of the boudoir of a famous courtesan the place smelt of drugs and supplements. It was very late and the clear sky outside the window had darkened, but Shou'er was evidently neglecting her duties by failing to light the lamp in the room.

However, Xiaowan didn't have the mind to say anything about it. After more than ten days of grief, illness, and fright, she was so weak now that everything around her felt distant, strange, and irrelevant. Even her torso and limbs, which were numb and heavy, seemed to no longer belong to her. Fortunately, she could still feel her heart was beating, the lobes of the lungs were breathing, and the brain was active, but even these parts seemed to be declining—

"Well, am I going to die?" Dong Xiaowan thought stoically, surprised that this day had come so soon. "Dying at the age of nineteen. What does it mean?" She thought hard, but her mind was blank. She was so weak that she couldn't concentrate her mind by any means. And the harder she tried, the more elusive her thoughts became; finally only some blurred indistinct traces were left, hardly recognizable—

At this moment, Dong Xiaowan felt that she was alone, walking along a blurry path that was like a drifting belt across a dark bottomless abyss—if she was not careful, she would fall into that abyss and be gone forever. Her legs trembled in fear, but she had to move forward because she heard a kind, gentle voice calling out to her. She walked and walked and walked, her legs heavier and heavier. "Alas, I won't make it there. Let me take a rest and then go back home—" At that thought, she found herself standing in front of a dark wall, which had a small round hole instead of a door. She took a closer look and saw a bed, in which lay a naked girl who looked exactly like herself; the girl was surrounded by a pack of creatures that were neither humans nor beasts staring covetously at the snow-white body and a hideous-looking, butcher-like man was cutting off pieces of her flesh to feed them. Next to him stood a middle-aged woman whom she recognized as her own deceased mother, who, sleeves rolled up, waited with a sharp knife in her hand; when any of the neither-human-nor-beast creatures caught a slice of the girl's flesh, the woman took him by the

西夹脖子揪住，然后用干净利落而又冷酷无情的动作，把他的皮整张地剥下来，剩下那具血淋淋的躯体，就随手往地下一丢，让他们在那儿哀号、狂笑、跳闹、痛哭……董小宛瞧得毛骨悚然，双腿发软，正想离开墙洞，不料给屋子里的人发现了。那群被剥了皮的东西立即一个个从墙缝里钻出来，围着她欢呼大笑，硬要把她拖进屋子里去。董小宛吓坏了，连忙用力一挣，转身就逃。不知怎么一来，就骑上了一匹毛驴。这毛驴长着两道白眉毛，下巴上还拖着一把胡子。它撒开四蹄，跑得风驰电掣一般。董小宛害怕起来，也不知这驴子要把她带到哪里去，只好死死抓住缰绳，闭上眼睛。跑着跑着，突然驴子猛地一掀，把她抛出好远。等她爬起来，驴子不见了，眼前却出现了一座高山。她仔细一看，原来不是高山，而是无数死人堆在一起。那些尸体一具具都断头折臂，血肉模糊，惨不忍睹。一群顶盔贯甲的人还在上面挥舞刀枪，苦苦厮拼，时不时发出一两声疯狂的怒吼和惨厉的呼喊。突然，刀光一闪，一颗脑袋飞上了半空，随即疾速向山下飞来。董小宛正想躲避，谁知那颗脑袋突然变大了无数倍，龇牙咧嘴地向她砸来。董小宛心口一凉，闭着眼睛等死。然而，就在这时，她听见了先前那个召唤她的声音。它变得更加温柔、亲切，而且越来越近，使董小宛觉得无论如何也要瞧一瞧他再死。于是她又睁开了眼睛，却意外地发现，那个可怕的脑袋已经不见了，那座用尸体垒成的高山和在山上恶斗的人也不见了。如今，她已置身于春光明媚、鲜花盛开的原野上，黄莺在耳边娇柔地啼啭，蝴蝶在周遭翩翩飞舞。一个身穿白夹春衫、姿容绝世的美少年正在朝她走过来。“哦，我已找了你很久了！”他用美妙悦耳的声音说，伸出手，

neck and with a clean and ruthless movement stripped off the skin and threw it to the ground, where they wailed, laughed, jumped and cried, their bodies turned into gory masses. Dong Xiaowan was so terrified that her hair stood on edge and her legs softened. As she was about to step away from the hole in the wall, she was noticed by the ones in the room. The pack of skinned creatures immediately emerged from the wall cracks one after another, and cheering and laughing, dragged her toward the room. In sheer fright, she struggled, turned around and took flight. Somehow she got on a donkey with white eyebrows and a beard. When it spread the hooves and galloped, it ran like a gust of wind or a bolt of thunder. In utter fear, she held fast to the reins with her eyes closed, not knowing where the donkey was going to take her. As the donkey galloped, it suddenly snapped and threw her away. When she stood up, the donkey was gone. A high mountain appeared in front of her. She took a closer look and found it was not a mountain, but a huge mound of countless gory dead bodies of humans that had been decapitated, amputated or maimed. On the mound, a crowd of armored men were wielding their swords and spears in close combat, from time to time howling battle cries or letting out painful screams. Suddenly, with a flash of a sword one human head rose into the air and then flew quickly down the mountain. She tried to dodge it, but that human head suddenly grew many times bigger to come at her with a grin. Her heart grew cold and she closed her eyes to wait for death. However, at this moment, she heard the same voice that had previously called out to her. This time, it became softer and friendlier, and closer to her so that she felt obliged to have a look at him before dying. She opened her eyes again only to find the terrifying head was gone and so were the high mountain made of corpses and the people fighting on the mountain. Now, she was in an open field where spring was in full glory and the flowers were in full bloom, yellow warblers whispering softly in her ears and butterflies joyously flying around. A young man in a white shirt—one of unmatched beauty—was walking towards her. "There you are! I've been looking for you for ages," he said in a beautiful and pleasant voice, reaching out his hand to gently help

把她轻轻地扶起来。“我们现在回家去吧。我要用最华美的屋子安顿你，用最漂亮的衣裳打扮你，用最精致的食物供养你，我再不同你分离，再不让你受苦了！”他娓娓地说，不胜爱怜地瞅着她。董小宛顿时感到心头宁帖了，泪水涌上了眼眶。她想告诉他，她并不需要这些。只要他肯让她跟在身边，做一名卑微的奴仆，她就心满意足了。她还想告诉他，她是那样爱慕他。为了他，她可以去死……可是，她说不出来，因为她的喉头哽咽得厉害。她只是信赖地依偎着他，寸步不离地跟着他走……

然而，渐渐地，远处响起了呜呜的风声。那美少年站住了，抬头望了望天空，笑着说：“这风来得正好，我们可以早些到家了。”话刚说完，原野上已经天昏地暗，飞沙走石，那少年“呼”的一声，被风刮上了天空。董小宛猝不及防，慌乱中用手一抓，扯住了那少年的一根衣带，也被带上了空中。但是，衣带那样柔弱，它显然承受不住董小宛身体的重量，转眼之间，就被拉得又细又长，最后竟成了一根绷得紧紧的细丝。董小宛万分焦急，低头一望，只见下面阴风阵阵，惨雾沉沉，什么花啦，草啦，黄莺啦，蝴蝶啦，全都无影无踪。那些半人半兽、被剥了皮的“东西”，那些在尸山上恶战的甲士，以及那个硕大无朋的脑袋，又重新出现，并且张牙舞爪地向她扑来。董小宛害怕极了，竭力抓紧那根细丝。谁知这么一用劲，细丝“噗”地断了，董小宛立即高速向下堕去。她绝望地悲呼：“冒郎救我！”全力向上一挺，蓦地惊醒过来，原来是做了一个梦。只觉得浑身冷汗淋漓，一件里衣已经湿透了……

说也奇怪，现在董小宛觉得心里清爽了许多，身子虽然像是加倍的疲倦，却不似先前的麻木沉重了。她睁大眼睛望着绸帐的

her up. “Let’s go home now. I want to settle you in the most beautiful house, dress you up with the most beautiful clothes, and feed you the best food. I’ll never be separated from you again and never let you suffer anymore,” he looked at her lovingly and said. Dong Xiaowan’s heart calmed down, and tears welled up in her eyes. She wanted to tell him that she didn’t need those things. As long as he was willing to keep her in his company and let her be his humble servant, she would be satisfied. She also wanted to tell him that she admired him so much that she was willing to die for him—but she couldn’t say it because her throat was badly choked. She simply cuddled with him in trust and followed him every step of the way—

However, gradually, a whining wind came from the distance. The beautiful young man stopped to look up at the sky, and said with a smile, “The wind was just right. We can get home sooner.” Shortly after he said that, the open field was engulfed by darkness, sand flying and rocks rolling, and whoosh he was blown into the sky. Dong Xiaowan, caught off guard, panickedly grabbed a riband of the boy’s garment and was also lifted into the air. However, the riband was so slender that it obviously couldn’t bear her weight; in the blink of an eye, it was stretched thin and long and finally turned into a tight filament. In sheer fright, Dong Xiaowan looked down and saw that there was a gusty gloomy wind and a heavy ghostly mist below and that all the flowers, grasses, yellow warblers, butterflies had disappeared. The half-human half-beast skinned creatures, the armored warriors who had fought fiercely on the mountain of corpses, and the huge head without rival reappeared and came at her with all teeth and claws. She frightfully tried to hold on to that filament. To her dismay, with that effort, snap, the filament broke, and she fell at high speed. She desperately cried, “My lord, please help me!” She lifted herself up with all her strength and suddenly woke up. It was a dream. She was dripping with cold sweat that had already soaked her undershirt.

Strangely, Xiaowan’s heart felt lighter; although her body felt doubly tired, it was not as numb and heavy as before. She opened her eyes wide and looked at the top of the silk bed canopy, silently

方顶，默默地回想着适才的梦境，一颗心还在扑通扑通地直跳。“啊，那美少年我分明认识，那就是他，是他！他说找了我很久，这是真的吗？三年前，他确实同方公子来访过我几回，却只见到一面。记得那一天我碰上闹酒，正在里间睡着，还是娘把我推起来，扶出去见他的……可是，那以后他再没有来过。后来就传说他同陈圆圆相好得不得了。不过，听说圆圆这一次到底给田皇亲抢去了。那么，他如今又在哪里？他还记得我吗，他会来吗？嗯，会来吗……”

她这样暗暗叨念着。忽然，说也奇怪，她分明听见了，从很远很远的地方，传来一种有节奏的“吱扭——吱扭——”的声响，那是一支船橹在摇动。她不能说出这船是什么样子，但是分明感觉到，它是冲自己而来的。现在，她还听见了船上有人在说话，其中一个嗓音就是在梦中呼唤过她的那个亲切、温柔的声音。

“小贱种，你反了天了！竟敢管起大爷的事。看我不打死你！”一声男人的怒骂蓦地从天井里响起。萦绕在董小宛耳边的幻觉一下子被驱散了，而代之以乒乒乓乓的竹棒击地声、追打声、哭叫声。接着，楼梯咚咚一阵乱响，寿儿——一个长着一张猫儿脸的十四岁小丫环，头发披散，跌跌撞撞地冲进闺房来，一下子扑到董小宛的床沿，跪在地上直叫：“娘快救我，老爹要打死我！”

董小宛还未开口，她爹董子将已经手执竹棒，气势汹汹抢了进来。他有五十出头，一个在青楼妓馆混了几十年的老篾片，长得又高又瘦，皱皱巴巴的脸上，透出一种灰不灰、蓝不蓝的所谓“晦气”。他这辈子除了会打一手十番鼓，外加逢迎拍马，再没有别的能耐。相反，游手好闲、吃喝玩乐那一套，却学得精熟。现在，他光着微秃的脑袋，没有戴头巾，正瞪着一双大而混浊的

recalling the dream, her heart still thumping. She thought to herself, "Huh, I recognize that beautiful boy! It's him! It's him! He said he had been looking for me for ages. Is it true? Three years ago, he did come to visit with me in the company of Fang Junior several times, but only met me once. I remember that day I was sleeping inside from a hangover and was awoken by my mother, who helped me out to see him— However, he's never been here again since then. Later, it was said that he and Chen Yuanyuan were very fond of each other. Then, it was heard that Yuanyuan had fallen into the hands of Mr. Tian, a relative of the emperor. Then, where is he now? Does he remember me? Will he come? Will he ever come again?"

As she murmured, suddenly came a rhythmic squeak-squeak-squeak, the sound of a scull in the water from far, far away—it was strange that she could hear it clearly. She couldn't tell what the boat looked like, but she clearly felt that it was coming for her very self. Now, she heard people talking on the boat, and one of the voices was the kind and gentle voice that had called out to her in the dream.

"You daughter of a bitch! How dare you meddle with my business! See if I won't kill you," suddenly came a man's angry shouts from the atrium. The auditory hallucinations were suddenly gone and replaced with the sounds of chasing, crying, and bamboo sticks hitting the floor. Then, flip flop, Shou'er, a fourteen-year-old girl with a cat face, came stumbling into the boudoir, her hair dishevelled, and knelt down on the floor, screaming, "Missus, save me! Grandpa will kill me."

Before Xiaowan replied, her father Dong Zijiang broke in mightily holding a bamboo stick. He was a lanky man in his early fifties, a failed scholar that had been muddling in bawdy houses for dozens of years, his wrinkled face carrying a so-called "aura of bad luck" that was neither gray nor blue. In this life, he was good for nothing except beating a *shifan* drum and kissing asses. On the contrary, he was quite good at idling, eating, drinking, and having fun. At this moment, the old man with a hatless bald head was glaring with bulgy, murky eyes and baring his teeth with uncontrolled rage, as if he

眼睛，狂怒地龇着牙，像是要把寿儿一口吃下去似的。吓得寿儿浑身哆嗦，连滚带爬地藏到床后。

“爹——”董小宛蹙着眉毛，有气无力地叫，声音里透着烦躁。这位亲爹的脾性，她是清楚的。过去，靠着小宛母女俩，他倒不愁没钱花。可是自从陈氏死后，小宛又因病闭门谢客，家中的用度，就渐渐紧张起来。这位董大爷却嗜好难改，仍旧三天两日摊着巴掌向女儿讨钱。给得少了，他就偷着拿家里的东西出去变卖。这事小宛也听寿儿唠叨过许多回，碍着是亲爹，也不好怎么说他。偏偏寿儿这丫头躲懒归躲懒，性子却颇为耿直。她看小宛不管，有时就忍不住当面数落董子将几句，惹得老董大为光火，又跳又骂，这种事也非止一回。适才，想必寿儿又刺中了董子将什么痛处，竟然一路追打进来。

董子将听见小宛的叫声，怔了一下，随后他仍然冲上来，挥棒朝寿儿打去。寿儿慌乱中举手挡架，竹棒“啪”地打在她的手指上。寿儿哀叫一声，护着痛弯下身去，朝床底下一钻，躲在角落里再也不敢出来。董子将还不解恨，他一面用竹棒朝床下乱捅乱戳，一面恶狠狠地喝叫：

“畜生！奴才！你妈妈的出来不出来？赶快出来！出来！”

董小宛被他们闹得头昏眼花，心中又急又气。她用尽全力，一连挣扎了好几次，才坐起了身子。她喘着气，抖抖索索地指着门说：

“你、你们出、出去！都出去！”

说完，她又挣扎着打算站起来，但她的两条腿颤抖得那样厉害，实在站立不稳，只好又坐了回去。不过这一来，总算引起了她爹的注意。董子将斜着眼睛瞅了女儿一会，终于把竹棒扔在地

were about to devour Shou'er at one gulp, sending Shou'er shuddering with fear and rolling to the other side of the bed.

"Dad—" Dong Xiaowan, knitting her brows, called feebly, with an edge of annoyance in her voice. She knew only too well the temperament of her own father. In the past, thanks to Xiaowan and her mother, he hadn't worried about money. However, since Miss Chen's death, Xiaowan had shut her door on clients due to her illness, and they had found their finances increasingly tight. Old man Dong's habits were hard to change, and he still spread his palms open and asked his daughter for money every two or three days. If he got less than he asked for, he would steal things in the house and sell them. Xiaowan had heard Shou'er nagging many times about it but didn't say anything because he was her own father after all. But Shou'er, lazy as she was, was an upright girl. Seeing Xiaowan didn't care, she sometimes couldn't help but admonish him in front of her missus, sending the old man stomping and swearing—this kind of thing had happened quiet a few times. A moment ago, Shou'er presumably hit Dong Zijiang on a sore spot again so that he was going after her with a vengeance.

Hearing Xiaowan's call, Dong Zijiang stopped for an instant and continued his chase, waving the stick at Shou'er. She raised her hand to protect herself and, bam, the bamboo stick fell on her fingers. Screaming in pain, Shou'er bent down to slip herself into a corner under the bed. Anger not yet assuaged, Dong Zijiang poked the bamboo stick aimlessly into under the bed and shouted in a coarse, rage-filled voice:

"Animal! Slave! Won't you come out? Come out quick! Come out!"

Plagued by the noise, Dong Xiaowan exasperatedly struggled to sit up and showed them the door, "Out! You, you, get out! Both of you!" she said out of breath.

She tried to stand up, but her legs trembled so violently that she had to sit back. This time, she succeeded in being noticed by her father. Dong Zijiang cast a glance at his daughter, dropped the bamboo

上，气哼哼地转身走出了屋子。

躲在床下的寿儿，一直听着老董下了楼，脚步声消失了，才轻手轻脚地钻出来。她侧着耳朵又听了听，断定董子将已经走远了，才长长吁了一口气，一边拍打着头上、身上的灰尘，一边嘟嘟哝哝地说："自己为老不尊，不要脸，还不许人家说……"她回过头，蓦地发现董小宛正扶着床靠坐着，一动不动地闭着眼睛，就连忙走近去，讨好地问：

"娘，你怎么啦？你身子不好，这么坐着怎吃得消？快躺下吧！"

董小宛摇摇头，仍旧一动不动地坐着。过了一会儿，她突然睁开眼睛，一边示意寿儿不要说话，一边支起耳朵，神情显得越来越专注和深沉，像是极力倾听什么声音，又像神游在某一个遥远的地方。

寿儿被弄得莫名其妙，又不敢打扰她，只好呆呆地望着。

终于，董小宛的睫毛颤动了一下，恢复了常态。

"哦，我有点饿了，想吃粥。"她说，疲乏地抓住床靠，把头抵在立柱上。

寿儿的眼睛睁圆了："娘是说，饿、饿了？啊，娘身子大好啦？"

董小宛点点头，又摇摇头："我只要半碗，两根水菜……嗯，吃完了，你替我梳梳头，我捉摸，这头有两天没梳了吧？一定难看死啦！"

寿儿又惊又笑："娘，你今儿个怎么啦？娘，婢子这就给你弄去！"

"还有，这屋子也该收拾一下。"董小宛继续吩咐，闭上了眼睛，"我觉着，今晚，说不定有人要来……"

stick onto the floor, and turned to leave the room, still furious.

Shou'er, hiding under the bed, didn't come out until the sound of footsteps disappeared downstairs. Then she tilted her ear and listened. After making sure Dong Zijiang had indeed gone, she heaved a long sigh of relief. Knocking the dust off her head and body, she murmured, "As an old man he's disrespectable and disgraceful, but he doesn't allow others to say it." She turned around to find that Xiaowan had sat up on the bed, reclining with the support of her hands, eyes closed; she walked over and said obsequiously:

"Missus, what's up? You're not well. Don't sit like that. Please lie down."

Xiaowan shook her head, not moving a muscle. After a short while, she suddenly opened her eyes and pricked up her ears as she motioned Shou'er to be silent, her expression increasingly concerned and serious as if she were listening for something or her mind had wandered to a far away place.

Shou'er was puzzled but, not daring to disturb her, simply stood by and watched.

At long last, Xiaowan's eyelashes gave a twitch and she returned to normal.

"Shou'er, I'm a little hungry and want some porridge," said she, wearily resting her head on a pillar of the bed, one hand holding the bed railing.

Shou'er said with widened eyes, "Missus, do you say you're hungry? Why, does that mean you're well?"

Xiaowan first nodded and then shook her head, saying, "I only need half a bowl of porridge, a few slices of veggies boiled in water. Um, after eating, I shall need you to comb my hair. I gather my hair hasn't been combed for two days. It must look horrible."

It was a big surprise. Shou'er laughed, "Missus, what's up today? No problem. I'll make it immediately."

"Also, this room needs cleaning," Xiaowan continued to give instructions, eyes closed. "I think someone might be coming tonight."

## 不速之客

“虽然辜负了一个女子，但父亲总算平安脱离险地。看来，这没有什么可遗憾的！”冒襄默默地想，“我不能为着一个风尘女子而丢开父亲不顾，这是无疑的。即使再从头经历一次，我的选择，也只能是如此！”

这是虎丘大会结束后的当晚，也即是董小宛向寿儿说她感到肚子饿的同一个时刻，冒襄正乘着一只小船，沿七里山塘，缓缓地向桐桥圩的方向摇来。张明弼照例陪在朋友的身边。不过，他们没有交谈，各自默默地坐在船舱里，已经有好长一段时间了。

晚春的夕阳，完全没入了地平线，周遭的暮色变得越来越浓；沿河两岸，亮起了星星点点的灯火；反映着最后一抹青灰色天光的河水，悄没声息地从船舷下流过。从后梢传来了轻柔而有节奏的橹声……

由于觉悟到存在着那样强有力的“理由”，冒襄在失去陈圆圆后的情绪混乱当中，开始重新找到了立足之点。他逐渐平静下来，甚至似乎有一种解脱般的轻松之感了。

说起来，冒襄还是在去年他到湖南去探望当时还在衡州做官的父亲途中，才同陈圆圆认识的。那时正是早春，夹岸的柳树刚刚有一点绿影儿，梅花却开得正好。他从同船的一位姓许的父执辈口中，头一遭听到陈圆圆的“芳名”，并且被这位父执的热烈推崇所打动，特意在杭州停留了几天，两人一道去寻访陈圆圆。徒劳往返了好几次，最后，才总算把她请来了。冒襄清楚地记得，那天陈圆圆穿了一袭长过膝盖的暗青色茧绸女衣，下衬八幅白地绣青花湘裙。当她从帘子后面款款地走上红氍毹来的时候，笑涡

## An Unexpected Visitor

"I've let down a woman, but my father is saved from danger. So there's nothing to regret," Mao Xiang thought silently. "I'll never leave my father alone for a woman in the dust no doubt. If I were to go through it again, my choice would be the same."

The night after the Tiger Hill Conference, exactly the same moment Xiaowan told Shou'er that she was hungry, Mao Xiang, accompanied by Zhang Mingbi, was moving slowly on the Seven-Li Waterway towards Tongqiao Market in a small boat. They silently sat in the cabin. Neither of them had spoken for a long time.

The sun in the late-spring evening had completely submerged under the horizon, and the surrounding twilight became thicker and thicker; along the banks of the river, lanterns lit up here and there; the water of the river, reflecting the last touch of blue-gray skylight, quietly flowed along the sides of the boat. A soft rhythmic sound of a rowing scull came from the rear end of the boat.

There being such a powerful reason, Mao Xiang began to find a new anchor after experiencing the emotional turmoil that had come with the loss of Chen Yuanyuan. Having gradually calmed down, he now even felt somewhat relieved.

Mao Xiang had first met Chen Yuanyuan a year ago, on his way to visit his father, who was then an official in Hengzhou, Hunan Province. It was early spring. The willow trees on the river banks had just begun to green and the plum trees were blooming. He heard the name Chen Yuanyuan from a coeval of his father traveling in the same boat, who was named Xu, and was impressed by how the elderly gentleman admired and spoke of a young thing called Chen Yuanyuan, so he decided to stay in Hangzhou for a couple of days to find this fabulous woman together with Mr. Xu. After several failures, they finally succeeded to invite her over. Mao Xiang clearly remembered that that day Chen Yuanyuan wore a dark cyan wild-silk outfit that reached down to her knees and was lined with an eight-folded Hunan-style embroidered dress featuring blue flowers on a white background.

在她的腮边忽闪着，她像是无意，又像是有意地朝冒襄瞟了一眼，随即含羞地旋过脸去，侧转腰肢，回顾了一下拖在身后的裙裾。那美妙优雅的姿态，真像在烟雾缭绕当中一只翩然起舞的青凤。当时，冒襄虽然意识到其他人的在场，脸上依然保持着惯常那骄矜的微笑，可是内心深处，却分明地震颤了一下，被这女子不寻常的魅力所打动，不由自主地用眼睛去追随她那妙曼的姿影。

从这一刻开始，他俩的感情就飞速地交流起来。在陈圆圆出人意料地用当时已经不流行的弋阳腔，演出《红梅记》一剧的时候，冒襄怀着少有的兴趣和热情，自始至终关注着台上的演出；而陈圆圆也把含情脉脉的目光，频频投向他的座上。冒襄还记得，当演出的间歇，陈圆圆擎着玉壶，向座上的客人劝酒，却没有首先走向他时，他心里是多么地失望和不快；而后来，当陈圆圆在他身边明显地停留得最久，同他悄声低语时又挨得那么近，以至他可以清楚地看到她那蝉翼样的鬓影在轻轻颤动，嗅得着她那小嘴所发出的唇脂的馨香。这时候，他又是多么地得意和愉快——啊，直到现在回想起来，那仍然是令人心荡神飞，如醉如痴的奇妙境界！是冒襄多年来出入风月场所从未经验过的……

事实上，从那时起，冒襄就觉得离不开她了。待到酒阑人散，他立即提出了留宿的邀请。陈圆圆似乎有点为难，但还是应允了。直到天快亮时，她才登舟回去。当时，他是那样的难分难舍。而她反倒有点淡淡的，只告诉他打算到光福山去寻梅赏雪，如果他也去，可以有半月的盘桓。当时他考虑行程紧迫，无法久留，踌躇再三，只好约定到桂子飘香时节，与她在姑苏再见。

冒襄直到现在还记得，在那历时半年的往返旅途中，他对她

When she walked up to the red carpet from behind the curtain, dimples flickering on her cheeks, she glanced at him consciously or unconsciously, and then turned her face shyly to look behind at the train of her own skirt. The beautiful and elegant posture resembled that of a green phoenix dancing merrily in the mist. In that instant, even though his face still kept the usual proud and contained smile as he was aware of the presence of others, his heart gave a shiver. He was captivated by her extraordinary beauty, and his eyes involuntarily moved with her beautiful figure.

From this moment on, they quickly started an exchange. When Yuanyuan surprisingly sang in the Yiyang style—which was no longer popular at the time—in the performance of the opera *The Story of Red Plum* Mao Xiang watched from beginning to end with unusual attention; and in her turn, Yuanyuan affectionately cast her eyes on his seat from time to time. Mao Xiang still remembered how dejected and unhappy he was when Chen Yuanyuan held the jade decanter and proposed toasts to the guests at the table without approaching him first, and how delighted and proud he was a short while later when she sat beside him and kept whispering to him—they were so close that he could clearly see her temple hair, which was fluttering gently like a cicada wing and smelt of the sweet scent of lipstick from her little mouth. That was a wonderful and intoxicating moment, one that he had never had in his previous visits to places of pleasure.

In fact, from then on, Mao Xiang felt attached to her. When the party was over and everyone else had left, he immediately asked her to stay the night. A little embarrassed, Chen Yuanyuan agreed nonetheless. She stayed until dawn when she boarded her boat. He was reluctant to see her go but she was rather placid. She merely told him that she planned to go to Guangfu Mountain to see the plum blossoms and the snow there, and that if he cared to go they would be able to hang together for fifteen days or so. Since he had a tight schedule and was unable to stay long, he made a date with her to meet in Gusu City in the sweet olive season.

By now he still remembered clearly how he missed her during

的思念是怎样的强烈，怎样唯恐不能再见到她。他历历在目地回味着那一个暂短良夜的旖旎风情——那摇曳的灯影、低垂的罗帐、火热的眼神、潮湿的鬓发以及胳臂上疯狂的齿痕……这一切，都在时时刻刻挑动着他的情欲，使他在同别的女人在一起时味如嚼蜡。而且，也许因为这缘故，他还平生第一次不无妒意地想到，他离开期间，其他狎客将会代替自己的位置，而陈圆圆也会照样同他们厮混，一如那天晚上她对待自己一样……

不过，尽管如此，当半年之后，他护送母亲回来，路经苏州，陈圆圆出乎意料地表示她要嫁给他，从此完全、永远属于他的时候，冒襄却感到十分惊讶和突然，觉得这种要求未免过于天真，而且轻率得有点不知自量。因为在他看来，寻欢作乐是一回事，承担家庭义务又是另一回事；而且，就凭着那短短一夜的交情，对方也没有权利提出这种要求。所以他当即拒绝了她。然而，陈圆圆却不是那种容易摆脱的女人。她用不着苦苦哀求，她有的是聪明的手段。到了后半夜，再次领略到她的全部魔力的冒襄，就主动回心转意了。虽然，他提出了一个条件，必须等他把营救父亲的事情办妥之后，才从长计议这件事。

后来，冒襄就全副心神投入到营救父亲的事情当中去了。大半年来，没完没了地奔走、投诉、请托，加上还要不断劝解日夜忧伤的母亲，冒襄简直把陈圆圆完全抛在脑后。此外，他还多少有点儿后悔：不该这么容易就答应了她。所以有时候，他尽管也会忽然想到陈圆圆，想到是否该去看望她，可是出于一种多少感到丢了面子，因而想挽回一下的心理，他终于又打消了这种念头。半年来，他甚至连信都没有给她写过一封。谁知道，由于这一念之差，结果就永远失去了她……

“哎，这样的结果是好，还是不好？好，还是不好呢？”冒襄不由得反复自问。可是越问，心中越乱。他一阵烦躁，猛地站

the six-month-long trip and how he feared never being able to see her again. He ruminated on every moment of intimacy in that short beautiful night—the flickering lamp, the draping bed canopy, the fiery eyes, the wet hair on her temples, and the imprint of her teeth on his arm ... all these titillated his appetite for her and rendered all other women flat and tasteless as raw potatoes. Probably on that account, for the first time in his life, he was jealous, thinking that in his absence, other men would fill his place and she would sleep with them the way she slept with him that night ...

Despite the infatuation, he was quite alarmed when Chen Yuanyuan suddenly announced to him that she wanted to marry him and live happily ever after when he stopped by Suzhou City on his trip home with his mother; he thought that request too naive, too flippant to be taken seriously. To him, seeking pleasure and making merry was one thing, but to take familial responsibility was quite another. It was a one-night stand after all. She was not qualified to make that demand. So he turned her down outright. However, Chen Yuanyuan was not a woman to trifle with. She didn't plead; she had plenty of ploys to get what she wanted. In the second half of the night, after experiencing again the thrill of all her magic powers, Mao Xiang surrendered, on condition that the matter should be seriously considered only after he had successfully rescued his father.

Later, Mao Xiang dedicated himself body and soul to the rescue efforts. For a good part of a year, he went around pleading for his father and seeking help while comforting his sorrowful mother, leaving Chen Yuanyuan completely in the back of his mind. Besides, he more or less regretted having made a promise to her. He sometimes thought of her and wondered whether he should pay her a visit, but always dismissed the idea in the end, out of pride and self-esteem. Over the past six months, he hadn't even written a letter to her and that negligence had resulted in his losing her forever.

"Holy shit! Is such an ending a good one or bad? Is it good or bad?" Mao Xiang kept asking himself, but the more he asked of himself the more confused he was. As he grew increasingly unsettled

起身子。就在这时，他看见了一片繁密的灯火、一座拱形的石桥，以及桥头耸立的石塔。桐桥圩到了。

“辟疆，你做什么？”被冒襄的突然举动吓了一跳的张明弼问。

冒襄定了定神，清醒过来。为了掩饰自己的失态，他随手指着岸边一个带小楼的院落说：“哦，那幢小楼临水而筑，亭亭如画，唯是灯火俱无，不知是何人所居？”

张明弼顺着他的手势望去，“噢”了一声，说：“那不就是董小宛的家嘛，你怎么就忘了？前几年，我还陪你来过的！”他仔细看看，又说，“楼上影影绰绰的像是有灯火，嗯，她必定还在。”

听说是董小宛的家，冒襄倒愣住了。他朝那阁楼上依稀的灯火注视了一会儿，忽然回头向后梢叫道：

“船家，靠岸，我们要下船。”

“啊，做什么？”张明弼问。

“上去看看！”

“只是，只是听说小宛刚死了娘，她自己又病得很重，一直闭门谢客。瞧这灯火零落的样子，想必还不曾好，又何苦去打扰她！”

可是冒襄不理会张明弼的劝阻，他紧盯着越来越近的河岸，显出迫不及待的样子。船家一放下跳板，他就抢先一步跨上去，很快地上了岸。等无可奈何的张明弼从后面跟上来时，他已经站在竹篱笆前，开始打门了。

冒襄先轻轻地敲了几下，见里面全无应声，下手就重起来。可是敲了一阵，仍然毫无动静。张明弼说：

“辟疆，敢情他们都睡死了。算啦，我们还是回船吧！”

he stood up and saw a stretch of lights and an arched stone bridge with a stone tower at the end. It was Tongqiao Market.

"What are you doing, Pijiang?" asked Zhang Mingbi, startled by Mao Xiang's sudden movement.

Mao Xiang woke up from his trance. In order to cover his loss of composure, he pointed randomly at a yard with a multi-storeyed house and said, "Lo and behold! That riverside house is quite picturesque but unfortunately there's no light. Whose house is it?"

Zhang Mingbi looked in the direction of his finger and said, "Ah Hah! Isn't that Dong Xiaowan's place? I went there with you a few years ago." After looking more carefully he said, "There seems to be a lamplight. She must be there right now."

Hearing it was the residence of Dong Xiaowan, Mao Xiang evidently had a surprise. He set his eyes on the flicker of light in the attic and then turned around to call out to the boatman at the tail of the boat:

"Man, move close to the bank. We need to get off."

"Why, what are you up to?" asked Zhang Mingbi.

"I want to go and have a look."

"Problem is, it's said Xiaowan has recently lost her mother and she's seriously ill herself. Therefore her door is closed to clients. That her place is so dark suggests she's not well yet and we'd better leave her alone."

However, disregarding the dissuasion, Mao Xiang stared at the riverbank that was coming closer and closer with eagerness in his heart. As soon as the gangplank was lowered he quickly stepped on it and landed ashore. When the unwilling Zhang Mingbi caught up with him from behind, he was already standing in front of the bamboo fence and knocking on the gate.

At first he knocked lightly but getting no response from inside the knocking went louder. After a long while there was still no response. Zhang Mingbi said:

"My dear friend! Maybe they're all dead asleep. Forget it. Let's go back to the boat."

可是冒襄十分固执，他一声不响，捏起拳头，在门上咚咚咚地猛擂起来。

终于，门内传来了细碎的脚步声，接着响起了一个女孩儿清亮的嗓音：

“门公，是谁在打门呢？”

“莫理他！反正姐儿不见客，让他敲不应，自己去了算！”一个苍老的声音瓮声瓮气地回答，听来很近，就在门房内。

“那也得瞧瞧是谁啊！刚才老爹又出去了，若是他回来，叫门不应，又该骂人了。”

“不是，老爹他会喊我。只怕是东家的张小四，要不就是隔壁的王婆，又来借钱借米的。准没好事儿，不用理他！”

冒襄在外面听见，又好笑又好气。他又打了两下门，高声说：

“我们是如皋冒襄、金沙张明弼，特来拜望宛娘，快快开门！”

这一次总算有了反应，只听那女孩儿在门里“嗳”了一声，但是又不来开门，却埋怨门公说：“瞧你，估错了吧，是客人哩！快起来开门！”

冒襄同张明弼对瞧了一下，嘴上不说，心中都想：这鬼丫头也真够促狭，你自己来开一下不就完了，偏要支使门公！

门房里的床“吱扭吱扭”地响了一阵，大约是门公爬起来，只听他不满地咕哝了一句什么，估计是说那丫头不替他开门。果然，那丫头立即唱歌似的反驳说：

“这是你的事情，编排是该你干！我又没吃你的一份粮，凭啥要替你动手？”

……

终于，门“咿呀”一声打开了，露出了门公年老的、骨骼粗大的脸和矮小结实的身躯。

冒襄早就一百个不耐烦，见门一开，立即径直往里走。那门公想拦阻，但又不敢，只好求援地望着寿儿。

But Mao Xiang was a stubborn man. Without saying a word, he clenched his hand into a fist and pounded on the gate.

Finally, from inside came the sound of mincing steps and then the crisp voice of a young woman:

"Mr. Janitor, who is it pounding on the gate?"

"Let them be. Missus will receive nobody today. When they get no answer, they'll leave by themselves," an ancient male voice grumbled from the watch room.

"But we should have a look to know who it is. Grandpa went out just now. In case he's back and gets no answer he'll fly into a rage again."

"It can't be him. If it were him he would call out to me. I'm afraid it's Zhang Xiaosi or Grandma Wang next door coming to borrow money or rice. There won't be anything good. Let them be."

When Mao Xiang heard it from the outside, he was amused and annoyed at the same time. He pounded on the gate again and said at the top of his voice, "Mao Xiang from Rugao and Zhang Mingbi from Jinsha are here to see Xiaowan. Open the gate, please!"

This time, they finally had some response from inside. The girl said "oh" but did not come to the gate; instead, she grumbled to the janitor, "See? You were mistaken! They're our guests. Get up and open the gate!"

Mao Xiang and Zhang Mingbi looked at each other in the eye with the same understanding: this little girl was wicked indeed. Instead of opening the gate herself she asked the janitor to do it.

The bed in the watch room creaked and groaned as the janitor rolled out of it mumbling something, probably a complaint about the servant girl not opening the gate on his behalf. Sure enough, the servant girl retorted in a singsong voice:

"It's your business and you should do it. I'm not paid for that job of yours and why should I do it for you?"

...

Finally, the gate creaked open and revealed the janitor's old, rugged face and short, sturdy body.

Mao Xiang, long impatient, went straight in. The janitor wanted

寿儿却不慌不忙。她迎着客人先道了个万福，仍旧用唱歌一般的嗓门说："两位姐夫，远来辛苦了，请到堂上奉茶。待婢子通报去来。"

冒襄摇摇头："我们不吃茶，到楼上看看你娘就走。"

"多谢两位姐夫美意。"寿儿说，忽然露出戚然的样子，"只是我家阿娘病重，只怕、只怕不能见客。"

"啊，宛娘病得很重么？"张明弼问。

"嗯，重！重得简直不能再重。连人，她都快认不得了。"寿儿的声音甚至有点呜咽。

张明弼默默地点着头，望了一眼冒襄，意思是：怎么样？还要上去么？

冒襄没有作声，但显然也有点动摇了。他抬起头，犹豫不决地望着阁楼上昏暗的灯光。

寿儿闪动着一双黑眼珠子，在他俩身上溜了几下，忽然抿着嘴儿问：

"这位姐夫，可是如皋冒公子？"

"啊，正是小生。"

"若是如皋冒公子，我家阿娘倒必定是认得的。"

"……？"

"适才阿娘吩咐说，若是等闲俗客，一概不见。若是冒公子，你可得千万好好儿请上来。"

"啊！她怎么知道我要来？"

"这个么，婢子可就不知道啦！"寿儿狡狯地说，不待冒襄再问，她就转过身去，当先引路。冒襄同张明弼交换了一个莫名其妙的眼色，满腹狐疑地跟在后面。

## 倾诉悲喜

由于吃了半碗粥，许多天来，董小宛第一次感到多少有了点

to stop him but dared not. He looked at Shou'er for help.

Yet Shou'er was in no hurry. She curtsied to the visitors and said in a singsong voice, "Welcome, my brothers-in-law. Please come in and have some tea. I'll report your coming to Missus."

Mao Xiang shook his head and said, "No bother with tea. We'll leave soon after seeing your missus."

"Thank you for your kindness, brothers-in-law," said Shou'er, who suddenly became gloomy, "I'm afraid Missus won't be able to see you because she's very ill."

"Is that so? Is it serious?" asked Zhang Mingbi.

"Yes, very serious. Can't be worse. She's so ill that she can hardly recognize anybody," she said with a sob.

Zhang Mingbin nodded his head in silence and took a look at Mao Xiang, meaning "What then? Do you still want to go up?"

Mao Xiang didn't say a word but was evidently wavering. He lifted his head to look at the dim lamplight in the attic.

Shou'er, rolling her black bright eyes, studied the two men for an instant and then said with a laughter muffled by her hand, "Is this brother-in-law Young Master Mao from Rugao County?"

"Yes, it's me."

"If you're Young Master Mao from Rugao County, Missus will surely recognize you."

"—?"

"Missus told me just now that if it is anybody else just leave them alone but if it is Young Master Mao from Rugao County, let him in."

"Well, how does she know I'm coming?"

"That I don't know," said Shou'er slyly. Without waiting for more questions from Mao Xiang, she turned around and led them in. Mao Xiang and Zhang Mingbi exchanged a look and followed her suspiciously.

## The Heart of a Girl

Having had a half bowl of porridge, for the first time in days, Dong Xiaowan's spirits began to lift. She asked Shou'er to comb her

精神。她让寿儿替她梳了头，把乱糟糟的屋子收拾了一下。出于一种奇怪的预感，她还吩咐寿儿：要是如皋冒相公来访，马上告诉她。不过，随后她就意识到这种念头是多么可笑可怜了。哎，世上哪有这样好的事？你想着一个人，他就会立刻来到你的身边？何况人家是家财万贯的翩翩公子。纵然没有陈圆圆，也会有别的女人。就凭三年前那匆匆一面，能指望人家记得住你？怕早就把你忘个一干二净啦！再说，梦里不是已经把这事指点得明明白白了么？就别再费这份心思啦！这样一想，董小宛又觉得自己完全没有指望了。从今以后，她就像那荒原旷野上随风飘转的一株蓬草，孤苦伶仃，无依无靠……终于，她把脑袋深深地埋在被窝里，压抑地、凄苦地哭起来。

渐渐地，她听见有人走上楼来了。不是一个人，是好几个。陌生的、粗重的男人脚步声从过道里一路响过来，在门外停了一下，然后跨进屋来。

“谁？”董小宛问，竭力止住抽泣。

“哦，三年前，在此楼下曲栏杆畔，曾有幸与小娘子醉中一晤的那个人，今日特来拜候，不知小娘子可记得否？”一个优雅清亮的声音说。

有片刻工夫，董小宛弄不明白，为什么一听到这声音，自己的心像是突然停止了跳动，仿佛凝住了似的。“啊，他说什么？他说什么呀？这是什么意思？”她艰难地思索。蓦地，她的心狂跳起来，血液一下子冲上脑门和双颊：啊，是他，是他，是他来了！她在心里大叫，感到一阵晕眩。但是，她没有立刻转过身子。她不敢，也没有力量那样做。谁知道呢？也许稍一动弹，一切便都化为乌有了！

“小生是如皋冒襄。这位是金沙张公亮。”大概是听不见董小宛答应，冒襄只好自我介绍了。

董小宛仍旧小心翼翼地保持着原来的姿势，但是泪水已经涌

hair and tidy up the messy room. Out of a strange anticipation, she said to Shou'er that if Young Master Mao from Gugao County came she should be notified immediately. However, she quickly realized how ridiculous and pitiable she was to have that idea. Humph, how on earth can there be a good thing like that? Just because you think of someone, they would immediately come to your side? Besides, he's a wealthy man. If not Chen Yuanyuan, he would have another woman. How can you expect him to remember you merely on the basis of a passing encounter three years ago? He might have completely forgotten you. Besides, didn't the dream tell it all? Do not waste your time dwelling on that idea anymore. Thus thinking, Dong Xiaowan relapsed into despondency. From now on, she would be alone and lonely, like a blade of grass whirling in the prairie wind. Finally she buried her head in the quilt and let out sobs of pent-up sorrow.

A short while later, she heard the sound of footsteps moving up to her attic. It was not one person, but several. The sound of heavy, unfamiliar male footsteps came all the way up the staircase, stopped outside the door, and then entered the room.

"Who is it?" Dong Xiaowan asked, trying to stop herself from sobbing.

"Um, do you remember, three years ago, by the curved railing downstairs here, a man was lucky enough to join you in drunkenness? He's coming to see you," said an elegant and melodious voice.

Upon hearing that voice her heart stopped beating as if it had frozen. She didn't know why. "What did he say? What did he say? What does that mean?" She thought hard. Suddenly, her heart started beating wildly, blood rushing to her forehead and cheeks. Oh good heavens, it's him, it's him, it's him for sure. She yelled silently, delirious with joy. However, she didn't turn to him immediately, not daring do it or not having the strength. Who knows what's next? Maybe if she moves, everything will evaporate.

"It's me, Mao Xiang from Rugao County. This is Zhang Gongliang from Jinsha County," Mao Xiang introduced himself. There was no response from Xiaowan.

Xiaowan cautiously maintained her posture while tears welled up

上了眼眶。

“奴家……不敢忘记公子……”她颤着声儿回答，觉得冒襄已经走近床头。她不由得缩紧了身子，仿佛怕触着什么容易破碎的东西似的，一边哽咽地说：“……三年前，有劳公子几番临顾，仅得匆匆一晤，但阿娘背后说起公子，总是称赞不绝于口，说她见的人不少，从未有像公子这般人品的。娘还因奴家未能与公子多盘桓些日子，深为惋惜……如今阿娘死了，看见公子，奴家就想起阿娘。她的话，就像昨天对奴家说的一样……”

董小宛说到伤心动情之处，终于转过身子，撩开罗帐。于是，她看见了冒襄的脸。

这确实是一张俊美得令人惊叹的脸。如果说，早在三年前，它就给董小宛留下了鲜明美好的印象的话，那么，经过岁月的冲刷，它的许多细节部分在记忆中已经变得模糊之后，董小宛此刻重新面对它，却不禁怅然若失。因为她发现，自己三年来对于这张脸的一切想象和补充，竟然是如此蹩脚、平庸、俗气。而它其实是那样的空灵微妙，出人意料，而又完美无缺。它的美，绝不是用“弯曲秀长的眉毛、顾盼含情的眼睛、笔直高耸的鼻梁，以及线条优美的口辅”这样一些似是而非的描写所能表达的。它的非凡之处，首先在于那种天生的高贵气质，那种被传统的道德文化高度地充实和细致琢磨过的内在情感，以及充分意识到自己的身份和力量的雍容气派。当这一切，同俊美的外貌充分地糅合在一起，并且在一颦一笑当中自然而然地显露出来的时候，确实具有一种勾魂摄魄般的魅力。董小宛觉得自己的心跳得那样厉害，简直快要从胸膛里蹦出来似的，她赶紧垂下头去，不敢再看。

冒襄也在注视董小宛。三年不见，他发现记忆当中的那个娇痴懒慢、醉态可掬的女孩子，已经成熟为一个清丽绝俗的少女。也许因为正在生病的缘故，她看上去瘦了一些，却比当年更美了。

in her eyes.

"How, how dare I forget your young lordship?" she said in a trembling voice. Feeling Mao Xiang had stepped to her bedside, she unconsciously shrank her body as if afraid to touch a fragile object and said with a sob, "Three years ago, I only had the honor to meet you once though you came many times. My mother always praised you before me. She said of all the many men she had ever seen there was no one as good as you. She always regretted not having tried to make you stay with me for a few more days. Now she's passed away and your presence reminds me of her as if her words were said yesterday."

As she lamented, she turned and opened the canopy net. Then she saw Mao Xiang's face.

It was unmistakably a face of amazing beauty. That face had left a delightfully beautiful impression on her three years ago, but with the passage of time many of its details had become blurred in her memory. At this moment, when facing that face again, Xiaowan was surprised to find it was so ethereal and subtle and out of the ordinary. It was a perfect face. In comparison, the copy that she had tried to keep alive in her imagination in the past three years was so lame, cheap, and tacky. The beauty of the face was definitely not to be described by specious expressions such as "curved long eyebrows", "dewy eyes", "a straight and tall nose bridge", and "beautifully-lined mouth corners." What made it remarkable, first of all, was the natural noble temperament, the inner tenderness that had been highly enriched and refined by the traditional moral culture, and the graceful style that represented a full awareness of one's own identity and strength. When all this was fully blended with the handsome appearance and revealed naturally in a frown or in a casual smile, a fascinating charm was produced. Xiaowan felt that her heart was beating so fast that it was going to pop out of her chest, so she drooped her head quickly, not daring to look again.

At the same time, Mao Xiang was also watching Dong Xiaowan and found that the innocent drunken little thing in his memory had matured into a graceful young lady of alarming beauty after three

她的肤色变得更白净，相形之下，头发和眉毛显得更黑。配上梦幻似的妩媚而忧郁的眼睛，小巧玲珑的鼻子和嘴唇，使她足以置身于秦淮河畔最顶尖儿的一批名妓当中，而毫不逊色。但这不是主要的。主要的是，在这张脸上显示出一种与她的绝大多数同行姐妹不同的驯良神情，一种过于端庄娴静的气息。冒襄此刻还说不上对这种气息喜欢还是不喜欢。只是不知什么缘故，他忽然想到了陈圆圆，想起了她那恶作剧的眼神，那令人哭笑不得的任性，以及层出不穷的花样，并不由自主地为这突然闪现的记忆而微笑了……

"哦，张老爷、冒公子，二位请坐……"董小宛的声音在耳边响起。冒襄蓦地惊醒过来，他回顾了一下，发现张明弼已经在靠墙的一张椅子坐下，也就走过去，在旁边坐了下来。

这当儿，寿儿已经端上茶来，并且换过了两盏明亮的斗色晶灯。于是三个人便一边喝着茶，一边交谈。冒襄和张明弼详细地询问了小宛母亲陈氏的死，着实咨嗟感叹了一番；接着又问到董小宛的病，对她已见好转感到宽慰；随后，冒襄又约略地谈了一下别后的情形，谈到大半年来，怎样为着父亲的事四方奔走，现在有了结果。但是，他连一个字也没有提到陈圆圆。这并不是怕给董小宛知道，会引起猜疑和嫉妒。事实上，他对董小宛毫无别的想法。他今晚到这儿来，无非是满心的苦闷无聊打发不掉，想借此散散心而已。但是，他却不想提起陈圆圆，因为那毕竟是一件不痛快的、有损脸面的事……

不过，冒襄的这种心理，连他的好友张明弼也暂时捉摸不透。在这一阵子交谈中，张明弼很少开口。他一直在观察冒襄的言语、举动，猜测他的朋友如此坚执地要来拜访董小宛，到底有什么目的。当发现董小宛对冒襄流露出明显的、异乎寻常的依恋之情，

years. She looked thinner than before, maybe because she was ill, but she was even more beautiful. Her complexion had become fairer, so in contrast her hair and brows appeared darker. The pair of phantasmic, watery and melancholic eyes, an exquisite nose, and a little mouth, would place her well among the top courtesans on the Qinhuai River, but none of those was the most defining elements of her beauty. What made her different from most of the other girls was that her face showed an expression of docility and an excessive breath of dignity and calm. Mao Xiang couldn't say whether he liked or disliked that breath at this moment. For some unknown reason, he suddenly thought of Chen Yuanyuan—the mischievous eyes, the ridiculous willfulness, and the endless tricks—and involuntarily smiled upon this sudden flash of memory.

"Welcome, Lord Zhang and Young Master Mao. Please sit." Xiaowan's voice entered his ears. Mao Xiang, waking up from his reverie, looked back and found Zhang Mingbi already seated in a chair close to the wall. He walked over and sat beside him.

By now Shou'er had brought tea and lit up two bright crystal lamps. The three people conversed while drinking tea. Mao Xiang and Zhang Mingbi inquired about Xiaowan's mother's death in detail, and sighed over her fate. They also asked about Xiaowan's illness and felt relieved that she had improved. Then, Mao Xiang gave a brief account of his own experiences after their parting—how he had been going around to attend to his father's affairs for over half a year and how things had turned out. However, he didn't mention Chen Yuanyuan, not because he was afraid of causing suspicion and envy in Xiaowan but because he didn't think Xiaowan was in any way related. He came here tonight just to seek a respite from his boredom. He didn't want to mention Chen Yuanyuan, because after all, it was an unpleasant and inglorious thing.

Yet his best friend had no clue what he was thinking. Zhang Mingbi kept silent while the other two talked, taking note of every word and movement of Mao Xiang and trying to guess why he had insisted on coming. When Mingbi found Xiaowan obviously had

而冒襄对于同陈圆圆的那段关系又讳莫如深时，张明弼就认定，冒襄已经把物色如夫人的目标，转移到董小宛身上来。他本来就一直为好朋友的痛苦忧郁而担心，同时，还为自己没能及时找到冒襄报信，致使陈圆圆被田弘遇抢去，多少感到有点内疚，但又苦于无法补救。现在发现了冒襄的这种“意向”，他不禁大为欣慰，于是决心要尽力促成它。因此，当谈话告一段落，张明弼就趁机站起来，拱着手说：

“我差点儿忘了，适才下船的时候，原不曾说清要不要船家等着。只怕他等得不耐烦，自己回去了。辟疆、宛娘，你们先谈着，我去吩咐一声就来！”

说完，也不等冒襄答应，他就叫寿儿提灯引路，匆匆出门，下楼去了。

“冒郎，你到这边来坐，这边暖和些。”当张明弼的脚步声在楼下消失了之后，董小宛忽然伸手拍了拍床沿，这样招呼说。正在为老朋友突然走开而感到疑惑的冒襄，怔了一下，茫然地回过头来。

“哎，来呀，把灯也拿过来，奴家有话要对你说哩！”董小宛娇嗔地催促着。

冒襄这一下听明白了。他目光灼灼地瞅了董小宛一会儿，微微一笑，站起来，先去桌上擎起一盏晶灯，把它放到董小宛床头一张方凳上。然后，侧身在床沿上坐下来，就势抓起董小宛的一只小手，把它放在嘴唇边轻吻着。

“唔，记得么？周清真的妙句：‘弄粉调朱柔素手，问何时重握’……”

董小宛把手抽回来，“啊，不，奴家的手脏！”她急急地说。

可是冒襄又一次捉住了它，“管它呢，嗯，管它呢，只要我喜欢！”他任性地说，挨个儿吻着那细嫩圆润的指尖；随即伸出

an unusual attachment to Mao Xiang and that Mao Xiang was very secretive about his relationship with Chen Yuanyuan, he decided that Mao Xiang was considering Dong Xiaowan for a concubine. Having been worried by his good friend's sorrow and melancholy and feeling more or less guilty for failing to give notice to Mao Xiang in time to stop the kidnapping of Chen Yuanyuan by Tian Hongyu and for his inability to make remedies, Zhang Mingbi was greatly relieved and decided to make it happen. Therefore, when the conversation paused, Zhang Mingbi took the opportunity to stand up and excused himself, saying:

"Oh, no! I've almost forgotten it. I didn't tell the boatman whether he should wait for us. I'm afraid he'll leave after waiting for too long. Pijiang and Xiaowan, just go on with the conversation and I'll be back shortly."

Without waiting for a response from Mao Xiang, he asked Shou'er to light the way for him and went downstairs.

"Sweetheart, come and sit beside me. It's warmer here," said Xiaowan after Mingbi left, beckoning to Mao Xiang by tapping the edge of her bed with one hand. Mao Xiang, who was puzzling over his friend's departure, gave a start and turned his head to her.

"Come, sweetheart! Move the lamp here. I want to tell you something," Xiaowan urged coquettishly.

Mao Xiang suddenly understood. He looked at Xiaowan with scorching eyes for a while, and, with a smile on his face, stood up, took up a crystal lamp from the table, and placed it on the square stool at the end of the bed. Then, he sat on the edge of the bed sideways, took hold of Xiaowan's hand, and put it on his lips.

"Um, do you remember that famous line from Zhou Qingzhen, 'When can I hold it again, that hand for beauty powder and paint pigments?'"

Xiaowan took back her hand and said worriedly, "Oh no! My hand is dirty."

But Mao Xiang caught it again. "It doesn't matter, um, it doesn't matter, as long as I like it," he said willfully, kissing the delicate and

胳臂，把董小宛揽进怀里，用腮帮在那娇养的脸蛋上轻轻挨擦起来。他微眯着眼睛，陶醉于这种愉快的、令人意荡魂销的接触当中。

“可是，可是奴家真的有话要问你……”董小宛无可奈何地说，脸红了。

“你问嘛……”

“那你说，圆圆她当真被抢走了么？”

像冷不防被人刺了一下似的，冒襄的表情变了。他放开董小宛，愠恼地盯着她，一会儿，才把眼光移开。

“哼，不错，抢走啦！”他冷冷地说，“你问这做什么？”

董小宛似乎没有注意冒襄情绪的变化，她点点头，露出悲戚的神情：“奴家也听说了，还有点不信。那么这是真的了——唉，陈家姐姐又漂亮，又能干，那份聪明伶俐更是万中无一。平日里姐妹行中理论到谁个将来最有出息，大家第一个就推她，却不道竟是这般命苦！”董小宛说着，声音哽咽了，泪水沿着脸颊流了下来。

冒襄没有作声。因为董小宛此时此刻突然提起这件事使他颇为恼火，而且他还有点怀疑她这样做的用意。哼，别看她假惺惺地故作悲态，说不定心中正幸灾乐祸，在变着法儿挖苦陈圆圆，以发泄她的妒火哩！风月场中，这样的娘们儿他见得多了。

渐渐，董小宛停止了流泪。她怔怔地望着床头的灯焰，半晌，低声地说：

“要是陈家姐姐不曾被抢，她同公子可是天生地设的一对。真的。只是，唉……”

冒襄忽然笑了。这嘴角上的笑容表示着他对这样的“表演”是多么熟悉，而且已经不想再“欣赏”下去了。他站起来，居高临下地望了望董小宛，说：

“你正病着，我本不该来打扰，又劳你陪了我这许久，实在

fleshy fingertips one by one; then he stretched out his arm, held her close, and gently rubbed his cheek on her tender face. Squinting his eyes, he reveled in the pleasant and titillating contact.

"But, but I really want to ask you—" said Xiaowan helplessly, blushing.

"Ask away then."

"Tell me, has Yuanyuan really been kidnapped?"

Mao Xiang's expression changed as if he were stabbed in a surprise attack. He let go of Xiaowan and stared at her in annoyance, and after a while, he looked away.

"Huh, yes, she's been taken away," he said coldly, "Why do you ask?"

Xiaowan didn't seem to notice the change in Mao Xiang's mood. She nodded her head with a sad expression. "I've also heard of it but I still don't believe it. It's true then—oh, what bad luck for her! Miss Chen is beautiful, able and more intelligent than anyone else. When the girls discussed who had the best prospects, everyone thought it was her. No one had ever thought she would have such mishap," Xiaowan said, her voice choking and tears flowing down her cheeks.

Mao Xiang was silent, quite annoyed by Xiaowan's sudden mention of Yuanyuan at this moment and wondering what her intention was. Humph, forget about your feigned sadness. Who knows if you're not gloating in your heart, if it's not sourness and jealousy. In the bawdy houses, he had seen too many women of this kind.

Gradually, Xiaowan's sobbing came to a stop. She blankly stared at the flame of the lamp on the bedside, and after a long while, murmured:

"If Sister Chen hadn't been kidnapped, she would have been a perfect match for you. Really. It's just, aw—"

Mao Xiang suddenly smiled. This smile on the corner of his mouth showed how familiar he was with such acting, and he didn't like it anymore. He stood up and, looking at Xiaowan condescendingly, said:

"You're ill, I shouldn't have disturbed you. I'm sorry to have you

过意不去。你歇着吧，回头我叫人封五十两银子过来，给你将养身子。过些日子我再来看你。”

“……公、公子要走……”董小宛颤着声儿问。由于惊愕和着急，脸孔一下子变得煞白。

“嗯，时候不早了。”

董小宛忽然露出惨然的神色，她拼命咬住嘴唇，垂下头去。

“请公子不要送银子过来。”她哑着嗓子说。

“啊！怎么？”

董小宛张了张嘴，只说出“奴家……”两个字，就哽咽住了。她拼命地摇一摇头，立刻用袖子使劲堵住嘴巴，眼泪却“吧嗒吧嗒”地掉下来。

看见她这个样子，冒襄倒奇怪起来。他犹疑了一下，重新坐下，稍稍缓和了口气，说：“不是我不肯多留，实在是派到襄阳去向家大人报告喜讯的人，明朝一早就要出发，我得赶回下处向他交代许多事。今日，我是偶然路过这里，听说你病着，就进来看望一下。现在见你好了点，就放心了。这点银子，无非是我们相识一场，聊表心意，你就收下吧！”

也许这温言解释发生了作用，董小宛很快地平静下来。她低着头，拭着泪，驯顺地听完冒襄的话，然后说道：

“适才奴家出语不逊，请公子休怪。不是奴家不晓事，要苦留公子。实在是奴家自从娘死之后，十有八日，寝食俱废，一天到晚昏昏沉沉，净做些颠三倒四的噩梦。有时梦见自己已经死了，每一次都是公子忽然来到，才救了我。今天公子真的来了，奴家一见，便觉得心情宁帖，精神爽旺。如此看来，公子实在是奴家的救命恩人。所以，银子奴家是决计不能收的。便是公子强要奴家收下，奴家也会一生一世不得安心的。公子若是可怜奴家，就请再稍坐片刻，待奴家举酒，为公子恭祝福寿双全。能这样，奴

with me for such a long time. Just rest, and I'll ask someone to seal fifty taels of silver for you. You need to eat well. I'll see you again in a couple of days."

"Are—are you leaving, my young master?" Xiaowan asked in a shaky voice, her face pale with consternation and anxiety.

"Well, it's getting late."

Xiaowan's face darkened. Biting her lip, she lowered her head. "Please don't send me money," she said in a husky voice.

"Why, what's the problem?"

Xiaowan opened her mouth, and choked up after saying "I—". Shaking her head desperately, she immediately covered her mouth with her sleeve, but her tears rolled down her cheeks like rain.

Mao Xiang was startled to see her like that. He hesitated for an instant, sat down again, and said in a friendlier voice, "It's not that I don't want to stay longer, but the man who's going to Xiangyang to report the good news to my father will leave early tomorrow morning and I have to rush back to my place to arrange for things. I happened to pass by your place today and heard that you're unwell, so I came in to see you. Now that I see you're better, I feel relieved. This little bit of money is nothing more than a gift for you, a token for our acquaintance. Please accept it."

Xiaowan quickly calmed down, probably because these soft words had produced an effect. Head lowered, she listened docilely to Mao Xiang as she wiped her tears. Then she said:

"Sorry I've displeased you. Please pardon me. It's not that I'm not reasonable and want you to stay against your will. Since the death of my mother, I haven't been able to eat or sleep well and have been sleepy from morning to evening, having nightmares of all kinds. In some of them, I was dying but was finally saved by your sudden appearance. Today you've really come. When I see you I suddenly feel much better. This means you're really my savior. So I shouldn't take your money. If you insist on giving it to me, I won't feel good for the rest of my life. If you have pity on me, please sit a while and let me raise the cup to toast to your happiness and longevity. If you do me

家明儿就是死了，也于心无憾了！”

冒襄当初看见董小宛眼泪汪汪的样子，满以为她必然照例要撒娇撒痴，又哭又闹。刚才他之所以缓和了态度，无非是以退为进；他说那一番话，也多半是随口敷衍。他已经准备着，倘若对方还要纠缠不休，他便抽身就走，毫不客气了。可是，没想到董小宛竟是一哄便听，温驯老实得出奇。接着，又听她说出那样一篇情真意切的话，更是大出冒襄的意料，反而使他不知如何应付才是了。

“只是、只是张兄正在船上等着我，去迟了怕不好……”冒襄犹犹豫豫地说。

“这个么，公子倒不必挂心！”寿儿那唱歌似的嗓音忽然在门帘外接口说，“张老爷临出门时曾吩咐婢子，说今儿是初三，星朗风清，他要沿河闲步，观赏夜景，半时一刻不会回船，他请公子在这楼上多坐些时，不必急着就走！”

由于寿儿这样说，冒襄也就无法再推托。他只好听凭董小宛吩咐寿儿置酒备肴，暂时留下来不走了。

## 苦留后约

直到三更以后，冒襄才从董小宛的闺房告辞出来。酒席之上，他被董小宛不断地殷勤相劝，着实喝了不少。不过，他还能保持头脑的清醒，没有忘记张明弼还在船上等他，也没有忘记明天一早要办的事。所以，尽管董小宛一再挽留他住下，他都坚决谢绝了。董小宛不敢过分勉强，只好起身送他下楼。当董小宛奇迹般地不用别人搀扶就站立起来，并且步履如常地走出闺房时，冒襄还没怎样在意，站在旁边瞧着的寿儿，却惊奇得瞪大了眼睛。

such a favor, I won't have regrets even if I die tomorrow."

A moment ago, when seeing Xiaowan full of tears Mao Xiang had thought she was going to make a show of herself. He had softened his tone simply as a perfunctory gesture. In fact, he had been prepared to leave immediately should she continue to mess with him. To his surprise, Xiaowan had been docile and submissive, believing in every word of his. To his greater surprise, she had told him how much love she had felt for him. He was suddenly at a loss as to what to say and what to do.

"The problem is, Brother Zhang is waiting for me on the boat. It's not good to keep him waiting for too long," said Mao Xiang awkwardly.

"That isn't a problem, my young master," said Shou'er in a singsong voice from outside the door curtain, "When Mr. Zhang left, he said, 'It's the third day of the month, the stars are bright, the wind is cool, and I'll take a stroll along the river and won't be back very soon. Tell Young Master Mao that he can stay in the house as long as he likes and shouldn't hurry to go."

Mao Xiang no longer had any excuse, so he stayed. Xiaowan bade Shou'er to prepare wine and food.

## A Promise

It was not until after the third watch that Mao Xiang took leave of Dong Xiaowan. At the drinking table, Xiaowan had persistently offered him wine, and he had drunk quite a great deal. However, his mind was sober. He hadn't forgotten Zhang Mingbi was still waiting for him on the boat and what he had to do early tomorrow morning. Therefore, even though Xiaowan had repeatedly asked him to stay the night, he had resolutely declined. Xiaowan, not daring to insist on making him stay against his will, stood up to escort him downstairs. When Xiaowan suddenly stood up without being supported by anyone and walked out of the boudoir, Mao Xiang didn't notice anything unusual, but Shou'er, who had been standing by and watching, opened her eyes wide in surprise.

灿烂的银河已经移到中天，朦胧的银辉洒满了整个院子。湿润的、微冷的风，从七里山塘上吹来。在房顶的茅草上、在花树的梢头和草丛里，露珠儿在闪烁。四邻早已灯火全无，一片沉寂。偶尔，从远处的深巷里，传来一两声狗儿低沉的吠叫……

董小宛到了楼下，在屋檐前站了一站，等寿儿赶上来，把披风披在她的身上，她就陪着冒襄，缓缓地向大门走去。

“公子此去，不知何时才能再来？”不声不响地走了十来步之后，董小宛终于打破了沉默。

冒襄有点醉了。他乜斜着眼睛，微笑说：“人生何处不相逢。要来也容易，只要我想得起，就……来了；若是……我想不起，也不打紧……你托人来——说，提醒我……哈哈，不就来了？”

“只怕，只怕奴家托人去说，公子也不肯来呢！”董小宛的声音透着幽怨。

“不……不会的。只要你，托人来说……要不，你，到如皋，来找我，呃，也行！”

“到如皋？那——老爷、老太太不会骂你？还有少奶奶……”

“啊哈，这个，你就不知道了。爹妈最宠我，从、从来不拂我的意。少奶奶么，最是贤惠不过了，她还劝、劝我讨、讨小哩！”

“啊，公子这话当真？”

“谁、谁骗你！骗你，我、我就不是冒襄！”

这话刚说出口，门楼下的阴影里忽然有人拍着手笑道：“好呀，辟疆已经有约，宛娘还不赶快道谢！”

随着话音，两个人走到星光下来，却是张明弼和冒成。冒襄一见就站住了，指着张明弼大声大气地问：

“好你个张公亮，刚才躲到哪、哪儿去了？这会子却又钻、

The bright Milky Way had moved to the middle of the sky, and a hazy silvery light had been sprinkled all over the courtyard. A humid, slightly cold wind was blowing from the Seven-Li Waterway. Dewdrops flickered on the straws on the thatched roof, on the tops of the flowering trees, and on the bushes. All lights were out in the neighborhood in a dead silence. From time to time, from a deep alley far away came a low-pitched dog bark or two.

Xiaowan went downstairs. She stood in front of the eaves and waited for Shou'er to catch up and put the cloak on her. Then she accompanied Mao Xiang to walk slowly towards the gate.

After quietly walking ten steps, Xiaowan finally broke the silence and said, "I'm sorry to see you go. When will you come again, sir?"

Mao Xiang, a little intoxicated, squinted his eyes with a smile and said, "Life is full of surprises. It can be any time. I'll come whenever I think of you. If I forget to come, it doesn't matter. Just send someone to remind me and haha, here I will be."

"I'm afraid, I'm afraid that you won't come even if I send someone to you," said Xiaowan in a pathetic voice.

"No, it won't happen that way. Just send someone, or rather, you come to Rugao to see me, uh, that will work too."

"To Rugao? In that case, won't your parents be angry with you? There's also her ladyship your wife—"

"Haha, you don't know about this. My parents are most indulging to me and never say no to what I want. My wife is the most virtuous woman in the world. She's even persuading me to take a concubine."

"Is that so? Are you serious?"

"Who, who lies? If I lied to you, I, I weren't Mao Xiang."

At this moment someone in the darkness downstairs suddenly clapped his hands and laughed, saying, "That's a good one. Now you have a promise from Pijiang. Say 'thank you', Xiaowan."

Following that voice, the two walked down into the starlight. It was Zhang Mingbi and Mao Cheng. Mao Xiang stopped when he saw them and howled at Mingbi:

"Zhang Gongliang! Where, where the hell have you been hiding?

钻出来！”

“唉呀，辟疆，你还说哩。你赖在宛娘房里老是不出来，害我等得好苦。三番两次差冒成来打听，好容易才打听到这会儿散席了，我才巴巴地赶来接你。你一声儿不谢倒还罢了，反来埋怨我，这真是从何说起哟！”张明弼摆出一副委屈的样子，随即自己又笑起来。他转向董小宛说：

“宛娘，你身子瞧着像是大好了，恭喜恭喜！辟疆我们接走就行了。夜寒露重，你就不要远送了！”他瞧了瞧冒襄，又走上前来，向董小宛咬耳朵说：“你放心，明儿，我一定让他再来！”

董小宛本来打算把冒襄一直送到河边上。听张明弼这样说，她就没有再坚持。不过，她仍旧一手扶着寿儿的肩膀，站在门前，默默地目送着张明弼和冒成一边一个，搀扶着醉态可掬的冒襄，由门公提着灯笼引路，朝岸边泊着的小船走去。直到人影都看不清了，小船也离开了河岸，舱里的灯火颤动着，消失在迷茫的夜色深处，这才慢慢地走回院子来。

董小宛刚走进堂屋，她爹董子将就像从地里冒出来似的，出现在她的面前。

“阿囡，你可大好了？真叫爹高兴呀！”董子将笑嘻嘻地迎上来说，瘦刮刮的脸上现出多时不见的兴奋神情。

“爹还没睡？是的，孩儿觉着这会儿好多啦，有劳爹爹挂心。”董小宛疲乏地微笑着，行了一个礼，走向楼梯。

“呃，爹一心记挂着你的身子，哪儿睡得着哇！”董子将讨好地说，跟了过来，“呃，这么说，冒公子走啦？”

“嗯！”董小宛漫声应答着。强自支撑了大半宿，这会儿，

And now you come out at this moment."

"Oh? Pijiang, then you're complaining against me? You stayed in Xiaowan's boudoir and kept me waiting for ages and ages. Again and again I sent Mao Cheng to check on you and finally he reported your dinner party is over, so I've hurried here to pick you up. Instead of thanking me, you're complaining against me. Where should we start?" said Zhang Mingbi, who put on an aggrieved look and laughed again. Then, he turned to Xiaowan and said:

"Xiaowan, you look well again, congratulations! We're picking up Pijiang now. It's rather cold with heavy dew outside. Just stop here and don't stay out too long." With that, he cast a look at Mao Xiang, walked over to Xiaowan and whispered into her ear, "Don't worry. Tomorrow, I'll let him come again."

Xiaowan had intended to escort Mao Xiang all the way to the river, but hearing that, she no longer insisted. However, she didn't immediate return to the yard. One hand on Shou'er's shoulder, she stood in front of the gate silently seeing him off. The lovably intoxicated Mao Xiang, supported by Zhang Mingbi and Mao Cheng and led by the janitor carrying a lantern, walked to a boat mooring at the riverbank. She watched until the flickering light of the boat disappeared into the depths of the mysterious night.

Just as Dong Xiaowan entered the drawing room, her father Dong Zijiang appeared in front of her as if popping out of the ground.

"My girl, are you much better now? Your dad is so happy," Dong Zijiang smiled and said, his skinny and pale face showing an expression of excitement that hadn't been seen for quite some time.

"You haven't gone to bed yet, Dad? Yes, I think I'm much better now. Thank you Dad for being so caring," said Xiaowan, who smiled languidly, bowed and walked toward the stairs.

Dong Zijiang caught up with her. "Uh, I am worried about your health and can't go to sleep," he said obsequiously. "So, Young Master Mao has left?"

"Hum," Xiaowan replied nonchalantly. She was exhausted by now. If Shou'er hadn't helped her, she might not have been able to

她实在已经筋疲力尽，要不是寿儿搀扶着，她也许就爬不上楼梯了。可是，她的精神仍然很兴奋。忽然，她停住脚步，回头问：

“爹，你说，冒郎他怎么样？”

“啊，啊，好，很好，好呀！如皋首屈一指的大富翁，有财有势，花起银子来像撒灰似的，从来不皱眉头！你不见他前时在南京，偌大一所桃叶河房，他一个人就全包下来，在那里天天摆酒宴客，哪一顿不招待个一百几十人的！唉，说起他家的银子来，真是拔根汗毛也比我们的大腿粗——海着咧！”

“爹！我不是说这个，我是说人！”

“人？嘿，人也好！小白脸，美男子，风流倜傥，人称‘东海秀影’。听说多少女儿家都为他神魂颠倒，说是‘宁为冒郎妾，不做富家妇’！嘿，阿囡，不是爹夸你，今晚他竟肯亲自来访，可见你福缘不浅哩！”

听爹这样一说，董小宛的心里也自甜滋滋的。她一转身，也不用寿儿搀扶，噔噔噔地独自上了楼。董子将一见，连忙紧赶几步，把寿儿搡到一边，抢先跟进闺房去，气得寿儿冲着他背后直做鬼脸。

董子将踏入闺房，看见董小宛已经坐在梳妆台前，正对着镜子怔怔地瞧。她一只手搭在腮边，轻轻地抚摸着，嘴角荡漾着微笑。董子将蹑手蹑脚地走近去，在离女儿三尺远近的地方站住，轻轻地叫唤：

“阿囡，阿囡！”

见女儿没有反应，董子将只好干咳一声，提高声音叫：“阿囡！”

董小宛愣了一下神，蓦地回头，脸上闪过一丝惊讶的神色，然后，立即就绽开笑脸。

“爹！”她做出撒娇的样子，欢快地叫，站起来，扯着董子

climb the stairs. However, her spirits were still very high. Suddenly, she stopped and asked:

"Dad, what do you think of Young Master Mao?"

"Ah, ah, good, very good, good indeed. He's from the wealthiest family in Rugao. Rich and powerful, spending money like dust, without blinking. You didn't see how he took the whole of the Peach Leaves Riverhouse all to himself in Nanjing a few days ago and banquet there every day, entertaining more than a hundred people every time. Boy, speaking of his family's wealth, take a hair from his calf and it's thicker than my thigh. He's incredibly rich."

"Dad! I don't mean that. I mean the person."

"The person? Oh, the person is good too. A fair, clean face—a beautiful man, a charming prince. He's known as 'the man in the mirage'. I hear that many girls fall in love with him and say, 'I'd rather be a concubine of Young Master Mao than the wife of another rich man.' Hey, my girl, I'm not flattering you but his patronage tonight does show you're very fortunate."

Hearing those words, her heart was filled with joy. She turned around and went upstairs alone, without Shou'er's support. Seeing that, Dong Zijiang quickened his steps, pushed Shou'er aside, and followed his daughter into the boudoir, leaving Shou'er grimacing at his back in displeasure.

Stepping into the boudoir, Dong Zijiang saw Xiaowan was already seated in front of the dressing table, staring into the mirror without moving—one hand touching her cheek indulgently—and beaming with happiness all across her face. Dong Zijiang tiptoed forward and stopped three feet away from his daughter.

"My girl, my girl," he whispered softly.

Seeing that his daughter didn't respond, Dong Zijiang let out a dry cough and raised his voice: "My girl!"

Xiaowan gave a start and turned her head suddenly. A look of surprise flashed across her face, followed by a broad smile.

"Dad!" she yelled gleefully like a baby. Then she stood up and pulled Dong Zijiang to a chair by the sleeve. "Dad, sit, please

将的袖子，把他拉到椅子旁边，“爹，你坐嘛，坐呀！”等董子将坐下之后，她也紧挨着他坐下来，用手指替他拈去粘在袖子上的一丝蛛网，说：“爹，女儿病了这许多天，劳你们操心不少，如今大好了，你可高兴？”

董子将神气起来。他皱着眉，正儿八经地点着头：“嗯，阿囡，你这些天可把爹吓坏了！也怪，怎么不迟不早，姓冒的那小子一到，你就好了？哼，倒像害的是相思病似的！”

董小宛脸一红，娇嗔地背过身子不依说：“爹，瞧你胡说些什么呀！”

“哦哦，胡说，是胡说，不说了，不说了！”董子将连忙改口，随即凑过来，压低声音问，“那么，你莫骗爹，他到底给了多少？”

“什么给了多少？”

“咦，你别装糊涂呀，当然是……”董子将把拇指和食指圈起来，做了个表示银子的手势。

“没有。”董小宛摇摇头。

“阿囡，你莫骗爹。爹知道你今儿个赚了不少，你这是拼着命儿挣的，多了爹也不要你的。这十两八两的零头，就算给爹买盅酒喝吧！”

“爹——真的没有嘛！”

“笑话！有道是‘窑门半爿开，有 × 无钱莫进来！’他不带个百儿八十的，敢进我董家门？阿囡，快给我！”

董小宛摇摇头。

“哎，阿囡，我知你要攒体己。实话说吧，若不是爹近来手气背，一连两天输得摸大门弗着，也不会巴巴地赶着屁股来向你讨。晌午我到半塘寺去求了根签，说我今夜准定翻本，你可不能

sit." After Dong Zijiang was seated, she sat down next to him, and, removing threads of a cobweb sticking to his sleeve, said, "Dad, I've been sick for so many days and you've worried about me. Aren't you happy to see me well now?"

Dong Zijiang became very proud of himself. Knitting his brows he nodded in seriousness, saying, "Well, my girl, you've scared me out of my wits these days, but strangely, why are you well again when Young Master Mao appears, not sooner or later? Huh, it's like lovesickness."

Xiaowan blushed, and turning her back in a feigned anger, said, "Dad, what nonsense you're talking?"

"Oh yeah, nonsense, it's nonsense, I'll stop, I'll stop talking." Dong Zijiang stopped the subject quickly, leaned over and said in a whisper, "Then, don't you lie to me. How much did he give you?"

"How much what?" said Xiaowan.

"Well, don't you pretend not to understand my question. Of course, the—" Dong Zijiang said, making a circle with his thumb and index finger to suggest silver.

Xiaowan shook her head and said, "None."

"My girl, don't lie to your old man. Dad knows that you've made a lot of money today. You're earning it with your life. I don't ask for more than some small change, like ten taels or eight for a cup of wine."

"Dad, there really isn't any silver."

"You're kidding me. There's a saying, 'The bawdy house door is half open. If you have no money, don't come in.' Without bringing a hundred or eighty taels of silver, how dare he enter the door of the Dongs? My girl, give it to me."

Xiaowan shook her head.

"Well, my girl, I know you want to save for yourself. To tell the truth, if it weren't for bad luck at the *mahjong* table recently, if I hadn't been losing for two days in a row with nothing left, I wouldn't have come to beg from you. I went to Bantang Temple and drew a fortune stick. It said I'm going to regain my money tonight, and you can't

见死不救！好，十两不行，那就五两怎么样？五两！”

“……”

“妈的，这样的女儿！那就三两，总行了吧？”

“……”

“啊，二两……”

“一两也没有。”董小宛终于说道，口气很平静，“冒公子是要给我些钱将息身子，可孩儿没有要他的。”

董子将迷惑地瞅着女儿，仿佛不明白她说什么。到后来，他眨眨眼睛，嘻嘻地笑起来：“阿囡，你别吓唬爹。爹胆子很小，不禁吓，一吓就吓坏了！”

“孩儿不是吓爹，这是真的。”

董子将的脸色忽然变成死灰，他斜着眼睛，丧魂失魄地在原地转了一个圈子。当目光重新落在女儿身上时，他的脸就由于失望和怨恨而变得狠巴巴的了。

“混账！”他咆哮起来，随手抓起一把茶壶，“啪”地摔碎在地上，“你、你鬼迷心窍！连自己是什么货色，都忘得一干二净了！你以为你是太太小姐，闲得发慌，找个小白脸来偷情吗？我们是做现钱买卖。一文钱，一文货！你这是卖的哪门子的春风人情！给钱也不要，不要钱你喝西北风去！”

董子将越骂越上劲，又拿起桌上还没来得及收拾的酒杯、汤匙，一只一只地往地上狠摔。顿时碎瓷片和残酒、汁水溅满了一地。寿儿在门外看见，又急又气，但是不敢走过来，只好拼命地朝董小宛使眼色。

董小宛一动不动地站着，紧抿着嘴唇，根本没有留意寿儿的招呼。她的脸色变得越来越苍白，忧郁地望着暴跳如雷的爹，脸

leave me broke. Well, then, if you can't give me ten taels, what about five? Five taels."

"..."

"Damn, what a daughter! Then two or three. Is that all right with you?"

"..."

"Then, two taels—"

"There isn't one single tael," Dong Xiaowan finally said in a calm tone. "Young Master Mao wanted to give me some money so that I can eat better to boost my body, but I didn't accept it."

Dong Zijiang looked at his daughter in bewilderment as if he hadn't understood what she had said. Then, he blinked his eyes and smiled grinningly, "My girl, don't scare your old man. Your dad is timid as a mouse and can't bear being scared. You'll scare the shit out of him."

"I'm not scaring you, Dad. It's true."

Dong Zijiang's face suddenly turned dead gray. Slanting his eyes he paced around in dispair. When his gaze fell on his daughter again, his face hardened with disappointment and rage.

"Bastard girl," he snarled, grabbed a teapot at hand, and smashed it to the ground. "You, you're possessed by the devil and forget what a—! You think you're a lady looking for a young lover to kill time? We're doing a cash business. One penny of cash for one penny of value. What kind of stupid favor are you giving? They give you money and you don't accept it. Go live on the northwest wind!"

As his fury grew, Dong Zijiang took the wine cups and spoons on the table and smashed them to the ground one by one. Instantly, the floor was littered with residual wine, leftover food, and shards of broken porcelain. Shou'er saw it from outside the door. She was angry and worried but didn't dare to come close, so she winked desperately at Xiaowan.

Xiaowan stood motionless, her lips pressed tightly together, oblivious to Shou'er's signal. Her face becoming paler and paler, Xiaowan stared gloomily at her thunderous father with a desperate

上流露出一种绝望的、坚决的神情。等董子将把两个酒杯、两只汤匙全摔完了，又拿起饭碗要摔的时候，她忽然冷冷地说：

“你摔吧，全摔完了也没什么。反正，我明儿也要走了！”

“什么？你要干什么？”董子将的手一下子停在半空，瞪着眼睛问。

“明儿冒公子来时，我要跟他去，再不回来了！”

“啊，胡说，不行！”董子将大叫一声，一下子蹦到女儿跟前，气急败坏地挥舞着手中的碗，“我不准你走，不准！听见没有？你是我养大的！我是你的爹！你得养我、侍奉我，给我挣钱、挣钱！谁都休想把你带走！休想……”

可是，任凭他怎么叫骂、蹦跳、哀求，董小宛却再也不开口了。

## 矢志相从

虽然董小宛拿定主意要跟冒襄走，可是冒襄却丝毫没有这种意思。夜来的一段邂逅，在他来说，无非是一时无聊，逢场作戏，绝没想到要承担什么责任。次日醒来，他已经把昨夜醉中的那一番戏言忘个干净。等赴襄阳向父亲报信的家人一走，他也收拾行装，准备返回如皋。只是挡不住张明弼再三提醒督促，冒成也在一旁帮腔，他才勉强命船家把船绕到半塘来，向董小宛辞行。

船刚靠岸，董小宛就匆匆迎出门来。显然，她早就在妆楼上守候着了。她今天特意打扮了一番，乌云般的头发梳得整整齐齐，到顶上用金环束住，向后挽成一个坠马髻。鬓边插了一组经过精心选择的珠翠首饰。病后苍白的脸色，被敷得很匀净的脂粉巧妙

but determined look. Having smashed the two wine cups and the two spoons, Dong Zijiang picked up the rice bowl and was going to smash it. Dong Xiaowan suddenly said, coldly:

"Smash them! It doesn't matter if you smash them all. After all, I'm going to leave tomorrow."

Dong Zijiang stopped his hand in the air and asked, opening his eyes wide, "What? What do you want to do?"

"When Young Master Mao comes here tomorrow, I'll go with him and never come back."

"Whoosh, nonsense! No way!" Dong Zijiang yelled. He leapt to his daughter, and, waving the bowl in his hand furiously, said, "I forbid it. No way. Did you hear me? You were raised by me. I'm your father. You have to provide for me, take care of me, and make money for me. No one can take you away. Don't you even think about it."

However, no matter how he shouted, jumped, and pleaded, Xiaowan never spoke again.

## Woman Bound for Love

Although Dong Xiaowan had made up her mind to go with Mao Xiang, the latter had no intention to take her with him. For him, the encounter last night was nothing more than a moment of pleasure-seeking on the spur to beguile the time with no thought of obligation. When he woke up in the morning, he had forgotten all the beautiful words he had said in drunkenness last night. As soon as the servant left for Xiangyang to report to his father, he packed up and prepared to return to Rugao. It was simply because of Zhang Mingbi's persistent persuasion and Mao Cheng's echoing from aside that he reluctantly asked the boatman to detour to Bantang to bid farewell to Xiaowan.

As soon as the ship docked, Xiaowan enthusiastically came out to greet them. Obviously, she had been waiting upstairs for a long time. She was beautifully dressed up for the occasion. Her hair as dark as night was neatly combed and tied up with a golden ring on the top, a falling bun at the end, and a cluster of carefully selected bead jewellery on the sideburns. Her face pale from the illness was cleverly remedied

地补救过来了；淡淡地描出的眉毛，则相得益彰地衬托出她那双妩媚的眼睛。她穿了一袭桃红色薄绒女衣，紫色衬里，下面是八幅白地紫花滚边湘裙。在等待船上放下跳板的时候，她略带不安地站在岸边，紧闭着嘴唇，没有望冒襄，神情显得有点严肃。寿儿拎着一小捆行李跟在她的身后。

"唔，她的确是别具风致，非寻常女子可比！只是，她为什么要带行李来？这是什么意思？"冒襄疑惑地想，一边走到船旁，伸出手去，把董小宛搀上船来。

"二位相公真是信人！深蒙一再垂顾，教奴家不知如何答谢才好！"董小宛在船头站定之后，就敛着衣襟，侧着身子，深深地行着礼说。

"岂敢，岂敢！只为小生在姑苏的事情已经办毕，要返回如皋去了，特来向小娘子辞行。"冒襄随口回答，一边仍旧怀疑地打量着对方。

"啊，公子就要回去了？"

"正是。"

"不知何时启程？"

"即刻便要启程。"

"张老爷也一起去么？"

"科考之期将届，小生尚要赴海陵就试。张兄意欲偕小生到如皋盘桓数天，便回金坛去了。"

"如此，奴家有一事相恳，不知公子能俯允否？"

"啊，请讲不妨！"

一直到说这句话的时候，冒襄的脸上始终带着和蔼的微笑，但是，心里却越来越警惕。以他多年来出入风月场所的经验，他十分清楚同这一类"名妓"交往，要提防些什么。别看她们一副

by the evenly spread powder; the slightly groomed eyebrows perfectly complemented her charming eyes. She wore a pink velvet coat with a purple lining, and underneath was an eight-panel Hunan-style skirt with purple flowers on a white background and a folded edge. While waiting for the boat to lower the springboard, she nervously stood on the bank without looking at Mao Xiang, her lips closed tightly, her expression serious. Shou'er stood behind her with a small bundle of luggage.

"Um, she does have a special charm. But, why does she bring her luggage? What does it mean?" Mao Xiang thought puzzledly as he walked to the side of the boat and stretched out his hand to help her aboard.

As soon as Xiaowan stood at the bow of the boat, she held her skirt and leaned sideways to bob a curtsy and said, "You're true to your words indeed, sirs. I'm so obliged to you for your visits that I can never thank you enough."

"How dare I oblige you, how dare I? My business in Suzhou is over and I have to return to Rugao. I'm here to say goodbye to your ladyship," Mao Xiang replied in a flat voice, still watching her suspiciously.

"So, you're returning home, sir?"

"Exactly."

"When do you leave?"

"Right now."

"Is Lord Zhang going too?"

"The date for the imperial exam is near and I need to go to Hailing to take the exam. Brother Zhang wants to spend a few days with me in Rugao and then go back to Jintan."

"If so, may I ask you a favor?"

"Well, ask away then."

Mao Xiang, who had been wearing a congenial smile on his face until now, grew increasingly vigilant. Based on his many years of experience in pleasure land, he was very clear about what to beware of when dealing with the so-called "famous courtesans." Regardless of

楚楚可怜的模样，却都不是寻常之辈。她们都有相当的身价，有很广的社会联系，有她们的崇拜者和捧场者。同她们打交道时必须小心，既不可过于古板迂执、傲慢无礼，也不可轻易地允诺什么。这两方面如果有哪一方面处置失当，传扬开去，都会为名士圈子里的同人笑话，有损名声。现在冒襄凭着董小宛今天的打扮，还带着行李，已经估计到她是有准备而来。联系昨天晚上她对自己苦苦相留的态度，他就多少猜测到对方的用意了，“哼，莫非你指望我就这样把你带走？可没那么容易！”他冷冷地想，同时考虑着她一旦提出这样的要求，将如何拒绝。

“二位相公屡顾之恩，奴家愧无以报。如不嫌弃，宁愿随船相送一程！”董小宛说，又一次恭恭敬敬地行下礼去。

如果董小宛一开口就提出要委身相嫁，那么冒襄自然很容易加以拒绝，可是她现在只要求“随船相送一程”；如果她提出是专门为了送冒襄，那么冒襄也还可以设法推却，可是她一开口就点明是送的“二位相公”，这就把张明弼也包了进来；而刚才冒襄又亲口说过，张明弼打算同自己一道回如皋去，这就更加使冒襄不便自作主张了。

“嗯，公亮兄，你看……”当冒襄终于发觉这个请求无法立即加以回绝之后，他只好回过头去，先征求张明弼的意见了。

“啊，便是冒兄与小生也以来去匆匆，未能与宛娘多盘桓些时日为憾。如此甚妙，只是偏劳宛娘，却是不当！”张明弼兴冲冲地说。

冒襄本来指望张明弼能帮他一把，所以事先不住使眼色。谁知这位把兄一心想当撮合山，却装作看不见。他不但自己表示同

their pitiable appearance, they were no ordinary women, each having a price tag, a wide network of social connections, and a flock of admirers and patrons. Caution must be exercised when you deal with them. You shouldn't be rigid, arrogant, or rude, nor should you easily promise them anything. If you make a mistake either way, you'll be a laughing stock in the celebrity circles and ruin your reputation. Judging from the luggage and the way she dressed today, Mao Xiang gathered she had an agenda. Thinking of her begging him to stay last night, he more or less understood her intentions. "Huh, do you expect me to take you away like this? It's not that easy," he thought coldly, fumbling for an excuse to refuse her should she make such a request.

Xiaowan gave another respectful curtsy and said, "I'm much obliged to your lordships for your kindness in coming to see me, a kindness I can't repay. If you don't mind, I'd like to escort the two of you for part of your journey."

If she proposed to marry herself to him he would be able to turn her down easily, but now she only asked to escort them for part of the journey; if she proposed specifically to escort Mao Xiang, then he would also be able to refuse her. Problem was, she said "the two of you," which also included Zhang Mingbi; and to make matters worse, Mao Xiang said from his own mouth just now that Zhang Mingbi was going to Rugao with him and that made it all the more difficult for him to give a refusal.

"Well, Brother Gongliang, what do you think?" When Mao Xiang finally realized that this request couldn't be rejected immediately, he looked back to solicit Zhang Mingbi's opinion.

"Um, Brother Mao and I come and go in a hurry. We have been regretting not having more time with your ladyship. Of course you're welcome to join us, but it's just not quite right for you to take the bother," Mingbi said cheerfully.

Mao Xiang, expecting his friend to help him out, had been winking before Mingbi spoke. Yet to his disappointment, this friend of his was bent on being their matchmaker and pretended not to see it. Not only did Mingbi agree, but he also suggested that Mao Xiang was

意，还把冒襄也说成早有此心。冒襄不好立即否认，唯有苦笑。

“这么说，冒公子也不见弃了？”董小宛问，目不转睛地望着冒襄。

冒襄迟疑了一下，终于说：“多蒙宛娘错爱，小生不胜感激。不过此事尚须从长计议。这儿风大，请——”说着，他就彬彬有礼地侧过身子，伸出手去，把董小宛搀进前舱的小厅里。

冒襄乘坐的这条船，是三吴地区常见的那种“浪船”。这种船不论大小，都装配有厅、房、门、窗，布置得颇为雅洁。船桅上虽然挂着风帆，却只是巴掌大的一块小席，全不管用。它航行时主要靠船尾的一支大橹，由两三个精壮汉子合力摇动，或者靠人上岸拉纤前进。更有一样，乘船时人和物都必须保持两边平衡，不能有超过一石的偏重，否则船身就会倾斜，所以又叫“天平船”。这种船一般只在方圆七百里的水道内航行，偶尔也冒险过次把长江，至于沿江而行，那就得改乘大江船了。

当冒襄把张明弼和董小宛让进前舱的小厅里坐定之后，有好一会儿，他望着窗外的景色，没有立即开口。他并非傻子，自然不至于看不出董小宛所说的“相送一程”，无非是一种借口，一旦让她随船之后，下一步，她就会提出更高的要求，例如要他娶她之类。而这是绝不可能的。不要说现在他正急于回家去安慰母亲，还要应付迫在眉睫的科考，还有八月的乡试，根本没有心思来考虑处理这种事。而且，即使他真的要纳妾，董小宛也不是他心目中的理想人选。这个风尘女子身上所表现出来的过于温驯端

thinking the same way. Unable to deny it immediately, Mao Xiang smiled a bitter smile.

"So, Young Master Mao won't mind my company either?" Xiaowan asked, looking at Mao Xiang intently, who hesitated for an instant and said, "I'm much obliged to your ladyship for your favor, which I'm unworthy of. We have all the time in the world. It's windy here. Please—" Then he turned aside politely and reached out a hand to help her step into the small common room of the front cabin.

The boat Mao Xiang took was a typical "wave-rider" common in the Sanwu area. Regardless of its small size, it was elegantly decorated and complete with bedrooms, a common room, doors and windows. A sail was hung on the mast, but it was just a small patch of fabric with no practical value. The boat was mainly propelled by a large scull at the stern worked by two or three hardy men, or by multiple men pulling it along the bank with ropes tied to their bodies. One thing was particularly important: people and objects had to be balanced on the two sides and the difference of weight between the two sides should be no more than one *dan*, otherwise the hull would tilt, so it was also called a "balance boat." This kind of boat generally only sailed in the waterways in a small area of seven hundred square miles and only occasionally took the risk of sailing in the Yangtze River. As for travel along the Yangtze, it was the business of a large river boat.

After Mao Xiang seated Mingbi and Xiaowan in the small room of the front cabin, he looked out of the window for a while without speaking. He was not a fool who didn't understand Xiaowan's offer to escort him for part of the journey was nothing more than a pretext. Once she was allowed to accompany him on the boat, she would put up a higher demand in the next step, such as asking him to marry her, something totally impossible. Besides, he was in no mind for a thing like that while having two more important things to do: to go home to comfort his mother and to prepare for the coming imperial recruitment examination, whose local primary took place in August. Moreover, even if he really wanted to take a concubine, she was not the ideal

庄的气质，那种一心向慕做一个贤妻良母的古怪念头，都使冒襄不喜欢。虽然未至于讨厌她，但他认为，那样的角色，有他的妻子来充当就足够了。他心目中的如夫人，除了美貌和技艺之外，还应当会撒娇撒痴，会使小性儿，会嫉妒、恶作剧，会把人捉弄得啼笑皆非、心痒难熬——总而言之，应当有那么一点“坏”，才够味儿，就像陈圆圆那样……

一想到陈圆圆，冒襄的心又隐隐作痛起来：“哦，她是出类拔萃的、罕有的、宝贵的！这样的女子，一辈子最多只能遇到一个！她已经几乎永远属于我，却让我把她丢失了！但毫无疑问，她是无法代替的！”

冒襄猛一抬头，发现有两双眼睛正关切地期待地望住自己——那是董小宛和张明弼。他一下子清醒过来，定了定神，垂下眼睛说道：

“宛娘，你的一番盛意，小生已是心领。只是你病体初愈，第一要紧的是将身子养好，这车舟劳顿，却是不宜。往后日子正长，相见机会还很多，何必拘执于眼前？依小生之见，这相送一程，不如就免了吧！”

“可是，可是，奴家自己觉着精神健旺，已是大好了！”董小宛急急地说。

“今日是大好了，可是路上一劳累，又安知不会反复？还是以静养为宜。”

“啊，奴家卧病十有八日，药石无灵；得公子昨夜枉顾，顿觉身心俱泰，霍然而愈。此皆公子洪福相庇之故。奴家、奴家只恐一旦离了公子，‘二竖[1]’重来，那时，便是想再求公子相救，已是不能了。还望公子怜奴危病之苦，准许随船盘桓几时，奴家毕生铭感公子大德大恩！”

---

① 二竖，指病魔，出自《左传·成公十年》。

candidate. He didn't like the excessive docility and ladylikeness in this woman in the dust who wasn't supposed to entertain the strange idea of being a good wife and a good mother. She was not bad at all but his wife was good enough to fulfill such a role. In his mind, a concubine, in addition to beauty and talent for art, should also be coquettish, idiotic, and capable of throwing little tantrums, being jealous, and playing hoaxes—all in all, there should be a little bit of badness as in Chen Yuanyuan.

At the thought of Chen Yuanyuan, Mao Xiang's heart ached again. "Um, she's outstanding, rare, and precious. You can only meet such a woman once in a lifetime. She has almost belonged to me, but I've lost her. There's no doubt that she can't be replaced," he thought to himself.

Mao Xiang looked up and found that two pairs of eyes were looking at him concernedly and expectantly. They were the eyes of Dong Xiaowan and Zhang Mingbi. He suddenly woke up. Then he collected himself, lowered his eyes and said:

"Xiaowan, I really appreciate your kindness, but you haven't quite recovered from your illness yet and shouldn't travel in boats and carriages. At present, the first important thing is to take care of your own health. There're long days ahead and there're plenty of opportunities for us to meet, why limit yourself to the moment? In my humble opinion, you'd better stop here and go no further."

"But, but, I do feel well enough," Xiaowan said anxiously.

"You're well today, but who knows if you won't relapse when you're exhausted from travel? Please don't go."

"Aw! I've been ill for eighteen days and the medicine doesn't work; but your visit last night has cured me body and mind because I'm blessed with your kind protection. I'm really afraid that once you leave me the demons will come back and that by that time, if I want to ask you for help again it'll no longer be possible. I hope your lordship will have pity on me and spare me from the demons that have caused my illness. I'll be obliged to you for life if you allow me to hang around with you for a couple of days."

冒襄听她这样说，呵呵地笑起来：“宛娘也太言重了。哪里就有如此神妙之理！你无非是就医多时，药力到了，你自己虽然未觉，其实病已见愈。却撞着我来访，便把医师之功错算到小生身上。昨夜即便小生不来，你也一样会好的。”停了停，他又接着说，“不瞒小娘子说，非是小生执意不允，皆因眼下科考之期已届，小生此去，是日夜兼程，一天也耽搁不得。万一小娘子的贵恙在船上反复起来，到那时停船料理又不是，不停船料理又不是，却怎生区处？”

“啊，若是果真如此，奴家必当自行离船，决不敢耽搁公子们一日行程！”董小宛回答得很坚决。

冒襄漫不经心地摇摇头：“这话现时好说，到时我们又岂能……”他忽然看见董小宛神色惨然，眼圈红红的，嘴唇也在可怜地抖动着，马上就要哭出来的样子，就顿住不说了。

“辟疆！”坐在旁边许久没有说话的张明弼终于开口了，“宛娘既是一片至诚，你又何苦执意相拒？我瞧她今日身子确是大好了，陆路奔波怕还不行，船是尽可坐得的。倘若你还不放心，那么到时有什么事，都包在愚兄身上便是！”

冒襄对于这位把兄不同他商量，就自作主张一个劲儿地煽风牵线，本来就十分不满。适才张明弼又不理会他的暗示，一口答允让董小宛随船送行，更使冒襄恼火。这两口气还未出，现在听他又来讨好卖乖，便把脸一沉，回过头，紧盯着张明弼问：“这么说，公亮兄是不打算随弟回如皋去啰？”

这次他们结伴去如皋，本是张明弼的主意，其中包含着他作为冒襄的盟兄，专诚前往拜谒冒母，向她表示敬意和慰问这样一种用意。现在冒襄忽然提出这样的问题来，张明弼就知道冒襄生气了。他历来有点怕这位才貌出众的兄弟，总是顺着他，不敢违

Hearing that, Mao Xiang laughed and said, "You're flattering me, my dear lady. There isn't such a magical power. It's nothing more than the efficacy of the medicine. You've been seeing the doctor for a long time and the medicine has finally worked. You've actually been cured by the physician without realizing it yourself. When I happened to visit, you mistook the physician's curing power to be mine. Even if I hadn't paid the visit last night, you would've still recovered." After a pause, he continued, "To tell you the truth, it's not that I insist on not taking you along but that the imperial exam is near and I have to travel day and night to get home and there's no single day to lose. In case your ladyship becomes ill again, should I get off the boat to take care of you or continue the journey regardless of your illness?"

"Aw! If that's the case, I'll leave the boat on my own and won't dare to delay your trip by one single day," Xiaowan replied firmly.

Mao Xiang shook his head dismissively and said, "It's easy to say. When it happens, how can we—" He stopped as he suddenly saw her sad expression, her eyes red and her lips compressed pitiably, ready to cry.

"Pijiang," said Mingbi, who hadn't spoken a word for a long time. "It's very kind of her ladyship indeed, why insist on refusing her? I see she's indeed very well today. She won't be able to travel by land but a boat will be good. If you're still not sure, then you can count on me when anything happens."

Mao Xiang was very dissatisfied with this good friend of his for matchmaking without his consent and the chap's deliberate disregard of his hints in allowing Xiaowan to take the boat and accompany them annoyed him even more. Now before his anger was vented, this man came to please him. He twisted his face sullenly, turned his head, and stared at Zhang Mingbi. "So, you're not going back to Rugao with me?" he asked.

This joint trip to Rugao was originally Mingbi's idea because, as Mao Xiang's sworn brother, Mingbi wanted to pay tribute to Mao Xiang's mother. Now that Mao Xiang suddenly asked such a question, Mingbi knew his friend was angry. In fact, Mingbi had always been a

拗他的意思。见他发了怒，张明弼只好讪讪地住了嘴。

一度重新燃烧起希望的董小宛，现在似乎完全绝望了。她不再说话，眼圈又开始发红。她垂下头去，久久地盯着自己的裙裾，可是到底没有哭出来。

看见她这个样子，冒襄倒也有点不忍。他站起来，走近董小宛的身边，柔声地劝解说："非是小生薄情，其实行程紧迫，这也是为小娘子着想，没有办法的事。你好好儿回去吧，可别想不开。秋后我说不定还要来，到时一定多盘桓些时日，好不好？"

在冒襄说话的当儿，董小宛似乎也拿定了主意。她仰起脸，严肃地瞧着冒襄，眼睛里现出果决的神情。等他说完之后，她也站起来，说：

"既然公子实在为难，奴家也不敢相强。只是奴家已决意离开此地，不再回来。如今既有此便船，奴家这就向船家说，情愿租借那烟篷底下一席之地，附搭而行。奴家既不敢相送公子，路上奴家是死是活，公子亦一概不必理会。"

董小宛说完，朝冒襄和张明弼深深行了一个礼，就转过身，朝舱外走去。

这一着大出冒襄的意料，他没想到董小宛的意志竟如此坚决。自然，他可以吩咐船家，不准她附搭，但那样做不但显得太绝情，而且同一个风尘弱女这样相斗，也未免过于小气，有失自己的身份。那么听凭董小宛住到烟篷底下呢？更加不行。因为她并非一名普通的妓女，在江南的名士圈子中，她早就艳名远播，无人不晓。若是传扬开去，董小宛在冒襄的船上竟然遭受如此虐待，势必引起舆论哗然，自己也难免为人们所笑骂……

这样一想，冒襄反而着忙起来。他张嘴想喊，又觉得不太妥

little afraid of this beautiful and talented sworn brother. He had always listened to him and never dared to contradict him. Seeing that Mao Xiang was angry, Zhang Mingbi went silent.

Xiaowan, whose hope had been rekindled a moment ago, now seemed completely desperate. She no longer spoke. Her eyes began to flush again. She lowered her head and stared at the edge of her skirt for a long time but held her tears in check.

Mao Xiang couldn't bear to see her like that. He stood up, went over and consoled her in a soft voice, "It's not because I'm cruel-hearted. I do have a tight schedule. It's for your good too. I have no choice. Please go back and don't resent me for it. I might be able to come again in autumn and spend some more time with you. How does that sound?"

As Mao Xiang spoke, Xiaowan made up her mind. She raised her face and looked at Mao Xiang sullenly, with a determined look in her eyes. When he finished speaking, she stood up and said, "Since you have concerns, I dare not oblige you. It's just that I've decided to leave this damn place and will never come back. Now that there's a boat, I'll ask the boat owner for a lift. I'd like to borrow a space under the cooking tent. Since I don't have the honor to be your company, you don't have to do a thing on the trip whether I'm dead or alive."

After Xiaowan said that, she gave a deep bow to Mao Xiang and Zhang Mingbi, then turned and walked out of the cabin.

That was quite unexpected. Mao Xiang had never thought Xiaowan was so determined. Of course, he could tell the boat owner not to allow her to take the boat, but that would seem too unsympathetic; besides, it was also too mean and beneath him to fight against a weak woman in that manner. Then, allowing Xiaowan to sit in the cooking tent? It was even worse. She was no common whore. In the celebrity circles in River South, she had been famous for a long time, and no one didn't know her. If word spread that she had been abused on Mao Xiang's boat, it would be scandalous and he would be a laughing stock.

Thus thinking, Mao Xiang started to worry instead. He opened

当，于是只好朝正在一旁紧盯着他的张明弼做了个手势，意思是请他快点把董小宛招呼回来。

不一会儿，董小宛跟着张明弼重新走了进来。她低着头站在冒襄跟前，默不作声。冒襄板着脸把她上上下下打量了一阵，终于无可奈何地问：

“嗯，你是说只要随船送我们一程？”

董小宛点了点头。

“就送一程，没有别的了？”

董小宛犹豫了一下，想说什么，但终于仍旧点点头。

“好吧，那么你就留下。到下一站，你可一定得回来！”

冒襄说完，就朝舱外叫：“冒成！”

冒成应声出现在舱口。

“你去——把这位小娘子的行李搬进来。然后吩咐船家马上开船！”

“是！”冒成答应着，但是身子却没有动弹。

“去呀！呆着做什么？”

“是——呃，启禀大爷，刚才外面来了个人，他说他是小娘子的爹……”冒成垂着手说。

“唔？”冒襄的目光顿时闪动起来。他怀疑地瞧了董小宛一眼，问冒成，“他来做什么？”

“他说、呃、他说……”

“快说啊！”

“是！他说，这位小娘子是他一手养大的，大爷不能就这样把她带走了，他求大爷念他年老孤贫，好歹赏他几个钱。”

这要求来得如此突然、意外，有半晌工夫，舱里变得一片静默：冒襄双眉紧皱，一言不发；张明弼微低着头，在慢慢地捋他的胡子；董小宛则显出一副又急又气的样子。她大睁着一双惊惶的眼睛，瞧瞧这个，又瞧瞧那个，当发现似乎谁都不打算听她的

his mouth to give a loud cry, but felt that it was not appropriate, so he gestured to Mingbi, who had been watching him all the while, to bring Xiaowan back.

After a while, Xiaowan came back into the cabin with Mingbi. She stood in front of Mao Xiang, drooping her head, not saying a word. Mao Xiang studied her up and down for a while, and finally asked resignedly:

"Well, you mean you just need to accompany us for part of the trip on the boat?"

Xiaowan nodded.

"Just accompanying us for part of the trip and there's nothing else?"

Xiaowan wanted to say something but instead gave a nod.

"Good. Then you can stay. At the next stop, you must turn back."

After Mao Xiang said that, he yelled from the cabin, "Mao Cheng!"

Mao Cheng appeared at the cabin door. "Go bring in her luggage and tell the boat owner to set off."

"Yes, sir!" said Mao Cheng without moving.

"Go! Why don't you move?"

"Yes-uh, sir, but just now a man came and he said he's the father of her ladyship—" Mao Cheng said with his hands down.

"Huh?" Mao Xiang was puzzled. He glanced at Xiaowan suspiciously and asked Mao Cheng, "What's he here for?"

"He said, uh, he said—"

"Say it!"

"Yes! He said he's brought up this young lady by hand and you shouldn't take her away like this. He begs you to have pity on a poor old man and give him some money."

The request came so suddenly and unexpectedly that the cabin became silent. Mao Xiang frowned without saying a word; Mingbi tilted his head forward and slowly stroked his beard; Xiaowan looked anxious and angry. Her panicked eyes darted between the men in front of her, and when she realized that no one cared to listen to her

解释时，她的表情就由情急变成绝望了。

终于，冒襄慢慢地抬起了头，冰冷的目光笔直地射向冒成，后者哆嗦一下，赶紧低下头去。

“胡说！”冒襄蓦地吼叫起来，“宛娘不过是跟船送我们一程，一两日内就要回来。什么‘把她带走了’？他说这话想敲诈谁！以为本公子会吃这一套？笑话！告诉他，钱，有！可就是不给他，半个子儿也不给！让他赶快走，别耽误了开船！”

说完，冒襄就转过身，狠狠地盯了董小宛一眼，快步走进与小厅相连的卧室里，“砰”地关上了门。

explanation, her expression changed from panic to despair.

Finally, Mao Xiang slowly raised his head, and his icy gaze shot straight towards Mao Cheng, who shuddered and quickly lowered his head.

"Nonsense," Mao Xiang roared abruptly. "Xiaowan is just traveling with us on the boat for a while and she'll be back in a day or two. What does 'take her away' mean? Who does he want to blackmail by saying so? He thought I'll buy that? Kidding! Tell him, money, yes, I have it, but I just won't give it to him, not even half a penny. Let him go as quickly as possible and don't let him delay our boat."

Then, he turned around, gave Xiaowan a hard look, and walked quickly into the bedroom connected to the small common room, slamming the door shut behind him.

汉英对照

# 白门柳

## 第一部 夕阳芳草 下

## Willows of the White Gate I

# Romance in the Setting Sun

## Part 2

刘斯奋 著　　褚东伟 译

by Liu Sifen　　translated by Chu Dongwei

广州新华出版发行集团

广州出版社

GUANGZHOU PRESS

# 目 录

# Table of Contents

# 第七章

# 钱谦益心灰意冷，柳如是妇唱夫随

## 舌剑唇枪

虎丘大会之后的第三天，即农历三月三十日夜里很晚的时候，钱谦益和柳如是乘船回到了常熟。随他们一道回来的还有陈在竹等三位族人，以及一群男女仆役。当由灯笼、伞盖、大轿、小轿和各式箱笼行李组成的这支队伍浩浩荡荡进入半野堂时，钱府上下都从睡梦中惊醒，忙碌起来。从大门、二门、大堂、二堂一直到内宅偏院，灯光接二连三地亮了。几个执事头儿几乎是同时出现在门厅里，神色惊惶的仆人来回奔跑，两顶专供宅内行走的肩舆已经抬出轿厅来准备着。一个睡眼惺忪的年轻门班糊里糊涂地走错了方向，被班头夹脖子揪住，用力一搡，趺趺撞撞奔回队列里。

钱谦益在轿厅下了四人抬大轿。他显得憔悴而疲惫，黝黑的脸明显变瘦了，头发胡子也似乎白了不少。在等候其余几个人下轿的当儿，他闭着眼睛，一动不动地站着。几名执事头儿的殷勤问候，也没能使他打起精神。直到陈在竹等人默默地走过来，征

Chapter Seven

# In Which Qian Qianyi Was Demoralized and Downcast and Liu Rushi Steadfastly Stood By Him

## Bandying of Words

Late night, the thirtieth of March in the lunar calendar, three days after the Tiger Hill Conference, Qian Qianyi and Liu Rushi arrived back in Changshu by boat. Together with them were three clansmen—one of them was Chen Zaizhu—and a flock of male and female servants. When the train of lanterns, canopies, sedan chairs, trunks, and baskets marched into the Half Wild Estate, people in the Qian house were woken from their dreams and quickly acted. Lights went on one after another from the main gate, through the second gate, the main hall, the second hall, and all the way to the inner courtyard. A few head servants appeared in the doorway almost simultaneously and other servants hurriedly to and fro. Two small sedan chairs for home use were placed in the doorway to await the master and the mistress. A sleepy boy servant went in the wrong direction, and a head servant took him by the neck and dragged him back into line.

Qian Qianyi stepped off the four-bearer sedan chair. He looked haggard and weary, with more white hairs on his head and in his beard, his darkish face apparently thinner than ever. As he waited for his clansmen to dismount from their sedan chairs, he stood still with closed eyes. The enthusiastic greetings of the head servants at home didn't raise his spirits. He didn't open his eyes until the clansmen in

询地望着他时，钱谦益才勉强睁开眼睛，摆摆手：“嗯，你们都回去吧！”说完，他就转过身，同柳如是各自上了一顶肩舆，由两名小厮提着灯笼在前头照路，慢慢地向内宅行去。

今夜没有月亮，几颗闪烁的星星，只眨了眨眼，就隐没在薄翳中了。宅院里一片幽暗，远近疏落的灯火在夜气中颤动着，更鲜明地凸现出来；肩舆两旁，廊柱、栏杆，以及栏杆外花树的影子不断闪过；大门那边的人声渐远渐小，听不见了，耳畔只剩下训练有素的轿夫们又轻又匀的脚步声……

也许是回到了家的缘故，钱谦益觉得紧张的心情开始松弛下来。虽然肢体加倍的倦怠，但这些天来拼命撕扯着他的神经的那只利爪，终于松开了。他仰靠在椅上，默默地瞅着长廊外的那一道黑糊糊的、城垛似的高大院墙，忽然感到：天地固然很大，但是一个人只需要有一角之地，就完全可以躲开扰攘的人世，自得其乐地生活下去。而自己的这个家是安全的、可靠的。在这坚固高大的院墙之内，绝对不会有自己的地位和权威遭到蔑视那种情形发生。这就够了，至于院墙外面的风风雨雨，大可置之不理。“哼，让他们爱怎样拨弄就怎样拨弄好了！所谓名声，所谓威望，无非是博取高位的一种本钱。如果做不到这一点，还有什么用！”他冷淡地想，开始觉得近两三天来，自己为此而惊慌失措，寝食不安，实在没有必要。接着，他又想到，这一次无疑十分倒霉而且扫兴，但同天启元年主试浙江，被人告发纳贿舞弊，以及前几年本乡奸民张汉儒上京诬告自己那两桩事比较起来，毕竟幸运得多。那两次都被弄得锒铛入狱，几乎性命不保；这一次大不了复官不成，白赔几千两银子，外加被人指责非议一阵子，如此而已。“哎，‘唾面自干，韬晦待时’，古人尚且难免，又何况我钱谦益！”这样暗暗说了一句之后，他似乎终于找到一条自我解脱的退路，

his company walked up to him for directions. "Well, you can all go now," he said. Then he and Liu Rushi each stepped into a home sedan chair and moved slowly toward the inner quarters of the residence, two boy servants lighting the way with lanterns.

There was no moon. A few stars twinkled and quickly disappeared into the hazy clouds. Darkness had taken the residence, with a few dim lights here and there flickering with the breath of night. Pillars, railings, and flowering trees outside the railings flickered past on either side of the sedan chairs. The voices at the gate gradually became distant and inaudible, and there was only the sound of light, rhythmic footsteps of the well-trained chairmen.

Having arrived home, Qian Qianyi finally relaxed. His limbs were still weary but the claw that had gripped his nerves in the last couple of days finally loosened. As he lay in his recliner looking out at the dark, tall, courtyard wall that fortified the place, he suddenly realized that a small corner of the big world would be sufficient for a man to be away from the crowd and enjoy life and that he was already very fortunate to have such a safe haven. Inside this tall, solid wall, there was no challenge to his position and authority. That was enough. He might as well ignore the wind and rain outside. "Let them be. The so-called good name and influence are no more than one's capital for high office. If he doesn't get it, what's the use of them all?" he thought coldly. All the anxieties, all the restlessness in the last couple of days were really unnecessary. True it was bad luck, but compared with two previous experiences—being charged with bribe-taking and abuse of power in his capacity as head examiner in Zhejiang Province and being framed by his townsman Zhang Hanru—it wasn't that bad. In those two situations, he had almost lost his life, but this time around, in the worst case scenario, it would be nothing more than a failure to get reinstatement to office, a loss of a few thousand taels of silver, and some damage to his reputation. "If someone spits into your face, let it dry by itself. Hide your edge and wait for your opportunity. The ancients knew it, so should I." Thus thinking, he seemed to have found an excuse for himself. He was no longer worried. He had planned to

不再像原先那样烦恼。本来，他还打算广派人员，四出打探士林当中对于这件事的反应，如今也觉得派不派都无所谓了……

第二天早上，钱谦益在我闻室里一直睡到辰时。

在外面的起居室里，柳如是踮着脚走来走去，显得心神不定。她早就起来了，梳洗之后，到毗邻供奉观音大士的龛堂里上过香，又袖着手儿瞧了一会红情、绿意两个丫环浇花。她本想等钱谦益起来一起用早点，后来等不及，只得先用了。用完早点，钱谦益仍旧酣睡不醒，她便研墨展纸，临了几行宋徽宗的《女史帖》，终于觉得全无兴致，又丢下了。

“莫非这件事就这样完了？”她想，“这么快，这么容易！……老头儿其实也太胆小了，被人一吓唬就慌了神！本来应该破釜沉舟试一试的，他却不敢。结果功败垂成，多少心思全白费了……今后怎么办？莫非当真要老娘陪他这样过一辈子不成？莫非这一辈子再没有出头露脸之日了？哼，不行，当初老娘嫁他可不是为的这个！……但是，那又怎么样呢？有什么办法？有什么——哎，到底是怎么回事！这死老儿怎么还不爬起来？”

柳如是转过身，犹豫了一下，正要朝寝室走去。这时，红情的声音在院子里响起来：

“啊，老夫人来了！婢子给老夫人请安！给少爷请安！老夫人请屋里坐，老爷这会儿还睡着未醒呢！”

柳如是怔了一下，站住了。只见门帘掀起，钱谦益的元配夫人陈氏，在一群丫环仆妇的簇拥下，走进起居室来。

陈氏是一位面目慈和的老妇人，头发已经微微见白，圆圆的、平扁的脸上，嵌着一对杏核眼，眼皮像是老睡不醒似的耷拉着，再加上扁扁的小鼻子和两片厚嘴唇，使人觉得这张脸即使在年轻的时候也不漂亮。但出身名门，自幼深受诗书礼教的熏陶却使她

send his men to find out how the other gentry scholars reacted to this incident, but now he didn't think it really mattered.

He had a very good sleep in the Wowen Chamber that night and didn't wake up until late in the morning.

Outside in the drawing room, Liu Rushi tiptoed to and fro apprehensively. She had woken up early. Earlier on, after washing and dressing up, she went to the shrine to offer incense to Bodhisattva Guanyin. Then she watched her maids Hongqing and Lüyi watering flowers for a while. She wanted to have breakfast together with Qian Qianyi but after some waiting she decided to eat first. After she had breakfast, he was still sound asleep, so she ground some ink on the inkstone, spread the writing paper and copied a few lines from Song dynasty emperor Huizong's *Copybook for Ladies*. Then she became bored and gave it up.

"Is this the end?" she thought. "It has come too soon. The old man is timid as a mouse. He's lost all wits upon being scared. He should burn the bridges, but he doesn't dare to do it. What a shame to stop like that while success is at hand! All the efforts have been in vain. What about my future? Should I spend the rest of my life like this? Will I ever see the light? Oh, no! I didn't marry him for this. But what can I do? Is there anything I can do, anything at all? Woe! What on earth has happened? Why doesn't this damn old man get up?"

She turned around, paused for an instant, then decided to walk back to her bedroom, when suddenly came the voice of Hongqing:

"Good morning, mistress. Good morning, young master. Mistress, please get seated. His lordship is still sleeping."

Liu Rushi startled and stood still. As the door curtain was lifted, in came Qian Qianyi's wife Lady Chen, accompanied by a few female servants.

Lady Chen was an unassuming old woman whose hair had started to gray. In her oval, flat face were embedded a pair of apricot kernels, over which drooped her sleepy eyelids. She had a flat, small nose and a pair of thick lips. One could tell that, even when she was young, that face had never been beautiful, but born of a notable family with a good

的言行举止之间，自有一种大家闺秀的雍容气派。这一点，恰恰无论是朱姨娘还是柳如是都无法仿效的。她今天穿了一身茶褐色绣蓝花茧绸女衣，梳着一个老式的圆髻，髻上插着几支珠翠。由于满脸细碎的皱纹已无法掩盖，她干脆只薄薄地涂了一层脂粉。陈夫人高大肥胖，与柳如是的矮小灵活恰好是鲜明的对照。

同陈夫人一道进来的，还有少爷钱孙爱、大丫环月容和两个有身份的老妈子。

“姐姐来啦，姐姐请坐！”当柳如是看见已经躲不开时，她只好迎上前去，行着礼说。本来，按照规矩，当姨太太的应当每天早上到上房去给太太请安。可是柳如是嫁进来时，是坐的八人抬的花轿，举行过大吹大擂的婚娶典礼，加上钱谦益又吩咐家人称她作柳夫人。论身份地位，她都不能算姨太太。算什么，谁也说不清。不过以柳如是的性子，她就认为，第一，按年岁大小，称陈夫人一声“姐姐”就足够了，没有必要像其他姬妾婢仆那样，称之为“老夫人”；第二，那些每日请安、逢节磕头之类的玩意儿，自己就更加无须沾边。为了这个缘故，不少亲友以至婢仆私下里都为陈夫人愤愤不平。倒是陈夫人逆来顺受，安之若素，从未提出过抗议。所以大半年来，彼此还能相安无事。

“那么，老爷还没起来么？”陈夫人由月容扶着，在起居室正当中的一张椅子坐下之后，抬起眼睛，安详地望着柳如是，问。

“哦，还没哩！”柳如是细眯着眼睛，迎着对方的目光，用同样不慌不忙的口吻回答。以往，她同陈夫人相对时，不知为什么，总是不由自主地有点紧张和慌乱，仿佛做了什么亏心事似的。这使她事后回想起来，十分气恼。现在她决心改变这种状况。

“哎，你也坐啊！”陈夫人温和地说，又朝站在身旁的钱孙

education in poetry, the classics, and etiquette, she had the elegant demeanor of a lady, which was lacking in the concubines: Lady Zhu and Liu Rushi. Today, she was wearing a dark brown cocoon silk dress embroidered with blue flowers; on her head was an old-fashioned bun with a few pearl hair pins stuck into it. She had merely applied a thin layer of powder on her face now that the fine wrinkles could no longer be concealed. She was tall and stout, exactly the opposite of Liu Rushi, who was short and slim.

Together with Lady Chen were Qian Sun'ai the young master, servant girl Yuerong and two older maids.

"Welcome, Elder Sister! Pray take a seat." Now that she was unable to dodge the first lady of the house, Liu Rushi walked up to Lady Chen and bobbed a curtsy. As a concubine, she was supposed to pay tribute to the mistress first thing in the morning every day according to the rules of the house, but Liu Rushi was no ordinary concubine. She had been properly married to Qian Qianyi with a decent wedding; she entered the house in a bridal sedan chair carried by eight men. Besides, Qian Qianyi had asked everyone in the house to call her "liu furen" (her ladyship Liu). So she was not exactly a concubine. Then, what was she? No one could tell. According to her own understanding, she should address Lady Chen as Elder Sister based on age instead of *laofuren* (venerable mistress) and it was not her business to pay daily morning tribute and kowtow to Lady Chen on important days. Many relatives, friends, and servants felt sorry for Lady Chen, but Lady Chen herself, having always been a humble woman, never protested. Therefore, over the past six months, they had been living in peace.

After sitting down in a chair in the middle of the drawing room with the help of Yuerong, Lady Chen lifted her eyes and looked at Liu Rushi calmly, saying, "So, his lordship has not woken up yet?"

Liu Rushi met her gaze with narrowed eyes and said in an equally calm tone, "Not yet." Previously, whenever she met Lady Chen, she had always been involuntarily nervous as if she had done something wrong, and she had always hated herself for that. Now, she had made up her mind to change it.

"You take a seat too," said Lady Chen in a soft voice. Then, she

爱点点头，“孙爱，你也坐下。”

钱孙爱很快就坐下了。他还是那样苍白、瘦弱。从一进门起，他就目不转睛地瞅着柳如是，眼里闪出狂喜的光，时时露出要同她说话的样子。

柳如是却没有坐。按照钱府的家规，在正室夫人面前，姨太太只能坐凳子，而不能坐椅子。凳子比椅子要矮一截，这无非是维护上下尊卑传统之意。如今柳如是自然用不着去坐凳子，但是陈夫人招呼她坐下时，只是以“你”相称，却撩起了柳如是心中的愤慨。她早就发现，尽管自己口口声声称陈夫人作“姐姐”，对方也不曾就此提出过异议，可是这个老太婆却始终不肯回称自己一声“妹妹”。这常常使柳如是尖锐地、屈辱地想到：对方实际上仍然不肯承认彼此的平等地位，哪怕她嘴巴上并不这样说……

“咦，怎么不坐？坐啊！”陈夫人催促说，她对于柳如是的踌躇显然有点奇怪。

“是呀！柳太太，太太让你坐哩！”钱孙爱也热心地帮腔。

“哼，再不坐，她就会当我不敢呢！”柳如是想，只好憋着一口气，在陈夫人右边的一张椅子上坐下来。

这之后，为着保持一种起码的家庭气氛，她们开始谈起天气、柳如是这次随钱谦益到苏州去的见闻、车舟的劳顿，以及家中的一些琐事等等。陈夫人的脸上始终挂着蔼然的微笑，她耐心地听着，从不打断柳如是的述说。柳如是则显得过分的兴奋和快活，她用苛刻的、批评的口吻谈到她所见到的一切，不断地在谈话中引进各种各样深奥的典故和古人的名言，她还常常无缘无故地发笑，随后就突然停下来。

“昨天晚上老爷很晚才睡么？”陈夫人不动声色地问，回头

turned to Qian Sun'ai beside her and said, nodding her head, "Sun'ai, you sit too."

The boy quickly sat down. He was still pale, thin, and fragile. He had been looking at Liu Rushi intently since he came in, his eyes twinkling with rapture, as if ready to speak to her at any moment.

Liu Rushi didn't sit. The Qians had a rule: a concubine should sit on a stool instead of in a chair. A stool is shorter than a chair. Such a rule was meant to maintain family order. Liu Rushi of course didn't have to sit on a stool, but she was utterly annoyed by Lady Chen addressing her as "you". She had been addressing Lady Chen as Elder Sister, but the old lady, having never objected to it, had never addressed her as Younger Sister. In fact, she had been aware of it since quite some time ago. To her, it was humiliation enough, because it for all intents and purposes represented a refusal to accept her as an equal, though the old lady had never said it.

"Sit. Why don't you sit?" urged Lady Chen, surprised by Liu Rushi's hesitation.

"Your ladyship, Mistress asks you to sit," Qian Sun'ai echoed zealously.

"Well, if I don't sit, she will think that I don't dare to," Liu Rushi thought as she sat down in a chair on the right side of Lady Chen, restraining her anger.

To maintain superficial harmony as family, they started a conversation. They first talked about the weather. Then, Liu Rushi told Lady Chen about the recent trip to Suzhou—what she had seen and heard and the boats and carriages she and their husband had taken. They also talked about some trivial family matters. Whenever Liu Rushi spoke, Lady Chen always patiently listened with an agreeable smile on her face, never interrupting the younger woman, who, overly animated and very talkative, spoke of everything with a harsh, critical tone, using literary allusions and quoting a few lines from the classics from time to time, sometimes giggling for no good reason at all, and often stopping abruptly.

"Did the lord go to bed very late last night?" asked Lady Chen

瞧了瞧寝室的门。

柳如是斜了陈夫人一眼。“她为什么总是摆出这副样子？好像这府第里唯有她才是名正言顺的主子似的！”柳如是愤愤地想。为了表示对这种可恨的“尊严”的鄙视，她故意歇了一会儿，才慢条斯理地回答：“昨天么，老爷一回府就睡下了。嗯，他呀，就是这么个怪脾气，要么不睡，要么一睡就睡个没完！我劝过他多少回，这样不好，会伤身子的哟！当时，他还真听了。可过得十天半月，又忘啦！”她顿了顿，瞟着陈夫人，“老爷这脾气，姐姐还能不知道？”

“是这样的么？我当真还不知道哩！”陈夫人老实地回答。

“啊哟，姐姐这话可是在骂我了！”柳如是大惊小怪地嚷起来，“姐姐怎会不知道？若是姐姐说不知道，就是骂我随口喷蛆了！”

陈夫人怔了一下，随即微微一笑：“怎么会？这些年，都是你们服侍老爷。他的脾性儿怎样，自然该是你们比我知道多些。”

柳如是不作声了。她眨眨眼睛，感到有点失望：“哦，她为什么不生气？我明明在挖苦她，难道她听不出来？不，她是打心底里瞧不起我！对啦，她是大家小姐，我不过是下贱的娼妇。她想必觉着，连同我生气也有失她的金贵身份！”这样一想，柳如是仿佛给人兜头浇了一瓢冷水似的，呆住了。她茫然若失地瞅着陈夫人，渐渐现出一种绝望的、怨毒的神情。

“老爷暂且不醒也好，有一桩事，我原要先与你商量的。”陈夫人说，仿佛没有留意柳如是的神情。

“……”

“是这么回事，三姨太她有过错，得罪了你，我已经教训过她了。闻得老爷也很生气，要将她赶出去，让她到城东老屋去住。这原也应该。只是乃念她服侍老爷十几年，又有生养孙爱这份功

placidly, who turned to glance at the bedroom door.

Liu Rushi gave her a sidelong glance. "Why does she always put up airs like this, as if she were the only mistress of the house?" Liu Rushi thought resentfully. To show her contempt for such hateful airs of authority, she didn't reply immediately. After a long silence, she said slowly, "Well, the lord went to bed as soon as we came home. Well, he either stays up all night or sleeps endlessly, as is his habit, a weird one. I've told him many times that it's not good for his health, and he's always listened, but he always relapses after a few days." After a pause, she looked at Lady Chen and said, "My dear sister, don't you know this strange habit of his?"

"Is it so? I don't know it," said Lady Chen honestly.

"Ah, are you criticizing me?" said Liu Rushi in feigned alarm. "How come you don't know it? Saying you don't know it's like criticizing me for lying."

Lady Chen flinched. Then, she said, "By no means. It's you and the others that have been taking care of the lord over the years. Of course, you know his habits better than I do."

Liu Rushi went silent. She blinked her eyes, feeling a little disappointed: "Oh, why is she not angry? Doesn't she hear I'm mocking her? No, she's looking down on me from the bottom of her heart. Yes, she's a lady from a big family and I'm just a despicable prostitute. She must have felt that losing temper with me is beneath her status." Thus thinking, Liu Rushi was stupefied, as if someone had poured a bucket of cold water on her head. She stared dazedly at Lady Chen with a look of despair and resentment.

"Let the lord go on sleeping, then. I have something to discuss with you first," says Lady Chen, who didn't seem to be paying attention to Liu Rushi's expression.

"..."

"Here's the thing. Admittedly, the Third Lady has made a mistake. She shouldn't have offended you that way. I've already given her a lesson. The lord is also very angry. He wants to send her away to the old house in the east of the city. She deserves it. Because she's served

劳。常言道，不看僧面看佛面。我想向你讨个情，饶恕了她这一次，下次再犯，加倍责罚，我也决不维护于她。你瞧，这样成不成？”

陈夫人垂下眼睛，缓缓地说着。以她的身份，用这样的口吻向柳如是说话，在旁人看来实在是低声下气得过分。站在旁边的大丫环月容和两个老妈子惊异地瞧着她，又望望柳如是，脸上都现出愤愤不平的神色。

柳如是自然不会看不见这一点。本来，这件事她已经答应钱谦益暂且作罢，不过怕朱姨太知道后，愈加神气起来，才一直故意拖着，不给她说清楚。至于陈夫人，她从娘家回来时，钱谦益同柳如是已经上了苏州，自然也不知道。如今她显然是听了朱姨太的投诉，出面来说情的。不过，老太婆的这种态度和口气，却使柳如是十分恼火。“哼，你这是故意让我难堪、出丑、下不来台！我可不是傻瓜！”她想。于是冷笑一声，说：“姐姐这话，我可是万万不敢承当！我是什么人？怎敢如此大胆，起意要把三姨太撵出府去？纵然这大半年，我在老爷身边的时候多些，但老爷的事情，我是一星半点也不敢过问。三姨太骂我、咒我，背地里阴损我，我心里不痛快，辩驳几句也是有的。可是大婆小婆拌嘴斗气的事，哪户人家少得了？吵过就算了，我可没往心里去。我也不知老爷要把三姨太赶出府去是何用意，眼见老爷火气大了，吓得想问也没敢问。如今姐姐不知受了哪些个黑心瞎眼的丫头妈子撺掇，突然来向我讨情，真叫我吃惊不小！瞧这样子，我岂非成了那轻贱狂妄、没教没养的人了？姐姐你心里有气，骂我、打我都行，可千万别提这讨情的事！”

这一番话带枪夹棒，既尖酸又决绝，听得陈夫人面上红一阵、白一阵，怔在那里，没有了主意。就连站在她身后的两个老妈子

the lord for over ten years, and she is the birth mother of Sun'ai, I'd like to beg you a favor. Please spare her this time. As the saying goes, 'it's for the sake of the Buddha if not the monk.' If she ever makes that mistake again, you can double down on the punishment and I shall not defend her. What do you think?" said Lady Chen in a reserved tone, her eyes lowered. Such a tone was below herself. Yuerong the servant girl and the two old maids standing by looked at her bewilderedly, then at Liu Rushi, with an expression of indignation on their faces.

Of course, that didn't escape Liu Rushi's attention. She had already promised Qian Qianyi to drop the issue for the time being, but, afraid that Lady Zhu would become proud of herself again after knowing it, she didn't tell her outright. Lady Chen obviously didn't know it, because when she returned from her parents' home, Qian Qianyi and Liu Rushi had already gone to Suzhou. She came to mediate upon hearing Lady Zhu's complaint. Yet her attitude and tone of voice annoyed Liu Rushi greatly. "Hmph, you are embarrassing and making a fool of me. I'm not a fool," she thought. So she said with a sneer, "My dear Elder Sister, I dare not take what you said. Who am I? How dare I be so bold as to drive Third Lady out of the house? True I've spent more time with the lord in the last six months, but I've never dared to intervene in the lord's business. When Third Lady swore at me, cursed me or slandered me behind my back, I was not happy and there were some arguments, but wives and concubines argue in every big family. Such arguments shouldn't be taken seriously. I'm also wondering why the lord decided to drive Third Lady out of the house. Seeing him so angry, I was so scared that I didn't even dare to ask. It must be some servant girl or old maid with bad intentions who has been backbiting me so that you've come to me to speak for Third Lady. I'm really shocked. Now you're speaking as if I were a contemptuous, arrogant, uneducated person. My dear Elder Sister, if you're not happy with me, you can criticize me or give me a beating, but don't say you've come to ask me for mercy."

These words were like bullets and daggers. Lady Chen was nonplussed, her face blushing and paling alternately. The two old

也面面相觑，倒抽一口凉气。最后，还是大丫环月容乖觉些，她悄悄扯了扯孙爱的衣袖，又努努嘴，意思是要他出面去说。

钱孙爱自从见了柳如是，就时时想同她说话，只是插不上嘴。被月容提醒，他就忙不迭地跳起来，走到柳如是跟前，恭恭敬敬地行了一个礼，说："孩儿给柳太太请安。许久不见柳太太，柳太太可好？"

柳如是瞥了他一眼，淡淡地问："嗯，少爷有什么事吗？"

钱孙爱兴冲冲地说："哦，没……没什么，孩儿只是许久不见柳太太，心中想念得很。前些日子听说柳太太身子欠安，孩儿一直担心着，如今见柳太太好好儿的，孩儿就放心了！"

钱孙爱这话说来谦卑有礼，一片真诚，倒使柳如是有点意外。她凝视着他，忽然微微一笑："嗯，你口口声声喊我做太太，就不怕你三娘打烂你的小屁股？"

"怕什么！"孙爱脸红了一下，随即理直气壮地说，"这是爹吩咐的，你是太太，我自然该这样叫，没错！"

柳如是点点头，笑得更加柔和："你不是再不进我这门了么？怎么今天又来啦？"

"不，那是三娘不许我来，其实孩儿很想来的。今天是太太带我来，她、她就拦不住啦！"

"嗯，要是没人带，你就不敢来了？"

钱孙爱犹豫了一下，他显然还没考虑过这个问题。但是，当看见柳如是微眯的眼睛现出轻蔑的神情时，他就情急起来："不，我敢，谁说不敢？只要我喜欢，哼，谁也管不着我！"

"这样说，你是喜欢我啰？"

"是……孩儿、孩儿，喜欢……"兴奋得满脸通红的钱孙爱结结巴巴地说。

maids standing behind her looked at each other and gasped in fear. In the end, the quick-witted servant girl Yuerong pulled on Sun'ai's sleeve and pointed at Liu Rushi with her pressed lips to mean he should go talk to her.

Qian Sun'ai had been waiting for an opportunity to speak to Liu Rushi. Following Yuerong's hint, he jumped up, walked over to Liu Rushi, bowed respectfully, and said, "Accept my tribute, Mother Liu, are you doing well?"

Liu Rushi cast a glance at him and asked placidly, "Well, what's up, young master?"

Qian Sun'ai said cheerfully, "Oh, no—nothing. It's just that I've been missing you, Mother Liu. I haven't seen you for a long time. I heard that you were not well a few days ago, so I am worried. Seeing you're well now, I'm really happy for you."

Qian Sun'ai spoke with humility, politeness, and sincerity, which surprised Liu Rushi. She stared at him, and suddenly smiled slightly, saying, "Well, you keep calling me 'mother', so you're not afraid your third mother will spank your ass?"

"Why should I be afraid?" Sun'ai blushed, then said confidently, "Dad has asked me to call you 'mother'. You are a mother, so I must call you 'mother'. There's nothing wrong with it."

Liu Rushi nodded and smiled more gently, "Haven't you decided never to come again? Why are you here again today?"

"No, I've always wanted to come. It's just that Third Mother forbids me to. Now that First Mother has brought me here, Third Mother can't prevent it."

"Oh? If no one takes you here, you won't dare to come?"

Qian Sunai hesitated for an instant. Clearly, he hadn't thought about it before. Seeing the expression of contempt in Liu Rushi's slightly closed eyes, he became anxious. "Of course I dare. Who said I dare not? As long as I like it, hum, no one can prevent me from coming."

"So, you like me?"

"Yes, I do. I—I like—" stammered Qian Sunai, his face red with excitement.

“那么，”柳如是歪着头，高高地挺起胸脯，并且风骚地摇摆着腰肢，“你说说，喜欢我哪儿？唔？”

“这个……孩儿，不，不知道……孩儿只是觉得……喜欢……”钱孙爱羞涩地瞧了柳如是一眼，低下头去。可是，他立刻又抬起头来，狂热地盯着柳如是看。

在同孙爱说话的当儿，柳如是一直暗暗注视着陈夫人的反应。当她发现这位自命高贵、循规蹈矩的可恶的老太婆，被自己的行为吓得目瞪口呆，不由自主地浑身发抖时，她尝到了一种报复的、恶意的快感。

“那么，好吧。难得你有这份孝心。我回头要好好打赏你！”柳如是终于结束道。她已经把陈夫人狠狠地捉弄了一番，并且亲眼看见了对方的恐怖和慌乱，也就不想再理会钱孙爱了。

钱孙爱却不明白这一点，而且他又一次受到月容的催促。

“娘，不要，孩儿不……什么打赏，不要！孩儿只要你……一件事，答应我。”他语无伦次地说。

“哎，什么事？”

“孩儿……呃，你若是真疼孩儿的话，求你向爹说，别把三娘赶出去。”

柳如是怔了一下，顿时沉下了脸：“你这孩子真不懂事，刚才我不是说了吗，这不关我的事！”

“哦，关的，关的，我知道关的！我要你答应我！”钱孙爱一把揪住柳如是的衣袖，扭着身子，撒起娇来。

柳如是有点恼火了。她心想：“亏你这涎脸的孱头刚才嘴巴子比糖还甜，老娘还当你真的向着我。原来你们都串通好了，来做戏给我看。哼，老娘岂是受人耍的角色。你便求到塌天，也休想我松口！”拿定主意，她就用力把袖子一挣，说：“你歪缠什么！看把衣裳弄皱了，快快松手！”

“不嘛，我要你答应我！”钱孙爱一边说，一边把袖子攥得更紧。

"Then," said Liu Rushi, tilting her head, lifting her breasts high, and swaying her waist. "Tell me, what do you like about me? Huh?"

"That—that I don't know. I only feel—I—like—" Qian Sun'ai gave Liu Rushi a shy look and lowered his head, but he immediately raised his head and stared feverishly at Liu Rushi.

While talking to Sun'ai, Liu Rushi kept watching Lady Chen's reaction. She had a vengeful, malicious satisfaction when she saw the pretentious, well-behaved, hateful old woman dumbfounded by her actions and shuddering involuntarily.

"Well, then. I appreciate your filial piety. I'll reward you well later." Liu Rushi finally said. Seeing the horror and panic on Lady Chen from the practical joke, she didn't feel it necessary to go on speaking to Qian Sun'ai anymore.

Qian Sun'ai didn't know that. When he was urged by Yuerong again, he said, "Mother, don't—I don't—I don't want any reward. I just want you to do, to do one thing. Pray agree. I beg you," he said incoherently.

"Oh? What is it?"

"Mother, um, if you really care about me, pray tell Father not to drive Third Mother out of the house."

Liu Rushi cringed and her face suddenly sank. "You are really a child. Didn't I say it just now that it isn't my business?"

"Oh, yes, it is. I know it is. Pray promise me." Qian Sun'ai grabbed Liu Rushi's sleeve, shaking his body coquettishly.

Liu Rushi was irritated. She thought to herself, "What a drooling brat you were just now! Your mouth was sweeter than a honeycomb. I thought you were really defending me. It turns out that you've all teamed up to set me up. Hmph, who am I to be set up? I won't promise anything, no matter how you plead with me." Having made up her mind, she pulled her sleeve from him and said, "Take your hand off me. You have wrinkled my garment."

"No, I want you to promise me," said Qian Sun'ai, holding her sleeve even tighter.

柳如是当真生气了，她瞪起眼睛，喝道：“混账东西，你松手不松手？”

钱孙爱犹疑了一下，但是柳如是先前的亲昵态度显然给他造成了错觉。他不但不松手，反而大胆地把柳如是的胳膊抱住。

“我不嘛，我……”

然而，怒不可遏的柳如是不等他说下去，便扬起右手，“啪”地扇了他一记耳光。

这一下，钱孙爱立即松了手。他后退两步，呆呆地望着柳如是，脸上现出茫然、惊诧的神情，渐渐这神情变成恐怖。蓦地，他尖叫一声，转过身去，发疯似的推开赶过来保护他的月容以及另外两个老妈子，飞奔出了门。两个老妈子连声叫唤着，也慌里慌张地奔了出去。

这当儿，陈夫人早已站了起来。她气得浑身直打哆嗦，指着柳如是，一迭声地说：“你、你、你你……”却什么也说不出来。

柳如是也满脸通红，她悻悻地理着衣袖，激怒地叫：“你们自己没脸面，却使出这等下作的诡计，支派个孩子来上阵，让他挨打。这可是你们自招，怨不得谁！”

陈夫人显然完全不会对付这种无法无天的侍妾。她不知怎么办才好，半晌，才喘着气说：“好，我、我找相公去！”

“不用找了。我都听见了！”一个低沉的嗓音说。大家蓦然回过头去。不知什么时候，钱谦益已经披着一件长袍，脸色阴沉地站在寝室的门口。

“古语说，‘国必自伐，然后人伐之。’家亦如此，必先自败，然后人败之！”他怒声说，走出起居室来，“同是一个家中的人，尚且不能和睦相处，偏要争斗不休。你们说，这样怎能抵挡外人的侵侮和欺凌，怎能应付非常之变？你们纵然不用为这种事操心，

Liu Rushi was angry. She stared at him and shouted, "You bastard! Will you take your hand off or not?"

Qian Sun'ai hesitated for an instant. Liu Rushi's previous friendly attitude had clearly created an illusion for him. Instead of letting go of her, he boldly embraced Liu Rushi's arm.

"No, I won't. I —"

Yet, Liu Rushi was furious. Before he finished his words, she raised her right hand and slapped him in the face.

Qian Sun'ai immediately let go of her. He stepped back and stared blankly at Liu Rushi, with an expression of bewilderment and shock on his face, which gradually turned into one of fear. Suddenly, he screamed, turned around, pushed Yuerong and the two old maids who had come to protect him, and fled the room like a maniac. The two old maids called out to him and ran out in panic.

By this time Lady Chen had already stood up. Trembling with anger, she pointed to Liu Rushi and said, "You, you, you, you ..." She stuttered and could not go on.

Liu Rushi blushed. She tidied her sleeve in resentment and shouted angrily, "What cowards you are to think of such a trick and let a child bear the brunt! It's all your doing and no one else is responsible."

Lady Chen, of course, had no idea how to deal with such a lawless concubine at all. She was nonplussed. After a long while, she said out of breath, "Alright, then. Let me find our husband."

"You don't have to find me. I've heard it all," said a low voice. Everyone turned around abruptly. Qian Qianyi was standing gloomily at the door of the bedroom with a long gown.

"As the old saying goes, 'A country is defeated by itself before being finally defeated by the enemies.' The same goes for a family. A family is defeated by itself before being defeated by others," he said angrily as he walked out of the sitting room. "As family, you are supposed to live in harmony, but instead you are fighting each other nonstop. Tell me, how can we defend the family against incursion and bullying by others, and how can we survive disasters? True you don't

可是我要！你们还让不让我有片刻的安宁？啊！”他发火地吼叫起来，严厉地瞪着陈夫人。直到后者满心委屈地低下头去，掩着面孔倒在椅子里，他才转眼看看柳如是，发现她咬着唇儿，还在皱眉瞪眼地生气，就放缓和了声调，说：“现在，可不是争闲气、泄小忿的时候，须得和衷共济，以渡难关——今天这事，我看就算了。朱姨娘嘛，还让她留在府里，可不准她再闹！至于孙爱，年纪不小了，该懂点事了。连他也跟着混闹，成什么话！嗯，回头叫他来见我！”

## 访友消愁

“不知老师枉顾，请恕弟子失迎之罪！”罢官在家的前户科给事中瞿式耜，身穿礼服迎出大门外来，拱着手说。他那高大健壮的身躯微弓着，浓眉下面一双精光闪烁的眼睛专注地望着阶下，长方形的脸上现出恭敬严肃的神情。

这是钱谦益回到常熟之后半个月的一天下午，偏西的太阳从幽静狭长的巷子上空照下来，把高大漂亮的瞿府门楼的影子，清晰地勾画在大门对面的白粉影壁上，那影壁盖着讲究的瓦顶，还有雕砖镶边。

刚刚从四人抬大轿里走下来的钱谦益，听见这熟悉的招呼，抬起了头发花白的脑袋，黝黑的脸上露出亲昵的，几乎是讨好的笑容。

“哎，太亲翁，何必客气！”他大声说，迎上去，同趋步下阶的主人行礼相见，“说真的，一路上我还叨念着，怕你出门了呢！”

“没有——二冯兄弟，还有云美、子长他们都来了，正在卿

have to worry about such things, but I do. Can you give my mind a moment of peace? Woe!" He roared angrily and stared at Lady Chen sternly until she lowered her head aggrievedly and collapsed into the chair, her hands cupped over her face. Then, he turned around to see Liu Rushi, who was still burning with rage, so he softened his tone and said, "Now isn't the time to fight for trivial matters and vent little fits of anger. We need to help each other to overcome our difficulties. Let's forget about what has happened today. Lady Zhu shall stay in the house on condition that she shouldn't make trouble. As for Sun'ai, he's no longer a kid and should know better. He shouldn't be involved in a thing like this. Um, I'll talk to him later."

## Seeking Consolation in the House of a Friend

"My dear teacher, what a great honor to have your visit!" said Qu Shisi, who came out in formal attire and greeted Qian Qianyi with a salute. Qu Shisi was Royal Liaison Officer of the Department of Revenues discharged from office. While he put his hands together in salute, his tall and yet rotund body bent slightly forward with an expression of deference on his rectangular face, his sparkling eyes under the thick brows looking intently at his guest ascending the stairs.

It was one afternoon half a month after Qian Qianyi returned to Changshu. The sun in the west shone from above the quiet narrow alley and cast the shadow of the tall, majestic gatehouse of the Qu residence on the white screen wall opposite the gate. The screen wall had an arty tile roof on top and was laced by carved bricks.

Upon hearing the familiar greeting, Qian Qianyi, who had just stepped off the four-bearer sedan chair, raised his head of gray hair with an intimate, almost flattering smile on his dark face.

"Hey, *taiqin*[1], no ceremonies," he said in a loud voice as he went forward to meet the owner of the residence, who was walking down the stairs. "To be honest, I was afraid you had gone out."

"No, I haven't. The Feng brothers, Yunmei, and Zichang are

---

① *taiqin*: grandpa of daughter-in-law

云阁里看字画呢！”

“噢，他们都来了么？”

“要是老师有事……”

“没事、没事！我也是随便走走。嗯，听说你新近收到一幅赵子昂，我正想瞧瞧！”

“是，请——”

“请！”

这样说完之后，两人便并肩朝宅子里走去。

在常熟城里，瞿式耜可算是同钱谦益关系顶深的一个人。他不仅是钱氏早年的学生，而且他的孙女儿又许给了钱孙爱。论学业渊源，他该称钱谦益作老师；论姻亲关系，钱谦益却得反过来尊他一声“太亲翁”。不单如此，他们还曾一起在朝共事，一起在崇祯二年被温体仁排挤罢官；十多年间，他们同样一直在家赋闲，得不到起用。前几年，有个叫张汉儒的本地帮闲，秉承温体仁的意旨，入京告发钱谦益在家贪肆不法，把瞿式耜也告了进去，结果师生二人又同时被捉拿进京，下狱问罪。幸而温体仁很快就倒了台，他们才逃过危难。因了这种种缘故，二人的关系，就确实非比一般。不过，瞿式耜生性耿直，对钱谦益是恭敬而不阿谀。所以有些见不得人的事，钱谦益也避免找他商议。不过，既然落到了目前这种倒霉的境地，瞿家却又成了钱谦益寻求慰藉的理想去处了。

当钱谦益在瞿式耜的陪同下步入卿云阁时，先到的几位本地名流或坐或站，正在那里指手画脚地品评字画。看见钱谦益进来，大家便住了口，一齐迎上来同他相见。这些名流，平时也都是钱府的常客，彼此熟悉得很。可是此刻钱谦益见到他们，却不由自主感到有点心虚。“嗯，不知他们可已听说那桩倒霉事？”他想，

all here. They're having a look at the calligraphy and paintings in Qingyun Pavilion."

"Oh, are they here too?"

"My dear teacher, if you have anything serious—"

"No, I don't . I'm just stopping by. Well, I heard you recently received a work by Zhao Zi'ang and would like to have a look."

"Yes, please."

"Please!"

After this exchange, the two walked side by side to the house.

In Changshu City, Qu Shisi was one of the closest persons to Qian Qianyi. He was not only a former student but also the future father-in-law of Qian Sun'ai. As a former student, he should call Qian Qianyi "teacher"; as the two were related by a future marriage, Qian Qianyi in turn should respectfully address him as *taiqin*. And not only that, but they had also worked as colleagues at court, both having been ousted from office in the second year of the reign of Emperor Chongzhen[AD 1629] as a result of Wen Tiren's persecution; both had been staying at home for over ten years without reinstatement. A few years ago, a local idler named Zhang Hanru, who, acting on Wen Tiren's instructions, went to Beijing to report Qian Qianyi's "illegal activities" at home which involved Qu Shisi. Consequently, both teacher and pupil were arrested and sent to a Beijing prison. Fortunately, Wen Tiren soon fell from grace, and they survived the crisis. For these reasons, the relationship between the two was fairly close. Qu Shisi was an upright man by nature, who was respectful but not obsequious to Qian Qianyi, who cautiously kept secrets from him. Now that Qian Qianyi had sunk so low, the house of the Qus was an ideal place for him to seek comfort.

When Qian Qianyi walked into the Qingyun Pavilion with Qu Shisi, several local celebrities who had arrived earlier were judging the paintings and calligraphy works with gesticulations, some standing, some sitting. When they saw Qian Qianyi coming in, everyone stopped and came to meet him. These celebrities were also regular visitors to Qian's residence. But when Qian Qianyi saw them, his mind was not at ease. "Well, I'm wondering if they've heard of the

脸上尽力装出从容镇定的样子，暗地里却十分注意每个人的神情。直到发现大家都没有异常的表示时，他才稍稍放下心来。“毕竟是交往多年，所以……”于是，他开始分外热情地同大家行礼、寒暄，侧着耳朵倾听每一个人所说的每一句话，然后，带着亲切的微笑，回答哪怕是最微不足道的问题……

“啊，牧老，你来，你来瞧这画！他们说是宋徽宗，怎么会是宋徽宗！”一个兴冲冲的声音蓦地叫起来。那是一位名叫冯班的本地名士。他长着一个可笑的红鼻子，和一双狂热的、醉醺醺的眼睛。秃而亮的脑门上歪扣着一顶半新不旧的方巾，下面露出乱蓬蓬的头发，直裰的胸前尽是星星点点的油污酒迹。不过，别看他外表邋里邋遢，却写得一手好诗，对书法也颇有研究，在江南文坛上薄有名气，与他哥哥冯舒并称“常熟二冯”。

“咦，牧老，你快过来瞧啊！”冯班又叫，不管钱谦益正同别人说话。

“定远，你总是火烧眉毛似的！”钱谦益微笑着责备说，离开了交谈者，走到挂在墙上的一幅绢本宋画跟前。

这是一幅《芙蓉锦鸡图》：一枝盛开的木芙蓉自画的左上方斜伸下来，枝上伫立着一只羽毛璀璨的锦鸡。它的重量把花枝压得微微弯垂。一丛萧疏的秋菊安排在画的左下方，右上角则对称地翩飞着一双彩蝶。蝴蝶下面用瘦金书题着一首五言绝句：

秋劲拒霜盛，峨冠锦羽鸡。
已知全五德，安逸胜凫鹥。

右下方靠边署着：宣和殿御制并书

incident," he thought, straining to give a calm look on his face while secretly watching everyone's expression. It was only when he found that no one had any unusual expression that he felt relieved. "After all, we have known each other for years, so ..." He then began to greet everyone and exchange pleasantries with them in good cheer. He tilted his ear to listen to every word, and, with a friendly smile, answered every question, even the most trivial ones.

"Oh, Elder Mu, come here, come look at this painting. They say it's by emperor Huizong of the Song dynasty. How can it be Huizong?" said an excited voice. It was a local celebrity named Feng Ban. He had a ridiculous red nose and a pair of feverish, drunken eyes. An old headscarf sat askew on his bald, shiny head, his hair unkempt and his long gown full of oil and alcohol stains. Despite his sloppy appearance, however, he was a decent poet and calligrapher. He was well-known in the literary circles in River South as the younger one of the Feng Brothers of Changshu, the elder one being Feng Shu.

"Hey, Elder Mu, come have a look," called Feng Ban again, interrupting Qian Qianyi's conversation with somebody else.

"Dingyuan, you're calling as if it were an emergency," Qian Qianyi admonished with a smile. Then, he stopped the conversation and went to a Song dynasty silk scroll painting.

It was titled "Golden Pheasant and Hibiscus". A flowering cotton rose[①] branch extends downward obliquely from the upper left corner; on the slightly-bent branch stands a golden pheasant in colorful plumage; in the lower-left corner is a bunch of sparsely-scattered autumn chrysanthemums; in the upper-right corner fly a symmetrical pair of multicolored butterflies; under the butterflies is a five-character quatrain written in "thin print":

*qiū jìn jù shuāng shèng, é guān jǐn yǔ jī.*
*yǐ zhī quán wǔ dé, ān yì shèng fú yī.*
which says:

---

① cotton rose: hibiscus mutabilis

钱谦益漫不经心地望着画幅。这幅画他在瞿式耜家里已经看过多次，而且反复讨论过它的真伪。要在以往，他会立即说出自己的意见。不过此刻出于一种周到的考虑，他却想给冯班一点面子。

“定远，你说这画不是徽宗御笔，所据何来？”他侧过头问。

“咦，牧老你瞧那首题诗，第一句，‘秋劲拒霜盛’的‘盛’字，显系‘威’字之误！此处下一‘盛’字，不唯平仄欠工，而且不通！须是‘威’字方诗意畅达，而且谐韵。岂有堂堂御笔，而荒谬不经若此！必系赝品而又出于极端下流无知者之手无疑！”

冯班说“盛”字是误字，钱谦益倒不曾注意到。他走上前去再仔细瞧一下那首题画诗，随即微笑起来。但他也不立刻说破，反而点点头：“定远的话不错，这画或许并非道君皇帝真迹。”

“喂，怎么样？怎么样？啊？”一直瞪大眼睛等他回答的冯班，兴奋地跳起来，胜利地大叫。

“可是……”“不过……”好几个声音同时表示不服气。钱谦益摆摆手，让他们安静下来。

“我说这画并非道君真迹，是说可能如此。皆因宋时画院中，确有画师曾为道君代笔，所谓‘供御画’便是。不过，倘若此画

*In deep autumn, the blooming cotton rose defies the frost.*
*A multicolored pheasant proudly raises his steeply-crowned head.*
*Complete with all five virtues,*
*One is peaceful and quiet like the bird.*

In the lower-right corner was written:

*Painting and calligraphy made for the Xuanhe Palace*

Qian Qianyi looked at the picture absent-mindedly. He had seen it many times in Qu Shisi's house and had repeatedly discussed its authenticity. Instead of immediately expressing his opinion as usual, he decided to withhold it for the moment, because he wanted to save Feng Ban some face.

"Dingyuan, you said that this painting isn't by emperor Huizong himself. What is your basis?" He turned to Feng Ban and asked.

"Well, Elder Mu, take a look at the inscription poem. In the first line, 'In deep autumn, the blooming cotton rose defies the frost', the word *shèng* (blooming) is obviously the word *wēi* (powerful) in error. The meter isn't right, nor does it fit in terms of meaning. It must be the word *wēi*, which is poetic and in keeping with the rhythm. Such a lowly work can't be from the hand of Emperor Huizong. It must be a fake by a vulgar, ignorant artist."

Qian Qianyi hadn't noticed the word *shèng* before, so he stepped forward and took a closer look at the inscription poem. Then, he smiled, but didn't say his own opinion immediately. Instead, he nodded and said, "You're not wrong. This painting may not be an authentic copy of Emperor Huizong, the Taoist Prince."

"Haha, how is my judgment? How is my judgment?" Feng Ban, who was waiting for Qian Qianyi's comment, jumped up excitedly and exclaimed triumphantly.

"But ..." "But ..." Several voices expressed disapproval at the same time. Qian Qianyi gestured to calm them down.

"I just said it might not be an authentic copy of the Taoist Prince, because back then, in the Royal Academy of Art, there was indeed an artist who did some hackwork called 'works for the emperor' for the

果属此类，则题诗内断不致出现误字。即使当时确有误题，亦必不敢以之进呈天子，更不敢任其流传，而必当即时毁去。”说到这里，他稍稍停顿了一下，望望大家，才又接着说，“其实，‘拒霜’，乃木芙蓉之别称。‘拒霜盛’，是谓此花盛开。故‘盛’字并无不通。若改作‘威’字，反而不妥了……”

这样一说，持不同看法的几个人都频频点头。冯班却像被人掐住了喉颈的公鸡似的伸着脖子，瞪着眼睛，再也神气不起来。

“不过世上之事，阴差阳错，未可以常理度之者正复不少，所以亦不能以此论定。”钱谦益瞧了一眼冯班，又补充说，“但我观此画布局严谨，宾主分明，疏密有致，色泽鲜妍，渲染精妙。即便是左下角上那丛不惹眼的小菊，亦摇曳多姿，刻意求工，故此画纵非道君御笔，亦当系北宋院画之精品——鄙人浅见如此，未知诸位以为如何？”

这一席议论，说得大家都点头称是。只有冯班仍不服气，他咕咕哝哝地说：“我瞧那锦鸡就画得差劲儿，怪模怪样的，活像只断头鸡！”

这当儿，瞿式耜已经命人把《芙蓉锦鸡图》收起，亲自从箱子里挑了一幅，交给小厮挂上，一面对钱谦益说：“老师，这便是学生新近购得的那一幅赵子昂的《双马涉溪图》了。”

钱谦益一听，顿时来了精神。他忘了答瞿式耜的话，瞪大眼

Taoist Prince. If this painting were one of such works, there shouldn't have been an error in the inscription poem. Even if there were indeed an error, they wouldn't have dared to present it to the emperor, nor would they have dared to circulate it. Instead, it would have been destroyed immediately." He paused for a moment and scanned the celebrities. Then, he continued, "Actually, *jù shuāng* is another name for hibiscus. *Jù shuāng shèng* means this flower is in full bloom. Therefore, the word *shèng* isn't implausible. On the contrary, if it were changed into *wēi*, the poem definitely would sound odd."

The men holding different views from that of Feng Ban's nodded in agreement. Feng Ban, however, was suddenly dispirited, stretching his neck like a rooster being strangled at his throat, with his eyes popping out of the head.

"However, there're things in this world that may be wrong but can't be explained by common sense. Therefore, there shouldn't be simple conclusions." Qian Qianyi looked at Feng Ban and added, "Look at this painting. The layout is meticulously done with due emphasis on the important details, everything in good order, and the colors and hues in a good array. Even the bunch of inconspicuous little chrysanthemums in the lower-left corner are exquisite and variegated. So, if the painting isn't the result of the imperial brush of the Taoist Prince, it should be a masterpiece from the Royal Academy of Art in the Northern Song dynasty. A masterpiece of painting. What do you think of my humble opinion?"

Upon hearing such a comment, everyone nodded, except Feng Ban. Not yet convinced, he mumbled, "In my eyes, the golden pheasant is poorly drawn. It looks strange, like a decapitated rooster."

Qu Shisi ordered a servant to put away "Golden Pheasant and Hibiscus", took out another painting from the box, asked a servant boy to hang it on the wall, and said to Qian Qianyi, "My dear teacher, this is Zhao Zi'ang's 'Two Horses Crossing the Creek' I've recently bought."

Qian Qianyi's eyes lit up. Forgetting to reply to Qu Shisi, he stared at the wall with wide-open eyes. As the servant boy unrolled

睛，全神贯注地瞧着墙上。只见画轴在小厮手里缓缓转动着，首先露出一个仰着的马头，那用简练遒劲而又富于变化的线条勾勒出的马头，筋肉毕现，鼻孔张开，眼睛里闪射着桀骜不驯的光芒，端的是神采焕发，顾盼惊人。然后是健壮的脖颈、飞扬的鬃毛……第二匹马出现了，那是一匹花骢马。它正低着头，顽强地向前行进，下面，是八条强有力的腿，或屈或伸，在一道宽阔湍急的溪涧上蹴踏起飞溅的水花……

全场人都被这幅杰作的不寻常魅力吸引住了，静静地观赏着，谁都没有说话。钱谦益更是如醉如痴。他一会儿退得远远地拈着胡子，眯起眼睛欣赏全貌，一会儿又走上前去，几乎把鼻尖贴着画面作细部的观摩，许久，才连连点头，叹道："神品，神品！"

"若是老师喜爱，学生就此相赠。"瞿式耜说。

钱谦益蓦地一惊，忙不迭地回头瞧着主人，结结巴巴地问："你说、你说……"

"学生想将此画送给老师！"

"啊，这、这、这如何使得！太亲翁莫要作耍，不……这，我……"

瞿式耜摆一摆手，淡然说："区区一画，何足挂齿！"说着，回头吩咐小厮，"把这画收拾好了，待会儿，给钱老爷送过去！"

钱谦益不再推辞了，但是嘴里仍然喃喃地说道："罪过、罪过！"同时，斜起眼睛瞧着两个小厮把画收起来，装进一只长形的黄杨木盒子里，另外放到一张单独的桌子上，这才放了心似的，回过头去，向主人深深地作揖称谢。其他客人见了，也围上来，带着羡慕的神情，纷纷向钱谦益道贺。

这时，一个声音蓦地叫起来："啊哟，不得了！臭！臭不可闻！混账，收起！听见没有？快收起！"

大家吃惊地回过头去，发现冯班站在一幅刚刚挂起来的书法

the scroll in his hands, the lifted head of a horse was revealed. The horse head, drawn with concise, rigorous, and variegated lines, was vivid in every detail: bulging muscles, wide-open nostrils, and unruly, sparkling eyes. Then came out the thick, long neck, the flying mane ... then appeared the second horse, a five-colored steed, which, bending its head, was treading strenuously forward. Down below were eight strong legs, bent or stretched, sending up splashes of water on a wide and fast-moving stream.

Everyone was arrested by the unusual charm of this masterpiece and stared at it silently. Qian Qianyi was mesmerized. He now stepped back to admire the whole picture, now stepped forward to study the details, almost sticking the tip of his nose to the picture. After a long while, he nodded his head and said excitedly, "A great masterpiece! A great masterpiece indeed!"

"My dear teacher, if you like it that much, let me give it to you," said Qu Shisi.

Qian Qianyi was surprised. He turned to look at the host and stammered, "You're saying, you're saying—"

"I'd like to give it to you."

"Oh, no. It's too precious. You're kidding me, *taiqin*. No, this, I—"

Qu Shisi waved his hand and said calmly, "It's a mere painting, no big deal." He turned around and said to the servant boy, "Pick up this painting and take it to Lord Qian later."

Qian Qianyi no longer refused, but still mumbled, "Shame on me, shame on me!" At the same time, he squinted at the two servants and watched as they placed the painting in a long wooden box and put them on a separate table, and then, as if relieved, turned around and thanked the host with a deep bow. Seeing this, the other guests came over and congratulated Qian Qianyi admiringly.

At this moment, a voice suddenly shouted, "Oh, this is outrageous! It stinks! It stinks badly! Bastard! Put it away! Do you hear? Put it away!"

Everyone turned around in surprise and found Feng Ban standing in front of a work of calligraphy that had just been hung up, jumping

跟前，用袖子拼命地捂着鼻子，另一只手气急败坏地挥舞着，又跳又叫。大家好奇地走前一看，原来挂出来的是一幅宋代黄庭坚的自书诗《登快阁》。那书法苍劲瘦硬，笔笔有力举千钧之势，一望而知是幅精品。大家正有点摸不着头脑，只见冯班像是再也忍受不了，他从人丛中一下子冲了出去，远远地站着，兀自掩鼻挥手，呜呜不休。

众人又惊奇又好笑。顾苓忍不住高声问："定远兄，你这是怎么了，莫非这又是那下流无知之徒弄出的赝品？"

冯班远远地摇着头，但又不肯把衣袖从鼻子上放下来。大家只听见他咿咿唔唔地说着，却听不清他说什么。这时，他的哥哥冯舒说话了。

"小弟已知定远之意——"他慢吞吞地说，"只是，他持论太偏，见解虽奇，却有失忠恕温厚之道。他一生志业，只怕就吃亏在这一点上！"说到这里，他十分惋惜地叹了一口气，却停住了。这个冯舒，长得又高又瘦，性格同他的弟弟恰恰相反，说话行事总是慢条斯理，往往绕了半天圈子，还到不了点子上。大家都深知他的脾气，明白催他也没用，都静静地等他说下去。

"他还嗜酒如命，这就更不好了。"冯舒又说，仰起头，瞧着屋梁，"比如去岁科考，他醉酒迟到，还侮辱宗师，结果，考了个六等……"

听见他这样慢条斯理地揭着弟弟的短处，大家都暗暗好笑。冯班远远听着，眼睛瞪圆了，他忽然把袖子放下来，大声说："不用你说！我说！"

冯舒顿住了，他把目光从屋梁转移到弟弟身上，"你说，自然我就不用说了。"他同意道，于是，重新退到一旁，不再开口了。

and screaming, desperately covering his nose with a sleeve, and his other hand angrily waving. Everyone stepped forward curiously and saw that it was "Dengkuai Pavilion", the handwriting of a poem by Huang Tingjian in the Song dynasty. The strokes were rigorous, edgy, and forceful. One could see it was a masterpiece at a glance. While everyone was confused, Feng Ban could stand it no longer. He stormed out of the small crowd and stood far away. Holding his nose with one sleeve and waving the other hand, he whined unstoppably.

The crowd was surprised and amused. Gu Ling couldn't help asking, "Brother Dingyuan, what's wrong? You have found another forgery by a vulgar ignoramus?"

Feng Ban shook his head from a distance but refused to remove his sleeve from his nose. He kept mumbling, but no one could hear what he was saying. At this time, his brother Feng Shu spoke.

"I know what Dingyuan means—" he drawled. "But he's too biased in his views. His ideas are original but ungracious. It's not good for his career development, I'm afraid." Then he stopped with a sigh. Feng Shu, a tall and thin man, showed exactly the opposite temperament. He always spoke and acted slowly. He would ramble on and on without getting to the point. Everyone knew his temperament and understood that there was no use to urge him. They quietly waited for him to make his point.

"Besides, he's addicted to drinking, to make matters worse." Feng Shu added, as he raised his head and looked at the roof beam above. "For example, he was late for last year's imperial exam because he was drunk. He even profaned Confucius, the Great Master. As a result, he only made it to Level Six, the lowest level ..."

Hearing him revealing his younger brother's shortcomings in such a way, everyone secretly laughed. Feng Ban listened from a distance, his eyes widening. Suddenly, he let go of the sleeve and said loudly, "You don't have to say it. Let me say it."

Feng Shu stopped, and he shifted his gaze from the roof beam to his younger brother. "If you say it, of course I don't have to say it," he said. Then, he went silent and stepped aside.

“列位，小弟平生论诗，第一等讨厌的，便是那劳什子江西派！”冯班气呼呼地说，“江西之体，大抵有如农夫之指掌、驴夫之脚跟，本臭硬可憎，却自夸什么‘强健’！又如老僧娶女之床席，奇臭恼人，却自夸什么‘孤高’！再如老妪之教新妇、塾师之训弟子，语言面目，无不可厌，却自考什么‘我正经’！这个姓黄的老家伙，乃是江西派第一个奇臭可憎之人。不意今日觌面相逢，却不是老大的晦气！”冯班说完，又把鼻子掩上了。

大家忍不住笑起来。孙永祚打趣说：“想不到天不怕地不怕的冯定远，却被江西派吓得只差没跳墙而走！”

冯班摇头说：“冒犯了天地，不过粉身碎骨而已；碰上江西派，却教人如堕粪窖，五脏翻腾，求生不得，求死不能！这黄老头儿万一有再起之日，我必远避，否则别寻生计，永不作有韵之语！”

瞿式耜微笑说：“既然定远兄如此说，这幅字竟是再也挂不得了，快快收起！”

待到小厮把字幅取下，重新收藏好，冯班才走回来，叹着气说：“经此番浊臭一冲，必损我三日诗思！”

在这番闹腾的当儿，钱谦益一直没有插话。因为他的整个心思，都关注在那幅赵子昂的《双马涉溪图》上了。从冯班逃开去的一刻起，他就退坐在一张花梨木圈椅上，脸上虽然也跟着大家一起微笑，眼梢却不住地往搁着画匣的方向瞄，恨不得立即就把那幅现在已经属于他的宝贝抱回家去，关起门来细细地重新欣赏。只是考虑到礼貌，他才勉强忍住了。好容易挨到关于黄庭坚和江西诗派的这场风波告一段落，他就站起来，准备告辞。然而，这时候，瞿府的一名家人扬着拜帖，走进来禀告说：

“许大相公求见，说有要事马上面陈钱老爷！”

"Comrades! To me, the so-called Jiangxi School of Poetry is most hateful," Feng Ban said angrily. "The style of the Jiangxi School is as rustic as a peasant's palm or a donkey's heel and yet they praise themselves for being rigorous. It stinks like a corpse, and yet they call it 'aloofness'. It's as boring and hateful as an old woman giving a lesson to her son's bride or a school teacher telling his students to behave, and yet they consider themselves guardians of propriety. This Mr. Huang is the most stinking and most hateful member of the Jiangxi School. What bad luck to see his work today!" Then he covered his nose with his sleeve again.

Everyone laughed. Sun Yongzuo said jokingly, "It turns out the most fearless Feng Dingyuan who defies the gods is scared the hell out of him by the Jiangxi School."

Feng Ban shook his head and said, "Offending the gods results in death at most but the Jiangxi School is like a huge cesspool from which there's no escape. It's worse than death. Should Mr. Huang's style comes in vogue again, I would keep away from it, or pursue a different career altogether instead of writing poems."

Qu Shisi smiled and said, "Since Brother Dingyuan doesn't like it, let's put it away."

After the servant boy took off the scroll and put it away, Feng Ban came back and said with a sigh, "This stink has killed my inspiration. I won't be able to write poetry in the next three days."

During this uproar, Qian Qianyi never cut in a word, because he was deeply obsessed with Zhao Zi'ang's "Two Horses Crossing the Creek". Earlier, when Feng Ban fled, he stepped back and sat down in a rosewood armchair. While he smiled like the others, his eyes kept looking in the direction where the storage box was placed. Now that the painting was his, he couldn't wait to take it home, close the door, and study its every detail. He stayed out of politeness. When the unrest over Huang Tingjian and the Jiangxi School of Poetry finally came to an end, he stood up, ready to leave, but at this moment, a servant of the Qus came in waving a calling card and said:

"Mr. Xu came and said that he has something important to tell

这位许大相公，名叫许隽，是本县的一名老秀才。因为会写几句诗，尤其善于把眼前的事物七拼八凑地弄进诗句中，造成一种离奇滑稽意味，使人读来，往往忍俊不禁，所以钱谦益平日同他也时有来往。如今听说他巴巴地追踪到瞿府来，说有什么要事相告，倒教钱谦益吃了一惊。他回头望了望大家，只好暂时打消告辞的念头，重新坐下来。

许隽很快就出现了。他头发花白，戴着一顶旧毡帽，一身玄色布直裰洗得发白，右边袖子的手肘处还打了个大补丁，脚下一双旧黑布鞋有好几处都脱了线，露出白袜子。不过，他的表情却十分神气，红扑扑的一张脸，宽颧骨、狮子鼻，走路时微昂着头，大摇大摆，显出目空一切的样子。

“哦！牧老，你原来躲在这儿快活，却叫我好找！”许隽气咻咻地叫，同大家行过礼，然后一屁股坐在椅子上。

“茶！”他大声说，不客气地瞅瞅瞿式耜。

瞿式耜朝小厮做了个手势，茶端来了。许隽接过，一口喝干，用袖子擦擦胡子，这才像喘过了一口气。

“牧老，这江南的士习，是越来越不成话了！”他说。

“啊，怎么？”

“他们造作谣言，无事生非，由来已久，这也罢了。可是，这一回竟造到你老哥头上，你说可气不可气！哼，还亏他们是复社！”

听了这话，大家都不由得“啊”了一声。钱谦益的脸却一下子红了，他动了动嘴巴，想说句什么，可是终于没有勇气说出口。

“前几日，弟上姑苏去了一趟，”许隽接着说，显然没有发现钱谦益的神情异常，“那一天，闲着无事，便到书坊走走，想

Lord Qian in person."

This Mr. Xu was Xu Jun, an old *xiucai* scholar in the county. He was a poet of sort, especially good at improvising by putting things in front of him in the lines, which were bizarre and amazing. Qian Qianyi had met him from time to time. Hearing Mr. Xu was here and had something important to tell him, Qian Qianyi was surprised. He looked back at the others, and, dropping the idea of leaving, sat down back into his chair.

Xu Jun appeared soon. He wore an old felt hat on his head of gray hair, a black long gown whitened from constant washing with a large patch on the elbow of his right sleeve, and a pair of old black cloth shoes on his feet that were threadbare in several places, revealing his white socks. He appeared, however, rather animated, with a blushing face, broad cheekbones, and a lion's nose, and an overbearing posture.

"Dear Elder Mu, you're having fun here. I've been looking for you everywhere," Xu Jun shouted in a fake anger, bowed to everyone present and then sat down on the chair.

"Tea, please!" he exclaimed, looking at Qu Shisi without ceremony.

Qu Shisi made a gesture to the servant, and tea was brought. Xu Jun took it, drank it in one gulp and wiped his beard with his sleeve. His breath began to return.

"Elder Mu, the milieu of the literary circles in River South is getting worse and worse," he said.

"So, what has happened?"

"They spread rumors and make trouble. That's no big deal. But this time, they're spreading rumors about you. Hateful! Hmph, it's a shame that they're Fushe members!"

That shocked everyone. Qian Qianyi's face suddenly turned red. He moved his mouth and wanted to say something but finally didn't find the courage to say it.

"A few days ago, I went to Gusu," Xu Jun continued, apparently not seeing Qian Qianyi's unusual expression. "When I had nothing to do, I went to the bookstore to buy some new books, where I overheard

拣两本新选的墨卷，却碰到两个方巾朋友在那里闲讲。弟起始也没在意，后来听他提到牧老，便留了心。谁知不听犹可，一听，真差点没给他气死！——那个不知是姓方还是姓汪的小畜生，竟造出一段漫天撒谎的奇闻来，说牧老如何同京里周阁老串通，想替阮圆海翻案开脱，怎样给周仲驭、陈定生识破，上门问罪。说得活龙活现，煞有介事。是弟气不过，上前同他争辩，说：'牧老是我的老友，我们天天在一块儿，怎么就没听说这事？你们快快闭嘴，没的在此污人清白！'谁知那两个小畜生笑嘻嘻地说：'若要人不知，除非己莫为！如今这事江南各府县都传遍了！可不是我们随口乱道！'他们、他们还说：'钱牧老怕是想入阁想疯了，所以做出这等事来！'牧老，你说，这可气人不气人！"

许隽这么没遮没拦地一口气说下来，客人当中像冯氏兄弟这些不知情的，都惊愕地张大了嘴巴，仿佛听到了什么海外奇谈。至于瞿式耜、顾苓、孙永祚等人，或者是参与其事，或者多少听到点风声，只是碍于情面，在钱谦益面前装作一无所知，这时都不禁变了脸色，担心地窥伺着钱老头儿的神情，估计他立即就会暴跳起来，大发雷霆。

然而，出乎意料，钱谦益却没有这样。他只是呆呆地望着许隽，眼睛露出绝望的、黯然的神情，脸色也变得越来越苍白。终于，他低下头去，喃喃地说："不，不是这样，不是这样！"

"当然不是！"被这个惊人的消息唬住了的冯班，忽然跳起来，高声大叫，"他们凭什么这样诬赖人，可恶！牧老，不要怕，有我冯班在，决不容那伙无耻之徒胡作非为！"他奔向许隽，"伯彦兄，你说，那两个混账畜生是谁，我明儿就上姑苏去找他算账！我要……"

他还要说下去，可是瞿式耜做了个手势，把他拦住了。瞿式耜走到钱谦益跟前，沉默了一下，说："至人之虑，自非群愚所

a conversation between two scholars in square headscarves. I paid them no attention until they spoke of you. I listened and was shocked to hear what they were talking about. A little bastard named Fang or Wang was spreading a rumor: You're colluding with His Lordship Mr. Zhou, the Prime Minister, to reverse the Ruan Yuanhai case. Zhou Zhongyu and Chen Dingsheng discovered the plot and went to your house to remonstrate with you. He spoke as if it were real. I was outraged and went forward to argue with him, saying, 'I'm an old friend of Elder Mu and have never heard a thing like this. Please shut up! Don't slander him!' But that little bastard said, 'Don't do it if you don't want it to be known! I've not made it up. It's being spread in all the counties and prefectures in the River South area.' They also said that you're doing such a thing because you're desperately trying to enter the Cabinet. It's outrageous, isn't it?"

Xu Jun said it directly in one breath. Some of the guests, like the Feng brothers, having no knowledge of the matter, opened their mouths in surprise, as if they had heard some strange tales from abroad. Some, like Qu Shisi, Gu Ling, and Sun Yongzuo, who, either having played a part in it or heard it from others previously, had been pretending to be ignorant for the sake of respect for Qian Qianyi, now changed their countenance. They worriedly watched old man Qian's expression, expecting him to fly into a rage.

Yet Qian Qianyi didn't do so. He merely stared blankly at Xu Jun with a look of despair and sadness, his face growing paler and paler. Finally, he lowered his head and mumbled, "No, it's not like that, it's not like that!"

"Of course it isn't!" shouted Feng Ban, startled by this shocking story. "Why are they slandering Lord Qian? Damn it! Elder Mu, don't be afraid! I won't allow the shameless thugs to run at large!" He ran over to Xu Jun and said, "Brother Boyan, tell me who those two bastards are. I'll go to Suzhou tomorrow to fix them. I'll ..."

As he spoke, Qu Shisi made a gesture and stopped him. Then, Mr. Qu walked to Qian Qianyi, and after a moment of silence, said, "The thoughts of great men are not understood by fools. My dear teacher,

能省知。老师德高望重，难免为居心叵测之徒侧目，是以蛾眉招谤，古今同慨。然而亦无非蚍蜉撼树，适足见其不自量而已！何况如今国事蜩螗，已不堪问！不出数年，当有大变。老师正无须与彼辈争一日之短长。依学生之见，不如暂且仍作东山高卧，静以观变。直待九重诏下，登车揽辔，拯社稷、济苍生，犹未为晚！”

接着，顾苓、孙永祚也走过来，竭力劝慰。钱谦益的心情这才慢慢舒展了一点。他叹了一口气，说：“我已是垂暮之年，什么拯社稷、济苍生，此生是不敢企望了！但求能优游林下，读书养性，清清静静地过上几年，也就心满意足了。只是，唉……”

“哦，说到读书养性，牧老的拂水山庄，那可是第一等的！”顾苓连忙凑趣说，“都道‘徐家戏子瞿家园’，乃系我常熟二美，可是学生总觉着，拂水山庄只需稍加修葺，只怕未必便让稼老专美呢！”

瞿式耜也说：“我那个破园子算什么！不过枉得虚名罢咧！被人一个劲儿地起哄，也真想花点工夫把它修一修。前些日子我已经着人到留都去请计无否来帮我踏勘，若是老师想修拂水山庄，到时便让他一块儿瞧瞧！”

钱谦益抬头瞧瞧瞿式耜，又瞧瞧顾苓，却没有作声。他适才那番“读书养性”的话，本来是聊以解嘲的敷衍话，现在被他们煞有介事地一说，倒提醒了他，觉得这也不失为忘却眼前处境的一种办法。他若有所悟地捋着胡子，终于，缓缓地点了点头。

## 家仆之累

“老爹，老爷现在书房里，命你去见他。”李宝走进账房间来说。

被称作老爹的那个人——钱府的大管家何思虞从账本上抬起

since you're a greatly respected man of importance, there are certainly little men who are jealous of you. Such things have repeatedly happened in history. Yet, it's nothing more than a mayfly shaking a tree and not worth a grain of thought. The country is now in chaos and things change quickly. In a couple of years, there'll be opportunities. So, don't be disturbed by the little men. In my opinion, you just relax and wait for your opportunity. In time, you'll rise again to save the country and the people!"

Gu Ling and Sun Yongzuo also came over and consoled Qian Qianyi. Now he felt better. "I am too old to hope to be of any service to the saving of the country and the people. All I want is to be able to stroll in the woods, enjoy reading, and live a quiet life for a few years, but, alas ..." he said with a sigh.

"Well, speaking of reading, your lordship's Waterside Villa is the perfect place for it!" said Gu Ling obsequiously. "As they say, there're two best places in Changshu: the theater of the Xus and the garden of the Qus. However, in my humble opinion, if Waterside Villa were renovated a little bit, it wouldn't exclusively belong to you!"

Qu Shisi said: "Oh, my garden isn't that great. It doesn't deserve the praise. People are flattering me. I'm planning to have it renovated. A few days ago I sent for Ji Wufou in the Legacy Capital. If my dear teacher wants to have Waterside Villa renovated too, I can ask him to have a look when he comes."

Qian Qianyi raised his head and looked at Qu Shisi and then Gu Ling, but said nothing. His "to enjoy reading" was merely self-mockery. The echoing of his friends reminded him that to enjoy reading was indeed a good way to get out of his current predicament. As if suddenly enlightened, he stroked his beard and slowly nodded his head.

## Thieving Servants

"Old man, his lordship is now in the study and asks you to see him," said Li Bao as he walked into the accounting room.

He Siyu, called "old man" by Li Bao, lifted his head from the

头来，用躲藏在白眉毛底下的一双锐利的眼睛瞧着来人：“嗯，什么事？”

李宝摇摇头，赔着笑脸说：“只是请老爹即刻过去。”

“好。”何思虞说，重新低下头去。“你瞧好了——”他伸出一只干枯弯曲的、戴着嵌绿玉金指环的手，指着账本，对鼻梁上架着玳瑁眼镜的账房先生说，“这些，还有这些，你都好生再盘一下。怎么会只剩这一点儿？亏得太多了，这样不成！懂吗？好，回头我再来。”

说完，他就直起身子，疑惑地瞅了一眼还在等候他的李宝，向外走去。李宝连忙跟着他。

“老爹，老爹！”

“啊？”何思虞没有回头。

“我那——”李宝急急赶上来，“我那五两银子，老爹跟邹老爹说了么？”

“还没哩！”

“可是、可是听说就这几日，船便出海了呀！”

“慌什么，还没定呢！再说，你那几两银子，邹老爹未必就瞧得上眼！”

“怎么？”

“你也不想想，他现赁着二三十号海鳅船，哪一次出海，不是三万五万的生意。区区五两银子，在你自以为老大一笔帮衬，但到他手里，不算你一股吧，不行；算你一股吧，他还真嫌零碎费事！”

“可是……”

“算了！你想发外洋财，过几年再说。那五两银子，回头你来拿回去！”何思虞断然地说。

这之后，两人都没有再说话。走了一段路，何思虞斜眼瞅了瞅李宝，见他耷拉着脑袋，噘着嘴巴，一副不乐意的样子，便微

ledger and looked at the comer with sharp eyes hidden under his white eyebrows. "Well, what's up?" he asked.

Li Bao shook his head to mean he didn't know and said with a smile, "He just told me to get you right away."

"I see," He Siyu said. Lowering his head, he held out a dry, crooked hand with an emerald gold ring, pointed to the ledger, and said to the accountant wearing tortoise shell glasses, "Look carefully, here, and here! Calculate again. Too little is left. The deficit is way too big. It won't work out. Understand? I'll be back later."

Then, he stood up, cast a quizzical glance at Li Bao who was still waiting for him, and walked out. Li Bao quickly followed him.

"Old man, old man!"

"Yes?" He Siyu said without looking back.

"What about my —" said Li Bao, who hurried to catch up. "My five taels of silver? Did you tell old man Zou about it?"

"No, not yet."

"But, but I hear that the boat will go to sea within a couple of days!"

"Don't hurry! It's not decided yet! Besides, old man Zou may not think the few taels of silver of yours is worth the bother."

"Why?"

"Just think about it. He's rented a fleet of up to thirty sea boats. Each voyage involves thirty to fifty thousand taels' worth of goods! You think your five taels of silver is a great contribution, but to him, it's a problem. If he doesn't count you in, it doesn't seem good, but if he counts you in, it's not worth the trouble."

"But ..."

"Forget it! If you want to invest in foreign trade, you need to wait for a few years. I'll give the money back to you," said He Siyu in a resolute tone.

Then, both went silent. After walking for a while, He Siyu cast a glance at Li Bao, who was sulking with his head drooping and mouth pouting. He Siyu smiled slightly and said, "Young man, if you want to make some money so that you can get a wife, why insist on investing

微一笑："小伙子，你想混几两银子讨媳妇儿，何必非得往通番贸易上打主意？那可是风险买卖，我是为你好，怕你赔不起哟！你如今既进了这钱府的大门，又承老爷看得起，让你早晚跟着他，这便是你这辈子的财气到了！今后只要你乖觉些，我自会把些门道来慢慢点拨你！"

李宝抬起头，呆呆地瞧着眯着眼睛、在他旁边傲然而行的瘦小老头儿。渐渐地，他脸上的神情发生了变化，一丝希冀的、贪婪的光芒在他眼睛里闪动起来。突然，他大步跨到何思虞的跟前，"扑通"跪下去。

"老爹在上，今后老爹便是我的干爹！李宝如若负心背义，天地不容！"

何思虞左右瞧了一下，连忙把李宝扯起来，"傻小子，谁让你在半路上来这一套！"他低声责备说。于是，两人继续往前走。

"嗯，这样吧，"何思虞沉默了一阵子，终于说道，"眼下有一桩现成的买卖，不过，做得成做不成，就瞧你的本事了。"

"啊，干爹请讲！"李宝惊喜地睁大眼睛。

"我问你，老爷跟前，你说话能到什么地步？"

"这个……"

"好，这我不管。我只告诉你，现在下房里，正锁着两个人，一个是金花桥头的机户王之善，一个是小东门外竹木行的张胜。王之善六年前借去银子五十两，到今年连本带利该还一百九十两；张胜五年前借银三十两，到今年该还一百零二两。但二人至今分文未还。前两日我说起，老爷很生气，命人把他们叫来，责骂了一顿，关在下房里，说是一日不还清，就一日不放人。昨天这两家央人来向我求情，说是情愿各出五两银子赎人。现在，你如能说通老爷放了他们，这十两银子，我分文不取，全数归你。

in foreign trade? It's a risky business. For your good, I'm telling you the truth. I'm afraid you can't afford to lose the money. Now that you've entered the Qian house, and his lordship likes you to be with him all the time, you're in luck and will have money. Just listen to me and I'll let you know what to do."

Li Bao raised his head and stared numbly at the skinny old man who, with narrowed eyes, walked proudly beside him. Gradually, the expression on his face changed, and a light of hope and greed flickered in his eyes. Suddenly, he stepped in front of He Siyu and knelt down.

"Old man, please accept my respects! From now on, you'll be my substitute father! I swear by the names of the gods!"

He Siyu looked around and quickly pulled Li Bao up. "What a silly boy! Don't do this!" he admonished in a low voice. Then, the two moved forward.

"Well, here's something," He Siyu said after a moment of silence. "There's a done deal, but whether it can be actually done depends on your ability."

"Oh, Father, please tell me about it!" Li Bao opened his eyes wide in surprise.

"Tell me, how much does his lordship trust you?"

"That —"

"Forget it. Here's the thing: There're now two men locked in the basement. One is Wang Zhishan, a silk fabric maker by the Jinhua Bridge, and the other is Zhang Sheng from the bamboo and wood shop by the Little East Gate. Wang Zhishan borrowed fifty taels of silver six years ago and is supposed to pay a hundred and ninety taels of silver in principal and interest; Zhang Sheng borrowed thirty taels five years ago and is supposed to pay a hundred and two taels this year, but they've paid nothing so far. Two days ago, I told his lordship about it. He was very angry. He summoned them here, scolded them, and locked them up in the basement, saying he wouldn't let them go before the debt is paid. Yesterday, the two families begged me to help them through an acquaintance, saying each family would give me five taels of silver if I could help them redeem the two men. Now, if you can

如何？”

“啊！”李宝的眼睛蓦地发亮了，可是随即又担心地咕噜，“只是，只是不知老爷答应不答应。”

“我不是说了吗，那就看你的本事啰！”何思虞冷冷地说。这之后，他就闭上嘴巴，再也不谈它了。

……

当何思虞登上荣木楼，踏入匪斋的时候，钱谦益正站在书房中央，望着墙上的《耦耕堂读书图》出神。那是不久前柳如是在苏州画的一幅画，虽不甚工，却颇饶淡远之致。钱谦益为着讨柳如是的欢心，特意命人精工装裱后，拿来挂在书房里。

听见何思虞的脚步声，钱谦益很快地转过身来。他点点头，算是回答对方的行礼，随即在一张椅子上坐下来。

“嗯，我让你带我的信去见何先生，这事办了么？”

“禀老爷，已经去过。”何思虞恭敬地回答，从袖子里摸出一封信来，双手呈上，“这是何相公的复信，请老爷过目。”

“唔，可是你亲自去的？——他可应允？”钱谦益一边拆信，一边问。

“是小人亲自去的。只是何相公一味推却，说他才疏学浅，万万不能与黄陶庵先生相比，生怕教不好，耽误了少爷的前程。”

钱谦益草草看了一下信，把它扔在一边：“哼，我岂不知黄陶庵无人能及。只是他已辞馆而去，我再三苦留，却留他不住，又有什么办法？总不能让少爷天天这么荒废着！你——明儿再去一趟，替我反复道达恳聘之意，请何先生务必应允。”

“是！”

“嗯，你坐！”钱谦益摆了摆手。但是，等何思虞告了坐，

persuade his lordship to release them, the ten taels of silver will all be yours. I won't take anything. What do you think?"

"Is it so?" Li Bao's eyes suddenly brightened, but then he murmured with trepidation, "It's just, just that I'm not sure if his lordship will agree or not."

"As I said, it depends on your ability," He Siyu said coldly. Then, he closed his mouth and went silent.

...

He Siyu climbed up to the Hibiscus House and entered the study called the Fei Chamber. Qian Qianyi was standing in the middle of the study staring at the "Reading in the Hall of the Farming Duo" on the wall, lost in thoughts. It was a painting made by Liu Rushi in Suzhou not long ago. It was not glorious in terms of artistic perfection, but it had a unique appeal. To please Liu Rushi, he had it framed and hung up on the wall of the study.

Hearing He Siyu's footsteps, Qian Qianyi quickly turned around. He nodded in response to the salute, and then sat down in a chair.

"Well, did you take my letter to Mr. He?"

"Yes, I did, my lord," He Siyu replied respectfully. He took a letter from his sleeve and handed it to his master with both hands, saying, "This is Mr. He's reply letter for your lordship."

"Good! Did you go yourself? Has he agreed?" asked Qian Qianyi as he opened the letter.

"I went there myself, but he insisted on not accepting the offer, saying he was not as learned as Mr. Huang Tao'an, he was afraid he wouldn't make a good teacher, and he'd better not waste the time of the young master."

Qian Qianyi quickly scanned the letter and threw it aside. "Hmph, of course I know that Huang Tao'an is unmatched. It's just that he resigned and left. I've tried to make him stay, but he insists on going. What else can I do? We must have a teacher for the young master. Go talk to Mr. He tomorrow and let him know my sincerity."

"Aye, my lord!"

"Well, take a seat," Qian Qianyi gestured. However, after He Siyu

用半个屁股在一张凳子上就座了之后，他并没有立即说话，却转过脸去，又对墙上那幅《耦耕堂读书图》出起神来。

“你说，这拂水山庄，若是重加修葺，所费须得几何？”他沉思地问。

“啊，老爷想重修拂水山庄？”

“嗯，”钱谦益点点头，“我打算把它下点工夫修修好，待弄得像个样子之后，就搬到那边去，关起门来，清清静静读几年书。”他瞧了瞧何思虞，见对方露出疑惑的神情，就提高了声音，像是解释又像是训斥似的说，“息影田园，读书养性，乃是我的素志！好多年前，我就与程松圆订下此约，无奈杂务纷扰，未能如愿。如今松老已经作古，这归隐读书之约，我却不曾暂忘。”

“是！”何思虞拱手应诺着，迟疑一下，问，“只不知老爷之意，是小修？中修？还是大修？”

“不修则已，要修就得像样点——便是大修，如何？”

“这，只怕须得六七千金之数。”

钱谦益仰起头来，考虑了一会儿，斜瞅着何思虞：“当真要这么多？”

何思虞的表情严肃得不能再严肃：“禀老爷，这还是往少里估的，老爷不信……”

“好，六七千就六七千！”钱谦益下决心地说，“回头，你先找人通盘算一算，拟出个大概单子。待过几天我亲自踏勘之后再定。”

“是。不过……”

“什么？”

“六七千两银子数目非小，眼下家中的账面已经很紧，只怕……”

“又是拿不出来！是不是？”钱谦益不耐烦地打断他，“不就是修个园子这么点事，偏你有许多推搪！”他生气地说。

gingerly sat down on a stool with half of his bottom, he didn't speak immediately, but instead turned to stare at the "Reading in the Hall of the Farming Duo" on the wall.

"Tell me how much it will cost to renovate Waterside Villa?" he asked thoughtfully.

"My lord, are you going to renovate Waterside Villa?"

"Yes." Qian Qianyi nodded. "I'm thinking of having it renovated. When it's good enough, I'll move there, close the door, and read quietly for a few years." He cast a glance at He Siyu, and when he saw the quizzical look on the servant's face, he raised his voice and said, as if explaining to him or rebuking him, "I've always longed to retire to a quiet place and enjoy reading for the rest of my life. I promised Cheng Songyuan years ago that I would accompany him, but have failed to do so because there have been too many things to attend to. Although Songyuan has passed away, I've never forgotten my promise."

"I see," said He Siyu, clasping his hands. Then he asked hesitantly, "My lord, do you want a small renovation or a big one?"

"Now that we decide to renovate it, let's make it decent. What about a big one?"

"That, I'm afraid, is going to cost six or seven thousand taels of silver."

Qian Qianyi raised his head, pondered for a moment, and then, looking at He Siyu slantingly, said, "Will it really cost that much?"

He Siyu said in a serious voice, "My lord, that's the minimal cost. If you don't believe it ..."

"Well, let it be six or seven thousand," Qian Qianyi said determinedly. "Calculate all the costs with your men and give me a detailed list later. We'll make a decision after I study it."

"Aye, my lord, but ..."

"But what?"

"Six or seven thousand is no small amount. Our finances are already very tight. I'm afraid ..."

"We don't have that money, right?" Qian Qianyi impatiently interrupted. "It's just renovating a garden. Why do you make up so many excuses?" he said angrily.

“小人不敢，小人只求老爷赐示良策。”

钱谦益冷笑说：“我有什么良策？良策该由你们去想！”说完，他随手拿起案头的一本书，打算就此结束这番谈话。

何思虞本能地站起来，却拖延着不走。他低头站了片刻，为难地说：“启禀老爷，非是小人……这几年家中的情形，老爷是知道的……”

钱谦益睁大眼睛瞧了他一会，突然把手中的书重重一放，霍地站起来，怒声说：“我知道！我还知道这几年你着实捞了一把！”

这句话果然见效。何思虞哆嗦一下，畏缩地抬起眼睛。

“有没有？你说！有没有？嗯？”钱谦益厉声追问。

何思虞“扑通”一下跪在地上，叩下头去：“求老爷息怒，小人知错了，小人不该顶撞老爷，小人该死！小人该死！”

钱谦益一声不响。直到何思虞快要把脑门碰破了，他才悻悻地说：“去吧！园子的事，过几天我可得问你！”

何思虞得了这一句话，才如获大赦地爬起来，却不敢抬头，道了谢之后，就连忙退了出去。

钱谦益重新拿起书本，举到眼前，随即又放下了。他倒背着手，开始在室内徘徊起来，心里很不愉快。近几年，由于吃了一场大官司，加上为着迎娶柳如是、谋划起用、陈夫人许愿重修佛寺等等，着实花了不少银子，这一点他是知道的。另一方面，去年江南一场大旱，弄到赤地千里，饿殍载道，手中白白捏着几千亩良田，租子却全收不上来；加上各地兵荒马乱，道路不通，虽有七八间商号，也是连年亏损，难以支撑；特别是去年与人搭伙出海贸易遇上风暴，一下子漂没了三艘满载货物的双桅大船，其

"I don't dare to, my lord. Pray tell me what to do."

Qian Qianyi said with a cold sneer, "I don't know what to do. You should know it." Then he picked up a book from his desk, meaning to end the conversation.

He Siyu instinctively stood up but didn't leave immediately. He stood silently for a moment, his head lowered, then said hesitatingly, "My lord, it's not that I ... but as you know, the situation hasn't been that good in the last couple of years ..."

Qian Qianyi stared at him for a while with wide open eyes. Then he suddenly slammed the book on the desk, stood up, and said angrily, "As I know! As I know, you've really made a fortune over the past few years!"

That really worked. He Siyu trembled and lifted his eyes timidly.

"Haven't you? Tell me, haven't you? Huh?" Qian Qianyi exploded.

Plop! He Siyu went on his knees and kowtowed. "Pardon me, my lord! I'm very sorry. I shouldn't have contradicted you. Damn me. Damn me."

Qian Qianyi was silent. He Siyu kowtowed so hard that he almost broke his forehead. Then, Qian Qianyi said sullenly, "Go! I'll ask you about the garden in a few days."

As if having received an amnesty, He Siyu stood up, and not daring to look up, quickly withdrew.

Qian Qianyi picked up the book again, held it in front of him and then put it down. Putting his hands behind his back, he started to pace around the room gloomily. He knew he had spent a lot of money in recent years, clearing himself in a corruption case, marrying Liu Rushi, running about for his reinstatement, contributing to the renovation of a temple as promised by his wife Lady Chen ... True that he had a few thousand acres of fertile land, but the great drought in the River South area the previous year had resulted in a crop failure and a great famine. Consequently, there was no rent income from the tenants. He had seven or eight trading firms but they had hardly survived the endless wars; to make matters worse, a big storm in the previous year had swallowed up three shiploads of goods at sea and

中一艘又恰恰是自己占的大股……这一切，他也是知道的。可是若说他大半辈子辛辛苦苦积攒起来的这一份家产，几年工夫就亏空到连六七千两银子都拿不出来的地步，他还真有点不怎么信。前些日子，他也曾亲自查看过账本。账面上倒写得清清楚楚，瞧不出什么破绽。不过，他知道，像何思虞这种老奸巨猾的家奴，作弊营私的办法多得很，而且上下左右都是暗中串通好了的，一切漏洞都堵得严严实实。他们早已形成了一个看不见的网，要冲开缺口固然很难，甚至想抛开它也不行，因为这样一来，情况只会更糟。那些堆积如山、永远也处理不了的难题，立即就会像冰雹一般地倾泻到你这个当主子的头上，弄到你手忙脚乱，寸步难行，结果只会加速家业的败亡。所以，过去钱谦益眼见他手下的豪仆们一个个都置田买屋，鲜衣怒马，暴发起来，明知此中有鬼，也唯有抱着“水至清则无鱼，人至察则无徒”的宗旨，采取睁一只眼闭一只眼的态度。有时某个豪仆在外面作恶犯法，被官府拘去，他还得写帖子、递保状，凭着自己的面子交情，把他设法赎出来……不过，现在发现这些狡猾凶悍的家伙，只管自己发财，大有置他这个主子于不顾，听凭其败落之势，钱谦益不禁又惊又怒，觉得这种状况，再也不能任其发展下去了。

“不过，那又该怎么办呢？这伙鬼东西，可是难轧得很！弄不好，就会未见其利，先见其害……”他想，猛一抬头，发现不知什么时候，李宝已经走了进来，正毕恭毕敬地垂手站在一旁，目不转睛地瞧着自己，露出有话要说的样子。

也许是这个贴身仆人恭谨侍立的姿态，也许是他那年轻的富有生气的样子，使得钱谦益的心忽然动了一下。他记起来，李宝是半年前才进府当差的。当时也曾问过，他家里是慧日寺前开绸绒店的。因为被徐孝廉家的绸绒店欺凌，几乎无法立足，所以情愿循常例缴纳八十两“献身银”，让儿子到钱府来充当奴仆，以求得庇护。这李宝小时也读过几年书，能写会算。钱谦益因为老

he was a major stakeholder of one of the big trade ships. He was aware of all these things but would not believe his lifetime savings had dwindled to less than six or seven thousand taels of silver. He had checked the books a few days ago. Everything was clearly recorded. Nothing seemed wrong. But he knew He Siyu was a cunning servant with no lack of stealing methods. This damned servant was certainly colluding with others to commit perfect thefts.They had formed an invisible net. He could neither break it or get rid of it. Things would get worse should he do so. The heaps of unsolvable problems would rain down on him like sleet, disorient him and cripple his actions, and accelerate the downfall of the family. Previously, seeing some of his servants suddenly become rich and buy land, houses, and good clothes, he knew they had been stealing, but thinking it was part of human nature he had turned a blind eye to it. Sometimes, when one of the rich servants committed a crime outside and was arrested by the *yamen*, he would use his connections to bail them out. However, these ungrateful, cunning, merciless men were so bent on fattening themselves at his expense that they had no regard for his interests at all and were ready to see the ruin of the house. Qian Qianyi was shocked at the realization and became very angry. He decided to do something to stop them from stealing from him.

"But what can I do? These devilish men are not to be reckoned with. Confronting them may bring more harm than good," he thought. When he lifted his head, Li Bao was standing at attention beside him, looking at him with fixed eyes, as if going to say something.

Qian Qianyi cheered up a little, perhaps because of the respectful posture or the youthful vigor of the body servant. The boy had come half a year ago. His father owned a silk and velvet shop by the Wisdom Sun Temple. Back then, because they were often bullied by another silk and velvet shop owned by Xu Xiaolian, his family paid Qian Qianyi eighty taels of silver in protection money, as was the practice, and sent Li Bao to the Qian house to serve as a servant boy. Li Bao was literate and knew some arithmetic. Seeing that the boy was honest and intelligent and thinking Qian Sheng would leave the house

仆钱升的儿子考中了秀才，不便长留府内，又见李宝为人老实勤快，就让他跟了自己。现在钱谦益正因家中的悍仆难以驾驭而烦恼，骤然看见李宝，倒生出一个念头来，觉得这小伙子不失为一个可造之材。若加以培养，历练几年，说不定会成为自己得力的臂膀。他又仔细瞧了瞧年轻的仆人，发现他还是一个长得满俊的小伙子，唇红齿白，眉眼鲜明，身材健壮，衣服帽子也干净整洁。钱谦益心中愈加喜欢，紧绷的脸随之松弛下来，和蔼地问：

“你——有什么事吗？”

李宝畏缩了一下，脸红了。他的嘴巴动了动，却没有说出话来。

“说嘛！”

李宝的脸更红了。他讷讷地说：“小人、小人想求老爷一件事。”

“嗯？”

“下房里现关着两个人，小人想求……求老爷放了。”

“啊，为什么？”

“那、那两个人与小人原有些认得。他家里人来寻小人说，所以、所以……”

钱谦益一声不响地盯着李宝，面容渐渐又变得严厉起来。这种求情放人的事他见得多了。他根本不相信这类事情会是白做的，对方必定已经许给李宝多少钱。“没用，一切都是白费心机，谁都不能相信！刚才，我还那样满心满意想提挈他，真是走了眼！”他阴郁地想。

“老爷……”李宝又说。但是，现在他那恭谨的姿态、那俊俏的外表，在钱谦益眼中已经变得那样可憎可厌，就连他恳求的声音也充满着捉弄的意味了。

“胡说！”钱谦益蓦地吼叫起来，“那两个家伙是欠债不还的无赖泼皮！我不拿帖子把他们送官，已经够便宜了！放人？休想！”

说完，他就把袖子一拂，怒气冲冲地走出门去，把吓得不知

sooner or later as the old servant's son had become a *xiucai* scholar in the county school, Qian Qianyi agreed to take the boy. As Qian Qianyi was plagued with the thought of his unruly servants, Li Bao's appearance gave him an idea. He might as well make this boy a good helper. Given proper coaching, in a couple of years, the boy might be very useful. Qian Qianyi looked up and down the young servant, who was a handsome lad with red lips, bright teeth, sharply defined eyes and brows, a robust body, and clean and tidy clothes. He liked the boy. His strained face relaxed.

He asked in a gentle voice, "What's up?"

Li Bao gave a start and blushed. His mouth moved, but nothing came out.

"Say it."

Li Bao's face became even redder. He said shyly, "My lord, I want to ask you a favor."

"Um?"

"There're two men locked up in the basement. I'm wondering if you can release them."

"Oh, why?"

"I'm familiar with those two men. Their families came to me for help, so, so ..."

Qian Qianyi stared silently at Li Bao, and his face gradually became stern again. Having seen this kind of intercession too many times, he didn't believe that this kind of thing would be done for free. There was surely a promise of reward for Li Bao. "He's no use. I've wasted my time. There's no one to trust. I was thinking he's worth my trust. It turns out I'm wrong," he thought gloomily.

"My lord, ..." Li Bao said. But now his respectful attitude and attractive appearance had become disgusting in Qian Qianyi's eyes, and his pleading voice was irksome.

"Nonsense!" Qian Qianyi bellowed. "Those two men are thugs who don't pay their debts. They should thank me for not sending them to the *yamen*. Release them? Don't even think about it."

Then, he flapped his long sleeves and angrily walked out the

所措的李宝丢在书房里。

## 收服李宝

就在钱谦益决定重修拂水山庄之后半个月，一个名叫惠香的年轻女子来到常熟半野堂。她是盛泽归家院一名颇有名气的歌妓，当年同柳如是的交情很不错，这次路过苏州，便特意来拜访老朋友。

为了接待这位昔年的手帕姐妹，柳如是着实忙碌了一番。她把惠香安排在西院一幢最好的房子里住下，又亲自指挥一群丫环、老妈子给惠香布置房间，帐褥摆设都是最新的最好的，还让人到匪斋去向钱谦益讨了那个西洋自鸣钟来摆上。那钟是精铜造的，大小不过一寸多，镶在一个雕成贝多罗花式样的紫檀座上，每隔一个时辰，就会自动报响一次，是钱谦益花了重金向西洋商人购来的。当这钟摆出来时，把惠香吓了一跳，说什么也不肯留下。

“姐姐，我怕丢失了，没得赔哟！”惠香说。

“怕什么，我这院子四面八方都有人守着呢，谁敢来偷！要不，我再派绿意和两个老妈子来专门给你守着，夜里就睡在这钟旁边，白天也让你有多把人手使唤。妹妹，说真的，你带的那老妈子，又老又聋，快不中用了，真不知你怎么就受得了？”

“姐姐，你如今阔气了，同旧时不同了！”惠香说。

“笑话罢咧！讲阔气，可轮不着我们。虽说十万八万的，即时也还拿得出，再多就不成啦！嗯，妹妹，你尝尝这荷叶蒸卷，还是热的。你也知道我这肚子常闹病，吃不得半点冷食。前些时碰上寒食，举不得火。老头儿就吩咐头天夜里把吃的预先弄好了，

door, leaving Li Bao in the study, paralyzed with fright.

## Buying Off Li Bao

Half a month after Qian Qianyi decided to rebuild Waterside Villa, a young woman named Huixiang came to the Half Wild Estate in Changshu. She was a famous singsong girl in the Homecoming brothel in Shengze. A good friend of Liu Rushi, she stopped by on her current visit to the city.

Liu Rushi received this former "handkerchief sister" with great enthusiasm. She arranged for Huixiang to stay in the best house in the west yard and personally instructed a group of young and old maids to furnish Huixiang's room, giving her the best mosquito net, the best beddings, and a petite automatic foreign clock—which had been taken from Qian Qianyi's study by one of her maids upon her order—made of fine copper, embedded on a red sandalwood stand carved into a spider lily. It struck every hour. Qian Qianyi had spent a huge sum of money to buy it from a Western trader. When the clock was put in the room, Huixiang was alarmed and refused to take it.

"Sis, I'm afraid I can't afford to pay for it if I lose it," said Huixiang.

"No worries. The yard is closely guarded in all directions. No thieves dare to come. Or, I can send Lüyi over to you and two older maids to guard it for you. They will sleep beside the clock at night and serve you during the day. Sis, seriously, the old maid you've brought with you is old and hard of hearing. She will expire soon. I really don't understand how you can stand it."

"Sis, you are a rich lady now, very different from what you were in the old days," said Huixiang.

"You're making fun of me. I'm far from being rich. We do have something like eighty to a hundred thousand in savings, but that is all we have. Sis, try this steamed lotus leaf roll while it's hot. You know that I can't eat cold food because my stomach isn't good. The night before the Cold Food Festival fire ban, the old man ordered the cook to prepare some hot food, put it in two boxes, and wrap each of

盛在盒子里，裹上几层棉絮，由两个老妈子坐在暖窖里，轮流这么抱在怀里焐着，等第二天我吃时还是暖的！”

“啊，钱老爷待姐姐真是好！”

“妹妹，嫁人吧！姐姐劝你，还是挑个老的好！姐姐什么滋味都尝过了，比过了。什么宋辕文、陈卧子，到头来还是觉着这个钱老头儿会疼惜人！你别笑，这可是真的！哦，对了，你来得正好。明儿老头儿说要同我到拂水山庄去游玩，你自然也去！他是想连带把山庄踏勘一下，说是想好好修一修，从此同我读书偕隐，白头终老……”

“姐姐真是好福气！”

“福气个啥呀！我才不乐意呢！一辈子窝在这穷乡下，有什么味道？其实哩，老头儿也不是那等没志气的人，他是一时不顺心，才生出这等高蹈出世的念头……”

说到这里，柳如是就站起来，对望着她发呆的惠香说：“时候不早了，我还得回去上香。妹妹你先歇着，明儿你要是起得早，就过我闻室来找我！”她行出几步，又走回来，伸出指尖儿轻轻拧了拧惠香的脸蛋，“告诉你，我那鬼老头儿别看他今年六十一了，可是人老心不老，明儿你若是把他勾引上了，我可不饶你！”说完，“扑哧”一笑，款摆着腰肢，当真走了。

第二天，惠香起了个早。梳洗完毕，就由绿意引路，到我闻室去。

柳如是看来起床还不久，正坐在妆台前，手里玩弄着一把梳子，由红情替她梳妆，一边同一个年轻俊俏的男仆说话。那仆人低着头，红着脸，站在离妆台远远的一个角落里，显得很局促不安的样子。

只听柳如是说：“李宝，我问你，昨儿一整夜，老爷当真都是在书房里过的？”

them with layers of cotton. Two old maids each held a box in her lap and sat in the warm basement all night long. When I had the food the following day, it was warm enough."

"I envy you. Lord Qian is really good to you."

"Sis, you should get married. Listen to my advice, pick an old man and marry him. I know what's best because I've known too many men–Song Yuanwen, Chen Wozi, and others. In comparison, none of them is as caring as old man Qian. Do not laugh. It's true. Well, by the way, you've just come in time. The old man is going to take me to Waterside Villa tomorrow, so of course you'll go with me. He wants to have a look at the villa before deciding how to rebuild it. He says we'll be reading there together in peace and quiet for the rest of our lives ..."

"You're a fortunate girl, sis."

"Fortunate? No, I don't want to live a life like that. What fun is there to hide in the damned countryside? Actually, the old man is not without ambitions. He's come up with this recluse idea simply because he's downcast at the moment ..."

Then, Liu Ruyi stood up and said to Huixiang, who was staring at her puzzledly, "It's getting late. I have to go back to offer incense to the gods. Sis, you can sleep now. If you get up early tomorrow, just come to the Wowen Chamber." After a few steps, she suddenly came back, reached out her fingertips and gently pinched Huixiang's cheeks, saying, "Mind you, this old man of sixty one isn't that old in his heart. If you dare seduce him tomorrow, I won't forgive you." She chuckled after saying that and walked away, swaying her waist.

The next morning, Huixiang got up early and after getting washed and dressed went to the Wowen Chamber guided by Lüyi.

Liu Rushi, apparently having just got up a moment ago, was sitting in front of the dressing table playing with a comb in her hand and talking to a handsome boy servant while Hongqing dressed her, the boy standing in a corner far from the dressing table and looking very nervous with his head lowered and face blushing.

Liu Rushi said, "Li Bao, tell me, did his lordship really spend the whole night in the study last night?"

李宝低低地回答了一声："是！"惠香因为站得近，听见了。柳如是却听不清，她回过头来，看见了惠香，就招呼说："妹妹，你来啦，先坐着，我这就来！"又唤李宝，"浑小子，我听不清，你站过来些说，我吃不了你！"

李宝勉强向前移动了两寸，又提高嗓门说："启禀夫人，老爷昨夜是睡在书房里。"

"嗯，你不是骗我？"

"小的不敢欺骗夫人。"

"哼，不敢？那怎么有人告诉我，他昨夜出门了，是到城南秦寡妇家去了？"

"啊？没、没有呀！昨儿小的一直侍候在老爷身边，不曾离开半步。"

"真的？"

"是真的，小的不敢欺骗夫人。"

"好，我暂且信了你，过后若是我查访出来你说假话骗老娘，仔细你的皮！"

"小的不敢！"

这之后，柳如是没有再说话，可也没有让李宝走。直到红情替她梳完头，把最后一支珠翠插好之后，她就轻盈地站起来，先朝惠香点点头，然后走到李宝跟前，瞅着他问："前儿，你挨老爷骂啦？"

李宝怔了一下，不由自主抬起头。可是一接触到柳如是那似笑非笑的目光，他又慌忙低下头去。

"是。"他红着脸低声说。

"为了十两银子，求老爷放人，他不答应，是不是？"

"啊，夫人都、都知道！"李宝的脸孔顿时变得煞白。由于害怕，他的额上开始冒汗，身子也在微微发抖。

"我什么不知道！"柳如是傲然说，眼睛并没有离开年轻的仆人，"哼，没出息的东西，老爷不答应，为什么不来找我？"

Li Bao replied in a low voice, "Yes, he did, my lady." Huixiang heard it because she was standing nearby, but Liu Rushi didn't hear it clearly. As she turned around to face the boy she saw Huixiang and said, "Sis, good morning! Come over and sit." Then she called to Li Bao, "Bloke! I can't hear you. Come closer. I'm not going to eat you."

Li Bao inched forward and raised his voice. "My lady, his lordship did sleep in the study last night."

"Are you lying to me?"

"No, my lady. How dare I?"

"Hmph! How dare you? Then, why did I hear that he went to Mr. Qin's widow in the south of the city?"

"No, there's no such thing. I was with him all the time."

"Is it true?"

"It's true. I dare not lie to you."

"Okay, I believe you for the moment. If I find out later that you've lied to me, watch your skin!"

"I dare not lie to you."

Liu Rushi went silent but he didn't let Li Bao go. After Hongqing finished combing her hair and inserting the last pearl, she stood up airily, first nodded to Huixiang, then walked over to Li Bao, looked at him and asked, "Were you reprimanded by his lordship the other day?"

Li Bao startled and lifted his head involuntarily, but as soon as he saw Liu Rushi's half-smiling expression, he hurriedly lowered his head again.

"Yes, my lady," he said in a low voice, blushing.

"For the sake of ten taels of silver, you begged his lordship to release the debtors, but he didn't agree, did he?"

"Ah? You know it all?" Li Bao's face suddenly turned pale. Out of fear, his forehead began to sweat and his body trembled slightly.

"What don't I know?" Liu Rushi said disdainfully, without taking her eyes off the young servant. "Hmph, useless thing! His lordship doesn't agree, but why didn't you come to me?"

"Ah?" Li Bao lifted his head in surprise, clearly unable to believe his ears.

“啊！”李宝惊愕地抬起头，显然不敢相信自己的耳朵。

“你要早跟我说了，人早放了，你也不用挨骂。十两银子嘛，也到手了。”柳如是慢条斯理地说，又瞟了李宝一眼，“这么着吧，我看你可怜巴巴的，就帮你这一回。不过，往后你可得听话，乖乖儿的，多孝顺着我点，知道啦？”

“这、小……”李宝被这出乎意料的结局弄得不知所措。终于，他“扑通”跪在地上，叩着头说，“多谢夫人恩典。小的誓当感激图报，没齿不忘！”

柳如是摆摆手说：“好啦，你去吧！”然后，她就转过身，堆起笑脸，对惠香说：“妹妹，让你久等了。非是姐姐有心怠慢你，让你坐冷板凳，实在是偌大个家，事无巨细都得我管，而且还不能出错！上上下下都瞪大眼睛瞧着你哟！你不曾当管家婆，这份难处你是不知道的——好啦，时候也不早啦，用过早点，我们就过去。你难得来一趟，今儿我们可要玩个痛快！”

## 交易不成

李宝没有欺骗柳如是，前一天夜里，钱谦益确实是在书房里过的。当天傍晚，瞿式耜摆酒给从南京赶来帮他修园子的计成接风，把钱谦益请去作陪。待到酒阑人散，回到府来已经很晚，他便没有再过我闻室来，就近在匪斋歇下了。从计成的口中，他了解到，阮大铖听说虎丘大会那桩图谋，由于周镳、周钟兄弟出面干预，已告失败，十分伤心，捶胸顿足地痛哭了一场；后来就致书周延儒，请求起用马士英来代替自己。据说此事已有眉目，马瑶草不日便会东山再起云云。听到这个消息，钱谦益心里很有点酸溜溜的。“啊，马瑶草到底又上去了！可是我钱某人呢？难道真的注定就这样一沉到底？难道真的应了几年前周延儒说的那句

"If you had told me, the debtors would have been released and you wouldn't have been scolded. And you would have got the ten taels of silver." Liu Rushi said slowly as she glanced at Li Bao, "Well, since you're a pitiable creature, I'll help you once, but in the future, you have to behave and listen to me and serve me well. Understand?"

"This, I ..." Li Bao was nonplussed by the unexpected turn of events. Plop! He went down on his knees, kowtowed, and said, "Thank you for your mercy, my lady. I swear I shall be grateful and never forget your great kindness."

Liu Rushi gestured to him and said, "You can go now." Then she turned around, put on a smile, and said to Huixiang, "Sis, sorry to have kept you waiting. I didn't mean to let you sit on a cold bench. The house is too big. I have to take care of everything. No mistake allowed. All eyes are on me. You've never managed a house before, so you don't know how difficult it is. Well, it's no longer early. Let's have breakfast and leave. I'm really happy to have your precious company. Let's go enjoy ourselves."

## Deal or No Deal

Li Bao hadn't lied to Liu Rushi. Qian Qianyi had indeed spent the night in the study. On the previous evening, Qian Qianyi came home very late and went to the Fei Chamber. He had been invited by Qu Shisi to attend the welcome party for Ji Cheng, who came from Nanjing to help with the rebuilding of Qu Shisi's garden. At the banquet, he learned from Ji Cheng that Ruan Dacheng, who was heart-broken after hearing that his plans had failed at the Tiger Hill Conference due to the intervention of the Zhou brothers, Zhou Biao and Zhou Zhong, had written to Zhou Yanru to restore Ma Shiying to office instead of himself. It was said that the request was granted and that Mr. Ma would make a return soon. Hearing that news, Qian Qianyi was sour. He thought, "Ma Yaocao has risen again, but what about me? Am I really destined to sink to the bottom never to rise again as Zhou Yanru sarcastically said a few years ago—that I'm only good for a leader in the mountains? Well, now I'm afraid I can't

挖苦话——‘钱牧斋只堪领袖山林’？嗯，如今只怕连山林领袖都当不成了。近一个月来，到半野堂来登门求见的士子比过去已经明显地减少了……”这样一想，钱谦益就变得垂头丧气，只剩下苦笑。虽然他仍旧同计成约定，趁第二天他们全家要上拂水山庄去游玩，先过来替他瞧瞧该如何规划，可是已经兴致大减。回到匪斋之后，他思前想后，在床上折腾了大半夜，今早起来，勉强打起精神，正打算走过我闻室来瞧瞧柳如是，却碰上何思虞带了个人来，说是要“献产”，临时又耽搁住了。

现在，钱谦益坐在花厅里，正心不在焉地听来人介绍情况。那人看上去有三十岁出头，露骨鼻、瓦刀脸，一双眼珠子滴溜溜地转个不停。他自称姓徐，名正，家住徐镇小油坊。据他说，他家有良田四十顷、庄园一所、牛二十头、织机九部，还有其他一些财产。因哥哥去世，家中人丁稀少，同族中人乘此机会，图谋篡夺。他自度人孤势单，难以抗拒，现在情愿将财产献给钱谦益，以换取保护。同时，希望钱谦益能荐举他到衙门内做事……来人轻快地说着，那声音听来就像一只旋转着的陀螺，中间还不时夹杂着低低的、谄媚的笑声。钱谦益默默地瞅着他，心里越来越不感兴趣。虽说在现时，这种通过“献产”来换取豪势之家的赏赐和荐举，早已不是什么新鲜的事儿，事实上，他过去也接受过多宗。何况目前家中亏空，正急需得到几笔“横财”来补充，这个徐正所报的数目虽不算太大，可是三四千两银子总是有的，能够拿到手，重修山庄的开支，便能解决大部分。这在他来说，本来正是求之不得。不过，钱谦益也知道，这种事情，比较麻烦费事。因为其中关系复杂，内幕很多，往往远不是投献人所说的那样简

even be a leader in the mountains as recently the number of scholars who have come to see me is much smaller than before ..." he thought. Thus thinking, he smiled a wry smile dejectedly. Although he kept his promise to meet Ji Cheng at Waterside Villa while he was visiting it with family so that Ji Cheng would be able to advise him on how to rebuild the garden, his enthusiasm was gone. Back in the Fei Chamber, he threw himself into bed and tossed and turned for most of the night. After he woke up in the morning, he lifted his spirits to see Liu Rushi in the Wowen Chamber, but was delayed by He Siyu, who brought a man to "donate properties" to him.

Qian Qianyi sat in the Flower Hall and listened absent-mindedly to the visitor, a man in his early thirties, with a bald nose, and a square face, whose eyes nervously moved nonstop. The man called Xu Zheng lived in the little oils mill in Xus Town. According to him, his family owned forty acres of fertile land, a mansion, twenty heads of cattle, nine looms, and some other properties. After the death of his elder brother, his clansmen took advantage of the lack of men in the family and tried to seize his family property. Single-handed, he was unable to fend them off and would rather hand over his properties to Qian Qianyi in exchange for protection. Meanwhile, he also hoped that Qian Qianyi could recommend him for a job in the *yamen* ... The visitor spoke at a fast speed, in a voice that sounded like a spinning top, intermittent with subdued obsequious laughter. Qian Qianyi watched him silently and became increasingly disinterested. There was nothing wrong with this kind of property offering in exchange for favors or recommendations from a powerful family, as was the practice. In fact, he had received many property offerings in the past. Besides, because of his tight finances, he was in desperate need of some windfalls. Though Xu Zheng's offering was no more than three or four thousand taels of silver in value, it would be able to account for the greater part of the costs of rebuilding his garden. He was supposed to welcome such an offering. However, he had concerns. He knew that this kind of thing was more complicated than it seemed. There were often untold relationships and stories. From what Xu Zheng had just said, it was

单。从徐正刚才的话来推测，显然那些财产本来是属于他哥哥的。如今哥哥死了，这徐正便趁他嫂子孤儿寡妇，没有主意，怂恿她献产。甚至是他背着嫂子，私自前来投献也未可知。钱谦益当然不必理会这一点，但那样一来，势必会在他们徐家的族人当中引起轩然大波。派人查收时，一场流血械斗固然不可避免，还会惊动官府。虽说这一点钱谦益也不怕。不过倘若闹得沸沸扬扬，远近皆知，那就不妙了。因为目前自己正大受士林非议，处境已很难堪；倘若再加上这么一桩，只怕更加吃不消。所以，直到徐正说完了好一阵子，他仍然沉着脸，没有表示态度。

看见主人不说话，站在一旁的何思虞不禁着急起来。自从前些天受到钱谦益严厉申斥之后，何思虞一直惴惴不安。他自天启二年起，一直担任钱府的大总管。十多年来，贪污受贿，巧取豪夺，积下的私产少说也有二三万。他自以为手段高明，神不知，鬼不觉，没想到却被钱谦益一句话就戳穿了。这使他大为恐慌，生怕主人乘机报复，或者把他一脚踢开。所以这几天他费尽心思，到处奔走，好容易才找到徐正这个门道，满以为可以平息一下钱谦益的不满和怒气，兼以显示自己的忠心能干。现在看见钱谦益迟迟不作声，脸上也没有高兴的表示，他就有点沉不住气了。犹豫了一下，他终于问：

“老爷，您看……”

“没有什么好看的，不行！”钱谦益断然地说，站起来，尖利地瞧了何思虞一眼，径直往外走去。

clear that those properties had originally belonged to his elder brother. Now that his brother was dead, Xu Zheng, taking advantage of his sister-in-law and the half orphans, had cajoled his sister-in-law to give up the property, and it was not unknown whether he was actually disposing of their properties without their knowledge. Of course, Qian Qianyi didn't need to take this into account, but if that be the case, it would definitely cause a commotion among the Xu relatives. A bloody battle would be inevitable during the transfer, and even the intervention of the *yamen* had to be sought. Although Qian Qianyi was not afraid of that either, the uproar would not benefit him. Currently under siege from the gentry scholars, he was already in an awkward situation. Such a scandal would make matters worse. Therefore, he gave no opinion and his expression remained stoic long after Xu Zheng finished speaking.

Seeing his master was silent, He Siyu, who was standing nearby, became anxious. He had had his heart in his mouth since he was reprimanded by Qian Qianyi a few days ago. This man had been steward of the Qians since AD 1622, the second year of the reign of Emperor Tianqi. For more than ten years, he had accumulated a wealth of at least twenty to thirty thousand taels of silver in value through various methods of grafting—embezzlement, taking bribes, stealing, and extortion. He thought he was smart, never expecting to be discovered by any one. That Qian Qianyi directly pointed out his dishonesty panicked him. Afraid that the master would take the opportunity to get revenge on him or kick him away altogether, in the past few days, he had been running about and finally found Xu Zheng, whose offering of properties might help alleviate his master's anger and at the same time prove his loyalty and competence. Now, seeing Qian Qianyi's silence and stoic expression, he could no longer hold his nerve.

After hesitating for a while, he finally asked, "My lord, what do you think ..."

"What do I think? No!" said Qian Qianyi flatly, who stood up, gave He Siyu a sharp look, and walked straight out.

何思虞错愕了一下，本能地打算拦阻，可是随即就清醒过来。他默默地瞅着钱谦益的背影，眼里现出一丝怨恨的神色。然后，他回过头来，对怔在一旁的徐正冷冷地说：

“徐二秀，你哪天都不挑，偏挑今天来，八成是碰上鬼了！另找主儿吧！”

## 遁迹园林

拂水山庄坐落在常熟城的西北郊，正当虞山南麓与尚湖之间，从钱府出门不远，便有水路可通。虽说头两天已经做好郊游的准备，钱家的眷属人丁仍然拖延至辰时才正式出门。钱府是数代单传，人口本来不多，但临时来了几个客人，再加上一大群奴婢，数目也就相当可观。现在，全部人员分乘四艘大船，第一艘坐的是钱谦益、计成、顾苓、孙永祚，以及新聘的塾师何云；陈夫人、钱孙爱、朱姨娘和老尼姑解空坐了第二艘；柳如是本来也要坐第二艘，但因为要陪惠香，而且用她的话来说，也是乐得清静宽敞，所以甘心委屈一下，带着红情、绿意和几名老妈子坐了第三艘；第四艘是载运用具杂物的船。至于其余男女仆役，则按照不同的身份职责，分别安排在各条船上侍候。

当船队荡开碧绿的河水，一只接一只地向着城外缓缓摇去时，“十里青山半在城”的秀丽景色，就在人们的眼前展开了：苍翠的虞山，像一道长长的屏风，横架在城墙之上。城内这边，是鳞鳞万瓦，袅袅炊烟，以及纵横的街道，络绎的行人，看上去，

He Siyu was dumbfounded and instinctively tried to stop him but immediately woke up. He looked quietly at Qian Qianyi's back with a hint of resentment in his eyes. Then he turned around and said coldly to Xu Zheng, who was also nonplussed by the situation.

"Xu Erxiu, what a bad day you've chosen! It's a damned day. Go find someone else to negotiate a deal."

## Respite in the Country Garden

Waterside Villa was located in the northwest suburb of Changshu City, between the southern foot of the Yu Mountain and the Shang Lake, not far from the Qian residence, from which there was a waterway. Although preparations for the outing had been made two days before, the Qian family tarried until it was fairly late in the morning. There having been only one male heir in the family line for generations, the Qian family itself was a small one, but the convoy was rather spectacular with the guests and servants going together. They were seated in four large boats. Qian Qianyi, Ji Cheng, Gu Ling, Sun Yongzuo, and the newly hired family tutor He Yun sat in the first boat. Lady Chen, Qian Sun'ai, Lady Zhu, and Jiekong the nun took the second one. Liu Rushi was supposed to take the second one, but instead condescended to take the third one with Hongqing, Lüyi, and a few old maids, because she wanted to be in the company of Huixiang, and in her own words, she was happy to have more quiet and space. The fourth boat carried utensils and miscellaneous supplies. The other men and women servants were placed in the other boats according to their responsibilities.

As the boats plowed their way toward the suburb one following another, a vista of "ten miles of green mountains, half in the city"[1] unfolded before their eyes. The green Yu Mountain was like a long screen placed squarely over the city wall. The rows of tiled houses with rising and drifting kitchen smoke and the crisscrossing streets with swarms of pedestrians inside the city constituted a moving

① It is a quote from a poem by Shen Xuan.

就像镌刻在屏风上的一幅活动图画。待到航船出了城外，景色就更加令人着迷：一片肥沃而平坦的原野，从山脚下延伸开去，巨大的、半月形的尚湖，在远处闪闪发光。而在这样的背景当中，则是棋盘似的青青稻田，间杂着一丛一丛的绿树、一个一个的村庄；牛羊在河岸上踯躅，白云在蓝天上浮荡……这一片得天独厚的土地，活力确实惊人。仅仅是去年，它还曾遭受到大旱和蝗灾的严重袭击，但是入春以来，几场透雨，几度熏风，它又出人意料地迅速复苏过来，并且急急忙忙地重新展现出秀丽的姿容。如果两岸的田舍不是那样的低矮破败，在田间劳作的农夫不是那样衣衫褴褛、形容憔悴，它给人的印象，必然还会更加美好一点。幸而，钱府船上的男女主人们，并没有因此影响了游兴。他们根本没有留意到这些，依旧在那里兴致勃勃地指点观赏，坦然地、尽情地享受着这块属于他们的土地的殷勤奉献……

在钱府的船上，如今最兴奋的，要数计成。这不仅是由于他那双经验丰富的敏锐眼睛，立即就发现这片负山面湖的地带，实在是修建大型园林的理想处所，而且还因为他现在很穷，很需要通过承办一两项大型工程来积攒一笔钱。事实上，作为一位造诣很高的叠山师，数十年来，他受聘于豪门富户，负责建造的园林不少。像武进吴元的独乐园、扬州郑元勋的影园、仪征汪机的寤园等，都是他的得意杰作。不过，他虽然因此而名声大噪，却并未因此富有起来。譬如，他早就希望能够买一块地，替自己精心构筑一个小小的园林，作为暮年的归宿，可就是一直拿不出这笔款子。他也认识不少有钱的主顾，同其中一些人还颇有交情，但是谁都不曾认真关心过他的这个愿望。倒不完全是他们不够慷慨，而是他们或许根本就没有想到计成真有这种想头，他也应当有自己的园子，虽然一般来说，他只能算是一个穷人。计成是懂规矩

picture on the green screen. Once the boats were out of town, the view was even more spectacular: A large stretch of fertile, flat prairie land extended from the foot of the mountain to the vast, crescent Shang Lake glistening in the distance. Against this backdrop was a chessboard of verdant paddyfields interspersed with villages and groves of lush green trees; cattle and sheep roamed the riverbanks, and white clouds drifted in the blue sky ... This prestigious land was teeming with an incredible vitality. Having been hit hard by a severe drought and a locust plague in the previous year, it had quickly recovered at the beginning of spring after some rainfalls and was now eager to reassert itself. If the farmhouses on the sides of the river hadn't been so low and dilapidated, and the farmers working in the fields hadn't been so ragged and haggard, it would certainly have looked even better. Fortunately, such a blemish didn't spoil the fun of the men and women on the boats who didn't notice it at all as they excitedly pointed here and there and commented on what they saw, indulgently enjoying to the fullest measure the best the land had to offer ...

Of all those aboard, Ji Cheng was the most excited, because for one thing his seasoned eyes quickly discovered this belt between the mountain and the lake was a perfect place for a grand garden and for another he was broke and destitute and needed to do one or two more major projects to fill his pockets. In fact, as a highly skilled landscape architect, he had built a great number of gardens for wealthy families in the past few decades, including such masterpieces as the Single Joy Garden of Wu Yuan in Changzhou, the Shadow Garden of Zheng Yuanxun in Yangzhou, and the Wakefulness Garden of Wang Ji in Yizheng. Despite his fame, he hadn't become rich through building them. He had long hoped that he could buy a piece of land and build a good garden for himself to spend old age, but he just couldn't come up with the money. He was a friend to quite a few wealthy clients, but no one had ever cared about his wish. It was not that they were not generous enough, but that they perhaps had even never thought that a poor man like Ji Cheng should have a garden of his own. Ji Cheng knew what was proper to do, so he had to keep his wish

的，他只好继续把愿望悄悄藏在心里。不过最近，也许是已经年逾花甲的缘故，这个愿望渐渐变得越来越强烈和迫切了。“无论如何，我得设法攒一笔钱，自己修个园子，哪怕很小一个园子也罢！”他想。恰好这时候，瞿式耜派人送来了请他修葺园子的聘书。计成十分高兴，立即赶到常熟来。接着他又听说钱谦益也想请他负责改建拂水山庄，更是喜出望外。他素仰钱谦益大名，觉得这于自己是一种难得的荣耀，“只不知他肯出多少价钱？他无疑是很有钱的！当然，我不应当一下子就想到这个，特别是对这样一位大名鼎鼎的人物，不应该！可是……”一路上，计成被这种念头弄得十分兴奋，又有点不安。他殷勤地同大家周旋，同时偷偷窥伺主人的神情。当他发现主人对自己十分尊重、十分信赖时，这种不安又转化为惭愧和感激了。

终于，船队靠了码头。山庄的总管钱斗——一个衣着华丽的圆脸胖老头儿已经领着两名执事人员在岸上候着。于是钱谦益上了四人抬大轿，其余女眷和客人则改乘小轿，由一名头戴毡笠、身穿红背心的伞夫扛着一把黄色的轻绫大伞，在前头开路，其余的仆人就挑的挑、提的提，络绎跟在后面。

现在，队伍在稻秧摇曳的田野中缓缓穿行。因为早就过了清明踏青的时节，所以这条路上的行人并不多。偶尔有几个挑担提篮的农夫农妇，见了这支浩浩荡荡的队伍，早就吓得闪避一旁；只有一两个不懂事的小牧童，被队伍的仪仗排场所吸引，抛开牛儿，远远地奔过来，咬着手指，瞪大眼睛，好奇地站在路旁观看。

走完了田野，队伍爬上了一道傍溪而筑的土堤。这溪从北边虞山脚下蜿蜒而来，到脚下拐了个弯，径直向西流去。溪的这边

secret. Recently, however, as he passed sixty this desire had gradually become stronger. "I'll save money by all means and build a garden of my own. Even a small one will be good," he thought. Qu Shisi's appointment letter just came in time. Ji Cheng was happy to take the offer and came to Changshu without delay. Then he heard that Qian Qianyi wanted to have the Waterside Villa rebuilt by him. He was even more gladdened. Having heard Qian Qianyi's big name, he felt it was a great honor for him. "I just don't know how much he's willing to pay. He's undoubtedly rich. Of course I should not think about money first, particularly when the invitation came from such a famous man. I shouldn't think about money first, but ..." he thought. Ji Cheng was both exhilarated and apprehensive. He approached everyone with care and caution but his apprehension turned into shame and gratitude when he realized that Qian Qianyi had great respect for him and great trust in him.

Finally, the fleet moored at the pier. Steward of the villa Qian Dou, a chubby old man with a round face in gorgeous clothes, was waiting on shore with two head servants. Qian Qianyi stepped into the big sedan chair with four bearers, and the guests and the female members of the family took the small sedan chairs. An umbrella holder with a felt hat and a red vest led the way in front of them. All the other servants followed with luggage in their hands or on their shoulders.

The procession moved slowly through the paddyfields amid swaying rice seedlings. It was long past the season for spring excursions, so there were not many pedestrians on the way. Once in a while, there were some men and women farmers carrying baskets in their hands or with a shoulder-pole, who stepped aside timidly to dodge this mighty army. One or two herder boys, who had no sense of fear, attracted by the great array, came running over, leaving their cattle behind, and fingers in their mouths, eyes wide open, watched curiously from aside.

After passing the fields, the cortege climbed onto the dam of a stream, which meandered from the foot of the Yu Mountain in the north, made a turn where they were and flowed straight west. On this

是杨柳和桃树，溪的那边是茂密的翠竹。计成根据经验，知道翠竹之内，应当就是山庄了。果然，不久轿队就在一处酒肆前停了下来。钱谦益同男客们都下了轿子。至于陈夫人和柳如是等女眷，不便同男客们混在一起游览，没有停轿，一直朝山庄大门那边去了。

计成站在轿前，抬头打量了一下，只见迎面是一幢三开间的平房。房檐下伸出一根长竿，上面飘着一面青色的酒旗。平房里安着一个柜台、十来副桌椅。不多的几个游客正在那里喝酒。平房后面，耸立着一幢两层的红色小楼。楼上悬着一个黑漆横匾，上面写着“花信楼”三个金色大字，在两旁翠竹垂杨和远处虞山的映衬下，倒也颇饶画意。

“计先生，这道长堤名唤‘月堤烟柳’，这楼名唤‘酒楼花信’，乃系敝庄八景中之二景。是学生闲时胡乱想出来的名目，却是可笑得很了！”钱谦益走过来，用了一种听起来像是随随便便的口吻介绍说。

计成喝了一声彩，来不及说话，顾苓已经在旁边插口说：“计先生，你不知，牧老所题这山庄八景，可谓景景精切，不可移易！除眼前此二景外，尚有‘秋原耦耕’‘梅圃溪堂’‘锦峰清晓’‘香山晚翠’‘春流观瀑’和‘水阁云岚’。山庄胜境，竟是给他这三十二字，轻轻道尽了呢！”

孙永祚也点着头说：“不错，牧老还替这八景一一写的有诗，俱是高华俊爽的传世之作。我记得题这‘酒楼花信’的一首是‘花压高楼酒泛卮……’”

他本想念下去，可是看见大家已经移动脚步，只好临时闭了

side of the stream were willow and peach trees, and on the other side was a lush growth of green bamboos. Experience told Ji Cheng that the villa was inside the bamboo grove. Sure enough, the sedan chairs soon stopped in front of a tavern. Qian Qianyi and the male guests got off their sedan chairs. The ladies, who didn't feel it appropriate to mingle with the gentlemen, continued to move forward in the sedan chairs toward the gate of the villa.

Ji Cheng stood in front of the sedan chair and looked in front of him. It was a bungalow with three rooms. A long pole protruded from below the eaves, with a blue wine flag blowing in the wind. Inside the bungalow there was a counter and a dozen tables with chairs. A few tourists were drinking there. Behind the bungalow stood a two-storey red building. The building carried a horizontal black lacquer plate with three golden characters that said "House of Blooming Flowers". It gave a rather picturesque view with the green bamboos and tall poplars on both sides and against the backdrop of the Yu Mountain in the distance.

"Mr. Ji, this long embankment is called 'Moon and Willows Bank', and the building is called 'House of Blooming Flowers'. They're two of the eight views in the villa. Such names just occurred to me. They sound stupid, do they?" Qian Qianyi came up and explained in a casual tone.

Ji Cheng said, "Excellent names!" Before he gave further comments, Gu Ling cut in, "Mr. Ji, the eight views of the villa each have a unique appeal. Apart from the two in front of you, there're six others: 'Farming in Autumn', 'The Creekside Plum Grove', 'Hills at Dawn', 'Mountain at Dusk', 'Waterfall in Spring', and 'Waterside Pavilion under the Clouds'. The picturesque beauty of the villa is vividly captured in these thirty-two characters."

Sun Yongzuo also nodded, saying, "Yes, Elder Mu has written a poem for each of these eight views. All of them are masterpieces to be handed down to posterity. I remember the one for the House of Blooming Flowers is 'Blossoms weigh down on the tall house and wine overflows from the pot ...'"

He stopped reciting when seeing that everyone was moving again

嘴，跟着大家朝酒肆走去。

原来，这酒肆后面紧挨着溪涧，从上面的一道石板桥走过去，进了东角门，里面是一个花木扶疏的小庭院，这才是花信楼的真正所在。

由于刚才这楼的外观给计成的印象颇好，所以此刻他特别留神察看。他发现这庭院的布局却很是一般，无非是方池石山、合抱小廊。当中是楼，楼旁一树梨花，高达四丈。虽然花期将过，雪白的、带五瓣的花朵仍然密密层层缀满枝头，几乎遮住了半爿楼宇。计成心想："这梨花倒是难得！只是院墙太低，又没有遮拦，酒肆里的声音全跑进来了。若是把院墙加高一尺，溪边再植上几排翠竹，这样外边的声音还能听见，却已变得依稀隐约，那意趣便大不相同了！"不过，出于谨慎，他决定暂时不指出来。"虽然主人有意让我主持改建山庄，但是当着这许多人，指摘原筑之非，总是有损他的脸面的。"他对自己说。

这当儿，大家已经登上花信楼的二楼，跨进一间朝西的厅房里。

"哎，一登上这楼，便教人又想起牧老那首诗，真是绝妙好辞——'花压高楼酒泛卮，登楼……'"孙永祚又吟诵起来。显然，他对于刚才未能把这诗念完，一直有点不甘心。

可是钱谦益又一次打断了他。

"计先生，你瞧敝庄这格局规模，该当如何改作才是？"他兴冲冲地走向窗前，问。

计成朝孙永祚抱歉地点点头，然后走到窗前，向外望去，发现这山庄范围着实不小。它紧挨着虞山脚下，门前隔着一片平坦

and followed them to the tavern.

Behind the tavern was a creek. They walked across a stone bridge over the creek and entered the east corner door. Inside was a small courtyard with flowers and trees, where the House of Blooming Flowers was located.

As Ji Cheng had been impressed by the exterior of the two-storied house a moment ago, now he paid special attention to it. He found that the layout of this courtyard was rather commonplace with nothing more than a square water pool, a stone hill, and a small corridor. In the middle was a two-storied house, next to which was a forty-foot-tall flowering pear tree. Although the flowering season was almost over, the branches were still densely covered with five-petaled snow-white flowers, which hid half of the house. Ji Cheng thought to himself, "The flowers are beautiful indeed. It's just that the courtyard wall is too low and without hindrance all the sounds from the tavern came in. If the courtyard wall were raised by one foot, and a few rows of green bamboo were planted by the creek, there would be a different vibe. The sounds from the outside could still be heard, but they wouldn't be so loud." However, he decided out of prudence not to point it out for the time being. "Although the owner of the place intends to have me preside over the renovation of the villa, it is not appropriate to criticize the original work in front of so many people," he said to himself.

They came to the second floor and walked into a hall facing west.

"Ah, it reminds me again of Elder Mu's poem, an excellent one: 'Blossoms weigh down on the tall house and wine overflows from the pot ...'" Sun Yongzuo said, resuming his reciting. Clearly, he had taken it to heart that he hadn't been able to finish his reciting earlier.

But once again he was interrupted by Qian Qianyi, who walked excitedly to the window and asked, "Mr. Ji, have a good look at the layout and tell me what changes should be introduced to such a large place."

Ji Cheng nodded apologetically to Sun Yongzuo, then walked to the window and looked out. He found that the villa was indeed a very large one, situated at the foot of the Yu Mountain, separated from the

的田野，不远就是烟波浩渺的尚湖。一道回环的溪水把方圆数十亩的山庄围绕起来。庄上照例种着些古松、银杏、梧桐、桂花、垂杨一类的树木。那些楼堂馆榭就掩映在林木之中。虽说离得远，细微之处瞧不太清楚，可是，以计成老练的眼光，仍然立即发现，这山庄初创时显然比较草率，后来虽经改造，却缺乏通盘的规划，而且是分几次施工，所以布局上问题不少。他沉吟了一下，拱着手说："宝庄负山面湖，风景奇秀，且深得自然天成之趣，就形势气象而言，似犹在松江横云山别墅之上。唯是改作之事，学生不才，非经实地踏勘之后，却未敢妄言。"

钱谦益注意地听着，又深深地瞧了计成一眼，似乎明白了叠山师的细微用心。他点点头，不再追问。于是大家顺着计成的话头，谈论了一阵在山林地建园的种种优点，把横云山别墅同拂水山庄比较了一番，又到北厅去瞧了瞧利用拂水岩作借景的情形，就一起动身下楼。

楼下庭院的左侧，有一道贝叶式的角门。出了角门，是两条分岔的石子路，一条往北，一条往西，各自蜿蜒于花木丛中。钱谦益主张先去瞧拂水岩，于是大家便取道往北，慢慢行去。

现在，月堤上的人声已经听不见。四下里静悄悄的，只有微风吹动树木，发出沙沙的声响。一群灰色的麻雀，正栖息在长廊的栏杆上，发现有人走近，便匆匆飞进蔷薇丛中，不见了。隔着溪涧，传来了牛的呜叫声……因为这山庄属于钱府私有，普通百姓未经许可是不能进来的。平日钱谦益不来时，偌大一座山庄就

expansive Shang Lake nearby by a belt of flat fields. A circular creek surrounded the villa with an area of dozens of acres. Ancient pine trees, ginkgo trees, phoenix trees, sweet osmanthus trees, and weeping willow trees populated the villa as was the custom. Various other structures were scattered amid the trees. Although Ji Cheng didn't see the details clearly from a distance, with his sophisticated eye, he nevertheless immediately discovered that this villa had been poorly built and that later renovations, for lack of a master plan, created some blemishes in the layout. He thought for a while, then folded his hands and said, "With the mountain behind and the lake in front, your villa commands the best view offered by nature. I can say that the milieu is much better than that of the Hengyun Mountain Villa in Songjiang, but I dare not say how to rebuild your villa without making a thorough investigation."

Qian Qianyi, who was listening attentively, cast a glance at Ji Cheng, as if he understood the subtle thoughts of the landscape architect. He nodded and stopped his query. The others continued from where Ji Cheng left off. They talked for a while about the benefits of building a garden by a mountain, with a thorough comparison of the Hengyun Mountain Villa and the Waterside Villa. Then, they went to the north hall to have a look at how the Waterside Rock was used to "borrow scenery". Finally, they left the second floor together.

To the left of the courtyard below was a corner door in the shape of a pattra leaf. Outside the corner door was a pebble path forked into two, winding through flowers and trees, one leading to the north and the other to the west. Qian Qianyi suggested that they should see the Waterside Rock first, so they moved slowly north.

There was no more human sound on the Moon Bank. It was quiet all around, except for the rustling of the trees in the breeze. A flock of gray sparrows were perched on the railing of the corridor. Seeing some humans approaching, they hurriedly flew into the rosebushes and disappeared. From across the creek came the mooing of cows ... Because the villa was privately owned by the Qians, ordinary people couldn't enter it without permission. Such a large villa lay idle most

闲闭着，只有钱斗领着二三十个奴仆负责收拾照料。前两天，听说主人要来，才特意又打扫了一遍，并且把各处门户都开了锁。计成跟着大家看了几处亭台轩榭，其中有他认为还可以的。不过，他自始至终都避免公开提出批评，相反还挑了一两处有特色的处所，着实称赞了一番。他的这种谦和态度，显然博得了主人很大的好感。

“牧老，此廊甚是不俗，与适才团桂阁那段复廊相较，却又别饶意趣哩！”计成说。这时，他们正从梅圃溪堂里转出来，走在一道长廊上。这长廊先斜向左，接着又斜向右，然后又斜向左，成“之”字形走向。廊外的景物则随着每个转折而不断变换，时而花木丛集，时而碧水远山，时而又奇石耸峙、楼阁玲珑……

“啊，计先生称许此廊？”钱谦益似乎有点意外。

“不错！你瞧它随形而弯，依势而曲，或蟠山腰，或萦水际，穿花渡涧，蜿蜒不已，令游者目不暇给，兴味无限。可谓深得造园三昧！”

钱谦益眯缝着眼睛听着。末了，他微微一笑：“说来却是笑话一件，这廊是我让他们改的。原来不是这样子，原来是笔直的——曲尺形。可是前些日子有个年友来，他说曲尺形是古制，如此一改，便全无古意了。”

“古之曲廊，确是曲尺形。”计成认真地说，“唯是曲尺形典重则有余，灵变则不足，施之于殿堂尚可，若家居之园，实不若‘之’字形为佳。譬如仪征寤园的‘篆云廊’，便是取的此种

of the time. It was taken care of by twenty or thirty servants led by Qian Dou. Two days ago, hearing that the master was coming, they had given the villa a thorough cleaning and unlocked all the doors. Ji Cheng carefully studied the terraces, pavilions, corridors, and cottages and thought some of them were good. However, he cautiously avoided open criticism and tried to find something good to praise. So, he praised the few spots he found good. Such a humble attitude, of course, won the favor of the villa owner.

"Elder Mu, this corridor is truly remarkable. Compared to the double corridor of the Osmanthus Pavilion, it has a different appeal," said Ji Cheng. They went across the Plum Garden and walked into a long corridor, which went to the left front and then to the right front and then again to the left front in a zigzag course. The scenery outside the corridor changed with each turning point, flowers and trees, flowing water and distant mountains, strange rocks and bizarre stones, and small cottages and exquisite pavilions coming to view in succession.

"Oh, you like this corridor?" Qian Qianyi looked slightly surprised.

"Yes, I do. Look! It twists and turns in perfect keeping with the natural features, meandering along, now on the hill, now alongside the creek, now through the flowers and trees, and now across a rivulet, keeping your eyes busy all the way. It's a good piece of work," Ji Cheng said.

Qian Qianyi listened with narrowed eyes. When Ji Cheng finished, he smiled slightly, saying, "It's like a joke. Originally, it was not like this. It was straight, like a right angle ruler. I asked them to change it. A few days ago, a friend my age came. He said the right angle ruler design is that of the ancients and that such a change has just killed the quaintness."

"The ancient curved corridor is indeed in the shape of a right angle ruler," Ji Cheng said in a serious tone. "The problem is, the right angle ruler shape is too stiff and not capable of accommodating nuances of the landscape. For a palace, it's good, but not as good as

式样，识者无不称之！”

“正是，正是！”钱谦益连连点头，兴奋起来，“寤园我尚未曾有缘一游，不过经先生如此一说，学生我已是疑虑全消了！”

这样说完之后，有一会儿，钱谦益停住脚步，一言不发地瞧着计成，目光闪动着，像是在考虑什么。

这时，站在一旁很久没有说话的孙永祚忽然环顾了一下，随即紧张地盯住站在他对面的塾师何云：“士龙兄，你可曾拜读过牧老的《酒楼花信》？确是高华俊爽，令人心折！”

“哦，莫非就是子长兄适才没念完的那一首？”有着一个大得出奇的鼻子和一部乱蓬蓬的黄胡子的何云，微笑着问。

“不错，你听我念完，诗是这样的——”孙永祚急急地说，随即大声吟诵起来：

花压高楼酒泛卮，登楼共赋艳阳诗。
人间容易催花信，天上分明挂酒旗。
中酒心情寒食后，看花伴侣好春时。
秾桃正倚新杨柳，横笛朱栏莫放吹。

他念完了，又由衷地赞美了一句：“好诗，真是好诗！”这才如释重负地退到一边去，同时偷偷地注意着钱谦益的反应。当发现老师不仅没有表示高兴，反而皱起眉头时，他就露出困惑的神情。

“计先生，”钱谦益终于开口了，“学生有一事意欲与先生商量，不知当否？”

a zigzag shape for a home garden. For example, the Cloud Corridor of the Wakefulness Garden in Yizheng has taken the right angle ruler design and everybody likes it."

"Exactly, exactly!" Qian Qianyi nodded excitedly. "I've not had a chance to visit the Wakefulness Garden yet, but what you say has cleared my doubts."

Qian Qianyi stood still and pondered for a moment and stared at Ji Cheng without saying a word, his eyes flashing, as if thinking of something.

At this point, Sun Yongzuo, who hadn't spoken for a long time, looked around and stared nervously at the home school teacher He Yun standing in front of him, saying, "Brother Shilong, have you ever read Elder Mu's poem 'Flowers Bloom at the Tavern'? It's elegant and graceful."

"Is it the one Brother Zizhang was going to recite?" asked He Yun smilingly, who had a surprisingly large nose and a disheveled yellowish beard.

"Correct! Listen to me. Here's the poem —" Sun Yongzuo quickly replied. Then, he recited:

*Blossoms weigh down on the tall house and wine overflows from the pot.*
*On the balcony of the house we dedicate our poems to the sunny day.*
*Down below is the human world with flowers in bloom and a tavern flag blowing in the wind.*
*After wining and dining in the Cold Food Festival*
*We're here to admire the flowers in the good spring.*
*Peach blossoms lean against weeping willows*
*Like a column of pink musicians singing and playing flutes."*

After reciting, he said with great sincerity, "A good poem. What a good poem!" Then he stepped aside as if relieved, secretly watching Qian Qianyi's reaction. When he found that his former teacher was frowning instead of being delighted, he looked confused.

"Mr. Ji," Qian Qianyi said. "I have something to discuss with you."

“啊，牧老只管吩咐！”

“先生的大作《园冶》一书，学生前时也曾拜读……”

“啊，那是晚生胡乱涂鸦，不意竟污清盼，尚希牧老指谬！”计成连忙拱手回答，脸不由得红了。因为那部书，虽然是他平生建造园林的经验心得的结晶，却是阮大铖出钱替他刻印的，上面还有阮氏的序言。他曾经因为这缘故在士林中颇受诟骂，现在钱谦益忽然提起这本书，计成便不禁惊疑起来了。

“我记得先生于书末‘自识’中，曾有‘唯闻时事纷纷，隐心皆然，愧买山无力，甘做桃源溪口人’之叹。不知这‘买山’之愿，如今已了却否？”

计成又是一惊！他没有想到钱谦益读书如此细心，而且记性又如此之好。不错，他确实在跋语中写过这么几句。那是他刚完成书稿，一时感触，随手写下的。如今十年过去了，他的这部书也早已传遍了大江南北，可是从来没有人留意到他的这个卑微的愿望，更别说帮助他实现了。“那么，他为什么要问这个？他想做什么？……啊，莫非，莫非……”计成的心忽然一动，随即猛烈地跳动起来，“啊，不是，不是的，不会！”他在心中大声地否定说，竭力使自己镇静下来。然而，他的情绪被震荡得那样厉害，以致无法马上回答主人的问话。

钱谦益瞧了他一眼，又说：“学生如今却有个冒昧之请，意欲就在本庄侧畔划出数亩之地，请先生自建一园，移居其中，以便日夕过从，请教造园叠山之学问，不知先生意下如何？”

钱谦益说这话时，虽然声音不高，而且显得有点踌躇，可是在计成耳朵里听来，却无异是仙乐齐鸣。他的脸顿时变得煞白，直愣愣地瞧着钱谦益，几乎不敢相信自己的耳朵。

“啊，莫非先生不允？”钱谦益似乎有点失望。

"I'm all ears, Elder Mu."

"I've read your book *On the Building of Gardens* some time ago ..."

"Have you? I'm so much flattered that you've bothered to read such a sloppy book. Pray pardon me if there's anything wrong in it," said Ji Cheng, blushing, his hands pressed together. The book represented the essence of his art, but, since Ruan Dacheng had paid for the lithographic printing and written the preface, he was widely criticized in the circle of gentry scholars. Qian Qianyi's mention of the book immediately put him on alert.

"In the afterword, you said, 'In such a world of chaos, I would like to be a recluse too, but without the means to buy a piece of land in a mountain for myself, I choose to be a man building gardens for others, wandering in the peach groves and by the creeks.' I'm wondering if you've had your wish."

Ji Cheng was surprised that Qian Qianyi had read his book so carefully and even remembered such a detail. Yes, he had indeed written those words in the afterword in self-pity after finishing the manuscript. Now ten years had passed. The book had spread across the country, but no one had ever noticed his humble wish, let alone helped him realize it. "Then, why does he ask about that? What does he want to do? ... Is it, is it ...?" Ji Cheng's heart suddenly gave a jolt, and then beat violently. "Oh, no, no, no!" He rejected those thoughts and tried to calm down himself, but his emotions were so turbulent that he was unable to reply to Qian Qianyi immediately.

Qian Qianyi looked at him and said, "I have an idea. If you agree, I can give a few acres of land of my villa to you so that you can build a garden of your own next to mine and live in it. Thus we'll be able to meet day to day and I'll be able to learn from you the art of landscape architecture. What do you think?"

Qian Qianyi spoke in a small, hesitant voice, but in Ji Cheng's ears, those words were like a chorus of drums, cymbals, xylophones, gongs, bells, and rattles. Ji Cheng's face went white with astonishment. He stared at Qian Qianyi, unable to believe his ears.

"You won't agree?" Qian Qianyi said, looking a little disappointed.

“啊！不……”计成用微弱的声音说，觉得泪水马上就要涌上眼睛。他想大声表示答应，又想扑倒在对方的脚下，但是又觉得出于礼貌，应当先辞谢几句。正在拿不定主意，忽然，传来了急促的脚步声，李宝神色紧张地出现在长廊里。在他的后面，还跟着两名轿夫，扛着一顶肩舆。

长廊里的气氛一下子被扰乱了。钱谦益和客人们都诧异地回过头去。

李宝奔到离大家还有几步远时，就站住了。他行过礼，瞧了瞧客人们，犹豫了一下，径直走到钱谦益身边，低声说了几句。只见钱谦益的眉毛皱了起来，神情也变得十分古怪。他抬头瞧了大家一眼，想了想，终于无可奈何地说：

“耦耕堂那边有点小事，须得学生去料理。烦三位先陪计先生游着，学生转身便来。”

他走向肩舆，行了几步，又走回来，对计成说：“计先生，适才之事，回头再议，尚祈应允！”说完，这才拱一拱手，上了肩舆，匆匆去了。

计成眼泪汪汪地张了张嘴，很想高声告诉他，自己已是十二分的同意，可是到底没有说出来。“啊，等他回来再说吧，反正也不忙着这半晌一刻，是的！……”他唏嘘地想，颤巍巍地走前几步，以无限崇敬、感激的心情，拱手目送着钱谦益的背影，直到肩舆在花树丛中拐了个弯，看不见了，才默默地转过身来。

## 借诗励志

钱谦益之所以中断游园，匆匆赶往耦耕堂来，是因为听李宝禀告说：柳如是同朱姨太又争吵起来了，闹得不可开交。陈夫人气得差点没昏过去，正在那里哭泣垂泪哩！这教钱谦益又是吃惊

"Oh, no, but ..." Ji Cheng said in a weak voice, feeling that tears were about to come into his eyes. He wanted to say "of course I do" in a loud voice, and he wanted to throw himself at Qian Qianyi's feet, but he felt that according to etiquette he shouldn't immediately accept the offer. As he was hesitating, there suddenly came the sound of hurried footsteps. Li Bao appeared in the hallway with a nervous look. Behind him was a sedan chair carried by two bearers.

The atmosphere in the hallway suddenly changed. Qian Qianyi and the guests turned around in surprise.

Li Bao came over and stopped a few steps away from them. He saluted his master from a distance, looked at the guests, and then walked straight to his master and said something in a low voice. Qian Qianyi frowned upon hearing it and his expression became very strange. Then, he lifted his head and said to the others apologetically, "There's a trifle in the Hall of the Farming Duo. My friends, pray take care of Mr. Ji for a while. I'll be back shortly."

He walked toward the sedan chair but turned back after a few steps and said to Ji Cheng, "Mr. Ji, we'll discuss the matter later. I hope you can agree." Then, he excused himself and left hurriedly in the sedan chair.

Ji Cheng opened his mouth with tears in his eyes and wanted to say it out loud that he had a hundred and twenty percent agreed, but eventually held it back. "Well, we can talk about it when he comes back. Anyway, there's no hurry. Yes, there's no hurry ..." he thought with a sigh. Then, he gingerly took a few steps forward, and, pressing his hands together, watched with infinite reverence and gratitude as Qian Qianyi left until the sedan chair made a turn amid the flowering trees and disappeared.

## Allusions in a Poem

Hearing from Li Bao that another fight was going on between Liu Rushi and Lady Zhu, Qian Qianyi interrupted his garden tour and hurried to the Hall of the Farming Duo. That Lady Chen had almost passed out from the bickering shocked him and made him angry.

又是生气。本来，他以为经过前些日子那一番调停，她们总该会体谅一下自己的处境和难处，稍稍变得互相忍让一点。可是没想到，才安静不几天，又闹将起来，甚至连这么个日子也不让自己安生地过。“啊，这些女人！”他恼火地想，同时又担心：这会儿她们不知闹得怎样了？若是互相厮打起来，柳如是只怕要吃亏。她是那般娇小荏弱，而朱姨娘却身强力壮！随后他又想到：周围还有许多人劝架，也许不至于闹到这种地步，“不过，也难说，如是的性子烈得很，倒不如当初下决心把老三送到城东旧宅去的好……”一路上，钱谦益就是这么胡思乱想，直到他所乘坐的肩舆来到耦耕堂。

大堂内静悄悄的，一点声音都没有。钱谦益撩开轿帘向外望了望，“嗯，莫非她们吵完了？”他想，随即下了轿子，走上大堂来。

可是出乎意料，大堂内竟是空空如也，不但陈夫人、柳如是和朱姨娘不在，就连钱孙爱和随身侍候的婢仆们也全都无影无踪。钱谦益不由得奇怪起来，正想回头询问李宝，忽然听见一个熟悉的嗓音说：

“妹妹，不错吧，我说准是他哩！”

随着话音，只见东边旁间的门帘掀开，柳如是款款地走了出来，后面还跟着一个年轻女子，那是她的手帕姐妹——惠香。

“啊哟！老爷可来啦！”柳如是笑吟吟地迎上来，行着礼说。

“你——”钱谦益怀疑地打量着她。他本想问：你们怎么又吵起来了？但发现柳如是不像是刚吵过架的样子，所以临时又改了口，“你们——原来在这儿！”

“我们一直守在这儿，不敢离开半步，专等老爷来哩！”柳如是歪着头儿说，又回顾惠香，“妹妹，你说是不是？”

“哦……”钱谦益瞅了瞅惠香。还在第一次看见惠香时，他

Previously, he had intervened in a fight and explained his situation to them, asking them to be tolerant of each other. To his disappointment, they were fighting again after a few days, leaving him no peace. "These women!" he sighed with irritation. Meanwhile, he was deeply concerned. If they had taken to fists, the delicate and fragile Liu Rushi was definitely no match for the large and strong Lady Zhu. Then he thought, they might not have gone that far as there were so many others with them. He wasn't sure. Liu Rushi had a tempestuous temper. He regretted not having sent Lady Zhu to the old residence in the east of the city. Along the way, Qian Qianyi struggled with such thoughts until the sedan chair he was in pulled up at the Hall of the Farming Duo.

The antechamber was quiet. There was no sound of any kind. Qian Qianyi lifted the curtain of the sedan chair and looked out. "Well, it looks like they've finished the squabble," he thought. Then, he got out of the sedan chair and walked into the antechamber.

To his surprise, the antechamber was empty. Neither Lady Chen nor Liu Rushi nor Lady Zhu was there, nor Qian Sun'ai and the servants. Qian Qianyi felt it strange. He was about to turn around and ask Li Bao when suddenly he heard a familiar voice: "Sister, it's him, as I guessed."

As the voice fell, the curtain of the east room was lifted and Liu Rushi walked out gracefully, followed by a young woman, her handkerchief sister Huixiang.

"Welcome, my lord!" Liu Rushi greeted him with a smile and a curtsy.

"You—" Qian Qianyi looked at her suspiciously. He wanted to say "You're fighting again?" but seeing Liu Rushi didn't seem to have just quarreled with someone, he changed his words, "You're all here!"

"We have been here all the time without daring to move a single step, in case you may come any moment. We're waiting for you." Liu Rushi said, tilting her head. She looked back at Huixiang, "Sister, am I right?"

"Oh ..." Qian Qianyi looked at Huixiang. The first time he saw

就觉得她同柳如是有几分相像，也是细长的眼睛，淡淡的眉毛，只是左眉梢上多了一颗黑痣。现在他又发现她比柳如是更年轻娇嫩，也更文静，正在含羞带笑地躲避着他的视线……“那么——夫人和孙爱他们呢？”钱谦益神思不属地问。

“他们？”柳如是撇撇嘴，“谁知道！兴许是等老爷不来，腻烦了，全都到外头摘花斗草，耍子去啦！”

“你们没有——”钱谦益不无留恋地从惠香的身上移开眼睛，“没有吵架？”

“吵架？”柳如是显得十分惊奇，“吵什么架？今儿我们可是一直有说有笑，亲热得紧哩！”顿了顿，她又斜睨着钱谦益，微微冷笑，“再说，我这位妹子来了，她长得又漂亮，又水灵，我生怕有人对她起了什么坏心眼，光是寸步不离地守着她都忙不过来，哪有工夫同人吵架！”

钱谦益错愕了一下，随即掩饰地哈哈一笑，转过身去，大声叫：“李宝！”

李宝其实就站在他身后，马上答应。

钱谦益沉下了脸：“你——刚才胡说些什么？谎报情由，诓骗于我，是何道理？嗯？！”

李宝显然早就预料到会出现这种局面。他立即双膝跪下，磕着头说：“禀老爷，这不关小人的事。小人便有天大的胆子，也不敢诓骗老爷……”

“混蛋！你竟敢诋毁主母，戏弄老爷，无法无天，你该当何罪！”钱谦益的声音严厉起来。

李宝吓得浑身一抖，更加频繁地磕着头：“老爷容禀，这不关小人的事，确实不关小人的事！”他反反复复地说，可是到底

Huixiang, he felt she and Liu Rushi looked alike, both having narrow eyes and light eyebrows, except that there was a mole on a tip of her left eyebrow. Now he found that she was younger, juicier and of a quieter disposition. She avoided his gaze with a shy smile ... "Then— where are Lady Chen and Sun'ai?" asked Qian Qianyi absent-mindedly.

"Where are they?" Liu Rushi said, twisting her mouth. "Who knows? Since they're tired of waiting for you, they're now out picking flowers, gathering herbs[①] and having fun."

"You have not—" Qian Qianyi said, looking away reluctantly from Huixiang, "quarreled?"

"Quarreled?" Liu Rushi said in alarm. "Why should we quarrel? We talked and laughed together and had a good time." After a pause she looked into Qian Qianyi's eyes and scolded him slightly, "Besides, my friend is here. She's so pretty and juicy. I'm afraid someone will have designs on her. While I'm so busy keeping a watch on her, how can I have time to quarrel with others?"

Qian Qianyi was at a loss for an instant, then laughed in embarrassment, turned around and shouted, "Li Bao!"

Li Bao, who was actually standing right behind him, immediately replied.

Qian Qianyi said with a sunk face, "What did you say? Why did you lie to me, huh?"

Li Bao, of course, had long expected this to happen. He immediately knelt on his knees and kowtowed, saying, "My lord, it has nothing to do with me. How can I be so bold to lie to you?"

"You scum! How dare you slander your mistress and tease your master? What kind of punishment do you want?" Qian Qianyi said in a stern voice.

Li Bao trembled with fright and kowtowed harder. "My lord, it

---

① Gathering herbs (*doucao*, or herb gathering competition) is an ancient game for women and children, in which the winner is the one who gathers the greater variety of herbs.

关谁的事，又不说出来。

这种态度，更加激怒了钱谦益。他“哼”了一声，正要说出更严厉可怕的话来。这时候，柳如是开口了：

“哎，相公！你这是生的哪门子的气哟！告诉你，这不关李宝的事，是我！是我叫他这样去说的！这可明白了吧？我见那几个糟老头儿无味得很，相公陪了他们大半天，我只怕你都腻烦了，所以才使这么个法儿把你接出来，散散心。再说，我的这位惠香妹妹，来了这么几天，你还不曾好好儿招呼过她哩。她是个厚道人，嘴上不说，可心里也难免埋怨你了——”她又一次回头瞅着惠香，诡谲地一笑，“妹妹，你说是么？”

钱谦益噎住了。虽然他也已经猜到这件事是出于柳如是的主使，但是一来，他对于这种过于放肆的玩笑颇不喜欢；二来，李宝这奴才一边倒的态度，也使他有一种被叛卖、被愚弄的感觉，所以就借着机会爆发出来。可是，现在听了柳如是这么俏声软语的一番解释，他那满腔怒火不知怎么一来，便忽然失去了适才的势头，再也旺不起来了。他瞧了瞧惠香，又瞧了瞧柳如是，终于说道：

“是你——”

“是我，是我，当然是我！”柳如是变得像个淘气的小姑娘，她走过来，挽住钱谦益的手，“老爷，你瞧——花柳争荣，山光如泼，如斯美景，你竟忍心撇下我们姐妹不管么？”

“可是还有客人在等——”

“这我不管！我只要你陪我！”柳如是跺着脚，撒起娇来。

钱谦益没有办法了。“好，好，我陪你们走走就是！”他说，回头瞅了瞅还跪在地上等候发落的李宝，喝道：“欠打的奴才！今儿若不是夫人讨情，非打折你的狗腿不可！你去，找到计先生他们，传我的话，就说我眼下一时还分身不开，请他们先慢慢游着，我随后便来！”

has nothing to do with me. It really has nothing to do with me," he said repeatedly. But he didn't say whose idea it was.

This attitude further angered Qian Qianyi. He snorted and was about to say something harsher, when Liu Rushi said, "My dear husband, why are you so angry? It has nothing to do with Li Bao. It's me. It's me who told him to say it that way. Now you see? Those old men are boring as hell and you've spent enough time with them. I've thought out this method to get you away from them so you can relax for a while. Besides, Sister Huixiang has been here for many days without getting enough attention. She's a nice lady and doesn't complain, but she must've been complaining in her heart —" She looked back at Huixiang and gave a sly smile, saying "Sis, did I say it correctly?"

Qian Qianyi became speechless. The hoax went too far and he didn't like it at all. Meanwhile, he felt betrayed and humiliated when he saw Li Bao was siding with her. Although he had already guessed that Liu Rushi was behind the hoax, upon hearing Liu Rushi's gentle voice, for some reason, the momentum of his anger abated. He looked at Huixiang, then at Liu Rushi, and finally said,

"It's you—"

"It's me, it's me, of course it's me!" Liu Rushi became a naughty little girl, came over and took Qian Qianyi's hand, saying, "My lord, lo and behold! Blooming flowers, weeping willows, and green mountains, what a beautiful day! How can you be so heartless as to leave me and my sister alone?"

"But I have guests waiting for me —"

"I don't care! I only want you to be with me," Liu Rushi said, stamping her feet coquettishly.

Qian Qianyi had to yield to her. He said, "Okay, okay, I'll walk with you for a while." Then, he looked back at Li Bao, who was still kneeling on the ground waiting for his order, and shouted, "You deserve a flogging. If not for your mistress, I would break your legs. Go find the guests and tell them I'm busy at the moment and will be back with them shortly. Ask them to go on with the garden tour."

李宝连忙答应了，又叩头谢过，慢慢地站起来。这时，红情和绿意早已走出庭院来伺候，于是一行人便簇拥着，慢慢向外走去。

刚刚走到院门外，柳如是摸了摸发髻，忽然说："啊哟，我的一支珠钗不在了，想是失落在里面了！"说着，便要回身进去寻找。

钱谦益说："何必你亲自去？叫红情替你找就行了。"

柳如是摆摆手："不行！她不知道！"便匆匆进去了。

钱谦益便不阻拦，趁等候的当儿，他的眼睛又在惠香的身上溜起来。

"小娘子此来，想是要多盘桓些时候了？"他问。

"啊，不，奴家打算明日便家去了。"惠香敛衽回答，向院门内溜了一眼。

"怎么？小娘子难得老远的来一趟，如何便说要去？一定要多住些日子才好！"

"多谢姐夫美意，奴家在府上已是打搅多日，心下甚觉不安！"

"小娘子哪里话来！如是适才还埋怨我不曾好好儿招呼客人，我是甘受此责！所以打算回头命人把含晖阁收拾一下，就请小娘子长住，也好日夕亲近哩！"

惠香分明吃了一惊，连忙说："这如何使得，奴家、奴家明日当真要家去了。"

钱谦益笑嘻嘻地说："小娘子走不得！便是你姐姐放你走，我也不……"话未说完，忽然看见柳如是从里面匆匆走出来，他便立刻住了嘴。

"嗯，你刚才说什么来着？"柳如是怀疑地瞧瞧他们，问。

"没有，没说什么！"钱谦益连忙说。

"没有？"柳如是一边往前走，一边表示不相信。

Li Bao hurriedly said "aye, sir.", kowtowed in gratitude, and slowly stood up. By this time, the two servant girls Hongqing and Lüyi had come. Together, they slowly moved out.

When they came out of the courtyard, Li Rushi suddenly touched her hair bun and said, "Sorry. A hairpin is missing. It must've been left in the bedroom." Then, she turned around to look for it.

Qian Qianyi said, "You don't have to go yourself. Hongqing can find it for you."

Liu Rushi waved her hand and said, "No, she can't. She doesn't know where it is." Then, she went in hurriedly.

Qian Qianyi didn't stop her, and while he waited, his eyes fell back on Huixiang.

"My dear lady, are you staying with us for a while this time?" he asked.

"Oh, no, I plan to go home tomorrow," Huixiang replied, glancing back at the gate.

"What? After taking all the bother to come here, you're leaving so quickly? You should stay longer."

"Dear brother-in-law, thank you for your kindness. I've already disturbed your quiet for too many days."

"Don't say that. Rushi criticized me for not having paid enough attention to her guest just now. I accept her criticism. I'll have the Hanhui Chamber cleaned up for you so that you can stay there and spend more time with us."

Huixiang was clearly surprised. She said, "You're too obliging. I'm really leaving tomorrow."

Qian Qianyi said with a smile, "Please don't go, my dear lady. Even if your sister lets you go, I will not ..." Before he finished speaking, he suddenly saw Liu Rushi coming from inside, and he immediately stopped.

Liu Rushi looked at them suspiciously and asked, "Well, what did you say just now?"

"Nothing. I didn't say anything," Qian Qianyi promptly replied.

"Nothing?" said Liu Rushi in disbelief as she came forward.

“哦，姐夫要留我多住几天，可是妹妹已是决意明儿便家去了！”惠香坦然说。

柳如是“哼”了一声，狠狠地盯了钱谦益一眼，吓得钱谦益连忙别转脸，一声儿也不敢出。

这之后，柳如是便故意不搭理他，只顾和惠香有说有笑。有时钱谦益厚着脸皮搭讪几句，也被她不是抢白，便是挖苦，弄得老大没趣。就这样，一直来到了秋水阁。

秋水阁筑在一个绿竹环抱的小岗阜上，高两层，四面都开着窗子，南窗正对尚湖，北窗则靠着虞山。阁内没有扶梯，但是左侧有一座带石磴的假山，与第二层连接。楼上当中一张罗汉榻，榻后立着一架屏风，上面酣墨淋漓，龙飞凤舞，却是祝枝山手书的南宋辛弃疾词《哨遍——题秋水观》，那词从第一句“蜗角斗争”起，到最后一句“清溪一曲而已”止，足足有二百零三字，把整片屏风填得密密麻麻，端的是飞腾磅礴，气势惊人。在榻的左右是二几四椅，四个角落里还各供着一架盆景。

天气晴朗，远处尚湖上来往的渔船和飞舞的白鸥历历可数。钱谦益等一行人从阁旁的假山登上二楼之后，照例先走到南窗前眺望了一会，又绕着阁巡行了一周，然后就随意坐了下来。

柳如是正坐在榻左侧的一张椅子上。她仰着头，老半天地瞧着屏风上那一首词，忽然“吃吃”地笑出声来。

钱谦益和惠香感到莫名其妙，一齐回头瞧着她。柳如是只是笑，却不说话。钱谦益忍不住了，赔笑地问：“夫人如此发笑，

"Oh, my brother-in-law wants me to stay for a few more days, but I said I've already decided to go home tomorrow," said Huixiang calmly.

Liu Rushi snorted and stared at Qian Qianyi, who quickly turned his face away, not daring to say a word.

After that, Liu Rushi deliberately ignored him, talking and laughing with Huixiang. Sometimes Qian Qianyi cut in brazenly, but she either criticized or ridiculed him. This continued until they came to the Autumn Water Pavilion.

The Autumn Water Pavilion was built on a small hilltop surrounded by green bamboos. It was two stories high and had windows on all sides. The south window overlooked the Shang Lake and the north window faced the Yu Mountain. There was no staircase in the pavilion, but there was an artificial rock hill with stone steps on the left, which was connected to the second floor. In the middle of the second floor was an Arhat couch with a screen standing behind it. On the screen was a poem titled "To the Autumn Water Temple" by Xin Qiji of the Southern Song dynasty handwritten by Zhu Zhishan, whose strokes were like flying dragons and dancing phoenixes. The poem, consisting of two hundred and three characters, starting with "the fight of snails" and ending with "a little stream, a little song" filled the screen, which looked majestic because of it. There were two short side tables and four chairs on the sides of the couch, and a bonsai in each of the four corners.

Under the clear sky, the fishing boats traveled to and fro on the lake, white gulls circling, loving, and diving. After Qian Qianyi and his guests climbed from the artificial rock hill beside the pavilion to the second floor, as usual, they went to the south window to overlook the distance for a while, then walked around the place to admire the view on all other sides before finally sitting down at random.

Liu Rushi sat on a chair to the left of the couch. She stared at the calligraphy on the screen for a while and suddenly laughed out loud.

Qian Qianyi and Huixiang felt confused and turned around to look at her. Liu Rushi just smiled without speaking. Qian Qianyi

莫非辛稼轩此词，有何不妥？”

柳如是摇摇头。

“那么，必定是祝枝山这书法有可议之处了？”

柳如是又摇摇头。

“然则夫人何故发笑？”

“我笑把稼轩此词写在这屏风上，不甚切当！”

“啊，此阁为山庄最古之物。当初兴建时，曾祖父因慕辛稼轩之为人，以其瓢泉居第中有秋水观之筑，遂亦名此阁为‘秋水’，并请祝枝山题此词于屏上，却有何不当？”钱谦益的口气有一点急促，显然对于柳如是肆意指摘先人遗泽，颇为不悦。

柳如是却微微一笑：“当日如此安排，自无不妥。唯是就今日而言，却是未免失当了！”

“此话怎讲？”

“稼轩集中，佳作甚多，依妾之见，大可另选一阕，书于屏上，未必就不如此词切当哩！”

“请道其详！”

“譬如，他那首《水龙吟——登建康赏心亭》就脍炙人口，妾亦甚赏之！”柳如是说，顿了顿，忽然又皱起眉毛，“不过此词用典颇多，其中‘求田问舍，怕应羞见，刘郎才气’几句，我就不知何解。”

钱谦益本来准备她提出什么稀奇古怪的说法来，听她这样一说，倒不由得笑起来：“夫人莫非是装糊涂？这几句有何难解！无非是说，那种留恋家室、热衷于经营安乐窝的行为，若与那英雄豪杰的胸襟抱负相比，恐怕是要自惭形秽的了。那几句话，出于《三国志·陈登传》，是刘备教训许汜的话——‘君有国士之名，

couldn't help but ask, all smiles, "Why do you laugh, my dear lady? Is there anything wrong with Xin Jiaxuan's poem?"

Liu Rushi shook her head.

"Is it about Zhishan's calligraphy, then?" Liu Rushi shook her head again.

"Then, why are you laughing, my dear lady?"

"I'm laughing because it's not quite right to have this poem by Jiaxuan on the screen."

"Oh? This pavilion is the oldest thing in the villa. When it was built, my great-grandfather, in admiration of the poet's personality, named it "Autumn Water" after the Autumn Water Pavilion in the Ladle Spring House of Xin Jiaxuan and asked Zhu Zhishan to inscribe the poem on the screen. What's wrong with it, then?" Qian Qianyi said in an irritated tone, obviously dissatisfied with Liu Rushi's impudent criticism of his ancestors.

Liu Rushi smiled slightly, saying, "There's nothing wrong with such an arrangement. It simply doesn't fit this occasion."

"Please explain."

"In my opinion, there're many great poems in the Collected Poems of Jiaxuan. There should be a better poem than this one for this screen."

"Tell me more."

Liu Rushi said, "For example, the poem 'A View from the Joyful Heart Pavilion' is very popular, and I love it too." But she paused with a frown. "But it has too many literary allusions. I don't understand lines like: 'Acquiring land and buying houses, you should be ashamed to see the talent of the young Mr. Liu.'"

Hearing that, Qian Qianyi, prepared to hear something extraordinary, laughed in amusement. "You're pretending not to understand it, aren't you? These lines are pretty easy to understand. They mean that love of the comfort at home is not to be compared with the ambition of the great heroes. They're from "Life of Chen Deng" in *The Chronicles of the Three Kingdoms*, in which Lord Liu Bei of the Shu Kingdom, admonishes Xu Si, "Now the nation is in chaos

今天下大乱，帝王失所，望君忧国忘家，有救世之意；而君求田问舍，言无可采，是元龙所讳也，何缘与君语！如小人，欲卧百尺楼上，卧君于地，何但上下床之间耶！’”

柳如是不动声色地听着，等钱谦益背完了，她就站起来，拍着手笑道：“不错，不错！就把这几句写在屏风上，岂不切当之至！”

钱谦益怔了一下，随即“啊”的一声，也笑起来：“好哇，闹了半天，原来你是拐着弯儿骂我！”

“我岂敢骂相公！”柳如是的神情变得很严肃，“妾身是为相公担忧哟！”

钱谦益望了望柳如是，不再笑了。他静默了一下，迟疑地问：“你、你是说——”

柳如是点点头：“妾身见相公打姑苏回来之后，心也散了，神气也没有了，起用的事也不再提了，同往日像是换了一个人，一天到晚就叨念着修园子、修园子，仿佛天下再没有比这更要紧的事了。这样一蹶不振，怎不教人担忧！”她叹了一口气，看见钱谦益没吱声，接着又说，“如今天下大乱，国步维艰，虽未如汉季之甚，然而来日大难，实未可料。妾身虽系女流，也欲以国士期待相公，望君能忧国忘家，有救世之意！不想相公如今也竟学起许汜之流来，一心求田问舍，正应了刘玄德之所讥而不自知，岂不令妾身大失所望！”

钱谦益起初不以为然地听着，到后来，他的眼睛渐渐睁圆了，眉毛也竖了起来。一种愤急、气恼的神情从他那张黝黑的脸上呈现出来。他动了动嘴唇，显然想说几句激烈的话。可是，发现惠

and the emperor has no place to live. As National Adviser, you should share the destiny of the nation, forget your own family and help save the nation from the crisis, but instead, you're acquiring land, buying houses, and giving no good advice. This is what Chen Deng hates most. How can he speak to you? If it were someone like me, I would sleep atop a hundred-foot tower and let you sleep on the ground—far beyond merely the difference between an upper and lower bed!"

Liu Rushi listened quietly. When Qian Qianyi finished reciting, she stood up, clapping her hands. She said with a smile, "That's perfect. Those words should be inscribed on the screen."

Qian Qianyi mused and then laughed. "Now I see. You're beating around the bush to criticize me."

"How dare I criticize my dear husband?" said Liu Rushi, whose expression became serious. "I've always been worried about you."

Qian Qianyi looked at Liu Rushi and stopped smiling. He was silent for a while and then asked hesitantly, "You, you mean ..."

Liu Rushi nodded and said, "Ever since you came back from Gusu, you've been looking depressed and troubled, without mentioning the matter of reinstatement to office. You have become completely a different person. All you care about is the rebuilding of the garden, as if there were nothing more important in the world than rebuilding the garden. How can I not be worried when you are so downcast?" She sighed, and seeing Qian Qianyi was silent, she continued, "The world is in chaos and the country is in great difficulty. Although it's not as bad as the end of the Han dynasty at the moment, who knows what lies ahead? I'm a woman, but I want my husband to forget the home and do great things for the country in this hour of national crisis. Instead, you're learning from Xu Si, acquiring land and buying houses without knowing that you're exactly the kind of man ridiculed by Lord Liu Bei. You don't know how disappointed I am."

Qian Qianyi listened nonchalantly at first, but later his eyes gradually opened and his eyebrows rose. A look of indignation and annoyance crossed his dark face. He moved his lips to say something harsh, but when he saw Huixiang was watching them silently, he gave

香正在一旁默默地注视着，他就放弃了这种打算，低下头去，半晌，才懊恼地说：“我又何尝甘心如此。不过事到如今，又有什么办法！”

这一次，柳如是没有马上回答。她不客气地瞧了瞧惠香，吩咐道：“红情、绿意，你们先陪惠姑娘到楼下去走走，我们随后就来！”

待惠香等人的脚步声在楼下消失了，她才回过头来，目光灼灼地瞅住钱谦益：“说真的，这一次，我看相公是太胆小！什么周仲驭、陈定生，不就是那几个人么！说他们有多大能耐，我还真不相信！你不见前些日子，陈、钱二位老爷到外面跑了那一阵，附和相公主张的人又何尝少了？此番之败，依妾之见，不败在周仲驭势力太强，而败在相公心志不坚，实行不力。而一败之后，又自甘退守，不图振作。如此谋事，只怕一百年也是枉然！”

“你不知道！”钱谦益也站了起来，烦躁地在阁子内走来走去，“姓周的对我嫉忌甚深，这一次他是故意指着火坑让我跳。就算真办成了，又安知他不会另生枝节！我想过了，与其让他拴着脖子当猴儿耍，倒不如在家管山管水图个清静！”

柳如是冷笑一声：“相公也忒眼浅！你不见崇祯元年至于今，才只十五年，宰辅已换了四十余人。凡领此衔者，多则一载，少则半月，便又去职。我就不信他周阁老能久占此位！相公若不预作绸缪，还埋头修这劳什子山庄，只怕到时又要坐失良机哩！”

钱谦益被她一言点醒，顿时不作声了。他呆了半晌，才喃喃地问：“嗯，那么，该怎么办？”

“依妾身之见，”柳如是胸有成竹地说，“眼下周仲驭之流

it up, lowered his head, and, after a long while, said with vexation, "I don't want to be resigned to fate like this, but things having come to such a state, what else can I do?"

This time, Liu Rushi didn't immediately respond. She looked unceremoniously at Huixiang and said, "Hongqing, Lüyi, you take Miss Huixiang for a walk. We'll come later."

When the footsteps of Huixiang and others receded down the stairs, she turned and looked at Qian Qianyi with burning eyes. "Seriously, this time, I think you're too timid. You don't have to be afraid of Zhou Zhongyu and Chen Dingsheng. They're but a handful of men. I really don't believe they'll amount to anything. Don't you realize that after Mr. Chen and Mr. Qian's trips there have been more supporters for you? The current setback, in my humble opinion, isn't the result of Zhou Zhongyu's powerful influence but the result of your lack of will and action. It's just one setback and then you've lost heart and started retreating. Doing things like this, you wouldn't succeed even in a hundred years."

"You don't underhand." Qian Qianyi also stood up. He paced around in the pavilion irritatedly. "This Zhou guy is very jealous of me. He's setting me up. Even if it went well, there would be no guarantee that he wouldn't do something to thwart it in the end. So, I'd rather take care of the garden at home than be led by the nose."

Liu Rushi said with a sneer, "How come you're so short-sighted? Don't you see that in the fifteen years from the first year of the reign of Emperor Chongzhen [AD 1628] to this day the Prime Minister has changed more than forty times? Nobody holds the position for more than a year, some as short as half a month. I don't believe he'll hold it long either. Get prepared and don't waste your time on the mountainside residence so that you won't miss another good opportunity."

She was right. Qian Qianyi went silent. He mused for a long time and then muttered, "Well, then, what should I do?"

"In my opinion," Liu Rushi said confidently. "The likes of Zhou Zhongyu are currently publicizing what happened at the Tiger Hill

正四处播扬虎丘之事，相公决不能坐视其猖獗，须得赶快派人出去，联络当初附和我们的人，力斥其非。如此，方不至于株守自困，受制于人！”

“对！”钱谦益兴奋地站起来，“夫人真不愧女中豪杰！好，我这就去回绝计无否，然后就……”

柳如是微微一笑：“相公不必去了。妾身早已命李宝把他们打发走了！”

钱谦益吃了一惊：“啊，你——什么时候，怎么我不知道？”

“就在刚才——我回身去寻珠钗的时候。”柳如是得意地说，“那时相公正在打我那惠香妹子的主意哩，哪里会知道！”

Conference. You shouldn't sit by and watch it escalate. You must defend yourself by sending someone as soon as possible to contact those who have agreed with us in the beginning and explain the situation to them. This way, you can turn the tide and take things into your own hands."

"Well said!" Qian Qianyi exclaimed excitedly. "My dear lady is a wise woman indeed. Yes, I'll tell Mr. Ji that I am not going to rebuild the garden home, and then ..."

Liu Rushi smiled slightly, "Don't bother. I've asked Li Bao to send them away."

Qian Qianyi was stunned. "Ah? You — when? Why don't I know it?"

"A moment ago. When I left to look for the pearl hairpin," Liu Rushi said proudly. "When you were obsessed with Sister Huixiang. How can you know?"

# 第八章

# 游金山泪承谑吻，走尸林悲动长吟

## 金山遇友

黄宗羲终于决定同方以智结伴北上，到京师去游历，并且就近在那里参加今年八月的乡试。三月底，他离开苏州上嘉兴去，找到正在那里访友的二弟黄宗炎，筹措了一笔旅费，并把老母和家事托付给宗炎和另一个弟弟宗会照料。随后，黄宗羲便带着书童黄安重新北上，计划在四月底赶到镇江，同约定在那里等候的方以智会合。黄宗羲这一次赴京应考的目的，固然是打算把他那个上书朝廷的计划付诸实施，而在此之前，还想亲眼瞧一瞧朝廷的情形，估计一下时局将会如何发展；但另一方面，经历了虎丘大会那一场风波之后，也使他决定暂时改换一下环境。

那件事，对黄宗羲的震动和刺激确实很大。他做梦也没想到，这桩卑鄙阴谋的策划者不是别人，恰恰就是自己一向崇敬和信赖

Chapter Eight

# In Which Mao Xiang Was Teased Into Kissing the Tearful Dong Xiaowan on Their Tour of Jinshan Island and Huang Zongxi Was Deeply Saddened to Walk Among the Dead in an Elm Grove on His Way to the Northern Capital

## An Appointment at Jinshan

Huang Zongxi finally decided to go north with Fang Yizhi. They would travel to the capital and sit for the provincial session of the imperial examination in August. At the end of March, he left Suzhou and went to Jiaxing, where he found his second younger brother, Huang Zongyan, who was visiting friends there. He took some money from Zongyan for his travel expenses and told him to take care of their mother and family matters together with another younger brother Zonghui. After that, Huang Zongxi continued his journey north, accompanied by his page Huang An. He planned to arrive in Zhenjiang at the end of April to meet Fang Yizhi, who had agreed to wait there. The reason why Huang Zongxi had decided to take the exam in Beijing instead of his home province was of course that he wanted to carry out his plan to petition to the imperial court, but before doing that, he wanted to size up the situation of the court with his own eyes. Besides, after the turmoil at the Tiger Hill Conference, he needed a break.

That incident had indeed shocked and upset Huang Zongxi. He had never expected the mastermind of such a diabolical conspiracy

的钱谦益！仅仅在事情大白的前一天，自己还不辞辛苦地跑去拜见他，恳求他出来主持大局。一想到自己是如此愚蠢幼稚，对方又是如此虚伪奸诈，黄宗羲的心里就充满了愤怒、痛苦和羞愧的感情："哼，仅仅为着复官起用，为着他自己的功名富贵，便置天下大义于不顾，干出这等寡廉鲜耻的事情来！还亏他是个东林耆宿，怎么配！怎么对得起以身殉志的东林列位先贤！这些年，我真是瞎了眼，错看了他，完完全全地错看了……"近两个月来，黄宗羲一直被这种心情困扰着。他不止一次地想到，应当赶到常熟去，当面向钱谦益提出质问，并毫不客气地表明，如今自己是多么鄙视他！甚至要说的话，黄宗羲都准备好了。他一再兴奋地想象着他们一旦见面时的情景：自己如何声色俱厉，义正词严；对方则丧魂落魄，呆若木鸡……不过，说也奇怪，当他认真地考虑要采取行动时，心里又踌躇起来。他发现自己其实并不愿意看见钱谦益，甚至还有点怕看见他。"嗯，不，不是害怕，而是讨厌！对的，这样的人，如果出现在我的面前，我只怕会作呕的！"他这样自我解释说。所以，这一次，当他乘坐的天平船行经苏州时，也就没有绕道到常熟去，而是继续沿运河北上，径直前往镇江。

不过，说实在的，即使不是那样，黄宗羲此刻也没有心思再去理会钱谦益。因为一路之上，到处都在哄传着令人吃惊的关于时局的种种噩讯，把他的情绪弄得十分激动、紧张。这些消息照例分成两类：一类是关于"流寇"的。说是李自成数万大军围困明朝总兵左良玉于河南郾城，朝廷命陕西、三边总督汪乔年率兵驰援，结果在襄城兵败。李自成攻破城池，活捉了汪乔年，把他

was none other than Qian Qianyi, whom he had always respected and trusted. Just a day before the conspiracy came to light, he had been to the old man's home to beg him to come forward and watch over things. As he thought how stupid and naive he was and how hypocritical and treacherous the old man was, Huang Zongxi's heart was filled with anger, pain and shame. "Hmph, he's done such a shameless thing for his reinstatement to office, for his own fame and fortune, with no sense of right and wrong at all. And he's a respected East Wood elder! How can he be worthy of the respect? How can he answer to the East Wood martyrs? How blind I've been all over the years! I've been completely blind ..." he thought to himself. For the past two months, Huang Zongxi had been tormented by such thoughts. More than once, he wanted to rush to Changshu and interrogate Qian Qianyi in person. He should tell the old man without ceremony how much he now despised him. He had even prepared what to say. Time and time again, he excitedly imagined the scene of their encounter: how indignant he would be and how stunned and dumbfounded the old man would be ... But curiously, when he was going to take action, he hesitated. He found that he actually didn't want to see Qian Qianyi, and was even a little scared to see him. "Well, no, it's not fear, but disgust. Yes, when such a person appears before me, I'll be nauseous," he explained to himself. Therefore, when the transport boat he was riding passed Suzhou, he didn't detour to Changshu, but instead continued to go north along the canal and went straight to Zhenjiang.

To be honest, even if it were not so, Huang Zongxi would not have had the time to think about Qian Qianyi at this moment, because along the way, all sorts of shocking bad news about the current situation came. He was concerned and worried. As usual, there were two categories of news. One was about the rebels. Tens of thousands of Li Zicheng's rebel troops were said to have besieged Chief Commander Zuo Liangyu and his troops in Yancheng, Henan Province. The court had ordered Wang Qiaonian, chief commissioner to the northwest border, to reinforce Zuo Liangyu. However, Wang Qiaonian was defeated at Xiangyang. Li Zicheng had broken through

杀死在城外，左良玉则逃到湖广去了。如今李自成连陷西华、陈州、睢州、太康、宁陵、考城、归德之后，再次进围开封。与此同时，张献忠、革里眼、左金王等“贼”军则攻陷了安徽的含山、和州、庐州。南京为之震动，已宣布戒严云云。另一类是关于“建虏”的。据说山海关外的松山城已于二月十九日最后失守，总督洪承畴死战力竭，被俘不屈，已经壮烈殉国；同时被害的还有巡抚邱民仰、总兵王廷臣、曹变蛟等。又说，位于松山附近的锦州也被清军攻陷，守将祖大寿率众投降。这一连串的噩耗，把黄宗羲惊得目瞪口呆。虽然这些年来，他听到的全是这一类的坏消息，几乎已经习以为常，而且像松山陷落这种结局，本来也是预计到了的。可是几件事合在一起，突然传进耳朵里，黄宗羲仍然感到异常震惊。特别是松山一战，实在关系重大。如今一败，山海关屏障尽失，形势便岌岌可危了。黄宗羲痛心焦虑之余，对洪承畴的壮烈殉国，又非常钦佩赞叹，觉得大丈夫立身处世，正当如此。他并不认识洪承畴，而且前些日子，他同朋友们谈到松山战事时，还激烈地攻击过洪承畴，说他这一次全军覆没，全在于指挥无能、畏敌如虎之故。可是那一切，如今似乎都不重要了。洪承畴的形象在黄宗羲的心目中忽然变得高大起来，并且被赋予不平凡的意义。“不管怎么说，作为社稷重臣，他是竭尽孤忠，完了大节！同他相比，钱牧斋真该愧死了！”他感慨地想，希望知道更多一些洪承畴就义的情形。可是打听的结果，说法却很不一致，有的

the city, captured Wang Qiaonian alive and killed him outside the city, while Zuo Liangyu had fled to Huguang Province. Li Zicheng, after successively capturing Xihua, Chenzhou, Suizhou, Taikang, Ningling, Kaocheng and Guide, was laying siege to Kaifeng again. At the same time, Zhang Xianzhong, He Yilong the Popeye, "King of Zuojin" He Jin, and other rebel leaders had captured Hanshan, Hezhou, and Luzhou in Anhui Province. Nanjing was shaken by it, and martial law was declared. The other category was about the Jurchens. Songshan City outside Shanhai Pass was said to have finally been lost on the nineteenth of February. Governor Hong Chengchou, after failing to defend the city, had been captured and martyred together with Governor Qiu Minyang, commanders Wang Yanchen and Cao Bianjiao, among others. It was also said that Jinzhou, which was close to Songshan, had also been captured by the Qing army, and garrison commander Zu Dashou had surrendered with his troops. Huang Zongxi was shocked by the series of bad news. Although he had been used to this kind of bad news and the fall of Songshan was something expected, when things came together, he was still shocked. The Battle of Songshan was of great importance. The loss of Songshan meant the loss of the protection of the Shanhai Pass. The situation was dire. While being worried about the situation, Huang Zongxi admired Hong Chengchou's heroic death and felt that it was exactly what a man should do under such circumstances. He didn't know Hong Chengchou personally. A few days ago, when he was talking to his friends about the Songshan war, he had vehemently attacked Hong Chengchou, saying that it was the incompetence and lack of courage on the part of the commander that had led to an entire army being wiped out by the enemy. All that didn't seem to matter now. The image of Hong Chengchou suddenly became larger in Huang Zongxi's mind, and was endowed with a great significance. "No matter what, as one of the country's most important officials, he's done his utmost to stay loyal to the country and has died a martyr. Compared to him, Qian Muzhai should be ashamed," he mused. He wanted to learn more about Hong Chengchou's heroic death only to find the stories were

说是死于城破后的巷战，有的说是被俘后绝食而死，还有的说他绝食未死，是后来自缢殉国的。“嗯，赶快到镇江去，那里来往的人多，一定能打听到！”这样拿定主意之后，黄宗羲觉得自己的心情仍然平静不下来，忠臣烈士们舍身报国的崇高行为久久激动着他，使他热血沸腾，心神震荡。“啊，我得赶快抓紧，而且，要更认真一些！”他想，于是立即吩咐黄安从行囊里拿出他的那一份上书的草稿。他靠坐在船舱前，定一定神，然后埋下头去，一字一句地推敲起来……

直到农历四月的最后一天，黄宗羲乘坐的船，才来到镇江城北的北固山下。因为事先同方以智约定的会合地点是金山寺，所以黄宗羲没有进城，吩咐船家径直往西，摇到金山去。

金山又名龙游山，是矗立在长江上的一座小岛，离城也有五六里远近，与焦山、北固山崎角相望。山上树木扶疏，雄伟壮观的金山寺从山下一直修到山顶，远远望去，只见一重一重的台阶，一段一段的院墙，一幢一幢的殿宇，一道一道的廊阁，向两旁迤逦延伸，把整座山层层包裹起来。飞檐和高阁上的彩绘，被上午的阳光照耀得闪闪发光。山顶上的慈寿塔，在晴空下巍然屹立，显得分外肃穆庄严。

“大爷，《白蛇传》说的‘水漫金山’，可就是这个金山？”黄安伸长了本来就细长的脖子，睁大一双圆鼓鼓的眼睛，盯着越来越近的金山，好奇地问。他是头一回上镇江来，对周围的一切都感到格外新鲜。

“不错，是这山。”黄宗羲点点头，同时对今天山上游人之

very inconsistent. Some said he had died of street fighting after the fall of the city, some said he had starved himself to death after being captured, some said he hanged himself after failing to starve himself to death. "Well, I'd better hurry to Zhenjiang. There're a lot more people coming and going there and I'll definitely be able to find out." Having made up his mind, Huang Zongxi still couldn't calm down. His blood was boiling and his heart was racing, moved by the sublime deeds of the martyrs who had sacrificed their lives for the country. "Oh, I should hurry and do the best as I can," he thought. Then, he asked Huang An to take the draft of his petition letter out of his luggage and sat down in front of the cabin to study it word by word with his head lowered, making a correction from time to time ...

On the last day of April, Huang Zongxi's boat arrived at the foot of Beigu Mountain in northern Zhenjiang city. Because the place to meet Fang Yizhi was the Jinshan Temple, Huang Zongxi didn't enter the city. He ordered the boatman to go straight west and row to Jinshan.

Jinshan, or the Gold Mountain, also known as the Dragon Mountain, was actually a small island in the Yangtze River, five or six *li* away from the city, forming a triangle with the Jiao Mountain and the Beigu Mountain in the distance. The island was densely populated with trees, and the majestic Jinshan Temple had been built from the bottom of the mountain all the way to the top. Seen from a distance, it was a series of stairs, courtyard walls, temple palaces, corridors, and pavilions snaking around the mountain in close layers. The colorful paintings on the cornices and the high pavilions sparkled under the morning sun. The Longevity Pagoda on top of the mountain, which stood majestically under the clear sky, looked serene and sublime.

"My young master, is this the Gold Mountain flooded in *The Legend of the White Snake*?" asked Huang An curiously, gazing at the mountain that was coming closer and closer, his slender neck stretched, his bulging eyes opened wide. It was his first visit to Zhenjiang, and he was curious about everything around him.

"Correct! It's the same mountain," Huang Zongxi nodded,

多感到有点惊奇：嗯，瞧这密密麻麻的样子，只怕少说也有好几千人哩！他们都是做什么来了？

“那么，禅杖还在么？”黄安又问。

“什么禅杖？”

“自然是法海禅师的禅杖呀，会变金龙的！”

“蠢材，哪有什么变龙的禅杖！一个话本故事罢咧，你也当真了！”

黄安眨眨眼睛：“那么，韩蕲王[1]大破金兵——也是没有的了？”

“嗯，这却是有的。”

“那么黄天荡……”

“在那边。”黄宗羲朝西一指，“远着呢，你瞧不见。”

“哦——小人听说，本朝洪经略相公文武双全，也是韩蕲王一流的人物哩！”

黄宗羲“唔”了一声，没有马上回答，脸色变得阴沉起来，半晌，才叹了一口气：“洪经略自是难得的帅才，可惜……”他正要说下去，忽然，天平船剧烈地摇晃起来，一艘涂饰得红红绿绿的大游船正挨着船舷驶过。船上坐着几个缙绅模样的男子，正围着一个浓妆艳抹的妖冶女人在吃酒打闹。江风拂处，传来一串吃吃的艳笑。黄宗羲不由得皱起眉头，重重“哼”了一声。

黄安兀自愣愣地目送着如飞而去的游船，只听船家在舱外大声说：“今儿是四月三十，这些人莫不是来瞧赛龙船的？”

端午节虽说是五月初五，可是这一带向来的习惯，龙船总是提前好几天就开始出动。“怪道今天山上游人如此之多！”黄宗

① 韩蕲王：指南宋抗金将领韩世忠。

slightly surprised at seeing so many people on the mountain today. "Well, look at the crowds! There're thousands of people, I'm afraid. What are they doing here?"

"Then, is the Zen staff still there?" Huang An asked.

"Which Zen staff?"

"That of Zen Master Fahai, of course. The one that can turn into a golden dragon."

"Idiot, there's no Zen staff that can turn into a dragon. It's just a legend and you're believing it."

Huang An winked, saying, "Then, the story of Han Shizhong[①] defeating the Jin invaders isn't real either?"

"Well, that one is real."

"What about the Battle of the Huangtian Swamp[②]..."

"The Huangtian Swamp is over there," Huang Zongxi said, pointing to the west. "It's too far. You can't see it."

"Oh. I hear Viceroy Hong of our time is also a good scholar and a great warrior in one person like Han Shizhong."

Huang Zongxi said uh and didn't immediately respond, his face gloomy. After a while he sighed, "Viceroy Hong is a great commander, but unfortunately ..." As he spoke, his boat started to shake violently. A large painted cruise boat passed by. On the boat, a few men who looked like officials were eating, drinking, and frolicking with a richly-dressed and heavily-powdered woman, whose wanton laughter drifted over with the wind. Huang Zongxi knit his brows and snorted.

As Huang An's gaze followed the cruise boat flying away, the boatman said loudly from outside the cabin, "Today is April 30th. Probably they're here to see the dragon boat competition."

Although the Dragon Boat Festival was on May 5th in the lunar calendar, it was a custom in this area that the dragon boats came out

---

① Han Shizhong (AD 1089–1151), also known as Han Zhongwu and Han Qiwang, among other names, was a military commander of the South Song dynasty.

② Huangtian Swamp is an ancient place name. The Battle of Huangtian Swamp took place in AD 1130 between the Southern Song army led by Han Shizhong and the Jin army led by Wushu.

羲恍然想道，这么一来，心里更感到不快："屈原忠心为国，遭小人谗害，屡遭斥逐而矢志不渝！他忧伤宗国沦亡，悲愤自沉，欲以一死以励后人，高风亮节，千古共钦！不期今日，却反成了醉生梦死之辈寻欢作乐的题目，真是可恨可叹！"想到这里，他不由得又"哼"了一声。

这当儿，天平船已来到金山脚下。因为挤聚在码头上的船只很多，上岸时着实费了不少工夫。黄宗羲领着黄安，在人丛中挨挤着，进了山门，穿过天王殿，从大殿后绕过去，刚刚登上一道带石栏的台阶，就听见江面上响起了"咚咚锵！咚咚锵！"的鼓钹声。周围的游人"哄"的一声，都朝山上拥去。黄宗羲立脚不住，被一下子挤到角落里。回头一看，却不见了黄安。他急了，提高嗓门喊了几声，倒是有了答应。原来那小书童因为挑着担子，转身不灵，又一心想瞧赛龙船，反而被挤到了栏杆边上，主仆二人现在相距就七八步远。可是人群不知为什么又停住不动了。黄宗羲挤了几下，挤不过去，不禁情急起来，大声嚷道："哎，你们堆在这儿做什么，快快让我过去！"近旁的几个人回头瞧了瞧，见他是个儒生，倒也稍稍向两旁让了让。可是一来游人实在太多，而且看来前头又给堵住了，无法动弹。也有些人见黄宗羲不过是个衣着朴素的穷秀才，没把他放在眼里，仍然挤着不动。黄宗羲哪有心思瞧什么赛龙船，他眼见自己过不去，黄安又出不来，心想：这一耽搁，不知要拖延多少时候！于是，又跺着脚叫嚷道："你们听见没有？快快让我过去！听见没有？"

"哎，这位相公，非是小人存心不让，实在人太多……"站

a few days in advance. "No wonder that there're so many people in the mountain today," Huang Zongxi suddenly understood, looking gloomier. "Qu Yuan was a great patriot. Slandered by little men, he was exiled again and again, but his loyalty to his kingdom never wavered. When his kingdom fell, he drowned himself in great sorrow, hoping his death would wake up his people. His glorious act has been remembered and he's been worshiped by all posterity. Yet deplorably, the memorial day has become an occasion for these hateful men to seek pleasure." Thus thinking, he couldn't help but give another snort.

The transport boat came to the foot of the Gold Mountain. Because there were many boats crowded at the pier, it took quite some time to get ashore. Huang Zongxi and Huang An, jostling with the crowd, entered the mountain gate and passed the Palace of Four Heavenly Kings. As they climbed a flight of steps with stone railings on both sides, drums and cymbals sounded on the river. The tourists swarmed up the mountain. Huang Zongxi lost balance and was pushed to a corner. He turned around and found Huang An missing. In a panic, he called out to the boy, who replied from the crowd. It turned out the boy, who was unable to move with the luggage on his shoulder pole while eager to see the dragon boat competition, had been pushed onto the railing. Master and servant were merely seven or eight steps away from each other. For some reason, the crowd stopped. Huang Zongxi tried to elbow his way toward Huang An without success. He became worried and shouted loudly, "Hey, what are you doing here? Let me pass." A few people nearby looked back and, seeing that he was a young scholar, stepped to the sides. However, there being too many tourists, his way was blocked again and he couldn't move. Some people ignored him and continued to jostle, seeing that he was no more than a poor scholar in ordinary clothes. Huang Zongxi couldn't go over to Huang An, nor could the servant boy come over to him. He didn't care about the dragon boat competition. He was worried about the delay that would be caused. So, he stomped his feet and shouted, "Do you hear me? Let me pass. Do you hear me?"

"Sorry, sir! I don't mean to stand in your way. There're simply

在跟前的一个店伙模样的小伙子被他迫急了，回过头来，委屈地说。

“嘻嘻，这龙船又不是他家的，人人都看得，凭什么要人家让道？莫非那船上坐得有他的干娘么？”一个油腔滑调的声音说，周围的人听了，倒有一半哄笑起来。

“尔等休得放肆！”一个深厚的声音制止说。那是位衣着华丽的中年儒生，长着一部浓密的大胡子，他回头对黄宗羲点点头：“尊驾请勿焦躁，你我既置于此地，正所谓形格势禁，只有安心等候而已。”

黄宗羲仿佛没有听见，他睁大了眼睛，怒气冲冲地环视着众人，突然厉声叫道：“大明的江山就要亡了！你们还这等安心么？”

这句话，犹如炸响了一记霹雳。人们哆嗦了一下，都惊悚地回过头来，呆呆地瞪着黄宗羲，一个个脸上都现出错愕、恐怖的神情。站在近旁的几个，更是不由自主地向两旁闪开，给他让出一条道来。黄宗羲紧咬着嘴唇，一声不响地走过去，扯住黄安，回头就走。这一次，没有任何阻碍，人们畏缩地退向两旁，呆若木鸡地目送着这个来历不明的、在此时此地向他们发出可怕预言的奇怪书生，摸不透这一主一仆究竟是疯子，还是秉承天帝意旨来向人间示警的神人。要不然，他怎敢在大庭广众之中说出这等不顾死活的话来呢？

黄宗羲挤出了重围之后，领着黄安又登上一重石阶，然后向右一拐，正打算绕过妙高台后面，径直上楞伽台去。忽然前面起了骚动，像刚才争看龙船那样，人们猛地向前挤拥了一下，随即又忙不迭地后退，照例又把黄宗羲挤在一边。黄安这一次倒有了经验，寸步不离地跟着主人。“哎，又是怎么回事？”黄宗羲气恼地想。这时候，人们继续向两旁后退，让出当中一条道来。与

too many people..." A young man standing in front of him, who looked like a shop assistant, turned around and aggrievedly replied to his urging.

"He-he, the dragon boat doesn't belong to him. Everyone can see it. Why should anybody give way to him? Is his adopted mother sitting on the boat?" said an oily voice, and many of the people around laughed.

"Don't be rude," a deep voice said to them. It was a decently dressed middle-aged scholar with a bushy beard, who turned to Huang Zongxi, nodded to him and said, "Don't worry, sir! Now that you and I are here without being able to move, we can do nothing but wait with patience."

As if not having heard it, Huang Zongxi angrily looked around with wide-open eyes and suddenly shouted sharply, "How can you be so happy while the Great Ming is in danger of ruin?"

That sentence was like a thunderclap. People shivered and turned around. Stunned and frightened, they stared at Huang Zongxi. The ones who stood nearby involuntarily stepped aside to make room for him. Biting his lip, Huang Zongxi walked quietly over, grabbed Huang An, and turned to leave. This time, there was no more hindrance, because people had coweringly stepped to the sides. They dumbfoundedly stared at this strange young scholar of unknown origin, who had given them a terrible prophecy, wondering whether he and his servant were lunatics or messengers sent by Providence, because no ordinary person dared to say such dangerous words in public.

After Huang Zongxi broke through the siege, he and Huang An ascended another flight of steps, then turned right to pass the Wonderful Heights Terrace from behind and go straight to the Lanka Terrace. Suddenly there was a commotion in front of them, like the one about the dragon boat just now. People suddenly rushed forward, and then hurriedly stepped back and like a moment ago jostled Huang Zongxi aside. Huang An, now experienced, followed his master every step of the way. "Ah, what's this one about?" Huang Zongxi thought with irritation. People kept stepping back to the sides, leaving a path in the

此同时，全场变得鸦雀无声，大家都伸长脖子，瞪大眼睛，仿佛着了魔似的，一动不动地瞧着正从妙高台那边走下来的一男一女。那个女郎约摸十八九岁，穿一袭薄如蝉翼的西洋红夏布短衫，退红衬里，皮肤白皙，体态轻盈。虽然她手里拿着一柄生绡白团扇，轻轻遮住了半张脸蛋，只露出一双略带几分忧郁的、梦幻似的大眼睛，可是一望而知，必定是位绝色丽人。不过，如果仅仅是她，也许还不至于引起这样的轰动，因为尤其令人惊叹的，是与她并肩同行的那个男子，竟然也是个美得令人目眩的人物。他儒生打扮，一身素白，手上摆弄着一柄折扇，俊美的脸上带着一种漠然的、懒洋洋的神情。他微微昂着头，在人们自动让出来的路上不慌不忙地走着，就像漫步在自己家中的庭院里那样自然。而对于周围投来的惊愕、叹赏、妒羡的目光根本不当一回事。显然，这一切对他来说早已习以为常，既不会使他不安，也不能令他产生任何兴奋了。

"啊，原来是他！他也来了镇江——只不知那女子是谁？是陈圆圆？不，一定不是。那么……"当黄宗羲认出这位风度翩翩的美男子便是一个月前在苏州分手的冒襄之后，心里本能地冲动了一下，打算走上前去同他相见。可是只一瞬间，这种冲动就消退了。与此同时，一种阴沉而有力的思想抓住了他："哼，国事败坏到如此地步，一面立志要拯救社稷苍生，一面却迷恋于醇酒妇人，这是荒唐的！以往我同他们混在一块的时候太多了，今后决不能再这样！"所以，尽管冒襄就在眼前经过，黄宗羲却别转了脸。等游人稍稍散开之后，他就领着黄安循路登山，径直找方以智去了。

## 各怀心事

黄宗羲的反感，冒襄无疑是不了解的。他甚至不知道黄宗羲站在人从当中注视过他，因为他压根儿没有留意周围的人。他正一心一意在考虑：到底用什么办法，才能把身边这个董小宛打发走。

middle. At the same time, everyone was silent, and as if possessed by demons, craned their necks with their eyes wide open to stare at a man and a woman walking down the Wonderful Heights Terrace. The young woman, fair-skinned and sprightly, eighteen or nineteen years of age, wore a blouse of scarlet ramie cloth with a pink lining. Although a white fan made of unbleached silk in her hand hid half of her face, only revealing a pair of melancholic, dreamy eyes, one could see at a glance that she was a great beauty. More importantly, the man walking beside her was of even greater beauty. He was a young scholar dressed in white, with a folding fan in his hand and an expression of nonchalance and lethargy on his handsome face. His head slightly raised, he walked unhurriedly on the path that people had yielded to him, as if he were walking in his own courtyard, totally oblivious to the surprise, admiration, and envy, to which he was so accustomed that they could neither disturb him or excite him in any way.

"Oh, it's him! He has also come to Zhenjiang—I just don't know who that woman is. Is it Chen Yuanyuan? No, it can't be. Then ..." When Huang Zongxi recognized this handsome young man as Mao Xiang, who he had met in Suzhou a month ago, he instinctively wanted to greet him, but soon that impulse subsided. He was stopped by a ponderous thought: "Hmph, what hypocrisy it is to be obsessed with wine and women while vowing to save the country from ruin and the people from suffering in this hour of national crisis! Having wasted too much time hanging out with them, I won't do it again in the future." Therefore, when Mao Xiang passed him, Huang Zongxi turned his face away. When the tourists began to disperse, he climbed up the top of the mountain to look for Fang Yizhi.

## Two Men, Two Minds

Mao Xiang no doubt had no idea that Huang Zongxi was disgusted with him. He didn't even know that Huang Zongxi was standing in the crowd watching him, because he didn't pay any attention to the people around him at all. He was thinking what method he could use to get rid of Dong Xiaowan.

现在冒襄颇为后悔，当初他一时心软，竟答应让董小宛随船相送。他是这样想的：尽管董小宛的动机十分可疑，但只要自己把得稳，她到头来也只能是枉费心思而已。可是，随着旅程的推移，冒襄越来越意识到，这个想法过于简单了。因为董小宛显然不是那种容易摆脱的女子。这倒不在于她是多么地善于胡搅蛮缠；而是由于她的坚定和固执，以致在长达二十七天的旅途中，冒襄试图劝导她离船的一切努力都归于白费。她不仅像一个最温柔体贴的妻子、一名最驯良服从的奴仆那样侍候着冒襄，使他领略到包括在同陈圆圆一起时，都不曾有过的舒服和适意；而且，她还像一位最知心而多才多艺的腻友、一位最忠实而聪明的学生那样，同冒襄娓娓谈心，陪他弹琴、下棋、抹牌、度曲，怀着专注和崇敬的神情，聆听着冒襄的教诲，并时不时以一两句令人解颐的妙语来表示她的颖悟……恰恰是这样一些缘故，迅速消解了最初冒襄因她强行相送所引起的恼怒，使她在冒襄的感觉中不再是一个陌生、隔膜、居心叵测的风尘女子，而变得较为值得亲近和可以理解了。所以，每当她坚持着要再送一程时，冒襄竟然感到很难板得起脸孔、狠得下心肠。不过，这也就使他暗暗吃惊，觉得事情有点不妙，意识到有堕入对方设置的感情陷阱里去的危险。哪怕现在已经弄清楚，这是一个不含恶意的陷阱，但他仍然不愿意。“这是不可能的！无论如何，她比不上圆圆，比不上！况且，我既然失去了最好的，又岂能退而求其次，白白招人笑话！”他冷冷地想。所以，抵达镇江之后，冒襄就决定当机立断。今天一早，他特意带了董小宛来登金山，打算尽兴一游之后，就此把她打发走。谁知刚才在妙高台上，没等他提出来，董小宛就像猜测到他的心思似的，竟抢先指着大江发誓，说什么“妾此身有如江水东下，断不复返吴门！”他大吃一惊，当即板起脸孔，严词拒绝。随后，也不管小宛已是神色惨淡，仿佛马上要哭出来的样子，他立即就动身下山。不过，虽然已经把话说清楚，但董

Now Mao Xiang regretted succumbing to Dong Xiaowan's request to accompany him on the boat. He had thought her calculations would be a waste of time as long as he was determined, but as the journey progressed, he increasingly realized that he was too naive, because she was obviously not the kind of woman to get rid of easily. Not that she was unreasonable, but that she was so determined that during the twenty-seven-day boat trip all his attempts to persuade her to leave the boat were in vain. Not only did she serve him like a tender, loving wife or a loyal and obedient servant, giving him comfort and consolation he had never had with Chen Yuanyuan, but also conversed with him, attended him while he composed music, played chess, cards, or the zither with dedication and deference, listening to his pedantry attentively and from time to time cutting in one or two witty words, like a most understanding friend or a highly-intelligent and most dedicated pupil ... It was precisely for these reasons that his anger caused by the imposition of her will on him was quickly dispelled so that he felt she was more lovable and pitiable than a strange and incomprehensible prostitute with a motive, which he had thought she was. Therefore, when she insisted on accompanying him further, he felt it difficult to refuse her outright. He was surprised to find he had almost fallen into an emotional trap she had set for him. Even though the trap might not be malicious, he didn't want to fall into it. "It's impossible. She's by no means to be compared to Chen Yuanyuan. Besides, I'll be a laughing stock when I take the second best after failing to get the best," he thought coldly. After arrival at Zhenjiang, he made up his mind to let her go. Early in the morning today, he came with her to the Gold Mountain, intending to send her away after the tour. To his dismay, on the Wonderful Heights Terrace just now, before he broached the subject, she pointed to the river and swore, as if having guessed what he was thinking, "I'll never go back, like the water flowing downward." That stunned him. He immediately pulled a long face and refused her with no kind words. Her expression suddenly dimmed and tears welled up in her eyes. He didn't care and decided to go down the mountain immediately. However, he continued

小宛是否就会听从，冒襄却仍旧有点吃不准。所以，一路上，他都在继续打主意。他已经下定决心，无论如何，这一次决不能让步了。

现在，他们已经走出了山门，站立在三间四柱石坊之下。时近晌午，江面上龙船的钲鼓声经过前一阵子的大敲大打之后，正沉寂下去。江岸上依旧人头攒拥，大约是在等候观看第二轮的比赛。今天游金山，本来张明弼也同他们一块儿来了，不过他知道冒襄有要紧的话要同小宛谈，船一靠岸，就借口去访本寺的住持，管自走了。这会儿，冒襄估计他可能已经回船了，便也朝码头走去。

“公子，”行出几步之后，默默地跟在身后的董小宛忽然叫住他，“龙船很快又赛起来了，我们顺着这岸边再走走，好么？”她嫣然微笑着，要求说。

冒襄瞅了瞅她，倒感到有点意外。“嗯，莫非她到底想通了？”他想。本来无心再走，但对方既然提出来，冒襄也不想显得过于小气。而且，只要对方不提婚嫁的事，别的他倒无所谓。于是他点点头，还特意停了一下，等小宛走到同他并肩时，才一起沿着岸边的石堤，慢慢向前走去。亲随冒成和一名挑食担的仆人见主人不回船，也只好继续在后面跟着。

这当儿，“咚咚锵！咚咚锵！”的鼓钹声重新响起来。五艘龙船冲波激浪，出现在江面上。这些龙船，都安装着精工雕刻的龙头和龙尾，一条条昂首奋鬣，鳞甲鲜明。船上搭起了漂亮的彩篷，前后插着旗、幢[①]和绣伞之类，迎风飘扬。后梢的兵器架上，刀枪剑戟森然罗列。二十名精壮汉子，扎缚得紧凑威武，分两排坐在又狭又长的船舱里。每人手中都拿着一柄大桨，应和着本船

① 幢：古代原指支撑帐幕、伞盖、旌旗的木杆，后借指帐幕、伞盖、旌旗。

to ponder on the matter all the way, since he was not sure whether Dong Xiaowan had taken in what he had clearly said. No matter what, he would not give in this time. He made up his mind.

They walked out the mountain gate and stood under the three-section four-pillar stone arch. It was almost noon, and the sounds of cymbals and drums on the dragon boats were trailing off. The riverbank was still full of people who were probably waiting to watch the second round of the competition. Zhang Mingbi had come with them on this current trip to the Gold Mountain, but knowing that Mao Xiang needed time to have a serious conversation with Dong Xiaowan, he left alone as soon as the boat docked, excusing himself by saying he was going to see the abbot of the monastery. Thinking that Mingbi might have returned to the boat by now, Mao Xiang walked toward the pier.

After a few steps, Dong Xiaowan, who was quietly following behind, stopped him. "Sir," she said, smilingly. "The dragon boats will start racing again shortly. Let's walk along the bank."

Mao Xiang gave her a glance and was a little surprised. "Well, she's finally given it up," he thought. He had no plan to do more walking, but now that she requested it, he should not be too ungracious. Besides, as long as she didn't mention the subject of marrying him, he was fine. Then, he nodded his head and paused for her to catch up with him before walking forward along the stone embankment. Seeing the master was not going back to the boat, servant boy Mao Cheng and the servant carrying food on a pole followed him onward.

"Bom, bom, bom! Clang, Clang, Clang!" The drums and cymbals sounded again. Five dragon boats appeared on the river, racing through the waves with beautifully carved dragon heads and tails, flying manes, and shining scales. Each boat had a colorful canopy, with flags, banners, and embroidered umbrellas in front and behind, fluttering in the wind. On the weapons rack on the stern was an array of sabers, spears, axes, and halberds. Twenty muscular men in tight warrior attire sat in two rows in the hull, and with the large paddles in their hands rising and falling in unison to the rhythm of the gongs

的锣鼓点，齐起齐落，把船划得如脱缰的马，如离弦的箭。每一只船的龙头上，还头朝下、脚朝天地倒立着一个小伙子，龙尾下面还用绳索悬吊着一个八九岁的孩童，他们在龙船的高速前进中显得那样从容自若，不断做出种种惊险的姿势，使旁观的人叹赏之余，都禁不住为他们捏上一把汗。

不过，此刻沿堤岸一带的游人已经忘了瞧赛龙船，他们的目光都被缓缓而行的冒襄和董小宛吸引去了。这一对儿恍如天仙临凡般的仪容和风度，如此令人惊叹、着迷，以致无论他俩走到哪里，哪里的人们都像生怕亵渎了他们似的，纷纷自动让开。待到他们走过之后，才又合拢来，远远地跟在后面瞧。而这一骚动，又招引了更多人的注意，情不自禁地参加进来。今天金山上的游客，少说也有好几千，到后来倒有一大半都在若即若离地跟着他们的身影移动……

"公子，但愿你能记得今天。"董小宛向身后的人群瞥了一眼，幽幽地说。

冒襄怔了一下，明白了她的意思。他微微一笑："今天我们成了神仙眷侣啦，怎会不记得！"话刚出口，便觉得不妥，于是又改口说，"也难怪他们如此惊羡，须知'秦淮二董'，原不是浪得虚名！"

董小宛摇摇头，叹了一口气："虚名也罢，实名也罢，奴家此生只盼公子垂怜，便死也甘心了，谁知公子……"

冒襄发现她又来了，顿时冷下脸，默不作声。

董小宛从团扇的边上窥伺着他，"扑哧"一笑："好了，奴家不说这个了，不说了！"她移开扇子，噘起嘴巴，轻声地、撒娇地说，"怎么哩，还不成么？"

冒襄"哼"了一声，半真半假地警告说："你要再说那些个扫兴的话，我可就……"

and drums, rowed their boat forward like a horse off the reins, or like an arrow from the bow. On the dragon head of each boat, there was a young man standing head over heels, and an eight- or nine-year-old child hung by a rope under the dragon tail, adeptly changing their posture and performing breathtaking stunts as the boat raced forward, astounding and enthralling the spectators.

However, the tourists along the bank moved their eyes off the dragon boats to Mao Xiang and Dong Xiaowan, who were passing them at a leisurely pace. The beauty and charm of this couple, who were like fairies visiting this world, were so enthralling and captivating that no matter where they went, people stepped aside to give way, as if afraid to desecrate them, reassembled after they passed, and followed at a distance. The commotion attracted more attention and more people joined in the procession. There were at least thousands of tourists on the mountain island. In the end, more than half of them came to follow in their footsteps ...

Dong Xiaowan cast a glance at the crowd behind them and said with enjoyment, "Sir, I hope you can remember today."

Mao Xiang froze for an instant and understood what she meant. He smiled faintly and said, "Today we have become a fairy couple. How can I not remember it?" As soon as he said that, he regretted, so he revised his words and said, "No wonder they're so envious. The 'two Dongs of the Qinhuai River' are not empty names after all."

Dong Xiaowan shook her head and sighed, "Whether the name is empty or substantial, in this life I hope for nothing more than your love and will die a happy woman if I get it, but you ..."

When Mao Xiang saw she was still the same, his expression darkened and he went silent.

Dong Xiaowan peeped at him from the edge of her round fan and chuckled, saying, "Alright, I'll stop saying it. I'll stop." She removed the fan from her face, pursed her mouth, and said coquettishly in a low voice, "Why, is that not enough? "

Mao Xiang gave a snort and warned half-seriously, "If you continue to say things that spoil the fun, I will ..."

董小宛连忙用扇子掩住他的嘴巴，“奴家知道，知道啦！”她挨近他，柔声地说。停了停，她又问：“大比之期将近，公子这一回去，只怕要到七八月才能再出来了？”

“嗯……”

董小宛眨眨眼睛，忽然笑道：“奴家可料准了，公子这一回，定能高中！”

“噢，何以见得？”

“这是神明告知奴的。”董小宛认真地说，“这些日子，奴家天天在神前烧香，默祝公子今科高中。昨儿夜里神明来托梦，说公子前身是杜牧之，一生风流倜傥，才华绝世，当年遭李德裕之忌，未能尽展襟抱。因此天帝垂怜，特遣公子重游人间，扶助大明真命天子，只应在今科了。”

冒襄瞅着她，现出半信半疑的神色，“嗯，岂有此理！”他说。

“啊呀，这可是千真万确。神明还对奴说，公子自降世以来，怜贫惜弱，广施仁义，又事亲尽孝，声闻朝野，天帝甚为嘉慰，已命增禄三秩。所以公子此去，岂止科甲连登，今后只怕还要入阁拜相呢！”

冒襄怔了片刻，随即呵呵笑起来：“更属荒唐，更属荒唐！”他摇着头说。不过，虽然如此，心中也觉受用。他抬起头，张望了一下，看见那几只竞渡的龙船，此刻正聚集在离他们不远的江边上，一个劲儿地击鼓鸣钲，却不怎么前进。冒襄早就发现，从他俩出现在堤上的一刻起，这几只龙船就一直有意无意地跟随着，他们走到哪里，它们也跟到哪里。这时他兴头起来，回头大声吩

Dong Xiaowan hurriedly put her fan on his mouth, leaned toward him, and said in a soft voice, "Sorry, sir. I'm sorry." After a pause, she asked, "Examination day is close. You won't be able to come out again until July or August, I'm afraid."

"You're right."

Dong Xiaowan blinked her eyes and laughed. "I'm sure you'll succeed in this exam."

"Oh? How do you know?"

"A god told me," Dong Xiaowan said seriously. "I've been offering incense to the gods every day these days, praying for your success in the exam. One god visited my dream last night, saying you're a reincarnation of Du Muzhi, who was handsome and talented but was unable to fulfill his ambition due to the suppression of the jealous Li Deyu. Now, by the grace of the Lord of Heaven, you're sent back to the human world to assist the Son of Heaven, the emperor of Great Ming, and the coming examination is the occasion for you to come out."

Mao Xiang looked at her with a doubtful look and said, "Well, that's funny."

"Trust me. That's absolutely true. The god also said to me, since your coming into the world, you've helped the poor and the weak, kind and just to all, and filial to your parents and loving to your family, and your great name has been heard across the country. The Emperor of Heaven is very delighted and has decreed that you be promoted. Therefore, you'll not only succeed in all the coming examinations, but also in the future, I am afraid, will enter the Cabinet to serve as a minister," Dong Xiaowan said.

Mao Xiang was silent for a moment, then laughed. He shook his head and said, "It's even more ridiculous, even more preposterous." He felt good nonetheless. He raised his head and looked at the river. The racing dragon boats were gathered near them, beating drums and gongs incessantly but not making much progress. He had long discovered that ever since his appearance on the bank with Xiaowan they had been following them intentionally or unintentionally. In a

咐冒成：

“你去——问问他们是些什么人，老跟着我们做什么？”

冒成答应了。他走到岸边，做了个有话要问的手势。那几只龙船立即停止击鼓鸣钲，等冒成大声传达了冒襄的询问之后，其中一只龙船就划了过来。从船上走下一个瘦高个儿的汉子，他来到离冒襄还有五六步远的地方，便跪倒在地，恭恭敬敬叩着头说：

“公子爷、奶奶在上，小人周阿六，给公子爷、奶奶请安！”

冒襄打量着这汉子，正觉得有点面善，冷不防听他这样称呼，倒愣了一下。

“罢了，起来吧！”冒襄摆摆手，然后又问，“我瞧你有点面善，莫非哪里见过？”

“启禀公子爷：旧年秋天，公子爷奉老夫人从衡州回来，便是小人撑的船。”周阿六低着头回答。

冒襄“哦”了一声，顿时记起来了，“不错不错！果然是你！”他高兴地说。那一次从湖南回来，正碰上大饥荒，盗贼蜂起，沿途风险还真不少。快走到苏州时，因为争航道，还同某太监的船冲突起来，双方干了一仗。当时虽说有兵卒护卫，但起航停泊等一应事宜，还真亏了周阿六小心安排维护，才得以平安到家。“哦，我记得你们总共有一二十人，他们可都好？”冒襄又问。

“托公子爷的福荫，他们都好。”周阿六说，又回头用手一指：“那不，都在船上哩！”

话音刚落，仿佛应和他的话似的，龙船上的鼓钲蓦地大敲大打起来。接着，全船的人放开喉咙，齐声高喊：

“恭祝公子爷阖府福泰安康！”

happy mood, he turned around and called out to Mao Cheng:

"Go ask who they are and why they follow us."

Mao Cheng said "aye, sir", walked to the riverside, and made a gesture of asking. The dragon boats immediately stopped their drums and gongs. After Mao Cheng loudly conveyed Mao Xiang's query, one of the dragon boats came over. A tall and thin man disembarked from the boat. When he was five or six steps from Mao Xiang, he knelt down on his knees, bowed his head reverently, and said:

"My young grandpa and my young grandma, I'm Zhou Aliu. Please accept my salute."

Mao Xiang was surprised to hear such a form of address as he looked at the man and wondered why he looked familiar.

"No ceremonies, please stand up." Mao Xiang waved his hand and asked, "You look familiar. I must have seen you somewhere."

"Yes, my young grandpa. In autumn last year, when you returned from Hengzhou with Her Ladyship your mother, you took my boat," Zhou Aliu replied with his head down.

Mao Xiang said "oh" and suddenly remembered. "Right! Sure enough, it's you," he said happily. That was when he came back from Hunan. It was a dangerous trip with robbers and thieves everywhere in the wake of the great famine. When they were about to reach Suzhou, they had a fight with a eunuch's boat over the route. Although they had soldiers on the boat to protect them, they had quite a number of other issues like anchoring and making their way through the congested waterway. Thanks to Zhou Aliu's efforts, they were finally able to make it home safe and sound. "Well, I remember there were a dozen of you on your boat. Are they all good?" asked Mao Xiang.

"Thank you for asking, my young grandpa. They're all doing well," Zhou Aliu said, pointing to his boat, "Look! They're all on the boat."

As soon as his voice fell, as if responding to him, the drums and gongs on the dragon boat suddenly sounded. All the boatmen shouted in unison:

"Peace and prosperity be with you and your family, my young

“哦，好，好！”冒襄点着头，高兴地说。他回头吩咐冒成：“你回船上去，封二十两银子，再把昨儿买的‘兰花三白’也挑两坛子，就烦周六哥带回去给大伙儿助助兴。”

周阿六听了，连忙重新跪下，叩头谢过，又走到江边，向伙伴交代了几句，这才随冒成去了。

龙船上的人显然知道了冒襄有所赏赐，鼓钲敲打得更欢了；随即把船划离江岸，同其余那几只龙船重新合在一起，在江上排成一字形。船夫们以更加响亮的呐喊，再一次朝冒襄欢呼致敬之后，五名倒立在龙头的小伙子，和五名悬挂在龙尾上的孩童就卖劲地表演起来——拿大顶、竖蜻蜓、金鸡独立……一招比一招惊险，一式比一式美妙，直把金山上下的数千名游客看得神迷目夺，如醉如痴。冒襄显得十分兴奋，他兴致勃勃地欣赏着这场专门奉献给他的精彩表演，时时发出响亮的、愉快的笑声，仿佛已经把身边的董小宛完全忘记了……

## 天意成全

董小宛虽然竭力设法讨好冒襄，但冒襄不自觉的冷淡，却加深了她的绝望和痛苦。作为一个风尘女子，她十分明白命运赐给她的机会是不多的。当机会一旦出现，就必须竭尽全力死死抓住。否则，一纵即逝之后，很可能就会落得个抱恨终生。事实上，近些年来，不但田弘遇迫抢这样一些事使她历尽惊恐，而且，在平常与狎客们的接触中，她也听到了许许多多关于时局越来越坏的可怕新闻。在酒阑人散、寒灯独对的时候，她不止一次心惊肉跳地想到，一旦大祸临头，自己这么一个无依无靠的风尘弱女，

grandpa."

Mao Xiang nodded and said happily, "Excellent!" He turned around and said to Mao Cheng, "Go back to the boat, get twenty taels of silver and two pots of white orchid wine you bought yesterday and let Brother Zhou take it to the boat to boost everybody's spirits."

Hearing that, Zhou Aliu knelt down again and kowtowed in gratitude. Then he walked back to the river, and said something to his boatmates, and left with Mao Cheng.

The men on the dragon boat, knowing that there was a reward from Mao Xiang, beat the drums and gongs even harder. Then, they rowed the boat away from the river bank and were reunited with the other dragon boats to form a line on the river. The boatmen hailed Mao Xiang again at the top of their voices. Then, the five young men standing upside down on the dragon heads and the five children hanging from the dragon tails began another series of astounding performances—spreading the legs in the air, raising the tail up like a dragonfly, standing like a golden rooster ... Each movement was more breathtaking than the last, and every posture was more beautiful than the other, captivating and mesmerizing the thousands of tourists up and down the Gold Mountain. Mao Xiang excitedly watched the wonderful show dedicated to him with great interest, letting out loud and merry laughter from time to time, as if he had completely forgotten Dong Xiaowan, who was standing beside him ...

## Love's Destiny

As Dong Xiaowan tried her best to please Mao Xiang, his unconscious indifference aggravated her despair and pain. As a woman fallen in the dust, she knew very well that fate had given her very few opportunities. When one arose, she had to do her best to seize it. Should she miss it, she would regret it for the rest of her life. In fact, over the past few years, she was not only worried by Tian Hongyu's relentless pursuit of her but also horrified by the bad news she had heard from her clients about the deteriorating situation of the country. When she was with herself in the dead of night after drinking and

怎么能应付？正是这种紧迫的危机感，使她觉得无论如何也不能放松眼前的机会。何况命运给她送来的，又正是她日夜想慕的冒襄！所以，近一个月来，为了获得这位贵公子的理解和怜悯，董小宛几乎运用了她的全部智慧。看来，这还是有效果的。冒襄的态度比起最初已经明显地变得热乎起来，他瞧她时，目光也亲切多了。有一次——那是在欢娱之后的枕上，他甚至抚摩着她的光胳臂，详细地询问起她的出身、家世，还问到历年来她所欠下的积债的数目，使她立即敏感地想到，他可能考虑替她赎身，顿时紧张得浑身颤抖，差点儿连话也说不出来。她没敢隐瞒，老实地告诉他，母亲在世时已欠下些债，后来母亲死时又借了一笔，加上父亲多嗜好、喜挥霍，一心把她当成摇钱树，平日里打着她的招牌到处借钱，如今算在一起，已欠下二三千两银子。冒襄听着，“噢”了一声，没有再说话。她还等着他再问别的，可是抬头一瞧，他已经呼呼地睡着了。从此以后，冒襄就再也没有提起这类的事，她也没敢再追问，可是心里却愈来愈焦急了。特别是船快到镇江时，她发现冒襄的神色愈来愈阴沉，说话也有点冷冰冰的。今天一早起来，他却忽然变得分外殷勤客气，并提出一定要来游金山。董小宛感到事情不妙，因此刚才在山顶上，她抢先指着大江发誓，表明决心要跟他回如皋。果然冒襄立即就变了脸，断然拒绝。他除了提出眼下忙着应付科试，以及要料理大半年来因替父亲奔走而荒废了的家务之外，还特别提到董小宛欠债很多，无法应付。她听了，犹如被兜头浇了一瓢冷水，浑身都凉了。不过，她也知道，对于冒襄这种公子哥儿，不能硬来，否则惹恼了他，随时都

merrymaking, she often worried about her own future. With no one to rely on, how could she get along in the world should the catastrophe come? With such a feeling of urgency, she was determined that she would not let this opportunity go, no matter what. What was more, this time, fate had brought her exactly the love of her dreams. Therefore, over the past month, Dong Xiaowan had used every possible means to make Mao Xiang understand her and sympathize with her. It seemed that her efforts had had some results. Mao Xiang's attitude was clearly better than before. When he looked at her, his eyes were friendlier. Once, when they were lying in bed after doing it, he even stroked her bare arm and asked in detail about her home, family, and how much money she owed. She immediately thought that he might be considering redeeming her from the brothel and became so nervous that she was shaking all over and could hardly speak. Not daring to hide anything from him, she honestly told him that it was two to three thousand taels of silver in total, including a posthumous debt owed by her mother, a loan for her mother's funeral, and her father's borrowings in her name for his wasteful life. Mao Xiang listened, said "oh", and went silent. She waited for him to ask her more questions, but when she looked up, he was already asleep. Since then, Mao Xiang had never mentioned the subject again. Not daring to mention it, she became more and more anxious. Earlier, as the boat neared Zhenjiang, she found Mao Xiang's countenance bleak and his tone cold, but when they woke up this morning, he suddenly became polite and cordial and even suggested a tour to the Gold Mountain. Dong Xiaowan felt something was wrong, so at the top of the mountain just now she pointed to the river and swore to go to Rugao with him. Sure enough, Mao Xiang's countenance immediately changed. He refused her categorically, citing the coming imperial examination, the need to put things right at home after his six-month absence, and her huge debts that he was unable to help pay. When she heard it, her whole body became cold, as if a bucket of cold water had been poured on her head. However, she knew that she should not rush a capricious young man from a big family like Mao Xiang, otherwise he would be irritated

会翻脸不认人。所以，刚才她强作欢容，极力讨好。但看来作用不大，董小宛的心情就愈来愈痛苦和绝望了。

当他们看完龙船，回到天平船上的时候，张明弼已经在舱里等候着。同他在一起的，还有方以智、余怀，和一位名叫张岱的中年儒生，四个人正围在桌子旁抹纸牌。看见他俩进来，方以智说声“算我输了！”便把纸牌一放，首先站起身，拱着手迎上来，呵呵笑着说：“神仙眷侣回来了！恭喜，恭喜！”

冒襄尚未答话，余怀已在旁边抢着说：“今日这金山上的风光，硬是给辟疆和宛娘双双占尽了。明日传扬开去，不知要令多少名士美人羡杀、妒杀、愧杀哩！”

“岂止侈美一时？我敢断言，今日金山此段佳话，已是长存于天壤之间，可以不朽了！”张岱一本正经地说。他是个衣饰华贵的儒生，有着一张聪慧的、讨人喜欢的脸，和三绺梳理得一丝不苟的小胡子。

方以智说：“王睿冲云，‘情之所钟，正在我辈’。原该如此！若是宗子兄此言果真应验，那么小弟这个媒人，却是功不可没呢！”

“哦，辟疆同宛娘相识，原来还是密之兄之介！”张岱瞪大眼睛问。

方以智神气地说：“不错！那是崇祯十二年，小弟应试南都，巧遇辟疆……”

张岱不等他说完，马上断然说：“那么密之兄也是不朽的了！”

“哎，那么小弟呢？”余怀插进来问。

and turn away from her completely. That's why she had put on a smile and tried her best to please him just now. It didn't seem to have much effect, though. Dong Xiaowan became increasingly depressed and frustrated.

When they returned to their boat after watching the dragon boat show, Zhang Mingbi was already waiting in the cabin. Accompanying him were Fang Yizhi, Yu Huai, and a middle-aged scholar named Zhang Dai, who were playing cards at the table. Seeing them coming in, Fang Yizhi said, "Well, I lose." He put down his cards, stood up, brought his hands together to salute them and said with a smile, "The fairy couple is back. Congratulations, congratulations!"

Before Mao Xiang replied, Yu Huai cut in, "Pijiang and Xiaowan have become the major attraction on the Gold Mountain today. When word spread tomorrow, countless men and women celebrities will be jealous."

"It's more than a sensation. I dare say that today's story in the Gold Mountain will be remembered by history," said Zhang Dai in a serious tone. He was a gorgeously dressed scholar with an intelligent, pleasant face and a mustache that was carefully groomed.

Fang Yizhi said, "Wang Ruichong said, 'The sages dismiss feelings of love. The lowly are not good enough to know them. It's us who are in the middle to have them.'① That's how it should be. If Brother Zongzi's words come true, then I should be thanked as the matchmaker."

"Oh, I see. It's Brother Mizhi who has brought Pijiang and Xiaowan together," said Zhang Dai, opening his eyes wide.

Fang Yizhi said proudly, "That's right. It was the twelfth year of the reign of Emperor Chongzhen [AD 1639], I went to sit for the imperial examination in the South Capital and happened to meet Pijiang ..."

Zhang Dai cut in abruptly, "So Brother Mizhi will also go down in history."

"Hey, what about me then?" Yu Huai cut in.

---

① It is a quote from "Biography of Wang Yan", *The Book of Jin* (Jinshu).

张岱瞧了瞧他，正要开口，方以智已经抢着说：“淡心兄自然也是不朽的！不止淡心兄，便是宗子兄、公亮兄，还有冒成和方才来船上领赏银的周阿六，都已是名垂千古，欲‘朽’不能了！”

大家“哦”了一声，都半信半疑地望着他。

方以智微微一笑：“诸位不妨想想，辟疆和宛娘既已不朽无疑，那么今后但凡有记载金山之游的，自不能不书及他们回船此节，若然书及回船，自不能不书及诸位，以及冒成、周阿六，故此辟疆和宛娘朽则已，若然不朽，我辈也无可奈何，唯有陪他一块儿不朽而已！”

大家听他说完，怔了一下，随即开怀大笑起来。余怀一跃而起，尖着嗓子大叫：“妈妈的！四大皆空，人身不过一具臭皮囊，名声也是骗人的玩意儿。我是只盼一死即朽，不留一丝一毫影迹在这世上！如今撞在辟疆网里，被他硬拖着朽不了，真是何等懊恼！不行不行，今儿非罚他们不可！”说着，他回头叫：“冒成，那些樱桃洗净没有？快快拿出来！”

只听冒成在后梢答应了一声，托出来一大盂樱桃，摆到桌子上。那樱桃少说也有五六斤，颗颗大如小枣，堆在宣瓷大盂里，一眼望去，红的血红，白的雪白，还衬着片片绿叶，十分鲜明可爱。冒成向冒襄禀告说：“这是周阿六特地送来的，说是请大爷、董姑娘和相公们尝个鲜。”冒襄点点头。本来，他有心向朋友们解释一下，他对董小宛并不存在他们所猜想的那种意思，可是一

Zhang Dai looked at him, and was about to speak when Fang Yizhi said, "Brother Danxin will go down in history too, of course. Not only Brother Danxin, but also Brother Zongzi, Brother Gongliang as well as Mao Cheng and Zhou Aliu, the boatman who came to receive the reward, will all go down in history. We'll all be immortal and won't die."

Everyone looked at him doubtfully.

Fang Yizhi smiled slightly and said, "Let's think it this way: since Pijiang and Xiaowan are already immortal, any future record of the Gold Mountain tour will document their return to the boat and therefore everyone here today, all of you, Mao Cheng, and even Zhou Aliu. If the story of Pijiang and Xiaowan today isn't remembered, we'll not be remembered. If they become immortal, we can do nothing but be immortal together with them."

When he finished, everyone laughed out loud after figuring it out. Yu Huai sprang up and shouted at the top of his voice, "Damn! The four elements[①] are all empty. The human body is nothing but a stinking skin bag, and a good name is just something to deceive people with. I just hope that I'll be forgotten as soon as I die and leave no trace in this world. What bad luck to be entangled in Pijiang's business and dragged by him into immortality! No, no, they must be punished today." He turned around and shouted, "Mao Cheng, have those cherries been washed? Hurry! Take them out."

Mao Cheng replied from the stern and soon came with a large bowl of cherries and placed it on the table. The cherries, as big as jujubes, some as red as blood, some as white as snow, weighing at least five or six pounds all together and with a few green leaves under them, looked very beautiful in the large Xuanzhou porcelain bowl. Mao Cheng reported to Mao Xiang, "These are from Zhou Aliu. He said he wants the young grandpa, Miss Dong and all the gentlemen here to try them while they're fresh." Mao Xiang nodded. He wanted to explain to his friends that he and

① The four elements are earth, water, fire, and air.

直插不上嘴，这时也就只好随着大家作过揖，先坐下来再说。

“淡心兄，你说要罚辟疆，不知怎生个罚法？”方以智不等大家坐定，就笑嘻嘻地问。

“我此罚却简单不过，题目就在这樱桃上！”余怀不慌不忙地说，向在座的人环顾了一眼，“自来这樱桃好有一比，比作美人香喷喷的朱唇；自来美人之唇也有一比，比作这红艳艳、甜滋滋的樱桃。此譬虽则来源甚古，却是妙到绝处，切到绝处。再过一万年，只怕也无以改易！不过譬喻归譬喻，究竟此二物之间，滋味有何不同，何者更胜，却从来未经人道过。今日适逢席上既有樱桃，又有美人，何不就罚辟疆当场反复尝试，作出品评，以解我辈之惑？”

这话刚说完，大家立即哄然叫好。小宛瞧了瞧冒襄，见他捋着胡子，一声不响，知他必定不会答应，心里一阵刺痛，站起来就要走开。方以智等人只当她害羞逃席，连忙一窝蜂地追过去，把她拖了回来。

正在闹哄哄的当儿，忽然张明弼大声说：“诸位先别闹，且听听辟疆怎么说！”

大家果然静下来，一齐望住冒襄。只见冒襄淡淡一笑，说：“淡心此谑，倒还不俗。若然小弟拒不受罚，不只辜负了他一番巧思，更辜负了这一桌樱桃，未免可惜——也罢，小弟便尝试一遭，又有何妨！”

大家见他答应得爽快，都欢呼起来。董小宛呆住了。“啊，怎么……”她想，同时心中依稀闪过一个念头，但冒襄那冷冰冰的神情使她立即又把它否定了。

“哎，宛娘，快过去嘛，这有什么可害羞的！”余怀柔声催促说，一边同伙伴们交换着狡黠的眼色。

Dong Xiaowan were not in the kind of relationship that they were thinking, but not having the opportunity to speak, he sat down after the exchange of salutes.

"Brother Danxin, you said you wanted to punish Pijiang. Let us know how," Fang Yizhi asked with a smile as they sat down.

"My punishment is very simple. We'll use the cherries," Yu Huai said calmly as he looked around at the people present, "A cherry has been compared to the red lips of a beautiful woman and the lips of a beautiful woman have been compared to a red, sweet cherry. Although such analogies are almost cliches, they're good ones indeed, so good that they'll continue to be used ten thousand years later. An analogy being an analogy, no one has ever told the difference in taste between the two or which one tastes better. Now that we have both cherries and a beautiful lady on the boat, why not let Pijiang taste them on the spot again and again and pass a judgement to clear the confusion in our understanding?"

Everyone cheered. Xiaowan looked at Mao Xiang. Seeing he was stroking his beard and said nothing, she knew that he wouldn't agree. With a tingling pain in her heart, she got up and was going to walk away. Fang Yizhi and others thought she was shying away from them and hurried to stop her from leaving and pulled her back.

Amid the commotion, Zhang Mingbi suddenly said in a loud voice, "Be quiet, everybody! Let's listen to what Pijiang has to say."

The party went quiet and looked at Mao Xiang in unison. Mao Xiang smiled lightly, saying, "Danxin's idea of having fun isn't bad at all. If I didn't accept the punishment, his good idea would be wasted and it would not be fair to the tableful of cherries either. So, let me try them. What's the harm?"

Seeing that he readily agreed, everyone cheered. Dong Xiaowan was stupefied. "Oh, how come ..." she thought. An embarrassing scene flashed through her mind, but seeing Mao Xiang's icy expression she quickly dismissed it.

"Hey, Xiaowan, hurry! Don't be shy!" Yu Huai urged in a gentle voice as he exchanged sly glances with his companions.

董小宛又瞧了瞧冒襄，只见他已经伸手从白瓷盂里拣起一桠带绿叶的樱桃，并用一个潇洒美妙的动作，扯了一颗放进嘴里，皱起眉毛斜睨着她，像是有点不耐烦的样子。

“无论如何，我得过去，对，我得过去！”她在心里说，不由自主地移动脚步，重新回到自己的位置上坐下来。

“好，现在开始！”她听见方以智恶作剧的声音。一刹那间，她无暇多想，匆忙中用了一个慌乱、笨拙的动作仰起了头。同时，觉得自己脸红了。“啊，我的样子这会儿一定很蠢，他一定更加不喜欢了！”她不知所措地想。可是情势已经不容她加以补救，第一记亲吻就落下来了。果然，熟悉的气息，熟悉的感觉，但是那意味却完全不同。它显得那样冷漠、勉强，只轻轻碰了一下，就逃也似的退了回去……

“好呀！”董小宛听见一声哄然的喝彩。

“喂，怎么样？什么滋味？”一个怪声怪调的嗓音问。还是那个余怀。

冒襄却没有回答。董小宛不敢睁开眼睛，她生怕一睁眼就会看见冒襄那张冷酷无情的脸孔。

很快地，第二记亲吻又来了。它比第一次更加冰冷、更加机械，而且有一种示威似的意味，仿佛在说：“嗯，你们瞧够了么？还想不想再瞧？想瞧我还可以再来！”董小宛的心一抖，随即因痛苦而紧缩了。尽管耳畔正在闹哄哄地回响着各种喝彩声和嬉笑声，可是她却感到泪水已经涌上了眼睛。当第三记、第四记亲吻来临时，它就顺着脸颊流淌下来了。

“啊，宛娘在哭哩！”一个声音忽然叫起来。霎时间，像听到一声命令似的，喧闹声戛然停止了。船舱里变得一片寂静。

“宛娘，你做什么？”方以智的声音问。

Dong Xiaowan looked at Mao Xiang. He reached out his hand and picked up a sprig of cherries with green leaves from the white porcelain bowl, and with a quick and beautiful motion took one and slid it into his mouth. Then, he furrowed his brows and squinted at her, as if a little impatient.

"Anyway, I have to go over, yes, I have to go over to him," she said to herself, involuntarily moving her feet. In the end, she returned to her seat and sat down.

"All right, let's start now," came Fang Yizhi's mischievous voice. It all came so suddenly that Xiaowan had no time to think. She hurriedly raised her head in a confused and clumsy manner. At the same time, she felt herself blushing. "Oh, my, I must be looking stupid now, and he would dislike me even more badly for that," she thought, nonplussed. But before she was able to take a remedy, the first kiss fell on her lips. Sure enough, it was the familiar breath, the familiar feeling, but the meaning was completely different. It felt so nonchalant and reluctant. It came and went too quickly as if trying to keep away from her ...

"Hooray!" Dong Xiaowan heard a loud applause.

"Hey, how is it? How does it taste?" asked a nasty voice. Again, it was Yu Huai.

Mao Xiang didn't respond. Fearing to see Mao Xiang's cold, expressionless face, Dong Xiaowan didn't dare to open her eyes.

Then came a second kiss. It was colder and more mechanical than the first one, and somewhat defiant, as if he were saying, "Well, have you seen enough? Do you want to see more? I can do it again if you want to see more of it." Dong Xiaowan's heart skipped a beat and twisted with pain. Amid the noisy hoorays and laughter, she felt tears well up in her eyes. When the third one and fourth one came, those tears burst forth and ran down her cheeks.

"Oh, Xiaowan is crying," a voice exclaimed. In an instant, the wild excitement suddenly stopped, as if the party had received an injunction. The cabin was quiet.

"Xiaowan, what's up?" Fang Yizhi asked.

董小宛的泪眼闪动了一下，随即低下头去，没有回答。

“哎，这是怎么回事？啊！”方以智转向冒襄，后者扭过头去，也是不吭声。

“嗨！你们说话呀！”方以智发急了。

“是这么回事！”张明弼在一旁开腔了，“宛娘要随辟疆回如皋，辟疆没答应。”

“哦，此乃绝佳之事，怎能不允！”方以智说。

“这是不可以的！”冒襄冷冷地说，“天下事哪有如此容易！”

“有何难处？”方以智不客气地追问。

冒襄把曾经对董小宛说过的那些困难又复述了一遍，并补充说：“况且金陵落籍，亦费商量。”

方以智摇摇头：“此等事并非难至不可解。如今弟要知道的，乃是仁兄到底有无娶宛娘之意？”

这一问，确实问中了冒襄心中的要害。他觉得说有意也不是，说无意也不是，不由得支吾起来。

方以智却仿佛看透了冒襄的心思。他“哼”了一声，说：“宛娘是空谷幽兰，淤泥菡萏。坊曲中人，论色、艺，胜于她的会有；若论人品，她却是第一。当今天下扰攘，大乱未已，阁下不于彼辈中觅如君则已，若欲有所物色，而弃宛娘不取，只怕会追悔不及哩！”

冒襄不作声了。他平日虽然有“翩翩浊世佳公子”之誉，备受各方面的推崇和称赞，他自己更是高傲自负，可是唯独对于方以智，却是十分信服。因为方以智不仅在吃喝玩乐和恶作剧方面，是一名头等的好手，他能想出种种出人意表的新鲜点子，把每一

Dong Xiaowan's teary eyes fluttered open but soon she lowered her head in silence.

"Hey, what's going on?" Fang Yizhi turned to Mao Xiang, who turned away and said nothing.

"Hey! Speak up!" Fang Yizhi became anxious.

"This is what happened," Zhang Mingbi said from aside. "Xiaowan wanted to go to Rugao with Pijiang, but Pijiang didn't agree."

"Oh, it's a beautiful thing. How can you refuse?" said Fang Yizhi.

"It won't do," said Mao Xiang coldly. "It's not that easy."

"What's the problem?" asked Fang Yizhi bluntly.

Mao Xiang repeated what he had said to Dong Xiaowan, adding, "Besides, it takes time to take her name from the register of prostitutes in Nanjing."

Fang Yizhi shook his head and said, "This kind of problem is not impossible to solve. What I want to ask is: Are you planning to marry Xiaowan at all?"

This question really touched the sore spot in Mao Xiang's heart. He could neither give an affirmative answer nor a negative one, so he stumbled.

As if having seen through Mao Xiang's mind, Fang Yizhi snorted and said, "Xiaowan is an orchid in a valley, or a lotus growing in the mud. In the courtesan houses, there might be girls who are more beautiful and talented than her, but in terms of character there's no match. Today, the world is in turmoil, and the chaos isn't over yet. If you are not looking for a concubine in their ranks, that's fine, but if you give up Xiaowan for another girl, you'll regret it for the rest of your life, I'm afraid."

Mao Xiang was silent. Highly respected and widely praised as "a brilliant young man in the murky world", he was rather proud and conceited. Fang Yizhi alone commanded his respect. Fang Yizhi was not only good at eating, drinking, merry-making and playing hoaxes—he could always come up with all sorts of unexpected and fresh ideas to make every party fascinating and lively—he was but also a first-class

次聚会弄得引人入胜，热闹非凡，而且他还博览群书，见解超卓，有着称得上当世第一流的学问。冒襄自觉比不上他。所以，现在听他正言厉色地这么一说，冒襄就不能不仔细考虑一下了。

“依我之见——”看见冒襄沉吟不语，张岱从旁插话了，“人决不如天决，现今放着有骰子在此，何妨让宛娘掷出彩来，看看天意如何，也免得辟疆兄多费踌躇。”

“不错，天决！天决！”余怀立即表示赞同。

在大家说话的当儿，董小宛一直默默地倾听着，身子不断微微打战。听见张岱这样建议，她就抬起头来，询问地望着方以智。看见方以智绷着脸，没有吭声，她也就不敢动弹。

“哎，宛娘，事到如今，你还忌讳什么！”余怀说，从桌上抓过骰子，塞在她的手里。

董小宛这才畏畏缩缩地站起来，用眼梢偷偷瞧了瞧正皱着眉毛呆坐在一旁的冒襄，然后赶快走到船窗前跪下，仰起脸，望着外面的天空，开始怀着深切的虔诚，喃喃地祝祷。她做得那样专注认真，以至满腔的悲苦和哀怨都被牵引起来，嘴唇在可怜地抖动着，泪水在眼眶里打转。一时间，周围的人都静静地望着，谁也不说话。终于，董小宛祷告完了。她站起来，用袖子揩了揩眼角，走到桌子跟前，双手捂住骰子，摇了又摇、摇了又摇。她的表情越来越紧张，眼睛睁得越来越大。突然，她像是横了心似的，双手一放，把骰子全投到桌面上。众人一看：其中三粒先掷出三个六点，第四粒滚动了几下，也停在六点上，还剩下一粒，却兀自滴溜溜地转个不停。大家都屏住气等着，终于“笃”的一声，

scholar, well read and highly intelligent. Mao Xiang felt inferior to him. Now that Fang Yizhi said so in such a serious tone, Mao Xiang had to consider the matter more seriously.

"In my opinion—" Zhang Dai cut in, seeing Mao Xiang was silent. "A human decision isn't as good as one by providence. There're dice here. Why not ask Xiaowan to throw the dice and let's see what the will of heaven is. Thus, Brother Pijiang won't have to worry about it anymore."

"Yes, a decision by providence! A decision by providence!" Yu Huai immediately agreed.

While the men were talking, Dong Xiaowan listened quietly, and her body quivered slightly. Hearing Zhang Dai's proposal, she raised her head and looked at Fang Yizhi inquiringly. When she saw he was pulling a long face and didn't say a word, she didn't venture to move.

"Hey, Xiaowan, since things have come to such a pass, what are you afraid of?" said Yu Huai, who grabbed the dice from the table and shoved them into her hand.

Only then did Dong Xiaowan stand up timidly. From the corners of her eyes, she glanced at Mao Xiang, who was sitting next to her with his eyebrows closely knit, then walked quickly to the boat window and knelt on her knees. Then, she lifted her face, looked up at the sky outside, and started to say her prayer in a whisper yet with all piety. She did it with such concentration that all her grief and grievance welled up, her lips quivered miserably and her eyes swirled with tears. In that moment, all the men went silent. Finally, Dong Xiaowan finished her prayer. She stood up, wiped the corners of her eyes with her sleeves, walked to the table, covered the dice with both hands and shook and shook and shook and shook. Her expression became tenser and tenser and her eyes opened wider and wider. Suddenly, as if resigned to her fate, she threw all the dice on the table. To the amazement of the men present, three of the dice were sixes, the fourth one rolled a few seconds and stopped at six, and one was still rolling. The men waited with bated breath, and finally with a "tuk" sound the die stopped, and the upside said six!

骰子停下来，这粒骰子朝上的那一面，竟然也是六点！大家凑前去一瞧，都愣住了。

“全六！全六！天意，天意！”余怀首先大嚷起来。他奔到冒襄跟前：“怎么样，辟疆，这下你可没得说了吧！”

冒襄也被这种上天显示的“奇迹”弄得目瞪口呆。半晌，他才回过神来，沉吟地望着方以智，说：“好吧！如果当真是天意成全此事，弟也没有话说。只是眼下不能操之太急，宛娘仍请先回姑苏，到秋天弟再去接她一起赴留都就试。待到中与不中都有个结果之后，才有空暇料理此事。”

方以智点点头：“这样也好，大家可都听清了？我们都是证人，此事就这么定了。宛娘，你就先回姑苏等辟疆的消息吧！”

董小宛没有立即回答。不过，在她的脸上，悲戚的神情消失了。她严肃地抿着嘴唇，用那双大眼睛瞅了瞅方以智，又瞅了瞅冒襄，轻轻地点了一下头。

## 抱负不同

把冒襄和董小宛分别送走之后的第二天，方以智同黄宗羲一起动身到北京去。

他们搭乘江船过了长江，从锣鼓喧天、龙舟云集的瓜州渡口重新进入大运河，到扬州后，换了一只官船，取道高邮、淮阴，迤逦北上。

一年一度的梅雨季节已经到来。从扬州起航后，日日阴雨连绵，天空变得惨淡无光。两岸平坦的原野上，水气弥漫，远远望去，灰蒙蒙、白茫茫的一片。偶尔闪现出一个村落、几丛杂树的影子，也是那般的冷落、荒凉。低矮的船篷上，沙沙的雨点日夜

Everyone stepped forward to look, and they were all stunned by what they saw.

"Perfect sixes! Perfect sixes! The will of heaven! The will of heaven!" Yu Huai shouted first. He hurried to Mao Xiang and said, "How is it, Pijiang? Now you don't have anything to say."

Mao Xiang too was dumbfounded by this miracle of providence. After a long while, he came to his senses, and looking pensively at Fang Yizhi, said, "Alright, then. If it really is the will of heaven, I have nothing to say. It's just that I can't be in too much of a hurry right now. Xiaowan should go back to Gusu first. I'll pick her up in autumn and take her to the Legacy Capital, where I'll be taking the imperial exam. I'll take care of the matter, whether I'll succeed in the exam or not."

Fang Yizhi nodded his head. "That's also good. Do you all hear it? We're all witnesses, so the matter is settled. Xiaowan, you have to go back to Gusu and wait for the news from Pijiang."

Dong Xiaowan didn't immediately respond, but the sad expression on her face disappeared. Pressing her lips together with a serious expression, she looked at Fang Yizhi and then Mao Xiang with her big eyes and nodded slightly.

## A Friend with a Different Flair

The day after they saw off Mao Xiang and Dong Xiaowan respectively, Fang Yizhi and Huang Zongxi left for Beijing.

They crossed the Yangtze River by riverboat and re-entered the Grand Canal from Guazhou Ferry, which was packed with dragon boats, on which gongs and drums beat thunderously, and after arriving at Yangzhou, they changed to a government boat and headed north by way of Gaoyou and Huaiyin.

The rainy season had arrived. After they left Yangzhou, it was rainy and cloudy every day, and the sky was dark. On the flat plains on both sides of the river, a high density of water vapor filled the air and formed a large curtain of gray mist. Occasionally there was a village or a few clumps of trees. Even those were bleak and deserted. On the low

响个不停。潮湿、发霉的气味从船舱的各个角落里散发出来，又一个劲儿往衣袖、领子里钻，使人浑身上下像是泡在无形的涎沫里似的，滑腻腻、黏糊糊，难受极了……

也许是受了这种讨厌天气的影响，两个朋友渐渐都变得有点闷闷不乐。本来，开头那七八天，两人还有说有笑，他们谈到了冒襄和董小宛的关系，谈到松山的失守和洪承畴的殉国，还谈到了复社内部的纠纷和面临的危机。不过，彼此的见解都不大一样。譬如：对冒、董的姻缘，方以智表现得颇为热心，黄宗羲却持冷淡甚至不以为然的态度；对于洪承畴之死，黄宗羲大表崇敬，方以智却认为松山之失，洪氏负有重责，他的死无非是逃避罪责而已；对于复社的前途，方以智认为人心已散，事不可为，黄宗羲却仍旧抱有很大的希望，认为经此一场波折，或者能使对立的各派消除误会，重新团结起来……就这样，谈来谈去，总是谈不大拢。最后，只好各自沉默下来，已经有好几天了。

现在，黄宗羲正靠在船篷上闷头看书。从另一个角落里，传来了金属轻轻碰击的声响——方以智在摆弄着一架不知从哪儿弄来的西洋千里镜。那是一尺来长的一柄金属圆筒，两头嵌有玻璃。昨天方以智把它一一拆开来，说是要研究一下它何以能将远处的物象移置眼前。他到底研究得怎样，黄宗羲也不大清楚。不过后来这千里镜却怎样也装不拢了。方以智虽然强作镇定，也已是额头见汗。昨儿半个夜晚，今儿一个早上，还没弄好，直到现在还与他的书童方理在那儿忙着。

“密之这人就是好奇太过！也不管懂不懂，拿过来就乱弄一

roofing of the boat, the rustling raindrops kept ringing in the early day and night. A damp, musty smell came from every corner of the cabin to assault them by way of the sleeves and collars, so that they felt as if they were soaked in a kind of invisible saliva, which was greasy, sticky and extremely uncomfortable ...

Maybe because of this nasty weather, the two friends gradually became gloomy. In the first seven or eight days, the two of them talked and laughed. They talked about the relationship between Mao Xiang and Dong Xiaowan, the fall of Songshan and Hong Chengchou's martyrdom, the internal struggles of the Fushe and its current crisis. However, their opinions often differed. Fang Yizhi, for example, was very enthusiastic about the romantic relationship between Mao Xiang and Dong Xiaowan, but Huang Zongxi was indifferent or even disapproving; Huang Zongxi spoke highly of Hong Chengchou's death, but Fang Yizhi believed that the man was accountable for the loss of Songshan and that his death was nothing more than evasion of punishment; Fang Yizhi believed that the Fushe had no hope because the Fushers were no longer united, but Huang Zongxi still had high hopes for it, thinking that this incident might be an occasion for the various factions to understand each other and get reunited ... In fact, there was little they could agree on. As a result, they didn't speak to each other for days.

Huang Zongxi leaned on the wall of the cabin reading a book. From another corner came the sound of metal grating upon metal. Fang Yizhi was playing with a telescope he had got from somewhere. It was a metal cylinder about a foot long, with glass embedded on both ends. The day before, Fang Yizhi had taken it apart, saying he wanted to study how it moved distant objects to in front of him. Huang Zongxi didn't know what exactly Fang Yizhi had found out. He only knew his friend was unable to reassemble it. Although Fang Yizhi tried to keep calm, his forehead sweated. Having been working on it from last night to this morning, with little sleep, he was still working on it with the help of his servant boy Fang Li.

"Mizhi is just too curious. Without caring whether he understands

气。瞧他那着急劲儿，这千里镜八成是不知向谁借来的，可是稀罕物儿。当真弄坏了，还不知怎么赔哩！”黄宗羲想，有心过去瞧一瞧，但转念一想，这玩意儿自己也不懂，过去也是白搭，便仍旧坐着没动。

然而，想重新安定下来却也不太容易。那些零件碰击的“笃笃”声，以及方以智主仆二人商量的零声碎语，不断地往耳朵里钻，而且变得越来越清晰、响亮，尽管黄宗羲努力收敛心神，他的视线仍旧有好几次在排得密密麻麻的仿宋字体中迷失了方位。最后，他忍不住了，转过脸去说：

“若弄不好，先放着，待到了京里，寻个待诏瞧瞧好啦！”

他这样说了，可是方以智也不知听见没有，他一不抬头，二不作声，只是把嘴唇抿得更紧，仍然在那里装了又拆，拆了又装。黄宗羲见说他不动，倒也没有办法，只好埋下头去，继续阅读；然而，终于又放下书本，站起身，慢慢地踱到方以智的旁边，开始打量着桌子上那一堆奇形怪状、神秘莫测的零件。“啊，若说这些东西搭配起来，便能将数十里外之景物移置目前，实在教人难以相信，然而却又千真万确。能发明此物之人，岂但技绝人寰，简直是巧夺天工哩！不道天下竟有心思灵通若此之人，实在匪夷所思！”他惊奇地想。他看了一会，不由自主就心痒起来，轻轻伸出手去，想拿起那片鸡蛋大的玻璃镜片，细细看一看。然而没等他触到镜片，就听方以智喝道：“别动！”

黄宗羲的手一抖，讪讪地缩了回来。他瞧了瞧方以智，只见他正在全神贯注地研究一只铜环，把它翻过来倒过去地看了又看，

it or not, he just toys with it. Look at his anxiety. This telescope must've been borrowed from someone. It must be very precious. If it's broken, he must recompense the owner," Huang Zongxi thought. He wanted to go over and have a look, but on second thoughts, he dropped this idea and stayed put, because, unfamiliar with the gadget himself, he would not be of any help at all.

However, it was not easy either to regain focus. The "tuk-tuk" sound of the parts colliding, as well as the occasional conversation between Fang Yizhi and his servant, kept entering his ears and became clearer and clearer, louder and louder. Although Huang Zongxi tried his best to concentrate on the book, he lost track again and again amid the closely arranged fine characters. Finally, unable to bear it any longer, he turned to them and said:

"If you can't get it right, leave it alone for now. You can find a royal technician-in-waiting① to help you when we get to the capital."

Fang Yizhi didn't raise his head, nor did he speak, as if he hadn't heard it. Pressing his lips even tighter, he took the telescope apart and put it together again. Now that he didn't listen, Huang Zongxi could do nothing but go on reading. After a while, Huang Zongxi eventually put the book down, got up, walked slowly to Fang Yizhi, and began to look at the disarray of mysterious parts laid on the table. "Well, it's hard to believe that when these things are combined, they can draw things from dozens of miles away to right in front of you, but it's absolutely real. The person who has invented this device is not just clever. He's a genius. It's amazing that there're people in this world who are so smart," he thought in awe. After looking at it for a while, he couldn't help reaching out his hand to touch the lens. Fang Yizhi shouted, "Don't touch it!"

Huang Zongxi flinched and recoiled in embarrassment. He watched from aside. Fang Yizhi was absorbed in a copper ring, which

---

① a royal technician-in-waiting: The original word is *daizhao*. A *daizhao* is a person (a talented person in the arts, classics, music, craftsmanship, etc.) to be appointed to office at court.

比了又比，似乎根本没有留意黄宗羲在场，或者虽然留意了，却丝毫没有把他放在眼里似的。站在旁边伺候的书童方理，却幸灾乐祸地做着鬼脸。黄宗羲的脸蓦地涨红了，他把袖子一拂，气鼓鼓地走回他的位置去，一屁股坐下来，重新拿起书本。不过，即便是这样，方以智也仍旧没有来理会他。黄宗羲愈加气恼。“哼，好你个方密之，竟然如此傲慢可恶！我倒要看看你到底有多大能耐，能把这千里镜装好！”他愤愤地想。

谁知，像是回答他似的，就在这时，方以智蓦地发出一声欢呼：“成了！”

接着，他立即动手，把桌上那堆零件一件接一件地装配起来。转眼工夫，一架伸缩自如，同原先一模一样的千里镜就擎在他的手里。他把它凑在眼睛上，试着瞧了几下，又奔到窗前，对着外面，调节好距离，从左到右，又从右到左地来回了望了一阵。终于感到满意了，他就把千里镜朝方理的手中一塞，倒背着手，哈哈大笑起来，一边笑，一边得意洋洋地在舱内走来走去。

“哈哈，我方某人到底还是行的！什么西洋奇器，不过如此！任他故神其技，我照样能无师自通！”他傲然地说，随即吩咐方理：“去，呈给黄相公鉴定鉴定！”又兴冲冲地对黄宗羲说：“太冲兄，经此一番，弟于此物不唯知其然，且更知其所以然了！他日倘有所需，弟照样能做出一个来！”

黄宗羲没料到方以智果然把千里镜装配成功，他有点意外，也有点佩服。虽然如此，对于方以智适才的傲慢无礼，他仍然感到恼火。所以，当方理把千里镜双手捧到他面前时，黄宗羲便气哼哼地背过脸去，不肯接受。

正在满心等待朋友赞扬的方以智，看见这情状，不禁愕然。方理走回去，凑在他的耳边咕哝了几句。方以智半信半疑地问：“我当真这等说？”看见方理肯定地点点头，他又回想了半天，

he turned in this hand to observe from all angles, totally oblivious to Huang Zongxi's presence or deliberately ignoring it. Fang Li the pageboy, who was standing next to him, made a grimace in mischief. Huang Zongxi suddenly blushed. He flapped his long sleeves, angrily walked back to his seat, sat down and picked up the book again. However, Fang Yizhi still ignored him. Huang Zongxi became increasingly irritated. "Hmph, what hateful arrogance! I'd like to see how you can reassemble the telescope," he thought angrily.

To his surprise, Fang Yizhi suddenly cheered, as if replying to him. "That's it!"

Then Fang Yizhi immediately started putting the motley of parts on the table together, one by one. In the blink of an eye, a retractable telescope exactly the same as it was before was held in his hands. He put it close to his eyes, peeped into it, then went over to the window, where he readjusted it and watched the distance from left to right and from right to left. Finally satisfied, he pressed the telescope into Fang Li's hands, put his own hands behind his back and laughed out loud as he triumphantly walked around the cabin.

"Haha, I can do it! What is called a clever device from the West isn't that difficult after all. No matter how clever it is, I can figure it out without a teacher," he said proudly. He said to Fang Li, "Take it to Mr. Huang and let him have a look." Then he excitedly said to Huang Zongxi, "Brother Taichong, after having done this, I not only know what it can do but also how it works. If there's any need in the future, I can make another one."

Huang Zongxi, not expecting Fang Yizhi to successfully reassemble the telescope, was both surprised and envious. Yet, he was still irritated by Fang Yizhi's arrogance and rudeness. When Fang Li held the telescope in front of him with both hands, he angrily turned his face away and refused to take it.

Seeing that, Fang Yizhi, who was awaiting his friend's praise, was puzzled. Fang Li walked back and whispered something in his ear. Fang Yizhi asked in disbelief, "Did I really say that?" Fang Li nodded affirmatively. Fang Yizhi thought back over a moment ago and

这才恍然大悟地一拍脑袋："啊，不错，我影影绰绰是说过这么句话。当时我眼看要弄通了，觉得身旁有人……原来是……哎，真该死！"他懊悔地跺一跺脚，连忙走过来，对黄宗羲又是打躬，又是道歉。

黄宗羲对这千里镜本来也产生了兴趣，只是被方以智一声断喝，扫了兴。现在见他一再赔礼，气也就消了。他一声不响地从方理手中接过千里镜，反复摆弄了一阵，又起身走到舱口去，学着方以智刚才的样子，对外面观测了半天，然后把千里镜交回方以智手里，淡淡地问：

"适才听兄自言，此镜可以仿制，莫非兄果已尽得其中奥妙了么？"

"这个自然——其实亦无大奥妙。"方以智连忙说，"弟已将此镜之构造绘成一图，只需觅良工数人，便可制作。"说着，他把黄宗羲引向他原来坐的地方，拿出一张纸来，铺在桌面上。黄宗羲看见上面写着"千里镜图说"五个篆体字，下面用毛笔描着一架千里镜，以及它的几个截面图形，还有各个零件的式样，尺寸、比例都注得清清楚楚。黄宗羲反复瞧了一阵，终于叹道：

"社兄真可谓聪明过人！我辈虽则也一样的读书，唯于此道，却是万万不及了！"

"啊哈，小弟不才，平生所自负者，也就是尚有此一点'聪明'！"方以智说。由于兴奋，他那张本来就红扑扑的脸孔，更加容光焕发了，"不过，西洋之学，只是详于'质测'，若言及'通几'，则往往疏拙浅陋。何况他那'质测'，也并未完备。小弟之志，其实并不在此哩！"

黄宗羲瞧了他一眼，没有搭腔。

方以智却没有觉察自己的话又引起了朋友的不快，他依旧兴

suddenly realized what had happened. He slapped his head and said, "Oh, yes, I said something like that. At that time, I almost hit upon the solution and felt there was someone beside me ... It turned out ... Hey, damn it!" He stamped his feet regretfully, hurried over, bowed and apologized to Huang Zongxi.

Huang Zongxi, who had developed an interest in the telescope, had been very unhappy after Fang Yizhi shouted to him. Now that Fang Yizhi apologized to him again and again, his anger was gone. He took the telescope from Fang Li's hands without saying a word, fiddled with it for a while, then got up and walked to the cabin door, and in the manner of Fang Yizhi, observed the outside for a long time, and then returned the telescope to Fang Yizhi and asked in a calm tone:

"Just now, you said you can make a copy of the telescope. Does that mean you already know it inside out?"

"Yes, of course. In fact, there's no great mystery," Fang Yizhi said. "I've already drawn a picture of the structure of this telescope, and we just need to get some good workers to make it." He led Huang Zongxi to where he had sat, took out a sheet of paper and spread it on the table. Huang Zongxi saw five seal-script characters that said "Diagram of the Telescope" on the top and below the title was a telescope with a few cross sections, drawn with a brush pen, the specifications of every part clearly marked. Huang Zongxi looked at it for a long time and finally marveled:

"You're a genius! Although we have been reading books like you, but none can compare to you in this regard."

"Aha, I'm no genius. This little skill is the only thing I'm proud of in my life," said Fang Yizhi. Because of his excitement, his red face became even more radiant. "Western learning, however, lies very much in physical inquiry. From a philosophical point of view, it's often shallow. Besides, the so-called physical inquiry isn't perfect in itself. Therefore, it's not what I'm after."

Huang Zongxi gave him a glance but said nothing.

Not realizing his words had made his friend unhappy again, Fang

冲冲地问："我辈生于当今之世，不知社兄以为是大幸耶？是大不幸耶？"

"哦，生当忧患丛集之世，恐怕只能说是不幸吧。"黄宗羲淡淡地说，管自走了开去。

方以智的眼神闪烁了一下，旋即暗淡下去。"小弟知社兄必定这般答我。"他点点头，叹了一口气，"便是弟亦每以辗转于这忧患之人生，延喘于这昏昧之乱世而咨嗟太息，竟至中夜难眠，悲愁泪下！"他声音低沉地说，神情抑郁地望着窗外的茫茫雨雾，以及那一队背着纤绳、在泥泞的岸边艰难前进的纤夫，许久没有说话。

黄宗羲本以为方以智接下来不知还会怎样自吹自擂，所以故意走开去表示不想听，没料到对方却发出这样凄苦低沉的叹息，反倒怔住了。

"然而，回心一想，又不尽然！"方以智忽然转过脸来，悲伤地、坚决地直视着黄宗羲的眼睛，"当今之世，无疑衰极乱极，病入膏肓，万难救治。但是，若以文明教化而论，却昌明鼎盛，远迈前代！推其故，实因已上承百代之智慧，积之蓄之，育之培之，乃能达此空前胜境。且更有西洋之学，入于中国，可与吾国之学相发明，遂使我辈生于今世，得以坐集千古之智，折中其间，成就一番空前之大学问、大见识，雄视一世，映照先后。如此说来，又是一大幸事了！"

"坐集千古之智，折中其间？"黄宗羲喃喃地重复说，疑惑地望着朋友，并没有立刻意识到这句话的全部分量。

"不错！"方以智坚决而自信地说，"以弟观之，历来所谓儒者，多有二病：一，穷理而不博学；二，闻道而不为善。无论拘守名教，以尊礼法，还是好作诡异言行，以超越礼法，二者都

Yizhi asked excitedly, "Are we fortunate or unfortunate to be born in this world, brother?"

"Oh, to be born into a world of many worries is a misfortune, I'm afraid," said Huang Zongxi placidly. Then he walked away.

Fang Yizhi's eyes flickered but soon dimmed. "I know you'll definitely answer me like that." He nodded his head and sighed, "Tossed around in this turbulent life and fighting for breath in this dark and chaotic world, I often feel so sad that I can't go to sleep at night with tears in my eyes," he said in a muffled voice. Then, he looked sullenly at the misty rain outside the window and the boat-pullers plowing forward on the muddy shore. A long silence.

Huang Zongxi, who had walked away a moment ago to show he was not interested as he anticipated that Fang Yizhi was going to brag about himself, was shocked to hear the deep, painful sigh.

"But things are not so bad when you think more about them." Fang Yizhi suddenly turned to Huang Zongxi and looked directly into his eyes with an expression of sadness and determination. "Today's world is no doubt turbulent and chaotic. It's terminally ill and cannot be cured. Yet the level of civilization is unprecedented, more advanced than in any of the previous dynasties, because the world as it is today is the result of hundreds of generations of wisdom. Besides, the introduction of Western learning reinvents Chinese learning so that we're able to attain to great learning and develop a great vision by sitting on the thousands of years of wisdom and leveraging it. Thus, we can also say we're very fortunate."

"Sitting on the thousands of years of wisdom and leveraging it?" Huang Zongxi repeated in a low voice as he looked quizzically at his friend, not aware of the full weight of this expression.

"That's right," Fang Yizhi said firmly and confidently. "In my view, the so-called Confucianists have always had two shortcomings: first, they're insightful but not knowledgeable; second, they know the importance of being good but never do good. Either clinging to the rectification of names to uphold the law of propriety or using cunning in what they speak or do to bypass the law of propriety is nothing more

无非为着求名，故意束缚矫扭其真性。至于科举之士，一年到头只知弄八股，此外懵懵然一无所知。彼一心所望者，无非‘利禄’二字，又安有心思博学深造？如今天下滔滔者，无非此辈！唯是学问二字，乃千秋之事，岂可无人任之？故弟于此立一大志愿：若得资财，当建草堂，养天下之贤才，删古今之书而统类之。举凡经解、性理、物理、文章、经济、小学、方技、律历、医药诸门学问，均审订真伪，发其精粹，清其条理，详其始末，编为百卷之书。不唯望其有用于当世，亦为千秋万代存一文明教化之真脉。如此，方不负此七尺昂藏，一身学识也！”

方以智越说越激动，洪亮的声音在船舱内嗡嗡回响。他不再看黄宗羲，并且开始威严地来回踱步。那睥睨一切的灼灼目光，那骄横而自尊的姿态，使他的形象在这一刻里变得那样不可一世，看上去，就像一位号令千军的统帅，或是一位君临万方的帝王。

黄宗羲睁大眼睛，仿佛不认识似的望着朋友。不过，使他感到惊愕的，与其说是方以智此时此刻所表现出来的非凡自负，不如说是这位才气过人的朋友所决心选择的那条道路——潜心著述，藏之名山，以待来者。不错，这是自古以来无数学者所共同走过的道路，本来无可非议。但是，黄宗羲一向认为，作为不幸而生于忧患时世的他们这一辈人，眼下却没有权利，也没有可能那样做。事实上，黄宗羲从来也没有忘记，自己是东林党人的儿子，是因为反抗魏忠贤阉党的暴政而被迫害致死的那批忠臣烈士的遗孤。他不只同阮大铖之流有着不共戴天之仇，而且强烈意识

than suppressing the true self to seek fame. An imperial examination taker only knows how to do eight-legged essays all year round and knows nothing else ... There's nothing but power and gain in his mind. How can he learn deeply and widely? The world is full of such men today. Learning is a never-ending human endeavor. There must be men to do it seriously. That's why I'm making a big wish: if I get the money, I'll build an academy of thatched houses to accommodate the best scholars from all over the country who will review and edit all ancient and modern books, put them into different categories—exegeses, theory of life, theory of things, literary works, government, philology, music, calendar, medicine and medical treatment—and then verify their authenticity, take out the best parts to put in good order with explanations of the origins and developments, and then compile a one-hundred-volume book. It will not only be useful for people today but will benefit posterity as well by preserving the gist of our civilization for them. That's what a real intellectual should do and what his learning should be for."

Fang Yizhi became increasingly excited as he spoke, his loud voice echoing in the cabin. He stopped looking at Huang Zongxi and started pacing back and forth majestically. With the scorching eyes that looked down on everything and the assertive and arrogant look, he looked invincible, like a commander of thousands of troops, or a king who ruled the land.

Huang Zongxi opened his eyes wide and looked at his friend as if he hadn't known him. What surprised him, however, was not so much the extraordinary arrogance that Fang Yizhi showed at this moment, but the path that this talented friend decided to choose: the writing of a multi-volume book to be kept in the mountains for future readers. Yes, this was the path that many scholars had traveled since ancient times, and there was nothing wrong with it, but in Huang Zongxi's mind, born in this unfortunate age of turmoil, they simply didn't have the right nor was it possible to do so. In fact, Huang Zongxi never forgot that he was the son of an East Wooder and the orphan of a martyr who had died of eunuch Wei Zhongxian's tyranny. Not only did he have a

到自己所肩负的使命。随着年岁和见识增长，他越来越明确地认定：国家的局面之所以会衰败到今天的地步，根本原因就在于天启年间皇帝昏庸，重用阉党，使国家的正气受到了严重的摧残。他参加复社，积极为社事奔走，就是为了在士林当中重新树立起一股正气，并运用“清议”的力量，推动朝廷改良弊政，防止阉党篡权的局面再度发生。尽管近年来国家的局势每况愈下，毫无起色，但黄宗羲始终没有忘记先人的遗志，也没有失掉复兴大明的信心。这一次，他不远千里赶到北京去，就是为了亲自观察一下，尝试一下……“不，他是不对的！如今当务之急是‘流寇’，是‘建虏’！在社稷苍生尚有一线生机之时，作为一个热血男儿，一个圣人之徒，如果不挺身而出，勇于承当救国拯民之责，那是可耻，是有损于为人品格的！”他不以为然地想。

黄宗羲抬起头，打算说出自己的看法，却看见方以智已经从行箧中拿出一部厚厚的书稿，兴冲冲地走到他跟前：

“这部《通雅》，是弟穷三冬之力写成的，自谓尚可一观，如今就请社兄指谬。”

黄宗羲瞧了瞧朋友，发现对方脸上，刚才那种不可一世的神气已经不见了，此刻正诚恳地望着自己。他犹疑了一下，只好把涌到嘴边的那些话暂且吞了回去，默默接过书稿，回到窗前的座位上，一页一页地浏览起来。

## 全家自尽

在运河航行了大半个月之后，他们乘坐的官船来到了徐州城下的黄河渡口。

这里离开梅雨地区已经很远，黄河上空，一碧如洗。几片轻

deadly hatred of the likes of Ruan Dacheng, but he was also keenly aware of the mission bestowed on him. As his age and experience grew, he became more and more convinced that the country had fallen into disarray because the Tianqi emperor had placed too much trust in the eunuchs so that morality had had no place. The purpose for his joining of the Fushe and active involvement in its affairs was to restore a sense of justice among the scholars, and help the imperial court correct the ills of government by the power of criticism and prevent eunuch politics from coming back. Although the situation in the country had been getting worse and worse over the past few years, Huang Zongxi had never forgotten the will of the forefathers, nor had he lost his confidence in reviving the Great Ming. Therefore, he was going to travel thousands of miles to Beijing to see with his own eyes and act if possible. "No, he isn't right. Now, the most urgent task is to deal with the guerrilla rebels and the eastern Jurchens. It would be shameful and disgraceful for a man with warm blood and a disciple of the sages not to stand up and bear the responsibility to save the country and the people while there's still a ray of hope," he thought contemptuously.

When Huang Zongxi raised his head to speak his mind, Fang Yizhi had taken out a thick manuscript from a box and walked excitedly toward him.

"This is *A General Guide to Civilization*. It has taken me three years. I think it's worth a read."

Huang Zongxi looked at his friend and found the proud expression had gone from his face and that he was looking at him earnestly. He hesitated for an instant and swallowed back the words that came to his mouth, took over the manuscript in silence, returned to the seat by the window, and browsed it page by page.

## A Family Suicide

After sailing on the Grand Canal for more than half a month, their boat came to the Yellow River Ferry at Xuzhou City.

It was far away from the plum rain area, and the sky above the

絮般的白云，在遥远的天际缓缓浮动着。五月的夕阳毫无遮挡地把绚烂的余晖，尽情投向空旷宽阔的河面。混浊的、闪耀着金光的滚滚洪流喷着白沫，打着回旋，犹如成千上万匹暴烈的野马，从西边的地平线上汹涌而来，又一刻不停地向东面的大海奔腾而去。几张灰色和褐色的船帆，在浊流里艰难地颠踬着。小山般的浪头一个接着一个，永不疲倦地拍击着荒凉的、赤裸的河岸，发出沉雷一般的可怕声响。

当航船横渡黄河的时候，黄宗羲和方以智并肩地靠在窗前，纵目远眺，谁也没有说话。虽然他们都不是头一次行经这里，但眼前这气吞万里的磅礴气势，仍然那样深深地震撼着他们，使他们的胸怀一下子扩展开来，并且被大自然伟大的、原始的、神秘的魅力所吸引，所陶醉，以至忘却了交谈，忘却了思考，甚至连自己的躯体似乎也被这原始的伟力所分解，所消融，不复存在了……

渡过黄河之后，登岸是一个大驿站，名唤“柳泉驿”。因为天色已晚，主仆一行便在驿站歇下了。第二天起来，收拾停当，用过早饭，方以智便命方理去交涉车子。方理去了半天，却空手跟着驿丞走回来。那驿丞诉苦说：“车子倒有，却因本地连年遭灾，骡马不足；加上粮饷匮乏，站里的驿卒裁了又裁，减了又减，只剩下十来二十人，到昨夜为止，能派的都派出去了，还没回来。只好委屈大人再住一天，明儿再走。”

方以智皱起眉头，不愿意在这鬼地方白白耽搁一天。他问明

Yellow River was blue and clear, with a few fluffs of white cloud slowly moving in the distant sky. The setting sun of a May day generously cast a rich glow on the open, broad river surface without reservation. A murky, glistening stream came mightily from the western horizon, foaming, swirling, and, like a drove of thousands of wild horses, galloped toward the sea in the east nonstop. A few gray or brown sailboats plowed their way ahead in the turbid stream. Hilly waves came one after another and tirelessly knocked on the deserted, bare riverbank with frightening, thunderous sounds.

As the boat crossed the Yellow River, Huang Zongxi and Fang Yizhi leaned against the window side by side and looked into the distance, neither speaking. Although it was not the first time for them to pass by this place, they were once again spellbound by the majestic view in front of them. Their minds suddenly opened to a great, pristine, mysterious charm of nature, and they ceased talking and thinking and even their bodies were dissolved and melted into the pristine greatness ...

After crossing the Yellow River, they landed where there was a major imperial post station[①] called Willow Springs Station. Because it was getting late, the masters and servants spent the night at the post station. The next day, after they got up, packed up and had breakfast, Fang Yizhi asked Fang Li to book a carriage. After a long while, Fang Li came back with the postmaster, empty-handed. The postmaster complained, "We do have carriages, but due to the natural disasters in this area in the past few years we don't have enough mules and horses. Besides, since we don't have enough funds from the government to cover food and wages for workers, the staff has been downsized again and again. There're only ten to twenty men left. By last night, all the available hands had been sent out. I'm deeply sorry you have to stay with us one more day and leave tomorrow."

Fang Yizhi frowned. He didn't want to waste a day in this damn

---

① Post station, or *yizhan*, is like a government relay station in the age of travel by horses.

驿站里还剩下两匹马，这个数凑一乘车子是不成，但倘若改为骑马，却还勉强凑合。于是，他同黄宗羲商量，决定不坐车子，就要了那两匹马。又同驿丞磨了半天，最后让他从站里那两个烧饭、挑水的老驿卒中，好歹抽出一个来跟着，便一齐动身出门，继续向北进发。

天色还早，四下里一片黑暗，只有闪烁的星星映在马眼上，反射出微弱的光芒。沙砾铺设的官道在脚下变得迷离一片，几乎难以辨认。拂晓前的风，从旷野上吹来，即使穿着风衣，戴着风帽，身上仍然感到凉飕飕的。这一带是南直隶[①]、山东、河南三省的交界，正当水陆交通的要冲，可是这些年来，由于饥民越来越多，其中铤而走险，落草当响马的为数不少。仅仅在去年，就有一个名叫李青山的强人，仿效《水浒传》中宋江的榜样，占住梁山泊，树起“替天行道”的旗号，经常攻陷州县，拦劫漕运粮船。投奔拥戴他的饥民很多，势力一直伸展到离这儿不远的韩庄，使南北交通几乎断绝。朝廷闻报，大为震动，急忙调派大批军队进行围剿，直到今年正月，才勉强把这场造反镇压下去。朝廷唯恐动乱再起，也曾下令对“就抚”的饥民加以赈济。但这几年，朝廷为着对付“流寇”，在过去每年征收几百万两“辽饷”之外，又接连加派了三百三十余万两的“剿饷”和七百三十余万两的“练饷”，眼下正恨不得把民间的每一滴脂膏都榨取出来，投入战场，哪有余钱去放赈？只好摊派给地方。而地方也正为应付

① 南直隶：明代称直隶于南京的地区为南直隶，相当于今江苏、安徽两省。

place. He found out that there were two horses left in the station. Two horses were not enough to pull a carriage but should be sufficient if they went on the journey by horse only. So, after consulting Huang Zongxi, he decided not to book a carriage but instead rent the two horses. Then, upon his insistence, the postmaster finally agreed to let him take one of the two elderly couriers, whose usual duty was cooking and carrying water from the well. Then, they set out for the north again.

It was still early, and it was dark all around, with only the dim echo of twinkling stars in the eyes of the horses. Under their feet, the imperial road paved with gravel was blurred and almost unrecognizable. Pre-dawn wind blew from the open fields, and the windbreaker and the hood didn't prevent it from being chilly. This area, the junction of three provinces—South Zhili, Shandong, and Henan—was a hub of land and water transportation. In recent years, it had seen more and more robbers as more and more starving men tried to survive. As recent as last year, there was a tough man named Li Qingshan, who, in the manner of Song Jiang in the novel *Water Margin* uprising in the Liangshan marshes, held up the banner of "let the will of heaven prevail", captured counties and prefectures and hijacked grain transportation boats. As more and more hungry people gathered around him, his influence expanded to Han Village in this neighborhood, so that the traffic between the north and the south was almost cut off. The imperial court was shocked to hear it and hastily sent out a large number of troops to put down the unrest. Not until January this year were gang crimes finally brought under control. Fearing that the unrest would resume, the imperial court had ordered relief to the hungry rioters who had surrendered. In the last few years, besides levying a special tax of millions of taels of silver a year for the military stationed in East Liao Province, a special tax of three million and three hundred thousand for the suppression of peasant uprisings, and a special tax of seven million and three hundred thousand for the training of soldiers, the imperial court had been struggling to squeeze every drop of fat from the people and inject it to the battlefield, how

“三饷”，弄得焦头烂额，同样拿不出钱来。何况那些官府衙门，上上下下都在千方百计捞钱敛财，即使有那么一点赈额，经过他们的手七克八扣，留给饥民的，到底能有多少，也就可想而知。更别说饥民实在太多，已经到了远远超出人力所能救济的地步。所以目前这一带，尽管官军加强了巡逻和弹压，但路上并不太平。正是考虑到这种情况，临出门时，方以智已经换上便服，还同黄宗羲各自挎了一柄宝剑，八名家丁和承差也各执刀棒，相随护卫，以防万一。

现在，黄宗羲在马上微微佝偻着身子，裹紧了风衣，在马蹄踩踏地面的单调而有节奏的声响里默默地想着心事，一边等待着第一抹曙色的出现。不过，由于黄安和方理在马后不停地同驿卒谈话，使他的思路时时被打乱，集中不到一个问题上。他一会儿想到离开余姚已经快三个月，家中的情形不知怎样，母亲好吗？看来应当修一封家书去问候一下了；一会儿又想到不久前同侯方域发生的一场口角，想到自己同这位社兄总是合不大来。记得自己曾在张自烈面前激烈地批评过侯方域一味花天酒地，而置父亲的生死于不顾。这个话，张自烈后来不知传达给侯方域没有？……过了一阵，他的思路又转到哲学问题上，想到“气”和“理”这两个概念，历来众说纷纭，莫衷一是，有一派人主张“理”在“气”先，另一派人又主张“气”在“理”先，可是在他看来，“理”和“气”本来是一个东西，并无区别，亦无所谓先后，人们硬要把它分开，实在毫无必要，也毫无道理……

然而，他渐渐觉得坐在鞍子上越来越不舒服。因为长久没有骑马，他已经大大生疏了。他不能让自己的身体自然地顺应着马

could it have the money to provide relief? So, it asked the local governments to give relief. The local governments, plagued by the three special taxes, didn't have the money either. Furthermore, the officials and *yamen* men were doing everything possible to make money for themselves. Even if there was a small amount of relief money, it was not hard to imagine how much could be left to the hungry after their handling, not to mention that there were too many hungry people to be fed. Therefore, in this area, despite the heavy military presence, the road was by no means safe. Given this situation, before they set out, Fang Yizhi and Huang Zongxi changed into plain clothes and each took a saber. The servants and the courier, eight in total, also took sticks and sabers with them just in case.

Huang Zongxi, wrapped tightly in his windbreaker and slightly hunched over his horse, mused in the monotonous and rhythmic sound of horse hooves hitting the ground, waiting for the first light to appear. However, because Huang An and Fang Li kept talking to the courier behind the horse, his thinking was disrupted from time to time, and he couldn't focus on any single issue. At one moment, he thought: It's three months since I left Yuyao. How are things at home? How is my mother doing? Maybe I should write a letter. At another moment, he thought of a recent argument with Hou Fangyu, with whom he didn't get along well. He remembered his bitter criticism of Hou Fangyu in front of Zhang Zilie for indulging in debauchery and not caring for his own father's life and death. Did Zhang Zilie tell it to Hou Fangyu?... After a while, his mind turned to philosophical issues. There're always different opinions on the two concepts, *qi* and *li*[①]. Some scholars maintain that *qi* precedes *li*, but in his view *li* and *qi* are originally the same thing, there's no difference, and there's no such thing as precedence between them. Separation of the two isn't necessary, nor does it make any sense ...

Having not ridden a horse for a long time, he felt increasingly uncomfortable sitting on the saddle. Because he was unable to timely

---

① *Qi* is the observable part of things. *Li* is the organizing principle of things.

儿走动时的起落颠簸，结果被马鞍子把股骨撞得生疼。“哎，看来我是越来越娇嫩了！”他想，“当年刘玄德因久不骑马，遂有功业未就而髀肉复生之叹，我如今的情形比他更糟！如此下去，怎么了得？”于是他把那些冥思遐想暂时抛开，一心一意练习起骑马来。他仔细分辨马的行走节奏，一边尽量放松身体去迎合它。开始他老是把握得不准，情况反而更糟，但他仍旧耐着性子坚持下去，慢慢就变得比较适应了。加上从前练习骑马时所学的那一套动作要领也重新被回忆起来，并且开始发挥作用，再走上十多里之后，他终于又熟练起来了。

这当儿，天已经破晓，一轮红日从右前方冉冉升起，照亮了雾气缭绕的广阔原野，给拖着长长的影子前进的旅人的脸上、身上，以及他们的行李、马匹上，抹上了一片淡淡的红晕。几只乌鸦呱呱地叫着，从路旁的树丫上飞了起来。黄宗羲为着试验一下自己的骑术到底恢复得怎样，就放松了缰绳，在马屁股上轻轻敲上一鞭，催着马越过方以智，顺着变得清晰起来的大路，向前慢跑起来。

这一次颇为顺利，黄宗羲按照回忆起来的要领，上身微微向前倾着，两腿用力夹紧马肚子，小心翼翼地控制着缰绳，居然跑得很平稳，转眼之间，已驰出三四里。他得意地勒住缰绳，回头望了望，看见方以智等人没有跟上来，便拨转马头，打算循原路驰回去迎他们。然而，就在这时，他听到了几声哭喊，声音尖锐而凄切，像是个女子，又像是孩子。听起来，人就藏在路旁不远的那片榆树林子里。黄宗羲勒住马，朝林子张望了一阵，却看不出什么名堂，但是，哭喊声又响起来。他皱起眉毛，想走过去瞧瞧是怎么回事，临时又想到：要是强盗在行劫，人多势众，自己对付不了，岂不更糟？迟疑了一下，他终于拨转马头，飞快地向原路奔去。

adjust his body to the bumping of the horse as he moved forward, his thighbones hurt from being hit by the saddle. "Hey, it looks I'm getting more and more delicate and fragile," he thought. "Back in the old times, Liu Bei, who hadn't ridden a horse in a long time, once sighed, 'The flesh on my thighs is back before I've achieved anything.' My situation is worse. It shouldn't continue." So, he put his thoughts aside and concentrated on practicing his horseback riding skills. He carefully felt the rhythm of the horse's gait as he tried to relax his body to accommodate it. At first, he didn't get it right and made mistakes. As he persisted, he became better and better at it, and to his delight, the set of horseback riding skills he had learned earlier gradually came back to him. Ten miles later, he became a proficient horse rider again.

It was dawn. A red sun was rising from the horizon in their front-right, illuminating the expansive, misty plains and casting a faint glow on the faces and bodies of the travelers moving forward—each with a long shadow dragging behind—and on their luggage rolls and horses. A few ravens cawed and flew up from the trees along the road. To test how well his riding skills had recovered, Huang Zongxi loosened the reins, gave a lash to the horse's backside, overtook Fang Yizhi, and trotted forward along the road that was becoming clear.

This time, it went pretty well. Leaning slightly forward with his upper body, clasping the horse's belly with his legs, and holding the reins tightly in accordance with the tips he recalled, he galloped steadily forward and, in the blink of an eye, he galloped three or four miles. Then, he proudly pulled the reins to stop and looked back. Seeing that Fang Yizhi and the others hadn't caught up with him, he turned his horse's head to gallop back to meet them along the same path. At this moment, however, he heard someone crying in a sharp and miserable voice like that of a woman or a child from the elm grove nearby. Huang Zongxi pulled the reigns and looked at the grove for a while but saw nothing. Then, the crying resumed. Knitting his brows, he wanted to go and find out what was going on, but stopped on second thoughts. If a robbery was taking place, he was no match for the robbers. He'd better let it go. After some hesitation, he turned

方以智正由仆人们簇拥着，缓缓地走过来。听了黄宗羲的报告，他回头问随行的那个老驿卒可知道出了什么事。老驿卒含含糊糊，也说不清楚。倒是黄安极力劝阻，说必定是响马在行劫无疑。方理也主张小心为妙。方以智瞧着黄宗羲，沉吟了一下，终于说："走，瞧瞧去。"

大家跟着黄宗羲，来到距榆树林子还有百步之遥的地方，方以智挥挥手，叫大家停止前进。他勒住马，远远朝林子观望了一阵，然后拔出佩剑，吩咐大家准备好，这才命一个名叫孙福的年轻承差过去打探。

孙福提着枣木棍，轻手轻脚地踅进树林子，很快，又重新走出来。他脸色发白，气喘吁吁地奔到方以智马前，禀告说："回、回老爷，里、里面全是死、死人！"

"响马呢？"方以智厉声追问。

"没、没有！"

"没有？"

"是、是没有。"孙福说，犹豫了一下，又补充说，"小人不曾看见。"

"那么死的都是些什么人？是怎么死的？"

"兴许是……是些饥民，小人没瞧清楚。哦，都是上吊死的！"

大家不禁"啊"了一声，这声音表示着吃惊，但随后，就放下心来。是的，眼前怕就怕遇上响马，弄清不是，便该谢天谢地。至于饥民自寻短见，反而用不着过于大惊小怪。这类事件近年来实在太多，已没有什么稀奇。而且作为过路人，也很难管得了，最多通知地方上一声，让他们派人来收尸就是了。所以，听孙福这样说了之后，方以智只是点点头，随即把剑收回匣里，准备继续赶路。

但黄宗羲还在沉吟着。

"里面——还有活着的么？"他问，向树林子瞧了一眼。

his horse around and galloped back along the same road.

Fang Yizhi was slowly moving forward, accompanied by the servants. After hearing Huang Zongxi's report, he turned around and asked the old courier if he knew what had happened. The old courier mumbled something they couldn't hear clearly. Huang An suggested they should not go, saying it was no doubt robbers at work. Fang Li also advocated caution. Fang Yizhi looked at Huang Zongxi, pondered for a while, and finally said, "Let's go and have a look."

The party, led by Huang Zongxi, came to a hundred yards away from the elm grove. Fang Yizhi waved his hand and they stopped. Holding the reins of the horse, he looked over at the grove for a while, and then took out his saber and told his company to get prepared. Finally, he asked a young servant called Sun Fu to go over and have a look.

A jujube wood stick in hand, Sun Fu tiptoed into the grove but soon came out. With a pale face, he breathlessly ran to Fang Yizhi's horse and reported, "Master, it's all dead people."

"Where are the robbers?" Fang Yizhi asked grimly.

"No robbers."

"No robbers?"

"No. There're no robbers," said Sun Fu. After hesitating for an instant, he added, "I didn't see any."

"So, who are the dead? How did they die?"

"Maybe, maybe some starving people. I didn't see them clearly. Um, they hanged themselves."

"Ah?" Everyone was shocked. Yet very soon they felt relieved, glad that it was not robbers. Hungry people committing suicide was not something to be afraid of. It was nothing unusual in recent years. Besides, as passers-by, there was nothing they could do except to give notice to the local *yamen* and ask them to take care of the corpses. Fang Yizhi nodded, put his saber back into the sheath and was about to go on with the journey.

But Huang Zongxi was still pondering.

"Is there—is there anyone alive inside?" he asked, looking at the

“没、没有。都死了。”孙福回答。

“可是，刚才我听见，有人在叫！”

“那——兴许当时有人还活着，后来就死了。”

“最好再细瞧一下，若是还有活着的……”

“啊，不错！”方以智表示同意，“孙福，你就再走一趟，若然还有活着的，就拿些干粮给他，再打发他点银子，叫他自寻活路——去吧！”

“是！”孙福应了，可是显然很不乐意，却又不敢违拗主人的意思，于是噘着嘴，去马背上取了一小袋干粮，慢吞吞地朝林子走去。

黄宗羲瞧着年轻承差的背影，脸上露出不满的神色。突然，他一俯身，跳下马来，把缰绳往黄安怀里一抛，大步赶上孙福，一把夺过对方手里的干粮，管自走向树林。孙福怔了一下，连忙跟了上去。

这片榆树林子不太大，弥漫着一股难闻的臭味。每棵树的树皮全都给饥民扒光吃掉了，只剩下赤裸裸的木质层，看上去，就像一具具被剥了皮的僵尸，张牙舞爪地挺立在那里，可怕极了，虽然已经是初夏天气，枝丫上也不见长出叶子来。只有成群的乌鸦“呱呱”地叫着，在树林子里乱飞乱窜。这些吃腐尸吃红了眼的畜生，一只只都长得又肥又大，而且不怕人。有好几次，要不是孙福及时挥舞棍棒，它们就会扑到头上来了。越往里走，那股臭味越大，地上的白骨也越多，东一堆西一堆抛得到处都是，稍不小心，就会碰到脚上。黄宗羲活了这么大年纪，还从来没有走进过这样阴惨可怖的树林子，从未置身于这种令人毛骨悚然的境地之中。虽然是大白天，心里也不由得直发毛。现在，他才明白，孙福为什么很不乐意再来一趟。不过，自己既然逞了强，已经不能后退，而且他也不想后退。所以尽管他已经想到，此举很可能是多余的，但仍旧掩着鼻子，硬着头皮往前闯。

grove.

"No, no. They're all dead," Sun Fu replied.

"But I just heard someone screaming."

"Then—maybe someone was alive at that point, and then died."

"It's better to look more carefully. If there's still someone alive ..."

"Um, that's right." Fang Yizhi agreed. "Sun Fu, you go there again. If there's someone alive, give them some food and money and tell them to go on living."

"Aye, sir," Sun Fu replied. He was obviously reluctant to go, but not daring to contradict his master, he pouted and took a small bag of food from the back of the horse, and walked slowly to the grove.

Huang Zongxi looked at the young servant's back with a disgruntled expression on his face. Suddenly, he leaned forward and jumped off his horse, threw the reins into Huang An's arms, caught up with Sun Fu, snatched the food from his hand, and headed toward the grove. Sun Fu was startled for an instant and then hurriedly caught up with him.

The small elm grove was pervaded with a gut-wrenchingly hideous stench. All the barks having been stripped off the trees and eaten away by the hungry people, the trees stood naked like skinned zombies with bared fangs and sharp claws. It was scary. It was early summer, but there were no leaves on the branches and twigs. Swarms of ravens croaked and flitted about in the grove. These big and fat scavengers feeding on human corpses were not afraid of living humans at all. Sun Fu had to swing his stick to keep them at bay. The further they went inside, the stronger the stench, and the more bones on the ground, which were littered around and would hit their feet if they were not careful. Throughout his life, Huang Zongxi had never seen such a terrifying wood and had never been in such a spooky place. He was terror-stricken, even though it was broad daylight. Now he understood why Sun Fu had been so reluctant to come again. However, since he was playing the hero, he could no longer withdraw, nor did he intend to. Knowing his trip might be unnecessary, he held his nose with a hand and pressed forward.

终于，孙福站住了，他用棍棒指着前面的树上，低声说：“喏，就在那儿！”

黄宗羲顺着他所指的方向抬头望去，果然看见树丫上挂着大大小小七八具尸体，有男有女，有老有少。一个个耷拉着舌头，全身僵直，显然已经死去多时。那些尸体的表情有的像在哭，有的像在笑，还有的眼睛睁得老大，龇牙咧嘴，形状十分可怖。黄宗羲不愿多看，他慢慢走过去，一面向四周打量着，看看有没有活的人还留在地上。可是，除了两捆破破烂烂的行李，和一些胡乱丢弃的粗碗破罐之外，再也看不见什么。“啊，都死了，一个也没留下！刚才还听见他们的叫声，要是我立时赶进来，也许他们就不用死了，然而……”他懊悔地想，不由得又抬头朝树上的尸体瞧了一眼，发现死者的衣衫虽然十分破烂肮脏，而且头发披散，没戴帽子，但从其中一两个人那宽大的袖子、长过膝盖的衣裙式样以及衣裳的质料来判断，显然不是普通的平民百姓，而应当是有一定身份的人家。这也没有什么可奇怪的，因为连年灾荒，再加上朝廷催索“三饷”逼得很紧，许多中产之家，也难以幸免于难。“嗯，看来他们有老有少，像是一家人。若在那太平时世，纵有天灾，也未至于流离道路，曝骨荒郊。可是，现在竟然弄到连这一类殷实本分的良民也走投无路，唯有以一死来求得解脱，就更别说那些贫苦无告的广大之众了……”这么一想，黄宗羲不禁垂头丧气，刚才急于救死扶伤的那一份热心也随之大减。所以，尽管孙福出于讨好他，建议再往林子深处找一找，他却摆摆手，悄然转过身，向外走去。

## 生灵涂炭

“似这等合家自尽的，还未算是最惨哩！”听完了黄宗羲的

Finally, Sun Fu stopped, and, pointing his stick at a tree in front, said in a low voice, "There! Over there!"

Huang Zongxi looked up in the direction he was pointing and saw seven or eight corpses of different sizes hanging from the trees. Some of the dead were male and some were female, some old and some young. Their tongues were drooping from their mouths and their bodies were stiffened. Apparently, they had been dead for a long time. Some had the expression of crying, some seemed to be laughing, and some were grinning horribly with bared teeth and wide-open eyes. Huang Zongxi didn't want to give them another look. He slowly walked over and looked around to see if there was anyone alive on the ground but saw nothing except two bundles of rags and some broken bowls and pots littering around. "Woe! They're all dead. There isn't a single one left! If I had rushed in right away when I heard their screams just now, they might not have had to die, but ..." he thought regretfully. He instinctively looked up at the corpses on the trees again and found that it was not an ordinary family, judged from the broad sleeves, the garments that reached to under the knees, and the fabric of the clothes of two of them, though their clothes were ragged and filthy and their heads were disheveled without hats. It was not surprising, because the years of famine, coupled with the imperial court's ruthless levying of the three special taxes, had impoverished many middle-class families. "Um, some are old, some are young. They should be family. If it were peaceful times, even natural disasters wouldn't have displaced them and exposed them to the elements in the wild. Now, however, even such a good family has come to such a tragic end—only death can liberate them—let alone the poorer families ..." Thus thinking, Huang Zongxi became very sad and his earlier enthusiasm for charity cooled down. So, when Sun Fu ingratiatingly suggested they go deeper into the grove to check, he waved his hand, silently turned around and walked backward.

## An Abyss of Misery

"Such family suicides are not the worst," said Fang Yizhi after

叙述之后，方以智说。这时，他们一行人已经重新上路，刚才那片榆树林子，也被他们撇下好远了。

“去年冬天，我从京里南下，途经此地，遇着一位社友，听他说起一事，委实骇人听闻！”方以智接着说，随即蹙起眉毛，就像通常人们说到一件极不愿意再提的揪心事那样，沉重地叹了一口气，“他是说去年秋冬——那时的情形比现今还要糟得多，满路都是饿死、冻死的人。剩下那些半死不活的，就像游魂似的一天到晚四处游荡，走到哪里都躲不开他们。啊，不知兄见过不曾？人到了那种境地，那眼神实在是可惊可畏！当他瞅着你时，不知怎地，便会闪出贪婪、狂乱的光芒，说不准什么时候，他们就会猛扑上来，把你拖去宰掉，吃了！其实，那时节到处都在吃人，什么易子而食、攫人而食，早已不算稀罕。竟有公然把妇人和孩童捆了，拿到市上出卖，专供人当猪羊一般屠宰，唤作‘菜人’的。那位社友起初还不甚相信。有一遭，他随一个姓周的客商上景城，时近晌午，到一间酒店去打尖。店伙过来说：‘肉刚卖完，请少待片刻。’那社友暗想：我这一路行来，连寻顿面食都甚难，如何此店却有肉？正疑惑间，只见有个小厮，带进来两名捆住双手的女子，一直入了后厨。那店伙便叫：‘客官已等候许久，可先取一只蹄子来！’那社友吓了一跳，连忙跟进去看，就听一声惨叫，一个女子的膀子已被齐肩斩下，倒在地上挣命。另一个吓得面无人色，筛糠也似的发抖，见有人进来，便痛哭求救；地上那个却只求速死。那姓周的客商看得不忍，当场出钱把她们都赎下，眼见断了膀子的活不成，便夺过刀来，分心一刺，

hearing Huang Zongxi's description. The group hit the road again, leaving the elm grove behind them.

"Last winter, when I was traveling south from the capital, I passed by this place and met a friend. He said something really appalling," Fang Yizhi continued. Then he knit his brows as people do when they speak of something disturbing that they don't want to mention. He sighed heavily. "According to him, last winter, the situation was much worse, with corpses of people who had died of starvation or cold littering the road all the way. Those lingering on the brink of death wandered around like ghosts. Have you ever seen such a terrible sight? When people are in that kind of situation, their eyes are really shocking and scary. When they look at you, for some reason, their eyes sparkle with greed and madness, as if at some point they would rush at you and take you away to be slaughtered and devoured. In fact, humans were eating humans everywhere at that time. It was not uncommon for people to eat each other's children or to kidnap other people to eat. There were men who bound up their wives and children and sold them in the marketplace to be slaughtered like pigs and sheep. Such victims were called 'human meat'. My friend didn't believe it at first. Once, he went to Jing City with a trader named Zhou. At noontime, they went to a restaurant for lunch. The waiter came and said, 'The meat has just been sold out. Please wait a moment.' My friend thought to himself, 'It has been difficult for me to find bread and noodles all the way. How can there be meat in this restaurant?' As he was wondering, he saw a helper bring in two women with their hands tied and take them into the back kitchen. The helper shouted, 'The guests are waiting for too long. Get a paw first.' The friend was shocked to hear it and went in to have a look. With a loud scream, an arm came off one woman, who writhed in pain on the floor. The other woman trembled with fear, her face colorless. Seeing someone come in, she cried for help. The one on the floor asked to be delivered as soon as possible. Mr. Zhou couldn't bear to see it and redeemed the two women. Seeing the one who had lost an arm was not going to live, he took the sword from the butcher and ended her misery. He took the other woman home to be his concubine.

让她少受点儿罪；却把另一个带回家去，做了偏房。只这般，当时不知多少人称赞周客商积了阴德，必得好报。你瞧，这可不是惨绝人寰的妖变么！”

在方以智叙述这桩令人毛骨悚然的故事当儿，黄宗羲一直阴沉着脸，一声不吭。直到方以智说完之后好一会，他才突然抬起头，用愤怒的、咬牙切齿的声音质问：“地方上发生此等令人发指之暴行，官府竟然坐视不管么？”

“管？”方以智冷笑一声，“彼辈既不能感动老天爷抛下无数牛羊粟麦，以救民困，又不愿割自身之肉以疗民之饥，也唯有‘不管’一法了！”

“我是说‘三饷’！”黄宗羲争辩似的大声说，“若只蝗、旱一端，而无‘三饷’之索，民生亦不致如此憔悴。天意不可测，天灾不可抗，诚难以此责备于人间之守、牧；‘三饷’却是朝廷所命，莫非官府也不将灾情申报朝廷，乞请皇上减免么？”

“灾情怕是会申报的，至于乞请皇上减免‘三饷’，只怕再饿死一倍人，彼辈也未必有此胆量！”

“哼，恋位畏死，唯知阿从上意，国事之坏，就坏在此辈愚庸怯懦之官吏手中！”

方以智没有立即回答，他回头瞟着黄宗羲：“足下以为，即使有人胆敢乞请减免，皇上会恩准么？”

“生民涂炭，至于此极，皇上以天下之忧为忧，又岂会置之不理？”

“当今皇上腹心之忧，只在流寇、建虏。”方以智依旧不慌

When people heard the story, they lauded the trader for doing a great charity, which would be rewarded in the future. Isn't this a horrible, inhuman world?"

While Fang Yizhi told this grisly story, Huang Zongxi kept a gloomy face and said nothing. When Fang Yizhi finished speaking, he suddenly raised his head and asked in an angry, raspy voice, "When such heinous atrocities happen in a place, does the *yamen* just sit by and do nothing?"

"The *yamen*?" Fang Yizhi said with a sneer. "They can neither persuade the Lord of Heaven to bestow upon the world numerous cattle and unlimited grains to save the people from the misery nor are they willing to part with what they have. The only thing they can do is to sit by."

"I am speaking of the three special taxes," Huang Zongxi said in a loud voice, as if in an argument. "If there had been the drought and the plague of locusts only and there hadn't been the three special taxes, people wouldn't have been deprived of their livelihoods like this. Nature is capricious and natural disasters happen. It's not fair to put the blame on human negligence. However, the three special taxes are levied according to imperial decrees. The *yamen* has a responsibility to report the natural disasters to the imperial court and ask for exemptions."

"They do report the natural disasters, I think, but I don't think they have the guts to plead for exemptions from the three special taxes on behalf of the people, even though the death toll doubles."

"Hmph, it's such power-hungry, death-fearing, ignorant and cowardly officials that have brought down the nation."

Fang Yizhi didn't immediately respond. After a moment of silence, he looked back at Huang Zongxi and said, "In your opinion, if someone pleads with the emperor for exemptions, will His Majesty approve it?"

"While people are suffering so, as one who worries about the worries of the people, how can His Majesty ignore it?"

"Today, His Majesty is only concerned about the guerrilla rebels

不忙，“时至今日，三军尚能用命，实赖有此‘三饷’支撑，一旦不继，战局便有立变之虞！兄以为皇上肯怜此一方之民，而听任社稷倾覆么？”

“依兄之见，如若无关于社稷之存亡，则四方之劳扰，民生之憔悴，亦不过是疥癣小疾，不值一顾了？”

“不敢！弟所欲知者，是倘若令足下秉政，该当如何处置？”

黄宗羲不响了。因为他发现自己正面临一个事实：一方面对建虏、流寇作战，需要粮饷；另一方面广大民众在天灾和“三饷”的双重重压下，又已经到了无法支持的地步。要是放松征饷，本来已经焦头烂额的军队就更加不能坚持作战，就有亡国的危险。要是不顾人民死活继续强征滥索，就会要么像刚才榆树林子里发生的情况那样，把他们逼上死路；要么就会促使越来越多的人铤而走险，参加到“流寇”队伍中去，同样会加速国家的覆亡。国事之难办之处正在于此。这是一种毫无希望的局面。“哦，莫非大明当真除了亡国一途，竟是没有出路了么？”这个可怕的念头在黄宗羲脑中一闪，但他立刻又把它否定了。“不，不对，不至于！出路还是有的，有的！”他怒气冲冲地对自己说，随即想起了自己正在准备的那份上书。“无论如何，民为邦本。民不思乱，则祸源自消，国家可定。而安顿民众，眼下之第一要务，便是从速恢复井田之制。这一次，就看朝廷肯不肯采纳，能不能实

and the Jurchens from Jianzhou," Fang Yizhi drawled. "To this day, the three armies① can still function exactly because there're the three special taxes. Once the three taxes are disrupted, the situation will worsen. Do you think His Majesty will be more interested in saving the people in a certain place than in saving his own regime from collapsing?"

"Does that mean, in your opinion, all the hardship and sufferings of the people, their life and death, are nothing compared to the rule of the emperor?"

"I dare not say so. What I want to know is, what would you do if you were put in charge?"

Huang Zongxi was silent. He was brought to a fact: On the one hand, food and money are needed to fight against the invaders and the insurgents; on the other hand, the common people have got to the point where subsistence is barely possible given the natural disasters and the three special taxes. If the tax collection effort is slackened, the already battered army will not be able to go on fighting and the country will fall. If people are exploited regardless of their lives, they'll either be driven to a dead end, like what just happened in the elm grove, or take up arms and join the insurgents. Either way hastens the downfall of the Great Ming. Such is the state of affairs in the country. This is a hopeless situation. "Woe! Does the Great Ming have no way out except ruin?" This frightening thought flashed in Huang Zongxi's mind, but he immediately dismissed it. "No, it shouldn't be so. It hasn't got to such a bad state. There must be a way out. There sure is!" he said angrily to himself. Then he remembered the petition letter he had prepared. "After all, people are the foundation of the state. If the people harbor no thoughts of rebellion, trouble won't arise and the country will be in peace. To pacify the people, the first priority at the moment is to restore the Well-Field System as soon as possible. Now, it's up to the imperial court to decide whether they'll accept my

---

① the three armies: the front army (for reconnaissance, bridge-building, etc.), the middle army (main force), and the rear army (for rear service)

行了……”

“太冲兄……”方以智平静的声音响起来。他显然想解释什么。

黄宗羲冷冷地望了他一眼。“国事如此，亏你还是个复社头儿，翰林院的编修，就这么沉得住气！”他想，突然在马屁股上加了一鞭，一声不响地向前奔去，把莫名其妙的方以智抛在后面。

晌午时分，他们一行人到了韩庄，打过尖，喂了马，稍事休息，又继续登程，打算在天黑之前，赶到陶庄。

现在已经渐渐深入山东境内，越往前走，周围的景象就越发荒芜、残破。虽然已是初夏，可是路旁的田野仍然大片大片地丢荒着，偶尔才看到几个衣不蔽体的农夫在低头干活。路旁的累累白骨，依旧无人收拾，东一堆、西一块，随处可见。有时出现一个村庄，也是房屋倾圮，人烟稀少。只有兀鹰在低空盘旋，野狗在街巷游荡。这些瘦骨嶙峋的野狗，显然是凭着凶狠和机灵，才得以在饥灾和战乱中保存了性命。它们一见来了行人，就迅速地退到一个随时可以逃跑的地方，然后狂吠起来。于是又惊动了在断壁颓垣之下藏身的乞丐，一个个露出须发蓬乱、面目浮肿的脑袋，远远朝这边张望……

方以智像是想起了什么，他用马鞭指着路旁的一个村子，回头问那个老驿卒：“数月前，我行经此地，见这村子还好好儿的，为何竟变得如此破败不堪？”

那老驿卒瞎了一只眼，头发胡子都花白了，神情木讷，举止迟钝。听了方以智的问话，他毫无反应，直到方理替主人大声重复了一次，他才“啊”了一声，低着头禀告说：“回大人的话，上月这村坊叫响马洗荡了！”

proposal to implement the Well-Field System ..."

"Brother Taichong ..." said Fang Yizhi in a calm voice. He clearly wanted to explain something.

Huang Zongxi gave him a cold look. "As a leader of the Fushe and an editor of the Hanlin Academy, how can you stay calm in such a moment of national crisis?" he thought. Then, he gave a lash to his horse and galloped forward, leaving Fang Yizhi behind, puzzled.

By noon, the company arrived at Han Village, where they had lunch, fed the horses, and rested for a while. Then, they resumed their journey, planning to arrive at Tao Village before dark.

Now, they were in Shandong Province. As they moved forward, the view in front of them became more and more bleak. It was early summer, but the land on both sides of the road was largely barren of crops. Occasionally, they saw a few peasants clothed in rags working in the fields with their heads bent. Piles of white bones lined the road, unclaimed, unattended. Once in a while, a village appeared, with broken houses and little sign of human habitation, and with vultures hovering around and wild dogs wandering in the lanes. The wild dogs had survived the famine and the wars, obviously through their ferociousness and cunning. When they saw strangers coming, they quickly withdrew to a safe place from which they could escape at any minute and barked savagely. The barking jolted the beggars awake, who were hiding amid the broken houses and collapsed walls. They stuck out their disheveled, swollen heads and peeped timidly at the strangers from a distance ...

Fang Yizhi seemed to have remembered something. He pointed with his horsewhip to a village by the roadside and turned around to ask the old courier, "When I passed this place a few months ago, I saw that the village was still good, but why has it become so dilapidated?"

The old courier was blind in one eye. His hair and beard were gray, his expression was dull, and his movements were slow. Hearing Fang Yizhi's question, he didn't respond. When Fang Li repeated it aloud on behalf of his master, the courier said with his head bent, "My lord, it was robbed by bandits last month."

方以智吃了一惊："难道是李青山余党？"

"回大人的话，不是李青山，是九山王。"

"什么九山王？"

"就是抱犊崮[①]的九山王。"

方以智"哦"了一声，他记起来了：上次行经这里时曾听人说过，虽然梁山泊的贼首李青山已投降朝廷，被斩首正法，但在花盘山和抱犊崮一带，还有另一伙响马，为首的不逞之徒名唤王俊，自称九山王，手下也有数千人马，却拒不投降，凭借崇山密林和饥民的掩护，继续与官军周旋。想不到如今竟闹到这边来了。

"嗯，那九……那强盗，可是常来此处骚扰？"他问。

"啥？"老驿卒听不懂。

"大人问你，那伙强盗是不是常来这路上杀人抢东西！"

"噢，噢！回大人的话，也不常来，不过他说来就来，神出鬼没的，俺也摸不清！"

方以智不由得皱起眉头，同黄宗羲交换了一个忧心忡忡的眼色。他正想再问，忽然前面传来一阵呐喊声。大家吃了一惊，抬头望去，只见从大路拐角上的树林子后面，一簇人马奔了出来，奔在前面的，是一群衣衫褴褛的人，后面还有手执刀枪的骑兵。大家被这突如其来的景象吓呆了。方以智叫了一声："糟糕，快跑！"就想拨转马头奔逃，却被老驿卒拦住了。

"大人莫慌，那是官军！"

"啊，官军？"大家再次回头望去，这才看清楚了：后面的那五个骑兵确实是官军打扮，奔在前头的那些人原来是用绳子反缚着串连在一起的。五个官军正嘻嘻哈哈地笑着，用鞭子驱赶他

---

① 抱犊崮：名山，坐落于现临沂市与枣庄市交界处，属沂蒙山区。

Fang Yizhi was stunned. "Was it the remnants of the bandits led by Li Qingshan?"

"No, my lord. It's not Li Qingshan. It's the King of Nine Mountains."

"What King of Nine Mountains?"

"The King of Nine Mountains from the Baodu Mountain."

"Oh," Fang Yizhi said. He remembered having heard that name last time he passed by the place. Li Qingshan, head of the Liangshan bandits, had surrendered to the imperial court and been beheaded, but in the area of Huapan Mountain and Baodu Mountain, there was another gang led by the outlaw Wang Jun, who, proclaiming himself King of Nine Mountains, had a following of thousands of men and, refusing to surrender, played cat and mouse with the imperial troops under the cover of the mountain forests and swarms of hungry people. That they had come here was not something Fang Yizhi had expected.

"Well, does the King of Nine Mountains—do the bandits often come to harass people here?" he asked.

"Pardon?" The old courier didn't understand.

"My master is asking, do those bandits often come here to kill and rob?"

"Oh, oh, they don't come here often, but they come and go like ghosts. I can't tell how often."

Fang Yizhi knit his brows and exchanged a worried look with Huang Zongxi. He was about to ask further, when suddenly came a scream from in front of them. Everyone was startled. They looked up and saw a group of people rushing out from behind the bushes on the corner of the road. It was a flock of men and women in rags, followed by horsemen with swords and spears. Everyone was astounded by this sudden sight. Fang Yizhi exclaimed, "Eek, run!" He wanted to turn his horse's head and run away, but was stopped by the old courier.

"Don't panic, my lord. This is the imperial troops."

"Ah, imperial troops?" Everyone looked back. It was indeed imperial troops. The five riders in the back were dressed in military uniform, and people who ran in front had their hands tied on the back

们向前奔跑。为了使这一长串男女老少都有、已经跑得精疲力竭的犯人不至于因快慢不一而互相牵扯跌倒，有一个官军还特意跑到前头，大声用口令控制着速度。然而，当他们快要奔到方以智他们站立的地方时，终于还是有人支持不住，猛地扑倒在地上。结果其余的人也被牵扯着，跌倒了一大片。那几个官军见了，顿时发起怒来，他们用最粗野下流的话叫骂着，鞭子唰唰地朝那些趴在地上的人劈头盖脸地抽去，于是又响起了一片呻吟和哭喊……

由于弄清了不是响马，方以智这会儿已经镇定下来。他皱起眉头，目不转睛地注视着眼前的情景，正考虑着怎样制止这种令人厌恶的暴行。

但是，黄宗羲显然忍耐不住了。他大喝一声："住手！"随即催马向前，朝离得最近的一名官军迎上去。

那官军气势汹汹地举起鞭子，正要向一名在地上挣扎的妇女抽打，蓦地发现眼前多了一个怒目圆睁的书生，倒呆了一呆，鞭子也停在半空。

"你、你不能这样打人！知道吗？"黄宗羲指着那官军说。由于情急和气愤，他的声音有点发抖，"你是人，她也是人。你为何这等打她？你这样打她，是会把人打死的呀！你知不知道？"

那官军搞不清他是什么人，又被他不顾一切的样子吓住了，倒畏缩了一下，不知所措地回过头去，瞧着他的同伴，仿佛在问：这是怎么回事？他是什么人？为什么要这样？

其余几个官军也注意到了这边发生的事情，并且显然觉得他们这位同伴的狼狈模样很滑稽。他们互相递着眼色，嘻嘻哈哈地笑着，却不过来帮他解围。

"你们身为国家干城[①]，受国之恩，食民之饷，应须对敌如罴

① 干城：盾牌和城墙，比喻捍卫国家的将士。

and were strung together with a strong rope. The five soldiers were laughing as they drove them forward with whips. To prevent this long line of exhausted captives of all ages, men, women and children, from falling over each other due to different paces, one officer even ran to the front and controlled the speed by shouting commands. However, when they ran to where Fang Yizhi and company were standing, one of the captives was too tired to move forward and fell to the ground. Many others on the same rope fell too, one after another. Seeing this, the soldiers became furious. They swore at them with the vulgarest language and ruthlessly whipped the fallen ones, who moaned and cried.

Now that it was not bandits coming, Fang Yizhi was relieved. Knitting his brows, he stared straight at the scene in front of him, thinking how to stop the gut-churning atrocity.

Yet Huang Zongxi could no longer bear it. He shouted loudly, "Stop!" Then he spurred his horse and cantered to the nearest officer.

The soldier angrily lifted his whip and was about to hit a woman who was struggling on the ground, when suddenly he saw a young scholar glaring at him. The whip stopped in midair.

"You, you can't beat people like that. Do you know?" Huang Zongxi said, pointing to the officer, his voice trembling slightly from worry and anger. "You are a human, and she is a human too. Why do you beat her like that? If you go on beating her like that, you'll kill her. Do you know it?"

Not knowing who he was and frightened by his indignation, the soldier cringed and confusedly turned around to his comrades as if asking, "What's up? Who's he? Why does he do this?"

The other soldiers also saw what was happening here and apparently found the awkward reaction from their comrade quite amusing. They winked at each other and laughed, but didn't come to help him.

"As guardians of the country, you are the recipients of imperial favors and live on contributions from the people, you must go at the enemies like bears and tigers and treat the people like fathers and

虎，对民如父兄才是。这些百姓已经受尽饥荒战乱之苦，憔悴不堪，纵然有罪，你们将他们捆缚押送也就是了，又何苦将他们如此戏弄，滥施箠楚？古语云，‘人皆有恻隐之心’。莫非你们没有？”黄宗羲振振有词地继续申斥着。

“啊，放你娘的狗屁！”被同伴们的讥笑弄得羞怒交集的官军突然大吼一声。他想必已经清醒过来，发现黄宗羲不过是一个过路的普通书生，“老子不懂！快滚开，要不老子的鞭子可不认人！”

“什么？你敢！”黄宗羲被这种当众的侮辱气歪了脸。他愤怒地大叫着，不顾一切地向那官军逼近。

那官军吼叫了一声，猛地扬起鞭子。站在后面的方以智大吃一惊，连忙高叫：“不得放肆！”几个仆人也一拥而上，要去救援。但是，已经来不及了。那鞭子夹着风声抽下来，眼看就要落在黄宗羲的头上。幸而他反应快，往旁边一闪，总算躲过了一击，可是头上的那顶方巾却让鞭梢打了下来，掉在尘埃里。

那官军仍不罢休，又一次举起鞭子。黄安、方理等一群仆人已经奔了过来，齐声叱喝着，护住了黄宗羲。

另外四个官军见了，互相使个眼色，也一齐拔出刀剑，各自从不同方向围拢来，一声不响地盯住了这伙多管闲事的旅客，大有一触即发之势。

这当儿，那群被押解的老百姓已经停止了哭喊，陆陆续续爬起来。他们像一群受惊的羔羊那样，紧紧挤在一起，呆呆地望着眼前这一幕，一个个脸上现出不安而又茫然的神情。

方以智凭着自己是朝廷命官，在事情发生以来，一直表现得十分镇定。可是，看见眼前这种凶险的情势，也不由得着忙起来。本来，为着旅途安全，他打算尽可能不暴露自己的身份，但事情

brothers. These unfortunate people are suffering from famine and war. If they're guilty of some crime, you can tie them up and take them away, but why do you abuse and torture them like that? As the old saying goes, 'Everyone has a heart of compassion'. Don't you have it?" Huang Zongxi reprimanded him sternly.

"That's bullshit!" the soldier, who had been ridiculed by his comrades, suddenly shouted in embarrassment and anger. Having woken up from the shock, he found that Huang Zongxi was just an ordinary scholar passing by. "I don't understand. Get out of the way, or beware of my whip!"

"What? You don't want to do it!" Huang Zongxi roared with anger as he took on the soldier like a mad man, his face distorted by this public humiliation.

The soldier howled and suddenly lifted his whip. Fang Yizhi, who was standing behind, was stunned and quickly shouted, "Hands off!" The servants also rushed to Huang Zongxi's rescue. However, it was too late. The whip came down with a whistle and was going to land on Huang Zongxi's head. Luckily, he responded quickly and dodged a blow, but his headscarf was knocked off by the tip of the lash and fell into the dust.

The soldier, who was not going to give up, lifted his whip again. By then, Huang An, Fang Li and other servants had come over. They shouted at the soldier and kept Huang Zongxi from his whip.

When the other four soldiers saw it, they winked at each other and drew their swords. From various directions, they silently surrounded the troublesome travelers. The situation was volatile.

By now, the captives had stopped crying and struggled to their feet one after another. They huddled together like a herd of frightened lambs, staring blankly at the scene in front of them, with nervous and puzzled expressions on their faces.

Fang Yizhi, who was an official appointed by the imperial court, had stayed calm from the beginning. However, when he saw the dangerous situation in front of him, he could no longer be composed. Originally, for the safety of the trip, he had planned not to reveal his

到了这一步，也就顾不得了。于是，他回头对老驿卒说：

“你去告诉他们，就说本官在此，叫他们休得放肆！”

老驿卒眨了眨那只独眼，拱手领命，走上前去，拿出一面号牌让那些官军看了，然后说：“这位是京里的翰林方大人，你们快快回避，休要在此惹是生非，可听见了？”

那几个官军听他这样一说，似乎颇觉意外，一齐向方以智投来怀疑的目光，随后又低声商量起来。只听一个火暴暴的嗓门——那是刚才同黄宗羲冲突的那个军士，大声说：“什么鸟大人，我瞧就不像！”

方以智的脸刷地红了。他正要发作，但看见其他几个官军把那个人制止了，心想：“只要快点把他们打发掉便好，又何必与这等粗鄙小人计较！”于是，又忍住了。

这时，一个像是小头目的官军把骨棱棱的脸转向他，抱拳说：“小军张吉，不知大人在此，冒犯车驾，祈请恕罪！”

其余四个官军也一齐抱拳欠身，却都不下马拜见。方以智心中更加不满：“这伙贱骨头，直恁无礼！”他恼怒地想，无可奈何，只好摆摆手，说：“嗯，去吧！”

几个官军正想走开，可是，已经重新戴好方巾的黄宗羲忽然叫道：“且慢！”他气冲冲地挤上前来，指着那群老百姓，质问张吉，“你说，他们所犯何罪？尔等竟如此折辱他们？”

张吉用冷冰冰的眼光瞧了他一会儿，忽然兜转马头，对同伴喊：“你们呆着干什么？走啊！”

等那群百姓被驱赶着重新上路之后，他才回过头来，嘲弄地说：“秀才想知道么？告诉你也无妨，他们是犯的——王法！”说完，双腿一夹，催着马，奔到那队“囚徒”行列旁边，“啪”

identity as best as he could, but when things got to this point, he had no more concerns. Then he turned around and said to the old courier:

"Go tell them, there's an official here, and they shouldn't act in such a brutal manner."

The old courier blinked with the eye that was not blind, put his hands together and said "aye, my lord," then stepped forward and showed the soldiers a name badge, saying, "This is Lord Fang from Hanlin Academy in Beijing. You must give way to him as soon as possible. Don't make trouble here. Do you hear me?"

The soldiers were stunned to hear it. They looked suspiciously at Fang Yizhi and talked to each other in a whisper. Suddenly, a big voice, that of the soldier having collided with Huang Zongxi a moment ago, said, "An official? He doesn't look like one."

Fang Yizhi's face turned red. As he was going to flare up, he saw the man was stopped by the other soldiers. He thought, "Get rid of them as soon as possible. There's no need to meddle with such lowly creatures." So, he held himself back.

At this point, a soldier who looked like a small-time officer turned to Fang Yizhi, clasped his hands and said, "I'm Zhang Ji. I didn't know you are here, my lord. Sorry for standing in your way. Please forgive me."

The other four soldiers also clasped their hands and bowed, but none of them got off their horses. Fang Yizhi felt even more offended. "These bastards are so rude," he thought angrily. Yet, he could do nothing but wave his hand and say, "Hmm, just move on!"

As the soldiers were about to leave, Huang Zongxi, who had put on his square headscarf, suddenly shouted, "Hold on!" He furiously rushed forward, and asked, pointing to the captured people, "Tell me, what crime did they commit? Why did you humiliate them like that?"

Zhang Ji looked at him coldly, then suddenly turned around and shouted at his comrades, "Why don't you move? Go!"

When the captives started to move forward, Zhang Ji looked back and said sarcastically, "Do you really want to know, Mr. Scholar? It doesn't matter if I tell you. They've broken the emperor's law!" With

的一鞭，把走在末尾的一个小伙子揍得打了个趔趄，随即同他的伙伴们一齐狂笑起来。

黄宗羲气得连眼眶都差点睁裂了，他一抖缰绳，打算猛冲上去，却被方以智拦住了。

“太冲，算了，何必同这些无赖之徒一般见识，有失我辈身份！”

“哼，莫非你当真以为这等不平之事，也是无关社稷的疥癣小疾么？”黄宗羲怒气冲天地质问。

方以智轻轻地摇着头，却不回答。直到走出好远一段路之后，他才仰起脸，神情抑郁地望着远处苍茫的暮色，曼声吟哦起来：

> 欸斯世之难处兮，又奚之而可适？
> 夜耿耿兮不鸣，睇东方兮何时明？
> 独储与不寐兮，长太息兮人生！
> ……

低沉、凄苦的声音在这一小队默默前行的旅人身畔盘旋着、纠结着，然后随着晚风飘散开去，越飘越远，终于在空寂、荒凉的旷野上消失了。

## 京师见闻

六月初旬，黄宗羲和方以智一行，终于抵达北京，并在宣武门外的方以智居第住了下来。

还在抵京的前一天夜里，黄宗羲就病倒了。先是发热，然后开始打寒战，已是初伏天气，盖上三层棉被，他仍然冷得抖个不住。好容易寒战停止了，而体温却急剧上升，热得吓人，面孔烧

that, he held his horse fast with his legs and spurred it to a trot. When he caught up with the captives, whoosh, he whipped the young man at the end of the line off balance and laughed madly with his comrades.

Huang Zongxi was so angry that his eyes almost burst. He flicked the reins to rush forward but was stopped by Fang Yizhi. "Taichong, let them go. Why should we lower ourselves to the level of these thugs?"

"Hmph, do you really think that this kind of injustice is a small matter that has nothing to do with the fate of the country?" asked Huang Zongxi angrily.

Fang Yizhi shook his head slightly but didn't answer. After they had traveled for a while, he lifted his face, and, looking sullenly at the hazy twilight in the distance, howled out loud:

*"How difficult it is to live in this world!*
*But where else can I go?*
*In a long, long night, the roosters don't crow*
*When will the light of dawn appear in the east?*
*Alone I am, and sleepless are my nights.*
*Woe, woe, woe is my life!*
*..."*

The low, plaintive voice hovered around the group of travelers, who moved forward silently, then drifted away with the evening wind, and finally disappeared into the empty and deserted wilderness.

## At the Capital

In the beginning of June, Huang Zongxi and Fang Yizhi finally arrived in Beijing and settled in Fang Yizhi's residence outside Xuanwu Gate.

The night before his arrival, Huang Zongxi became ill. He caught a fever and began to shiver shortly afterwards. It was early summer, and he was still shivering from the cold under three layers of blankets. The shivering from the cold finally stopped, but the body temperature

得通红，一个劲儿地嚷头痛，接着又呕吐起来。黄安一瞧这情形，知道主人的疟疾又犯了。当时已是半夜，黄安不好去惊动方以智，而且估计叫醒他也没有什么用，只好自己小心服侍着。挨到天明，黄宗羲的热也退了，头也不疼了，只是全身感到极度疲倦。这时，方以智也起来了，听说这事，便连忙走过来探视。他先问了病情，接着又让黄宗羲捋起袖子来诊脉。也不知他是从哪儿学来的一套，诊脉时那三根手指头不是搭在病人的手腕上，而是按在手肘弯上。只见他眯缝着眼睛诊了一会儿，满有把握地说："不碍事，这病须得隔日方再复发，明儿到了京里，我就有办法了！"进入北直隶地面之后，他们已经改乘了一辆大骡车，见黄宗羲这样子，方以智便吩咐另雇了一辆小点的，铺上褥子，让黄宗羲睡在里面，一直赶进北京来。

现在，黄宗羲就躺在方以智寓宅的客房内。时近正午，四下里静悄悄的。方以智因为要上翰林院去报到销假，一清早就出门了。黄安正在院子里给他煎药。那药是方以智临出门时亲自送过来的，据说来历颇不寻常，是几年前一位法力高深的茅山术士送的。方以智一直珍藏着，不肯轻易示人，因为是黄宗羲，他才慨然转赠，还说一经服下，必奏奇效。黄宗羲正苦于这疟疾几年来不断延医诊治，总是断不了根，见方以智说得郑重，自是喜欢，当即命黄安拿去煎煮。又因为方以智说，这药熬的时间愈长，功效愈高，所以黄安直到这会儿还在院子里忙着。

rose sharply. His body was frighteningly hot, his face burned red, and his head ached badly. Then, he began to vomit. Seeing this, Huang An knew it was malaria again. It was already midnight. Huang An didn't think it appropriate to disturb Fang Yizhi at this late hour. Besides, there was not much Mr. Fang could do. So, he attended his master alone. By dawn, Huang Zongxi's fever had subsided, and his head no longer ached, but his body felt leaden. After Fang Yizhi got up, he heard about and hurried over to have a look at Huang Zongxi. He first inquired about the symptoms, and then asked Huang Zongxi to roll up a sleeve and felt his pulse. Curiously, when checking the pulse, Fang Yizhi put three fingers on the crook of the patient's elbow instead of on the wrist. He closed his eyes and felt the pulse for a while, and then said confidently, "It's not serious, but the symptoms re-emerge every other day. I'll be able to deal with it after we arrive in Beijing tomorrow." They had been riding in a big mule carriage after they entered North Zhili Province. Now that Huang Zongxi was ill, Fang Yizhi asked the courier to additionally hire a smaller one with a mattress pad for Huang Zongxi to sleep in. Then, they came all the way to Beijing.

Now Huang Zongxi was lying in the guest room of Fang Yizhi's residence. It was almost noon, and it was quiet all around. Fang Yizhi had gone out early in the morning because he had to report his return to the Hanlin Academy. Huang An was stewing the herbs in the garden. Fang Yizhi had brought the herbs before he went out. The herbs, a gift to Fang Yizhi from a Taoist priest with magical powers in the Mao Mountain, were said to have come from an unusual origin. Fang Yizhi treasured them very much and had never showed them to anybody else. Earlier, because Huang Zongxi was a special friend, he generously took them out, saying that once taken they would perform miracles. Huang Zongxi, who had been suffering from malaria for years, was very glad to hear it and immediately ordered Huang An to take them to the yard for decoction. Since Fang Yizhi had said the longer the herbs were boiled, the more effective they would be, Huang An was still busy boiling them in the yard.

黄宗羲急于尽快把病治好，眼下还有另一个缘故。他这次千里迢迢地到北京来就试，目的在于亲眼瞧一瞧朝廷的情形，估量一下国家的局势到底发展到什么地步，以便把他的那份上书作进一步的充实修改，并在适当的时候呈递上去。所以他希望能尽快到外面去走一走，瞧一瞧，走访一些前辈和朋友，打听些最新的消息。可是这病一犯，他至少有一二十天别指望出得了门。这怎不教黄宗羲又是着急，又是气恼！

诚然，在快到北京的路上，他从来往官员的口中，已经陆陆续续听到不少消息。例如河南的开封自从四月被李自成再度围攻以来，形势日见危急，朝廷已将侯方域的父亲——前兵部右侍郎侯恂释放出狱，任命他为督师，率左良玉军火速驰援；又说张献忠的农民军已经攻克庐州，知府郑履祥被杀，兵锋所向，无为、庐江岌岌可危；还有，像皇上最宠爱的田贵妃病势日见沉重，可能不久人世啦，朝廷近日有令严厉禁毁煽惑犯上作乱的妖书《水浒传》啦，以及一些官员的任免等等。不过，其中最使黄宗羲震动的消息，却是朝廷已经查明：洪承畴自松山陷落之后，其实并未战死，也没有就义殉国，而是被俘后苟且偷生，竟然投降了东虏，如今在敌国很受礼遇。告知他这个消息的人还谈到，前些日子盛传洪承畴殉难时，皇上一度震悼异常，曾下旨隆重设祭，打算为他建祠立碑。钦天监还择定五月十一日上午巳时三刻由皇上亲临东郊致祭，文武百官一起陪祭。幸而及时查明了真相，才把

Huang Zongxi couldn't wait to be healed because there was something on his mind. This time, he had traveled all the way to Beijing to sit for the imperial examination because he wanted to see what the imperial court was doing with his own eyes, and with a better understanding of the situation of the country, he would revise his petition letter and submit it to the court at an appropriate time. He hoped he could go out as soon as possible, to look around and visit elders and friends, from whom he would be able to get the latest news. Now that his illness struck again, he would be confined indoors for at least ten to twenty days. He was deeply worried and exasperated.

During the journey to Beijing, he had heard a good deal of news from the traveling officials. For example: since Kaifeng in Henan Province was again besieged by Li Zicheng in April, the situation had become increasingly dangerous; the court had released Hou Xun from prison, father of Hou Fangyu and former Right Vice Minister of the Ministry of War, and appointed him military supervisor to be in charge of Zuo Liangyu's army reinforcing Kaifang's defense; Zhang Xianzhong's peasant army had taken Luzhou and killed Prefect Zheng Lüxiang, and as they moved forward, Wuwei and Lujiang were in danger; Lady Tian, the emperor's favorite concubine was seriously ill and would be dying soon; the imperial court had banned the seditious book *Water Margin*; so-and-so had been appointed to office and so-and-so had been discharged from office ... so on and so forth. The most shocking news was that the imperial court had found out that after the fall of Songshan, Hong Chengchou, instead of having been martyred in battle, had surrendered to the eastern Jurchens after being captured and was now enjoying a good life in the enemy country. The person who had told him the news had also said that His Majesty the emperor had originally been shocked and sad to hear Hong Chengchou's martyrdom and issued an edict that a mourning ceremony be held and a memorial temple be built to honor him. The mourning ceremony had been set for 9: 45 a.m., May 11, which was chosen by the Imperial Academy of Astronomy. His Majesty the emperor himself and all the major court officials and military commanders were supposed to be present. The

一切停止下来。虽然皇上天心仁厚，对洪氏的家属未予追究，但如今北京城里的官民百姓，已是无人不对洪承畴恨之入骨，骂声载道……这消息来得如此突然，犹如当头一棒，把黄宗羲打蒙了，仿佛心里有什么宝贵的东西被人一下子拿掉了似的，只剩下一片空虚和茫然。而当这种感觉，同受到钱谦益欺骗的旧创伤重叠在一起时，黄宗羲的愤怒就因为失望、痛苦而变得不可抑制。“啊，为什么他们都是这般的虚伪、懦怯，而又无耻善变？这些身负重望的衮衮诸公们！”他向方以智激烈地喊叫，“为什么他们要骗人？一次又一次地骗？啊，为什么？为什么！”自此以后，一连几天，他都变得很少说话，更没有半点笑容，一天到晚只是默默地坐在车子里赶路，弄得方以智莫名其妙，问了几次，都问不出缘故，只好由他去了。

不过，黄宗羲最初那一两天的沉默，如果说是由于愤怒和痛苦的话，那么，当情绪渐渐变得平静之后，他就陷入了对事情的深入思考之中。他想得很多，很杂。他竭力想弄清像钱谦益和洪承畴这样被人们寄予厚望的人物，何以到头来竟会置青史上的荣辱毁誉于不顾，做出这等厚颜无耻的事情来？难道仅仅是由于一个是迷恋乌纱，一个是贪生怕死？黄宗羲觉得，倘若是一个对自己所从事的事业有着坚强信念的人，富贵荣华和身家性命往往不是最重要的，特别是到了像钱洪二人这样的年纪、经历和地位的人，他们考虑得更多的，应当是身后的名声、历史的评价。除非，他们对于自身所从事和维护的事业已经完全丧失了信心！“啊，难道在他们看来，东林的事业、大明的江山都已经变得如此的没有希望，以至根本不值得留恋、顾惜了吗？”这个念头在黄宗羲的心中一闪，仿佛长期以来，他艰难而坚定地扛着的那个沉重的、巨大的、无形的包袱碰上了刀刃，突然裂开，原来里面装的并非

event was canceled thanks to the timely discovery of the truth. His Majesty the emperor was benevolent and had spared the Hong family from punishment, but the officials and the people in Beijing hated Hong Chengchou with a vengeance ... The news came so suddenly that it was like a bolt out of the blue sky. A sense of emptiness settled in Huang Zongxi, as if he had been robbed of something he had treasured. When this feeling was combined with that of being cheated by Qian Qianyi, he was disappointed, pained and filled with outrage. "Why are these eloquent, highly respected gentlemen all so hypocritical, so cowardly, so shameless and so fickle?" he yelled loudly at Fang Yizhi. "Why do they lie again and again? Why? Why?" After that, for quite a few days, he seldom spoke, nor did he smile. He just sat quietly in the carriage all day long. Fang Yizhi was puzzled and asked him what had happened, but he didn't reply. So, Fang Yizhi had to leave him alone.

Whereas Huang Zongxi's silence for the first two days was due to anger and pain, that silence became a contemplation of the heart of the matter. He thought and thought, trying to figure out why men like Qian Qianyi and Hong Chengchou, whom everybody had looked up to, had eventually sunk so low and done such shameless things disregarding their honor and reputation. "Is it as simple as love of power in the first case and fear of death in the second?" Huang Zongxi thought. "If a person has a steadfast faith in his noble cause, power, wealth, and life are often not the most important things, especially for men like Qian Qianyi and Hong Chengchou, who are old enough, experienced enough, and influential enough; they should think more about their own reputation and how they'll be judged by history, unless they've completely lost confidence in the great cause they've cherished and served. Hmph! Are they thinking that the East Wood dreams and the future of the Great Ming have become too hopeless to be worthy of their efforts at all?" The idea came to him as if the big, heavy, invisible baggage he had been carrying on his shoulders with good grace was suddenly pricked open by the tip of a knife only to reveal a pile of worthless rags unwanted by anybody instead of some precious

什么奇珍异宝，而是一堆毫无价值、谁也不要的破烂！黄宗羲被这意外的发现骇呆了。“啊，不，不是这样！这是荒谬的，可耻的，事情不致如此。等到了京里，就会弄清一切了！”他对自己说，尽快赶到北京的心情愈加迫切了。如今，倒是来到了，可是……

一股甜不甜、辣不辣的气味从窗上透进来，钻进了鼻孔。“嗯，那是什么？是腌菜？是煮豆子？哦，对了，是药，是黄安在煎药！”黄宗羲一下子清醒过来。他稍稍抬起身子，鼓起劲，朝院子里叫：

“黄安！”

黄安答应着奔了进来。

“快，我要吃药！”

“回大爷，还未好呢，方大人吩咐……”

“少啰唆，快拿来！”黄宗羲不耐烦地一挥手，由于乏力，又躺下了。

黄安瞧瞧主人，犹犹豫豫地应了声：“是！”走出去了，一会儿，把一碗药端了进来，嘟嘟囔囔地说，“方大人说，这药须得煎上三个时辰，如今才煎了两个时辰，怕还不成……”

黄宗羲不理他，重新支起身子，接过药尝了尝。药倒不苦，可是很烫口，只好暂时先放下。他正想重新躺回去，忽然院子里响起了一阵杂沓的脚步声，接着一个声音在叫：

“太冲，太冲，你在这儿吗？”

黄宗羲一怔，还没分辨出是谁，就见帘子掀起，三个儒生走进来。头里的一个，中等个儿，一张白净的长圆脸，眉毛胡子很黑，一双眸子闪闪发光。这是黄宗羲的好朋友陆符。跟在后面的是黄崇简，黝黑的圆脸，粗硬的络腮胡子，使他看上去不像一个文人，但从容不迫的举止，加上善良的细长眼睛，却足以改变他最初给人的印象。第三个是位清秀文弱的青年儒生，名叫冯道济。

treasures. Huang Zongxi was shocked at this sudden discovery. "Oh, no, I shouldn't think so. It's absurd and shameful. Things haven't come to such a bad pass. When we get to Beijing, everything will be clear," he said to himself, more anxious to get to Beijing. However, now that he was in Beijing ...

A sweet, spicy smell came through the window and entered his nostrils. "Well, what's that? Pickles? Boiled beans? Oh, yes, it's the decoction. The herbs Huang An is boiling." Huang Zongxi suddenly woke up. He lifted his body a little, and, with all his energy, called out to the yard:

"Huang An!"

"Yes, young master!" Huang An hurried in.

"Make haste! I want to take the decoction."

"Young master, it's not good yet. Mr. Fang said ..."

"No nonsense! Bring it here!" Huang Zongxi waved his hand impatiently, and lay down again because of lack of energy.

Huang An looked at the master and reluctantly replied, "Aye, young master!" After a while, he brought in an herbal decoction and muttered, "Mr. Fang said, it takes six hours to prepare the formula on the fire. It's only four hours now. I'm afraid it's not good yet ..."

Without responding to him, Huang Zongxi sat up again, took the decoction and sipped it. The decoction was not bitter, but it was very hot. He had to put it aside for a while first. When he was about to lie down again, suddenly there came a clatter of footsteps from the yard, and then a voice called out:

"Taichong, Taichong, are you here?"

Huang Zongxi was startled, and before he could tell who it was, the curtain was lifted and three scholars stepped in. The one in front was of medium height, with a fine oval face, black brows, a dark beard, and sparkling eyes. It was Huang Zongxi's good friend Lu Fu. He was followed by Huang Chongjian, who had a round, dark face and a thick, prickly beard that didn't befit a man of letters, but his quiet composure and friendly, slender eyes reversed the initial impression. The third was a polite, handsome young scholar named Feng Daoji.

“啊呀，原来是你们！”喜出望外的黄宗羲大叫一声，连忙挣扎起来，要下床同他们相见，却被陆符抢先一步，把他按住了。

“太冲，你身子欠安，不必起来，不必起来！”他说。

“那你们、你们怎么知道我在这儿？”黄宗羲在床上拱着手，结结巴巴地问，一边热切地瞅着这几位不速之客。

“自然是方密之！适才在魏家胡同吴骏公家里碰见他，说你在这儿，我们马上就赶来了。”陆符行着礼，高兴地说，“怎么，你这病——不碍事吧？”

黄宗羲摇摇头：“不碍事，老毛病了——哎，快坐下啊！”等客人们坐下，他就迫不及待地问，“眼下京里的情形怎样？朝廷有何新闻，快说给我听听！”

陆符同其他两位交换了一个微笑的眼色，好像说：“你们瞧，我没估错吧，太冲就是这么性急！”这当儿，黄安已经奉上茶来，陆符接过，揭开盖子，在杯沿上轻轻掠着杯里的水沫，思索了一下，说：“怎么说呢？眼下好像还算平静，自松山、锦州失陷后，东虏除了把松山、塔山、杏山三城平毁外，尚未闻有其他动静。至于流贼方面，据塘报说，驰援开封的我军丁启睿、杨文岳和左良玉等部，共二十万人马已经到了朱仙镇，准备合击李自成；侯司徒亦已离京南下，前往督师……”

“洪亨九——当真降了东虏？”黄宗羲皱着眉毛，打断对方的话问。

“哦，这事已无可疑。据细作报回的消息，他不止投降，而

"Oh, it's you chaps!" Huang Zongxi, who was delighted, said in a loud voice as he struggled to get out of bed to meet them. Lu Fu hurried forward and held him down.

"Taichong, you are not well. Don't get up! No ceremonies," he said.

Huang Zongxi bowed with clasped hands and said stammeringly as he looked eagerly at the unsolicited guests, "How, how did you know I am here?"

"Fang Mizhi told me of course. We just met him in Wu Jungong's residence on Wei's Hutong. He said you're here, and here we are," Lu Fu gladly said with a salute. "Well, how are you feeling? Is it serious?"

Huang Zongxi shook his head. "It's not serious. Just an old problem coming back. Please take a seat." When the guests are seated, he asked anxiously, "How is the situation in the capital? Is there anything new in the court? Tell me about it."

Lu Fu exchanged a smiling look with the other two guests, as if saying, "Look, didn't I say it correctly? Taichong is always anxious." At this moment, Huang An brought tea. Lu Fu took it over, lifted the lid, wiped the foam in the cup lightly over the edge of the cup, pondered for an instant, and said, "Where do I start? It seems calm at the moment. Since the fall of Songshan and Jinzhou, there have been no new developments other than the complete destruction of Songshan, Tashan, and Xingshan by the Jurchens. Regarding the guerrilla rebels, according to frontline reports, the reinforcements sent to Kaifeng, a total of 200,000 troops, consisting of regiments led by Ding Qirui, Yang Wenyu, and Zuo Liangyu, have arrived at Zhuxian Town, and are ready to launch an offensive against Li Zicheng. Mr. Hou has left the capital for the south to serve as frontline supervisor."

"Has Hong Hengjiu[①] really surrendered to the Jurchens?" Huang Zongxi frowned and interrupted Lu Fu.

"Yes, it's confirmed. According to the report of an undercover

---

① Hong Hengjiu is the literary name of Hong Chengchou.

且已经剃发改服，公然周旋于虏酋筵宴之上了！”

黄宗羲瞪大眼睛，只觉得一股厌恶、愤怒的情绪从心中喷涌出来，在身体内到处奔突冲击，却找不到宣泄的通道。终于，他一掌击在床上，叫道：“无耻！”

停了停，他又沉着嗓子问：“那么，洪逆在京的家眷，可处置了么？”

“这个么，皇上宽仁，对其家眷却未予追究。”

“不施惩处，何能以儆效尤！”

“听说，”坐在旁边一直未曾说话的那位名叫冯道济的年轻儒生插嘴说，“皇上之所以不办洪氏家眷，用意甚深，实欲借此羁縻洪亨九之心，使他知恩感戴，学那前秦王猛的榜样，令东虏不与我朝为仇。”

“哼，洪亨九是什么人？能与王猛相比？”黄宗羲怒声说，“指望他能阻遏东虏南进之心，简直是妄想！”

这话显然说得过于尖锐激烈，而且有直斥皇上之嫌。座上的客人你望我，我望你，都没有作声。过了片刻，陆符站起来，掀起门帘朝外面张望了一下，才走回来，凑近黄宗羲低声说：“京师不比外地，耳目甚近。兄说话须仔细些，若是给厂卫的人侦知，多有不便。”

黄宗羲见陆符神情郑重，知道不是在开玩笑。他自然明白厂卫的厉害，可是此刻他心头长期积郁着的那团苦恼的东西跃动得那样猛烈，以致他感到无法管束自己。要不是这当儿黄安插进来打岔，也许他还会说出更激烈的话来。

agent, he has not only surrendered but also been publicly mixing with Jurchen chiefs at banquets, wearing their hairstyle and dressed as one of them."

Huang Zongxi opened his eyes wide, feelings of disgust and anger welling up inside him without an outlet. Finally, he slapped his hand on the bed and hollered: "Shame on him!"

After a pause, he asked in a lowered voice, "Is his family punished in the capital?"

"By the graciousness of His Majesty the emperor, his family is spared of punishment."

"If there's no punishment, how can others be prevented from following suit?"

"I hear that," cut in the young scholar named Feng Daoji, who was sitting next to him and had been silent so far, "His Majesty the emperor has spared the Hong family out of consideration that Hong Hengjiu might be grateful and therefore persuade the Jurchens into stopping the hostility toward the Great Ming like what Wang Meng(AD 325–375) in the Qianqin Period did."

"Hmph, what kind of man is Hong Hengjiu? Can he ever be compared to Wang Meng?" Huang Zongxi said angrily. "To expect him to stop the Jurchens from advancing to the south is wishful thinking."

These words were, of course, too sharp, and contained a direct criticism of His Majesty the emperor himself. The guests at the table looked at each other without speaking. After a while, Lu Fu stood up, lifted the door curtain and looked outside for a while, then came back and said to Huang Zongxi in a muffled voice, "The Capital isn't like other places. There're eyes and ears around. Brother, you have to speak carefully lest you are heard by the secret agents and get into trouble."

Seeing Lu Fu's serious expression, Huang Zongxi knew his good friend was not kidding. He understood, of course, how powerful the secret police were, but at this moment he was unable to suppress the pain that had been tormenting him for a long time. If it were not for Huang An's interruption, he would have said something more outrageous.

“大爷，药凉了。”黄安说。

黄宗羲瞧了仆人一眼，又瞧了瞧炕桌上那碗已经不冒热气的药，把涌上喉头的一句话又强咽了下去。然后，仿佛唯恐它重新冒上来似的，他用了一个迅速的动作，端起那碗药，一仰脖子，“咕嘟咕嘟”地灌了下去，这才颓然地放下碗，沉重地喘了一口气。

“太冲，你吃的什么药？”一直注视着黄宗羲举动的陆符问，显然想把话题引开。

黄宗羲摇摇头：“是方密之送来的，也不知是什么药。”

“方大人说，这药可灵了，一剂就能断根！是一位茅山仙长送的。”黄安兴奋地补充说。

陆符似乎吃了一惊。他连忙问：“什么，你是吃的方密之的药？”看见黄宗羲主仆都肯定地点点头，他就“嗐”的一声猛地站起来说：“糟糕，你们可上了当了！”

这一次，轮到其他的人吃惊了。大家呆呆地瞪着他，不明白他这话是什么意思。

陆符长叹了一口气，说：“方密之这人才学过人，自不待言，只有一样不好，就是太好奇。越是稀奇古怪的事物，他越是弄得入迷。平日他收罗了一大堆乱七八糟的偏方奇药，也不知道灵不灵，就悄悄儿往人身上试。去年我得了腰痛症，他知道了就跑来看我，还给我带来了一把陈年草根，也说是得自什么崆峒山高僧，一服便愈。当时我信以为真，还着实谢了他一番。谁知一服下去，登时头晕目眩，耳鸣不已。后来幸得吴骏公请来沈太医，调理了整整一个月，才好了。这次他给你的什么茅山秘药，只怕也是那

"Young master, the decoction has cooled," said Huang An.

Huang Zongxi glanced at the servant, then looked at the bowl of liquor that was no longer steaming on the bed table, and swallowed the words that came up to his lips. Then, as if afraid that it would steam again, quickly picked up the bowl, tilted his neck and woo-loo-woo-loo drank it at one go, then put the bowl down and drew a deep breath of relief.

"Taichong, what kind of formula are you taking?" asked Lu Fu, who was watching Huang Zongxi's movements. Clearly, he was trying to divert the subject.

Huang Zongxi shook his head. "Fang Mizhi gave it to me. I don't know what formula it is."

"Mr. Fang said that this formula is very effective and one dose can cut the problem at the roots. It was given by a Taoist from the Mao Mountain," Huang An added excitedly.

Lu Fu was taken aback. He hurriedly asked, "What? You are taking Fang Mizhi's formula?" Huang Zongxi and his servant nodded affirmatively. Lu Fu suddenly stood up and said, "Oh no! You are fooled."

That startled everyone. They stared at him in puzzlement, not knowing what he meant.

Lu Fu gave a long sigh and said, "It goes without saying that Fang Mizhi is a highly talented person, but he has one shortcoming, that is, he has too much curiosity. The more bizarre something is, the more fascinated he is. He collects lots of strange herbs and secret formulas of dubious efficacy and tries them on other people. Last year, I suffered from low back pain. He came to see me when he heard of it and brought me a handful of old grass roots, saying that it was obtained from a monk in the Kongtong Mountain and my problem would be gone after one serving. I believed him and thanked him profusely. However, after I took it, I immediately felt dizzy and my ears rang non-stop. Fortunately, Wu Jungong brought me Royal Physician Mr. Shen. It took a whole month for me to heal. The Mao Mountain secret formula he's given you this time is more likely than

一路货色哩！”

黄宗羲听了，也不由得紧张起来。他轻轻摇了摇头，觉察不出晕眩，也没有耳鸣的现象，便迟迟疑疑地说：“嗯，这一次也许不至于……”一句话没说完，就觉得胃部突然翻滚了一下，喉头像被什么堵住了似的，直发闷，便连忙顿住不说了。

“岂有此理！”黄崇简一脸不以为然的神色，“你怎么不找方密之算账？”

陆符苦笑着把双手一摊：“怎么算哟！过后他知道坏事了，又跑来找我，一个劲儿地打躬作揖赔不是，还说不能让我白试了，一定要给我补偿。他也真舍得，即时把腰间佩的一把嵌了七颗珍珠的祖传宝剑解下来，硬是送了我……”

大家不由得“啊”了一声，显然对这个结局颇感意外，不由得露出了微笑。

黄宗羲却一点儿也笑不出来，因为现在他的胃部翻滚得越来越厉害，尽管他拼命抑制，却无济于事。他只好一手捂住嘴巴，一手向黄安挥舞示意。黄安吃了一惊，连忙奔向唾盂。就在这时，方以智兴冲冲的声音在门外响起来：

“太冲，吃药了么？可好些了？”

可是黄宗羲已经无法回答了。他猛地扑向床沿，俯身在唾盂上，开始大声地、猛烈地呕吐起来……

not the same kind of thing."

When Huang Zongxi heard it, he couldn't help but get nervous. He shook his head slightly, but there was no dizziness or tinnitus. Then, he said unsurely, "Well, maybe not this time ..." Before he finished speaking, he suddenly felt that his stomach rolled and his throat was blocked by something. He was struck speechless.

"That's downright absurd," Huang Chongjian said indignantly. "Why don't you hold Fang Mizhi accountable?"

Lu Fu spread his hands with a wry smile. "How can I hold him accountable? When he knew he made a huge mistake, he came to me, bowed his head, apologized, and offered to pay for the damage to my health. He generously took the seven-pearled sword handed down from his ancestors off his belt and insisted on giving it to me ..."

Everyone let out an exclamation of surprise and smiled.

Huang Zongxi was not able to laugh, for now his stomach churned and tumbled more and more violently. He was desperately trying to control it, but it was in vain. He covered his mouth with one hand and gestured to Huang An with the other. Huang An was scared and hurried to the spittoon. Just then, Fang Yizhi's excited voice sounded from outside the door:

"Taichong, did you take the decoction? Are you feeling better?"

But Huang Zongxi couldn't answer. He threw himself on the edge of the bed, leaned over the spittoon and started vomiting violently ...

# 第九章

# 惜遗才深忧重虑，应乡试意马心猿

## 苦候情郎

随着秋天乡试的日期愈来愈逼近，董小宛的心情也变得愈来愈焦急不安。

两个月前，在金山脚下的船上，多亏了方以智等人的热心撮合和督促，冒襄终于在最后一刻里回心转意，答允了董小宛的婚嫁要求。他还当着众人的面同董小宛约定，到秋天便来苏州接她，然后两人一起到南京去参加乡试；待考试有了结果之后，再来商办迎娶的事。现在五月早过，六月也结束了，七月已经过去了十天，可是冒襄仍旧音影全无……

董小宛是五月底回到苏州半塘的。一到家，她就申明两条：一、从此洗净铅华，不再接客，一心一意等待冒襄来接她；二、从当日起，她不再吃荤食，实行斋戒诵经，祈祷菩萨的保佑。本来，董子将自女儿走后，被债主一天到晚上门追逼，弄得焦头烂额，走投无路，忽见董小宛去而复回，不禁喜出望外。这一回他有了经验，知道事情到了这一步，硬拦是拦不住的，弄不好，还

Chapter Nine

# In Which an Elder Offered to Help Mao Xiang, Who Went to Take the Provincial-Level Examination, Leaving His Romantic Relationship Behind

## Dong Xiaowan Waited for Her Love

As the date of the autumn provincial-level exam was drawing near, Dong Xiaowan became more and more anxious.

Two months ago, on the boat at the foot of the Gold Mountain, Mao Xiang changed his mind at the last minute and agreed to Dong Xiaowan's marriage request thanks to the enthusiastic matchmaking efforts of Fang Yizhi and others. He promised Dong Xiaowan in front of everyone that he would come to Suzhou to pick her up in the autumn, and then together they would go to Nanjing, where he would sit for the provincial-level examination. They would discuss the wedding arrangements after the exam results were released. Now, May was long behind, June had passed too, and ten days had passed in July, but there was still no news from Mao Xiang ...

Dong Xiaowan returned to Bantang, Suzhou at the end of May in the Chinese calendar. Once she arrived home, she made two declarations: First, from now on, she would wash away the dirt by stopping receiving clients and wait for Mao Xiang single-heartedly. Second, from that very day on, she would go vegetarian, chant sutras and pray for the blessing of the bodhisattvas. Seeing Dong Xiaowan's sudden return, Dong Zijiang was overjoyed. He had been pursued by his creditors day and night every day since his daughter left. This

会落得个人财两空。所以他一反旧态，开始竭力讨好女儿，对董小宛申明的两条不但没有反对，而且自告奋勇，不辞辛苦地到如皋跑了一趟，求见冒襄，当面禀告这件事。结果，据他说，冒襄表示信守前约，立秋后便来接董小宛上南京，还打赏了董子将十两银子。董小宛得到这个消息，心志更加坚定，每日在观音娘娘跟前上香祷告，也更加勤快虔诚。不过，时至今日，冒襄还不来接她，甚至连信也没有一封，董小宛就开始觉得事情有点不对劲了……

董小宛刚刚吃过晚饭，照例又倚在闺房的小窗前，打起帘子，朝楼前不远的山塘河眺望。

火红的夕阳，已经落到了柳林后面，天色渐渐暗下来，几只回巢的鸟儿在水边匆匆飞过，河面上，除了三四只小划子外，暂时还看不见其他船只。眼下已是夏秋之交，天气本来就够热，加上这会儿连一丝风也没有，院子里的树木都静静地垂下枝叶，只有成群的知了，在看不见的地方，一齐发出震耳欲聋的鸣叫，更增加了人心上的烦闷。董小宛不停地打着蒲扇，身上脸上仍旧一个劲儿地淌汗。但她忍耐着，没有离开窗户。因为三个月前，冒襄到半塘来访她的时候，也是在傍晚。她觉得，这一次说不定他也会在这个时候来到。何况天气这样燠热，假若冒襄今天已经到了苏州城，也很有可能要待到傍晚凉快些再动身来访她。“哦，虽说他本来用不着拐到苏州去，可以径直从浒关到半塘来。不过谁知道呢？冒郎不比别人，需要应酬的朋友、处置的事情很多……”一想到冒襄也许到了苏州，却不急着首先来找自己，董

time, he knew better. Now that things had come to such a pass that there was no stopping her, should he try to stop her against her will, he would lose her completely and consequently his only source of income. Therefore, he abandoned his usual method and started to curry favor with his daughter. Not only did he have no objection to the two declarations of Dong Xiaowan, but he also offered to travel to Rugao to see Mao Xiang and told him about Xiaowan's resolutions. Mao Xiang said he would keep the promise and take Dong Xiaowan to Nanjing with him in early autumn and rewarded Dong Zijiang with ten taels of silver. Hearing that, Dong Xiaowan became all the more determined to marry Mao Xiang and all the more pious in daily incense offerings and prayers to Bodhisattva Guanyin. However, as of this day, Mao Xiang hadn't come to pick her up and hadn't even written her a letter. She began to feel that something was wrong ...

Dong Xiaowan had dinner, and as usual leaned against the small window of the boudoir, lifted the curtain, and looked out over the Shantang River in front of the house.

The fiery evening sun set behind the willow trees, and the sky gradually darkened. A few homecoming birds flitted past the waterside. On the river, there were no boats, save for three or four rafts. It was now the turn of summer and autumn, and the weather was hot in itself. Without a puff of wind at the moment, the trees in the yard quietly drooped their branches and leaves, and an army of cicadas sang in a deafening chorus from unseen corners, adding to the sense of gloom. Dong Xiaowan kept fanning herself with her palm fan, her face and body were still dripping with sweat. She didn't leave the window, though, for, three months ago, when Mao Xiang visited her in Bantang, it was also an evening. She had a hunch he might come at this hour. Besides, the weather being so hot, if Mao Xiang had already arrived in Suzhou City today, he would most likely wait until the evening, when it would be cooler, before coming to see her. "Of course, he didn't have to detour to Suzhou. He could come straight from Huguan to Bantang. But who knows? Young Master Mao is no ordinary person. He has lots of friends to meet and lots of things to do ..." When it

小宛禁不住有点埋怨:“哎，他是多么不懂得人家的心啊！”不过，随后她便责备起自己来：“你算个什么人？冒公子他答应娶你，肯这样远道迢迢来接你，就是天大的情分啦！别要不知足，只要他来了，迟一点早一点你可千万不能计较！”这样数落了自己之后，董小宛觉得心情平静了许多。她不再胡思乱想，睁大眼睛，热切而专注地向远处眺望，等待着航船的出现。

终于，在通往苏州那边的河面上，几点明亮的灯火闪烁着，从沉沉的暮霭里浮现出来。接着，出现了一艘船的轮廓。董小宛顿时紧张起来。她忘了打扇，全神贯注地盯着，一边在心里默默地祝祷。只见那船越驶越近，轮廓也越来越清楚，那是一只“七里舡”，船舱里坐着的，依稀是个方巾儒服的文士。“啊，那是他吗？是他吗？”董小宛惊惶地想，心里“扑通扑通”直跳，随后，一下子又像停止了似的，因为那只船已经驶近离院门不远的那个码头。董小宛觉得，它立即就要靠岸，她日夜思念的冒郎马上就要从放下的跳板上走下来了！

但是，那只船并没有靠岸，它在船尾那支轻快地摇动着的大橹催动下，拖着一条发亮的水线，不慌不忙地驶过去了。“不，不是的。”董小宛喃喃地对自己说，眼睛没有离开那只船。她还怀着一丝希望：谁知道呢？也许真的是他，只是由于船家一时疏神，走过了头还没觉察，马上就会转回来的……然而，那只“七里舡”并没掉转头来，它越去越远，终于消失在黄昏的薄暗里了。

董小宛失望地回过头来，“嗯，眼下时候还早，冒郎未必就能赶到。上一次，他也是齐黑以后才来的。”这样安慰自己之后，她感到站得有点累了，就去搬来一把椅子，在窗前坐下，一边打着扇子，一边继续守候。

occurred to her that Mao Xiang might have arrived in Suzhou without coming to her first, Dong Xiaowan grumbled, "Oh, woe! What an uncaring man he is!" However, she soon blamed herself. "What kind of person are you? Mr. Mao is obliging enough to agree to marry you and to come all the way from such a long distance to pick you up. Don't be greedy. Everything is fine as long as he comes. You shouldn't care whether he comes soon enough." After admonishing herself, Dong Xiaowan was at peace with herself. Leaving the disturbing thoughts behind, she opened her eyes wide, looked eagerly and anxiously into the distance, and waited for the appearance of his boat.

Finally, from the direction of Suzhou came a few flickering lights in the dusty twilight, then the silhouette of a boat appeared. Dong Xiaowan suddenly became nervous. Forgetting to cool herself with the hand fan, she watched intently and prayed silently in her heart. The boat came closer and closer, and its outline became clearer and clearer. It was a seven-*li* punt. In the cabin sat a scholar with a square headscarf and in a Confucian long gown. "Ah, is that him? Is that him?" Dong Xiaowan thought panickedly. Her heart pounded thunderously but soon stopped as the boat sailed to the pier in front of her courtyard. It was about to dock at the bank and the man of her dreams would soon step off the lowered springboard.

The boat, however, didn't dock, and propelled by the large, brisk oar, it sailed unhurriedly forward, dragging a shining trail of water behind it. "No, it isn't." Dong Xiaowan muttered to herself, her eyes not leaving the boat. Yet, she still entertained a glimmer of hope. Who knows? Maybe it is him, but it's just that the boatman is absent-minded and doesn't notice he's missed the destination. They'll turn around soon. However, the seven-*li* punt didn't turn around. It went further and further away and finally disappeared into the murky light of dusk.

Dong Xiaowan turned around dejectedly. "Well, it's early yet and Mr. Mao may not be able to show up right now. Last time, he arrived after dark." Thus comforting herself, she felt a little tired and brought a chair for herself. Then, she sat by the window and continued to wait

天色越来越暗，树上的知了也叫得愈来愈起劲，周遭的热浪紧紧地围裹上来，把人闷得连气也有点透不过了。可是董小宛下定决心无论如何要坚持下去，她的一双眼睛也始终没有离开山塘河面。这样又过了半个时辰，正当她觉得愈来愈闷热难受，快要支持不住的时候，脸上忽然像给一根鹅毛轻轻拂了一下，感到一丝凉意，接着又是第二下、第三下……说也奇怪，周遭的热浪仿佛遇到了什么难以对付的敌手似的，悄悄地、分明地退下去了。渐渐地，那鹅毛样的清爽感觉变得清晰起来，有力起来。董小宛的一缕鬓发开始摇摆。接着，她发觉衣衫也在飘动……蓦地，一道曲折的闪电划破了沉沉的夜幕，原来天空中不知什么时候已经乌云密布。这时，树上的知了早已停止了鸣叫，潮湿的空气到处弥漫，看来，一场大雨就要来临了。

董小宛长长地舒了一口气，正打算闭起眼睛歇息一下，忽然又想到：啊，要是下起大雨，冒郎不知道还能不能动身前来？一旦意识到这场雨对于她来说，很可能不是好事而是坏事，董小宛顿时又紧张起来，恨不得立即把眼前的凉爽赶跑，把刚才的闷热重新召唤回来。

“娘，陈小官又来了，你见他不见？”丫环寿儿不知什么时候走了进来，摆出一副公事公办的神气问。

董小宛错愕了一下，随即皱起了眉毛：“什么见不见？我不是早说了，他若再来，你只管替我赶走就是！”

“可是……”

“我不听，不听！让他走，快走！”董小宛厌恶地捂着耳朵叫嚷。

“是！”寿儿答应了一句，却仍旧挨延着。这时，董子将的喝骂声在楼下响起来：

“好呵，原来又是你这个臭叫花子！你来干什么？啊，你来干什么？”

while cooling herself with the hand fan.

It was getting darker and darker, the whir of cicadas on the trees grew louder and louder, and the surrounding heatwaves assailed and suffocated her, but Dong Xiaowan was determined to wait no matter what, and her eyes never left the Shantang River. After another half hour, when she couldn't hold out from the increasing heat anymore, she suddenly felt a goose feather gently brush her face with a soothing coolness, then a second time, and then a third ... Curiously, the surrounding heatwaves quietly and unmistakably retreated, as if they had encountered some formidable enemy. Gradually, that feathery, refreshing feeling became clear and intense. A tuft of Dong Xiaowan's temple hair began to flutter. Then, she noticed that her clothes were fluttering too ... Suddenly, a flash of lightning cut through the dark night sky where storm clouds had gathered. By this time, the cicadas on the trees had stopped chirping, and the air was permeated with dampness. It looked that a heavy rain was coming.

Dong Xiaowan let out a long sigh of relief and was about to close her eyes for a rest when she suddenly thought: Oh, if the rain is too heavy, I wonder if Mr. Mao will be able to set out and come here. As soon as she realized that the rain was probably a bad thing for her instead of a good one, Dong Xiaowan suddenly became nervous again. She wished she could drive the coolness away and call back the sultry heat.

"Missus, Chen Xiaoguan is here again. Do you want to see him or not?" Shou'er the servant girl came in and asked in business style.

Dong Xiaowan was stunned and said with a frown, "To see him or not? Didn't I tell you that if he comes again, just drive him away?"

"But ..."

"No buts. I won't listen. Let him go. Hurry!" Dong Xiaowan bellowed, covering her ears with her hands.

Shou'er said "yes, Missus" but stood still. At this point, Dong Zijiang's swearing came from downstairs.

"So, it's you again, stinking beggar! What are you doing here? Hey, what are you up to?"

只听对方含糊地应了一句什么。紧接着“啪”的一响，然后就是陈小官的惊叫：

“啊，你打人，你为什么打人？”

“老子就打你这个臭叫花，怎么样？你走不走？不走老子还打！”董子将得意地说，不难想象出他那副狞笑的模样。

寿儿瞧了董小宛一眼，连忙三步并作两步地走了出去，接着又“咚咚咚”地下了楼。

“哎，你还呆着干什么？走，快走呀！”只听她催促说。

好一阵没动静。然后，才听见陈小官说：“好，我走，我这就走——不过，你们可别得意过头了，小爷当初可是花过大钱的！如今把我榨干了，你们就翻脸不认人，只想挑那高枝儿攀。也不想想，人家姓冒的会要你？要你罢啦！哼，就摆出这么副面孔来了！”

他一边愤愤地说，一边走出后门去了。

董小宛侧耳听着，轻轻舒了一口气，重新在窗前坐下来。这个陈小官，说来可真是个轻贱骨头。他本是桐桥圩一户殷实人家的独生子，今年也才二十二三岁，天生不喜读书，只爱游荡玩耍。早年他爹在世，总还有个人管着；后来他爹一死，他娘又只知溺爱儿子，这陈小官就愈加放纵起来。不知怎地，几年前，他竟迷上了董小宛。初时也只是来喝杯茶，求幅画儿，偶尔也留宿一晚半晚。那时小宛的娘还在，见他舍得出银子，倒也以礼相待。谁知，他竟因此生出了妄念，想把董小宛娶回家去。其实小宛哪会看得上他？便是平日陪茶侍寝，也是被娘逼得紧了，没奈何敷衍他一下。但是陈小官却不知趣，一心以为是银子花得未足，从此便加倍挥霍起来。今儿二十、三十，明儿五十、一百。小宛的娘

There was a faint reply from another man, immediately followed by a slapping sound, and then Chen Xiaoguan's scream:

"Blimey! You're beating me! Why do you beat me?"

"I am beating you, you stinking beggar, so what? Do you leave or not? I'll beat you harder if you don't," said Dong Zijiang insolently. It was not hard to imagine his grinning look.

Shou'er looked at Dong Xiaowan and hurriedly went downstairs.

"Hey, why don't you move? Go, off you go!" She urged Chen Xiaoguan.

A long silence. Then Chen Xiaoguan said angrily, "Alright. I'll leave. I'll leave right away—but don't be too glad. I've spent a lot of money on you. Now that you've squeezed every last tael of silver from me, you're turning your back on me to court favor with someone more worthy, as if you had never known me. Do you really think Mr. Mao will condescend to marry you? He's merely playing with you and yet you're acting like that."

Then, he walked out the back door.

Dong Xiaowan cocked her ear and listened, then let out a sigh of relief and sat down at the window again. Chen Xiaoguan was really a despicable creature. The only offspring of a wealthy family at Tongqiao Market, twenty-two or three years of age, he loved fun and play instead of studying for a bright future. In the early years, when his father was alive, there was some form of discipline; later, after his father died, he was spoiled by his mother and became even more dissipated. Somehow, a few years ago, he fell in love with Dong Xiaowan. At first, he only came to drink a cup of tea or ask for a painting and occasionally stayed for an evening or a night. At that time, Xiaowan's mother was alive, and seeing that he was generous with his money, she treated him with courtesy. However, he had developed a wishful thinking that he might marry Dong Xiaowan, who would never give it a thought. Xiaowan's reception of him with tea or in bed was merely perfunctory given the pressure from her mother, but Chen Xiaoguan didn't know what she was really thinking and doubled down on his spending, twenty or thirty taels of silver today, fifty or one hundred

是个惯家子，见钱就收，还时时拿些暖心的话来笼络他，弄得陈小官愈加死心塌地，不到两年工夫，竟把好端端一份家业荡个精光。小宛娘眼见他已经穷态毕露，仍旧天天上门来纠缠，赶又赶不走，便干脆带了董小宛去跑黄山、白岳，一走就是两年，为的是让他死了这条心。今年初，董小宛回到半塘之后，听说陈小官已经连祖屋都变卖了，亲戚朋友谁也不肯收留他，只好带着老母住进了养济院，其实同乞丐差不多了。谁知，陈小官一听说董小宛回到了半塘，竟又巴巴地找上门来。起初，董小宛一时心软，也周济过他一两半两。谁知他就想差了念头，以为董小宛对他依旧有情，还疯疯癫癫地逢人就说，他好比唐人小说中的那个落难的荥阳公子，董小宛就是那个多情多义的妓女李娃，他们不久就会共谐琴瑟之好了。此后，他就不歇地上门。董小宛见不是头，叫她爹和寿儿下狠劲儿赶了他好几次，还吓唬要把他缚去见官，陈小官才来得少了些，不过，仍常常会冷不丁从后门踅进来，伸着巴掌讨钱。董小宛早就吩咐过，碰上这种情况，寿儿就该毫不犹疑地把他轰走。可是这个鬼丫头也不知得了他什么好处，仍旧一次一次地替他上来通报。

董小宛摇摇头，竭力摆脱这种烦心的干扰。她又把目光投向山塘河，“哎，莫非今天又是空等？”她不安地想，同时开始在心里计算着：今天已是七月初十，距八月初十的考期只剩下一个月了，除掉路上花去的时间，到南京也就只有两三天的宽余；还有许多事情要安排准备，两三天的时间是最起码的了。那么，就

tomorrow. Xiaowan's mother customarily took any money that came her way and from time to time spoke a few warm words to him, which made him even more determined in wooing the girl he loved. In less than two years, he squandered all his fortune in the brothel. Down and out, he came to harrass Xiaowan every day, so her mother took her away for a tour to the Yellow Mountains and the White Mountains①—where they stayed for two years—to get rid of him altogether. Earlier this year, after Dong Xiaowan returned to Bantang, she heard that Chen Xiaoguan had sold the home handed down by his ancestors and none of his relatives and friends would take him in so that he had to move into a charity home with his mother. He had practically become a beggar. However, when Chen Xiaoguan heard that Dong Xiaowan had returned to Bantang, he came to her door again. At first, Dong Xiaowan had pity for him and gave him some money, but he mistook her kindness for love and like a lunatic told everyone that he was like the young Mr. Xingyang in distress, Dong Xiaowan was the loving and righteous prostitute Li Wa, and soon they would be living happily ever after. Later, he kept coming to her door. Seeing there was no end to it, Dong Xiaowan asked her father and the servant girl to drive him away every time he came. They even threatened to send him to the *yamen*. Then, the harassment was less frequent. Once in a while, he came stealthily through the back door and begged for some money. At such moments, Shou'er was supposed to drive him away outright as she had been instructed to, but somehow she kept reporting his coming to her mistress. Maybe she had been bribed.

Dong Xiaowan shook her head to get rid of this annoying interference. She turned her eyes again to Shantang River. "Ssh, will my waiting be in vain again today?" she thought anxiously, and at the same time began to calculate in her mind, "Today is the tenth of July, and there's only one month to go before the exam date, which is the tenth of August. Excluding the days on the road, he'll have no

① the White Mountains (*baiyue*): modern-day Qiyun Mountains in Anhui Province

是说，除非冒郎临时决定不去应考——这是不可能的——否则，他必须最迟在这一两天内来到苏州。这一两天内他要是不来，就不用指望他会来了！这样一想，董小宛心里顿时凉了半截。“啊，难道真像陈小官所说的，他是在骗我？”这个念头一出现，她不由得呆住了。的确，这是她从来没有想到过的。说也奇怪，在苦苦追求冒襄的几个月当中，她尽管想得不少，想到过他会冷淡她、讥笑她、拒绝她，甚至骂她、打她，可偏偏不曾想到过他会欺骗她。即使是现在，她也仍然不大相信他会这样做。然而这个想法一旦产生了，要摆脱它却不太容易。

“哼，你只不过是个风尘女子，人家可是个贵家公子爷。他欺骗你一下有什么奇怪！这样的事情古往今来难道还少吗？”她听见心里有一个声音这样说。

“啊，不，不会的，冒郎可不是这样的人！”另一个声音急急忙忙争辩。

“你说他不是这样的人，凭什么？你究竟知道他多少？”头一个声音质问道。

“凭我的心！凭我同他一个月的朝夕相处。我知道他不会这样做，我相信他！”另一个声音自信地回答。

头一个声音：“纵然他本无心骗你，可是你把他逼得太紧了，他没有办法，扯个谎，哄哄你，好把你打发走，也是有的。”

另一个声音：“可是、可是当时有许多人在场，大家都是听见的呀！”

头一个声音：“听见又怎样，这些事儿，在他们眼里，本来就是闹着玩，成了也就成了，若要反悔，也只是一句话！又不是明媒正娶，莫非你还能到衙门去告他？”

另一个声音：“冒郎若真的这样对待我，可是太狠心了……”

more than three days in Nanjing and he needs at least two or three days to prepare. Unless Mr. Mao has suddenly decided not to take the exam—which is unlikely—he should be arriving at Suzhou within a day or two at the latest. If he doesn't come in a day or two, I shouldn't expect him to come anymore." Thus thinking, Dong Xiaowan's heart suddenly grew heavy. "Was he lying to me like Chen Xiaoguan said?" She was shocked by her own thought. Indeed, she had never had such a thought before. Strangely, in the few months of her arduous courtship with Mao Xiang, she had thought of many possibilities—he might be cold to her, ridicule her, reject her, criticize her or even beat her up—but it had never crossed her mind that he would ever deceive her. Even now, she still didn't quite believe he would do it. However, once such an idea came up, it was difficult to get rid of it.

"Hmph, you're merely a woman in the dust, and he's a gentleman from a noble family. What's so strange about him lying to you once? Is this kind of thing rare in the past and in the present?" one voice came from inside of her.

"Oh, no, it can't be that way, Mr. Mao isn't such a man," another voice hurriedly argued.

"Why do you say he's not such a man? How much do you know about him?" asks the first voice.

"Because my intuition has told me. Because I've spent a month with him day and night. I know he'll not deceive me and I trust him," replied the second voice confidently.

The first voice said, "Even if he didn't intend to lie to you, he couldn't help it, because you pushed him too hard. It's nothing unusual for a man to tell a lie and make you go happily."

The second voice said, "But, but many others were present at that moment, and everyone heard it."

The first voice said, "Many others heard it, so what? In their eyes it was part of the fun. If the word is good, it's good. If it's not kept, who will take it seriously? With no formal marriage with a matchmaker, can you sue him in the *yamen*?"

The second voice said, "If Mr. Mao really treats me like that, he's

头一个声音："哼，你现在才知道？公子哥儿没有一个是靠得住的，还是早早绝了这份痴心妄想吧！"

……

就这样，两个声音越往下争论，董小宛的心就越往下沉。她瞪大眼睛，失魂落魄地坐着，甚至雷声夹杂着闪电不断在窗前隆隆滚过，倾盆的暴雨开始在屋外咆哮翻腾，她都完全没有觉察到……

然而，就在这个时候，江面上隐隐约约传来了一阵笛子的吹奏声。宛转、悠扬的旋律穿越重重雨幕，飞进窗子里来。那是一曲古谱的《梅花三弄》。吹笛子的人显然是个高手，只听他不慌不忙地吹着，并没有故意提高调门，可是无论是雷的轰鸣，还是雨的喧阒，都始终不能把他的笛声掩盖住。相反，当你留神去倾听时，就会被那美妙的旋律所吸引，不由自主地让你的心去追随它，以至忘却了其他声响的存在。起初，董小宛呆呆地听着，渐渐，她的眼睛发亮了。

"啊，冒郎，冒郎！"

她尖声大叫，猛地跳起来，跌跌撞撞地向外奔去。刚奔到门口，就同一个人撞了个满怀，原来是丫环寿儿。寿儿想搀住她，可是董小宛粗暴地把她一把推开。

"啊，冒郎，冒郎！"她兴奋地、重复地嚷着，飞快地奔到楼下，连雨具也不去拿，光着脑袋冒着哗哗而下的大雨，穿过院子，一直向山塘河奔去。待到被女主人的举动吓了一跳的寿儿，撑着油纸伞赶出来时，董小宛已经被浇得浑身湿透，却仿佛毫无知觉，正在那里焦急地张望着，侧耳倾听着。

"娘，你、你这是做什么？"寿儿战战兢兢地问。

"吹笛子的人。"董小宛含糊地说了一句。

too cruel ..."

The first voice said, "Hmph, you've finally known it? None of the young noblemen are trustworthy. Stop your wishful thinking right now."

...

As the two voices argued, Dong Xiaowan's heart grew heavier and heavier. Eyes wide open, she sat there dejectedly, mindless of the sound of thunderbolts rumbling in front of the window, and the pouring rain outside the house ...

Just then, however, there came from the distance the sound of a flute playing on the river. The melodic, rhythmic tune broke through the heavy rain and entered the window. It was the ancient "Song of the Plum Blossoms in Strophic Form". The flute player was evidently a master of the art. He was playing calmly without exerting himself mightily, but neither the rumble of thunder nor the roaring of the rain could prevent his music from being heard. On the contrary, if you listened carefully, you would be attracted by the beautiful melody and your mind would automatically fly with it, oblivious to the presence of other sounds. At first, Dong Xiaowan listened impassively, but gradually her eyes lit up.

"Yes! Mr. Mao! It's Mr. Mao!"

She screamed ecstatically, sprang to her feet and went staggeringly out. When she ran to the door, she bumped into someone. It was the servant girl Shou'er, who tried to steady her, but she roughly pushed the girl away.

"Yes! Mr. Mao! It's Mr. Mao!" Shouting excitedly and repeatedly, she ran downstairs, and braving the heavy rain without an umbrella, trotted across the yard to the Shantang River. When Shou'er, who had been stunned by her mistress' action, came with an oil-paper umbrella, Dong Xiaowan was already spattered all over, but oblivious to it all, she stood there watching the river intently and listening anxiously, her ear cocked up.

"Missus, what are you doing?" Shou'er asked timidly.

"The flute player," said Dong Xiaowan pointlessly.

“吹笛子？谁在吹笛子？”寿儿莫名其妙。

董小宛没有回答。是啊，究竟是谁在吹笛子呢？刚才，她还以为是冒襄。可是，等她赶出来寻找时，码头上却空荡荡的，既没有船，也没有人，而且连笛声也忽然消失了……

董小宛失魂落魄地站着，呆呆地望着在潇潇暮雨的笼罩下，正变得愈来愈昏黑的河面，两腿一软，坐倒在泥地上。

## 放言无忌

董小宛的担心并非没有根据。冒襄确实临时改变了主意，没有依约到苏州去接她。他独自带了冒成和另外两个仆人早早到了南京。就在董小宛冒着倾盆大雨到山塘河畔去寻觅他的那个夜晚，冒襄正在秦淮河畔他下榻的桃叶河房里摆酒宴客。

他这次匆匆赶到南京来，与其说是为了准备应考的事宜，毋宁说是由于心绪不佳。说来也怪，尽管他父亲的事情算是彻底解决，朝廷已经下达调令，让冒起宗离开左良玉军，前往湖南宝庆上任。从此以后，他再也用不着风尘仆仆地到处奔走求告，去窥测权贵们的脸色。可是，这一切并没有使冒襄变得轻松起来。当最初那一阵激动和高兴过去之后，他又开始变得闷闷不乐。要说原因，也没有什么特别的原因。不是因为时局。虽然目前时局确实比较紧张，张献忠的农民军自从于五月攻克了庐州之后，又连陷无为、庐江，并在巢湖操演水师，大有进军江南之势。最近，监军太监卢九德命总兵官黄得功、刘良佐二军攻击，结果却在峡

"The flute player? Where is the flute player?" Shou'er was puzzled.

Dong Xiaowan didn't respond. Yes, where's the flute player? Just now, she thought it was Mao Xiang playing the flute on the river, but when she rushed out to look for him, the pier was empty. There was not a single boat or a single soul in sight, and even the sound of the flute had suddenly disappeared...

Dong Xiaowan stood in despair, staring blankly at the river surface, which was getting darker and darker under the cloak of the spattering evening rain, and then her legs gave way and she collapsed to the muddy ground.

## Freedom of Speech

Dong Xiaowan's worry was not unfounded. Mao Xiang did change his mind. Instead of going to Suzhou to pick her up as promised, he went direct to Nanjing with Mao Cheng and two other servants. The night Dong Xiaowan braved the pouring rain to look for him on the bank of the Shantang River, Mao Xiang was holding a banquet in the Peach Leaves Riverhouse by the Qinhuai River where he lodged.

He came to Nanjing in a hurry this time, not so much to prepare for the exam as to take an excursion from his sense of gloom. After the imperial court issued an order to allow his father Mao Qizong to leave Zuo Liangyu's army and take an appointment in Baoqing, Hunan Province, the matter was satisfactorily closed, and from then on, he no longer had to run around asking for help and reading the faces of those in high office, but curiously he didn't feel relieved at all. When the initial excitement and joy were over, he became sullen again. There was no specific reason for it. It was not because of the current situation of the country, although it was indeed highly volatile. Zhang Xianzhong's peasant army had captured Luzhou in May, and later Wuwei and Lujiang, and was now training their water units in the Chao Lake in preparation for an offensive towards the south of the Yangtze River and recently, eunuch Lu Jiude, supervisor to

山一线战败。现在黄得功已退守定远。不过，冒襄估计明朝在长江一线还有重兵把守，农民军还不至于一下子就攻得过来。他也不是因为陈圆圆，那已经是过去的事了。况且他冒襄也不会把一个女子看得这样重。至于董小宛，在冒襄的心目中，分量就更轻了……总而言之，连他自己也说不清是什么缘故，他只是打心里觉得烦闷、无聊，对什么也提不起劲头来。尽管眼下他正以主人的身份坐在宴席前，却怀着一种冷淡的、甚至是反感的心情，默默地注视着兴高采烈的客人们在那里觥筹交错，高谈阔论。只是到了迫不得已的时候，他才偶尔加插一两句，或者做出一丝淡淡的微笑。

本来，冒襄也没有心思摆酒宴客，只是顾杲和梅朗中巴巴地找上门来，说是最近许多社友都陆续来到南京，平日难得一见，要叙一叙，乐一乐，并且说明要敲他的竹杠。冒襄不好推辞，虽说由于乡里灾荒，加上为了父亲的事使了不少钱，如今他手头已远不如前时宽裕，也只好硬着头皮，拿出百把两银子来，由着他们去弄。结果，今天晚间来的客人还真不少，除了梅、顾二人外，还有吴应箕、陈贞慧、余怀、张岱和冒襄的拜把兄弟陈梁、吕兆龙以及其他一些认识和不认识的社友，总共有二三十人之多；又把顾眉、李十娘请来侑酒，就在水阁里设了五席。冒襄、陈贞慧、梅朗中、余怀、张岱和李十娘共一席。席上，大家东拉西扯地说些新闻、趣事，由于冒襄始终表现出一种冷冷的神态，同席的人受到他的影响，气氛始终热不起来。相比之下，倒是其他几席又是猜枚，又是行令，大笑大叫，好不热闹。陈贞慧早就发现了这

the imperial troops, had ordered the two front commanders, Huang Degong and Liu Liangzuo, to launch an offensive against the rebels, but unfortunately, they had been defeated at the Xiashan frontline and Huang Degong had retreated to Dingyuan. Since there might still be heavy troops guarding the Yangtze River, Mao Xiang gathered the rebels would not make it to the south of the river anytime soon. It was not because of Chen Yuanyuan, either. The relationship was a thing of the past, and besides, he would not take a woman so seriously. As for Dong Xiaowan, in Mao Xiang's mind, she carried even less weight ... All in all, even he himself couldn't tell the reason. He just felt tired and bored and couldn't bring himself to anything. Sitting at the table as host of the banquet, he silently watched in contempt and disgust as the guests drank and talked in good cheer, cutting in a word or two or giving a faint smile when he had to.

In fact, Mao Xiang was not in the mood to give a banquet. However, Gu Gao and Mei Langzhong came to him and said that now that many Fushe members had recently come to Nanjing they should get together and have some fun time, at his expense of course. Since it was not polite to say no, he took out about a hundred taels of silver against his own will for them to arrange the banquet. Having been affected by the famine and having spent large sums of money to solve his father's problem, he now had a very tight budget. There were quite a few guests today, twenty to thirty in total. Besides Mei Langzhong and Gu Gao, there were Wu Yingji, Chen Zhenhui, Yu Huai, Zhang Dai, and his sworn brothers Chen Liang and Lü Zhaolong, as well as some other Fushers, some of whom he didn't know. Gu Mei and Li Shiniang were invited to escort the guests. There were five tables lined up in the Water Pavilion. Mao Xiang, Chen Zhenhui, Mei Langzhong, Yu Huai, Zhang Dai, and Li Shiniang shared one table. At the table, the guests merely talked for politeness's sake, sharing some irrelevant rumors and anecdotes. The atmosphere never warmed up as everyone was affected by Mao Xiang's cold expression. In contrast, the other tables were very lively, with fun drinking games such as "drink-if-you-don't-guess-it-right" and "drink-if-you-can't-say-it-right". Chen

种情况，但是弄不明白冒襄为什么这样子，又不好问。余怀和张岱两个受不了这份冷清，借口敬酒，双双离开座位，走到旁的桌子去，赖在那儿久久不回来。这一下，席上的气氛更形冷落。末了，连梅朗中也有点坐不住，时时露出想要离开的样子。陈贞慧见状，只好一边用眼色止住梅朗中，一边起身去把余、张二人拖回来。但冒襄还是那副样子，毫不改变。陈贞慧一连几次投去询问的眼色，他都只当没看见。陈贞慧无可奈何，正想寻个题目，打破这种僵局，忽然听见有人大声说：

“你我也不用争，就请定生他们几位评一评！”

陈贞慧回头一看，方脸大眼的陈梁正扯着顾杲，步履蹒跚地走过来。两个人看来都喝得不少，陈梁从脸上一直红到了脖子，顾杲的脸却有点发青。他们各自一只手拿着酒杯，另一只手互相牵扯着，已是醉态可掬。

陈贞慧不由得一笑，问：“噢，你们要我做什么？拼酒我可不行！”

“不！”陈梁放开顾杲，摆了一下手，打了个酒嗝，“是这么回、回事！刚才我说，崇祯元年起，到今、今年为止，宰相一共已经换过四……四十三人，可他硬、硬说是四十四。小弟让他数，他又数——呃，数不出，小弟要、罚……他酒，他还不服气。定生，你、你来评评看，这酒该……不该罚？你说！”

陈贞慧“噢”了一声，笑着说：“这可让你问倒了，我还真

Zhenhui had sensed something was amiss. He was wondering what had happened, but didn't think it appropriate to ask. Yu Huai and Zhang Dai couldn't stand the cold atmosphere, so they both left their seats under the pretext of toasting others and walked to the next table, where they stayed for a long time without returning. Consequently, the atmosphere at this table got even colder. In the end, even Mei Langzhong couldn't sit still and tried to find an occasion to leave. When Chen Zhenhui saw it, he stopped Mei Langzhong with a wink and stood up to drag Yu Huai and Zhang Dai back to the table. Yet Mao Xiang's expression remained unchanged. Chen Zhenhui threw him a few incuiring glances, but he just turned a blind eye to them. Disappointed, Chen Zhenhui tried to find a topic to break the deadlock when he suddenly heard a loud voice:

"The two of us can stop arguing. Let Dingsheng and the others decide."

Chen Zhenhui looked back and saw that Chen Liang was pulling Gu Gao to their table, both of them intoxicated. Chen Liang's face was red down to his neck, but Gu Gao's face was slightly blue. Each holding a cup of wine in one hand, they held each other by the other hand in drunken excitement.

Chen Zhenhui couldn't help laughing and asked, "So, what do you want me to do? As far as drinking is concerned, I'm no match for either of you."

"No, it's not drinking." Chen Liang released Gu Gao, waved his hand, and hiccupped. "Well, here is the thing. I just said that from the first year of the reign of Emperor Chongzhen [AD 1628] up to, up to now, there have been forty-three prime ministers, but-but he insisted that it's forty-fcur. I asked him to count them one by one, and he counted. Well, he couldn't count them to forty-four. So, he shall-shall be punished with, with a cup of wine. He doesn't accept it. Dingsheng, you be the judge and tell us if he, he should be punished with this cup of wine."

"Oh, I see," said Chen Zhenhui with a smile. "This is a great question. I've never counted them." Then, he looked back at his table

没有细数过哩！”他回头问席上的人：“兄等有谁算过，到底是多少？”在座的几位听了，都面面相觑，又疑惑地摇摇头。陈贞慧只好转向其他桌子，大声问：“列位社兄！则良和子方适才问我，本朝十五年间，到底换过多少宰相？小弟蒙昧，无法回答，列位有谁知道的？”

其他几席的人听他这样一问，都停止了交谈；有些人不知就里，露出莫名其妙的神情。直到陈贞慧又重复了一遍，大家才窃窃私语起来。热心的，就开始计算。终于，有一个士子把桌子一拍，跳起来大声证实说：“是四十四人。”

陈贞慧回头一看，认得是冯班，便微笑起来，拱着手说：“啊哈！到底是定远兄记性好！敢问其详？”

冯班先不回答，端起酒杯，一饮而尽，又把方巾推到脑后，抓了抓乱蓬蓬的头发，这才屈着手指头计算道：“崇祯元年入相者有：施凤来、张瑞图、李国谱、来宗道、杨景辰、李标、刘鸿训、周登道、钱龙锡、韩炉；二年：成基命、孙承宗、周延儒、何如宠、钱象坤；三年：温体仁、吴宗达；五年：郑以伟、徐光启；六年：钱士升、王应熊、何吾驺；八年：文震孟、张至发；九年：林钎、孔贞运、贺逢圣、黄士俊；十年：刘宇亮、傅冠、薛国观；十一年：杨嗣昌、程国祥、蔡国用、方逢年、范复粹；十二年：姚明恭、张四知、魏照乘；十三年：谢升、陈演；十五年：蒋德璟、黄景昉、吴甡。一共四十四人！”

陈贞慧见冯班一口气地背下来，倒也佩服他记性好，正想夸奖几句，从另一张桌子上有人不慌不忙地说：“嗯，不对，还欠

and asked, "Brothers, has any of you ever calculated the number? How many are they?" Those at the table looked at each other and shook their heads puzzledly. Chen Zhenhui turned to the other tables and asked, "My Fushe brothers, just now Zeliang and Zifang asked me how many prime ministers there have been in the fifteen years under the current emperor. Since I'm not knowledgeable enough, I can't answer it. Does any of you know the answer?"

When the men at the other tables heard his question, they stopped talking. Not knowing what was going on, some looked puzzled. Chen Zhenhui repeated his question. The guests started to whisper among themselves. The enthusiastic ones started counting. Finally, a young scholar slammed the table, sprang to his feet, and said loudly and confidently, "Forty-four!"

Chen Zhenhui turned around and saw it was Feng Ban. He smiled and said, pressing his hands together in salute, "Aha, Brother Dingyuan, you have a good memory. Please let us know who they are."

Feng Ban didn't reply immediately. He picked up the wine cup, drank it, shoved the square headscarf to the back of his head, scratched his unkempt hair, then counted on his fingers, saying, "Year One of Chongzhen: Shi Fenglai, Zhang Ruitu, Li Guopu, Lai Zongdao, Yang Jingchen, Li Biao, Liu Hongxun, Zhou Dengdao, Qian Longxi, Han Kuang; Year Two: Cheng Jiming, Sun Chengzong, Zhou Yanru, He Ruchong, Qian Xiangkun; Year Three: Wen Tiren, Wu Zongda; Year Five: Zheng Yiwei, Xu Guangqi; Year Six: Qian Shisheng, Wang Yingxiong, He Wuzou; Year Eight: Wen Zhenmeng, Zhang Zhifa; Year Nine: Lin Qian, Kong Zhenyun, He Fengsheng, Huang Shijun; Year Ten: Liu Yuliang, Fu Guan, Xue Guoguan; Year Eleven: Yang Sichang, Cheng Guoxiang, Cai Guoyong, Fang Fengnian, Fan Fucui; Year Twelve: Yao Minggong, Zhang Sizhi, Wei Zhaocheng; Year Thirteen: Xie Sheng, Chen Yan; Year Fifteen: Jiang Dejing, Huang Jingfang, Wu Shen. Forty-four in total!"

Seeing Feng Ban recite such a long list in one breath, Chen Zhenhui was impressed with his good memory and was going to

一个。”

陈贞慧循声看去，说话的那个人长得又高又瘦，坐在椅子上也比旁的人高出几乎一个头，原来是冯班的胞兄冯舒。

陈贞慧还来不及开口，就听冯班气呼呼地说：“胡说！一个不欠，就是四十四人！”

“不对，是四十五人。”冯舒仍旧是那么慢条斯理。

“四十四！”

“四十五。”

“那好，你说，那一个是谁？你说！”

“你不妨再想想。”

“我想不出，我要你说！你说，听见没有？”冯班直着脖子嚷，眼睛瞪得像要从眶子里蹦出来，那个酒糟鼻子显得更红了，活像一只发怒的雄鸡。

冯舒却全不理会弟弟这一套。“要我告诉你，本来也未尝不可。”他慢吞吞地说，“但我的意思是要你自己先想一想，你却连想也不想，就来问我；那么我就得想一想，这样答应你好不好？自然，这是不好的。所以我就不能告诉你了。”

在座的客人们见他们兄弟这样抬杠，都忍不住笑。同时，也猜测起冯舒所说的那漏掉的一个是谁。有人说是黄立极，也有人说不是，甚至还有人对冯班已经数出来的人也提出异议。于是又各抒己见，互相争论，结果越算越糊涂。陈贞慧眼看争不出个结果，只好叹了一口气，苦笑着，对陈梁和顾杲拱手说：“十五年间，宰相换了四十余人。此事实属亘古未有。我辈生于斯世，尚且闹不清楚，后世之人只怕就更糊涂了。”

话刚说完，就听吴应箕冷冷地说：“十五年间四十余相，若

pass him a compliment when suddenly someone from another table drawled, “Well, that’s not right. One is missing.”

Following that voice, Chen Zhenhui saw a tall and thin man, who was almost a head taller than the ones sitting next to him. He was Feng Ban’s elder brother Feng Shu.

Before Chen Zhenhui spoke, he heard Feng Ban’s angry voice: “Nonsense! No one is missing. It’s forty-four, no more, no less.”

“Wrong! It should be fifty-five,” Feng Shu continued to drawl.

“Forty-four!”

“Forty-five.”

“Well, tell us, who is the missing one? You tell us!”

“Think hard.”

“I cannot think of anyone else. I want you to tell me. Tell me, do you hear?” shouted Feng Ban like an angry rooster, his neck straight, his eyes bulging as if they were going to jump out of the sockets, and his red nose even redder.

However, Feng Shu completely ignored the anger of his younger brother. “I can tell you, of course,” he continued to drawl. “I want you to think hard, but you’re asking me without even giving it a try. Then, I’ll have to think hard before I can tell you. What do you think? Of course, it isn’t good. So, I shouldn’t tell you now.”

The guests present couldn’t help laughing when they saw the brothers having such an argument. At the same time, they tried to guess who the missing one was. Some said it was Huang Liji, others said it was not, and some even raised objections about the ones who had been already counted by Feng Ban. Then, everyone had an opinion, and they argued with each other. The result was great confusion. Seeing it was unlikely to have a consensus, Chen Zhenhui let out a sigh and said to Chen Liang and Gu Gao with a wry smile, “Over forty prime ministers for fifteen years. It’s unprecedented. As men living in this age, we’re confused. You bet later generations will be even more confused.”

Hearing that, Wu Yingji said coldly, “Over forty prime ministers for fifteen years wouldn’t be a problem if the incoming were all good men

所进者都是君子，所退者都是小人，原也无妨。奈何十五年中，却是小人日众而君子日稀！”

大家静了一下，仿佛在体味这话的内涵。忽然有人把桌子拍得“砰”的一响：“不错！我瞧温体仁、杨嗣昌、薛国观这几个就是欺君误国的罪魁！”

“骂得好！还有王永光、蔡国用、谢升！”另一个大叫。

“钱士升呢？此公也不是好东西！”又一个深沉的声音响起来。

有人表示怀疑：“钱士升尚非小人……”

可是他立即遭到好几个人的同声反驳：

“他起用唐世济！”

“他逼走文震孟！”

“他同温体仁朋比为奸！”

“他……”

“喂，诸位，当今这一位怎样？我是说‘周’！”一个高亢的声音盖过全场。那是一个二十岁出头的士子，因为兴奋，他的那双年轻的眼睛闪闪发光。

大家忽然不作声了。因为周延儒目前正在朝中秉政，而近来对东林方面的人颇为优礼，多所起用。评判他不但不便，而且似乎有点困难……

“哼，这有什么？”在一片寂静中，吴应箕的声音像一柄刀子似的捅了出来，“‘周’也者，昏懦贪婪，沽名钓誉！”

大家怔了一下，随即哄然地附和起来，其间还夹杂着欢呼。这欢呼表示着对吴应箕胆量的钦佩，以及他们从这种肆无忌惮的议论中所获得的快意和满足。

面对着这热烈、兴奋的场面，冒襄始终静静地坐着，一言不发。要是在以往，他必定早就参加进去，并且会设法以最激昂的情绪，最深刻的判断，以及最出人意料的妙语去耸动全场，赢得

and the outgoing were all bad men. Unfortunately, all through the fifteen years, bad men are many and good men have become increasingly rare."

Everyone was silent as if trying to digest the meaning of these words. Suddenly, someone slapped the table with a "bang". "Quite right. I think Wen Tiren, Yang Sichang and Xue Guoguan are criminals who have cheated the emperor and caused havoc to the country. "

"Well said! And Wang Yongguang, Cai Guoyong, Xie Sheng too," another man shouted.

"What about Qian Shisheng? That man isn't good, either," a low-pitched voice said.

Someone raised an objection: "Qian Shisheng isn't a bad man ..."

But he was immediately refuted by several other voices:

"He reinstated Tang Shiji."

"He forced Wen Zhenmeng out."

"He colluded with Wen Tiren."

"He ..."

"Hey, blokes, what about this one? I mean Mr. Zhou," said a loud voice. It was a twenty-something, and his young eyes sparkled with excitement.

Everyone suddenly became silent. Because Zhou Yanru was the incumbent prime minister and was quite nice to the East Wood scholars, having promoted many of them, it was not prudent to judge him, nor was it easy ...

"Hmph, what's the big deal?" Wu Yingji's voice broke the silence like a dagger. "This Mr. Zhou is selfish, dastardly, and greedy."

Everyone was shocked to hear it. Then they started to echo him, with a few shouts of approval. The shouts represented their admiration for Wu Yingji's courage, as well as the joy and satisfaction they derived from such unbridled discussions.

Mao Xiang sat silently amid all the noise and excitement without saying a word. He should have joined in under normal circumstances and won applause from his comrades with his impassioned, compelling and witty speech, but now he was disenchanted and utterly bored. "A repetition of the same old stuff! Eating a bone whose meat has been

喝彩。可是如今，他觉得这一切都是那样平淡、乏味。“老是这么一套！啃来啃去就一块骨头，真是腻烦透了！”他默默地想，随手端起酒杯，却发觉已经喝干了。他正想伸手去取酒壶，旁边伸过来一只女人洁白柔软的手，轻轻把他按住了。冒襄回头一看，原来是李十娘。十娘文静地微笑着，起身端过酒壶，替他把酒斟满，一边低声地问：

“冒公子，听说你同小宛——可是真的吗？”

冒襄微微一怔，抬眼瞧瞧李十娘，发现她那双漂亮的细长眼睛正凝视着自己，他就移开了视线，含糊地应了一声。

“什么？”李十娘盯着他追问。

“嗯，还不定哩！”冒襄迫不得已，漫应了一句。之后，为了把话题引开，他抬头朝四面张望了一下，问：“你可知道，侯朝宗相公怎么没来？”

“哦，公子还不知道？这些天来，侯公子同香君打得火热，一天到晚躲在媚香楼里不出来。昨儿才听说他们游燕子矶去了，这会只怕还未回来哩！”

冒襄“噢”了一声，正想说：“我还以为他还在河南陪他尊大人哩，原来已经又藏进媚香楼去了！”忽然发现，李十娘不知怎地，眼皮儿发红了，脸上也现出黯然神情。他就临时住了口，同时觉得这种神情很熟悉，仿佛不久前在什么地方见过……蓦地，他想起来了，是董小宛！不错，在他同董小宛相处的那段日子里，她也常常流露出这样的神情。“这一次我没有依约去接她，不知道她会怎么样？恐怕她时至今日，仍然会在那栋小楼上盼望着，脸上也是这么一副神情吧？”他斜睨着李十娘，心里隐然漾起一丝不安。然而，没等这种感情扩大开来，就见仆人冒成匆匆走近他的身边，把一份朱红纸拜帖呈了上来。

冒襄心神恍惚地接过，打开一看，里面写着：

eaten. Boring like hell." Thus thinking, he picked up the wine cup, only to find that he had already drunk it. As he was about to grab the decanter, a woman's delicate and soft hand gently landed on his hand to stop him. Mao Xiang looked back and saw it was Li Shiniang, who, smiling politely, got up and took the decanter, filled his cup with wine, and asked in a low voice:

"Mr. Mao, I heard you and Xiaowan—is it true?"

Mao Xiang was a little surprised. He looked up at Li Shiniang, and found her beautiful slender eyes staring at him, so he looked away and gave an ambiguous reply.

"What?" Li Shiniang stared at him and asked.

"Well, it's not decided yet." Mao Xiang had to speak more clearly. Afterward, to divert the subject, he looked around and asked, "Do you know why Mr. Hou Chaozong has not come?"

"Why, you don't know it yet? These days, Mr. Hou and Xiangjun are very fond of each other and are huddling together in the Meixiang House all the time. I heard yesterday that they had an outing to the Swallow Ferry. I'm afraid they're not back yet."

"Oh," Mao Xiang said. As he wanted to say, "I thought he was still in Henan with his father. It turns out he's hiding in the Meixiang House again," suddenly, he found Li Shiniang's eyes were red for some reason and her expression was very sad, so he swallowed the words. At the same time, he felt that this expression was very familiar, as if he had seen it somewhere a short time ago ... Suddenly he remembered that it was that of Dong Xiaowan. Yes, in the days when he was with Dong Xiaowan, she often showed such an expression. "Since I didn't pick her up this time as promised, I don't know what has become of her. I'm afraid she's still looking forward to my coming in that little storied house with the same expression on her face." Glancing at Li Shiniang from the corner of his eye, he was somewhat guilty. Yet, before this feeling of his intensified, his servant Mao Cheng hurried over to him and handed him a scarlet calling card.

Mao Xiang took it absent-mindedly and opened it, which read:

通家侍弟史可法顿首拜

冒襄吃了一惊，问：“客人呢？”

当冒成回禀史可法的轿子马上要到时，他就着忙起来，站起身，凑在陈贞慧耳边嘱咐了几句，匆匆向外走去。

## 贵人援手

“史大人夤夜到访，不知有何要紧之事？他不是在扬州任上吗，怎么到了南京？又怎么知道我在这儿？”冒襄疑惑地想。这时，他已经把客人迎进河房的堂上，行过礼，分宾主坐了下来。

“弟因漕务来南都，已有七八日，明儿一早，便要回扬州去。适才在熊坛老府上，得知兄台已到了南京，特来拜候！”客人似乎猜出了他心中的疑问，一坐下，就微笑着解释说。

“啊！”冒襄连忙站起来，拱着手说，“老公祖言重了，晚生如何担当得起！”

“哎，坐下，坐下！你我之间，不必多礼！”史可法摆摆手。可是，等冒襄重新坐下之后，他却放下手中的茶杯，自己站了起来。

在灯光下看，这位素以精明干练著称的现任漕运总督兼凤阳、淮安、扬州巡抚是一个身材矮小的人。他面孔黧黑，举止利索，有一双精光闪烁的眼睛。据说他可以十天半月不睡觉地办公，实在累了，就用手中的笔杆抵住眉心，闭上眼睛养一会儿神。也许

*Salute from Shi Kefa, a humble family friend, ...*

Mao Xiang was surprised and asked, "Where's the guest?"

Mao Cheng replied that Shi Kefa was arriving in a sedan chair, so Mao Xiang quickly stood up, whispered a few words in Chen Zhenhui's ear, and hurried out.

## A Helping Hand

"Calling at such a late hour, Mr. Shi must have something important to discuss with me. He's supposed to be in Yangzhou attending to his duties. Why is he in Nanjing? How does he know I'm here?" Mao Xiang thought puzzledly as he welcomed the guest into the drawing room of the riverhouse. After the exchange of pleasantries and salutes, the two sat down as guest and host.

"I've been in the Southern Capital for seven or eight days to handle water transport[①] issues and will be leaving early tomorrow morning. Since I heard from the respectable Mr. Xiong Mingyu that you happen to be here, I think I'd better meet you," the guest explained with a smile after sitting down, as if understanding his doubt.

"Oh!" Mao Xiang stood up, pressing his hands together in salute and said, "Thank you for taking the bother. It's such a great honor to have your visit."

"Well, please sit. No ceremonies between you and me," Shi Kefa gestured. However, after Mao Xiang sat down again, he put down the teacup in his hand and stood up himself.

Under the light, Mao Xiang studied his guest. The current Supervisor of Water Transport and Governor of Fengyang, Huai'an and Yangzhou, known for his acumen and ability, was a short man with a dark face, sparkling eyes, and a neat way of doing things. It was said that he could work without sleep for over ten days. When he was exhausted, he put the stem of the brush-pen in his hand against

① water transport: *caoyun*, transportation of government grains on water courses

因为这个缘故，他今年才四十出头，前额上的头发却快掉光了，两鬓也已经一片斑白。现在，他头戴乌纱帽，身穿三品绯色圆领袍，袍背缀有一方显示品位的孔雀图案，束着一根金花腰带，脚下粉底皂靴。

史可法在堂内来回踱着，好一阵子还不开口说话。冒襄的目光追随着他，不知怎的，忽然有点不安。“嗯，他会不会为着父亲调职的事来责备我？”他想。随即忆起去年冬天，有一次，他上扬州去见史可法，想请他帮忙疏通，结果碰了一鼻子灰的事。现在这事到底办成了，他会怎么看，会不会不高兴？这样一想，冒襄就神经紧张起来，脊背也开始微微冒汗。

果然，史可法停止了踱步，转过身来。

“听说，令尊大人已调往宝庆，是么？”他问，语气是严厉的。

冒襄蓦地脸红了，“是的。”他轻声回答，避开了对方逼人的目光。

“这么说，到底让你办成了！”史可法说，像是在冷笑，又像在叹息。随后，他又踱起步来。

冒襄越加不安了。他已经看准，这位史世叔今晚来意不善，自己难免要挨他一顿数落，弄不好，还会挨骂。一想到自己堂堂“复社四公子”之一，如今却落得个被人责骂，而且似乎无法辩解的境地，他的自尊心就因痛苦而颤抖起来。“哼，你要骂就骂吧！反正，我就是这样！什么名声、地位，那些玩意儿，我早就腻烦了！”他自暴自弃地想，随即挑战似的抬起头，一言不发地盯着客人。

这当儿，史可法已经重新坐回椅子上。他用两根指头，轻轻

his forehead and closed his eyes for a while. Maybe because of this, the hair above his forehead had almost fallen out and his temples were already gray, although he was only in his early forties this year. At the moment, he was wearing a black gauze hat[①], a crimson round-necked robe for a third-rank official—on the back of which was a peacock pattern that indicated the rank level—with a golden floral-patterned belt and a pair of white-soled black boots.

Shi Kefa paced back and forth in the drawing room without speaking. Mao Xiang's eyes followed him. For some reason Mao Xiang was suddenly a little uneasy. "Well, will he blame me for my father's transfer?" he thought as he remembered that he had been to Yangzhou the previous winter to seek Shi Kefa's help only to be rebuffed. "Now that this thing has been done, what will he think? Will he be unhappy?" Thus thinking, Mao Xiang's nerves got tense, and his back started to sweat.

Sure enough, Shi Kefa stopped pacing and turned around.

"I heard that your respectable father has been transferred to Baoqing. Is it true?" he asked in a stern tone.

Mao Xiang blushed. "Yes, it is," he answered timidly, avoiding the other man's menacing gaze.

"So, you've got it done," said Shi Kefa, as if with a sneer or sigh. Then he started pacing back and forth again.

Mao Xiang became even more uneasy. He had already realized that this friend of his father's hadn't come with a good intention tonight and he would probably receive some lecturing or even scolding. When he thought that as one of the Four Young Men of the Fushe he had sunk so low as to be scolded by someone without being able to offer any explanations, his self-esteem trembled from pain. "Well, let him scold me. I'm the way I am. I'm tired of name and reputation," he thought in resignation. Then, he lifted his head defiantly and stared at the guest without saying a word.

Shi Kefa had sat back in his chair. Tapping on the armrest with

---

① a black gauze hat: a hat of an ancient Chinese official

敲打着扶手，终于开口了。

“时至今日，此事也不必再说了！”他慢吞吞地说，“虽则学生仍未敢苟同，唯是忠孝两全，自古为难，却也未可深责。弟如今所望者，是仁兄于尽孝之后，从此一心一意施展高才，忠心谋国，戮力王室，拯民水火，庶几不负男儿生于天地间之意！”

冒襄怔住了。本来，他正憋着一口气，等候挨对方的痛责，没想到史可法轻轻一句话，就把这件事放过了，而且对自己似乎仍然期望颇高。他不由得心头一热，冲口而出说：“晚生私意，也正是如此！”话刚出口，又觉得不够谦谨，就闭口不说了。

史可法却似乎并不介意。“如此很好！”他点点头说，停了停，又瞅着冒襄，微微一笑：“弟今晚匆匆而来，乃系有一事欲与我兄面商——”说着，他从袖子里掏出一封书信，递了过来。

冒襄连忙接过，只见封皮上还空着未写，也没有缄口。他疑疑惑惑地抽出信笺，展开一看，原来，是史可法写给本期南京乡试的主考官何瑞征的一封信，大意是说：彼此京华一别，已多年不见，十分想念，闻得老朋友这次主试南都，十分高兴，到时又可以把酒话旧了。接着，信中就向对方大力推荐冒襄，夸他年轻英俊，学富才高，是一个难得的栋梁之材，眼下国家多难，民生忧悴，正需要选拔像冒襄这样的人才出来报效社稷，共扶危局。末了，史可法希望主考大人阅卷之时，对冒襄的卷子能加以留意，倘有一点可用，尽量予以提携。

冒襄一边读信，心头一边怦怦直跳，浑身的血液也急剧地流动起来。待到把信读完，他已经激动得说不出话来了。他自然很明白，这封信的价值是多么宝贵；而一向以刚毅廉直出名的史可

two fingers, he said:

"Now that it has happened, let's forget about it," he drawled. "Although I don't approve what you've done, I shouldn't be hard on you, since loyalty to the country and filial piety don't always go together. I'm hoping, after you've performed your act of filial piety, you can be devoted to the country and the emperor heart and soul with your great talents to save the people from water and fire. That's what a man should do who stands between heaven and earth."

That surprised Mao Xiang, who had been prepared for a scolding. Not only did Shi Kefa drop the matter so easily, but he seemed to have high expectations of him as well. Greatly relieved, he said, "That's what I'm thinking too." As soon as these words came out of his mouth, he realized he should be more humble and stopped speaking.

Shi Kefa didn't seem to mind. He nodded and said, "Very good!" After a pause, he looked at Mao Xiang with a smile and continued, "I've come in a hurry tonight to discuss with you something else ..." he said, taking out an envelope from his long sleeve and handed it to Mao Xiang, who took it over.

The envelope was unaddressed, nor was it sealed. Mao Xiang puzzledly took out the letter from it. It was written by Shi Kefa to He Ruizheng, chief examiner for the coming provincial-level examination in Nanjing. The letter said in a nutshell: It has been many years since we last met in the capital, and I miss you very much. Hearing you are coming to Nanjing as chief examiner of the provincial-level examination, I am very excited and hope to be able to drink with you and share our stories ... I am strongly recommending to you a handsome, talented young man named Mao Xiang, who is a rare genius. In this hour of national crisis, he's exactly the kind of talent we're looking for ... I am hoping you can pay some special attention to this young man when you grade the papers. If you think he'll be of some use, please lend him a helping hand.

As Mao Xiang read the letter, his heart was pounding and his blood was racing. By the time he finished reading, he was too excited to speak. He understood how precious the letter was and what a

法，肯主动地替他写这样一封信又是多么地不容易！如果不是对自己确实特别的赏识，而且期望十分殷切，他根本不可能这样做。此刻，在冒襄的心里，半年前由于向对方请托父亲的事遭到拒绝的余怨，顿时烟消云散了，代之而来的是满腔的感激之情。他觉得心头发颤，泪水涌上了眼睛，只是用力咬住嘴唇，才勉强忍住了。

“以仁兄之卓荦高才，今科自能高中，原也无须弟多此一举。”史可法一边收回信件，一边说，“只是弟为朝廷求贤心切，生怕考官阅卷不细，以致埋没了仁兄的文章，使兄台为社稷效力之机又迟三年。是以不揣冒昧，出此下策，只怕我兄未免失笑了。今日特来奉商，仁兄倘以为可，此信不日便着人发出，如何？”

冒襄本来就感动万分，听了这番谦恭客气的话，再也忍不住。他猛地站起来，踉跄着走前几步，拜倒在地，哽咽说：

“晚生蒙老公祖俯赐栽植，没齿难忘！”

史可法连忙把他扶起来。“兄台何必如此！弟万不敢当！”他说，“仁兄既然应允，芜笺明日便可发出。”停了停，又叹一口气说：“国事蜩螗，已至于此！朝廷常叹老成凋谢，无材可用，却听凭许多英俊之才埋没草野，而不从速百计罗致振拔之。仍靠着三年一比，八股取士，从容矩步，不知祸之将至！到底这局面还容得几个三年？这八股文章又能出得几个济艰之才？啊，老天，老天！你庇佑我大明天下三百年，如今到底意欲何为啊！”

冒襄本来打算再说上几句感谢的话，可是见史可法说话时声

great favor it was for Shi Kefa, who had always been known for righteousness and integrity, to offer to write such a letter on his behalf. Without a genuine appreciation or a great expectation of him, the elder would not have done such a thing. By now, the resentment for the rebuff of his request for help in his father's transfer had completely disappeared. Instead, his heart was suddenly warm with gratitude. Tears welled up in his eyes and he had to bite his lips to stop them from flowing.

"Given your great talent, you'll succeed in the exam and there's really no need for me to take this extra step," Shi Kefa said as he took back the letter. "I am doing it just in case the examiners are not careful enough and fail to recognize the talent in you so that your recruitment for the service of the country will be delayed for another three years. It's not a good method but I can't think of anything else. If you have no objection, I'll send it tomorrow."

Hearing those words, Mao Xiang, who had already been deeply moved, stood up, staggered forward and knelt down on his knees. He said in grateful tears, "It's most obliging of you. I'll never forget your kindness."

Shi Kefa hurried to stand him up. "Brother Mao Xiang, please stand up," he said. "Now that you've agreed, I'll send the letter tomorrow." After a pause, he added, "While the country is in such great turmoil, the imperial court complains that it doesn't have enough talented men while the old ones have withered. The fact is, many talented young men lie waste. Instead of discovering them and putting them to good use, the imperial court still insists on the old ways, unhurriedly selecting talents through the 'eight-legged essays' system on a triennial basis, not knowing a big calamity is coming down on their heads. How many more periods of three years are there? How many talented men can they discover through the eight-legged essays? Oh, Lord of Heaven! You have blessed the Great Ming for three hundred years and what do you intend to do now?"

Shi Kefa got increasingly emotional as he spoke in a solemn tone as he looked up at the dark night sky outside the house with a

色俱厉，情绪变得异常激动，他悲愤地仰望着堂外的沉沉夜空，眼睛里闪动着晶莹的泪光——显然不是客套的时候，冒襄只得屏住气不作声。而且，渐渐他的情绪也受到了对方的感染。“是啊，国事坏到了这种地步，恐怕已非少数人之力所能挽救。那么，即使这一次我考中了，又能得意多久呢？万一不幸亡国，这一切还有什么意义呢？”这样一想，冒襄就不禁呆住了，虽然随后他又安慰自己：“嗯，只怕还不至于此，还有一丝希望……”可是，刚才那份兴奋的心情却消失了。

这当儿，史可法已经重新控制住了自己的感情。

“啊哈！”他朝冒襄转过脸来，微微一笑，“时候已经不早，此事就这样办了。愿兄台善自珍重！”说着，就站了起来。

“啊，老公祖这就要走？”

史可法点点头：“自我师败于峡山后，献贼有进窥江南之意，眼下沿江防务甚急。凤阳总督高公、安庆巡抚郑公已被朝廷撤职逮问。凤督一职，由马瑶草代任。诏令是昨天到的，适才弟已看了邸报。”

“什么？马瑶草起用了？”冒襄吃了一惊。

史可法瞧了瞧冒襄，似乎对于他的反应感到奇怪。

“马瑶草虽然同阮圆海私交颇厚，”史可法沉默了一下之后，说，“但此人并非阉党，心术人品尚称端直，而且素有知兵之名。这次朝廷起用他，以弟之见，可谓得人。”

冒襄本想提醒史可法，对马士英须得提防着点。可是听史可法言下之意，对马士英似乎颇为推重。他摸不透史、马二人的关

sad expression, his eyes glistening with tears. Mao Xiang, who had wanted to say a few more words of gratitude, held his breath and kept quiet, as it was obviously not fitting to say them now. Meanwhile, his mood was greatly affected by that of Shi Kefa. "He's quite right. The country has come to such a pass that a few individuals are not enough to correct things. Even if I can make it in the coming examination, how far can I go? When the country is no more, what's the point of it all?" He was shocked by his own thoughts, but soon consoled himself, thinking, "Well, maybe it's not that bad. There's still a glimmer of hope ..." Nevertheless, the excitement that had come to him a moment ago was now completely gone.

At this point, Shi Kefa had regained control of his feelings.

"Well, it's getting late." He turned to Mao Xiang and smiled slightly. "I have to go now and will send the letter tomorrow. Take care, Brother Mao." He stood up as he spoke.

"Why, must you go now?"

Shi Kefa nodded. "After the defeat of the imperial army in Xiashan, the insurgent Zhang Xianzhong is planning to go south of the Yangtze River, and now the defense along the river is an urgent matter. Mr. Gao, Governor-General of Fengyang, and Mr. Zheng, Governor of Anqing, have been discharged by the court and taken into custody for interrogation. Ma Yaocao has taken over the office of governor of Fengyang. The edict arrived yesterday, as I just read in the official communication."

"What? Ma Yaocao is reinstated?" Mao Xiang asked, shocked by the news.

Shi Kefa looked at Mao Xiang, apparently surprised at his reaction.

"Although Ma Yaocao has a good personal relationship with Ruan Yuanhai," Shi Kefa said after a moment of silence. "He isn't a member of eunuch Wei's party. He's basically an honest man and is a good war strategist. In my view, he's the right person for the job."

Mao Xiang wanted to remind Shi Kefa that he should be careful of Ma Shiying. However, judging from the tone, he felt Shi Kefa had high

系到底如何，觉得不便贸然进言，便只好拱着手，唯唯应着，不再说什么了。

## 背信疑云

正当史可法向冒襄谈到马士英的时候，在城南库司坊石巢园的大厅内，阮大铖和他的客人们都在心急火燎地等待马士英的到来。

阮大铖也是昨天才得到消息。虽然早在四个月前，也就是钱谦益为他开脱那件事失败之后，阮大铖眼见自己一场好梦化为泡影，无法可想，只好咬咬牙，当时就写信给周延儒，请他设法先把马士英弄上去再说。周延儒欠着阮大铖一万两银子的人情，自然难以推却，何况马士英不是逆案中人，事情好办得多，所以爽快地答应了。不过，到底又拖了好几个月，才算把这事办成。昨天，当马士英派了一名管事人来告知这个消息的时候，阮大铖着实高兴得手舞足蹈，心想："哈哈，这回到底让我钻通了，只要老马能上去，不愁他将来不拉我一把！"不过，这么个大喜讯，马士英竟不亲自登门向自己报告，又使阮大铖有点意外，也有点不满。他问明来人，知道是军情紧急，朝廷诏令即刻起程赴任，马士英正忙得团团转，实在无法分身，于是便点点头，吩咐立即备轿，前往拜谒。谁知，当他兴冲冲地赶到马士英府上时，却扑了个空——马士英出门拜客去了。阮大铖可就有点着恼。他也不管什么礼貌不礼貌，当着马府家人的面，就唠唠叨叨地数落起来，说什么这可是件大事啦，马士英本该先来找他啦，不来找他也应当在家里等啦，他也是靠六十岁的人，让他这样来回扑空多不好啦；还有，他如今有许多顶顶要紧的话要向马士英交代，现在找不到人，可怎么办啦，如此等等。马府的人知道这胡子老爹的脾气，尤其知道他同大老爷的交情，所以只是一个劲儿地应

regard for Ma Shiying. Not knowing what the relationship between Shi Kefa and Ma Shiying was, he felt he had better not speak his mind so quickly, so he just responded politely without saying anything.

## A Cloud of Mistrust

When Shi Kefa spoke about Ma Shiying to Mao Xiang, in the hall of the Stone Nest Garden in Kusifang in the south of the city, Ruan Dacheng and his guests were waiting anxiously for Ma Shiying's arrival.

Ruan Dacheng had got the news the day before. As early as four months ago, after Qian Qianyi failed to obtain a pardon for him, seeing that his good dream was going to burst like a bubble, Ruan Dacheng, who couldn't think of anything else, wrote to Zhou Yanru, against his own will, asking him to get Ma Shiying reinstated first. Zhou Yanru, owing Ruan Dacheng a favor of 10,000 taels of silver, was naturally unable to turn down the request. Besides, since Ma Shiying was not involved in the treason case, things were much easier, so Zhou Yanru readily agreed. However, it took several months to get it done. On the previous day, upon hearing the news from the man sent by Ma Shiying, Ruan Dacheng was exhilarated. "Haha, I've done it! As long as Old Ma makes it, I won't have to worry. He'll lend me a helping hand in time." However, Ma Shiying hadn't come to him in person to report the good news. Ruan Dacheng was a little disappointed and unhappy. Upon learning that Ma Shiying had to report for duty immediately and was too busy to come to him, he nodded his head and got his sedan chair ready for a visit to his friend. To his disappointment, when he excitedly rushed to Ma Shiying's house, his friend was not in. Ma Shiying had gone out to visit someone. Ruan Dacheng was a little annoyed. Not caring whether it was rude or not, he complained in front of the Mas: for such a matter of great importance he should have visited me in person or at least have been waiting for me at home because it isn't good to let a sixty-year old make a trip in vain, I have many important things to say to him but can't find him, what can I do, blah blah blah. The people at the Ma residence were well aware of the bearded old man's temper, especially his close relationship with the

着，并不回嘴。阮大铖发了一通牢骚，到底等马士英不着，只好又回来了。到家之后，他越想越不甘心，又生出个办法：命管家阮庆写下六七份请柬，分送给平日气味最相投、来往最密切的几个好友——中山王府的二公子徐青君、南昌建安王府镇国中尉朱统𨪱、罢职漕运总督田仰、前江宁知县杨文骢，以及一位姓王的总兵官，请他们前来饮宴。另外又写了一份给马士英，就用以上几个人、再加上他阮大铖的名义通知对方，说定于第二天，也就是今晚，在石巢园摆酒，给他饯行，请马士英务必赏光。请柬送出去之后，阮大铖心想："看你马瑶草来不来？你若是乖乖儿前来便罢，若还推三阻四，我老阮可跟你没个完！"结果，这一次马士英答复得倒爽快，说他一定前来。阮大铖听了，这才稍稍消了一点气，同时，也就想好了一大通到时要对马士英说的话，其中包括一系列的要求和约定，准备都要在酒筵上提出来，并且当场取得对方的许诺和保证。鉴于马士英自昨日以来，这几下子的表现颇不漂亮，阮大铖已经警惕起来，觉得对他的这位"债户"不能放松，而要抓得很紧很紧。

现在，客人们早已到齐，最初那一阵子快活、热烈的寒暄和交谈也已经结束。大家默默地喝着茶，围着从旧院请来侑酒的两位秦淮名妓——马婉容和王小大，听她们轮流着唱小曲儿，也听得有点腻烦了。厨房的管事好几次出来打听什么时候才开席，可是，马士英仍旧不见踪影。

"哎，圆老，怎么回事？瑶老到底还来不来啊？"徐青君终于打了一个呵欠，问。他显然已经不耐烦了。

"哼，你问我，我又问谁去？请柬是昨夜送去的，今天一早又派人去问过他，都说要来，来！谁知道！"由于长久地扭转脑袋，眼巴巴地看着门外，阮大铖觉得脖子累得好酸。听了这话，

master, so they just kept agreeing without talking back. After venting his complaints for waiting for Ma Shiying in vain, Ruan Dacheng had to go back dejectedly. After he returned home, the more he thought about it, the more unsettled he became. Finally, he came up with an idea. He ordered his housekeeper Ruan Qing to write six or seven invitation letters and send them to his best friends, including Xu Qingjun, the second son of the Prince of Zhongshan, Lieutenant Zhu Tonglei in Jian'an Palace of Nanchang, Tian Yang, ousted Governor of Water Transport, Yang Wencong, ex-magistrate of Jiangning County, and an army officer named Wang, inviting them to a banquet. In addition, he wrote another letter of invitation to Ma Shiying in the name of these men and himself to ask Ma Shiying to come to the send-off party at the Stone Nest Garden this very evening. After the invitations were sent out, Ruan Dacheng thought to himself, "Mr. Ma, I'll see if you dare turn me down. If you come, it's good. If you don't, wait and see." Ma Shiying agreed immediately. After hearing it, Ruan Dacheng's anger abated and he was prepared to put forward his demands and requests at the banquet and get a promise. Based on his experience in the past few days, he began to doubt Mr. Ma's trustworthiness and decided to act as quickly as possible so that this debtor of his would live up to his expectations.

All the guests had arrived. After the exchange of pleasantries and the jovial, casual conversations were over, they sat down to sip tea. In the middle were two famous courtesans from the Qinhuai River, Ma Wanrong and Wang Xiaoda, singing songs in turn. Everyone listened quietly until they were bored. The head chef came out several times to ask when to serve the food. However, there was still no sign of Ma Shiying.

Finally, Xu Qingjun yawned and asked, "Hey, Elder Yuan, what's happened? Is Elder Yao coming or not?" He was clearly impatient.

Having looked outside the door too long with his head turned, Ruan Dacheng felt his neck get sore. Hearing that, he turned to Xu Qingjun and answered irritatedly, "Hmph, you are asking me. Who do I ask? The invitation was sent last night, and I sent a servant this

他就回过头来，没有好气地回答。

“既是瑶老说过要来，那么他一定会来的，诸位不必担心！”有人很有把握地说。那是马士英的远房亲戚田仰，他身材矮小，肩膀很窄，瘦削衰老的脸上，却奇怪地长着两道漆黑的、年轻的眉毛。

“可现在都什么时候了呀！”徐青君不高兴地说。

“只怕，叫什么事情临时绊住了吧？”体格健壮、脸孔却很瘦的王总兵小心地说，“眼下军情很紧，听说献贼已经……”

“哼，事情再多，也该来了！”坐在对面的杨文骢打断他的话。杨文骢是马士英的妹夫，同田仰也算是亲戚。他有四十五六岁的样子，衣服穿得很华丽；小眼睛，细鼻子，淡眉毛，配着一张胖胖的圆脸，脾气一向挺温和。可是不知为什么，现在他却有点愤愤然：“昨儿我巴巴地上门访了他两回，今儿一早访了他一回，都没见着——哪里就有这么多事了？今晚我们大家都在这里等他，他又不是不知道！”

“龙友兄，你说这话，可就太不体谅瑶老了！”田仰不以为然地微笑着。显然，同样作为亲戚，他所选择的立场同杨文骢恰恰相反，他决心充当马士英的坚定维护者，并且认为这样做是聪明的，“瑶老新膺重任，百事纷拿。他为人又最是认真严谨，事事都讲究亲力亲为，一时忙开了，对我们这些老友照应不到，也是有的。兄又何必耿耿于怀，责备于他？”

“我不是说我们！”杨文骢吵架似的说。由于被对方隐藏着圈套的话所激怒，他的圆脸涨得通红，“我是说圆老！他们二人的交情谁不知道？再者，这次他马瑶草东山再起，还不是全靠圆老帮的大忙！光冲着这情分，他就该哪儿不去，头一个先得来拜谢圆老！也用不着我们白白候上这大半晚，还不知道他来不

morning to ask him again. He said he would come, but who knows?"

"Since Elder Yao said he's coming, he'll be here. Don't worry," someone said reassuringly. It was Ma Shiying's distant relative Tian Yang, a short-statured man with narrow shoulders, whose saggy, aging face curiously had a pair of dark, youthful eyebrows.

"But it's so late now," growled Xu Qingjun.

"Maybe he's delayed by something urgent," said Mr. Wang, the army officer, a sturdy man with a thin face, in a timid voice. "The situation at the front line is very tense. I hear the rebels led by Zhang Xianzhong ..."

"Hmph, no matter how busy he is, he should be here by now," interrupted Yang Wencong, sitting across from him. Yang Wencong was Ma Shiying's brother-in-law and also a relative of Tian Yang. A well-dressed man, he was about forty-five or six years old with small eyes, a thin nose, sparse eyebrows, a plump, round face, and a gentle temperament. For some unknown reason, he was now a little agitated. "I called at his house twice yesterday, and this morning I called again, but I didn't see him. Are there so many things for him to do? We're all here waiting for him and he knows it."

"Brother Longyou, please be understanding of Elder Yao." Tian Yang smiled in disapproval. Obviously, as a relative of Ma Shiying, he chose a position opposite that of Yang Wencong. He had decided to act as a staunch defender of Ma Shiying, and thought it wise to do so. "Elder Yao has taken on great responsibilities, and there're so many thorny issues ahead. As a meticulous man, he does everything himself to make sure it goes well. Maybe he's too busy to come and meet the old friends in time. Such things happen. Please don't be too harsh on him."

"I don't mean us," said Yang Wencong as if in a row. Furious at what he perceived to be a hidden trap, he said, as his round face blushed red. "I mean Elder Yuan. Who doesn't know the friendship between the two of them? Besides, Ma Yaocao's reinstatement is the result of Elder Yuan's efforts. For that great friendship alone, he should not go anywhere else. Elder Yuan is the first person for him to thank. If he had come in time, we wouldn't have been waiting for so long, and

来呢！”

“哈哈，不错！”正浑身散了架似的歪在椅子上、转动着一双小眼睛瞧着大家争论的朱统𨰿，突然蹦起来，“八成是马老头儿乌纱帽儿一戴，就把我们这伙老朋友给忘啦！”他喜气洋洋地叫，挥动着长长的胳臂。朱统𨰿是明朝的宗室，本来封在江西，不久前为着躲“流寇”，搬到南京来住，他看中了石巢园有得吃，有得玩，主人又格外热情大方，便一头钻了进来，很快同阮大铖等人打得火热。若论长相，他那高高凸出的前额，以及相应地向前钩着的下巴颏，同老皇帝朱元璋还真有几分相似，说明他确实是一颗“龙种”。现在，他大步走到阮大铖跟前。

“我们同他交情浅，没说的。可是你呢？圆老，你不是常说，你同老马是二十年的过命交情么！怎么今天也叫他给甩啦！咦？啊！”他嘲弄地问，显得兴高采烈，随后就哈哈大笑起来。他笑得那样厉害，以至到后来不得不双手捂着肚子，倒在椅子上打滚，惹得周围的人不由得露出茫然的微笑。

阮大铖没有作声，可是他的脸色却分明变了。一种混杂着怀疑和怨恨的灰白色从他那张滚圆的胖脸上呈现出来，一双乌溜溜的眼睛也顿时失去了光彩。

“马瑶草不会弃我，不会！”他喃喃地说。

“不会？”朱统𨰿一翻身又站了起来，他显然还没有尽兴，“那么，你就等着吧！看老马今晚还来不来！别瞧他昨儿还糖豆儿似的黏着你，可今天不同喽，人家又上去喽！你对他还有什么用！不错，是你帮的大忙，可那又怎样呢？如今是他在上头你在下头，他愿不愿意帮回你，还不知道哩！再说你的事连周老头儿都帮不了，还能指望他马瑶草有办法？没准儿，还把你看成累赘咧！哈哈，这回呀，你老就认栽吧！”

now we don't even know whether he'll come at all."

"Haha, well said!" Zhu Tonglei, who was lying askew in the chair like a bundle of loose bones and watching the others argue with his small eyes, suddenly jumped up. "Most probably as soon as old man Ma put on the black gauze hat, he forgot all these old friends of his," he exclaimed in good cheer, gesticulating with his long arm. Zhu Tonglei was a member of the royal family of the Great Ming. His estate was in Jiangxi, but he had moved to Nanjing some time ago to keep away from the guerrilla rebels. Seeing that he could eat and play in the Stone Nest Garden and the host was especially generous, he immediately moved in upon arrival in Nanjing and mingled with Ruan Dacheng's circle of friends. In appearance, he did somewhat resemble the founding emperor Zhu Yuanzhang with his protruding forehead and the curved lower jaw, which indicated his royal birth. Now he strode to Ruan Dacheng.

"It's no big deal to us because he doesn't know us well. But what about you? Elder Yuan, aren't you always saying that you and Old Ma are friends of twenty years? How come he's dumped you today? Huh?" he asked mockingly, looking amused. Then he burst into laughter. He laughed so hard that he put his hands on his stomach, fell on his chair and rolled in it, which made everyone around him laugh.

Ruan Dacheng said nothing, but his expression clearly changed. A pale color mixed with suspicion and resentment appeared from his round, plump face, and his dark bright eyes suddenly lost their spirit.

"Ma Yaocao won't let me down. No, he won't," he muttered.

"No?" Zhu Tonglei turned to Ruan Dacheng and stood up, clearly having not had enough fun. "Then, just wait. Let's see if Old Ma comes tonight. He was glued to you like a jelly bean yesterday, but today it's different. He has risen up. You're no use for him now. Yes, you were a great help to him, but so what? He's above and you're below. There's no knowing whether he's willing to help you back. Even Old Man Zhou cannot help you with your case, so how can you expect Ma Yaocao to do anything? Maybe he'll consider you a burden. Haha, this time, you'll have to take the bad luck."

“大恩不报，自古已然！”许久没有说话的徐青君忽然冒出一句，又打了一个呵欠，并且做出打算起身告辞的样子了。

阮大铖慢慢地抬起头，望望这个，又望望那个，仿佛问：会这样吗？真会这样吗？然而，大家还没来得及说话，他却猛然一跃而起。“不，不会的！不会！你们说，不会！是不是，说啊！”他厉声追问，恶狠狠地环顾着。大家被他这突如其来的举动吓慌了，都不由自主地后退了一下。

就在这时，像是回答他似的，大堂外响起了急促的脚步声。门公引着一名家仆打扮的人一步跨了进来。那人环顾了一下，认出阮大铖之后，就走过来，跪下禀告说：

“小人马六儿，是抚台马大人的长班。奉我家老爷之命，来见阮老爷——我家老爷说，承阮老爷和诸位老爷盛情相邀，本拟前来领教，唯是军务紧迫，即刻便要登程，实在无法停留。特命小人前来转知列位老爷，并致歉意！”

大家听了，顿时面面相觑，一句话都说不出来。过了一会，杨文骢定了定神，勉强问道：

“嗯，可有瑶老手启？”

“回大人，我家老爷说行色匆匆，就不写信了，让小人口头转达。”

“那么——瑶老可尚有其他话说？”

“回大人，没有了。”

杨文骢同其余的人交换了一个眼色，看见大家都不作声，他就朝马六儿摆摆手说：“嗯，知道了，你回去多多拜上马大人，就说我们这些知交好友恭祝他此行一帆风顺，马到功成。我们在此静候他的破贼捷报！”

马六儿叩了头，退出去了。杨文骢这才转过身来，却看见阮大铖失魂落魄地呆在椅子上，不动，也不说话。他沉吟了一下，

"There have been ungrateful men since ancient times," said Xu Qingjun suddenly, who hadn't spoken for a long while. He yawned in a posture to stand up and leave.

Ruan Dacheng raised his head slowly, looked at one, then another, as if to ask: How can it be so? How can it be really so? Before anyone could speak, he suddenly jumped up. "No, it can't be. No. Tell me, it can't be so, can it? Tell me," he shouted desperately, looking around in anger. Everyone was baffled by his sudden outburst and involuntarily stepped back.

Just then, as if to answer him, from outside the hall came the sound of hurried footsteps. The janitor ushered in a man who looked like a servant. The man looked around, and upon recognizing Ruan Dacheng, he came forward, knelt down and said:

"I'm Ma Liu'er, servant of Governor Ma. I'm here by order of my master to see your lordship. My master said that he was grateful for the invitation from your lordships and had planned to meet with you here and listen to your advice, but unfortunately he has to leave right away to attend to urgent military matters with no delay. He asked me to let you know and apologize to you."

The guests looked at each other. None was able to say a word. After a while, Yang Wencong calmed down a little and asked:

"Well, do you have a letter from Elder Yao?"

"Your lordship, my master said he didn't have time to write a letter and asked me to pass the message in person."

"Then, did Elder Yao ask you to say anything else?"

"No, my lord."

Yang Wencong exchanged a look with the other guests, and seeing that everyone was silent, he waved to Ma Liu'er and said, "Well, I see, you go back and send our regards to Lord Ma, and tell him that all his good friends here congratulate him and wish him a good journey and great success. We're waiting here for the great news of his victory against the insurgents."

Ma Liu'er bowed and left. Yang Wencong turned around and saw Ruan Dacheng sitting despairingly on the chair, not moving or talking.

打算走前去劝慰几句，到底迟了一步，阮大铖忽然狠狠地一扯胡子，用力跺着脚，呜呜大哭起来……

## 整装赴试

南京乡试的考场，坐落在城南淮清桥和武定桥之间的秦淮河西岸，离应天府学不远，与名妓聚居的旧院，也只是隔河相望。

这个可以容纳上万举子同时应试的江南第一大考场，规模与格局都与众不同。当门一片大空地，用木栅栏三面围了起来。栅栏的东西两侧，各有一个斗拱结构的辕门。从辕门走进去，是两座鼓楼，分立在坐北朝南的大门两旁。鼓楼后面是两座石牌坊，分别用朱漆在右边的牌坊上写着“明经取士”，在左边的牌坊上写着“为国求贤”。牌坊当中，是一座庄严肃穆的大门楼，上面悬着一块黑字横匾，工楷大书写着两个字“贡院”，下面并排横着三个门洞，这是考场的大门。进了大门，接着是仪门，这是举子们领取试卷的地方。仪门之后又是一道门，名叫“龙门”，顾名思义，自然是暗喻着连登金榜、飞黄腾达的意思。龙门内，平列着四道较小的门，却是取的《虞书》“辟四门”之义。走完这一道道门之后，就来到考场之内。一条宽阔的露天通道，从门

He mused for an instant, and was going to say a few words of comfort, but he was one second too late. Ruan Dacheng suddenly pulled his beard hard, stomped his feet and cried out loud ...

## Mao Xiang Was Prepared for the Imperial Exam

The examination court for the provincial-level imperial examination in Nanjing was located between Huaiqing Bridge and Wuding Bridge on the west bank of the Qinhuai River in the south of the city. It was adjacent to the Yingtian Academy and across from the Old Yard on the other side of the river where the famous courtesans lived.

This examination court, the largest test center in River South, which could accommodate tens of thousands of candidates at the same time, was very different from other test centers in size and layout. In front of the examination court was a large open space surrounded on three sides by a wooden stake fence. At the east and west ends of the fence were two outer gates with bow-shaped load-bearing structures. After entering a side gate, one could see two drum towers with a south-facing main gate in between. Behind the drum towers were two stone arches. On the right arch was written in red lacquer RECRUITING SCHOLARS LEARNED IN THE CLASSICS, and on the left arch SEEKING TALENT TO SERVE THE COUNTRY. Between the arches was an imposing turreted gate. On the top of the gate hung a black horizontal plaque which read The Academy of Examinations, written in standard script, and below the plaque were three door holes aligned evenly in a horizontal row. That was the main gate of the examination court. The main gate was followed by the ceremony gate, where the candidates received their test papers. Behind the ceremony gate was another gate called "dragon gate", which as its name suggests symbolized the threshold to entering the realm of the dragon, or in other words, the threshold to success. Inside the dragon gate were four smaller gates in a row, which symbolized the four doors for success in the *Book of Yu*. After one passed all the gates, they arrived at the examination court. A wide, open-air corridor extended from the entrance inward. On either side of the corridor was an eight-

边一直向内伸延。通道两旁，是八尺高的砖墙，墙上是一个个带栅栏的门，每个门的距离也是八尺左右。数以百计的这样的门，都按《千字文》的顺序一字一门地编着号。每号门内，是一条仅可容二人并肩通过的狭长小巷。那些有顶无门的小斗室，就一间接一间地排列在巷的一侧，每巷总有上百间之多，这就是“号舍”——举子们答卷和住宿的地方。

为着能够随时监视考场的情况，在露天通道当中，建有一座“明远楼”。楼高三层，飞檐轩窗，气象颇为雄伟。有了这座楼，再加上考场四角上的望楼，举子们在考试期间的一举一动，都逃不过监考人员的眼睛，企图作弊就不那么容易了。

如果说，这还不够保险的话，那么考场周围还另有防范的措施。首先是围墙，它不是一道，而是两道。内围墙高一丈，外围墙高一丈五尺，每一道的墙头，都布满了带尖刺的荆棘，它们把考场同外界严格地隔绝开来。其次，到了考试期间，还专门有差役兵丁在围墙之间来往巡逻。这样，即便有哪个作弊者铤而走险，竟然翻越棘墙，也必定会落入巡逻兵丁之手。

贡院的前半部分，也就是考场部分的情形，大体就是这样子。至于试卷的誊抄、批改、推荐乃至录取，都在贡院的后半部分进行。那里面还有许多院落馆舍，戒备也更加森严。只靠着交卷的地点至公堂的东西两栅栏同前半部分发生关系，应试举子那是绝对禁止进入的。

乡试的试期，照例从八月初九日开始。按规定，每个举子必

foot-tall brick wall, on which were a row of small gates, protected by wooden stake fences and eight feet away from each other. Hundreds of such small gates were numbered with characters as they appear in *The Thousand-Character Text*. Inside each small gate was a narrow lane that allowed passage of two persons side by side. Each lane was lined on one side with as many as a hundred roofed roomlets that had no doors, and these roomlets called "numbered rooms" were where the candidates wrote their test papers and slept in the night.

A watchtower was built in the open-air corridor to monitor the situation of the examination rooms at any time. The tower, consisting of three stories with wide, projecting eaves and protruding rectangular windows, was a majestic presence. With this tower and the turrets on the four corners of the examination court, no movement of the candidates during the examination could escape the eyes of the invigilators, and cheating would not be easy.

In case that was not safe enough, other precautions were taken around the examination venue. First of all, there were the fence walls, the inner wall as tall as ten feet and the outer wall as tall as fifteen feet, each covered with sharp thorns, which effectively isolated the examination court from the outside world. In addition, during the examination period, special soldiers were installed to patrol between the walls. This way, should a fraudster dare to take the risk and climb over a thorn wall, he would definitely fall into the hands of the patrolling soldiers.

That constituted the examination court, which was the frontal part of the Gongyuan. Copy-making, marking, recommendation and admission procedures took place in the rear part of the Gongyuan, where were many courtyards and buildings under tight security. Communication with the frontal part only took place between where the examination papers were collected and the two fence walls at the east and west sides of the common room. Candidates were absolutely forbidden to enter the rear part.

The provincial-level imperial examination normally started on the ninth of August in the lunar calendar. According to the regulations, each candidate had to sit for three sessions, the first one on the ninth,

须考满三场——初九日为第一场正场，十二日为第二场正场，十五日为第三场正场。每场考试，都是提前一天点名，并发卷进场。所以，到了八月初八这一天，冒襄早上起来，梳洗完毕，就开始准备上考场去。

自从那一天夜里史可法来访，主动提出要替他向主考官说项疏通之后，冒襄对于这一次乡试，就变得重视起来了。本来，在过去整整一年中，由于烦心的事太多，他一直脱不出身来认真准备。这一次虽然循例到南京来，却多少抱着姑且碰一碰运气的想法。但是，如今他的想法不同了。他不仅下决心全力应考，而且志在必得。这倒不在于史可法的推荐，势必会有助于他的成功，而是史可法这一行动本身所体现出来的、对他异乎寻常的关怀和重视，促使他振作起来。

这位史大人，作为雄镇淮扬、声威素著的一位封疆大吏，向来是复社士子们推崇景仰的偶像。他早年家境清贫，曾受知于著名的东林党领袖左光斗。入仕后，以清廉正直、干练有为著称。他推诚御下，赏罚严明，能与部卒同甘共苦。每次出发作战，都是将士们先食，他自己后食；将士们先穿，他自己后穿，颇有古贤将之风，在腐败已极的明朝军队中，显得十分难能可贵。他的军队，也因此具有较强的战斗力，曾多次挫败农民军的进攻，为明朝把守住江南富庶之区。同时，作为漕运总督，他还大力整顿，锐意改革，使积弊很深、混乱已极的南北漕运大见起色，保证了江南地区的钱粮能源源不绝地运往京师。这一切，都使史可法在

the second one on the twelfth, and the third one on the fifteenth. The day before each session, a roll call was made and the test paper was handed to the candidates, who were required to enter the examination court immediately. So, on the eighth of August, Mao Xiang got up early in the morning, washed and dressed up, and was prepared to go to the examination court.

After Shi Kefa offered to communicate with the chief examiner, Mao Xiang became more serious about the provincial exam. For almost a year, he had had no time to prepare for the exam because he had too many things on his mind. This time, he had come to Nanjing as a routine, more or less to try his luck. The visit from Shi Kefa had changed his mind. Not only was he determined to go all out for the exam, but he was resolved to win as well, not because Shi Kefa's recommendation would surely contribute to his success, but because the special attention he had received from Shi Kefa had deeply inspired him.

The respectable Mr. Shi, as an official appointed by the imperial court whose name resounded in the lower reaches of the Huai River and the Yangtze River had always been an idol admired and worshiped by the scholars of the Fushe. He came from a poor family and in his early years studied under Zuo Guangdou, a famous leader of the East Wood Party. Ever since he became an official, he had been known for his cleanness, integrity, and ability. Treating his subordinates with sincerity and sharing in their joys and sorrows, he enforced rules of rewards and punishments strictly and fairly. Every time they went out for a military action, he let the soldiers eat and be clad first in the manner of virtuous military commanders in ancient times. That quality was very valuable in the corrupt Ming armies. As a result, his troops excelled in combat and successfully defended the rich and prosperous River South region for the Great Ming by repeatedly repelling the peasant insurgents. At the same time, as Governor of Water Transport, he also instituted a series of reforms so that transport through waterway between the South and the North, which had been previously very chaotic, was greatly improved to enable money and grains from the south of the Yangtze River to be continuously

朝野人士、特别是复社士子当中备受赞誉，被看作是具有高尚的道德品质和杰出的政治军事才能的典范人物。如今，正是他，而不是别人对冒襄如此关怀和器重，为着使他能够尽快获得施展才干、为国效力的机会，竟不惜冒着可能招致非议的风险，毅然采取非常的行动，这确实使冒襄受宠若惊；而当他深入体味对方这一行动所包含的殷切期待时，又止不住热血沸腾、情怀激越。“这些年来，国家的局面越来越坏，朝廷中那些当权的大老们确实不行了！大明中兴的希望，如今已经落到了我们肩上！看来只有实行我们所主张的一套，才有可能把社稷从水深火热中解救出来。这些年，我们上去了一些人，但远远不够，还需要上去更多，才能真正掌握大局。史世叔无疑正是看到了这一点，才如此热心地提挈我。既然如此，我也应挺身而出，当仁不让！我为什么只想着碰运气？我冒襄岂是那等平庸之辈？不，我一定要中，一定能中！”

这样下了决心之后，他就变得空前热心起来，开始全力以赴地投入紧张的准备。他摒绝了一切交游，也不再去弄诗词歌赋，集中精力钻研揣摩八股文的写作。他把自己前几次乡试的试卷以及平日的习作又翻了出来，同那几部最著名的八股文选集，像钱禧、杨廷枢选的《同文录》、马世奇选的《澹宁居集》、艾南英选的《明文定》，以及一些有名的程墨、房稿的选本仔细对照参

transported to the capital unimpeded. Because of all this, Shi Kefa was highly regarded among the court officials and gentry scholars, especially members of the Fushe, as a model figure of high moral caliber and outstanding political and military talents. Now, this man, not anybody else, cared about and appreciated Mao Xiang so much as to run the risk of incurring criticism by resolutely taking an extraordinary action for the young man to have an opportunity to serve the country with his talent. Mao Xiang was very grateful. As he reflected on the earnest expectations symbolized by this action, he couldn't stop his blood from boiling with excitement. "Over the years, the situation of the country had gotten worse and worse, and the ones in power in the imperial court are truly incompetent. The hope of the Ming dynasty's revival now rests on our shoulders. It seems that only by implementing our plan, can the dynasty be saved from the crisis. In the past few years, some of us have been employed by the imperial court, but it's far from enough, and more of us are needed to take control of things. Uncle Shi has no doubt seen it, so he's helping me out enthusiastically. That being the case, I must take up the responsibility and do my part. Why do I just leave everything to chance? Am I such a mediocre person? No. I have to win. I'll definitely be able to win."

Having made up his mind, Mao Xiang was more enthusiastic about the exam than ever and began to devote all his energy to the intense preparations. He gave up all socializing and stopped writing poetry, lyrics, and odes to concentrate on studying the eight-legged essay. Putting his practice writings and the papers of the previous exams side by side with the most famous anthologies of eight-legged essays, such as the *tong wen lu* (*Anthology of Essential Writings*) compiled by Qian Xi and Yang Tingshu, the *dan ning ju ji* (*The Danning House Collection*) by Ma Shiqi, and the *ming wen ding* (*A Definitive Collection of Ming Essays*) compiled by Ai Nanying, as well as some well-known *chengmo* (eight-legged essays by chief examiners and famous scholars) and *fanggao* (eight-legged essays by *jinshi* scholars) anthologies, he studied with a vengeance with special attention to how to introduce the topic, how to explore the

详，特别在如何题前盘旋、如何抉发题中神理、如何实力发挥等关键之处下工夫。这样弄了将近一个月，自觉眼光和手笔都有了突飞猛进，与一个月前大不相同。他得意之余，自负地想：“哼，除非是试官瞎了眼。否则，以我今日这种文字去应考，再不中便是没有天理！史世叔要替我关说，自是一番好意。不过其实我文字火候已到，关说不关说，又是其次了！”

所以今天，他准备前往考场的时候，显得十分从容镇定，先换了衣服，又命冒成取出一顶新方巾来戴上；然后开始检点进场行李，不外是铜铫、号顶、门帘、火炉、烛台、烛剪、枕褥之类；接着又察看了一下场食，看见三屉格考篮里，上层是米盐、酱醋、鸡蛋等食料，中层是些精巧点心和补品，像月饼、蜜橙糕、莲子、龙眼肉、人参之类，最下的一层放着笔墨、砚台、挖补刀、糨糊等，都已准备停当。他又坐下来吃了一盏茶，正要起身出门，临时记起还应当照例卜一卦，问个吉凶。于是先去重新盥了手，焚起一炷线香，然后把书案上一个小小的锦盒拿来，从里面拈出五十根蓍草，先抽出一根，再把其余的四十九根随手分作两部分，按四根一组来数数，数来数去，得了个“贲卦”。冒襄心想：“贲者，文明之象也。”心里已有几分喜欢。再细看卦象，只见内外两爻，相对发动，似乎预兆着此去会一举两得。冒襄倒疑惑起来：这次

theme contained in the topic, how to demonstrate one's potential, and other important aspects of essay writing. After doing this for almost a month, he felt he had made significant progress over a month ago in terms of both argument and writing skills. He was very proud of himself and even thought with a bit of conceit, "Hmph, unless the examiner is blind, with this quality of writing, there's no reason for me to fail the exam. It's very kind of Uncle Shi to want to speak for me, but actually it isn't necessary. Now that my writing has come to such perfection, whether he speaks for me or not is not that important."

So today, when he was going to set off for the examination venue, he looked calm and collected. He changed his clothes, ordered Mao Cheng to take out a new scholar's headscarf and put it on, then checked the items to be used in the examination room: a small copper wok, a mosquito net, a door curtain, a stove, candlesticks, a candle stand and a candle fuse cutter, a pillow, etc. Then he examined the food to be eaten during the exam in the three-layer exam basket with ingredients like rice, salt, soy sauce, vinegar, eggs, etc. in the top layer, some snacks and supplements in the middle layer such as moon cakes, orange pudding, lotus seeds, longan flesh, ginseng, etc., and a brush pen, an ink bottle, an inkstone, a knife, paste, etc. in the bottom layer. Everything was there. He sat down and drank a cup of tea. As he was about to get up and leave, he suddenly remembered that he had to make a divination as was his habit to see whether his luck would be good or bad. Then, he went to wash his hands, burned a stick of incense, and from the table took a small brocade box, which contained fifty straws. He took one out and then divided the other forty-nine into two bundles at random. He counted them in groups of four. The resulting hexagram of the counting was a "grace"[①], which means "small success." Mao Xiang thought to himself, "A grace is a good omen." He was glad at heart. He took a closer look at the hexagram and saw that the lines of the lower (internal) hexagram and upper (external) hexagram were aligned in perfect harmony, as if suggesting

① grace: *bi*, the 22nd of the 64 hexagrams in the *I Ching*

考得再好，也只得一个举人，莫非还能考回两个举人来不成？想来想去，始终有点摸不着头脑。最后他想：“无论如何，总不是个凶兆。”于是放下心来，起身出门。

桃叶河房离贡院并不太远，过了淮清桥，往南一拐就到了。这时，路上人员拥挤，都是赶赴考场的士子。有年轻英俊、步履矫捷的，也有老态龙钟、须发俱白的；有的穿得讲究华美，有的则衣衫破敝；有的空手而行，自有健仆替他扛箱提笼，有的自己携带行李，累得弯腰曲背、满头大汗。脸上的神气，也因人而异：那东张西望、表情紧张的，必定是初上举场的生员；那心事重重、低头走路的多半是久困场屋、累试不中的老秀才；至于那些从容镇定、神态昂然的举子，若不是自视甚高，以为稳操胜券，就是暗中打通了关节，已经胜利在握。冒襄就属于最后一种。由于冒成照例跟在后面替他扛行李，所以他十分轻松自在地走着，脸上挂着微笑，时不时朝路旁那些摆卖闱墨文集、各式文具以及古玩字画的摊子瞧上一眼。

当他快走到贡院的时候，背后忽然响起了急促的脚步声，还没来得及回头，一个人影就“呼”的一声，擦着他的肩膀冲了过去，要不是躲得快，就会被撞倒了。冒襄一瞧那高大的背影好熟悉，便扬声招呼道：

“朗三！”

那人停了一下，回过头来，果然是梅朗中。只见他方巾歪了，头发蓬松着，跑得满头大汗，上气不接下气。当认出是冒襄时，他便气急败坏地挥了一下手：“哎，完啦，小弟要迟到……”说着，又领着仆人飞奔而去。

that he was going to kill two birds with one stone. However, he was puzzled. No matter how well he would do this time, he could only get one *juren* degree. No one could get two. He thought and thought, but still didn't get a clue. Finally, he said to himself, "Anyway, this isn't a bad omen." So, he relaxed, got up and set out.

The Peach Leaves Riverhouse was not too far from the Gongyuan. Mao Xiang had only to walk over the Huaiqing Bridge and make a south turn to get there. At this time of day, the road was crowded with scholars rushing to the exam court. Some were young and handsome walking with fast steps while some others were old and slow with white hair and beard; some were gorgeously dressed while some others were poorly clad; some were empty-handed, with their boxes and baskets carried by their servants, and some carried their luggage on their own and hunched forward with their heads sweating. Everyone had a different expression. The ones nervously looking around were first-timers; the ones hanging their heads pensively were mostly old scholars who had failed again and again, trapped in the examination court; those who were calm and collected either were confident of themselves, or had had things secretly arranged for them. Mao Xiang belonged to the last category. With Mao Cheng following behind carrying his luggage as usual, he walked in a light spirit with a smile on his face, and from time to time cast a glance at the stalls selling books, stationery, antiques, paintings, and calligraphy.

When he was about to reach the Gongyuan, there was a sudden sound of hurried footsteps behind him. Before he turned around, whoosh, a figure brushed against his shoulder and ran forward. If he hadn't dodged quickly, he would have been knocked down. Seeing the tall figure looked like one of his friends, he called out to him:

"Hey, Langsan!"

The man stopped and looked back. It was indeed Mei Langzhong, who was out of breath and sweating profusely, his square headscarf tipped askew and his hair fluffy. When he saw it was Mao Xiang, he waved his hand vexedly and said, "Damn, I'm late ..." Then, he continued to run forward with his servant.

冒襄有点莫名其妙，但随即就醒悟过来。前几天，他上贡院看过贴出的告示，知道今年点名进场，头一批是点的太平府的生员，冒襄所属的扬州府排在最后。梅朗中那个县属于宁国府，记得也是比较靠前的，难怪他如此惶急。“朗三这家伙，总是这等冒冒失失！”冒襄皱着眉毛想，不由得微笑起来。

“老兄听说了么？今期乡试，谁该中式，那头十名的单子，都已在主考大人的夹袋里了！”忽然，他听见有人在身边这样说。

“啊，有这等事，那我们岂不是白考了么？”另一个人吃惊地问。

“白考倒不全是白考。只这头十名，阁下休去想它就是了。”头一个人冷冷地说。

冒襄心中一动，回过头去，发现说话的是一胖一瘦的两个举子。

“买一个举人，”胖举子眨着眼睛，“不知要多少银子？可惜我没门道，要不，拼着把那三间祖屋卖了，好歹也要捞他一个！”

“卖祖屋？”瘦举子鄙夷地说，“那济什么事！你想中举，倒不如把脸皮磨厚点，跑到太仓州去，在那个什么西张夫子大圣人张天如的灵前，恭恭敬敬叩上九个响头，再给那些个什么四配、十哲、十常侍、五狗之流的伪君子们响响地拍上一通马屁，甜甜

Mao Xiang was a little confused at first, but woke up immediately. A few days ago, he read the notice posted at the Gongyuan and knew that this year's roll call would start with candidates from Taiping Prefecture. Candidates from Yangzhou Prefecture, to which Mao Xiang belonged, would come last. Mei Langzhong's county belonged to Ningguo Prefecture, which would come early on the roll call. No wonder he was so anxious. "This guy is always so reckless," Mao Xiang thought with a frown. Then, he smiled.

"Man, have you heard that the top ten list is already in the examiner's pocket?" someone next to him suddenly said.

"Oh? Is it so? Then, what do we take the exam for?" asked another man, alarmed.

"The exam is still useful, but don't think about top ten," said the first man coldly.

Mao Xiang was startled and turned around. It was two *juren* candidates speaking, a stout man and an underweight one.

"How much silver," said the stout man, "does it cost to buy a *juren* degree? If I had the connections, I would buy one by selling the three houses I've inherited, no matter what."

"Selling your inherited houses?" the underweight candidate said contemptuously. "How much does it help? If you want to be successful, you can just as well thicken your face, go to Taicang Prefecture and reverently kowtow nine times to the shrine of the great sage Zhang Tianru the West Zhang and then kiss the asses of hypocrites the likes of the Four Disciples Equal to Confucius (*si pei*)①, the Ten Outstanding Disciples (*shi zhe*)②, the Ten Permanent Attendants (*shi chang shi*)③ , and the Five Dogs of the nephew of

---

① Four Disciples Equal to Confucius: Yanhui, Zeng Sen, Kong Ji, and Meng Ke

② Ten Outstanding Disciples: Yan Yuan, Min Ziqian, Ran Boniu and Zhong Gong for virtue and conduct, Zai Wo and Zigong for eloquence, Ran You and Ji Lu for government, and Zi You and Zi Xia for literature

③ Ten Permanent Attendants: a group of twelve eunuchs that controlled political power during the reign of emperor Lingdi in Eastern Han dynasty—Zhang Rang, Zhao Zhong, Xia Yun, Guo Sheng, Sun Zhang, Bi Lan, Li Song, Duan Gui, Gao Wang, Zhang Gong, Han Kui, and Song Dian

地叫上几声干爸干爹，求他们让你加入复社，保管你不出三年，定能高中！”

“啊，莫非又是复社捣的鬼？”

“哼！”

“我找过他们，可是他们不要我。”胖举子怔了半晌，垂头丧气地说。

“他们不要，我还不稀罕呢！什么君子，狐群狗党罢咧！别看他们现在挺神气，总有一天……”瘦举子话没说完，忽然发现冒襄正有意无意地跟在后面，他就住了嘴，扯了胖举子一把，两人紧走几步，在人丛中一混，转眼就不见了。

听了这番刺耳的议论，冒襄不觉暗暗吃惊。如今世风日下，科场腐败，黑幕重重，早已怨声载道，他是知道的。加上这种八股文章其实又考不出什么真才实学，遂致许多贤能之士长期困于场屋，郁郁不得志。正是有感于此，复社同人才群集起来，试图扭转颓风，通过互相援引，使贤能之士得以扬眉吐气，发挥才干。经过整整十年的努力，总算陆续上去了一些人，但招致的非议和怨谤也着实不少。特别是那些社外的士子，更是疑神疑鬼，把复社看成是扰乱科场的魔头灾星，碰到什么劳什子事情，总要往复社身上猜、往复社身上推。这样一来，复社无形中反成了代人受过的众矢之的。“瞧吧，这才真叫一峰崛起，群山皆妒呢！”冒襄冷冷地想。同时，心里油然升起了一股傲气：“哼，不错，我们复社的人就是要中，该中！你们越是不服气，我越要中给你们瞧瞧！无非就是这些八股时文，我不信就弄不过你们！”这样一想，他就抖擞精神，加快脚步，向贡院走去。

Empress Wu Zetian, call them dad or pop and beg them to admit you to the Fushe. Then, within less than three years, you are guaranteed to succeed in the exam."

"Ah? Is it Fushe again?"

"Of course."

"I approached them, but was rejected," said the stout candidate depressedly.

"Rejected? I don't care to join them at all. They're no gentlemen, but a pack of hypocrites. One day, all their arrogance will ..." As he spoke, the thin man suddenly found that Mao Xiang was following them deliberately or inadvertently, so he shut his mouth and pulled the fat man forward. The two of them quickened their steps and disappeared in the blink of an eye.

Mao Xiang was alarmed to hear this unsettling conversation. He knew that nowadays the social milieu was degenerating and the imperial civil service exam system was very corrupt with countless shady deals that had given rise to widespread complaints. Moreover, the eight-legged essay was no good for the discovery of real talent and scholarship. Instead, it had trapped many talented and capable men in the examination court. It was precisely because of this reason that the Fushers had come together to make a change by helping each other in the advancement of their careers. Over the past ten years, they had managed to send some of them to positions of power, but meanwhile they had incurred a lot of criticism and slander. Scholars outside the society were particularly suspicious of the Fushers. They regarded the Fushers as devils who disrupted the imperial civil service exam system and blamed the Fushe for anything bad that had happened. Thus, the Fushe had always been a scapegoat for the fault of others. "See, when a peak is too prominent, all the mountains are jealous," Mao Xiang thought coldly. At the same time, a sense of pride suddenly rose in his heart. "Hmph, yes, the Fushers shall succeed. We must. The more you are unconvinced, the more I want to show you. It's just eight-legged essays. You will be defeated." As he thought, his spirits rose, and he quickened his pace toward the Gongyuan.

## 考场百态

“哎，辟疆，你可来了！累得我满场子地好找！”

冒襄刚刚走进贡院的辕门，余怀就兴冲冲地迎上来。

“哦，什么事？”冒襄边问，边打量着四周。他发现，尚未进场的举子还很不少，栅栏内外，依旧挤得满满的，少说也有二三千人，再加上他们的仆从，人数就更多了。一部分举子正拥挤在贡院的大门前听候点名，其余的则东一堆西一群地随意站着。有的正起劲地交谈，有的则抱着书本，还在那里临阵磨枪。各种形状、各种颜色的考篮和行李丢得满场子都是，耳畔回响着一片接连不断的、嗡嗡的说话声响。

“嗯，什么事？”冒襄把目光收回来，瞧着余怀，又问了一句。

余怀却不立即回答，他拉着冒襄离开人来人往的辕门，才神秘地低声说：“告诉兄，兄可不要心慌哟！——嗯？”

“到底什么事？”

“兄不妨猜猜——有一个人来了。”

“谁？”

余怀挤眉弄眼地：“你不妨猜猜嘛！”

“我没工夫猜！”

“那——”余怀无可奈何了，他瞅着冒襄，犹疑了一下，“好，告诉你吧，董双成——的仙驾到啦！”

冒襄吃了一惊：“什么？小宛她来了？”

“瞧嘛，我不是叫你不要慌……”

“谁叫她来的？她在哪儿？我怎么不知道？”

“你当然不会知道，人家对老兄可是体贴得很，怕扰乱你首场文思，一直留在三山门外的船上，没有进城哩！”

# Faces at the Examination Court

"Hey, Pijiang, finally you're here! I've been looking for you everywhere."

Yu Huai greeted him eagerly as Mao Xiang stepped through the outer gate of the Gongyuan.

"Oh, what's up?" Mao Xiang asked, looking around. He found that a great many candidates hadn't come into the examination court yet. At least two or three thousand candidates were crowded at the fence on the outside or the inside. If the servants were counted, the number was even greater. Some candidates gathered in front of the Gongyuan gate waiting for the roll call, while others stood in random groups talking or doing last-minute cramming. Exam baskets and luggage rolls of all shapes and colors were littered all over the place. From the crowd came an incessant, buzzing sound of men talking.

Mao Xiang took his eyes back, looked at Yu Huai and asked again, "Well, what's up? "

Without immediately responding, Yu Huai pulled Mao Xiang away from the overcrowded outer gate, and mysteriously whispered, "Brother, when I tell you, don't panic, all right?"

"What's the matter then?"

"Brother, you might as well guess. Someone has come."

"Who?"

Yu Huai winked and said, "Just guess!"

"I don't have time to guess."

"Then—" Yu Huai had to give in. He looked at Mao Xiang and hesitated for an instant. Then he said, "Well, let me tell you. Dong Shuangcheng the fairy lady is here."

Mao Xiang was stunned, "What? Xiaowan? Is she here?"

"Look, didn't I tell you not to panic ..."

"Who has got her here? Where is she? Why didn't I know?"

"Of course you don't know. She's very considerate of you, brother. Afraid to distract you from the exam, she didn't enter the city and is now staying on the boat outside the Sanshan Gate."

“那，你怎么知道？”

“自然是有人告知我啰！咦，辟疆，那天在金山下的船上，你不是当着大家的面说得好好的，要到姑苏去接她来南京就试，怎么到时又不去了！嗯，这可不大好哇！哈哈！”余怀嬉皮笑脸地说。

“这你不用管！”冒襄一挥手，烦恼地走开去，忽然又走回来，“你可知道，她来做什么？”

“来做什么？问得出奇！自然是要同老兄配洞房花烛耍子来啦！”余怀摊开双手，依旧笑嘻嘻地说，随即又摇头晃脑地吟诵起来，“哎，‘洞房花烛夜，金榜题名时’！如此快事，真是几生修得！辟疆兄，小弟这厢恭喜了！”说着，他拱手当胸，深深地作下揖去。

冒襄面孔一红：“休要胡说！”

“什么？胡说？”余怀惊讶地说，“这消息可是千真万确。我好心好意来告诉兄，你不谢我倒也罢了，还……”说到这里，像突然想起什么，他回头瞧了瞧辕门旁那杆号旗，立刻叫起来，“不好，点到我们了！”说着，他就慌里慌张地丢下冒襄，一溜烟地跑了。

“这么说，她到底追到南京来了！我本来就担心她会这样，果不其然！现在该怎么办？怎么办？”当只剩下冒襄一个人时，他烦躁不安地想，并且背着手，徘徊起来。

说实在的，他没有依约到苏州去接董小宛，是有他的考虑的。虽然几个月前，在镇江金山脚下，他被董小宛苦苦缠着不放，再加上方以智、余怀等一班社友帮着起哄，在迫不得已的情况下，他勉强同意考虑娶董小宛，但是内心深处，却并不当真就这样定

"How did you know it then?"

"Someone told me, of course. Why, Pijiang, didn't you promise, in front of everybody on the boat at the foot of the Gold Mountain that day, that you would go to Gusu and pick her up on your trip to Nanjing for the exam? Why did you go back on your word? Well, well, that's not very good. Haha!" Yu Huai said with a bad smile.

"You don't have to worry about that." Mao Xiang dismissed Yu Huai with a wave of his hand and walked away, deeply annoyed, but suddenly came back and said, "Do you know what she's doing here?"

"What is she doing here? What a strange question to ask! To play with you in the bridal room, of course," Yu Huai said, spreading his hands, with a smirk on his face. Then he continued, rocking his head from side to side, "Well, a candlelit wedding night and the day the list of successful candidates for the civil service is unveiled are the best moments of a man's life. Your good luck is the result of lifetimes of cultivation. Brother Pijiang, my congratulations to you!" As he spoke, he clasped his hand before his chest and bowed deeply.

Mao Xiang's face turned red. He said, "Don't talk nonsense."

"What? Nonsense?" Yu Huai said in puzzlement. "This news is absolutely true. Instead of thanking me for my good intentions in letting you know, you're ..." Before he finished, he suddenly remembered something. He turned his head to the signal flag next to the outer gate and exclaimed, "Oh, no, it's time for us to report for the roll call." With that, he ran away in a hurry, leaving Mao Xiang behind.

"So, she's eventually come to Nanjing. I was worried she would be like this, and sure enough she is. What should I do now? What should I do?" he thought irritatedly when he was left alone. Putting his hands behind his back, he stopped moving forward and paced around pensively.

To be honest, he didn't go to Suzhou to pick up Dong Xiaowan as promised for a reason. Sure, he had agreed to consider marrying Dong Xiaowan at the foot of the Gold Mountain in Zhenjiang upon the insistence of Dong Xiaowan and under the persuasion of his fellow Fushers including Fang Yizhi and Yu Huai, but deep down he

了。他回到如皋家中之后，冷静一想，就更加觉得别扭。在他看来，董小宛无论如何也比不上陈圆圆。仪容、风度姑且不论，光拿性格脾气来说，董小宛就远远缺乏陈圆圆那种魅力。陈圆圆，即使他们已经有了迎娶之约之后，冒襄仍然常常有一种担心，生怕她会突然改变了主意，弃他而去。虽然，正因为这缘故，他常常故意地冷淡她，但骨子里却在于更紧地维系住她！可是对董小宛，他却全然没有这种感觉。她太驯顺、太死心塌地了！诚然，她很爱慕他，这点是无可怀疑的。可是她太笨拙了，笨拙得令人腻味……如果说，陈圆圆像一匹美丽的、不羁的小马的话，那么董小宛就像一只羔羊。羔羊只会使人可怜，而美丽不羁的马却会挑动人征服她驾驭她的欲望。"我失去了圆圆，也不能娶小宛。我不能让人家笑话我无能！"于是冒襄便决定违背成约，不到苏州去接董小宛。因为他想到乡试期间，四面八方的社友都会聚集到南京来，如果董小宛在场，他们难免又会一窝蜂地起哄，把自己闹得更加无法下台……

"可是真糟糕，她竟然自己跑来了！哎，真是岂有此理！"冒襄又生气，又着急地想。不过，也只一会儿，他就不能再想下去了。因为一群同县的举子发现了他，都纷纷围上来向他招呼、问候，冒襄只好暂时把心事放下，同大家周旋起来。

一直到傍晚，才轮到点扬州府的举子进场。大家穿着又宽又大的白布直裰，在八月的酷暑骄阳下足足候了三个时辰，虽然打着伞，也已经一个个汗流浃背、头昏脑涨、疲惫不堪。谁都懒得再说话，只一个劲儿地叨念着快点进场。

自从冒襄来到之后，考场内已经发生了几起不大不小的事件。一件是贡院二门内搜检时，查出了两名夹带作弊的举子。其中一

hadn't taken it seriously. When he thought about it after returning to his home in Rugao, he felt all the more uncomfortable. In his opinion, Dong Xiaowan was not to be compared with Chen Yuanyuan not only in appearance and demeanor but also with regard to personality and temperament. With Chen Yuanyuan, even an engagement couldn't stop him from worrying that she might change her mind and leave him, and because of that intense love and fear of losing her, he often deliberately kept a distance from her. With Dong Xiaowan, it was completely different. He didn't have such a feeling. She was too submissive and obedient. There was no doubt that she adored him, but she was too clumsy, to the degree of being boring ... If Chen Yuanyuan was like a beautiful and rebellious pony, then Dong Xiaowan was like a little lamb. A lamb invokes pity, but a beautiful and rebellious horse invokes a desire to conquer. "I've lost Yuanyuan, but I shouldn't marry Xiaowan lest people should laugh at me for being incompetent." Mao Xiang therefore had decided to break his promise to go to Suzhou to pick up Dong Xiaowan, knowing many of the Fushers would come to Nanjing for the provincial-level exam and should Dong Xiaowan be present they would make fun of him and there would be no escape from it ...

"But who knows she comes here herself! It's outrageous," Mao Xiang thought angrily and anxiously. After a while, however, he was not able to think about it anymore, because a group of candidates from the same county caught sight of him and gathered to greet him. Mao Xiang had to put aside his thoughts and talk to them.

It was not until evening that the Yangzhou candidates started to enter the examination court. Having waited for six hours under the scorching August sun in a large white long gown, everyone sweated profusely in spite of the umbrella and felt dizzy and fatigued. No one wanted to talk anymore. All they wanted was to enter the examination court as soon as possible.

Inside the examination court, a few incidents of no small account had taken place since the arrival of Mao Xiang. One was the discovery of two fraudsters at the checkpoint at the second gate of the

个事先请人写好了几百篇文章，各种题目都有，然后用蝇头小楷写在极薄的金箔纸上，卷折成很小的纸头，有的塞在笔管里，有的藏在镂空的砚台底下，显然打算到时拿出来照抄；另一个更巧妙，把事先准备好的文章用药汁写在青布衣袄上，外面抹上一层青泥，只要把泥一擦掉，字迹就立即显现出来。这两人的手段都不可谓不高，不知怎地，竟然给发现了，结果被剥掉衣帽，戴枷示众。这一下，可把场外的举子轰动了。那些身上不干净的害怕起来，登时就散掉了一二百人。第二件是天气太热，有五六个举子支持不住，当场中暑昏迷，被考场的军役抬出去救治了。还有一件，是不知哪来的一个狂士，喝得醉醺醺，跑进辕门来捣乱，又嚷又叫，还念着一支曲文：

读书人，最不济，
滥时文，烂如泥，
国家本为求才计，
谁知道变作了欺人技。
三句承题，两句破题，
摆尾摇头便道是圣门高弟，
可知道三通四史，是何等文章？
汉祖唐宗，是哪朝皇帝？
案上放高头讲章，店里卖新科利器。

Gongyuan. One of them had hundreds of essays written in advance, with all kinds of topics, in small script on thin sheets of gold foil rolled into small balls and stuffed into writing-brush pipes or hidden under the hollowed-out inkstone, apparently to be copied in time. The other one was more ingenious. The prepared essays were written on the gray cloth robe in a chemical solution with a layer of gray mud smeared on the outside. When the mud was wiped off, the handwriting immediately appeared. Though the methods were clever, they were discovered nonetheless. Consequently, the two men were stripped of their gowns and caps and displayed in public, with shackles on their wrists and ankles. This sent a shock wave through the candidates outside the examination court. Those who were not clean panicked and in an instant about two hundred candidates vaporized. In a second episode, five or six candidates fainted from the heat and were carried out by the military servicemen for treatment. A third episode involved a madman who, coming from nowhere and horribly drunk, ran in through the outer gate to make trouble, shouting, screaming, and chanting:

"How useless are the scholars!

How worthless are the essays!

What the imperial court uses for the discovery of talent becomes a wholesale scam.

'Three sentences to accept the title, two sentences to break the subject' — Rocking their heads and wagging the tails

They claim to be disciples of the sage

Do they know what kind of books the *santong* and the *sishi*① are?

Do they know to what dynasties belonged

the Gaozu emperor of Han and the Taizong emperor of Tang?

They read explanatory notes by famous scholars and essays by the latest successful candidates bought from the bookstores

① *santong*: three history books—*tong dian*, *tong zhi*, and *wen xian tong kao*; *sishi*: four history books—*shi ji*, *han shu*, *hou han shu*, and *san guo zhi*

读得来肩高背低，口角唏嘘，
甘蔗渣儿，嚼了又嚼，有何滋味？
辜负光阴，白日昏迷，
就教骗得高官，也是百姓朝廷的晦气！

他一边念，一边嘻嘻地笑，羞得那班举子脸上红一阵、白一阵。最后，大家心头火起，一拥而上，把他逮住，交给巡绰官拘押起来……

现在，冒襄终于听见站立在东门的提调官点到了自己的名字。他答应一声，回头从冒成手里接过考篮和铺卷，走进如皋县的行列里，直到点齐后，才在手执高脚点名牌的县差引导下，登上台阶，走进大门。这时，天已昏黑，大门内的院子两边，堆起了两垛芦柴，熊熊的火光一直亮到天上。冒襄放下行李，同其他举子一样，照例解开衣服，脱下鞋袜，用手提着，然后到二门的栅栏领取试卷。

"嗯，刚才搜出了两个身藏夹带的，这一回只怕连累我们都得受罪了。"他一边想，一边走进二门。果然发现里面的气氛不同往常，四个搜检官每人负责一个角落，正虎视眈眈地坐在椅子上。一见冒襄走进，就有两个衙役过来，将他解衣剥裤，翻笼倒箧地大搜特搜，不但文具全都经过敲打查验，夹被夹衣要拆开，就连糕饼饽饽也用刀切开来瞧一瞧。冒襄给折腾得满肚子火，但又不能发作，好不容易检毕放行，走进龙门。他看看试卷上的座位编号，正巧，就编在"地"字第一号。他知道那是龙门东侧第

*Until their backs are sore and their mouths are dry.*
*Chewing the chewed sugar cane, again and again*
*What taste do they enjoy?*
*Wasting their time, sleepy in the day*
*Their rise to high office through this dishonest means is a curse for the imperial court and the people."*

He giggled as he chanted, and the candidates nearby blushed in embarrassment. In the end, they flared up, rushed forward, caught him and handed him over to the inspector for detention ...

Finally, Mao Xiang heard an exam administrator standing at the eastern gate calling his name. He replied, turned around and took his exam basket and luggage roll from Mao Cheng, and then stepped into the line of candidates from Rugao County. When the roll call was over, they ascended the steps and went in through the gate following the county officer holding a freestanding name list. By this time, it was already dark, and two stacks of dry reeds had been piled up on either side of the courtyard inside the gate with the flames lighting up the sky. Mao Xiang put down his luggage and, like the others, unbuttoned his clothes, took off his shoes and socks, and carried them in his hands, as was the requirement, and then went to the fence wall at the second gate to get his test paper.

"Two candidates carrying hidden paper notes were caught just now and I'm afraid we'll all have to go through additional scrutiny," he thought as he walked in through the second gate. Sure enough, the atmosphere inside was different from usual. Four inspectors were installed in the four corners, watching like tigers eyeing their prey. As soon as Mao Xiang walked in, two *yamen* men came over, unbuttoned his clothes, emptied his basket, and did a thorough search. Not only were all the stationery items tapped one by one, every article of clothing with a lining was ripped open as well. Even the cakes were cut open and examined. Mao Xiang was full of rage, but had to keep himself under control. Finally, the checking was over and Mao Xiang walked through the "dragon gate". He looked at the seat number on the test paper, which

一个门，又名“东龙腮”的，也就不去看墙上所悬的“席舍图”，径直出了龙门，向右一拐，进了“地”字号门，在第一间号舍安顿下来。

原来这号舍宽才三尺，深也只有四尺，每个举子住一间。为了便于监视，故意建成有顶无门，也没有窗户，只有一个放油灯的小壁龛，两边墙上各有两行突出的砖托。至于桌子和床，其实只是两块可以合并的木板。要答卷时，把两板分开，在上下两层砖托上各放一块，就成了桌子和椅子。睡觉时，两块并排放在下面那两道砖托上，就成了床。因为地方很狭小，举子只好曲膝而卧，加上没有门，只能临时挂一张油帘，碰上刮风下雨，景况就十分狼狈了。就算不下雨，像现在这样炎天酷暑，也简直同坐在蒸笼里差不多。不过冒襄已经顾不上这些。他知道马上就要鸣炮封门，留给他作准备的时间已经不多。他赶紧到过道里向“号军”——一个负责料理举子起居饮食的老兵讨了一点水，泡起一杯茶，狼吞虎咽地塞了两件点心，就动手磨墨。这时候，号栅已经关上，四下里变得静悄悄的，再也看不见有举子在走动，就连监考人员那威严的咳嗽声和脚步声也暂时听不见了，整个考场呈现出一派严肃的、不安的气氛，就像是一个马上就要展开生死搏杀的战场。不过，冒襄却相当镇定，他依旧动作轻快地磨着墨。已经是第四次参加乡试，对于这种气氛，他可以说是相当熟悉。诚然，前三次都是铩羽而归，但这一次毕竟不同，他经过近一个

happened to be number one in the lane labeled "earth". He knew it was the first gate on the east side of the "dragon gate", known as "the east gill of the dragon", so without checking the seating chart hanging on the wall, he went straight out of the "dragon gate", made a right turn, entered the "earth" lane, and sat down in the first booth.

The roomlets were only three feet wide and four feet deep, one for each candidate. They were roofed structures designed to prevent cheating, with no door or window. There was only a small niche on the back wall for an oil lamp, and two rows of protruding bricks on each side wall. The writing desk and the bed were actually two wooden planks that could be fit together to become one. When the candidate was going to write the test paper, he separated the two planks and placed them respectively on the top and bottom layers of bricks to form a desk and chair. When he was going to sleep, he placed both planks side by side on the two brick supports at the bottom to make a bed. Because the place was cramped, he had to sleep with his knees bent, and since there was no door, he had to temporarily hang an oil curtain where the door was supposed to be. When there was wind and rain, it was a disaster. Even without wind and rain, it was not pleasant either. Sitting in the roomlet in such hot weather was like sitting in a steamer pot. However, Mao Xiang had no time to dwell on this. He had to hurry to make his last-minute preparation as the signal gun would be fired soon and the lane gate would be closed. He got some boiled water from the old soldier providing logistics support, made some tea, gulped down two food items, and started to grind ink. Then, the gate of the lane was closed and the place suddenly went quiet. There was no more movement of the candidates. Nor was there the weighty coughing or sound of footsteps of the examiners. The examination court suddenly became solemn and tense as if a life-or-death battle was going to take place. Mao Xiang was composed and calm, briskly grinding his ink. It was the fourth time for him to take the provincial-level examination and he was only too familiar with it all. True he had failed three times, but this time, it was going to be different, having achieved a breakthrough in the art of eight-legged essay writing after

月的苦心钻研，自觉对于八股文的写作，已经取得了飞跃突破，眼界和手笔，都远非昔日可比。何况史可法又事先替他通了关节。除非老天爷故意捣蛋，否则断无不中之理。事实上，老天爷看来也是肯帮忙的，他不是已经在卦象里显示吉光了么……

“轰！轰！轰！”封门的号炮响了起来。冒襄的思绪跳动了一下，断了。他本能地把墨条放下，向外张望了一下，坐正身子，等候分发试题。可是，那轻快的思绪，仍然在他脑子里跃动。

“……如果这一次中了的话，那么明年就该到北京去参加会试。哼，我倒不怕会试！虽说会试中式要比乡试难得多，但好就好在考官的学识眼光也会高得多，相信他们更能识得我的文章！……若是会试、殿试也都中了，最好能争取进翰林院，像方密之那样，当个编修之类，干好了，就有机会入阁当值，参与机务，将来路子就会顺当得多。要不然，给外放到穷乡僻壤去，当个劳什子县太爷，那就毫无意思了！对，到时我一定要设法入翰林院！……”这样暗自决定了之后，他就开始想象自己一旦跻身于权力中心，将如何施展才干，取得皇上的信赖，然后大力整顿朝政，毫不留情地撤换那些昏庸无能之辈，把与自己志同道合的一批人提拔起来，安插到各个重要部门。然后通过他们，坚决贯彻自己的一套政治主张。这样，不出数年，就一定能把国家的局面彻底改变过来。到那时，流寇荡平，建虏扫灭，大明中兴，自己也将作为一代名臣而流芳青史……冒襄就这样沉浸在雄心勃勃的悬想里，脸上带着微笑。他想得那样兴奋，那样入迷，以至巡绰官把试题发到他手中时，都差点儿没反应过来。

a month of intensive study, with heightened awareness of issues and enhanced writing skills. Besides, there was the help from Shi Kefa from behind the scenes. Unless Providence was not with him, there was no reason why he shouldn't succeed this time. In fact, Providence was ready to help. Didn't He show it in the hexagram? ...

Boom! Boom! Boom! The cannon sounded for the closing of the lane gates. Mao Xiang's train of thought was interrupted. He instinctively put down the inkstick and looked out. As he sat up straight and waited for his test paper, that jumping train of thought resumed.

"... If I succeed this time, I'll be able to go to Beijing for the national examination. Hmph! That won't be a problem either. True, the national examination is much more difficult than the provincial examination, but the examiners are more learned and wiser. They surely will appreciate my writings ... If I pass both the national examination and the palace examination, I should try to enter the Hanlin Academy as an editor, like Fang Mizhi, and if I do well as a Hanlin Academy editor, I shall have an opportunity to serve in the Cabinet to participate in important decisions. In that case, the road ahead will be a bright one. Otherwise, should I be sent to a remote place to serve as a county magistrate, it would be utterly meaningless. Right! I'll try my best to enter the Hanlin Academy ..." Having thus made up his mind, he started to imagine how he would win the confidence of the emperor by making full use of his talents at the center of power, how he would be able to reform the government by ruthlessly removing the incompetent and actively promoting the likes of himself to important positions, who would steadfastly enforce his ideas of government. Thus, the decline of the dynasty would be reversed. By then, the insurgents would be crushed, the invaders would be defeated, and the Great Ming would be rejuvenated, and he would go down in history as a great hero ... Immersed in his ambitious thoughts, he smiled. He was so deeply engrossed in his thoughts that he barely noticed that the test paper had been handed to him by the test administrator.

试题一共二十三道，其中《四书》出三题，《五经》每经出四题。按照规定，除了《四书》那三题必须全做之外，《五经》的二十题，举子只需做自己所报考的那一经的四题便可。每题一文，合成“七艺”之数。要在不到两天的时间内做成七篇文章，而且要做得好，还要工楷誊正，实在是一桩极紧张极辛苦的差事，常常有不少举子无法终篇，或者因紧张过度而当场昏厥。

所以冒襄不敢再胡思乱想，他拿着题纸，首先很快地浏览了一遍。他知道，由于《四书》《五经》这几部古书的篇幅不多，字数有限，一般地抽取其中的句子来做题目，时间一长，就难免重复。所以如今的试官都是想方设法地变花样，或在每章每节内择取数句，或者把一章分成几节，或者从一节中截取一句，或者把几章几节连在一起，这样来出题目，使人无从预测。不过，举子也有相应的对付办法，那就是把习作的数量成倍地加大，把那几部经典割裂又割裂、拼凑又拼凑，预先做它几十题，乃至上百题文章，记牢、背熟。这样，往往总有那么一两题，甚或三四题给碰中。为了应付这次考试，冒襄事先也准备了一批文章。现在，他希望能在这二十三道试题里，发现有他做过的题目……然而，没有。甚至连最易碰巧的《五经》题目，也全是他未曾做过的。看来，他想的题太偏、太巧，而这一次，主考官却仿佛有意同举子们捉迷藏，出的题目偏偏全是比较普通的。

There were a total of twenty-three questions, of which three were about the "Four Books" and four about each of the "Five Classics". As per the instructions, all three questions about the "Four Books" had to be answered, of the twenty questions about the "Five Classics", the candidate only had to answer the four about the classic he had registered for. One essay for each question. All together, seven essays should be written to correspond to seven topics. Writing seven essays in less than two days in good quality and in a clear copy was a stressful task. Many candidates had failed to complete them or fainted on the spot due to excessive stress.

Mao Xiang stopped his wild thoughts and flipped through the test paper. The test questions were often based on sentences from the "Four Books" and the "Five Classics", which consisted of very short books, and there was not much room for the test question writers to maneuver. Over time repetitions had been unavoidable. Therefore, test question writers were doing their best to avoid repetition by using varying methods. They would write a question based on a few sentences from a chapter or a section, or an individual sentence from a chapter or section, or a combination of sentences from different chapters or sections of a chapter. Thus, the test questions became increasingly unpredictable. However, that didn't prevent the candidates from guessing. They multiplied their practice writings by making various combinations of sentences from those classics and writing dozens and hundreds of essays and committing them to memory. Thus, chances were great that in the actual exam they would meet one or two, or even three or four test questions they had prepared. Mao Xiang knew the trick. So, he had also prepared some essays for this exam. Now, he was browsing the test paper to see if there were any questions for which he had prepared in the twenty-three test questions ... but to his disappointment, there was none. Even "Five Classics" items, which were easier to guess, were all new to him. He had been too smart and had gone too far out of the ordinary. This time around, the test maker, as if playing hide-and-seek with the candidates, gave the most ordinary test questions.

终于，冒襄呆住了。固然，他不至于因此就做不出文章来，但事先经过精心准备、反复推敲的那一批得意之作，如今竟连一篇都用不上。也就是说，七篇文章全都得重新构思、写作、修改、誊正。这样一来，能否真正充分发挥出自己的本事，可就有点难说了。“哦，我何以没想到这一层？何以一个劲儿去钻那些怪题、僻题？我本该想到，出了那些年的怪题、僻题之后，也许会倒过来一下，可是我竟失算了！”他懊悔地想，又看了一遍试题，不知是着急还是心慌，他忽然觉得：这些题目无疑都很平常，唯其如此，要翻出新意、显出本领，却又非常之难。这一次，他似乎注定是无法把它写好的了……

“嘿，我还满心想夺它个头名，谁知还没下笔就先栽了个跟头！这一个月来，我没日没夜，把心血全泡在这上面，若还只考得个四五十名以后，那还有什么意思？还有什么意思！”他在心里恼火地叫，一阵烦躁，猛地抬起头。就在这时，他看见一双眼睛。这是一双年老的、混浊的、丑陋的眼睛。它在一动不动地、怀疑地瞅着自己。冒襄不由得一惊！

瞅着冒襄的是个年老的号军。他之所以这样，大约是冒襄的举止神情引起了他的注意。老号军发现冒襄也在看他，就收回了目光，抬起头，向遥远而神秘的子夜星空望了一眼，走开去了。

“啊，他为什么这样？这是什么意思？”冒襄想，不由自主地把视线投向天幕。蓦地，他脑际灵光一闪，仿佛听见一个声音在说：“天意！一切自有天意，你又何须自寻烦恼？”这声音是如此威严，如此仁慈。冒襄的心情忽然变得平静了。在他的眼前，仿佛呈现出一股无比伟大的、支配一切的、无法抗拒的力量，而人世间万事万物的生灭、兴衰、因果都早已由它作出了最合理最严格的安排，一个尘世的人，是无法加以窥度的。那么，又怎知这种安排就一定对自己不利呢……

Mao Xiang was at a loss. Of course he was able to answer the questions, but the essays he had carefully conceived and meticulously polished were no use now. That meant he had to conceive and write all seven essays from scratch, revise them and copy them in print. Then, whether he would do a good job or not hung in the balance. "Whoops! Why didn't I think of this before? Why did I concentrate on the unlikely, off-the-track questions? I should have thought of the possibility of a sudden return to the familiar after years of deviation from the beaten path. Poor me! What a miscalculation!" he thought remorsefully. Then he read the test paper again and thought nervously: These questions look easy but to answer them well with good arguments and argumentation is difficult. I'm afraid I won't be able to answer them well ...

"Well, well, I'm stumbling in the very beginning while I'm thinking of coming out number one. I've been exerting myself day and night for a whole month. Should I come out number fifty or even worse, what a joke that would be!" His heart crying in anguish, he looked up. Just then, he saw a pair of eyes staring at him suspiciously. It was a pair of old, murky, and ugly eyes. He was shocked.

It was the warden staring at Mao Xiang, whose movement and expression had probably caught his attention. When he saw that Mao Xiang was also looking at him, the old soldier withdrew his gaze, raised his head, looked away at the distant and mysterious starry midnight sky and left.

"Why, why is he like that? What does that mean?" Mao Xiang thought, inadvertently casting his gaze at the dark sky. Suddenly, a light flashed across his mind as if a voice were saying, "The will of heaven! Everything is decided by the will of heaven. Why do you worry before worry finds you?" The voice was so reassuring and kind that he suddenly calmed down, as if an awesome, all-pervasive, irresistible power had presented itself before him that had reasonably and perfectly designed all life and death, all rise and fall, and all causes and effects, unfathomable to an ordinary human being. How could he know that the design was certainly to his disadvantage?...

他不再烦躁，轻轻拈起笔，饱蘸了墨，伏下身去，开始在试卷上一个字一个字地书写起来……

## 卖婆点拨

董小宛确实已经到了南京。她知道眼下正是考试最紧张的几天，怕扰乱了冒襄的心思，所以没有进城，还暂时留在三山门外的船上。

由于一直盼不到冒襄的音讯，在惶急无计的情况下，董小宛终于下决心到南京来寻他。而促成这个行动的，则是现在正同她在一起的这位姓陆的卖婆。

陆卖婆是个已届中年的小户妇女。鹅蛋脸，小尖鼻，细眉细眼，颇有几分姿色；加上生就一张巧嘴巴，能言会道，便不甘寂寞，单身匹马出来闯江湖。她专门出入大户人家，做那一类兑换金珠首饰、贩卖包帕花绒、篦头插带、牵线说媒的帮闲活计，混得久了，也就见多识广，胆大心雄。她住在姑苏半塘，离董小宛的家不过隔着十来间房子，平日常有来往。那天，陆卖婆接了几件首饰，想找主儿兑换，顺脚过来问一声，看见董小宛在独自流泪，问起情由，得知是这么回事，便竭力撺掇她到南京来找冒襄，还自告奋勇陪她一道来，只要董小宛肯担当她的一应花销脚仪就行。董小宛眼见等候无望，也曾动过这念头，只苦于自己孤身一人，她爹董子将又要守着家，分身不开，忽然听说陆卖婆答应相陪，自然十分感激。当下立刻打点行李，择日出门。一路上晓行

Then, his anxiety was gone, and he dipped his brush pen in the ink, bent over the desk, and started to transcribe his ideas word by word ...

## A Woman Peddler's Advice to Xiaowan

Dong Xiaowan had indeed come to Nanjing. Knowing these were the most stressful days before the exam, she didn't enter the city lest Mao Xiang be disturbed. She stayed on the boat outside Sanshan Gate for the time being.

Before she came to Nanjing, she had been waiting for Mao Xiang, but he never turned up. In desperation, she finally made up her mind to go to Nanjing. She had been coaxed into taking this action by Miss Lu, a lady trader, who was accompanying her now.

Miss Lu was an eloquent middle-aged woman from an ordinary family. With an oval face, a small pointed nose, thin eyebrows and slender eyes, she was a beauty of a sort. Not the type to be confined at home, she came out to see the world all by herself and frequented big families, bartering, buying and selling sundry goods, jewelry and accessories or occasionally doing matchmaking. Knowing the ways of the world, she was able to come up with bold ideas. Her home was in Bantang, Gusu City, about ten houses away from Dong Xiaowan's place. The two had seen each other very often. That day, having been commissioned to barter away some jewelry, she came to ask if Dong Xiaowen happened to be interested. Seeing Xiaowan was weeping, she asked what had happened. Upon learning the story, she encouraged Xiaowan to go to Nanjing to see Mao Xiang and offered to travel with Xiaowan, who should pay her travel costs. Earlier on, that idea had also crossed Xiaowan's mind when she saw her waiting had been in vain, but she had eventually given it up, as she was afraid of traveling alone and besides, her father Dong Zijiang had to take care of the house and couldn't go with her. The sudden offer from Miss Lu helped her make up her mind. She was very grateful to Miss Lu and immediate set about preparing her luggage. On the carefully selected date, they left Gusu, traveled by day and slept at night, and finally

夜宿，终于在八月初六这天，来到三山门外。

现在，她们在船上已经住了三天。陆卖婆从不曾来过南京，她这次自告奋勇陪董小宛，一半是出于情分，一半也是想乘机见见大世面。所以船到第二天，她便扯着董小宛上岸游逛。董小宛本没有这份心情，但拗陆卖婆不过，只好倒过来陪她。前天和昨天，她们已经游了莫愁湖和凤凰台，可是陆卖婆毫不满足，游兴越来越高。她不知听谁说，石城门内的关帝庙求签最灵验，今天又嚷着要去。董小宛实在有点厌烦了，便推辞不肯。不过，陆卖婆却不是那么轻易摆脱得了的。她心眼儿又多，嘴巴子又会说，何况有许多事情，董小宛还得靠着她。所以最后，董小宛依旧只好乖乖儿吩咐船家解缆向北，撑到石城门去。

“啧啧，瞧，这才是我的好妹子嘛！”陆卖婆顿时高兴得眉开眼笑，她把头探出舱外，朝船家一扬手，“喂，老大，怎么还呆着？快开船！你奶奶我今儿要上石城门去游耍，你若荡得快时，那两盅儿黄汤，少不了你！”说完，一扭身，又坐到董小宛身旁，拉着她的手：“好妹妹，你只管放心好了，有老姐姐在，你那宝贝冒公子他飞不上天去！”

“可是、可是他宁可自个儿来，也不去接我！”董小宛可怜巴巴地说。一提起冒襄，她的眼圈就红了，差点没掉下泪来。

“哎，我不是说了吗，他不来接你，兴许是给事情绊住了，分身不开，兴许是临时一忙，就忙忘了，兴许……”

“不！”董小宛悲戚地摇摇头，“他是成心这样子，我都想过了！”

“啊，怎么？”

“他若不是成心，就该给我捎个信。这两三个月，我不歇央人

arrived at the Sanshan Gate on the sixth of August.

By this time, they had stayed in the boat for three days. Miss Lu had never seen Nanjing before. She had offered to accompany Dong Xiaowan for the current trip partly to help a friend and partly to see a big city. The day after their arrival, she asked Xiaowan to go ashore with her to see places. Xiaowan was in no mood for fun, but upon her insistence became her escort instead. They had already toured the Lake of No Sorrow and the Phoenix Terrace in the past two days, but Miss Lu was still not satisfied. Her spirits went higher and higher. She had learned from somewhere that the General Guan's Temple inside the Stone City Gate answered prayers and insisted on going there today. Xiaowan had enough and decided not to go. However, Miss Lu was not a woman to give up easily. She was canny and had a good tongue. Besides, Xiaowan counted on her for many things. So finally, Xiaowan asked the boatman to row the boat north all the way to the Stone City Gate.

"Haha, look, this is my good sister!" Miss Lu beamed with joy, sticking her head out of the cabin and gesturing to the boatman. "Hey, boss, why don't you move? Row your boat! Your lady is going to see the Stone City Gate. If you row fast enough, I'll award you with two cups of yellow wine." Then, she turned and sat down beside Dong Xiaowan and held her hand. "My good sister, don't you worry! Since your elder sister is here with you, your sweetheart won't run away from you."

"But, but he's come alone without picking me up on the way as promised," Dong Xiaowan said sadly. Speaking of Mao Xiang, her eyes turned red, and tears almost fell.

"Well, didn't I say maybe he was too busy to pick you up? Maybe, he's been stuck on something and couldn't withdraw himself from it. Maybe he was too busy to remember it. Maybe ..."

"No!" Dong Xiaowan shook her head sadly. "He did it on purpose. I've thought about every possibility."

"Oh, why do you think so?"

"If he hadn't done it on purpose, he should have sent me a letter.

带信给他，叮嘱提醒这事。起初他还答应得好好的，可后来……”

“后来他就不答理了？”

董小宛点点头，随即又摇摇头：“也不是全不理，就是……”

“答应得不那么爽利了，对不？”

“嗯……”

陆卖婆斜睨着董小宛，转了半天眼珠子，末了，“扑哧”一笑，安慰说：“妹妹，瞧你急的！只要他不曾把口儿封死，事情就完不了！哪怕他封了口，我们也还有法子拆开它！你愁什么！”说着，她探身从矮几上抓了两把瓜子，塞了一把给董小宛，一边嗑着，一边说：“好吧，如今你再把这事从头到尾给姐姐说上一遍！”

“姐姐不是都知道了么？”

“不成！前时你回我话的样儿，像煞那阔小姐偷汉，说一半，留一半，吞吞吐吐。今儿我要听个有根有蒂、有枝有叶，才好给你出主意！”陆卖婆随口吐掉一瓣瓜子壳，立即又拣了一颗瓜子搁在嘴里嗑着。

董小宛呆呆地瞅了陆卖婆一会儿，终于叹了一口气，低下头去，幽幽地说起来。她从三年前如何第一次认识冒襄起，说到今春的冒襄再度来访，她如何挽留他，后来又怎样随他到了镇江。冒襄开始怎样拒绝她，后来由于朋友们的督促他又怎样回心转意，这一次他又怎样突然反悔，背约不来……一五一十向陆卖婆和盘托出。她还特别谈到了冒襄同陈圆圆的关系，最后哽咽说：“我知他心里想着陈姐姐。我自问万万不敢同陈家姐姐比，若是陈家姐姐还在，我也不敢存这份心思。只是现在……”说到这里，她再也忍不住了，用双手掩着脸，背过身去，失望地、凄苦地哭泣

In the past two or three months, I kept sending him letters to remind him. In the beginning, he replied that he would keep his promise, but later ..."

"Later, he no longer replied to you?"

Dong Xiaowan nodded, but soon shook her head. "It's not that he didn't reply to me. It's just that ..."

"He became evasive?"

"Yes ..."

Miss Lu squinted at Dong Xiaowan for a long time, rolling her eyes, and finally laughed and comforted her, saying, "Sis, look how worried you are! As long as he doesn't shut the door, the matter won't end. Even if he shut the door, we would have a way to open it. Don't you worry." Then, Miss Lu leaned over and grabbed two handfuls of melon seeds from the short table, put one handful into Dong Xiaowan's hand, and said as she cracked a melon seed between her teeth. "Well, now tell me the whole story from beginning to end."

"Haven't you already known everything?"

"Not everything. The way you spoke was like that of a young lady from a wealthy family caught sleeping with a lover. Half of the story was told and half was hidden. I must hear all the details before I can give you any advice." She spat out the seed coat and put another seed into her mouth.

Dong Xiaowan stared blankly at Miss Lu for a while, lowered her head with a sigh and told the story without reservation in a pathetic tone: how she first met Mao Xiang three years ago, how Mao Xiang came to visit her again this spring and how she tried to make him stay, how she later followed him to Zhenjiang, Mao Xiang initially rejected her but later, coaxed by his friends, changed his mind, and how he had suddenly gone against his word by not coming to pick her up ... She particularly emphasized the romantic relationship between Mao Xiang and Chen Yuanyuan. Finally, she sobbed, "I know he doesn't forget Miss Chen and I never dare to compare myself to her. If she were still available to him, I wouldn't have dared to harbor such a thought, but now ..." Unable to continue, she covered her face with her hands,

起来。

陆卖婆却没有劝止她，仍旧管自嗑着瓜子。待到把最后一颗嗑完了，她就站起身，用蒲扇兜着瓜子壳从船篷下往外一倒，又在船帮上扑打了两下，这才放下扇子，转过脸来，拍了拍董小宛的胳膊，说：

“好了好了，莫哭了，哭肿了眼睛，待会儿上岸怎么见人？如今合计合计，怎样摆布你那心上的人儿是正经！——妹妹，不是姐姐要说你，这事弄成今天这局面，妹妹你也有不是哩！”

董小宛已经渐渐停止了哭泣，听了这句责备，她不由得抬起头，迷惑地瞅着陆卖婆。

“你那位什么陈家姐姐，我没见过。”陆卖婆继续说，“她到底怎么个天上有、地下无，妹妹到底比得上她比不上，我也不晓得。不过，这些年姐姐我在江湖上走动，绝色的美人儿也见过几个，未必妹妹就不如她们。若论文才品位，妹妹反觉高出一头。只一样，妹妹却差得太远。你降不住冒公子的心，原因只怕也就在这上头了！”

“哦？”

“妹妹，我问你，那些公子哥儿，有财有势，吃穿不愁，家里又都放着三妻四妾的，怎么还要出来找你们姐儿白相胡缠，你想过么？”

“这……”董小宛的脸红了一下，她想解释说，冒襄家里只有妻子，尚未讨妾，但是动了动嘴，却没有说出来。

陆卖婆也不理会她，只管自己说下去：“哼，无非是想换个口味儿罢咧！这也如同吃腻了山珍海味的人，便想尝尝山桃野杏，图个泼辣新鲜。对付这等主儿，你不放出那轻狂风骚的骚劲儿，把他撩拨得爱又不是，恨又不能，丢不开，放不下的，还能指望

turned around and cried out desperately and miserably.

Without trying to stop her from crying, Miss Lu continued to crack melon seeds. When the last one was cracked, she stood up, put the seed coats on the rattan fan and flipped them into the river from under the boat roof, banged the fan on the edge of the boat, put it down, turned around, and patted Dong Xiaowan on the arm, saying:

"It should be fine. Don't cry! If your eyes become red, how do you see people when we get onshore? The important thing is to think a way to handle your beau. Sis, allow me to speak frankly, things have come to such a pass partly because of your own fault."

Dong Xiaowan gradually stopped crying, and upon hearing this rebuke, she lifted her head and look puzzledly at the peddler woman.

"I've never seen Miss Chen," said Miss Lu. "And I don't know if she is really such a rare beauty that you can't compare to. I've seen quite a few other beautiful things over the years in my travels and I don't think you are any less beautiful. In terms of talent, they can't compare to you. There's one thing that is missing in you: the ability to enter Mr. Mao's heart. That's probably the reason."

"Oh?"

"Sis, let me ask you, why do those young men from big families, who have money and power, don't worry about food and clothes, and have three wives and four concubines at home, come out to play with you? Have you ever thought about that?"

"That—" Dong Xiaowan blushed. She wanted to say that Mao Xiang only had a wife and no concubine yet, but swallowed the words that came to her lips.

Miss Lu ignored her and said to herself, "Hmph, they just want a different flavor. It's like someone who's tired of eating mountain goodies and precious seafood trying a wild peach or apricot. They're looking for something new, something that excites them. For some men, you'd better show them the slut in you so that they're drawn to you, unable to go away, not knowing whether they should love you or hate you. Only that way you can make them marry you. Sis, your problem is that you are too meek, too submissive, and too serious

他死心塌地娶你？妹妹，你输就输在太文静服帖，一本正经呢！”

听了陆卖婆这番开导，董小宛才有点如梦初醒。本来作为自幼在妓院里长大，而且开门接客也有好几年的小娘，对于这个道理她也未尝不知。只是，秦淮河上的名妓，向来是讲究各人有各人的风度派头。像顾眉的雍容华贵、李十娘的柔弱妩媚、寇白门的风流放诞、李香君的机灵狡黠等等，而文静端庄、清高自命，则正是自己之所以显得与众不同的一种特色，曾经使许多风流狎客大为倾倒。她虽然不想故意做作，但总以为像冒襄这样见多识广的公子哥儿，尤其会喜欢这一套，却没想到……她不由得回想起与冒襄相处的那些情景，越想越觉得陆卖婆的话有理。她着急起来：“啊，那、那该怎么办？”

“怎么办？”陆卖婆撇撇嘴，“拿出你的手段来啊，莫非还要姐姐教你？”看见董小宛面现难色，她就奇怪地皱起淡淡的眉毛，“怎么，连这都不会？你那死鬼老娘，当年可是远近闻名的骚姐儿哩！难道就不曾点拨你几下子？”

“哦，不——”董小宛慌乱地说，连脖子都羞红了。她怕陆卖婆再说下去，只好使劲点点头。

“嗯，这就对了！”陆卖婆神气地挥了挥手，“这是第一要紧的，若再见到冒公子时，你可得记住了！嗯，还有，你这冒公子必定是个名士头儿什么的啰？”

“姐姐怎么知道？”

“哼，什么瞒得过我！若他不是名士头儿，你这小妮子会这等恋着他？我瞧那冒公子虽则心气高傲，脸皮子却薄——你不见他在金山时明明回绝了你，后来叫他那帮子朋友一起哄，就顿时软了。嘿，如今这世道也越变越奇了！我在姑苏常听人说：要当大名士，光有文章还不够，连逛窑子也得格外知情识趣，才会受人抬举奉承！好嘛，他越是怕人起哄，你就越要把这事张扬开去！赶明儿你就回你的曲中去，寻着你那帮子什么手帕姐妹、干

about them."

Miss Lu's words jolted Dong Xiaowan awake. Having grown up in a brothel from a young age and having been receiving clients for quite a few years, she was aware of it. It's just that the famous courtesans on the Qinhuai River all made a point of having a unique style. For example, Gu Mei was graceful, Li Shiniang was wily, Kou Baimen was wild, and Li Xiangjun was cunning. Being quiet and aloof was Xiaowan's unique style that had captivated many romantic men. Although she didn't want to affect that style, she thought it might work for such a worldwise rich young man like Mao Xiang. She was wrong ... As she recalled the moments she had had with Mao Xiang, she increasingly felt Miss Lu was right. She started to worry. "Then, then, what should I do?"

"What should you do?" Miss Lu said with a grin. "Use your wiles. Do you need me to teach you?" Seeing Dong Xiaowan's awkward expression, she knit her brows eerily and said, "Why, you don't have them? Your deceased mother used to be a famous cunning slut. Didn't she teach you anything?"

"No, she didn't—" Dong Xiaowan said embarrassedly, blushing to the neck, but afraid Miss Lu would continue, she nodded forcefully.

"No wonder," Miss Lu said proudly with a wave of her hand. "It's the most important thing. Next time you see Mr. Mao, remember my words. Well, by the way, your Mr. Mao must be a leading celebrity, isn't he?"

"How do you know, Sis?"

"Hmph, nothing can escape me. If he were not a leading celebrity, would you be so madly in love with him? I can see Mr. Mao is thin-faced though he's a proud man. He rejected you at first at the Gold Mountain but immediately compromised when coaxed by his friends. The world is getting more and more strange, isn't it? I often heard in Suzhou that a respectable celebrity not only has to write well but also needs to behave well, even in brothels. The more afraid he's of being laughed at, the more necessary it is for you to spread the word. Tomorrow, go back to the courtesan house to which you belonged

爹婶娘，逢人便说这事，闹它个满城风雨、人人皆知。只要四面八方这一哄起来，就不怕那冒公子不乖乖儿就范啦！”陆卖婆一口气地说完了，得意地瞅着董小宛，“妹妹，你瞧，姐姐这条计策如何？”

董小宛耷拉着脑袋，没有立即回答。她在心里掂量来掂量去，觉得这确也是一个办法。但她又担心，万一被冒襄发现了，会弄巧反拙。不过，如果不这么办，事情只怕就更加没有希望……她犹豫了又犹豫，最后轻声说：

“但凭姐姐做主。只是姐姐可千万别说是我……”

陆卖婆眼珠子一转，似乎明白了，她笑起来：“妹妹只管放心，一切都算在姐姐身上，妹妹只当不知道就是！”

## 武庙求签

“妹妹，我们姐俩好不容易来上一趟，待会儿，你可得在帝君跟前诚心诚意地求根签哩！我也要求一根。”陆卖婆掏出一把铜钱，把围拢上来的几个乞丐打发走，一边回头对董小宛说。

这时，她们已经来到关帝庙，正站在大殿的石阶前。这关帝庙就坐落在石城门内。石城门又叫汉西门，是南京西南面的一个主要城门，出门不远就是一个大船码头，来来往往的轿马行人很是不少，所以这关帝庙的香火也颇为兴盛。如今庙前的空地上，除了前来拜神的人们外，还摆起一个一个的茶档，以及出售香烛元宝的摊子，那些走索卖解的、占卜算命的、卖小吃的、拉皮条的，也混迹其中，招徕生意，显出一片熙熙攘攘的景象。

自从听了陆卖婆一番开导，董小宛如今觉得心里踏实了一点，情绪也开朗起来。她见陆卖婆兴头十足的样子，就说：“姐姐觉着这地方好么？可惜我们来迟了几天，若是赶上七月二十九的地藏胜会，那才热闹呢！”

and find your handkerchief sisters and the older men and women you know, tell them your story and let everyone in the city know it. When everyone talks about it, Mr. Mao will have no choice but to honor his words." Miss Lu said it in one breath and looked at Dong Xiaowan self-indulgently, "Sis, what do you think of my plan?"

Dong Xiaowan didn't immediately respond, her head hanging low. She weighed it in her mind and felt it was worth trying, but she was worried that if it was discovered by Mao Xiang she would make a fool of herself. If she didn't do that, she wouldn't have any chance at all ... She hesitated for a long time and finally said in a low voice:

"I'll listen to you, Sis, but don't say it's my ..."

Miss Lu rolled her eyes, laughed, and said knowingly, "Sis, just don't worry! It will be my doing, and you just pretend not to know it."

## Xiaowan Drew a Fortune Stick in General Guan's Temple

"Sis, now we're here, I suggest you draw a fortune stick in front of Lord General Guan. I'll also draw one," said Miss Lu as she took out a handful of copper coins and handed them to the beggars around to send them away.

They were standing in front of the steps leading to the main hall of the temple. General Guan's Temple was situated inside the Stone City Gate, also known as the Hanxi Gate. It was a major city gate on the southwest of Nanjing, close to a ferry port. Since the part of the city was bustling with vehicles and passengers, the temple had flourished. At this moment, the little square in front of the temple was crowded with pilgrims, tea sheds, and stalls selling incense, candles, and sacrificial gold ingots while acrobats, fortune-tellers, snack sellers, and pimps were hawking their wares.

Miss Lu's advice made Xiaowan feel better. Seeing Miss Lu was so excited, she said, "Do you like the place? Unfortunately, we're here a few days too late. If we had been here on the twenty ninth of July, you would have had seen more people."

“是么？好妹妹，你倒说给我听听哟！”

“嗯，若到这一天，南京人各家各户，都要在门前搭起两张桌子，点上两支通宵风烛，供上一座香斗，从大中桥到清凉山这七八里路上，就像游着一条银龙，一夜的亮，香烟不歇，大风也吹不熄。到其时，满城的人都出来烧香赶会，直闹到天亮哩！”

“哟！那一定交关好白相啰！”

“不过说来呢，也好笑。原来这地藏菩萨一年到头把眼闭着，只有这一夜才睁开眼。所以不知谁就想出这主意，让满城都摆开香花灯烛让他瞧见，哄得那菩萨只当一年到头都是如此，便欢喜这些人好善，乐意保佑人了。姐姐你瞧，这不可是使奸诓骗么？”

陆卖婆笑得眼睛只剩一道缝：“我说么，如今人人都话我姑苏人么心术弗正、专会使奸，原来南京人胆子更大，连菩萨都敢骗！”

两人一边说着笑话儿，一边走到场子边上的小摊前，买了两扎线香，转身正要登上大殿，忽然发现不知什么时候，身后已经围了一群人，都是些油头粉面的年轻小伙子，也有一两个年纪较大的，一个个都打扮得花里胡哨。有的摇着折扇，有的托着鸟笼，正在那里指指点点、交头接耳，不时发出一阵轻薄的哄笑。

董小宛瞧出这是冲自己来的。凭着这些年的风尘阅历，她知道这伙人都是些浪荡无赖子弟，平日闲得发慌，经常成群结队到处转悠。碰上有些姿色的年轻妇女，便一窝蜂地追着不放，评头品足、疯言疯语，甚至调戏侮辱。她怕被他们一旦缠住，难以脱身，连忙扯了扯陆卖婆的衣袖。陆卖婆也是乖觉人，立即会意，

"Is that so? Sis, tell me about it."

"On that day of the year, every household in Nanjing puts up two tables in front of their door, lights two all-night candles and places an incense burner on a table to form a shining eight-mile silver dragon from the Dazhong Bridge to the Qingliang Mountain. The light and smoke lasted all night despite the winds. Everyone in the city comes out to pay pilgrimage to the temple and hangs out at the night market all night long."

"It must be fun, then."

"The interesting thing is, the Earth Womb Bodhisattva① has his eyes closed all year round except this night. Therefore, someone has come up with a brilliant idea: to fill the whole city with lights, flowers, incense, and candles so that he'll think the city is like that all year round and the people are really nice and will be happy to bless them. Sis, don't you think it's cheating the gods?"

Miss Lu laughed, eyes crinkling at the edges. "Oh my! Everyone says people from my hometown Gusu are wilful, but it turns out Nanjing people are more audacious. They dare fool the bodhisattvas!"

As they joked, they came to a stall at the edge of the square, where they bought two bundles of thin incense sticks. When they turned to ascend the main hall, they suddenly found a crowd had built up behind them. It was mostly oily young men wearing fancy dress, with one or two older ones in their midst. Some of them waving folding fans, some holding bird cages in their hands, they were gesturing and whispering, letting out bursts of wanton laughter from time to time.

Dong Xiaowan knew they were after her. Based on her years of experience, she knew that they were young ruffians who hanged around in groups to kill time. When they saw a pretty young woman, they chased after her in a swarm, giving rude remarks, teasing her, or even assaulting her. Afraid that she would be harassed, she tugged at

---

① "Earth Store (Kṣitigarbha)" from Sanskrit is also translated as "Earth Treasury" or "Earth Matrix".

便同董小宛一起转身，匆匆向大殿走去。刚行出几步，忽然有人迎面拦住去路，怪声怪气地叫：

“啊哟，好妹妹，哥哥到处寻你不着，原来妹妹到这儿耍子来了，怎么也不告诉哥哥一声？”

董小宛一看，原来那伙人当中的几个，已经站在阶前等着，说话的那人长得小眼睛、短眉毛，当中嵌着一个难看的蒜头鼻子，瞧模样不过十六七岁的年纪，却一脸的淫邪轻薄劲儿。董小宛一声不响，低着头往斜里走，想绕过他们。

可是那少年却不罢休，又一次跟过来，嬉皮笑脸地张开双手拦住说：“哟，好妹妹，怎么，不理哥哥了？莫非生哥哥的气了？嘻嘻，别走嘛，哥哥给你赔个礼好不？”说着，当真作下揖去。但是，又不马上直起身来，却像发现了什么似的，斜瞅着董小宛的裙裾，笑嘻嘻地说：“好妹妹，你这，嗯，你这脚儿真小，真好看！让哥哥仔细瞧瞧，好么？”

董小宛心中一跳，脸顿时红了。虽然她明知自己的脚藏在裙子里，对方不可能瞧见，但是仍然不由自主地往里挪了挪。周围的那些浪荡子弟早已大声喝彩起来：

“拿出来瞧瞧嘛，怕什么！”

“不过是瞧瞧，又不会把你瞧大了！”

“瞧这小妞的模样，她的脚，嘻嘻……”

“也难说，须得瞧过才知道！”

“对，瞧瞧！再不让瞧，我们可要动手啦！”

“……”

陆卖婆虽然见多识广，可是看见这种阵仗，心里也有点发毛。她一面用身子遮护着董小宛，一面用最粗鄙难听的话叫骂着。可是那伙浪荡子弟见她是个外地女人，加上那一口苏白，即便骂起

Miss Lu's sleeve. A woman of quick intelligence, Miss Lu immediately understood and turned to leave with Xiaowan. They quickly walked toward the main hall of the temple but were stopped by someone from in front, who said in a fishy voice:

"Pretty girl, I've been looking for you everywhere, and you are here. Why didn't you let me know?"

Following that voice, Xiaowan saw some of the ruffians were standing ahead blocking their ascension to the steps. The one speaking was a small-eyed, short-browed, garlic-clove-nosed youngster who was merely a sixteener or seveteener but had wantonness written on his face. Xiaowan silently stepped aside to dodge them as she moved forward, her head lowered.

But the boy didn't give up. He came over, opened his hands to stop her and said with a grin, "Oho, good sister, why are you ignoring your brother? Are you angry with me? Hey, hey, don't go! Let me apologize to you," he said with a deep bow. However, he didn't straighten up immediately. As if having discovered something, he looked at Dong Xiaowan's skirt and said with a disgusting smile, "Good sister, your, um, your feet are so small and beautiful. Let your brother take a closer look."

Dong Xiaowan's heart jumped, and her face suddenly turned red. Although she knew her feet were hidden in the train of the skirt and it was impossible for him to see them, she involuntarily retracted them. The other ruffians around cheered loudly:

"Take them out and let us have a look! What are you afraid of?"

"Let us have a look, and they won't grow bigger from our looking."

"Look at the chick, her feet, hee hee ..."

"It's hard to say. You have to see them to know."

"Right. Let us have a look! If you don't let us see them, we'll have to help ourselves."

"..."

Miss Lu, despite her worldly experience, felt a little nervous when she saw a thing like this. While covering Dong Xiaowan with her own body, she swore at the ruffians in the vulgarest language, but

人来也像唱歌儿似的，哪里会怕？还有些人见她徐娘半老，泼得有趣，趁她指手画脚，没遮没拦，倒先在她身上捡起便宜来……

在这当儿，董小宛反而显得比较镇定。作为一个青楼女子，她对于自己将会落到一个什么样的处境，倒不太担心。现在她一心考虑的是如何尽快摆脱这种下流的纠缠，以免传到冒襄的耳朵里，引起不必要的误会。因为她自从在金山下与冒襄有了成约之后，一直闭门谢客，并向冒襄一再表示洁身以待的决心。如果今天这事闹得不清不楚，被人加油添酱地传扬开去，只怕有点不妙。事实上，眼下冒襄对她已经三心二意，而且他俩这件事，背地里心怀嫉妒、伺机中伤的人只怕也不少……这样一想，董小宛就紧张起来，虽然眼前这伙人那副流氓无赖的样子使她感到害怕，可是也只好强自镇定，凑在陆卖婆的耳边说：

“姐姐，你叫他们别吵，我有话说！”

陆卖婆正招架不住，一听这话，连忙对那伙人大声说：

“你们弗要叫，我妹妹有话说哩！”

连叫了几声，那伙人才听清楚了。他们没想到董小宛如此大胆，还敢答话，倒有点意外，不由得静了下来。

董小宛侧着身子，先向众人深深道了个万福，然后说：“众位哥哥……”

话刚出口，立即有人怪声喝起彩来：

“叫得结实！”

“这才对嘛，多热乎！”

“哎，好妹妹……”

可是更多的人却目不转睛地瞅着，等着她说下去。“嘘——

since she was not a Nanjing native and her Suzhou accent sounded more like singing than swearing, the young ruffians were not afraid at all. Seeing that she was a milf and an interesting shrew, they began to take advantage of her instead while she was busy gesticulating with her body unguarded ...

At this point, Dong Xiaowan seemed relatively calm. As a woman from a brothel, she was not worried about what might happen. Now she was just thinking about how to get rid of this nasty entanglement as soon as possible so that it would not get to Mao Xiang's ears and cause misunderstanding. Since her engagement with Mao Xiang at the foot of the Gold Mountain, she had shut her door on all clients and repeatedly told Mao Xiang that she would wait for him with a clean body. Should she be involved with these ruffians today and the story be embellished, there might be consequences. In fact, Mao Xiang was only half-hearted towards her, and there were many men who were jealous and were ready to slander her with the least evidence ... Thus thinking, Dong Xiaowan became nervous. Though at heart she was very much scared by the thugs in front of her, she remained calm and composed.

She whispered in the ear of Miss Lu, "Sis, ask them to stop the noise. I'd like to have a word with them."

Hearing that, Miss Lu, who could hold out no longer, said to the ruffians, "Stop shouting! My sister has something to say to you."

She had to repeat it several times before the ruffians heard it. Surprised that Dong Xiaowan was so bold as to confront them head on, they quieted down.

Dong Xiaowan curtsied to them with one knee bent and then said, "Brothers ..."

As soon as the word "brothers" came out, someone suddenly cheered in a sinister tone:

"Brothers, yeah, bravo!"

"That's right! We're your brothers."

"Hey, good sister ..."

But most of them were merely watching, eyes glued to her, and

听她说什么。”有人说道。

“今天承蒙众位哥哥抬举，到这儿捧奴家的场，奴家这厢谢过了！”董小宛说着，又行了一个礼。

这一次，却没有人再作声，他们显然感到情形有点不对劲，但是却不知道是怎么回事，这楚楚动人的小妞儿怎会这样说话?

“众位哥哥只怕还不认得奴家，”董小宛停了一下，又说，“奴家姓董，贱名白，草字小宛。早先也曾在秦淮河旧院里住过几年，后来去了姑苏。这一次是奉如皋冒辟疆相公邀约，到南京来访他的。如皋冒相公，众位哥哥想必也是认得的，他是‘复社四公子’之一，同南京六部的大人们都是极相熟的……”

董小宛估计，那帮浪荡子弟还不知道她是什么人，只从衣着打扮不像缙绅之家的女眷这一点，把她误认作一般的小家碧玉，所以敢于大胆围着调戏。如今她说出自己的身份是个妓女，而且是复社大名士冒襄请来的，或许他们就会觉得相错了对象，扫兴而去。果然，听董小宛这样自我介绍之后，有不少人就露出了愕然和没趣的神色。只有最先向她调戏的那个蒜头鼻子的少年，却似乎仍不甘心，他阴阳怪气地说：

“噢，原来是大名鼎鼎的董小娘子，那就更好啰。难得今日有缘一见，就请到外间去陪我们喝酒吧！”

“多谢哥哥盛情！”董小宛连忙行礼说，“只是奴家难以从命。”

“怎么?”蒜头鼻少年顿时瞪起了眼睛，“莫非你以为小爷出不起价钱?告诉你，小爷有的是银子！你要多少，说吧！”

“哦，不是银子，是奴家今儿委实不得空。”

“什么得空不得空！不就是拜神烧香的事嘛！告诉你，今儿

waited for her to continue. "Hush! Listen to what she has to say," someone said.

"Today, thanks for your kindness. I do appreciate your coming to see me. Thank you very much, brothers," said Dong Xiaowan, who bobbed another curtsy.

This time, no one made a noise. They obviously felt something was wrong, but they didn't know what was going on. How could this charming little chick talk like that?

"Dear brothers, I don't think you know me yet." Dong Xiaowan paused, then added, "My family name is Dong, given name Bai, and literary name Xiaowan. I lived in the Old Yard on the Qinhuai River for a few years, but then moved to Gusu. This time, I've come to Nanjing to meet with Mr. Mao Pijiang from Rugao. I had an appointment with him. Have you heard of Mr. Mao from Rugao, brothers? He's one of the Four Young Men of the Fushe and knows all the top officials in the six ministries in Nanjing ..."

Dong Xiaowan reckoned that the gang of thugs didn't know who she was, and came to tease her just because they considered her a girl from an ordinary family. She was not dressed like a young lady from a powerful family. Now that she said she was a prostitute invited over by Mao Xiang, a famous scholar in the Fushe, they might feel they had chosen the wrong target and go away. Sure enough, after hearing Dong Xiaowan's self-introduction, many of them were overpowered. Only the garlic-clove-nosed boy who had teased her seemed unresigned. He said in a sarcastic tone:

"Oh, you're the famous Lady Dong. It's even better. We're so lucky to see you. Let's go out of here and have a drink."

"Thank you for your kindness, brother," Dong Xiaowan said with a curtsy. "It's just that I can't accept your invitation."

"Why?" The garlic-clove-nosed boy stared at her. "Do you think I can't afford it? Let me tell you, I have lots of money to spend. How much do you want? Just tell me."

"Oh, it's not about money. It's just that I'm occupied today."

"Occupied? It's just worshiping the gods and burning incense.

小爷这顿酒是吃定了。你不来也得来！”那少年蛮横得可以。

“对！叫你来就得来，别敬酒不吃吃罚酒！”他的一个同伙帮腔说。

“咦，瞧她架子还挺大的呢！”“装模作样罢咧，哪有姐儿不爱钞的？”“对，对，她们不就是干的收钱卖货的营生么！”另外几个也七嘴八舌地说。

“哈哈哈哈！”更多的人哄笑起来。

“嗳哟！你们这是做什么呀！”许久没有说话的陆卖婆突然挥舞着双手叫了起来，“人家又不是一定不肯随你们去，只是今儿不行罢咧！常言道，‘头头不了账账不清’，今儿是冒公子和复社的相公们早就请了的，自然得先轮到他们！你们硬要横插一杠子，窑子上也没这规矩！各位老爹少爷如果有心帮衬，赶明儿到秦淮河去！我们谢都来弗及呢，哪有把进门的买卖往外推的道理？只是今儿不行，冒公子和复社的相公们，这会儿正在石城门外的船上等着我们呢！啊哟！不同你们闲嚼蛆了，我们烧炷香就得回去，迟了，只怕要落一顿埋怨呢！”

陆卖婆一边说，一边扯着董小宛往殿上就走。

也不知到底是因为陆卖婆的一番话打了圆场，还是因为听说冒襄和复社的人就在外面的船上，给吓住了，这一次，那伙浪荡子弟却没有追上来。不过，当她们登上台阶，来到殿门外时，陆卖婆却发现董小宛低着头，两行泪水正顺着脸颊默默地流下来。那是痛苦的、屈辱的泪水。陆卖婆担心地回顾一下，半带劝解半带吓唬地说：

“妹妹，快别哭了。若是给那帮瘟星瞧见了，姐姐好歹糊起这张窗纸儿，说不定又给捅破啦！”说着，紧拽几步，把董小宛拖进了大殿。

这是一座歇山顶的殿堂，殿内九梁六柱，十分宽敞。当中供

That's no big deal. I tell you, you must come with me whether you like it or not," the young man said resolutely.

"Yes! You must come when you're wanted. Accept the invitation or face the consequence!" echoed one of his comrades.

"Hey, look at her! She pretends to be a lady." "She's just pretending. Is there a whore who doesn't like money?" "Yes, yes, isn't she in the business of taking money and offering service?" others also echoed.

"Haha, haha!" The thugs guffawed.

"Ayo! What are you doing?" Miss Lu, who hadn't spoken for a long while, suddenly shouted, waving her hands. "It's not that she doesn't want to go with you, but that she can't go today. As you know, first things must be first. Today, since Mr. Mao and the boys of the Fushe have invited her first, they must be first. You can't break the rule even in the brothel. If you really want to patronize her, go to the Qinhuai River tomorrow. We'll be only too happy to receive you. How can we push business out the door? Today isn't good. Mr. Mao and men of the Fushe are waiting for us on a boat outside the Stone City Gate at the moment. Sorry, we shouldn't delay too long by talking with you. We have to go back immediately after the incense offering. If we're too late, they'll complain."

As Miss Lu spoke, she pulled Dong Xiaowan toward the main hall.

Either having been persuaded by Miss Lu or scared upon hearing Mao Xiang and the Fushe men were on the boat outside the Stone City Gate, the bunch of young rascals didn't follow them this time. However, as the two ladies climbed to the door of the temple hall, Miss Lu found Dong Xiaowan's head was drooping and two lines of tears were flowing down her cheeks. It was tears of pain and humiliation. Miss Lu worriedly cast a backward glance and then turned to Xiaowan and said, partly to comfort her and partly to scare her:

"Sis, don't cry! If the bad boys see it, they'll see us through." As she spoke, she dragged Dong Xiaowan into the hall.

It was a temple with a hip-and-gable roof and with nine beams

着一尊一丈来高的关圣帝君坐像，塑得赤面美髯，凤眼蚕眉，栩栩如生。他的两侧还各有一座较小的塑像，左侧是一位白面无须的青年将军，手里捧着一方印；右侧站着一位黑面虬髯的壮士，肩上扛着一柄大刀。那自然便是关平和周仓了。神前的香案上，照例陈列着各式供品，香烛围绕，烟雾腾腾。一些善男信女正俯伏在蒲团上顶礼膜拜。

当董小宛把三炷点燃了的线香在香炉上插好，双膝跪倒在蒲团上时，有片刻工夫，她抬起还残留着痛苦的眼睛，仰望着神龛里的那尊关圣帝君像。她觉得帝君的面容是如此威严，如此美丽，他的眼神又是如此智慧，如此慈祥。他仿佛在说："你前世作下了孽，所以今生合该遭受如此磨难。不过，只要你一心向道，乐善不渝，是可以赎清前愆，从苦海里获得超生的……"

董小宛的心忽然觉得平静了："是啊，我今生受苦受难，都是前世作孽的报应！但愿我的债已经偿清，从此脱离苦海，同冒郎白头偕老！"

于是，她合掌当胸，虔诚地祝祷了一会儿，叩下头去，然后站起身，把供桌前的一个签筒拿过来，开始使劲地摇着，一边继续默默祝祷。她不停地摇着，随着她的手势，竹签在签筒里发出悦耳的沙沙声响。渐渐地，董小宛的整个心灵也沉浸在这美妙而神秘的旋律里，仿佛已经同冒襄一起踏上了去如皋的归途。那沙沙的声响便是江水在船舷旁流过，是轿夫轻快的脚步，是冒郎在她耳边喁喁细语……

and six pillars in the hall, which was very spacious. Inside was a lifelike statue of General Guan, about 10 feet tall, with a red face and a lush, beautiful beard, phoenix eyes and silkworm eyebrows. There was a smaller statue on each side of General Guan. On the left was a young general with an unbearded fair face holding a seal in his hand. On the right stood a muscular warrior with a bearded dark face, and a large sword on his shoulder. They should be Guan Ping and Zhou Cang. On the incense table before the gods, like in other temples, various offerings were displayed, surrounded by incense sticks and candles, with incense smoke wafting into the air. Some pious men and women were kowtowing to the statues on the futons.

When Dong Xiaowan put three lit incense sticks on the burner and knelt down on the futon, she raised her agonized eyes and looked up at the statue of General Guan in the altar. She felt that the General Guan's face was so majestic and beautiful, and his eyes so full of wisdom and kindness, as if he were saying, "You have committed sins in your past life, so you have to suffer such hardships in this life. However, as long as you are dedicated to the pursuit of the good path and perform good deeds unwaveringly, you can redeem your past sins and be liberated from the sea of suffering ..."

Dong Xiaowan's mind suddenly calmed down. She thought, "Yes, my suffering in this life is retribution for my past sins. I hope my debt is paid, and from now on I'll be free from the sea of misery and live happily with Mr. Mao ever after."

So, she folded her palms on her chest, prayed for a while, bowed her head, then stood up, took a fortune holder from the sacrificial table and shook it hard as she continued to say her prayers in her mind. She kept shaking the fortune holder, and in response to her movements, the bamboo sticks made a pleasant rustling sound in it. Gradually, Dong Xiaowan's whole heart was immersed in this wonderful and mysterious melody, as if she had already embarked on the return journey to Rugao with Mao Xiang. The rustling sound was the sound of the river flowing along the boat, that of the light footsteps of the sedan bearers, or the whispering of her beau in her ear ...

终于，签筒“笃”的一响，这是神明显灵的信号。董小宛反射似的睁开眼睛，果然，一根签已经脱筒而出，掉在地上。她赶紧弯腰把它捡起来，“啊，不知神明怎么说，不知他怎么说？”她匆遽地、惊惶地想，把签抓在手里，慌里慌张地站起来，到右首的柜台上，纳了一文钱，向庙祝取了签纸。可是她的手抖得那样厉害，以至无论如何也看不清楚写在签纸上的那几行字。她只好停下来喘一口气，待到稍稍平静一点时，才重新去读签文。这一回，她不仅看清了，而且像猛地挨了一记似的呆住了。签文上写着这样一首七言绝句：

忆昔兰房分半钗，
如今忽把信音乖。
痴心指望成连理，
到底谁知事不谐。

Finally, there was a sound of "tuk" from the tube that held the fortune sticks, which was a sign of the gods manifesting themselves. Dong Xiaowan intuitively opened her eyes, and sure enough, a fortune stick came out of the tube and fell to the ground. She hurriedly leaned forward and picked it up. "Oh, what does General Guan say? What does he say?" she thought nervously. Then, holding the fortune stick in her hand, she stood up in a panic, went to the counter on the right, donated one *wen* to the temple and got the written interpretation of the fortune stick. Her hands trembled so badly that she couldn't see the words on the slip clearly. She had to recollect herself, and when she was a little calmer, she read the result slip again. This time, she saw it clearly and was stunned as if she had received a blow. On the slip was a seven-character quatrain which read:

*yì xī lán fáng fēn bàn chāi,*
*rú jīn hū bǎ xìn yīn guāi.*
*chī xīn zhǐ wàng chéng lián lǐ,*
*dào dǐ shéi zhī shì bù xié.*

which means:

*In the boudoir, they gave each other a token of love.*
*But now, there's no news from the man.*
*How she longs to be married to him!*
*But in the end, things have gone wrong.*

# 第十章

# 借戏班小计赚胡子，斥阉孽私语动侯生

## 用计撮合

乡试的第三场，即最后一场，按规定是八月十六日结束。但十五日是中秋佳节，贡院照例提前一天放牌，让已经交卷的举子先行出场。在第一批出来的举子当中，有吴应箕、陈贞慧、梅朗中、顾杲、侯方域、余怀、陈梁、吕兆龙、冯舒、冯班、张岱、孙永祚以及其他一些复社社友。冒襄也在其内。现在，他们兴冲冲地聚集在桃叶河房里，一边愉快地交谈着，一边准备摆酒赏月，唱戏谢神。

七天前，冒襄刚进考场时，虽然一度被意外的挫折困扰过，可是当那神秘的、来自上苍的启示使他平静下来之后，情况就改变了，握管下笔之际，竟是出奇的顺利，仿佛有神鬼相助似的，文思源源涌出。那七篇八股时文，当真做得理真法老、花团锦簇，连自己看着，也不由得惊异起来。第二、三场考的是论、判和时务策，情形也一样。而且每一场，都是才放头牌他就已经交卷出

# Chapter Ten

# In Which Zhang Dai Borrowed a Drama Team from Ruan Dacheng and Hou Fangyu Was Moved by a Private Remark

## Gu Mei's Contrivance

The third and final session of the provincial exam was scheduled to end on August 16th, but since August 15th was the Mid-Autumn Festival, the Gongyuan announced one day earlier that those who had already submitted their papers could leave first. Among the first batch of candidates that left the examination court were Wu Yingji, Chen Zhenhui, Mei Langzhong, Gu Gao, Hou Fangyu, Yu Huai, Chen Liang, Lü Zhaolong, Feng Shu, Feng Ban, Zhang Dai, Sun Yongzuo, and some other members of the Fushe. Mao Xiang was among them. Now, they happily gathered in the Peach Leaves Riverhouse, talking and preparing for a drinking and moon-viewing party, at which everyone would sing an opera song to the gods that had blessed them.

Despite the disturbance that took place upon his entering the examination court, when Mao Xiang finally sat down, a mysterious inspiration immediately came to him and words poured out spontaneously, as if a divine spirit were helping him. He wrote the seven eight-legged current affairs essays at one go, and all of them were compelling, coherent, and elegant. He was amazed at how well he did. Likewise, he did very well in the second and third sessions, in which the candidates were tested on theory, judgment, and strategic thinking. In all three sessions, he was among the first batch of

场。待回到河房，把试文逐篇默写出来交给几位相知的社友传阅，又博得大家的击节叹赏，同声推许，就连评点名家、爱挑眼的吴应箕读了之后，也点头不语。瞧着这种情形，冒襄表面虽然不露声色，依旧一副淡淡的神气，内心却十分得意，觉得这一次虽不敢说必能夺魁抡元，但入闱中式，恐怕是没有疑问了。

也许因为这个缘故，当董小宛在顾眉和李十娘的陪伴下，带着陆卖婆突然来到桃叶河房时，冒襄并没有表现出任何惊愕和不快。相反，就在董小宛径直向他走来的一刹那，冒襄甚至露出了愉快的、抱歉的笑容。不过，董小宛显然没有领会这笑容的含义。她那严肃而苍白的脸孔，那双大睁着的惊惶的眼睛，以及变得僵硬了的身姿，说明了她内心的紧张不安；而那紧闭着的小嘴，那毫不迟疑的步态，又显示出她的勇气和决心。不过，最令冒襄感到惊异的，却是此刻董小宛整个姿态所显示出来的那种殉道者般的悲壮动人的意味，以致他忽然感到有一点畏怯，有一点慌张。虽然几句照例的应酬话已经溜到了嘴边，却像一下子给施了魔法似的，再也说不出来。

董小宛来到冒襄跟前，就站住了。她仰起头，睁大那双梦幻似的大眼睛，一言不发，只管呆呆地望着冒襄。她望得那样专注，那样长久，似乎忘记了她此刻在什么地方，也忘记了周围还有许多人在场……

终于，冒襄被她瞧得有点不自在。他转动了一下身子，发现社友们的目光都集中在他俩的身上，一个个都露出意味深长的微笑。冒襄的脸微微一红，正想打个哈哈，把这尴尬的场面掩饰过去，一个清脆悦耳的女人嗓音已经在人丛中嚷了起来：

“啊哟，大家快瞧瞧这两口儿！一个在如皋，一个在姑苏，千辛万苦地约定到南京来相会，可是见了面，光顾着你瞧我、我瞧你，一句话儿也不说！这是唱的哪一出子戏哟！”

candidates to be allowed to leave. When he returned to the riverhouse, he wrote out the test essays from memory and handed them over to several acquaintances. They all marveled at his writings. Even Wu Yingji, who was well known for being very picky as a critic, nodded his head in approval. Seeing that, Mao Xiang was very proud of himself, although he remained calm and composed on the surface. He knew he would be one of the successful candidates, if not the best.

Perhaps because of that, when Dong Xiaowan, accompanied by Gu Mei and Li Shiniang, suddenly came to the Peach Leaves Riverhouse with Miss Lu the peddler, Mao Xiang showed no surprise or displeasure. On the contrary, the moment Dong Xiaowan walked straight toward him, Mao Xiang even gave a pleasant and apologetic smile. However, Dong Xiaowan obviously didn't understand the meaning of this smile. Her solemn, pale face, her wide, panicked eyes, and her stiffened figure, spoke of her inner nervousness, but her tightly shut mouth, her unwavering gait showed her courage and determination. What surprised Mao Xiang was the look of a martyr that her entire posture gave. He was suddenly scared and apprehensive. The customary words of greeting that had risen to his lips stuck, as if he were suddenly bound by a spell.

Dong Xiaowan came over to Mao Xiang and stopped. Then, she lifted her head and silently gazed at Mao Xiang with her wide dreamlike eyes for a long time, as if she had forgotten where she was at the moment and that there were many other people around ...

Finally, Mao Xiang felt a little awkward under her gaze. He turned around and found that the eyes of the Fushe comrades were all focused on her and him, with meaningful smiles on their faces. Mao Xiang flushed slightly, and just as he was about to give a laugh and cover up his embarrassment, a clear, crisp female voice shouted in the crowd:

"Haha, look and behold! One from Rugao, one from Gusu, and the two finally meet in Nanjing as agreed after all the hardships, but when they actually meet, you look at me, and I look at you, and neither says a word! Which opera scene is this?"

那是顾眉。她一边说，一边摇摇摆摆地走了过来。顾眉和李十娘都是董小宛的手帕姐妹。前几天，董小宛带着陆卖婆到旧院去寻着她们，把她同冒襄的事原原本本地说了，恳求姐妹们帮忙。顾眉听了，满口应承，并对陆卖婆那个通过大肆张扬此事，造成舆论迫使冒襄就范的主意十分欣赏。她说："哼，你别说，这事还真得这么办才成！如今这世道，我们当婊子的要走红，自然得有他们名士捧场；可他那个大名士，若离了我们婊子，只怕也当不神气哩！"她果然说干就干，一面让董小宛搬进城里，就在眉楼住下，一面串连了一伙姐妹，逢人便说冒襄和董小宛的事，加油添醋，竭力张扬。结果，到如今，这事在名士圈子里已弄得人人皆知，不少人还答应了顾眉，要尽力设法促成这段姻缘。所以，此刻顾眉已是心中有数。不过，她也知道，这事到底成不成，最后还在于冒襄怎么拿主意。因此她一进来，就十分注意冒襄的表情反应。发现冒襄并无厌烦不快的表示，她就先松了一口气；接着又看见这一对儿傻怔怔地在那里四目交视，无语相看，顾眉差点儿没有笑出来。"哼，我还道这位冒大公子拿班作势的，有多难轧，敢情儿不过'银样镴枪头'！可笑我这位董家妹妹也忒多心胆小，一天到晚地担惊受怕。待我如今略施手段，把这门亲事给撮合了，看她拿什么谢我！"这么一想，她又笑吟吟地说：

"噢，敢情儿是怕我们听了去不成？好好好，我们这就走。若再碍着，还不知他们心里怎么咒死我们哩！"

顾眉说着，转身就向堂外走去。走了几步，回头看看，大家都还站着没动，她又叫："咦，怎么啦！你们倒是走呀！"

"你不说到哪儿，我们怎么走？"李十娘微笑着说，"莫非姐姐要去投秦淮河，我们也得跟着不成？"

It was Gu Mei. As she spoke, she came over, swaying her body. Gu Mei and Li Shiniang were Dong Xiaowan's handkerchief sisters. A few days ago, Dong Xiaowan went to the Old Yard with Miss Lu the peddler to see them. She told them her story and begged for help. Gu Mei agreed immediately and liked Miss Lu's idea that they should make the romantic relationship widely known so that Mao Xiang would have no choice but to compromise. She said, "Hah, that's a good idea. It's actually the only way to do it. In today's world, if we bitches want to get anywhere, we must rely on the celebrated men, but meanwhile a celebrated man like him would lose his glamor without a bitch like us!" She acted immediately. First, she let Dong Xiaowan move into the city and stay in Mei's House. Then, she contacted other prostitutes and let them spread the story about Mao Xiang and Dong Xiaowan, with embellishment of course. As a result, the affair was quickly known in the circle of gentry scholars, many of whom promised Gu Mei that they would help to make the marriage happen. Gu Mei was now confident of her contrivance, but she also knew that the decision was Mao Xiang's after all. Therefore, when she came in, she watched Mao Xiang's expression. Seeing that Mao Xiang was not showing any signs of irritation or displeasure, she breathed a sigh of relief, and seeing Mao Xiang and Dong Xiaowan stupidly staring at each other in silence, she almost laughed out loud. "Hmph! I thought Mr. Mao is a very difficult person, but it turns out he's merely a bogeyman. Miss Dong is too timid. Let me use some tricks, and he'll be tamed. By then, she will never thank me enough."

Thus thinking, she said with a smile, "Oh, they're afraid of being heard by us. Alright, then. Let's go now. If we stand in their way, they'll hate us."

With that, Gu Mei turned around and walked out of the main room. After a few steps, she looked back. Seeing nobody had moved, she shouted at them, "Hey, what's the matter? Move!"

"But you haven't told us where to go," Li Shiniang said with a smile. "Should we follow you too if you're going to jump into the Qinhuai River?"

“死丫头！这还用问？当然是上水阁去啊！”顾眉跺着脚说，随即眼珠子一溜，又嫣然笑道，“谁个听话，乖乖儿跟我去，我等会儿甜甜地唱支小曲儿给他听；谁还赖着不走，哼，我同冒公子、小宛，还有这位陆卖婆，可要拿扫帚子夹屁股的赶啦！”

“噢，有小曲儿听，我当然去的！”站在近旁的顾杲首先蹦了起来，他扯着李十娘，笑嘻嘻地经过冒襄和董小宛跟前，做了个鬼脸，然后三步并作两步，走出堂屋。

于是，其余的人也纷纷笑着，向外走去。转眼工夫，堂屋里就只剩下冒、董二人。

当顾眉连哄带逼地往外赶人的当儿，冒襄一直没有动弹，也没有开口阻拦。他刚考完试，眼下那种如释重负的愉快感觉还没有消失，同时，对于自己背约不去苏州又多少有点不好意思，而董小宛这样不辞辛苦地巴巴赶来，又使他多少有点感动。说也奇怪，在见到董小宛之前，他丝毫也没有这种感觉，甚至对她这样苦缠不休感到恼火；可是，此刻，当董小宛就站在眼前，而且又是这么一副楚楚可怜的模样，冒襄就觉得，自己过去那样对她，是不是有点过分了？

“嗯，你——到底自己来了。”沉默了一阵，冒襄终于开口了。没等董小宛回答，他又急忙说，“这次我没到姑苏去接你，你一定怨我吧？其实，我倒一心想去，就是试期迫得太紧，没有办法。不过，我打算好，考完了还是要去——没想到你倒先来了，正好。只是难为你啦！”

“奴家不怨公子。公子忙着应考，这是要紧的大事，不去姑苏是应当的。如今奴家已见着公子，又听说公子考得很好，奴家心里只觉得喜欢。”董小宛低着头，轻声地说。

“啊，你也知道了？”

“这些天来，奴家夜夜对着月亮烧香叩头，求神保佑公子今科高中。刚才在眉楼听人说起，公子头场这几篇文章，好得什么

"Damn girl! Do you need to ask? Of course, it's Water Pavilion!" Gu Mei said, stomping her feet. Then she suddenly rolled her eyes and said with a broad smile,"Those who listen to me, come with me and I'll sing a song for you shortly. Those who don't , beware of broomsticks from us: me, Mr. Mao, Xiaowan, and Miss Lu!"

"Hah, I want to hear you sing!" Gu Gao, who was standing nearby, jumped up. He held Li Shiniang's hand, made faces at Mao Xiang and Dong Xiaowan as he passed them, and quickly walked out of the main room.

The others laughed and followed them. In the blink of an eye, the room was empty, with only Mao Xiang and Dong Xiaowan left.

During all the time that Gu Mei coerced and coaxed the others to leave, Mao Xiang stayed still and silent. Having come out of the examination court, he was still indulging in the pleasurable sensation that came after a relief from a heavy duty. More or less sorry for breaking his promise by failing to go to Suzhou, he was now moved to see Dong Xiaowan had come all the way to see him. Curiously, before meeting Dong Xiaowan, he didn't have the slightest bit of this feeling. Instead, he was even annoyed by her persistent pestering. Now, when she was standing in front of him and looked so pitiable, he began to feel guilty.

"Well, you—finally, you've made it here." After a moment of silence, Mao Xiang opened his mouth. Before Dong Xiaowan answered, he hurriedly said, "Sorry, I didn't go to Suzhou to pick you up. You must hate me for it. In fact, I wanted to go, but since the examination was so close, I was unable to go. I was thinking I would have to go anyway after the exam. Now you're here. It's excellent! Thank you for the trouble."

Dong Xiaowan said in a soft voice, her eyes downcast, "I don't blame you for it. Nothing is more important than the exam. You didn't have to go to Gusu. Now that I see you and know you've done well in the exam, I'm very happy for you."

"Ah, you've heard it too?"

"In the past few days, I offered incense and kowtowed to the moon every night, praying for the gods to bless you with success in

似的，还未曾放榜，书坊已经着人来打探，要拿去翻刻印行。奴家便想，果是上天有灵，公子得中，奴家纵然半路上遭了不测，也……”说到最后这一句，董小宛的嘴唇忽然颤抖起来，声音也开始发哑，随即咽住了。

冒襄目不转睛地瞅着董小宛。他本以为，自己这次失约，难免会招来对方一把眼泪一把鼻涕的责备，至少也会埋怨几句，谁知董小宛不但一点责备的意思都没有，反而处处为他设想、开脱。他没想到对方会这样体谅自己、关怀自己，一时大为感动，情不自禁地伸出手去，把董小宛柔软洁白的小手轻轻握住，怜惜地说：

“这……可真是难为你啦！我没想到……真的。嗯，刚才你说什么——遭了不测？这可是怎么回事？”

“没……没什么。”

“不，你快说，我要你告诉我！”

“真的没什么。就是……我们来时，半路上遇到强盗了，要抢东西，还要……我们拼命地跑，好不容易躲进了芦苇荡，才没叫他们搜着。可是舵坏了，船开不动，又不敢上岸，怕再遇见强盗。船上的东西吃没了，只好挨饿，一直过了三天，船家才偷偷上岸，把舵修好。那会儿奴家一个心思就想，自己天生命苦，死了，也没有什么好恨的；又是死在来寻公子的路上，到底也算有福了。只是不明不白，临死也不能给公子捎个信，却是……怎么……也不甘心！”董小宛强挣着说完，再也忍不住了。她蓦地挣脱了冒襄的手，使劲掩着嘴巴，倒在椅子上，悲苦地、委屈地哭泣起来。

冒襄呆呆地站在原地，瞅着董小宛，没有动弹，也没开口劝解。不知为什么，他觉得心里有点乱，拿不准主意该怎么办和说一些什么话才好。不错，柔声软语地说上一些安慰劝解的话——自己虽然并不许诺什么，但听起来仍然亲切——这并不困难，而且过去他就曾不止一次地用这种办法来应付对方，每一次都十分

this exam. I heard in Mei's House just now that your essays in the first session are so good that, although the examination results are not announced yet, the bookstores are competing to publish them. I was thinking, should my prayers be answered and you succeed in the exam, even if I encounter some mishap during the trip, it would be worth the while ..." She stuck as her lips quivered and her voice shook.

Mao Xiang gazed at Dong Xiaowan. He had thought his failure to keep his promise would incur a tearful reprimand or at least some complaint. To his surprise, she didn't blame him at all. On the contrary, she was thinking in his shoes and trying to find an excuse for him. Moved by her consideration and love, he reached out his hand and gently held her soft, creamy hand, and said with pity in his voice, "I—I'm sorry for all the trouble you've been through. I haven't been considerate enough. Um, what did you say just now? What mishap?"

"Nothing."

"Well, just say it, you must tell me!"

"Nothing really. It's just ... halfway during the trip, we met some robbers. They not only robbed but also wanted to ... We ran and ran and finally escaped by hiding ourselves in the reeds. When we came back to the boat, the rudder was broken and the boat couldn't move. We didn't dare to go ashore for fear that the robbers might come back again. We stayed on the boat and starved when the food ran out. After three days, the boatman stealthily went ashore and fixed the rudder. At that time, I thought, since I'm born an unfortunate girl, dying like this is fine, and I should be happy dying on the way to find my love, but I wouldn't be reconciled if my love doesn't know it." Dong Xiaowan struggled to finish the story. Finally, unable to hold herself together, she broke free from Mao Xiang's hand, covered her mouth with her own hand, collapsed into the chair, and sobbed woefully.

Mao Xiang stood there dumbfounded, staring at Dong Xiaowan. He didn't move, nor did he try to comfort her. For some reason, he felt a little confused, not sure what to do and what to say. Yes, saying a few soft, kind words of comfort without promising anything was not something difficult. He had used this method before, and it worked

灵验。可是时至今日，到底还该不该这样做呢？冒襄却感到有点犹豫了。他十分清楚，董小宛所需要的是真诚的许诺，而不是空泛的安慰。如果自己仍旧用那种办法，来敷衍这么一个对自己一片痴情的弱女子，那就未免太欺负她，而且不够光明正大。但是当真答应娶她呢？困难也确实不少。先别说自己是否当真喜欢她这一层，就拿替她还债和赎身这两件事来说，没有一两千两银子在手，只怕难以打发得清。而家中自从经过父亲那件事之后，景况已经大不如前。现在一下子要拿出两千两银子来讨妾，只怕父母也未必会同意。“哎，即便娶的是圆圆，事情也说不定办得成办不成，何况是她！”这样一想，冒襄又泄了气。他回头瞧了董小宛一眼，正想走过去胡乱劝解几句，冷不防顾眉带笑的嗓音在门外响了起来：

“怎么？还没说完么？唉呀，这可真是‘剪不断、理还乱’哟！”

顾眉一边说，一边走了进来。蓦地看见冒襄正皱着眉毛站在堂屋中央，又瞧瞧董小宛，发现她正歪在椅子上哭泣，顾眉倒吓了一跳，忙问：“怎么啦，怎么啦？刚才还好好儿的，怎么会闹成这模样？——哼，冒公子，八成是你瞧我这妹子脾气儿好，不知又怎地欺负她了吧？”

说着，她连忙走到董小宛身边：“妹妹，不要哭。告诉我，冒公子他怎么欺负你？待姐姐跟他评理！”

董小宛本来已经哭得差不多了，只是希望冒襄能过来，向她说上几句温柔体贴的话，所以才拖着。她看见顾眉走进来，就连忙自己揩干眼泪，一边站起身，一边说：“不是冒公子，是妹子自己要这样子。”

“这话可是真的？”

董小宛点点头。

顾眉这才松了一口气。她瞧瞧冒襄，又瞧瞧董小宛：“那边都备办妥了，大家都等着你们入席呢！若没什么，就过去吧！”

every time. But should he do the same today? He was hesitant. He knew very well that what Dong Xiaowan needed was a sincere promise, not empty platitudes of comfort. To use such an old method to perfunctorily console such a vulnerable woman who was infatuated with him was not fair to her and was tantamount to bullying. It was beneath him. What about giving her a promise to marry her? There were indeed many difficulties. First, he was not sure whether he really liked her. Second, it would cost him one or two thousand taels of silver to repay her debts and redeem her from the brothel. That was a fortune he could hardly afford after having spent so much money on his father's transfer. His parents probably would not allow him to spend one or two thousand taels of silver taking a concubine. "Even if it were Yuanyuan, they probably wouldn't agree. Her chances were even slimmer," he thought dejectedly. He cast a backward glance at Dong Xiaowan and wanted to move close to her and offer her some words of consolation, when suddenly rang the laughing voice of Gu Mei, "Hah, you haven't finished yet? Oh, feelings, what feelings of love ..."

Gu Mei walked in. When she saw Mao Xiang standing in the center of the main room with knitted eyebrows, she looked at Dong Xiaowan and found that she was crying in the chair. Startled, Gu Mei hurriedly asked, "What's the matter, what's the matter? You were fine just now. Why are you like this? Hmph, Mr. Mao, are you bullying my good-tempered sister again?"

She hurriedly walked to Dong Xiaowan's side, "Sis, don't cry! Tell me, how did Mr. Mao bully you? I'll reckon with him!"

Dong Xiaowan's crying had waned. She was simply waiting for Mao Xiang to come over and say a few kind words. When she saw Gu Mei come in, she quickly wiped away her tears, stood up and said, "It has nothing to do with Mr. Mao. I just felt like crying."

"Is it true?"

Dong Xiaowan nodded.

Gu Mei breathed a sigh of relief. She looked at Mao Xiang, and then at Dong Xiaowan and said, "Everything is ready over there. Everyone is waiting for you two to sit at the table! If you're fine,

看见冒、董二人没有反对的表示，她就对董小宛说：“妹妹，瞧你，这模样怎么去见人！快，隔壁屋里有妆奁，你去匀匀脸再来，我们等你！”

董小宛答应着，顺从地走进隔壁去了。趁这当儿，顾眉把冒襄扯到一边，悄悄儿问：

“嗯，怎么样，公子拿定主意没有？”

冒襄瞧了她一眼，知道骗她不过，只好老实地摇摇头。

顾眉本来眯缝着眼，嘴角漾着笑影，一见他这样，眼睛顿时睁圆了，“怎么，到这会儿你还想着陈圆圆？”她生气地说，“你说，我这妹妹哪里比不上圆圆？圆圆她会这等死心塌地待你？她肯这等不要命地来寻你？她肯为你去死也心甘情愿？”

冒襄没有吱声。顾眉所说的这些，他也曾想过，他也觉得在这个方面，陈圆圆确实比不上董小宛。但他现在所考虑的，并不是这个。

“你少扯圆圆的事！”他不高兴地说，“我是说的落籍、还债！”

“噢，敢情是为的这事发愁呀！”顾眉一听，倒高兴起来，“这有什么难，大不了就是那么一两千两银子么！你堂堂冒公子，还怕拿不出？”

“哼！你哪里晓得！”冒襄冷笑说，“一年前你说这话还差不多，可现在——”他闭住嘴巴，摇摇头。

“这……”顾眉眨巴着杏子样的大眼睛，似乎有点为难了，她不由得沉吟起来。然而，当目光重新落到冒襄的身上时，她就露出了微笑：

“冒公子，你真是聪明一世，糊涂一时！亏你平日里自尊自

please go and join the others!" Seeing that Mao Xiang and Dong Xiaowan didn't object, she said to Dong Xiaowan, "Sis, look at you, how can you meet people like this! Hurry up! There's a mirrored dressing case in the next room, go and get your face fixed. We'll wait for you."

Dong Xiaowan agreed and walked into the next door obediently. Taking advantage of this moment, Gu Mei pulled Mao Xiang aside and asked in a whisper, "Well, how is it going? Have you made up your mind, sir?"

Mao Xiang glanced at her, and knowing that he couldn't lie to her, he shook his head honestly.

Gu Mei, who had been squinting her eyes with a smile at the corners of her mouth, opened her eyes wide when she saw him like that. "Why, are you still obsessed with Chen Yuanyuan now?" she said angrily. "Tell me, why is my sister not as good as Yuanyuan? Can Yuanyuan be so devoted to you? Can Yuanyuan risk her life to look for you? Can she die for you?"

Mao Xiang was silent. What Gu Mei said had also crossed his mind. He also felt that Chen Yuanyuan was indeed not as good as Dong Xiaowan in this respect. But that's not what he cared about at the moment.

"Don't speak of Yuanyuan!" he said irritatedly. "It's about paying her debts and buying her out from the brothel!"

"Oh, is that what worries you?" Gu Mei lit up when she heard it. "It's no big deal. Just one or two thousand taels of silver isn't a great fortune. As the young master of the Maos, of course you have it."

"Humph! You don't understand," Mao Xiang sneered. "You could say it that way a year ago, but not now—" He closed his mouth and shook his head.

"Oh?" Gu Mei blinked her big apricot-like eyes with a tad of embarrassment. She was puzzled. However, when her eyes fell on Mao Xiang again, she smiled and said, "Mr. Mao, you're a wise man confused! You have always behaved decently and have your own opinion on things, but when it comes to a thing like this, you forget

重，挺有主张的，事到临头，却又把自个儿的分量给忘了！”

“……”

顾眉撇撇嘴：“若是那些个阿猫阿狗之流的无名小辈，奴家也没办法。可像您老这样大名鼎鼎的复社公子，说句笑话——就拿这名字上当铺儿去，也能当它个千儿八百呢！还用得着为银子发愁？”

“……”

“你不信？”顾眉的眼睛变得闪闪发光，“你俩这事如今在秦淮河上已是人人皆知，你若是把它认实了，赶明儿我们就索性把它再闹腾开去，闹它个江南轰动，万口争传，越轰烈越好！到那时——瞧吧，自然会有人愿当那黄衫客、古押衙①，替你掏腰包儿！你信不信？”

停了停，她见冒襄沉着脸，没吱声，摸不透他的心思，于是又掩着嘴儿，“扑哧”一笑：“公子可别着恼，奴家是跟你说笑话儿！不过，说真的，如今好名之徒多得很，他瞧你俩名士美人，这段风流佳话，若然成了，人人羡煞自不必说，没准儿还能流传千古！只要花上那千把两银子，就能攀上个黄衫、押衙的美名，他只怕还觉着很划得来哩！”

也不知冒襄到底是在听，还是没有听，他一动不动地站着，慢慢地捋着那乌黑漂亮的胡子，仍旧没有说话。

## 馋猫借戏

阮大铖愁眉苦脸地坐在石巢园的书房里，望着墙上那幅《百子山樵笠屐图》发呆。这幅画是十年前，他从怀宁家乡搬到南京来住下不久，花了二十两银子，央一位写真名手画的。画中那个头戴青箬笠、身披绿蓑衣的大胡子中年人，就是阮大铖本人。当

① 黄衫客、古押衙：两者在此均指设计救人者。

your own weight."

"..."

Gu Mei curled her lips. "If it were someone insignificant like a dog or cat, I wouldn't do anything. But a well-known young scholar of the Fushe like you, allow me to put it in a joke, if you took your name to a pawnshop, you could get a thousand or at least eight hundred! In that case, do you still need to worry about money?"

"..."

"You don't believe it?" Gu Mei's eyes twinkled. "The romantic relationship between you and Xiaowan is now known to everyone on the Qinhuai River. If you take it seriously, I can make it more widely known tomorrow and create a riot in the south of the Yangtze River. The more people talk about it, the better! By then—let's wait and see—there'll be no lack of obliging men ready to pay for you! Do you believe it or not?"

She paused. Mao Xiang was silent, his face sullen. Not knowing what he was thinking, she covered her mouth and laughed. "Don't be angry, sir. I was kidding. But, to be honest, there're so many men craving for fame nowadays. If anyone can play a part in bringing the union of a famous young scholar and a great beauty, everyone would be envious of him, and maybe his name will be passed down in history. One thousand taels of silver for the reputation of a great lovers' patron is a good deal."

Mao Xiang stood motionless and slowly stroked his beautiful black beard without responding. Maybe he was not listening.

## A Greedy Cat Came to Borrow the Drama Team

Ruan Dacheng sat in his study in the Stone Nest Garden with a mournful face, staring blankly at the picture on the wall captioned "Portrait of Baizi Mountain Woodcutter in Straw Hat and Clogs". Ten years ago, shortly after he moved to Nanjing from his hometown Huaining, he found a master figure painter and spent twenty taels of silver for it to be made. The bearded middle-aged man wearing a green bamboo hat and a green straw raincoat in the picture was Ruan

时画成之后，不少人看过，都说十足就像阮大铖的模样，岂止像而已，简直是“形神兼备，气韵生动”！阮大铖听了，十分高兴，特地派人拿去精工装裱好，把它挂在书房正当中的墙上。每逢有新来的客人参观到这里，他就特意指点给客人看，同时喋喋不休地说起自己如何“少负向、禽之志”，一心向慕山林，如今遭到罢官斥逐，倒成全了自己的“初志”，实在是一件大幸事！然后，他就用乌溜溜的眼睛斜睨着对方，神秘地压低声音问：“听说朝廷不久就要开放党禁，平反起用一批人，真担心我到时又悠闲不成了！嗯，你可有什么消息吗？”不过，这只是起始几年才这样，到后来，时光一年一年地过去，开放党禁却毫无影迹，阮大铖就不由得焦急起来，渐渐怀疑当初挂这样一幅画是否明智；如果一开始就把画中那个自己画成头戴乌纱帽、身穿圆领绯袍的话，会不会好一点？不过，他也没有马上把画收起来，而是作为补救措施，在画的两旁挂起了一副对联，写上“有官万事足，无子一身轻”两句话。意思是：儿子可以没有，官不可不做。希望老天爷根据他前世的表现来安排今生的命运时，能尊重他的这一选择。然而，几年又过去了，儿子固然照旧的养不下来，复官起用的活动也一再受挫，毫无希望。这就不由得阮大铖不感到既焦急、又沮丧。虽然上个月初，他的生死之交马士英在自己的全力帮助下，终于获得起用，出任凤阳巡抚。可是再好的朋友也只是朋友，朋

Dacheng himself. Back then, after the picture was completed, many people who saw it said that the man in the picture looked exactly like him in both form and spirit. Ruan Dacheng was very happy to hear it, so he got it framed and hung it on the wall in the middle of the study. Whenever a new visitor came to the study, he would point at the picture and tirelessly told them that since childhood he had been admiring two ancient recluses Xiang Changping and Qin Qing and wanted to live in the woods, his current exile fortunately had made it happen, and it was indeed a blessing in disguise, and then, he would squint at his guest with his black eyes and ask in a mysterious low voice, "I hear that the imperial court will soon lift the party ban and rehabilitate a batch of ousted officials. I'm afraid that by then I won't be able to enjoy peace and quiet like now. Well, have you heard any news?" It was like that only in the first few years. Later, as time passed year by year, there was no progress in the lifting of the party ban. Ruan Dacheng became anxious and started to doubt whether it was wise to hang such a picture after all. Maybe it would have been better if his image in the picture were wearing a black gauze hat and a round-necked red long gown. However, he didn't put the painting away immediately. Instead, as a remedy, he hung a couplet on both sides of the painting, which read:

WITH HIGH OFFICE EVERYTHING COMES
WITHOUT CHILDREN THERE IS NO BURDEN

It means that one can do without sons, but not without office. He hoped that providence would respect his choice when arranging his fate in this life, considering his performance in the past life. However, several years had passed, his efforts for reinstatement were thwarted again and again, although he still had no sons. There seemed to be no hope at all. He was desperate and despondent. At the beginning of last month, Ma Shiying, his "friend in life and death", with his unreserved help, was finally appointed Governor of Fengyang, but no matter how good a friend is, he's just a friend. After all, a friend being an official

友有官做毕竟不同于自己有官做。这里头的含义、作用、滋味都大不相同。何况马士英又走得那么匆忙，连见上一面都办不到。到底他现在怎么想，会不会一朝得志，就翻脸不认人？这些此刻都闹不清楚。尽管这一个多月来，阮大铖已经接连派人送去两封信追问，但结果，要不是回禀说潜山一带兵荒马乱，道路不通，信无法送到，就是说马士英忙于指挥作战，行踪不定，根本见不着他，所以一直没有回音。这就更使阮大铖惊疑之余，又添了几分气闷……

已是傍晚时分，天色开始暗下来，咏怀堂那边静悄悄的，既听不见锣鼓响，也听不见唱曲子的声音。要在平日，戏班教习臧亦嘉常常这会儿还领着那班伶人在排戏。可今日是中秋节，夜里还要张罗演出，所以早早就叫了歇。本来，平常愁闷涌上来时，只要听听唱曲，看看排戏，阮大铖的情绪就会渐渐又变得兴奋起来，并且情不自禁地沉浸在其中，暂时忘却周围的一切。可是偏偏碰上这莫名其妙的中秋节，可教阮大铖此刻内心的一份冷清和懊丧怎生排遣？

“啊，这全是复社那伙恶人闹的！是他们，全是他们！”阮大铖猛地跳起来，“呸！混账！猪！王八蛋！”他双手攥紧拳头，恶狠狠地骂出声来。骂过之后，感到还不解恨，于是又大声地使劲骂了一遍，这才觉得胸中的闷气稍稍排除了一些，不再像先前那样堵得慌。然后，他重新回到书案前坐了下来，抽笔展纸，开始给马士英写第三封信。

在信中，他也像前两次那样，首先大大恭维了马士英一番，说他是个“王佐之才”，更兼兵机谙熟，调度如神，此次拥“熊

is very different from oneself being an official. It's not the same either in terms of what it means, or what it can bring, or what it feels like. Besides, Ma Shiying left in such a hurry that there was no time for the friends to meet before his departure. There was no knowing what Mr. Ma was thinking now. Would he turn his back on an old friend now that he had got what he wanted? It was not clear at the moment. Over the past month, Ruan Dacheng had sent two letters to Ma Shiying. One never made it to Fengyang because the road was blocked by the fighting in the Qianshan area, and the other did make it to Fengyang, but since Ma Shiying was fully engaged on the frontline and his whereabouts were uncertain, it couldn't be delivered to Ma Shiying himself. Thus, besides fears and suspicions, Ruan Dacheng was also plagued with frustrations ...

It was dusk. The sky began to darken, and it was silent in the Playhouse, the home theater, with neither the sound of gongs and drums nor the sound of singing. Normally, Zang Yijia, the musical director, conducted the rehearsal there. But today the rehearsal had stopped earlier than usual, since it was the Mid-Autumn Festival and there was going to be a performance in the evening. When he was downcast, he would cheer himself up by watching the rehearsal and listening to the singing of the actors and temporarily forget everything else, but now, he was unable to assuage his loneliness and depression because of this damn Mid-Autumn Festival.

"Hmph! This is all caused by the bad men in the Fushe! It's them, it's them!" Ruan Dacheng jumped up abruptly. "Bah! Bastards! Pigs! Sons of bitches!" He clenched his fists and cursed vehemently. Not soothed by the cursing, he raised his voice and cursed again until his depression was alleviated a little bit and his chest was no longer as congested as before. Then, he returned to the desk, sat down, drew a brush pen, spread the paper, and began to write a third letter to Ma Shiying.

He started the letter, like the previous two, with lavish praises, saying, "You have the talent of a prime minster. With your expert knowledge of the art of war and an army of devoted and fearless warriors,

罴之士”，旌旗西指，定能一鼓破贼，克奏殊勋。然后，就用了整整两页信笺，逐一回顾了彼此的交情，用谦逊然而却是明白的口吻，提醒对方不要忘了自己给予的两次巨大帮助。在信的最后一段，他是这样写的：

我公行前，曾命专人驰告，反复周详。足见关怀旧雨，情谊殷拳。分虽隔夫云泥，情不忘于沆瀣，是用感激，聊申芜函，倘于为国宣劳之余，时怀俯赐栽植之意，俾效驰驱，则大铖有生之日，皆图报之年也！

写完之后，阮大铖自己又摇头晃脑地大声吟诵了一遍，自觉音节铿锵、情深辞切。到后来，他自己竟先感动起来，泪水在眼眶里直打转转，“啊啊，这样的文字，这样的才华！若是马瑶草还有点良心，就无论如何也该设法拉我一把！”他唏嘘地想着，慢慢擦去眼泪，又把信折好，装进已经写好的封套里。做完这一切之后，他站起身，一边考虑着该派谁去送信合适，一边转过脸来。就在这时，他看见院公站在门口。

“禀老爷，有一位张相公来拜。”院公行着礼说。

“哦？”这个时候还有人来访，使阮大铖感到有点意外。而且他记不起相熟的人中，有哪一个姓张的。不过，他还是把帖子接了过来，只见上面写着：

眷晚生张岱顿首拜

“嗯，张岱？这名字倒像听过，他是什么人呢？”阮大铖侧着脑袋，竭力回想着，却怎么也回想不起来。最后，只好摇摇头，吩咐门公：“外堂有请。”说完，他走进里间，换过衣服，慢腾腾地跟了过来。

you'll be victorious wherever you go." Then, he used two entire pages to recall anecdotes of their friendship, and in a humble but clear tone, reminded Ma Shiying not to forget the two great efforts he had made to help him get reinstated. In the last paragraph of the letter, he wrote:

*My friend, it was very considerate of you to send your servant to let me know before you left. That shows you are a true friend indeed. Although you've risen to the clouds, you've not forgotten an old friend who is still staying in the mud. I am writing to you to express my heartfelt thanks for your kindness. Meanwhile, I am hoping that in your less busy moments you'll remember to find an opportunity for me. If I can have my wish and serve you in any capacity, I'll be grateful to you for the rest of my life.*

After he wrote the letter, he read it aloud, rocking his head. The cadence and sincerity of tone moved himself, and tears welled up in his eyes. "Hooray! What beautiful words and what talent! If Ma Yaocao still has any conscience left, he'll have to find an opportunity for me," he thought. Then, he wiped his tears, folded the letter and put it into the envelope, which had already been addressed. Finally, he stood up. As he turned around, thinking who might be the best person to deliver it, he caught sight of the janitor, who was standing in front of the door.

"My lord, there's a Mr. Zhang waiting to see you."

"Oh?" Ruan Dacheng was a little surprised to hear someone had come to visit him at such a time. He couldn't remember having a Mr. Zhang among his acquaintances. Nonetheless, he took over the calling card, which read:

*Kowtow from Zhang Dai, a relation of the younger generation.*

"Well, Zhang Dai? This name sounds familiar. Who's he?" Ruan Dacheng tilted his head and tried to remember him, but failed. In the end, he shook his head and said to the janitor, "Invite him to the outer room." Then, he walked into the inner room, changed his clothes, and slowly came out.

阮大铖来到外堂，就放轻了脚步。他且不进门，先趴在窗棂上偷眼一瞧，看见里面站着一个方巾道袍的中年儒生，正倒背着一只手，在逗弄架子上那只白毛黑嘴的鹦哥儿。自从复社发表《留都防乱公揭》以来，同阮大铖交往的士子已经很少，现在瞧这儒生的背影并不熟悉，阮大铖愈加犯疑。他本想再瞧清楚一点，又怕被对方发觉，只好轻轻咳嗽一声，跨进大堂。

张岱听见响动，回头望了望，顿时展开了笑脸：

“圆老，你这鹦哥儿，甚有意思呢！”他喜滋滋地说。

“啊呀，原来是张兄！”阮大铖亲热地招呼。瞧清楚张岱的脸后，他觉得似乎有点面善，却想不起曾在哪儿见过。但对方一点都不客气拘束，阮大铖也就不好意思显出自己健忘，只好跟着装出一副熟稔的样子，“啊啊呀呀”地应酬着，分宾主坐下，一边希望从言谈中弄清对方的来历。

“啊，圆老，瞧见你这鹦哥儿，晚生就想起我家的‘宁了’来了！”张岱一边接过小厮奉上来的茶，一边兴致勃勃地说，“‘宁了’——圆老想必不曾听说过吧？难怪。此乃我家二十年前所珍养的一只异鸟。身小如鸽，黑翎如八哥，能作人言。其时晚生年纪尚幼，听见祖母唤婢妾，它便传呼道：‘某丫头，太太叫！’有客来，又叫：‘太太，客来了，看茶！’其音朗朗，绝不含糊。后来，家中来了个新娘子，爱睡懒觉。那鸟每天清晨便叫唤：‘新娘子，天明了，起来吧！太太叫，快起来！’不起，它就骂：‘新娘子，臭淫妇，浪蹄子！’那新娘子恨这鸟入骨，有一回，偷偷

As Ruan Dacheng came to the outer room, he lightened his footsteps. Instead of entering the room immediately, he leaned on the window lattice to take a peek and saw a middle-aged scholar in a square headscarf and a Taoist robe standing inside, and, with a hand behind his back, teasing the white-haired and black-billed parrot on the shelf. Since the Fushe published the "Public Denunciation of a Treasonist in the Legacy Capital" there had been very few scholars to mix with him. Now that from the back view this scholar didn't look familiar to him, Ruan Dacheng became even more suspicious. He wanted to see more clearly, but, afraid of being noticed by the visitor, gave a light cough and stepped into the room.

Hearing the sound, Zhang Dai looked back and beamed with a big smile.

"Elder Yuan, you have an interesting parrot!" he said cheerfully.

"Oh, it's Brother Zhang!" Ruan Dacheng greeted the guest warmly. When he saw Zhang Dai's face clearly, he felt it familiar but couldn't remember where he had seen it before. The guest appeared quite at home, not like a stranger at all. Ruan Dacheng didn't want to give the impression of being forgetful, so he pretended to know him well. After exchanging pleasantries with the guest, Ruan Dacheng invited him to a seat, hoping to remember him by talking to him.

"Elder Yuan, your parrot reminds me of Ningliao, which we used to keep," Zhang Dai said cheerfully while taking over the tea from the servant. "Ningliao—maybe you've never heard of it. No wonder. It was a rare bird that my family kept twenty years ago. It was as small as a pigeon, had the dark feathers of a starling and could talk like a human. At that time, I was a young child. When my grandma called out to a maid or concubine, it echoed, 'So-and-so, Old Lady wants you!' When a guest came, it said, 'Old Lady, the guest is here. Tea, please!' Its voice was clear and fully intelligible. Later, we had a bride in the house. The bride always slept too much. The bird called out to her every morning, 'Bride, it's daytime, get up! Old Lady calls. Get up!' If she didn't get up, it would swear at her, saying, 'Bride, stinky whore, slut!' The bride hated the bird very much and secretly mixed

在饲粮里掺了药，把这鸟毒死了！”

张岱说着，语调低沉下去，神气之间，大有不胜惋悼之意。阮大铖却莫名其妙，不知道他喋喋不休地说这些不相干的事情做什么。只听张岱又说：

“世间之异物，也着实不少。譬如晚生外祖家那头白骡，取名‘雪精’的，也妙不可言。此骡四蹄都白，日行二百里，唯服晚生一人驱策。旁人想骑它，必定又踢又咬。最奇的，是此骡之尿，可治噎嗝之疾，比仙丹还灵……”

正说着，只见小厮捧出一个托盘来，上面盛着三碟点心：一碟月饼，一碟山楂糖，还有一碟是带骨鲍螺。张岱的眼睛顿时亮了，他忘了说话，直勾勾地盯着，喉核儿一下一下地动，分明是在咽馋涎。等点心一摆到方几上，他就老实不客气地抓起筷子，先夹了一块月饼送进嘴里，嚼了几下，“咕嗞”一声吞了下去。他点点头，又去夹带骨鲍螺。

阮大铖冷眼瞅着。现在他已经断定，此人纵然见过，也无非一面之交。根据他的经验，这种不速之客，越是一坐下来就东拉西扯地胡诌，越是有所谋而来。像混几两银子使啦，骗顿酒饭吃啦，诸如此类，因为不好意思立即提出，就没话找话。别看这个姓张的穿得还蛮光鲜，可是如今肚子饿得咕咕响，外头还硬撑着穿绸着缎的穷酸有的是！这样一想，阮大铖原先的敬畏之意就顿时大减，打心里生出一种轻蔑之情。不过，他倒不打算把张岱轰走，因为此人好歹也算个秀才，如今穷极来投，不妨趁此收为己用。可是张岱接下来说的那句话，却又使阮大铖动了气。

在这当儿，张岱已经一连吃了两只带骨鲍螺。只见他皱起眉

poison into the bird food and killed it!"

Zhang Dai's tone saddened as he spoke with a mournful expression. Ruan Dacheng was puzzled, not knowing why he babbled on about something so irrelevant.

Zhang Dai continued, "There're many amazing creatures in the world. For another example, the white mule in my maternal grandfather's house. Its name is Snow Spirit. It's also an unusual creature. All its hoofs are white, and it can travel two hundred *li* a day. Interestingly, it only allows me to ride it. When others try to ride it, it will kick and bite them. The most amazing thing about it is that its urine can be used to treat hiccups, and it's more effective than an elixir ..."

While he was talking, the servant brought over a tray with three plates of snacks: a sliced moon cake, hawthorn candy, and abalone steaks. Zhang Dai's eyes suddenly lit up. He stopped speaking, stared straight at the plates, and his Adam's apple moved, obviously swallowing his saliva. As soon as the snacks were placed on the square table, he grabbed his chopsticks, took a slice of the moon cake, put it in his mouth, chewed a few times, and gulped it. Then, he nodded his head and reached for the abalone steaks.

Ruan Dacheng looked at him coldly. Now he had concluded that even if he had met this man before, he was just a passing acquaintance. According to his experience, the more nonsense this kind of uninvited guest talked after sitting down, the more dubious his motive, which might be to ask for a meal, a few taels of silver, or the like. They talked and talked because they dared not directly say it. This Mr. Zhang was decently dressed, but Ruan Dacheng had seen too many men wearing silk and satin outside actually had empty stomachs. Thus thinking, Ruan Dacheng's original feeling of respect was replaced with a feeling of contempt. Despite that, he didn't want to drive Zhang Dai away, because this man was a scholar after all and might be of some use now that he had come to seek shelter. However, what Zhang Dai said next greatly angered him.

By now, Zhang Dai had eaten two abalone steaks. Knitting his

头，摇头叹气说：“到底不是出于姑苏过小拙之手的，滋味便差得太远！”

阮大铖斜眼瞧着张岱那副馋猫似的模样儿，心想：“哼，我好意款待你，你白吃了不算，还拿腔作势地不领情，却想吓唬谁来！”于是，他翻了翻白眼，挖苦地说：“姑苏过小拙家的带骨鲍螺，学生也曾尝来，同是乳酪所制，却难得美味如斯，不知以何法为之，方能至此？仁兄既是食家，必知其妙，可以见告么？”

张岱摇摇头，一本正经地说：“此点在晚生亦是老大疑问。因晚生家中养有乳牛一头，也喜自制乳酪，曾试以种种办法，始终有所未及。也曾叩问过小拙，唯是他吞吞吐吐，只拿些虚文支应。后来晚生急了，拿出十两银子朝桌上一掷，才买下他一句话，说是要用蔗浆霜掺和。唯是回家一试，依旧不成。听说，他制酪时甚是诡秘，锁入密室，还用纸封门，虽父子亦不轻传。”

阮大铖见他说得煞有介事，倒也有点意外，只好随口说道：“原来仁兄精于易牙之道，难怪寒舍这寻常之物，难入法眼了！”

“啊，不敢！”张岱似乎被搔着痒处，顿时变得眉飞色舞，“晚生平生无他嗜好，于各地特产却搜求不遗余力。如北京之苹婆果、黄鼠马牙松，山东之羊肚菜、秋白梨、文官果、甜子，福建之福橘、福橘饼、牛皮糖、红腐乳，江西之青根、丰城脯，山西之天花菜，苏州之带骨鲍螺、山楂丁、山楂糕、松子糖、白圆、橄榄脯，嘉兴之马交鱼脯、陶庄黄雀，南京之套樱桃、桃门枣、地栗团、莴

brows and shaking his head, he sighed, “It’s not from the hands of Guo Xiaozhuo in Gusu after all. The taste is far from right.”

Ruan Dacheng squinted at Zhang Dai, who was like a greedy cat, and thought, “Hmph, I treat you with kindness, but you’re so ungrateful after eating it free. To hell with your presumptuousness!” So, he rolled his eyes and said sarcastically, “I’ve also had abalone steaks at Guo Xiaozhuo’s restaurant. It’s also made of cheese, but it tastes so much better. I wonder how they make it. Since you are a gourmet, you must know the secrets. Can you tell me?”

Zhang Dai shook his head and said seriously, “I also wonder how they make it. Since we have a milk cow in our house, we often make cheese at home. We’ve experimented with various methods without success. Once, I went to ask Guo Xiaozhuo, but he was reluctant to tell me and just said something irrelevant. I was annoyed and put ten taels of silver on the table. Then he opened his mouth and said, ‘It must be mixed with powdered cane sugar.’ I went home and tried. There was still no success. It’s said that his cheese-making process takes place in a locked secret room with a security seal on the door. He hasn’t even taught the skill to his sons.”

Surprised at his seriousness, Ruan Dacheng said, “Oh, I see. You’re a great chef. An ordinary food like this of course won’t impress you.”

That hit the spot. Zhang Dai suddenly became elated. “Well, I dare not say that,” he said. “I have no other hobbies than visiting places and searching for special delicacies, like preserved apples and young yellow horse-dung naga cabbage in Beijing, sheep tripe mushrooms, white autumn pears, civil official fruit, and sweet plums in Shandong, Fu citrons, Fu citron cakes, ox skin candy bars, and red fermented bean curd in Fujian, green roots and Fengcheng dried fruit in Jiangxi, broccoli in Shanxi, abalone steaks, hawthorn sticks, hawthorn pudding, pine nut candy bars, white ball mushrooms, dried olives in Suzhou, preserved mackerel in Jiaxing, yellow orioles in Taozhuang, bush cherries, Taomen jujubes, water chestnut balls, lettuce balls, hawthorn candy bars in Nanjing, and, in Hangzhou,

笋团、山楂糖，杭州之……”

他一口气地数下来，把阮大铖听得目瞪口呆，其中有许多名目阮大铖不但没有见过，甚至没有听说过。他蓦地想起：曾经听人说，复社有个张宗子，是天字第一号的馋嘴之徒，莫非便是此人？

“啊，请恕学生健忘，”阮大铖连忙打断张岱的话，问，“不知仁兄的雅篆，可是叫宗子的么？”

张岱怔了一下，说：“不敢，正是晚生。”

他说话的声音不大，态度也很温和。可是阮大铖的脸色立即变了。他飞快地朝门外溜了一眼，当看清没有别的陌生人时，就沉下了脸。

“你——来做什么？”他恶狠狠地问。

“圆老不必吃惊！”张岱连忙说，“晚生此来别无他意，只是奉了吴次尾、陈定生二位社兄之命，来向圆老借戏而已。”

“什么？”

“借戏！就是……”看见对方似乎仍不明白，张岱就扬起袖子，扭转腰身，做了一个舞台动作，“哎，这个！”

“啊，借戏？”阮大铖陡地睁大了乌溜溜的眼睛，“你们——向我？”

“对！对！只因眼下秋试已毕，适逢中秋佳节，敝社诸同人宴集于桃叶河房之内，言及圆老近有《燕子笺》新剧，无不渴欲一睹为快。因命晚生前来，与圆老面商，欲借贵家班前去搬演一夕……”张岱毕恭毕敬地拱着手。看见阮大铖摇着头，慢慢地揉搓着大胡子，一声不响，他就露出焦急、恳求的神色，把刚刚说过的话，又一字不漏地重复了一遍，然后深深作下揖去：“不情

there're ..."

He counted all the delicacies in one breath, to the amazement of Ruan Dacheng, who hadn't seen or even heard of many of them. At this point, Ruan Dacheng suddenly remembered that someone had said that there was a Fushe member called Zhang Zongzi, who was the number one glutton in the world. It might be this man in front of him.

"Please forgive my forgetfulness," Ruan Dacheng interrupted Zhang Dai and asked. "I don't remember your style name. Is it Zongzi?"

Zhang Dai paused for in instant and then said in a low and humble voice, "Yes, it is."

Ruan Dacheng's expression changed immediately. He glanced at the door, and when he saw that there were no other strangers, his face sank.

"What are you—what do you want to do here?" he asked sternly.

"Elder Yuan, don't be surprised," Zhang Dai said hurriedly. "I have no other intentions than to borrow your play on the order of Wu Ciwei and Chen Dingsheng."

"What?"

"To borrow your play. It's ..." Seeing that the host still didn't understand, Zhang Dai raised his sleeves, twisted his waist, and made a stage move. "Your play, like this."

"Oh? You come to borrow my play?" Ruan Dacheng suddenly widened his dark eyes. "You chaps—from me?"

"Exactly! Because the autumn examination is over and it's the Mid-Autumn Festival, the comrades of our society is having a banquet in the Peach Leaves Riverhouse. Someone spoke of your new play *Letter from Swallow*, and we're all eager to see it. So, they sent me here to borrow your cast and crew for a performance there ..." Zhang Dai clasped his hands respectfully. Seeing Ruan Dacheng shaking his head and slowly rubbing his beard with his fingers without saying a word, Zhang Dai was worried with a beseeching look. He repeated what he had just said word by word, and then gave a deep bow, saying, "I know we're asking too much, but, if you can kindly agree, we all

之请，尚祈俯允！”

## 当众允诺

“定生，你说，阮胡子他肯借戏给我们么？”侯方域扭过头来，怀疑地问。

陈贞慧微微一笑，显得胸有成竹：“若是别人去借呢，兴许当场闹翻也难说。如今宗子肯去，我瞧准成。他惯会认低服小，又是那一副无可无不可的脾气，这一层，你我都不及他！”

“可你瞧，月亮都升起来了！”侯方域不耐烦地说。

陈贞慧回头望去，东窗外，沉沉的夜色已变得有点透明，青苍色的雾霭浮荡着。远处的城墙上，那星星点点、因戒严而增设的灯笼和火把暗淡了下去，一轮银盘样的满月正从女墙上露出头来，几片薄薄的云彩，边缘上镶着银白色的光辉，冉冉地浮动着……

陈贞慧的目光不无忧虑地在城墙上停留了一下，随即回过头来：“别急别急，我算准了。阮胡子听说是我们借戏，别说一晚，便是十晚，他也会满口应承哩！快去想你的诗吧，看轮到你了！”

“这有何难，我早就有了！”侯方域说着，踱了开去。

他一直走到水阁上首，那里并排摆着三张八仙桌、几副笔墨砚纸，许多人围在那里。有的正皱着眉头默想出神，有的在胸有成竹地执笔挥写，还有的则在咿咿唔唔地吟哦推敲……这也是顾眉出的主意，要大家都来给董小宛写诗捧场。那已经写好的一二十首诗，就一张接一张地贴在墙上，供大家浏览品评。这当中，顶活跃的要数梅朗中和冯班。他们如鱼得水似的在人缝中钻来钻去，两双闪闪发光、因兴奋而变得出奇相似的眼睛，前后左

will be obliged to you."

## A Promise in Public

Hou Fangyu turned his head and asked doubtfully, "Dingsheng, do you think Big Beard Ruan will lend us his drama team?"

Chen Zhenhui smiled slightly, looking confident. "If someone else had gone, there would probably be a fall-out on the spot. Now that Zongzi has accepted the task, I think it will be done. He can lower himself and meanwhile doesn't take things too seriously. For such things, we're not as good as he."

"But you see, the moon has risen," Hou Fangyu said impatiently.

Chen Zhenhui looked back, and outside the east window, the dark night had become a tad transparent, and a blue mist was floating in the air. On the city wall in the distance, the lanterns and torches installed for the curfew dimmed. A full moon in the shape of a silver plate was emerging from the fortress wall. A few thin clouds with silver linings sailed slowly across the sky ...

Chen Zhenhui's gaze rested on the city wall for a while, not without worry, and then he turned around, "Don't worry! I'm sure Big Beard Ruan will agree immediately upon hearing it's us who want to borrow his drama group whether we want it for one night or ten nights. Go compose your poem. It'll be your turn soon."

"That's not a problem. I already have it," Hou Fangyu said. Then he paced away.

He went all the way to the top of the Water Pavilion, where were three *baxian* tables with a few writing sets, and many people gathered around them. Some were contemplating with knitted brows, some were writing with confidence, and some read aloud to see if their composition sounded right ... It was also Gu Mei's idea. She had asked them to write poems to create the right vibe for Dong Xiaowan. Twenty poems were already completed and posted to the wall to be read and commented on. Of all the participants, the most active ones were Mei Langzhong and Feng Ban. Like ducks taking to water, they darted to and fro through the gaps of the crowd, their eyes shimmering

右地忙个不停，一会儿对这首诗称赞几句，一会儿又对另一首诗大摇其头，再一转身又热心地替别人推敲斟酌起句子来，甚至干脆一把夺过笔，把人家的稿子改得一塌糊涂。

“嗯，这首诗好！好就好在纯乎唐音，绝无半点江西派臭脚丫子气！”冯班站在一首诗前，大声称赞说。

梅朗中撇撇嘴：“纯乎唐音，谈何容易！只这‘雄浑高华’四字，今人便是学足一生，此境也永不能到。何况这诗虽刻意求工，终伤绮靡，结句更已近隐僻。老兄如此推许，只怕有些儿走眼哩！”

“什么，我老冯也会走眼？”冯班顿时瞪大了眼睛，“此诗决无绮靡、隐僻之处，即便是绮靡、隐僻，也不定就不是唐音！我问你，温飞卿绮靡不绮靡？李义山隐僻不隐僻，是不是唐音？”

“那是晚唐，而非盛唐！”

“啊，盛唐是唐，晚唐难道就不是唐？”

“虽则是唐，唯是唐音却应以盛唐为正格！”

“既然是唐，便是唐音！”

“终非正格！”

“也是唐音！”

他们你一言我一语，面红耳赤，各不相让，越争越激烈，弄得大家头昏脑涨，只好都停下来，怔怔地瞧着他们。顾眉见了，不禁大皱眉头。她看见侯方域走近，就连忙朝他打眼色。

侯方域却装作没看见。不过，他也知道梅朗中是有名的“诗痴”，而冯班却是天字第一号的“诗狂”。这两个宝贝凑在一块，如果无人制止，只怕吵到天亮也停不下来，于是便分开人丛，走

and strangely looking alike because they shared the same excitement. They now praised a poem, now shook their heads at another one, and now turned around to enthusiastically give suggestions to a comrade. Sometimes, they even grabbed the brush pen and scribbled something on someone else's manuscript.

"Mm-hmm, this poem is really good! It's pure *tangyin*, the sound of Tang, and absolutely has no stench of the Jiangxi School of Poetry," said Feng Ban approvingly, who stood in front of a poem.

Mei Langzhong pouted, "Pure *tangyin*? It's easier said than done! A modern man can never reach the level of 'rigor, elegance, grace, and beauty' in a lifetime, no matter how hard he tries. Besides, although this poem aims at it, it ends up being too ostentatious. The last line is abstruse. Your praise shows your misjudgment, brother."

"What? I've misjudged the poem?" Feng Ban suddenly widened his eyes. "This poem is by no means ostentatious or abstruse. Even if it is, it may still be Tang dynasty style! Let me ask you, isn't Wen Feiqing ostentatious? Isn't Li Yishan abstruse? Aren't they Tang dynasty poets?"

"It's late Tang, not the heyday of Tang!"

"Well, the heyday of Tang is Tang, but isn't late Tang also Tang?"

"Although it is, the sound of Tang typically refers to the style of poets in the heyday of the Tang dynasty as the right form!"

"Since it's Tang, their poems are the sound of Tang!"

"After all, those poems are not typical of Tang style!"

"But they *are* the sound of Tang too!"

They argued, their faces red from ear to ear, and neither giving in to the other. They argued and argued until everyone was annoyed and stopped to look at them. Gu Mei frowned. When she saw Hou Fangyu approaching, she winked at him.

Hou Fangyu pretended not to see it. He knew that Mei Langzhong was a famous poetry addict and Feng Ban was the number one poetry maniac. Now that these two lovely men had met, they probably would not stop arguing until dawn, so Hou Fangyu separated the crowd and walked over. He read the poem that had caused the controversy. It

过去，先瞧一瞧那首引起争论的诗。原来是一首七绝：

温柔婉丽复冰清，
水入山塘便有情。
微雨凭君舟上望，
小帘人影正盈盈。

下面的落款是“金沙吕兆龙”。

侯方域心想：“这诗小有情致，却非唐音，但并不见得绮靡、隐僻。可笑他们却乱争一气。这一痴一狂，只怕已是入魔了！”于是，他大声说：“你们都不要争！等我写出一首来，也让你们瞧瞧是唐音不是唐音！”

说完，他就大步走近桌子，拿起一支兼毫湖笔，把已经酝酿好的一首诗，龙飞凤舞地写了出来：

水阁金荷斗日曛，
双凫惊起隔花闻。
北涛南走三千里，
不解飘零哪识君。

turned out to be a seven-character four liner:

*wēn róu wǎn lì fù bīng qīng,*
*shuǐ rù shān táng biàn yǒu qíng.*
*wēi yǔ píng jūn zhōu shàng wàng,*
*xiǎo lián rén yǐng zhèng yíng yíng.*
which means:
*Gentle and graceful, pure and clear,*
*The river enters the Mountain Lake for the sake of love.*
*In the light rain, the beau looks across the water from his boat, and sees the moving shadow of his love on the small curtain.*

At the end of the poem was an inscription: "Written by Lü Zhaolong from Jinsha."

Hou Fangyu thought to himself, "This poem is nicely written, but it's not the sound of Tang, and it's not ostentatious or abstruse, either. It's ridiculous that they're fighting over meaningless claims. An addict vs. a maniac. They're both possessed by demons, I suppose." So, he said in a loud voice, "Stop arguing! Let me write one and tell me if it's the sound of Tang or not."

With that, he strode over to the desk, picked up a Huzhou brush pen made of a mixture of wolf hair and lamb hair, and quickly wrote out a poem that he had already hatched in his mind:

*shuǐ gé jīn hé dòu rì xūn,*
*shuāng fú jīng qǐ gé huā wén.*
*běi tāo nán zǒu sān qiān lǐ,*
*bù jiě piāo líng nǎ shí jūn.*
which means:
*The golden lotus at the Water Pavilion fights the setting sun.*
*Two startled mallards flit across the flowers.*
*The waves from the north have traveled three thousand miles south.*
*Not knowing the life of wandering, how can one understand you?*

侯方域刚刚抛下笔，站在旁边瞧着的社友们已经哄然叫起好来。侯方域笑了一笑，回头瞅着两个争吵的人，意思是说：“怎么样啊，这可是唐音！”

两个争吵者也显然被这诗的不同凡响吸引住了。冯班一声不响，狂热的脸上现出茫然若失的神情；梅朗中则用贪婪的目光死盯着诗笺，“啊，朝宗，真有你的！”他嫉妒地喃喃说。

这当儿，几个社友已经把坐在一边的冒襄和董小宛拖了过来。

“辟疆，你快来瞧——‘北涛南走三千里，不解飘零哪识君！’朝宗这诗，可是把你俩一笔儿写出来了哩！”一个社友兴冲冲地叫。

“是啊，宛娘若不因飘零，便不会识得辟疆；但既识了辟疆，从此便不必飘零了！妙！”另一个摇头晃脑地说。

“可别放过了‘不解’二字！”有人高声指出，“唯宛娘深解飘零之苦，是以对辟疆一往情深！若不解飘零之苦，哪得如此情深？而情既愈深，则自必愈欲早脱飘零之苦。区区二字，已把宛娘的心事和盘托出，这便是‘诗眼’了！”

“辟疆，莫要辜负了宛娘生死相随之志啊！”几个声音同时敦促说。

“我们写了这许多诗，如今也该辟疆来和一首了！”又一个声音提议。

“对，对！”大家同声附和。

冒襄没有立即作声。自从同董小宛来到水阁之后，他一直很少说话。虽然顾眉那一番话，确实给他指出了一个可行的办法，

When Hou Fangyu dropped his brush pen, and the Fushe comrades who were standing beside him wowed. He smiled and looked back at the two quarrelling men, meaning, "How is it? Is it sound of Tang?"

The two men who had been arguing were obviously attracted by the unusual charm of the poem. Feng Ban was silent, with a look of loss on his previously fervent face. Mei Langzhong stared at the poem with envious eyes. "Chaozong, you're really good, man!" He mumbled jealously.

At this moment, a few Fushe comrades dragged Mao Xiang and Dong Xiaowan to the desk from where they sat.

"Pijiang, come and have a look! 'The waves from the north have traveled three thousand miles south. Not knowing the life of wandering, how can one understand you?' Chaozong has brought the two of you together in one stroke!" someone said.

"Yeah, if Xiaowan hadn't had a life of wandering, she wouldn't have known Pijiang; but once she knew Pijiang, she wouldn't have to wander from now on! It's a wonderful poem," said another man, rocking his head.

"Don't let go of the two words *bù jiě*," someone said in a loud voice, pointing at the two words meaning "not understanding." "Xiaowan understands deeply the pain of wandering in loneliness, so she has a deep love for Pijiang! Without an understanding of the pain of wandering in loneliness, how can she have such a deep love for Pijiang? The deeper the love gets, the stronger the desire to get rid of the misery of wandering. All Xiaowan's thoughts are captured in these two syllables, which are the eyes of the poem!"

"Pijiang, don't let down the girl who wants to follow you in life and death," several voices spoke in unison.

"We've written enough poems, and now it's time for Pijiang to share one," another voice proposed.

"Yes, yes!" everyone echoed.

Mao Xiang didn't respond immediately. Since he came to the Water Pavilion with Dong Xiaowan, he had seldom spoken. Although

来解决由于经济拮据所面临的困难，可是他仍然拿不定主意是否这样做，尤其拿不定主意娶不娶董小宛。然而，当他来到水阁之后，眼前的气氛却使他吃惊了。社友们上自吴应箕、陈贞慧，下至一般同人，都异口同声地推许董小宛，夸奖她不仅色艺无双，而且品格超群，是风尘中一位极难得的奇女子。他们尤其对董小宛不避艰险，千辛万苦地到南京来寻冒襄这一行动赞不绝口，认为能获得这样一位女子的心，是冒襄的莫大福气。接着，大家就一窝蜂地题诗赠句替董小宛捧场，鼓励她不怕挫折，追求到底。这一切，都使冒襄感到有点意外。他原以为，在名士圈子中，董小宛的身价，无论如何也比不上陈圆圆。他既然失去了陈圆圆，如果退而求其次，娶董小宛的话，难免会为人所笑。但现在看起来，情况并非如他所料的那样。经过了这次反复和波折之后，冒襄也渐渐看清了，董小宛有不少好的品质，恰恰是陈圆圆所欠缺的。而且，事情已经到了这一步，看来如果自己仍执意不允，就显得太过褊狭和无情，不仅多少有点对不起董小宛，而且还会大大地扫了社友们的兴。万一董小宛伤心绝望之余，干出诸如自寻短见一类的傻事来——这是很可能的——那么就很难得到社会上的谅解，自己的声誉也势必会受到影响。这样一想，冒襄就感到一种压力。这是一种柔软的，然而坚韧的压力，就像一张网，而自己则成了网中的一条鱼。他似乎能够逃脱，但事实上却没法逃脱……

“哎，冒公子，你倒是快写呀！我们都等着瞧哩！”一个女人清脆的嗓音在耳边响起。冒襄一回头，发现顾眉那双带笑的、大有深意的眼睛，正在很近的地方紧盯着他。

“嗯，一切都是命中注定！”冒襄觉得心里有一个声音这样

Gu Mei's suggestion did point out a feasible solution to the financial issue, he was still undecided as to whether he really wanted to do so, especially whether to marry Dong Xiaowan at all. However, when he came to the Water Pavilion, the atmosphere surprised him. The Fushe comrades, from Wu Yingji and Chen Zhenhui to the less familiar ones, all praised Dong Xiaowan unanimously, saying such a woman was very hard to find among the courtesans, with her unparalleled beauty and outstanding character. They especially praised Dong Xiaowan for going through all the hardships and dangers to be united with him in Nanjing, believing that it was a great blessing for him to have won the heart of such a woman. Then, they swarmed to the desks to write poems in support of Dong Xiaowan, encouraging her to be undaunted by the setbacks and persist to the end. It really surprised him. He had thought that in the eyes of his scholar friends, Dong Xiaowan was not as desirable as Chen Yuanyuan and if he married Dong Xiaowan as a substitute for Chen Yuanyuan, they would laugh at him. But now it seemed that things were not like what he had thought. After all the twists and turns, Mao Xiang gradually realized that Dong Xiaowan had many good qualities that were lacking in Chen Yuanyuan. Moreover, since things had come to such a state that if he continued to turn her down it would seem too cruel and heartless, and not fair to Dong Xiaowan either, and besides, it would also disappoint his Fushe comrades, who were so enthusiastic. Should Dong Xiaowan do something stupid in sadness and despair such as committing suicide—this kind of thing did happen—it would be difficult for him to be pardoned by public opinion, and his reputation would inevitably be damaged. Thinking of that, Mao Xiang felt a pressure. It was a soft yet tenacious pressure, like an invisible net, and he was a fish caught in that net. He seemed to be able to escape, but in fact he couldn't ...

"Hey, Mr. Mao, please write your poem! We're all waiting to read it!" A woman's crisp voice sounded in his ear. Mao Xiang turned around and saw Gu Mei's smiling and meaningful eyes were staring at him from a very close distance.

"Well, it's all destiny." A voice spoke in Mao Xiang's head. Then,

说。于是，他点点头，拿起笔，沉吟片刻，慢慢地在诗笺上写出了这样几句：

白门柳色向江分，
一棹烟波溅练裙。
莫道啼鹃啼不歇，
皋云犹得似巫云。

他一边在写，梅朗中就在一边大声地读出来，所以不仅站在旁边的人瞧得清楚，站得稍远的人也都听到了。冒襄刚写完，大家就不约而同地欢呼起来：

“好了好了，辟疆已经答应了！”

“‘皋云犹得似巫云’！就是说，今后辟疆和宛娘的巫山阳台之会，要移到如皋去了。好句，妙句！”

“喂，这‘皋云’可有出典？”

“老兄何其健忘——‘飞云冉冉蘅皋暮’，便是贺方回《青玉案》里的一句。辟疆移用于此，他又家在如皋，正是一语双关哩！”

“哎，可惜今日不曾请得柳麻子来！”

“怎么？”

“他惯喜说什么时事书。今日这‘众名士大宴秦淮河，冒公子新题巫山咏’便是绝好的一个关目了。”

he nodded his head, picked up the brush pen, pondered for a moment, and slowly wrote the following lines on the writing paper:

*bái mén liǔ sè xiàng jiāng fěn,*
*yī zhào yān bō jiàn liàn qún.*
*mò dào tí juān tí bù xiē,*
*gāo yún yóu dé shì wū yún.*
Which means:
*Lines of willows at the White Gate part at the riverside,*
*A white skirt stands on a boat amid the splashing misty water.*
*A cuckoo cuckoos nonstop.*
*The cloud of Gao is the cloud of the Wushan Mountain.*①

Since Mei Langzhong read every word out loud as Mao Xiang wrote, the ones who couldn't see it also knew what he was writing. As soon as Mao Xiang finished, all those present cheered in unison:

"Hooray! Pijiang has agreed!"

" 'The cloud of Gao is the cloud of the Wushan Mountain' means that in the future, Pijiang and Xiaowan's conjugal union at the Sun Terrace of the blissful Wushan Mountain will find a permanent home in Rugao. It's a good line indeed!"

"Hey, is *gāo yún*, 'the cloud of Gao', a literary allusion?"

"How forgetful you are! 'fēi yún rǎn rǎn héng gāo mù', the clouds are sailing in the evening twilight, is a line from He Fangyu's 'The Green Jade Bowl'. Pijiang lives in Rugao, so it's a pun here."

"What a shame! Mr. Pockmarks has not been invited here today."

"Why do you say so?"

"He loves to tell real stories on the stage. If he were here today, he would have another story to perform: 'Famous scholars feast on the Qinhuai River and Mr. Mao composes a new poem about his Wushan Mountain romance.'"

---

① The Wushan Mountain or the Wushan Mountain cloud and rain is a metaphor for sexual intercourse.

“那么，其中自然非说到老兄不可啰？”

“老兄何必取笑。你倒说说，这秦淮河上若然少了我辈，又安得有如许风流！”

“哈哈哈哈！”

“快，快拿酒来！”一个洪亮的声音盖过了愉快的逗乐，那是冒襄的拜盟兄弟陈梁。很快地，酒拿来了。乱纷纷当中，冒襄只觉得陈梁把一只酒杯塞在自己的手里，另一个人端着酒壶把它斟满。

“你们两个先饮个交杯儿！咦，小宛，快过来啊，还害羞什么！”那是顾眉得意的嗓音。

直到这时，冒襄才忽然想起：“是啊，我怎么忘了小宛？现在，她自然该高兴了，只不知是什么模样？”他不禁用眼睛寻找着，随即发现董小宛就站在他左边不远的地方，手里也端着一杯酒。不过，出乎冒襄的意料，她并不是在笑，也没有显得怎么激动。她平静地站着，目不转睛地瞅着冒襄，那澄澈的、略带忧伤的大眼睛仿佛在问：“你这一次是真心的么？不会再变了么？可是，我却有点担心，真的，担心……”

## 借戏骂奸

陈贞慧的估计不错，在酒宴快要开始的时候，张岱终于带着阮大铖家的戏班子和全副行头回到了桃叶河房。他一边用手帕拭着额上的汗，一边兴冲冲地向陈贞慧报告他如何在阮大铖家吃了月饼、带骨鲍螺和山楂糖，如何大谈各地土特产，把阮大铖听得一怔一怔的。当他提出借戏时，阮大铖如何吃惊，不敢相信，后来又怎样高兴得眉开眼笑，手舞足蹈。

"Then, naturally, he'll mention you in the story performance, brother."

"Don't make fun of me, brother. But honestly, without us, the Qinhuai River wouldn't have been so romantic a place!"

"Haha, haha!"

"Hurry, bring the wine!" A loud voice drowned out the pleasant amusement. It was Chen Liang, Mao Xiang's sworn brother. Soon, the wine was brought. Amid the chaos, Mao Xiang found that Chen Liang had slipped a wine cup into his hand, and another man filled it with a wine decanter.

"You two do a lovers' crossed-cups first! Hey, Xiaowan, come here, why are you so shy?" It was Gu Mei's prideful voice.

That reminded Mao Xiang of Xiaowan. He thought, "Yeah, why have I forgotten Xiaowan? Now, she should be happy, but I'm wondering what she looks like now." He couldn't help but search for her with his eyes, and then found Dong Xiaowan standing a few steps to the left. She was also holding a cup of wine in her hand. However, unlike what he had expected, she was not smiling, nor did she appear excited. She stood placidly, staring at Mao Xiang, as if her clear, melancholy eyes were asking, "Are you serious this time? Are you going to change your mind again? I'm still worried. Really, I'm worried that ..."

## Damning the Playwright

Chen Zhenhui was right. When the banquet was about to start, Zhang Dai finally returned to Peach Leaves with Ruan Dacheng's drama team and all the costumes and props. While wiping the sweat on his forehead with a handkerchief, he excitedly reported to Chen Zhenhui how he ate a moon cake, abalone steaks, and hawthorn candy bars at Ruan Dacheng's residence, and how he talked about local specialties across the country, how Ruan Dacheng was agape with curiosity, and, when he put forward his request to borrow the drama team, how Ruan Dacheng was first overcome with disbelief and then elated with pride.

“啊哟，定生，你要是亲眼看见老阮那巴结劲儿才好哩！又打拱又作揖，就差没摇尾巴罢咧。他一直把我送出大门外，还拉着手，再三嘱我有空常去玩儿，亲热得什么似的！”

陈贞慧笑了笑，说：“辛苦你了，宗子，快坐下歇歇，喝杯茶！”

他们说话的当儿，其余的社友在一旁听着，脸上都露出惊讶、困惑的神情。他们大多数人事先并不知情，这时都弄不明白，陈贞慧怎么会想出这样的怪念头？为什么放着许多戏班子不请，偏偏去借阮胡子的家班？他们还担心这样做会不会引起外间的误会？会不会给阮胡子乘机拣便宜？诸如此类。但是也有人说：“久闻阮家班训练严格，演技出色，看一看也无妨！”对于这些议论，陈贞慧一概不回答，他只摆摆手，让大家少安毋躁，开桌入席。随后就打发那个捧着戏单伺候的花衣末角下去，马上排演起来。

中秋的圆月，已经升上东天。冉冉飘动着的几朵浮云，不知什么时候已经消散了。清明的月色从天幕上倾泻下来，照亮了香风十里的秦淮河；两岸河房临水的露台上，坐满了饮酒赏月的人们，快活的笑声、细碎的谈话声和悠扬的乐曲声在夜风中回荡着；河道上，张灯结彩的游船来来往往，每当柔橹摇过，灯光和月色的倒影就像蛇一般在碧滢滢的水面蜿蜒跃动起来……尽管江北一带的战事还处于胶着的状态，南京城也尚未解除戒严，可是耽于逸乐的人们，仍旧不愿放弃这一年一度的好时光，何况又是象征团圆的中秋节。人们嘴上不说，心里不免都在想：“团

"Dingsheng, I wish you had been there and seen how ingratiating he was! He bowed and held his hands toward me in the humblest gesture, and would have wagged his tail if he had one. He walked me to the gate and, when parting, held my hand and told me that I should visit him often, like a very good friend."

Chen Zhenhui smiled and said, "Well done, Zongzi, thank you very much for the good job. Sit down and have a cup of tea!"

The other Fushers listened with surprise and puzzlement. Most of them wondered why Chen Zhenhui had such a weird idea and why he had singled out Ruan Dacheng's while there were so many drama teams out there, afraid that in so doing they might be misunderstood by others and give Big Beard Ruan an opportunity to take advantage of them ..., but some others said, "Since it's said that Mr. Ruan's drama team is rigorously trained and super good, there's no harm to have a look." Without responding to their doubts and comments, Chen Zhenhui gestured for them to quiet down and take their seats. Then, he asked a *mojiao*① player in colorful clothes waiting aside with a menu in his hands to get the actors ready.

The full moon of the Mid-Autumn Festival had risen in the eastern sky. The few floating clouds had by now dissipated. Clear moonlight poured down from the sky, illuminating the romantic Qinhuai River. On the patios of the Riverhouses on both sides of the river sat men and women drinking and talking as they admired the moon. Joyous laughter, noisy chatter, and the melodious sound of music reverberated in the night wind. Pleasure boats with colorful lights came and went. As a boat passed by with the swinging of the soft oar, the reflections of the lights and moonlight swayed and danced like snakes on the translucent water ... Although the warfare north of the Yangtze River was still intense, and the martial law in Nanjing City hadn't been lifted yet, people indulging in pleasures were unwilling to give up this once-in-a-year opportunity for fun, not to say it was now the Mid-Autumn Festival, the annual day of reunion. "Reunion,

① *mojiao*: an old male character in a traditional Chinese play

圆，团圆，还有几年团圆的日子可过呢？还是过得一次，就算一次吧！”

因为照例要谢神，水阁上首，已经供起了两架纸马——一幅是文昌帝君像，另一幅是关圣帝君像。大家一齐起身，由吴应箕领头，排了班，在神像面前叩过头，祭献了一番，然后各自入席，照例先点了四出单折的短戏演着，待献上汤来之后，才正式上演《燕子笺》。

现在，开场的锣鼓已经打响。前排席位上，同陈梁、吕兆龙坐在一起的冒襄也停止了交谈，准备看戏。对于陈贞慧今晚的安排，冒襄虽然也感到疑惑，不过他早就听说，这《燕子笺》是阮大铖苦心经营的一本新剧，看过的人都赞不绝口，所以倒有心见识一下。

锣鼓越敲越上劲，门上帘子一动，走出来一个青衣小帽的副末。他摇摇摆摆地走到台前，开口唱起了一首〔西江月〕：

老卸名缰拘管，闲充词苑平章。春来秋去酒樽香。烂醉莫愁湖上。燕尾双乂如剪，莺歌全副偷簧。晓风残月按新腔，依旧是张绪当年景况。

reunion. How many more days of reunion like this do we have?" they thought, without saying it.

As was the custom, sacrifices were made to the gods. Two paper horses were offered respectively to the statue of the God of Literature and the statue of the God of War at the high altar of the Water Pavilion. The scholars stood up, and led by Wu Yingji, lined up, kowtowed to the statues, and said their prayers before returning to their seats. They chose four one-act plays from the menu to be performed as preludes. The main show, *Letter from Swallow*, would start when soup was served.

Gongs and drums sounded. Mao Xiang, who was sitting in the front row together with Chen Liang and Lü Zhaolong, stopped talking to watch the performance. Although Mao Xiang was also puzzled about Chen Zhenhui's arrangement tonight, knowing that *Letter from Swallow* was a new play that Ruan Dacheng had been working hard on and everyone who had watched it was full of praise, he'd like to have a look.

As the sound of gongs and drums intensified, the curtain moved, and a supporting character in a green coat and a small hat appeared. He came swayingly to the front of the stage, and sang a *xi jiang yue*[①] song:

*Now that the Old Man gets rid of the reins of fame and power,*
*He devotes his time to the art of play writing.*
*Day after day, year after year, his cup smells of sweet wine*
*And he gets drunk on the Lake of No Sorrow.*
*The swallow, whose forked tail is like a pair of scissors, and the oriole, who sings beautifully,*
*Are sources of his inspiration.*
*In the morning breeze or under the light of the waxing crescent moon,*
*He writes a new song while he himself is still like the pure-hearted Zhang Xu, who was starving because he had given away his wealth.*

---

① *xi jiang yue*, Moon of West River, is a musical score.

这支上场小曲，照例是编剧人用以说明本剧的缘起、意图。冒襄听了，心想：“虽然‘老卸名缰拘管’一句，显属说谎，其余八句也处处文饰标榜自己，总算他还不敢过于放肆。”于是，接着听下去，曲调已变成了〔汉宫春〕：

扶风才子，嫖姚后裔，霍姓都梁。挈友长安取应，为试期尚远，追欢笑，暂过平康。丹青笔，听莺扑蝶，小像写云娘。不料朱门有女，与青楼一样，窈窕相当。把春容笺咏，燕子衔将。被同侪计构，更名姓，决策勤王。二美并，麒麟高阁，走马状元郎。

按照写戏惯例，这第二首曲属于“家门”，具有提要全剧内容的作用。冒襄听了，便知道这戏大抵是写两个长得一模一样的女子，一个是青楼妓女，一个是官家小姐，由于燕子衔笺牵合，共同爱上了一个名叫霍都梁的书生。却被他的朋友——一个小人

The opening song, as was the convention, told the background and purpose of the play. After hearing it, Mao Xiang thought to himself, "Although the line 'Now that the Old Man gets rid of the reins of fame and power' is obviously a lie, and all the other lines are also intended to embellish and advertise himself, he doesn't have the audacity to be too presumptuous after all." So, he went on listening. The next song was a *han gong chun*①:

*Huo Duliang, talented young man from Fufeng, a descendant of Huo Qubing,*

*Went to Chang'an City to take the imperial examination together with a friend of his.*

*Since it was too early yet, he decided to have fun in a pleasure house in Pingkang District.*

*He made a portrait of the famous prostitute Xingyun*

*And gave it a caption "Listening to the Orioles and Chasing the Butterflies".*

*Coincidentally, Feiyun, a daughter of the Minister of Rites, looked exactly like the beautiful prostitute.*

*She sent a letter to Mr. Huo through a swallow to tell him her feelings of love.*

*After being framed by his friend, Mr. Huo served in the imperial army under a pseudonym and became a national hero.*

*The story had a happy ending: Mr. Huo regained his stolen title as zhuangyuan② and lived with both beauties happily ever after.*

As a norm in playwriting, the second song is a brief summary of the whole play, putting the plot in a nutshell. Upon hearing it, Mao Xiang understood it was about two young women who looked identical, one a prostitute, the other a young lady from a powerful family. A love triangle was formed between the two ladies and a young scholar named Huo Duliang through a letter delivered by a swallow. A friend of the young scholar was a little man and ruined the relationship, but because the young man came out number one in the imperial examination and

---

① *han gong chun,* Spring in the Han Palace, is another musical score.

② *zhuangyuan*: number one winner in the imperial examination

从中破坏，几经波折，最后由于书生勤王有功，又高中状元，结果一男二女，团圆结合，皆大欢喜。

“嗯，就关目来看——”冒襄又想，“倒还罢了。只是阮圆海此人，心术极是不端，每于戏文之内，暗藏讥诋攻讦之语，发泄其私愤。向者《春灯谜》《牟尼合》诸剧，便是显证。却是不可不防！”由于对董小宛那件事最后表明了态度，这一年多来，使冒襄困扰不安的各种个人私事，至此算是都理出了眉目。他于是又稍稍有心思来关注一下社里的事务了。他估计，陈贞慧今晚之所以特地去借这本《燕子笺》来演，十之八九也是想瞧瞧阮大铖有没有在戏中捣鬼。为着不要等到别人发现了纰漏，自己仍旧糊里糊涂，茫无所知，冒襄便摒除杂念，集中精神看起戏来。

冒襄的这种想法，坐在另一张桌子旁的陈贞慧自然是不了解的。如果知道了，他就会告诉冒襄，今天晚上他这样做，用意还要更深一些。自从发生了钱谦益企图替阮大铖开脱事件之后，陈贞慧内心的震动很大。一方面，他更加清楚地认识到，由于东林、复社的坚决斗争，阮大铖之流的阉党余孽，近几年来虽然似乎已经老实得多，不敢再嚣张妄为，但是，事实证明，他们始终没有死心，还在暗中积极活动，妄图死灰复燃。另一方面，像钱谦益这样的东林领袖，竟然不惜自毁名节，勾结朝中权贵，干出这等出卖东林、复社的无耻勾当，这也使陈贞慧于震惊之余，产生了一种深切的忧虑，一种危机感。因为很清楚，像这么一件冒天下之大不韪的勾当，如果不是已经得到社内相当一部分人士的默许和支持，钱谦益是绝不敢贸然从事的。现在，这个阴谋虽然已经被揭露和制止了，但它所造成的恶劣影响，它对社内人心所起的冲击和瓦解作用，却是不容低估的。如果不急图振拔，后果将不堪设想。正是基于这样一种担心，几个月来，陈贞慧已经同吴应箕、张自烈、侯方域、梅朗中等人分头出发，走访各地社友，做了不少坚定人心、激励斗志的工作。上个月，陈贞慧还专程到松

became a national hero in the crackdown on a rebellion, all was well that ended well, with a happy reunion of one man and two wives.

"Well, the plot is okay," Mao Xiang thought. "It's Ruan Yuanhai's motive that is doubtful. He often hides ridicule and slander and vents his personal anger in his plays. *Riddles on the Spring Lanterns*, *The Muni Pearls* are obvious examples. We must be cautious." Now that he had made up his mind on his romantic affair with Dong Xiaowan, he was somewhat relieved and relaxed, so he turned his attention to the affairs of the Fushe. He gathered that in borrowing the drama team tonight, Chen Zhenhui probably also wanted to see if Ruan Dacheng had a hidden motive in this play, so he concentrated on watching the play so that he would not be embarrassed if someone else caught the issues first.

Chen Zhenhui, who was sitting at another table, naturally didn't know what was going on in Mao Xiang's mind. If he had known it, he would have told Mao Xiang that he did this tonight with a deeper meaning. Qian Qianyi's attempt to exonerate Ruan Dacheng had greatly shocked Chen Zhenhui. On the one hand, Chen Zhenhui was now more keenly aware that the remnants of eunuch Wei Zhongxian's party, like Ruan Dacheng, hadn't given up their ambitions, although they were much quieter thanks to the efforts of the East Wood Party and the Fushe. On the other hand, in addition to the shock, he was aggrieved and deeply worried with a sense of crisis by the self-debasement of an East Wood leader like Qian Qianyi, who colluded with powerful courtiers and shamefully betrayed the East Wood Party and the Fushe. He knew that such inglorious doing, without the acquiescence and support of a great many Fushers would not have taken place. Now, the conspiracy had been exposed and stopped, but the damage had been done. Its adverse effect on the morale of the Fushers was irrevocable. If he didn't do anything to boost the spirits of the Fushers, the consequences would be great. Therefore, in the past few months, Chen Zhenhui and his friends—Wu Yingji, Zhang Zilie, Hou Fangyu, and Mei Langzhong—had respectively paid visits to other Fushers all over the River South to boost their morale. In

江走了一趟，找到了几社的领袖陈子龙、周立勋、徐孚远、李雯、彭宾等人，推心置腹地谈了几次，消除了彼此间的不少隔阂和误会。今天晚上，他特地派张岱去借阮大铖的家班到桃叶河房来演《燕子笺》，也是出于同样的考虑。刚才，他已经同吴应箕、侯方域、梅朗中、顾杲等人暗中合计好，准备借此机会狠狠揭露阮大铖一下，给社内同人敲响警钟，并激励大家的斗志。陈贞慧本来也想把这个计划告诉冒襄，但见冒襄被董小宛缠住不放，弄得昏头转向，六神无主，只好作罢。现在，因为还不到发难的时候，陈贞慧也不着急，一心一意先看戏。他发现，这本《燕子笺》虽然不外是才子佳人，小人拨弄，几经波折，终获团圆一类的套套，但编排布局却较一般传奇来得曲折复杂，遣词造句也务求绮丽华美，还运用了"飞燕"一类新奇别致的道具，再加上阮大铖的家班确实训练有素，演技不同凡响，所以依旧颇能吸引观众。董小宛、顾眉和李十娘几个，竟看得目不转睛，如痴如醉。其余的人，也都忘记了喝酒吃菜，静静地停杯观看。

现在，戏已经演到《写笺》一折。只见台上那个尚书小姐郦飞云，借故把丫环支使开去之后，便独自对那幅画着一双亲密情侣的画儿，偷偷地看一回又猜一回、猜一回又看一回，终于春情难禁、神魂颠倒地唱起来：

〔四季花〕画里遇神仙，见眉棱上，腮窝畔，风韵翩翩。天然，春罗衫子红杏褲香肩，那人偎半边。两回

the previous month, Chen Zhenhui made a special trip to Songjiang, where he met with the leaders of the Jishe such as Chen Zilong, Zhou Lixun, Xu Fuyuan, Li Wen, and Peng Bin to clear misunderstandings between them. For the same reason, he had sent Zhang Dai over and invited Ruan Dacheng's drama team to perform *Letter from Swallow* in the Peach Leaves Riverhouse. Just now, he had secretly planned with Wu Yingji, Hou Fangyu, Mei Langzhong, and Gu Gao to take this opportunity to expose Ruan Dacheng, sound the alarm to their fellow Fushers, and reboost their fighting spirit. He wanted to tell Mao Xiang about this plan, but seeing that Mao Xiang was being pestered by Dong Xiaowan and looked dazed and helpless, he had to give up. Since it was not time to launch an offensive yet, Chen Zhenhui was in no hurry. He turned his attention to the show. He found that, although *Letter from Swallow* is nothing more than the story of a talented young scholar and a beautiful woman, in this case two beautiful women, who, after some twists and turns, were finally reunited, since the plot of the play was more complicated and intriguing than most other plays of the same kind, the language was particularly beautiful, many of the props—such as a flying swallow—were novel and unique, and the drama team was indeed well-trained, the audience simply loved it. Dong Xiaowan, Gu Mei, and Li Shiniang were all fascinated by the performance. The others also stopped eating and drinking and watched attentively.

Now it was the scene of "Writing a Letter". Li Feiyun, daughter of the Minister of Rites, sends her maid away and secretly admires the picture in which two lovers are huddled together. She looks at the picture again and again and imagines the happiness they have. Finally, she becomes so overwhelmed with thoughts of love that she sings in delirium:

*[To the tune of "Flowers of Four Seasons"]*
*Here is a fairy princess in the picture.*
*Her eyes and face glow with charm.*
*She is a great beauty endowed by nature.*

眸，情万千，蝶飞锦翅，莺啼翠烟，游丝小挂双凤钿，光景在眼前。（那些要）阳台云现，纵山远水远人远，画便非远。

〔浣溪沙〕麟髓调，霜毫展。方才点笔题笺。这巢间小燕忒刁钻，蓦忽地衔去飞半天。天天未必行方便，便落在泥边水边。（那些）御沟红叶荡春烟，（只落得）飞絮浮萍一样牵。

〔柰子花〕二三春月日长天，往常时几自淹煎，那禁闲事恁般牵挽，画中人几时相见？待见，才能说与般般……

这几支曲子，不但文辞华美，而且情意缠绵。加上那个扮演郦飞云的旦角，又天然生就一副好嗓子，她用流丽悠远的昆山腔这么轻挑慢吐地唱出来，当真是千娇百媚，令听众意荡魂销。直到她把最后一个字唱完了好一会儿，大家还静静地侧着耳，追寻品味着那仿佛还在耳畔梁间萦绕摇曳的袅袅余音……

“好！”顾杲首先回过神，大声喝彩说。然后，他把长鼻子转向陈贞慧，交换了一个眼色，又怪声怪气地接着称赞：“好一

*Wearing a silk shirt, and red apricots reaching down to her scented shoulders from the trees,*

*She lies in the arms of her beau and the two stare into each other's eyes with love and passion.*

*The butterflies flutter their colorful wings.*

*The orioles chirp in the mist.*

*Thoughts of love are like the gossamers that catch the double phoenix headdress.*

*Love is real, love is earnest,*

*No mountain and no river can prevent its consummation like in the picture.*

*[To the tune of "Washing Light Fabric in the Creek"]*

*Having ground the ink, I picked up my brush pen*

*and started to write a letter to my beau.*

*This mischievous little swallow didn't want to help me at all.*

*She snatched the paper, flew around for a long time,*

*And dropped it at the waterside.*

*I was thinking to send a message to my beau*

*Only to find it floating in the moat before it was completed.*

*[To the tune of "The Jasmine Flowers"]*

*Day after day, night after night,*

*I am tormented by a longing,*

*By the thoughts of love.*

*When can I see the man in the picture?*

*And when can I meet him and tell him that I love him so? ...*

These songs were not only beautiful in language, but also intense in emotion. Sung frivolously and slowly by the *danjiao*[①] who played Li Feiyun in the metallic and melodious Kunshan accent, they cast a spell on the audience. Long after she finished the last line, they still lingered in the ears of the audience ...

"Hooray!" Gu Gao woke up and cheered loudly. Then, he turned his long nose to Chen Zhenhui, winked at him, and then said in a

---

① *danjiao*: a man or woman playing a female character

个‘画中人几时相见？待见，才能说与般般’！如此妙句，真亏他想得出来！”

“不错，”显然早有准备的梅朗中接口说，“此出直唱到这一句，那无情中之情，方始尽出。想不到可憎可厌的阮胡子，倒是一名绘风绘月的能手！”

“朗三此誉，何其太低。”侯方域一本正经地眨着眼睛，“似他这等文藻、这等才情，又岂止‘能手’而已！”

“噢，倒要请教。”梅朗中装出惊讶天真的样子。

“弟瞧此戏，非但结构奇妙，词采华赡，格局谨饬，且宾白、科诨，无不生动自然，曲曲传神，足与曲文相得益彰。时下词曲家竟喜以临川、吴江高自标榜。吴江一派且不论，若临川一派，其真能窥玉茗堂之精奥而传者，依弟之见，只怕除了这阮圆海，已无第二人了！”

“朝宗言之有理。”陈贞慧微笑地加了进来，“据弟所知，阮圆海不止词曲精妙，便是文章诗赋，也是极好的。”

“我见过他万历四十四年会试那几篇制艺，”吴应箕瓮声瓮气地说，“也算得理真法老，字字痛切。”

“喂，喂！”顾杲兴奋起来，大声说，“弟有八字之评，专道阮圆海的才情——‘文章宗匠，艺苑班头’。列位以为如何？”

陈贞慧点点头：“也还相称。不过，若再添八字，凑成四句，便更觉妥帖。”

strange voice, " 'When can I see the man in the picture? And when can I meet him and tell him that I love him so?' What wonderful lines! How can he write something so beautiful?"

"It's good indeed," said Mei Langzhong anxiously. "The feelings of frustration and helplessness culminate in this line. The hateful and spiteful Big Beard Ruan turns out to be a master in the expression of romantic feelings."

"Langsan, you're too stingy in giving your praise." Hou Fangyu said with a serious expression, blinking his eyes. "With such use of language and such skill, he's more than a master!"

"Oh? Would you please explain," Mei Langzhong said with feigned surprise and innocence.

"In my view, not only are the structure, the lyrics, and the music great, the spoken lines and the movements are good too and go perfectly with the music and the lyrics. The lyricists and music composers today vie with each other to claim to be followers of the Linchuan School and the Wujiang School. Very few get the true spirit of the Linchuan School, let alone the Wujiang School. In my humble opinion, Ruan Yuanhai is the only one who has achieved this. There is no second person."

"You're quite right, Chaozong," Chen Zhenhui cut in with a smile. "As far as I know, Ruan Yuanhai not only excels in lyrics and music but also writes good poems and essays."

"I've read his eight-legged essays written in the imperial exam in the forty-fourth year of the reign of Emperor Wanli[AD 1616]." Wu Yingji said in a low, muffled voice. "They're well crafted essays with good arguments, and every word is accurate."

"Well," Gu Gao, who became excited, said loudly. "I have an eight-word comment for Ruan Yuanhai's talent: *wén zhāng zōng jiàng, yì yuàn bān tóu* (a great master of language and a leading artist). What do you think?"

Chen Zhenhui nodded, "It's commensurate with his achievements. However, if you add eight more words and make it four phrases, it will be more accurate."

“噢？”

“我这八字便是：‘若主骚坛，可执牛耳。’”

“啊，‘文章宗匠，艺苑班头；若主骚坛，可执牛耳’——不高？”

“不高！”

“当得起？”

“当得起！”

“啊，啊，啊！哈哈哈！”他们齐声大笑起来，把戏台上那个书生霍都梁吓了一跳，差点儿没唱岔了喉。其他社友更是莫名其妙，都回过头来怔怔地瞧着他们。

“嗯，若是当真让阮圆海出来主骚坛，执牛耳，列位社兄捉摸他敢呢？不敢？”待大家笑得差不多时，陈贞慧捋着胡子，考究地问。

顾杲的目光一闪，顿时收敛起笑容：“我瞧他不敢！”

“怎么？”

“哼，他叛卖东林，投靠魏阉，认贼作父，残害忠良，那一档子猪狗不如的臭事、脏事，谁个不知，谁个不晓！除非是那不辨香臭的昏虫、屎里觅道的什么‘前辈’‘元老’，谁又会买他的账！”顾杲的声音越来越高。

“对，对！”梅朗中也跳起来，“他乖乖儿做个缩头乌龟，老老实实躲在龟窝里过日子便罢，若敢不知好歹，抛头露脸，瞧我老梅不把他那狗贼胡子捋个精光才怪哩！”他装出一副凶猛的样子，还做了一个拔胡子的手势。

“朗三兄果然勇气可嘉。”侯方域慢悠悠地转动着一只杯子，“只是你以为阮圆海必不敢出来，那又未免小觑于他了。你不见

"Oh?"

"My eight words are: *ruò zhǔ sāo tán, kě zhí niú ěr* (If poets gather at the sacrificial altar, he should be the one to hold the bull's ears). "

"Ah? A great master of language and a leading artist? Isn't it too high a praise?"

"No."

"Does he deserve it?"

"Yes, he does!"

"Hahaha! Hahaha!" They laughed so loud that the actor playing Huo Duliang on the stage was startled and almost lost his lines. The other members of the Fushe were startled too and turned around to stare at them blankly.

"Well, if Ruan Yuanhai is really invited to lead the Poets' Society, do you think he dares to accept it?" Chen Zhenhui asked when the laughing stopped, stroking his beard thoughtfully.

Gu Gao blinked his eyes and said solemnly, "I don't think he dares!"

"Why?"

"Hmph, he betrayed East Wood and joined Eunuch Wei's party, identifying himself with the evil, persecuting the good, and doing all kinds of dirty and inglorious things. Who doesn't know it? No one but some stupid worms that make their living in a dunghill and can't tell the difference between a good smell and a foul one will care to mix with him," Gu Gao said, his voice rising higher and higher.

"Yes, yes!" Mei Langzhong also jumped up. "He'd better go on living his life as a turtle with his head shrunken into his shell! If he knows no decency and comes out in public, I'll tear out all the hairs in his beard!" He feigned a ferocious expression and made a beard-pulling gesture.

"That is very brave of you, Brother Langsan," Hou Fangyu said, slowly turning a wine cup, "But you're underestimating Ruan Yuanhai by saying he doesn't dare to come. Haven't you heard that he spent ten thousand taels of silver last year trying to get Premier Zhou, through

他去年刚刚才花了一万两银子，想打通周阁老的关节，让钱牧斋替他开脱翻案？又不见上个月，他到底还是把马瑶草活动了上去？慢说是‘主骚坛、执牛耳’，只怕他还要入阁拜相呢！”

“朝宗，你未免言之过甚了吧？”许久没有说话的冒襄，忽然插嘴说。自从侯方域等人一唱一和地称赞《燕子笺》的时候起，冒襄就一直在揣摩他们这样做的用意。他十分了解这几个朋友的品性，知道他们无非是故弄玄虚，真章儿还在后头。到了他们突然反过来痛骂阮大铖，冒襄就明白了：“哼，敢情儿你们是借阮胡子来做下酒物，寻开心啊！”但他们竟把这事瞒着自己，却使冒襄有点着恼。这时，《拾笺》一折又已经演完。冒襄趁锣鼓声停下来的当儿，又说：“马瑶草不是逆案中人，自然起复，但未必阮圆海也能起复，老兄又何必危言耸听，杞人忧天！”

“不错！”冯舒慢条斯理的声音从左边的角落里传来，“便是钱牧老替阮圆海开脱之事，也只是传闻而已，未必便有真凭实据。”

“嘿嘿，”侯方域轻蔑地一笑，没有转过脸去，“已苍兄，你是钱牧老的高足，他有无此事，你尽可去叩问于他，小弟在此恕不多言。”说完，他又斜睨着冒襄，“辟疆兄以为小弟是危言耸听么？小弟却担心老兄近日做了桃源中人，便忘却了世事哟！”

冒襄被当面揶揄，脸顿时红了。陈贞慧见他瞪大眼睛，像要发作，便连忙站起来说：“大家不要斗嘴——辟疆、已苍，二位莫误解弟等之意。阮圆海这次力举马瑶草，实指望他日马瑶草得志，能带挈于他。这自然未必能得逞，唯是这胡子贼心不死，于

Qian Muzhai, to reverse his case? Don't you know that last month he finally got Ma Yaocao reinstated through his efforts? To lead the Poets' Society as 'holder of the bull's ears' is nothing compared with his ambition to become a Cabinet minister."

"You are exaggerating, Chaozong," Mao Xiang, who hadn't spoken for a long time, suddenly interrupted. As Hou Fangyu and others praised *Letter from Swallow*, Mao Xiang was trying to guess their intentions. He knew very well what kind of men his friends were. It was just another moment of their deviousness and their real motive would be revealed later. When they turned to damn Ruan Dacheng, Mao Xiang suddenly understood. "Hmph, you're making fun of Big Beard Ruan as an appetizer!" he thought, a tad annoyed that they were hiding it from him. By now, the scene "Picking Up the Brush Pen" had ended. In the lull of the gongs and drums, Mao Xiang added, "Ma Yaocao was not involved in the treason case, so his reinstatement is something understandable, but Ruan Yuanhai may not be so lucky. Don't be an alarmist, brother, you're scaring yourself."

"That's right," came the calm voice of Feng Shu from the left corner. "That Elder Qian has helped exonerate Ruan Yuanhai is just another rumor. There's no evidence."

"Hmph," Hou Fangyu snorted contemptuously without turning to look at Feng Shu. "Brother Yicang, you're a favorite pupil of Elder Qian, so you can ask him if he has anything to do with it. There's no need for me to provide evidence." Then, he squinted at Mao Xiang, saying, "Brother Pijiang. Do you think I am an alarmist? I am worried that you've forgotten the world as you are enjoying yourself too much in Peach Land!"

Mao Xiang's face suddenly turned red from the teasing. Seeing that his eyes were wide open and ready to explode, Chen Zhenhui quickly stood up and said, "Stop the banter, men! Pijiang and Yicang, please don't get me wrong. Ruan Yuanhai has gone all out to get Ma Yaocao reinstated this time, because he hopes to get Mr. Ma's help in return. He may not get what he wants, but it's clear he's not reconciled to his fate yet. This isn't worth worrying about in itself. What is worth

此可见。此事本不可怕，倒是近年来，我同人君子，见国事日亟，忧心如焚，无暇内顾，遂对阮圆海渐生姑息宽贷之意，此诚一可惊可畏之变。是以贞慧于此，不得不披肝沥胆，大声疾呼！”

说到这里，他停了一下，目光灼灼地扫过全场，仿佛要用这种办法，把话送进每一个人心里去。看到大家都屏息听着，一个个脸上都现出严肃的神情，他才接着说下去：

“今晚弟特地烦宗子兄去借了这本《燕子笺》来演，便是让列位亲眼见识，阮圆海实为一有才之小人。若容此种狡狯有智之奸徒死灰复燃，必定危倾家国，祸延社局。凡我同人，务必同仇敌忾，打击之、禁制之，绝不能容他有出头之日！列位或尚不知，这狡险之徒直至近日，仍在蠢动钻营，欲图一逞。此事说来虽不值一哂，唯其用心却极险极毒———朝宗兄，你且把那件事也对社友们说说！”

侯方域沉着脸，摇摇头，显然对于冒襄适才说他“危言耸听”仍余气未消。梅朗中在一旁看见，便自告奋勇地站起来：“让小弟替朝宗说好了。事情是这样——开试之前几日，朝宗正在媚香楼同香君饮酒，有位王将军也在座。他与朝宗本属世交，因罢职在此闲居，便常来走动。朝宗知他家境亦非富裕，却见他出手甚是豪阔，本已有点疑心，只是不好问得。偏是香君那妮子乖觉，却将这事来提醒朝宗。朝宗便认真起来，逼着姓王的定要追根究底。那姓王的吃问不过，才屏去从人，说出底蕴。原来他是受了阮圆海之托，来求朝宗向社里说情疏通，将他开脱。那每日使用的银两，都是老阮的开支。朝宗这才恍然，当时再不理他。姓王的没奈何，只得灰溜溜地跑了。诸位请看，这狗贼胡子到底可恶不可恶、可恨不可恨呢？”

梅朗中的话音刚落，余怀就蹦了起来：“蠢，蠢！蠢透了！”

worrying about is that our comrades are too busy thinking about the national crisis and have relaxed our vigilance against him. That's why I stand out to sound the alarm."

He paused and scanned the room with his hot eyes, as if to strike these words into everyone's heart. Seeing that everyone was listening with bated breath and a serious expression on their faces, he continued:

"Today, I asked Brother Zongzi to borrow his *Letter from Swallow* so that all of you can see with your own eyes that Ruan Yuanhai is really a bastard with a talent. If we allow such a cunning man to have an opportunity, he would definitely endanger the Fushe and the Great Ming. All the Fushe comrades must be united against him and leave him no opportunity to be reinstated. You may not know yet that this cunning and dangerous man has never given up his ambition. You may think it's amusing, but what he did days ago does show how treacherous he is. Brother Chaozong, tell our friends that story."

Hou Fangyu shook his head with a sullen face, apparently still angry at Mao Xiang, who had called him an alarmist. Mei Langzhong saw it from beside him and stood up, saying, "Let me say it on behalf of Chaozong. Here's the thing: a few days before the imperial examination, Chaozong was drinking with Xiangjun in the Meixiang House, and a General Wang was also present. He was a family friend of Chaozong. Ousted from office, he resided in this neighborhood and frequently visited Chaozong. He was not a rich man but was spending money generously. Chaozong was a little suspicious but never asked him about it. Xiangjun was wary and cautioned him about it. Chaozong was on alert and bent on finding out about it. Mr. Wang, unable to dodge his questions, asked for the servants to be sent away and honestly told the truth. He was sent by Ruan Yuanhai to ask Chaozong to intercede with the Fushe for the exoneration of the bastard. All his expenses were covered by Old Ruan. Having learned the truth, Chaozong stopped speaking to him. Mr. Wang left in abashment. So, brothers, don't you think Big Beard Ruan is abominable?"

As soon as Mei Langzhong finished speaking, Yu Huai jumped

他大叫。

“淡心兄，你说谁蠢？”顾杲问。

“当然是阮胡子啊！他以为花几两臭银子，就能把我们买了，真是天字第一号的蠢材！”

“他能写出这《燕子笺》，倒也不是蠢材。”陈梁讥讽地说，“不过利令智昏，那是确定无疑的了！”

“对，他是昏了头！”“白日做梦！”“这胡子如此可恶，果然轻饶他不得！”好几个声音同时叫起来。

“对，对，饶他不得！”更多的人附和说。

可是，那几个同钱谦益关系较深的人，像冯氏兄弟、孙永祚、顾苓等人，仍旧一声不响。

这时候，侯方域慢慢地站了起来，他完全收起了惯常的那种傲慢不逊的神情，低着头，沉默了一下，才说：“适才朗三所言，尚有可补充之处——当时香君见王将军说出底蕴，曾私下对小弟说：她自少便因阿娘得识定生兄，深敬其高义，又闻次尾兄亦铮铮之士，嘱小弟决不可因阮圆海负此二位至交好友。又说：‘以公子之世望，怎能替他阉党儿子办事？公子读书万卷，见解可别连我们区区女流还不如！’”侯方域用深沉、感动的声音说着，抬起头，望着大家，“小弟在此转述此语，不独是此语曾令小弟深为感佩，也是想教列位社兄知道，青楼之中，尚有此等人物！”

同刚才梅朗中说话时的情形不同，这一次侯方域说完了好一阵子，大家仍旧静静地坐着，没有作声，一个个脸上现出沉思，甚至惭愧的神情。

“香君此语，可以不朽了！”不知是谁，忽然赞叹地说了一句。

“今夕得闻此语，自此之后，我再不敢看轻旧院人物了！”另一个说。

up. "Idiot, idiot, what an idiot!" he yelled.

"Brother Danxin, who are you calling an idiot?" Gu Gao asked.

"Of course it's Big Beard Ruan! He thought he could buy us for a few taels of stinking silver. He's a big idiot!"

"Since he can write a play like *Letter from Swallow*, he's not an idiot," Chen Liang said sarcastically. "He's simply blinded by his own ambition."

"Right! He has lost his head!" "Daydreaming!" "Big Beard is so hateful. Let's not spare him!" several voices shouted at the same time.

"Yes, yes, don't spare him!" more voices echoed.

However, those who had a close relationship with Qian Qianyi, such as the Feng brothers, Sun Yongzuo, and Gu Ling, remained silent.

Hou Fangyu stood up slowly, having put away his habitual arrogant expression, lowered his head in silence, and then said, "I'd like to make an amendment to what Langsan said just now. After hearing General Wang's confession, Xiangjun whispered to me, 'I've been acquainted with Dingsheng through my madam and have always admired him for his noble character, and I've also heard that Ciwei is a reputable gentleman. Don't break up with these two good friends of yours because of Ruan Yuanhai. She also said, 'Given your reputation, don't get involved with Eunuch Wei's running dogs. As a well-read scholar, you should know better than a little woman like me.'" Hou Fangyu added in a deep, emotional voice, as he lifted his head to look at the others. "I'm repeating her words to you, not only because she has deeply moved me, but also because I want you to know that even a prostitute can have great wisdom."

Unlike a moment ago when Mei Langzhong spoke, when Hou Fangyu finished speaking, everyone was sitting still without making a sound, with a contemplative or even ashamed look on their faces.

"By saying these words, Xiangjun will be immortal!" someone exclaimed in admiration.

"From now on, I won't dare to look down on the Old Yard girls!" said another.

“香君此语，只怕有些人不便与闻呢！”

“哦，怎么？”

“他们枉自饱读诗书，自夸圣贤高弟，却全无骨气，若闻知此语，岂非活活愧死？”

“我们且休说别人！”冯班忽然气冲冲地站起来，吵架似的说，“我们如今不也在快快活活地瞧阮大铖的《燕子笺》么？这会儿戏也停了，我们也不用再看了，竟是散了吧！”说着，就要往外走。

大家经他这样一提醒，才发觉，戏不知什么时候已经停了下来。

“哎，定远兄，何必要走！”陈贞慧连忙起身挽留。眼见今晚的安排已经完全达到预期的目的，而且由于侯方域最后这一下即兴陈述，把大家深深地打动，这使陈贞慧尤其满意。

“社友们难得聚首一趟，何不就拿阮圆海这戏做下酒之物，该赞则赞，该骂则骂，谋彻夜之欢呢！”他竭力劝说着，又回头大声问台上：“咦，怎么都停下了？快快演起来！”

“定远兄，不要走！”“急什么？”“等会儿还要同你唱和一番哩！”许多人也帮着挽留冯班。

可是，冯班尚未挽留住，却连冯舒、孙永祚、顾苓等人也一齐起身要走。大家知道他们都是钱门弟子，对于今晚这样处处拿钱谦益作话柄，自然老大不舒服，即使再挽留，只怕也是白费劲，所以便不再勉强，让他们走了。

在大家乱纷纷地送冯班等人出门的时候，冒襄却坐着没动。刚才侯方域转述李香君的那一番话，使他既意外又吃惊。他不只见过李香君，而且还相当熟识——一个身材矮小、肤色白净的小女孩儿，外号“香扇坠”。平时也无非觉着她人还机灵，小嘴巴子叽叽呱呱的，挺会捉弄人，却想不到她能说出这等深明大义的话来。“怪道朝宗如此迷恋于她，原来竟是一位奇女子！”冒襄

"I'm afraid some men wouldn't be happy to hear such words from Xiangjun!"

"Oh, why is that?"

"They're well read in the classics and pride themselves on being the worthy disciples of the sages but none of them has a backbone. If they hear this, won't they be ashamed to death?"

Feng Ban suddenly stood up angrily. "Let's stop talking about others," he said as if in a quarrel. "Aren't we enjoying Ruan Dacheng's *Letter from Swallow* now? Now that the show has stopped, let's disband." Then, he turned to leave.

Then, the others realized that the play had stopped at some point.

"Hey, Brother Dingyuan, don't go!" Chen Zhenhui quickly stood up to stop him from leaving. Seeing that tonight's arrangement had fully achieved the expected effect and his comrades were deeply moved by Hou Fangyu's impromptu remark, Chen Zhenhui was greatly satisfied.

"Now that we're gathered here, why don't we have fun all night long? Let's take Ruan Yuanhai's play for an appetizer. Praise it if you like it or criticize it if you don't ," he said. Then, he turned around and shouted at the stage, "Why have you all stopped? Go on!"

"Brother Dingyuan, don't go!" "What's the hurry?" "I'll sing with you later!" Others joined in the persuasion.

Feng Ban didn't listen. Feng Shu, Sun Yongzuo, and Gu Ling also stood up to leave. Since they were all pupils of Qian Qianyi and were annoyed by the disrespect for their teacher, they would not stay any way. Seeing there was no use persuading them to stay, the others let them go.

While everyone else went to the door to see off Feng Ban, Feng Shu, Sun Yongzuo and Gu Ling, Mao Xiang sat still. Li Xiangjun's words repeated by Hou Fangyu just now had surprised him. He had met Li Xiangjun. In fact, he knew her only too well. Nicknamed Fan Tassel, she was a young girl with a short stature and a fair complexion. He knew that she was smart with a sharp, quick tongue, and was very good at teasing others, but he never thought that she was capable

肃然起敬地想。他忽然觉得，自己理想中的女子，要么是陈圆圆那样的，不然，至少也应当像李香君这一类，但是偏偏碰上了董小宛，她与上面这两种类型全无一点相近……想到这里，冒襄不由得朝董小宛那边望了望，却意外地发现，原来董小宛也在含情脉脉地望着他。“哼，她就会这个！仿佛除此之外，她再也没有什么事情好干似的！”冒襄恼火地想，随即别转脸，整个晚上，再也不去瞧她了……

of making such wise remarks. "No wonder Chaozong is so taken with her. She's such a talented girl!" Mao Xiang thought in great admiration. He suddenly felt that the ideal woman for him was either a Chen Yuanyuan or a Li Xiangjun at least, and Dong Xiaowan belonged to neither type ... Thus thinking, he looked toward Dong Xiaowan and found she was also looking at him, with affectionate eyes. "Hmph, that's all she is good for, as if there were nothing else to do other than that!" Mao Xiang thought sullenly. Then, he turned his face away and never looked at her again for the rest of the night ...

# 第十一章
# 乱象纷呈上书碰壁，奇器迭出传教有方

## 满腔赤诚

来到北京之后的最初一个月里，黄宗羲是在异常兴奋、忙碌和期待的状态中度过的。

虽然十五年前——那时他还是一个十七岁的少年，曾经为着申雪父亲的冤案来过北京一次，但事后这座城市在他脑子里留下的印象却是如此零碎、模糊，除了宏伟壮观的紫禁城、森严肃杀的刑部衙门、怪模怪样的四合院之外，似乎就只有在大街上悠然蹒跚的骆驼，和又甜又酸的冰糖葫芦了。但是，这一次却完全不同。从他进入北京的那一天起，他就立刻感受到这个全国最大的城市——政治和经济中心的那种非凡格局和气派，它那君临一切的气息。特别是疟疾过去之后，他开始出门四处走动，这种感觉就更加强烈了。

是的，在这里居住着至高无上的皇帝，拥有着令人生畏的生杀予夺的大权，聚集着来自全国各地最优秀的人物，可以最快地了解到关于时局的重要消息，准确地把握朝廷决策的脉搏；自然，也存在着实现自己的主张和理想的最大机会……正是这一切，强烈地打动了黄宗羲的心，使他情不自禁地被吸引、被征服，陷入了一种陶醉狂喜、忘乎所以的状态之中。

Chapter Eleven

# In Which Huang Zongxi's Petition Met with a Rebuff and a Foreign Missionary Opened Eyes with Exotic Gadgets

## A Sincere Heart

In his first month in Beijing, Huang Zongxi was excited, busy, and full of hope.

He had been in Beijing once. Fifteen years ago, when he was a seventeen-year-old boy, he came to Beijing to seek redress of the wrongs his father had suffered, but his impression of the city was fragmented and vague. Apart from the magnificent Forbidden City, the fear-inspiring Yamen of the Ministry of Punishment, and the bizarre courtyards, there was nothing but camels slowly moving on the streets and the sweet and sour candied haws. However, this time, the city looked completely different. The day he entered Beijing, he immediately felt the awe-inspiring grandiosity and grandeur of the largest city in the country as the political and economic center. When he recovered from malaria and started going out and walking around, the feeling was even stronger.

Yes, here lived the emperor who held the power of life and death over all and gathered the elites of the country, from whom he could quickly learn everything about the current situation and feel the pulse of the imperial court. Naturally, this was also a place to put his ideas into practice ... Thinking of this, his heart was filled with awe, rapture, and euphoria.

由于三月松山失陷、洪承畴降敌的余震逐渐过去，从那时以来，关外的清兵一直未见有进一步的行动；而南方的农民军，又似乎始终被遏制在河南、湖广一带，尚不能对京师构成威胁，所以近几个月来，北京的局面暂时还保持着相对平静。黄宗羲在方以智、陆符、黄崇简等一班朋友的陪伴下，先后瞻仰了紫禁城，逛了棋盘街、东西四牌楼、城隍庙、灯市口等有名的热闹繁华去处；游览了包括什刹海、文丞相祠、首善书院等一些名胜古迹；还特地到城墙上去，站在一尊尊巨型铁炮和堆积如山的灰瓶和滚木当中，向守城的将官详细询问以往清军三度入寇、逼近京畿的战斗情形。不过，在这期间，他更忙碌而频繁的，是去拜访一些在京做官的前辈和朋友，向他们打听消息，交换关于时局的意见，并且出人意料地成了一位“乐观派”，经常以他热烈的言谈和高昂的情绪使大家感到惊讶。

“列位，”他不止一次这样说，“小弟在江南时，曾道听途说京里之种种情形，俱是摇头叹息者多，而鼓舞欢忭者少。听来听去，亦以为国事真不可为矣！然而此次北来，方知以往所闻，未免言过其实。诚然，国步维艰，于今为极！但尚未至于无望。其最要者，今上天聪明敏，宵旰忧勤，励精图治之志，困而愈坚，此其一；朝中君子仁人，鼎力扶持，直言谋国，正气未堕，此其二；更兼我朝三百年恩泽在民，感激图报之心，处处可见。譬如前时洪亨九降于建虏，消息传来，京中之民怒不可遏，不待上命，便将其祭棚一夜拆平；更有人以狗屎涂抹洪逆之门，戟指痛骂，

In the past few months, the situation in Beijing had been relatively stable, now that the tremors of the fall of Songshan and the surrender of Hong Chengchou to the enemy in March were over, the Qing troops outside the Shanghai Pass had stopped advancing, and the peasant army in the south seemed to have been contained in Henan and Huguang, posing no immediate threat to the capital. Accompanied by Fang Yizhi, Lu Fu, Huang Chongjian, and other friends, Huang Zongxi visited bustling places such as the Forbidden City, Qipan Street, East Sipai, West Sipai, the City God Temple, and Dengshikou, and famous attractions and places of historical interest such as the Shicha Lake, the Wen Tianxiang Temple, and the Shoushan Academy. He even climbed up the city wall, where he stood among the giant iron cannons and the huge piles of lime bottles and wood logs and asked the commanders guarding the city in detail about the three battles with the Qing invaders encroaching on Beijing. He spent most of his time, though, visiting elders and friends serving as officials in Beijing for updates on the situation, and in the sharing of his views, he surprised them as an utter optimist with his ardent language and enthusiastic voice.

"Dear Sirs," he often said. "When I was in River South, I heard many stories about the capital. Most of them are demoralizing and few are encouraging. Now that I am here, I know those rumors are not true. The Great Ming is indeed in crisis, but it's not entirely hopeless. For one thing, His Majesty the emperor is wise and works diligently to correct things with a strong determination. For another, good men still prevail at court and are doing their best to help the emperor. Besides, the benign government of the Great Ming has lasted three hundred years and the grateful people are ready to defend it with their lives. For example, when news came that Hong Chengchou had surrendered to the Jianzhou Jurchens, the people in the capital were so angry that before the emperor issued an edict they immediately removed all memorial altars overnight. Some even put dog feces on the gate of his residence and cursed him. His family members were so scared that they dared not come out. This is the wrath of the people, which will

使其家人震慑不敢出。这便是民气！荡寇平虏赖此，家国中兴赖此！弟所以知大明还是有望的！”

当然，黄宗羲的议论并不仅仅停留于此，他常常紧接着就指出目前政治、经济、军事乃至文化教育方面的各种弊端，并且兴奋而自信地提出一系列的改革主张：第一、第二、第三……不过，当他这样说的时候，人们的反应大都比较冷淡，或者拈须微笑，或者沉默不语，再不然就干脆摇头表示反对，同意并支持他的人却少而又少。看到这种情形，黄宗羲有点意外，也有点扫兴。“嗯，也许我不会说话，他们没听明白我的意思。确实，我的这些主张绝不是三言两语能说清楚的！”他想，于是又恢复了自信，开始着手把他的那份上书的初稿重新加以修改、补充，尽量使之更加明确完善，切实可行，准备一旦有机会就呈送上去，让朝廷加以考虑和采纳。

当然，在这段时间里，黄宗羲还继续不断听到有关时局和朝廷的各种各样的新闻。比如他听说，最近皇上见国事日坏，忧心如焚，越来越迷信上神佛，每日子时亲自上城南的佛阁拈香诵经不算，还招来一批道士，加以优礼供奉，让他们装神弄鬼。好几位言官都曾上疏切谏，以为非治国之道，可皇上就是不听。又如，黄宗羲还听说，辅臣贺逢圣，最近已被批准告老还乡。在临走前那几天，每次见到皇上，他都放声痛哭，叩头不止。问他为什么这样，他又不肯说。大家都感到十分奇怪。再如，还听说，最近皇上不知听了谁的谗言，认为这一次推举内阁大臣时有徇私作弊的行为，十分震怒，当即把吏部尚书李日宣等六人逮捕下狱。现在这六人已经流放的流放，罢官的罢官，就连刑部侍郎惠世扬也以执法不严获罪，被撤了职。当然，还有别的一些新闻，像皇上最宠爱的田妃病得越来越重啦，马士英被起用为凤阳总督啦，朝廷调派援救开封的各路大军已经云集朱仙镇，结果不知会怎样啦，

kill the insurgents, drive away the invaders, and bring the Great Ming back. Therefore, I know there's still hope for the Great Ming."

Of course, Huang Zongxi's argument didn't stop here. He often went on to point out the ills of the political, economic, military, cultural, and educational institutions and propose a series of reforms, first, second, third ... However, when he was speaking, there was no warm reaction from anybody at all. Some smiled noncommittally, stroking their beards, some kept silent all the time, and some shook their heads in disapproval. There were very few who shared his views and supported him. Seeing that, Huang Zongxi was surprised and disappointed. "Well, maybe I didn't put it right. They don't get my point. Indeed, it's not easy to put my proposals in a few words." Thus thinking, he regained his confidence and started to revise and amend his petition letter to make it clearer and more cogent. Once he had the opportunity, he would submit it to the imperial court.

During this period, more news of the court and the situation came to the ears of Huang Zongxi: the emperor, in his desperation, had turned to deities and was visiting the Buddhist Temple in the south of the Forbidden City at midnight every day to burn incense and chant sutras—he had even invited many priests to perform Taoist services—and a few royal consultants petitioned against it, but he didn't listen; before retiring to his hometown on account of old age, Prime Minister He Fengsheng cried and kowtowed to His Majesty every time he went to court, keeping his mouth shut when asked why he was like that, and everyone was puzzled; His Majesty, outraged upon hearing a false report that there had been some misconduct in the selection of Cabinet ministers, immediately ordered for the arrests of six officials including Li Rixuan, Minister of Personnel, and they were now exiled or became commoners, and even Hui Shiyang, Vice Minister of the Ministry of Punishment, had lost his job for negligence of duty; the illness of the emperor's favorite concubine Lady Tian had worsened; Ma Shiying had been reinstated to office and now became Governor of Fengyang; the reinforcements to Kaifeng had assembled in Zhuxian Town, and it was not known yet if they could break the siege ... Though Huang

如此等等。对于这些事件和消息，黄宗羲也照例发表过一些直言不讳的看法。不过，由于他正一心一意埋头修改那份陈述政见的上书，对于这类无关宏旨的消息也就不想分心去探究了。

这样，一直到了七月。一天上午，黄宗羲正在宣武门外方以智的寓宅里给朋友陆符写信，准备告诉对方，自己暂时不打算搬到万驸马的北湖园去住。这件事陆符虽然已经提出过好多次了，但黄宗羲是这样考虑的：北湖园在城的尽西头，那里确实比较清静，适宜专心温书应考；可是离开城中心太远，消息不大灵通，有什么事要找个人商量也不容易。而黄宗羲目前修改给朝廷的上书，却必须随时了解时局的最新动向，并不时要向有关的人请教切磋。再三考虑之后，他还是决定谢绝陆符的邀请。

不过，结果他却未能把这封信写完。因为刑部左侍郎徐石麒忽然派了个承差来传话，让黄宗羲立刻上他那儿去一趟。徐石麒是黄宗羲父亲的门生。天启年间，黄尊素因触怒魏忠贤，被捕下狱。当时徐石麒任工部营缮主事，曾经极力奔走，设法营救，结果也被牵连罢官。直到魏忠贤垮台后，才重新被起用。他曾经在南京任职多年，对黄家始终十分关怀照顾，并且坚持把整整比他小了三十二岁的黄宗羲当作小弟弟看待。因为这个缘故，黄宗羲以往到南京，总要去拜望他。这一次来北京也不例外。不过，徐石麒的脾气有点古怪，一张铁青色的方脸，很少笑容，有时同客人面对面地坐着，老半天也不说一句话，也闹不清他到底想什么。

Zongxi had made a few remarks on those events, since they were not directly related to the great cause, he let them go and concentrated on the revision of the petition letter that included his important political views.

One morning in July. Huang Zongxi was writing a letter to his friend Lu Fu in Fang Yizhi's residence outside the Xuanwu Gate. He was going to tell that friend of his that he was not going to move into North Lake Garden, the residence of Prince Wan, son-in-law of the emperor. Lu Fu had invited him many times, but he had his considerations. True that North Lake Garden was a perfect place to prepare for the imperial examination, because, located in the west end of the city, it was very quiet. The thing was, it was too far away from city center. Isolated from the outside world, he would not be able to receive timely updates on current events and would find it difficult to approach anyone from there for the discussion of important matters. The petition letter called for a good understanding of current affairs and the exchange of views with relevant persons. Therefore, he decided to decline Lu Fu's kind offer.

However, before Huang Zongxi could finish the letter, a servant of Xu Shiqi, Left Vice Minister of the Ministry of Punishment, suddenly came with a message that Mr. Xu wanted to see him immediately. Xu Shiqi was a former student of Huang Zongxi's father. During the Tianqi period, Huang Zunsu was arrested and imprisoned for angering Wei Zhongxian. At that time, Xu Shiqi was the head of the Construction Department of the Ministry of Industry. Because of his efforts to free Huang Zunsu, he was ousted from office. After Wei Zhongxian's downfall, he was reinstated to office. Mr. Xu had worked in Nanjing for many years, where he was very caring to the Huangs, treating Huang Zongxi, thirty-two years his junior, as his younger brother. For this reason, every time Huang Zongxi went to Nanjing, he would pay a visit to this great family friend. This current trip to Beijing was no exception. However, Xu Shiqi had a weird disposition. His iron-gray square face rarely smiled. Sometimes he would sit face to face with the guest without saying a word for a long time, and it

所以黄宗羲轻易不去打扰他。现在忽然听见传唤，黄宗羲不敢怠慢，连忙放下笔，换了衣服，跟着刑部衙门的承差出门上马，向宣武门内行去。

正是接近入秋时节，天气不凉不热，抬头望去，晴空一碧如洗，阳光耀眼。这一带是中下级官员聚居的地方，一幢接一幢的四合院，大门一律开在东南角上，门内是带雕饰的影壁。房屋虽不甚宏丽，总算还比较整齐。这一带还是有名的花市，特别是上、下斜街，常年靠种植花木出售为生的居民，很是不少。现在透过竹篱笆，可以看见一行一行排列得很整齐的花盆和苗圃，种满了各种各样应时的花木。其中有黄色六瓣、花朵大如碗口的秋葵，有小巧玲珑、黄色的花瓣上带赤紫色斑点的小种万寿菊，有青色、紫色和红色的蓝菊，有娇艳可爱的木莲，有朱红色的、蓬勃烂漫的草本夹竹桃，还有秋海棠、璎珞鸡冠，以及其他一些叫不出名字的花木，都在秋阳下静静地开放着。几只白色的小蝴蝶，正绕着花丛上下飞舞。时不时，可以看见一个年老的花匠，或者带着孩子的妇人在花丛中忙碌着，听见马蹄声，他们就不慌不忙地直起腰来……

“凉飔乱翻千簇艳，初阳静映一篱秋！”黄宗羲愉快地瞅着街旁的景致，心里油然冒出这样两句诗。随即又想：“啊，这样烂漫多彩的秋色，这样平静悠闲的岁月，又怎能想象可以听凭流寇和建虏来把它毁掉！”于是，他又一次想到他的那一份上书，“我得尽快把它修改出来，无论如何，我也要试一试！也许皇上果真会采纳呢？”他暗暗想着，又兴奋起来，紧一紧缰绳，加快速度，向前行去。

was very hard to know what he was thinking. So, Huang Zongxi didn't go to see him unless necessary. Now that he was summoned, Huang Zongxi quickly put down his pen, changed his clothes, and following the servant of the *yamen* of the Ministry of Punishment, hurried toward the Xuanwu Gate.

It was almost autumn. The weather was neither cold nor hot. The sky was clear, and the sun was shining. This was a neighborhood where lower and middle-level officials lived. It was lined up with courtyard houses, whose doors were all on the southeast corner with a carved screen wall inside. They were not gorgeous but looked rather neat. There was a famous flower market here. Many residents of the Upper Oblique Street and the Lower Oblique Street made a living by growing flowers and selling them all year round. Now through the bamboo fence, one could see the neat rows of flowerpots and the nurseries of various seasonal flowers such as autumn dish-sized sunflowers with six yellow petals, signet marigolds with mauve spots on the tiny and exquisite yellow petals, felicia amelloides in cyan, purple and red, mango lotus, which was delicate and lovely, lush herbaceous oleander with a romantic vibe, as well as begonia, amaranthaceae, and many other unnamed flowers, all quietly blooming in the autumn sun. A few small white butterflies were flying up and down around the flowers. Occasionally, one could see an old gardener or a lady with children around working amid the flowers, calmly straightening up upon hearing the sound of the horse hoofs ...

"A chilly wind ruffles a thousand flowers. The morning sun silently shines on the autumn garden." Two lines of a poem suddenly occurred to him. He thought, "What a romantic and colorful autumn! What a peaceful and quiet life! How can we allow the insurgents and Jurchens to take it all from us!" Then, he thought of his petition letter again. "I must finish it as soon as possible. For better or worse, I'll have to give it a shot. Maybe His Majesty the emperor will take my advice. Who knows?" Thus thinking, he brightened up, tightened the reins in his hand, and sped up.

## 当头棒喝

位于刑部街的徐石麒衙门，今天气氛有点不寻常，大门外，排列着好几柄官扇，七八匹鞍鞯鲜明的骏马歇在墙影下，一群皂隶打扮的人正站在一旁静静地守候着。显然，衙门里来了什么重要官员，而且不止一个。“嗯，不知谁来了？瞧样子不像是请客宴会，那么，为何偏挑这么个时候召我来呢？”黄宗羲疑惑地想，在门前勒住马，跳下地来。

“启禀相公，我家老爷眼下有客，吩咐说，黄相公来时，请先到私衙小花厅奉茶。”那个承差到门上问明情况之后，走回来这样说。

黄宗羲点点头，知道这几个客人只是碰巧来到，与自己无关。于是把缰绳抛给承差，自己跟着迎出来的院公往私衙里走。他早就听人说，徐石麒自任刑部侍郎以来，因为执法严猛，守正不阿，眼下颇受皇上信用。刚才他在路上忽然想到，正好趁此机会把自己准备上书朝廷的事同徐石麒商量，如果可能，干脆就托他代为呈递。现在，黄宗羲被这种念头弄得愈来愈兴奋，虽然他明知不能马上见到徐石麒，却仍旧一边走，一边睁大眼睛朝里张望，希望能意外地发现主人的身影。

果然，事有凑巧，刚进二门，就听见了说话的声音，三位纱帽青袍的官员正从大堂上走下来。在他们的后面，是身材高大的徐石麒。他头戴乌纱，身穿绯色三品补服，看样子正往外送客。

黄宗羲犹豫了一下，拿不准主意是否上前相见，随即发现徐

# A Rebuttal

At Xu Shiqi's *yamen* on the Ministry of Punishment Street, the atmosphere was a bit unusual today. In front of the gate were aligned several large ceremonial fans. Seven or eight steeds with bright saddles and appurtenances were resting in the shadow of the wall. A group of *yamen* men were standing quietly aside. Obviously, there were some important officials visiting the *yamen*. "Um, who are here? It doesn't look like a banquet, so why does he choose such a time to summon me here?" Huang Zongxi thought doubtfully as he stopped his horse in front of the gate and landed on the ground.

"Dear sir, his lordship is seeing guests at the moment. He told us to welcome you to the private flower hall, where you can have some tea first," said the servant, who had checked with other servants at the gate.

Huang Zongxi nodded his head, knowing that it was just a chance encounter and these guests had nothing to do with him. So he threw the reins to the servant and followed an older servant to the private flower hall. He had long heard that Xu Shiqi had been greatly trusted by His Majesty after being appointed Vice Minister of Punishment for strictly enforcing the law. On his way here, it had suddenly occurred to him that he might take this opportunity to discuss his petition with Xu Shiqi, and if possible, ask the elder to submit it on his behalf. Now, Huang Zongxi was getting more and more excited by this thought. Although he knew that he would not be able to see Xu Shiqi right away, he looked around with wide eyes as he walked in, hoping the host would suddenly turn up from somewhere.

Sure enough, by a mere chance, when he passed the second gate, he heard the voices of the three officials in black gauze hats and green robes walking off the main hall and behind them was exactly Xu Shiqi, a man of huge stature, who was wearing a black gauze hat and a crimson Rank Three official uniform and was apparently seeing off his guests.

Huang Zongxi hesitated, not sure whether he should go up to

石麒冷冷地朝他一瞥，并无任何表示。黄宗羲便不敢孟浪，连忙闪过一旁，让他们过去。

那几位客人并没有注意黄宗羲。他们管自走着，显得心事重重，而且神情沮丧，似乎碰了什么钉子。快要走出二门时，其中一个长着一只骨棱棱的鼻子和两撇八字胡的官员忽然回头说：

“此事干系重大，还望徐大人三思！”

但是徐石麒一声不响，那张青灰色的长方脸板得紧紧的，仿佛根本没有听见这句话。那官员眨眨眼睛，脸上闪过一丝怨恨的神色，但终于无可奈何地垂下头，快快地走出去了。

黄宗羲目送着他们的背影，心中有点纳闷。不过他也明白，以自己目前的身份地位，朝廷里的事情还轮不到他来操心究问。于是，他不再理会，依旧脚步轻快地往里走，一边考虑着如何把自己的打算向主人提出。

黄宗羲刚刚在小花厅坐下，徐石麒就跟着走进来了。看样子，他还在为刚才那一幕内容不详，但显然并不愉快的会见而生气。任凭黄宗羲站起来行礼、问候，他却沉着脸，一声不响，只略拱一拱手，就示意黄宗羲坐下，自己也在一张花梨木六方扶手椅上坐了下来。

“嗯，不知把我唤来，有什么事？”黄宗羲想。看见主人尽自皱着眉，不开口，他不禁有点奇怪，也有点不安，想开口动问，临时又忍住了，只是热切地睁大眼睛，微微向前倾着身子，现出探询的、洗耳恭听的神情。

终于，徐石麒慢吞吞地开口了。

“这些日子，贤弟都在做些什么啊？”他问，语气是淡淡的，脸上没有一丝表情。

“哦，有劳兄长垂问，”黄宗羲赶紧拱着手回答，“小弟这些日子——也没干什么。刚到时病了几天，后来好了，便在城里

meet Xu Shiqi, but seeing the latter glancing at him coldly, without saying anything, Huang Zongxi didn't dare to intrude, so he quickly stepped aside and let them pass.

The guests didn't notice Huang Zongxi. They were walking dejectedly, as if they had met with a rebuff. When they passed the second gate, one of the officials who had a bony nose and a mustache suddenly turned to Xu Shiqi and said:

"This matter is very important. I hope your lordship can think it over."

Xu Shiqi kept silent, his gray rectangular face pulled tight, as if he hadn't heard those words at all. That official blinked his eyes, and a look of grievance flashed across his face, but he finally lowered his head and walked out in dismay.

Huang Zongxi watched them as they left and was a little puzzled. However, he understood that given his current status, it was not his business to worry about matters in the imperial court. So, he let it go and briskly walked inside as he thought how to present his plan to the host.

Shortly after Huang Zongxi sat down in the small flower hall, Xu Shiqi came in. It seemed that he was still angry about the obviously unpleasant meeting, whose aim was unclear. Huang Zongxi stood up to salute and greet him, but he kept silent with a sullen face and merely bowed with clasped hands and gestured for Huang Zongxi to sit down. Then, he himself sat down on a rosewood hexagonal armchair.

"I wonder why he summons me here," Huang Zongxi thought. Seeing the host knitting his brows in silence, he was puzzled and uneasy at the same time. He wanted to ask but immediately held himself back. Instead, he just widened his eyes anxiously and leaned forward slightly with an eager expression.

Finally, Xu Shiqi slowly opened his mouth.

"What are you doing these days?" he asked in a flat tone, with no expression on his face.

"Thank you for asking, Elder Brother," Huang Zongxi quickly answered, pressing his hands together. "I—haven't been doing

到处瞧了瞧，顺便走访几个朋友。另外就是准备应考的事。还有、还有……”

“嗯，你的应酬好像也不少，我听说了。”徐石麒提醒道，同时，仿佛不想过早暴露这句提示的锋芒似的，他垂下了眼睛。

黄宗羲本想接下去就谈到他的那份上书，忽然对方冒出来这么一句，倒把他噎住了。

“是的，他们都来邀请小弟，盛情难却，所以……”他迟疑了一下，老实承认说，同时心里想：“莫非兄长对我多所应酬不以为然？这可是误解！”他正想作些解释，可是徐石麒已经抛开了这个话题。

“那么，准备得怎样了啊？”他依旧不动声色地问。

“啊，兄长是说……”

“自然是乡试！”

“这个……小弟尚在准备之中。”

“如何准备，可以见告否？”

“也……也就是照常准备罢了，其实，没有什么……”黄宗羲含糊地回答，忽然脸红了。事实上，这大半个月来，他几乎把应试抛到了脑后，“反正还有一两个月，过些日子再说吧！”他想，刚才他提到正在准备，无非是随口说说，没想到会被认真追问起来。

徐石麒尖利地瞅了他一眼：“贤弟觉着，今科可有把握必中？”

“啊，小弟岂敢！”

“然则是否望其能中？”

“这个——自然……”

“既然望中，而又无必中之把握，”徐石麒的语气变得严厉起来，“却日日忙于应酬，沉酣宴席。这样子，可合适么？”

黄宗羲错愕一下，顿时羞得满脸通红：“兄长责备得是，不过……”

anything these days. I was sick for a few days after I arrived. When I recovered, I went to some places and visited a few friends. Then, I began to prepare for the exam. And, and ..."

"Well, you also went to quite a number of banquets, I hear." Xu Shiqi said. As if trying not to sound too blunt, he lowered his eyes.

Huang Zongxi, who was going to bring up the subject of his petition, shrank from such a remark.

"Yes, they all came to invite me. It's hard to decline their kind invitations, so ..." He admitted it honestly after hesitating for an instant. Meanwhile, he thought to himself, "He thought I love banquets. It's a misunderstanding." As he was going to explain, Xu Shiqi switched to another topic.

"So, what about your preparations for the exam?" he asked stoically.

"Oh, you mean ..."

"The provincial exam, of course."

"Well ... I'm still preparing for it."

"How do you prepare? Could you tell me about it?"

"Just ... just as usual, in fact, there isn't ..." Huang Zongxi replied vaguely and suddenly blushed. In fact, for the past half month, he almost forgot about the exam. "Anyway, there's still a month or two, I can start preparing in a couple of days," he had always thought. His reply that he was preparing was merely perfunctory. Xu Shiqi had taken it seriously.

Xu Shiqi stared at him and said, "Are you sure you can succeed this time, my younger brother?"

"No."

"But do you want to succeed?"

"Of, of course ..."

"You want to succeed, but you are not sure you can ..." Xu Shiqi's tone became stern. "Then, do you think it right to meet people and attend banquets every day?"

Hong Zongxi blushed with shame. "I do deserve your criticism, elder brother, but ..."

但是徐石麒做了个不容他置辩的手势："我本不想责备于你！"他气呼呼地说，"可听说这些日子你在外面任性胡闹，很不像话。念及老师在世时对我恩深义重，却又不能不说！"

"啊，请兄长只管教训，小弟无不凛遵！"黄宗羲连忙站起来，毕恭毕敬地拱着手，同时心里暗暗吃惊，不知道自己犯了什么错，使得对方大动肝火。

徐石麒却没有立即说下去。他似乎在极力压制自己的怒气，过了一会，才冷冷地问："我听说，这些日子，你在外面全不知收敛，说出许多没遮没拦的话，甚至出言不逊，非及皇上，可有此事？嗯？"

黄宗羲本来正在垂首聆训，听了这话，不由得抬起头，迷惑地望了望主人。他没想到对方是为的这个事而生气，相反，他还满心指望能得到对方的支持和帮助哩！事实上，黄宗羲一向认为：开放言路，把判断朝政是非得失的权利扩大到广大有识之士当中，使人们能对国家大事直言不讳地提出意见，这对于集思广益，补偏救弊，以振兴国家来说，是十分重要的一环。最近以来，他对时局是发表过一些见解，但他自问没有一丝一毫出于私心，全是为的社稷安危、家国存亡着想，而且他记得似乎也没有非议过皇上。何况即便是皇上的意见，也未必一点都不错；直言敢谏，也正是臣子应尽的职责。为什么徐石麒却把这种事看得如此严重，大动肝火？黄宗羲对此颇感意外，并且有点失望，不由得呆住了。

看见黄宗羲默不作声，徐石麒又激动起来。他站起身，向前走出两步，忽然转过身来，压低声音训斥说："这里是京师重地，辇毂之下，可不是江南，懂吗？在江南，任凭你们放言高论，胡说一气，也没人管你。可这儿是京师！一言一行，都须小心谨慎，循规蹈矩！可你——"他提高了声音，"已经年过而立，还是如此不知天高地厚，率性胡来。万一遭逢不测，叫我如何维护于你？

Xu Shiqi made an unequivocal gesture. "I didn't mean to criticize you," he said angrily. "But from what I hear, you've gone too far in your wild behavior. Now that I hear it, I must warn you as a pupil of your father, who was very kind to me in his lifetime."

"Please don't hesitate to educate me, my dear elder brother." Huang Zongxi quickly stood up and bowed, wondering what mistake he had made to make Xu Shiqi so unhappy.

Xu Shiqi didn't respond immediately. He seemed to be trying his best to suppress his anger. After a while, he asked coldly, "I hear that these days you have been talking to people without knowing the limits and have even criticized the emperor. Is that true?"

Huang Zongxi, who was listening with head bowed, raised his head and looked at the host with puzzlement. He hadn't expected Xu Shiqi to be angry for this. In fact, he was looking forward to the friend's support and help. Huang Zongxi had always believed that opening up the speech channel to give all wise people the right to judge the government and propose solutions to the problems was very important for national rejuvenation. He had indeed expressed his opinions on the current situation recently, but they were all out of concern for the safety of the Great Ming and survival of the country and none of them were out of a selfish motive. He didn't remember having ever criticized the emperor. Besides, the emperor was not necessarily correct all the time, and it was the duty of a subject to speak his mind. Why did Xu Shiqi take this kind of thing so seriously and get angry? Huang Zongxi was quite surprised and a little disappointed too, so he kept silent.

Huang Zongxi's silence annoyed Xu Shiqi. He stood up, took two steps forward, turned around suddenly, and admonished in a low voice, "This is the capital with strict surveillance, not River South, understand? In River South, you can say whatever you like, but this is the capital. You must be careful in your words and deeds, and follow the rules, but you—" He raised his voice as he spoke. "You are now a grown-up man and yet are still so imprudent and rash. How can I protect you when something unexpected happens? How can I be

又如何对得起地下的恩师？”

“兄长责备得是。不过，小弟之议论，自以为光明正大，并无不可告人之处。”黄宗羲沉静地回答。现在，他已经从最初的惊愕中恢复过来，并且准备有所申述了。

“你——”被对方的执迷不悟大大激怒了的徐石麒睁圆了眼睛。他的嘴巴抖动着，显然打算给予更严厉的申斥，但临时又改变了主意，只从袖筒抽出来一份手折，扔到桌子上。

“你自己看吧！”他冷冷地说，随即叉着腰，气哼哼背过身去，似乎打算再也不理会这件事了。

黄宗羲疑惑地瞅了瞅主人的背影，慢慢地捡起那份手折，打开来瞄了一眼。忽然，他心头一震，忙不迭地把手折举到眼前，一行一行地看下去。终于，他大吃一惊地呆住了。原来，这些天来，他在社交场合所说的每一句涉及时局的话，都被一字不漏地记录在这份手折里！

蓦地，一个狰狞可畏的名字闪过黄宗羲的脑际：“啊，东厂！毫无疑问，这是东厂的缉事人干的！要不，就是锦衣卫。可是这份机密的手折怎么又会到了兄长的手里呢？”黄宗羲震悚之余，又感到疑惑不解。他不由得抬起头，却发现，徐石麒也正好回过头来。

徐石麒严厉地瞅着他：“哼，看清楚了吧？要不是行人司的熊鱼山大人同锦衣卫的骆指挥有同乡之谊，知道这事，替你说情，把折子压下来，这会儿，只怕你早已身陷囹圄了！”

“……”

“熊大人今早特地把这折子拿来给愚兄，嘱我转知贤弟，今后务须检点言行，切不可率情任性，自干法网。熊大人还说，贤弟若再蹈覆辙，他就爱莫能助了！”也许因为看见黄宗羲低头不

worthy of my late teacher?"

"Dear elder brother, thank you for your criticism. However, my views are sincere and honest, and there's nothing to hide." Huang Zongxi replied calmly. Now he had recovered from his initial consternation and was ready to defend himself.

"You—" Xu Shiqi, who was greatly infuriated by the young man's stubbornness, widened his eyes. His mouth was quivering, obviously to give a more severe reprimand, but he changed his mind before he spoke and only took out a folded document from his sleeve and threw it on the table.

"See for yourself!" he said coldly, then with hands akimbo, turned his back angrily, as if to drop the matter altogether.

Huang Zongxi glanced at the back of the host in bewilderment, slowly picked up the folded document, opened it, and took a glance. Suddenly, his heart trembled, and he hurriedly moved the document closer to his eyes, and read it line by line. In the end, he froze in shock. Every word he had said on current affairs was recorded in this document!

Suddenly, a scary name flashed across Huang Zongxi's mind. "The East Factory! There's no doubt that it's the doing of the spies of the East Factory or the Jinyiwei Special Forces. But why is this confidential document in the hands of Brother Xu?" Huang Zongxi was shocked and puzzled at the same time. He lifted his head and saw that Xu Shiqi was turning around to him.

Xu Shiqi looked at him sternly. "Hmph, do you see it clearly? If it were not for the intercession of Mr. Xiong Yushan of the Communication Department, who is a fellow provincial of Commander Luo of the Jinyiwei, I'm afraid you would have already been in prison."

"..."

"Mr. Xiong came this morning and gave me the document. He asked me to tell you that in the future you must discipline yourself in words and deeds and mustn't be self-willed and be caught in the meshes of the law. Mr. Xiong also said that if you make the same mistakes again, he won't be able to help." Seeing Huang Zongxi kept

语，到后来，徐石麒稍稍缓和了语气。

“可是，小弟自问立心纯正，所言所行，无一不是为的社稷苍生着想，小弟实不知何罪之有！”黄宗羲抬起头，迎着徐石麒的目光，眼睛里充满苦恼的神色。

“胡说！你刚来一月，能知道多少京中情形、朝廷底细，便高谈阔论，肆口诋讥？”

“这个，小弟确实不知！”黄宗羲突然爆发似的高声说，“但小弟却知道，若是人人重足而立，侧目而视，钳口不言，离亡国便不远了！”

徐石麒没提防他会这样，反而吓了一跳。他本能地向窗外张望了一下，随即回过头来。

“好啊，照阁下这么说，今日之事，倒是愚兄不是了？”他恼羞成怒地问，一张青灰色的脸气成深紫，“好，既然如此，老夫不管就是！”他朝门外一指，“阁下请便吧！”

黄宗羲愣了一下，脸色不由得变了。他默默地瞅着徐石麒，神情显得愈来愈倔强、固执。终于，他慢慢地跪下去，趴在地上叩了一个头，然后站起来，一声不响地向外走去。

徐石麒倒抽一口凉气，目瞪口呆地瞧着黄宗羲跨出门槛，走下台阶。突然，他使劲地一跺脚，气急败坏地大嚷：

“站住，给我回来！”

## 危机四伏

当黄宗羲最后离开刑部衙门的时候，已经是下午。

不知是终于明白这位小弟并不是可以简单地压服的呢，还是被他那一腔凛凛正气所感动，徐石麒从盛怒地要把黄宗羲轰走，到最终又收回成命，态度发生了很大的变化。他不仅把黄宗羲留了下来，而且怀着对这位小弟的新的了解和爱重，同他谈得很多，很深入。他列举了种种事实，说明朝廷的黑暗和腐败，以及处身

silent with his head lowered, Xu Shiqi softened his tone a little.

"But my intentions are all good, and whatever I say or do is all for the sake of the country and the people. I really don't know what crime I'm committing." Huang Zongxi lifted his head to look at Xu Shiqi, his eyes full of distress.

"Nonsense! You have only been here for one month. How much did you know about Beijing and the imperial court before you made your comments and criticisms?"

"Surely I don't know much," Huang Zongxi said. Then suddenly he raised his voice. "But I do know that if everyone stands still, looks sideways, and says nothing, then the collapse of the Great Ming won't be far away."

Xu Shiqi was taken aback. He instinctively glanced out the window, then turned around.

"So, according to what you say, sir, the mistake is mine?" he asked exasperatedly, his gray face turning purple with anger. "Alright then, fine. I'll leave you alone." He showed Huang Zongxi the door and said, "You take care of yourself, sir!"

Huang Zongxi was stupefied. He looked at Xu Shiqi with a stubborn and rebellious expression. Finally, he slowly knelt down on the ground and kowtowed, then stood up and walked out in silence.

Xu Shiqi was taken aghast and stared at Huang Zongxi dumbfounded as he stepped across the threshold and walked down the steps. Suddenly, he stomped his foot and shouted angrily:

"Stop, come back!"

## Jeopardy

When Huang Zongxi left the *yamen* of the Ministry of Punishment, it was already afternoon.

Either having finally realized that this little brother was not to be easily subdued or having been moved by the righteousness of the young man, Xu Shiqi's attitude took a sudden turn. After showing Huang Zongxi the door, he called him back. Huang Zongxi stayed. With respect for and a new understanding of the little brother, Xu

在这样一个环境当中，应当怎样小心谨慎，绝不可任性胡来。为着说服黄宗羲，徐石麒甚至把朝廷最近发生的一件尚未完全公开的大事，也同他谈了。据说事情是这样的：原来，自从松山失守之后，皇上十分恐慌，一心设法同清军媾和，但又担心群臣知道，会起来反对阻挠，所以私下同兵部尚书陈新甲商量，决定背着外廷，派遣兵部员外郎马绍愉一行四人为使节，携带敕书到沈阳去同清方秘密交涉。这件事本来做得极为机密，一丝风儿也不透。不过，大约皇上也知道陈新甲的嘴巴不大牢靠，所以曾经反复叮嘱他绝对不能向外泄露。谁知陈新甲仍旧忍不住，把这件事悄悄告诉了当时奉命赴陕西对“流寇”作战的总督傅宗龙，傅宗龙临行前又告诉了内阁大学士谢升，谢升又向外廷的言官作了透露。消息就此传开了。起初言官们还半信半疑，于是一窝蜂地弹劾谢升，说他造谣惑众，用意却在试探皇上的态度。皇上查知是陈新甲露的底，心中自然恼火，但还是宽容了他，只把谢升罢官了事。不料偏偏事有凑巧，就在前几天，马绍愉把一份关于和谈情况的秘密报告送给陈新甲。陈新甲看过之后，随手放在书案上就离开了。他的家童误以为是日常战报，竟冒冒失失拿去给外面传抄。于是一下子真相大白，满朝哗然。皇上正为清军方面提出的苛刻条款而苦恼踌躇，冷不防外廷闹将起来，不禁又惊又气，一查泄密的原因，顿时火冒三丈，震怒异常，立即下严旨切责陈新甲，今天又把陈新甲逮捕入狱。看样子，大有要把他置于死地之意。

Shiqi held an in-depth discussion on a variety of issues with Huang Zongxi. He enumerated a number of facts to let the young man understand how decadent and corrupt the imperial court was and how one should be cautious in such circumstances. In order to convince Huang Zongxi, Xu Shiqi even divulged a latest event that hadn't been made public. After the fall of Songshan, the emperor panicked and wanted to make peace with the Qing army. For fear that the court officials would object upon hearing it, the emperor decided, after consulting Chen Xinjia, Minister of War, to send a group of four duly authorized delegates headed Ma Shaoyu, a department chief at the Ministry of War, to Shenyang to secretly negotiate peace with the Qing army without the knowledge of other court officials. It was meant to be a closely guarded secret. Knowing Chen Xinjia's tongue was not good at keeping secrets, the emperor had repeatedly told him not to divulge it to anybody else. However, Chen Xinjia couldn't help disclosing it to Governor General Fu Zonglong, who had received the edict to go to Shaanxi to fight against the insurgents. Before departure, Fu Zonglong told Xie Sheng, Secretary of the Cabinet. Xie Sheng told the supervisors of the Outer Court. Thus, it was quickly spread. At first, the supervisors didn't quite believe it, so they swarmed to impeach Xie Sheng, saying that he had spread rumors to delude the public, but their intention was to see the emperor's attitude. After finding out that it was Chen Xinjia who had leaked the secret, the emperor was very angry, but he pardoned him and dismissed Xie Sheng from office instead. Sometimes coincidences happen. Just a few days earlier, Ma Shaoyu had sent a secret report on the peace talks to Chen Xinjia. After Chen Xinjia read it, he put it on the desk and left. His servant boy mistakenly thought it was a daily war update and took it to the outside to be copied. So, all of a sudden, the truth came out, and there was an uproar in the court. The emperor, who was being deeply troubled by the harsh terms proposed by the Qing army, was very angry. When he found out about the reason for the leak, he flew into a rage and immediately issued an edict ordering the punishment of Chen Xinjia, who was arrested today and was very likely to receive

黄宗羲进府时所碰见的那三位官员，就是陈新甲平日的好友，特地来向徐石麒求情，请他帮忙设法从轻发落的。

说完这件事，徐石麒捋着胡子，沉重地喘了一口气："按说呢，陈某身为大司马，执掌兵部数年间，无尺寸之功，反使边关重镇四座、内地重镇七十二座，分别沦于建虏、流寇之手，藩王七人遭杀戮，可谓罪有应得。唯是议和之事，显系奉皇上之旨，不过如今败露，他纵欲申辩，又有何用？便是愚兄审理，也唯有判他一个'蔽主专擅，私款辱国'而已！所以贤弟口口声声说为臣之道，在于直言不讳，又岂知审时度势，尤为重要！陈新甲不识时务，事发之后，他不深自引罪，还直陈其功，这就无异是拿皇上的过失来张扬，所以非死不可了！此事近在眼前，贤弟难道还不该深省么？"

不知道是因为这件新闻太令人震惊，还是徐石麒的劝说起了作用，自此之后，黄宗羲没有再坚持原来的见解。他顺从地留在徐府吃了午饭，等新的一批说情者一到，他就辞了出来。

现在，黄宗羲骑着马，独自走在归途上。刚才在徐石麒衙里听到的那件新闻，在他心里所引起的吃惊和震动一直没有消失，毋宁说，使他的心情变得更加混乱了。因为朝廷和清军秘密议和的消息，尽管已经风传了好些日子，但是黄宗羲却一直希望这不是真的。事实上，黄宗羲也如同当时相当一部分朝野人士那样，认为山海关外的辽东以及奴儿干地区，本来就是大明疆土的一部分，如今在那里大胆妄为地建国称帝的女真族人，本来是明朝的

the death sentence. The three officials that Huang Zongxi had met when he entered the *yamen* were Chen Xinjia's friends, who had come to plead with Xu Shiqi for a lighter punishment.

After he finished speaking, Xu Shiqi stroked his beard and let out a heavy breath. "As the top military officer, Mr. Chen has been in charge of the Ministry of War for several years without any record of victory. Instead, he's lost four important border towns and seventy-two key towns in the heartland to the Jurchens and the insurgents. Seven vassal kings have been killed. So, the punishment just serves him right. The secret negotiation of peace with the enemy is obviously the decision of the emperor. Now that it's known, he must be the scapegoat. Even if I am chosen to try him, the only thing I can do is to convict him of 'cheating the emperor and colluding with the enemy'. You keep saying speaking up one's mind honestly is the responsibility of a loyal subject to the emperor, but you don't know how important it is to be aware of the circumstances. Chen Xinjia didn't understand this. After the incident broke, instead of reflecting on his own mistake, he was proclaiming his contribution, which was tantamount to publicizing the Emperor's faults, so he must die! I hope you can take a lesson from this."

Either because the news was too shocking, or Xu Shiqi's persuasion worked, Huang Zongxi no longer insisted on his views. He obediently stayed in the Xu residence for lunch, and when a new batch of intercessors arrived, he took his leave.

Now, Huang Zongxi was going back on horseback. He hadn't yet recovered from the impact of the news he had heard in Xu Shiqi's *yamen* just now. To be more exact, his mind was turbulent. The rumor that the imperial court and the Qing army were negotiating a peace deal had been around for quite a few days, but he had always wished that it were not true. As a matter of fact, Huang Zongxi, like quite a few others in and out of the imperial court, believed that the Liaodong and Nuergan area outside the Shanhai Pass was originally part of the Ming territory, the Jurchens who had started a new country with an emperor there were originally subjects of the Great Ming, their

臣民，他们对明朝的无情进逼，是一种犯上作乱的叛逆行为，对他们决不能饶恕，更不能承认他们的政权。而一旦同他们和谈，就无异于把他们置于同明朝平等的地位，这是万万不可以的。所以朝廷上下，一向以和谈为耻辱。加上崇祯皇帝又是一个极要面子的人，也十分忌讳和谈。不过如今的问题在于，恰恰就是皇帝本人，竟然也暗中派人向建虏输款。在黄宗羲看来，这实在是一个极其不祥之兆。“啊，难道局面已经到了这样严重的地步，连皇上也觉得除了输款，再没有别的办法了么？”黄宗羲惶惑地想。这种突然暴露的内幕，仿佛一下子清除了这些天来在黄宗羲眼前的许多迷离恍惚的遮蔽物，使他比任何时候都更加清晰地看到：那道日夜危及大明政权生存的可怕裂缝，到底有多深。这一发现，同自己竟然成了锦衣卫鹰犬们侦查搏击的对象那件事交缠在一起，黄宗羲的心情就变得更加阴暗了。

如今，他已经出了宣武门，本该一直朝南，回方以智的住宅。但他坐在马背上只顾想心事，竟不知不觉走差了方向，直到马儿在一堵坍塌了的破墙面前停住不走，才猛然惊醒过来。

“啊，我怎么会走到这里？这是什么地方？”他茫然四顾，发觉自己不知什么时候，已经走在一片废墟之间。前面的去路被瓦砾堵死，两旁是接连不断的颓垣败壁，丛生的野草灌木，还有满地的破砖碎瓦，却难得看见有梁柱和门窗。大约这片废墟已经存在多年，可利用的木料都早已被人取走了。如今，在断墙残壁之间，横七竖八地搭起了一些低矮肮脏的窝棚，还开出了几畦菜地。自然，也住了不少居民。不过，看来他们都是一些来自城郊的流民，无处栖身，迫不得已才麇集到这片废墟上，所以景况特

ruthless attack on the Great Ming was an act of rebellion and should never be forgiven, and their government should never be recognized. Negotiating with them was tantamount to placing them on an equal footing with the Great Ming, which should absolutely be forbidden. That was also why everyone in the court had always regarded any peace talk as shameful, and Emperor Chongzhen, who was a face-loving person, had also regarded the subject of negotiating a peace deal as taboo. The problem now was, it was the emperor himself who was secretly bribing the Jianzhou Jurchens. Huang Zongxi saw it as a bad omen. "Have things come to such a pass that even the emperor himself thought there's no other solution than to bribe the Jurchens?" Huang Zongxi thought bemusedly. This sudden exposure of the inside story seemed to have cleared away many of the objects that had obstructed his vision these days and enabled him to see more clearly than ever how deep the terrifying crack that threatened the Ming edifice day and night was. This discovery, coupled with the fact that he had become the target of investigation and persecution of the Jinyiwei spies, sent Huang Zongxi into a greater despondency.

He was supposed to head south for Fang Yizhi's place after passing the Xuanwu Gate, but since he was too obsessed with his thoughts, he unknowingly went in the wrong direction and didn't realize it until the horse stopped in front of a collapsed wall.

"Why am I here? What is this place?" He looked around nervously, realizing that he was walking among ruins. The road ahead was blocked by rubble. On his both sides were broken walls standing amid weeds, shrubs, and shattered bricks and tiles, with almost no beams, pillars, doors and windows. The ruins had probably been there for many years, and all woodwork of any use at all had long been taken away. Between the broken walls were some low and dirty shacks and a few patches of vegetables. Evidently, there were quite a few residents in the neighborhood, who were refugees from the outskirts of the city. They had nowhere to go to and had to live in the ruins as a last resort. It was a pathetic sight. There was no single person that was decently dressed. All the people here, either the ones who were

别可怜。此刻，黄宗羲竟看不见一个衣着哪怕稍为光鲜一点的人。不论是挑担的、提篮的、徒手的，还是蹲在墙基上捉虱子聊天的，全都穿得那样破烂肮脏，而且大多数神情麻木、心事重重。即使偶尔响起一两声嬉笑，也都摆脱不掉绝望、凄凉的意味，只有那些个衣不蔽体的野孩子，似乎比较容易忘却人世的辛酸。他们成群结队地在风沙飞旋的瓦砾上撒欢，忽然又厮打起来，发出了响亮的、粗野的喧闹……

“啊，原来京城里还有这么一个地方，我却从来不知道。”黄宗羲惊奇地想，一边打量着周围的情景，发现不远的路旁，有一个小小的茶寮，几个人正坐在里面喝茶。他想了一下，便驱马过去，跳下地来，对那个卖茶的中年汉子拱一拱手，问：

“请教大哥，这儿是什么地方，怎么会成了这样子，敢是遭了兵火么？”

那卖茶汉子长得腰粗体壮，神气粗豪。他打量了一下黄宗羲，却先不回答，伸出毛茸茸的左手，拿起一个粗瓷大碗，右手提起茶罐子，哗哗地满满斟了一碗茶，往黄宗羲面前一放，说：

“秀才，你问的可是件了不得的大事儿，少说也该值他娘的三两银子！你若要我答你，须得喝了我这碗茶！”

黄宗羲怔了一下，疑疑惑惑地问：“不知大哥这茶……”

那汉子哈哈大笑起来：“秀才放心！我纵然想诈你三两银子，你也未必拿得出；就算拿得出，你也未必肯！告诉你，我这茶只要一文大钱！”

黄宗羲这才放下心来。他伸手在袖筒里摸索一会，掏出一个铜钱，放在桌上，又拱着手说：“不敢请教大哥……”

那汉子拿起铜钱，瞄了一眼，又放在手里掂了掂，撇着嘴冷笑说：“如今这种‘崇祯通宝’又轻又薄，只怕丢到水里都浮得起，

carrying things with a shoulder pole or a hand, or who were empty-handed, or who were squatting at the foot of a wall catching lice while talking to each other, were dressed in dirty rags, and most of them looked numb and dejected. The occasional laughter didn't disperse the despair and desolation. Only those wild children who were barely clothed seemed to be mindless of the suffering of the world. They frolicked on the rubble and amid the flying dust, in twos and threes, and suddenly fought each other, shouting and screaming ...

"Why haven't I heard of such a place in the capital before?" Huang Zongxi wondered. He looked around and saw a small tea house on the roadside ahead of him, where a few men were drinking tea. After a moment of hesitation, he rode over, got off the horse, bowed to the middle-aged tea house owner, and asked, "Sir, what's this place? Why is it like this? Is it because of the war?"

The tea house owner was a burly man of a large build. He looked at Huang Zongxi, and without immediately replying to the young man, he picked up a large porcelain bowl with his hairy left hand and lifted the teapot with his right hand, filled the bowl, put it in front of Huang Zongxi, and said, "Oh, Mr. Scholar, you are asking something very important. It's worth at least three taels of silver. If you want me to answer you, you must drink this bowl of tea."

Huang Zongxi was startled. He asked in bewilderment, "Sir, is your tea ..."

The man laughed loudly and said, "Don't worry, Mr. Scholar! Even if I want to defraud you of three taels of silver, you might not have it; even if you have it, you might not want to give it to me. Honestly speaking, it only costs one *wen*."

Huang Zongxi was relieved. He fumbled in his sleeve for a while, took out a copper coin, put it on the table, and then clasped his hand and said, "So, sir, can you tell me ..."

The burly man picked up the copper coin, glanced at it, weighed it in his hand, curled his lips, and sneered, "Nowadays, this kind of Chongzhen mint coin is so light and thin that it can even float on water. This one is no use. Let me give it to the kids and they can play

有个屁用，只配给小孩玩儿罢啦！”说完，他伸出头去，扯着嗓门吆喝了一声，把铜钱朝街心抛去。那群正在戏耍追逐的野孩子顿时一拥而上，喧呼争夺起来。

黄宗羲脸红了一下，感到有点不好意思，只好又把手伸到袖筒里，想挑个好点的钱给他。那卖茶汉子见了，却摇摇手说：“行啦，你秀才就别摸了！如今京城里，也就剩下这种‘鹅眼钱’啦！只怕你摸穿了袖子，还是一样！”

“哎，我说郝大哥，你别瞧不起这‘鹅眼钱’！赶明年，怕就要使到铁钱、铅钱啦！到时你再想找它，还没有哩！”一个上了年纪的茶客沙哑着嗓子插嘴说，他有一个又红又大的酒糟鼻子，头上扣一顶满是破洞的旧毡帽，下面露出乱蓬蓬的白发。

“怎么没有？”一个瘦瘦的、长得蛮俊的后生笑嘻嘻地接上来，“兴许到时这种崇祯鬼子钱统统都要废了，另造一种又亮又大的新钱呢！”

“嗯，要真这样，那敢情好！”老茶客眯缝着眼睛说，溜了黄宗羲一眼。

听着这两人一对一答，黄宗羲似懂非懂：“嗯，要把这些钱都废了，另造新钱，这是什么意思？”他想，不过，随后又自己笑起来，“瞧你！无非是市井愚民几句闲扯淡，你倒认真起来了。”

“秀才，你不是要问这地方怎么会成了这样子么？告诉你，这是天启六年那一场大地震弄的。打这儿一直往北，到刑部街，周围十多里地，都是这样。你只怕是头回到这鬼地方来，所以不知。”那个叫郝大哥的卖茶汉子瞅着他，瓮声瓮气地说。

黄宗羲“哦”了一声，忽然想起来了：天启六年，也就是他

with it." Then, he popped his head out of the tea house and threw the copper coin towards the middle of the street with a "Hey, there!" and a flap of his arm. The bunch of wild children who were chasing each other suddenly swarmed toward it.

Huang Zongxi blushed in embarrassment and put his hand back into his sleeve, trying to find a better coin. Seeing that, the tea house owner waved his hand and said, "That's alright. You can't find it. Now in the capital, there's only this kind of 'goose-eye coin' left. I'm afraid you can't find anything better than that even if you break your sleeve by fumbling hard."

"Hey, listen, Brother Hao, don't look down on this 'goose-eye coin'! I'm afraid we'll have to use iron coins or even lead coins next year. By then, if you want to find such coins, they don't exist." interjected an elderly customer with a large, red bumpy nose in a hoarse voice, who was wearing an old felt hat full of holes on his head, with bushy white hair underneath.

"Why don't they exist?" a thin, handsome young man took it up with a smile. "Maybe by then all this kind of Chongzhen ghost money will be abolished and a new, bright and big coin will be created."

"Well, if that be the case, then it's good," the elderly customer said with narrowed eyes, glancing at Huang Zongxi.

As the two men bantered, Huang Zongxi understood the situation a little bit. "Well, what do they mean by 'all this kind of Chongzhen ghost money will be abolished and a new, bright and big coin will be created'?" he thought, but then he laughed, "Look at you! It's nothing more than a gossip of some idiots in the marketplace, but you're taking it seriously."

"Mr. Scholar, aren't you asking how this place has become like this? Let me tell you now. It's the result of the great earthquake in the sixth year of the reign of Emperor Tianqi[AD 1626]. Ten *li* from here all the way north to the Ministry of Punishment Street, it's all like this. I'm afraid that you're in this damn place for the first time, so you don't know it," said the tea house owner called Brother Hao in a throaty voice, looking at Huang Zongxi.

Huang Zongxi said "oh" and suddenly remembered the curious

父亲被魏忠贤迫害，死于狱中的第二年，听说北京发生了一场奇特的大震灾，毁坏房屋无数，还震死了不少人。当时都传说是上天示警……

“这个——在下也曾闻说。不过，都整整十六年了，怎么还是这样子？”他半信半疑地问，一边回头去看那片废墟。

郝大哥呵呵笑起来：“秀才，你可问得真逗！怎么还是老样子？它不是这样子，还能怎么个样子？莫非你还想皇帝老儿大发慈悲，把‘三饷’全免了，好让大伙儿把房子建起来不成？”

黄宗羲怔了一下，脸顿时沉了下来：“不错，这话也许是事实，可是此人说到皇上的那种口吻神情，却大是不敬！”黄宗羲觉得有必要告诫对方几句。但是接下来听到的话，却更使他吃惊。

这是那个俊俏后生。他笑嘻嘻地瞅着黄宗羲：“要它不是这个样子也不难，不过，那可得等到——”说着，他憋起嗓子，用河南小调唱起来，“吃他娘，穿他娘……”

他本想唱下去，那个郝大哥回头狠狠地盯了他一眼，他就临时停住了。

然而，黄宗羲已经听懂了。还在江南时，他就听说，李自成为着煽惑群众，收买民心，不久前曾造了几句民谣，道是：“吃他娘，穿他娘，闯王来了不纳粮！”现在这青年唱的，不就是那支民谣吗？蓦地，一个可怕的念头在黄宗羲心中一闪：“啊，他们是流贼的细作！”他的脸色不由得变了，一刹那间，吃惊得连心脏也仿佛停止了跳动，随后又差点儿要拔腿飞奔，但是理智告诫他：千万不能有任何异常的表示！要不，在这个地方，他们随时都能把你杀了！于是，为了掩饰自己的慌乱，也为了镇定一下，他端起那一碗本来嫌脏、不打算喝的茶，咕嗞咕嗞地灌了下去，放下碗，抹抹嘴，偷窥了一下对方的神色。随即装出微笑，道过

earthquake in Beijing that destroyed countless houses and killed a lot of people in the sixth year of the reign of Emperor Tianqi, the year after his father's death from Wei Zhongxian's persecution. It was rumored at that time that it was a warning from Providence ...

"I—I've heard of it. It was sixteen years ago, but why is it still like this here?" he asked in disbelief, looking back at the ruins.

Big Brother Hao laughed. "Mr. Scholar, your question is so funny! Why is it still like this here? If it were not like this, what could it be like? Do you still want the emperor to show mercy and free us from the three taxes so that we can rebuild the houses?"

Huang Zongxi was struck speechless and his face suddenly sank. "Yes, this may be true, but the way this man speaks of the emperor is very disrespectful," Huang Zongxi thought. He felt like admonishing the tea house owner, but what he heard next surprised him even more.

It was the handsome young man. He looked at Huang Zongxi with a smile, saying, "It isn't difficult to change the situation, but we would have to wait until—" As he spoke, he raised his voice and sang in a Henan Opera tune, "We have nothing to eat, and nothing to wear ..."

Big Brother Hao turned to him and gave him a fierce look, so he stopped.

Huang Zongxi was shocked. He had heard back in River South that Li Zicheng had recently made a ballad to incite the masses, which said "We have nothing to eat, and nothing to wear. When the Rebel King comes, we'll be free from the taxes ..." What the young man was singing was exactly that ballad. Suddenly, a terrifying thought flashed in Huang Zongxi's mind. "These are the spies of the rebels," he thought. His countenance changed suddenly, and he was so scared that his heart stopped beating. As he was going to take to his heels, his better sense told him that he should stay calm, or, in this place, they could kill him anytime. So, in order to cover up his panic and calm down, he picked up the bowl of tea, which was dirty and he hadn't intended to drink, and poured it down his throat. Then, he put down the bowl, wiped his mouth, took a stealthy look at the men in the tea house, and immediately put on a smile. "Thank you, sir," he said, and

谢，转身离开茶寮。由于心慌，他上马时很费了点事，好不容易爬上马背，又不敢立即奔逃，慢慢地走出几十步远，估计那伙人再也赶不上了，这才在马屁股上使劲抽了一鞭，纵辔狂奔起来。“常听人说，流贼细作已经遍布京师，我还不信，不想今日当面碰上了！”黄宗羲心忙意乱地想，不断加鞭，等马儿一直跑出了废墟，进入上斜街时，他才渐渐收紧了辔头。

不知是当年受震较轻呢，还是由于靠近大街，恢复得较快，这一带的房屋虽然也十分简陋，总算还像个样子，路上的行人也较多，整个气氛已不似先前那样荒凉诡秘。黄宗羲惊魂稍定，松了一口气，但随后又感到十分气愤：“真是岂有此理！京师重地，怎么连流贼的细作混了进来都没人管？那些厂卫的缉事人都是干什么的？为什么不赶紧来个全城大搜查，把这些家伙统统抓起来，该关的关，该杀的杀！照这样子闹下去，万一流寇真的打进来，怎么得了！”

他越想越感到情况严重，觉得有必要马上向巡捕营报告，让他们派人先把茶寮里的那几个人抓起来。“对，可别叫他们跑了！”黄宗羲想，顿时亢奋起来。可是，巡捕营在哪里呢？他焦急地四处张望，想找个路人询问一下。没等他拿定主意，在街道的另一头，远远响起了一阵尖锐的呼啸。那是一种凄厉的、惊骇的声浪，仿佛是屠夫追逐着牛羊，又像是烈风摧折着树木。那呼啸越来越近，越来越响，渐渐变成了路人走避的脚步声，店铺关门的乒乓声，爹娘和儿女的呼唤声，以及东西被碰翻、打破的声音……黄宗羲被这突如其来的混乱景象弄糊涂了。他本能地打算跟着躲避。

turned to leave. Because of his panic, he had great difficulty getting on the horse. When he finally climbed onto the back of the horse, he didn't dare to run away immediately. Instead, he moved at a very slow speed at first until he reached a safe distance. Then, he whipped up the horse, loosened the reins, and galloped forward. "When people said that the spies of the insurgents are all over the capital, I didn't believe it, but today, I've seen it with my own eyes," Huang Zongxi thought, rather disturbed, as he kept whipping the horse until it took him out of the ruins and entered the Upper Oblique Street. Only then did he tighten the reins.

The houses in this neighborhood were much more decent, though the structures were crude. Maybe they hadn't been much affected by the earthquake. Maybe they had been quickly rebuilt after the damage because they were close to the main street. There were quite some pedestrians on the road, and the bleakness and terror that he had had a moment ago didn't belong here. Huang Zongxi was relieved and breathed a sigh of relief, but then he couldn't help getting angry again. "This is outrageous. Why do they allow the spies of the insurgents to enter the capital at all? What's the use of the secret agents of the East Factory, the West Factory, and the Jinyiwei? Why don't they search the city to arrest and kill all the spies? If things go on like this, the consequences will be serious when the insurgents finally come to the capital."

The more he thought about it, the more worried he was. He felt it necessary to report it to the patrol station immediately. The spies in the tea house should be arrested first. "Yes, don't let them escape!" Huang Zongxi thought with excitement. But where is the patrol station? He looked around anxiously, looking for a passerby to ask. While he was hesitating, a sharp whistling sounded in the distance on the other side of the street. It was a shrill, terrifying sound, like that of a butcher chasing cattle or sheep, or a gale breaking trees. The whistling got closer and closer, louder and louder, and gradually turned into a din of pedestrians dodging, shops closing, parents and children calling each other, and things being knocked over and smashed ... Huang Zongxi was befuddled by this sudden chaos. He instinctively dodged

忽然，一切声音都停止了，路上的行人也全不见了。他正在不知所措，渐渐地又有了响动。不过，那是急骤的马蹄声，错杂而单调，一队人马风驰电掣般奔了过来。马上的甲士，个个衣履鲜明，神情冷傲，对于他们出现所引起的惊慌和混乱仿佛早已习以为常，不屑一顾。他们在离黄宗羲还有十来步远的地方突然停住，随即跳下马来。

黄宗羲定神一看：“咦，这不就是锦衣卫的缇骑吗？好了，这下可不用到处找了！”黄宗羲想，连忙驱马上前，打算向他们报告刚才遇到的情况。

缇骑们却根本没有注意他。他们一下马，就向路旁的一个带篱笆的院子走去。头里的一个一抬腿，“砰”地踹开了院门，其余的人跟着冲了进去。紧接着，屋子里就传出了喝骂声、哭喊声和乒乒乓乓摔家伙的声响。一个女人带哭的嗓音尖叫：

“天哪！我们可是本分人家，怎么敢去做强盗哇……”

黄宗羲吃了一惊：“怎么，莫非这里也藏着流贼奸细不成？”他连忙走过去，隔着篱笆往里瞧去，顿时呆住了。原来，这是一个靠种花出卖为生的人家。黄宗羲还记得很清楚，今天上午，他上徐石麒的衙门，行经这里时，还曾经怀着平静而愉快的心情，眺望过园子里的烂漫秋色，对那些五彩缤纷的秋葵、蓝菊、草本夹竹桃、海棠和璎珞鸡冠表示过由衷的喜悦。可是，如今这些花木正遭受着最无情的摧残，两个顶盔贯甲，全副武装的缇骑，正在不声不响地以最冷静而干脆的动作，对花园进行着彻底的破坏。他们用利斧砍倒花木，用铁锤砸毁假山，还用沉重的战靴在苗圃上践踏过去……

黄宗羲被眼前的情景弄糊涂了。他直瞪瞪地望着那些断头折臂的花木，那些五颜六色、狼藉满地的花朵。其中，在一株被齐

like the others. Suddenly, all sounds stopped, and all the pedestrians on the road disappeared. As he was wondering what was happening, another sound arose. It was the sound of hurried hooves, cluttered and monotonous. A fleet of horse riders rushed over at a gallop. The armored soldiers on the horses were all dressed in uniform and looked stern, oblivious to the panic and confusion they had caused. They stopped abruptly at a distance of about ten steps from Huang Zongxi and jumped off their horses.

Huang Zongxi looked over. "Isn't this the Jinyiwei cavalry? Good. Now, I don't have to look for them," Huang Zongxi thought as he hurriedly went forward to report to them what he had seen just now.

The cavalrymen didn't pay attention to him at all. They got off their horses and walked to a fenced courtyard by the road. The one in front raised his leg and kicked open the courtyard gate with a "bang", and the rest rushed in. Then came the sounds of shouting, swearing, crying, and smashing. A woman screamed with a crying voice, "Blimey! We're good people. How can we be bandits ..."

Huang Zongxi was taken aback. "What? Are there rebels and spies hiding here too?" He hurriedly walked over and looked in through the fence. He was stunned. It was a family who made a living by growing and selling flowers. He clearly remembered that he had admired the beautiful autumn scene in the garden in a calm and happy mood and the pageantry of sunflowers, signet marigolds, felicia amelloides, mango lotus, herbaceous oleander, begonia, and amaranthaceae had filled him with joy when he passed this place on his way to Xu Shiqi's *yamen* in the morning. However, these flower plants and trees were now being ruthlessly destroyed. Two fully armed cavalrymen, clad in helmet and armor, were quietly and determinedly erasing the garden with the fastest movement. They chopped down the flower plants and trees with sharp axes, smashed the rockery with hammers, and trampled the nursery with heavy combat boots ...

Huang Zongxi was confused by the scene in front of him. He stared at the flower plants and trees, whose heads and arms were broken and whose flowers were littering the ground. On the bare stalk

腰砍断的秋葵的光秆上，伏着一只白色的小蝴蝶，大约它在这一场突然降临的灾难中躲避不及，受了伤，飞不起来了。现在，它正抖颤着翅膀，在葵秆上艰难地爬行着，在它的身子后面，还拖着一条黏糊糊的“肠子”……黄宗羲瞅着瞅着，渐渐眼前的景象变了，仿佛此刻在他面前的不是花园子，而是阴森可怖的诏狱。那些被砍倒在地的也不是花木，而是被锦衣卫拘拿入狱的东林党人。其中有杨涟、左光斗、魏大中、周朝瑞、顾大章、袁化中、周顺昌、高攀龙以及自己的父亲黄尊素，而且似乎连他——黄宗羲本人也在内……他们有的断颈，有的折臂，有的拖出肠子在挣命。地上那些五颜六色的东西，就是他们流出的脓和血……蓦地，黄宗羲发出一声低沉而钝浊的呼叫，用双手掩着脸孔，回头便走。他跌跌撞撞地奔到马前，爬了上去，挥动马鞭，直到跑回方以智的住宅，他都没有回头再看一眼。

第二天一早，黄宗羲就吩咐黄安收拾行李，跟着陆符搬到城西的万驸马北湖园里去了。

## 共赏秋菊

崇祯十五年九月下旬，也就是距黄宗羲搬走之后两个多月，方以智收到在丰台做官的一位同年送来的十几盆名种菊花。他赏玩之余，一时兴动，便备下酒席，写了帖子，邀请平日要好的两位同僚——詹事府谕德吴伟业和兵科给事中龚鼎孳过来饮酒赏花。吴、龚二位都是老复社成员，吴伟业还是复社领袖张溥的得意学生。三人在江南时，就已经彼此认识。不过，后来方以智到了京里，同吴伟业相处的时间久些，关系也比较密切。至于龚鼎孳，因为一直在湖北做官，不久前才调到北京来任职，过去方以智同他虽然有过联系，但是相知不深。而且对于这位合肥才子，

of a sunflower plant that was cut off in the middle lay a small white butterfly that had failed to escape from this sudden disaster and had been seriously wounded. Now, it strenuously crawled on the sunflower stalk, dragging a sticky, smashed body, fluttering its wings ... As Huang Zongxi watched, the scene gradually changed from a garden into an eerie and terrifying interrogation chamber and the flower plants and trees became the East Wooders who had been arrested by the Jinyiwei. Among them were Yang Lian, Zuo Guangdou, Wei Dazhong, Zhou Chaorui, Gu Dazhang, Yuan Huazhong, Zhou Shunchang, Gao Panlong, his own father Huang Zunsu, and even himself ... Some of them had broken necks, some had broken arms, and some were dragging their intestines and struggling to live. The colored spots on the ground were their blood ... Suddenly, Huang Zongxi let out a low and dull cry, covered his face with his hands, and turned around to leave. He stumbled to his horse, mounted it, waved his whip, and fled all the way back to Fang Yizhi's residence without ever looking back.

Early the next morning, Huang Zongxi packed up through Huang An and followed Lu Fu to Prince Wan's North Lake Garden in the west of the city.

## Viewing Chrysanthemums

Late September, AD 1642, the 15th year of the reign of Emperor Chongzhen, that is, two months after Huang Zongxi moved out, Fang Yizhi received a dozen pots of rare chrysanthemums from a coeval of his, who was an official in Fengtai. He loved them so much that he prepared a banquet and sent for two colleagues, Wu Weiye, morality teacher to the crown prince, and Gong Dingzi, Secretary of Military Supervision. Both were veteran members of the Fushe, and Wu Weiye was also a favorite pupil of Zhang Pu, leader of the Fushe. The three had met in River South. After Fang Yizhi arrived in Beijing, he spent more time with Wu Weiye, so the two had a closer relationship. Since Gong Dingzi had been an official in Hubei and only had been recently transferred to Beijing, Fang Yizhi didn't know him very well. Moreover, Fang Yizhi didn't like this "genius from Hefei" very much,

方以智还说不上太喜欢，总觉得他过于八面玲珑，多少有点装腔作势的味道。不过，方以智也不是那种心地浅狭的人，他看见对方经常上门，对自己颇为尊重，再加上吴伟业当面背后都一直在说龚鼎孳的好话，于是对这位新朋友也就渐渐热乎起来。

如今，方以智同两位客人坐在书房的明间里。那十几盆名种菊花就分成两排，陈列在台阶下。其中有什么“醉杨妃”“银鹤翎”“鸡冠紫”“留仙绉”“霓裳羽衣”等等，名色不同，姿态各异，正在晴和的九月阳光下，舒展着五彩缤纷的花瓣。阵阵清香，随着清爽的秋风飘到筵席上来。三位朋友已经着意观赏赞叹过一回，还分韵赋了几首诗，如今一边坐着闲谈，一边继续饮酒赏花。龚鼎孳是个爱说话的人，更兼交游广阔，消息灵通，所以照例大部分时间，都是他和方以智高谈阔论。吴伟业则在一旁静静地听着，很少插嘴，清秀的脸上始终带着温雅的微笑。

现在，他们已经转移了好几个话题，因为是随意而谈，所以也没有什么次序，一会儿谈起七月中田贵妃的病逝和她妹子入宫顶替，一会儿又扯到抄手胡同华家的专煮猪头肉，扯到不久前南京皇宫所发生的一桩离奇的失宝案，然后又回到北京，说最近有人在田弘遇府上见到了陈圆圆，比在江南时仿佛清瘦了些，却是更美艳了。接着，他们就把陈圆圆同董小宛比较了一番。龚鼎孳认为董小宛无论如何比不上陈圆圆，冒襄皆因平日过于自负，这次落得了哑巴吃黄连，也怨不得谁；方以智却不同意，认为董小

because he felt that the man was too sophisticated and somewhat pretentious. However, Fang Yizhi was not the shallow and narrow-minded sort. Since Mr. Gong often came to see him and appeared very respectful, and Wu Weiye kept speaking well of him either in his presence or behind his back, Fang Yizhi gradually began to accept this new friend.

Now, Fang Yizhi was sitting on the patio of the study with the two guests. The dozen or so pots of precious chrysanthemums were divided into two rows and displayed under the steps. Among them were The Drunken Lady Yang, Silver Crane Feathers, Rooster Crown Purple, Crepe Skirt, and Neon Feather Dress, each with a different name, color pattern and posture, stretching their colorful petals under the warm September sun. Waves of sweet aroma drifted to the table with the cool autumn wind. The three friends watched and praised them for a while and composed a few poems in different rhymes, then conversed while continuing to drink and enjoy the flowers. Gong Dingzi was a talkative person with extensive contacts and a wealth of information. So, most of the time, he was doing the talking to Fang Yizhi. Wu Weiye listened quietly and rarely interrupted, always wearing a gentle smile on his delicate face.

They switched from one topic to another. Because it was a casual conversation, they didn't have to follow any sequence. At one moment, they talked about the death of Royal Concubine Lady Tian in July and her sister's entering the palace as a replacement. At another moment, they spoke of the specially boiled pig head meat of the Hua's Restaurant on Chaoshou Alley. Then, they veered to the bizarre theft of a precious treasure that had recently taken place in the Nanjing Imperial Palace. Then they switched back to Beijing, saying that someone had recently seen Chen Yuanyuan at Tian Hongyu's mansion, that she looked thinner than when she was in River South but more beautiful. They compared Chen Yuanyuan with Dong Xiaowan. Gong Dingzi thought that Dong Xiaowan was not as good as Chen Yuanyuan by any means and Mao Xiang had to accept her as a result of his self-conceit, but Fang Yizhi disagreed, saying that although Dong Xiaowan

宛也许色艺稍逊，难得的却是人品端庄，没有陈圆圆那么多风尘气味。最后，照例是吴伟业出来打圆场，说陈董二人各有千秋，也正如眼前这菊花——“醉杨妃”和“银鹤翎”，观赏者可以各有偏爱，其实却未易轩轾，才把这场争论平息下来。这之后，他们就把话题转到战局方面，从不久前朝廷派出的援军在朱仙镇遭到惨败，谈到河南开封已经危在旦夕，又谈到兵部的昏庸无能。末了，话题回到眼下轰动朝野的那件大新闻——兵部尚书陈新甲一案上来。

“说来可笑之至！”方以智说，“陈老头儿自从在狱中上疏，乞求宽宥，被皇上驳回之后，如今又里外上下地一个劲儿送礼请托，昨儿竟送到我这儿来了！”

“那么，方兄必定是拒之门外无疑啰！”龚鼎孳微笑地问，白皙的脸上现出凑趣的神情。

方以智摇摇头：“小弟是照收不误！”

“哦？”

“龚兄奇怪么？”方以智瞅了他一眼，一本正经地说，“据小弟看，陈老头儿今番自取其败，只怕是神仙下凡也救他不得了——只是可惜这一百两银子！他既然着人巴巴地送上门来，小弟若不受他，自必会有旁人承受。与其让别人承受，何如由小弟承受？譬如今日，小弟欲请二位老兄来此饮酒赏花，这银子便正好充作酒资，比之让那些俗物得了，拿去求田问舍，放债积谷，岂不胜似多多！何况，陈老头儿平素贪婪得紧，这银子本非光明正大之财，就算白送一点给我们，他也没有什么可埋怨的！”

might be less beautiful and less talented, she had a better character and didn't have the dusty smell of Chen Yuanyuan. In the end, as usual, Wu Weiye intervened to settle the dispute, saying, Miss Chen and Miss Dong each had their own merits, and just like the chrysanthemums in front of us—Drunken Lady Yang and Silver Crane Feathers—viewers can have their own preferences, but in fact, their preferences won't undermine the charms of either. After that, they turned the topic to the war and spoke of things like: the reinforcement troops sent by the imperial court to Zhuxian Town had suffered a serious defeat, Kaifeng in Henan Province was in a precarious situation, the Ministry of War was filled with corrupt and incompetent men ... In the end, they returned to the breaking news that was causing a stir in and out of the court at the moment—the case of Chen Xinjia, Minister of War.

"It's like a joke," Fang Yizhi said. "Old Man Chen wrote a letter to His Majesty from prison begging for forgiveness but met with a rebuttal. Now he's bribing everyone for intercession on his behalf. You know what? He actually sent money to me yesterday."

"Then, you must have rejected it," Gong Dingzi asked with a friendly smile on his fair face.

Fang Yizhi shook his head, saying, "No. Of course I've accepted it."

"Oh?"

"You must be wondering why I took it, Brother Gong." Fang Yizhi said solemnly, glancing at Dong Dingzi. "In my view, Old Man Chen deserves what he gets. I am afraid that even if the gods came down to earth, they would not be able to save him. Poor guy! He shouldn't have thrown away this hundred taels of silver. Since he wants to spend the money, if I don't take it, someone else will. Isn't it better for me to take it than to see somebody else do? Now that the money comes into my hands, I can invite you over for flower viewing parties like this one. It just comes in handy for the wine and food. If it had come into the hands of some vulgar person, he would invest it in a new house, more land, more grains for storage, or simply loan it out to collect high interest. Besides, Old Man Chen is very corrupt and the money isn't clean after all. He has nothing to lose after giving it to us."

龚鼎孳眨巴着眼睛，似乎一下子没听明白，随后就大笑起来。

“好，好！密之，亏你做了几年京官，原来一点儿没变，还是江南名士的本色！佩服，佩服！”说着，举起酒杯，同方以智对饮了一杯，又回过头，打算敦促吴伟业，却发现这位吴大诗人皱着眉毛，一脸不忍的神色。

“咦，骏公，怎么了，你？”龚鼎孳奇怪地问。

吴伟业轻轻叹了一口气：“陈大司马虽然有罪，却其实未至于死，你们又何必……”

“啊哈，这一回，只怕他是死定了！”龚鼎孳笑嘻嘻地说。

“倘若他果真已是难逃一死，”吴伟业温和地责备说，“你们就更加不该如此。”

龚鼎孳怔了一下，随即睁大了眼睛：“喂喂，这一次可是他咎由自取，怨不得我们！”

“可是……”

“可是什么？”龚鼎孳立即反问，他显然感到方以智的在场，而吴伟业的责备是冲着他们两个人来的，“可是我们不该幸灾乐祸，落井下石是不是？不过，只怕你可怜他，到头来他却未必感恩戴德，还要反咬你一口！”他尖刻地说。

“其实、其实，他也没怎么得罪我们。”吴伟业红着脸分辩。

“没得罪我们？那么，‘二十四气’之说是谁捣鬼？主使者又是何人？哼，你别看他面子上同我们敷衍，骨子里邪门着哩！我就从来不信他！”

龚鼎孳所说的这个“二十四气”之说，是指不久前，有人因周延儒再度出任内阁首辅后，起用了不少东林人士，心怀忌恨，于是编造了一个“二十四气”的假案，把包括吴伟业在内的

Gong Dingzi blinked his eyes, trying to figure out what was meant, and then laughed out loud.

"Well done, Mizhi! You haven't changed much after serving in Beijing for so many years. You're still what you were, a wise gentleman from River South. Bravo!" He raised his wine cup, toasted to Fang Yizhi, and turned around to urge Wu Weiye to toast too, only to find that the great poet was knitting his brows in distaste.

"Hey, Jungong, what's wrong with you?" Gong Dingzi asked with puzzlement.

Wu Weiye sighed slightly, "Mr. Chen is guilty, but he's not punishable by death. Why have you ..."

"Aha, this time around, I'm afraid he's as good as dead," Gong Dingzi said with a smile.

"If he really has to die," Wu Weiye said in a mild admonishing tone. "It's more wrong of you to act like this."

Gong Dingzi was silent for an instant, then his eyes widened. "Hey, this time around, it's his own fault, and he can't blame it on us."

"But ..."

"But what?" Gong Dingzi asked. He obviously felt Fang Yizhi's presence and the brunt of Wu Weiye's rebuke, which was directed at the two of them. "But we shouldn't be gloating over his misfortune and kick him when he's down, right? However, I'm afraid that if you have pity on him, in the end, he may not be grateful at all, and will turn against you instead," he said acidly.

"Actually, he hasn't done anything to harm us," Wu Weiye argued, blushing.

"He hasn't? Then, who is behind the 'twenty-four conspirators' rumor? Who's the mastermind? Hmph! He seems polite to us, but who knows what he's planning in his mind? I've never trusted him."

The "twenty-four conspirators" rumor that Gong Dingzi spoke of involved a trumped-up charge against twenty-four officials including Wu Weiye by those who were not happy with Zhou Yanru, who had become prime minister again and had reinstated a great number of East Wooders. The rumor had even reached the ears of the emperor,

二十四位官员罗织进去，指为私党，说得煞有介事，还到处散播。结果弄得皇上也知道了，降下旨来，命百官有则改之，无则加勉；其中还特别严词责备了言官们一顿，弄得人心惶惶。这件事，至今也闹不清是谁捣的鬼。不过龚鼎孳本人是言官，职责又是监察兵部，加上前一阵子言官们对兵部的攻击尤其猛烈，所以他便疑心是陈新甲在暗中报复，其实未必有根据……

吴伟业不响了。他显然不善于争论，而且害怕争论。看见对方来势汹汹，他就气馁了。

“好，我们不谈这个，不谈了。”他委屈地、无可奈何地说，懊丧地低下头去，“其实，唉……”

龚鼎孳眼珠子一转，也立即表示同意：“对，算了，不谈，不谈！”他哈哈大笑起来，“喝酒，喝酒！”

在他们争论的当儿，方以智始终没有插话。吴伟业的责备，使他多少有点扫兴。固然，对于陈新甲，方以智没有丝毫好感，但是朝廷上无休无止的党争，说实在的也使他越来越厌倦了。不错，穷凶极恶的魏忠贤阉党，虽说早在十多年前就被打了下去，其后继起与东林为敌的前内阁首辅温体仁、薛国观等人也相继因罪垮台。周延儒复出之后，不少受排挤打击的东林旧臣都获得起用。但目前朝廷之上，各个山头派系的斗争，仍旧异常复杂激烈。就拿陈新甲来说，他虽然不属于温薛一党，但也并不买东林这边的账，而是凭借皇上的宠信，一直在自拉山头，竭力扩充本身的势力。更兼他身为兵部尚书，却指挥无能，丧师失地，又背着朝廷暗中向清军求和。这些，都引起东林方面的强烈不满，早就想

who issued an edict that all the officials should reform themselves if they were involved in such a plot and warn themselves not to if they were not. In the edict, the emperor particularly reprimanded the imperial counselors, who therefore were filled with fear. It hadn't been known who was behind all this. Gong Dingzi himself was an imperial counselor, and his duty was to monitor the Ministry of War. Besides, the imperial counselors had previously lashed out against the Ministry of War. So, he suspected it was Chen Xinjia retaliating behind the scenes but he wasn't sure ...

Wu Weiye was silent. He was clearly not good at arguing. In fact, he was very afraid of arguing. While Gong Dingzi was inflated with steam, he was deflated.

"Well, let's not talk about that. Let's forget about it," he said aggrievedly and helplessly, lowering his head in frustration. "Actually, alas ..."

Gong Dingzi rolled his eyes and immediately agreed. "Yes, forget it. Let's not talk about it," He laughed loudly. "Drink, drink!"

While they were arguing, Fang Yizhi never cut in a word. For him, Wu Weiye's rebuke spoiled the fun. Of course, Fang Yizhi had never had any liking for Chen Xinjia, but the endless partisan strife in the court made him increasingly sick. It was true that eunuch Wei Zhongxian's evil party had been crushed ten years ago and those who continued to befoe the East Wood Party, such as Prime Minister Wen Tiren and Xue Guoguan had been ousted one after another, and many veteran East Wood-affiliated officials who had been persecuted had been reinstated after Zhou Yanru came back to power, but at present, the struggles between the parties in the imperial court were still complicated and intense. Take Chen Xinjia for example. Although he didn't belong to Wen Tiren and Xue Guoguan's party, he was by no means friendly to the East Wooders. Instead, as a favorite courtier of the emperor, he was doing everything possible to expand his own power. As Minister of War, he proved to be an incompetent commander, having lost much of the army and a large part of the territory. He even secretly negotiated peace with the Qing

把他轰下台，只是由于皇上一味回护，才无可奈何。现在好不容易来了机会，当然不肯放过。刑部左侍郎徐石麒之所以坚决主张惩办陈新甲，与此可以说不无关系。不过，方以智也明白，战局到了目前这一步，其实是由来已久、积重难返，绝不是陈新甲一人所能扭转的。陈老头儿固然不是安邦定国之才，可是换一个人，难道就有办法么？这样一想，方以智对于当前这一场党争到底有什么意义，就不能不感到怀疑。刚才，他颇有点玩世不恭，内心其实是苦闷的。正因如此，他现在完全能够理解吴伟业的心情。他不但不打算附和龚鼎孳，去讥笑这位好好先生的善良和软弱，相反有心替他打打圆场，说上几句慰解的话。

但是，他没来得及这样做。因为长班孙福匆匆走了进来，呈上一份拜帖，并禀告说："兵部左堂冯爷的轿子快到门外了！"三位朋友一听，不由得你望我，我望你，都颇感意外。

"莫非是为的陈新甲？"龚鼎孳冒出一句。

方以智沉吟了一下，吩咐："外堂奉茶！"随即放下杯子，站起来，走进里间换过公服。又朝吴、龚二人做了个"稍待"的手势，匆匆地迎了出去。

这位来访的"兵部冯爷"，就是兵部左侍郎冯元飙。他是天启二年的进士，做过几任京官，也外放过许多次，仅仅三个月前，

army without the knowledge of the imperial court. All these had caused strong dissatisfaction among the East Wooders, who wanted to have him ousted, but could do nothing, because the emperor always protected him. Now that the opportunity had finally come, they certainly would not let it go. Therefore, it was understandable why Xu Shiqi, Left Vice Minister of the Ministery of Punishment, insisted on having Chen Xinjia punished. However, Fang Yizhi also understood that the situation had come to such a pass not without a reason. It was the result of a long-lasting problem, not to be corrected by Chen Xinjia alone, even if he wanted to put things right. Old Man Chen was certainly not the man to save the country, but was there anybody else to do it? Thus thinking, Fang Yizhi began to question the meaning of the struggles between the two parties. He had appeared rather unconcerned a moment ago, but his heart was heavy. Therefore, he could now fully understand Wu Weiye's feeling. He was not going to go along with Gong Dingzi and ridicule the kind-heartedness and weakness of will of this good gentleman. Rather, he wanted to help him out of the awkward situation and say a few words of consolation.

Before he had the time for it, Sun Fu the servant hurriedly came in, presented him with a calling card, and said, "The sedan chair of Lord Feng of the Left Chamber of the Ministry of War has come to the door." When the three friends heard this, they looked at each other in surprise.

"He's also here to intercede for Chen Xinjia?" Gong Dingzi said intuitively.

Fang Yizhi thought for an instant, and then said to the servant, "Invite him to the outer room and serve him tea." Then he put down the cup, stood up, went into the inner room, and changed into the official uniform. After that, he made a "wait a moment" gesture to Wu Weiye and Gong Dingzi, and hurriedly went out.

The visiting "Lord Feng of the Ministry of War" was Feng Yuanbiao, Left Vice Minister of the Ministry of War. He became a *jinshi* in the second year of the reign of Emperor Tianqi [AD 1622] and had served as an official in Beijing several times. He had also

还在南京任通政使。他为人喜智术，有权谋，早年曾上疏弹劾周延儒，攻击不遗余力；这一次进京后，看见周延儒有改弦更张之意，他也就一反旧态，同周延儒密切交往，关系拉得很好。冯元飙目前是东林派中坚之一，而且一向以复社的后台自任。所以他突然来访，并没有使方以智感到惊疑不安。相反，当老头儿那又矮又胖的身躯和那张生动的、乐呵呵的圆脸映入眼帘时，方以智内心的愉快、亲近的感觉便油然而生了。

“哈哈，学生还愁着吃闭门羹哩！如此秋光，兄翁不去登高、赏菊、饮酒，原来还有耐性守在家里！”冯元飙一见方以智，就兴冲冲地拱着手说。

“彀老来得正巧！”方以智一边还礼，一边笑着说，“饮酒、赏菊，却不须远求，眼下舍间便有，就请进去共饮三杯如何？”

“噢？”

“只因一位年友日前送来十几盆菊花，晚生见它尚属不俗，今日便备了几杯薄酒，邀骏公、孝升两位过来赏玩，如今他二人就在书房里。”

“原来如此！有此雅事，兄翁如何便忘了学生？厚彼薄此，该罚，该罚！”冯元飙摇晃着脑袋，又哈哈笑起来，满庭院都响彻了他洪亮的嗓音。

“晚生甘愿受罚三大杯！”方以智爽快地说，随即在通往书房的侧门前停下来，“那么，请彀老这就过去？”

冯元飙眼珠子一转：“嗯，你说孝升也在里面？”

“是的。”

served in other places. Three months ago, he had been general commissioner in Nanjing. He liked calculating and scheming. In his early years, he had impeached Zhou Yanru and spared no effort in attacking him. However, after entering Beijing this time, he decided to befriend Zhou Yanru instead when he saw that Zhou Yanru wanted to switch course. Feng Yuanbiao was currently a key member of the East Wood Party and had always considered himself a patron of the Fushe. Therefore, his sudden visit didn't surprise Fang Yizhi at all. On the contrary, when the old man's short and stout body and his animated and cheerful round face came into view, a pleasant feeling of affinity quickly rose in Fang Yizhi's heart.

"Hah, I've been worrying that I won't see you. I thought you might have gone out to climb the mountain, view chrysanthemums, and drink wine on such a clear, crisp autumn day instead of staying indoors." Feng Yuanbiao said excitedly as he saluted Fang Yizhi with pressed hands.

"You've just come in time, Elder Tao," Fang Yizhi said with a smile as he returned the salute. "There's no need to go anywhere else to drink wine and view chrysanthemums. I have them all in my house. Please go in and drink with me."

"Oh?"

"A coeval of mine sent me a dozen pots of chrysanthemums a few days ago. Since they're really good, I prepared a few cups of thin wine today, and invited Jungong and Xiaosheng over to enjoy the flowers together. Now they're in the study room."

"I see. How can you forget me when there's such a beautiful thing? You should be punished." Feng Yuanbiao rocked his head and laughed, and the whole courtyard resounded with his loud voice.

"Sure. I'll drink three cups of wine as punishment," Fang Yizhi quickly agreed. Then, he stopped in front of the side door leading to the study room and said, "Then, please go in, Elder Tao."

Feng Yuanbiao rolled his eyes, saying, "Well, you said that Xiaosheng is also inside?"

"Yes."

“噢，那就罢了，那就罢了！”冯元飙忙不迭地说，拉着方以智往前走，又回过头来，狡黠地眨眨眼睛，“学生现今叨掌兵部，他是本科言官，在这当口上，还是扯开些为好！”

方以智“哦”了一声。他当然明白，龚鼎孳作为兵科给事中，职责就是对兵部衙门实行稽查，将其办事的情况、好坏得失，随时向皇上报告。双方的关系向来是既尖锐对立，又时有勾结，颇为微妙。如今陈新甲一案尚未了结，冯元飙作为他的副手暂掌兵部，对于龚鼎孳自然不便过从太密，以免招来闲话。不过，既然此刻是在自己的家里，而且彼此其实又早就是同一个圈子里的人，方以智就觉得冯元飙似乎小心得过分了。

冯元飙大概从眼神里瞧出他的心思，又哈哈笑起来：“兄翁，学生我是同你说笑话儿，其实哪有工夫饮酒赏菊！我这就要上周阁老那儿，经过这里，顺脚进来瞧瞧你，马上就要走的！”

这当儿，他们已经来到堂上，于是重新行礼见过，分宾主坐了下来。

“兄翁，这些天，可见到太冲么？”冯元飙一边接过小厮奉上来的一杯茶，一边言归正传地问。

“哦，前日他曾同恺章、道济二兄过访舍下，约晚生明日到天主堂去访汤若望，并说不日便返江南去了。”方以智回答，一边想起对方是浙东慈溪人，同黄宗羲也算得上同乡。

“嗯，听说，他今科又未考中？”

“是的。”

"In that case, I'd better not go," Feng Yuanbiao said hurriedly as he continued to walk forward, holding Fang Yizhi's hand behind him. Then, he turned around and said, "I'm now in charge of the Ministry of War, and he's the imperial counselor overseeing the ministry. So, I'd better not meet him here in such a time."

Fang Yizhi said "oh". Of course, he understood that Gong Dingzi's duty as a military affairs supervisor was to monitor the *yamen* of the Ministry of War and to report everything good or bad to the emperor in time. The relationship between them two was very subtle, involving both conflict and collusion. Since the case of Chen Xinjia hadn't been concluded yet and Feng Yuanbiao was temporarily in charge of the Ministry of War as his deputy, it was naturally not convenient for him to be too close to Gong Dingzi, so as not to incur gossip. However, since they were in his own home at the moment, and both men had actually been in the same circle for a long time, Fang Yizhi felt that Feng Yuanbiao's concerns were not necessary.

Feng Yuanbiao, who probably had seen Fang Yizhi's thoughts, laughed again, saying, "Elder Brother, I was joking with you. In fact, I don't have time to drink and enjoy chrysanthemums now. I'm just stopping by on my way to Elder Zhou's place. I'll be leaving in a moment."

They arrived in the main room, saluted each other again and sat down in the host and guest seats respectively.

"Elder Brother, have you met Taichong these days?" Feng Yuanbiao asked as he took a cup of tea from the servant.

"Um, the day before yesterday, he came with Kaizhang and Daoji and we agreed to visit Tang Ruowang[1] tomorrow at the cathedral. He said he's going back to River South very soon," Fang Yizhi replied, remembering that Feng Yuanbiao was from Cixi, East Zhejiang, Huang Zongxi's native place.

"Well, I heard that he failed the imperial exam again."

"Yes."

---

① Tang Ruowang: Johann Adam Schall von Bell (AD 1592–1666)

“今年是朱锐锦主考，私下走他关节的人听说多得很嘛，太冲怎么也不托人去说说？”冯元飙的表情很认真。他收起了笑容。

方以智苦笑一下：“太冲的脾气犟得很，他哪里肯做这种事。”

冯元飙摇摇头：“他这人就吃亏在什么都太认真！其实八股到了今日，哪里还考得出什么真才实学？不过是虚应故事罢咧！他这一认真，自己落第不算，朝廷也少了个可用之才。如今反让那些竞进无耻之徒占了便宜去，可谓不值！”

“弢老所见甚是。便是晚生也曾这等劝他来，唯是太冲不肯听从，也真教人无可奈何。”

方以智这样说了之后，好大一会儿，主客二人都没有再说话。冯元飙慢慢地捋着他那几根稀疏的黄胡子，仰着下巴颏儿，像在考虑什么。

“听说，太冲打算上书朝廷，可有此事？”终于，他又问。

“哦，弢老也知道了？”

“弟是听小儿辈闲谈言及，却未得其详。”

“这个，晚生倒曾看过。大抵太冲的意思，是国事至此，非急谋改革，不足以图存。而改革之急务，在于压抑豪强兼并，恢复井田之制，即：平均全国之田，按户授给，每户五十亩。剩余者，始由富民占有。此外，更须免除繁苛赋役。古时之田，不许买卖，国家十一而税；后世之田，准许买卖，则更可放宽，比如三十而税一。若谓当今战祸未息，为助饷计，赋税难以骤减，亦须严限于十五税一之内。如此，则富者不困，而贫者亦能稍稍安

Feng Yuanbiao stopped smiling and said with a serious expression, “Zhu Ruijin was the Chief Examination Officer. There were many candidates who tried to influence him privately. Why didn’t Taichong use some help?”

Fang Yizhi gave a wry smile. “Taichong is a stubborn person. He wouldn’t do a thing like that.”

Feng Yuanbiao said, shaking his head “He has failed because he’s too serious about everything. In fact, by this day, the eight-legged essay can no longer measure the talent of a scholar. It’s just a formula. Because he takes it too seriously, he’s failed the exam and the imperial court has failed to discover a talent. He’s simply given up his opportunity to some shameless guy. What a pity!”

“You’re quite right, Elder Tao. I’ve also tried to persuade Taichong, but he wouldn’t listen. There’s nothing we can do about him.”

After Fang Yizhi said that, both host and guest were silent for a long time. Feng Yuanbiao slowly stroked his sparse, yellow beard, tilting his chin upward, as if thinking about something.

“I heard that Taichong is going to submit a petition letter to the imperial court. Is it true?” Finally, he spoke.

“Oh, you’ve also heard it?”

“Some young men spoke of it, but I don’t know the details.”

“I’ve read it. It’s to the effect that since things have come to such a pass, only drastic reforms can save the Great Ming. The most imperative task of the reforms is to stop the rich and powerful from amassing land and to restore the well-field system, in which all land in the country is divided into equal shares to be distributed on household basis, fifty acres for each household. Only the surplus land is to be kept by the rich families. Besides, taxes and corvée should be reduced. In the old system, land cannot be traded, and the applicable tax rate is 1/10. In the new system, land can be traded, and a 1/30 tax rate applies. Since drastic reduction of taxes is impossible while the war is going on and a lot of money is needed to sustain the army, the tax rate should be limited to below 1/15. Thus, the wealthy won’t become poor, and the poor will get some protection. When the root cause of

居。乱源一去，贼自易平，贼平国定，则建虏亦无能为矣！”

方以智说到这里，偷眼瞧了瞧客人，发现冯元飙皱着眉，抿着嘴，样子像是要笑，又像是要哭，便赶紧接着说：“太冲亦知当今南北交煎，天下糜烂，此议无法骤行。故拟议先于江南数省试行之。该处虽亦艰困日甚，所幸尚未经兵燹，或者较易收效也……”

他本来还要说下去，见冯元飙做了个制止的手势，便顿住了。

冯元飙摇摇头：“纯属空论！莫说朝廷必不采纳，即使采纳，照他这一套去弄，只怕江南就先自大乱起来——不过，有这么一份东西，总比没有的强。明儿，兄翁就让太冲拿来，告诉他，别忙着走了，由学生替他转给周阁老。老头儿也未必有工夫看，无非做个由头，学生再从旁撺掇，让他把太冲留下，分派个差事干干，总还是可以的！”说着，站起身来。

“哦，弢老，陈新甲之事，眼下不知怎样了？”方以智一边往外送客，一边问。

“听说皇上还有点踌躇，到底是他亲手晋拔起来的人嘛！老陈在狱中好像也听到点风声，正在到处送礼，托人说情。他的那些党羽也四出运动。学生已经对徐大人说了，此人不除，岂止国无宁日，亦终是我东林之患！——嗯，在这节骨眼上，朝廷公论还是顶要紧的。兄翁在内廷走动，也须警醒着点，该说的还是得说！”

方以智点点头，走了几步，忽然笑着说：“老陈一去，大司

the uprising is gone, putting it down is just a matter of time. When the rebellion is put down and peace and order are restored in the country the Jurchens will go nowhere."

Fang Yizhi glanced at the guest as he spoke and found that Feng Yuanbiao's brows knit and lips pressed as if trying to contain a laugh or a cry, so he quickly added, "Taichong understands that this plan cannot be implemented immediately, because the situation both in the north and in the south is dire and the country is in chaos. Therefore, he proposes to try it out in some provinces south of the Yangtze River. Though life is increasingly hard in those provinces too, there's no warfare going on there, so there's a good chance that the plan may work out ..."

He was about to continue when he saw Feng Yuanbiao make a gesture to stop him, so he paused.

Feng Yuanbiao shook his head and said, "It's sheer empty talk. The imperial court won't accept his proposal. If it did, I'm afraid River South would be thrown into chaos first—but such a thing is better than nothing. Tell Taichong to bring it here tomorrow. He should stay in Beijing. There's no hurry to leave. I'll forward the letter to Elder Zhou. The old man probably won't have time to read it, but it may lead to something. I'll speak a few good words from beside him and ask him to let Taichong stay and have a job. That should be no problem." After speaking, he stood up.

"Oh, Elder Tao, what's going on with the Chen Xinjia case now?" Fang Yizhi asked as he saw off his guest.

"I heard that the emperor is still in two minds. After all, Chen Zhenjia has been promoted by His Majesty himself. Old Chen seems to have heard something in prison and is sending money to everyone he knows, asking them to intercede on his behalf. His henchmen are also doing everything possible to help him. I've already told Mr. Xu that if this person isn't eliminated, the country will have no peace, and East Wood will continue to be threatened by him. Um, at this juncture, publicity at court is still very important. As you move about in the inner court, you must be aware of opportunities to speak."

Fang Yizhi nodded his head and walked a few steps forward, then

马一职，只怕就非老先生莫属了！”

冯元飙停了一下脚步，回过头来，眨眨眼睛：“噢，兄翁这样以为么？这是别人说的，还是兄翁自己这么想？”他随即继续往前走，一边摇着白发皤然的脑袋，叹息说：“若然果真如此，那恰是我所最最不愿的！试问十余年间，但凡坐上这把交椅的，哪一个有好下场！”

## 西洋教士

第二天，黄宗羲依约来到了。同他一起来的还有冯道济和他堂兄冯恺章。至于陆符，因为这一次乡试，他暗中买通了主考官的关节，果然高中举人。这几天又是拜房师[①]，又是会同年，正忙得不亦乐乎，所以没有同来。

方以智把他们接进堂屋之后，先不忙出门，却把昨天冯元飙的那番意思向黄宗羲说了。谁知黄宗羲听后，脸上毫无喜色，只淡淡地说：

“弢老盛情，小弟感激心领。只是小弟归意已决，上书之事，也作罢论了。”

方以智怔了一下，还没有开口，坐在旁边的冯道济迫不及待地插了进来：

“哎，太冲兄，回江南有什么好？家父既肯开这个口，料想必定是有把握的。好不容易到京师来一趟，你就干脆住下，等三年后，再考他个头名！”

冯恺章也说：“不错，这一回没考中，不怨天，不怨地，更不是自家文章不好，就怨朱锐锦那老昏虫公行贿卖，暗通关节！如今外面骂声载道，听说有人在贡院门上贴出一副对子，道是，‘不用孔子，不用孟子，只取公子；不要古文，不要今文，只取

① 房师：明清两代，举人、贡士对荐举自己试卷的同考官的尊称。

suddenly said with a smile, "Now that Mr. Chen is gone, I gather the Minister of War position is surely yours."

Feng Yuanbiao stopped still, turned to Fang Yizhi, and said, blinking his eyes, "Do you really think so, Brother? Is it what others say or what you think?" He then continued to walk forward. Rocking his white-haired head, he sighed, "That's the last thing I would hope for. Just think, in the past ten years, who in that position has ever had a good end?"

## Johann Adam Schall von Bell, the Foreign Missionary

Huang Zongxi came the following day, as appointed. Along with him were Feng Daoji and Feng Daoji's cousin Feng Kaizhang. Lu Fu, who had bribed the examiners and won a *juren* degree, was very busy visiting the examiners and other successful candidates and therefore was unable to come with him.

After welcoming them into the main room, Fang Yizhi was in no hurry to depart immediately. He told Huang Zongxi what Feng Yuanbiao had said the day before. Unexpectedly, after hearing it, Huang Zongxi merely said lightly with no joy or smile on his face, "It's very kind of Elder Tao, and I'm grateful. It's just that I've already decided to go home and not to submit the petition letter."

Fang Yizhi went silent. Before he spoke again, Feng Daoji, who was sitting next to him, couldn't wait to cut in, "Well, Brother Taichong, what's the point of going back to River South? Now that my father said it, he must be sure it can be done. Because you're already in Beijing after a long, arduous journey, I suggest you just stay and take the exam again three years later. You'll come out Number One."

Feng Kaizhang said, "Exactly! You have failed this time, not because your luck isn't good or your essays are not well written, but because of the corruption of Zhu Ruijin who openly abused his power. Everyone is damning him. It's said someone has posted a couplet on the gate of the Gongyuan, which says:

*No use for kong zi* [Confucius], *no use for meng zi* [Mencius], *only gong zi* [rich man's son] *counts,*

真纹！’话虽说得忒过分些，我们不也算公子？不是照样没考中？不过，这等老昏虫还是该骂骂他才解气！”

可是黄宗羲只是坚决地摇摇头，却不作声。

“太冲兄，莫非你听说是周阁老，所以……”方以智瞅着他问。

“噢，若是为的周阁老，太冲兄尽可放心！”冯道济又一次插了进来，“周阁老以往曾同我东林为难，这是不错的。不过他这次复出，却大异于前，对我东林倒甚是优礼。听家父说，上月有一次，他在御前讲读，皇上拿了一个奏本问：‘张溥、张采是何等人？’周阁老当即答道：‘读书的好秀才！’皇上又问：‘张溥已死，张采小官，科道官如何说他好？’周阁老答说：‘他胸中颇有学问，文章也好。科道官做秀才时，见过他的文章，今以用之而未尽其才，所以可惜。’皇上说：‘也不免偏激！’周阁老说：‘张溥、黄道周皆有些偏，只是会读书，所以人人惜他。’——你瞧，他维护复社也算尽心尽意了！”

冯恺章也说：“听说，幼老[①]这次得以复官，也全仗周阁老在皇上面前一席话哩！”

这些消息，黄宗羲大约是第一次知道。他仰起脸，呆呆地听着，神情变得柔和了一点；可是只一忽儿，又复归于冷淡，依旧摇摇头。

方以智很清楚黄宗羲的执拗脾气，知道一时也劝他不转，便站起来，说：“此事慢慢商量。时候不早，只怕汤若望等得久了，我们这就去吧。”

于是，四个人一齐出门，各自上马，穿过金井胡同，沿着上

---

① 幼老：指黄道周，字幼平。当时因罪罢官。

*No need for gu wen [classical essay], no need for jin wen [modern essay], only zhen wen [sterling silver] is taken.*

It's not accurate, because we also belong to the category of *gong zi*, but such corrupt officials do deserve to be damned."

But Huang Zongxi just shook his head resolutely without speaking.

Fang Yizhi looked at him and asked, "Brother Taichong, is it because it's Elder Zhou ..."

"Well, don't worry about Elder Zhou, Brother Taichong," Feng Daoji interjected again. "Sure Elder Zhou was once an enemy of East Wood, but now he's a changed man after his reinstatement to office. My father said: When Elder Zhou was giving a lecture at court last month, the emperor picked up a document and asked, 'Who are Zhang Pu and Zhang Cai?' Elder Zhou replied, 'Two well-read scholars.' The emperor asked, 'Zhang Pu is dead and Zhang Cai is just a small-time official. Why do you say they're good?' Elder Zhou replied, 'They're learned and write beautiful essays. When I was a *xiucai* scholar, I read their essays. It's a pity that their talents haven't been fully made use of.' The emperor said, 'They must be stubborn.' Elder Zhou said, 'Both Zhang Pu and Huang Daozhou are stubborn and only good at reading books, but for that reason people think it's a pity.' So, you see, he's been trying to defend the Fushe."

Feng Kaizhang said, "I hear that Elder You's reinstatement to office is also the result of the influence of Elder Zhou, who has put in a good word for him in front of the emperor."

Huang Zongxi raised his head and listened with interest, as such information was novel to him, and his expression brightened a little, but quickly darkened again. He shook his head.

Fang Yizhi was very aware of Huang Zongxi's stubbornness. Knowing that he couldn't change the young man's mind, he stood up and said, "We'll discuss this matter later. It's not early. I'm afraid Tang Ruowang has waited too long. Let's go now."

Then, the four of them went out of the house and mounted their horses. They passed through Jinjing Alley, veered to Upper Oblique

斜街，向东行去。

天主堂位于宣武门内东面城墙下的一个角落里，是万历年间神宗皇帝特许意大利籍耶稣会教士利玛窦兴建的。以后，就一直成为西方传教士们聚居并进行传教活动的场所。那是一座有着半圆形屋顶的罗马式建筑，当中一扇带石阶的门，四面开着许多窗子，周围装饰着许多稀奇古怪的花纹图案。天主堂旁边另建有宅邸，供教士们居住。当方以智等四人在院门外下马，通报之后，汤若望很快就出现了。

这是一位身材高大的德意志人，有着虬结的胡须和高高隆起的鼻子。突出的眉骨之下深藏着一双古怪的、碧荧荧的眼睛。不过，他那头金黄色鬈发，却按中国式样直梳上去，并且也像中国儒生那样，戴了一顶方巾，身上穿一件白色的布直裰。他曾经在北京专门学习，又在中国住了十多年，其间还到西安去传过教，一口中国话说得十分流利。

一见方以智，汤若望就大声欢呼起来：“啊，方先生，幸会，幸会，小弟已经恭候多时了！”又转向其余三人：“不敢动问这三位先生高姓大名？”等方以智介绍之后，汤若望又连说几声“久仰、幸会！”然后，他就按照中国的方式同大家一一作揖寒暄。

“道未兄，这位黄先生和两位冯先生今日一则是久慕尊颜，特来拜望；二则是意欲瞻仰贵教的宝刹，并一聆汤兄雅言。”方以智说。

“啊，不敢当，不敢当！倒是小弟亟望列位先生不吝赐教！”汤若望谦逊说，又殷勤地问，“不先过舍下奉茶么？”

方以智回头望了望，看见三位朋友都露出疑虑的神色，就

Street and headed east.

The cathedral was located in a corner at the foot of the eastern city wall inside the Xuanwu Gate. It was built by Matteo Ricci, an Italian Jesuit priest, during the Wanli period with the special permission of Emperor Shenzong. Since then, it had always been a place for Western missionaries to meet and carry out missionary activities. It was a Romanesque building with a dome, a door with stone steps, many windows on the four sides, and various strange patterns around. Beside the cathedral were the living quarters of the priests. The four visitors dismounted at the courtyard gate and announced their visit through the janitor. Tang Ruowang appeared shortly.

He was a tall German with a knotted beard and a high nose. Beneath the protruding browbones were a pair of bizarre, blue eyes. However, his golden curly hair was combed straight up in the Chinese style, and he also wore a square headscarf and a white long gown like a Chinese scholar. He spoke Chinese fluently, having lived in China for more than ten years, during which he had studied Chinese in Beijing and been to Xi'an on Jesuit missions.

Upon seeing Fang Yizhi, Tang Ruowang cheered loudly, "Hah, Mr. Fang, it's such a pleasure to see you. I've been waiting for your visit." Then he turned to the other three and said, "May I ask your names, sirs?" After Fang Yizhi introduced his friends, Tang Ruowang said, "I've been looking forward to meeting you. It's such a pleasure." When the introductions were over, he bowed and exchanged pleasantries with everyone according to Chinese etiquette.

"Brother Daowei, Mr. Huang and the two Mr. Fengs are here today because they've been looking forward to seeing you on the one hand, and on the other hand, to pay homage to the sacred temple of your religion and listen to your precious teaching," Fang Yizhi said.

"Oh, I feel flattered. I'm looking forward to learning from you." Tang Ruowang said humbly. Then he asked politely, "Would you like to go to my room and have some tea first?"

Fang Yizhi looked back and, seeing the hesitant look of his friends, said, "Thank you for your kindness, but let's see the sacred

说："不必了，先瞻仰宝刹吧！"

"好的，那么，请！"

等大家移动脚步，汤若望在旁边陪着，一起穿过院子，步上台阶，进入天主堂内。

在这小半天里，黄宗羲很少说话。刚才，在方以智家里，他拒绝了冯元飙的建议和大家的劝说。这件事，至今还影响着他的情绪。是的，此时此刻，他不希望也不需要别人来怜悯他，哪怕是冯元飙这样的东林前辈。虽然自己这一次到北京来，可以说事事失意，一败涂地，乘兴而来，扫兴而归。但越是这样，他越觉得接受别人的任何怜悯和恩赐，即便对方出于真心诚意，对自己来说，也是一种羞辱，是没有骨气的表现。"哼，我自然还要来北京，可那得等考中之后，理直气壮，堂堂正正地来。眼下何必赖着不走，让人笑话！"他想。可是这种话，当时不便马上说出口，他本想等上路之后，再慢慢向方以智解释。谁知方以智仿佛有意作弄他，偏偏绝口不再提这件事，一路上只顾同冯氏兄弟有说有笑，弄得黄宗羲愈加气闷。

不过此刻，他的这种烦恼暂时被对于天主堂的好奇心所取代了。他发现，这幢按照西洋式样设计建造的大堂又狭又长，顶上装着天花板，看不见屋梁，两边排列着带雕饰的窗，正当中是一个用香灯和帐幔装饰起来的神龛，供着一幅耶稣的油画像。画中的那个耶稣，长得高鼻梁，大耳朵，须发蓬松，容貌清癯，头顶上有一轮"圣光"。他左手捧着浑天图，右手雄辩地向前方伸出，嘴巴微微张开，仿佛在热烈地讲述着什么伟大的真知灼见。

黄宗羲头一次看见耶稣的肖像。不过使他惊异的，不是这位西方救世主那种咄咄逼人的姿态，而是西洋绘画的准确和逼真。

temple first."

"Well, then, please!"

So, everyone moved. Tang Ruowang escorted them by their side. They passed through the yard, walked up the steps, and entered the cathedral.

During all this time, Huang Zongxi seldom spoke. Earlier in the day, he had rejected Feng Yuanbiao's suggestion and refused to be persuaded at Fang Yizhi's residence. He was still feeling bad from it. Yes, at present, he neither wanted nor needed anyone to pity him, even a senior East Wooder like Feng Yuanbiao, although everything had turned out the wrong way contrary to his wishes and he had failed miserably in Beijing this time. In a situation like this, he felt that any pity or help from anybody, even if he was sincere, would be a form of humiliation to him, and accepting it would be a sign of weakness. "Hmph, of course I'll come to Beijing again, but that will be after I pass the exam. I'll come here again with grace and dignity. Why should I stay here now to be a laughingstock?" he thought. Finding it was not a proper moment to say a thing like that at Fang Yizhi's residence, he planned to slowly explain it to Fang Yizhi on the way to the cathedral. Unfortunately, Fang Yizhi kept talking and laughing with the Feng brothers along the way and never mentioned it again, as if deliberately ignoring him, which made him even more distressed.

At this moment, his distress was temporarily replaced by the curiosity about the cathedral. He found that the hall of the cathedral, designed and built in the Western style, was long and narrow, with a ceiling on top, no beams visible, carved windows on both sides, and a shrine with an oil painting of Jesus Christ in the center and decorated with lamps and drapery. The Jesus in the painting had a tall nose, big ears, fluffy beard and hair, a clear face, and a circle of holy light around his head, his left hand holding a map of the sky and his right hand stretching imposingly forward, his mouth slightly opened as if he were passionately explaining some great truth.

It was the first time for Huang Zongxi to see a portrait of Jesus Christ. What amazed him was not the imposing posture of this

他有好一阵子目瞪口呆，疑心那不是绘画，而是一尊彩塑。接着，他情不自禁地走近去，细细观看。“啊，原来世上竟有这等神奇的写真妙技！可知世界之大，确实未可管窥蠡测！”他叹服地想。

这当儿，汤若望已经在一旁热心地布起道来。他从亚当和夏娃如何偷吃了伊甸园的禁果，由此繁衍出了有罪的人类说起，一直说到耶稣降生，布道救人，如何被钉死在十字架上，死后三日又如何复活升天等等。说得绘声绘色，煞有介事。方以智大约早已听过，虽然没有打断他，嘴角上却挂着一丝不以为然的微笑。冯氏兄弟则听得津津有味，不时要求对方讲得详细一些。至于黄宗羲，他是本朝大儒刘宗周的学生，历来主张“气外无物”，包括天地鬼神在内。他对于汤若望这套说法，当然不相信。“这不过也如佛氏之有释伽，道教之有李老君一般，未必无其人，却是故神其说。其实所谓主宰者，纯是一团虚灵之气，草木之荣枯，寒暑之运行，地理之刚柔，象纬之顺逆，人物之生死，俱由这气自为主宰。鬼神之说，俱属其次！”他想，一边跟着大家，步入右侧的一间圣母堂内。

圣母堂的布置同正堂差不多，里面也供着一幅画像，上面画着圣母玛利亚——一位童贞女，怀里抱着一个婴儿。据说那就是刚刚诞生的耶稣。黄宗羲照例转了一圈，心想：“童女无夫而孕之说，中国也有，不过却是周厉王误失龙漦，童女践之而有孕，

Western savior, but the accuracy of detail and lifelikeness of Western painting. He was struck with awe. Wondering whether it was a picture or a colored statue, he went forward to have a closer look. "How come there're such miraculous portrait-making skills in the world? The world is really too big to be seen through a pipe hole or to be gauged by a spoon," he marveled.

Now, Tang Ruowang started his sermon enthusiastically. He told the story of how Adam and Eve stole the forbidden fruit in the Garden of Eden and thus became the progenitors of sinful human beings, how Jesus was born, spread the word of God and saved people, how he was crucified, and how he was resurrected and ascended to heaven three days after his death ... He told the story vividly and in all seriousness. Fang Yizhi had probably heard it before. Although he didn't interrupt him, there was a disapproving smile on the corner of his mouth. The Feng brothers listened with relish, and from time to time asked the priest to explain in more detail. Huang Zongxi, a former pupil of Liu Zongzhou, a great scholar of the day, had always believed that there's nothing except *qi*. There are neither devils nor gods. Therefore, he didn't believe Tang Ruowang's story. "This is just like the story of Sakyamuni in Buddhism, or Lao-tse in Taoism. The person may have existed but the story is an embellishment. The absolute ruler is purely a mass of formless breath that dictates the life of plants and trees, the cycle of the seasons, the geography of the earth, the position of the stars, and the life and death of human beings. The story of gods and spirits is really irrelevant," he thought as he stepped into the Hall of Our Lady on the right.

The layout of the Hall of Our Lady was similar to that of the main hall. There was also a portrait inside, that of the Virgin Mary holding in her arms a baby said to be the newly born Jesus. Huang Zongxi toured the room, thinking to himself, "There's also a story in China about a virgin giving birth to a baby, but it's a very different story: King Li of Zhou broke the bottle of saliva of a holy dragon by accident. A virgin maid stepped on it and became pregnant. As a result, she gave birth to a beautiful girl, who was the cause of the downfall of

结果生下了个亡国的褒姒！中外传闻，竟是如此之异，亦可谓一奇了。只不知这位汤先生闻知，作何感想？”

参观完天主堂，汤若望又一再邀大家到宅邸里去用茶，二冯兄弟同传教士已经混熟，一口答应。黄宗羲踌躇了一下，也表示同意。于是大家又跟着汤若望往回走。

“太冲，你觉得如何？”方以智忽然凑上来悄声问。

黄宗羲瞥了他一眼，顿时想起一路上被对方故意冷落的那一场哑巴气。他有心回敬一下，急切间却想不出该说句什么才解气，只好沉着脸，一声不吭。

方以智显然心里有数，他狡猾地眨着眼睛，笑嘻嘻地说：“这——其实不算什么。待会儿，更有匪夷所思的呢！”

说话的当儿，已经进了宅邸的大门，从影壁转西，经前院进入二门，穿过方砖铺地的后院，来到北边正房的起居室里。

“弟是单身，没有家小。所以凡有客来，弟都请进这儿来坐。”汤若望解释说，随即请大家坐下。一个年轻仆人奉上茶来。黄宗羲看他也就二十多岁，青衣小帽，眉目清秀，分明是个中国人，胸前却悬着一个小小的十字架，同汤若望胸前所悬的一模一样。“瞧样子他是已入了教的。闻得已故徐阁老[①]、李之藻等人，均曾入其教，公行弥撒之礼，不知确否？”他想问，又觉得唐突，只好忍住了。

这时，冯氏兄弟已经被屋子里的几件新奇别致的摆设吸引住了，那是摆在墙边的一架风琴、炕桌上一个香盒大小的自鸣钟、方几上的一台显微镜和竖在墙角的一支滑膛枪。冯氏兄弟仿佛成

① 徐阁老：指崇祯初年内阁大学士徐光启。

the kingdom. It's amazing two virgin mother stories can be so vastly different. I wonder what Mr. Tang will think if he knows the Chinese story."

After showing the guests around the cathedral, Tang Ruowang insisted on inviting them to his residence for tea. The Feng brothers, now feeling quite at home, immediately agreed. Huang Zongxi hesitated for an instant but also agreed. So, they followed Tang Ruowang and exited the cathedral.

"Taichong, what do you think?" Fang Yizhi suddenly came up and asked Huang Zongxi in a low voice.

Huang Zongxi glanced at him and suddenly remembered he had been humiliated by this guy's deliberate ignorance of him on the way here. He was determined to retaliate, but couldn't think of what to say to avenge his anger, so he kept silent with a sullen expression.

Fang Yizhi obviously knew what was happening. He blinked his eyes slyly and said with a smile, "This is really nothing. You'll be alarmed shortly."

They entered the main gate of the residence, turned west at the screen wall, passed through the front yard, the inner gate, and the backyard paved with square bricks, and then came to the drawing room of the main house on the north side.

"I'm single and don't have family. So, whenever there're guests, I invite them here," Tang Ruowang explained as he asked the visitors to sit down. A young servant brought tea. He was a twenty-something with beautiful features, dressed in a blue gown and wearing a small hat. He was clearly Chinese but wore a small cross on his chest, exactly the same as the one on Tang Ruowang's chest. "He seems to have joined the church. It's said that the late Prime Minister Xu and Mr. Li Zhizao also joined the church and attended Mass services. I wonder if it's true," Huang Zongxi thought. He wanted to ask the priest, but thinking it might be inappropriate, he held himself back.

The Feng brothers were attracted by the curious gadgets in the room: an organ by the wall, a self-ringing bell the size of an incense box on the heated *kang* table, a microscope on the small

了走进玩具店的孩童，不停地转动着闪闪发光的眼睛，脸上露出惊讶、狂喜的神情。等主人放下茶杯，微笑着发出邀请，他们立即站起来，一个奔向风琴，一个奔向滑膛枪，并且同时地提出一连串夹杂着惊叹的问题，弄得汤若望穷于应付，不知该回答哪一个好。正在不可开交，忽然传来了一阵悠扬的音乐，那乐声有点像鸟鸣，但鸟声没有它悦耳动听；像乐器齐奏，但周围又看不见乐队。而且那旋律有点奇特，全然不像中国的音乐。大家正在纳闷，就看见那个年轻仆人双手捧着一个闪闪发光的鸟笼，从隔壁慢慢走出来，小心翼翼地把它挂在门旁的一只铁钩子上。

大家仍旧呆呆地站着，显然不相信耳畔的这种美妙的乐声，同笼子里的这只小鸟有什么关系。

“噢，列位先生，这是一只会唱赞美诗的鸟儿，请过来欣赏它的歌唱。它在赞美全知全能的天父和基督哩！”汤若望伸出一只手，用感动的、热烈的声音说。

大家疑疑惑惑地围上去，仔细一看，发现不只笼子是用金属细丝编成的，连笼子里的那只小鸟也是金属制作的。它虽然张着嘴巴，站在那里，却一动也不会动。大家正猜不透这只假鸟怎么会发出声音来，音乐声忽然终止了。那个年轻仆人立即从怀里摸出一把式样特别的钥匙，插进笼子底座的一个小孔里，旋转了几下，音乐声重新响起来。

“啊，汤先生，贵邦之制作，可谓巧夺天工，令人耳目全新！只不知如此奇技，系何人所授？”冯道济又惊又喜地问，他显然已经佩服得五体投地。

“冯先生下问，小弟正欲奉告。”汤若望举起一根指头，庄严地回答，“这启迪我们以无穷智慧者，并非血肉之躯的凡夫俗子，

square table, and a musket standing in a corner of the room. They kept rolling their sparkling eyes, with expressions of surprise and wonder on their faces, like children who had walked into a toy store. When the host put down the teacup and said "please have a look" with a smile, they immediately stood up. One ran towards the organ, the other towards the musket, and both kept asking many questions interposed by exclamations of surprise. Tang Ruowang, bombarded with the questions, didn't know which one to answer first. Amidst this excitement suddenly came a burst of melodious music, which sounded somewhat like a bird singing, but a bird would not sing that well, or a chorus of various musical instruments, but there was no band in sight. The melody was exotic, not at all like Chinese music. As everyone was wondering, the young servant slowly came out of the next room with a gleaming birdcage in his hands and carefully hung it on an iron hook by the door.

The guests stood dumbfounded, obviously not believing that the beautiful music in their ears had anything to do with the bird in the cage.

Tang Ruowang stretched out a hand and said with a warm and enthusiastic voice, "Oh, gentlemen, this is a bird that can sing hymns. Please come over and enjoy its singing. It's praising the omniscient and almighty Heavenly Father and Jesus Christ."

Then, the guests went over to the cage, and after a closer look, they found that not only the cage was made of metal filaments, but even the bird in the cage was also made of metal. It stood there with its mouth open but couldn't move. As everyone was wondering how the fake bird could make that sound, the music suddenly stopped. The young servant immediately took out a curious-looking key from under his arm, inserted it into a small hole at the base of the cage, turned it a few times, and the music sounded again.

"Mr. Tang, such exquisite artifact from your country is mind-boggling indeed. May I know who has invented it?" Feng Daoji asked in awe.

"I was just about to tell you before you asked," Tang Ruowang

乃系慈悲万能的上帝！是上帝教导我们一切，还谕示我们不应将此智慧据为私有，要传授给居处于世界之上、哪怕最遥远地域的人民！”

“那么，汤先生远涉重洋，长驱万里，来游中国，其意也在此啰？”冯恺章问，肃然地望着主人。

汤若望点点头，把炯炯的目光转向他：“正是。皆因我辈俱系天生之罪人，我们的灵魂都沾满邪恶与不洁。唯有慈悲万能之上帝能够拯救我们！”

在他们对答的当儿，黄宗羲在一旁默默地听着。他见汤若望一本正经、咄咄逼人的样子，心想：“仁义之性，与生俱来。天下之理皆非心外之物。要拯救自己，也唯有反求本心，努力内省——‘致良知’而已矣，又何必求助什么上帝！”不过，虽然这样，汤若望作为一位“夷狄僧侣”，为着传播和实行自己所崇信的“道”，不惜背井离乡，变俗易服，来做一名异国的臣民，时至今日，仍然保持着饱满充沛的热情，这一点，却使黄宗羲惊异之余，心中不无触动。“要是换了我，处于他的地位，能够这样做么？”他暗中问自己，随即又吃了一惊，“哎，我为什么要这么想？为什么会这样想？”他隐隐约约感到，自己正接近一种可怕的、危险的想法。他不敢，也不愿意再深究下去了。

“哎，道未兄，这些话，还是留待你做弥撒的时候去说吧！”大约是瞧见黄宗羲的神色有点不对头，方以智从旁插进来说，“这位黄先生是位嗜书如命的人，阁下还是把那些奇书秘籍拿出来，让我们见识见识！”

汤若望正说到兴头上，忽然被打断，不免有点扫兴。他张了张嘴，似乎打算分辩，终于失望地摆一摆手，说：“请稍候！”然后悻悻然走进隔壁的房间，一会儿，同那年轻仆人各自抱了一

replied solemnly, raising a finger. "The one who enlightens us with infinite wisdom isn't a mortal man of flesh and blood, but the merciful and almighty God. It's God who teaches us everything and tells us that we shouldn't keep such wisdom to ourselves but instead should pass it on to other people, who might be living in the most distant corners of the world."

"Then, Mr. Tang, is that the reason why you've traveled thousands of miles to China?" Feng Kaizhang asked, looking at the host in deference.

Tang Ruowang nodded and turned his glowing eyes to him, saying, "Exactly. All of us are born sinners, and our souls are full of evil and impurity. Only the merciful and almighty God can save us."

At the same time, Huang Zongxi listened silently. Seeing Tang Ruowang's serious and assertive look, he thought, "Benevolence and righteousness is innate in human nature. The law of things is never outside the mind. To save oneself, one can only turn to their original mind and look inside for the good ideas. Why should we turn to God for help?" As a foreign monk, Tang Ruowang was respectable nonetheless, as he had left his home, adopted the native customs, dressed like the natives, and became a subject of a foreign country in order to transmit and practice his faith with unabated enthusiasm. "If I were him, would I be able to do the same?" he asked himself secretly. Then he was taken aback by his own thoughts. "Well, why do I have such thoughts? Why do such thoughts come to me?" He vaguely felt he was walking a dangerous line of thinking. He didn't dare and didn't want to go any further.

"Hey, Brother Daowei, save these words for the Mass," Fang Yizhi interjected, seeing Huang Zongxi didn't look quite right. "Mr. Huang is a book addict. So, you can show us your precious books."

Tang Ruowang felt a tad disappointed when he was suddenly interrupted. He opened his mouth, as if to argue, but finally waved his hand in disappointment and said, "Please hold on." Then he sullenly walked into the next room, and after a while, he and the young servant came out each with a large stack of books and placed them on the

大摞书出来，都堆在桌上，说：“请吧！”

黄宗羲听说有书可观，精神为之一振。他连忙走过去，先翻看一下书目。他发现这些书，绝大多数都是自己所不知道，或者仅仅听说过名字，却没有机会读到的。其中有徐光启与教士利玛窦合译的《几何原本》、李之藻译的《圜容较义》、徐光启的《测量法义》——这后两种是谈几何原理的实际应用的书，还有汤若望本人著的介绍西洋光学的《远镜说》，教士熊三拔著的专论水力机械的《泰西水法》，至于王征与教士邓玉函合译的《远西奇器图说》则是介绍物理学中重心、比重、杠杆、滑轮原理及简单机械构造的书。此外，还有介绍世界五大洲之说的《万国舆图》、介绍世界地理知识的《职方外纪》，以及介绍西洋天文学的《浑盖通宪图说》等等。黄宗羲越翻越兴奋。虽然有许多书他根本看不懂，但正因为这样，却激起了他越来越强的求知欲望，激起了他要把它们读懂、钻通的热情。“哎，这些都是经世致用之学！学者所须知。与那些个风琴、雀笼音乐真是不可同日而语！”他兴奋地想。随即，也不管还有其他人在场，先挑了一本比较容易读的《职方外纪》，退回椅子上埋头翻阅起来……

这一天，由于黄宗羲的坚持，他们在汤若望的宅邸里一直逗

table. "Please!" he said.

Hearing there were books to see, Huang Zongxi immediately brightened up. He hurried over to look at the titles first. Most of the books were unknown to him. He had heard of some of the titles but had had no chance to read them. Among the books were *ji he yuan ben* (*The Elements of Geometry*) co-translated by Xu Guangqi and priest Matteo Ricci, *yuan rong jiao yi* (a chapter of *In Sphaeram Ioannis de Sacro Bosco Commentarius*) co-translated by Li Zhizao and Matteo Ricci, Matteo Ricci's *ce liang fa yi* (*Techniques of Measuring*) translated by Xu Guangqi, the latter two being books on the practical application of geometric principles, *Explanation of the Telescope* written by Tang Ruowang himself, which introduces Western optics, *tai xi shui fa* (*Hydromethods of the Great West*) written by priest Sabatino de Ursis① on hydraulic machinery, and *yuan xi qi qi tu shuo* (*Illustrated Explanations of the Wonderful Machines of the Far West*) jointly translated by Wang Zheng and German priest Johann Schreck, whose Chinese name was Deng Yuhan, a physics book that introduces concepts such as center of gravity and specific gravity, principle of the lever, working principle of the pulley and simple mechanical structures, *Atlas of the World*, which describes the world's five continents, *zhi fang wai ji* (*Introduction to World Geography*), which is an introduction to the geography of foreign countries, and *hun gai tong xian tu shuo* (*An Illustrated Explanation of the Universe and the Sky*), which introduces Western astronomy. Huang Zongxi became more and more excited as he browsed through the titles. There were many books that he couldn't understand at all, but his curiosity for knowledge was aroused. "These books involve practical learning, very different from the music from the organ and the birdcage. A real scholar should read them," he thought, full of zest. Then, as if the others hadn't been present, he picked up the *Introduction to World Geography*, a relatively easy book, and returned to the chair to read ...

Because of Huang Zongxi's insistence, they stayed in Tang

① Sabatino de Ursis: Xiong Sanba(Chinese name), AD 1575–1620

留到下午很迟的时候才告辞出来。汤若望留他们用了午饭，出门时，又殷勤地一直把他们送到路口，才挥手告别。

在夕阳映照的归途上，方以智拍马走到显得既疲倦、又兴奋的黄宗羲身旁，悄悄地问：

“如今，你不急着走了吧？这位老汤还精通火器制造，朝廷近日颇有用他督造火炮之议，听说他还有一部《火攻挈要》，更是当今一大奇书。哼，就为的读一读它，你也值得留下来！”

## 谒见首辅

由于方以智和冯氏兄弟一再劝说，黄宗羲终于同意把那份上书交给冯元飙转呈周延儒。

半个月之后，他得到通知，说周延儒已经看到他的上书，并决定接见他。于是，黄宗羲在十月初八日下午申牌[①]时分，依约来到周延儒的府邸。

如果在三个月前，黄宗羲得知他的上书受到这位当朝首辅如此重视，那么，尽管他对周延儒的为人有种种不满，也必然会大为兴奋，十分感激。不过，时至今日，情况已经不同了。他这一次从同意呈递，到依约来见，与其说是出于对自己那份上书依然抱有热情和信心，不如说主要还是出于对冯元飙的尊重，以及不想过于拂逆朋友们的一番盛意。事实上，自从七月的那一次，徐石麒把他找去谈话之后，黄宗羲的心情就改变了。他再也无法像先前那样盲目乐观和自我陶醉。而当他一旦用变得清醒了的目光环顾四周时，这个庄严肃穆的帝王之都那黑暗、腐败、病态、没落的一面，就立即清楚地显现出来。他发现，在这里居住着至高无上的皇帝，但是这位皇帝正处于内外交困、焦头烂额的境地，而且变得越来越刚愎自用，喜怒无常；在这里拥有着令人生畏的

① 申牌：下午三时至五时。

Ruowang's residence until late in the afternoon. Tang Ruowang treated them to lunch, and when they left, he graciously escorted them all the way to the intersection before finally waving goodbye.

On the road lit by the setting sun, Fang Yizhi patted his horse and went to the side of Huang Zongxi, who looked tired but excited, and asked in a low voice:

"Now you're no longer in a hurry to go? Old Tang is also an expert at making firearms. The imperial court plans to ask him to supervise the making of cannons. It's said that he has a book called *Guide to Firearms*. For this book alone, you should stay."

## Seeing the Prime Minister

Through repeated persuasion by Fang Yizhi and the Feng brothers, Huang Zongxi finally agreed to give the petition letter to Feng Yuanbiao, who would take it to Zhou Yanru.

Half a month later, he was informed that Zhou Yanru had read the letter and decided to meet him. So, Huang Zongxi came to Zhou Yanru's residence in the late afternoon of October 8th in the lunar calendar as scheduled.

If it were three months ago, Huang Zongxi would have been very excited and very grateful when learning that his petition letter was so important in the eyes of the current prime minister despite all his dissatisfaction with the old man's conduct. Today, however, things were different. This time, he had agreed to submit the letter and come to meet Zhou Yanru not so much because he still had hopes for his petition but because he felt obliged to be respectful to Feng Yuanbiao and didn't want to let down his friends. In fact, he had completely changed his mind after Xu Shiqi talked to him in July. He could no longer be as blindly optimistic and self-absorbed as before. And as soon as he looked around with sober eyes, the dark side of the solemn imperial capital, which was corrupt, morbid, and decadent, immediately appeared before him. Here lived an emperor with supreme powers who was battered by inside and outside troubles and became increasingly self-willed and bad-tempered. Here lay

生杀予夺的大权，但这个大权却操纵在东厂和锦衣卫这样一些阴森可怕的衙门手里，被用来对付忠心谋国的人士和广大无辜的百姓；在这里聚集着来自各地的优秀人才，但这些人目前正卷入你死我活的党派之争，互相指责掣肘，以致少数有为之士也无法施展才干；这里还可以迅速听到有关时局的最新消息，把握朝廷决策的脉搏，但是这些消息却一个比一个倒霉，一个比一个更令人灰心丧气；至于朝廷的所谓决策，更是完全陷于仓皇应付，挖肉补疮，一片混乱……再加上这一次乡试，公行贿卖、徇私作弊的情况，比以往任何一次都要严重得多，而朝廷对此竟然毫无办法，听之任之。这更使得黄宗羲愤慨之余，感到深深的绝望。所以，直到此刻，当他越过一队又一队的轿车马匹，来到首辅官邸的大门前时，从表情到内心，都始终是冷淡而又迟疑的。

“哎，太冲，你到底来了！小弟足足候了你半个时辰哩！”一个喜滋滋的声音大声招呼说。

黄宗羲抬头一看，认出是周延儒的幕客顾麟生。

顾麟生是常熟人，今年也就三十出头，长得眉目挺拔，精明强干。他本是复社成员，因为他父亲顾大章是周延儒的老师，所以这一次周延儒复出，就把他聘作幕僚，参与机密之事，颇为信用。上一次就是他看到周延儒的来往书信，知道钱谦益密谋为阮大铖翻案开脱，写信告诉了冒襄，才把那件事彻底揭穿。黄宗羲同顾麟生本来就认识，而且交情不错，这次到北京后也互访过几次。他知道黄宗羲今天要来，所以先到门上来守候。

顾麟生这一出现，黄宗羲还不觉得怎样，周围那些先到的人却顿时骚动起来。他们都是为着各种各样的公事或私事来求见周

the awful power of life and death, but that power was controlled by the East Factory men and the Jinyiwei guards, who relentlessly persecuted the loyal and patriotic as well as the innocent common people. Here gathered the best minds from all over the country, but they were engaged in an endless life-or-death partisan struggle that made everything impossible for the few capable men who still wished to correct things. Here, he could hear the latest news and feel the pulse of the court, but it was all bad news. The decisions of the imperial court were all bad ones, ill-informed, hastily made, unable to address the real problems at all. It was all a chaos ... and in the latest imperial examination, corruption was rampant and more serious than before, and yet the imperial court could do nothing but let it go. Huang Zongxi was saddened and disappointed. So, when he finally arrived at the gate of the official residence of the prime minister after making his way through entourages of sedan chairs and horses, his expression and mind remained anxious, and he was not sure he was doing the right thing.

"Hi, Taichong, glad you are here. I've been waiting for you for an hour." A cheerful voice greeted him loudly.

Huang Zongxi looked up and saw it was Zhou Yanru's staff adviser Gu Linsheng.

Gu Linsheng was from Changshu. This smart-looking thirty-something with defined features was also a member of the Fushe. Because his father Gu Dazhang was Zhou Yanru's teacher, when Zhou Yanru was reinstated to office, the old man hired him as a staff member to participate in confidential matters. It was him who had learned from Zhou Yanru's correspondence that Qian Qianyi was plotting to reverse the Ruan Dacheng case and written to Mao Xiang. Having known each other for a long time, Huang Zongxi and Gu Linsheng had a very good relationship. There had been several mutual visits since Huang Zongxi arrived in Beijing. Gu Linsheng had come to the gate to wait for Huang Zongxi because he knew the friend was coming today.

Huang Zongxi didn't feel there was anything unusual when Gu Linsheng appeared, but the men who had arrived earlier stirred when

延儒的。有的手本已经递进去好久了，始终不见答复，眼见时候不早，正在着急，好不容易盼出来个人，当然不肯放过，纷纷围上来，七嘴八舌地打听消息。

顾麟生显然十分熟悉这种场面。他板着脸，挥挥手，说声：“周相公接客未完，请列位安心守候！”然后，挽着黄宗羲的胳膊，头也不回地往里走。

碰了这个钉子，多数人都泄了气，只有一个胖胖的、留着一把长胡子的绅士仍旧不甘心，他紧赶几步，在大门前赶上了顾麟生。

“顾先生，小弟并非求见周相公，乃是来访董先生的。相烦转知一声，不胜感激！”胖绅士赔着笑脸，乞求地说。

顾麟生回顾一下：“哦，阁下要访董先生？”他问，停住了脚步。

“正是正是！”胖绅士连忙拱着手说，“小弟近刻得新书两部，意欲送上一部请董先生过目，另有一部——若顾先生不弃，就敬请先生指教！”

“这个……”

“尚希哂纳！”

在他们对答的当儿，黄宗羲只是冷冷地听着。他早就听说，周延儒有一个心腹幕客，名叫董廷献，为人狡狯贪婪，借着主人的权势，卖官鬻爵，贪赃受贿，早已秽声载道。这位胖绅士要找的，大约就是此人。至于所谓“送书”，无非是行贿的隐语，这些书后面，照例都附得有金子、银子，叫作“书帕”。这胖绅士不知急于谋求什么，如今竟打算连顾麟生也一并讨好拉拢。“哼，我倒要瞧瞧玉书怎么办！”黄宗羲想。

they saw someone coming out. They had come to see Zhou Yanru for various public or private matters. Some of them had submitted their calling cards long ago and were anxiously waiting for a reply. When someone finally came out of the residence, they of course would not let him go and quickly surrounded Gu Linsheng to make inquiries.

Gu Linsheng was obviously very familiar with such a scene. With a stern face, he waved his hand and said, "The Prime Minister is receiving a guest. Please wait patiently." Then, holding Huang Zongxi's arm, he walked in without looking back.

Having met with a rebuff, most of the visitors were crestfallen. A chubby gentleman with a long beard didn't give up. He hurried forward and caught up with Gu Linsheng at the gate. "Mr. Gu, I'm here to see Mr. Dong, not the Prime Minister. If you can tell Mr. Dong, I'll be very grateful," the fat gentleman begged with an obsequious smile on his face.

Gu Linsheng stopped and looked back. "Oh, you want to see Mr. Dong?" he asked.

"Yes, sir," the fat gentleman hurriedly replied, putting his hands together. "I'm taking with me two copies of a newly published book. I want to give one to Mr. Dong for his advice, and if you are interested, I want to give the other one to you and hear your advice too."

"This ..."

"I'll be honored if you accept it, sir."

Huang Zongxi listened gravely as they talked. He had heard Zhou Yanru had a trusted staff adviser called Dong Tingxian, who was avaricious and greedy and notorious for monetizing his connection with his patron by selling official positions and titles. The chubby gentleman might have come to see him. The giving of a book was no more than a euphemism for the giving of a bribe. To the back of the book was attached some gold or silver wrapped in a kerchief called *shupa* (book sticker). The chubby gentleman had obviously come for something and was eager to get it, so he was now even courting favor with Gu Linsheng by giving him a "book" too. "Hmph, I would like to see what he does with the books," Huang Zongxi thought.

“好吧，我给尊驾转知董先生就是！”顾麟生回答得十分干脆，拉着黄宗羲继续往里走。

“啊，那么这书？”

“先寄在门房里，待会儿我来取！”顾麟生说，没有回头。

“玉书，”沉默着走了十来步之后，黄宗羲终于忍不住问，“这多半年来，你都是这样子的么？”

“什么？”

“自然是‘书帕’，还有……”

顾麟生“噢”了一声，满不在乎地说：“这算个什么？你不见姓董的，那才叫会家子哩！不管是谁，想谋个总兵、巡抚什么的，都得巴巴地先来拜他。要不，就休想办成！这些年，他可是捞得够肥了。别瞧那几本破书，只怕他未必就能看得上眼！”

“不过，这怎么可以……”

顾麟生“嘻嘻”地笑起来：“若说不可以，也真不可以。但要那样子，除非你不来这官场上混！如今的风气，人家倒不恨你要钱，却恨你不要他的钱。你一不要钱，得罪的人可就多了！”

“啊，怎么？”

“你要了钱，把事给办成了，他到地方上去，就能五倍十倍地捞回来，何乐而不为？你若不要钱，他的事办不成，岂非绝了财路，又怎能不恨你！”

黄宗羲不由得“哼”了一声，心想：“国先自伐，然后人伐之！政事之坏，就坏在这伙无孔不入的蛀虫身上！连顾玉书这样的人，初涉官场，便立时为习气所染，亦可见颓风之溺人，何等可骇可惊！”虽然他明知根由不在顾麟生身上，而且即使顾麟生洁身自好，也还有其他的人，他们比顾麟生恐怕更贪婪十倍，像董廷献

"Alright, I'll let Mr. Dong know," Gu Linsheng said, taking Huang Zongxi's hand as he continued to walk inside.

"Then, what about the books?"

"Leave it with the concierge. I'll pick them up later," Gu Linsheng said, without looking back.

"Yushu," Huang Zongxi finally asked after walking about ten steps in silence. "Have you been always like this over the past six months?"

"What do you mean?"

"Of course I mean the *shupa*, and ..."

"Oh," Gu Linsheng said calmly. "It's no big deal. You don't know how good Mr. Dong is at doing business with his prestige. Whoever wants to become an army general or a governor or anything has to go through him. Otherwise, they won't succeed. Having made a whole lot of money over the years, he may not even cast a glance at this book."

"But that is illegal ..."

Gu Linsheng laughed. "If you say it's illegal, it's illegal, but you must do it unless you don't want to enter officialdom. Nowadays, people don't hate you for taking their money but will hate you for not taking it. If you don't take the money, you'll end up having more enemies."

"Ah, how is it so?"

"If you take the money and the thing gets done, he'll be happy, because he can make five times as much after he's appointed to a position in a province. If you don't take the money, his hope is frustrated, and he'll hate you for blocking his way to wealth."

Huang Zongxi snorted, thinking to himself, "A country destroys itself before it's destroyed by others. The crisis of the nation is exactly caused by these parasites, who take every opportunity to fatten themselves. It's shocking to see that the government is so corrupt that even a newcomer in politics like Gu Yushu immediately sinks into the muddy waters." Huang Zongxi knew that the root cause was not in Gu Linsheng, and even if Gu Linsheng was clean, there were other men who were probably ten times more corrupt, like Dong Tingxian and

之流那样。但是，黄宗羲仍然觉得有必要劝谏一下朋友，提醒他不要忘了做一个正人君子的准则。“嗯，等见过周阁老之后，我得好好说一说他！”他严厉地想。

这当儿，他们已经从前院东边的一道侧门走进了别院。当他们从一间花厅的门外经过时，黄宗羲看见三四个纱帽补服的官员正在那里默默对坐，像在等待着什么。顾麟生附在耳边告诉黄宗羲：陈新甲一案，由于主持审理的刑部左侍郎徐石麒坚持要按失误军机、私款辱国的死罪来论处，判定当斩，举朝为之震动。据说眼下皇上还在犹疑。花厅内的这几个官员，就是来求周延儒设法营救的。黄宗羲早就在徐石麒那里听说过陈新甲的案情，觉得此人确实罪大恶极，死有余辜；而且对于朝廷上至今仍有一部分大臣在替陈新甲辩护说情，极力开脱，心中颇为不满。他望了一眼顾麟生，淡淡地问：

“周相公可肯援手？”

顾麟生微微一笑：“援手是要援手的。不过周相公侍候皇上多年，皇上的脾气心思他比谁都摸得透……”他四面望望，忽然凑上来，压低嗓音说，“皇上其实杀心已决，只是他不想做丑人，所以……”

黄宗羲听他说得厉害，倒吃了一惊，连忙使个眼色制止他。顾麟生吐一吐舌头，马上住了口。

这之后，两位朋友便不约而同地沉默下来。又走过几道门，来到一所小斋前，顾麟生让黄宗羲在门外稍等，独自走进去。一会儿，他重新走出来，说：

“相公有请！”然后又咬着耳朵叮嘱说，“今日早晨，相公最心爱的一只波斯猫儿难产死了，直到这会儿还很不开心，外面丢着一大堆客人，他都不想见。是我再三替你说了情，他才勉强

many others, but he felt the need to persuade his friend and remind him not to forget the code of conduct for a good man. "Well, I'll talk to him after meeting Elder Zhou," he thought sternly.

They entered the side courtyard through a side door on the east side of the front courtyard. When they passed by the door of a flower hall, Huang Zongxi saw four men in official caps and uniforms sitting there silently, on two sides, as if waiting for something. Gu Linsheng whispered in his ear and said: Xu Shiqi, Left Vice Minister of the Ministry of Punishment, who was presiding over the trial of Chen Xinjia, had decided to behead Chen Xinjia for negligence of duty and colluding with the enemy, but that shocked the imperial court; it was said that the emperor was still hesitating; the officials sitting in the flower hall had come to plead with Zhou Yanru. Having heard of the Chen Xinjia case from Xu Shiqi before, Huang Zongxi knew that the death penalty just served Chen Xinjia right. Sickened to learn there were still some ministers in the court to defend and intercede for the man, he glanced at Gu Linsheng and asked apathetically, "Is the Prime Minister going to intercede?"

Gu Linsheng smiled slightly. "Sure he will, but having served the emperor for so many years, he knows the emperor's temperament and thoughts better than anybody else ..." He looked around, suddenly came close and said in a low voice, "The emperor has actually made up his mind on the death sentence, but he doesn't want to appear to be a heartless man, so ..."

Huang Zongxi was surprised to hear it, and since it involved the emperor, he hurriedly winked to stop him. Gu Linsheng stuck out his tongue and immediately stopped.

After that, the two friends both went silent. After passing a few more doors, they arrived at a small study room. Gu Linsheng asked Huang Zongxi to wait at the door and went in alone.

After a while, he came out and said, "now you can see the Prime Minister," then with a whisper, "Since his favorite Persian cat died in labor this morning, he's still very sad and doesn't want to see any of the guests waiting outside, but I've persuaded him to see you.

肯了。待会儿，他说什么，你都听着，千万不要辩驳，可记住了？只要他肯把你留下，往后一切都好办，有我呢！”

这时黄宗羲也多少有点紧张。毕竟，这是他头一遭来谒见这位当朝首辅。“嗯，不知道他是什么样儿？脾气怎么样？我该怎样对待他？”他匆忙地想。对于顾麟生的叮嘱，他听了进去，却来不及反应过来，只是机械地点着头，随着顾麟生步上台阶，进了小斋。

这是一间小小的、布置得异常雅洁的书斋。骤眼望去，斋内的一切，都以小巧别致为特色——小巧的屏风，小巧的桌椅，小巧的卧榻。当中一张古制的狭边书儿，上面陈设有笔砚、香盒、熏炉之类，也无一不是小巧玲珑，式样别致。四面的墙壁看不见一幅字画，却有一个小小的佛橱，里面供着一尊镏金小佛。因为已是十月之交，天气渐凉，椅子上都垫上了古锦褥，小榻上铺了一张斑斓的虎皮。

黄宗羲没有心思观察斋内的布置，他睁大眼睛，四处张望，希望能尽快见到主人。这时，响起了官靴踩地的橐橐声响，身穿一品补服、头戴纱帽的周延儒从屏风后面慢慢走了出来。他是个中等身材的人，虽然上了年纪，而且似乎有点闷闷不乐，却依然颇有风度，一张肌理细腻的长圆脸，再加上细长的眉眼，笔直的鼻梁，使人不难想到，这位当朝首辅年轻时必定是一个美男子。即使是现在，那梳理得一丝不苟的花白胡子，那始终不见发胖的腰身，也还处处显露出优雅。当然，作为身负重任的大臣，他同时又是自信而从容的。要在平时，他的目光想必坚定有神，但不知为什么此刻却毫无光彩，向前突出的下巴两旁，也现出两道深沟，使整张脸显得忧郁失神，缺乏它所应有的威严和气派。

Whatever he says, just listen. Don't argue, remember? If he decides to let you stay in Beijing, everything will be fine. Trust me."

Huang Zongxi was a little nervous. After all, it was his first visit to the Prime Minister. "Um, I wonder what he looks like. What is his temperament like? How should I speak to him?" he thought apprehensively. He heard what Gu Linsheng said, but unable to respond immediately, he merely mechanically nodded his head, and on the heels of Gu Linsheng, went up the steps and entered the small study.

It was a compact, nicely arranged study. Everything in it was small and exquisite—a mini screen, a short table, some undersized chairs, a pygmy couch, and a narrow edge desk, on which were placed a brush pen, an inkstone, an incense box, and an incense burner, all of them small, exquisite and stylish. The only thing on the walls was a niche, in which sat a gold-plated statue of the Buddha. Because it was already the beginning of October, and the weather was getting cold, the chairs were padded with brocade cushions, and the pygmy couch was padded with a striped tiger skin.

Huang Zongxi had no mind to observe the layout of the study. He opened his eyes wide and looked around to find the host when suddenly came the sound of official boots stepping on the floor. Zhou Yanru slowly emerged from behind the screen, wearing an official's long gown and an official's hat. He was a man of medium height, whose old age and sullen expression didn't reduce his decorum. A delicate, long, round face, slender eyes and brows, and a straight nose bridge suggested that he had been very handsome when he was young. His meticulously combed gray beard and his healthy body that had never been overweight were still permeated with beauty and grace. Of course, as the prime minister, he was also confident and calm. At the moment, his eyes that were supposed to be bright and resolute for some reason lacked the luster as they should have, and two deep ditches showed on the sides of his raised chin, so that his face appeared melancholy and bleak, without the solemnity and grace as it should have.

黄宗羲愕然地望着这张脸，有片刻工夫，不大相信这就是周延儒。说来也好笑，大约是出于一种反感的心理，过去他一直把这位首辅想象成为一个瘦小阴鸷的人，一双蛇样的眼睛里永远闪动着贪婪和猜忌的光芒……不过，他很快就清醒过来，因为顾麟生已经开始介绍。于是黄宗羲松了一口气，怀着对周延儒的新鲜的，甚至有点可亲的印象，上前拜见，并在主人的搀扶下站起身，重新叙过礼，分宾主坐了下来。

“嗯，也许他并不如我想象的那样贪鄙忮刻？他既然两度入相，这后一次，还是东林方面给出的力，想必自有其过人之处。比如我的那一份上书，送上来才半个月，他就不仅看了，而且还立即予以接见，只这一点，就不容易！”黄宗羲一边继续打量主人，一边想。他的心情渐渐变得开朗了一些，觉得说不定周延儒当真对他的那个改革计划感兴趣。他甚至开始考虑，要是对方询问起来，将如何对答。

“玉书兄，待会儿烦你替我翻检一下，把古人的咏猫诗找那么一二十首出来。我想瞧瞧他们是怎么写的。”宾主寒暄了几句之后，周延儒忽然回过头，对顾麟生这样说。

“是！”后者拱着手答应。

“什么？咏猫诗？他要咏猫诗做什么？”黄宗羲迷惑地想，目光不由得投向那张狭边书几。他刚才曾注意到，那上面的笔砚尚未收起，笺纸上还依稀有书写过的痕迹。蓦地，他记起顾麟生的那一番叮嘱，心想：“对了，听玉书说这位周相公死了一只什么波斯猫，伤心得很，这会儿想必正打算写诗哭它哩！”

由于忽然发现，直到此刻，周延儒虽然似乎是在和颜悦色地接待自己，其实他一心惦念着的，却是那心爱的玩物，黄宗羲不由得愣住了。随后，一股受到侮辱的感觉从心底里渐渐冒出来。他那瘦小的脸孔由于恼怒而涨红了。

Huang Zongxi stared at that face in consternation. For a moment, he hardly believed that this was Zhou Yanru. Funnily, he had always imagined the Prime Minister as a short, thin, sinister man with eyes like those of a snake that always twinkled with greed and suspicion ... However, he soon woke up, because Gu Linsheng had begun to introduce him. He breathed a sigh of relief, and with a fresh, favorable impression of Zhou Yanru, went forward to kowtow to the host, who now looked amiable to him, and stood up with the help of the old man. After exchanging pleasantries, they respectively sat down in their seats.

"Well, maybe he's not as mean as I thought. Since he's become Prime Minister twice and even has had the backing of the East Wooders, he must have something special to recommend himself. It has only been a couple of days, and he's not only read my petition letter but also has arranged this meeting with me. This alone shows he's a very serious man," Hong Zongxi thought, regarding the host. He gradually cheered up a little bit, thinking that perhaps Zhou Yanru might be interested in his reform plan. He even began to consider how to answer his questions.

After the exchange of pleasantries, Zhou Yanru suddenly turned around and said to Gu Linsheng, "Brother Yushu, can you please find me ten to twenty ancient cat poems when this is over? I want to see how the ancients wrote about cats."

"Aye, sir," said Gu Linsheng.

"What? Cat poems? Why does he ask for cat poems?" Huang Zongxi thought, puzzled, as his eyes involuntarily turned to the narrow edge desk. He had noticed just now that had an ink stone and sheets of paper with lines of writing. Suddenly, he remembered Gu Linsheng's advice. "Um, Yushu said that the Prime Minister is very sad because he's lost a Persian cat, so he's writing a poem to mourn his cat," he thought.

Realizing Zhou Yanru was actually thinking about a pet all the time while talking to him affably, Huang Zongxi was annoyed. A feeling of humiliation rose from his heart, his thin, small face flushing in anger.

“哎，太冲兄，你不知道，玉老此猫乃是去年粤督沈公从濠镜屿波斯商人处购得，专程送到京里来。本是一对，通体纯白，无一杂毛，缱绻依人，甚是可爱。那雌猫尤为奇物，左右两眼，颜色不同，一金一银，顾盼莹然，见者无不称异。不料今早竟死于难产，着实教人痛惜呢！”大概看见黄宗羲神情不对，顾麟生连忙解释说，一边朝他直使眼色。

黄宗羲却只装没有瞧见。他朝主人拱一拱手，直冲冲地问：“老师相，半月前晚生托请弢老转呈的那一封上书，不知已蒙钧鉴否？”

“哦，兄台的上书么？冯少司马已经转到了。”周延儒点点头，奇怪地瞧了客人一眼。

“不知已蒙钧鉴否？”黄宗羲又问。

“这个……嗯，学生我也曾拜读……其中见解，大体是不错的，不过……”周延儒含糊地说。

但黄宗羲毫不放松：“尚祈明教！”他又一次拱着手。

周延儒显然觉察到对方态度的咄咄逼人，而且对这种谈话的方式感到不快。为了使对方明白这一点，他挥了挥手，用变得威严的口吻说：“这个，以后再说吧！”

这样断然地把问题了结之后，他就立即把交谈转到了其他方面。他开始问黄宗羲最近读些什么书，问他有没有见过钱谦益，还问到江南的灾情，而不管是在询问，还是在听的时候，他都始终保持着一种淡漠的、莫测高深的神情，而且常常是不等黄宗羲说完，他就提出另一个问题来打断他。这就造成了一种印象，似

"Well, Brother Taichong, you don't know how precious this cat is. Mr. Shen, Governor of Guangdong, bought it from a Persian merchant stationed in Haojing Island[1] last year and made a special trip to Beijing to give it to Elder Yu. In fact, it's two cats, both immaculately white. They're very attached to humans and very cuddly. The female one is especially rare. She has a golden left eye and a silvery right eye shining brightly. Everyone loves her stunning beauty. Unfortunately, she died in labor this morning." Seeing that Huang Zongxi's expression was not right, Gu Linsheng hurriedly explained and winked at him at the same time.

Huang Zongxi just pretended not to see the winking. He bowed with clasped hands and asked pertly, "My dear teacher, I wonder if you've read the petition letter forwarded by Elder Tao."

"Oh, is it the letter from you, brother? Mr. Feng has given it to me." Zhou Yanru nodded and glanced at the guest with a curious look.

"Have you read it yet, your lordship?" Huang Zongxi asked again.

"Um, I've read it. The arguments are basically good, but ..." Zhou Yanru said hesitantly.

But Huang Zongxi didn't give up. "But what? Please kindly tell me." He clasped his hands and bowed again.

Zhou Yanru obviously felt intimidated by the young man and was very displeased with the way he spoke. In order to make Huang Zongxi understand this, he waved his hand and said in a dignified tone, "Well, let's talk about it later."

After categorically closing the topic, Zhou Yanru immediately turned the conversation to other things. He asked Huang Zongxi what books he had read recently, whether he had seen Qian Qianyi, and what the natural disasters were like in River South. When he was asking a question or listening to the reply, he always maintained an indifferent and lofty air. He often interrupted Huang Zongxi by asking another question before the young man finished speaking, to give the

---

① Haojing Island: now Macao

乎黄宗羲所说的那些情况都是他早已掌握、毫无价值的，而他这样问，仅仅是出于一种礼貌而已。

起初，黄宗羲还十分认真地回答主人的问话。但是很快地，他就变得兴趣索然，而且越来越清晰地意识到，自己在对方眼里，其实是多么卑微和幼稚。他开始脸红心跳，局促不安，回答问题也一次比一次简短，最后只剩下“是”和“不是”。

看见这种情形，坐在一旁的顾麟生暗暗着急。他接连朝黄宗羲使了几次眼色，但黄宗羲固执地低着头，只装没瞧见。顾麟生没有办法，正想开口替他打几句圆场，忽然回廊里响起了脚步声，接着，长得又干又瘦的老幕客董廷献出现在门口。顾麟生只好临时咽住了。

董廷献先向斋内张望了一下，然后耸着肩，弓着腰，迈着轻而急的步子，走到周延儒身边，俯下头去，低声说了几句什么。

只见周延儒面无表情地听完，摆了摆手说：“让他们先等着，就说我这会儿还没工夫见他们。”

“是！”董廷献恭顺地应诺着，却不退下。他用眼梢斜了斜黄宗羲，稍稍提高声音：“不过听说徐大人已经入奏，就怕圣旨随时会下……”

周延儒横了他一眼，不耐烦地说：“慌什么？没见我这会儿有客人吗！”然后，他便不理会幕客，重新转向黄宗羲，堆起笑容问：“刚才，我们说到哪儿了？——对，听说钱牧斋到盛泽迎亲时，给人赶着飞瓦片，这可是怎么回事？”

“阁老大人既有要务，晚生就此告退了。”已经变得垂头丧气的黄宗羲，连忙站起来说。

impression that the reply was something he had already known and therefore worthless, and he was just asking out of politeness.

At first, Huang Zongxi answered the questions very seriously, but soon he became less enthusiastic, aware of how stupid and naive he was in the eyes of Zhou Yanru. He began to fret and blush, and his reply became shorter and shorter, until finally he merely answered "yes" or "no".

Seeing that, Gu Linsheng, who was sitting beside him, became worried and kept winking at Huang Zongxi, but the latter pretended not to see it, with his head stubbornly drooping. Gu Linsheng could do nothing but leave him alone. As he was going to smooth it out for his friend, he suddenly heard the sound of footsteps from the corridor. Then, Dong Tingxian, a withered old staff adviser, appeared at the door. Gu Linsheng had to hold back the words that came to his lips.

Dong Tingxian first glanced at the study, then shrinking his shoulders and tilting forward, walked to Zhou Yanru's side with light but fast steps, bowed his head, and said something in a low voice.

Zhou Yanru listened with no expression on his face, then waved his hand and said, "Let them wait and tell them I don't have time to see them right now."

"Aye, sir!" Dong Tingxian said submissively. Instead of backing out immediately, he added in a slightly louder voice, squinting at Huang Zongxi from the corner of his eye, "But I hear Mr. Xu has already gone to the court to talk to the emperor. I'm afraid that the edict will be issued any time soon ..."

Zhou Yanru glanced at him and said impatiently, "What's the hurry? Don't you see I have a guest now?" Then, ignoring the staff adviser, he turned to Huang Zongxi and asked with a smile: "Where were we just now?—Yes, I heard that when Qian Muzhai went to Shengze to welcome his bride, he was chased with bricks. What has happened?"

Huang Zongxi, who was downcast and sullen, quickly stood up and said, "Since your lordship has important matters on hand, I must excuse myself now."

“噢，兄台这就要走？”周延儒的表情有一点惊讶，也有一点惋惜，但是并不挽留，跟着站起来送客。直到走出门口时，他才眯起眼睛，欣赏地望着对面墙头上正在秋风夕阳里忽闪着的几根枯草，用漫不经心的口吻说：

“学生之意，是想奉屈兄台到阁里来，协理文牍之事——自然，这事也不急，先生回去权衡轻重之后，若肯俯就，便通知玉书，让他告诉我。”

“Ah, must you go now, big brother?” Zhou Yanru asked with an expression of surprise and disappointment. Without intending to keep Huang Zongxi longer, he stood up to see off the guest. When they walked out of the study, he said in a flat tone, narrowing his eyes to look at the few withered blades of grass on the opposite wall that were fluttering in the autumn wind and the setting sun.

“I’m thinking you can work in the Prime Minister’s Office to help with the processing of paperwork if you don’t mind. Of course, there’s no hurry. You can think about it, and if you agree, just ask Yushu to tell me and I’ll take care of it.”

# 第十二章
# 施援手三招制恶，谈时局一夜惊魂

## 勾引道姑

自从三月底回到家中之后，整整半年里，钱谦益的足迹再没有离开过常熟。

由于同周延儒之间的那桩秘密交易全盘失败，他对于起用的事已经心灰意冷；何况外间的舆论，对他又颇为不利，就更使他疑神疑鬼，轻易不想出门。

他也曾打算，干脆把拂水山庄着意改建一番，从此隐居养老，也就算了。偏偏柳如是竭力阻拦，坚决反对，结果只好作罢。

不过，说也奇怪，由于不再胡思乱想，钱谦益反而能专下心来过日子。他鉴于家里近几年亏空越来越大，下决心整顿财务；又自觉年纪大了，精神不济，便把这事同柳如是商量。柳如是也不推辞，把家里的财权一手揽了过去。别瞧她是个风尘弱质，女流之辈，行事处置，真还有点魄力。她用恩威并施的手法，先把一批地位较低但能干可用的管事人员收作心腹，让他们反过来监视何思虞、邹志之类的大管家；接着又制定出一套严格的财务制度，随时随地检查、督促；还杀鸡儆猴地狠狠处置了几个桀骜刁

## Chapter Twelve

# In Which Qian Qianyi Subdued the Villains with Tact and Bad News Disrupted the Dinner at Mao Xiang's Home

## A Secret Date with a Nun

Since his return at the end of March, Qian Qianyi had never left Changshu for the past six months.

He didn't want to go out, because he no longer entertained any hopes for his reinstatement to office after the secret transaction with Zhou Yanru completely failed, and he suspected everyone was talking about it behind his back.

He had planned to renovate the Waterside Villa and spend his old age as a recluse from now on but eventually gave it up because of Liu Rushi's strong objection.

Curiously, Qian Qianyi suddenly calmed down and was able to concentrate on family matters. As his family had had a huge deficit in the past few years, he decided to put the finances in order. Feeling he was too old to handle such matters, he talked to Liu Rushi, who without hesitation gladly took over all family finances. Although she looked fragile, she was in fact a very capable woman, who acted very quickly and resolutely. First, she used a combination of reward and punishment to secure the allegiance of some lower-ranking but capable servants, making them her trusted aides, who, in turn, reported to her on their superiors such as He Siyu and Zou Zhi. Then, she made some strict rules about the spending of money and made sure they were

顽的豪奴。就这样，不到两个月，她居然把原来混乱不堪、漏洞百出的账房整治得井井有条，使那些心怀不轨的人至少暂时不敢轻举妄动。至于朱姨太，因为眼见大势已去，加上在整肃财务的当儿，有好几件案子本来都牵连到她，柳如是却宽大为怀，不予深究，这使朱氏惊愧之余，不由得对柳如是顿生感激之意，渐渐反倒设法巴结起她来。看到这种情形，钱谦益心中十分欣慰，对柳如是也更加宠信。他既不用操这份心，便集中精力去做他的学问。他把自己早年所写的诗词文章，重新认认真真地修改润色了一次，分门别类地编排起来，分为一百一十卷，定名为《初学集》，准备一旦弄到款子，就拿去刻印出版；另外，又动手将佛教的有名经典《楞严经》详加注疏；闲下来时，就同柳如是写诗唱和，或是下棋作画，翻书赌茶，日子倒也过得优游自在。

这样，一直到了农历十月。

这天上午，钱谦益照例在匪斋里注释他的《楞严经》。当注到“于时世尊顶放百宝无畏光明，光中生出千叶宝莲，有佛化身，结跏趺坐”这几句时，心中油然涌起一阵感触：“是啊，佛家言一叶宝莲便是一世界，千叶宝莲便是千世界。而大千世界中的一切，都如梦幻泡影。人生在世，唯其能作如是观，便可少却无限烦恼！”正呆呆地想着，忽然，李宝送进来一批信札。钱谦益放下笔，随手捡起一封，见是苏州寄来的最新塘报抄件，就先丢下不看。因为近几年来，时局越来越坏，塘报上难得有什么令人鼓舞的消息——不外是哪个城镇又被“流贼”攻陷了，哪个官员又

strictly observed. Besides, she punished some cunning and unruly servants as a warning to others. Thus, in less than two months, she quickly put the previously chaotic and leaky accounting office in order, so that those who had been stealing from the house had to behave, at least for the time being. However, she was very lenient to Lady Zhu, who was involved in several cases of stealing and didn't investigate those cases further. Seeing the situation had changed and grateful to Liu Rushi for the kindness, Lady Zhu, who had been scared and ashamed, gradually began to curry favor with Liu Rushi. Qian Qianyi was relieved to see it and trusted Liu Rushi even more. Now that he no longer needed to spend his time on financial matters, he began to concentrate on his academic and artistic pursuits. He carefully revised and polished the poems and essays written in his early years, arranged them into one hundred and ten volumes, and named them *The Writings of a Beginner*. Once he got the money, he would get them lithographed. He also set about annotating the famous Buddhist classic *The Surangama Sutra*. In his free moments, he bandied poems or played chess with Liu Rushi, or the two painted a picture or played the "turn a page and drink a cup of tea" game together. It was a rather quiet and leisurely life.

That life lasted until October in the lunar calendar.

One morning, as Qian Qianyi was annotating *The Shurangama Sutra* as usual in his study, he came across these lines: "Then, the World-Honored One emitted from the top of His head a bright and awe-inspiring halo in which appeared a thousand-petalled lotus, on which sat an avatar of the Buddha with crossed legs." He was deeply touched. "Yes, according to Buddhist teaching, a single petal of a lotus is a world, a thousand petals are a thousand worlds, and everything in the thousand worlds is like a dream or a bubble. Living in this world, one has to think this way to save themselves from infinite troubles," he thought to himself. While he was pondering, Li Bao brought in a batch of envelopes. He put down his brush pen and picked up one. Seeing that it was a copy of the latest official communication from Suzhou, he put it down. It was not worth reading. The situation had been worsening

战死或者被杀了，以及损失了多少人马等等。不看还好，越看越令人灰心丧气，老半天都舒坦不过来。虽然如此，钱谦益到底又忍不住，迟疑了一下，依旧把塘抄捡了起来，带着厌恶、冷淡的神情拆开，瞄了一眼。忽然，他的眼睛睁大了——塘抄上面，赫然写着一行大字：

潜山我师大捷

“什么？大捷！”他心头一喜，连忙看下去。消息的内容是这样：据凤阳总督行辕“加急飞递”送到的战报称，新任总督马士英率属下总兵官黄得功、刘良佐二军，于长江以北凤阳、庐州、安庆一线，与张献忠、左金王、革里眼等农民军相持两月，乘敌方并力进攻桐城之际，分进合击，转战十余日，已于九月二十四日大破张献忠于潜山县境，击毙闯世王、马武、三鹞子、王兴国等。目前，张献忠率其余部退走湖北蕲水，革、左残兵亦向北逃散，已不能再对江南构成威胁。历时一载的南京紧张状态亦因此宣告解除。

“啊，总算把张献忠赶跑了，谢天谢地！”钱谦益心中一阵兴奋，不由自主地站起身子，把塘抄仔细地又从头到尾看了一遍。直到证实没有理解错之后，他才如释重负地透了一口气，重新坐了下来。的确，自从今春以来，张献忠会合革里眼贺一龙、左金王贺锦两支农民军，连陷长江北岸的含山、和州、无为、庐江等

over the past few years, and there had rarely been any encouraging news in the official communications other than the fall of another city to the insurgents or the death of another commander in battle or the loss of more soldiers and horses. He would feel better by not reading them. After some hesitation, however, he picked it up again, opened it, and glanced at it with an expression of disgust and aversion. Suddenly, his eyes opened wide. A line in a mighty big script caught his eye:

GREAT VICTORY IN QIANSHAN

"What? Great victory?" He was overjoyed and eagerly read the communication, which said: According to the frontline report sent through expedited delivery by the Governor of Fengyang's temporary *yamen*, the new Governor Ma Shiying and his two subordinates, Commander Huang Degong and Commander Liu Liangzuo, after a two-month stalemate at the Fengyang-Luzhou-Anqing frontline north of the Yangtze River with the peasant armies led by Zhang Xianzhong, He Jin nicknamed King of Zuojin, and He Yilong nicknamed Popeye, finally defeated Zhang Xianzhong in Qianshan County and killed Ma Wu and Wang Xingguo on September 24 in a ten-day-long battle by taking advantage of the vacuum in the rear of the enemy forces laying siege to Tongcheng City. Now, Zhang Xianzhong and the remnants of his troops had retreated to Qishui, Hubei Province, and the remnants of the troops of He Jin and He Yilong had also fled north. They no longer posed any threat to River South. The one-year-long alert in Nanjing was thus lifted.

"Oh, thank goodness! Finally, Zhang Xianzhong is gone." A strong feeling of excitement rose inside him. He stood up involuntarily, and read the communication carefully from beginning to end. After making sure there was no mistake, he breathed a sigh of relief and sat down again. Indeed, Qian Qianyi had been deeply worried since spring. Zhang Xianzhong had joined forces with two other peasant armies, led by He Yilong and He Jin respectively, and captured several cities on the north bank of the Yangtze River, including Hanshan, Hezhou, Wuwei, and Lujiang. They were now training their soldiers

地，并在巢湖操练水军，大有进兵江南之势，而明朝官兵屡战屡败，抵敌不住的时候，钱谦益实在很担心过一阵子。虽然他知道明朝在南京外围，还驻有重兵防卫，农民军未必就能攻得进来，但是战局如果发展到那一步，毕竟就很危险了。如今偌大一个中国，除了一些边远的地区，就只剩下江南这一小片尚可称作“乐土”。万一被那些杀人不眨眼的“流贼”攻了进来，像自己这种家大业大的官绅人家，别说安居乐业，只怕连可以逃跑活命的地方都没有。所以，前一阵子，钱谦益虽然煞有介事地在整顿财务，著书立说，内心却曾不止一次阴沉地想到：这其实是白费心机，说不定哪一天“流寇”一来，一切便都完蛋了账！甚至两个月前，他听到朝廷起用马士英，代替已经逮捕下狱的高斗光任凤阳总督时，也并不感到有任何值得乐观之处。然而，出乎意料，马士英刚一出马，就大破张献忠于潜山。“嘿，瞧不出马瑶草还真有点本事，竟然一战成功！”钱谦益惊奇地想，同时，心里不期然地涌起一股酸溜溜的感觉：“是啊，这一下马瑶草该得意洋洋了！如今打个胜仗不容易，何况又是大胜。就凭这一仗，马瑶草这把凤督交椅不只算是坐稳了，没准儿还会升迁哩！”不过，也只是一会儿，随后他就想到，这其实也没有什么好羡慕的，十余年来，凭借剿“寇”有功而爬上高位的幸运儿固然也有一些，但更多得多的，却是在空前残酷激烈、没完没了的战斗中送了命。而那些侥幸爬上去的人，也并没能得意多久，便又一个一个地跌落下来，不是毙命于“流寇”的枪炮之下，就是因逃脱不了最终的惨败，而被震怒的朝廷逮捕入狱，纵然不死，也已是饱受凌辱。如今马士英虽然打了个胜仗，又怎知他日后不会因此而倒霉获罪，甚至不得好死呢？“哎，任他大千世界，苦乐人生，俱如梦幻泡影！”

for river crossing. It seemed that their advancement to River South was imminent. Meanwhile, the armies of the Great Ming suffered repeated defeats and couldn't stand against the enemy. True that there were Ming troops stationed on the outskirts of Nanjing and the peasant armies might not be able to break the strong defense, but should things come to that stage, it might be too late. River South was now the only peaceful place left in the vast territory of China, together with a few remote corners. Should the ruthless insurgents, who plundered and killed without blinking an eye, break the defense, big, wealthy families like his would have no place to escape to, not to say to continue to enjoy a happy and peaceful life. Therefore, in the past few months, while he was putting family finances in order and writing his books, he knew everything might be in vain, since the insurgents might come any moment. He was so disheartened that even when news came two months ago that the imperial court had reinstated Ma Shiying to office to fill the vacancy left by Gao Douguang, Governor of Fengyang, who had been thrown into prison, he was not happy at all. Ma Shiying's defeat of Zhang Xianzhong in Qianshan was really a big surprise to him. "Well, I've underestimated him. He's a capable man. Victory at one blow," Qian Qianyi thought, amazed and jealous at the same time. "Um, with this success, he should be very proud of himself. There're hardly any victories nowadays and his victory is a big one. Not only the governorship is secured, but also he'll have good chances for a promotion." Soon, however, he laughed at himself for that jealousy. It was nothing good, he thought, as there were much more men who had died in the endless fierce battles than the lucky ones who had made it to the top, and besides, even the lucky ones were not so lucky when they fell one after another, either at the gunpoint of the enemy or from the favor of the imperial court after inevitable defeat in battle, and in the latter case, even if they escaped death, they couldn't escape humiliation. Ma Shiying's victory was no guarantee of his exception from punishment for his future defeats. There might be no good end for him after all. "Alas, all pleasures and sufferings in the thousand worlds are but dreams and bubbles. Let them be." He kept repeating

这样默默地叨念了两遍之后，钱谦益又变得心平气和，于是把塘抄抛开，伸手去拿另外一封信……

这一天，钱谦益在匪斋里一直工作到下午。当他把本日所做的疏稿检点一下，发现已经积有三千字之多，这才舒展一下身体，站起来，一边用手轻轻捶打着发酸的腰部，一边怀着愉快而充实的心情，慢慢下了楼，走过我闻室来。

我闻室里静悄悄的。由于柳如是身体本来就不大好，加上前些日子操持家政，过于劳累，结果病倒了。近一个月来，一直卧床不起。当钱谦益放轻脚步，走进庭院时，看见堂屋门帘一掀，红情从里面送出一位道姑来。那道姑有三十二三年纪，头戴一顶鱼魫冠儿，脸上薄施脂粉，身上的杏色道袍纤尘不染，一条黑丝绦带，紧紧束住依然窈窕的腰身。她手里拿着一柄拂尘，虽无十分颜色，却也自饶风韵。钱谦益认得她叫潘灵飞，一年前才从别处云游来此，专门出入大户人家，讲经论道。刚好碰上南门外修静观的老道姑死了，她也不知使了什么法儿，就顶替做了住持。钱谦益平日见她眼波流荡，言语巧俏，有心勾搭她，只是未得机缘。

潘道姑一见钱谦益，就含笑站住，行着礼招呼说："钱老爷……"

钱谦益知道她是来看望柳如是的病的，连忙满面春风地迎上去，彬彬有礼地客套了一番，这才目不转睛地瞅着潘道姑问：

"仙长瞧贱内这病……"

"老爷放心，夫人这委厥寒热之症，皆因以往疏于护理，身底子已是偏弱，加以近日又操劳过甚——不过也无妨，只需将息几时，再由小道传授她些导引之法，便可无碍了。"

it before he finally restored his peace of mind. Then, he put that communication aside and took up another envelope.

One day, Qian Qianyi worked in the Fei Chamber until afternoon. He counted the words in his manuscript and found he had already written three thousand Chinese characters. Then, he stood up and slowly descended the stairs to go to the Wowen Chamber with an indescribable sense of fulfilment, patting his back with his right hand.

The Wowen Chamber was quiet. Liu Rushi, suffering from poor health, was taken ill after days of busy work. She was bedridden for a month. As Qian Qianyi stepped into the courtyard with lighter steps, the door curtain of the main room was lifted open and a Taoist nun came out, followed by Hongqing. The nun looked thirty-two or three, with a Taoist fish bone hat on her head, a thin layer of powder on her face, a spotless Taoist robe with a black silk band tied around her slender waist, and a *fuchen* whisk in her hand. She was not an extraordinary beauty but was attractive enough. Qian Qianyi knew she was Pan Lingfei, who had come to this place from somewhere else a year ago. She traveled between rich men's homes to provide Taoist services. When the old nun in the Xiujing Temple outside the South City Gate died, she somehow took over as the abbot of the temple. Qian Qianyi had always wanted to hook up with her, because he had found a slut in her eyes and in the way she spoke, but he hadn't had a chance yet.

When the nun saw Qian Qianyi, she stopped with a smile, and greeted him with a salute. "Lord Qian ..."

Knowing that she was here to help with Liu Rushi, Qian Qianyi walked up to her with spring breeze on his face, and politely greeted her. Then, he stared at the nun with unconcealed attention and asked:

"Dear Sister, what do you think my wife's illness ..."

"Don't worry, my lord. Madam's symptoms of cold and fever are caused by the lack of care in the past. While her body is already weak, she's overworked herself recently, but it doesn't matter. As long as she rests for a few days and follows my method to guide the breath, she will be fine."

钱谦益“噢”了一声，笑嘻嘻地说：“久闻得‘导引神气，以养形魂，延年之道，驻形之术’。原来仙长深通此术。可知贱内毕竟有福，所以得遇高人！”

说完，他向我闻室那边看了一眼，又左右望了望，发现红情还站在一旁伺候着，就侧转身，做出送客的姿态。等潘灵飞走出七八步，估计红情听不见了，他才凑近去，悄声说：

“怪道仙长雪肤花貌，原来深谙驻颜之术。几时一并收我做个弟子，也好日夕领教！”

潘灵飞的眼睛闪烁了一下，乖巧地躲开身子，却用眼梢瞟着钱谦益，轻声说：“我这导引之术，须是人定[①]之后，三更之时，来我观里，于密室之中，方可传授。只怕老爷未必有这份诚心？”

钱谦益一听，半个身子都酥麻了。他连忙赌咒说：“但得仙长垂怜，小生便是死了也甘心！”又结结巴巴地问，“那么，那么就是今夕？”

潘灵飞却只是微笑，并不回答。待到走出月洞门，她才转过身来，像是有意，又像无意地把手中的拂尘朝钱谦益轻轻一点，瞅了他一眼，随即飘然向外走去。害得钱谦益伸长脖子，睁大眼睛，目送着她的背影，好半天，才擦一擦鼻子，喜滋滋地回过头来。

## 抱病理财

当钱谦益匆匆穿过庭院，向寝室走去时，忽然想到，刚才自己那些举动，会不会被柳如是在屋子里看见了？于是，就怀了一份小心，放轻脚步，先隔着门帘偷瞧了一下。他发现柳如是依旧躺在床上，却把一张书案移到床头，案上堆满了一厚本一厚本的

① 人定：指夜里的21—23时。

"Oh," Qian Qianyi said with a smile. "I've heard that 'Guiding the breath to regulate the body and the spirit constitutes the secret to a long life and a healthy body.' I'm glad that you know this art. My wife is blessed indeed to have met a friend with such great powers."

He glanced at the Wowen Chamber and then looked left and right. Seeing that Hongqing was still standing by, he turned to make a gesture of farewell. When Pan Lingfei walked beyond the range of Hongqing's hearing, he caught up with her, leaned over and whispered in her ear, "No wonder you have a snowlike skin and flowerlike face. It turns out you know the secret to beauty. Do you mind taking me as a student so that I can learn from you from time to time?"

Pan Lingfei's eyes sparkled. As she shyly dodged contact with Qian Qianyi, she glanced at him from the corner of her eye and said in a soft voice, "My breath-guiding technique must be taught in perfect quiet at midnight in a secret room in my temple. I'm afraid you're not serious."

Qian Qianyi was mesmerized to hear it and quickly said, swearing, "Upon my life! I'll die a happy man if you can kindly take me, Sister." Then he added, stammering, "So, what about tonight?"

Pan Lingfei just smiled and didn't answer. When she walked out the moon-hole door, she turned around, and gently gestured towards Qian Qianyi with the *fuchen* whisk, either intentionally or inadvertently, glanced at him, and then drifted out of the Qian residence. Stretching his neck and opening his eyes wide, Qian Qianyi watched her receding figure as she left. After a long time, he wiped his nose and turned around, full of joy in his heart.

## A Sick Woman Handled Family Finances

As he hurried across the courtyard toward the bedroom, Qian Qianyi suddenly thought that Liu Rushi might have seen what he had done just now. So, with a sense of caution, he lightened his footsteps and peeked through the curtain first. He found that Liu Rushi was still lying in bed, but a book table had been moved close to the head of the bed. On the table were piled a huge stack of thick account books.

账册，她自己怀里也抱着一本，正在那里静静地翻阅，对于刚才屋子外发生的事似乎毫无知觉。钱谦益放下心来，正要撩开帘子走进去，忽然听见“啪”的一声，账本合上了，柳如是恨恨地骂：“都是蠢货！没有一个争气的！”

钱谦益吓了一跳，本能地停住脚步。急切之间他闹不清这话是冲谁说的，迟疑了一下，只好硬着头皮往里走，一边小心翼翼地问：

“哎呀，你这是怎么了，好端端的又生谁的气？噢，还把这些破账册都搬来了！你身子不好，该好好歇着才对，又弄这些劳什子做什么？”他一边责备地摇着头，一边偷眼打量对方的神色。

“哼，不管，不管行吗？都快气死人了！”柳如是圆睁着眼睛，怒声地说。

“哎，到底是怎么回事？”

“怎么回事！前一回派出去的那四个人，原来都回来了，都不敢来见我。今日一查这账，才知道他们全都把本钱消折了！每人一百两银子出去，弄几个月，只剩得个三五十两回来，有两个还说留在行里，不曾结得账，只怕连这个数也不够！你说气死人不气死人！哼，亏他们临去时赌咒发誓地说得好听，如今折了我的银子不算，连我这脸也给丢尽了！”

钱谦益慢慢地捋着胡子。当弄清柳如是的火气不是冲自己而来，他就放了心。他知道柳如是自从接管了家中的财权之后，急于有所建树，前几个月亲自挑选了四个她认为得力可靠的家人，各带银两，分别到山东、浙江和福建去经商，满指望能大大赚几注彩头，一来填补家中的亏空，二来也显示她理财有方。谁知竟

She was holding one in her hands and quietly flipping through it, oblivious to what had been going on outside the house. Qian Qianyi was relieved, and just as he was about to lift the curtain and walk in, suddenly he heard a slap and the account book was closed. Liu Rushi cursed angrily, "They're all idiots. None of them is good."

Qian Qianyi was frightened and stopped instinctively. Not knowing who she was speaking of, he hesitated for an instant, but then decided to go inside and bite the bullet.

He asked gingerly, "Oh, what's up, dear? Who's it that has made you so angry? Oh, you have all the account books here. You're not well and should take a good rest. What are you doing with all this shit?" He shook his head reproachfully and watched Liu Rushi's expression from the corner of his eye.

"Hmph, can I turn a blind eye? It's such a horrible mess," Liu Rushi said angrily with her eyes wide open.

"Hey, what's going on?"

"What's going on? The four servants who were sent out earlier have all returned, and they don't dare to come to me. After checking the account today, I found out that they all have a capital loss. Each of them went out with 100 taels of silver, and after a few months, only 30 to 50 taels are left. Two of them said the money is in the bank and the account isn't cleared yet. I'm afraid they've lost even more. It makes me mad. Hmph, they swore beautifully when they left, but now they've not only lost my money but also my face."

Qian Qianyi slowly stroked his beard. When he found that Liu Rushi's anger was not directed at him, he was relieved. He knew that Liu Rushi was eager to make a difference since she took over the finances of the family. Several months ago, she handpicked four trusted servants and sent them to Shandong, Zhejiang, and Fujian to do business, each carrying a hundred taels of silver. She hoped they would make some money to fill the deficit hole and meanwhile she could show her competence in the management of family finances. However, they returned with a capital loss. No wonder she was so frustrated and angry. Qian Qianyi wasn't interested in this kind of

折本而回，也难怪她又急又气。不过，钱谦益这会儿却没有心思来管这种事，因为同潘道姑今晚的私会又开始来挑动他的思绪，使他不由自主地露出了微笑。

“哎，你倒是说话啊！”柳如是生气地嚷。

钱谦益错愕了一下，“哦，算了！”他摆一摆手，“如今时局不靖，生意难做，也未可全怪他们。何况这几个人，又不是惯做生意——自然，你亲自挑选的人，必定是得力可靠的。如今乡下有几个庄子，庄头都老了，我久想换下来，不如就委了这几个人去，却是正好。”

柳如是冷冷地说：“这几年不是水就是旱，光守着那几亩田，能有几多入息？而且也太慢！如今想快赚大赚，还得靠经商这条路！”

钱谦益摇摇头：“你别小看那几千亩田！说到底，那才是根本。有了它，吃喝穿用全有了。只要守得住，便是一辈子不出去，也冻不着，饿不死。出外经商不是不好，到底是没准头的事儿，若赚得到时便好，万一消折起来，倾家荡产也只是一年半载的工夫！如今都说徽州人善会经商，出了几个大富翁，便人人眼红起来，都要学他的样。不知徽州地方，向来山多田少，地又瘦瘠，不宜稻粱。为求活命，不得已才出外经商。由此暴富的也有，但本钱蚀尽，漂泊而死的又岂在少数？我们现守着六七千亩田，经不经商本属其次，又何必把这事看得太重呢？”

可是柳如是十分固执：“不管怎么说，我那几个人是决计不去做庄头的！”

钱谦益瞧了她一眼，无可奈何地说：“那么，你还打算让他

thing at the moment, though, because he was obsessed with the coming secret meeting with the nun tonight, which made him smile despite himself.

"Hey, please speak," Liu Rushi said angrily.

Qian Qianyi jolted. "Oh, forget it." He waved his hand. "Nowadays, since the general situation is bad, it's very difficult to do business. We can't blame it all on them. Besides, these servants haven't done business before, though they must be reliable men, as you've handpicked them yourself. We have a few farms in the countryside and the managers are all old now. I've wanted to replace them for a long time, so we might as well send these servants over."

Liu Rushi said coldly, "In the past few years, it has been either flood or drought. How much income can those few acres of land generate? And it's too slow. Now, if you want to make a lot of money quickly, you must do business."

Qian Qianyi shook his head, saying, "Don't make light of those thousands of acres of land. In the end, that's what we rely on. It gives us everything we need, food, clothes, and other daily necessities. As long as we can keep it, we're free from cold and hunger for the rest of our life without having to go anywhere. It's not bad to go out to do business, but it's a matter of chance. If you can make money, it's good, but the risk is great too. We can also go broke easily. We all know people in Huizhou are good at doing business and there're quite a few millionaires from there. Everyone envies them and wants to follow suit, but they don't know that Huizhou has more mountain than arable land, and the land is bare and barren, not suitable for the cultivation of rice and grains so that, in order to survive, they have to go out to do business. True that there're a few successful ones, but who knows how many have lost all their capital and died in a wandering life? We have six or seven thousand acres of land, and doing business isn't a must. Why should we take it so seriously?"

But Liu Rushi was very stubborn. "Anyway, those servants of mine shouldn't be sent to the farms," she said.

Qian Qianyi glanced at her and said helplessly, "Then, are you

们出去？”

柳如是点点头，沉思地说：“不过，这一回我不是让他们走内地……哼，我要打发他们出海！”她说，蓦地抬起头，目光闪闪地瞅住钱谦益。见他没有作声，她就用了突然兴奋起来的大声说：“听我说呀！如今内地是兵荒马乱，生意难做，可是海外不打仗，也没闹饥荒，正好做生意！顶多就是风波凶险一点。可是我派人分几起出去，这趟不着那趟着，只要有一起人回来，就不蚀本；两起回来，就是一倍的赚头！要是运气好，弄到些犀角、象牙、苏木、胡椒，或者别的什么稀罕宝贝回来，还怕不奇货可居！这样一年别说去三回，就是两回吧，已经非同小可。再营运数年，哼，我担保还你钱牧斋老爷一个货真价实的常熟首富，你信也不信？”

柳如是越说，越被这个突然闪现的诱人计划所激动。她一挺腰坐了起来，苍白的脸上现出两片红晕。仿佛她已经把一根魔力无穷的网绳攥在手里，只要轻轻扯动一下，大批的财富就会源源而来似的……

钱谦益见她这样子，却不由得暗暗摇头。出海贸易，那自然是最能获利的买卖。以往钱谦益也一直在做，还一度拥有过十多艘大海鳅船。可是后来几次出海遇上了风暴，那些船沉的沉、毁的毁，损失了大半，剩下几艘，前几年因为吃官司，急着要银子用，都卖掉了。以现在的经济状况，想重新去造船，真是谈何容易！而自己没有船，想要出海经商，就只能去搭伙。这样就得受船主和主商的剥削和控制，更别说还得缴纳很重的引税和水陆两饷了。而且弄不好，随时都会给人扣上“结盗”“通番”的罪名，

planning to let them go out to do business again?"

Liu Rushi nodded and said pensively, "However, this time I'm not going to send them to the inland ... Hmph, I'm going to send them out to sea." As she spoke, she raised her head abruptly and stared at Qian Qianyi. Seeing that he didn't make a sound, she said in a suddenly loud voice, "Listen to me. Now the inland is war-torn, and it's very difficult to do business there, but there's no war or famine overseas, perfect for business! The only risk lies in the waves. I can send the servants in batches. If one mission fails to bring profit, I'll send another. As long as one batch comes back, we'll not lose money; if another batch comes back, the income will be doubled. If we're lucky enough and get some rhino horns, ivory, logwood, pepper, or other rarities, we can sell them for a lot of money. We'll make two or three voyages a year and in a couple of years, I promise you'll be the undisputed top rich man in Changshu. Do you believe it or not?"

As she spoke, Liu Rushi became increasingly excited by the alluring prospect that suddenly occurred to her. She sat up straight, with two flushes of red on her pale cheeks, as if she had already grasped a rope with infinite magic powers in her hand, and a large fortune would flow in with a little tug ...

Seeing her like that, Qian Qianyi couldn't help shaking his head. Overseas trade was of course the most profitable business. Qian Qianyi had done it in the past and once owned more than ten sailboats. However, after several voyages, most of those boats had been lost in the storms. The few remaining ones had been sold a few years ago when he needed money badly to get him out of trouble in the legal case. Given his financial circumstances now, it was not possible for him to build new sailboats. Without sailboats of his own, if he wanted to go to sea to do business, he could only team up with others. In that case, he would have to be exploited and controlled by the boat owner and the principal trader, not to mention the heavy Boat-Guiding Tax and land and water tolls. There was also the danger of being charged with "working with pirates" and "colluding with foreigners". Previously, Zhang Hanru, a troublemaker in this county,

上一次，本县奸民张汉儒向朝廷诬告他，就是把这当成一条罪状，使他受了许久的追查。钱谦益是栽过跟头的人，实在再也没有柳如是那种雄心勃勃的劲头。不过，他也不想立即扫她的兴，只好含糊其词地说：

“嗯，这也是个好主意……不过，再从长计议吧！”这样说完之后，为着转移话题，他就从袖子里把那份塘抄掏出来，“我倒差点忘了，这儿还有个好消息哩！”

“怎么？真的把流贼打跑啦！”柳如是接过塘抄一看，顿时欢快地叫起来，“这下可教人放心啦！你别说，前些时风声紧张那阵子，可把我担心死了，夜里翻来覆去净做些噩梦，真可怕！”

“哼，这回呀，马瑶草可是得意喽！”钱谦益冷冷地说，在一张椅子上坐了下来。

柳如是怔了怔，随即眼波一转，似乎明白了。她沉默下来，半晌，问：“这马大人，不知相公可认识？”

钱谦益依旧沉着脸：“倒不曾见面，不过我知道他，他也知道我。天启时，我曾在徐元叹那里见过他给元叹集子写的一篇序，文章是会做的。”

“嗯，这马大人倒是一位不可小看的人物哩！”

“……”

柳如是微微一笑：“相公，说句你不爱听的话，妾觉着前些年，你未免把复社那伙书生瞧得太重。其实他们一无权，二无兵，光凭两片嘴皮子整天穷嚷嚷，到底成不了什么大事！”

柳如是说到这里，故意顿住了。钱谦益的眼睛却渐渐亮了起来：

“你是说，我应当下点工夫去联络马瑶草？”

“相公说呢？”

“唔，有道理，很有道理！”钱谦益把膝盖一拍，站了起来，“其实又何止马瑶草！如今天下方乱，真正有力量的还是那等手

falsely reported him to the court, citing his trading activities as a crime, and as a result, he was investigated for a long time. Having had a bitter lesson, Qian Qianyi was not as enthusiastic about doing business as Liu Rushi, but in order not to displease her, he merely said perfunctorily: "Well, that is a good idea, but let's think further ahead," he said, taking out the copy of the communication from the frontline to change the subject. "I almost forget there's good news here," he said.

"What? The insurgents have been driven away?" Liu Rushi shouted with joy after reading the communication. "Now I'm relieved. You know how worried I was when bad news came a few days ago. I tossed and turned in bed and had nightmares. I was scared."

"Hmph, this time, Ma Yaocao must be very proud of himself," Qian Qianyi said coldly, and sat down on a chair.

Liu Rushi was puzzled for a moment, and then her eyes rolled as if she had understood it. After a long silence, she asked, "Do you know this Mr. Ma, my dear husband?"

Qian Qianyi said, his face still sullen, "I haven't met him in person, but I know of him and he also knows of me. I once saw his preface to *The Collection of Writings* by Xu Yuantan in Mr. Xu's place in the Tianqi period. It's well written."

"So, this Lord Ma is a man not to be overlooked."

"..."

Liu Rushi smiled slightly. "My dear husband, maybe you don't like to hear it. I feel that in the past few years, you've taken the Fushe scholars too seriously. In fact, they have no power and no army. All they're good at is lip service. They won't amount to anything after all."

Liu Rushi deliberately paused as she spoke. Qian Qianyi's eyes gradually lit up. "You mean, I should make some effort to contact Ma Yaocao?"

"What do you think, my dear husband?"

"Well, it makes sense, it makes sense." Qian Qianyi slapped his hand on his knee and stood up. "Not only Ma Yaocao, in fact. This is a time of war, so the real power lies in the hands of the generals and

握兵权的将帅……对，这主意好！”他连连点着头，倒背着手，兴冲冲地在室内踱了几步，忽然又站住，“只是，我与马瑶草素无交往，这‘联络’二字，却又从何措手？”

柳如是叹了一口气：“我的相公，你平日的聪明机警到哪儿去了？这眼前不就是绝好的一个题目么——潜山大捷！”

钱谦益不说话了。他捋着胡子，斜瞅着柳如是，仿佛在考虑什么，然后慢慢地踱开去，绕了一个圈子，又一个圈子……最后，他在书案前停了下来，随手拿起笔，蘸了蘸墨，在一张锦笺上很快地书写起来。

“嗯，你听啊——”他说，放下笔，兴冲冲地拿起锦笺，“《鹅行——闻潜山战胜而作》，这是题。下面是诗：

督师堂堂马伏波[1]，
花马刘亲斫阵多。
三年笛里无梅落，
万国霜前有雁过。
捷书到门才一瞥，
老夫失喜两足蹩。
惊呼病妇笑欲噎，
炉头松醪酒新蓺！

唔，就先把这诗给马瑶草寄去，算是祝捷。你看如何？”钱谦益说着，得意地把诗笺递给柳如是。

“嗯，把马大人比作东汉马援，仿佛高了些儿。不过既想哄他高兴，也只能如此。”柳如是一边看诗，一边说，“那么这花

---

① 马伏波：真名马援，东汉开国功臣之一，因功累官伏波将军。

commanders who are leading the army ... Yes, that's a good idea." He nodded his head, again and again, his hands behind his back, and excitedly paced in the room. Then, he suddenly stopped, saying,"It's just that I've never had any contact with Ma Yaocao before. How do I contact him now?"

Liu Rushi sighed, "My dear husband, where have all your wits gone? Isn't this the perfect opportunity? You can congratulate him on the great victory at Qianshan."

Qian Qianyi was silent. He stroked his beard and squinted at Liu Rushi, as if thinking about something, then slowly moved away and paced around the room ... Finally, he stopped in front of the desk, picked up a brush pen, dipped it in the ink, and quickly wrote on a sheet of brocade paper.

"Well, listen—" he said excitedly, as he put down the pen and picked up the paper. "'The Wild Goose Comes, written on hearing the Qianshan Victory'. That is the title. Here is the poem:

*Superintendent Ma Fubo,*
*Together with Liu the Colored Horse fought many great battles.*
*For three years, there was no falling of plum flowers in the sound of the flute*
*And then suddenly came a wild goose in the sky*
*Bringing the message of victory to the door.*
*The old man jumped up with joy and sprained his ankles,*
*And the sick lady cheered up and almost killed herself by laughing.*
*They hurriedly heated the Songlao wine on the stove and drank to the great heroes.*

Well, let's send this poem to Ma Yaocao first as a congratulatory message. What do you think?" Qian Qianyi said as he proudly handed the poem to Liu Rushi.

"Well, to say Lord Ma is Ma Yuan in the Eastern Han dynasty is an exaggeration. But if you want to make him happy, that's all you can do," Liu Rushi said while reading the poem. "Then Liu the Colored Horse must be Liu Liangzuo. Why do you single him out without

马刘想必是刘良佐了？何以相公独点出他来，而不及黄得功？”

钱谦益笑了一笑：“夫人果然心细！我自然有意如此。须知自崇祯五年，山东莱登巡抚谢琏陷于贼之后，一直废而不设，到去年才重新增置。莱登二州与辽东隔海相望，位置异常重要，我对此职瞩望已久，唯是苦于缺乏有力者推荐。这花马刘乃系前漕运总督朱大典之旧部，当年平定莱登一役，花马刘战功卓著。我若有朝一日出抚莱登，对此种人物自不能不加以留意。”

柳如是点点头：“那么，这‘病妇’自然是说我了。相公送诗给马瑶草，却把妾扯进去做什么？”

“啊，这个么？”钱谦益凑过来，笑着说，“那是要让马瑶草知道，我这河东君柳夫人，乃是一位身在病榻，而心忧天下的奇女子呀！”

“啐，我可不稀罕！”柳如是撇撇嘴，随即佯嗔地板着脸儿说，“相公须得另外谢我！”

“行啊，请夫人只管道来！”

“真的么？你说这话可不许反悔——我要的是，你答应我派人出海经商！”

钱谦益的笑容僵住了。他本能地打算反对，可是一接触到柳如是变得冰冷起来的目光，他就决定妥协了。

“噢，可以可以！只要夫人喜欢。就是别太操劳，千万保重身子，才是顶要紧的！”说完他眼珠子一转，又赔笑说，“我还得赶紧写封信给马瑶草，连这诗一道寄去。另外，左良玉那里，我也想给他去封信。那么，今儿晚上我就歇在书房那边，不来陪夫人了？”

mentioning Huang Degong, my dear husband?"

Qian Qianyi smiled. "You're really perceptive, my dear wife. I do have a purpose. The position of Governor of Laizhou and Dengzhou in Shandong Province was abolished after the death of Xie Lian in the battle against the insurgents in the fifth year of the reign of Emperor Chongzhen[AD 1632] and was restored last year. The two prefectures, Laizhou and Dengzhou, which look across the sea at Liaodong Province, are very important strategically. I have been looking forward to filling this position for a long time but don't have strong recommendations. Mr. Liu the Colored Horse used to be a subordinate of Zhu Dadian, former Governor of Water Transport, and stood out as a great fighter in the battle against the insurgents in Laizhou and Dengzhou. If I want to serve in Laizhou and Dengzhou one day, I must pay attention to men like him."

Liu Rushi nodded her head. "Then, this 'sick lady' must be me. You are sending a poem to Ma Yaocao, but why do you bring me in?"

"Hah, about this?" Qian Qianyi came over and said with a smile, "That's to let Ma Yaocao know that Lady of River East, wife of Mr. Qian Qianyi, is an extraordinary woman who is concerned about the world while lying on her sickbed."

"Humph, I'm not flattered," Liu Rushi said, pouting her mouth and feigning a sullen face. "My dear husband, that's not enough. I want something else."

"Say it then, my dear lady."

"Really? Then, you must promise you won't go back on your word. What I want is, promise me to send your men to do business overseas."

Qian Qianyi's smile froze. He instinctively wanted to say no, but when he met Liu Rushi's cold gaze, he decided to compromise.

"Well, agreed. As long as my dear lady likes it, I'll do it. Don't work too hard. The most important thing is to stay healthy," he said with a smile, rolling his eyes. "I have to write a letter to Ma Yaocao to accompany the poem. Besides, I need to write a letter to Zuo Liangyu too. I'll sleep in the study and won't come to stay with you tonight."

## 码头绑架

不知道是潘道姑的导引之术不灵，还是为着张罗派人出海的事操心太过，到十一月，柳如是的病不但没有丝毫起色，反而有加重的趋势，这使钱谦益不由得着忙起来。他虽然背着柳如是又勾搭上了潘道姑，但那不过是兴之所至，偶一为之——潘灵飞在钱谦益生活中的位置，当然绝对无法同柳如是相比。他眼看继续留在常熟就无法使柳如是安下心来静养，加上他本人自从觉悟到应当改变目标，设法去联系那些手握兵权的将帅之后，也有心出外走一走，所以，到了十一月中旬，钱谦益就带着柳如是，还有顾苓、何云、钱曾等几个心腹门客，乘船到了苏州，依旧下榻在阊门外的徐氏东园里。

本来，钱谦益以为，经过这半年来闭门不出，虎丘大会的那一场风波应当已经过去，自己又可以恢复正常活动了。然而，来到苏州之后，他才发现，士林当中，对自己持抵制态度的仍旧不少。他们不但不像过去那样争着来谒见这位“东林前辈”，甚至钱谦益主动去拜访，有几次竟然吃了闭门羹。这使他颇为懊丧。幸而并不是所有人都这样子，何况钱谦益如今也不把士林的作用看得那样重要，所以，他一方面延请名医替柳如是治病，另一方面继续同那些气味相投的人来往。日子倒也不难打发。

这一天，钱谦益打听到吴江县的大名医郑钦谕到了苏州，现住在虎丘。郑钦谕是名门后裔，医术得自祖传，名为“带下医”。到了郑钦谕之手，他又把这门医术加以深入研究，发扬光大，如今在江南地区声誉很高，许多名公巨卿都争着延请他。此外，这

# Kidnapping at the Pier

Either because Pan Lingfei's induction methods didn't work well, or Liu Rushi had worked herself too hard arranging for the business mission overseas, Liu Rushi's health hadn't improved at all by November. Instead, it became worse. So, Qian Qianyi became busy. Though he sometimes visited Pan Lingfei surreptitiously, it was just an adventure. The nun was not to be compared with Liu Rushi after all and occupied no position in his life. Seeing Changshu didn't have the quiet for Liu Rushi to recuperate, and having realized that he should turn to the military leaders for support, he decided to make a trip away from home. So, in the middle of November, he went to Suzhou by boat, taking with him Liu Rushi and a number of his proteges: Gu Ling, He Yun, and Qian Zeng. As usual, he lodged in the East Garden of the Xus outside the West City Gate.

Qian Qianyi had thought the Tiger Hill incident should have been forgotten after he stayed out of sight for six months and that by now he should be able to resume his activities. However, after he arrived in Suzhou, he found there were still many scholars who were boycotting him. His friends no longer swarmed to him like before, and many of them even didn't receive him when he called. He was very sad. Yet, he was not entirely frustrated, because not all of them were like that and he no longer thought the scholars were that important in his reinstatement to office. There, he did two things: getting good physicians for Liu Rushi and meeting friends who didn't desert him.

One day, Qian Qianyi learned that Zheng Qinyu, a famous physician from Wujiang County, had arrived in Suzhou and was now staying at Tiger Hill. Mr. Zheng was from a hereditary medical family. His medical skills were inherited from his ancestors, and as a gynecologist, he was said to be "born a physician". In his hands, the medical art handed down by his ancestors was further developed. He enjoyed such a high reputation in River South that many celebrities and dignitaries vied to invite him to their homes. In addition, he was also a sociable great scholar, who was well-read in studies on the

郑钦谕还精研程朱理学，能诗会文，豪爽好客，又是个大名士。过去，钱谦益同他也有数面之缘；这一次听说他来了，自然十分高兴，本打算先去拜访，然后请他过来瞧瞧柳如是的病。但柳如是在徐氏东园里窝了许多天，早已闷得慌，听说上虎丘，就坚持要跟去。钱谦益拗她不过，只好吩咐收拾一只大船，又招呼顾苓、何云、钱曾三个也跟着，一齐在山塘河码头下了船，慢慢向虎丘摇去。

如今，柳如是被安顿在内舱里，由红情、绿意两个丫环伺候着。钱谦益同三位门客坐在前舱，一边品茶闲谈，一边眺望着两岸的景色。

已经是初冬时节，本来碧绿清澈的河水，开始有点发蓝，而且明显地浅落了。晴爽的天空却变得愈加高朗。随着寒霜不断施展威力，两岸树木的叶子纷纷掉落。西风掠过光秃的枝丫，发出呼呼的声响。幸而这儿那儿的堤坝上、码头旁，或是人家屋宇的背后，会冷不防冒出一株两株枫树，却依然殷红如火，好歹给这个萧瑟寂寥的天地，增添了一点色彩。

不过，即使如此，船舱内的客人也很快就厌倦起来。他们开始把更多的时间用在谈话上。他们谈到了前些时候的潜山大捷，还谈到了张献忠一度退往湖北蕲水之后，最近又重新袭破太湖、黄梅二县，大有卷土重来之势。接着，他们又谈到了河南的重镇开封，被李自成的农民军重重围困数月之后，明朝援军于九月中掘开黄河堤坝，打算用水灌淹农民军；农民军也掘堤反灌，结果碰上倾盆大雨，河水暴涨。一日之内，朱家寨口和马家口同时溃决，洪水从开封北门涌入，穿东南门出，城中近百万户人家都被

Theory of Principle (*lixue*) proposed by Cheng Yi and Zhu Xi and wrote beautiful poems and essays. Having met the physician several times in the past, Qian Qianyi was very glad to hear he was also in Suzhou and decided to pay him a visit and meanwhile invite him over to treat Liu Rushi's illness. However, Liu Rushi also wanted to go, because she was bored after staying too many days in the East Garden of the Xus without ever going out. Upon her insistence, he had to take her with him. He also took Gu Ling, He Yun, and Qian Zeng. Together, they embarked on a big boat at the Shantang River pier and slowly sailed toward Tiger Hill.

Liu Rushi sat in the inner cabin and was served by two maids, Hongqing and Lüyi. Qian Qianyi and the three proteges sat in the front cabin, drinking tea and chatting while looking at the scenery on the sides of the river.

It was early winter. The clear, greenish water became bluish and had evidently diminished, and the clear sky became even clearer. In the cold frost, leaves were falling off the trees as the west wind whistled across the tree tops. Fortunately, there were a few flaming maple trees now and then on the banks, beside a pier, or behind a house to give a little color to the desolate and deary world.

However, that didn't prevent the passengers on the boat from feeling bored. They started to kill time with conversations. At one moment they talked about the great victory in Qianshan. At another, they discussed the possible comeback of Zhang Xianzhong, who, after retreating to Qishui in Hubei province, had now recaptured Taihu County and Huangmei County. They also discussed the situation in Kaifeng, Henan Province, a city of great strategic importance. North of Kaifeng, the Ming reinforcement troops had blown up the bank of the Yellow River in September to drown Li Zicheng's insurgent army after the city had been besieged for a few months. The peasant army had done the same to fend off the Ming troops. Worse still, a huge rain had come and the river had been flooded. In one day, the Yellow River bank had broken at both the Zhujiazhai Ferry and the Majia Ferry, and the deluge had entered Kaifeng from the north city gate, swept across

洪水席卷而去，只有周王府一家以及巡抚以下官民不到二万人侥幸逃脱，农民军也被卷走了一万余人，据说已经拔营而去。当大家谈到这一场骇人听闻的空前惨祸时，都感到垂头丧气，叹息再三。接下来，他们又谈到了陈新甲一案，没想到皇上的态度如此坚决，周延儒、谢升等阁臣交章求情，都毫无结果，最后还是用的押赴市曹，当众斩首的方式处决。大家虽然认为陈新甲死有余辜，但对于皇上的刻薄寡恩，也不禁摇头咋舌；只是随后谈到兵部尚书一职，已任命漕运侍郎张国维继任，而张国维又是钱谦益的门生，大家才又多少变得活跃起来……

在这阵子谈话当中，钱谦益绝大部分时间只是默默地听着，很少插话。不知为什么，近些日子来，他每逢听到这一类消息，心情总是变得很恶劣。而这种“恶劣”，又不像过去那样，仅仅是对于明朝的前途、自身的命运感到担心和焦急而已。相反，这方面的担心，如今他倒是减轻了些，却增加了几许怨恨、几分冷嘲。他隐隐约约觉得，目前这种政治格局如果照旧不变地维持下去，他这一辈子恐怕再也难得有出头之日；只有出现大的变动，甚至当真闹出一场大乱子，他才有可能在权力的重新结构和利益的重新分配当中，扭转自己目前倒霉已极的处境。正是基于这样一种日益清晰起来的想法，如今钱谦益对于北京那个朝廷的命运，已经不再看得那样生死攸关，似乎没有它的存在就不行。“哼，如果它注定要完蛋的话，那么就让它完蛋吧！它完蛋之后，我们还可以凭借南京为中心，在江南富庶之地重新建立起一个朝廷，再度开创大明的中兴！”他内心深处曾经不止一次这样冷冷地想。而且事实上，据他所知，这种准备北方一旦陷落，便在江南谋求建立偏安之局的想法，也并不仅仅属于他钱某一个人。像南京兵部尚书熊明遇、南京都察院右都御史李邦华，以及福建帮官僚首领黄道周等人，都有这种想法。只不过彼此所抱的目的不

the city and exited through the southeast gate. As a result, nearly a million homes had been swept away by the flood. Less than twenty thousand people had managed to escape. Among the survivors were the family of Prince Zhu Su, the family of the governor, a few other officials, and some common people. The peasant army had lost more than ten thousand lives and was said to have left. When they spoke of this horrifying tragedy, they were very depressed. Then, they spoke of the Chen Xinjia case. They hadn't anticipated that the emperor was so resolute that neither Zhou Yanru's nor Xie Sheng's plea had had any effect. Chen Xinjia had finally been beheaded in public at a crossroads in the city. Although Chen Xinjia was punishable by death, everyone shuddered at the ruthlessness of the emperor. At long last, the atmosphere was somewhat enlivened when they spoke of Zhang Guowei, former student of Qian Qianyi and current Vice Minister of Water Transport who had been newly appointed to fill the position of the Minister of War.

While the others talked, Qian Qianyi merely listened silently most of the time and rarely cut in. For some reason, in recent days, whenever he heard anything like these, he felt very bad. Such a bad feeling didn't come from a worry for the fate of the Ming dynasty or himself like before. Rather, it was more about hate and resentment than worry. He sensed he would never see the light again if the current political status quo didn't change, and that only in a drastic change or even a turmoil that would cause a redistribution of power and a reshuffle of interests was it possible for him to come out of his current predicament. Because of such an increasingly clear realization, Qian Qianyi no longer cared about the fate of the imperial court in Beijing, which he had previously regarded as indispensable. "Hmph, if it's doomed, then let it be. When it's finished, we can revive the Great Ming in the prosperous land of River South with a new imperial court in Nanjing," he thought coldly, again and again. In fact, he knew he was not alone in harboring such an escapist idea of setting up a new imperial court in Nanjing. Others included Xiong Mingyu, Minister of War in Nanjing, Li Banghua, censor of the right arm of the Censorate

尽相同，暂时还心照不宣罢了。所以，当钱谦益看见眼前这几位门生，还糊里糊涂地一心指望北方战局能够好转，指望北京朝廷能有什么非凡的作为，他就不禁在心里发出冷笑，有心想点醒他们一下，又觉得还不到时候，只好依旧沉默着，无聊地把脸转向窗外。

开始，他这样做只是为了消遣。然而，渐渐地他的目光就变得专注起来。因为他发现如今岸上的情况有点异常，一群人，少说也有三五十个，正聚在前边一个码头上，乱哄哄地谈论着什么，一边谈，一边回头张望。远处的河堤上还不断有人奔来。

“嗯，莫非出了什么事？”钱谦益想，目不转睛地瞧着越来越近的码头。忽然，站在高处的几个人齐声高叫：

“来哉！来哉！”

那群人顿时紧张起来，纷纷四散分开。有的人还抄起棍棒，一副如临大敌的样子。其中一个人——青衣小帽，长得浓眉大眼，敏捷地跳到水边的石阶上，大声招呼：“船，快，摆过来！”

现在，钱谦益的船已经撑到与码头平行的地方。顾苓等人也发现了岸上的情形，都停止了交谈，一齐望着舱外。

这当儿，只见两个汉子扛着一顶轿子奔到了码头。刚刚停下，旁边的人就拥上去，七手八脚地把一个女子从轿子里推了出来。那女子被绳子捆住了手脚，嘴巴也塞了布团，只是没有蒙脸。钱谦益骤眼一看，觉得有点面善，正疑惑间，隔壁内舱里的柳如是忽然惊叫起来：

“啊，小宛！”

钱谦益吃了一惊，仔细一看，果然像是董小宛。只见她被那些人从码头上扛下来，很快地塞进了一只小船里。那船显然是预

in Nanjing, and Huang Daozhou, head of the Fujian Fellowship of Officials. They all shared the same idea without saying it, but each had a more or less different motive. Therefore, when Qian Qianyi saw these proteges of his were still stupidly hoping the situation in the north could be reversed and the imperial court in Beijing could do something extraordinary, he couldn't help letting out a cold sneer in his heart. He wanted to wake them up, but thinking it was not time yet, he kept silent and looked out of the window for something interesting.

It was just a casual look, but gradually his eyes were arrested by something unusual ashore. It was a small crowd of thirty to fifty people gathering at a pier in front, talking noisily about something and looking back from time to time at the people coming over from behind.

"Is there anything wrong?" Qian Qianyi thought, staring intently at the pier that was coming closer. Suddenly, several men standing at the top shouted in unison:

"There! There!"

The crowd suddenly acted quickly and stepped away. Some even picked up sticks as if the enemy were coming. One of them, a young man with thick eyebrows and big eyes, wearing a blue robe and a small hat, jumped agilely to the stone steps by the water, and shouted loudly, "Hurry up! Push the boat here!"

Qian Qianyi's boat came to the side of the pier. His proteges also noticed the commotion on shore. They all stopped talking and looked out of the cabin.

At this moment, a sedan chair carried by two men rushed to the pier. As soon as it stopped, the few men nearby went forward and dragged a woman out of the sedan chair. The woman's hands and feet were tied with ropes, and her mouth was stuffed with cloth, but her face was not covered. Qian Qianyi felt he had seen her somewhere. While he was thinking, Liu Rushi, who was in the other cabin, suddenly exclaimed:

"Ah, Xiaowan!"

Qian Qianyi was taken aback. Sure enough, it was indeed Dong Xiaowan. She was carried off the pier and quickly shoved into a

先准备好的，待到那个粗眉大眼的汉子也登上去之后，艄公就立刻挥动长篙，迅速掉转船头，随即驾起大橹，飞快地向阊门那边摇去……

这一切，都发生在很短的时间里，没等钱谦益和他的学生们清醒过来，那只劫持者的小船已经驶出好远，岸上那群人也一声呼哨，纷纷走散，转眼都不见了。

“老爷，柳夫人请老爷派人上岸去，打听一下是怎么一回事。”红情的声音从背后响起。

钱谦益怔了一下，回过头来。他犹疑地瞧着丫环，却没有马上表态。因为一来，他不想多管闲事——他自己的事情就够多的了。二来，他还听人说过，董小宛打算嫁给冒襄。这使他想起大半年前的虎丘大会，最后就是由于冒襄拿出了周延儒的幕客顾麟生的那封信，才把自己弄得当场出丑，一败涂地。为此，钱谦益至今仍耿耿于怀，恼恨不已。不过，他还想到：董小宛同柳如是过去是手帕姐妹，上一次她遭到田弘遇的迫抢，躲进了徐氏东园，自己由于心情不好，硬是赶走了她。为这事柳如是一直不开心。这一次如果又拒绝……

“牧老，此处离董小宛的家已是不远，不如就让晚生上岸打听一下，如何？”也许是看见老师还在踌躇，顾苓便自告奋勇地说。

钱谦益又沉吟了一下，终于点点头：“嗯，也好，如此就烦云美辛苦一趟。”

于是，等船靠半塘，顾苓就独自上了岸。过了约摸半个时辰，他把事情打听清楚回来了。原来是这样：十天前，冒襄的一位拜把子兄弟名叫刘履丁的，受冒襄的委托，带着七百两银子和几斤人参，从润州来到姑苏，准备替董小宛还债、落籍。起初，刘履

small boat, which had been obviously put there in advance. After the man with thick eyebrows and big eyes boarded the boat, the boatman immediately pushed the boat with the long push pole, turned the boat around, took up his big oars, and quickly rowed the boat toward the West City Gate ...

All this happened in a very short period of time. Before Qian Qianyi and his pupils woke up, the hijacker's boat had sailed far away, and the crowd on shore had scattered with a whistle and disappeared in the blink of an eye.

"My lord, Lady Liu wants you to send someone ashore to find out what's going on," Hongqing's voice sounded from behind.

Qian Qianyi turned around and looked at the maid. He didn't give an immediate reply because, for one thing, he didn't want to be involved in other people's business while his own was worrying enough, and for another, he had heard that Dong Xiaowan was going to marry Mao Xiang, which reminded him of the Tiger Hill Conference six months ago. It was Mao Xiang's disclosure of the letter from Zhou Yanru's staff adviser Gu Linsheng that had caused his loss of face and the abortion of his plan. For this reason, Qian Qianyi was still resentful of Mao Xiang. Yet, Dong Xiaowan and Liu Rushi had been handkerchief sisters, after all. He had let down Liu Rushi once previously by turning Dong Xiaowan away from Xu's Garden, where she was hiding from Tian Hongyu's pursuit. Liu Rushi had never forgiven him ever since. If he turned down her request again this time ...

"Elder Mu, this place isn't far from Dong Xiaowan's home. I can go ashore and ask about it." Gu Ling volunteered, seeing his teacher was hesitating.

Qian Qianyi thought for a while and finally nodded his head. "Well, that's good. Please go and find out."

When the boat reached Bantang, Gu Ling went ashore alone. An hour later, he found out about the situation. Ten days ago, Liu Lüding, a sworn brother of Mao Xiang, came from Runzhou to Gusu on Mao Xiang's behalf to pay off Dong Xiaowan's debts, carrying with him seven hundred taels of silver and several catties of ginseng. At first,

丁把事情看得很容易，待到把债主找来一谈，才知道这个“黄衫客”“古押衙”并不好当。那群债主全是些地头蛇，又凶又刁。他们认定冒襄是个大阔佬，存心要狠狠敲他一笔。双方谈判了好几天，连个还债的方案都没谈成。刘履丁不禁焦躁起来，仗着自己是个官儿，就拍起桌子吓唬他们。这一下可就坏了事。那群债主显然早有准备，立即一哄而散，而且临走时连董小宛也绑架了去，大约打算把她藏起来做人质。刚才钱谦益他们瞧见的那一幕，就是这么回事。

大家听了，这才恍然。钱谦益拈着胡子，慢吞吞地说：“噢，想不到冒辟疆还真的肯娶董小宛。不过，他既有心娶她，就该让刘渔仲把银子带够，也用不着闹得这样人仰马翻！”

顾苓摇摇头：“我瞧辟疆其实也是半心半意，无非是被他那伙朋友逼狠了，有点无可奈何。听说，他这次一个子儿也没有出。那几斤人参，是刘大人从京里带来的；那七百两银子，是一位姓陈什么的大将军替他掏的腰包！”

钱谦益又“噢”了一声，却转口问：“听说刘渔仲在粤西的郁林做知州，怎么会到了这里？”

“哦，他三年前就因母亲辞世，回到漳州家中守制，今已满服，正在待缺候补，所以有空出来走动——对了，刚才他在董家，正一筹莫展，见了我，高兴得什么似的，还一个劲地问起老师。看样子，像是想求老师出面替他斡旋似的。”

钱谦益瞧了他一眼，皱着眉毛问：“你可曾告诉他我在这里？”

“没有。学生未知老师的意思，自然不会贸然告知他。”

“哼，我看他是活该！”没等钱谦益再开口，钱曾突然迸出来这么一句，随即又闭嘴不说了。

Liu Lüding thought it was a piece of cake but when he negotiated with the creditors, he found it was not so easy to be a brave hero, for he found they were all tough and cunning local rogues, who were bent on extracting a large sum of money from Mao Xiang, whom they believed to be super-rich. The negotiation lasted for days without any result. Liu Lüding, who was a small-time official, was irritated and slapped his hand on the table to scare them, but that ruined the negotiation, and the creditors, who had prepared for this, immediately left and kidnapped Dong Xiaowan as a hostage. That was all the commotion was about.

Having learned the situation, Qian Qianyi said slowly, plucking at his beard, "Good for Mao Pijiang. He has finally made up his mind to marry Dong Xiaowan. Now that he's serious about it, he should have asked Liu Yuzhong to bring enough money to avoid a hectic situation like this."

Gu Ling shook his head. "Pijiang is actually half-hearted. He's doing it against his own will. That bunch of friends have kept urging him to marry Dong Xiaowan. I hear that he hasn't given a single coin this time. The ginseng was brought by Mr. Liu from Beijing and the seven hundred taels of silver were given by a Mr. Chen, an army commander."

Qian Qianyi said "oh", and asked, "I hear that Liu Yuzhong is a prefect in Yulin, Guangxi Province. How come he's here?"

"His mother died three years ago, and he returned to his hometown in Zhangzhou on a mourning leave. Now, the mourning period is over and he's waiting for a vacancy, so he has the time to travel around. By the way, he was at Dong's House just now, and he was at a loss as to what to do next. When he saw me, he suddenly brightened up and asked about you. I think he wants to get your help."

Qian Qianyi looked at him and asked, knitting his brows, "Did you tell him I'm here?"

"No. I didn't tell him, since I didn't know what you would think."

"Hmph, I think he deserves it," said Qian Zeng before Qian Qianyi spoke again. Then, he fell silent.

“哦，却是何故？”坐在他旁边的何云偏过脸，故作不解地问。

“士龙兄——”看见钱曾咬着牙不吭声，乖巧的顾苓插了进来，“那还用问？要是他姓冒的不活该，可就轮到我们活该了！”他一边说，一边用眼睛去溜钱谦益。

何云却拿起杯子，呷了一口茶，说道：“过去的事，已经过去了！有道是‘破甑不顾[①]’——倒也不必再耿耿于怀，有伤和气！”

他这么一说，钱谦益和顾苓虽然都感到意外，但还没有什么表示，钱曾的脸色却陡然变了。他慢慢回过头，用那双能把人看得心里发毛的眼睛盯了何云一会儿，末了，“嘿嘿”地冷笑起来：“好吧，你就拍姓冒的马屁去吧，可我没忘记自己是钱门弟子！”

何云毫不着恼。他依旧不慌不忙：“话不是这等说。所谓‘冤家宜解不宜结’么！何况同是清流中人，能解，还是设法解了的好。今日这番巧遇，据我瞧，倒不失为一个机会……再说，辟疆同宛娘的事，如今已是尽人皆知，八方瞩目，若因惧惮债主气焰之故，而终竟不成，也怕见得我们江南名士，未免过于无能哩！”

何云一边说，一边意味深长地注视着钱谦益，显然是暗示老师应该考虑出面干预这件事，以便通过笼络冒襄，进一步同陈贞慧那一伙人讲和。不过，看见钱谦益冷着脸不吱声，何云也就摸不透老师的想法。他正打算作进一步的劝说，忽然看见红情正从里面走出来，只好临时又顿住了。

“老爷，柳夫人请老爷内舱说话。”红情垂着手说。

钱谦益抬起头，瞧了丫环一眼，又瞧了瞧言犹未尽的何云，现出怫然不悦的神色，随即站起身，朝大家拱一拱手，向内舱走去。

---

① 破甑不顾：意指犯错之后不必介意，应从中吸取教训，防止下一次犯错。出自《后汉书》。

He Yun, who was sitting next to him, turned to him and asked in exaggerated puzzlement, "But for what? "

"Brother Shilong," seeing Qian Zeng grit his teeth without saying a word, the respectful Gu Ling cut in. "That's obvious. If Mr. Mao doesn't deserve it, we do." He studied Qian Qianyi's expression as he spoke.

However, He Yun picked up the cup, took a sip of tea and said, "Let bygones be bygones. There's an old saying 'Leave a broken pot alone.' We should forget about the grudges and look to the future."

Both Qian Qianyi and Gu Ling were surprised to hear it but they still didn't say anything. Qian Zeng's expression suddenly changed. He slowly turned to He Yun and stared at him with his piercing eyes for a long while. At last, he let out a cold sneer, "Go and kiss Mr. Mao's ass if you like, but don't forget you're a pupil of Mr. Qian."

He Yun was not angry at all. He calmly said, "Well, I wouldn't say that. It's better to have a friend than a foe, as the saying goes. Besides, we're all good men and we'd better be reconciled. I think the chance meeting today is a good opportunity for reconciliation. Furthermore, the romance of Pijiang and Xiaowan is known to all. If it doesn't have a good ending simply because of the obstruction of the creditors, we all lose face as famous scholars of River South."

As he spoke, he looked meaningfully at Qian Qianyi, clearly hinting that the teacher should consider intervening in this matter so as to make peace with the likes of Chen Zhenhui by befriending Mao Xiang. However, as Qian Qianyi kept silent with a cold face, He Yun didn't know what the teacher was thinking. As he was going to argue further, he suddenly saw Hongqing coming out, so he had to stop.

"My lord, her ladyship wants to speak to you," Hongqing said with her hands down.

Qian Qianyi raised his head, cast a glance first at the servant girl then at He Yun with a look of displeasure, before he stood up, bowed at his company, and walked toward the inner cabin.

## 好事多磨

吴江县的县城又名松陵镇，从苏州往南，要走上好几十里的水程。那地方紧挨着大运河，人烟稠密，商业兴盛，店铺子不少。董小宛被债主们绑架之后，秘密送到这里，囚禁在一座宅院内。这宅院又大又深，外人很难找得到她，何况周围还有人严密把守。不过，债主们也没有再特别为难董小宛，一到就替她松了绑，又派了一个叫田婆的老妇人来侍候她，每天照常供她吃喝，只是不许她擅自下楼。

债主们这样做的用意，董小宛自然是懂得的。所以，从被关进来的那天起，她就望眼欲穿地盼望着外面的消息。她估计，刘履丁既然受了冒襄和朋友们委托，照理不会因此就罢手不管，应当还会再来。然而，三天过去了，五天过去了，今天已经是第八天，刘履丁仍旧杳无音讯。董小宛就不由得着急起来了。

虽然，她一再说服自己：刘履丁纵然再来，也不能这么快。他也许还要回如皋去找冒襄商议，筹措款子，再赶回来，最快也得一个月才行。如今自己落到这个地步，只有耐心守候。但是，焦急和担心仍然越来越强烈地煎熬着她。特别是想到三个月前，她在南京关帝庙求过的那根签——“忆昔兰房分半钗，如今忽把信音乖。痴心指望成连理，到底谁知事不谐！”董小宛就更加感到心惊肉跳，坐卧不安了。

# A Good Ending That Came Late

The seat of Wujiang County was also known as Songling Town. From Suzhou to Songling Town, it was a journey of a few dozen miles by boat. Adjacent to the Grand Canal, the town was densely populated and packed with shops. After Dong Xiaowan was kidnapped by the creditors, she was secretly sent here and confined in a large and deep courtyard. It was very difficult for anyone from the outside to find her, not to mention that there were men around who closely guarded her. However, the creditors were rather sparing to Dong Xiaowan. They untied the rope as soon as they arrived in the courtyard and even gave her a servant called Mrs. Tian. They gave her food but forbade her to go downstairs without permission.

Dong Xiaowan understood the intentions of the creditors in their leniency. Therefore, from the day she was locked up, she eagerly waited for news from the outside, knowing that since Liu Lüding was entrusted by Mao Xiang and the friends, he would not give up. However, three days passed, five days passed and there was still no news. Today was the eighth day, and nothing was heard from Liu Lüding. Dong Xiaowan couldn't help feeling anxious.

Meanwhile, she repeatedly tried to convince herself that Liu Lüding might not come so quickly. If he had gone to Rugao to see Mao Xiang and get the money for her redemption, it would take a month at least. Now that things had come to such a pass, all she could do was to wait patiently. But anxiety and worry continued to torment her with increasing intensity. She was particularly disturbed as she recalled the fortune slip from General Guan's Temple in Nanjing three months ago:

*In the boudoir, they gave each other a token of love.*
*But now, there's no news from the man.*
*How she longs to be married to him!*
*But in the end, things have gone wrong.*

她是在南京乡试放榜之后，被冒襄又一次赶回苏州来的。本来，八月十五中秋节那一天，在桃叶河房里，冒襄已经当众题诗，正式许诺要娶她。当时，董小宛以为事情从此会顺利一些了。“哦，谢天谢地，那根签到底不灵！”她欣喜之余，曾经这么想。谁知仅仅过了两天，还没等她高兴过来，新的打击又接二连三地来了。首先是八月十七那天，冒襄突然不辞而别，连话都没留下一句。董小宛又惊又急，连忙雇船，拼命追赶，一直到仪征才赶上了。虽然最后弄清楚，那是冒襄的父亲冒起宗决定弃官不做，返回家乡，途经这里，派人把儿子召去见面。但已经把董小宛差点吓掉了魂……此后大半个月里，董小宛再不敢离开冒襄一步，就跟着他留在銮江上等候放榜。她想起陆卖婆的开导，有意改变以往过于文静端庄的态度，稍稍放出些狡狯轻狂的手段来对付冒襄。特别是在一次宴会上，她表现得那样泼辣，那样刁蛮，把座上的客人支派得团团转；还接二连三地大杯拼酒，一下子就压倒了所有的歌姬。这一手果然有效，她发现冒襄惊奇得睁大了眼睛，仿佛发现了什么稀罕事物似的，从此对她明显亲热起来……

谁知这一次仍然好景不长，到了九月初七，突然晴天一记霹雳——南京贡院放榜，冒襄的名字竟然落到了副榜上。副榜是正榜之外的附加名额，属于安慰性质。纵然被录取，也不能算做举人，下科仍须再考。与正榜相差甚远。董小宛至今还清楚记得，那天，冒襄正和汪汝为等一班朋友，在銮江口的梅花亭子上饮宴，

She was sent back to Suzhou by Mao Xiang after the results of the provincial exam in Nanjing were released. Previously, on the day of the Mid-Autumn Festival, Mao Xiang wrote a poem in the Peach Leaves Riverhouse in front of his friends and officially promised to marry her. At that time, Dong Xiaowan was very happy and thought that things would go well from then on. "Oh, thank goodness, that sign on the fortune stick is wrong," she said to herself. Unfortunately, two days later, as she was still rejoicing in her heart, new blows came one after another. The first one came on August 17th, when Mao Xiang suddenly left without saying goodbye. Dong Xiaowan panicked and hurriedly rented a boat to chase after him. She didn't catch up with him until she reached Yizheng. It turned out that Mao Qizong, Mao Xiang's father, who had resigned his official post and was going back to his hometown, was stopping by and wanted to see his son. Though a false alarm, it had scared the hell out of Dong Xiaowan ... For the greater part of a month, she stayed with Mao Xiang on the Luan River and waited for the examination results without daring to leave him for a minute. Following the advice of Miss Lu the peddler, she sometimes turned from a graceful lady into a wily and naughty bitch. Once at a banquet, she was so wild and nasty and gave orders to everyone, who obeyed her blindly. She drank in full glasses, one after another, and quickly outshined the other singsong girls. This method really worked. She found that Mao Xiang's eyes widened in surprise, as if he had discovered something curious, and that since then he had clearly grown fond of her ...

However, good times don't last. On the seventh day of September in the lunar calendar, there was a thunderclap on a sunny day. The Gongyuan in Nanjing released the examination results and the name Mao Xiang fell on the sub-list. The sub-list was a supplement to the main list, equivalent to a list of consolation prizes. Being on the sub-list didn't mean being a *juren*. To become one, the candidate had to retake the exam the following year. There was a whole lot of difference from the main list. Dong Xiaowan still clearly remembered the day when Mao Xiang, Wang Ruwei and a bunch of other friends wined and dined at the Plum Blossom Pavilion at the mouth of the Luan

一边等候发榜的消息。当时，大家都说冒襄必中无疑，冒襄自己也显得很有把握，谈笑风生。甚至当报录人举着报帖，一路嚷着“恭喜高中”，奔上亭子来时，冒襄仍旧自信地微笑着。然而一刹那间，他的脸色变了，愕然地瞅着报帖，仿佛不认识上面的字似的。随后，他的脸就涨红起来，渐渐又转为煞白，由于肌肉在发抖，他那张俊美的脸扭曲了，变得十分难看和怕人。末了，他猛地一拂袖子，扭头就朝亭子外走去。他走得那样快，当董小宛慌里慌张地跟着赶到江边时，冒襄已经吩咐开船。见了董小宛，他那铁青地板着的脸孔，就露出了憎厌冷酷的神情。只是亏了随后赶到的冒成不由分说，一下子就把她扶上了船，冒襄才没来得及说什么。可是，此后一路上，他都阴沉着脸一声不响，也不再搭理董小宛。看到这种情形，董小宛自然不敢再惹他生气，她想：“无论如何，他肯让我跟着他，这就够了！”

然而，她未免想得太顺当。当船到了如皋城郊的朴巢时，冒襄的逐客令就下来了。理由除了还债、落籍的老问题之外，又加上父亲刚从外地归来，未曾禀告；以及他自己考试失意，无心顾及其他等等。总而言之，要董小宛仍旧回苏州去等着。董小宛好不容易才争取到这一步，眼看就要进城，怎肯轻易返回？何况她还担心一拖下去，说不定冒襄又会变卦，所以放声痛哭，表示绝不离开。然而，冒襄的意志是不可改变的，一切眼泪、哀求都打动不了他的心。到头来，董小宛仍旧只有服从。

River while waiting for the examination results. At that time, everyone said there was no doubt that Mao Xiang would succeed in the exam, and Mao Xiang himself looked very confident, talking and laughing all the time. When the messenger holding a report card and shouting "Congratulations!" all the way rushed to the pavilion, Mao Xiang was still smiling confidently. In an instant, however, his expression changed as he stared in astonishment at the report card, as if he didn't recognize the words on it. Then, his face reddened and gradually turned pale, and because of the convulsion of the muscles, that beautiful face was twisted and became ugly and scary. Finally, he suddenly waved his sleeves, turned around and walked out of the pavilion. He walked so fast that the panicked Dong Xiaowan was left far behind. By the time she rushed to the river bank, Mao Xiang had already ordered the boatman to row the boat. Seeing Dong Xiaowan, his dark face showed a look of disgust and resentment. Thankfully, Mao Cheng, who arrived later, helped her onto the boat before Mao Xiang had the time to say anything. However, Mao Xiang kept a gloomy face all the way and didn't say a word, nor did he pay any more attention to Dong Xiaowan. Seeing that, Dong Xiaowan didn't dare to say anything, lest he be angry again. She thought, "Anyway, he hasn't turned me away."

However, she was too optimistic. When the boat arrived at Puchao on the outskirts of Rugao City, Mao Xiang's eviction order came. In addition to the old issues of debt repayment and de-registration of her prostitutehood, he cited some other reasons as well: his father had just arrived home from a remote place and he hadn't reported their relationship to him yet, he had failed the provincial exam and was not in the mind for other things, and so on. All in all, he wanted Dong Xiaowan to go back to Suzhou and wait. After all she had done and having come thus far, just a short distance away from Rugao City, how could she give up so easily? Besides, she was worried that if she didn't insist now, he might change his mind again. So she burst into tears and said she would never leave. However, Mao Xiang's will was immutable, not to be shaken by tears and pleas. In the end, Dong Xiaowan still had to submit to that will.

那时候，她是多么伤心哟！当船儿撑离码头，冒襄由一群仆从簇拥着，站在岸上，纯粹出于敷衍地朝她扬一扬手，就匆匆背转脸去，董小宛的心像被刀子扎一样，痛苦得几乎想往水里一跳，就此死掉算了。只是想到冒襄还没有彻底回绝她，似乎还存在一线希望；而负责护送她的冒成，又在一旁竭力慰解，她才勉强抑制住悲痛。随后，她就拿定了主意：从这一天开始，她身上的一套衣裳不再更换，要是到了冬天冒襄仍不来迎娶，她宁可冻死！她让冒成这样转告冒襄，也当真这样做了。回到半塘之后，她就天天守候着，一直挨到十月底，眼看冬天已经过去三分之一，冒襄那边仍旧全无消息。董小宛几乎已经绝望了。就在这时候，刘履丁忽然来到了半塘。他不仅带来了冒襄的问候，而且带来一大笔钱……如今董小宛已经记不清，一刹那间，她说了些什么，做了些什么。她只记得自己像是昏过去了，随后，又醒转来。此后一连好几天，她都像是生活在梦中似的——她笑，她哭，她收拾东西。她逢人便告诉冒襄已经派人来接她了。随后，就……

“啊，莫非，莫非我真的是在做梦吗？”董小宛想，心里一急，猛地站了起来，“不，不会，不是的！冒公子是托了人来要接我去，他还带了银子、人参，这是千真万确的。不，这不会是梦！”她在心里大喊。然而，当她向周围环顾的时候，又渐渐迷惑起来。“可是，如果不是梦，我怎么会到了这里？周围为什么一个人都没有？连田婆也不见了？这是什么地方？这到底是什么地方！”她着急地、出声地问，慌里慌张地奔向窗户。然而，在那里等着她的，只是一角幽暗的天空，一钩昏黄的淡月，和一片荒烟迷漫的废园，树木黑糊糊的影子在淡蓝色的烟雾中若隐若现。鸱枭一类的夜鸟不时发出几声怪叫，听来像是鬼魂痛哭，又像妖魔在狂笑，却依旧看不见一个人影。董小宛更加惊慌起来。她愈

How distressed she was at that moment! When the boat pulled away from the pier, Mao Xiang, surrounded by the servants of his family, stood on the bank and waved goodbye to her perfunctorily, and then hastily turned away. Dong Xiaowan's heart smarted as if a knife was stabbed into it. It was so painful that she even thought of ending it all by jumping into the river. Mao Cheng, who was escorting her, kept comforting her from aside. When she thought that Mao Xiang hadn't completely rejected her after all and there still seemed to be a glimmer of hope, she began to feel better. Then, she made a resolution: From today on, I won't change my clothes. If he doesn't come to marry me in winter, I'd rather freeze to death. She asked Mao Cheng to tell it to Mao Xiang, and she did what she said. After returning to Bantang, she waited and waited. It was the end of October. One third of winter had passed, and there was still no news from Mao Xiang. Dong Xiaowan had almost despaired. Just then, Liu Lüding suddenly came to Bantang. He not only brought greetings from Mao Xiang, but also a lot of money ... Now Dong Xiaowan couldn't remember what she said and did at that moment. She just remembered that she passed out but then came to later. For days afterward, she lived in a dream, laughing, crying, packing her belongings. She told everyone that Mao Xiang had sent for her. Then ...

"Is it really just a dream?" Dong Xiaowan couldn't bring herself to believe it. In a panic, she suddenly stood up. "No, no, no! Here is a man sent by Mr. Mao to pick me up, and he's brought silver and ginseng. There's no mistake. No, it isn't a dream," she said loudly in her mind. However, when she looked around, she became confused again. "But, if it isn't a dream, why am I here? Why is there no one around? Where is Mrs. Tian? What is this place? What on earth is this place?" she asked anxiously, panicked. She rushed to the window desperately. What awaited her, however, was only a corner of the dark sky, a dim yellowish moon, a misty deserted garden, and the dark shadows of trees looming in the bluish mist. Owls or some other nocturnal birds hooted from time to time like ghosts crying woefully or demons laughing wildly. There was still no one in sight. She panicked

来愈担心这真是一个梦。如果真的是梦，那么醒来之后，就一切都没有了，没有刘履丁，没有冒襄的信，也没有替她还债落籍的事。她还得像几个月来那样，苦苦地守下去，守下去。“啊，不，不能！”她迷乱地想。现在，她觉得最重要的，就是要尽快弄清：这不是梦！她连忙捋起衣袖，把胳臂凑在嘴上，使劲地咬了一口。顿时，感到了一阵尖锐的刺痛，被咬的地方出现了两排深深的齿印，随后就渗出殷红的血来。她还不放心，又接连咬了两口，都感到疼痛，这才变得清醒了一点。“哦，不是梦，真的不是梦！”她喃喃地说，一边轻轻地抚摸着被咬过的地方，一边在椅子上坐了下来。

然而，这种平静并没有持续多久。渐渐地，她又想起了那根要命的签。不错，就算不是梦，就算一切都是真的，刘履丁是真的，还债落籍也是真的，可是，为什么结果仍旧这样倒霉呢……难道、难道真的像那根签所说的，“到底谁知事不谐”么？这样一想，董小宛又开始不安起来。是的，在过去，她一直以为，事情这样艰难的根源，就在于冒襄的高傲和薄情。所以她才决计用柔情蜜意去感化他、维系他，利用社会舆论去督促他，试图迫使他就范。大半年来，她可以说是费尽了心机，竭尽了气力。好不容易，冒襄总算答应了，甚至不管怎么说，他真的派人来办理迎娶的事了。然而，到头来仍旧办不成！这就不能不使董小宛怀疑：她是不是想错了？以往她屡受挫折，也许并不在于冒襄本人，而是冒犯了另外一种神秘的、命运的力量。过去冒襄的种种冷漠、狠心、不近人情，其实都是这种可怕力量所作出的安排，是想让她知难而退。她却毫不觉悟，一个劲儿地苦苦追求。因此，那种神秘的力量才在这最后一刻里再次发出警告……

even more, worrying that it really was just a dream. If it was really a dream, then everything would be gone after she woke up. There would be no Liu Lüding, no letter from Mao Xiang, no one to repay her debts and redeem her from the brothel, and she would have to continue to wait as she had done in the past few months. "Oh, no, it shouldn't be like that," she thought confusedly. She felt that the most important thing at the moment was to confirm it wasn't a dream, so she rolled up a sleeve, put her arm to her mouth and bit it with her teeth. A sharp pain immediately rose and two deep indentations appeared where she had applied her teeth, blood oozing out of her skin. Still unconvinced, she took another two bites, and she experienced the same pain. Until then was she certain. "Oh, it's not a dream. It's real," she murmured to herself, gently caressing the bitten spots as she sat down in the chair.

However, the calm of mind didn't last long. She soon remembered the ominous sign on the fortune stick again. Yes, even if it isn't a dream, even if everything is real—Liu Lüding is real, and repayment of the debts is real—the result isn't so good after all ... The prophecy "but in the end, things have gone wrong" on the fortune stick seems to have come true. Thinking of that, Dong Xiaowan began to feel uneasy again. Yes, in the past, she had always thought that the main issue was Mao Xiang's arrogance and lack of warmth, so she had tried to conquer him with tenderness and cement their relationship with public opinion. After having exhausted all her wiles and energy in the past six months, she had finally succeeded in extracting a promise from Mao Xiang, and in spite of everything, he had really sent for her and set about marrying her. However, it still didn't work out in the end. Dong Xiaowan couldn't help wondering: Have I been wrong from the very beginning? Maybe my setbacks have nothing to do with Mao Xiang himself. They're more the result of my having offended destiny itself, a mysterious, powerful being. The indifference, cruelty, and lack of warmth of Mao Xiang in the past are actually out of the design of this formidable power. It wants me to retreat. Yet, I've unwittingly persisted in my courting. Therefore, that mysterious force issues another warning at this last moment ...

董小宛被这新的、可怕的发现骇呆了。虽然，在过去，她也曾模模糊糊地想到过这个问题，但从来没有现在这样清晰而深入。一刹那间，她心里凉了半截，“啊，要真是命中注定，刘大人就算回来，又有什么用？而且，说不定他根本就不会再回来了！”她绝望地想，挣扎了一下，试图站起来，却出乎意料地感到那样疲倦、无力。终于，她颓然地靠在椅子上，用双手掩住脸孔……

现在，她觉得眼前一片黑暗，仿佛又回到了大半年前那个梦境当中：那位答应要带她回家的美少年，也就是冒襄，正在向天空飞去，而她只抓住了他的一根衣带，那衣带被坠得又长又细，成了一根细丝。最后，细丝断了，她急速地向下掉落。下面是一个无底的深渊，一群似人非人的妖怪，正在那里等候着，马上就要猛扑过来，把她剥光、撕碎、吃掉……

“啊哟，这可是怎么啦？哭什么哩？”一个尖尖的女人嗓音大惊小怪地问。原来，田婆回来了。这个老太婆，长得又干又瘦，有一双人称为“绿豆眼”的小眼睛，和一张向前啄出的、鸟喙似的嘴巴。她本是个插带婆[①]，因常到这所宅院来走动，便被临时指派来服侍兼监视董小宛。她显然十分乐意这个差事，把董小宛管得死死的，不但不准她下楼一步，甚至董小宛站在窗前多瞧上一会，她都要干涉。至于平时拿班作势，冷言冷语就更不必说了。说是让她来服侍董小宛，倒差点儿没让小宛反过来服侍她。刚才，她不知跑到哪儿去了，而且喝了酒，这会儿红着脸走上楼来，却现出一副少见的兴冲冲的样子。

“莫哭莫哭，我说姐儿，你的造化到了！快，去换身衣裳，装扮装扮，跟我走！”田婆说着，伸手推了推董小宛。

董小宛只顾默默垂泪，没听清，也没搭理。直到“跟我走”

① 插带婆：指梳妆女工。

Dong Xiaowan was shocked by her new, terrifying thought. She had vaguely had that thought before, but it had never been so clear. In an instant, her heart became cold. "If it's really fate, what's the use of Mr. Liu even if he comes back? Besides, maybe he won't come back at all," she thought in despair, struggling to stand up but unable to because she was too tired and weak. Finally, she sank back into the chair and covered her face with her hands ...

The vision in front of her dimmed, and she sank back into the dream of six months ago. The beautiful young man who has promised to take her home—that is Mao Xiang—is flying to the sky and she is holding a ribbon from his robe. The ribbon grows longer and longer, thinner and thinner, until it becomes a long, long thread. In the end, the thread breaks and she plummets toward a bottomless abyss down below, where a horde of humanlike monsters are waiting to pounce on her, strip her of all her clothes, tear her into pieces and devour them ...

"Hey, what's up? Why are you crying?" came a high-pitched, alarmed female voice. It was Mrs. Tian, a skinny and thin woman with small eyes called "mung bean eyes" and a beak-like mouth protruding forward. She made a living by arranging head accessories for ladies and came to the courtyard quite often. Now she was sent over as a temporary servant and meanwhile to keep watch over Dong Xiaowan. Obviously, she enjoyed the new role that gave her power, which she exercised unsparingly. Not only did she forbid Dong Xiaowan from going downstairs, but also interfered when Dong Xiaowan stood at the window for too long. Besides, she had always treated Dong Xiaowan disdainfully and spoken to her harshly. Instead of serving Dong Xiaowan, she had almost made Dong Xiaowan her servant. Having disappeared into nowhere a while ago, she now came back with a blushing face, evidently intoxicated. "Don't cry, sister, don't cry, Your luck has come. Hurry, change your clothes, fix your hair, and come with me," Mrs. Tian said as she reached out her hand and gave Dong Xiaowan a push.

At first, Dong Xiaowan didn't hear clearly and ignored the old woman as she was weeping, but when the words "come with me"

三个字钻进了耳朵，她才蓦地一怔，抬起头来。

“快去梳头换衣裳，跟我走呀！”田婆又催促说。

“啊，上哪儿去？”

“你别问，去了你就知道了！”

“不，我不去！”董小宛忽然害怕起来。

“咦，这倒奇了！不叫你出去，你天天嚷着要出去，如今让你出去，你倒不肯了？”

“不，我不去，我不去！”董小宛站起身来，倒退一步，身子紧贴着桌子，惊恐地睁大眼睛，仿佛唯恐田婆硬把她拖出去似的。

田婆疑惑地瞅着她，随即绿豆眼一转，有点明白了。她说：“哼，敢情是怕那边把你甩了，这边留着你没用，才让你出去吧？告诉你，不是，是来了客人！”

“啊，莫非，莫非冒郎他……”

田婆撇撇嘴：“客人嘛，倒是有好几位，有没有姓冒的，我可不知道。”

董小宛怔怔地瞅着田婆，她的神情渐渐起了变化，一种兴奋的、狂喜的光芒从她的眼睛里闪现出来。

“是的，是的，一定是他！”她尖声叫道，猛地离开了桌子，“冒郎来了，冒郎接我来了！啊，这可好了——不灵！那根签到底不灵！”她一边嚷，一边慌里慌张地朝楼梯奔去，却被田婆一把揪了回来。

“你做什么？快让我走，我要见冒郎！”董小宛生气地说。

田婆冷冷地道：“瞧你这身打扮，能去见客人么？”

董小宛错愕了一下，低头瞧了瞧自己身上，虽然自从刘履丁来到半塘后，经过劝说，她已经重新开始替换衣裳。可是这几天，

entered her ear, she was suddenly awake and raised her head.

"Groom your hair, change your clothes, and come with me," urged Mrs. Tian.

"Where are we going?"

"Don't ask. You'll know when you are there."

"No, I'm not going." Dong Xiaowan suddenly became fearful.

"Well, that's strange. You wanted to go out every day when you were not allowed to. Now, you're asked to go out, and you won't!"

"No, I'm not going, I'm not going," Dong Xiaowan stood up, took a step back and leaned against the table, her eyes widening in horror, as if afraid that Mrs. Tian would take her out by force.

Mrs. Tian looked at her, puzzled, then rolling her mung bean eyes, she suddenly understood why Dong Xiaowan acted like that. "Hmph! Are you thinking you have to go now because you are dumped by your beau and you're no longer useful here? Let me tell you, it's not like that. We have guests!"

"Oh? Is it Mr. Mao ..."

Mrs. Tian said, twisting her lips, "Well, there're several guests. I don't know whether there's a Mr. Mao or not."

Dong Xiaowan stared blankly at Mrs. Tian, and her expression gradually changed. Her eyes sparkled with excitement and anticipation.

"Yes, it's him, it must be him!" she exclaimed as she suddenly left the table. "Mr. Mao has come! Mr. Mao has come! Thank goodness! Wrong! The fortune stick is wrong!" She shouted and hurried toward the stairs but Mrs. Tian pulled her back.

"What are you doing? Let me go! I want to see Mr. Mao," Dong Xiaowan said angrily.

Mrs. Tian said coldly, "Look at the way you dress. Can you see the guests like that?"

Dong Xiaowan quieted down and lowered her head to look at her clothes. She had begun to change clothes after she was persuaded to by Liu Lüding, who came to Bantang on Mao Xiang's behalf, but she did look out of shape these days, because, tortured by sadness and

由于愁苦和绝望的情绪越来越重，她一直无心修饰打扮，这会儿确实不成样子，难以见人。

“啊，不错，可不能让冒郎瞧见我这模样！”她想。于是，连忙转过身，迅速地向妆奁匣子走去……

## 酒席圈套

一顿饭工夫之后，打扮得整整齐齐的董小宛由田婆提着灯笼引路，喜滋滋地出了院门，沿着一条花树掩映的小径往前走。

“嗯，不知到底是刘大人来，还是冒郎也来了？田婆说有好几位客人，或许真有冒郎在内也未可知。不过，若说是刘大人回如皋去把冒郎请来，又绝不能这么快；想必是冒郎自刘大人走后，放心不下，随后亲自赶来。这么说，冒郎对我确是一片真心，从前他那样子，看来确是有为难之处，迫不得已。我竟是错怪他了！”这么一想，董小宛感到又喜欢，又惭愧，觉得自己以往徒然对冒襄一片痴情，其实却并不真正了解他，尤其不懂得体谅他。相反，由于自己的固执任性，给对方添了许多烦恼。“哦，从今以后，我一定不再这样，我一定要更加体贴他，顺从他。为着他，让我干什么都行，哪怕是死！”她偷偷用手帕拭着涌到眼角来的泪水，感激地暗暗发誓说。

这当儿，她们已经走完曲曲折折的回廊和石径，来到一处单门独户的小小院落里。董小宛不认得路，糊里糊涂地只跟着田婆走。如今她觉得这地方同囚禁她的那个地方一样，也颇为偏僻隐秘，离正院好像也很远。不同的是它并不荒凉，院子里的花木池石都布置得错落有致。一幢三开间的小平房，掩藏在浓密的树影里；低垂着的窗幔透出灯光，传来了叮叮咚咚的音乐声，那是一面琵琶在弹奏……

“原来冒郎不是在大堂上，却在这个地方候我。”董小宛想，

despair, she hadn't been in the mood to dress up. Indeed, she shouldn't see people like that.

"Ah, yes, she's right. I can't let Mr. Mao see me like this," she thought. So, she quickly turned around and walked over to the makeup box ...

## Trap at a Banquet

In the time for a meal, Dong Xiaowan got dressed, and led by Mrs. Tian, who held a lantern in her hand, happily stepped out of the courtyard and walked forward along a path lined by flower trees.

"Is it Mr. Liu or Mr. Mao? Mrs. Tian said that there're several guests, and maybe Mr. Mao is among them. However, it can't be Mr. Liu bringing Mr. Mao from Rugao, for he wouldn't have been back so quickly. It should be Mr. Mao coming himself after Mr. Liu's departure because he was deeply concerned. This shows how much he loves me. He acted as if he hadn't cared for me because he indeed had difficulties. I shouldn't have wronged him," she thought. She was gladdened by her own thought and felt guilty at the same time. She felt that she has loved him without truly understanding him and being considerate of him. On the contrary, her stubbornness and willfulness had caused him much trouble. "From now on, I won't be like that anymore. I'll be more considerate and more submissive. I'll do anything for him, even if it means death," she vowed silently as she secretly wiped the tears from the corners of her eyes with a handkerchief.

They walked along the winding colonnade and stone path and came to a small, separate courtyard. Not knowing the place, Dong Xiaowan simply followed Mrs. Tian passively. She felt this courtyard was as secluded as the one where she was kept and that it was very far from the main courtyard. The difference was that this one was not deserted and the flowers, trees, water pool, and stones in the yard were neatly arranged. From between the drapes of a small three-room bungalow hidden in the dense shadows of trees came the light of a lamp and the tremolando of a *pipa* ...

"Oh, Mr. Mao isn't in the main room. He's waiting for me here,"

跟着田婆匆匆踏上台阶，走进堂屋去。

这堂屋不大，当中一架曲屏，前面一张圆桌，桌上酒肴杂陈，三个衣饰华丽的人围坐在桌旁饮酒，下首坐着一个浓妆艳抹的瞎先生，怀抱着一面琵琶，正在那里边弹边唱。看见董小宛和田婆跨进门槛，酒席上的一个人“啊”了一声，站起身来，其余两人也一齐抬起了头。

也许因为太兴奋，加上从幽暗的院子忽然来到灯火明亮的屋子里。有片刻工夫，董小宛虽然觉得冒襄就在座位上，却分不清楚究竟是哪一个。她竭力睁大眼睛，把席上的三个人看了一遍，又看一遍，依然无法确定。她十分着急，正想开口叫唤。蓦地，她清醒过来，席上的三个人中，并没有冒襄。除了那个长着一把大胡子的胖老头是这所宅子的主人，她被关进来时见过一面之外，其余两个她都不认识。

“啊，冒郎呢？他在哪儿？他到哪里去了？”董小宛想，焦急地转动眼睛寻找着，却看不见。

这时，那个叫张员外的主人说话了：

“呵呵，难得小娘子光降草筵，幸之何如！快请入席！”

“可是冒公子呢？”董小宛迫不及待地问。

张员外一怔：“冒公子？哪个冒公子？”

“就是，就是如皋的冒公子，托刘大人替奴家还债的。他不是来了么，奴家要见他。”也许是忽然意识到自己的举止过于冲动，有失礼仪，董小宛脸红了。她低下头去，行着礼轻声地说。

张员外却越加摸不着头脑：“什么，冒先生来了么？怎么我不知道？”

Dong Xiaowan thought as she hastily followed Mrs. Tian up the stairs and into the main room.

The main room was not very big. It had a curved screen in the middle and a round table in front of it. On the table was a motley of dishes. Three men in gorgeous clothes were sitting around the table drinking, and next to them was a blind musician with heavy make-up playing a *pipa* and singing. Seeing Dong Xiaowan and Mrs. Tian come in, one of the men said "hah" and stood up, and the other two raised their heads simultaneously.

Either because of the inner blindness caused by her own excitement or the transition from the darkness in the courtyard to the bright light in the room, Dong Xiaowan, staring at the three men in front of her, couldn't tell which one was Mao Xiang, although she was convinced he was among them. She scrutinized the three men at the table with wide-open eyes again and again, but still couldn't see clearly. As she worriedly opened her mouth to call Mao Xiang, she suddenly woke up to reality and found none of them was Mao Xiang. Of all the three men at the table, she only knew one: the fat old man with a big beard, who was the owner of the house and whom she had met when she was first brought in. The other two were total strangers.

"Where is Mr. Mao? Where is he? Where has he gone?" Dong Xiaowan thought, anxiously turning her eyes around to search for him, but in vain.

Then, the owner of the house, who was called Squire Zhang, spoke.

"Hah, welcome to my humble dinner party, my dear lady. It's such a pleasure. Please come and sit."

"But where is Mr. Mao?" Dong Xiaowan asked impatiently.

Squire Zhang looked surprised. "Mr. Mao? Which Mr. Mao?"

"Mr. Mao from Rugao, who asked Mr. Liu to pay my debts. Isn't he here? I want to see him." As she spoke, Dong Xiaowan blushed and lowered her voice after realizing her own impertinence.

Squire Zhang was even more confused. "What, is Mr. Mao here? Why don't I know it?"

这时，田婆在一旁插嘴了："嗳，哪有什么冒公子！都是这妞儿自己想出来的。小妇人早先领了员外之命，去叫她来侑酒助兴。她就自作多情，以为什么冒公子到了，这不是笑死人了么！"

张员外这才恍然省悟。他点点头："田婆说得不错。冒先生尚未有消息，更不曾光临寒舍。在下今晚请小娘子来，是因为这两位知交——"他指着坐在上首的一位白面长须的中年绅士，介绍说："这位是海盐冯江老。"又指了另一位高颧骨、尖下巴的青年人，"这位是毗陵杨世兄——久慕芳名，渴欲一晤。还望小娘子赏光，入席共饮三杯，一申积悃，请！"张员外说着，作了一揖。他这样彬彬有礼，显然是因为董小宛虽然身遭囚禁，毕竟是一位江南名妓，而且很可能不久要成为复社头领冒襄的姬妾，不便过于得罪的缘故。

这时，冯江老也站了起来，拱着手说："在下久闻小娘子芳名，如雷在耳。只恨僻处海盐，未能一睹仙颜。今夕一见，方知盛名之下，绝无虚誉。就请入席如何？"

可是尽管他们婉言温语，又捧又哄，董小宛却似乎既没有看见，也没有听见。她失魂落魄地站着，脸色变得越来越苍白，嘴巴也闭得越来越紧了。

座上三个男人交换了一下眼色。张员外摸着络腮胡子，忽然哈哈一笑："我知道小娘子的意思了。莫非你怕今晚同我们饮酒，万一传到冒先生的耳朵里，多有不便么？只管放心！这两位是我极信赖的知交，这位瞎先生——"他指了指那个弹琵琶的盲女，"又是长住我家的。其余也都是我的心腹，我包管不会传出去！何况，小娘子进府多日，在下尚未好生款待。如今就请宽心入席，尽此一夕之欢好了！"

在他说话的当儿，董小宛似乎终于从最初的打击中恢复过来。她慢慢地抬起头，绝望地瞅着张员外。终于，仿佛下了决心似的，等对方说完，她就行了一个礼，平静地说："多谢员外美意，奴家虽是风尘陋质，却也知道为人须讲信义。妾身已许冒郎，便须

Mrs. Tian cut in, "Hah, there's no Mr. Mao. She's made it up. Upon your order, I went to get her to accost you at the drinking party and she thought Mr. Mao is here. It's ridiculous wishful thinking."

Squire Zhang suddenly understood. He nodded, saying, "Mrs. Tian is right. There's no news of Mr. Mao, and he has not come to my shabby house. I've invited you here tonight because of these two good friends." He pointed to a fair-complexioned and long-bearded middle-aged man sitting at the fore seat and said, "This is Mr. Feng Jiang from Haiyan." Then, he pointed to a young man with high cheekbones and a pointed chin and said, "This is Brother Yang Shi from Piling, who has long heard about you and wants to see you. Please do us a favor by joining us to drink a few cups of wine. Please come and sit." Squire Zhang said with a bow. He was polite to the hostage because, after all, she was a famous courtesan in River South and the likely concubine of Mao Xiang, leader of the Fushe.

Mr. Feng Jiang also stood up and said with a bow, "I've long heard about your resounding name, but living in Haiyan, I've been unable to see you. Now, your presence makes me understand why you are so famous. Please take a seat."

Dong Xiaowan stood there paralyzed, her face turning paler and paler and her lips pressed tighter and tighter, as if she hadn't seen them and heard their compliments and flattery.

The three men exchanged glances. Squire Zhang rubbed his beard and suddenly laughed. "I understand what you are thinking. You are afraid Mr. Mao might hear of your drinking with us and get angry. Just don't worry. These two are my trusted friends and the blind musician," he continued, pointing to the blind girl who was playing the *pipa*, "lives in my house. All the others are trustworthy too. No one will tell others. Besides, I owe you a proper reception. Please sit down at the table and drink with us tonight."

As he spoke, Dong Xiaowan gradually recovered from the blow. She slowly raised her head and looked at Squire Zhang, as if she had made up her mind. When Squire Zhang finished speaking, she bobbed a curtsy and said calmly, "Thank you for your kindness, sir. Although

矢志相守，虽暗室亦不敢有欺。今日之事，请恕奴家难以从命！”

张员外愕然地望着神色严肃的董小宛，不由得脸红了。“哼，要是冒先生经此挫折，便弃你而去，从此不来了呢！”他恼羞成怒地问。

董小宛呆了一下，惨然道：“若是冒郎果真见弃，奴家只有死而已！”没等把话说完，泪水已经涌了出来。她用袖子掩着脸，急急向门外走去。

“慢着！”张员外大喝一声。等董小宛站住之后，他却不立即说话，沉吟着在室内走了两步，这才转过身来，傲然地说：“你——听着！你历来欠我的债，连本带利，合共纹银一百二十八两。只要你今晚肯留下来，陪我们喝一夜的酒，这账就算一笔勾销，怎么样？嗯？”

张员外这话刚说出口，田婆已经在一旁叫起来：

“哎呀！这真是从何说起哟！陪一夜的酒，就是一百几十两的银子！天下哪有这样便宜的买卖？我说姐儿，你真是不知几生修得的福气，遇上了员外这样的大善人、活菩萨！像他这样轻轻易易就把这老大一笔账给你勾销了，我瞧着都心疼！咦，你还拖延什么？快应承呀！还要叩头谢恩。唉呀，唉呀，一百二十八两哟！我瞧着都心疼！”

田婆一边嚷嚷，一边手舞足蹈，急得什么似的，也闹不清她是为董小宛着急呢，还是为张员外心疼，还是为自己没碰上这好运道而不平？

这一次，董小宛没有立即回答。要在往日，这区区一百多两银子，她自然未必放在心上，可是现在她已经变得很穷，更主要的，这一次刘履丁之所以没能把事办成，不就是因为手头的银子不够，无法应付债主们的敲诈吗？如今只要自己答应陪酒一夕，就能省掉一大笔钱，事情也许就会好办得多，自己也能早日脱离苦海，同冒襄从此永远厮守了。相反，要是放弃这个机会，万一冒襄当真筹措

my origins are humble, I know that a woman must be faithful. Since I've given myself to Mr. Mao, I should stay faithful to him forever. Even if I'm in a dark room, I won't hide anything from him. Please forgive me for not accepting your invitation."

Squire Zhang looked at Dong Xiaowan in consternation, his face reddening. "Hmph, what if Mr. Mao gives you up and never comes back after the setback?" he asked exasperatedly.

Dong Xiaowan thought for an instant and then said sadly, "If Mr. Mao really gives me up, I'll have to die." Tears welled up as she spoke. She covered her face with her sleeve and hurried to the door.

"Hold on!" Squire Zhang shouted loudly. When Dong Xiaowan stopped, he didn't immediately speak. After pacing in the room for a while, he said coldly, "You—listen! You have owed me 128 taels of silver in total, principal and interest. If you stay tonight and drink with us, this debt will be written off. How about that? Huh?"

Mrs. Tian exclaimed, "Wow, what a deal! Over one hundred taels of silver for one night of escort service? How can there be such a good deal in the world? Sis, you're in luck. You've met a very kind man, a living Bodhisattva. What a generous man he is to write off such a large sum of debt like that! Don't tarry. Accept the deal. Oh my, oh my, what a fortune to throw away!"

She gesticulated as she spoke excitedly, as if she were worried for Dong Xiaowan, who should jump up to the offer, or sorry for Squire Zhang, who was throwing away a fortune, or complaining against her own fate, which didn't give her an opportunity like that.

Dong Xiaowan didn't reply immediately. In the past, she wouldn't have cared a fig about a hundred taels of silver, but now was different. She was impoverished, and Liu Lüding's failure to redeem her from the brothel was exactly the result of lack of money. Here came an opportunity to settle part of the debt. If she took it, things would be easier and she would be able to get out of the sea of troubles and be united with Mao Xiang sooner. If she gave up the opportunity and Mao Xiang unfortunately failed to raise the money, the planned marriage would be aborted and she would end up deploring her fate

不到款子，不得不停止迎娶，那么自己活着的唯一希望，就会被彻底葬送，落得个抱恨终天……但是，她又想到，自己已经明明白白向冒襄保证过，绝对不再接客，洁身相守，又怎能自毁誓约，做出这种对不起冒襄，有损他名声的事来呢？正是这样两种念头，在董小宛的心中激烈地争斗着，使她一时之间无法作出抉择。她好几次想横一横心，冲出门去，却到底拿不出勇气来……

“嗯，怎么样啊？”张员外不耐烦地催问了。

“算了，就破例这一次吧，就一次！要知道，这笔钱有多重要啊！”董小宛心忙意乱地想，转过身来。

然而，就在此时，她忽然听见了一声叹息。这叹息很轻、很柔，就像微风飘过，几乎令人觉察不出。但董小宛觉察到了，不仅觉察到，而且分明地感觉得出其中所包含的惋惜和失望。她不由得一怔，回过头去，却意外地发现，那位怀抱着琵琶的瞎先生正把脸朝着她。这位靠卖唱为生的盲女，有着一张善良而忧郁的圆脸，要是不瞎的话，她很可能还是一位相当俊俏的姑娘。现在她的一双眼睛却显得死气沉沉，毫无光彩。不过，虽然如此，她却似乎凭着敏锐的感觉，知道周围所发生的事情，而且洞察到董小宛的内心活动。正当董小宛打算迈出很可能是错误的一步时，她就发出了劝阻的信息。

董小宛站住了，她目不转睛地瞅着瞎先生那张善良而忧郁的脸。瞎先生似乎立即感知到了。她的嘴角轻轻一动，朝董小宛做出一个充满抚慰意味的微笑，仿佛在说：“你何必着急呢？我算准了，你的冒郎不会抛掉你，他一定会来接你的！”

董小宛的心忽然宁帖了。她定了定神，回头朝张员外和那两个客人瞧了一眼。“啊，不，他们是在骗我，他们想必是算准了：我不敢让冒郎知道这件事，那么，到时他们就可以赖账了！”她想，开始变得清醒起来。

她不再犹疑，默默地行了一个礼，又朝瞎先生感激地、轻轻地点一点头，然后转过身，向门外走去。尽管田婆气急败坏地提

for the rest of her life ... However, having promised Mao Xiang never to take a client again, how could she break her oath and do anything that would hurt Mao Xiang and damage his reputation? Torn between these thoughts, Dong Xiaowan couldn't make a quick decision. She wanted to rush out the door several times, but couldn't muster up the courage ...

"Well, what do you think?" Squire Zhang urged impatiently.

"Forget it! Let me make an exception this time, just one exception. This money is really important to me," Dong Xiaowan thought, her heart fluttering. She turned around.

At this moment, she suddenly heard a sigh. It was a light and soft one, coming like a breeze, almost inaudible. Dong Xiaowan not only heard it, but also clearly felt the pity and disappointment in it. She jolted to find it was the blind musician with the *pipa*, who was facing toward her. The blind lady musician had a kind, melancholy, round face. If she were not blind, she would have been a great beauty. Her eyes were lifeless and listless, but her hearing was good. She knew everything that happened around her and could see through Dong Xiaowan's mind. When Dong Xiaowan was going to take the wrong move, the blind girl sent out a warning.

Dong Xiaowan stopped still and stared at the blind girl's friendly and melancholy face. The blind girl seemed to have sensed it immediately. The corners of her mouth moved slightly, and she gave Dong Xiaowan a soothing smile, as if to say, "Why are you in such a hurry? I'm sure your Mr. Mao won't give you up, and he'll definitely come to pick you up."

Dong Xiaowan suddenly calmed down. She took a breath and looked back at Squire Zhang and the two guests. "No, it won't do. They're lying to me. What if they don't keep their promise, knowing I'm afraid Mr. Mao might hear of it?" she thought. Now, her mind was clear.

She stopped vacillating. Then, she bobbed a curtsy, nodded a grateful nod at the blind musician, who couldn't see it, turned around and walked out the door. Mrs. Tian, lantern in hand, called her name

着灯笼从后面呼唤着赶来，她也没有放慢脚步。

## 辣手制恶

“渔仲兄，现时会作诗的女子中，这黄皆令——阁下以为如何？”钱谦益把玩着手中的一把诗扇，微笑着问，同时，漫不经心地朝正聚在码头上等候的那群债主瞥上一眼。

这是他在赴虎丘途中，偶然碰上董小宛被劫持之后第九天的上午。由于柳如是的再三要求和督促，钱谦益终于接受了何云的建议，决定插手过问冒襄和董小宛的事。他们找到刘履丁，问明情况之后，已于昨天派人通知债主方面，让他们立即把董小宛送来。今天一早，钱谦益就约齐刘履丁，还有一班门客，分乘三只大船，浩浩荡荡来到了半塘董小宛的家门外，在码头上停泊下来，只等董小宛一送到，就开始处理债务。

“啊，秀水黄氏二女，皆德、皆令俱有才名。书、画且不论，这诗毕竟是好的。”刘履丁回答，同时瞧了瞧钱谦益。他显然有点不解：岸上的债主们纷纷云集，一场大争执已经迫在眉睫，怎么这位钱牧老还有闲心谈诗论文！刘履丁吃过债主们的苦头，知道这伙地头蛇的厉害。九天前，谈判决裂之后，他也曾想过回如皋去向冒襄求援，但一来当初自己夸下了海口，有些不好意思；二来也有点不甘心就此认输。加上考虑到一来一往，费时太久，所以才决定留下来，就地想办法。此后一连许多天，他四处奔走请托，哪知一听说是这么一件事，谁都摇头摆手，表示难轧得很，惹不起。刘履丁这才着急起来，颇悔当初自己过于孟浪。正在彷徨无计，忽然听说钱谦益愿意出面承担，干预这件事，刘履丁真

and ran toward her exasperatedly, but she walked off without looking back.

## A Heavy Hand on the Villains

"Brother Yuzhong, of all the women poets now, how is Huang Jieling?" Qian Qianyi asked with a smile, fiddling with a poem fan in his hand, and casting a glance at the creditors waiting on the pier.

It was the morning of the ninth day after he witnessed the kidnapping of Dong Xiaowan on his way to Tiger Hill. Pestered by Liu Rushi, Qian Qianyi finally accepted He Yun's suggestion and decided to intervene in the matter regarding Mao Xiang and Dong Xiaowan. They first found Liu Lüding, and after finding out about the situation, sent a message to the creditors and asked them to send Dong Xiaowan back to her home immediately. Early this morning, Qian Qianyi, Liu Lüding, and the proteges arrived massively outside Dong Xiaowan's home at Bantang in three big boats and docked at the pier. They were set to clear the debts as soon as Dong Xiaowan arrived.

"Jiede and Jieling, the two daughters of the Huangs in Xiushui, are both talented. Regardless of calligraphy and painting, their poems are good." Liu Lüding replied and looked at Qian Qianyi at the same time, wondering how this old man could still talk about poems while the creditors had gathered on the river bank and a major dispute was imminent. Having had an unpleasant experience before, Liu Lüding knew how bad the local villains were. Nine days ago, after the negotiations broke down, he thought of going back to Rugao to seek help from Mao Xiang but finally decided to stay and try to solve the problem with local sources. For one thing, he had boasted that he could do it. And for another, he didn't want to admit failure. Besides, the trip would take too much time. For many days he went around asking for help, but when hearing the story, everyone shook their heads and waved their hands in dismissal. Liu Lüding became worried and regretted being too confident at the outset. While he was at a loss as to what to do next, he was overjoyed to hear Qian Qianyi would like to help and intervene in this matter, for he knew that Qian

是喜出望外。他知道钱谦益久住家乡，名高望重，同各方面都有联系，在这一带很有势力。他肯出面，局面自然大不相同。不过，刘履丁仍然担心，事情未必就能顺利解决。事实上，他本人也并非那种无能之辈，在郁林知州任上时，素有精明干练之称；可是碰上眼前这伙人多势众的地头蛇，竟然处处形格势禁，施展不开。这些人，不少都是惯打官司的老手，不只不怕见官，而且还能言善辩。上一次，刘履丁就领教过一个姓郝的讼师，那条三寸不烂之舌，真是波澜翻飞，能把死的说活，活的说死。刘履丁口才本来不错，也被他弄得张口结舌，穷于应付。所以这一次钱谦益到底能有多大把握，刘履丁始终暗暗悬着一份心。此刻见他临阵之际，仍旧兴致勃勃地谈诗论文，一副漫不经心的样子，刘履丁的疑虑就更重了。

“那么渔仲兄以为，这皆德、皆令两姐妹，是姐胜于妹呢，抑或妹胜于姐？”钱谦益接着又问。

刘履丁怔了一下，老实地回答：“皆德自嫁贵阳朱太守之后，深自韬晦，其诗遂少流传于世；而皆令身为杨氏之妇，仍时时乘舆四出，奔走于权势之门，名声亦因之而大噪。不过以晚生愚见，皆令未免有风尘之态，不若皆德冰雪聪明也！”

钱谦益瞧着手中的诗扇，微笑地听着，没有立即接口。过了一会，他才把诗扇递给刘履丁，说：“你瞧瞧，这也是皆令的诗，可有风尘之态？”

等刘履丁把扇子接过去，他就仰起头，捋着胡子，津津有味地吟诵起来：“‘灯明惟我影，林寒鸟稀鸣。窗中人息机，风雪初有声……’这种诗，其声凄清，其韵寂寥，有如霜林落叶，午

Qianyi was a man with great influence, who had been living in the hometown for a long time and had a wide range of contacts. With his intervention, the situation would obviously be very different. However, Liu Lüding was still worried that even so, the issue might not be resolved smoothly. In fact, he himself was not the incompetent sort. When he took office as prefect in Yulin, he was known to be shrewd and capable, but overwhelmed by the local villains in number, there was no room for him to maneuver here. Many of these local villains were veterans in lawsuits, who were eloquent and unafraid to go to court. Earlier, Liu Lüding had been crushed by a seasoned litigator named Hao, who could prove the dead were alive and the living were dead with his glib tongue. An eloquent man himself, Liu Lüding was often made tongue-tied and speechless. Therefore, he was not sure how much Qian Qianyi could do and became all the more suspicious of Qian Qianyi's ability in resolving this issue when he saw the old man was so unhurried as to be talking about poetry at this critical juncture.

"Then, Brother Yuzhong, which one do you think is better, the elder sister or the younger one?" Qian Qianyi asked.

Liu Lüding paused for an instant and answered honestly, "Since Jiede married Prefect Zhu of Guiyang, she's been very much secluded and her poems have rarely been seen by the outside world. Jieling, however, has been very famous, because she's often been seen in sedan chairs visiting families of other officials as wife of Mr. Yang. In my opinion, Jieling has some mundanity in her poems while Jiede remains crystal clear."

Staring at the poem fan in his hand, Qian Qianyi listened with a smile and didn't immediately comment. After a while, he handed the poem fan to Liu Lüding and said, "Look at this one. It's one of Jieling's poems. Do you see any mundanity in it?"

When Liu Lüding took over the fan, he raised his head, stroked his beard and recited with relish: "'In the light of the lamp, there's only a shadow of me. In the cold woods, birds have stopped chirping. In the other windows, human activity has stopped. From somewhere,

夜梵钟，何尝有半点风尘之态！贱内河东君曾说：‘皆令之诗近于僧。’可谓确评！至于姚叔祥之辈，集古今名媛淑女，比拟皆令，全不识其神情气理，安可谓知诗，又安可谓知皆令！”说到这里，他瞧了瞧刘履丁，见对方低着头不吱声，钱谦益意识到自己只顾说得痛快，对刘履丁却未免有点不客气，就闭嘴不说了。

刘履丁这时也意识到过于认真会有损彼此合作的气氛，为着掩饰这种尴尬的场面，他笑了一下，接着对方的话茬儿说：“能诗会文之女子，虽说历代都有，唯是数量之多，却无过于本朝。尤其近数十年间，名门淑女不必论，便是青楼脂粉、商妇贫婆，竟然也拥鼻咿唔，讲什么‘蜂腰’‘鹤膝’、平仄、拗救，而且颇不乏出类拔萃之辈，这也可算是一大异事了！”

钱谦益点点头：“这也皆因本朝文运昌明盛极之故。所以许多聪明尤物，便乘时而生。也不必远说，譬如辟疆兄的这位未来如君，便是不可多得的一位奇女子哩！”

刘履丁正为今天这事担忧，见对方提起董小宛，便连忙接口说：“不错，否则，以辟疆那心高气傲的性儿，又岂会轻易许诺于她？只是，那帮债主着实贪婪险狠，简直可恶之极，只怕未必便肯轻易就范。”

钱谦益摇摇头，不在意地说：“兄台尽管放心，此事包在学生身上。辟疆兄是我平日极爱重的一个人，论才华学问，当今世上能与他颉颃的，也就是那么屈指可数的三数子而已！所以，学生这次不只必定要为他玉成此事，而且，到时还要在虎丘大排宴

the sound of wind and snow has arisen.' There's pathos in the tone and bleakness in the prosody, like leaves falling in the frosty woods, like a temple bell chiming in the midnight. Is there any mundanity in it? My wife Lady of River East has said, 'Jieling sounds like a bhikshuni in her poems.' It's an accurate description. The likes of Yao Shuxiang compare Jieling to the famous court ladies in history, but they've all missed the spirit of her poems. They neither understand poetry nor Jieling," Qian Qianyi said. As he spoke, he cast a glance at Liu Lüding, who was looking at the floor silently. Realizing that he was a little rude to Liu Lüding by speaking honestly, he stopped his comment.

At the same time, Liu Lüding also realized that being too serious would damage the atmosphere of harmony. To cover the embarrassment, he smiled, and said, following the subject, "There're women poets in every dynasty, but there're more in this current one. In the past few decades in particular, not only famous ladies, but also prostitutes and wives of businessmen have been writing poetry, talking about 'a bee's waist' and 'a stork's knee,' meters and the correction of a bad meter, and the like. Some of them are quite good, actually. It's a wonderful development."

Qian Qianyi nodded and said, "This is all because it's a great era for literature. Many artistic souls have seized the opportunity and seen the light. Mao Pijiang's fiancée, for example, is one of them. She's really brilliant."

Now that Dong Xiaowan was mentioned, Liu Lüding, who had been anxious about today's business, quickly took up the subject and said, "Yes, she is. Otherwise, given Pijiang's pride, he wouldn't have promised her. Problem is, those creditors are really greedy and wicked. They're abominable. I'm afraid they won't give in so easily."

Qian Qianyi shook his head and said slowly, "Brother, don't worry. I'll take care of it. I like Brother Pijiang very much. In terms of talent and learning, very few men can compare with him. I can count them on my fingers. So, this time, I will not only help him get united with Xiaowan but also hold a banquet at Tiger Hill to bid farewell to

席，遍邀四方名士，为小宛把盏饯行哩！”

“啊，劳烦牧老如此费心，何以克当！晚生先此代辟疆向牧老谢过了！”喜出望外的刘履丁连忙站起来，拱着手说。

钱谦益微微一笑：“区区微劳，何足挂齿？到时渔仲兄若是也去如皋，学生倒想烦你代我向辟疆兄致意哩！”

“这个自然，一定转达！”

这之后，刘履丁重新坐下来，两人又谈了些其他的事。终于，船身微微晃动了一下，只见顾苓兴冲冲地走进舱来说：

“牧老，宛娘的船到了！”

钱谦益“噢”了一声，回头朝刘履丁做了个谦让的手势，说：“请！”

于是两人站起来，走出舱门。

这时，岸上聚的人更多了，少说也有三五百，其中一部分是债主，以及他们的仆从打手之类，也有不少是赶来瞧热闹的人。看见钱谦益和刘履丁出现在船头上，本来正东一群西一伙凑在一块闹闹嚷嚷、指指点点的人们顿时静了下来，一齐回过头来，伸长脖子朝这边观望。

刘履丁到底放心不下，迫不及待地用眼睛寻找着。他发现载着董小宛的那只小快船已经靠了岸，却泊得很远，离自己这只船最少也有三四丈。两个仆妇模样的女人正在搀扶着董小宛下船，岸边还有五六个壮汉各执棍棒准备着。等董小宛一踏上码头，他们就立即把她严密护卫起来，完全是一派如临大敌的架势。显然，如果债主们的要求得不到满足，他们随时随地都会把董小宛重新劫走。

这时，钱谦益也已看清了形势，却不动声色，只是侧过头，向身边的顾苓低声问：“嗯，都准备好了么？”得到了肯定的回答，他就点点头，对刘履丁说：

“渔仲兄，且回舱中宽坐，看学生发落。请！”

Xiaowan upon her departure."

"That would be too much trouble for you, dear Elder Mu. Let me say 'thank you very much' on behalf of Pijiang." Liu Lüding, who was overjoyed, quickly stood up and bowed to Qian Qianyi.

Qian Qianyi smiled slightly and said, "That's no big deal. Don't mention it. Brother Yuzhong, when you go to Rugao, please send my greetings to Brother Pijiang."

"Of course I will."

After that, Liu Lüding sat down again, and the two talked about some other things. Finally, the hull swayed slightly, and Gu Ling cheerfully stepped into the cabin and said, "Elder Mu, Lady Xiaowan's boat has arrived."

Qian Qianyi said "oh", turned around, humbly gestured to Liu Lüding and said, "Please!" Then the two stood up and walked out the cabin.

Now, there were more people gathered on the bank, at least three or five hundred. They were creditors, their servants and henchmen, and idlers who came to spectate. Seeing Qian Qianyi and Liu Lüding appear on the bow of the boat, these people, scattered here and there, talking noisily and gesticulating, suddenly quieted down, turned around and gazed at the boat, their necks stretched.

Liu Lüding worriedly searched with his eyes for Dong Xiaowan and found the small fast boat she was in had already docked at least thirty or forty feet away from his own boat. Two women servants were helping Dong Xiaowan off the boat. There were five or six muscular men waiting on shore with sticks in their hands, ready to surround her as soon as she landed, as if an enemy were coming. Obviously, if the demands of the creditors were not met, they would continue to hold Dong Xiaowan hostage.

Qian Qianyi, who also saw the situation, remained calm. He tilted his head to Gu Ling beside him in a low voice, "Are you ready?" When he heard "yes," he nodded his head and said to Liu Lüding, "Brother Yuzhong, please go sit in the cabin and watch me deal with them. Please!"

等刘履丁移动脚步之后，他回头叮嘱顾苓：“一切听我号令行事，不可孟浪！”说完，这才不慌不忙地走回舱里。

刘履丁和钱谦益刚刚在各自的位子上坐下，就听见顾苓在外面大声叫道：

“岸上的人等听着：今日虞山钱牧斋老先生来到这里，是专门为的排解董家同各位的债务纠葛。钱老先生声望久著，信誉昭然，诸位想已知晓，不须在下多说。承他应允主持此事，实乃乡邦之福。各位尽可放心，保管人人满意，各得其所！如今，先请董姑娘上船说话。”

顾苓的话音刚落，就听岸上“哄”的一声骚动起来，几个声音同时高叫：

“不行，不能把人给他！”

“不把债还清，我们决不放人！”

“我们又不是三岁孩儿，谁会上当！”

刘履丁在舱里听见，心想：“光凭一句话就想让他们把小宛交出来，只怕未免把对手想得太驯良了！”

他瞧了瞧钱谦益，却发现老头儿神气安闲地捋着胡子，似乎一点也不紧张。等顾苓在外面同债主们又交涉了一阵，仍旧没有效果，钱谦益才回过头，对侍立在身边的李宝低声吩咐了一句什么。李宝答应着走出舱外。于是，只听顾苓不再坚持，却又大声说：

“列位必定要先清偿欠债，也可以。那么如今这里有三只船，为快当起见，决定同时清偿——二十两以下的，可以到左首这只船，由钱遵王先生发放；二十两到六十两的，可以到右首这只船，由何士龙先生发放；六十两以上的，请上在下这只船，由钱老先生亲自发放。请啊！”

听顾苓这样说，刘履丁又不禁暗暗摇头：“这样处置无非是

After Liu Lüding began to move, he turned around and said to Gu Ling, "Do as I say and don't ruin the plan." With that, he calmly walked back to the cabin.

Liu Lüding and Qian Qianyi had barely sat down in their respective seats when they heard Gu Ling shouting loudly outside, "Everyone, listen! Mr. Qian Muzhai from Yushan came here today to solve the debt issue of the Dongs. As you all know, and I don't want to elaborate, Mr. Qian is a man of great repute, and obviously doesn't really need my introduction. I'm glad he's agreed to handle this issue. We're really blessed. You can be assured that everyone will be satisfied with what you'll get. Please send Miss Dong to our boat for a discussion."

After Gu Ling spoke, he heard a commotion onshore, and several voices shouted at the same time:

"No, don't give her to him."

"We won't let her go unless the debt is paid."

"We're no three-year-olds to be fooled."

Liu Lüding heard it in the cabin and thought to himself, "They won't be so kind as to hand over Xiaowan by mere persuasion, I'm afraid."

He looked at Qian Qianyi but found that the old man was calmly stroking his beard and didn't seem worried at all. After Gu Ling negotiated with the creditors outside for a while to no avail, Qian Qianyi turned around and whispered to Li Bao, who was standing next to him, in a low voice. Li Bao said "aye, sir" and went out of the cabin. Then, Gu Ling stopped arguing and said loudly:

"Sirs, if you insist the debts be paid off first, that's fine. Now, here are three boats. To save time, we've decided to pay off the debts in three groups. If your amount is below twenty taels of silver, go to the boat on the left and get it from Mr. Qian Zunwang. Between twenty and sixty, go to the one on the right and get it from Mr. He Shilong. Above sixty, come to my boat and get it from the venerable Mr. Qian. Please!"

Hearing Gu Ling say this, Liu Lüding secretly shook his head, thinking, "It's divide and conquer. Although the idea is good, I'm

想分其势力，各个击破，设想虽妙，只怕对方仍未必肯就范。”

果然，没等他想下去，岸上又早已嚷成一片。一会儿，只见顾苓气咻咻地一步跨进来，说：“牧老，他们还是不肯，说什么也要先应承一律按原定本息发放，方肯上船，怎生处置？”

本来，按原定本息发放，似乎也很合理，但这些放债的富人，大多是乘人之危，大肆敲诈，不少利率当时就定得过高，加上拖欠了许多年，利上滚利，竟有超过本钱好几十倍的。如果按这样偿还，刘履丁带来的那几百两银子和几斤人参，绝对不够应付。现在钱谦益既然不打算代冒襄掏腰包，唯一的办法，就是说服对方压减利息。但是看来债主们认定冒襄是个大阔佬，决不肯放过这个大捞一把的机会。上一次，刘履丁就是这样谈崩的。现在他眼看钱谦益听了顾苓的报告之后，沉吟不语，就不由得着急起来，斜倾着身子说道：

“据晚生所知，这伙人中有个姓郝的，是个积年讼棍，一切坏主意全是出在他身上。此人伶牙俐齿，凶险狡诈，极难对付。”

钱谦益点点头，却没有答话。他又沉吟了一下，才对顾苓说：“嗯，好吧，让他们推出两个人来，上船议事！”

顾苓应诺着，到外面去传达了钱谦益的话。这一次，债主们没有再吵闹。过了一会，只听顾苓的声音说：

“噢，是你们二位哪，请！”

随着话音，船身摇晃起来，接着鱼贯走进来两个人。头里一个是五十开外的胖绅士，长着一把大胡子和一双金鱼样的鼓眼睛，

afraid they won't take the bait."

Sure enough, as he was thinking, there was a commotion onshore. After a while, Gu Ling stepped in exasperatedly and said, "Elder Mu, they still don't agree. They insist on the payment of principal and interest according to the original terms before they can get on the boat. What should we do?"

Payment of principal and interest according to the original terms sounded plausible. However, most of the creditors were rich men taking advantage of the vulnerability of their debtors and had set the interest rates too high at the outset. With interest on interest over the years, sometimes, the debtor had to pay dozens of times the principal. Thus calculated, the several hundred taels of silver and a few catties of ginseng that Liu Lüding carried with him was only a fraction of what was needed. Now that Qian Qianyi had no intention of paying off Mao Xiang's debts with his own money, the only way to solve the problem was to ask the moneylenders to reduce the interest. The creditors, however, believed that Mao Xiang was a rich man and would not let go of such a great opportunity to make a fortune. That's why Liu Lüding's negotiation with them had broken down previously. Seeing Qian Qianyi was silent upon hearing Gu Ling's report, Liu Lüding became anxious and bent toward the old man, saying, "One of them is a seasoned litigator named Hao. He's a long-time litigator, and all the bad ideas come from him. This man is cunning, glib-tongued and very difficult to deal with."

Qian Qianyi nodded his head without speaking. He thought for a while and then said to Gu Ling, "Well, fine, let them send two men to the boat to negotiate with me."

Gu Ling said "aye, sir" and went outside to convey Qian Qianyi's message to them. This time, the creditors made no more noise. After a while, Gu Ling's voice said, "Oh, it's you two. Come aboard!"

As Gu Ling spoke, the boat shook, and two men entered the cabin, one following the other. In front was a fat gentleman in his fifties, with a large beard and a pair of bulging eyes like those of a goldfish. It was Squire Zhang, who was responsible for keeping Dong

正是负责囚禁董小宛的那位张员外；另外那一位儒生打扮，方脸大耳，显得精明强干的，也恰好就是那个姓郝的讼师了。

“学生张秀，拜见两位大人！”张员外似乎有点怕钱谦益，畏畏缩缩地拱着手说。

那个姓郝的讼师却显得沉着机警。他一进舱，就目光闪闪地打量着周围的情形。等张秀说完了，他才彬彬有礼地一揖，说：“在下郝思平，见过二位大人。”

钱谦益没有马上说话，默默地瞅着对方，把他们挨个儿掂量一番之后，他才满脸堆笑地站起来。

“哦，原来是二位先生，久仰！”他回着礼说，又回头瞅着刘履丁，“这二位，不知渔仲兄可曾会过？”

这两个人正是上一次代表债主方面出面谈判的头儿，又凶又刁，刘履丁一见他们就头皮发麻。他红着脸，悻悻地说：“怎么，张员外、郝讼师，又是你们二位，好啊，哼！”说着，一拂袖子，气呼呼地管自坐回椅子上。

钱谦益微微一笑，他既已弄清来人的身份，心里也就有数。于是不再客套，指一指椅子，让张、郝二人坐下，他自己也重新坐了下来。

“二位先生，适才学生听说列位东翁定要按原定本息发放，以冒辟疆先生之财力，实在难以办到，还望列位东翁压减一二才好！”钱谦益单刀直入地说，他知道对方必然不会答应，所以也不想多绕弯子。

果然，早有准备的张秀马上拱着手说：“哦，难得二位大人屈尊赏光，出面主持这事，实乃吾辈之福。适才压减息金之议，本当承命，唯是各券所定息金，俱系双方当时讲妥，两相情愿，更无异辞。时至今日，却要压减，只怕人情惊诧，徒滋纷扰，未

Xiaowan hostage. The other one, who had a square face and big ears and was dressed like a scholar, was the litigator named Hao.

"I'm Zhang Xiu. Pleased to meet you, sirs!" Squire Zhang said timidly as he saluted Qian Qianyi with clasped hands.

The litigator named Hao looked calm and alert. The moment he stepped into the cabin, he stared at the surroundings with watchful eyes. After Zhang Xiu spoke, he bowed politely and said, "I'm Hao Siping. Pleased to meet you, sirs."

Qian Qianyi didn't speak immediately. After studying the two men carefully, he stood up with a smile on his face.

"Oh, I can't wait to see you two, sirs," he said, returning their salute. Then he looked back at Liu Lüding, "Brother Yuzhong, have you ever met these two gentlemen?"

These two men were exactly the same negotiators for the creditors. They were hard and cunning. When Liu Lüding saw them, his scalp tingled. He blushed and said sullenly, "Why, Squire Zhang and Litigator Hao, it's you two again, good, hmph!" As he spoke, he waved his sleeve and sat back down on the chair resentfully.

Qian Qianyi smiled slightly. Having found out who they were, he knew what to do next. Ceremonies over, he pointed to the chairs and asked Mr. Zhang and Mr. Hao to sit down, and he sat down in his own seat.

"Gentlemen, I heard just now that all you creditors insist on payment of principal and interest according to the original conditions, but given Mr. Pijiang's financial resources, he won't be able to do it. I hope that you can give him a reduction," Qian Qianyi said upright. Since they would not agree anyway, there was no need to beat around the bush.

Sure enough, Zhang Xiu, who was prepared for this, immediately folded his hands in salute and said, "Sirs, we appreciate your coming to mediate between us. We're greatly honored and should agree to a reduction as you've proposed. The problem is, now that the interest rate on every debenture was agreed to in the beginning by both parties, the reduction will set a bad precedent and create chaos. It won't work

易实行。”

“嗯，向来国家律例：私放钱债，每月取利并不得超过三分。如今我瞧这债目，不少竟高至四五分的；且更有将利做本，转算几年，便借一取百，未免太过！若不压减，又怎么成！”钱谦益板着脸说。

按照明朝的律例，确有月利限于三分，违者笞四十；并有不准以利滚利，违者以坐赃论罪，杖一百等条目。但实际上早已成为一纸空文，很少有放债者会去遵从。除非某个官吏出于这样那样的原因，想惩治一下放债者，才会偶尔把它抬出来。现在张秀听钱谦益这样说，一时弄不清他的真正意图。不过张秀知道这位钱老头儿可不是刘履丁，他在本地很有势力，同官府也勾结得很紧，若惹得他认真起来，真要这样干也不是不可能，所以一下子给唬住了，讷讷地不敢回答。

钱谦益看见三言两语就把对手给吓住，心中暗暗高兴。他正想进一步劝说，忽然，坐在张秀旁边的那个讼师郝思平哈哈一笑，开口了：

“钱老先生所见甚是！就债目而观之，息金果然定得高了些，理应压减才是。岂止应当压减，其实放债这事，每每足以助长豪强之家兼并之权，挫损小民生存之气，积弊颇多，简直就该严令禁止！”他一本正经地说，瞅了瞅座上的两位主人，发现他们都露出留神倾听的神气，就得意地微微一笑，接着说，“不过，话又得说回来，此事其实又是禁不得的，何故？因富者乃系贫者之母，贫者一旦有事，必要求助于富者；而富者则凭借日积月累，

out."

"Well, the national law says, for private loans, the monthly interest mustn't exceed three percent. Now I see that many of these debentures carry as high as four to five percent. On some of them, interest is converted into capital and in a couple of years, one tael of silver borrowed becomes one hundred to be paid off. It's outrageous, isn't it? If you don't agree to a reduction, how can the debts be paid off?" Qian Qianyi said with a stern face.

The Ming law did limit monthly interest to three percent, and anyone breaching the law was punishable by forty whippings. It also forbade interest on interest, and those breaching it should receive one hundred whippings. Since no moneylender complied with the law, it was basically a dead letter. The law was only occasionally applied when an official wanted to punish someone. Zhang Xiu didn't know Qian Qianyi's real intention in citing the law, but he knew this old man, who had a large network of connections including the *yamen* and held sway in this place, was not to be trifled with like Liu Lüding. "No one is sure he isn't able to do it if he means what he says," he thought. So, the bluff worked and Zhang Xiu was so scared that he dared not reply.

Seeing Zhang Xiu was taken in with the bluff, Qian Qianyi was amused in his heart. As he was going to press further, Hao Siping, the litigator sitting beside Zhang Xiu suddenly laughed and said:

"You're quite right, Mr. Qian. When we look at the debentures, the interest rates are indeed too high, and they should be lowered. In fact, not only the interest rates should be lowered but such loans should be banned altogether since they encourage the deprivation of the weak by the strong and lead to serious social problems," he said solemnly. Seeing the two hosts were both listening attentively, he smiled smugly and added, "However, on the other hand, they shouldn't be banned. Why? Because the rich are parents to the poor. When the poor become helpless, they turn to the rich. The rich have become rich because they've built their wealth through years of hard work and saving. Poor and rich are like left hand and right hand to each other.

方能有所盈余。这一贫一富，也正如人之左右手，右不富，则无力助左。若禁绝放债，使富者不富，则犹如砍去右手，举国俱成废人矣！何况，国家之法，本在利民。如今凶岁连年，兵戈未已，穷民愈多而富民愈少；借债者愈多，而放债者愈少。若仍拘执于三分之薄利，势必令放债之家心灰意馁，将钱钞另谋出路。如此，富者或无大碍，而贫者从此告贷无门，生计俱绝矣！此压减息金之大害也，还望老先生三思！”

郝思平这么滔滔不绝地一口气说下来，连钱谦益听了，都不由得暗暗点头，心想：“刘渔仲说此人巧舌如簧，不易对付，如今果然！”事实上，钱谦益又何尝真心维护三分利息的律例？他自己在常熟放债，也同样是实行高利息、利滚利的一套。不过，此刻他既要替冒襄主持还债，自然就顾不上许多了。现在，他看得更加清楚：张秀好对付，难轧的是郝思平这个讼棍，不尽快把此人制住，事情就无法进行。于是他瞅着郝思平，不动声色地问：

“郝先生果然辩才不凡，想必是位‘状元’啰？”

他这样问，是因为苏州一带，打官司的风气十分盛行，讼师也最多，内中也分别等级，最高级的称作“状元”，最低的称作“大麦”。这伙人最喜招揽是非，操纵官司，从中发财。

郝思平怔了一下，拱着手说：“不敢。”

“那么，董家欠下郝先生多少本息？”

“哦，董家与在下并无债务瓜葛。”

“然则阁下今日来此作甚？”

If the right hand isn't rich, it doesn't have the ability to help the left hand. Banning money lending altogether would be like cutting off the right hand, and the whole nation would be crippled. What's more, the purport of the law of the Ming is to protect the people. After years of natural disasters and war, there're more and more poor people and fewer and fewer rich people. There're more and more borrowers and fewer and fewer lenders. If we insist on a marginal interest rate, the rich will be discouraged and find other outlets for their money. Thus, the rich won't have a problem, but the poor won't be able to borrow money from anyone and their very survival is at issue. Thus, reducing interest rates isn't a good idea. Please think about it again, sir."

Hao Siping delivered a long, eloquent speech in one breath. Qian Qianyi nodded as the litigator spoke and thought to himself, "Liu Zhongyu said this man is glib-tongued and hard to deal with. He's right." In fact, Qian Qianyi had no intention to safeguard the provision of the Ming law that prescribed the three percent interest rate. As a moneylender in Changshu, he was also a beneficiary of high interest rates and interest on interest. He took the opposite position now because he was helping Mao Xiang to pay off Dong Xiaowan's debts. "Zhang Xiu isn't a problem. The litigator is a hard nut to crack. I must defeat him. Otherwise, we can't move ahead," he thought. Then, he looked at Hao Siping and asked placidly:

"Since you speak so well, you must be a top scholar, I gather?"

He asked this question because lawsuits were very common in the Suzhou area, and there were more litigators here than anywhere else. The litigators were divided into different ranks. The highest rank was called "top scholar" and the lowest rank was called "barley". These litigators manipulated lawsuits and profited from them.

Hao Siping was startled at first but soon folded his hands and said: "I dare not say so, sir."

"So, tell me, how much does the Dong family owe you, principal and interest, Mr. Hao?"

"Oh, they owe me nothing."

"Then why are you here today?"

“这——是他们请在下来协理此事，所以……”郝思平似乎意识到对方口气不善，变得有点紧张，不像刚才那样神气活现了。

这时，钱谦益可就不容对方躲闪了。“胡说！”他猛地一拍桌子，黝黑的脸上顿时像罩了一层严霜，“你与董家既无债务瓜葛，便该回避远引，如今却硬来从中插手，百计煽惑，兴风作浪，竟至劫人做质，以图要挟，胡作非为，至于此极！分明是个刁顽不逞之奸徒。若不严惩，王法何在！”他回头叫：“来人哪！”

话音刚落，只听通往内舱的门里暴雷也似的应了一声，随即门帘掀起，四个衙役打扮的汉子如狼似虎地扑了出来，手中铁链一抖，把郝思平的脖子套住了。

这一手来得如此意外，不但张、郝二人猝不及防，就连刘履丁也惊讶得张大了嘴巴，半天合不拢。

钱谦益斜了一眼张秀，发现那大胖胡子脸色大变，浑身筛糠也似的抖个不住，便“噢”了一声，换过一副和颜悦色的脸孔，对他说：“学生知此事全是这姓郝的奸徒从中捣鬼，与尊驾无干。不过，尊驾若仍扣住人质不放，却也难免担着干系。如今就请去吩咐贵价，把人质送上船来，慢慢再谈不迟。”

张秀本来十分害怕，听说与他无干，心中顿时宽了一半，哪里还敢违拗，连忙走出舱外，大声招呼手下那几个仆人，把董小宛送上船来。

正聚在岸上等候消息的那群债主只听见船里大呼小叫，却弄不清发生了什么事情，忽然看见要放人质，有几个机灵的便大声鼓噪起来，表示不同意。但是负责看守董小宛的那几个汉子，是张秀的家仆，自然服从主人。他们反而大声叱喝着，用棍棒挡开

"Um, they invite me to help, so ..." Hao Siping became nervous and less confident as he had been, having sensed the sharpness of the question.

Yet Qian Qianyi allowed no room for him to dodge. "Nonsense!" The old man slapped the table angrily, as if his dark face were suddenly covered with a layer of frost. "Since you have nothing to do with the debts of the Dongs, you should have stayed away, but now you've come in to meddle with the case by inciting the creditors to trouble-making and even to hostage-taking. You are a treacherous man and must be punished to do justice to the law." Then he turned around and shouted, "Come and get him."

A thunderous response erupted from the inner cabin, the curtain was lifted and four *yamen* men pounced upon Hao Siping like tigers and tied him up with an iron chain.

It all came so suddenly that not only Zhang Xiu and Hao Siping were caught off guard, but even Liu Lüding was alarmed as well, his mouth agape, unable to close for a long time.

Qian Qianyi cast a glance at Zhang Xiu. Seeing the stout, bearded man was trembling in fear, he said "oh" and changed into an amiable face, saying, "I know it's all the doing of the treacherous man named Hao and has nothing to do with you, but if you continue to hold the hostage, you're definitely involved. Please go and ask your men to send the hostage to the boat and let's talk about it then."

Zhang Xiu, who was scared out of his wits, was suddenly relieved upon hearing that he had nothing to do with the matter. Without hesitation, he hurried out of the cabin and asked his servants in a loud voice to send Dong Xiaowan to the boat.

The creditors waiting on the bank heard the turbulence on the boat but didn't know what was going on. When they suddenly saw that the hostage was going to be released, some vigilant ones shouted their disapproval. But the men keeping watch over Dong Xiaowan were Zhang Xiu's servants and only listened to their own master. They quickly moved, shouting loudly and waving sticks to fend off the creditors who rushed over to stop them and finally delivered Dong

那些拥过来试图制止的债主，把董小宛送上了船。

这当儿，钱谦益已吩咐衙役把恨得咬牙切齿的郝思平暂且押到后舱看管起来。看见董小宛走进船舱，他就喜滋滋地站起来。董小宛这一次绝处逢生，自然感激得热泪交流，呜咽着跪拜下去。钱谦益把她扶起来，着实抚慰了一番，然后吩咐跟上船来的董子将和寿儿，把她扶到内舱去歇息。

当做完这一切之后，他才回过头来，瞧了瞧张秀。发现那大胖胡子正愁眉苦脸地呆在一旁，钱谦益便同刘履丁交换了一个眼色，微微一笑，对张秀说：

“张兄不必过虑，钱某不才，尚能分清是非好歹。那姓郝的怙恶不悛，自应惩处；至于张兄，若不嫌弃钱某，倒想借重大力呢！”

张秀眼见郝思平被锁去，人质又被迫送回，今日已是一败涂地，心中正在七上八下，不知钱谦益下一步会怎样处置自己，忽然听见对方说出这么句话，他不由得一怔，疑惑地抬起头来。

“嗯，请坐着说话。”钱谦益指一指椅子，随即自己也坐了下来。

“弟素知张兄乃信诚君子，凡事都易商量。”钱谦益一本正经地说，目不转睛地瞅着张秀，“只是岸上那些人良莠不齐，其中难免杂有一二刁顽之徒。弟诚恐待会儿发放交割之时，此辈又来吵闹放泼，令人不欢。故此想请张兄届时在此作陪，助我督促弹压。以张兄在彼辈中之威望，此事当不难办到，不知能应允否？”

张秀本来正睁着一双金鱼般的鼓眼睛，疑惑地瞅着钱谦益。听了这话，他的脸色变了，猛地站起来，气急败坏地摇着手说：“啊，这个、这个……”他分明想拒绝，但在对方目光的逼视下，却始终不敢说出口。

坐在一旁的刘履丁，这时对于钱谦益的手腕和魄力已是由衷

Xiaowan to the boat.

Seeing Dong Xiaowan come in, Qian Qianyi stood up, all smiles, the hateful Hao Siping having been taken to the aft cabin. Having been rescued from the illegal confinement, Dong Xiaowan was very grateful and kowtowed to Qian Qianyi tearfully. Qian Qianyi helped her up and comforted her for a long while. Then he asked Dong Zijiang and Shou'er, who came with Dong Xiaowan, to take her to the inner cabin for a rest.

After that, he turned and looked at Zhang Xiu. Seeing the fat bearded man was standing aside with knitted brows, Qian Qianyi exchanged a glance with Liu Lüding, smiled slightly, and said:

"Brother Zhang, there's no need to worry. I'm not a wise person, but I can still distinguish between right and wrong, good and bad. The man named Hao is a villain and should be punished. You're different, and I hope you wouldn't mind giving me some help."

Now that Hao Siping was locked up and the hostage was sent back, Zhang Xiu felt defeated and was at sixes and sevens, not knowing what Qian Qianyi would do to him next. Hearing that, he was surprised and looked up suspiciously.

"Well, please sit. Let's talk about it." Qian Qianyi pointed to a chair, then sat down himself.

"I know that you're a good man I can talk to," Qian Qianyi said solemnly while staring at Zhang Xiu. "It's just that the men on the bank are mixed, and some of them are unreasonable and will make trouble when the money is paid. Therefore, I'd like to ask you to accompany me and prevent them from making trouble. With your influence, it shouldn't be a problem. What do you think, Brother Zhang?"

Hearing that, Zhang Xiu, who was looking suspiciously at Qian Qianyi with his eyes bulging like those of a goldfish, stood up in panic and waved his hand exasperatedly. "Oh, this, this ..." He clearly wanted to refuse, but under the gaze of Qian Qianyi, he dared not to say it out.

Liu Lüding, sitting nearby, was completely convinced by Qian

地信服。他看见张秀狼狈万状，倒也不想迫之太甚，便劝阻地说了一声："牧老——"但是，钱谦益伸出一只手把他挡住了，同时斜眼看了看站在旁边的顾苓。

顾苓会意，走过来笑吟吟地说："张兄何必见外？此事我们已合计好了。若然张兄应允时，阁下名下的这一百二十八两的本息，便仍按原券所定，照发不误。而且事完之后，另有酬劳。如此安排，不知尊驾意下如何？"停了停，他又凑上去，咬着耳朵补充说，"这事只有此间局内数人知晓，决不会传到外间去！"

张秀听说他那份债券可按原定本息发放，眼睛先是一亮，随即又收敛起来。他没有说话，低下头，沉默了许久，终于，轻轻地点了一点头。

一直紧盯着对方的钱谦益，目光闪动起来，黝黑的脸上掠过一丝胜利的微笑，马上又变得异常兴奋。他敏捷地站起身，得意洋洋地望了刘履丁一眼，然后脸向着舱门外，用威严的声音大声说：

"来人哪！吩咐下去，开始发放！"

## 警报频传

崇祯十五年闰十一月，黄宗羲回到了扬州。因为临离京时，方以智有一封信托他带给冒襄，所以黄宗羲没有立即过江，而是带着黄安，沿运盐河买舟东下，先到如皋去。他抵达冒家时，已是闰十一月十五日，冒襄听说他来访，十分高兴，立即把他迎进府里，两人各自谈了些别后的情况，其中自然也包括这次乡试的失意。不过大家都不愿多揭这块伤疤，互相安慰了几句，就把话

Qianyi's skill and courage. Seeing that Zhang Xiu's predicament, he became sympathetic and cut in, "Elder Mu—" However, Qian Qianyi reached out a hand to stop him from speaking and meanwhile squinted at Gu Ling, who was standing aside.

Gu Ling understood immediately. He came over and said with a smile, "Brother Zhang, don't make a stranger of yourself. We've already figured this out. If you agree, the one hundred and twenty-eight taels of silver under your name in principal and interest will still be paid according to the original terms specified in the debenture. And when this is over, there'll be a reward for you as well. I hope you're satisfied with this arrangement." After a pause, he leaned to whisper in his ear, "This is between us and no one else will know."

Hearing his debenture will be cashed, principal and interest, according to the original terms, Zhang Xiu lit up, but only for a brief moment. Then without speaking, he lowered his head and kept silent for a long time before finally nodding his agreement.

Qian Qianyi's eyes flickered and a triumphant smile flashed across his face. His spirit was back. He stood up nimbly, glanced proudly at Liu Lüding, then turned to look out the cabin door and said in a majestic voice:

"Someone come in! Tell the other boats to start making payments."

## Bad News

In December, 1642, or the second November in the lunar calendar in the fifteenth year of the reign of Emperor Chongzhen, Huang Zongxi returned to Yangzhou. Because Fang Yizhi had asked him to bring a letter to Mao Xiang before he left the capital, he didn't cross the river immediately. Instead, he and Huang An hired a boat and went east to Rugao first. When he arrived at the residence of the Maos, it was already December 15. Mao Xiang was delighted to hear his coming and immediately welcomed him into his home. They shared with each other their own stories after they parted, including their failure in the provincial-level examination. It was a painful experience

题转到了别的方面，像南北的战局啦，冒襄和社友们在南京作弄痛骂阮大铖啦，黄宗羲来回途中的见闻啦，京里的新闻啦，如此等等。随后，黄宗羲就交出了方以智的信。

这封信其实也没有什么特别要紧的事，只不过方以智当日在镇江金山下同冒襄分手之后，一直记挂着董小宛的事，特意来信追问督促一下。冒襄自从上月底托刘履丁到苏州去处理这事，至今一直得不到音讯，也不知办得成办不成，正在心神不定，看了这封信只有暗暗苦笑。黄宗羲本想问一问信中说什么，但瞧见冒襄神色不佳，像是有什么心事，看完信后一言不发地折好，放进袖子里，也没有告诉他的意思，他也就不好问了。

到了傍晚，黄宗羲正在客房里看黄安收拾东西，冒襄忽然又走进来，说他的父亲冒起宗知道黄宗羲来了，很想见一见。今晚就在拙存堂摆酒，请黄宗羲过去见面。黄宗羲自然不能推辞，吩咐了黄安几句，便跟着冒襄走过拙存堂来。

冒家是如皋县的首富，除了城中的这一座大宅第外，城内城外的园林别墅还有好几处，其中最优美讲究的要算位于城东北的那座水绘园。前些年，黄宗羲曾经在园里住过几天，发现确实是因势出奇，极尽工巧。至今黄宗羲还记得那些林林总总的名目，什么妙隐香林、壹默斋、枕烟亭、寒碧堂、洗钵池、雨香庵、水

and neither of them wanted to dwell on it. They comforted each other with a few words, and then the topic turned to other things, such as the wars in the north and in the south, the teasing and damning of Ruan Dacheng by Mao Xiang and other Fushers in Nanjing, and things Huang Zongxi had heard and seen during his trips, happenings in the capital, and so on. Then Huang Zongxi handed over Fang Yizhi's letter.

In fact, there was nothing particularly important in this letter. It was merely a reminder of Mao Xiang's promise to Dong Xiaowan. After parting with Mao Xiang at the Gold Mountain in Zhenjiang, Fang Yizhi had always been remembering the Dong Xiaowan matter. After Liu Lüding left for Suzhou to handle the matter at the end of last month, Mao Xiang hadn't heard from him and didn't know the results. While in an uneasy mind, Mao Xiang smiled a bitter smile after reading the letter. Huang Zongxi wanted to ask what was in the letter, but when he saw that Mao Xiang didn't look well, as if there was something on his mind, as this friend of his folded the letter and slid it into the sleeve not saying a word nor showing any intention to disclose its content, he decided not to ask.

In the evening, Huang Zongxi was watching Huang An handle their luggage in the guest room, when Mao Xiang suddenly came in and said that his father Mao Qizong heard that Huang Zongxi was here and wanted to see him. A welcome dinner party would be held in Huang Zongxi's honor at the Zhuo Cun Tang. Of course, Huang Zongxi couldn't refuse. After giving Huang An some instructions, he followed Mao Xiang to the Zhuo Cun Tang.

The Mao family was the richest one in Rugao County. Apart from this large downtown mansion, there were several garden villas in and outside the city. Among them, the most grandiose was the Water View Garden located in the north-east of the city. A few years ago, Huang Zongxi had stayed in that garden for a few days and found that it was indeed a great work of architecture with a beautiful landscape. To this day, Huang Zongxi still remembered the various names, such as Miaoyin Forest, Yimo Library, Zhenyan Pavilion, Hanbi Hall,

明楼、小浯溪、鹤屿、小三吾、目鱼基、波烟玉亭、湘中阁、悬溜山房、因树楼、涩浪波、镜阁、碧落庐等等。当时黄宗羲就住在水明楼上。那楼由前轩、中轩、阁楼组成，其间用长廊连接，廊前、轩侧点缀着竹树和假山，非常别致；楼前就是洗钵池。那几晚正好有月亮。楼前伫望，但见滢滢的碧水荡漾着清冷的银辉，把庭院映照得明亮而迷蒙。当时，黄宗羲不由自主地念出了杜甫“五更山吐月，残夜水明楼”的名句，并为眼前的良辰美景所深深陶醉了……“哦，今日也正好是十五，水明楼前的月色想必依旧美好吧？可是当此疮痍满目、大厦将倾的时候，这良辰美景到底还能维持多久呢？”这突然涌起的思绪，使黄宗羲的心紧缩了一下，随即又变得沉甸甸的，脚步也迟缓起来，连冒襄同他说话，都懒得搭理了。

他们到了拙存堂，已经有两三个清客先在那里等候。彼此见过，谈了几句闲话，冒起宗就出来了。这位弃官归里的宪副大人，身材不高，两鬓已微微见白，穿着打扮一丝不苟。他的脸称得上富态而秀气，现在却显得有点憔悴。他由两个丫环搀扶着，从屏风后面慢慢地走出来，看见客人，他的一双细长的眼睛就在疏朗的眉毛下眯缝起来，露出蔼然的微笑。

黄宗羲一见，连忙趋步向前，口称“世叔”，跪拜下去。

Xibo Pond, Yuxiang Temple, Shuiming Tower, Little Wu River, Stork Island, Little Sanwu, Fish Basket, Pavilion upon Waves, River Cabin, Mid-Hill House, House-among-Trees, Young Waves, Mirror Pavilion, Biluo Cottage, and so on. Huang Zongxi had been put in the Shuiming Tower. The building consisted of a front hall, the main hall, and the attic connected by a long corridor. The corridor and the sides of the halls were beautifully decorated with bamboo trees and artificial rock hills; in front of the building was the Xibo Pond. Those happened to be moonlit nights. The clear water in the pond rippled with cold silvery light, rendering the courtyard mysterious and misty. Huang Zongxi was intoxicated by the beautiful view and couldn't help but recite Du Fu's famous lines:

*"The mountains spit out the moon in the fifth watch,*
*And the tower is made bright by the water in the waning night ..."*

"Um, it's the fifteenth day of the month. The moonlight scene in front of the Shuiming Tower must still be beautiful, but when the country is ravaged by disasters and war and the great edifice is about to collapse, how long can the beautiful scenery last?" Huang Zongxi's heart stopped at the sudden thought and then grew heavy, and his footsteps became slow. When Mao Xiang spoke to him, he didn't want to reply.

When they arrived at the Zhuo Cun Tang, three squires were already waiting there. After the exchange of pleasantries, Mao Qizong came out. The former deputy head of justice of a province, who was of a short stature, was meticulously dressed. He had resigned his office and returned to his hometown. Now, his temples were slightly white and his plump face with well-defined features looked a little haggard. He had slowly walked out from behind the screen with the support of two servant girls. Seeing his guest, he immediately smiled, his slender eyes squinting.

"My dear uncle!" Huang Zongxi said. He hurried to the elder and knelt down to salute him.

冒起宗弯腰扶起，拉着黄宗羲的手，把他细细端详了一阵，又亲切地询问了他家中的一切情形。听说黄宗羲的母亲健康在家，四个弟弟宗炎、宗会、宗辕、宗彝都已成家立业，他就点点头，感慨地说："十余年间，宦途奔波，碌碌风尘，所历所闻，无一可喜。所幸者，便是故人之子，俱已长大成器。纵使来日大难，亦继起有人。老迈无能如我辈，可以从此息肩了！"

冒起宗一番话说下去，已是神色黯然。冒襄见了，连忙走前去劝慰说："爹爹，何须说这些？太冲兄远道而来，京里新闻，所知甚多，适才孩儿还来不及打听。如今就请入席，请太冲细细道来。"

这样说完之后，他就请黄宗羲和清客们先行，他亲自搀扶冒起宗，同大家一起步入西厅。

这西厅不大，紧挨着正堂隔壁，当中已经摆起了一席，顶上一盏六角形宫灯，四面还点着明晃晃的红烛。冒襄代表主人，奉觞送酒，客人们照例又是行礼，又是谦让，挨延了一阵，这才分宾主各自就座。

于是，大家一边饮酒，一边叙谈。冒起宗问起北边的情形，黄宗羲便把京中政局混乱、厂卫横行、朋党倾轧、民不聊生，以及皇上暗中同建虏议和，陈新甲因泄密下狱处死等情形约略说了一遍。大家着实咨嗟叹息了一番。黄宗羲急于了解南方的战局，他知道冒起宗不久前曾在湖北一带对农民军作战，必然十分熟悉

Mao Qizong bent down to help Huang Zongxi up, took his hand, studied him for a long while, and then inquired about his family. When he heard that Huang Zongxi's mother was well and the four younger brothers, Zongyan, Zonghui, Zongyuan, and Zongyi, were all married with their own careers, he nodded and said emotionally, "Over the past ten years, I've been moving around in the performance of my official duties, and there's nothing enjoyable in what I've experienced and seen. Fortunately, the sons of my old friend have grown up and will take up the responsibilities in the event of a major crisis. Old and useless men like me can rest assured now.

Mao Qizong looked very sad when he spoke. Seeing that, Mao Xiang hurriedly comforted him and said, "Dad, please don't say this. Brother Taichong has come a long way from the capital with a lot of stories to share with us. I haven't had time to hear him yet. Let's sit down at the table and hear the stories."

Then, he asked Huang Zongxi and the squires to go in front, and he and his father followed, one supporting the other. Together, they walked into the west hall.

The west hall, which was not very big, was next to the main hall. There was a dinner table in the middle, a hexagonal palace lantern above, and bright red candles on all sides. Mao Xiang, taking the decanter in his hand, poured wine into the cups and presented them to the guests on behalf of his family. The guests bowed and yielded to others, as was the etiquette. After the ceremonies, the host and the guests finally sat down in their seats.

Then, they drank and talked. Mao Qizong asked about the situation in the north. Huang Zongxi gave a brief account of the political chaos in the capital: the East Factory, the West Factory, and the Jinyiwei spies rampaged in the streets, the political parties fought vehemently, people were suffering, the emperor secretly negotiated peace with the Jurchens, and Chen Xinjia was put to prison and beheaded for leaking the secret ... Everyone sighed. Huang Zongxi was anxious to hear about the situation in the south. Knowing Mao Qizong had fought against the peasant army in Hubei a short while ago

那边的情形，于是，等有关北京的话题稍为停顿下来，他就迫不及待地问：

“小侄在京里时，常闻议论，说建虏固然可虑，而大明之心腹大患，实在流寇。前时听说开封之役，贼与官兵决河互灌，死者不下数十万，遂令数百载名城，一朝残破，心甚震悚。及至归抵扬州，复闻陕督孙公近有柿园之败，南阳为贼所屠。中原糜烂，一至于此！不敢请教老叔，这流贼所凭者何，竟能如此猖獗！莫非已是无法制御了么？”

有好一阵子，冒起宗都没有回答。他把弄着手中的酒杯，眼睛直愣愣地瞅着某个无形的东西，神情变得越来越忧郁，终于，叹了一口气，说：“这事说来只怕也是天降妖变，惩此下民。以往我亦是耳闻其状，未得亲见。直至去秋调职襄阳，日夕往来战阵之间，始稍知其详。大抵此寇横行肆虐二十余载，旋仆旋兴，久不能荡平者，富室暴殄，天灾盛行，固然是其根本；不过贼之魁首，实亦有非常过人之处。即以李自成而论，我曾询及贼之降将射塌天李万庆等辈，俱谓其不好酒色，不贪金帛，布衣粗食与部下共之，坚而能忍，有容人之量，士卒乐为之死，故于众贼之中，势力日强，又造‘三年免征，一民不杀’之语，四处播煽，愚民不察，风靡而从……”

“啊，‘三年不征，一民不杀’，不知此贼果能实行否？”黄宗羲脱口而出地问，显然被关于李自成其人的这种闻所未闻的

and was supposed to be very familiar with the situation there, when the topic of Beijing came to a temporary stop, he immediately said:

"When I was in the capital, I often heard that while the Jurchens are definitely a concern, the real problem of the Great Ming is the insurgents. It was said that in the Battle of Kaifeng the insurgents and the imperial army blew up the Yellow River banks to flood each other, resulting in the death of hundreds of thousands of people and the destruction of the famous historical city. I was greatly shocked. When I stopped at Yangzhou on my return trip, I heard that Mr. Sun, Governor of Shaanxi, was defeated at Shiyuan, and a massacre by the insurgents took place in Nanyang. The Central Plains region is going to the dogs. My dear uncle, can you tell me what has made the insurgents so strong? Is there no way to beat them?"

Mao Qizong was silent for a long while. He fiddled with the wine cup in his hand, his eyes staring at something invisible, his expression growing increasingly wistful. Finally, he sighed and said, "I think it's a devil coming from heaven to punish the people. I had heard about the situation long ago but had never seen it in person until I was transferred to Xiangyang in the autumn, when I began to know more about it. The primary reason why the insurgence has lasted for twenty years, now ebbing, now waning, without being wiped out, is of course the ruthless exploitation of the poor by the rich and frequent occurrence of natural disasters, but the leaders of the insurgence do have certain qualities to recommend them. Li Zicheng, for example, as I found out from a surrenderer called Li Wanqing the Sky Shooter, with no interest in wine, women, gold, and silk, is clad in rags and shares his meager food with his underlings. He has a strong will and a magnanimous heart, and his men are ready to die for him. Therefore, of all the major insurgents, he has stood out over time. Besides, he's made a slogan—'No levies for three years and no killing of ordinary people—and spread it around. The witless people, who are blind, gather around him one after another ..."

"Ah, no levies for three years, no killing of the ordinary people? Does he do what he says?" Huang Zongxi blurted out, obviously

描述吸引，并感到惊异了。

冒起宗瞧了他一眼，似乎对他提出这个问题感到有点意外。

“世侄以为他能实行否？”他反问。沉默了一下，看见黄宗羲没有反应，他又缓缓地说：“去冬襄城之破，闯贼怒贡生李永祺迎陕督汪公拒守，大捕城中士子一百九十人，削鼻断足，并尽屠永祺之族，彼又安能不杀！”

“哎，太冲世兄！”一个姓吕的老清客看见冒起宗似乎有点不高兴，赶紧帮腔说，“杀人放火，乃贼之本性；他若能不杀，这贼岂不就做不成了么？”说出这句自以为得意的“妙语”之后，他就捋着山羊胡子，嘿嘿地笑起来。

黄宗羲没有理他，眨了眨眼睛，又问：“不过，适才世叔说，那李闯‘三年不征，一民不杀’之语一出，四方愚民竟风附影从。若彼嗜杀如故，又安能至此？”

冒起宗想不到黄宗羲会这样提问，一下子倒被弄得张口结舌，不知怎样回答。加上他还不了解黄宗羲这种凡有疑问非要寻根究底不可的脾气，只当对方同情流寇，有意顶撞自己，于是把酒杯轻轻一放，脸色也跟着沉了下来。

坐在下首的冒襄却十分熟悉他的这位社友，看见父亲的神情不善，连忙插进来说：“太冲兄，怪不得人人都说你是个打破沙锅的性儿，什么都要问到底。不过，似这等显而易见之理，你怎么还想不透？”

“哦，小弟确实弄不明白。”黄宗羲老实地回答。

“此理至简单：闯贼之意，无非是归附者可以不杀罢了。我听说，闯贼每攻一城，束手迎降者不杀不焚，守一日者杀十之三，

attracted and surprised by the novel description.

Mao Qizong cast a glance at him, surprised by the question.

"Do you think he can do it, my dear nephew?" he asked back. After pausing for an instant, and seeing that Huang Zongxi didn't respond, he continued slowly, "Last winter, after they took Xiangcheng, they captured a hundred and ninety scholars and cut off their noses and feet, and slaughtered scholar Li Yongqi's entire clan because Li Yongqi had welcomed Mr. Wang, Governor of Shaanxi, into the city. Is that 'no killing'?"

"Well, Brother Taichong," said an old squire named Lü, who saw Mao Qizong was a little unhappy. "Murder and arson are in the nature of insurgents. If they don't kill, how can they be called insurgents?" After saying what he considered a maxim, he stroked his goatee and laughed proudly.

Huang Zongxi ignored him and asked again, blinking his eyes, "But just now, Uncle said that when Li Zicheng's slogan 'no levies and no killing' spread, the witless people swarmed to him like wind and were attached to him like his shadow. If he kills like the previous insurgents, how can he be so popular?"

Hearing this unexpected question, Mao Qizong was tongue-tied. Not knowing Huang Zongxi had a habit of getting to the bottom of things when there was a doubt, he thought that the young man sympathized with the insurgents and deliberately contradicted him, so he lightly put down the wine cup, and his face sank.

Mao Xiang, who was sitting in the end seat, was very familiar with his fellow Fusher. Seeing his father's unfriendly expression, he hurriedly cut in, "Brother Taichong, no wonder everyone says that you love to get to the bottom of things. You have a question for everything. The answer is obvious. Why don't you get it?"

"I really don't get it," Huang Zongxi answered candidly.

"It's very simple. Li Zicheng means whoever follows him will be spared. I hear that when they come to a city, if it surrenders immediately, there's no killing or setting of fires. If it holds out for one day, three out of ten are killed, for two days, seven out of ten, and for

守二日者杀十之七，守三日则一城尽屠之。愚民畏死，所以便闻风归附了！”冒襄一边说，一边朝冒起宗使眼色。

黄宗羲这才恍然大悟。他点着头，朝冒襄拱一拱手说：“原来如此，承教了！”

这一下，倒引得冒起宗和清客们微笑起来。

于是，接下去冒起宗又说了一些同农民军作战的情况，并在黄宗羲的追问下，特别解释了农民军的“三堵墙”阵法，和“放进”攻城法。据他说，所谓“三堵墙”，就是临阵时，以三万骑兵做前锋，分成三队，前队若擅自溃逃，后队就可杀之；若久战不胜，则诈败散开，让敌人追进来，由步兵三万，各挺长枪拒敌，骑兵再突然回头夹击，十分厉害。至于“放迸法”，就是攻城时候，不采用传统的架设云梯的办法，而是在城墙下挖洞，放置火药罐，把城炸开。没有火药时，就把洞口加深加大，大至可以容纳上百人；每隔三五步留一土柱支撑，待洞挖成后，就用粗绳拴住土柱，外面用几千人扯住绳子，只听惊天动地一声呐喊，立时柱折城崩。这个办法也相当厉害，李自成曾用它攻陷了无数城池。

冒起宗语调低沉地说着，其余的人都停了杯箸，静静地听，一个个脸上都现出悚然惊惧的神色。他们虽然不曾亲身经历这种境地，但是不难想象当时惊心动魄的惨酷情景；同时，不由自主地想到，有朝一日这种奇祸巨变降临到自己头上来时，将会是怎样一种可怕的结局，而事实上，这并不是不可能的……

three days, the entire city is wiped out. The ordinary people are afraid of death, so they surrender immediately upon hearing wind of his arrival," said Mao Xiang, winking at his father.

Huang Zongxi suddenly understood. He nodded his head and said with a clasped-hands salute, "I see. Thanks for your explanation."

Mao Qizong and the squires laughed.

Mao Qizong shared his experience of fighting the peasant army, and Huang Zongxi continued to ask questions. He explained the peasant army's "three-wall" battle formation and the "break open" method, which goes as follows:

The so-called "three walls" consist of 30,000 horsemen as vanguard, divided into three units. In case the unit in front retreats without permission, the unit behind it can kill them. If the battle isn't won after a long period of fighting, the horsemen will feign defeat and scatter. When the enemy rush in, the 30,000 foot-soldiers, each with a long spear, will come out to meet them, and then suddenly the horsemen come back to ambush the enemy from behind. It's a powerful strategy. The so-called "break open" method is a replacement of the traditional method of setting up tall ladders. The peasant army dig holes at the bottom of the city wall, put bottles of explosives in the holes, and then blow open the city. When they have no explosives, they make deeper and wider holes, each of which can hold a hundred people, leaving an earth pillar every three or five steps. When the bottom of the wall is hollowed out they wind thick ropes around the earth pillars and a thousand men pull the ropes together, and boom, the pillars break and the city wall collapses. This is also a powerful method, and Li Zicheng has taken numerous cities with it.

Mao Qi Zong spoke in a low voice, and the others listened quietly without eating and drinking, with a look of horror on their faces. Although they had never experienced anything like it before, it was not difficult for them to imagine the terrifying scene; at the same time, they couldn't help but imagine what kind of a terrible end they would one day meet when such a great tragedy befell them, and in fact it was not impossible ...

终于，冒起宗不说了。他望了望大家，勉强地一笑，补充说：“虽然国家不幸，生此妖孽，不过扰攘至今，此妖恐亦气数已尽，不久便当败灭了！”

说到这里，他停顿了一下。可是刚才大家的情绪被压迫得那样厉害，并没有因为这句话而立即解脱出来。冒起宗看见大家只是投来惊疑不定的目光，都没有作声，便举起酒杯，呷了一口酒，神情严肃地说，“这事该算得已故陕督汪公的一件大功！据说，闯贼之祖墓，在米脂县万山中，其墓穴为异人点定，当年曾置铁灯一盏于墓室之内，并造语说：‘铁灯不灭，李氏当兴。’汪公侦知后，申报朝廷，于是派人入山，百计查明墓址，掘开之后，果见灯火尚明，于是立时扑灭；又在其先祖骸骨脑后，发现一小洞，大如铜钱，有赤蛇一尾，盘曲其中，长约三四寸，有角，见日而飞，高达丈余，以口迎日色，吞吐六七次，然后返伏穴中。于是一并杀死。汪公命将此蛇腊制后，连同闯贼先祖之颅骨一道函封，送呈朝廷。你想，闯贼之能横行天下，实全仗此一灯一蛇护佑，如今已是蛇死灯灭，他还能长久作恶么？”

冒起宗这话一说出来，在座的人都不禁“啊”了一声，随即又不响了，仿佛在默默品味这个消息所包含的不寻常意义。渐渐，大家的脸色变得开朗起来，有的人甚至露出了微笑。终于，那个姓吕的清客首先站起来，兴冲冲地举起酒杯，尖声说：

“好！这叫作天亡逆贼，物极必反。大明中兴有望了！来，

Finally, Mao Qizong stopped. He glanced at his guests and smiled a wry smile, adding, "Although it's very unfortunate of the Great Ming to have a monster like this one, after all the havoc he's created, he's exhausted all his energy and his days are numbered."

After that, he paused, but that optimistic remark didn't immediately lift the spirits of his guests, who were temporarily traumatized by the story. Seeing the puzzled look of his guests, he silently raised his cup, took a sip of wine, and said with a serious expression, "The credit should go to the late Shaanxi Governor Mr. Wang. It was said, the ancestral tomb of Li Zicheng was in the Wanshan Mountain, Mizhi County, and the tomb was sanctified by a Taoist priest, who had placed an iron lantern in it and spread the word 'If the light in the iron lamp doesn't go out, in time the Li family will rise.' The late Governor Wang got wind of it and reported it to the imperial court and meanwhile sent some *yamen* men into the mountain to find the tomb. When it was dug open, sure enough, the lamp was still burning, and the *yamen* men immediately extinguished it. They saw a hole the size of a copper coin in the back of the skull of Li Zicheng's ancestor, and in it sat a coiling red snake about three or four inches long with horns on the head. When it saw the light of sun, it flew up to a height of more than ten feet. Its mouth went for the sunlight, and after taking six or seven gulps, it returned to the hole in the skull. Then the *yamen* men killed it. Governor Wang dried the snake and sent it to the imperial court together with the skull of Li Zicheng's ancestor. Since Li Zicheng's victories are dependent on the protection from the lantern and the snake, now that the light is out and the snake is dead, how much more evil can he do?"

Everyone present exclaimed in surprise, but soon went silent, as if digesting the significance of the news. Gradually, they lit up and some even smiled. The squire named Lü stood up, raised his cup and said in a high-pitched voice:

"Excellent! This is the destiny of a trouble-maker. Things will reverse when they come to an extreme. Now the revival of the Great Ming can be expected. Cheers to Lord Mao for sharing the good

为东翁这非常喜讯浮一大白！”

“对，对！”其余的人也凑兴地举起了酒杯。

唯独黄宗羲坐着不动。他低着头，眉毛皱得紧紧的，一言不发，对于周围发生的情形，似乎根本听不见，也看不见。

“嗳，太冲，快来呀！”冒襄催促说。

黄宗羲仍然毫无反应。

冒襄同大家交换了一个莫名其妙的眼色，正想再催促，突然，黄宗羲抬起了头。

“可是，这难道是真的么？”他问，满脸都是苦恼的神色，“这样，李自成果真就会败亡了么？不急图改革，进贤用能，兴利除弊，救灾赈民，消弭祸源，光是毁掉一个李自成的祖墓，又有什么用？啊，又有什么用？”他的声音高亢起来，怒气冲冲地瞪着大家，眼睛却开始发红，并且冒出了泪水。

在场的人全都愕住了。冒襄瞧了瞧默然放下酒杯、慢慢踱开去的父亲，又转向黄宗羲，想劝解几句，急切间却不知道说什么好。正在犹豫的时候，忽然看见冒成的脑袋出现在窗棂上，朝他直打手势。冒襄只好暂且放下黄宗羲，向冒起宗禀告了一声，匆匆走出外间来。

“少爷，来了！”冒成一见他，就迎上来紧张地说。

“什么来了？”

“咦，刘大人呀！”

冒襄心中猛地一跳：“什么？刘大人来了？在哪里？”他急忙问。

“就在东厅里。小的见少爷正陪着老爷，不知好不好通报，所以……”

冒襄已经没有心思听他解释。他连忙迈开大步，迅速地向东厅走去。

news!"

"Yeah! Cheers to Lord Mao!" Others echoed.

However, Huang Zongxi sat motionlessly. Head lowered and brows knit, he kept silent, as if he hadn't heard or seen what was happening around him.

"Hey, Taichong, come over," urged Mao Xiang.

There was still no response from Huang Zongxi.

Mao Xiang exchanged a look with the others and was going to urge again when Huang Zongxi suddenly raised his head.

"But, is it true?" he asked, with a stricken expression on his face. "Will Li Zicheng really be defeated this way? What's the use of destroying Li Zicheng's ancestral tomb without eradicating the root causes by making reforms to bring in the talented, enact policies that promote the well-being of the people and cure the ills of society, and provide relief to people suffering from the disasters?" He spoke in an increasingly loud voice as he glared at the others, his eyes reddening and shining with tears.

Everyone present was confounded. Mao Xiang looked at his father, who quietly put down the wine cup and slowly walked away, then turned to Huang Zongxi to comfort him but didn't know what to say. As he was hesitating, he suddenly saw Mao Cheng appear at the window, beckoning to him. So he had to leave Huang Zongxi alone for the moment. After excusing himself from Mao Qizong, he hurried into the outer room.

"Young master, here he comes," Mao Cheng said upon seeing Mao Xiang.

"Who?"

"Mr. Liu."

Mao Xiang's heart jolted. "What? Mr. Liu has come? Where is he?" he asked anxiously.

"He's in the east hall. I saw you were with the master and wasn't sure if I should report his coming, so ..."

Mao Xiang was in no mind to hear his explanation. He hurriedly walked to the east hall.

刘履丁果然正在那里。也许因为这一个多月来着实辛苦，加上车舟劳顿，灯光下，他显得疲惫而憔悴，不过，表情仍旧是兴奋的。一见冒襄，他就兴冲冲地迎上来。

“幸不辱命，报喜来迟，尚祈恕罪！”他作着长揖说。

“嗯，她呢？”冒襄匆匆还过礼，问。

“别急嘛，莫非弟还能把她带到这儿来不成？我们的船到了码头，就派人向兄报信儿，却寻兄不着。阿嫂听说了，便即时派了丫环老妈，打了灯笼，抬了轿子来接，这会儿想已安顿好了——辟疆，不是愚兄夸奖，像阿嫂这等贤慧的，真是难得呢！”

“哦！”冒襄这才松了一口气。他定了定神，重新向刘履丁行礼道谢。

刘履丁摇摇头：“你可别谢我！应该好好谢钱牧斋才是。这一次，不是他热心出面主持，这事只怕还真的办不成。”

“啊，怎么？”

“一言难尽，你先看看信吧！”刘履丁说着，从怀里掏出一封信，“这是钱牧老托我捎给兄的。”

冒襄疑疑惑惑地拆开信，只见上面写着：

> 眷侍生钱谦益顿首拜。双成得脱尘网，仍是青鸟窗前物也。渔仲放手做古押衙，仆何敢贪天功。他时汤饼筵前，幸勿以生客见拒，何如？嘉贶种种，敢不拜命！花露海错，错列优昙阁中。焚香酌酒，亦岁晚一段清福也……

“那份谢礼是我临时命人采办，用你的名义送他的。”刘履

Liu Lüding was indeed there. In the lamplight, he looked weary and worn after a month of drudgery and travel, but he was in good cheer. Seeing Mao Xiang, he quickly came over.

"Mission accomplished. Forgive me for being so late to report the good news to you," he said with a deep bow.

"Where's she, then?" said Mao Xiang with a return salute.

"Don't worry, brother. Are you thinking I should have brought her here? When the boat arrived at the pier, I sent my servant over to you first, but he couldn't find you. Your kind wife heard it and sent the sedan chair over to pick her up and the maids to light the way with lanterns. She should've been taken good care of. Pijiang, I'm not flattering you. You do have a good wife."

"Oh!" Mao Xiang breathed a sigh of relief. He calmed down and saluted Liu Lüding again.

Liu Lüding shook his head, saying, "Don't thank me. You owe a 'thank you' to Qian Muzhai. If it weren't for him to intervene, I wouldn't have been able to do it this time."

"So, what has happened?"

"It's a long story. Read the letter first," Liu Lüding said as he took out a letter from inside his gown, "Elder Qian asked me to bring it to you."

Mao Xiang puzzledly opened the letter, which read:

*Salute from an older relation Qian Qianyi!*

*Once Dong Shuangcheng from the celestial world escapes the snares in this dusty world, she is still the beautiful fairy whose figure is seen through the green bird window. Lüding the scholar has turned into a knight to rescue her, and I dare not take the credit for what he's done. In the future, when she gives birth to a child, and you hold a celebration banquet, please don't exclude me. Now that you've brought me such great gifts, how can I not accept them? I'll put the wines and produce of the sea beside each other in the Youtan Tower. To light an incense stick and have a cup of wine is a great way to celebrate myself at the end of the year.*

"I bought some gifts through the servant and gave them to him

丁解释说，随即将这一次在苏州的一番周折大概说了一遍。看见冒襄默不作声，像在思考什么，他又微微叹了一口气，补充说：

“是啊，这件喜事来得有点不是时候，正碰上建虏大举入寇，不知要乱到什么地步呢！”

冒襄没有作声，似乎还沉浸在自己的思绪里。蓦地，他回过神来：

“啊，什么，你说什么？”

“建虏已于上月初六分道大举入塞，京师戒严。朝廷下诏征诸镇率兵入援。塘报已于半月前到了。如今外间传说纷纷，道是长城已经失守，建虏分东西两路长驱直入，前锋已进抵蓟州了——怎么，兄还不知道？”

冒襄大吃一惊，像晴空炸响一个霹雳似的呆住了。过了好一会儿，他才摇摇头，倒退一步，颓然坐在椅子上；随即，又猛地站起身，也不招呼刘履丁，管自跌跌撞撞地向西厅奔去。

1981 年 5 月—1983 年 5 月初稿

1983 年 12 月改毕

1994 年 10 月修订

2011 年 7 月再修订

in your name," Liu Lüding explained. Then he briefly recounted the long story in Suzhou. Seeing that Mao Xiang was silent, as if thinking about something, he sighed slightly and added:

"Well, the good news doesn't come at a good time. The Jurchens are invading on a massive scale. There's no knowing when all this chaos will end."

Mao Xiang didn't respond, as if immersed in his own thoughts. Suddenly, he woke up.

"What, what did you say?" he asked.

"The Jurchens broke through the fortresses at the border via different routes on the sixth of last month, and the capital is now under martial law. The imperial court sent garrison troops from other locations to reinforce the front. The front line report arrived half a month ago. Rumors say that the Great Wall has been lost and the Jurchens, having split into two groups, are advancing rapidly, and their vanguard has reached Jizhou. Why, haven't you heard it?"

Mao Xiang was taken aback, as if thunder had cracked in the clear sky. After a long while he shook his head, took a step back and sat down on the chair; then he suddenly stood up, and instead of taking care of his friend, stumbled to the west hall.

*Original writing by Liu Sifen:*
*May 1981–May 1983 first draft*
*Completed in December 1983*
*Revised October 1994*
*Revised July 2011*
*English translation by Chu Dongwei:*
*April 28, 2021–October 26, 2022, first draft*
*Midnight, December 7, 2022, second draft*
*February 10, 2023, final draft*